LIFE IN PARIS

BY

VIDOCQ.

LIFE IN PARIS;

OR THE

ADVENTURES OF A MARQUIS.

INTRODUCTION.

OF the chateau built at Choisy-le-Roi, in 1682, from the designs of the architect François Mansard, and successively inhabited by Madame de Louvois, the Grand Dauphin, son of Louis the Fourteenth, and the Princess de Condè; and of the small chateau, constructed by the architect Gabriel, in 1739, a short distance from the former, and which was purchased by Louis the Fifteenth for Madame de Pompadour, there remains nothing at the present time, but a few minor buildings, and the remains of a delightful terrace, against which the water of the river Seine still beats, and from whence the eye wanders over a country eminently beautiful.

Time and revolutions have, however, respected the ancient Pavilion of the Guards, situated formerly at the entrance of the Court of Honour. The coquettish style of the ornaments of this pavilion, which are due to the chisel of the most eminent sculptors of the epoch at which it was built, is more remarkable from the edifice being placed in the centre of a panorama, whose picturesque beauty the inhabitants of the country seem but little to appreciate.

The route from Versailles runs under the window of this small edifice; but, passing at this place through a forest of noble trees, is but little frequented. It is a source of real pleasure to recline at the foot of an old chesnut tree, or a stately oak, the inhabitants of the forest, without fearing that the discordant chaunt of the countryman, or the noisy interruption of some half-inebriated idler, in a merry mood, might approach to interrupt the castle-building dreams in which we are revelling.

The Court of Honour, behind the pavilion, is at present a kitchen garden; succulent vegetables now rear their heads where formerly trod the obsequious and spirited courtier, the noble and handsome dames, and the pretty little pages of the time of Louis the Well-beloved. Alas! they spin wool, dye cloth, and make *lucifers!* in what now remains of the building of the chateau once occupied by Madame de Pompadour. Had any one predicted to the proud marchioness, that, in less than a generation from her death, there would remain nothing of her noble mansion but a few ruins, and a poor and isolated pavilion, and which no doubt will soon disappear in its turn, such a one certainly would have been received with a smile of incredulity. Was it, in fact, possible to believe that the princely castle, so solidly built, would endure for less time than the engravings made at the era of its splendour, and of which we have seen a sample encased in a modest frame of ebony, in the possession of an inhabitant of Choisy-le-Roi, who preserves it as a precious relic?

The railroad from Paris to Orleans has usurped a great portion of the magnificent terrace which formerly existed in front of the castle, by the side of the river Seine. That which remains is still, at the present day, the most elevated point of Choisy-le-Roi: no landscape can be more cheerful, more animating, or more attractive, than the one which strikes the view of the spectator from this terrace on a fine summer's day.

The land bordering the Seine is here covered with a luxuriant vegetation, and studded with charming villas, rising up in almost a snowy whiteness from the green carpet of the landscape, and are reflected in the river, whose silvery waves glide smoothly between two flowery banks; the frequent clacking on the water, and a column of smoke, curling as it rises, announce the approach of a steam-boat, which conveys to Corbeil, to Ris, or to Soisy-sous-Etiolles, the good citizens of Paris, who endeavour to forget, by a promenade in the forest, the anxieties of the present and those of the morrow.

The pavilion, of which we are now speaking, had been repaired and decorated with taste by the care of a speculating proprietor; and a short time before the commencement of this history, an elegant calèche had brought there the parties who had rented it.

These were two men, whose costume and manners announced persons of distinction; the youngest wore at the button-hole of his coat the red riband of the Legion of Honour; the eldest possessed one of those cheerful and healthy countenances which indicated that its owner was perfectly contented with his lot. The rotundity of the whole of his person, the convenient amplitude of his dress, fashioned without pretension, the magnificent pin which attached his cravat to the bosom of his fine holland shirt, and his gold chain, the numerous rings of which sparkled against his white waistcoat, all gave him the appearance of a rich financier. These two men, after examining with the most scrupulous attention the habitation, of which the proprietor did the honours with that obsequious politeness which characterizes the speculator who has terminated an excellent bargain, appeared perfectly satisfied with what they had seen; and the youngest gave an order to the liveried chasseur, who followed him at a distance, to see charge of the carriages which had just arrived, and which had also transported there a host of servants and upholsterers.

The proprietor waited, with a certain impatience, the opening of the packages which contained the furniture for the mansion: he was satisfied, from the first, that they were of more than sufficient value to answer for the rent; he was, nevertheless, delighted to have a glimpse of them, and his wish was gratified: the whole of the goods were new and in the first style. Several other boxes contained magnificent crystals, painted and gilt porcelain, plate services, and other valuables. The upholsterers and decorators, aided by the servants of the new tenant, had soon placed everything in order. That finished, the strangers having surveyed the whole with the glance of a master, and having seen to the alteration of what did not please them, retired in the same stylish carriage which had brought them.

During the continuance of the season they entertained at their pavilion a large and fashionable society: but at the commencement of the autumn which followed, the whole of the services were repacked and transported to Paris; the strangers appeared but rarely at Choisy-le-Roi; and the doors and windows of the pavilion remained constantly closed.

CHAPTER I.

THIS history commences towards the evening of a sombre day in the month of February. The picture of the landscape, of which we have endeavoured to sketch the principal outlines, was much changed; the loriot, with its golden plumage, no longer warbled amongst the green boughs; the steam-boat no longer glided cheerily on the smooth waters of the Seine; the sun no longer poured its brilliant rays on the habitations which crowned the two sides of the river. The grey, dull looking sky, resembled an immense sheet of lead; a close thick rain, which had fallen since the morning with a continued monotonous sound, had completely drenched the ground, which was covered with large pools of water; the wind howled among the leafless trees; the waters of the river, so limpid when reflecting the azure of a clear sky, was now become dull and muddy.

Two men, miserably clothed, wandered for some minutes about the Pavilion of the Guards. With the night, the cold had become more severe, and had converted into sparkling stalactites each drop of rain which had settled on the despoiled branches.

There was no appearance of any light in the interior. The two men, who walked together, arrested their footsteps almost at the same moment, as though each had obeyed the same impulse. Every thing round them was quiet, except that at rare intervals was heard the sharp whistle of the waggon drivers, or the baying of the watch dog of some isolated farm.

"You see, I am not deceived," said one of the two men to his companion, in an under tone; "the crib is not inhabited."

"You are quite right, it only remains to force an entrance: you have the tools?"

"As you say, Fifi."

The man pulled up an old frock or blouse of blue linen, which, in addition to a pair of worn-out linen trousers, completed a costume little adapted for defending him against the rigours of the season; he then showed to his companion a cord, of tolerable thickness, tied round his waist.

"There's the cord," he said.

"'Tis all that is necessary. I have a dark lantern, lucifers, and false keys in the pockets of my redingote."

"You are lucky in having a redingote, for it's devilish cold."

In fact, the frost fell upon the almost naked limbs of the miserable wretch, who had disencumbered himself of the cord round his body : small flakes of ice hung from the untrimmed moustaches which shaded his upper lip; his teeth chattered loudly, and he continued beating his sides without being able to bring any warmth to his benumbed limbs.

"Come, courage," said his companion to him ; "if the booty is heavy, you can get a new rig-out to-morrow morning at the Temple."

"Yes, yes; I'll go to the Black Forest, and get a new costume, lined with silk, for ready cash."

While speaking, the man had searched upon the ground, and had picked up a stone of a certain weight.

"This, I think, is what we want," he said.

The other individual, who had made several knots in the cord, tied the stone to one of the ends, and had slung it over the coping of the wall. The stone fell on the other side; he pulled the cord towards himself, tried its strength, and, when assured that it was well fixed—

"On horseback," he said.

He swung himself by the cord, and, in an instant, he attained the coping of the wall, on which he placed himself crossways; his comrade followed his example. In order to descend the other side, they had only to repeat the same manœuvre.

After traversing the court, they found themselves under an elegant peristyle, in front of an oaken door, which appeared very solid. On each side of this door were windows breast-high, and which they first examined. These windows were closed by Venetian blinds, fastened with large bars of sheet iron and strong bolts, and secured on the inside by secret padlocks.

"There are secret locks to the windows; impossible to get in that way; let us look at the door."

"Stop; it's a puzzling entrance."

"Pierced?"

"No; a rim lock."

"Good; we can get in that way, perhaps."

The two thieves had tried nearly all the false keys of their bunch, when the door turned on its hinges. They hesitated a few moments.

"Let us listen," said one of them, "before we determine to enter."

"I hear nothing," replied the other; "hand the light, and let's go to work."

"The house is well furnished, there ought to be plenty to handle here."

They had just closed the door of the vestibule, and fancied themselves at home, when they heard the sound of steps as of two persons walking on the gravel of the road, and who stopped before the iron grating which defended the entrance to the court. A key turned in the lock, the grating opened, and two men, enveloped in large cloaks, entered the court, and directed their steps towards the house, after closing the gate firmly behind them.

The first comers had observed all that took place through a small wicket, or opening, cut in the panel of the door.

"Ah! we are caught in the net," said the most miserable of the two; "let us conceal ourselves."

"You are always trembling, Delicat; haven't we our knives well sharpened?"

"Yes; but these two men seem likely to defend themselves. The surest way is to lie concealed; we shall find our reward, perhaps, when they are in bed; and if we must cool them, my faith, why I shan't turn coward."

After these few words, exchanged rapidly and in an undertone, they hid themselves behind the door of a small passage, after extinguishing the light of their dark lantern.

It was quite time they did so, the new comers entered the room the latter had just left, and in a few moments lighted a lamp.

The thieves, concealed in the small passage, could see nothing, but heard all that passed.

"Which of us shall go to the cellar?" said one of those last arrived.

"It shall be you, Monsieur le Marquis."

"Be it so! In the mean time, Mr. Intendant, you will make a fire, for really this weather makes one chilly."

The Marquis took a key hanging on the wall near the door of the passage, and left the room.

"Did you hear?" said Delicat to his comrade, "it seems they are nobs,—a Marquis and his intendant. Ah! plenty of cash!"

"Will you never hold your tongue? Hark! the Marquis is returned."

In fact, the Marquis entered the room he had just quitted. The fire blazed on the hearth. He took a couple of glasses and some biscuits from a cupboard.

"Here," said he, "is one of the old bottles of Vougeot, which we never uncork but on grand occasions. To the health of Father Loiseau!"

"The poor goldsmith is not quite so happy as we are at this moment."

"I must confess, this Viscount de Lussan is quite a godsend; he is like a solitaire,—he sees all, knows all, and is everywhere."

"You have given him his share?"

"Yes; 10,000 francs in bank notes, and he is contented with it. The viscount is reasonable."

"And prudent; the bank notes tell no tales"

"Let us see the *merchandise*."

"Do you hear how they speak the *argot*?" said Delicat; "they are in the trade."

"You are right; they are members, and topping ones too."

"And they have just made an excellent affair, the beggars."

"Look at these earrings," said the Marquis to his intendant, whilst Delicat and his companion conversed quietly in the passage, "and the rings, chains, pins, and diamonds in paper. Why, they must be worth more than 50,000 francs."

"You see, my dear Marquis, that I always work well enough; between ourselves, a jade is never a good horse."

"Quite true!"

"The false keys performed well enough, didn't they?"

"Old Loiseau himself would not have opened easier with his own keys!"

The Marquis took out his watch.

"Almost nine o'clock," he said. "It is time to go; we have plenty to do to-night; place the merchandise in safety, and let us go; we will dispose of them shortly to our *friend*."

The intendant replaced, in the crown of his hat, several small cases of green and red morocco, which he had taken out, and left the room.

"'Tis done," he said, re-entering after an absence of some minutes. "Now, let us start."

"What a chance! my old Coco-Desbraises; they are decamping."

"Yes! let them go, and I'll say two words about this hiding place and its riches."

After the departure of the Marquis and his intendant, Delicat and Coco-Desbraises left their lurking place, in the hope of discovering the secret deposit of the treasures they had heard spoken of.

They proposed breaking open the bureaus, &c., but the keys were in the locks, and every drawer was empty. They searched in a savage mood, without finding anything; they determined, at length, to revenge themselves on the cellar, and opened the door with the key hanging in the dining-room; but the cellar, like the furniture which they had already ransacked, was completely empty; all they discovered was a single bottle of white wine, which they finished at one turn each.

"This is what I call queer, almost criminal! not a sou in the house of a marquis," said Delicat; "there's the devil mixed up in this."

"It's not quite natural," replied Coco-Desbraises, "but where, then, have they planted the merchandise of the goldsmith they have robbed?"

"I'm quite mystified; if you like, we'll begin to rummage again; the plunder is here to a certainty; we must find it."

A fresh search was equally unsuccessful.

"Nothing!" said Coco-Desbraises, who seemed worked up to a violent rage.

"On the faith of an honest comrade," said Delicat, "if you like, we'll set fire to the house, since we can find nothing!"

"That would not be fair; they are not, perhaps, the proprietors."

"Why shouldn't they be, since one of them is a marquis, and the other his intendant? There's something droll in the idea of the nobility turning thieves, and clever ones into the bargain."

"'Tis quite true that it's strange; for if they are rich, why risk their necks by plundering."

"Well, then! suppose they should be spies?"

"Spies, forsooth! If they were spies, would they be marquis and intendant? Ah! I'm sorry I didn't examine them better."

"Did you remark how they spoke? One would think they were Gascons."

"At all events, they are spiteful, the rogues, to have so well secreted their haul."

"You're right; but when so rich, to expose one's self to the galleys, is next door to madness."

"Perhaps 'tis a passion, a humour, with them; but when the plunder is worth 50,000 francs, one might well risk something. D'ye call that nothing? But they are lucky, the dogs!"

"You do well to fret, you will not prevent its ever being so; the water draws always to the river."

Whilst conversing, Delicat and Coco-Desbraises had searched the house in every corner; but to their great regret they found nothing worth taking, except that Delicat, having discovered in a drawer a redingote and a pair of pantaloons, long since forgotten and covered with dust, would absolutely take possession of his treasure, and at once invest his person in his new acquisition.

Delicat and Coco-Desbraises, in order to leave the pavilion, employed the same means which had served them to enter it; and having followed, for some minutes, a narrow path, which led through the grounds, found themselves on the high road which conducts the traveller to Paris.

"We have a long start of it from hence to Paris," said Coco-Desbraises.

"No matter," replied Delicat, "I don't fear the cold now. I could go to the end of the world, now I have pantaloons and a good redingote over my shoulders."

The Marquis and his intendant, who had taken the railroad to return to Paris, left one another at the station; the intendant entered a cabriolet, and the Marquis continued his road on foot, his face nearly concealed with a large wrapper, and his person well covered by his cloak. Arrived at the Boulevard de l'Hôpital, he stopped a few minutes; he then retraced his steps. Having continued this manœuvre several times, he entered a house without a porter, the door of which was fastened by a secret lock; he mounted slowly the four stages, and entered a small square room, and carefully closed the door.

Without losing time, he exchanged the almost elegant costume in which he had lately appeared, for one habitually worn by the patrons or conductors of the boats; that done, he went out, and having traversed the quay, descended to the beach, detached a boat from the stake to which it was fastened, and abandoned himself to the tide of the river. Arrived at the end of the place of the Hotel de Ville, and having securely made fast his boat to one of the large rings of iron inserted in the parapet, he directed his steps to the dark and narrow street known by the name of the Teinturiers.

CHAPTER II.

MADAME SANS REFUS.

PARIS each day loses some of the traits of its primitive physiognomy; thanks to the efforts of our Edilité, wide and airy streets continually replace the narrow and sombre alleys of the old Parisian city. The artists regret the ancient mansions, with the gable ends, arched windows, and small and conceited towers of the middle age, the last traces of which will soon disappear; our modern constructions, nearly resembling each other, and wide streets, accommodated with pavements and lighted with gas, have not, we must confess, that fantastic appearance which so much pleases the imagination of the antiquary. We can thus comprehend the regrets of the lovers of the picturesque and the archæologists; but we shall admit, at the risk of being thought a little prosaic, that we prefer the things of to-day to those of former times.

The capital, especially within the last ten years, has singularly improved; still there exist, here and there, buildings, and even streets, which strongly remind us of the Paris of our worthy forefathers; these streets and buildings, elbowed on all sides by the new city, will not long hesitate to disappear in their turn.

Who, among our readers, having promenaded the evening in a quarter well built, populous, and lighted by the thousand luminous rays from the gas, does not feel struck with surprise on finding himself, on a sudden, at the turn of a street, in one of those narrow passages where he can only pass by a mere chance, and even the name of which is unknown? Such are the streets of Clos-Georgeot, les Trois Sabres, la Masure, la Tuerie, la Vieille Lanterne, Grenier sur-l'-Eau, Saint Bon, Brise Miche, &c. &c.

The street of la Tannerie is one of those which it is impossible to pass without feeling such a sensa-tion of uneasiness, that we mechanically hasten our pace without an effort to give any account of the sentiment we obey. At night the darkness is rendered more dismal by the pale and flickering light of a common lamp, while by day it is still more dull and disagreeable.

The houses in this street appear so unsteady on their foundations, that at the least shock,—the slightest gust of wind,—we are astonished not to see them tumble one upon the other, like a house built of cards, breathed upon by a child.

These decayed buildings have no resemblance to the ruins encountered by chance in the midst of a noble country; and which, at certain hours, are burnished by the rays of a summer's sun, and over which spreads the large-leafed and dark-green ivy, and the bind-weed, with the blue harebell, and which seem placed there by the hand of the Creator, to remind us that nothing here below can perish without being replaced by a substitute. The decayed houses of the street of la Tannerie have nothing in appearance *venerable*, they only remind us of the *decrepitude of vice*.

They are entered by low misshapen doors; are lighted by that species of bay windows which the people, during our first revolution, christened *à la guillotine*,—no doubt, because their shape recalled to them the terrible instrument which then performed its dreadful office on the *Place Publique*.

The humidity which decimates the miserable inhabitants of these kennels (individuals are born, live, love, and die, in the street la Tannerie, and in all those which resemble it) leaks through the scarcely plastered walls, and slides away in black streams, which leave behind them a most disagreeable and unhealthy odour.

In the street la Tannerie, there is not a single workshop—not a single warehouse, consecrated to the industry exercised by day. The species of cellars, to which the presumptuous proprietors have given the name of shops, are wholly occupied by persons who carry on a doubtful trade, salesmen of the lowest grade, vendors of old clothes, rag merchants, dealers in old iron, and gin shops; nor is there in this street (if we except the one which occupies the corner of the street Planche-Mibray) a single wine merchant; wine is not consumed in this street; but brandy! there is a good supply of that.

The street de la Tannerie is crossed by another, so narrow that two persons cannot pass abreast,— 'tis the street of the Teinturiers: this one commences at that of la Vannerie, and opens on the river Seine, passing under the quay of the Gèvres; but for some years past, the part which leads from the street la Tannerie to the side of the river has been closed up by strong iron railings.

One end of this railing is securely fastened in the thick wall of the house numbered 31, in la Tannerie-street. This house has four stages. An arched oaken door (bound with iron work, and in which is a small wicket defended by three iron bars, and closed by a small door of strong sheet-iron) discovers, when opened, a spiral staircase, which leads to the superior stages, and, in lieu of bannisters, is provided with a black and slimy cord; this door, and the shop which occupies the ground floor, is painted green.

The windows of this house have been covered with a thick coat of whitening; they have left, however, in one of those belonging to the shop, a small round space, at which frequently appears a most provoking eye, charged to indicate to the inexperienced passengers the sort of industry exercised at No. 31, la Tannerie-street.

The shop is divided into two parts, separated by a partition formerly glazed, but the glass of which, long since broken, is replaced by oil paper. The shop, properly called, is simply furnished with some tables covered with oil cloth, which are never brushed except with the sleeves of the consumers, a few chairs, and several heavy stools. The bar, or counter, upon which proudly stand some bottles, chipped glasses, and a file of pewter measures, is composed of the moiety of an old buffet of worm-eaten oak; the arm-chair of madame, placed behind, is covered with a sheep-skin once black, but now nearly red; it has lost an arm in one of the battles which frequently take place there, and from the numerous wounds which are visible, escape the different materials of its interior.

This modest throne is occupied by a woman about fifty years of age, tall and thin, with pale blue eyes; an immoderate use of snuff has considerably enlarged the orifices of her long and pointed nose; her mouth, unusually large, is garnished with black and ill-shaped teeth; her lips are pale and thin; her hair is a mixture of red and grey; a scarlet handkerchief, *en marmotte*, decorates her head; the ornaments depending from her ears are composed of real brilliants; her thin and soiled fingers are bedecked with rings of no mean value; a chain *en jaseron*, making five or six circles round her neck, supports a large gold watch, and at her waist hangs a silver chain which encloses her keys and a knife.

This woman has a bottle of absinthe within easy reach, to which she pays very frequent and maternal attentions.

The odalesques of her modest harem are differently occupied; many are drinking; some play at cards; and others, from a lack of cigarettes, console themselves with *du caporal** and their short pipes.

With the reader's permission, we will not linger in the company of these unhappy girls, but enter the back room; when our eyes can pierce the thick cloud of smoke which envelopes the chamber, we shall have leisure to examine the individuals assembled in it.

Their appearance offers nothing remarkable; they are habited pretty nearly like the rest of mankind, unless it is that they seem to have a singular predilection for colours of a gaudy hue; the toilette of some would be irreproachable, if the large gold chains and toys, which are too visible, did not appear quite out of character; the costume of others is that of honest workmen in their Sunday's best; those who can boast merely of a frock or blouse and large linen pantaloons, keep themselves in the back ground; for the rest, whatever might be their dress, they all seemed perfectly to understand each other; and why? because we are now in a *real tapis franc*, and the men amongst whom we have introduced the reader, are the frequenters of this place, the name of which is at present known by every one.

There are *tapis francs* in the most fashionable quarters of the capital, as well as in the dirty and tortuous streets of the city, of those of the Hotel de Ville, of some faubourgs, and of the place Maubert. There are some for every description of felon—from the prigger of a handkerchief, up to the titled and decorated burglar of an exclusive society.

We must not attempt to conceal it, but there exist certain villains who consider themselves dis-

honoured—yes, dishonoured! is the word—if they condescend to drink in a place similar to that in which the necessity of our subject has compelled us to introduce the reader.

The *tapis francs* of *la grand Bohême*, which we shall presently describe, are fitted up luxuriously, lighted *à giorno;* we encounter none who do not wear kid gloves, and well polished boots. Is this the reason they escape the surveillance of the police? or is it that the police only declare war against vice covered with rags?

There exists a great difference between the *tapis francs* and those ignoble cabarets frequented not only by thieves, who visit nearly every place, but also distressed workmen, drivers of the public vehicles, the nominal supporters of women and vagabonds. The name of *tapis franc* is not applicable to these latter establishments; it is not necessary, in fact, to be *franc* or *affranchi*, to be at the head of an establishment which is limited to the serving liquors to its frequenters.

The police, who often visit these cabarets, fish, as we might say, in troubled water; at every sweep of the net which they cast in, they enclose a thief who is *wanted*, or a criminal who has broken his ban; sometimes, however, they fail in their attempt. When this happens, they contrive some trap; but the proprietor of the cabaret (whose interest it is to protect those by whom he lives, and who knows that the police give sufficient extension to the proverb, " *that which is good to take is good to keep*,") makes use of some well-known word or signal to apprise his company that the police is amongst them;—a bottle placed in a certain position, a large loaf placed against the window, &c.

The *real tapis franc* (the number of these dangerous establishments, in all the great centres of population, is much more considerable than is generally supposed) is a place known to the police, who exercise a continual surveillance over it, which seldom, however, leads to any good result; for the parties at the head of these rendezvous are also constantly on their guard, and use every effort to prevent any measures which to them might be fatal ones.

The profession of a master or mistress of the *tapis franc*, whether it be to let lodgings, to sell liquors, or exercise any nominal trade, is, nevertheless, to conceal the one which they exercise in reality—that of receivers: 'tis at the *tapis franc* that the thieves leave their tools, as well as manufacture them, where they disguise themselves, transport their plunder, divide the spoil, take refuge under false names when too sharply pursued.

The proprietors of the *tapis franc* are to the thief by profession, what là Mère is to the Companion of the Tower of France; the criminal, escaped or liberated, who wishes to continue his trade, finds there (without opening his purse, if he is known, or if he has merely a recommendation from some noted thief whom he has left at the galleys or in prison) a lodging, a dress suited to the kind of industry he exercises, passports, certificates, and necessary instruments; the man who has already suffered condemnation is admitted, of right, to take a part in the first *affair;* if he wishes to decline it, he receives a benefit of twenty-five per cent. on the produce of the sale of plunder.

"Silence!" said a man seated at the end of the room, addressing those who were present: "listen!"

The whisperings of private conversation ceased at once, and each approached the man who had spoken.

* Tobacco.

The speaker, tall and well-made, appeared about thirty or thirty-five years of age; his face, furnished with a well-trimmed beard, and handsome moustaches, had a peculiar character of distinction, and it required all the perception of a close observer to discover in his physiognomy a certain expression of firmness, which might escape the eyes of the vulgar. His dress was composed of a blue jacket with black buttons, wide pantaloons of canvas, with red stripes, supported, in lieu of braces, by a waistband, *en escot*, of the same colour; his shirt, of cottonade, was attached over his bosom by a small silver anchor, *en facettes;* and from beneath his hat of varnished leather, with a low crown and large brims, escaped his flowing locks of hair, as black as ebony.

This person, who wore the costume of the conductors of the boats, was not, however, one of those laborious workmen, for his hands did not betray any signs of the rough labour of the boatman.

"Twelve o'clock strikes in the city—it is time to depart," he continued; "advance in order, and let each endeavour to profit by what I am about to say to him; and first to you, Messieurs the *Divers*."[*]

Two men, well dressed in the French style, hat from Gibus, polished boots, and so on, approached near him.

"Messieurs Mimi and Lenain, you are to look after the pockets at the waiting-room of the opera; Dejean la Main d'Or and Petit Crepine will remain at the entrance; Maladetta and Lion le Taffeur, at the sortie. You can without fear mix in the crowd; every measure is taken in consequence; of all the spies sent by the police to the opera, there is but one to be feared, and that is *Le Coup de Deux;*[†] besides, he is the only one who knows you; but the Grand Richard is charged not to quit him, and when he sees him about to approach you, you will have the *Saint Jean*,[‡] and will remain quiet—the *rousse*[||] must be clever indeed if he catches you at work; here are your entrance tickets, disguise yourselves with *les doubles Vanternes*,[§] and success to you. You, Robert and Cadet Vincent, put a blouse over your dress; watch about at leisure, but take particular notice of those shops worth emptying; here are your working tools, of which you will give me a good account. The *Charrieurs à la Mecanique*[¶] will not turn out until two or three o'clock, to catch the nobs who may leave the ball on foot. The *Goupineurs de Poivriers*[**] and the *Santedessus* can take the air. Delicat and Coco-Desbraises will explore the Boulevards, and quarter of the Temple; Biscuit and Cornet-tape-dur, the streets in the neighbourhood of the markets; the two *momes*[††] and Lassaline will go in search of cloaks. Above all, my friends, no deception, and let all respect our motto: ' Honesty.'"

This discourse, from the man habited as a mariner, which we have only reported as it gave us oc-

casion to name some of the personages who must figure in this history, was expressed almost in a breath, in a quick voice, and with an accent which did not allow the observation any place; it was listened to with the most serious attention; and, when finished, each disposed himself to enter upon the post indicated for him.

The mariner left, after saying a few words to the old woman behind the bar. " 'Tis well, Rupin, 'tis well," she replied, " your orders shall be executed, my boy; here's a key. Come, my chickens," she continued, addressing the girls, " the larder will be well furnished to-night."

The women retired to bed, and there only remained in the room to which we have introduced the reader, those whose time for leaving had not yet arrived.

The mistress of the house had not quitted her arm-chair, and still continued her attentions to the bottle. The loud talk which came from the further room did not in the least disturb the old woman, who knew by experience the noisy character of her guests.

An individual, whose physiognomy betrayed his odious character, took up the conversation after the departure of Rupin; it was Delicat, who was exchanging a few words with Coco-Desbraises.

" Are we the lackeys of Rupin, that he gives himself authority to send us out to walk? ' Go,' he says to us, ' murder the bourgeois, throw them in the river, but bring here the cash, the watches, the plate, the merchandise. I'll sell the whole of it, and take a double part for my share.' Is that just?"

" No, no; it's not fair," replied those who had listened to Delicat.

" But that's not all," he continued; " we must do the bidding of these directors, who only work with the head; they give us something to do worth the trouble, but as for the means we find what we want in our walks."

" It's equally true," answered the man whom the others called Mauvais Gueux, a cognomen which he well merited. "To allow them to be our masters we run the risk of being condemned for life or to the scaffold; it's coming it a little too strong to play so deep a game for men who despise us, if they meet us in the street."

" And who say to you, ' Sir, I have not the honour of knowing you,' if we offer them a slight recognition," added Coco-Desbraises.

" If you were as determined as I am, you would give nothing to these idlers. We must not risk our lives for such poltroons."

" Poltroons!" cried an individual who had not yet spoken, " poltroons! you would not utter such folly if you were to see them at work. Poltroons! who would murder the holy father himself sooner than be taken; besides, it's not in their absence that we should slander them; they will be in purgatory quite soon enough."

" Listen! Vernier les bas Bleus," replied Delicat; " if you wish to get yourself murdered, you are welcome to do it. Rupin and this Brigand de Provençal will manage you as they have Le Grand Louis and Charles la belle Cravate."

" You put me quite in a sweat with your discourse," said Mauvais Gueux; " is it so difficult, then, to get rid of these Messieurs? If you will lend me a hand I'll undertake to get their account settled."

" Are you in earnest?" said Coco-Desbraises; " if so, I'll give you an idea which might be useful."

" Let us hear your idea then," cried the company.

" Well! if you are all agreed, there will be a good

[*] Pickpockets.
[†] The name given by thieves to an active agent of police, who generally arrested two at a time.
[‡] A signal to warn an accomplice to cease, that he is in danger of being taken.
[||] Policeman.
[§] Spectacles.
[¶] Thieves, who, with a handkerchief, seize a person by the neck, carry him in this manner on their shoulders, while a comrade rifles him, and leaves nearly naked and half dead in the public street.
[**] When the victim dies, which often happens, the *charrieurs à la mecanique* throw the body into the canal; for it is generally in these environs they exercise their horrible trade. Thieves who attack parties who have fallen down dead drunk in the streets.
[††] Boys.

LIFE IN PARIS.

haul and no danger. We will follow these game-cocks till we know where they roost; we'll lie hid very late, and the next morning be at their door at six o'clock to see them turn out; at the first chance we'll attack them, and when they're stiff we'll visit their crib."

"Bravo, bravo," cried the whole band.

"Let those who are for disposing of the Rupins hold up their hands," said Delicat.

All, with the exception of Vernier les bas Bleus, imitated Delicat. This opposition to the general desire brought on a tempest against Vernier.

"So! you would murder your comrades to plun-der them," he said to the brigands; "they command you, you say, and that doesn't suit you; well, then, work alone; but to murder the men to whom you are indebted every day for lessons by which you can rob almost with impunity, is what I call gra-titude à la Capahut;* but you will not accomplish your project, that I can promise you, for I shall give Rupin timely warning."

"If we don't stop you," said Coco-Desbraises.

Whilst this discussion was going forward, many jugs of wine had been emptied, and their passions were getting excited; the opposition of Vernier les bas Bleus was not received with any appearance of favour.

"No, we'll not give you the time to apprise the Rupins," said Delicat.

"That's just it," said Mauvais Gueux, "we must silence him."

Vernier les bas Bleus was not a man to be intimidated; all the bandits, armed with knives, approached, led on by Delicat, Mauvais Gueux, and Coco-Desbraises, to throw themselves upon him; he saw the folly of the slightest effort to resist alone a dozen men under the influence of wine and rage; he retreated to the door of the shop, which he quickly opened, and escaped by the small street of the Teinturiers.

The aggressors, who had no desire to engage in a struggle in the street, which would infal-libly attract persons to the spot, never dreamt of following Vernier les bas Bleus; the latter, however, supposing he had the whole band at his heels, ran with so much velocity that he upset two females in traversing the street de la Tan-nerie.

The surprise, their suffering, and their fears, compelled the two women to utter some piercing cries; they demanded succour, but the most profound silence reigned in this deserted and dimly lighted street, the suspicious appearance of which increased their anxiety; one of them, at length, having got on her feet, tried in vain to assist her companion to raise herself. The latter finding her senses leaving her, said to her friend—

"Make haste, my dear Laura, and knock at the nearest door; I shall die if I do not soon have assistance." Laura, at her wit's end, ran at first the length of the street to find the driver of the fiacre which they had hired. Unfortunately she failed in so doing; she returned directly to the spot where she had left her friend, whom she found in tears

from actual suffering and anxiety. Laura, upon looking about her, fancied she perceived a feeble light in the interior of the house from whence had issued the man who had upset them; she knocked at the door with her knuckles: no person answered; impatient, she picked up from the ground a piece of rubbish, and repeated her summons.

"Holy Mother! who knocks so late?" answered from within a voice whose very note seemed broken; "what is it you seek here?"

"Assistance for a lady who has met with an accident!" replied Laura, in a supplicating tone.

"Hold your tongues, some one knocks at the door!" said the same voice.

The door was opened, and the same woman whom we already know appeared on the threshold; she held in her hand a sort of lamp, whose flickering light seemed ready to disappear. A movement of surprise and interest, at the same time, appeared on the visage of *Mother Sans Refus* (the mistress of the tavern had received from her customers this surname, from her constant good nature) at the sight of the young female, whose gracious phy-siognomy, reflected by the pale and feeble light of the lamp, recalled the delicious creation of Esteban Murillo.

Laura was on the point of flying from the ignoble and repulsive countenance of the woman, but she recollected that her friend waited for assistance, and overcame the repugnance she felt towards her.

"Where, then, is the lady, that I may take her something to revive her? I'm glad, my little kit-ten, to be useful to such pretty demoiselles like you."

After saying this, Mother Sans Refus took a bot-tle, poured some brandy into a glass, carried the lamp in the other hand, and said to Laura—

"Now, let us go and see the lady, that we may assist her."

Laura conducted her to her friend, who had en-veloped herself in her cloak, and waited with re-signation for some assistance.

The old woman placed her lamp on the rubbish, which also served as a seat to the Countess Lucie de Neuville (such was this lady's name); she then offered the liquor she had brought.

"Thank you, thank you, good dame, but I want nothing," she replied, refusing the glass, "only assist me to regain my carriage."

Mother Sans Refus tossed off the brandy, and put the glass in the pocket of her apron.

"Enter my house a moment," she said, "you will be better there than in the street."

Laura and Mother Sans Refus helped up the countess, who was introduced into the shop, lighted simply, at that moment, by the feeble glare which entered through the squares of oil paper, in lieu of glass, in the partition.

Mother Sans Refus having replaced her lamp in the niche of the partition wall, examined, with some interest, the features of the countess.

"Holy Mother!" she said to herself, she is handsome indeed—as handsome as my poor Nichon. What earrings and chains, and such a superb cloak upon her shoulders! What a chance that she has not been seen by the comrades; they would have robbed her by authority, but they get nothing now, the rogues!"

The countess finding herself somewhat better, proposed leaving, but Mother Sans Refus objected to it.

"Don't be in a hurry," she said to her, "you will hurt yourself; you are safer here than with the curate of the parish; your friend and myself

---

* A robber named Capahut, who for a long while laid waste the evirons of Paris, and who has terminated his career on the scaffold, had a custom of travelling always on horseback. When he returned from work, (a robbery,) and was accom-panied by one of his comrades, bad luck to the latter if the spoil had been divided! When Capahut and his accomplice arrived at a distant place, the former dropped something on the road, he then spurred his horse so as to make him cara-cole; at the moment he was about to dismount, his comrade would stoop to save him the trouble, Capahut would seize a pistol, and his accomplice ceased to live.

will find your coachman, and then see you into the carriage; we won't be long; for the rest be not afraid, I'll close the shop."

Mother Sans Refus knocked against the partition, and said simply the word, "Silence."

That done, she left, taking Laura with her.

Lucie remained alone, and waited some minutes with resignation; she was not, however, at ease; she felt a sensation of uncomfortable terror, which was still further increased by the miserable appearance of every thing round her. On a sudden, the confused noise of several voices, from the room beyond the partition, struck her ear; she exerted all her strength to approach it, and, concealing herself behind the bar, near which her singular hostess had made her sit down, and holding her breath, trembling with fear and anxiety, she listened.

The individuals beyond the partition spoke in a low tone; Lucie could, therefore, only catch some few of their words, but which, indeed, were perfectly unintelligible; they were, to her, a confused jargon in an unknown tongue—the expressions of vice, mixed with horrible blasphemies.

More and more terrified, Lucie at length comprehended the frightful position in which she was placed; she expected, every instant, to become the victim of the wretches in the neighbouring room. At this moment the door of the partition opened; Lucie fancied herself lost; she had still sufficient presence of mind to retain her position; a man approached to light his pipe at the lamp which Mother Sans Refus had placed in the niche, and was still in the act of replying to an individual in the room behind.

"On the faith of Coco-Desbraises! if she makes any grimaces I shall soon stop her blinking."

Lucie, without well understanding the sense of these words, guessed, from the accent of the man who uttered them, that they inferred some horrible measure; she made a slight movement; the man turned his head towards the countess, as though attracted by the noise; the flame of the lighted paper with which he lit his pipe, and had then thrown upon the ground, caused a momentary glare in the place where Lucie was seated, and she saw distinctly, under the bar, behind which she was partly concealed, the body of a man, still young, enveloped merely in an old packing cloth. The bandit waited a moment, and then returned to the next room, saying—

"Come, my jewels, a glass of cogniac!"

A cold perspiration seized upon Lucie, and showed itself in the moisture which instantly bedewed her face; the blood flowed back to her heart; but gaining courage—even in the excess of danger —she preserved the use of her senses; every moment, however, she looked upon as her last; minutes appeared ages; a thousand frightful ideas haunted her imagination:—why had they shut her in?—why taken away her companion?—she was to be robbed, murdered, perhaps. At length her fears increased to such a degree, that she was on the point of crying out for assistance, when the sound of a key turning in the lock recalled her to herself. Anxious to ascertain if it was her friend and the old woman, she raised her head, and by the faint light of a lamp, which entered through the half-open door of the partition, she observed a man standing on the threshold; ('twas the one to whom we have heard Mother Sans Refus give the name of Rupin;) his right hand still rested on the key, which remained in the lock; in the other he held a coil of rope, or small cordage, constantly

in use amongst mariners; he stood motionless on the step of the door, as if waiting the arrival of another person.

The sound of several voices, and also of a carriage, came very opportunely to revive the drooping courage of poor Lucie, whom so much agitation had quite unnerved. She made a sudden movement; the attention of the man was attracted; he turned round and looked towards the place occupied by Lucie; her white dress, and the brilliancy of her diamonds, at once betrayed her.

Rupin quickly approached, and seized her two hands, saying, "My faith, but this is a prize; 'tis something new to see a lady of your rank in the tapis of Mother Sans Refus. Fear not, beauteous stranger, we know, too well, how to pay proper respect to *les calèges;** you shall receive attention and politeness."

"For pity's sake, allow me to leave this place," replied Lucie; "let me go, I implore you."

"Yes; you shall go, my angel, but, before leaving, you must pay your passage: come, kiss me;" and, suiting the action to the word, he took Lucie by the waist.

The countess uttered a piercing cry, the door of the adjoining room was opened, and the shop was, in a moment, filled by a crowd of individuals whose features were any thing but encouraging: one of them, who held a candle in his hand, approached Lucie, and already extended his hand to seize her necklace.

Rupin repulsed him briskly, and, suddenly changing his manner and language—

"Pardon me, madame," he said to Lucie, "but by what hazard has a lady of your rank found herself in such a place, and at such an hour?"

Lucie had no time to reply; Laura and Mother Sans Refus entered the shop at this moment, followed by several individuals attracted by their cries; one of them attempted to seize Rupin, but, endowed with great strength, he soon rid himself of the impudent aggressor, who fell heavily on the counter; —the fall was so rough that the glasses, bottles, and measures tumbled on the floor in the midst of the uproar.

Mother Sans Refus heard in the distance the measured steps of the patrol.

"Enter the cave, the patrol is close upon us!" she exclaimed.

Rupin and the other bandits disappeared by the back room, and all that remained in the shop, when the patrol arrived, were those whom curiosity had attracted to the spot.

Lucie, supported and guided by Laura, profited by the confusion to escape, and reached her carriage; she gave her purse, however, to Mother Sans Refus, whose strange and dangerous hospitality was liberally repaid.

Half an hour after this scene, which occupied less time than it has taken us to describe it, Lucie and Laura arrived at their hotel.

CHAPTER III.

ARISTOCRATIC THIEVES.

LA haute pègre† is an association of men, who, in the war they have declared against society, have

---

* The calège is not met with in the public street; she is not, however, an honest woman; her charms are the merchandise she retails, but obtains a high price for that which others of the same class, though in an inferior degree, dispose of at a moderate return. Her toilette is fresher, her manners more polished, but her *morals* are the same.

† An association of thieves of celebrity.

afforded to one another proofs of a devotedness and capacity, exercised for a long time, or who have invented or practised with success any peculiar species of robbery. The pègre de la haute* will plan a theft, but will not, himself, commit one of any minor importance; he would think he compromised his dignity as an experienced man; he only acts in affairs of magnitude, and despises those who pilfer trifles; indeed, these are his slaves.

At an epoch not far distant, the pègres de la haute had their own laws; laws which were never written in any code, but which, nevertheless, were more closely observed than many of those which regulate our social well-being; these laws are now fallen into disuse, but even at present, the pègre de la haute, who has not betrayed his companions in the moment of danger, is not abandoned by them when, in his turn, he finds himself in trouble;† he receives assistance in prison, at the galleys, and sometimes even at the foot of the scaffold.

The pègre de la haute is met with everywhere—at the Coq Hardi,‡ at the Maison Dorée, at the Bal Chicard,‖ and in the balcony of the Italian theatre; whether dressed in an elegant costume, a round jacket, or simply in a blouse, his exterior is suited to the necessities of the moment, which he is forced to adopt; he knows how to assume all shapes, speaks all languages, that of good society being as familiar to him as the *argot* of the prison and the galleys.

The pègre de la haute is attached to his profession, and the excitement it procures him; and a quality which we cannot deny him, is that of being an able juris-consult; he thus, as we might say, walks with the code in his hand; and if he has adopted any peculiar kind of robbery, he soon acquires such a dexterity that he can almost practise it with impunity. This is so true, that it is only from unforeseen circumstances, or secret information, that the arrest of those who appear before the bar of justice is due.

Many shades distinguish, amongst themselves, the *pègres de la haute;* the most easy of remark is, that which separates the Parisian thieves from those of the provinces; the former only adopt affairs which demand address and dexterity, *la tire*,§ *la detourne;*¶ the latter, on the contrary, less expert, but more audacious, will be caroubleurs,** vauterniers,†† or roulottiers.‡‡ But there exists an intermediate society, in which the head members of the corporation exercise indifferently every species of theft; nothing appears difficult to them—they will attempt any thing. Their life is often the stake they hazard in the game they play against society.

Let us now introduce the reader into a small cabinet or study, which forms part of a pretty little hotel of the Faubourg Saint Honorè; the hangings and curtains are of a dark tint, but relieved by silver fringe and tassels; the walls are hung with some pictures of the best masters; the chimney-piece, of veined Italian marble, on which is placed a pendulum in a frame of black marble, and two cups beautifully chiselled, is surmounted by an immense glass, incased simply by a thin moulding of silver

plate. The different articles of furniture are inlaid also with silver; on the shelves of an elegant library are ranged, richly bound, the best works in our literature; in a word, the most exquisite taste has been expended in the furnishing and decoration of this cabinet.

In front of a circular table, covered with papers, journals, pamphlets, and the thousand superfluities necessary to constitute a luxury well understood, sits a man enveloped in an elegant robe de chambre; he holds in his hand a small tablet or card-case, richly inlaid with gold, which he examines with much attention.

At some distance, occupying a fauteuil* à la Voltaire, with the easy freedom of an intimate friend, is a man somewhat older than the former; still his unceremonious manners might appear somewhat extraordinary, for his black costume, from head to foot, his knee-breeches and silk stockings, his shoes with small gold buckles, announce, if not a domestic, at least a subaltern.

The man in front of the table is Monsieur le Marquis de Pourrieres, auditor of the council of state, and knight of the royal order of the Legion of Honour. This man, however, is not unknown to us; we have encountered him at the house of Madame Sans Refus, giving instructions, under the name of Rupin, to the band of thieves.

One moment, reader! Whatever might be your incredulity or astonishment, exclaim not yet against the reality; we do not meet, it is true, scions of nobility in the infamous dens of modern Paris, unless, indeed, they are led there for the purpose of studying the *exclusive* manners of the inmates; but it often happens that the tenants of these dens quit of a sudden their retreat, to assume the character of great personages, without, however, renouncing their former trade.

'Tis a deplorable fact, but no less true. There are, in the highest circles, in the best society, men who have left the prisons or the galleys; at every step we take in the saloon we are liable to be elbowed by a swindler, a thief, or even an assassin. An old galley slave, who had certainly well merited the punishment to which he was condemned, Guy de Chambreuil, was, in 1814, director-general of the stables of France, and head of the police at the chateau. Who does not remember the famous *Cognard*, who, under the name of the Count de Pontis de Saint Hélène, contrived to get himself named colonel of the Legion of the Seine?†

Monsieur the Marquis de Pourrieres, auditor of the council of state, and knight of the Legion of Honour, in spite of his hotel, his equipages from the most fashionable builders, his splendid team, his name and his decorations, which gave him the entrée to the most aristocratic hotels, was neither

---

* A fashionable thief.
† Suffering a condemnation.
‡ A small public-house, of bad reputation, at Courtille.
‖ A house of the same description at the Place Maubert. We shall have occasion to speak of this house, which is one of the greatest pests of the capital.
§ Picking pockets.
¶ Robbery of the interior and stalls of shops.
** Housebreakers, who make use of jemmies, false keys, &c.
†† Thieves who introduce themselves through windows into the apartments they intend robbing.
‡‡ Men who steal boxes, portmanteaus, &c. from the public vehicles, &c.

* Arm-chair.
† Most persons are acquainted with the man Cognard, a criminal who several times made his escape from prison. Cognard was so well received at court, that the Duke de Berri himself presented him to Louis the Eighteenth, who attached on the bosom of the pretended Count de Pontis de Saint Hélène his own cross of Saint Louis. Guy de Chambreuil was an individual of the same species. These two individuals were not the only ones who, at the same epoch, occupied places at court. We shall cite, among many others whose names escape us, the following: De Fénélon, who pretended an alliance to the family of the illustrious author of Telemachus. This personage, who had been detained seven years at Bicêtre, was gentleman of the chamber. Jalade, a liberated forger, after suffering eight years with hard work, director of fireworks; Morel, escaped from the prison at Brest, employed in the secretaryship of the king's orders; Stevenot, escaped from the same prison, colonel of a regiment of the line; Ménégant, called de Maugenest, who, after suffering five or six condemnations, was made court poet, and sung the praises of the Bourbons, after adulating the republic and the empire.

more nor less than one of the most distinguished members of *la haute pègre.*

He still had in his hand the small carnet.

"Can you comprehend all this," he said to his companion, "to meet a countess at the house of Madame Sans Refus; on my faith, a real countess!"

"A real countess! a real countess! it's possible; but the contrary is also possible; it's not all gold that glitters; we are ourselves a proof of the truth of the old proverb."

"But, blockhead! haven't I told you the circumstance which forced this lady there?"

"You spoke to me about a fall or an accident, certainly; but can you tell me what the countess came to seek, past midnight, in the street de la Tannerie?"

"No; I only know that this countess is very capable of inspiring a sentiment of passion in an honest man; for the rest, I was there very apropos to prevent Delicat committing a vile act towards her—the brilliancy of her diamonds had dazzled the miserable."

"But what you did was not very prudent, if really these diamonds were as valuable as you say; 'twas a good opportunity lost, and they become scarcer every day."

"But, Mister Stupid, don't you know that Mother Sans Refus, with whom we must keep on good terms, for we shall find with difficulty a tapis more convenient than hers, sets her face against drawing blood at her house; and, besides, the good woman was much taken with this pretty countess, who, as she pretends, resembles her daughter."

"Is it true?"

"Something like it."

"In that case you ought to fall in love with her yourself; it is what generally follows when you meet a woman who, far or near, resembles the little Nichon."

"You know, my dear Roman, I never allow pleasures to interfere with my business."

"Is it really your intention to see this woman again?"

"Beyond a doubt."

"Bah! she will recognise you."

"I think so."

"She will blab."

"What's that to me; do you think I shall find it difficult to explain my presence at Mother Sans Refus's, and also my disguise? formerly the grand nobles went to the Porcheron, and to Ramponneau; they might well go now in such places, it's quite simple; but as I must, above every thing, give the pretty countess a good opinion of myself, I am going to return her this bijou, in which I have found her cards and these two notes of a thousand francs each."

The Marquis who, whilst conversing with Roman, had written a few lines on a sheet of ambered note paper, impressed with his arms, placed the carnet, the two bank notes, and his own note, in an envelope, and rung the bell; a servant in an elegant livery presented himself.

"Go," said he, "to the hotel of Madame the Countess de Neuville, and deliver this; if you are asked any questions, make no reply; you will not even say in whose service you are."

The servant bowed and retired.

Roman sighed when the servant left; the restitution of the two notes of a thousand francs appeared to him an unheard of imprudence.

The Marquis de Pourrieres and Roman continued the conversation, for a moment interrupted, when the Viscount de Lussan was announced.

"Request him to enter," said the Marquis. "Richard could not arrive at a fitter moment," he added, addressing Roman.

The Viscount de Lussan was a handsome young man, much above the middling height, but which was somewhat relieved by the freedom and grace of his manners.

"Good day, Marquis," he said, saluting de Pourrieres with an aristocratic politeness; "you see I am punctual; I bring you your share, and that of your faithful Achates," he added, smiling graciously to Roman.

"Is it fat?" inquired the latter.

"Really, my dear Roman," cried the Viscount de Lussan, "you are insupportable; can't you, when we are alone, employ the language of honest men? I don't know if you are like me, Marquis, but I cannot hear a word of *argot* pronounced without feeling my nerves set on edge."

"Come, dear Viscount, don't make war on this poor Roman. Let us talk of business. What have you brought us?"

"Two thousand francs for you and Roman."

"It's not much," said the latter.

"The harvest at the ball of the opera has not been so good as we hoped; Maladetta and Lion were not at their post."

"That surprises me," said Roman again; "Maladetta and Lion are generally very punctual."

"Their absence has been very prejudicial to us; Robert and Cadet Vincent have been pretty lucky, they have completely emptied the shop of a goldsmith in la Rue Pastourelle; the two boys and Lassaline have brought a few manteaus; they have drawn six thousand francs for the whole; the third is for you and Roman, one thousand for myself, and the remainder has been divided between the others."

"Have the Charrieurs à la Mecanique and the others obtained any thing?"

"They did not go out. Really, Marquis, you ought to rid us of these rabble."

"Why? They are intrepid fellows, who are contented with a little, and will be very useful if an occasion to employ them presents itself. But let us change the subject. You are acquainted, no doubt, as one who frequents the best society, with Madame the Countess de Neuville?"

"I am at all her assemblies."

"So that you can present me to her."

"Not at her house, dear Marquis, but at the hotel of the Marchioness de Villerbaune, her husband's aunt; but excuse me—for what reasons do you wish an introduction to Madame de Neuville?"

"This countess has a resemblance to Nichon," said Roman; and de Pourrieres, who has seen her by chance, has become desperately in love with her."

"The devil! the devil! why, I am myself in the same situation, and I don't know if I ought to furnish de Pourrieres with arms to fight against myself."

"How, Viscount, are you afraid of me?"

"Why, it's not without some pain that I shall do what you so much desire."

"Come, de Lussan, we will each do our best, the luckiest or the most dexterous will succeed; but as you are a younger and a handsomer man than I am, the chances are all in your favour."

"So much the better, dear Marquis; for the rest, what you desire shall be accomplished."

Roman, who for some minutes had been reading a journal which he had taken from the table of the

Marquis, suddenly uttered an exclamation of surprise.

"What's the matter, then?" demanded at the same time de Pourrieres and the Viscount.

"I am no longer astonished that Maladetta and Lion were not at their post!" said Roman. "They are dead!"

"Dead!" cried de Lussan.

"Yes, dead!" added Roman, "if ever any one died. Listen to this—

"'Paris, 10th Feb., 1830.

"'A young woman, endowed with a most pleasing physiognomy, occupied, with a young man, a modest lodging in the Rue des Lions, Saint Paul. For some time past, this young woman, who was at first remarkable for her liveliness and gaiety, has appeared quite out of spirits; and the neighbours frequently remarked, in the morning, the extreme paleness of her countenance, and the traces of tears—the unwilling witnesses, no doubt, of her troubles during the night.

"'She never replied to the questions kindly put to her. It was, however, soon known that the young man, with whom she lived, ill-treated her in a most brutal manner.

"'Yesterday morning, she had a violent altercation with him, during which a neighbour, attracted by the noise, approached the door, and distinctly heard the young man pronounce these words—"I will not change my conduct to please you." This neighbour could hear no more. The door of the apartment, in which were the two young persons, was opened with precipitation, and the young man went out, saying, "Don't wait for me to-night; I am going to the ball at the opera." At nine o'clock in the evening, a man, supposed to be a working locksmith, who carried on his shoulders a bag commonly known as a sac en ville, and who had a hammer in his hand, came to the house, and inquired for a young woman named Elizabeth Neveux. The porteress replied she knew no one of that name; but the workman so exactly described the features, the manner, and the usual costume of the person to whom he gave the name of Elizabeth Neveux, that the porteress sent him to the young woman of whom we speak, but who was only known in the house as Madame Lion.

"'The workman remained with her about an hour and a half, when the Sieur Lion returned, accompanied by a young Italian named Maladetta, who often came to see him. These young men were not intoxicated, but it was easy to perceive that they had partaken of some copious libations.

"'Some instants after, there were heard in the apartment of Lion the sobs and groans of the young woman, and then some piercing cries. The neighbours hastened there, when a man, the one who had inquired for Madame Lion under the name of Elizabeth Neveux, descended the staircase, upsetting those who opposed his flight, and escaped.

"'A most horrible sight presented itself to those who entered the apartment of the Sieur Lion; the two men who, within a short half hour, were seen full of life and spirits, were stretched on the floor, both dead! and horribly disfigured from the dreadful wounds they had received.

"'The police were instantly apprised of it, and a deputy of the Procureur de Roi attended at the house, accompanied by a judge of instruction.

"'The young woman was placed in the hands of justice, but the circumstances which attended this dreadful murder are not of a nature to show her guilt in a positive manner; still, when they demanded of her if she knew the author of the crime, she positively refused to give up his name, although it is certain he was not unknown to her.

"'An unforeseen event has tended to increase the mystery which already envelopes this tragical event. In a cupboard, concealed behind a secretary, they have discovered an enormous quantity of watches, snuff-boxes, and jewellery of all sorts. Must we conclude, from this discovery, that the two victims belonged to that gang of thieves who, in the police vocabulary, are called tireurs or fourlineurs, or were they merely receivers? This is a question which the evidence will decide.

"'The assassin left on the scene of his crime the instrument which served him for the commission of it; it is one of those heavy hammers generally made use of by locksmiths. They have also found his sack, in which are his tools.'

"There is nothing more," said Roman, interrupting his recital, to which de Pourrieres and de Lussan had listened with much attention, "than the obliging commentaries of the journalist:

"'This crime, committed with such audacity at half-past ten in the evening, in the very centre of a populous quarter, has produced amongst the inhabitants a feeling of insecurity. Every one demands the utility of a police,' &c. &c.

"It is not an escarpe* who has settled the account of our friends," said Roman, when he had finished reading the paper.

"I do not regret these two individuals," replied de Lussan; "the necessity of our business compelled me to associate with them often, and I assure you, my dear Marquis, that I suffered much from it; they were men without education, who had no elegance in their manners; I was interested, however, in Lion, I had introduced him to my tailor, a real artiste—a trouble completely thrown away, my dear fellow."

"They were brave boys," added de Pourrieres, "but, after all, I had rather know them to be dead than arrested; it's much safer—the dead are discreet."

The conversation continued for some minutes, when de Lussan quitted de Pourrieres and Roman, after saluting the Marquis and his friend with that grace and urbanity, the usual appanage of a well-bred man.

CHAPTER IV.

THE COUNTESS DE NEUVILLE.

MADAME DE NEUVILLE, and Laura de Beaumont, her friend, occupied, in the Rue Saint Lazare, near that of Larochefaucault, one of those ancient and vast hotels, which resemble in nothing the buildings of the present day, in which a parsimonious hand seems to have measured out space and air. The Count de Neuville, a gentleman of a good family, was, at the time this history commences, colonel in the royal corps of the staff; his rank had been acquired in the field of battle, the decorations which glittered on his breast had been purchased with his blood or by some glorious action; circumstances not very common at the time we write.

The Count de Neuville was gifted with that frank and open nature generally acquired by men who have lived long in camps; and the only defects with which it was possible to reproach him, with

---

* An assassin by trade.

any reason, was an extreme susceptibility of temper, and a certain hastiness of character, which might have passed unnoticed in many individuals, but which his age and position in the world caused to be remarked.

As we may well suppose, Lucie, in espousing the Count de Neuville, had not contracted a marriage of inclination; but as, before her nuptials, she had never left the school in which she had been educated, she had accepted, without making any objection, a man whose estimable qualities, and an exterior which, although not seducing, was not without a certain charm, sufficiently recommended him.

Thanks to the enlightened person who had the care of her education, she had not read the loose productions of the characterless women of our age; thus she had supported her station without repugnance, and the good qualities of her husband coming to her assistance, she felt towards him that calm affection which often endures beyond that of passion, and mostly leads to a haven of repose after a perfectly happy life, when no unforeseen events intervene to mar the course of ordinary existence.

The Countess Lucie de Neuville was very young and very handsome; a little capricious, perhaps, and liked to have her own way, but kind, spirituel, endowed with that noble generosity, and that perfect distinction, which seems only to belong to certain individuals.

Lucie had lost her father some months after her marriage; her eldest brother, brought up at some distance from her, had lost his life in Africa whilst she was yet an infant; her husband, then, was the only man in the world whose protection she had acquired.

Laura de Beaumont was an orphan; but a maternal uncle, who lived in a distant country, took a great interest in her, and every half-year forwarded to the mistress of the school in which she had been educated with Madame de Neuville, a sufficient sum to provide her with every comfort she might require.

When Lucie married the Count de Neuville, not wishing to be separated from Laura, to whom she was sincerely attached, and equally loved in return, she offered the latter to share her hotel, and had made her a friend and companion, as well as confidant in every thing.

The uncle of Laura, whose consent the Count de Neuville had solicited, approved the arrangement, which permitted his niece to leave school, and placed her in a desirable position in society.

Laura was eighteen years of age; she was a charming blonde, nothing could be more fascinating than the graceful pliancy of her movements; the blue azure of her eyes excused the paleness of her countenance, and her features, imprinted with that distinction so remarked among some privileged races, bespoke a soft and kind heart; it was impossible to listen to her voice without a pleasing sensation accompanying it. In a word, this young female appeared to realise one of those delicious dreams which cross our imaginations when twenty years of age—those golden dreams whose remembrances last for ever.

Such were the two ladies whom we have met at the house of Mother Sans Refus; we must now inform the reader of the circumstance which had led Madame de Neuville and her companion into this miserable place.

Monsieur de Neuville, whom the Minister of War had named chief of the staff of a division employed in Algiers, had departed some days before to occupy his station. This departure had greatly affected his young wife, who feared the dangers he was about to face; but the colonel, at parting, had reassured her as far as lay in his power; and, not wishing that his absence, during the season of balls and reunions, should deprive his wife of the pleasure she had no doubt anticipated, he had made her promise to mix in society, and for that purpose had especially recommended her not to neglect his relation, the Marchioness de Villerbaune.

The saloons of the Marchioness de Villerbaune, who inhabited an hotel in the Place Royale, were neutral ground, in which assembled the most distinguished men of the Parisian society; the private gentleman, the artiste, military man, literati, and diplomatist, were equally well received there, when their personal qualities rendered them worthy of the position they occupied in society; thus, these reunions were always brilliant, animated, and, what is still more rare, *ennui* was a stranger at them.

Madame de Neuville and Laura,—both handsome, though differing in their beauty,—both young and full of grace, were the belles of this hotel; at which, however, it was no rare matter to meet very pretty, very young, and very amiable women.

Where is the woman, however gifted with wisdom, who is not flattered at being the object of the homages of a crowd of distinguished men, especially when this adoration may appear disinterested, and presented solely from a strong feeling of admiration?

We shall not be surprised, then, to know that of all the recommendations which Monsieur de Neuville had given his wife, that of not showing any neglect to Madame de Villerbaune was the most closely observed.

Madame de Neuville and Laura, after giving to their toilette that rigid attention which a handsome woman never neglects, and which added still more to their brilliant charms, waited in their saloon whilst their horses were being harnessed, when Paolo entered.

Paolo was thirty-five years of age; he had been for several years in the service of the Baron de Noirmont, the father of Madame de Neuville, when the latter was married. He was a native of Savoy, and a long residence at Paris had not changed his primitive manners; honest, frank, loyal, full of devotedness—a type of those domestics at present only met with in romances or operas-comiques—he considered himself a member of the family whom he served; he respected Monsieur de Neuville—he loved his young mistress.

He entered the saloon to announce that the carriage would be ready in a few minutes; that said, he remained. Lucie guessed he had something more to say to her.

"You have something to tell me, Paolo," she said to him, accompanying her words with a most gracious smile.

"It's true, Madame la Comtesse, but I don't know if I ought."

"Come, fear nothing, and explain yourself at once."

Paolo brought forth a letter from his waistcoat pocket. "I have been requested to deliver you this letter; but it is from a person against whom Monsieur de Neuville has closed the door of his hotel, Mademoiselle de Mirbel, and I dare not——"

"A letter from Eugenie, after what has passed," said Lucie.

"This letter was given me by an old woman in rags; Mademoiselle de Mirbel is, as she assures me,

LIFE IN PARIS.

RUPIN PROTECTING LUCIE IN THE HOUSE OF MOTHER SANS REFUS.

very ill and very unhappy, and I thought that your ladyship——"

The eyes of the faithful servant were full of tears; Madame de Neuville saw that he hesitated saying all he knew.

"You have done right, Paolo," she said to him, "give me the letter, and leave us now; I will ring when I want you."

"You have not forgotten Eugenie de Mirbel," said Madame de Neuville, after reading the letter she had opened.

"Eugenie de Mirbel!" replied Laura, " a pretty brunette, who entered society a few months after my arrival at school?"

"Yes, the same; I am now aware why Monsieur de Neuville objected to my seeing her. Ah! the men show but little indulgence to the faults they cause us to commit. Listen, Laura,—

"'Have you forgotten her who was your friend, when a laughing and innocent young girl? I do not think so. If I am right, if you have preserved any remembrance of the poor Eugenie de Mirbel, in the name of all you hold most dear in this world, I implore you come to my assistance, or rather hasten to the succour of my infant. I must, indeed, Lucie, be very, very miserable to have the boldness to write to you after what has passed; if I suffered alone, if I had not at my side, and on the bed which I shall no more leave, a feeble and innocent creature, who will also share my fate if I receive not assistance, I should have sufficient courage to quit life without pressing the hand of friendship, or meeting an affectionate regard to ease my dying moments. But if I am a mother! Lucie, may you never experience the horrible sufferings of a mother who can do nothing for the child, who is dying of cold and hunger by her side. Cold and hunger, Lucie! If you fear to disobey Monsieur de Neuville, read him my letter; kneel before him; tell him that much is pardoned to those who are dying, and he will let you come; but in the name of heaven, in the name of your worthy father, who was the friend of mine, hasten to me; my breasts are dry, my poor little daughter cries, and I have not a sou! a sou! to purchase her a cup of milk.'"

"Let us go directly, Lucie," said Laura, when Madame de Neuville had finished reading the letter, "let us go at once; if Monsieur de Neuville was here, I am sure he would accompany us."

"Oh! yes," replied Lucie, "Monsieur de Neuville has forbidden my seeing Eugenie, and he was right; but she was not unhappy then."

Lucie and Laura threw a cloak over their shoulders; Madame de Neuville then rang the bell, which was answered by Paolo.

"You must get me a fiacre from the nearest stand, conduct it to the small door of the garden, in the street Larochefoucault, where you will wait for me," she said to him.

Although Madame de Neuville would not have concealed from her husband the step she was about to take, she thought it best to engage a public vehicle, in order to prevent herself being under the necessity of giving to her servants the reasons which induced her to visit a person who lived in the street de la Tannerie, instead of passing the evening at Madame de Villerbaune's.

The evening was already advanced when Lucie and Laura took their seats in the carriage, after crossing the vast garden of the hotel.

"This poor Eugenie," said Madame de Neuville, stepping into the coach, "she must be very unhappy to bring her mind to write such a letter as

the one I have received. Oh! my friend, how happy ought we to think ourselves if we compare our lot with that of the poor Eugenie de Mirbel!"

The countess said no more during the time it occupied in riding from the street Saint Lazare to that of la Tannerie; the miserable situation of her old friend appeared to affect her sensibly; and Laura, who seemed to imbibe the sadness of her companion, did not venture to disturb her reflections.

They were demolishing at this time, in la Tannerie-street, the old ruins which have made way for the new buildings which are now contiguous to the place of the Hotel de Ville. The street, narrow enough before, was now encumbered with rubbish, which rendered it impassible to carriages, so that it was at this time blocked up; the two ladies, therefore, were compelled to leave their fiacre at the corner of the street Planche Mibray.

They found, without difficulty, the dwelling of Eugenie de Mirbel; the poor girl had not exaggerated the picture of her frightful misery, the appearance of which deeply pained the sensitive heart of Madame de Neuville.

The walls of the garret occupied by Eugenie were naked, and the keen and frosty wind forced a passage through them, despite the plugs of rags with which they had endeavoured to replace the absent glass from the arched window, which lighted this miserable attic. Eugenie was reclining on a thin straw mattress, placed on a truckle bedstead, and covered merely by a light counterpane of cotton, once white; she pressed in her arms a pretty little infant, about three months old; the eyes of its poor mother, deeply sunk in their orbits, and surrounded with a black circle, announced that she was a prey to a burning fever.

"Ah! you are come," she said, as Madame de Neuville entered, followed by Laura; "I was afraid you would not come, I was so miserable."

"My poor Eugenie!" exclaimed Lucie, melting into tears. "Oh, yes! you are very miserable. But why didn't you write to me sooner?"

"Listen, Lucy! I am dying," said Eugenie, drawing towards her the countess, to show her the infant; "I am dying; but you will take care of my daughter; you will promise me, won't you?"

"No, you will not die, my poor friend; you are young, and nature is strong at your age."

Eugenie drooped her head in sadness.

"Take an interest in my child," she said, placing the infant in the arms of the countess.

Lucie ordered a physician and a nurse to be sent for, and purchased every thing necessary until Eugenie could possibly recover sufficient strength to be removed to a Maison de Santè; she gave some money to the old woman who had brought the letter of her friend; these attentions necessarily took some time, so that it was near midnight when she quitted Eugenie, promising to pay her another visit in the course of the following day. The reader has been informed how she and Laura were thrown down by Vernier les bas Bleus, in escaping from the effects of a quarrel, and what were the results of the accident.

Half an hour after leaving the house of Mother Sans Refus, the Countess de Neuville, as we have observed, entered her hotel with Laura, by the small door of the garden, near which, faithful to the directions he had received, Paolo was stationed like a sentinel.

The wound of Madame de Neuville, although not dangerous, required immediate attention; she requested the attendance of Dr. Matheo, the ordinary physician of the hotel.

The remedies of the doctor had greatly relieved her, but, as it often happens, after being subject to violent emotions, she passed a very restless night; dreams, which recalled to her mind the events which had taken place, troubled her sleep, and when she awoke, with her features bathed in perspiration, the thought of the dangers she had encountered, and to which she had exposed her young friend, produced a feeling of painful anxiety.

Her inquietude, however, increased, when she discovered that she had lost or been robbed of a small inlaid card-case or tablet, which contained, besides her cards, two bank notes of a thousand francs each.

Laura, who had passed the night near her friend, and to whom this fact was made known, and the anxiety it had produced, used her efforts to console her. "We have," the countess said to Laura, "committed a great imprudence, in trusting ourselves at such an hour in a deserted neighbourhood."

"Have we the time to think of every thing when we are about doing a good action?" replied Laura. "Besides, you are wrong to trouble yourself so; he who stole your case will attach no other value to it than that of the two thousand francs."

"But this man, at first so brutal, and who assumed so suddenly the tone, the manners, and the language of a man in good society, and who prevented one of those who came from the next room taking my necklace—who can he be?"

"Doubtless some honest workman, who would not see a theft committed in his presence if he could prevent it."

"You deceive yourself, Laura, this man is not a workman; and I know not why, but what I fear the worst is, that it might be into his hands that my case has fallen."

"For gracious sake, tranquillise yourself, my dear Lucie; 'tis a thousand to one that what you so much fear will not happen."

Laura was still speaking, when a femme de chambre announced the valet who had been despatched by the Marquis de Pourrieres. Madame de Neuville broke the seal, bearing a coat of arms, of the packet delivered to her, and, with a trembling hand, opened the envelope; it contained the case, the two bank notes, and among the cards a small note, with the following contents: "I thank providence, which has thrown in my way the case lost by you in the house in which I encountered you; I hope, madame, I shall be permitted to present my homage to you at a more convenient opportunity."

The countess could draw nothing from the servant, whom she questioned herself; he scrupulously obeyed the directions he had received.

The arms which embellished the letter, and the hand which had traced it, were perfectly unknown to Madame de Neuville.

CHAPTER V.

THE DEBUT OF A GREAT CHARACTER.

A MERCHANT de noveautes* and his wife occupied for many years a lovely little house in the Rue des Consuls, at Toulouse.

Success had crowned the constant activity and

* Silks and articles for the toilette.

well known honesty of this merchant, who by degrees had become a negotiant of credit, and had acquired a fortune which increased every day. Father Salvador (such was his name) had long wished for an heir to succeed him; at length providence listened to his prayers, and after a union of ten years, his lively and industrious partner gave birth to a son, whose arrival in this world was celebrated by a fête to which were invited all his friends and neighbours.

One of these homeric repasts, which are only known in the provinces, and occupy several hours, and at which are uncorked the oldest bottles reserved for the greatest occasions, and the remembrance of which is preserved for years, had crowned the fête.

The son of father Salvador, at fourteen, was so tall and well made, that he had the appearance of eighteen years. The young women already remarked the regularity of his features, his handsome blue eyes, and the magnificent fair hair, whose curling locks fell almost upon his shoulders.

Nature had lavished upon the young Salvador her most precious favours; his intelligence kept pace with the charms of his person, and he had obtained at college the most signal success. At fifteen, he passed his examination as a bachelor of letters, and his parents, of whom he was the pride and joy, wished him to become an avocat. "Our son will certainly become a distinguished lawyer, and in these times a distinguished lawyer can hope for any thing," was often the remark, to his affectionate wife, of the good father Salvador, who read the journals of the day, and was not quite so simple as the neighbours supposed him.

The house of father Salvador was large enough to allow some of the chambers to remain unoccupied. The honest merchant, who knew how to turn most things to a profit, had furnished these rooms, which he let occasionally to foreign negotiants, or the officers of the garrison. But father Salvador did not admit indiscriminately any one as a lodger: respecting merchants, he only received those who were recommended by one of his correspondents; and as for the officers, he took care to have those only whose age and rank was some guarantee for their conduct. Upon a single occasion only had he infringed upon his custom: a man, who called himself a negotiant from Marseilles, and whose passports were in addition perfectly correct, presented himself to him without the usual recommendation; father Salvador hesitated to comply with his request, but the man possessed such an honest countenance, and expressed himself with so much politeness, that he could not determine to refuse him.

This man had revisited him several times, and his exemplary conduct, which had been consistent for many years, and the regularity of his habits, had acquired for him the confidence of Salvador and his wife, who often consulted him when engaged in any important affairs.

The stranger, who called himself Duchemin, appeared very fond of the young Salvador, who, in return, welcomed him to his father's house with new pleasure at every visit. He spoke to him often of his studies, made him recount his numerous voyages which he mentioned as having made; and the young man, who longed for an adventurous life, was excited at the recitals, combined with sufficient art to awaken his imagination, without wounding the susceptibility of his parents. The latter, charmed at the opportunity afforded their son of advancing the knowledge he had acquired, transferred to the stranger a slight portion of the attachment they had devoted to their only child. Duchemin, whose commercial business brought him two or three times a-year to Toulouse, found himself at their house at the period their son had chosen to pass his examination as bachelor of letters. Duchemin, who had announced his departure, deferred it, to assist at the triumph of the young man; the latter gained his degree, to the surprise of no one; the joy, however, of his parents was beyond bounds, and Duchemin was invited to take part in the little fête which was given on the occasion.

The next morning, Duchemin announced that he must go to Murret, where he should remain three days; he persuaded the young man to request of his parents the permission to accompany him. Father Salvador could refuse nothing to his son after the signal success he had obtained, and immediately granted the slight favour he solicited; and the next morning, at seven o'clock, a hired carriage came for the travellers.

The weather was superb, and the blue sky, lined with silvery clouds, promised a fine day; every one seemed happy, and yet, on seeing her beloved and only son quit, for the first time, the paternal roof, his mother could not refrain from weeping, for a still and secret voice, which she in vain endeavoured to smother—a presentiment which nothing had given rise to, and which nothing justified—whispered that she would not again behold her dear child; she tried her utmost to chase away the sad thoughts which agitated her mind, and she was on the point of declaring that she could not consent to the separation, when the horse started off at a trot, and the carriage was out of sight.

"May the Almighty and the Holy Virgin protect him!" said the fond mother, as the vehicle which hurried away her son disappeared in the clouds of dust which it stirred up on the road.

Providence did not, however, listen to the prayers of the poor mother; the sun, which was to brighten the day of his return, rose in all its splendor, but the son came not. Weeks, months, years passed away, without the unhappy parents hearing the mention of his name; and at length, broken with grief at the loss of their only joy, they succumbed, after shedding their last and bitter tear.

Duchemin (we shall learn hereafter the real name of this individual) belonged to an honest family of the south of France; he had received a good education, and was endowed with a capacity sufficiently eminent to take an honourable position in society.

His parents died whilst he was still an infant; his guardianship was confided to a man too much of an egotist to comprehend the duties which are imposed by such a trust; this guardian, however, administered the small fortune of his ward with great honesty and zeal, and when the pupil attained his majority, remitted him his account in pounds, shillings, and pence, received the proper discharge, wished the young man every prosperity, and occupied himself no farther about him.

Duchemin found himself in consequence, at twenty, the absolute master of his actions, and the possessor of a considerable sum, which he hastened to dissipate.

The result might have been expected, and it arrived at last.

After some years, during which he allowed himself no time for reflection, Duchemin discovered one morning that his coffers were empty. He must now bid adieu to his pleasures, endeavour to employ his talents, and seek, in constant work, for a fortune, less perhaps than the one he had so quickly dissipated. Duchemin had not the courage to do this.

It was not the calls of an honourable commerce that led Duchemin to visit Toulouse; he went there simply to dispose of, to a Hebrew jeweller, the plate and jewels, the fruits of the depredations of an association of malefactors who infested the wood of Cuges, and of which he was a member.

Wishing to exercise in security his dangerous calling, Duchemin well knew that his first care must be to avoid those suspicions which, right or wrong, generally follow a stranger whose presence in a provincial town does not seem sufficiently accounted for, especially if he has not taken the precaution to lodge himself in a house of good repute. For this purpose he changed a small part of the proceeds counted to him by the jeweller, for merchandise, which he afterwards sold at a loss in a neighbouring town ; and at his first visit to Toulouse, he immediately thought of procuring himself the rooms he desired.

The Jew indicated to him the house of father Salvador, whose honest exterior and urbanity of manners had induced to open his doors to the supposed negotiant.

Duchemin, who was a keen observer of the virtues and vices of mankind, discovered, among the brilliant qualities of the young Salvador, the germ of many vices. This discovery, and the hope it inspired him with, of making a useful accomplice upon whom he might count in all the events of his adventurous life, determined him to lead the young man entirely from his family.

He had not much trouble in gaining the friendship and confidence of the young Salvador, who soon forgot his parents, and launched, with all the ardour of youth, into the midst of those seducing pleasures, which Duchemin, as by magic, conjured up under his very feet.

Salvador, in order to escape the active researches of his family, at first took the name of D'Aymard. It was under this name that he first tried his hand in the way of crime. Arrived, after travelling over a great part of France, in one of the towns of the north, he was received into the house of a young and rich widow, and in whom he inspired a sentiment of affection, if not love ; he robbed her, at the instigation of Duchemin, of a casket of considerable value. The young widow dreamt not for an instant of accusing the man she secretly loved, and his first and successful attempt having hardened him, Salvador forged several notes, by which considerable sums were drawn from the different bankers of France and Belgium.

At length fortune wearied of favouring the enterprises of the young man, he was arrested at the moment of committing a robbery at a rich bourgeois at Valenciennes; but, assisted by his comrades, who, luckier than himself, were not taken, he contrived to escape from the custody of the gendarmes.

Duchemin and Salvador were quickly pursued ; they were known to be the authors of numerous forgeries, which had nearly paralyzed commerce, and the description of the criminals was forwarded to every department of the kingdom. But in order to baffle justice for a time, they quitted France, which they crossed, and embarked at Marseilles in a packet boat on the point of sailing for Italy.

They stood in no want of cash, and arrived at Turin in grand style. Salvador took the name of the Viscount de Lestang, and passed himself off for a young man of noble family, who was travelling with his tutor to complete his education. The best frequented houses were open to the young French gentleman, whom every one, and especially the ladies, admired for his beauty and pleasing manners. Salvador had captivated the good graces of Madame Carmagnola, one of the most distinguished women of the place; this lady, although still very desirable, had, however, attained an age at which a woman might, without compromising herself, show some little interest for an amiable young man. Salvador became one of the most intimate of her small circle. Duchemin, in the quality of tutor, accompanied his pupil every where; he examined the different rooms, took an impression with exactness, false keys were made, and presently the whole city was in consternation at the information of a robbery, which the unexercised talents of the Turinaise police could not divine the means of execution.

Duchemin and Salvador found many of their accomplices at Turin, with whom they had arranged to meet in that city; they formed the project amongst themselves to rob the treasury of the house of Carmagnola. Every thing was prepared for the success of the project; false keys were procured, and, at the time agreed upon, the accomplices assembled near the place of attack; the night was obscure, and, thanks to a heavy rain, the streets were deserted. All the doors of the house of the rich banker Carmagnola were opened with a surprising dexterity, and the burglars arrived without obstacle at the room which contained the chest—the object of attack, and intended to be emptied. It was a coffer in oak-wood, strongly bound with iron, and fastened to the wall with cramps of iron, and secured with three locks, the impression of which Duchemin had not been able to obtain. It was necessary to force them: the bandits endeavoured to do so by using a jemmy and wedges of box-wood; they began to yield under the united efforts of four strong men, who already fancied they had possession of the gold and bank notes, when of a sudden a violent report was heard.

The thieves took to flight. The discharge of the pistol which had caused them such dismay, and had arrested them at the moment the robbery was about to be completed, was not, however, directed against them. Carmagnola, the banker, who was to start the next morning on a journey, had given his pistols to the servant, desiring him to put them in order, and the latter had imprudently discharged them in the garden, which was just beneath the window of the room in which the robbers were at work.

The latter, in making their escape, nearly upset the servant, who, astonished at encountering, in the middle of the night, four individuals in his master's garden, went immediately in pursuit of them; he had nearly reached the hindermost, and his cries would infallibly have drawn others to his assistance; the bandit turned round, planted himself firmly, and dealt him in the breast a blow with a poniard, which stretched him on the ground.

Being rid of the domestic, the robbers, whom nothing intercepted in their flight, escaped from the hotel *Carmagnola*, and dispersed themselves without further trouble.

"You go a good pace, my boy," said Duchemin to Salvador, when the pair found themselves comfortably seated before a cheerful fire in a room of the hotel *de la Bonne Femme*, where they lodged; "you improve mightily; 'tis only rendering you justice; a man wounded, perhaps killed!"

"Must I allow myself to be taken?" replied Salvador; "I would murder ten men sooner than become acquainted with an Italian prison."

"Very well, my dear pupil, you will one day, I hope, surpass your tutor; but what will be the result of all this?"

"Nothing; this servant, if he is not dead, could not recognise any one, as, according to our custom, we were masked."

Duchemin and Salvador were interrupted in their conversation by the entrance of a waiter of the hotel, who announced that a stranger wished to speak to them. Salvador requested that he might be shown into their room.

"Get post horses and start immediately," said the stranger, on being introduced, and who was no other than one of the accomplices of the attempted robbery; "go, if you would not be arrested in a few hours. Public rumour, corroborated by the assertions of the domestic you have wounded, and who pretends to have recognised Monsieur the Viscount de Lestang, openly accuses you."

"But that's impossible," exclaimed Salvador, "we were all masked."

"Your mask might have been deranged, or perhaps you spoke a few words; all that I can tell you is, that you are recognised—that I am certain of what I advance—and, moreover, that the officers of justice are actually at the banker's at this moment. Do now just what you please."

Salvador wished to remain and face the danger, but Duchemin thought it the wisest plan to decamp.

"When you carry butter on your head," he said to his companion, "you must not approach the sun; the butter melts and stains."*

The advice of Duchemin prevailed, and in a few minutes after the conversation just reported, a carriage of the Messieurs Bonnafours started with Salvador and his two companions.

They had scarcely re-entered France when they robbed the receiver-general of the Var, at Draginnan, of a sum amounting to nearly 35,000 francs, under the most singular circumstances, which we shall narrate, in order to give our readers an idea of the audacious character of Salvador and his accomplices.

Salvador, in exchanging his coin for bills drawn upon several receivers-general, and which are discounted with facility every where, had taken the certain impressions which were necessary to his plan. Duchemin, on his part, who, from being the tutor of the Viscount de Lestang, had now become his valet de chambre, had manœuvred so adroitly that he had contrived to make acquaintance with the confidential domestic of the receiver-general.

The servant slept in the room in which the chest was deposited. He was a good and honest man, and Duchemin saw at once that it would be useless to offer him a bribe

To attack him, to place him not perhaps out of the way, but at least beyond the possibility of opposing the success of their plan, Salvador and Duchemin would not have hesitated for a moment; but the domestic, like the faithful dog mentioned by la Fontaine, was of sufficient size and strength to make a valiant defence. Duchemin thought it best, therefore, to approach him in a different shape. A few bottles of wine of Jurançon, offered apropos, loosened the tongue of the retainer, who recounted his whole history to Duchemin.

* An axiom of the Israelitish fraternity of thieves, the sense of which is too clear to require explanation.

This history was that of most others; still it included the announcement of a fact which Duchemin hoped to turn to some account. The valet, in the course of his narration, speaking of an old chateau in his native country, and in which, according to him, ghosts had appeared, Duchemin laughed outright.

"If you had, like me, seen these spirits, you would not be inclined to laugh," said the valet.

"Really!" said Duchemin, who already saw the means of succeeding in the enterprise, and had resumed a serious manner; "you have really seen these spirits?"

"As plain as I see you."

And the valet recounted one of those lengthy and lamentable chronicles, which often consume a whole evening in the narration.

The night had approached, and Duchemin and the valet, who had been comforting themselves in a small public-house in the environs of Dragingnan, bethought them of returning to the city. The day had been warm, and at certain intervals the light of the Will-o'-the-wisp, or *ignis fatuus*, so common in the south, appeared at a short distance from the road. The valet, still under the influence of the tale he had just recited, seemed a prey to the greatest fear.

"I have always thought," he said, seizing the arm of Duchemin, " that those small blue flames were souls in purgatory."

" You might well be right," said Duchemin.

Arrived in town, they separated.

Salvador approved the idea which Duchemin had conceived.

The two comrades, habited in a complete suit of a black penitent, introduced themselves by stealth into the bedroom of the valet, and in which was the chest. Their companion acted as a watch on the outside.

The poor guardian, whose dreams were full of the images which had occupied him all day, having awoke, was seized with so much fear at the sight of two such hideous phantoms standing in front of him, that he had not the strength to utter a single cry. Salvador and Duchemin lost no time; whilst the former opened the chest with the false keys which they had fabricated, the latter threw lycopode powder in the flame of a candle which he held in his hand.

The unfortunate valet, who would have defended himself with courage had he known he was being the victim of a couple of bandits, could not cope with spirits. He lost completely the use of his senses.

Salvador and Duchemin retired without obstacle; but, singular fatality, the morning after the commission of this robbery, the two friends were arrested by an active gendarme, at the moment they were about to mount the diligence.

Brought before the court of assizes at Aix, they were both condemned to ten years of hard labour, and conducted to the prison of Toulon.

When a criminal who, in the course of his career, has distinguished himself by any action of notoriety, arrives at the prison, he has the privilege, which no one thinks of disputing, to choose the best place in the *banc*.* The *brave garçons*† bring him all the minor articles which are necessary to one condemned to labour; they deprive themselves even of their blanket to ameliorate the condition of the new comer.

The galley sergeants, who are also at present the

adjutants, observe towards these men a sort of respect and attention which they do not accord to a criminal who is expiating a crime of small importance.

The entrance of Salvador and Duchemin in the cell No. 3,* was saluted by an unanimous exclamation of delight; the prisoners surrounded them, the wine flowed in abundance, each recounted his history, and, as we might suppose, the greatest criminals obtained the most applause.

Salvador, when Duchemin had recounted his exploits to the dons of the chamber No. 3, received a slight portion of the consideration which had been accorded to his companion; they highly applauded, more especially his courage and presence of mind in the attempted robbery of the banker Carmagnola.

The two friends obtained, on their arrival, every thing necessary to a forçat, and conducted themselves, in a word, as men perfectly resigned to submit to a punishment which they *appeared* to consider as merited; this, however, was not their intention. Duchemin had in his possession a considerable sum of money in bank notes, which he knew how to conceal from observation; and as at a prison, as elsewhere, one can procure whatever is desired, when in a condition to pay for it, he had no trouble in providing himself with one of those cases of tin or ivory, about four inches long by about twelve lines in diameter, which could contain his passports, a saw, and the different mountings, and to which the *profession* has given the name of *bastrigue.*

The youthful appearance of Salvador had interested the commissaire of the prison, who gave him the berth of one of the *sous-payot*.

The places of *payot* and *sous-payot* are the best and most lucrative of all those which are distributed to the criminals, who by their conduct or education show themselves worthy of the favour of the administration. The *payot*, as well as the other *sous-officers* of the galleys, is *deferrè*, (free from restraint,) does no labour, and, in addition, has the permission to walk freely about the interior of the prison.

Duchemin and Salvador had prepared every thing to facilitate their escape, and waited with patience for the favourable moment; when, from some indication which could not escape the sharp eyes of Duchemin, they discovered that their project was half suspected by one of their companions of misfortune.

Duchemin had not obtained the same favours as Salvador; he was chained and put to work. His fellow-workman in chains, who was suffering a condemnation of five years, was a young man of about twenty-three or twenty-five years of age, strongly built; his features, perfectly regular, had a remarkable expression of resolution. We shall mention the cause which had transferred to the prison of Toulon this man, who plays a very conspicious part in the course of this history.

CHAPTER VI.

A SIREN.

THE traveller who, after journeying through the countries of the north and east of France, arrives in one of our cities of the south, might fancy himself transported into a strange land, if the uniform

---

* Dormitory.   † Kind theives.

* This cell is set apart exclusively for the most dangerous criminals.

of the custom-house agents and the gendarmes were not there to remind him that he has not quitted the royal kingdom of France. The people of the south, excited no doubt by the heat of the noon-day sun, which shines so intensely above their heads, admit the different passions with the greatest facility; their imaginations, of an extreme flexibility, wander without cessation for opportunities to present themselves, in which they can find an occupation, if only for a few moments. Let one of the wonders of the age, whether a brave officer, a celebrated artist, or a popular writer, arrive in any town of Languedoc, Provence, or of Guienne; if the *star* has *a name*, the whole population combine in one universal *vivat;* sufficient instruments will not be found in the town to suffice for the serenades; and if the sky is clear, and a hand by chance encounters another which *might* be near it, a simultaneous farandole is executed on the instant at the Place Publique.

It is from the country of the south that we have imported the fashion of presenting to the dramatic artists, those weighty ovations which leave the object under the fear of being buried alive under an avalanche of flowers ; a fashion, by-the-by, which has travelled further than liberty, for at the present time it has already made the tour of the world.

After this slight sketch of the character of our compatriots of the south, our readers will not be astonished when we tell them that the début of a young vocalist, who, to speak in the words of the announcement, *has not yet appeared upon any theatre*, occupied the whole population of the ancient Phocean town. They recounted wonders of the young female; she was, they said, more beautiful than the mother of the loves; her voice would throw into the shade that of Henriette Sontag, the celebrity of the age; she had not as yet had an opportunity of showing the powerful talents she possessed, and they already feared that the capital, which they cursed by anticipation, would interfere to steal away from the town of Marseilles the brightest jewel in its crown.

The day of the début arrived, the whole town congregated in the Rue de la Comédie; the speculators, who since the morning obstructed the avenues of the ticket offices, reaped a rich harvest; they fought at the door of the theatre; more than one of the lions of Marseilles left on the field of battle the most essential part of his attire; there were shoulders dislocated, hats uncrowned, arms and legs broken, and coats and paletots made shorter by a moiety. At length she appeared.

One exclamation broke from all quarters when the curtain rose: "The *débutante!* the *débutante!*" The audience would not listen to the short piece which was to precede the play. They maintained a rigid silence while the orchestra commenced the first notes of the overture to the opera, in which the débutante was to appear. Despite the benevolent expression remarked on the physiognomy of the greater part of the individuals assembled, they would most certainly have expelled from the benches the first who should dare to be visited by a sudden fit of coughing; for it takes but little to raise the bile of the good people of Marseilles. *Braves gens,* wherewithal, if they were not constantly in a passion, and ready to fight when they discuss amongst themselves the affairs either of business or of pleasure.

The debutante appeared at length ; she was a very handsome person, tall and well made, hair as black and glossy as the raven's wing, and her long curls falling over shoulders of a dazzling whiteness, with the face of a perfect oval ; her features, artistically regular, reminded one of those delightful creations left us by the chisel of the ancient sculptors; her blue eyes, half concealed under long and silky eyebrows, seemed to lanch out flashes of lightning.

She sung; the expectation she had created was not disappointed ; her rich and remarkably pure voice reached without effort the most elevated notes ; it was a deluge of pearly cadences, and admirable *furitures* constantly changing succeeded each other with marvellous rapidity.

Violent passions, in general, when the event which is to cause the explosion acts upon a nature easily impressed, spring up in the heart of him who is to be the victim of its effects : thus a young man, whom chance had led to the theatre, had still before his eyes the whole night the image of the enchanting singer.

This young man, whom we shall call Servigny, had realised a sum of about 20,000 francs, which he had deposited with a notary of Paris, who was to forward it to him at Marseilles; and he waited in that town for a vessel sailing to the East Indies, a country he had a great desire to visit, when the appearance of Silvia (the name of our cantatrice) came at once to change the resolution he had taken.

It is not difficult to obtain a presentation to a provincial actress ; obliged to manœuvre a crowd of *little authorities*, she is forced to open her saloons to all those who directly or indirectly exercise over public opinion a certain influence. Servigny, then, could easily approach her whom he had seen but once, but whom he already loved.

Silvia received him with much grace. Actresses (it is as well to remember there is no rule without its exception) extend, in general, great indulgence towards those who seem disposed to bow their heads before the powerful attraction of their charms. Servigny was young, handsome, and his introducer, as much to relieve himself as to serve Servigny, had of his own authority given him the fortune of an Indian nabob ; and, caught by the bait, Silvia employed for his seduction the most ravishing coquetry, and the most provoking glances. She would positively sing to him the prettiest songs in her collection, and when the unfortunate young man had more than half lost his reason, she squeezed his hand, gave him one of her most gracious smiles, and *congéd* him from her saloon a thousand times deeper in love than when introduced to her.

Silvia had much greater experience than her extreme youth would have led us to suppose, and we might admit that she was not at all indisposed to make her charms a means of attracting a fortune. Servigny, whom she supposed much richer than he was in reality, seemed to her a prey she ought not to neglect.

There exist families in which crime seems transmitted from generation to generation, and whose existence is merely to prove the old proverb, which says, " A true bred dog hunts by instinct."

The tavern-keeper of the street de la Tannerie, the hideous Sans Refus, was the natural daughter of a robber named Comtois, broken alive in 1788 in the court of Bicêtre, and of the girl Marianne Lempave, who shortly after was condemned for a theft to several years in prison.

Two bandits of the lowest grade, named Nifflet, and Dubois *the insolent*, claimed the paternity of a little girl to whom her mother, Sans Refus, had given the names of Desiree Celeste Comtois, and whom

No. 4.

LIFE IN PARIS.

SERVIGNY FLOGGING THE OLD FORCAT IN THE PRISON AT MARSEILLES.

we have lately encountered as Prima Donna of the theatre of Marseilles, under the name of Silvia.

The beauty of this girl (to whom for the present we shall still give the name of Silvia) was admired from her birth ; she was especially remarkable for the extreme purity and whiteness of her skin, and her faultless shape.

She was placed to nurse at Crepy, in Valois, where she remained until five years of age; the nurse was proud of having brought up the little girl, whose excellent health and great beauty were the living witnesses of the attention she had given to her nursling.

The revenue which the *honest* industry of Mother Sans Refus procured for her, was amply sufficient to permit her to hope that she might one day retire from business with a handsome fortune.

Mother Sans Refus loved nothing in the world compared to her child, and we have seen her prodigal in the most disinterested kindness and attention to the Countess de Neuville, simply because the features of this lady reminded her of those of her daughter, who had been withdrawn from her under circumstances which we will now relate.

A certain Monsieur de Preval encountered one day at the Tuilleries a young girl, about fifteen or sixteen years of age, and was struck with her extreme beauty; the girl was accompanied by a lady of a respectable age and appearance. De Preval, who on this day had nothing to occupy him, followed the two women to pass away the time. On the terrace, by the waterside, they accosted a man, decorated, who seemed waiting for them; they seated themselves, de Preval did the same, and, protected by the pedestal of the statue, against which were placed the chairs occupied by the three individuals whom he was watching, he could, without being perceived, hear the whole of their conversation. He learned that the decorated man was the father of the young person, and that the latter was being educated at the institution of Saint Denis, in her quality as the daughter of an officer of the Legion of Honour. De Preval was profoundly astonished at what he heard; he was well acquainted with the decorated man, who conversed with the two females he had followed; he knew him to be a widower, and that the only daughter of his marriage had been long since apprenticed to a linen draper at Ramboiullet.

De Preval, who knew where to find his decorated friend when he had occasion, left without further troubling himself; he knew all he wished to know.

The same evening, then, Preval accosted the officer of the Legion of Honour in a saloon privately opened to the amateurs of roulette and *trente et un*, and the following *tête-à-tête* took place:

"Well, Monsieur Fontaine, are you fortune's favourite to-night?"

"I am not displeased with her, my dear Preval," replied Fontaine, raking towards him a certain quantity of gold pieces.

"If you continue at this rate, you will be enabled to bestow a very handsome dowry upon Mademoiselle Fontaine."

"Destiny and the tides are changeable!" replied Fontaine, from whom an announcement of the dreaded *un après*, or *thirty-one*, had just withdrawn a portion of his former winnings; "if my daughter defers her marriage until I give her a dowry, I am afraid she'll be under the necessity of dying a virgin."

"Saint Catharine weaves no crown for those who have such beauty as Mademoiselle Fontaine."

"Catharine Fontaine beautiful!" cried the old officer of the Legion of Honour, greatly astonished. "I am very sorry on her account to be forced to differ from you; but Catharine Fontaine resembles her father;" and he placed himself in the position of a soldier under the inspection of his superior officer.

Fontaine was not handsome, and if what he said was true, the poor Catharine would not be likely to meet with many admirers.

"If your daughter is so plain, as you say she is," added de Preval, "who then is the charming person I heard in the Tuilleries this morning call you her father?"

Fontaine was greatly surprised, so much so that he forgot to mark the card he held in his hand, with the colour which had been just announced as having won.

"Oh! you saw my daughter this morning?" he said, stammering.

"Yes, Monsieur Fontaine, and I have also seen your new wife. I didn't think you would have married again without inviting me to the wedding."

Fontaine burst into a loud laugh.

"Monsieur de Preval," he said, when this excess of hilarity had passed, "I guess your intentions; the little creature you saw this morning pleases you, and you wish to inspire her with an affection for yourself; nothing more easy, my dear Preval; I will, if you promise me to keep the secret, make you acquainted with all that is necessary in order to succeed in your project."

De Preval made all imaginable promises, and Fontaine recounted to him as follows:

"I had requested, at the institution of Saint Denis, for my daughter, a place to which my quality as an officer of the Legion of Honour gave me a right. When they granted this request, I thought my daughter would be much happier if, instead of educating her at Saint Denis, I placed her in a house in such a manner that I might have no further cause for trouble on her account. This determination taken, I knew not what to do with the order of admission which I had obtained for my daughter, when a respectable woman, who wished to give her daughter a genteel education—"

"The one, no doubt, who accompanied the young female this morning."

"No, my dear Preval; the female of this morning is simply one of those attached to the institution. The mother of the young girl in question keeps one of those establishments not mentioned in good society; she lives in la Rue de la Tannerie, No. 31, and the frequenters of her house have surnamed her *Mother Sans Refus*."

"But I know that woman," said de Preval.

"Oh! you know her," added Fontaine, much astonished. "I am very glad of it. This woman then proposed to me to purchase for her daughter the place which was intended for mine; she would absolutely make a fashionable woman of her daughter, whom she never sees from the fear of compromising her. I was in want of money; I accepted, and now the young Desiree Celeste Comtois is brought up at Saint Denis under the name of Catharine Fontaine. You desire after this, no doubt, that I should give you some details of the character of this young female? She is handsome; that you know, as you have seen her; she has plenty of talent; she is an excellent musician; she sings delightfully; these are her virtues: she is deceitful, vindictive, and jealous; these are her defects. If at present you wish to make her your mistress, I shall not oppose it."

"You would not assist me?"

"It is not in my power."

"In that case I will act alone. One more question: have you ever written to Saint Denis?"

"Never."

"In that case it is all for the best, in the best of all possible worlds."

De Preval left Fontaine to his hazardous combinations, and returned home to ripen the plan he had conceived, to render himself master of the young Celeste. The following morning, having finished his best toilette, and procured an elegant carriage and servants, he repaired to Saint Denis, and requested to speak to the directress of the institution.

The possessor of a fashionable turn out, and a gracious exterior, is always well received. De Preval, who thought proper to ornament the button-hole of his surtout with a collection of decorations, was admitted at once into the cabinet of Madame the directress; he informed her that Fontaine had obtained the protection of the general of whom he (de Preval) was the aide-de-camp, and that the general, who wished to present to his wife the daughter of his protégé, had charged him to find at Saint Denis the young Catharine. The rules were opposed to the request he had made; it was, however, consented to; but the directress, who wished to satisfy the great personage in whose name de Preval had presented himself, without failing in respect to him, would not allow Celeste to leave unless accompanied by an instructress.

"So! must I also carry off the old one?" said de Preval to himself, when he saw the respectable matron who was to accompany him.

De Preval handed the two females into the carriage, and placed himself modestly in front of them; and appeared so reserved in his discourse, so full of slight and delicate attentions, that the old lady, who at first had regarded him rather as an enemy whom she must be on her guard with, finished by granting him the most gracious smiles. The carriage having stopped before a magazine of elegant novelties, de Preval said to the instructress that the general had charged him to make some purchases which he intended to present to Catharine, and requested the ladies to descend that he might have the benefit of their taste and advice.

Propose to a woman to visit a shop to examine the rich stuffs and the thousand futilities for their toilette, whether young or old, ugly or pretty, she will not require much pressing. The ladies entered the magazine with de Preval; the shopmen brought to the carriage every thing they took a fancy to; to them it was a complete fête. Preval paid, without bargaining, for all they had chosen. The purchases were stowed away; Celeste, as happy as a bird, had taken her place in the carriage, when a shopman, to whom de Preval had given the word, called the instructress, saying she had left something behind, and drew her to the other end of the warehouse; de Preval placed himself instantly by the side of Celeste, and, at a sign to the coachman, the horses started at a gallop.

"You are not conducting me then to the general you spoke of?" said Celeste, after a few moments' silence.

De Preval stammered out a few excuses.

"You endeavour in vain to deceive me," said Celeste. "If you were taking me to my father, you would not have left my instructress behind; besides, I recognised you directly, it was you who followed me yesterday to the Tuilleries."

"Ah! you recognised me?" said de Preval, whom the few words and decided tone of Celeste singularly astonished.

"Yes; and now instead of taking me to a general who is hardly aware of my existence, you are carrying me perhaps to some distant place, or small house, perhaps; this is just what is practised in the romances I have read in secret."

Celeste commenced laughing in earnest; the surprise of de Preval was so complete that he knew not how to act.

"As for the rest, it's equally the same to me; I fear nothing; and you will act just as I please."

"Ah! that's it, is it?" said de Preval, to himself; "I think I have made a conquest more precious than I expected. Shall I," he said to Celeste, "order the coachman to return with us to Saint Denis?"

"Leave the good man to continue his road, I do not wish to return to Saint Denis. I shall see presently what it will be possible I can do for you."

De Preval conducted Celeste to the rooms he had prepared for her, and having installed her in them, left the house.

"Peste!" said he some days after to Fontaine, who inquired of him if his enterprise had succeeded, "what a galliard this girl is! she has more spirit than many men, and if she had fallen into the hands of my friend de Lussan, she would get on apace if not prevented; but never mind, as she is very handsome, I think it possible to make something of her yet."

Monsieur de Preval, the elegant young man, with the most gracious manners, was not above turning to a profitable account the charms of the woman he had betrayed. You must not be astonished at this, reader. We meet in all classes of society with men of this stamp. The girl on the pavé *let out by* men whose name may be found in *la Pucelle* of Voltaire; the *lorette*, by the man who possesses her heart, but who we must not confound with *Arthur*; the *actrice* lends her money to *unappreciated* artists and unknown journalists; the woman of fashion distributes amongst her protégés places and decorations. Thus goes the world.

De Preval, who supported, though not in ignorance of it, (he was too experienced for that,) the yoke which all who knew Celeste had to submit to, and who wished, besides, to conceal from his friends the precious conquest he had made, took her to the Isles of Hyères.

The young girl allowed herself to be vanquished without the show of a defence; but de Preval was not satisfied with his victory; Celeste had yielded, without hesitation, to a deliberate proposal, because she could not do otherwise. De Preval saw clearly that it was not any love he had inspired, which had induced the fall of his mistress; he then endeavoured, by all the means in his power, to conquer the heart of her whose person he already possessed.

"But you do not love me then?" he said to her one day.

"I do not love you as I could love," replied Celeste; "if you leave me I shall not do you the slightest injury."

De Preval was a thorough gambler; he well understood, even, when necessary, how to *correct fortune;* but he had not, as he hoped, found at the Isles of Hyères an occasion of exercising his talents in that way; his purse being thus almost empty, he ordered Celeste to hold herself in readiness to depart for Paris.

"You wish then to return to Paris?" she said to him; "as you like, my friend, but for me, I remain here."

"You will remain here!"

"Without doubt—am I not at liberty?"

"But what will you do?"

"Don't let that disturb you, I am not at all embarrassed about my person."

"You know not what you say; you will follow me to Paris, I desire it, we will see which of us two will yield."

"That will not be me."

A violent quarrel ensued, and de Preval, who held in his hand a small riding whip, raised his hand and struck Celeste a blow with it.

She moved not a step—spoke not a word—but her brilliant eyes flashed like the lightning; her cheeks became frightfully pale. De Preval found he had gone too far, and attempted some excuse.

"'Tis well!" said Celeste to him; "'tis well; if you go, *I will go with you.*"

A few hours after this scene, de Preval left the circle where he passed his evenings; at the turn of a small street he had to pass in order to arrive at his hotel, he was accosted by a man enveloped in one of the cloaks usually worn by the fishermen of the provinces.

"If you go, *she* will go with you," said the man to him, and without allowing de Preval the time to recognise him, he dealt him a violent blow with a poignard, which laid him on the ground.

The passengers assisted de Preval, and carried him to his hotel; the wound he had received, though dangerous, was not mortal. Celeste was gone. De Preval, who feared above all things to be obliged to put justice in the confidence of his affairs, said nothing which could compromise him, and when recovered, returned to Paris.

We shall know, shortly, the events which from this moment preceded the début of Celeste at the grand theatre of Marseilles, where, under the name of Silvia, we have seen her obtaining the greatest success.

Let us suppose for an instant that several days have elapsed during the time we have taken to recount the preceding occurrences, and we shall hear Servigny, whom we shall find in the boudoir of Silvia, addressing this question to her—

"But you do not love me then?"

Silvia did not reply to Servigny with the same frankness she had used when de Preval had put a similar question to her; she had at the moment at which we are now arrived, a very different object in view.

"If I did not love you would you be here, when I have shut my door to every one?"

"But if you loved me, Silvia, why don't you confide your thoughts to me?"

"But I have really nothing to confide to you," said Silvia, glancing at Servigny with one of her winning smiles.

"You deceive me, Silvia; for some days you have been sad, preoccupied; I intreat you, leave me no longer ignorant of your troubles."

"Since you demand it, I will satisfy you; but remember I forbid you to laugh at me."

"I am listening with the most serious attention."

"It is a very happy life, you fancy, no doubt, that of a comedian to whom the public allows some little talent?" she said after a slight hesitation; "an actrice does every thing she pleases; she can listen to the compliments addressed to her; the most distinguished men hasten round her; it's very agreeable, no doubt; 'tis the happy side of the medal, of which you shall now see the reverse. If, taking time as it flies, we seek in a real affection some distraction to the incessant ennui of our profession, we are despised; if we remain prudent, we are slandered, we are forced, especially in the pro-

vinces, to submit to a thousand little influences; we must receive a crowd of persons who displease us, because they would hiss us at the theatre if we did not admit them to our saloons; but shall we find among our fraternity what we seek for in vain from the public? Oh! believe it not: those of our profession who have less talents than ourselves are jealous of us, those who possess superior ones despise us, and all endeavour to destroy us: the men, by their efforts to render useless our entrées, and the results we depend upon; the women, either in exciting against us those who are their lovers, and those who seek to become such, or by endeavouring to crush us by a luxury to which we cannot attain."

Silvia wept in finishing this little discourse, the conclusion of which Servigny could not imagine; her tears, which appeared sincere, touched the heart of the unhappy lover.

Silvia enjoyed the result she had produced, and saw that she might continue, which she did in these words:

"I have a suite of opals and emeralds of some beauty; I am attached to these ornaments, not on account of their value, which is not considerable, but because they belonged to my poor mother (here a pause and a renewal of the tears). However, at the time of my début, not having sufficient money to purchase the costumes which were indispensable, I confided them to a Jew, who lent me the sum I stood in need of; it was agreed that if I did not return him this sum at a certain time, the suite was to become his property. I hoped to have been in funds by the appointed time; I knew not then, that at the commencement of our career we were to be *farmed* by our directors. This morning the Jew came to me, he will wait no longer, and this evening, if, in the meantime, I do not pay him a pretty round sum, my jewels will be sold."

"Calm yourself, my dear Silvia, calm yourself, I will go and see this Jew, and he really must wait a few days longer."

"He will listen to nothing. I know that the Marquis de Roselli, whom I do not wish to receive, because I love you, Servigny, would buy these jewels to present them to the second cantatrice."

If Servigny had had at his disposition the small fortune that he possessed, he would quickly have dried the tears which bedewed the fair cheeks of the woman he loved; but not wishing to raise hopes in her which probably he might not have been enabled to realise, he left, confining himself to an entreaty to bear with resignation what she could not prevent. Silvia, who had remarked the preoccupation of his mind, and guessed that it related to her, delivered herself of a hearty laugh when left alone.

"'Tis well!" she said to herself, "'tis well! I think that I might, without committing myself, pray heaven that it will favour your success in what you are about to undertake."

The Jew, who acted merely as a confederate with Silvia, for the suite of jewels had only been deposited to bring about the comedy she wished to play, had all the qualities of the children of Israel. He was ugly, dirty, rusé, and a fripon; and every opportunity which presented itself of playing a good turn to a Goi,* whilst also gaining a few crowns, he seized with avidity and joy.

This modern Shylock, who was, besides, the sheet anchor of all the fashionables of Marseilles, inhabited the oldest den, of the dirtiest street, of

* Christian.

the worst quarter of Saint Jean. He received Servigny with a satisfaction which augured a good result to the latter.

"You wish to redeem the jewels of Ma'mselle Silvia," he said, when the young man had informed him of the nature of his visit ; "you are right, my young master ; she is a very pretty woman Ma'mselle Silvia, and loves you much, according to report."

"Ah! they say that?" replied Servigny, inwardly flattered at its being supposed he was in favour with such a handsome woman as Silvia.

"Here is the suite of jewels," added the Jew, placing on a table before which he was sitting a small box of morocco, which he had taken from a drawer ; "and such a set would not remain long in my hands if Ma'mselle Silvia had wished. Monsieur the Marquis de Roselli, a young Italian signor, was disposed to make every sacrifice for her."

He opened the small box ; Servigny thought to himself how much more beautiful Silvia would appear when adorned with the jewels, which reflected all the brilliant hues of the Iris ; he made a step forward, and, his body mechanically obeying his desire, he tendered his hand to receive them. The Jew covered the small box with his two long and bony hands.

"You must count me down 5,000 francs," he said.

"I have not the money," said Servigny, "but——"

The Jew allowed him no time to say more ; he replaced the small box in the drawer. which he closed, and put the key in his pocket.

"You must count me down 5,000 francs," he said again.

"Will you take the trouble of listening to me, sir?" said Servigny. The manners, the look, the voice of the Jew had all changed since Servigny had allowed to escape from his lips those fatal words, "I have not the money !" From being obsequious, they became almost insolent ; he made a sign, however, that he was ready to listen.

Servigny gave him to understand that if he had not at his immediate disposition the sum necessary to satisfy him, he was not entirely unprovided with resources ; he informed him that he possessed a considerable sum, deposited with a notary at Paris, and that he could dispose of this sum.

"I comprehend very well," replied the Jew, "I comprehend ; but as I can, even this very day, receive my money by selling to the Marquis of Roselli this suite, which will be my property this evening, why should I wait at least eight days longer ? If, however, you will offer me security, and a reasonable interest, we might, perhaps, arrange the matter." The Jew had examined with the most serious attention the papers which attested the truth of what Servigny had stated.

"Are you satisfied ? If you will be content with a bill of exchange at fifteen days' sight, for 5,500 francs——"

"You can't mean it ; I can receive my money to-night, and gain more than you offer me by selling the jewels to the Marquis of Roselli."

"Tell me, then, what you require ?"

"Well, then, the papers you show me are quite in order, and attest, it is true, that Monsieur Bernard, notary at Paris, holds in his hands a sum of 20,000 francs, which belong to you, and which he is to remit when you require it ; that is perfectly right. There are your papers ; and I am perfectly satisfied with your word ! You will give me simply a bill of exchange at fifteen days' sight for 7,125 francs ; the capital 5,000 francs ; interest on the capital at five per cent. for six months, 125 francs ;

and a profit of 2,000 francs, which I should make by selling the jewels to the Marquis de Roselli, and which I cannot lose even to oblige you, although I feel a great interest in you."

"Cursed be this infamous usurer !" thought Servigny. "But I cannot do otherwise. I accept your terms," he said.

"You are quite sure to pay me at the expiration ?" continued the Jew.

"Quite sure ! Parbleu ! I shall write this very evening to my notary to send me the necessary sum."

"It might then, perhaps, be indifferent to you to add another name to your own ; that of Monsieur Mathieu Durand, for example"—the Jew named a very creditable merchant of Marseilles—"whose signature you will imitate as well as you can on the note you are to make to my order."

"But it's a forgery you wish me to commit, miserable that you are !" said Servigny, who could not listen to such a strange proposition without feeling somewhat startled.

"You refuse ! Let us say no more about it then ;" and the wily Jew drew from the drawer the small box, and so managed that the rich stones sparkled in the burning rays of the sun, which forced themselves with some difficulty through the enormous bars of iron which defended the narrow window of his den. "But I have often, however, effected similar affairs ; and besides, what you consider as an imprudent action, will not in reality cause wrong or injury to any one. In taking your note I know that it's a forgery ; you are certain to pay it when due ; it will not leave my hands ; we are now at the 25th June, I will return it to you on the 10th July, in exchange for the sum of 7,125 francs. It is also well understood that you will remit me at once 100 francs for the expenses of the act and registering, which will be necessary as a commission, to my profit, on the sum deposited with your notary in case we take any farther step."

Servigny hesitated a long while ; still, in doing what the Jew required, he had no intention of offending against any law of honour or honesty, and he felt quite sure of paying, even before its expiration, the bill of exchange, on which he was to place the name of the merchant Durand. He signed.

Servigny, taking away the suite of emeralds and opals, had hardly left the house, when the Jew hastened to the residence of Silvia, to whom he recounted what had passed. "I know well," he said to her, "that this is the only feather you can pluck from the bird which is taken in your web ; the young man is not so rich as you suppose him ; he possesses at present but about 10,000 francs at the most."

"That might last pretty nearly a month," replied Silvia.

"I think you will do well to leave this young man what remains to him, and occupy yourself with the Marquis de Roselli, whom your obstinacy begins to weary."

"You are wisdom itself, worthy child of Abraham ; I shall perhaps take your advice into consideration."

"Eh ! eh !" said the Jew, inwardly laughing, like Fennimore Cooper's Nathaniel Bumppo, "we could together arrange some excellent affairs, but in that case we must play open-handed."

Silvia glanced at the Jew with a regard so keen that he bent his looks to the ground.

"Which of us two shall deceive the other, honest Josuè ?" she said.

"Really I don't know," replied Josuè, giving vent to the hilarity he could not restrain. "Ah! if you were but a daughter of Jacob!"

"Let us remain as we are. You will no doubt teach me many things worth learning; but I have remarked that masters wish to profit by their pupils, and that does not suit me. I have travelled nearly throughout Europe in the company of a man, with whom, perhaps, I might have remained, if he had been content to take his share and leave me mine. If I find one who is more just and equally capable as the Duke of Modena, we might, perhaps, understand one another."

"The Duke of Modena is a great man," said the Jew; "he has already *planted* me once."

The same evening Servigny, who had in the morning restored the jewels to Silvia, met the Marquis de Roselli in her box. He dared not, however, complain. Silvia, when the marquis had retired, expressed so much gratitude to Servigny for what he had done for her, she appeared so gracious, so delighted, that he feared to do her an injury in suspecting her.

The next morning, the Marquis de Roselli was leaving her house just as Servigny entered; he tried to persuade his mistress that she ought not to receive this man, whose intentions were known throughout the town. Silvia replied to him that she cared but little for the thoughts of such idlers, and commenced laughing; and added that she was delighted to be enabled to withdraw an admirer from her rival, the second chanteuse.

"And so you will receive again this Italian marquis?"

"If it pleases me, my dear; am I not free?"

"No, you are not at liberty to do that which displeases me, and hurts me."

"Ah! tyranny already! I give you notice I do not like those who are jealous."

"You think, then, that you may receive all the handsome fellows in the town, and that I shall not be allowed to oppose it? It shall not be thus, I promise you!"

"Ah! ah! you wish already that I should pay you interest for your money!" and Silvia regarded Servigny with a look of the most insulting contempt.

The young man started under this look as though he had been electrified; a sudden flash which crossed his brain showed him in a moment what were in reality the events which were passing. He left, in order to avoid a storm. Silvia advanced not a step to retain him. Still he only attributed at first to caprice—to one of those fantastic ideas which so often trouble the imagination of women—the conduct of his mistress.

"In paying what I owed to the Jew Josuè, you have rendered me a very great service; be assured then of my gratitude; but you are too well acquainted with the usages of good society, to claim a title for this service. I have loved you, I have proved it to you as much as it has been in my power to do; yesterday I loved you still, to-day I love you no longer; and I write thus, in order to escape the pain of telling you so; visit me no more, you might, perhaps, meet the Marquis de Roselli here."

Silvia signed this letter, which was delivered to Servigny when he returned home. He ought, no doubt, to have considered what had happened to him as a lesson by which he might profit, and occupy himself no more about Silvia. But if we recollect that he was not yet in possession of that experience which is only acquired by time, and especially that he really loved Silvia, we might, perhaps, find his conduct quite natural. His reason, it is true, condemned this woman; but his heart, deeply smitten, endeavoured to excuse her. He could not believe she had acted from her own sentiments; according to him, she had obeyed some strange influence. He would see her again. She would not dare to avow to him that she was the author of so odious a letter as the one he had received. "It is not possible," he thought, "that, so young, so beautiful, she has already attained to such a degree of corruption." Then again reading the letter he had received, he commented upon it with the most scrupulous attention, and this examination strengthened his opinion.

He went immediately to Silvia; the cantatrice received him in her boudoir; she was reclining on a divan, and arrayed simply in a black satin robe, which admirably contrasted with the pure carnation hue of her features. On beholding her so handsome, his first impulse was to throw himself at her feet; he restrained himself, however.

"It is not you, without doubt, Silvia, who has written this letter?" he said to her.

When Servigny addressed this question to her who had been his mistress, he no longer expected a denial; the cold irony which sparkled in the eyes of Silvia, gave him a presentiment of her reply. His expectations were not deceived. She did not, however, reply in a direct manner.

"I did not wish to see you again," she said to him; "I thought you would easily have understood me."

"And so you believe all that is written in this sheet of paper?"

"Without doubt; I loved you—at least I thought so; I love you no longer, that I am sure of. Is there anything in all that which ought to astonish you?"

Servigny had too honest a heart, and too much energy of character, to attempt a reply to words which accused her who uttered them of a barrenness of soul, and a cynisme really inexplicable. He was about quitting the boudoir of Silvia, when the latter, who no doubt had hoped for a scene of despair and weeping, and who seemed to find a pleasure in agitating the poignard in the wound she had caused, said to him—

"'Tis just so, my dearest; go; but make haste, for I expect the Marquis de Roselli."

It was too much; the infernal malice of Silvia merited an exemplary punishment. Servigny struck her in the face, and fled, frightened at the odious action he had been guilty of.

"Look to yourself," said Silvia.

"It seems they all quit you in the same way," said a man, who had concealed himself behind the curtains of the boudoir during the last scene; "must I also murder this one?"

This man wore the costume of the fishermen of the provinces.

"What do you want with me?" exclaimed Silvia, who, despite the audacity of her character, could not help trembling under the revengeful regards of the man before her.

"I came to kill you," replied the fisherman, showing a well polished knife.

Silvia seized a bell rope which was within her reach.

"Fear nothing," said the fisherman to her, "I'll not murder you to-day," and then disappeared by the window with the agility of a wild cat.

Left alone, Silvia wrote a short note which she did not sign, and forwarded it to the substitute of the Procureur de Roi.

The next morning at six o'clock Servigny was arrested at his residence, accused of forgery in a commercial transaction.

He replied with frankness to all the questions put to him; he told under what circumstances he had given to the Jew Josuè the letter of change on which he had placed the signature of the negotiant Mathieu Durand, and which he had afterwards endorsed; but the Jew, who preferred that justice should not be let into the secrets of his trade, deposed that he had discounted the note of hand honestly, believing that it had been signed by the person whose signature it bore.

Servigny, quite sure of being in a condition to pay it in a few days, had no fears as to the result of the fault he had committed; but an event, which he little expected, arrived, which plunged him at once into misery and despair. Instead of the money upon which he reckoned, he received a letter, which announced to him that the notary to whom he had confided his small fortune had taken flight, carrying away with him the funds his clients had trusted him with.

Servigny appeared before the court of assize at Aix; his youth and the candour of his confession interested every one; he was, however, as we have already observed, condemned to five years hard labour without exposition.

Men endowed with a certain amount of energy, frequently retain a calmness even in the excess of their misfortunes. Servigny was one of those men; he faced, without recoiling, the dark and dreary future, which dropt like a curtain before his eyes, and when alone in the cell he occupied in prison, he exclaimed to himself:

"That which pleases the Almighty to ordain will certainly be accomplished; but I will not submit to the punishment to which I have been condemned." Such was his philosophy!

CHAPTER VII.

THE ESCAPE.

As we have before observed, Duchemin, from suspicions which could not escape his keen foresight, had perceived that the project which he meditated was known to his companion in chains; he feared, therefore, that this man might report it, to obtain some favours; he communicated to Salvador his fears on the subject, who equally participated in them.

"There are still means," said Duchemin to him; "this man appears strong and resolute; could we not entirely confide our plans to him, and let him benefit by our means of escape? If he is afterwards in our way we shall know how to get rid of him."

Salvador, much more prudent this time than Duchemin, observed, that he whose indiscretion they feared, after all knew nothing positive, and that it would be much wiser to wait a little. Duchemin listened to this advice.

Several days elapsed without any thing happening which could lead them to suppose they had been betrayed.

An event, however, took place during this time, which not only determined them to inform Servigny of the means they had arranged for their evasion, but which also induced them to wish for his joining them.

An old forçat, whose prodigious strength and ferocity of character had rendered the terror of all the unfortunate inhabitants of the prison, wished, one day, that Servigny and Duchemin should assist him to commit a robbery in the arsenal. Duchemin, who feared, that in case this robbery should be discovered, he would be chained more securely, had no desire to be in the affair; Servigny positively refused to do so, and did not even condescend to give any reason for his refusal. All the rage of the old criminal was turned against the latter.

"Ah! you won't assist me!" he said to him; "very well, you cowardly *fagot*, you shall assist no one then, for I'll murder you"—

And, suiting the action to the word, he threw himself upon Servigny. The latter received him with a firm footing, and, without seeming to employ all his strength, *floored him*; and pressing his throat between his two hands, he forced him to demand pardon.

Men who are disposed to make an abuse of their strength invariably feel a certain respect towards those who appear organised, in a manner, to hold them at defiance. Duchemin, who had seen Servigny vanquish with ease a man whom he himself would not have attacked without a slight portion of fear, although knowing himself endowed with more than usual strength, was subject above all others to this influence.

"Tudieu! what a galliard you are," said he to Servigny.

Then addressing the old forçat, who was still on the ground under the effects of the pressure of Servigny's hands to his throat—

"You did not expect," he said to him, "to receive such an embrace to-day?"

"I'll murder him," replied the latter.

"We'll see about that," continued Servigny, as he quitted the scene of action with Duchemin.

The latter was enabled, before the day finished, to speak a few words with Salvador, to whom he recounted what had taken place.

"I assure you," he said to him, "he's a man who is no coward; and if he remains with us, he could upon occasion give us a helping hand."

"But will he remain with us? That is just what we must find out."

"What can he do on leaving this? He seems to me not overloaded with money; and as, probably, he has not been sent to Toulon for his *good* actions, he will be too happy to find with us the means of procuring some."

"I see that you will not allow to escape this opportunity of procuring a fresh pupil; but since we are now three instead of two, we must arrange a new plan."

"Have you seen Matheo?"

"Not to-day."

"You will not see him, probably, until the day after to-morrow; between this and then I will tell you what we shall require of him."

"Are you quite sure of this man, Duchemin?"

"As sure as I am of myself. He is interested, I give him money; he is a coward. I could make him cut his own throat."

This conversation between Salvador and Duchemin had taken place in an under tone, and so that Servigny, who, from discretion, had remained at the extent of his chain, could hear nothing. When Duchemin rejoined his companion, after quitting Salvador, the criminals entered their respective cells.

After the distribution of the wine, Duchemin and Servigny held the following conversation:

"You have guessed," said Duchemin, "that I intend to make my escape with the *payot* Salvador?"

THE INTRODUCTION.

LIFE IN PARIS.

"Yes," replied Servigny; "but it was by chance alone I learnt your intentions."

"I know it; you might, by denouncing us, have obtained some favours—have been *deferré*,* for example."

"I have not denounced you, because I would not prevent your doing that which I should like to be enabled to do myself."

"For what have you been condemned?"

Servigny, in whom the honest countenance of Duchemin had inspired confidence, recounted to him the whole of his history.

"Ah! you are a *man of letters*,†—there are plenty here, they are all very honest men," said Duchemin, with a certain expression of disdain, which did not escape Servigny.

"Whatever might be your opinion of me," replied the latter, "you can act without fear—I shall not betray you."

"Listen to me," continued Duchemin, after reflecting a few minutes. "We can very well manage the flight between us three. You have courage, resolution; if you like, you shall leave with us; when we are at liberty we'll see if we can come to some understanding."

Servigny, as we have already said, was fully determined not to submit to the punishment to which he had been condemned; he accepted then the proposition made to him, reserving to himself *en petto* the right of quitting his companions, if, as he had every reason to suppose, their company was not agreeable to him.

The forçat who, for any particular reason, desires to enter the hospital of the prison, will attain his end sooner or later; he knows so well how to simulate all the appearances of a serious illness, that the most expert physicians are often deceived.

Servigny, Duchemin, and Salvador were protected by one of the assistant surgeons attached to the hospital, the events of whose past life compelled him to obey Duchemin; (this surgeon was born in the Island of Malta, and named Matheo;) they could easily, then, obtain their admission.

But as they had no wish to compromise their protector, they did everything necessary to avoid the slightest suspicion.

Servigny, who had received from Duchemin the necessary instructions, entered the hospital first, to be treated for the scurvy; it is, of all diseases, that which the criminals can feign the best. Duchemin, who appeared the subject of a devouring fever, followed him; two days after, Salvador, apparently attacked with a complicated hemorrhage, rejoined his two companions.

The criminals who perform the offices of overseers in the hospital, are unchained, and can walk freely about the interior of the prison; they are generally the elders, who have made the prison a sort of adopted country, and who know how to manage with sufficient address to see nothing which the patients, or pretended patients, whom they have to nurse, wish to conceal, although apparently taking note of every thing; so that it is very rare that one of these men reveal to the superiors a project of escape.

They are mostly old foxes, who are up to every ruse of the trade, and who comprehend in half a word, without the necessity of letting them into the secret; they understand, by means of a finesse current every where, how to procure for their patients whatever they wish to improve the somewhat meagre regimen of the hospital; that done, they trouble themselves no further.

* Unchained.   † Forger.

Matheo, who did the service of the ward in which were placed Servigny, Duchemin, and Salvador, took care to regulate the prescriptions, &c., as to create a belief that they were really ill. The sergeants suspected nothing; the guard-slaves had received no orders to be more severe than usual; all went on to their wish, and Duchemin contrived to deliver a letter every day to Matheo, who, on his part, delivered the reply. At length what he had waited for arrived. Matheo informed him that every thing was prepared.

There is at the end of the largest ward in the hospital, and in which were confined our three worthies, a small room which serves as a dead-room. The overseer possessed the key of this room, which was opened merely for a moment to deposit the new guests there. Duchemin contrived to obtain the impression of this key; that accomplished, it was not difficult to manufacture a similar one.

Provided with this key, Servigny, Duchemin, and Salvador were enabled, upon every favourable moment, to enter into the small chamber. Under one of the tables of black marble, destined to receive the corpses, they dug a hole, through which, by means of their sheets twisted into a cord, and fastened one to the other, they descended at the propitious moment into the magazines for sea-stores, which are situated on the ground floor of the building, of which the hospital of the prison occupies the first stage.

When they had all three arrived in safety, Duchemin lighted a small candle, whose feeble light was hardly sufficient to dispel the darkness about them, and with the aid of the instructions he had received from Matheo, he commenced searching for the box which was to contain every thing they required for a complete disguise. He found it in one of the furthest corners of the magazine, and hastened to open it; it contained two complete suits of uniform of the gendarmes, arms and equipments, wigs, cords, and a small crow-bar to force one of the doors of the magazine which opened upon the arsenal.

Salvador and Duchemin equipped themselves in the two uniforms of gendarmes, and Servigny retained his dress as a forçat, to which he added a kind of wallet, strapped on his back; they tied his hands, and at the break of day, when the report of a cannon, which announced the opening of the port, was heard, the door of the magazine nearest the grating of the arsenal was forced.

"Let us now charge our arms," said Duchemin, who had found in the box several cartridges. "We don't know what may happen."

Salvador and Duchemin, in their uniform of gendarmes, and leading Servigny, who had the appearance of a forçat brought from the prison to attend before some court of assize as a witness, favoured by the crowd of workmen hastening to their daily labours in the different yards, passed, without being discovered, the gate of the arsenal.

They were in the city, which they traversed with the greatest rapidity. They then took the route to Beausset. At some distance from Toulon, they entered a path in the middle of a thick wood, in which they intended to repose for a short time; they had hardly arrived, when *three* reports of the cannon, repeated *three* times at equal intervals, announced to the inhabitants of Toulon and its environs that *three forçats* had made their escape, and that a sum of one hundred francs would be the recompense of whoever among them might bring back to the prison either of the fugitives.

"We shall do well," said Duchemin, "to remain in this wood during the day, in order not to pass, till night, through the *bourg* of Beausset."

"But if we should be discovered here by some of these man-hunters," replied Salvador; and he showed to his companions several peasants, armed with old rusty carbines and guns, who were clambering up a hill which overlooked the small copsewood in which they were concealed.

"They would not have the shrewdness to imagine that the uniform of a gendarme concealed the game they are in search of. What we must especially avoid, is the meeting any of our brothers in arms of the brigade of Beausset; the moment we have reached the wood of Cuges we are safe."

When the weather is neither too warm nor too cold, messieurs the gendarmes (if, however, they have nothing better to do) mount their horses towards the evening, and take a survey in the neighbourhood of their residences.

Duchemin, perfectly aware of the habits of these gentry, thought he had nothing to fear, seeing that when he quitted the wood with his two companions, there fell one of those continued rains, which, in the southern countries, appear still more cold and more disagreeable than in other places.

Unfortunately for the fugitives, the brigadier of the gendarmerie of Beausset had been having a dispute with his housekeeper; this had put him in a bad humour, and, as a matter of course, some one must feel the effect of it; he chose, by way of preference, the gendarmes who were under his authority. He ordered them to mount their horses, and led them to commence a patrol.

The fugitives, having left the wood in which they had passed most part of the day, followed, as much as possible, cross roads and out-of-the-way paths; at length, the night having arrived, and finding they were but a quarter of a league from Beausset, they fancied they might regain the high road. They entered upon it, when they encountered the patrol commanded by the brigadier of whom we have just spoken. Their surprise caused them a sudden movement. However, they did not lose countenance, and continued their route, though hastening their pace, after a "*bon jour, camarades,*" pronounced by Duchemin in a tone which evinced not the slightest emotion.

They fancied they had escaped this unlucky rencontre, but they were soon cruelly disappointed. The brigadier immediately recollected the reports of the cannon which had resounded during the day; and as he could not bring to his remembrance any name to apply to the physiognomies of the gendarmes he had encountered, although they ought to belong to the district of Toulon, a crowd of suspicions came across his mind, and which he commenced to clear up.

"Comrades!" he said to the pretended gendarmes, who had already passed him some distance, "comrades, stop a moment, we wish to speak with you."

"Shall we run," demanded Salvador of Duchemin, "or shall we stop?"

"We must continue to walk at the same pace; they will think we have not heard them, and, perhaps, will leave us alone."

"Look!" said Servigny.

Salvador and Duchemin turned their heads; the gendarmes, upon the order of their brigadier, had gathered bridle, and arrived, at a gallop, in such a manner as to cut off the retreat of those whom they suspected, if it became necessary.

"Courage! and fire on the gendarmes, or we shall be taken," exclaimed Salvador. "Leave the brigadier to me." He fired, and the brave old soldier fell, mortally wounded by a ball in his breast; Duchemin had imitated Salvador, and a gendarme had received the same fate as the brigadier.

Servigny having rid himself of the bands, which only secured him in appearance, escaped on one side; Duchemin and Salvador, who, while running, reloaded their arms, and who knew where to rejoin each other if they escaped the dangers which menaced them, had each taken an opposite direction. The two gendarmes exchanged a few rounds of carbine with the two bandits, but one of the former being slightly wounded, and those whom they pursued having taken to the enclosures, in which they could not follow them without abandoning their horses, and leaving the wounded unassisted, they ceased the pursuit, and returned to the high road, to relieve their comrades.

Salvador and Duchemin were thus enabled to arrive at a lonely inn, a short distance beyond Beausset, at which Matheo had deposited for them all that was required for a change of costume.

There are in all the provinces, and especially in the neighbourhood of those towns in which the prisons and houses of correction are situated, inns kept by a host *who has passed the chair*, and ready to do every thing, provided he finds his account in it. The man who kept the one in which Salvador and Duchemin found what had been left for them, was associated with the band, which, at this time, had infested for several years the forest of Cuges, and he rendered it, because he found it to his profit, the most essential services.

Duchemin and Salvador, after a night's repose, continued their route, in good spirits, after an excellent breakfast, provided with a couple of good horses, and suitably attired. They reached the forest of Cuges without meeting with any obstacles.

Duchemin, who was perfectly cognisant of the different rendezvous, since, as we have before mentioned, it was himself who was charged to sell, at Toulouse, and the other towns, the booty of the band, easily discovered those whom he wished to rejoin.

They received him with the greatest friendship; and, for several months, he took a share, as well as Salvador, in the honourable labours of his ancient friends.

The band was composed, in a great measure, of the inhabitants of the country; some, millers; others, cultivators or weavers; those who, like Duchemin and Salvador, were not established in the country, lived sometimes with one, sometimes with another. The chief of the band (which comprised a force of ten men, including the new comers) frequently assembled at his house his subordinates, either to proceed to a division of the booty, or to apprise them of circumstances which interested their safety.

The *aubergiste* of Beausset having apprised him, one day, that a general battue was to take place at the forest of Cuges, by several brigades of gendarmerie, the chief convoked the whole band, in order to impart this news to them. Salvador and Duchemin did not arrive until late at the house of the chief. They knocked, no one replied to them; and yet, the room in which their comrades were to sup appeared lighted. This house had a second door, known only to those in confidence, and which had been made in order to effect an escape into the country, in case of a surprise; this door was open, which strangely surprised Duchemin.

"Let us enter," said Salvador, "something extraordinary has taken place here."

"Let us enter, then," replied Duchemin, after examining if his pistols were in order.

They entered the house, and arrived without interruption in the lighted room.

The chief, his wife, his two daughters, and their seven comrades, were stretched pell-mell on the ground.

"They are dead drunk," said Salvador; and he approached one of them. "Dead!" he exclaimed, examining successively all the rest. "Dead! they are all dead! What is the meaning of all this?"

"The meaning is," replied Duchemin, who had in his turn examined the bodies, "that our friend Matheo has undertaken the work of the executioner."

Salvador and Duchemin could remain no longer in the country. After taking the little money which they had found at the farm, they bade adieu to Provence, and turned their steps towards Paris, where we shall shortly rejoin them.

We shall presently inform the reader what became of Servigny.

CHAPTER VIII.

A TAPIS OF THE GRANDE BOHEME.

THE cafés are, without contradiction, the places in which the numberless varieties of the national manners are observed, in the most unreserved and decided manner. Each of these establishments, putting aside the mass of individuals who have no physiognomy, and who are met with every where, has its frequenters, its manners, and its usages. An Englishman, travelling in France as a gentleman, was forced one day, in consequence of an accident happening to his travelling carriage, to put up at the worst auberge of a poor village of the Pyrennees; an ignoble hostess served him with a miserable dinner, and he was abused by a guest half drunk, as he was mounting his carriage. This Englishman wrote in his memorandum book these words: "They do not know how to provide a decent dinner in France, all the women are ugly and dirty, all the men drunkards and clownish." This Englishman, like many other men easily to be met with, without being obliged to cross the channel which separates us from the United Kingdom, formed his judgment from the label on the sack. Well! conduct this same man, on the same day, to the Café Tortoni, to the Estaminet Hollandais, to the Café de la Regence, and he will tell you seriously, that the Parisian population is composed of speculators, officers on half pay, who dream of the arrival of another Napoleon, and of chess players.

We have at Paris, the Café des Varietés, the general rendezvous of men who make, who sell, or who purchase the vaudevilles, or entire dramas, or halves or quarters of the same property; the Café du Cirque, where you may be sure of meeting, at all hours, minor authors, minor comedians, or second-rate musicians; the Café Desmares, who opens his doors every day to the modern Solons; the Café des Epiciers, that of the comedians, even that of the ——; we cannot print the word, which serves as a title to a romance of Monsieur Paul de Kock.

There exists yet, in that vast pandemonium called Paris, establishments decorated with as much, and even more luxury than those just named, which are situated in the most brilliant quarters of the capital, and which are no less frequented by the great Parisian Bohème; if we had no fear of a process for defamation, nothing would be easier to us than to name these establishments.

The Bohême Parisienne (let us observe in passing that this denomination, like that of lorette, for which we are indebted to the sprightly author of the Nouvelles á la Main, in a recent creation,) is naturally divided into the great and little Bohême; we shall only speak at present of the great Bohême.

A crowd of men exist at Paris, who reside in magnificent apartments, have fine horses, keep opera dancers, but who possess neither rents nor property; these gentry, swindlers, grees,* or chevaliers d'industrie, compose that society (among other societies) to which they have given for some time past the name of grande Bohême. These gentry, however, are looked upon much better in the world than those who content themselves with being openly, and frankly, thieves. We receive in our saloons, we admit to our tables, we salute in the street, such or such an individual, whose profession is perhaps no secret to any one, and who is indebted neither to his labour nor his fortune for the gold which shines through the net-work of his purse; while we curse, despise, or vilify the man who has abstracted from the counter of a shop an object of little value, a small loaf, for example. Is it because the members of the la grande Bohême possess more polished manners, a language more flowery, a costume more elegant than the common martyrs, that we act thus? Certainly not; it is that, egotists that we are, we believe ourselves endowed with sufficient wisdom and foresight to defend our purses against those from whom we have to fear no violence.

The chevalier d'industrie, the grees, the swindlers, whatever may be the name given to the members of la grande Bohême Parisienne, are, we think, more dangerous and more guilty than the other exploiters of society: more dangerous, because they escape nearly always the preventive laws of the country; more culpable, because the major part of them, men endowed with a certain capacity, might obtain by their talents, that which they obtain by fraud and indecency.

Necessity is generally the cause; (if we except some few individuals similar to those whose portraits we shall endeavour to delineate in this work;) it is generally necessity, we say, which leads the hand of the thief to commit his first crime, and often, when this necessity is not beyond control, he corrects himself and returns to an honest life. The Bohêmiens, on the contrary, are mostly young men of good family, who, often madly dissipating a fortune tardily acquired by their fathers, have no disposition to renounce the ease and comforts of a fashionable life, and the habits of luxury which they have contracted. They never amend themselves, for the very simple reason that they can easily, and generally with impunity, exercise their pitiable industry.

Whatever may be the virtues of the Bohêmiens which distinguish the nineteenth century, they do not attain the celebrity of their predecessors. The Cagliostros, Casanovos, the chevaliers of St. George and of la Molière, the counts of St. Germain, and a hundred others whose names we could refer to, have left behind them no worthy successors.

* Gentlemen who well understand how to palm a card or correct fortune.

The Bohêmien who would walk, even at a distance, in the steps of these great men of the corporation, should possess a lively and cultivated imagination, courage beyond all dispute, an unalterable presence of mind, a physiognomy at the same time agreeable and imposing, a person tall and well made.

The Bohêmien who possesses these qualities is but an old woman if he knows not how to make them available. Thus, he must, before appearing on the boards, provide himself with a convenient name; a Bohêmien cannot name himself Pierre Lelong, nor Eustache Lecourt.

His career will fail if he is foolish enough to take the name of a saint. The saints of our days are *used-up*, even to nausea.

Provided with a name, he must, if he is not so already, decide upon a fashionable tailor; his coats, cut in the newest style, must leave the hands of Roolf or of Chevreuil; he will purchase his gloves at Boivin's, his hat with Gausseran, his boots with Clerxs, his cane from Thomasin; he will only use handkerchiefs from Chapron, and will preserve his cigars in a case of Manilla straw.

He will lodge himself in one of the new streets of la Chaussée d'Antin; furniture de *pallissandre*, elegant draperies, bronzes, magnificent glasses, carpets from Sallandrouze, will embellish his apartments.

He will have English horses, his tilbury from the builder *à la mode*.

His servant will be neither too young nor too old; quick, foreseeing, audacious, and fluent, he will understand the proper moment to speak of the property of Monsieur, and of his old and rich parents.

An obsequious porter is the first care of the *Bohêmien de la haute*; his will therefore be flattered, made much of, and moreover generously paid.

The foregoing is but a slight sketch of the general traits which constitute the physiognomy of the Bohêmien de la haute, whatever may be the means he employs to procure the cash necessary to keep up the luxury with which he is surrounded, and to pay for the pleasures which are only purchased for ready money.

The Bohêmiens have no particular age, there are among them very young men, middle aged men, and old men with white hair; many have been dupes before they became knaves, and these are the most dangerous, and the most difficult to recognise, for they have preserved the manners and language of men of the world. As to the others, whatever may be the titles they assume, and despite the costume and the decorations they bedeck themselves with, there is always in their manners, in their habits, something which recalls the famous Baron de Wormspire; sometimes dangerous remarks will slide into their discourse, and often, although keeping on the defensive, they will make use of expressions which have not been borrowed from the vocabulary of good society. For the rest, if the diagnostics requisite to recognise them are not so ready at hand as those which more properly belong to the different categories of thieves, they are not the less visible, and it will be very easy to perceive them if we well observe these men.

There are many old officers in the *grand Bohême*, only that he who, under the colours, was but a sous-officer, calls himself captain; the captain is, at least, a colonel; the colonel is always a general of a division—he would be marshal of France if the government had rendered him justice.

It would be a hopeless enterprise to attempt to unveil all the ruses, or simply try a sketch of the principal traits of the physiognomy of the Bohêmiens of different ranks and classes; for then we should speak—

Of the *journalists* who exploite the dramatic authors, to whom they accord or refuse talents in proportion to the number of their subscriptions; of those who threaten if you do not remit them a certain sum, to include in their paper a notice *biographical* of yourself, your father, your mother, or your sister; or who offer you at a reasonable price a funeral oration of one of your great relations who has just rendered up his spirit. Bohêmiens!

Of the *pamphleteers*, who have *flous-flous* for every baptism. Bohêmien!

Of the *poet*, who has a dithyramd for every birth, and an elegy for every death. Bohêmiens!

Of the *chanteurs*,* by trade or occasionally, who sell their silence or their evidence; the honour of the woman they have seduced; a letter fallen by chance into their hands, and of a thousand others besides. Bohêmien!

Of the man who, when he disposes himself to play, first chooses the highest chair in order to overlook his adversary; who invariably places the cards as near as possible to the person against whom he is opposed, to cut them, that he may not observe the shuffle he has made, and who withdraws the cards with such a marvellous address. Bohêmiens!

Of those directors of companies, in partnership or by shares, whose coffer, like that of Robert Macaire, is always open to receive the funds of fresh shareholders, and always closed when requisite to pay the dividends become due. Bohêmiens!

Of those directors of agencies of dark affairs; of marriages, of places, or of interment—yes, of interment! you must not be astonished at it—Bohêmiens, or rather, swindlers; but swindlers musked, gloved, spurred, decorated, titled in every sense; to whom the procureur du Roi gives his hand, and who are saluted by the commissaire of police.

In one of the passages opening on the Boulevard, in the centre of one of the richest and most brilliant quarters of the good city of Paris, close to a theatre where the characters of noble fathers, of young lovers, and great coquettes, are filled by babes of eight or ten years of age, is an establishment in which, at all hours of the day and evening, we may be certain to meet some of the members of *la grande Bohême* Parisienne. This establishment, situated in the most obscure part of the passage in question, escapes the observation of the passengers. The honest man, who by chance enters it to take his half cup or can of beer, finds himself misplaced; he is constrained, without knowing why. He takes for diplomatists all these gentlemen so superbly dressed; the red ribands which sport at their button-holes dazzle him, and when he retires, he is ready to demand pardon of the lady at the bar for so great a liberty.

The establishment of which we are speaking, resembles in nothing that of the street de la Tannerie. Elegant tables, with slabs of white marble, are substituted for those covered with oil cloth; divans take the place of old stools; the counter is resplendent with gilding; and behind, on a seat which much resembles a throne, proudly sits a young and pretty woman. The master of the

---

* Thieves who levy contributions by threatening publicity to any wrongful act

café has no resemblance to the ordinary limonadier. He does not wear the white waistcoat and the muslin cravat which his fraternity seem to have adopted. He has never under his arm the indispensable serviette; his manner, the movements of his person, his grey moustaches, cut and brushed, give him the appearance rather of an ex-officer of heavy cavalry. He shakes hands with those of his guests whose purses seem for the moment well garnished; his voice is short, rude even, when he addresses those who may be momentarily out of luck. The sale of cans of beer, half glasses and glasses of absinthe, is the least branch of the commerce of this limonadier. If a young man of family, disposed to eat his white bread first, is led into this wasp's nest, he is flattered, fawned upon, fêted in every way. Monsieur will recount to him the campaigns he has never made; madame, who forgets not that she was once pretty, will bestow upon him her most gracious smiles. If the young man is in want of cash, "Eh! Monsieur! Monsieur," they will say to him, "why didn't you speak before? I would have lent you, without interest, the sum you wanted; but address yourself to such or such a one; if you like, I will introduce you to him;" and the young man is surrounded on all sides; he is left no time for reflection; he subscribes at length letters of change to the usurer, who gives him in return a small sum of money and a collection of less than doubtful pictures; the limonadier divides the profit, and the young man is despoiled of the remainder by the fraternity.

Monsieur —— is a first-rate hand at billiards; Monsieur —— plays exceedingly well at ecarté, and he has always at his disposition partners who are ready to serve him in all ways, provided they have their share of the pie; thus he is always ready to play the stake that is desired.

Monsieur —— advances money to those of his frequenters who have need of it to complete an *affair*, and shares with them the profits; he gives, or procures to be given, on their account, valuable information by means of cash, &c.; in fact, he has several strings to his bow, and his strings are constantly strung.

It was a little past six in the evening; the waiters lighted the gas in the establishment in question, and the guests were retiring to take their dinners. There only remained in the room those who were interested in a game at cards between the proprietor of the house and a handsome young man, and two strangers, engaged at a table near to that occupied by the players, who followed, with great attention and interest, the different phases of the game.

The presence of the two men seemed to annoy the players, who would probably have manifested the discontent they felt if the resolute mien and free-and-easy manners of these intruders had not imposed upon them a certain restraint.

"We are in a reunion of swindlers," said the eldest of the two in an under tone to his companion, "and the youngest of the players is a pigeon, whom the others are in train to pluck."

"It appears just so to me."

"There is not a doubt that little fellow, whom they call de Preval, makes *le sort** to him who holds the cards."

The game was finished; the young man had lost; in order to pay his adversary he drew out his note case, filled with bank notes.

"The dupe has the *sac*,"* said the youngest of the two strangers; "if we could do him, the contents would put us afloat."

"Let me act, and all will go well," replied the other. He then approached the limonadier with grey moustaches, and spoke a few words in his ear; the latter then looked at him in an angry manner.

"'Tis just so," said the stranger to him in an under tone, without appearing much affected at his menacing looks, "'tis just so; the same game again, but should it be the last, I will not allow a compatriot to be pillaged before my very eyes."

"Perhaps Monsieur would like to pluck him himself?" said de Preval, who had heard the few words we have just reported.

"Very likely, my young master!" replied Duchemin—our readers, no doubt, have already recognised him and his companion, Salvador—"does that displease you?"

De Preval took no notice of this indirect provocation, and the young man having lost the game with the same indifference as the former one, the combat finished for want of combatants.

Some moments after, the young man, Salvador, and Duchemin were nearly alone in the café.

"I think," said the latter, "that we are countrymen."

"We are, at least, from the same province," graciously replied the young man; "I am from the village of Pourrières in Provence."

"And I am from Tretz, less than two leagues from you; but perhaps you know my family; my name is Roman."

Salvador touched his friend by the elbow.

"What imprudence!" he said to him.

"Leave me alone," replied Roman; "my real name is no more compromised than my supposed one."

"I left the country very young," replied the young man; "but still I think I recollect a notary of that name, who lived at Pourrières."

"He was my uncle and my tutor."

Roman spoke the truth.

"My name is de Courtivon," said the young man in his turn, who could not, without being wanting in politeness, longer conceal his name from his compatriot.

"This youngster conceals his real name," said Roman to his friend. "No one at Pourrières bears the name of de Courtivon."

"Let him call himself Pierre, Paul, or Jean," replied Salvador, "our business is to get possession of his pocket-book."

"All things come to an end for those who have the patience to wait," continued Roman, who continued his conversation with the young man calling himself de Courtivon. He spoke to him of the beautiful landscapes of their country, of its blue sky, of the pretty girls of Arles, and the handsome men of Tarascon. Salvador took part in the conversation. De Courtivon, delighted at meeting such charming countrymen, requested their company at dinner. Salvador and Roman made some formal excuses, but de Courtivon having renewed his invitation, they followed him to the Café Anglais.

De Courtivon treated them handsomely. The most succulent dishes and the most generous wines were served to the convives, and at the dessert the greatest harmony reigned between these three personages. Salvador and Roman, who wished to procure the confidence of their Amphytrite, had

---

* A signal made by an accomplice to him who holds the cards, by which he indicates the play of the adversary.

* Plenty of money.

each recounted a history, a mere invention of the moment. De Courtivon, not liking to be less communicative than his new friends, commenced a recital in his turn.

CHAPTER IX.

THE MARQUIS DE POURRIERES.

"My name is Alexis de Pourrieres," said the young man.

"I had guessed that de Courtivon was not your name," said Roman.

"'Tis from habit I call myself so, as I have borne it for a long while; I have now, alas! no longer any reasons for concealing that of my family. Pourrieres, you know as well as I do, is a pretty considerable village in the department of the Var, between Brignoles and Saint Maximin. You may observe in the environs of this village the ruins of a monument raised, by Marius, to perpetuate the remembrance of the great victory which he gained over more than three hundred thousand barbarians, who came from the black forests of Germany to undertake the conquest of Spain; and the old chateau of the ancient lords of the village. The reparations which have been requisite to this ancient residence, has considerably altered its appearance of former times; the moats have been filled up, the drawbridge has been replaced by a grating, which is surmounted by the arms of the family, and recalls the reign of Louis the XV.; windows usurp the place of loop-holes; the old family portraits, the trophies which adorned the salle d'armes, which is at present a vast antichamber, were all dispersed during the time of the revolution; still, such as it is at present, the chateau de Pourrieres is not unworthy the attention of the tourist; we may still admire the graceful turrets which flank the heavy towers; the light columns, the chiselled architecture, and the magnificent stained windows of the chapel of the old feudal manor.

"This old chateau, escaped by miracle from the demolishing hammer of the black band, was restored to my family, with such property belonging to it as had not been sold during the first revolution, at the time of the return of the first emigrants into France. Although he had lost the greatest part of his fortune, my father, the Marquis de Pourrieres, was still in possession of a revenue of 80,000 francs when I was brought into the world. This fortune was more than sufficient to allow him to hold a distinguished rank at court, and the services he had rendered to the princes of the elder branch during the emigration, gave him a right to solicit an honourable employment. My father was one of those gentlemen whom their princes meet on the field of battle, but look for in vain among the crowd of their courtiers, when days of sunshine have replaced those of the storm. He made a journey, however, to Paris, in 1816, but his manners were, perhaps, a little abrupt; he knew not how to round his discourse with elegant periods; in a word, he made but a sorry figure amidst the courtisans of the modern œil-de-bœuf. He returned home without obtaining the service he had requested, and determined, without feeling any disappointment, to lead the life of a country gentleman.

"My father had confided the care of my education to a secular priest, who had been recommended to him by one of his brothers-in-arms of the army of Condè; he was an excellent man; his manners were pure, and he had acquired a vast erudition; in a word, he possessed every quality except the very one necessary to a tutor. He knew nothing of the world except from his books; his timidity of character was such that he had not the courage to reprimand me, or to inflict the punishment which I too often deserved; and the fear which my father inspired in him was such that he could not resolve to ask his intervention.

"Children, like all feeble beings, are generally disposed to make an abuse of the indulgence allowed them. As you may well suppose, I heeded but little the exhortations and reprimands of my worthy preceptor, whose weakness I was aware of; instead of studying, I passed the whole day with my young companions in wandering over the vast dependencies of the chateau. Thus, at the age of twelve years, if I was as strong as it is possible to be at that age, and endowed with the best of health, I was in return the most ignorant young rogue you could meet with. I knew how to read. I could write a little, I had retained some bits of Latin: this was all. My father, who better understood how to wield a sword than a pen, and had a greater veneration for *la curne de Saint Palaye, le miroir du vrai gentilhomme Français*, and *le parfait ecuyer*, than the *de viris illustribus*, having remarked that I improved in all the exercises of the body, had often congratulated my preceptor, who, I well believe it, was in the end persuaded that, thanks to his good counsels, I was become a very distinguished young gentleman.

"I was a little more than eighteen years of age, when my father and my professor, (my mother died a few years after my birth,) persuaded that it required some travelling to make an accomplished gentleman, resolved that I should visit the principal countries of Europe. My father would willingly have become my travelling companion, but the fatigues he had undergone during the emigration, had rendered him a valetudinarian, and the wounds he had received, chained him to the hearth of his patrimony. It was thus decided between my father and preceptor, that the latter should continue with me his functions of a mentor; a mentor very incapable, alas! and who had formed but a poor Telemachus.

"When my father, having called me into his cabinet, informed me of the decision which had been resolved upon, I felt at first, I must confess, a strong sentiment of delight; I was overjoyed to quit for some time the old chateau of my ancestors, which I knew by heart; the woods I had ranged in every direction, the hills I had so often climbed. The dreams of my young imagination were at length to be realised; I was about to visit countries, which, as I supposed, contained more marvels than those visited by Sindbad the Sailor. I should, in fact, see the world!

"Still, however great the delight I felt, when my father, having for a while pressed me in his arms, at length said 'Adieu.' I found my eyes filling with tears; I could not resolve to quit him. Was it an inward voice which I heard, but could not comprehend, which told me that I should not again behold him?

"Before commencing my tour in Europe, I was to reside for some months at Marseilles, with some relations of my mother, who were to guide my first steps in the world. These kind relations received me with a welcome; and the friendship they had formed for me, having, no doubt, blinded them to my faults, they were good enough to find me charm-

No. 6.

LIFE IN PARIS.

THE MURDER.

ing, at the same time agreeing that the voyages I was about to undertake would greatly improve me.

"My mother belonged to an ancient parliamentary family, of which all the members had preserved the severe morals, and cold and austere manners, of the ancient counsellors of the parliament of Provence. My great-uncle and my uncle, the sole relations who remained to me, (I do not reckon a crowd of cousins, of both sexes, of different degrees, whom I hardly had a glimpse of,) loved me much, no doubt; they inspired in me a great respect, but I was not pleased to be with them; I felt a chillness in their saloon; when I saw them walk or speak with a composed gravity, I figured to myself two family portraits, to whom the wand of a fairy had given life.

"I did not find, then, among these relations, the distraction in harmony with my age, and the manner in which I had been brought up.

"Continual movement was my ruling pleasure; I had a thirst for viewing sights which were not be found with them; I searched abroad, therefore, for the distractions I needed.

"When my preceptor attempted a remonstrance, I told him, with much indifference, that I only did as others of my age and station; that he ought not to show himself more severe than my father would be on similar occasions; that I knew well enough what was due to the dignity of my name, not to compromise it; that, in fact, I was old enough to do without a mentor. The honest man made no reply; he dreaded, above all, these discussions, and in order to have no more with me, allowed me a *carte blanche*. Behold me, then, at eighteen years of age, almost absolute master of my actions! (my uncles, who depended on my preceptor, occupied themselves no further about me, than to give me advice, to which I listened with all the appearance of the most profound veneration).

"Willing to profit by this delicious liberty, I began by frequenting the theatres and cafés. I joined the company of all the young patrons of these scenes of amusement. My name, highly esteemed throughout Provence, the fortune I should one day possess, gave me a certain authority over my young companions of pleasure, who formed round me a sort of little court, always ready to flatter me. I attended all the parties, all the fêtes; and as I did not show myself too severe in the choice of my companions, they generally voted me a very good fellow. I believe I have already told you that I was very expert in all the exercises of the body; that which I had the greatest predilection for, was fencing. My companions spoke to me incessantly of a master, named Louiset, called *Belle-Pointe*, whose room was frequented by all the rich and idle young men of the town, and who was looked upon as having great skill. I had no sooner manifested a desire to know him, than my friends introduced me there at once.

"Louiset Belle-Pointe was a master-of-arms in every sense; he spoke of nothing but tierces, quarters, and thrusts. He was a boaster, and loved his glass, which did not prevent his being as cunning as a monkey; and also passionately fond of money, (he only drank the wine he did not pay for,) and considered honest any means which procured it for him. Louiset received heartily the young Count de Pourrieres; he taught me all the finesse of his art, and, in a very few weeks, I became the most assiduous messmate, and the most intimate friend of the master-of-arms.

"It was not, I assure you, either my passion for fencing, or the pleasure of listening to the some-what loose discourse of the maitre d'armes, which attracted me to his house.

"I had remarked his daughter, and became desperately in love with her.

"Mademoiselle Jazetta Louiset was really a very pretty girl; she had one of those lively and striking physiognomies which fascinate at the first coup d'œil; a most seducing pair of beautiful black eyes, and hair of the same colour; her feet and hands were all of a size, quite aristocratic; she was, in fact, the most delicious creature I could imagine; gay, lively, always ready to sing the prettiest airs of our cheerful Provence, and scarcely seventeen.

"Jazetta had been brought up by a sister of her mother, as ugly and ungraceful an aunt as her niece was amiable and pretty; this woman was an Italian; the friends of Louiset said, but in a whisper, that she had exercised, at Genoa, her native country, a most ignoble trade, and that it was to evade the pursuits of justice that she had taken refuge in Marseilles. Whether a slander or not it is quite certain this woman was one of the most immoral of creatures. She had inculcated in her niece the most detestable principles; thanks to these lessons, Jazetta was as great a rouée at seventeen, as a woman at thirty who has seen much. What I now tell you, I did not know till afterwards; I viewed the things of life, at this time, through the glass which we hold before us when we are twenty years of age. I loved Jazetta as we love but once in our life. I loved her poor, I would have loved her rich; I believed her like myself; and really it was difficult to believe that such deceitful promises could leave a mouth so fresh and so rosy, or that there was nothing in that young breast but an old dry sponge in the place of a heart.

"Louiset, his daughter, and the old Genoese *farmed* me in concert; Jazetta wished that a superb toilette should add new charms to those she already possessed; she wished, she said, to be always handsome, so that she might always please me. I considered this quite natural, and gave her the option of choosing, amidst the richest tissues and most elegant bijoux, the articles of her dress. I lent money to Louiset, whose good graces I wished to preserve; and the aunt, who favoured my intentions with her niece, and who appeared to me a very worthy woman, discovered every day a fresh means of emptying my pockets.

"My unfortunate purse, from the force of pressure, became consumptive; I had borrowed of my new friends all they would lend me; my preceptor, who had no money, dared not request it of my father; it was in fact difficult enough to justify to him the total dissipation of a pretty considerable sum he had given us on our quitting Pourrieres. Jazetta, who had for several days requested of me an object of some value, which I had not been enabled to give her, turned sulky; Louiset, from whom they had claimed (at least he told me so) the payment of a note, abused me; the aunt had scruples. I was in despair.

"One morning, at the end of a slight altercation with Jazetta, I was more moody than usual. Louiset, who appeared as if he had drank a few glasses of wine too many, approached me. 'Don't be so dispirited,' he said, 'we must well submit to what we cannot prevent; do as I do, on the first day I am to be thrown into prison.'

"'My poor Louiset,' I said in turn to the maitre d'armes, who had given me a home thrust, and without leaving him time to finish his sentence, 'if I was master of my fortune you should not go to prison.'

"'I know it well, I know it well,' replied Louiset, 'but if the cause of your being so sad is that you have no money, why don't you endeavour to procure some?'

"'What means would you have me employ? Demand it of my father? he would not give it me. I have borrowed of all my friends.'

"'If I was the Count de Pourrières, I would place my signature at the bottom of a sheet of printed paper, and would go and find out Josuè, who would oblige me with an infinite deal of pleasure.'

"'Do you really think that this Jew—'

"'Josuè's trade is to oblige young men who find themselves momentarily in difficulties.'

"The words of Louiset were not dropped into the ears of a deaf man. The very same day he introduced me to the Jew Josuè, who readily lent me a pretty round sum, at a reasonable interest of *five per cent. per month!*

"When I had possession of this sum, Jazetta's good temper returned; Louiset, whose real or pretended debts I also paid, taught me an extra thrust, as yet unknown to any one; the aunt had no longer any scruples. Every thing went on well for some time. When my purse was again empty, the countenances became again cloudy. I made a fresh visit to the Jew.

"As you may well think, quite a prey to the love I felt, I neglected entirely my relations. I was oftener in the salle d'armes of Louiset than in the saloons of my uncles. They questioned my preceptor, who knew not how to reply, for the very reason that he knew nothing. They remonstrated, and I promised, for the sake of peace, to do every thing they required of me.

"The likeliest means of inducing me to forget Jazetta, was to persuade me to quit Marseilles. It was the one they adopted; but when the moment arrived to commence my voyages in Europe, I positively refused to go. My uncles had no expectation of the slightest resistance; they flew into a passion; I left them to take their walks, and having no further occasion for concealment, I gave myself up, without scruples, to every amusement. The friends of Louiset became my most intimate ones, I was seen every where with them, in the café, at the theatre, at the promenade; my connection with Jazetta was become a public scandal. Every respectable person was disgusted at meeting at the same time, the lover, the daughter, and the father. A similar state of things could not endure for any length of time. My father, who had been apprised of it, and who was chained to his bed by a severe illness, requested an order to incarcerate me for some time in a house of correction. This order would, no doubt, have been executed; but Josuè, who had been informed, I don't know how, of what was projected against me, gave me timely warning, and furnished me with the means of passing into Italy.

"Louiset, to whom I counted down a good round sum, was perfectly satisfied to allow me to take Jazetta, from whom I could hear of no separation. It is true he made me promise to bring her back, and marry her, as soon as my father should depart this life.

"Jazetta, who was not sorry to be at liberty, followed me with pleasure. I had no lack of money; and we visited, successively, Italy and Switzerland.

"We travelled for nearly two years, resting just where it suited us, and again taking up our route when ennui began to show itself; at length, Jazetta informed me that she was *enceinte*.

"This news caused me sincere delight. I was so devotedly attached to my mistress that, if I had not been aware of the inflexible character of my father, I should have hastened to throw myself at his feet and request his consent to my espousing her at once.

"When Jazetta announced to me that she was *enceinte*, we were at Bâle, in Switzerland; we journeyed a few months after. When she was near her time, we arrested our steps at Geneva, where her accouchement took place, and she was happily delivered of a boy, whom I acknowledged, and to whom I gave the name of Fortunè.

"I confided this infant to a worthy woman recommended to me by persons in whom I placed confidence. This woman undertook to bring him up with the greatest care, and to place him at school as soon as he attained the age of four years.

"Since this period I have not ceased to occupy myself about my son, who is now fifteen years of age, and the person to whom I have confided his education, informs me at the end of the year of all that concerns him.

"Josuè knew better than any one the extent of the fortune which would revert to me at the death of my father, so that he furnished me abundantly with the needful; but having gained experience with age, I had established my transactions with him on a different basis; I no longer borrowed, even at the rate of one per cent. per month; it was agreed between us, that he should furnish me with 12,000 francs a year, and that I should engage to repay him 15,000, and, that he should be reimbursed immediately after the death of my father.

"During the illness which followed the confinement of Jazetta, I had become acquainted with a young Englishman who resided in the same hotel; this man seduced my mistress, whom he carried away, I believe to Calcutta or Madras.

"We love sincerely but once in our lives, you know, and when 'tis at twenty years of age that we meet with the woman who is to inspire us with that sentiment, the remembrance of which is to last for ever, the deceptions which follow every event of life must appear much more cruel. No doubt, when I learnt the flight of Jazetta, I should have consoled myself with the knowledge that her conduct had rendered her unworthy of the love I still retained for her, and should have endeavoured to forget her; but do we always act as we ought to do? I must confess, I had but one regret, that of having lost her, and at the moment I am now speaking to you, I think, that if she were present, and asked my forgiveness, I should forget every thing that had passed.

"I do not know," said de Pourrières, at this moment interrupting the recital he was giving to Salvador and Roman, "if I ought to recount to you the events of my life up to the present moment."

"And why should you stop on such a good road?" replied Roman, accompanying his words with a provincial oath, which caused the count to smile; "your history interests us greatly; does it not Salvador?"

Salvador gave a sign of assent.

"I am afraid that what remains of my recital will lower me in the estimation which you are naturally disposed to accord to a countryman."

"Fear nothing," said Salvador, "we are indulgent."

"And we drink to your health, Monsieur le Comte," added Roman.

"The trouble I was in at being abandoned by Jazetta, brought on a severe illness, which lasted several months; for some time I was within an inch of the grave, but death I should have welcomed as a friend; at length youth proved stronger than disease, and I recovered my health.

"As some distraction to my sorrow, I visited the baths at Baden, and became acquainted at that town with a man who called himself the Duke of Modena."

"I know this man," exclaimed Roman, "his real name is Ronquetti."

"You are right," said de Pourrieres.

"The Duke of Modena possessed among other talents, that of rendering fortune favourable; after winning from me all the ready money I had, he thought he could not better prove his friendship towards me than by teaching me his means of success.

"He had no reason to complain of his pupil, who, after a few lessons, found himself equal to a contest with his master; but I hesitated to make the slightest use of the knowledge I possessed, and I mentioned this to the Duke of Modena.

"'Leave it to itself,' he replied to me, 'if ever you are on the point of being vanquished, you will not allow yourself to be thrown on the ground without using the arms in your possession;' and Ronquetti was right."

"But," said Roman, interrupting de Pourrieres, "you were allowing yourself to be plucked just now, head and tail, by that limonadier with the grey moustaches."

"I wanted to give him courage to stake a heavy sum against me, in order that I might punish him by the same means he has used to pillage others."

"I see, now, that I disarranged totally your intentions."

"Be assured, my dear countryman, that I appreciate your reason for having so acted.

"Fifteen years had elapsed since I had quitted the chateau de Pourrieres, and I had not, upon any occasion, written to my father. Ronquetti, who had long been my travelling companion, had just left me. Tired of the dissolute life I was leading, I thought of writing to my father to solicit from his indulgence the pardon of my faults and an oblivion of the past, when I received at Brussels, where I had resided for some time, a letter from Josuè, to inform me that he was dead, and that I must absolutely return, to be placed in possession of the inheritance to which I had succeeded. The Jew forwarded me 20,000 francs for my journey, and to make an honourable appearance on arriving in my own country. He also informed me that the cholera had carried off my two uncles, and that I was the last and only branch of the ancient family of de Pourrieres.

"I immediately quitted Brussels, and rested at Paris; I intended to have stayed some months in this city, which I had not then seen, before retiring from the world. I have been at Paris less than two months, and in a few days I shall quit this city without feeling the least regret. If ever you return to Tretz, rest a moment at the chateau de Pourrieres in your way; you will find me leading the life of a country gentleman, and occupying myself in the education of my son, whom I shall send for to be with me, and who will, I hope, be happier and wiser than his father.

"I am tired of running about the world; I have visited England, Switzerland, Italy, Holland, Spain, and Portugal, and I have observed every where the same vices and the same misfortune. To the misty atmosphere of old England, with its ships, its docks, and its tunnels, to the glaciers of Switzer-land, to the boasted hospitality and rustic virtues of the Helvetique peasants, to the lazzaroni of Naples, the marble palaces of Florence, to the gondolas and baracolles of Venice, to the brigands of Rome and the marvels of the Eternal City, to the canals and tulips of Holland, to the revolutions of Spain and the oranges of Portugal,—to all and each of these I prefer at this moment the blue sky and the green olive groves of our beautiful Provence.

"In a few days I shall give a grand farewell dinner to every person whose acquaintance I have made since I have been at Paris; if you will take a part in it you will afford me a sincere pleasure; and, if you are observers, you may study some curious physiognomies."

Salvador and Roman joyfully accepted the invitation of the marquis.

The evening was already advanced when they quitted the table at which they had dined. The marquis proposing to return to his residence at once, his two friends acccompanied him to the apartment he occupied alone, in a neat and small house in the Rue de Joubert, and only quitted him when he had retired to bed, and after making an appointment for the next morning.

"This might be useful to us," said Salvador to Roman, when they had gained the street, showing him a morsel of yellow wax.

"Ah! you have taken the impression; very well, but we shall have no occasion, I think, to make use of it; I have an idea which I will communicate to you presently."

Roman and Salvador arrived at the furnished room of the modest hotel which the poor state of their finances obliged them to choose. Salvador had taken a seat to rest himself a few minutes, whilst smoking a cigar; Roman, who remained standing, took off his hat, and made several profound and respectful bows or salutations to his companion, who regarded him with astonishment.

"I have the honour of presenting my respects," he said, "to Monsieur the Marquis de Pourrieres, and beg him to receive my most sincere compliments of condolence."

A flash seemed to sparkle in the eyes of Salvador; he comprehended his master.

"And when shall we execute your plan?" he said.

"I must mature it, and bring about a favourable opportunity; but it will not be difficult."

Salvador threw himself on the neck of his worthy comrade, and cordially embraced him. "It's charming," he added; "it's charming, my friend Roman; you are a great man."

CHAPTER X.

A FEW PORTRAITS.

If the patriotic deputés would discover at table the means of restoring to France her influence in Europe; if the men of letters would burn their own incense between the cheese and the dessert; if the Barbistes* desire, at the commencement of a new year, to recall the happy days of their youth, whilst jingling their glasses; if the philanthropist would argue as to the best means of allaying the miseries of the people, 'tis assuredly with the Restauroteur Lemardelay that they will assemble: this worthy successor of Baleine and Lejay possesses, in fact, the monopoly of the banquets which unite round the same table a considerable number of guests.

* Ancient pupils of the college of Saint Barbe.

The feast offered by the Marquis Alexis de Pourrieres, to those whom he had known at Paris, and at which Salvador and Roman were to be present, had been ordered some time before from this amiable culinary artist, and would leave nothing, it was said, to wish for.

At the day and hour indicated, the dinner was laid in a saloon elegantly furnished, and lighted by a reasonable quantity of perfumed wax-lights. Brillat-Savarin, Grimod, de la Reynière, Berchoux, d'Aigrefeuille, all the learned in gastronomy maintain, and we are of the same opinion, that an excellent repast can only be enjoyed by candle-light.

The table was covered with damask linen of a snowy whiteness; magnificent crystals and admirable porcelains reflected a thousand luminous jets; vases of gilded bronze, real artistic chefs d'ouvres from the workrooms of Denière, were charged with the most rare exotic flowers; the wines were refreshed in the coolers filled with ice; the chief and his assistants, the butler and his subordinates, were at their post; the guests might now arrive, every thing was prepared for their reception.

De Pourrieres, who would not leave to Lemardelay the care of receiving his company, arrived before his guests. Salvador and Roman soon followed him; he hastened to meet his new friends, and heartily shook hands with them.

It was at first the intention of de Pourrieres to invite but a few friends; but each of them, on its being known that the banquet was given to enable him to bid a final and solemn farewell to the world in which he had lived up to the present time, would absolutely bring a friend with him; it was afterwards discovered that no fête could be complete without the attraction of a few pretty women; thus the number of the guests was insensibly augmented, and the table, which at first was to have been laid out in a small cabinet, majestically lengthened itself in one of the largest and handsomest saloons of Lemardelay.

Salvador and Roman admired the luxury and perfect taste of the dinner table, and addressed some words to that effect to their Amphytrion, which seemed to flatter him. When his company began to arrive, there were old and young—many wore at their button-hole the revered sign of honour. Salvador remarked among them a handsome young man, much above the middle height, with a pleasing physiognomy, on which, however, one might remark an expression of haughty disdain. "Who," said he to the marquis, "is the young man who saluted you but slightly, and to whom most of those present seem to pay respect?"

"That, monsieur," replied de Pourrieres with a smile, "is one of the most curious phenomena of the Parisian capital. He is known to have neither rents or property either in the city or the country; neither places nor pensions; he is neither an artist, a merchant, or a man of letters; and still he gives the tone to the most distinguished lions of society. He has his box at the opera; he frequently changes his horses and equipages; he plays, and loses without a frown, considerable sums; he inhabits one of the most comfortable hotels of the new quarter of Europe; and when he leaves his house he demands of his valet, who constantly replies in the affirmative, if he has placed sufficient cash in his purse. Thus, Monsieur the Viscount Achille de Lussan sees the doors of the noblest and the best open before him; he is in all the clubs of good company, and all the philanthropic societies; the youngest and the prettiest duchesses raffle for him, and, if they dared, would dispute his heart with the opera

dancer he keeps—a very sweet creature, who will, perhaps, do us the honour to assist at the banquet."

"This Monsieur de Lussan," said Roman, "appears a galliard to be depended upon.'

"You are not deceived," said de Pourrieres; "he uses the arms with which nature has blessed him with as much address as the sword which his noble ancestors have bequeathed him; he has already killed a few whose curiosity induced them to pry into the sources of his fortune; so that at present he is held in very great respect."

During the time of this short conversation, several fresh guests had arrived, and after having saluted their entertainer, had mixed in the different groups who waited and chatted for the time to arrive for placing themselves at table.

De Pourrieres continued the conversation commenced with Salvador and Roman:

"If all these messieurs," he said, "would be sincere, and recount their history, you would listen to some singular confessions, and would learn more in one hour than all the familiar romances of the day would teach you in ten years. There are, you see, in the folds of the human heart, some bad passions and disgraceful vices, which the all-seeing eye can alone discover, and which will never be unfolded by the writers of romance."

"Oh! oh! Monsieur le Marquis, do you know that you moralise to perfection?" said Salvador, who was but slightly prepossessed in favour of the discourse which de Pourrieres had commenced.

"You are right, the time is badly chosen to enforce a moral; since we are met here to amuse ourselves, why let us do so; but, above all, be careful not to name me as de Pourrieres; those who are here all know me by the name of de Courtivon alone."

Roman glanced significantly at Salvador.

"While we are waiting for permission to do honour to the feast," he said, addressing the marquis, "continue, at least so far as lies in your power, to make us acquainted with the guests."

"With pleasure. That little man, who calls himself de Preval, is a satellite which gravitates round the star called de Lussan; but as the means which he employs to procure the luxury he enjoys, are pretty well understood, he is not accorded that consideration which they dare not refuse to the viscount. The women who are seduced by the neat figure, the graceful manners, and the sentimental tirades of Monsieur de Preval, whether duchesses, actresses, or kept women, are the mines which enrich him: an old Russian princess pays the expenses of his tilbury, an actress those of his apartment, and a young lady 'under protection' furnishes him with his pocket money. Monsieur de Preval, as a resource against the chances of his position, has a second string to his bow—he is, they say, more than lucky at play.

"This man, who seems nearly sixty years of age, with such a respectable physiognomy, and who wears at his button-hole the cross of the Legion of Honour, is one of the eagles of the bar, and a patriot of the elective chamber. The happy St. Yves, *advocatus et non latro res miranda*, was canonised, although an advocate; he is, perhaps, at present, the only one of his robe who has been admitted into the heavenly kingdom; it is for this reason, probably, that its bliss is so great, for if there was a second, the eternal father might not be sure of a tranquil end of his lease.

"However it may be, I will recount you a little anecdote, and very edifying, respecting this advocate and deputy, who might well, sooner or later, take a place by the side of his worthy patron, St. Yves, and carry off a portion of his celestial clients.

" 'Tis as follows. In order to render myself more intelligible, I shall adopt, if you will allow me, the form of a dialogue. You will observe, that the scene takes place in the cabinet of the advocate in question,—a room furnished with every possible luxury. The advocate is sitting before a circular table, enveloped in an elegant robe de chambre of flowered work, and his feet thrust in oriental slippers of red morocco ; a lady on the turn of life, but whose toilette is very elegant, enters and says to him :

" ' Eh! good morning, dear master; how are the five codes and their honourable commentaries?'

" She then takes a chair.

" ' Ah ! beauteous dame !' replies the advocate, ' all my jurisprudence I lay at your feet. On my honour, you are more beautiful every day !'

" ' Always gallant, dear sir, but a truce to your amiable compliments to-day, it is a serious business which has brought me here.'

" ' What is the affair ? I am all attention.'

" ' It is necessary to go back some little time ; excuse me if you find me prolix, it is a little failing of our sex. You recollect, dear sir, that for-ever-deplorable epoch of 1814, when a cloud of barbarians burst upon the already overwhelmed France; they gathered in their folds that famous king, who —thanks to a figure of rhetoric which is not yet defined—persuaded us, one fine day, that our enemies were our best friends.'

" ' Ah ! madame,' interrupted the advocate, sighing, ' what remembrances you conjure up! when I recall the grievances of my country I am ready to melt into tears.'

" ' It is easily conceivable,' thought the lady, ' he is so great a patriot, I might well have supposed I was putting his sensibilities to a great trial. Allow me to continue,' she said, after making this reflection. ' Among this crowd of barbarians there was a grand seigneur, a real uncouth bear, but who redeemed this slight defect by some millions of rubles. From his first arrival at Paris, he wished to be initiated into the Parisian manners, and for this purpose he wanted to rob the old man. After providing for the necessities of his toilette, he thought of those amiable nothings, of which the philosophers take so little account, but for which all the pretty women are mad ;—I mean the bijoux. It is here, my dear sir, that, in my turn, I must put my own sensibility to a very great proof; the mere remembrance of these misfortunes makes me weep, I loved my husband so fondly ! You recollect that I was a jeweller in the Palais Royal ; the barbarian came; he saw me, and *conquered*. A few months afterwards, and I belonged to the stranger; by means of a treaty made between my husband and this barbarian, I became the property of the latter. Alas ! he used his property *as a thing belonging to him*. But we know the results of *usage* in similar cases; you have guessed that I became a mother. The barbarian possessed some feeling ; he wished to recompense honourably my *fidelity;* in his last moments he called for a notary, and, by a will in the proper form, he left to the fruit of our loves, a considerable sum out of the millions in question. A short time after, the good man died ! The Almighty reclaimed his spirit.'

" ' *Amen!* Ah, sweet lady! how much this recital has affected me, and how sensible I am to your troubles !'

" ' Peste ! we must think of other matters ! It

remains now to harvest the crop left to my son by the old miser; but this succession is in Russia, and the Emperor Nicholas loves not that the millions pass the frontiers of his domains. It requires, therefore, nothing less than an advocate of your merit to remove the difficulties in our way. Will you undertake this mission ?'

" ' What! go to Russia?'

" ' Yes; to Russia.'

" ' Hum ! it's a long way; and during this time, what will become of my country and my clients ?'

" ' Oh! that's not my business; but if I make you an equivalent for what your profession may procure you, would you not, at this price, render me the service?'

" ' You know well, dear madame, that I can refuse you nothing.'

" ' Well, let us see: what do you require to undertake this affair and the necessary voyage?'

" ' Ah ! madame, what is it you demand of me? Is it money I think of ? But what will become of France in my absence ! Oh, my country !'

" The lady thought she should take into account, towards such a great patriot, the sacrifice he was about to make in exiling himself for her benefit.

" ' Well, dear sir,' she said, ' 25,000 francs ; is it enough ?'

" ' What is it you are saying? there, oh! France, what will become of you ?'

" ' But it seems to me that 25,000 francs ——'

" To be brief, the advocate accepted, and the lady brought him, the next morning, the 25,000 francs in handsome bank notes. After touching the cash, the advocate politely wished the lady good morning, assuring her that within a week he would be on his journey.

" But a month elapsed before our advocate bethought him of getting his passport. The lady, informed of this circumstance, paid him a visit and mentioned her astonishment ; but, like a man who is always prepared, he made a thousand reasons to justify his delay. The lady agrees to a fresh delay, at the expiration of which, another visit, and additional reasons for delay on the part of the advocate.

" The lady, at length dissatisfied, consulted : she was told, that if the advocate did not put himself *en route*, no doubt the want of cash prevented him, or obliged him to remain.

" Enlightened by this argument, she returns to her dear counsel: she questioned him if, by chance, the want of money was the obstacle which caused his delay in departing ? At the mention of the word money, the countenance of the advocate brightened up.

" ' Yes,' he said, ' it is so : I have bills abroad and I cannot absent myself until I have honoured them.'

" ' What amount is necessary ? Come, say the word frankly.'

" ' Frankly, then, 75,000 francs; but in the way of a loan.'

" ' You shall have them.'

" The next morning the lady brought the 75,000 francs. The advocate drew out two notes,—the one for 42,000 francs and the other for 33,000. We must do him this justice—he honourably *made the two notes.*

" Thus paid, cleared, and eased of his troubles, you will imagine that our advocate hastened to satisfy his client.

" Error !

" Our advocate is a deputy, and one of the first orators of the chamber ; it was not to be supposed he could travel as a simple advocate.

"He commenced his tour, then, by Goritz. He got himself presented to the king of France; (excellent king! he is, at present, very easy of access;) the king asked him if he *would eat a morsel.* Our advocate then quits his character, and assumes the man of politics; he accepts the breakfast of King Henry the Fifth, and then takes his flight towards St. Petersburgh. Hardly arrived there, a paragraph, neatly inserted in the Russian journals, announces the arrival of an illustrious personage. The Emperor Nicholas, informed of the breakfast at Goritz, allows him to be presented at court. Behold, then, our hero, admitted to the soirees, processions, reviews, parades, water parties, breakfasts, dinners, little suppers, and concerts of the Emperor Nicholas. Could an advocate, under such circumstances, find time to occupy himself with the affairs of his client, when the emperor himself devoted his time to him, and gave him so many and such agreeable occupations? 'Twas morally impossible! So, having passed two or three months at St. Petersburgh, and having dissipated as well the sum destined to bring to a happy conclusion the affair of the legacy, as the 75,000 francs, which we have not forgotten, our hero departed for his dear country.

"You may guess he was in no great hurry to receive a visit from his fair client, to render an account of his mission; he wished to escape the quarter of an hour of Rabelais. The lady, however, was informed of his return, and commenced the visits.

"'Eh! returned! and you have not been to see me?'

"'Ah! madame, what a voyage! what a country! I am destroyed, bruised, and broken.'

"'And yet it seems to me you had not that fresh colour and glow of health before your departure.'

"'Ah! madame, 'tis the effects of the cold climate, but still you may affirm that I am ruined in health.'

"'Come, come, courage! three months of our sweet air of France and you will recover.'

"'Oh! such a dreadful rheumatism!'

"'Let us talk a little about other matters; and the affair of my son, eh!'

"'Oh! oh! I wish the devil had all the pains of the stomach!'

"'Recover yourself; we'll talk about it another day. Drink freely and keep yourself warm.'

"The lady returned twenty times to hear the news she hoped for, respecting the journey to Russia; but twenty times the same scene was repeated: 'Oh! oh! my nerves! ouf! my rheumatism! ouf! the pains in my stomach!'

"The expiration, however, of the notes was approaching, the unpitying calendar marked the fatal date.

"The lady presented herself! No one. Her debtor, who for some time had merely been building castles in the air, had departed to pay his devotions in Galicia, and afterwards to Notre Dame d'Atocha.

"Returned from the latter country, the poor dear man forgot the notes made to his fair client, and a heap of others of the same nature, the means which such a good and honest patriot adopts to pay his debts.*

"That little stunted man, who is conversing at this moment with the Viscount de Lussan, with the grotesque shape, twisted legs, protruding stomach, and whose head seems to be buried in shoulders of unnatural size, whose arms are of an extraordinary length, the face covered with a thick and black beard, whose whole person, in fact, reminds one of the illustrious Sancho Panza, was formerly the curate of a village in the neighbourhood of Paris. Providence, it is true—

'En maçonnant les remparts de son âme,
Songea bien plus au fourreau qu'à la lame.'

Still, Monsieur the Abbé affects, as you may perceive, a grave and venerable appearance; he is only, however, one of those haughty priests who fancy themselves privileged to overreach wherever they may chance to be admitted; one of those priests without theory or practice, who only see the black side of matters, and who, whether from pride or folly, pretend to subject every thing to the shade of their hypocritical mummeries; one of those priests, in fact, who insinuate themselves every where, with the sole view of conveying a reprimand, and who become the plague of such as are good or weak enough to tolerate their revolting impertinences. As to religion, this personage cultivates it as a veritable disciple of Escobar; thus, those who know him well, tell us that he recites no other prayer than this:

'Pulchra Laverna,
Da mihi fallere, da justem sanctum que videri,
Noctem peccatis, et fraudibus objicere nubem.'*
HORACE.

"Observe that this man has launched into some extensive affairs—that he is crippled with debts—and to create some diversion to his embarrassments, he pays an assiduous devotion to the bottle.

"When he was curate of ——, he owed considerable sums to the banker P——, it was necessary to pay them, or at least give the banker some security in the shape of signatures, to assure him as to the fate of his balance. To pay was not so easy a matter, the principal element was wanting; to give good signatures, another difficulty; for who would consent to be security for an ecclesiastic, who had no other fortune than his curacy? To arrive at his object, therefore, he must have recourse to one of those unedited tricks,—to one of those turns, with which the devil inspires his friends and vassals, to extricate them momentarily from an awkward affair, but which they expiate sooner or later. Behold, then, that which Monsieur le Curé played to one of his honest parishioners, named, I think, Monsieur François.

"It was between Oculi and Latere of the year 18—.† The worthy Monsieur François presided, with all the grace he was master of, at the loading of the waggons with the soil from his court-yard.

"His education and his fortune, however, placed him above such vulgar attentions; but, encouraged by the example of Hercules, who formerly thought it no disgrace to cleanse the stable of Augea, he believed that every thing connected with agriculture was a matter of respectability.

"Besides, Monsieur François was not one of those ignorant and clownish peasants, whose vocabulary is in unison with the beasts they drive. Monsieur François had studied in his youth, the rudiments were not a stranger to him; and if the revolution had not taken place, he would be now a curate of a parish or canon of some fat chapel; but, arrested in his vocation by this great outbreak, he never could get beyond the minor orders, so that, in memory of the little collar and band which he had formerly worn, he is still called, in the coun-

---

* Historical.

* Kind Laverna, give me the means of deception, of passing for a man of wealth; hide with a thick veil, and dark midnight, my secret rogueries.

† These are the second and third Sundays in Lent.

No. 7.

LIFE IN PARIS.

DISCOVERED.

try, the Abbé François, although long since married, and the father of a numerous family. He further justifies this title of *abbé*, by a mania he possesses of quoting, in season or out of season, Latin citations, which are incrusted in his memory, and provokes a saying that he is as learned as Monsieur le Curé,—indeed, the labourers on his farm give him the priority.

"To return to the commencement: Monsieur François, following one of the servants who were conducting to the fields a load of soil, encountered, at the turn of a very narrow street, the abbé in question, curate of the parish. The latter profited by the warm rays of a spring morning to take his walk in the village; he had his *three-cornered* on his head and his breviary in his hand, and the rigorous costume of the holy canons.

"Monsieur François, according to Monsieur le Curé, was one of his best sheep; but the old chronicles add, that this same sheep had sometimes wandered from the fold, so that Monsieur le Curé had made many endeavours to bring him back to his shepherd. At this moment, and notwithstanding he had other views respecting his honest parishioner, he failed not to attack him on his weak side; elevating, then, his fore-finger with solemnity, he gave him his holy benediction, accompanying it with these words—

"'*Domine sit in animâ tuâ.*'

"Monsieur François, who possessed, as I have said, some sound learning, hastened to reply, by taking off his hat and making the sign—

"'*Ave Domine, gratias ago, Amen.*'

"The introduction thus terminated between the shepherd and his sheep, and both, no doubt, satisfied at showing the fruits of their studies, the curé continued in these words—

"'It is a long time, my good Monsieur François, since I have had the pleasure of seeing you at the presbytery; have I had the misfortune to incur your disgrace?'

"'Not the least in the world, Monsieur le Curé,' replied Monsieur François. 'I have always had occasion to speak well of your conduct towards myself; you possess the esteem of all your parishioners, and mine as well. But, shall I confess it? the nearer the time de Paques* approaches, the more I avoid the presbytery; it seems to me I know not how to appear there, without first regulating some accounts, very much in arrear—you know—'

"'Why, my good Monsieur François, do you think I preach religion in the street, and that I am intolerant enough to introduce it even in your labour? How very little you know me. If I complain of the rarity of your visits, my good Monsieur François, it is because you are an esteemed guest, and that, for a long time, I have not had the pleasure of seeing you at my house; in order to make amends, you must come some morning, without ceremony, and breakfast with me; I will give you a taste of a certain old wine, from behind the fagot-heap, of which you must give me your opinion; above all, be sure not to come on a fast-day, you know that Lent has already too many rigours, so we must indemnify ourselves together.'

"Monsieur François, flattered at such a polite invitation, and certain besides that Monsieur le Curé had no intention to take him in hand respecting the chapter of general confession, hastened to accept the proffered breakfast; the day was fixed for the Thursday following.

* Easter.

"The appointed day having arrived, the honest Monsieur François completed an extra toilette, and repaired to the presbytery. The first signs already induced a favourable augury; in fact, the surrounding atmosphere was agreeably perfumed by the odour of the viands preparing for the pious stomachs of our two personages.

"They take their seats; the table is laid out with propriety, even elegance, two dishes alone figure upon it, but the bottles are in much greater number. The curate, who has the means of putting his guest in good humour, does not fail to observe in pointing out the bottles: '*Album an atrum pota?*'

"'*Aut interlibet, aut alternis vicibus,*' replies Monsieur François. Hereupon our heroes, satisfied with themselves, commence their repast; the dainties succeed each other with rapidity, they moisten them frequently, animated conversation follows; to be brief, Rabelais has nothing better in his chapter on dinner table chit-chat.

"The second course disappears; Monsieur François seems slightly absorbed by the process of digestion, his unsteady eye has not the usual clearness; Monsieur le Curé, in order to return him thanks, salutes him with a '*nunc est bibendum, pulsanda tellus pede libero?*'

"'*Dulce est desipere in loco,*' bravely returns Monsieur François.

"Our convives having thus proved that they had not forgotten their Horace, commence the bout in reality; the colours are confounded, they drink alternatively red and white, and then white and red; then follows the coffee and its eternal accompaniments; the old Cognac, the kirsch of the Black Forest, and the anisette of Bordeaux. But for some time Monsieur le Curé had observed, that the eyes of his guest twinkled, that his legs were unsteady, in fact that his reason was buried in the depth of the bottles; it was exactly the state he had waited for: as for himself—younger, more robust, more in train, and especially more completely master of himself, the numerous bumpers he had swallowed had hardly made an impression upon him. In addition, he required all his presence of mind to arrive at his object. Having again assured himself that the words of Monsieur François grew thicker and thicker, that his sight was almost in a state of eclipse, and his reason on the eve of flight—

"'Monsieur François,' he said, 'before separating, I hope you will kindly render me a slight service.'

"'How, Monsieur le Curé? whatever you may wish, dispose of me; am I not your friend?'

"'Oh! I know it, but it is a trifling affair. I must tell you then, that Monseigneur the Bishop has required some information from me respecting the moral condition of the parish, and as to primary instruction, &c.; this information has been obtained, but it requires, besides my evidence, that it should be supported by the signature of one of the most active of the parish; but, who is more competent than yourself in such an affair, you who talk Latin to me like a Cicero, and are cited by every one as the most erudite in the country? Here are the papers, have the kindness to sign them.'

"In finishing this short discourse, Monsieur le Curé placed several papers on the table; Monsieur François, still under the influence of the flattering unction he had received, and the bumpers he had swallowed, armed himself with a pen, and five times surrounded his signature with his handsomest flourish.

"The game was played.

"'I must now say prayers, and visit my poor,

said Monsieur le Curé; 'adieu, my good Monsieur François; excuse me for leaving you so soon, but you know the necessity of our duties, especially in this holy time of Lent. My respectful compliments to your worthy wife and very respectable family.'

"They quitted each other the best friends in the world.

"Six months after this friendly breakfast, the worthy Monsieur François, surrounded by his family and domestics, was enjoying his patriarchal dinner, happy in the enjoyment of all around him, when a man with a repugnant mien presented himself; 'twas one of those sinister figures, known throughout the district as the bugbear of big and little. At the appearance of this uncouth personage, the process of masticating suddenly stopped; if a thunderbolt had dropped into the midst of the united family, they would have been less frightened !

"Monsieur François, however, rose up—

"'What's the matter, Master Tenanthon?' (the name of the personage, an honest bailiff in his way,) said he.

"'A mere trifle, my good Monsieur François; 'tis a little interested visit which I have made you, *for and in order* to receive from you a sum of ten thousand francs, besides the expenses, being the total amount of five notes drawn by Monsieur le Curé of your parish, endorsed by you, and protested in default of payment.'

"'How! what? what is it? what do you say?'

"'Why,' said Monsieur Tenanthon, in his most honeyed tone, 'those who have sent me are not fools. Look! is not that your signature?'

"'Ah! mon Dieu! what have I done?' exclaimed Monsieur François; 'I who imagined I was signing papers for the bishop—malediction! Yes,' he said at length to Master Tenanthon, ''tis sure enough my signature; but there are judges at Berlin, and I will be revenged!'

"A month afterwards, the abbé in question was condemned to a year in prison, as guilty of swindling and abuse of confidence; but Belgium is an hospitable land, where they make a collection of men of worth, the abbé went there for some time to increase the number.*

"Two men have retired in the embrasure of a window to converse more at their ease; the one is tall, thin, his complexion is bilious, his doubtful grey eyes are surmounted by thick black eye brows which meet above the nose; he is one of Messieurs the lawyers *de premiere instance* of the good city of Paris. The other is short and fat, with eyes *à fleur de tête*, a nose covered with spots; he is one of the members of the corporation of counsellors. These two men are no doubt ripening some dirty affair, they have none of a better sort.

"Master Ruinard, the name of the lawyer, lived while he was yet a student with a young woman who became pregnant by him; the unhappy girl, in concert with her lover, caused herself to miscarry.

"When the student married, he left his mistress, who lost no time in forming another attachment.

"Becoming again pregnant, she profited by the lessons she had received from her former lover; in consequence, she caused another miscarriage; but this time the crime was discovered, and she was cited before the court of assize of the Seine.

"By a singular coincidence, her ancient lover, he who had been her accomplice in the first crime, made one of the jury who had to decide on her fate. The woman, you might well suppose, made no use of her right to challenge a man upon whose indulgence she believed she could well rely.

"When, after the debates, the jury were assembled in the chamber of deliberation, the lawyer found himself called upon the last to give his vote; five voices were already favourable to the accused; you think, no doubt, that the addition of her lover's divided the vote, and that she would be acquitted? Well, you are mistaken; he voted with the jurors who had decided against the accused, who was condemned to six years of detention."

"Oh! what an abominable man !" exclaimed Salvador and Roman at the same time.

"After the judgment was pronounced," continued de Pourrieres, "the lawyer, who was leaving the assize court, was accosted by a well-known and creditable advocate, who was acquainted with all that had formerly taken place between the lawyer and the condemned.

"'You must have suffered greatly between the debates and the time at which the jury made up their minds?' he said to him.

"'What would you have, my friend?' replied the lawyer, with the greatest *sang froid;* 'she was guilty.'

"'Really, I admire your coolness; there wanted nothing to complete it but your voting against her.'

"'But that is just what I have done.'

"'How! you have voted against her who was once your mistress, and after what has taken place between you and her ?'

"'What would you have, my friend? I was the more convinced of her guilt, as she had caused herself to miscarry while she was my mistress; for the rest, my dear friend, I have obeyed my conscience.'

"The advocate, disgusted, turned his back without making a single word of reply to this Brutus of a novel kind, who consoles himself, by making a fortune, for the contempt with which every honest man looks upon him.*

"He who is conversing with the lawyer, has not yet attained to such an elevation as the deputy patriot. There exists between the two latter the same distance as between the Viscount de Lussan and de Preval; the advocate retains in the prisons, factors who are charged to procure him clients. It was proposed to him a short time ago to defend a young thief, accused of having stolen a considerable sum of money; the young hopeful expected he should be acquitted if he was cleverly defended, for no positive fact justified the accusation. The advocate saw the accused, and after listening to him, gave him great hopes, and demanded the retaining fee; the accused replied that he could not pay him until he was at liberty; the advocate thought it right to observe to him, that he would be no richer at liberty than he was in prison.

"'Oh! yes,' replied the prisoner, who knew by reputation the individual with whom he had to deal; 'when I am at liberty I shall be enabled to pay you liberally.'

"The advocate, who listened attentively after the signicative glance of the thief, pressed his client, who at length admitted to him that he was, in fact, the author of the robbery of which he was accused, and that the bag which contained the coin was hid under his mother's bed. The advocate pretended to disbelieve the thief; the latter, wishing to give him a proof of his good faith, invited him to withdraw the bag from its hiding place. 'Take the

* Historical.

* Historical.

magot,' he said to him, 'and retain a fourth of its contents, and return me the rest when I am at liberty.' The advocate repaired to Charentonneau, a small hamlet of Maisons-Alfort. As the mother was ignorant of her son's guilt, and of the place of concealment of the hidden treasure, it was necessary for our hero, before proceeding at his leisure, to rid himself of the presence of the honest woman, which he contrived by sending her to Maisons-Alfort, to obtain a sheet of printed paper. During her absence, the hiding place was easily discovered, and the bag taken out. The advocate defended the young thief, who was acquitted. But when he reclaimed the three-fourths of the stolen cash, the advocate claimed his retaining fee. The thief, as indignant as an old fox surprised by a chicken, swore, but a little too late, that he should not trap him a second time.*

"If ever I am accused," said Roman, "I shall confide my defence to this monsieur."

"You will do well," replied de Pourrieres; "but if, for reasons known to yourself, you wish to sell or let the pretty little cottage ornamented with the green vines, which you possess at Tretz, address not yourself to the individual with the pyramidical nose, who is lolling on the sofa. The dodges of the trade he exercises are numerous, and you may easily be caught. But as this individual does not spend in folly the money which he attains by swindling, he will soon have acquired a handsome fortune; he will then purchase a property, will be a captain in the militia, knight of the Legion of Honour, elector, juror, and will condemn, without pity, all who may appear before him.

"Discovering one day that his commerce did not produce him sufficient profits, a merchant of stockings and cotton nightcaps announced in all the journals that he would deliver, for the small expense of one franc, a seed, which, planted in a good soil, would produce a cabbage of extraordinary dimensions. Unfortunately for the horticulturists, the result proved to them that the grain of the colossal cabbage was but the seed of a fool, or something worse.

"The coloured complexion, carroty-looking hair, and the black coat with a tail like that of a stockfish, of the individual who is conversing with the inventor of the colossal cabbage, announce to you a native of the British Isles. This one sells to the good Parisians an unique specific, which will heal every disease, past, present, and to come. The panacea of this insulaire is quite simply flour of lentils, which they purchase because he sells it under his scientific name of Ervelenta.

"Here are two men, who I am astonished to see together, although countrymen. They are natives of the south of France. The first is about fifty-five years of age, he is corpulent, and of a good height; he possesses an agreeable physiognomy, although slightly marked with the small-pox; his manners are noble and winning; they say quietly, very quietly, that he finished his studies at a prison, where his comrades surnamed him 'the philosopher and advocate,' and that he carries on the right shoulder the witness of his ancient services. Since his liberation, three decorations, which he had not in prison, sport at his button-hole.

"The costume of this individual is always *recherché;* he plays the aristocrat admirably; one might say, without fear of contradiction, that he's a rogue of quality.

"The second is equally as fine a man as the for-

* Historical.

mer, but he is not, like him, possessed of a physiognomy adapted to the trade which they exercise between them. The small-pox, which has left but few traces on the visage of his friend, has visited him with heavy ravages. His beard is fair and bushy; he crops it after a *first affair,* and allows it to recommence its growth when he has completed a second. He declares in the gambling-houses, of which he is a constant frequenter, that he is of noble origin, ancient officer of cavalry, Count Paladin of the Holy Roman Empire; pretensions denied by the vulgar expression of his features, and an exterior very similar to that of a brothel-keeper. He is, in reality, nothing more than a knight of the enigmatical order of the Eperon d'Or, the brevet of which he purchased for fifty crowns from Sartorius Cortè; he would give away his brevet, I am told, for fifty cigars; I believe it. When he purchased this unlucky brevet, he fancied it would give him the right to place in his button-hole the riband of the order, which is of the same colour as that of the Legion of Honour. Alas! he was wofully disappointed.

"These two individuals, who are never separated, found themselves one day *tres sanglés* (the expression they make use of) both of them, that is to say, they had a very pressing need of money. The eldest said to the youngest—

"'Listen, I have found to-night a mine of gold, or rather, what is better, a mine of bank notes.'

"'How!' replied his friend, 'do you mean to forge bank notes? that doesn't suit me. I laugh at the police correctionelle, but I have a great respect for the court of assize.'

"'And who the devil speaks to you of forging bank notes or any thing else? is it not possible otherwise to procure real veritable bank notes?'

"'To get hold of a reasonable number, I only know of two modes; make them one's self, or rob the bank of France; and I confess to you, that either the one or the other of these actions terrifies me; you know that I am an honest man, and that the idea alone of committing a dishonest action, causes me a certain contraction of the muscles.'

"'But I assure you, it has nothing to do either with robbing or any thing like it; it is only necessary to know how to seize with dexterity a portfolio well filled with this agreeable and nicely printed paper.'

"'If it merely concerns the seizing a note-case with a little dexterity, I consent to assist you; but in the first place I wish to know your plan.'

"'My plan is simple, and if to-morrow is as fine as to-day, I am sure of succeeding.'

"'You kill me with impatience, with your repetitions! Tell me at once the project, I am all ears: speak!'

"'You observed the other day the healthy condition of the note-case of my banker?'

"'Yes, I remarked it and envied it too. But this portfolio is like the holy arch, no person can touch it.'

"'And yet if to-morrow's sun rises glorious like the present, and if you will second me, to-morrow, I say, we shall be the proprietors of the case.'

"'I think, my friend, that you are turned madman. It would be easier for us to take the moon by our teeth, than to appropriate the note-case of this worthy usurer.'

"'To-morrow, if it is fine, ('tis the condition, *sine qua non,*) you will be walking under the windows of the usurer in question, and if the note-case falls at your feet, you will pick it up and disappear; that's all I ask of you. Do you understand?'

" 'I hear, but I do not comprehend?'

" 'Do you consent, yes or no, to do what I ask you?'

" 'Well! Yes.'

" 'Be it so. In that case pray God that the morning of to-morrow may be a bright one ; and, if he answers your prayers, before midday we will both be at the fête.'

" 'We will meet then to-morrow morning at seven o'clock, at the Palais Royal, opposite the Rotundo.'

"The next morning found the two friends at the place and hour indicated. The sky was clear, the sun shone brilliantly, every thing announced a day free from storms. The eagerness was the same on both sides; they turned towards the residence of the usurer, and the eldest said to his friend—

" 'Before I enter the house, be attentive, and fortune will fall upon your head.'

"The Count Paladin of the Holy Roman Empire, promenaded on the pavement, waiting with impatience the lucky aerolite which was to tumble from above; at length, after an hour's expectation, which seemed longer than a day passed in a lock-up house, waiting the arrival of the needful, the envied note-case dropped; he picked it up and disappeared ; no one had observed what had passed.

"And now as to what took place in the cabinet of the usurer, who, as our swindler had anticipated, had opened one of his windows from the fineness of the day. The eldest of the two, for whom the usurer had often discounted certain notes, which were punctually discharged at their expiration, had presented to him two of 1000 francs each, at four months' date. The balance settled, there remained to our friend 1560 francs. The note-case was drawn from the strong box, and three notes of 500 francs each were extracted from it, turned and returned a dozen times, and presented after a long sigh; that completed, the usurer, as customary with him, placed the note-case at his side in order to drag from his chest the sixty francs, to complete the sum due to his client; at this moment the artful scoundrel seized the note-case, which he threw out of the window, which was immediately closed.

"The usurer was so surprised that he remained a minute without the power of uttering a word; at length he regained his senses, and called loudly; some persons entered. The swindler was seated in one of the corners of the room, his account of the notes discounted, and the three bank notes he had received, in his hand. 'I think,' he said to the parties who had entered the room, 'that this respectable monsieur is suddenly seized with madness.' The commissaire of police, sent for by orders of the usurer, at length arrived; our hero is searched, nothing is found upon him; he explains clearly his presence with the usurer, who at this moment recollects that the note-case was thrown out of the window; they all remark that it is firmly closed, and that the person accused is seated at the opposite extremity; on his part, he asserts that it was in the same state when he entered. The unfortunate usurer, who imagines that his money, which he holds the dearest in the world, is lost for ever to him, gives way to the greatest despair; his distress is so deep that he appears to have lost his reason. They question, however, the person he accuses. His manners and the decorations on his breast convinced every one of his innocence. They visited his domicile, obtained sufficient information, and he was at length released.

"As you may suppose, he was afraid of being followed, and used precautions in order to rejoin his friend; at length towards six o'clock in the evening, they met at the café which forms the corner of the Boulevard and of the Rue Montmartre; they saluted each other as acquaintances who have not met for some time, and then left to dine at Véfour's.

"Between the cheese and dessert the eldest says to his friend—

" 'Well! how much did you find? the usurer pretends that it contained 50,000 francs.'

" 'How! 50,000 francs, where?'

" 'Why, in the note-case this morning.'

" 'Of what are you speaking to me about, on my word of honour I do not understand you.'

" 'Come, a truce to joking, how much was there? that's the principal.'

" 'Why, you are certainly out of your mind!'

" 'You are an honest comrade, are you not?'

" 'Without doubt.'

" 'Well, don't keep me any longer in uncertainty; let us divide, and finish it.'

" 'Eh! by all the devils! is it to make a fool of me that you have paid for the dinner? explain yourself, I beg of you.'

"He did explain himself. When he had finished his discourse, the Count Paladin, after several bursts of laughter, replied, that he knew not what he meant; then, and then alone, the eldest of the two worthies discovered that his comrade resolved to appropriate to himself the contents of the note-case. He rose and said to him in a solemn tone: 'I believed until to-day that you were an honest man, I find I am deceived. Adieu, God will punish you.'*

"A genteel little actrice of a small theatre of the Boulevard du Temple had a lover. That is nothing astonishing, but what is extraordinary is, that she was sincerely attached to him. One fine morning the actrice and her lover were arrested while in bed. The young man was accused of a very serious crime, and they were ungallant enough to accuse the young devotée of Thalia of being his accomplice; but Dame Themis having discovered her error, she was restored to the patrons of her theatre. The young actrice was not one of those natures who forget their friends when in misfortune. Her sweetheart was under lock and key, she must endeavour to get him out of the scrape; she called upon the man who is sitting by the side of the two larrons† of whom I have just spoken. This man, who was a long time one of the pillars of the legitimist party, exercised in the provinces the profession of an advocate, when he was sent to the elective chamber. He tranquillised the young beauty who appealed to him, and pocketed a sum of 1500 francs; this done, the advocate troubled himself no further about his duped client, than if he never existed; he had really many things to attend to at this moment; but the young woman, who could support no longer the cruel torments of his absence, complained to the chamber of advocates; explanations were demanded by the secretary of the order. The Deputé Legitimiste, not having it in his power, as we must suppose, to give any satisfactory reply, begged his colleagues both of the one chamber and the other to accept at once his total resignation.

"He is conversing at this moment with one of the literati, to whom we might apply the lines of Voltaire against the Abbé Desfontaines:

> ' Au peu d'esprit que la bonhomme avait,
>   L'esprit d'autrui par complément servait,
>   Il compilait, compilait, compilait.'

---

* Historical.   † Swindlers.

"Do you require a history of any nation, no matter which, or some great man ; do you wish a romance of morals, a romance of the sea, or a romance of private life ; tales of any or every colour; a physiological treatise, a biographical sketch, an essay on physics, natural history or metaphysics, ask and you will have it. This illustrious unknown will arm himself with the large scissors which are laid in permanency in his bureau, and at the day and hour indicated, he will deliver you what you have demanded, provided, at all events, you have not paid in advance."

"I see that we are going to dine with all that Paris has collected of men whose characters are blemished," added Salvador.

"Undeceive yourself, my dear countryman ; apart some rare exceptions, all the men who are here are very creditable personages ; some are rich, or appear so, others exercise honourable professions ; some occupy situations which are generally bestowed upon honest men ; it is only in a whisper they speak of what I have been recounting to you, and when we meet these gentry in the saloons, we must put a good face upon it."

"Eh! good-day then, Monsieur de Courtivon," said a handsome young man who offered to de Pourrieres a hand neatly gloved, which the latter pressed in his own. The young man, after exchanging a few words with the Amphytrion, again mixed in the different coteries.

"Is it possible to refuse the hand offered you, when so perfectly gloved as the one I have just squeezed?" said de Pourrieres, smiling.

"It would in fact be difficult," replied Salvador, "especially if the individual should happen to be a little less of a rogue, than those whose history you have furnished us with."

"This young man is a clever physician ; but whatever may be the science he has acquired on the school bench, his knowledge will be always inferior to his wit, and his connection is consequently among the most distinguished and the most lucrative.

"A woman whose husband may be from home, and who may be doubtful as to the consequences of a conversation somewhat criminal with the nephew, the cashier, or intendant of her lord, calls to her assistance Dr. Delamarre, who undertakes to dissipate her fears ; young persons of noble families who would prevent a stain on their escutcheon, the lorettes who would escape the consequences of a supper at the Maison d'Or, the grisettes who wish to leave no traces of a boisterous evening passed at the Ile d'Amour, find with him assistance and deliverance, if the cash is forthcoming.

"Do you sigh for an heir, this skilful doctor knows how to procure you one; if you have one too many, he knows how to rid you of it; in a word, this gallant man is the providence of all the doubtful virtues and of every ambition. To finish the portrait of this personage, I will recount to you one of the least striking traits of his life :

"A Septuagenarian, a friend of his, who wished to mystify his nephews, and who probably had forgotten the refrain of the popular song:

'Jeunes femmes et vieux maris.
Feront toujours mauvais ménage.'*

rose one morning with the determination to be married. He cast his eyes at once on a young girl as pretty as she was innocent; and it is not saying too much, for she was very pretty: you may judge; her shape was light and well turned, her clear blue eyes, shaded with long silken lashes, seemed ready

* Old men with young wives
  Agree but badly, all their lives.

to melt like the setting sun; her hair, waving in the most beautiful flaxen curls, remind one of the virgins of Leonard de Vinci ; her skin is of a dazzling purity and whiteness, tinged slightly with the rose ; her mouth is perhaps somewhat large, but when she opens it to smile, you have a view of thirty-two little teeth well arranged, and by which you seem envious of being devoured.

"This young girl had been educated by the nuns, and she had quitted the village six months before, in order to live with an aunt, who concealed, under the appearances of a rigid severity, the hope which she had long since conceived, of making a market of the attractions of her niece; so that, when the gouty old fool demanded the hand of the young houri in question, she replied to him, that his choice did her great honour, and that her niece would be delighted to espouse so gallant a man.

"The marriage was concluded, but not consummated. The morning after the wedding, the unfortunate Septuagenarian called upon his friend ; his long face and disappointed looks announced a man whose hopes had been deceived.

"'Well ?' said the doctor to him.

"'Impossible ! my dear, impossible !'

"'The devil! but I cannot increase the dose without the risk of sending you into the other world.'

"'But I will not leave my fortune to my nephews,' cried the old man.

"'There is, luckily, a means,' replied the complaisant doctor.

"He whispered a few words into the ear of the old man.

"'I'll agree to it, and you shall have the 5,000 francs you demand, if the affair succeeds; but you assure me that afterwards it will be perfectly easy.'

"'Without doubt.'

"'Well, my dear, make the attempt.'

"'Give me a *carte blanche*, and all will go well ; I will answer for its success.'

"The physician communicated his plan to the old aunt, who, in consideration of a douceur, was willing to lend a hand to the most infamous immorality ; she induced her niece to believe that, in the present case, the physician had directions to consummate the marriage by procuration.

"The young girl, we may be allowed to suppose, found the substitute more agreeable than her husband; the doctor, on his side, was delighted to meet with such a charming windfall. At length, two lovely infants were the result of this pretty commerce, who proved the happiness of the good man in question, and the despair of the nephews.

"The respectable appearance and distinguished manners of that gentleman have, no doubt, induced you to take him for a negotiant of the first order: he is a *faiseur*. Do you know what a *faiseur* is ?"

"No," replied Salvador and Roman at the same time.

"Well! the *faiseurs* are individuals who assume to themselves the qualities of bankers, of merchants, or of commissionaires in merchandise, in order to entrap the confidence of honest merchants.

"The *faiseurs* may be divided into two classes ; the first is composed of efficient men of the corporation, of those who take the lead ; those poor devils, whom you may observe in the passage of the Palais Royal, which faces the café du Foy, compose the second. At the commencement of each year, they reappear on the horizon, pale and thin, their eyes dull and glassy; broken, although still young, for ever habited in the same habiliments, always sad and gloomy, they do little or nothing: their only trade is to lend their signature to their brethren of the higher branches.

"The latter (and Monsieur Roulin is one of the most distinguished of this corporation) proceed pretty nearly in the following manner:

"They engage, in one of the best quarters, a large house, which they contrive to furnish with a luxury adapted to inspire confidence in the most distrustful; their cashier often sports at his button-hole the red riband, and the comers and goers may remark in the offices, clerks who *appear* to be very busy, and bales of merchandise which seem ready to be forwarded to all the towns in the world.

"After being established some days, the house addresses letters and circulars to all with whom they desire to have relations. The number of letters never frightens one of these pretended merchants; Monsieur Roulin, especially, posted the same day 600 letters.

"In reply to the offers of service of the *faiseur*, he is forwarded some bills of exchange endorsed to him; in his turn, he sends others upon some good houses, among which he glides a few *kites*; the good ones serve as a passport to the *good*-for-nothings; and as the latter, as well as the former, are paid at the expiration, by the partners quietly *advised* on this head, the unknown names soon acquire a certain standing in the commercial world.

"The *faiseur*, wishing to avoid the appearance of a want of money, does not require his funds directly, he leaves them some time in the hands of his correspondents.

"When the *faiseur* has received a certain number of bills, he places them in his cash-box, or negotiates them; and, in exchange, he returns others, drawn generally on imaginary parties, or individuals who have never heard him mentioned, and notes of hand not worth the value of the paper.

"The sole industry of other *faiseurs*, who have not yet arrived at the same estimation as Monsieur Roulin, is to purchase merchandise, which they never pay for; these associate in parties of three or four, place some funds with a banker, start several commercial houses under different firms: one will be the house of Peter and Co., another that of Jacques and Co., and so on, in such a way, that there soon exists five or six, who act in concert and advise each other.

"When they are brought to a stand-still, the most expert deposit their account-books, and arrange with their creditors, who esteem themselves very lucky to receive ten or fifteen per cent.; the others disappear, leaving the key in the door of an empty apartment.

"To name all the partnerships that have died under the hands of that individual," continued de Pourrieres, pointing out to Salvador and Roman a short and fat man, with a merry countenance, whose little winking eyes were concealed by his gold spectacles, and who was easily recognised as a child of Israel, "would be attempting something impossible. That man would have invented the Ten Commandments, if they had not already existed; under his hands, the shareholder becomes a clay that he can mould at his pleasure, giving it all shapes and all colours; he is a great genius—he has invented 'guaranteed profits,' premiums without risk, though the dividends may be sought for and levied out of the capital. He has tried all things: he has worked coal mines, iron mines, gold and silver mines, bitumes of all sorts and all colours; railroads and **steam-boats**; journals, catholic, political, commercial, mechanical, and literary; women and youth; the chest of each enterprise is but rarely opened to

pay the interest and dividends due; but, in revenge, the cashier is always at his post to receive the funds of new shareholders; the profits of one affair serve to repair the losses of another. When the coffers are all empty, which happens too often to please this honest industrial, advertisements—and such advertisements!—are inserted in all the journals and every corner of France; new shareholders start up, eager to take their place at the banquet of this grand inventor and sleeping partner; in fine, this individual is a very great man."

All who were to take part in the festival had now arrived; de Pourrieres was about introducing to his friends a little old man, rather meanly clad, but whom every one saluted with marked respect, when the Viscount de Lussan approached him.

"I think," he said, after bowing to Salvador and Roman, "that all your guests are arrived. Shall we not do well, whilst waiting for the ladies, who will, doubtless, not keep us long, to adjourn to a small room, where we shall find, as M. Lemardelay assures me, every appetising liqueur possible?"

"'Tis an excellent idea of yours, M. le Vicomte," replied the marquis.

All the company, conducted by de Pourrieres, entered a small saloon adjoining the banquetting-room. On a round mahogany table were placed several decanters and elegant glasses of cut crystal; the absinthe with the reflection of the emerald, the Vermont, the Stoughton Madeira, were served to the guests with a generous profusion.

The ladies arrived.

The first was named Mina, a handsome and portly woman; her black and glossy hair hung down in ringlets on shoulders of a pearly white, her large and brilliant black eyes were lively as the eagle's; her lips, a little thick perhaps, but as red as the leaves of the pomegranate, enclosed a set of beautiful and well-arranged teeth. Although this woman was tall, her movements were graceful and pliant, and she had adopted a costume which added fresh charms to her marvellous beauty. A robe of cherry-coloured silk, trimmed with lace *en point d'Angleterre*, imprisoned a shape as faultless as that of the huntress Diana; her forehead was encircled by a gold band; and a necklace, composed of a magnificent opal and a triple row of pearls of middling size, set off a neck whose rising muscles gave evidence of considerable strength in the possessor.

She was accompanied by a female, who formed a striking contrast to her. Felicité Beaupertius was as frail and as mincing as her friend was strong and powerful; taken separately, her features were not faultless, but they formed a *tout ensemble* which pleased at the first sight. The calm expression of her physiognomy, the mildness of her regard, indicated an excellent temper; her hands and feet were remarkably elegant and small, her costume was simple but *recherché*. Mina was admirable, Felicité was lovely; we shall leave to our fair readers the task of deciding upon the respective values of these two eminent qualities.

The entrance of these ladies into the small saloon in which the guests of de Pourrieres had assembled, was acknowledged by a general acclamation. The old and the young pressed round them, and they received the homages with as much composure and ease, as a queen receives those of the most devoted of her courtiers; a slight blush, however, animated the features somewhat pale, of Felicité, when their admiration of her was expressed in terms a little too energetic.

LIFE IN PARIS.

THE THEATRE.

"That is a seducing little creature," said Salvador to de Pourrieres.

"Is she not?" he replied; "well, this young girl is as good as she is pretty, and perhaps if she had been placed in different circumstances, she would have been the ornament of the highest saloons. But who is the new divinity just arrived? Eh, parbleu! 'tis the opera dancer of the Viscount de Lussan."

The viscount, in fact, had hastened to meet a young female, no less a beauty than the others; her wearied-looking expression, the small brown circle which surrounded her deep hazel eyes, and the freedom of all her movements, made her resemble a beautiful lily, drooping on the ground after vainly striving against the storm.

Other females followed, all young, pretty, and richly dressed; each, on entering, was accosted by those of the guests whom she knew. One alone remained solitary, in the most obscure corner of the room, without any one seeming to think of her; this woman, it is true, was old, ugly, and less than modestly attired; the loneliness in which she had been left, appeared greatly to annoy the little old man, of whom de Pourrieres was about to speak to his two friends when de Lussan had accosted him; he shuffled about in every way, placed and replaced the three-cornered pad which balanced itself on his denuded head.

"Such a good woman!" he said, between his teeth; "they have no eyes except for these poppies gaily attired." At length he walked to the corner, and, taking the old lady by the hand, led her to the middle of the circle.

"Ladies and gentlemen," he said, "I have the honour of presenting to you my wife, Madame Juste."

Salvador and Roman imagined that the singular appearance of this couple would excite universal laughter; they were deceived. To their great surprise, the majority of those who surrounded the young and lovely women we have mentioned left them, to offer their respects to old Madame Juste.

"You must not be astonished at this," said de Pourrieres to them, "M. Juste is a very rich usurer, and lends money to most of the young men of family who are here."

"We have young men of family here, then?"

"Beyond a doubt, do you fancy for a moment that it is I who have invited here the swindlers I have mentioned?"

"If not, how is it they are present, then?"

"All these messieurs dabble in business; for this reason they endeavour to ally themselves with those young men who are entering life, and they often succeed; for we are not generally very dainty in the choice of our friendships, whilst we are without that experience which is only acquired by time. I am myself a living witness of the truth of what I advance: have I not told you that in my earlier career, I was connected with Ronquetti?"

Eight o'clock sounded from the magnificent gilt pendulum which ornamented the chimney-piece of the saloon.

"At table!" exclaimed the guests in one voice; "at table!"

De Pourrieres took the hand of Felicité Beaupertius. The French-Russian deputy advocate offered his to Madame Juste, and they adjourned to the banquet-room.

Lemardelay had levied his contributions on every country both foreign and domestic; the air, the sea, the rivers, the forest, and the garden, had furnished their best and most delicious productions; the plover with its golden plumage, the noble pheasant, the tempting quail, the roach from the Mediterranean, salmon from the Loire, the delicate smelt, the sturgeon, the sterlet from the Volga; the roebuck, the hare, the wild-boar's head from the Ardennes, the paw of the Greenland white bear, figured in all their different modes of cookery on the hospitable dinner-table.

CHAPTER XI.

HISTORY OF FELICITE BEAUPERTIUS.

THE first course of a grand banquet is habitually very silent; the guests, delighted at being at length enabled to satisfy a vigorous appetite, are too agreeably occupied to lose time in useless discourse; 'tis a wonder if even a few words escape in praise of the excellent crawfish soup or *potage à la Cressy*, or the odoriferous flavour of the excellent roast beef. At the second service, as the imperious cravings of nature become somewhat appeased, each commences to take notice of his neighbour, and political and literary discussions, lamentations on the last turn of the public funds, the eulogy of the danseuse à la mode, begin to mix themselves in the exclamations of admiration drawn from the guests by the unexpected appearance of a respectable *poularde* from Man's, artistically stuffed with those precious truffles ycleped *du Perigord*, or of a succulent carp from the Rhine. But at the dessert, when the generous wines of Bordeaux and Bordelais have not been spared during the previous courses, the conversation becomes general; then, if the guests are persons of a lively humour, and not too affected, 'tis a running fire of epigrammatic wit and humorous repartee; of eclats of laughter and refrains commenced without cessation, and never ended; amidst which are heard the detonations of the corks as they bound to the ceiling, and the bubbling of the divine champagne liqueur in the splendidly-cut glasses.

The banquet given by de Pourrieres was like most others. The first and second courses passed off agreeably, and if, during the time occupied in clearing them away, a stranger had entered the saloon, the respectable physiognomy of some of the guests, the air of good society, and the perfect deportment of all, would have made him fancy himself in the midst of a reunion of the peers of France, or at least the deputies. Let us, however, observe in passing, that the features of some, especially of the usurer, of his wife, and the Count Paladin of the Holy Roman Empire, produced a shade in the picture.

The appearance on the table of the finest dessert we can imagine, excited on the part of the guests a general burst of admiration. In fact, Lemardelay had surpassed himself, and this is not saying a little; he wished to gratify at once, all the senses of the convives; the perfumed odour of the lemons of Barbary, of the oranges of Setubal, of the pine apples from the tropics, agreeably pleased the smell; the lively colours of the cherries from Montmorency, and of the wood-strawberry, charmed the eye. One might certainly be allowed to feel a delicious treat, in carrying off from the magnificent peaches of Montreuil, and the white grapes of Fontainbleau, the velvet down they had not yet lost. The pastry, little *chefs-d'œuvre* of the illustrious Felix, the preserves and dried fruits of every kind, the confitures of Bar, cheese from all countries, amongst which the venerable cheese of Brie, which, thanks to M. de Talleyrand, obtained a triumph for

France at the celebrated congress of Vienna, occupied the place of honour; the raised dishes, so brilliant in their aspect, so elegant in their shapes, that it seemed next to sacrilege to destroy them, were placed upon the table at the same time.

Bottles, covered with a venerable dust, some rather lengthy, with a slightly swelling neck, the glass clear and thin, the colour somewhat golden, announce *the Johannisberg*, brought direct from the cellars of M. de Metternich, accompanied with a certificate of its growth ; others neatly enveloped in elegant basket-work, and on which, when the covering of green wax is taken off, we may read a sentence of the Koran, in Persian characters, and from whence escapes that liquor, so dear to the followers of the prophet, known by the name of Schiras wine, accompanied this unique dessert.

"Messieurs," said de Preval, "I propose the health of our Amphytrion, M. de Courtivon."

"To M. de Courtivon!" cried all the guests, raising their glasses ; "to M. de Courtivon!"

"We will not be so unjust as to forget the scientific artiste of the feast," said the Viscount de Lussan ; "I drink to Lemardelay!"

This toast, like the first, was received with unanimous approbation, and the esteemed *Master of Arts* was compelled to appear in the saloon to receive the compliments of the warm admirers of his culinary talents.

Thus far all had passed off agreeably ; but now the fumes of the precious wines, served in profusion to the company, taking possession of their heads, and the coffee and liqueurs, both French and foreign, having finished a work so well commenced, the conversation suddenly took a wider range. On this occasion, as it often happens, it was the ladies who gave the signal for the hazardous proposal and the whispered epigram.

"Well, M. de Courtivon," said the danseuse, "you are determined to quit the world, then?"

"Alas! yes, madame," replied de Pourrieres ; "I renounce Satan and all his pomps and vanities."

"'Tis very edifying," said Mina.

"And quite pastoral," added the danseuse.

"Shall you hold in your hand, when in the fields, a crook adorned with pretty rosy ribands?"

"Why, certainly, I shall have a crook, a flock of pretty sheep, and perhaps, in addition, a Phillis, if I can find one."

"Oh! M. le Comte, take me with you, I pray," said a lady who had not yet spoken ; "I assure you I will be faithful to you, and will not be led astray by the shepherds of the downs."

"I shall be sorry to deprive the quarter of Notre Dame de Lorette of its brightest ornament."

"You are not very gallant, my dear."

"Your flashes of wit are not so dazzling as the wine," said Doctor Delamarre. "Let us drink."

"More wine!" exclaimed the guests ; "and let us have some other glasses!"

Glasses of a monstrous size were brought, filled to the brim with champagne, and manfully emptied. The doctor filled his glass a second time, and swallowed at a gulp, without leaving a trace, the liquor it contained. His visage became horribly injected, his eyes were haggard, and his voice rank and inarticulate.

"That poor Delamarre is already drunk," said the Viscount de Lussan ; "'tis always his case. Delamarre !" he cried in his ear, "is it the shadows of the victims you have sent to purgatory, appearing to you, that make you so dull and morose?"

"Some wine!" said the doctor, whose head had fallen upon the table.

"This commences well," said Salvador to de Pourrieres.

"'Tis nothing," replied the latter ; he then made a sign to the waiters, who discreetly quitted the saloon.

The premature intoxication of the doctor produced on the guests an effect nearly similar to that recorded of the young Lacedemonians, on the exposure of the unhappy Iliotes after drinking beyond measure of the wine of Syracuse ; no one seemed inclined to finish, as it deserved, a fête so well commenced.

"Is it because this poor devil, who knows not how to manage the little strength he possesses, has fallen before the fight, that we should fear the combat?" said the Viscount de Lussan. "De Preval, come and assist me to transport into a corner this ignoramus ; his situation appears to sadden us."

De Preval hastened to do as de Lussan requested ; the doctor was carried into the embrasure of a window, and the folding drapery of crimson damask drawn round him.

"Now that we are at home," said the abbé, "and that M. le Vicomte has rid us of the sight of this drunkard, I shall take the honour, messieurs, of proposing to you the health of the ladies."

"Thanks to M. l'Abbé, and let us drink to the ladies," said the deputy-advocate patriot ; "I see with pleasure, my dear sir, that your religion is not intolerant."

"M. l'Abbé is a very estimable man," said the danseuse ; "'tis not of him, I can assure you, that they sing the famous lines—

Ou allez vous, Monsieur l'Abbé ;
Vous allez vous, casser le nez.' "*

"M. l'Abbé is very indulgent."

"And tolerant."

"He excuses, because he practises all the weaknesses of poor humanity."

"The spirit is willing, but the flesh is weak."

"Eh! l'Abbé, when shall you be nominated curé of a Parisian congregation?" said the deputy-patriot.

"When you again take your place in the elective chamber," replied the abbé, who now perceived that they were quizzing him.

"Well answered," exclaimed the guests, "well answered; let us drink."

Fresh bumpers were filled, and emptied all round.

"No personalities, messieurs, or our feast will end as sadly as that of the Lapithœ," said the Count Paladin of the Holy Roman Empire.

"M. the Count is right, we must not hunt the lice in our head."

"Oh! what an infamous comparison," exclaimed the majestical Mina. "It is quite evident you are indeed become a limonadier! Could you not employ an expression somewhat more agreeable?"

"Waiter, half a glass!"

"A bottle of beer!"

"A small glass!"

The limonadier with the grey moustaches, who was one of the guests, seemed a prey to a violent rage; his face, usually very pale, turned successively from white to red, from red to blue, from blue to green.

"Come, come, monsieur, if you get into a rage, I shall narrate to the company the anecdote of the lingot," said the Viscount de Lussan.

"Do so, tell us the anecdote of the lingot, 'twill help to pass the time."

"Must I?" demanded the viscount, of the unfortunate limonadier.

* "M. l'Abbé, where are you off to?
Your nose you are going to break too."

The latter made a sign in the negative.

"I think we had better request these ladies to entertain us with their histories," said a young man, whose languishing expression, long fair hair, and his manner, announced an unappreciated poet.

"Monsieur wishes for a subject for a vaudeville," replied the lorette.

"For a romance," added the danseuse.

"You are all burning with the desire to tell us your history," said the advocate, "and on our part we are all on the *qui vive* to hear it. Is it true, messieurs?"

"Without doubt," replied Salvador, Roman, and de Pourrieres, at the same time.

"Which shall we hear first," said the advocate, "the vaudeville or the romance?"

"The vaudeville," said the abbé.

"The romance," said Salvador.

"The votes are divided," added Mina; "suppose, to put all in humour, we have a drama?"

"Let it be the drama; but who will narrate it to us?" inquired Roman.

"Eh! parbleu! Felicité Beaupertius," replied Mina; "her history, I am sure, is a very touching one."

"Come, Felicité! commit suicide, my dear," added the danseuse.

Felicité hesitated some moments, before determining to proceed; but Salvador having filled her glass with champagne, which she slowly drank—

"Champagne is a delicious wine," she said; "when we have drank a few bumpers of the generous liquid, all the events of life appear to us *couleur de rose.*"

"Drink another glass, and commence your history," said the danseuse.

Felicité pushed away the glass of wine offered her.

"I am not thirsty," she said.

And leaning back on her seat, commenced as follows:

"You wish me to narrate my history, I will satisfy you; must I not subscribe my share, and pay for the dinner you have given me?"

"Felicité, you are malicious to-night," said the Viscount de Lussan.

"It's true, I was wrong."

"You are pardoned, my child; but the history, the history!"

"I was born at Dijon—"

"A village celebrated for its excellent mustard," said a young man, who seemed very proud of his coloured cheeks, his handsome teeth, his two large eyes; and also very much astonished that what he intended as an excellent joke had not produced universal merriment.

Felicité, thus suddenly interrupted, had hesitated.

"Continue," said Mina; "if this young monsieur recommences his witticisms, we will beg him to adjourn and play at loto."

"I was born at Dijon," continued Felicité, "at the place of the Hotel de Ville, opposite the ancient palace of the dukes of Burgoyne; you will see there a pretty little house, with the outside shutters painted green, and the walls hidden by a thick cluster of nasturtiums and sweet peas, which creep over a trellis work of brass wire. This house belongs to my family, I have passed there the best and happiest days of my life. At fifteen I was still as happy as any innocent young creature who has not been deceived by the illusions of the world. When I retired to my chamber after a well-spent day, and my father had impressed a hearty kiss on my fair forehead, dreams *couleur de rose* were the general companions of my undisturbed slumbers.

"I had attained my sixteenth year, when one day my kind father, after embracing me more tenderly than usual, asked me if I should like to get married.

"This word marriage, which generally produces so many and such sweet emotions to young females, I must confess to you, only caused me uneasiness. My first thoughts were, that when married I should be obliged to quit my father, whom I dearly loved; the pretty birds of my aviary, whose joyous notes woke me every morning; and the delicious flowers of my parterre, which I cultivated with such pleasure. Thus I burst into tears, threw myself on my father's neck, praying him to keep me near him.

"The kind and worthy old man kissed me and smiled.

"'What I have mentioned to you,' he said, 'must not cause you the slightest trouble; you may not, perhaps, be obliged to leave me, and it shall only be with your full consent that you marry the person I destine for you.' I wanted my father to promise me not to speak again about marriage, but he observed to me that he was already old, that the wounds he had received, and his many infirmities, did not permit him to hope for any long existence; that my brother, (I had a brother then,) compelled to follow his regiment in the quality of lieutenant, could not be of service to me as a protector; and that he should not die happy, if he quitted life and left me alone in the world.

"The man who had solicited my hand, was at length presented to me by my father; he was the senior surgeon of a regiment then in garrison in our town; he was a handsome young man about thirty years of age, with the manners and language of good society; his father had been the friend of mine. Although young, he had already made several campaigns, and the sign of honour hung at his breast. After he had spoken to me three or four times, I began to think I could marry him without grieving. Within a month I loved him to idolatry, his every word found an echo in my own breast; when he was absent from me, I wished his return; when I heard his footstep on the threshold, a cold perspiration bedewed my body, and my forehead became like fire. Well! do you know what happened? This man, whom his comrades esteemed, for he is brave, as I have heard; this man, to whom my father had accorded a place at his hearth, because he imagined (the poor old soldier!) that the cross which he carried at his breast was the safest guarantee of honour he could receive; this man, whose hand he pressed every morning in his own, well! this man employed all his seductions to mislead the heart and the principles of a young and innocent girl; he led her far from the paternal roof, and when he had obtained from her all she had it in her power to bestow, he cowardly abandoned her, without troubling himself further as to her fate.

"I had, then, followed my lover; and I must confess, it was only when he had quitted me, that I thought of my father, whom the disappearance of his daughter would plunge into despair.

"My seducer had abandoned me in a furnished hotel, at the moment I was about to become a mother. From this period a week, during which I know not what became of me, must be blotted from my life. When I regained my senses, I was in bed in one of the wards of a lying-in hospital; the events which had passed were wholly confused in my memory, I was determined to know them. It was then only I learnt, that, after reading the letter of my lover, in which he announced to me his departure, and advised me, by way of distraction he said, to form a fresh *liason*, I had fallen on the ground cold and senseless; for two days they kept me at the hotel I inhabited; but the physician who attended me, seeing I did not recover my senses, and that I was in want of every thing, had directed them to remove me to the hospital. Suddenly a confused suspicion flashed across me. 'And my child?' I exclaimed. From their silence, and the gloomy regards they fixed upon me, I understood them, it had died in its birth."

"Poor girl!" said the lorette.

"Oh! 'tis nothing," said Felicité; "help me to wine," she said, pushing her glass towards the Viscount de Lussan.

"Youth and an excellent constitution were more powerful than my illness; and with health I recovered my peace of mind; I no longer loved, I no longer even regretted, the man who had so basely abandoned me; I had no other feeling towards him than a contempt which his dishonourable conduct deserved.

"When they turned me from the hospital, I was still somewhat pale; I had not recovered all my strength; I was compelled to stop more than once to rest myself, before arriving at the hotel I inhabited before my entrance into the hospital. The mistress of this house seemed delighted at my recovery. I begged her to conduct me to the little room which had been mine. She asked me for money, and gave me clearly to understand that she would not return me the few things that I had left with her, until I had paid her the small sum I owed her. As I wept some bitter tears, she observed to me that I was wrong to afflict myself, and that, at Paris, a young and pretty girl need not be embarrassed about herself.

"I left my hostess, without knowing where to direct my steps; I wandered all day in the streets of Paris. Night arrived; it was cold; my teeth chattered against each other. I had taken nothing since the previous evening. I rested near a post, in a street I was ignorant of. I wept. The rain fell upon me, without my paying the least attention to it. An old woman, sheltered under an apology for an umbrella, approached me.

"She asked me the cause of my tears, and why I remained exposed to the rain. I knew not what I replied; but she took me to a wine-shop, and made me sit near a stove which held a good fire, when, thanks to the warmth, the blood again circulated in my veins. She ordered a cup of hot wine sweetened, and some biscuits. Half a glass of wine and a biscuit revived me a little, and I could recount to the old woman all that had happened to me. When I mentioned to her that I knew not where to pass the night, she told me to be easy on that score—that she would take me to her house, and that the next morning she would place me as a workwoman in a house where I should be made very comfortable.

"In fact, the next day she accompanied me to a house of a respectable appearance, and presented me to a female, who, after examining me with the most scrupulous attention, told her she would receive me; she then gave some pieces of money to the old woman, who advised me to do all that was required of me, if I wished them to continue their interest in me. I promised all that she requested of me. The old woman and the female to whom she had presented me seemed delighted with my docility; the old woman, before quitting, would absolutely kiss me.

"'You are very young,' she said, 'but be comforted, they will instruct you; you are in a good school here.'

"I did not comprehend then the terrible meaning she attached to these words.

"I was indeed at a good school. Still, during the first few days that I passed in the house of Madame Dinville, I found myself happy enough. This woman had taken away the plain garments I wore when I entered her house, and had replaced them by others which I considered far beyond the condition of a workwoman. I was served in my own room with the most nourishing dishes and generous wines, and she lavished on me the utmost attentions.

"She generally kept me company when I took my repasts; at such times she excited me to drink, and when the fumes of the wine began to rise to my brain, she would commence a singular discourse.

"I had been a week with this woman, when one morning she told me to dress myself and follow her. I hastened to obey.

"A carriage waited for us at the door. Madame Dinville took me to several shops, where she made some purchases; she bought neither a piece of silk nor a bijou without consulting me, and said she destined for me several of the items she had purchased; and as I exclaimed against this, she kissed me, saying, 'Hold your tongue, you little rogue, you are as pretty as an angel, you will make me regain all this.'

"The carriage deposited us in a dark and narrow street, before a house of mean appearance, the entrance to which was through a long passage. As I entered it, following my conductress, several mean-looking men were congregated before the door of a neighbouring wine-shop; one of these said to another of his comrades:

"'The debutanté is not ugly, she'll bring plenty of grist to the mill.'

"And the man glanced at me in such a manner that I was compelled to keep my eyes fixed on the ground.

"A few moments after this little event, I was with Madame Dinville in a tolerably large room, in which were assembled several other women who seemed waiting to be introduced into another chamber, where they remained a few moments, after which they hastened to quit the one we were in. These women were as different in physiognomy as in costume; some were young and pretty, others already past the meridian, were quite as ugly. Some were habited in silk and velvet, with elegant bonnets and expensive shawls; the others were barely dressed in a few old rags; and yet they seemed to be all on terms of acquaintance, and conversed together in the most friendly tone. Sometimes one of these women, who had entered laughing into the mysterious little chamber, left it in tears, accompanied by a municipal guard.

"I was not at my ease in this place, I felt terrified without knowing why; I said so to Madame Dinville, who replied that I was a child, and that I must not be frightened at what I saw.

"An old man, disgusting enough in appearance, to whom Madame Dinville on entering had given her own name and mine, called us. Introduced, in our turn, into the little room, we found there a man seated in front of an ebony bureau, and bending over a large register; he did not even lift up his head to look at us. He demanded my name, my age, the place of my birth. I replied mechanically to him; I was so astonished at every thing I saw, that I had no longer the consciousness of my actions.

"'Number 3797,' murmured the man, who finished transcribing on his heavy register my replies to his questions.

"This was not all. I was conducted into a cabinet where I found several men, whose appearance and features seemed very respectable; they were the physicians. As I remained before them, with my eyes fixed on the ground, and my countenance embarrassed, one of them observed to my conductress, that they had no time to wait my good pleasure. When she explained to me what they required, I fainted; the curtain which had blinded me was at length removed.

"When I came to myself, I was in the carriage which had brought us; Madame Dinville was at my side; she spoke not a word, the infamous shrew was quite aware that she must allow the bitter grief I felt, sufficient time to calm itself. When we arrived at her house, I wished her to restore me my poor wardrobe, and allow me to leave the house.

"She told me I was a fool, that I refused my happiness; she drew a frightful picture of the misery I should be subject to, the moment I left her door.

"As I would listen to nothing, she informed me, at length, that I was my own mistress no longer; that I was become, under No. 3797, the property of the police; that, in fact, I must either die of starvation, or remain attached to the soil of prostitution.

"Madame Dinville appeared touched at the bitter reproaches I made her; she told me she should not have acted thus, if the old woman who had brought me to her, had not deceived her. At length she proposed to me to remain there, but simply in the character of a workwoman. What could I do? where could I turn, except to die? And death to one who was as pretty as I was then, seemed a hard decree. I remained.

"The pensionaires of Madame Dinville were no longer concealed from me; and these women, no doubt to please their mistress, ceased not to boast of the enjoyments of their profession; and Madame Dinville was continually loading me with attentions.

"She placed in my hands some infamous books, which at first I threw away in disgust, but afterwards read, driven by that irresistible desire of curiosity which so torments every young girl. This reading, the conversation of my companions, the dietary regimen to which Madame Dinville had subjected me, at length produced the effect she had anticipated; ere a month had elapsed I was not the same person; I laughed and I wept without reason, and my nights were passed in dreams of love. I was half mad. At length one evening Madame Dinville made me drink some infernal drug, she dressed me in rich attire, and instead of shutting me in my room, as was her custom, I remained in the saloon, in which were also, as long as the evening lasted, those who were become my companions. The men arrived, they made us drink champagne, and the next morning I was a lost woman.

"From this period my life was a continued series of days of folly and nights of boisterous mirth. One evening Madame Dinville introduced several officers in our room; it was agreed that each officer should pass the night with one of us. As I was the youngest of all the élèves of Madame Dinville, I was the choice of the youngest of the officers, a captain of the African chasseurs. He was gifted with most amiable features, his large black eyes, which fell upon me with looks of compassion, were tinged with a remarkable expression of melancholy. Without the power of giving any reason for the sentiment I obeyed, I, who never accepted without doing violence to my feelings the temporary attachments to which I was condemned, waited with a degree of impatience the moment of retiring with the young officer. And yet I call heaven to witness, no thoughts, such as you probably attribute to me, had induced me to be thus anxious for the time.

"At length after drinking plenty of champagne, and emptying a reasonable number of bowls of punch, the hour of retreat arrived; all my companions were more or less unsteady, it was with some difficulty their cavaliers could support them on their legs; contrary to my custom, I had taken no part in their libations; I had remarked that the young officer scarcely moistened his lips from his glass, each time that his comrades swallowed large bumpers, and I had resolved to imitate him.

"The next morning when I awoke, the young officer who had passed the night with me, had apparently been up some time, for the cigar he was smoking was nearly half consumed; he looked at me with the same melancholy expression I had remarked the evening before; I know not how it was, but I guessed his thoughts, I buried my face in his bosom and shed some bitter tears.

"He kissed me on the forehead—'Poor, poor girl!' he said.

"I had at last found some one who pitied me; I still belonged to humanity then. These thoughts revived me; I continued to weep, but the tears I shed were sweet, they were no longer the burning tears which, after forcing themselves through my scalding eyelids, returned to consume my heart.

"The young officer, who had not ceased regarding me, exerted his utmost to contain himself, still a tear escaped from him, it rested for a moment on the deep scar which the yatagan of an Arab had marked upon his face, it then slid along his dark cheek, and remained suspended, like a brilliant dewdrop, on the extremity of his black and silky moustache. Oh! I would willingly have dried with a chaste kiss this precious tear; I dared not.

"How is it that between two beings who have never before met, there is established that mysterious community of feelings which produces a consciousness of fellowship, without the necessity of words; 'tis an enigma to which we shall never find the answer.

"I felt an irresistible desire of narrating to this man the events which had led me to the house in which he found me; I did not like him to quit me with the idea that I had sought it myself, and that I was pleased with Madame Dinville. I told him all that I have narrated to you.

"As I advanced in my recital, the features of the officer became overspread with an ashy paleness.

"'Where were you born? what is your name?' he said to me when I had finished; and as I hesitated—

"'Answer me!' he said, 'you must indeed answer me!'

"I told him the name of my father; a bitter groan escaped him, he hid his face in his two hands, and remained some moments without replying to me.

"He was my brother!

"Brought up in a military school, he had quitted the paternal mansion whilst I was still an infant, and the necessity of his profession had since constantly kept him at a distance; but the letters he had received from our father, had informed him of the circumstances of my flight with the surgeon I was to have married, and it was the resemblance of the events he had heard from the *fille publique*, to those which had happened to his sister, which had induced him to ask the name.

"I shall not attempt to picture to you the horrible despair which seized me when I made the dreadful discovery; my sobs burst out with such a force, that they attracted to my chamber my brother's comrades and their companions; we were then compelled to play a disgusting comedy, by pretending a disagreement on a very contemptible point, but which was of a nature to be believed by those who questioned us.

"They left us alone, in order that we might come to better terms."

After some moments of silence Felicité Beaupertius continued her history:

"When we were alone, my brother observed that, 'we could do nothing against *un fait accompli*; and that we had a right to hope that the Almighty would pardon us the crime we had committed, for we were in reality more pitiable than guilty. We must not allow ourselves to be crushed by despair; you must first quit this infamous house, and I shall directly employ myself to procure you the means.'

"My brother left with his comrades, after promising to see me again before the day finished. I had much to suffer during his absence; Madame Dinville and her pupils, who had observed on my cheeks the traces of the tears I had shed, continued to question me; and as I refused to reply to them, they made their own conjectures from appearances, as to what had taken place between myself and the young officer. Every supposition, every word, seemed to me, I know not why, a cruel insult, and I had to hear all without complaining.

"My brother returned, and informed Madame Dinville of his wish to take me to the theatre; as he offered to pay her liberally for this indulgence, she consented to my going.

"He conducted me to a small apartment in the hotel he inhabited, and from this period busied himself to seek for me an honest house into which I could be received. Fate, not yet wearied of pursuing me, was not willing that his efforts should be successful.

"The leave of absence he had obtained was on the point of expiration; he would be forced to part from me, without having settled any plan by which my lot could be alleviated; this thought haunted him day and night, and despair settled upon his hitherto gloomy countenance.

"I had reflected much during the last month, in which I had lived almost alone, and I had come to a resolution which I wished to communicate to my brother. One evening therefore, I begged him to enter my room; (he had only visited me when necessity compelled him;) I said to him that after what had passed, I had no wish to enter the world again, and that the wisest plan I could adopt would be to end my days in a convent. My brother made no effort to change my resolution; he saw that it was only induced by the necessity of my position, so without losing time, he obtained every information necessary, and the evening before his departure for Africa he conducted me to the convent of the sisters of Saint Vincent de Paule.

"I was employed for nearly eight months in one of the hospitals of Paris, and I acquitted myself invariably of the duties imposed upon me, in such a manner as to merit the esteem and praises of my superiors. The letters I received from my brother permitted me to hope, that at a period not distant I should be allowed to visit my father; so that, if I was not completely happy, I had at least recovered my peace of mind.

"All my hopes were destroyed in a moment, and I found myself on a sudden plunged again into a more frightful position than when I had met the woman to whom I owed all my troubles. One of the inmates of Madame Dinville, who was afflicted with a dreadful illness, was placed in one of the wards under my care. This woman, despite the costume I wore, and the change which a life of calmness and activity had produced in my features, recognised me. I begged her not to betray me, she promised not to do so; but two days had not elapsed, before every one was informed that, previously to my belonging to God, I had been the property of the police. One morning the abbess mother sent for me to her cabinet, and when we were alone, told me she was sensible that, since I had been under her authority, she had found no occasion to make me a single reproach, but that past events were opposed to my remaining longer among the holy daughters whose habit I wore.

"I did not attempt to soften the superior; her cold and harsh looks, her brief and dry tone, told me too well that my supplications would be in vain. I resigned myself.

"I quitted the garments of a nun, which were replaced by a plain but respectable dress, given me by the abbess.

"As I passed, on retiring, in front of the bed occupied by the woman who had betrayed me, '*Au revoir*,' she said to me. These words, and the malicious sneer which accompanied them, affected me more than the affront I had submitted to; they taught me that misfortune was an impassible circle round me, and that in this world there existed no escape by means of repentance.

"At this moment I came to a resolution to make this oracle belie itself.

"As I passed the threshold of the hospital, the porter gave me two letters; this man, on whom I had bestowed the most constant attention during the whole time of a severe illness, found means to render still more painful the wounds under which I was suffering: 'Give me your address, my sister,' he said to me, 'perhaps I shall come and see you,' and he accompanied his impudent words by a smile of still greater vulgarity.

"Arrived at the quay, I stopped to read my two letters; I had not till then remarked that they were both sealed with black. I was seized with a convulsive shivering; one of the letters informed me that my father had died after a long and painful illness; the other that my brother had been killed in Africa, charging at the head of his regiment a troop of Bedouins. I uttered not a cry, I shed not a tear, I looked gloomily at the Seine, whose waters glided calmly and smoothly; I said to myself that I had suffered enough to permit me to seek a refuge in death, and I remained a long time leaning on the parapet.

"I was aroused from the sombre reflections which overwhelmed me by the voice of an old woman, who demanded of me what I did there. 'I am waiting,' was my reply, 'for the night to advance, that I might plunge into the river.' This reply was the continuation of the thoughts which occupied my mind.

"The old woman seized me by the arm; I then recognised her as a servant I had had in my service some time before.

"'Are you mad, my sister,' she said to me, 'and what has happened to you?'

"In addressing this question to me, she regarded me with a look of affection. The ice which had till then frozen up my heart, melted before the mild and soothing tones of this poor woman; I wept. Already the idlers had congregated round us.

"'Come with me,' said the woman, 'we shall be more at our ease to converse.'

"She had not quitted my arm which she had placed in her own. I followed her without any resistance into the miserable garret of a poor house in the Rue des Rats.

"'Remain there,' she said to me, 'recover yourself; I must go out, but I shall not remain long; when I return you shall tell me what has happened to you, and perhaps I may be of some service to you. I am very poor, it is true, but when one has a good will, it is always possible to do some little good.'

"The old woman returned after being absent about an hour; she prepared, with an activity beyond her age, a slight repast, of which she begged me to take a part. My heart was too full to attempt to satisfy her, still not to disoblige her, I accepted a bason of soup and swallowed a few spoonfulls.

"The old woman had finished her humble meal.

"'Well! my child,' she said.

"I told her all that had happened to me, and made her read the two letters I had received.

"'You are very unfortunate,' she said, 'you have already suffered some cruel trials, and perhaps the future has in reserve for you others still more cruel; but that gives you no right to dispose of your life; it is from God you have received your existence, my child, and you must wait for your release, the moment it shall please him to recall that which he has given you. In quitting the house of your father to follow your lover, you committed a great fault; accept then, as an expiation, all the trials with which you have been visited.'

"I regarded with astonishment this poor woman, who evidently belonged to the lowest class of society, but who found, in order to console me, such eloquent words.

"'But must I then,' I exclaimed, 'return to that abominable house of Madame Dinville?'

"'No, no, my child,' replied the good woman, 'you shall not return to the house of this woman, it is not in vain that God has sent me to you at the moment you were about to commit a crime. As I have already told you, with good will we may accomplish much; so you need not despair, I shall look about, and it is probable I shall find something that may suit you. In the mean time, remain here, and pray God to give you sufficient courage to support the troubles of this life.'

"As she had promised, my worthy hostess went into the country, and after some days, she announced that she had at length found a place for me, and I accompanied her to an old gentleman and his wife, who, upon her recommendation, received me into their house.

"I had been nearly a month in their service, when one day I was accosted in the street by two individuals of shabby appearance, who asked me if my name was not Louise Durand. As this was not my name, I replied that they were mistaken; they insisted. Impatient at length with their obstinacy, I ended by telling them my real name. 'I was not wrong,' said one of them, suddenly changing his tone and manners; 'well, since you are Mamselle ——, you will have the goodness to come with us; you can boast, my little princess, of having led us a jolly good dance.' These two men were agents of that division of police to which they have given the name of *attribution des mœurs*.* They took me to a guard-house, where they registered the pro-

* Division of morals.

cess-verbal of my arrest. That done, they led me to the prefecture of police. I was thrown into the midst of half a hundred women, who appeared quite indifferent as to their fate.

"The black dress I wore, on account of the death of my father and brother, and which I had purchased with the little money given me by the abbess of the hospital on my leaving, drew upon me at first some jeers; but seeing I did not reply to their low witticisms, and that I did not stir from the corner in which I had taken refuge on entering the room, these women finished by leaving me at rest.

"The next morning my name resounded through the halls of the prison, and a jailer placed me in the hands of a municipal guard, charged to conduct me before my judge. I was obliged to traverse all the courts of the prison accompanied by my guide, to arrive at the house I had already visited with Madame Dinville. The passengers stopped to look at me, and they seemed astonished that I should conceal my face in my handkerchief.

"I was introduced into the cabinet of the examining commissare; I did not attempt to claim his pity for my fate; I knew too well that would be useless. I confined myself simply to replying by a 'yes,' or 'no,' to the questions he addressed to me, and I heard him, without feeling much emotion, condemn me to three months in prison.

"I was conducted to the prison of Saint Lazare. I met in this prison, which resembles most others, several women whom I had had occasion to know during my residence with Madame Dinville. These women pitied me, and severely blamed her who, in betraying me, had occasioned me the loss of my place in the hospital.

"'If by good luck,' said one of them, 'you had not been discovered by the agents until a month later, you would have been enabled to remain with the honest people with whom that good old woman had placed you; for, after a twelvemonth, you would have been exempt from their control.'

"This woman said true; one month more, and the police, to whom I belonged body and soul, would have been consented to release their prey.

"'How can you help it, my poor friend? 'tis exactly the case,' said this woman to me often, with whom I had made some acquaintance, as she appeared to me a little less shameless than my other companions in captivity; 'when once our name is inscribed in the *red book*, it must remain there, and the wisest part we can take, is to well employ our youth, and wait for our despair until we become old and ugly.'

"I began to think she might be right. I had in fact used all my efforts in the terrible struggle I had so long sustained: and these efforts had been all in vain. I was weary of suffering, and I did not wish to die; I threw, as they say, the handle after the axe, and as I received no succour from any one, I wrote to Madame Dinville to send me some, and I promised to enter her house as soon as I was at liberty. I did not wait long for her reply; it was more *affectionate* than I had expected, and accompanied with money and all the little bagatelles which might help to relieve my captivity.

"My life, from the day I was set at liberty, has been that of all women of my profession; but I can assert it, because I speak the truth, often, during the outrageous orgies in the midst of which I played a conspicuous part, often, I say, I regretted the days I had passed attending the patients of the hospital; but when these regrets intruded themselves, I sought consolation in the depth of a glass of champagne. Help me to a glass of wine, superb

Viscount de Lussan," said Felicité, interrupting herself.

The viscount hastened to obey her.

"'Tis really a strange circumstance," she continued, raising her glass above her head, "to see the last scion, as I am told, of one of the most illustrious families of Brittany, act as cup-bearer to a courtesan. Messieurs, I drink to your health ; you are no better than I am."

"Bravo, Felicité !" exclaimed the women ; "that's capital ! but finish your history."

Felicite tottered even in her chair ; her eyes wandered without the faculty of perception ; the poor girl began to feel the first attacks of the intoxicating liquors.

"Ah ! yes," she said, "I must finish my history. Well ! I, also, have enjoyed some happiness, like you, Mina ; like all of you, whether married or single ! I have found a man who pays my milliner, my jeweller, and my servants ; but this man, who is old and ugly, loves me not ; he has purchased me, as he would a well bred horse, or a handsome dog ; to him, I am an object of luxury, and he would quit me to-morrow if I ceased to be *á la mode*. But I am *á la mode!* I am, besides, well dressed. I have diamonds, and lacqueys, and I sleep on down. This will last as long as I can preserve my youth and my attractions—so long as I shall be merry, as Monsieur —— says ; after that—the hospital ; it is that which awaits us all. When I am there to die, they will not drive me away perhaps——"

Felicité took the glass, placed it at her side, and, although empty, attempted to raise it to her lips, but she had not the power to accomplish it ; it fell from her hand, and rolled to the ground, where it broke into a thousand pieces ; she then looked round in astonishment, her head dropped on her bosom, and she fell into a profound sleep.

The recital of Felicité Beaupertius made different impressions on the convives ; de Pourrieres, a few young men, and the females, were all disposed to believe her, and pity her ; the others thought she merely wished to render herself interesting.

"I like neither romances nor dramas," said the limonadier with the gray moustaches, "and if the ladies cannot entertain us with something better than the history we have just heard, they will do well to be silent—it was quite wearisome."

"You express yourself with much rudeness," said the danseuse.

"It is not rudeness, but honest military frankness."

"Come, come, you slander the military, they are in general very polished, even those who serve in the heavy cavalry."

"De Lussan, the history of the lingot !" said Mina.

"I am afraid I shall put our friend in a bad humour," replied the viscount.

"Never mind, he is not as humble as the animal they sing of, which, when attacked, makes no defence."

The limonadier quitted the seat he occupied without saying a word, and left the saloon ; creeping along the wall that he might not be discovered.

"An individual of more than doubtful probity," said de Lussan, when the limonadier was outside, "thought to himself one day, that it would be accomplishing something very droll, and would cause a smile even on the lips of Satan, if he could find the means of 'planting' our worthy friend ; after long reflection, he contrived, as follows, to attain his object. He called upon this honourable nego-

tiant, and requested of him a private interview. When alone, he said to him—

"'I exercised in a province the profession of a jeweller ; in consequence of some untoward affairs, I was compelled to quit the trade ; I have nothing remaining of all I possessed but a lingot of gold, which is worth about 10,000 francs ; the position in which I am placed prevents me from openly disposing of this lingot, composed of the bijoux which I found the means of subtracting from my creditors at the time of my failure. If you will purchase it of me, I will be reasonable enough to allow you the possibility of making a handsome profit.'

"Our friend could not refuse such a tempting offer, and a day was named to conclude it.

"The proprietor of the lingot observed to the limonadier, that they could not *coram populo* settle so delicate an affair. Our friend acknowledged the justice of this remark, and hastened to engage a small attic on the sixth floor of a very modestly furnished hotel, to which he repaired at the time agreed upon.

"'Have you brought what is necessary to prove the quality of the gold?' said the owner of the lingot.

"'My faith, no.'

"'How shall we manage, then?'

"''Tis very embarrassing.'

"'Eh! now I recollect, I have with me a small saw ; we will detach a morsel, which you shall take to the nearest jeweller, for the purpose of being assayed.'

"The lingot was drawn from the envelope, and placed on a table ; our friend took the charge of holding it whilst the other sawed ; a portion, removed by a few turns of the saw, fell on the floor ; the swindler stooped, picked it up, and gave it to our worthy friend, who examined it a few moments before leaving to get it proved.

"''Tis gold, and the best,' said the jeweller to whom he had taken it.

"Nothing being opposed to the conclusion of the bargain, our friend counted down six handsome bank notes of 1000 francs each, to the swindler in question, who retired as satisfied as a Jew who has taken in a Christian.

"Some days after, the lingot became the property of an honest banker, who had bought it in confidence ; but when they wished to use it, it was discovered to be nothing more than copper of the best quality. From this followed process, lawyers and bailiffs, so that at length our friend was compelled to restore the banker the sum he had received from him, and found that he had paid 6000 francs for a piece of copper weighing a few pounds.

"The unfortunate vendor of warm water had not observed that the fripon, when he stooped, had dexterously substituted a piece of the purest gold in the place of that he had detached from the lingot."

"The limonadier, no doubt, complained, and the swindler was punished?" said the young neglected poet.

"You are totally in error, my dear sir," replied de Preval ; "he made no complaint, and the swindler was not punished ; men who have any respect for themselves do not place justice in the confidence of their affairs. If, for example, we sought the procureur du roi every time we had to complain of a friend, we should not to-day see Pylades and Orestes sitting side by side at the same table." De Preval pointed out to the company the Count Paladin of the Holy Roman Empire, and his respectable friend.

"The past is a dream," replied the latter.

"It's true," said Mina, "let us merely look to the present, and beg this ex-legitimist to favour us with a history of his conversion."

"It is forbidden to mention politics in a reunion of more than twenty persons," replied the individual to whom Mina had addressed herself.

"Well, now, my honourable friend," said the deputy-patriot, "shall you not be a little embarrassed when the time arrives to render some account to your constituents?"

"Not more than yourself, my dear fellow; for it is whispered about, that since the lame and the blind have been your only visitants, all goes wrong."

"You are an impertinent scoundrel."

"At least I am very near one."

"There, there, messieurs! Have you forgotten that it is only at home we must wash our dirty linen?" said Roman.

"You are indebted to us a history," said de Preval, addressing the danseuse, "will you deliver yourself with as good a grace as your friend Felicité?"

"Certainly, I am quite ready to obey you; but if you are willing, Monsieur de Preval, you can recount to us a history much more interesting than any it is in my power to furnish you with?"

"And which may that be, bon Dieu?"

"Why, your own, parbleu! Do you fancy, then, we are ignorant of what passed at the Isles d'Hyères, between you and the young girl of the Legion of Honour?"

"Come, then, de Preval, it seems that it was a sort of mistress-wife?" said de Lussan.

"Are you suffering, at present, from the wound of the poniard she was the cause of your receiving from the provincial fisherman?" continued the danseuse.

"No, I am now quite recovered; but let us say no more about it, I beg of you."

"Is it true that this little creature is become a delightful vocalist, and that under the name of Silvia she has obtained immense success at Marseilles?"

"Is it true that she is the daughter of a woman named or surnamed Mother Sans Refus, who keeps a suspicious house in the Rue de la Tannerie?"

These numerous questions sadly annoyed the poor de Preval, who made several attempts, without success, to change the subject of conversation, but when they had tired of quizzing him, the danseuse was reminded of the promise she had made.

"Who, among you, recollects the ball at the Grande Chaumière?" she said.

"I do, I do," exclaimed those of the company who were devoted to medicine or law.

"Well!" replied the danseuse, "you will agree with me then that it is a charming place." La Grande Chaumière! At the mention of these words, like the old racer who feels the spur, the grave magistrate who dozes in his chair, the studious advocate who anxiously pores over the dusty papers of a lengthened suit-at-law, the skilful physician who seeks the solution of a problem in medicine, each and all raise their heads, and a smile cheers up their features, so serious but a moment before, and all the events of their past life spread themselves once more before their sight. These events are, the merry meetings of the parterre at the Odeon; the rendezvous under the old chestnut trees of the Luxembourg; the short pipes; and the garret in which they passed such happy hours with a pretty grisette.

"We have the honour of numbering among us two of the Celebrites of the modern bar and an honest physician, whose slumbers appear very agitated. Well! I am sure that these grave personages would give many things, if they were permitted to drink once more from the cup they have so often emptied.

"La Grande Chaumière, you see, is the *el dorado* of the disciples of Cujas, of Bartholo, and Hippocrates, and of those pretty birds of the Latin quarter, whose nest is found wherever the wine of Chablis, oysters, swings, and the cigarettes of Maryland, are procurable. Each finds there something agreeable—the students, smiling grisettes, who are not Lucretias—the grisettes, ardent attentions, foaming beer, and cakes every day, ices and recherché suppers the first day of every month.

"I was a modest little milliner when I was introduced into this place of entertainment by one of my companions of the work-room; I had never seen any thing so charming; the melodious sounds of the flageolet and the cornet-a-piston, the constant attentions of a handsome young man, who told me, between a waltz and a country dance, that he should die if I did not take pity on his sufferings, made me forget the hour at which I was to return home. My father was a poor workman, whose education had not corrected the faults he had received from dame nature; he was harsh—brutal even. Instead of making those observations to which I should have listened with respect, he ill-treated me in a horrible manner, and turned me from the door of the paternal roof, telling me to return from whence I came. My mother, who had already too often felt the cruel effects of my father's rage, wept in a corner, without daring to take my part.

"Outraged at the treatment I had received for a fault in reality slight, I quitted our house without very painful regrets, and I passed the night with my friend, who had taken me to the Grande Chaumière. She received me kindly, and told me I could live with her as long as I liked.

"The sweetheart of this young girl was the most intimate friend of him who had so pressingly courted me at the Grande Chaumière. I saw the young man again; he recommenced his attentions; I was young, inexperienced; he did not displease me; you have by this time guessed that he became my lover.

"To this attachment I brought a warmth of heart and a purity of sentiments, which my admirer was incapable of appreciating—so that before the expiration of six months he left me, to harness himself to the car of a new star, which has risen on the horizon of the Latin quarter.

"This abandonment, which nothing justified, wounded me deeply; but as I am, thank God, endowed with a reasonable dose of philosophy, I never for a moment dreamt of dying. I threw a glance behind, in order to examine my whole life, up to the moment at which I had arrived. I reflected as follows: To the age of eighteen, my conduct was irreproachable; I was gentle, modest, and industrious, and honestly brought my salary to the paternal roof; and yet, my parents, instead of aiding me to continue in the path I seemed willing to follow, appeared to take every opportunity possible to withdraw from me the desire of doing well; and because I one day passed a few hours more than I ought to have done at a public ball, my father, instead of sober remonstrance and efficient advice, which I had a right to expect, has struck me, and cast me from his door, in the middle of the night, without troubling himself as to what might become of me. He had not the right, however, of acting so severely towards me ; he who spends the best part of his days at the cabaret, and only replies by ill treatment to the just reproaches of his humble partner. Well ! a man sees me—tells me he loves me. I believe him; and this man, after robbing me of my innocence, my only wealth, has quitted me with as much indifference as a garment that he is tired of. Shall I continue for ever the dupe of my good qualities ? No; I am poor; there exists not in the world a person on whose friendship I can rely; but I am young, I am handsome, very handsome, indeed ; the future is before me; I will do as other women, who, because I am modestly dressed, regard me with such a disdainful air when I pass them ; as long as my youth and beauty remain, I will lead a happy life : when my beautiful black hair is turned to grey; when my figure, now so graceful, so well shaped, shall be bent with age; when the thirty-two pearls which adorn my pretty mouth shall turn to miserable tiny bones, and trembling in their gums, I shall not even then be unhappy, for I shall take care every day to put aside a part for the future.

"This resolution, taken at the moment I had been cowardly abandoned by the man I loved, has since been the guiding rule of every action of my life; I felt that if I wished to succeed in the career I had chosen, I must suffer myself to be loved by every one to whom it would be a pleasure, but that I must not love in return. I called to mind the celebrated beauties who have died in an hospital, after rolling in gold; thus I have loved no one, not even you, M. le Vicomte de Lussan, who are at this moment the fortunate possessor of my charms; and I have converted into good inscriptions in the public funds, the greatest part of the receipts obtained by my smiles, my glances, and my dulcet words.

"You will consider me, perhaps, as something very ignoble, very selfish; but what is that to me? Have you not all agreed, with some poet, that virtue without gold is a useless quality ? and are not all your actions the consequence of this maxim? Why then should I not be permitted to do as others?

"It is asserted that the ministers sell their country, that the deputies sell their conscience, that the electors sell their votes, that the generals sell their armies to the enemy; the pope, 'tis said, sells indulgences, dispensations, and the cross of the golden spur; M. l'Abbé sells absolution to his flock; they say that venal judges sell acquittals and condemnations; that the men in power sell the places, grades, and privileges of which they can dispose; the advocates, lawyers, and bailiffs sell their clients; the porters and servants sell their masters; I have purchased elegies from this illustrious Solon; I would purchase sonnets from this neglected poet, if his verses were of any value; Doctor Delamarre sells to ladies who are betrayed, advice which, sooner or later, will conduct him to the court of assize; this Englishman, who seems on the point of falling under the table, and this ex-merchant of nightcaps, sell fools' grain to the simpleton; this honest inventor of partnerships, sells to the shareholders the powder he throws in their eyes; husbands sell their wives, mothers sell their daughters; M. Justè sells silver for its weight in gold to young men of family. It seems, in fact, that in our modern Babylon, one half the world sells the other half; and I—I sell my smiles, my glances, and my honeyed words. Let those among you who find the merchandise not of good quality, say so, and the money shall be returned."

"Bravo, Coralie!" exclaimed M. Roulin, when the danseuse had finished this long tirade, "bravo! Let every one have his deserts, and the devil will be no loser."

"You are very ready to praise me; is it because I have forgotten you?"

"M. Roulin sells nothing, on the contrary, he buys whatever is offered him," said the Count Paladin of the Holy Roman Empire.

"Except your cross of knight of the golden spur."

"Messieurs," said Salvador, "what is the conclusion to be drawn from what we have heard?"

"Shall I reply to you with frankness," said the deputy Franco-Russe.

"You will do me a great pleasure."

"Well! the man who said that fools were sent on earth for the wise man's pleasure, has told a truth which is of all times, and of all countries."

"Amen," said the ex-curé.

It was now late, and the guests acknowledged the want of a few hours' repose. De Pourrieres ordered an enormous bowl of punch, each drank his share, and they separated.

"We will recount you our history another time," said Mina and the lorette, before quitting the Marquis de Pourrieres and his two friends.

CHAPTER XII.
TWO MURDERS.

ON the second morning from the feast, Salvador and Roman paid a visit to their Amphytrion. Although it was already late, de Pourrieres, who had so fêted Bacchus and Comus, on the night of the feast, was still in bed, and complained of having a drowsy head and disordered stomach.

"I am so ill," he said to his new friends, "that I really think it will be impossible for me to put myself en route to-morrow as I had intended."

"Well, you gave us a veritable Belshazzar's feast," replied Roman, "and you showed us an example worthy of being followed by your guests."

"Indeed I am astonished," said Salvador, "that we did not behold on the walls of the banquetting room, the three words which announced to the guests of Belshazzar the ruin of Babylon."

"That which did not happen yesterday, may happen to-morrow," said Roman; "but let us change the subject; the sky is clear, the sun shines gloriously; if you like, M. le Marquis, we will all go and breakfast in the country, with one of our compatriots, who lives at Villemonble, a pretty little village about two leagues from Paris."

De Pourrieres, who was really indisposed, would not at first accept the invitation given him, but Salvador and Roman having pressed it, and observing that a walk in the country would dissipate the clouds which obscured his brain, and renovate his strength, he determined to accompany them.

Salvador and Roman, since they had made the acquaintance of the Marquis de Pourrieres, had not allowed a single day to pass without making him a visit; and from simple acquaintances they became most intimate friends; Roman especially, whose quality of a countryman made him dear to the young man, had acquired his whole confidence; and the latter had, at length, got into the habit of consulting him on all matters he had in hand.

He had made him read all his correspondence with the Jew Josuè, and the woman at Geneva, who had the charge of his son; he read to him his father's will and the different codicils attached to it. The reading of these papers had proved to them that the idea of substituting Salvador for the Marquis de Pourrieres, by causing the dissappearance of the latter, could be realised. In fact, the cholera had carried off the nearest relations of the marquis, and all the old retainers of his family, with the exception of a single one, whose great age would render him an easy dupe.

"We shall be a little crowded, perhaps," said Roman to de Pourrieres, before mounting the vehicle, "but the cab will carry us as far as Bondy, when we will leave it and traverse on foot the park of Raincy. The walk will give us an appetite, at the same time that it will make you acquainted with one of the most agreable promenades in the environs of Paris, a noble chateau, and a superb avenue."

Salvador, the marquis, and Roman, took their places in the cab, which was found large enough to hold the three in comfort; Salvador, who was placed in the middle, took the reins, and they departed.

The horse, which seemed fresh enough to continue a much longer journey than the one required of him, trotted away in style, and the distance which separated the Rue Joubert from the pretty village of Bondy was cleared with rapidity.

After traversing the village, the voyageurs, as it had been agreed, descended from the cab; and after taking each a glass of Hollands with the aubergiste of the *Cheval Rouge*, in whose care they left the cab, put themselves *en route* for Villemonble.

It was a beautiful July morning, the sky was a deep blue, and strewn with little silvery clouds; the sun, which had risen in splendor, gilded the tops of the trees, on which still trembled the sparkling pearls of the morning dewdrops; the chaffinch and the linnet warbled under the leafy branches, in hopping from bough to bough; and each breath of wind brought with it the perfumed odour of the wild flowers.

When we quit a noisy city like Paris, the view of the country, when invested in her sweetest attire, and all in nature seems to smile, uniformly produces a lively impression; we feel lighter than we were an hour ago; we inhale the breeze with all the strength of our lungs, and are quite disposed to believe that we have taken a fresh lease of our life.

Such was the disposition of mind of Alexis de Pourrieres, who walked in front of Salvador and Roman, smoking his Havannah cigar.

He stopped of a sudden.

"Really," he said, "I am obliged to you for visiting me this morning, and especially for insisting upon taking me; if I had not accompanied you, I should be still in bed, as bad as 'tis possible to be after a heavy debauch; whilst now I am gay, active, and quite disposed to consider excellent, the simple meal with which our host is to furnish us."

"I would rather be forced to fight ten gendarmes to gain my liberty," said Salvador in a low tone to Roman, "than assassinate this man, in the cowardly manner we intend."

"How, scruples!" replied Roman in the same tone; "really the moment is well chosen for them; have you forgotten then that we have no money, and that we must absolutely keep ourselves quiet for some time if we have no desire to return *la bas?*"*

"Our position is embarrassing it's true; but this man places so much confidence in us—"

* Prison.

"Well! who the devil asks you to have a finger in the pie? When the moment to strike arrives, you will turn your head; it will be just as though you were not present."

"What is your conversation about?" said de Pourrieres, who still walked in front.

"Oh! of matters but little interesting," replied Roman; "of the rain and fine weather. You can, if you like, remain behind," he continued to his companion; "in five minutes the affair will be over."

They had arrived in the most obscure and least frequented part of the park.

"This way, M. le Marquis," said Roman to de Pourrieres, who had crossed the road to chase a butterfly, whose variegated wings glittered in the sunshine like a mosaic of precious stones; "this way; by following this path we shall arrive at Villemonble much sooner."

De Pourrieres retraced his steps, and Roman allowed him to pass the first into the narrow path he had indicated to him.

"I am as hungry as the devil," said de Pourrieres, after taking a few steps.

Roman took a survey about him, all was calm, the sky was serene, the linnet and chaffinch still warbled forth their loves under the foliage of the venerable oaks.

His hand fondled, in one of the pockets of his paletot, an instrument of death about ten or twelve inches long, composed of five or six pieces of whalebone strongly united together, and terminated at the extremities by a nob of lead of the size of an egg, each weighing a pound, and covered as well as the branch which united them by a texture of leather skilfully plaited. By an anomaly this instrument is denominated a *life preserver*.

He approached the marquis.

"Go and breakfast with Satan then," he said.

De Pourrieres fell as though struck with a thunderbolt.

At this moment the croak of a bird of prey, who winged his flight through the air, in pursuit of two innocent wood pigeons, sounded in the ears of the murderer; and by one of those changes in the weather, so common during the dog-days, the sky became lurid and overcast, the lightning furrowed up the clouds, the thunder groaned in the distance, and a heavy and continued rain had soon converted into a scene of desolation the landscape, which scarcely an hour ago had appeared so cheerful and so animated.

Salvador drew near to Roman, and regarded with terrified looks the body of the marquis, stretched on the ground.

"This sudden storm is no presage of good," he said, after a few minutes' silence.

"On the contrary, this storm is a lucky circumstance," replied Roman, who was perfectly composed; "it gives us a certainty that we shall not be interrupted; but let us make haste, we have not too much time for what remains to be done."

Roman drew from under a mass of dried branches and leaves heaped together at the foot of an old elm, one of those large earthen jars to which they have given the name of *dame-jean*, and when Salvador had taken the note-case and all that was found in the pockets of the Marquis de Pourrieres, he emptied the contents on the body, taking care to well saturate the garments of the corpse.

"'Tis spirits of turpentine," he said; "five minutes after we have set it on fire, there will remain nothing of the body but a shapeless mass, to which it will be impossible to give a name."

Let us not be accused here of painting a picture for the mere sake of terrifying our readers; we have already observed, and we here repeat it, the major part of the events that we narrate in this work are religiously true; and were we not afraid of augmenting the notes, already so numerous, we could adduce an authority for nearly every fact we advance.*

Salvador and Roman, after the latter had set fire to the heap of branches which he had placed round and upon the body, hastened to quit the scene of the crime they had committed, and regained at a hurried pace the auberge of Bondy, at which they had left their cab.

Salvador was still extremely pale; Roman left him on the step of the inn door, and went alone to get the cab, to which, as he had directed, the horse was already harnessed.

"You have been surprised by the storm, and it has disarranged your walk," said the host of the *Cheval Rouge.*

"'Tis a misfortune for which we shall easily console ourselves," replied Roman. He had brought the cab to the door of the court yard, under which Salvador was waiting. "Come, messieurs," he said, loud enough to be heard, "mount; adieu, friend."

"A pleasant journey, messieurs," replied the aubergiste, without even turning his head.

"If, on a future day, we may have to render an account before men, for the death of the Marquis de Pourrieres," he said to his accomplice, "this man will not be enabled to depose against us, he did not remark that we arrived three, and were only two at our departure."

The house in which was the apartment occupied by de Pourrieres, was composed of two parts, the one looking into the street, and the other into a garden which separated them; the apartment of the marquis was situate on the third floor of the former, and the porter's lodge was at the entrance of the latter; it was therefore very easy to enter this apartment without being seen.

Salvador and Roman, who, as we have said, had taken from the pockets of the marquis his note-case and keys, introduced themselves into his room towards the evening, after returning the cab to the person of whom they had hired it, in the Rue Basse du Rempart.

They took possession of all the bank-notes, money, jewels, and papers, letters and passports, which they found, and they were fortunate enough to meet with no interruption when they retired from the house.

After this expedition, the two accomplices, who were overcome with fatigue, hastened to their own hotel; Salvador was as pale as a corpse, a few convulsive movements, which he could not control, showed that he was the subject of a burning fever;

* In 1816, they discovered at Batignolles-Mouceaux, in a valley in which was situated the house of the mayor, ashes and the remains of branches and dry leaves, which must have been disposed in the form of a bed, and upon which were discovered the shapeless remains of a body; the bed had been totally consumed, and nothing more of the body remained, than the bones, completely calcined. Among these sad relics were found the blades of two razors, a few buttons of metal, and one of bone. The head of the corpse was not recognisable. Men of science maintained that the fire had been fed either by essences, or some inflammable matter; and in fact, it had been so considerable, that the foliage of the neighbouring trees were half consumed. This discovery induced, on the police, a lengthened search, which remained without results; it was never ascertained whether a crime had been committed, or whether a suicide had chosen such an extraordinary means of ending his life. However, it was never brought to light.

Roman on the contrary was as easy and as gay as usual.

"My dear pupil," he said to Salvador, when they had entered their little room, "we must try to change your features; if the sergeants of police, whom we have passed in coming here, had remarked your countenance, they would certainly have suspected that you had just committed some crime."

"Oh!" replied Salvador, "I shall always have the image of this unfortunate man before my eyes."

"If it was your first *coup d'escarpe*,* I should acknowledge that you might not be quite at your case, these sort of affairs disturb us a little the first time; but this is not your first. Have you forgotten the domestic of the banker Carmagnola, and the brigadier of the gendarmerie of Beausset?"

"Oh! they are not at all similar; if I struck them, it was in self defence; but this man, Roman, this man, whom we have murdered whilst he supposed us his friends !—"

"Talk no more about it, 'tis much the wisest, and let us busy ourselves about our little affairs. Behold yourself now, almost certain of inheriting the name and fortune of the Marquis de Pourrieres; shall you have sufficient courage and presence of mind to go on?"

"I hope you do not doubt it."

"You are younger than the deceased, but that's nothing; you have always seemed a little older than you are; you do not positively resemble him, but your features and your height have a similarity with his; you are fair, but thanks to the recent discoveries in chemistry, it will be easy to turn you into the handsomest brown possible. Your eyes are blue and his were black; but this difference will escape detection, much more easily as no one will dream of contesting your identity."

"But it appears there still remains an old domestic of the family?"

"It's true, but age must have weakened all the faculties of this man, whom we will get rid of, if it becomes absolutely necessary."

"We shall also be obliged to see the Jew Josuè."

"I shall present myself to him as your substitute; I shall not appear too severe when it concerns the chapter of interest; and with this, the Jew will be satisfied; the child of the deceased and of Jazetta is not a serious obstacle, he will become your son to-day; we shall see by and by what it will be necessary to do with him."

"Well, well, all is for the best, and behold me Marquis de Pourrieres, and the possessor of at least sixty thousand francs a year," exclaimed Salvador, who had resumed all his gaiety.

"You mean to say," added Roman, "behold us both Marquis de Pourrieres, and possessors of sixty thousand francs a year."

"That is a matter of course; we cannot now separate any more."

The first care of Salvador and Roman was to quit the hotel they inhabited at Paris, under false names, in order to lodge themselves more suitably; they had no fears as to the result of the researches induced by the discovery of the body of their victim, certain that such a shapeless mass could not possibly be identified.

They had often visited the cafè, in which they had first encountered the unhappy victim; no one among them inquired concerning him who had been known only as de Courtivon, and who besides had announced his approaching departure to all his friends.

* Murder.

SILVIA FOLLOWING ROMAN IN THE WOOD OF BOULOGNE.

LIFE IN PARIS

After having well studied their character, and when Salvador, who had great skill in forging, had learnt to imitate perfectly the writing of the deceased, they departed for Aix.

They had taken the post to arrive at this village; Salvador had all the papers of the Marquis de Pourrieres, which were perfectly correct; he had dyed his hair with the greatest nicety, and this operation had entirely changed the expression of his features; Roman took the name of Lebrun, and passed himself off as his intendant.

It was decided that Salvador should remain at Aix; and that Roman, bearing a letter exactly imitating that of the deceased marquis, should alone visit the notary who had the will, in order to take cognisance of the affairs of the succession; he was to appear satisfied with every thing, and approve of all that had been done, whilst having the appearance of being a careful steward of the interests of his master.

The notary, who besides was a very honest man, received him kindly; and within a week he felt a very great esteem for M. Lebrun; it was in fact difficult to meet with an intendant more honest or liberal.

The uncle and tutor of Roman, also a notary, had died some time before; and as the companion of Salvador had visited the village of Pourrieres but two or three times during the last fifteen years, he had no fears of being recognised. He was thus perfectly tranquil, and employed the time which was not passed with the notary, in collecting at Pourrieres and the neighbourhood all the information necessary to facilitate the appearance of his companion on the scene; he learnt with pleasure that the cholera had made such ravages in this part of Provence, that half the population at least had descended into the grave.

At his first visit to the chateau of Pourrieres, he was accompanied by the notary; it was, in some measure, an official visit; but wishing, as he said, to make more ample acquaintance with those who were to become his comrades, he returned there several times. The domestics, all new retainers, feared that the young marquis would not keep them in his service; emboldened by the good natured looks and joviality of M. the intendant, they resolved to mention to him their fears. Roman reassured them; his master, he said, would not cause trouble to any one, and, indeed, would find some mode of recompensing the services of those whom the deceased marquis had forgotten in his will. "As to you," he said often to old Ambrose, "you will not have to complain; M. the Marquis has informed me of his intentions towards you, and as you are not of this country, if you wish to retire to your own village, he will add a pension of 1200 francs to what the late marquis has left you."

"My young master is very good, M. Lebrun," was the constant reply of Ambrose to this intimation, but which was considered by the old man as a proof of attachment to him; "but I have lived at Provence since my infancy, and it is my intention to end my days here; at my age, you see, we require the sunshine."

"If any misfortune should happen to you it will be your own fault, you old imbecile," muttered Roman to himself.

Roman collected from the frequent conversations he held with Ambrose, much useful information, which he transmitted daily to Salvador, in order to give him time to engrave them in his memory. Ambrose, who had vowed to the house of de Pour-

rieres an attachment similar to that which old Caleb had shown to that of Ravenswood, was fond of narrating; he was, therefore, delighted when M. the intendant, having called him into his room, where he was sure of always finding a bottle of old wine, put him on the chapter of the family; and it was with feelings of honest admiration that he recounted the prowess of his old master in the army of princes, and the first pranks of the young marquis; and his eyes moistened when he spoke of the troubles caused to the old gentleman whom he had so long served by the protracted absence of his son.

Ambrose, very old as he was, seemed to possess an excellent memory; he recollected very well his young master, whom he had, he often said, frequently danced on his knees.

"I think I shall be sure enough to recognise him; still he must be greatly changed." This sentence generally terminated the discourse.

Ambrose was no doubt an obstacle, but this obstacle was not of a nature to induce two such audacious characters as Salvador and Roman to renounce their enterprize; it was at length decided that the former, who had had time to study well the game he was about to play, should no longer keep his vassals in expectation of the Marquis de Pourrieres.

Salvador therefore departed from Aix, but so late as not to arrive at Pourrieres until the night had commenced. He repaired at once to the notary, and when introduced, the ministerial official, who however had often seen Alexis de Pourrieres when about the age of ten years, showed an eagerness to recognise him, by way of showing his perspicacity.

Emboldened by the fortunate result of his first step, Salvador, who, at first, had been a little embarrassed, felt himself quite competent to proceed. After approving in his turn all that Roman had been satisfied with, he spoke to the notary of his travels, the waywardness of his youth, and the regrets which the death of his father had occasioned him, as he had hoped to have closed his eyes; he then made inquiries for Ambrose, that old and faithful retainer of the family, whom he hoped, he said, to find still full of vigour despite his advanced age.

The notary, to make his court to the new Seigneur de Pourrieres, proposed to him to send for the old domestic, and as Salvador eagerly assented to the proposition, a clerk was at once despatched, after receiving an order not to return without bringing Ambrose with him.

The first care of this young man, who had heard all that had taken place between Salvador and the notary, was to report to the old domestic, that his employer, who had not seen the Marquis de Pourrieres since he was ten years old, had however immediately recognised him; and that this circumstance seemed greatly to flatter the young marquis.

Ambrose appeared delighted at the return of his young master.

"If your employer has recognised him at once," he said to the clerk, "I am quite sure I shall also recognise him."

Ambrose, upon his arrival, was introduced into the cabinet of the notary.

"Ah! you are come, my old friend," said Salvador to him; "it is a very long time since we have met. Come, come and embrace me."

Salvador, who was dressed in a complete suit of mourning, appeared greatly affected. Ambrose, to whom his presence recalled many an old remembrance, threw himself into the arms of his young master, who held him a long time folded on his bosom.

At this moment M. Lebrun was announced. Roman, after saluting his master with great respect, took part in the conversation, and made a pompous elegy on the old domestic, who seemed overjoyed at the reception he had met with, and whose joy was carried to its climax, when the notary, having requested the marquis to share his supper, which was being served, he accepted it on condition that Ambrose joined the company, and took part in the repast.

During all the time the supper lasted, Salvador bestowed on Ambrose continual proofs of his attachment; and when the hour of retreat had arrived, and he returned to Pourrieres, with Roman, the old domestic was as contented and happy as possible.

The affairs of the succession were not difficult to manage ; the debt to the Jew was nearly 600,000 francs ; but the old marquis, who spent at the most but a moiety of his income, had left in ready money a considerable sum. Roman undertook to settle with the Jew, whom he found in his kennel in the quarter Saint Jean, occupied, as usual, counting the gold he had extracted from some unfortunate dupes ; so that after Josuè was fully indemnified, there remained to the Marquis de Pourrieres about 50,000 francs a-year in good stock.

"I thought," said Josuè, when Roman had announced his name and quality, "that I should have the honour to see M. the Marquis de Pourrieres ; but as you are his intendant, we may probably understand one another," he added, smiling.

The anticipations of the Jew were not deceived; M. the intendant showed himself so fluent in affairs, that Josuè, who could not divine the motive for his so acting, concluded that he was ignorant of his business.

"Say to M. de Pourrieres, that I am quite at his service," said the Jew, when he had received the sum due to him ; "my greatest pleasure is to oblige young men of noble family."

"I believe you," said Roman, taking leave of him. "If you always oblige at the same price, you ought to allow no occasion to escape of procuring yourself this pleasure."

Salvador, who, after his visit to the notary, had returned to Aix to terminate, as he said, some important affairs, took possession, in person, of the chateau de Pourrieres, as soon as his friend had informed him that he had arranged with Josuè.

"The old rogue," said Roman, in a letter he sent to his companion, "has plucked one of the handsomest feathers from our wing ; but he has not the slightest suspicion."

The old manor, when inhabited by the young and ambitious cavalier, took, all at once, an aspect more animating and cheerful; the ancient tapestries were replaced by fashionable papers; furniture of the newest taste usurped the places of the heavy chairs and gothic tables, which were bequeathed to the loft; handsome horses, a caleche, and elegant liveries, completed an ensemble quite in character.

The gentlemen of the neighbourhood had invited Salvador several times to their hunting parties and reunions, which he had eagerly attended, and had always attained the most flattering success.

We have naturally much indulgence for men who provide amusement for us; thus the neighbours of the chateau de Pourrieres, which was become the centre of all the country pleasures, were very friendly towards the proprietor ; the men found him a jovial companion—the women admired the aristocratic ease and perfect elegance of his manners.

Several of the distant cousins whom Alexis de Pourrieres had only casually seen at Marseilles, before commencing his travels in Europe, came to visit him. Salvador received them so graciously, and performed with so much politeness the honours of his house, that he contrived to make them forget that they had once hoped to share the fortune he possessed.

Salvador and Roman would have been quite at their ease, if they had not remarked that for some time the character of Ambrose was completely changed. The old domestic, usually cheerful and always ready with a laugh, was become moody and taciturn ; he seemed haunted by some overpowering idea, and he had been often surprised shaking his head, in a doubtful or negative manner, after regarding his master.

Roman, who possessed the whole confidence of Ambrose, had frequently questioned him with address. "Tell me," he said to him, "the cause of the sadness which overwhelms you; and if it is possible, M. the Marquis will do everything to put an end to it." Ambrose had long since avoided any reply to these questions ; but one day, Roman having been much more pressing than usual, Ambrose determined to make him a confidant.

"I am perhaps foolish, my dear friend M. Lebrun, but I suffer so that you will pity me. Figure to yourself that a month since, I had a dream, which I cannot drive from my memory. I dreamt that I was seated at the foot of the old mulberry tree which the late marquis had planted in the park, on the day of his son's birth. I had been there for some moments, when, of a sudden, I heard cries of distress. I rose quickly, and saw my young master, such as he was when he left the chateau to commence his travels, stretched on the ground; the blood flowed in large gushes from a severe wound in his breast. I was running to assist him, but was stopped by a man who said to me, placing his hand on my shoulder: 'Stop! 'tis I who am your master.' The features of this man are lost to my memory ; but I recollect that he had large blue eyes. I should certainly have forgotten this dream, if I had not remarked, by chance, that the eyes of M. the Marquis are blue, whilst I remember very well that he had eyes of a beautiful black, when he left the chateau. I am very unhappy, M. Lebrun; this dream follows me everywhere, and sometimes it causes in my mind some very strange ideas."

Ambrose leaned towards Roman, and whispered to him:

"Are you quite sure that our master is really the Marquis de Pourrieres?"

"You ask me a singular question there," replied Roman; "during the five years I have been in the service of M. the Marquis, I have always heard him thus named by the creditable persons with whom he has been in relation; and I must believe that he has a right to this name, since you yourself, as well as the notary, recognised him on his arrival here."

"It's true, it's true," replied Ambrose, sorrowfully nodding his head; "I am a fool ; we must not believe in dreams ; sometimes however dreams are warnings sent by Providence."

Roman employed all his rhetoric to reassure Ambrose, and did not leave him until he appeared somewhat calmer.

"We must absolutely find the means of ridding ourselves of this man," said Salvador, when Roman had reported to him the conversation he had had with Ambrose.

"Ah! if Matheo had not sent into the other world our friends of the forest of Cuges."

"We would not make use of them," said Salvador; "why leave to others the work we can do ourselves?"

"No doubt; but in order to avoid suspicions, the result of which might be disagreeable, the death of Ambrose must appear natural."

"Poison!"

"Poison leaves traces."

The two friends argued a long time, as to the means of attaining the end they desired, but without being enabled to discover any mode which seemed likely to be successful without leaving suspicions behind.

"But this man must absolutely die," said Salvador; "if he lives, we are lost."

Roman for some moments appeared to be reflecting.

"I have it," he exclaimed, at length suddenly, and striking his forehead; "I have it, my friend. In three or four days at the farthest we shall have nothing more to dread."

"What is your project?"

"You shall know when it is accomplished."

"But once more, I must know what it is."

"Eh, bon Dieu! M. the Marquis. Leave, I beg of you, your devoted servant to act at his pleasure; you know that he is a man of resources, and does not strain at a gnat."

Roman, a few days after, invited, in the name of his master, the neighbouring seigneurs and the notary we have mentioned, to pass the day at the manor of de Pourrieres. The invitations were all accepted; we know how well the marquis understood the mode of doing the honours of his table.

"I have assembled you, gentlemen," said Salvador to his guests, at the moment of placing themselves at table, "to taste a few bottles of excellent Tokay, and some gastronomic novelties that I have just received from Paris."

The breakfast was served with that comfort and luxury which adds another relish to the delicacy of the viands and the excellence of the wines. As usual, Salvador showed himself amiable and gracious, but yet an attentive examination would have allowed us to observe on his physiognomy the expression of an anxious and restless preoccupation. They remained long at table; Salvador, after the café and liqueurs were served to the guests, proposed to them a party at bowls. The game of bowls is much practised in the south of France, and particularly in Provence. The proposition was received with eagerness, and the guests adjourned to the bowling-green, situate in front of the principal entrance to the chateau.

They were arranging the game, when Ambrose, booted and spurred, and leading a horse by the bridle, approached Salvador and inquired if he had any commissions for Aix. The latter, who had received from Roman the necessary instructions, gave him an order for a hundred francs which he directed him to deliver to the librarian Aubin, who paid his subscriptions to the journals and reviews of the capital.

"Father Ambrose is still strong and vigorous," said the marquis to his guests, "and despite his great age, he is as good a cavalier as the best postilion in the country. But still I shall forbid Lebrun to give you such long rides."

"M. the Marquis is very good," replied Ambrose, "but as I have still a steady foot and a keen eye, I must make myself useful."

"Right, Ambrose, right; go my friend, and may Providence attend you."

Ambrose, who was in the saddle, gently spurred his courser, and departed at a slow trot.

"It is very lucky for me," he said to himself, letting the rein drop on his horse's neck; "every one recognises him; the notary who spoke to him but just now; the nephews of the late marchioness. But he has blue eyes," he said aloud, "and I am quite sure those of Alexis were black. Oh! my dream, my dream!"

Whilst the horse of Ambrose trotted along a narrow path which joined the high road leading to Aix, the party at bowls continued in front of the entrance of the chateau.

They prolonged the game until the hour of dinner, at which all who had assembled at breakfast again assisted. Towards eight o'clock in the evening, Salvador, having inquired for a key of which he pretended to be in want, Roman replied to him, before the guests, that Ambrose had carried it away, and that he was not yet returned. It was naturally supposed that the old man finding himself fatigued, had determined to sleep at Aix, and would not return till the next morning.

The chateau de Pourrieres was surrounded by vast dependencies, consisting of well-enclosed grounds, woods, vineyards, plantations of mulberries and olives, through which it was necessary to pass, in order to reach the village, at which was a cross-road that led to Aix; this road was the one used by all persons coming from the village; but the intendant of the chateau, whose affairs called him to Aix, had adopted another, which diminished the length by at least half a league.

The park of the chateau of Pourrieres, of immense extent and planted with trees like a forest, is crossed, at its extremity, by a rivulet, which takes its source in the mountains which crown the valley in which the chateau is built. This rivulet glides slowly between two rocks, nearly thirty-five metres high, at the summit of which you arrive by two gentle acclivities made expressly, one on each side of the park; these two rocks, and the rivulet they enclose, form at that part of the park which is contiguous to the manor, a natural barrier, which it would be impossible to overcome, if a bridge had not been established between the two least elevated crests of the rocks.

The width of the rivulet not being considerable, they have simply, to establish this bridge, placed some heavy beams across the rocks, and on these beams, which are kept in place by strong cramps of iron, are fixed some thick planks. When this primitive bridge is crossed, you follow a little path, which leads, after a few turns, to the high road from Aix to Marseilles.

Salvador and his guests were rising from table, when a domestic, whose troubled features and haggard eyes announced him as the bearer of some misfortune, entered the dining-room.

"Oh! M. the Marquis!" he exclaimed, "what an accident! what a dreadful misfortune! Ambrose! poor Ambrose!"

"Well!" said Salvador, "what has happened to Ambrose?"

"He is dead, M. the Marquis! I have just found his body in the rivulet of the park; the bridge broke, no doubt, at the moment he was passing over it on horseback."

And the domestic without waiting the reply of

his master, left him, to convey the sad news to the other inmates of the chateau.

All the guests had risen from table, when the servant had announced the fatal event which had caused the death of poor Ambrose, and Salvador had hastened to the scene, affecting all the signs of profound grief. His friends had followed his steps, and when they arrived at the place where the body was lying, Roman, who had mixed among the friends of his master, assumed a grief, which every one attempted to console.

The body of the faithful retainer was lifted with every mark of respect, and transported to the chateau; and the guests of Salvador, observing the grief which appeared to seize him, retired, after expressing their sorrow at the sad event.

The next morning Salvador and Roman were walking in a retired spot in the park. Roman, who seemed in great spirits, gaily rubbed his hands.

"Chance has served us," said Salvador, whom Roman had not put in the whole confidence of his plan, and who, since the evening before, had not found an opportunity to interrogate his worthy friend.

"Yes," said Roman, "but 'twas I who invoked this chance."

"How so?"

"I knew that every time Ambrose repaired to Aix, he took the route of the park, which greatly shortens the distance. Yesterday I directed him to go to the village, and I sent him to ask you for your commissions before the guests who were invited, expressly in order that it might be fully proved that he went of his own free will."

"But that does not inform me how it happened that the bridge broke just at the moment he was passing over it."

"Eh! my dear, nothing more simple. For some days past, I poured sulphuric acid on those parts of the planks which had most suffered from the ravages of time, in such a manner that they would of necessity give way, and carry with them the whole edifice, the moment they had to support the weight of a man and horse; and the portions of the rock on which this bridge was established, forming a sort of funnel, it was certain that Ambrose would be killed before arriving at the bottom of the precipice."

"Roman, I am satisfied with you," said Salvador, offering his hand to his worthy confederate; "you have acquired everlasting claims to my gratitude, and a moiety of the fortune of the family of de Pourrieres. Apropos, when shall we divide?"

"What's the use of dividing? you know I have a friendship for you; so I desire that we never separate. I am an enemy to luxury and grandeur, the position I occupy here does not displease me; I shall only appear, it is true, as the head of your domestics, but that's nothing to me, this perpetual comedy amuses me."

Roman, in his capacity of intendant, provided a magnificent funeral for Ambrose; Salvador assisted at the funeral-service and the procession, and all the inhabitants of the village of Pourrieres remarked his seeming affliction when they covered with earth the mortal remains of the faithful retainer. By his directions an humble monument, surmounted by an iron cross, was raised to his memory near the vault destined to serve as a sepulchre to the members of the family of de Pourrieres.

Roman received the farm rents and other revenues. When Salvador was in want of cash, he asked his companion for it, who gave it him without counting. One day, wishing to send a considerable sum to his coachmaker at Paris, he requested it as usual from Roman.

"I am very sorry to say it is not in my power to satisfy you, but you must wait till the next receipts, my chest is empty."

Salvador, who knew that Roman had touched, two days before, nearly fifteen thousand francs from different farmers in arrear, observed to him to that effect.

"The fifteen thousand francs," exclaimed Roman, "are far enough, if they still keep running. I played at baccarat, and lost them; but I shall regain them."

"You will do much better not to play again," replied Salvador, who seemed greatly annoyed by this contre-temps.

"And why should I debar myself from play, if I find a pleasure in it? Do I take you to task for purchasing horses and carriages?"

"A passion for the gaming table is soon followed by total ruin."

"When we are ruined we will take up with our old trade, we are too young yet to retire from business."

This little altercation had no results; the chain which attached these two men so firmly was much too strong to be broken by the first shock.

The recital of the facts which precede the period to which we are now arrived, has not given to our readers an exact idea of the character of Salvador. In fact, they have only seen him act up to the present, at the will of Roman; they have probably supposed that he was one of those natures without individuality; useful, at the most, at following any impulse given them; but it was not thus. Salvador, on the contrary, possessed as much if not more resolution than his companion; he knew how to examine things from their source; a quality in which Roman failed; and it would not have been impossible for a scientific phrenologist to discover in his cranium the bumps of organisation and foresight. We have already described the exterior accomplishments of his person, and his ready imagination. Roman, who had guided the first steps of Salvador in the career of crime, ought to exercise, and did exercise in fact, a certain influence over his mind; but his power was to cease the moment his pupil discovered that he was strong enough to fly with his own wings.

Salvador thought to himself one day, that, as the bearer of an honourable name, possessor of a handsome fortune, and endowed with a sufficient capacity to occupy an important place in society, he ought to attempt every thing to attain this position. The burglar wished to see the sign of honour glitter on his breast; the assassin would not find himself out of place in the seat of legislation; ambition began to gnaw his heart.

"You wish to become something," said Roman to him often, to whom he had confided his dreams of futurity; "as you like, each takes his pleasure where he finds it; but have a care, in attempting to mount too high we may fall."

"Whether we fall from the top or the bottom," replied Salvador, "what does it signify, when death will be the result in either case?"

"Whether you are a depute or peer of France, or remain simply the Marquis de Pourrieres, is a matter of perfect indifference to me, provided we can keep a good table, the best wines, and something to play at baccarat with."

"Be reasonable, do not lose more than a moiety of our revenue."

"Do not be alarmed, I am on the winning side at present."

The Marquis de Pourrieres, who had until now only visited the gentry of the neighbourhood, paid his respects to the public functionaries of his district; these advances were received with evident satisfaction; they were flattered to see rally in favour of the new order of things, a gentleman of the most ancient and venerated name of the province. Salvador caused it to be known that he should not be sorry to obtain an office in harmony with his name and fortune; and they replied that his desire to serve the state was too praiseworthy not to be gratified on the first occasion.

In the meanwhile the period for the election of the officers of the national guard having arrived, M. the Marquis de Pourrieres became a candidate. He was nominated, without opposition, commandant of the battalion of his district: Roman, to please his friend, had good humouredly accepted the modest rank of sergeant.

The ranks of the national guard of the district of Brignole was soon remarked for the great steadiness of its battalion, commanded by the Marquis de Pourrieres; the men who composed it were all dressed uniformly; their arms were in good condition; they continued to march in regular order. M. the Marquis had clothed, at his own expense, the most necessitous, and had presented his battalion with a band, whose music might satisfy ears more difficult than those of the good residents of the village and neighbourhood of Pourrieres.

When the period of the elections arrived, M. the Marquis, who had too much tact to place himself in the ranks, intrigued so cleverly that he was named at the first onset the government candidate.

Such services required a recompense, so that on the first of May after the elections, he was named knight of the Legion of Honour.

CHAPTER XIII.

FORTUNÉ AND SILVIA.

AMONG the numerous papers which Salvador and Roman had seized upon after the murder of the marquis, was a lengthened correspondence between the victim and the woman, Moulin, of Geneva, who had been charged to bring up the natural child of Alexis and Jazetta; all the letters of this woman bore simply, as an address, the initials A. de P., and were all addressed *poste restante* to the different towns in which the marquis had rested.

The most recent letter bore date about a twelvemonth previous to the death of the marquis, and acknowledged the receipt of a sum of 4200 francs, which was to pay for three years the pension allowed by his father to the young Fortuné.

Salvador had resided at the chateau nearly two years, and prepared to take a journey to Lyon, when he recollected that it was time to forward a fresh sum to Geneva.

"In a few years," he said to Roman, while folding the letter he had written, and in which he had placed three bank notes of 1000 francs; "in a few years this youth, who is now seventeen, will be quite a man, what shall we do then?"

"We will give him a small sum, and send him to one of those colonies from which he is not very likely to return."

"But will he go?"

"We shall see about it. For the rest we have three years or more before us, and I am not in the habit of troubling myself about matters until the moment of execution."

A few days after, instead of the reply of the woman Moulin, Salvador received a letter from the head magistrate of Geneva, nearly in the following terms:

"The woman Moulin having quitted our city more than three years ago, without leaving any indication of the place she has chosen for her residence, the letter you have written her has been handed to us; and we have thought it right to open it, in the expectation of finding in it some information of a nature to put us in the track of this woman, who has deceived many creditable persons of the town.

"We observe with pain that you have also been deceived by this intriguante, and we very sincerely regret to be obliged to inform you of facts which must necessarily cause you much trouble.

"The female, Moulin, had inhabited Geneva nearly five years at the time you confided your son to her; the parties who gave you a creditable character of her, did so in good faith; she enjoyed at this period the best reputation.

"This unhappy woman gave out to every one, that your son belonged to one of her nieces, who had died without leaving any fortune, and that she had taken charge of the infant to prevent his being placed in an hospital. This intriguante, who received from you more money than was necessary to bring up and educate suitably the young Fortuné, applied to her own use the pensions she received; for she was content to send him to a primary school, so that at nine years of age he was no better informed than the child of a village workman: and as from the letter before us you appear satisfied with his progress, we must believe that the letters which have been written you as coming from her, have been fabricated with the sole view of deceiving you.

"The young Fortuné was mild, kind hearted, and seemed gifted with a good share of intelligence; and was much liked by all the neighbours of his pretended aunt, and it was generally regretted that the fortune of Madame Moulin did not permit her to give her nephew a better education.

"Your son had attained his fifteenth year, when one day Madame Moulin directed him to go to Versoix, a village about two leagues from Geneva, to deliver a letter to sieur G. Piachaut, a carrier of goods, and to bring back the reply. When he arrived M. G. Piachant was absent; he was obliged to wait, and did not return to Geneva until seven o'clock in the evening. The door of the house inhabited by Madame Moulin was shut, he waited until nine o'clock for her he called his aunt, she did not come: at length he went, all in tears, and found father Humbert, a worthy man who had filled for more than twenty-five years the office of commissionaire at the Crown Hotel at Geneva. This man informed him that his aunt had been to seek him to carry her boxes to Vissel, who let out carriages, and that she was gone to Paris. As I was surprised at not seeing you with her, continued father Humbert, addressing Fortuné, she told me you were to meet her outside the town with one of your relations. The tears of Fortuné redoubled when he had listened to father Humbert. The good man, touched at his grief, accompanied him to the house of Madame Moulin, hoping he might collect some useful information. The neighbours informed him that Madame Moulin had sold all her furniture some hours only before her departure, which she had mentioned to no one. It was evident then that she had voluntarily abandoned her nephew, that the errand on which she had sent

all acknowledged that their sovereign was the most cherished mortal of the gods, and that fortune would never be weary of bestowing her gifts upon him. Crœsus drew from his finger a magnificent ring, and threw it into the sea. 'If I find this ring again,' he said, 'I shall believe all that you have told me.'

"Some days after, a splendid sturgeon was served at the table of the monarch, and in the belly of the fish he discovered his ring. 'You were not wrong,' he said to his courtiers; 'I am really the happiest of mankind.' A sage, who was by chance one of the guests, observed to him, that we are never so near falling into an abyss, as when at the height of prosperity; they all laughed at the wise man."

"And they were all right," said Roman; "why did this bird of evil omen, mix his croakings with the gay humour which, no doubt, seasoned the banquet?"

"They were all wrong, my dear Roman; for, listen to what happened.

"Sometime after, the great Cyrus attacked the dominion of King Crœsus; the latter tried in vain to resist the conqueror, he lost every battle he engaged in. At last he fell into the hands of his enemy, who, after overwhelming him with sufferings, had him flayed alive."

"And what is the moral of this history, or rather of this fable?"

"It is, that we must not reckon too surely on our destiny, and that the least event may undermine and destroy the scaffold upon which we have mounted."

"You are mad, M. the Marquis; our edifice is too strong to give way at the first breath of wind; and if the devil pleases, we shall die in our beds the Marquis de Pourrieres."

"I sincerely hope so; but is it possible to know what the future reserves for us?"

At this point the conversation finished.

A few days after, Salvador quitted the chateau, where he left Roman, to go to Lyons, to effect the recovery of some considerable sums due to the heir of the late marquis, and deposited in the office of Maitre Coste, notary. The steps he was compelled to take, put him in relation with persons who composed, at this period, the most distinguished society of the town.

After the termination of a dinner to which he had been invited, some young men, whom he frequently met, proposed to him to accompany them to the grand theatre. Salvador, after a little pressing, determined to follow them. These messieurs, on entering their box, made noise enough to disturb the play; and from the freedom of their manners, and the eccentricity of their toilette, they became in a few minutes the centre of attraction of all the opera-glasses. The lions of the provinces imitate, alas! all the whims of the capital.

These gents were each armed with a glass named a lorgnette. After putting in order these formidable instruments. they took a survey in their turn, and whenever they glimpsed an original physiognomy or a pretty face, observations full of malignity, or words of admiration, escaped their lips with the rapidity of lightning, and often reached the ears of those who were the objects of them.

Salvador for some minutes could not withdraw his eyes from a woman who had just entered a box, placed opposite that in which were him and his friends, and whose elegant toilette, and striking beauty, had attracted general attention.

The continued regards of Salvador appeared at length to confuse this female, who in turn looked at our hero with so much assurance and steadiness, that she nearly outbraved him.

"My faith!" he said to one of his friends, and pointing out the object of his admiration, "that woman is at least as impudent as she is handsome. What a look! it is as sharp as the point of a Malay poniard."

"Ah! you have remarked that handsome person?" said the young man to whom he had addressed himself; "she is very desirable, is she not?"

"Certainly," replied Salvador; "and if I were not afraid of encountering the whole of you, in my way, I would attempt to obtain her good graces."

"If it's only the fear of having one of us for a rival, you may, without any hesitation, attempt the adventure; but I think you will fail of success."

"You astonish me! is this lady endowed with a virtue beyond all proof."

"You are somewhat presumptuous, M. the Marquis; is it only the Lucretias who can withstand you?"

"Oh! you do not comprehend me; but answer me seriously, I beg of you, is this woman so virtuous that it would be a folly to attempt to create an attachment?"

"Have you read, M. the Marquis, an excellent romance of our most prolific romance writer, la Peau de Chagrin?"

"Without doubt."

"You recollect then a certain Countess Fedora?"

"What resemblance——?"

"Why! if this woman was a little older, we should all believe that she served as a model to M. de Balzac, when he drew the portrait of the Countess Fedora."

"So, in your opinion, this woman is——?"

"A woman without a heart, dear marquis, and we are too much your friends not to endeavour to turn you from the defile into which you seem willing to enter."

"Thanks for your good advice, monsieur, but in truth it is very difficult to follow it when we have before our eyes so seducing a creature as this is."

"We should require the strength of the god which animated the Galathea of the sculptor Pygmalion, if we were to become amorous of all the handsome statues we might meet in our path."

"If I were a less adventurous Paladin, I should quit the struggle without fighting, for your discourse is not of a nature to encourage me; but can you not tell me the name of this woman, and what authorises you to speak of her in terms so unfavourable?"

"We will inform you willingly of all you wish to know."

"I am all attention then."

"Madame la Marquise de Roselly has probably no intention of fixing herself in our city, for she has not furnished a house, and contents herself, since her arrival here, with the best apartments in the Hotel des Ambassadeurs; still, her equipages, which she has had from Paris, excite at once the admiration and the envy of all the wonder seekers.

"The extraordinary character, the original habits of this marchioness, (she smokes, fences like a pupil of Mathieu Colon, and is as good an equestrian as Baucher,) would have sufficed to close every door against her, if even the hundred-mouthed report had not taken care to enlighten us as to her history.

"The Marchioness of Roselly came from we know not where, when she made her début at the grand theatre of Marseilles under the name of Silvia."

"Silvia!" exclaimed Salvador, interrupting the narrator, "Silvia!"

"Do you know the Marchioness of Roselly?"

"Not exactly; but I have heard the cantatrice Silvia much spoken of. 'Tis singular," said Salvador to himself, who remembered what Servigny had recounted to him during his detention at the prison, and what he had heard at the dinner given at Paris by the Marquis Alexis de Pourrieres.

"Continue, I beg of you," he said, after a moment's silence.

"I informed you, then," continued his friend, "that Silvia came we know not whence, when she made her début at the grand theatre at Marseilles. As she possesses undoubted talents, and a beauty you can yourself judge of, she obtained the most brilliant success, and she soon counted as many admirers, as there are of rich, young, and handsome men at Marseilles. After a season with a young man of Paris, whose name escapes me, the results of which connection were fatal to the young man, who paid with his liberty and his honour for the short-lived pleasure of having pressed a pretty woman in his arms, she made the acquaintance of the Marquis of Roselly, a Venetian nobleman. This Italian, it appears, had but little sense, for ere three months had elapsed, to the great astonishment of the idlers of Marseilles, Silvia, after paying an enormous forfeit to her director, quitted the theatre, and announced to every one that she was about to marry the marquis.

"It was at first believed that the hopes of the young actress would not be realised; they could not suppose that such a noble gentleman as the Marquis of Roselly would consent to espouse an actress, whose reputation was more than equivocal; however, at the appointed day, the marriage was celebrated with much pomp and grandeur.

"Silvia, as marchioness, changed neither her character nor conduct, and her husband having been drowned in an excursion on the water, she was not very deeply afflicted at her loss; and after a voyage which she made to Italy to obtain the property of the marquis belonging to her, she reappeared at Marseilles, and without waiting the expiration of the usual time of mourning, she once more showed herself on the boards of that theatre. An insensibility, so openly paraded, disgusted every one, and instead of the bravos and transports of admiration which had welcomed her début, she received this time nothing but groans and hisses. The few friends who remained to her, (a pretty woman, whatever be her circumstances, has always some,) asserted that the succession of her husband was composed in a great measure of landed property, which, according to the laws that regulate the Lombard-Venetian kingdom, falling to the state for want of an heir, necessity had compelled her to resume the dramatic profession; but it was in vain, she was compelled to quit Marseilles. It was at this period she arrived here."

"But if, in reality, she has no fortune," said Salvador to those of his new friends who had informed him of the preceding circumstances, "what means does she employ to defray the expenses of the elegance and luxury with which she is surrounded?"

"You demand of me in this, dear marquis, the solution of a problem very easy to unriddle. Cannot a woman every day discover fresh resources?"

"Thus, you believe——?"

"That the handsome Marchioness of Roselly is, at the present moment, quite disposed to sell you very dearly, that which you can procure on much better terms, by addressing yourself elsewhere."

"Ah! you are really too bad."

"I hold the opinion of the philosopher of Geneva; you know what he said of the mistress of the king?"

"Enough, enough! spare a little this poor marchioness."

Silvia, or rather the Marchioness of Roselly, seemed to have guessed that Salvador and the young men around him were conversing about her, for she had not taken her eyes off their box—coolly balancing the bouquet of violets and camelias she held in her hand.

After the second piece, she left; not without bestowing on Salvador one of those looks, which enveloped by one glance the whole person upon which it was fixed.

Salvador, during the few days which followed this soirée, thought more than once of Silvia. He was not as yet positively in love with her, whose beauty alone had awakened a passion; but he felt himself attracted towards her by an undefined sentiment, and an irresistible curiosity.

Like all who have to reproach themselves with any crime, Salvador was extemely superstitious ;* he considered it was not *chance* which had placed before his path this woman, whose name he had already heard frequently pronounced; and that there existed between his destiny and hers, a mysterious connection. "To succeed in fixing this woman, who had attached herself to no one, and who rids herself in such an expeditious manner of those who displease her," he said to himself one day, "is a much more difficult enterprise, than to conquer when we hesitate not to employ certain means : a name and a fortune! Well, I will attempt the enterprise; and if I succeed, it will be a sign that no unfortunate event will again happen to me." This idea, which was at first only received as a folly, germinated in the mind of Salvador, and soon became its ruler.

Salvador presented himself several times at the hotel of the ambassadors, without being enabled to obtain the favour of being admitted to Silvia; and, as it often happens, the obstacles which presented themselves only added to his desire of succeeding.

A sharp-witted valet de place had been attached for several years to the Hotel des Ambassadeurs. This man, whom Salvador generously paid, informed him that the Marchioness of Roselly repaired nearly every evening to the place Belle-court, where the band of a regiment of the line, then in garrison in the town, attracted the elite of the Lyonnaise society.

One evening, therefore, Salvador made one of the crowd, already so numerous, of the admirers which the handsome Silvia carried everywhere in her train; and it was with some difficulty he contrived to obtain a seat near her. Silvia, who already knew his name, and was aware that he occupied an elevated position in society, was perfectly contented to forego in his favour, some of the rigours with which in general she visited those who wore her chains.

"I think," said Salvador, after the necessary preliminaries of every conversation, and which one of the partakers wishes to draw towards a subject

* Nearly all criminals, whether thieves or assassins, are excessively superstitious, they consequently believe in dreams, warnings, and the influence of particular days; many will never thieve on a Friday; or if, on quitting their rookery, they have met a priest, or even should upset a salt-cellar; but if they find a morsel of iron, they become audacious and enterprising.

more interesting than the one in which they are engaged, " that I had the pleasure of meeting you at the grand theatre some days since ?"

"It's true," replied Silvia, "and really, I must say, that you could not have examined with more attention, a valuable horse which you had the intention of purchasing."

"Ah ! madame, you punish very severely a fault which any one would have committed in my place. When once our eyes are fixed on yours, do you think it is possible to turn them away ?"

"Listen, M. the Marquis," said Silvia, after a few moments silence, "if I am sincere, will you promise me to reply with frankness to a few questions I am about to put to you ?"

"Yes," replied Salvador.

Silvia regarded him in a manner which seemed to question his most hidden thoughts.

"Do you love me?" she said.

Salvador had appeared on the field with the design of attacking, and it was the enemy who offered battle. This change in the game, which he had not anticipated, completely routed him ; so that he hesitated some moments before he could make a reply.

" Well!" continued Silvia, " do you love me ?"

" I believe so," replied Salvador.

"I will not be less frank with you ; I have as yet loved no one, not even my husband," she added with a smile ; "and I thought, up to the present day, that I should continue in the same humour ; it seems I have deceived myself."

"Ah ! madame ; is it a confession, and might I interpret it in my favour ?"

" You go a great deal too far in so short a time, M. the Marquis. I do not mean to say that I love you, but simply that it is possible I might finish by loving you ; but if you will believe me, we shall do well to remain there."

"Ah ! what you demand of me is impossible."

"I do not know if I am wrong, M. the Marquis ; but something tells me that no good will result from an attachment between you and me."

" Be assured, madame, that if my hopes should be realised, on my part, at least, your fears will prove groundless."

The conversation continued for some time on the same topics, and Salvador did not leave the handsome marchioness until he had obtained permission to visit her at the hotel.

Can love—that pure sentiment by which two hearts are joined as one—be felt by creatures so perverse as those who are now before us ; and is the sentiment which attracts one to the other, entirely the same as the one whose attacks we have all, more or less, experienced ? Alas! yes; tigers, as well as doves, seek out individuals of their species when the season of love arrives.

Love, when it has allied to one another two individuals, whose lives have been a continual course of profligacy and crime, is perhaps more violent, more constant, and more capable of devotedness, than that which springs up in the heart of an individual of ordinary stamp. This truth, once admitted, the events which are to follow the meeting of Salvador and Silvia, will appear no other than the results of a preceding cause.

It would have been very easy for us, in order to justify such of the events of this history as might appear at first sight somewhat extraordinary, to report a number of facts borrowed from real life. We have made use of this privilege with extreme reserve, for we are too well aware that an author only runs the risk of wearying his reader by laying open the stores of his information ; but still, the novel aspect under which we are forced to present Salvador and the daughter of Mother Sans Refus, induces us to bring to the remembrance of the reader some recent facts which are connected with a celebrated criminal.

Malefactors, to whatever class they belong, robbers or assassins by profession, (there exist assassins by profession, and we shall have occasion to pourtray some of these hideous individuals,) are, like all other men, even more, perhaps, than other men, governed by self-love ; but as they cannot boast of virtues they do not possess, they make a merit of their crimes ; thus, as we have already said, they despise those amongst themselves who only pilfer trifles, or who, after robbing, manifest any intention of repenting ; the publicity which is given to their crimes by the journals, flatters them, instead of annoying them; and they often arrive at the prison, having in their pockets the number of the journal which has recorded a faithful account of the evidence upon which they have been condemned. Indeed, since the journals of crime raise a pedestal to every great criminal, and ladies of fashion, dressed as for a ball, attend the trials at the court of assize, when the accusation promises details of blood, or, better still, the unhappy results of an unrestrained passion, miscalled love—all who are brought up at the bar of justice endeavour to assume a dramatic attitude, and to them the moment of triumph is when the audience appears frozen with horror.

Poulman is perhaps, of all the assassins who for some years have appeared before the court of assize at the Seine, the one who has shown the most revolting cynicism and the most degrading immorality. Well; this man, who enumerated, with a certain degree of enjoyment, all the different aspects of his crime, who described, without a frown, the horrible agony of his victim, was still a part of humanity, by the affection he bore to the woman Simonet, surnamed Louise with the cat's eyes, who, on her part, was madly fond of him. These two individuals, during their confinement at the Conciergerie, exhibited, every moment, proofs of an attachment without limit. Poulman, to whom Louise had given her hair, regarded it with rapture all day, and carried it constantly in his bosom ; he addressed to his mistress letters, in which he described his love in words of fire, and when he met her at the Avant-greffe,* he pressed her in his arms with unusual warmth. Louise had also enclosed in a little bag, which she carried in her bosom, all the letters she had received from Poulman ; she read them ten times a day, and the author of this work has often heard her address the companions of her captivity in these extraordinary words : " How unhappy I am ! my husband was a man of vicious habits, who rendered my life insupportable, and beat me continually; I quitted him ; I had the chance to fall into the hands of an honest man, who makes me happy and contented, and they must come and arrest him; what a fatality !"

The preceding abundantly proves that the most criminal women are, equally as the most virtuous, susceptible of affection. After this, our readers will not be astonished when we inform them, that within a week after Salvador and Silvia had met for the first time, they felt for each other a love (if we may be permitted to bestow this word on a sentiment between individuals of such a nature) as

* The place in the prison where prisoners are allowed occasionally to meet.

violent as that which united Poulman to the female Simonet.

We ought, before proceeding further, to give those of our readers who have followed us thus far, some explanation, which we hope they will receive with indulgence.

It is not simply to satisfy the vain curiosity of men of the world and idlers, that we have determined to write this book. Although not very expert in matters of literature, we are still aware that it is not sufficient to group together a certain number of persons, more or less eccentric, around one who may be more or less original, and to sprinkle the whole with some sketches of manners more or less exact, in order to make a useful book; we know also that useful works alone, are destined to hold a long career.

We have wished to provide a useful book.

Our strength is not equal to the task we have imposed on ourselves; but in default of other merit, we can claim that of intention, a merit of which honest readers will give us some credit.

It may perhaps be asked of us, why, of all the literary forms, we have adopted the most frivolous, that of romance. To this question we shall make a very ingenuous reply.

We had a wish to be read.

The public reader (pardon us the comparison) somewhat resembles those children who cannot be persuaded to drink the potion which is to save their life, unless the edge of the cup which contains it, has been previously spread with honey. First, find out the means to interest or amuse, you may afterwards instruct and moralise quite at your ease.

To prove that the slightest faults are almost generally followed by deplorable consequences; that there is no crime, however well planned, and however thick the clouds by which it is enveloped, which escapes its merited punishment ; that one crime is often punished by another ; that the results of every connection, which has not virtue for its basis, are always unhappy ; that there is no fall from which we may not rise if we possess courage ; that it is always possible to do good when there is no want of a desire ; such are the moral truths which this work is intended to enforce. We believe they will be abundantly proved by the facts which will be brought forward by the denoument of our work; for this reason we shall be very sparing of our reflections.

So far as the present, the persons we have brought in view, Salvador, Celeste-Comtois and her mother, Roman, and all the others, (excepting the Countess de Neuville, her friend, and Servigny, who remained but a moment before the reader,) are individuals essentially vicious. But let our friends be assured, we shall have some noble characters to relieve the picture, and more than one good action to recount.

Much has been written on the morals of criminals, and these morals, nevertheless, have never been as yet examined with fidelity. The majority of writers who have employed themselves on this subject, have endeavoured, above all things, to dramatise their facts; some have charged their palettes with colours either too dark or too light; others, blinded by their political ideas, have attempted to explain, by the organisation of society, all the vices of the class they intended to portray; others again, have only looked at them from the height of their official positions, and have only observed them under the influence of a prepossession, which the very nature of their functions necessarily impose on them.

We shall be told, perhaps, that the philanthropists have visited, in their minutest details, the places of detention, and that they have not used their pen, until they had conscientiously examined all. The author of this work would willingly believe these gentlemen, although in our time philanthropy has been made a stepping stone to procure worldly goods and chattels; but even admitting that these philanthropists have acquitted themselves of their mission, with all the honesty possible, still it is only *en toilette* that they have seen the prisons and houses of correction. On the visiting day, announced a long time before, the soup is nearly passable, the guardians are almost polite, and all the prisoners, desirous of obtaining either their pardon or a commutation of punishment, lambs without spot or blemish; and this is not all, there exists always, on the part of the condemned, a sort of fear, mixed with hope, and an humble respect, which prevents their showing themselves, such as they are, before those on whom is devolved a degree of authority, or who have not descended to their level; it is only when amongst themselves, and alone, they can be judged with effect, and should my opinion be thought too hazardous, I maintain, that were it necessary to write a work, in which should be described with minutia and exactitude the character and morals of criminals, the work should be written by one of themselves.

From circumstances which it is needless to mention here, since the preceding facts have sufficiently made them known, the author of this work finds himself placed in the most favourable position to execute the task he has undertaken; and to enable him to write the descriptions of character and morals introduced into this work, it has been merely requisite for him to recall the events of his life, and he can say that in default of other merit, it will at least possess that of exactitude.

In order to be thus exact, we must preserve to the individuals who have been brought forward, the language they habitually make use of, so that there are in the preceding pages, and those that follow, many slang words; and we shall be told, perhaps, that it was at least useless to initiate persons of education in the jargon of robbers and assassins. We should acknowledge, to a certain extent, this observation, had we been the first to do what we have done; but since, for a long time, we have been preceded in our career, the only care which has troubled us on the subject, has been, to carefully watch that our pen remained chaste. This is what we have done.

We owe to our readers the few preceding observations, and trust their length will be excused.

After a sojourn of some months at Lyons, Silvia and Salvador prepared to start for the chateau de Pourrieres, which the latter wished his mistress to visit, before putting himself *en route* for Paris, where he intended to fix himself.

The commencement of this connection had not been exempt from storms. Salvador, whom passion alone had attracted to Silvia, was the first to attempt to break the chains which attached him to this woman; Silvia, on her side, had endeavoured by every possible means to make of her lover, that which, up to the present moment, she had made of every man she had encountered, a plaything, always ready to submit to her caprices, and bow before the least of her wishes. They had neither succeeded in the attempt; a smile, a few soft words, or a few more tender regards than usual, brought back Salvador to the feet of Silvia when he showed an intention of breaking his chains; but when she attempted to make him feel the weight of the yoke he carried, the lover so tender, so submissive, some hours previous, totally changed his manners; and his bursts of anger terrified Silvia, resolute as she was.

"Listen," said Salvador to her one day, after a scene more violent than any which had preceded it; "do you wish that we should remain together?"

Silvia would have been inconsolable at the idea of her lover manifesting a desire to break with her, but the vicious nature which governed her, obstinately prevented the reply she had in her heart, coming to her lips; and she replied quite contrary to her real feelings.

"No," she said.

"You are quite determined?"

Silvia hesitated some moments before replying, but she could not belie her character.

"Yes!" she added.

Salvador was on the point of gaining a complete victory, but he could contain himself no longer.

"Ah! you wish to quit me; I might have expected as much from you, but do not count upon it."

Silvia had recovered, by a single blow, the advantage she had lost in the former struggles.

"I see that you are rather diverting," she said, "and you make use of some singular pretensions; because I have not as yet, probably, ceased to please you, you wish to keep me near you, in spite of myself. But it shall not be thus, M. le Marquis de Pourrieres. '

"It shall be thus, Madame la Marquise de Roselly."

"I am curious to know the means you intend to employ to force me to do your bidding."

"Stop, Silvia; you are grossly mistaken if you think you can make of me, what you have made of others. I am neither a de Preval nor a Servigny; from my heart, to the poniard of an assassin, there is, believe me, a space which you cannot clear; and I will not be the one to send you to a prison."

"Ah! you know what happened to me with these two men?" said Silvia, greatly astonished.

"I know many other things, besides; and I can, when it pleases me, pull down the scaffolding upon which you have risen. Has M. de Preval taken the trouble of informing you, that the name you bore at the institution of the Legion of Honour did not belong to you?"

"I have no talent for guessing riddles. I do not comprehend you."

"I will endeavour to make myself understood."

Salvador recounted to his mistress all he knew of her past life. How she had been educated at the institution of the Legion of Honour, under the name of Catharine Fontaine, which did not belong to her, and that she was the daughter of a woman who kept an infamous house. "You see," he added, "I can, if it pleases me, prove null and void your marriage with the Marquis of Roselly, which was contracted under a false name; you would then be forced to render an account to his heirs, of what you have received under the succession. You see clearly, Silvia, you are entirely at my discretion; do not force me to use my power."

"What you say might be true," replied Silvia; "you know sufficient of my character, to be convinced that, before I accorded an entire belief to your words, I should take care to assure myself of their truth. I am thus, to a certain extent, at your discretion; but that does not the least alarm me, whatever you may do, there will still remain something which you cannot deprive me of."

"And what may that be, if you please?"

"The talents I possess, youth, and perhaps some few attractions," added Silvia, smiling in her most seductive manner at Salvador.

"You are an infernal coquette," replied her lover, quite disarmed; "but, believe me, Silvia, let us try to walk on good terms, in the road we must follow together. No more of these struggles, the results of which will only be fatal to us both."

"You deceive yourself by just one half, my dear."

"How do you mean?"

"I mean, that if the battle is commenced again, the chances will be all in your favour, for you are in possession of all the secrets of the enemy; who, on her side, knows absolutely nothing regarding you."

"Oh! I assure you that you know all that it is necessary to ascertain of my life."

"Perhaps; but if you have secrets that you wish to conceal, act so that I do not discover them; if ever you deceive me, I shall perhaps make such a use of them as will be disagreeable to you."

"To a good understanding—success."

"And you will remain constant?"

"That I may adore you, and that you will not absolutely detest me; and that if ever I deceive you, you shall have acquired the right to revenge yourself."

"Agreed," said Silvia, offering her hand to Salvador, who impressed on it a burning kiss.

"And you will follow me to Pourrieres, and from thence to Paris?" he said, without quitting the hand of his mistress, and regarding her steadfastly as though guessing her thoughts.

"Wherever you wish," she replied; and this time, the deceitful smile which was always on her lips when replying to her admirers, came not, to belie the expression of her voice.

She was sincere.

Salvador immediately made preparations for his departure; and after several times recommending Silvia, whom the fear of offending against the usages of society had prevented his taking with him, not to tarry too long, he quitted Lyons.

Roman was absent when Salvador arrived at the chateau de Pourrieres, and when he demanded of the domestics where he was gone, they replied, that Monsieur the Intendant had left a week before, to rejoin, at Lyons, Monsieur the Marquis, and that since then they had received no news of him.

The absence of his accomplice would, at any other moment, have caused Salvador some uneasiness; but the impatience with which he waited for his mistress, and the preparations necessary to receive her, occupied his whole time, and left him not an hour to think of any thing else.

He knew it was impossible, without offending against society, to receive at his house, a woman whom he intended to get admitted into the circle he frequented. His first care, therefore, on arriving at the chateau de Pourrieres, had been to visit a neighbouring seigneur, whom the honours which he had obtained since his alliance with the new government had not alienated from him, in order to request his wife to receive into her house, for a few days, the noble Marchioness de Roselly, whom he had announced as the widow of an Italian gentleman with whom he had been acquainted during his travels.

Such services are seldom refused; so that Silvia, upon her arrival at Pourrieres, was received in the family of Salvador's neighbour, with that welcome and cordiality which they thought due to a woman whose youth, beauty, wit, and position of a widow, rendered very interesting.

Salvador had allowed it to be reported that he desired to captivate the good graces of the Marchioness of Roselly, whom he intended to espouse, if she would consent to it; on this account, the frequent visits he made to her appeared quite natural to the honest gentleman and his wife, who, without showing any affectation, seized upon every occasion to leave them together.

Salvador had arranged all the affairs which kept him at Pourrieres, and Silvia had announced to her hosts her approaching departure; they were to be *en route* on the following day but one, and to meet at Valence, where the first arrived was to await the other at the Hotel de la Poste, after a farewell fête to be given at the chateau de Pourrieres, and to which had been invited all the neighbours of the marquis. The latter, as much to please his mistress as to leave a good impression among his friends, determined that nothing should be wanting to this fête. A magnificent feast was to regale the party; the best musicians from Aix were put in requisition, to complete an orchestra worthy the noble dancers to whose pleasures it was destined; the entire park was to be illuminated with variegated lamps; and some splendid fireworks were to terminate the amusements.

The fête had arrived at its climax, and Salvador went to request Silvia to give the signal for the fireworks, which was to precede the supper, when a domestic came to him, in the part of the park where the orchestra had been established, to announce to him that Monsieur Lebrun had arrived, and that, after retiring to his apartment, he had requested that Monsieur le Marquis might be informed that he wished to speak with him.

The servant had delivered his message in the presence of Silvia, who had taken the arm of Salvador, who was doing her the honours of this fête; it seemed to her singular that an intendant should request his employer to attend him in his apartment, and she could not refrain showing her astonishment.

"Oh, my intendant is an old retainer of the family," replied Salvador to her observations, "and I permit him some trifling liberties, which I should not tolerate in another."

And, as the domestic waited for the reply of his master:

"Tell my intendant," he added, dwelling on the last word, "to attend me here."

The servant retired, to transmit to Roman the order he had received, and the latter, who had already doffed his travelling costume, was greatly annoyed at being obliged to discommode himself for the purpose of mixing in the crowd of guests.

"It seems there is something new," he muttered, "since he has not a moment to dispose of himself; we will go and see what it means."

After making a slight toilette, he repaired to the park; when he encountered Salvador, the latter made him a sign which, almost imperceptible as it was, did not escape the keen-sighted regard of Silvia.

"Could you not," said Salvador, "intrude a little upon your repose, in order to communicate to me what seems to be of such moment?"

"I beg Monsieur le Marquis will kindly excuse me," replied Roman, who had understood the sign of his friend; "but what I have to say to him admits of no delay, and only regards himself, and, every apartment in the chateau being occupied by the guests, I thought we should be more at our ease in my own room."

"You were right; and now you can explain yourself."

And, as Roman made no reply:

"You are at perfect liberty to speak in the presence of madame."

"I beg pardon of Monsieur le Marquis, but what I have to say to him being almost personal, it is necessary that I explain myself to him alone."

Salvador collected from the looks of his accomplice that it was to him alone that Roman would explain, he led Silvia to the part of the park reserved for the ball, and returned to join his friend.

"May I know," he said, when they were out of hearing of the crowd, "from whence you are come, and what you have done for the last fortnight, that you have been absent from the chateau?"

"Ah! my friend, I dare not say what has happened to me."

"I can guess it: you have remained at Aix during this fortnight?"

"Yes."

"You have gambled?"

"Yes."

"And no doubt you have lost considerably?"

"It is as much your fault as mine; why did you leave me? When I am alone, I find the time lie heavy on my hands, and to amuse myself I play; but what has happened will serve as a lesson to me."

"Yes; but it is now several times that you have held the same language to me. Well, how much have you lost?"

"Twenty-two thousand francs."

"Twenty-two thousand francs!" exclaimed Salvador. "Ah! tormentor," he added, "you have, then, promised the devil to be the ruin of us?"

"I confess it, the bleeding is a little strong; but you know, my friend, at cards, as at war, we may in *an instant* repair the losses of *a year*."

"So that you will not leave off this gambling?"

"Why shouldn't I attempt to regain what I have lost?"

"Ah! I wish that every gambler was at the bottom of hell!"

"Your wish is a charitable one; but will you allow me to make a short observation?"

"Willingly. Let me hear it."

"It has been said, if I remember rightly, that the fortune of the Marquis de Pourrieres belongs to us both?"

"Without doubt."

"Since we have been here I have lost about two hundred thousand francs. Well, do you think you have not dispensed more than that in objects of luxury, in horses, carriages, without taking into account the cost of the formation and music of your battalion of National Guard?"

"But, my friend, it is not so much the money you have lost that I regret, as the bad effect your conduct might produce in society; it will with difficulty be believed that an intendant can lose considerable sums; and they will suppose that you are a rogue, and that I am a fool."

"What you say is true; but show me, if you can, a means of overcoming a passion so imperious as the passion for gambling?"

"Listen, Roman! our position is a delicate one: the slightest accident might destroy the thick cloud which envelopes our crimes. The places you frequent are the rendezvous of all that is vile in society, and you might meet there some one who may recognise you."

"You lecture as well as the late golden-mouthed Saint John, and I promise for the future to follow your advice.

"I desire that this time you will keep your promise. Well, 'tis agreed, then, that you will not play again?"

" Allow me simply to regain what I have lost, and I will then bid an eternal adieu to the green cloth, to the dice, and to the cards."

" My good friend, cherish no longer a hope which conducts to suicide every gambler who would not die of starvation."

Silvia, whom Salvador had left with the wife of the noble seigneur her host, when Roman accosted him, had quitted this lady after a few minutes conversation, and, having followed a long avenue, hiding herself behind every tree, she had arrived at the little plantation in which Salvador and Roman had held their conversation.

At this moment she had placed herself near enough to hear what passed between them.

" My dear Roman," said Salvador, after a few moments of silence, " this cannot continue. Since we have been here you have lost more than two hundred thousand francs; a few years more of such a life and we shall be ruined, and forced, perhaps, to resume our ancient trade. Let us separate; it is the wisest plan we can adopt."

" Ingrate!" replied Roman; " you wish to quit me?"

" It is on my part a resolution taken, if you will not change your conduct. As I intend to fix myself at Paris, as you know, I shall borrow upon the estates belonging to the seigneury of de Pourrieres the sum necessary for furnishing my establishment in the capital; if you like, I will hand you over a sum equivalent to your share of what remains to us?"

" Hand me nothing, and let us remain as we are; you know well I cannot separate myself from you."

" Let us remain together, if that pleases you; but I shall keep from to-day the key of the coffer, and, when you wish to play, don't ask me for the money, for, I swear to you, I will give you none."

" Eh! what difference will that make to me? Do you think, by chance, that, if I determined to have some, it would be impossible to find means to procure it?"

" At all events, go no more to the gambling table."

" Good, good! time is a great master! Moreover, I am decided to play no more."

" If that is your resolution, all is forgotten. But I must leave you to attend to my guests; you will wait for me in my apartment, eh?"

Silvia, concealed behind a tree, had heard the latter part of the conversation between the Marquis de Pourrieres and his intendant; and this conversation proved to her that there existed a secret between these two men. But of what nature was this secret? This was just what she wished to know, and what probably she would have learned, if one of those sneezings which, despite all efforts, it is impossible to restrain, had not suddenly revealed to the two friends the presence of a third party.

" Some one is listening to us," said Roman, in a whisper, at the same time pointing to the place in which Silvia was concealed.

" Luckily we have said nothing which can compromise us," replied Salvador.

Silvia, from the movements of the marquis and his intendant, who, since her unfortunate sneeze, had spoken in a low tone, guessed that she had been discovered. Fearing to be recognised, and not wishing her lover to suppose she had been there for the purpose of listening, she left the place she had occupied, and came towards him.

" What! 'tis you, Monsieur le Marquis?" she said on meeting him, " I did not expect, I can assure you, to have the pleasure of finding you in this desert place."

" Ah! viper!" thought Salvador, biting his lips, " you watch us. Be assured, madame," he said, offering his arm to Silvia, " that the pleasure is all on my side. 'Tis well," he continued, in a short and commanding tone, addressing Roman, who, ignorant as yet of the connection which existed between his accomplice and the woman before him, was become the most humble and the most polished of intendants, " 'tis well, you can retire."

Roman made an inclination, and left Salvador and Silvia alone.

" You have been listening to us," said Salvador.

" I think you are mistaken," she replied.

" Why do you deny it? I saw you; you were there."

And Salvador pointed out to Silvia the tree behind which she had been concealed.

" And if it were so," she replied, " what right have you to reproach me? Thanks to the employment of some means I am ignorant of, you have contrived to learn more concerning me, than I know myself. Why should I be prevented taking the same advantage of you? For the rest, you need not be uneasy; I know nothing, I have heard nothing."

Salvador regarded Silvia steadily; he endeavoured to test her sincerity by her eyes; she sustained, without moving a muscle, the looks he fixed upon her, and then said to him smiling graciously—

" And even when I do discover any thing, what will the harm be to you? have we not made a sort of compact together? observe its conditions with as much fidelity as myself, and whatever happens I will not betray you."

" 'Tis well!" replied Salvador; " but let us rejoin the company, our absence might be remarked."

The hour for giving the signal for the fireworks had arrived, and the guests waited for their host with some impatience, when Salvador rejoined the company. After excusing himself for the short delay he had been guilty of, and when every one had chosen a comfortable seat, Silvia gave the signal, and suddenly a thousand fires of every colour launched into the air, and illuminated the darkest and most distant retreats of the park; and when the last sparks of the last rocket had been extinguished in the deep sombreness of the sky, the party returned to the dining-room, where a magnificent repast waited for those whom the pleasures of the evening had disposed to do it honour.

After returning to the Marquis de Pourrieres their thanks, which his generous hospitality had merited, and wishing him a speedy return, the guests separated, just as the first streaks of the morning gray commenced gilding the horizon.

Silvia was compelled to retire with the noble lady at whose house she was a guest.

Salvador, on entering his apartment, found Roman there, as it had been agreed. The latter was really sorry at having lost such considerable sums; he regretted especially that he might by his conduct have excited some suspicions; he offered his hand to his friend, who pressed it warmly.

Having concluded a peace, Salvador recounted to his accomplice what had taken place between himself and Silvia; and informed him that the Marchioness de Roselly and the cantatrice, whom their companion of the escape, Servigny, had spoken of at the prison at Toulon, were one and the same person; and that this woman was become his mistress. Roman recommended his friend to act with the greatest prudence in his relations with this syren, and added, that he feared love would supersede friendship. Salvador reassured his confederate, and they separated to obtain a few hours of repose.

The steps which Salvador was obliged to take to procure the sum necessary to defray the expenses of his journey and installation at Paris, were crowned with success; but they retained him at Pourrieres some days longer than he had intended. At length he put himself *en route*, accompanied by his friend, and after they had rejoined Silvia, who, as it had been agreed, waited for him at Valence, at the Hotel de la Poste, a handsome berline, with four active horses, conducted them speedily to Paris.

CHAPTER XIV.

SILVIA.

SALVADOR'S first care. on arriving at Paris, was to obtain a house suitable to the rank he wished to occupy in society; after visiting several, he fixed upon the little hotel in the faubourg Saint Honoré, in which we have introduced the reader at the commencement of this work.

The hotel being chosen, it only remained to furnish it with every object necessary to constitute an aristocratic existence, which was readily accomplished, with the assistance of the gold which was scattered by Salvador in profusion.

His own house being completely furnished, he occupied himself with that of Silvia; he engaged for her, in the Champs-Elysées, a sweet little villa, in quite a fairy style, which he had furnished with all the luxury and comfort necessary for such a pretty woman.

After choosing domestics who had left the service of persons in good society, renewed their equipages, and filled their stables with gay and handsome horses, Salvador and Silvia took possession of their new habitations. Roman, who wished, as he said to his friend, to continue for a few days longer to play the Grand Seigneur, had kept the little apartment which he occupied at the Hotel des Princes upon his arrival at Paris with Salvador and Silvia.

Silvia, who had upon several occasions met Roman with Salvador, and who had not forgotten the conversation of which she had heard some fragments in the park of de Pourrieres, had frequently put to him some insidious questions; but the old fox, who likewise had a memory, knew how to dissimulate, while preserving at the same time a good natured manner. The obstacles Silvia met with only increased her desire for information, and rendered her more enterprising to obtain it; she renewed with Salvador her attempts which had failed with Roman; but it was all in vain, she was compelled to wait a more favourable occasion, and which she felt convinced was not far distant.

Salvador, before quitting the chateau de Pourrieres, had taken care to furnish himself with letters of introduction from most of the noble families of Provence; thanks to these letters, which they felt they could not refuse to the last scion of an illustrious family, and to the strong recommendations from parties connected with those in authority in his department, every door was open to him, and he found himself received with a lively impression in the saloons of the noble faubourg Saint Germain, as well as in those of the ministers of the day. He made his court to an old duchess whom he had the happiness of pleasing, and this titled lady, willing to recompense a devotion worthy a grand eulogy, kindly took upon herself the charge of introducing into the best society, the pretty Marchioness de Roselly, whose beauty, grace, and sprightliness, made in addition a great sensation.

It was at this period that Salvador was nominated auditor of the Council of State.

Roman, after a sojourn of some weeks at Paris, and when Salvador, whom he had assisted in the arrangement of his house, had no further occasion for him, allowed himself one day, not knowing how to pass the time, to be introduced into one of those establishments known under the denomination of tables d'hote, and which are a hundred times more dangerous than the gambling houses of the defunct administration of M. Benazet.

The police carry on an active war against these sort of establishments, but all their efforts, as it appears, are without any results, for no sooner do they close one of these *tripots* at No. 4, Rue Richilieu, for example, than another at No. 6 immediately opens.

An excellent dinner is served every day at a certain hour, to the parties who frequent these houses; this is the honest pretext of the reunion; but when the guests pass into the saloon to sip their coffee, the tables for ecarté, rouge et noir, and even roulette, are already prepared.

These houses are generally presided over by veteran dames from the island of *Cytherea*, who are not wanting in wit, and by their tone and manners appear as belonging to good society. Every one of these women, if we were to believe them, is the widow of a general officer, or at the very least, of a superior officer; but it would be in vain to look for the titles and ranks of the defunct husbands which they claim, in the books of the Minister at War.

We have said that these sort of houses are more dangerous than the reunions formerly authorised; in fact, these latter were only tolerated on the condition that the authorities should be permitted to exercise a general control over them; the persons who frequented them could, in this manner, be easily kept under surveillance, and if all the chances of the game were calculated so as to assure the banker considerable advantages, when fortune seemed inclined to favor *un ponte*, they left him a clear field. In the houses we are speaking of, on the contrary, it is not merely against the fatal chances of the game we are forced to contend, but we must constantly be on our guard against the wiles of an infinity of rogues of all kinds, and of both sexes, to whom they are but places of reunion.

Many persons, who would never have put a foot in the dens of the Benazet administration, frequent, however, the houses to which the knaves, known under the denomination of *grecs*,* have given the name of *etouffes* or of *etouffoirs*.† 'Tis in order to attract these, that the widow of a general or a colonel opens the doors of her saloon to a crowd of charming women. It is not certainly for their virtue that these ladies are celebrated; but they are for the most part young, pretty, and well dressed, the mistress of the hotel requires nothing more from them.

---

* A person who makes gambling a trade, and at play swindles his adversary.

† A house for the purpose of play, and to "catch" inexperienced players.

Chevaliers d'industrie, *grecs, faiseurs*, constitute with these ladies the nucleus of the society of these establishments, which, in ordinary language, are called tables d'hote; a polished society, but assuredly, not too honest.

There are at Paris reunions of this description, composed principally of creditable persons, but it is exactly these latter which are chosen by swindlers of every degree, for where there are honest men, there are consequently dupes to be picked up.

The tables d'hote in which they gamble are not solely frequented by swindlers, *grecs*, and chevaliers d'industrie; you may also meet there the donneurs d'affaires;* these latter endeavour to discover the position and habits of the individual they wish to rob, the hours in which he absents himself from his apartments, and when they have learnt all that is requisite, they will give to one whom they call an *ouvrier*,† and who is no other than an expert *cambrioleur*,‡ the result of their information; that done, the *ouvrier* takes the impression of the lock, a false key is made, and at a favourable moment the *affair* is accomplished. It is unnecessary to add, that the donneur d'affaires knows well how to prove an incontestible alibi, which places him beyond any danger which might result from his hazardous questions and discreet visits.

After the former come the *emporteurs*,§ who are charged *á lever*; ‖ it is the latter who entice to the tables d'hote, where the play is, that crowd of young men without experience, who find there every thing to corrupt them; cards, exquisite wines, an easy chair, eager friends, agreeable women, and an extreme politeness when their purse seems well garnished, unite to dissipate their youth in mad orgies, and profligacy of every description!

The best frequented and most luxurious of all the houses of this description was patronised by an old general (a veritable general) who died a few years since, and whose name is often cited in the collection of *Victories and Conquests;* it is kept by a woman who is related by blood to a comedienne, who was, under the empire, the most lively, the prettiest, and the least cruel of all the priestesses of Thalia. It was into this house that Roman was introduced. Two individuals whom we have seen figure at the dinner given at Lemardelay's by Alexis de Pourrieres, the Count Paladin of the Holy Roman Empire, and his worthy friend whom he had met by chance, were the persons who introduced him.

Roman was sufficiently experienced to appreciate at the first glance the moral value of the individuals who composed the mass of frequenters of this house; but his cicerons, who fancied they had trapped a pigeon which they could easily pluck, were so extremely polite to him, that he could not avoid accepting a supper at the *Maison-doree.*

The good wines, the coffee, and the liqueurs having put the convives in good humour, the Count Paladin demanded of him his opinion of the house to which he was introduced.

"Do you wish that I should reply to you with candour?" he replied.

"You will give us great pleasure in so doing."

"My late kind father often told me that there were at Paris a number of individuals who decoyed rich strangers into gambling houses, kept

* Indicators of robberies.
† A thief.
‡ A thief who robs apartments with the aid of false keys.
§ Rogues who are commissioned to find out the dupes.
‖ Discover.

by women of gallantry, in order to pillage them at their leisure. I am very far from supposing that you are individuals of this sort; but I think the house into which you have introduced me is not too orthodox."

"And yet the general?"

"The general has the appearance, to me, of an old voltigeur of the army *de la Lune.*"

"But do not the ladies of the company appear amiable, pretty, and sprightly?"

"Ah! you endow them with too many virtues; they are only amiable when they win; pretty perhaps they *have been;* as to their wit, I have not been allowed to judge of it."

"And so, my dear sir, this house does not please you?"

"No, dear count, and unless you can show me something much better, I shall be compelled to keep in my note-case the few notes of a thousand francs which I had determined to lose."

"The government, in closing the old gambling houses has committed an intolerable abuse of power," said the Count Paladin, who had given up the hope of fleecing his new acquaintance; but since you are so greatly tormented with the desire to play, why don't you seek the remedy for your troubles in the place where it exists?"

"No doubt you wish to send me to some distance?" said Roman.

"How! you are ignorant," replied the Count Paladin, "that the worthy Mons. Benazet has transported to the hospitable territory of the Grand Duchy of Baden, his green cloth, his rakes, and his croupiers, and that the tax he pays to the sovereign of that country, forms the fairest part of the revenue of Prince Leopold?"

"I knew it, but I did not think of it," exclaimed Roman, who left with the speed of an arrow, after wishing a *bon soir* to his two companions.

Roman, when he quitted the Count Paladin and his friend, was determined to try his fortune at Baden. Like all who are governed by a passion for gambling, he only attributed to chance, which might yet turn in his favour, the numerous losses he had lately experienced; and accused his mal-address alone; and he was as persuaded as it is possible to be, that a martingal which he had just combined, would cause the ruin of the bank. After making the preparations for his departure, which did not long occupy him, for, as it has been easy to perceive, he was no friend to luxury or grandeur, Roman went to visit Salvador, whom he found at his hotel of the faubourg Saint Honoré, surrounded with every object of luxury, and with a crowd of upholsterers, horse-dealers, coachmakers, and furnishers, whose accounts he was arranging.

"And so you will not renounce this fatal passion?" said Salvador to his friend, when the latter had mentioned his departure.

"My dear friend, the love of luxury and pretty women, ambition, and pride, constitute a passion as costly at least as that of gambling."

"Perhaps you are right; but what can we do? We obey our destiny, and we shall probably arrive at the same termination after following different routes."

"Ah! still these foolish ideas. I leave you; I am not fond of listening to what the future might have in reserve for me. Adieu, my friend."

"Adieu, and manage so that you may return a millionaire."

Roman, before quitting Salvador, requested 50,000 francs of him, with which, he said, he should tempt

* Of the Moon.

fortune for the last time. Salvador, who, on his part, had gone to some enormous expense for his establishment and that of his mistress, who was perhaps more than himself governed by a licentious passion for luxury, and who could not dissemble from himself, that the rights of his accomplice, to the *bloody heritage* of Alexis de Pourrieres, were at least equal to his own, gave him this sum, without making any other observations than those he had before made at Pourrieres; and the two friends quitted each other, apparently quite satisfied the one with the other.

It was not, however, so. Salvador had by degrees accustomed himself to look upon his accomplice merely as a subaltern, and it was not without feeling a sensation of being greatly annoyed, a feeling of which, on reflection, he acknowledged the injustice, but which he obeyed unknowingly, that he saw him act with independence. Roman, for his part, did not contemplate with much satisfaction the connection which existed between his friend and Silvia; and he considered it rather unreasonable, that a fortune which ought to belong but to two individuals, should become the prey of three.

Salvador, after the departure of Roman, remained for some days gloomy and taciturn. Silvia seized this opportunity to attempt to learn something.

"Why then," she said to her lover, "is it, that this good Monsieur Lebrun has left you? you have no doubt sent him away without any motive, you are so hasty sometimes. You were wrong to let him go; one does not meet every day with an intendant so faithful, so devoted."

She dwelt on the last words with a sort of affectation, the intention of which Salvador perfectly understood, but pretended not to notice; and as he observed to her that his intendant had only absented himself for the purpose of arranging some affairs, and that he would return in a few days, Silvia seemed disposed not to believe him.

"If you will tell me where he is gone," she continued, "I will undertake to bring him back without wounding the feelings of either. Do accord me this favour, my friend. I much like Monsieur Lebrun, and if I do not see him again with you I assure you it will give me great uneasiness."

All the diplomatic address of Silvia failed against the reserve of Salvador, and this time also she dispensed all the treasures of her eloquence without obtaining any results.

A post chaise, with a pair of strong horses, attended Roman at the door of Salvador's hotel. The miserable man buoyed himself up with such strange illusions; he was so well convinced of the infallibility of the calculations to which he had submitted, the thing of all others the least susceptible of calculation, chance, that he would willingly, at one bound, have cleared the distance which separated him from the green cloth of Baden-Baden, and the only fear he had was, that some other, more diligent than himself, and the possessor of a secret similar to his own, might arrive before him, and break the bank of the gambling administration, which he looked upon already as his own property.

After crossing the Rhine on a bridge of boats, you arrive at Bischofshein, the first post on the great road from Rastadt and from Frankfort, from whence a branch railway conducts to Baden-Baden.

This route is at first as monotonous as a path through the fallow grounds of la Beauce, or the plains of la Champagne Pouilleuse; it is straight, sandy, and continues through an interminable line of poplars, and the right bank of the Rhine, which, from time to time, you just catch a glimpse of.

It is not until you have passed Stollhofen, that the aspect of the country changes; and that the road, until then insipid, suddenly improves, and offers to the view acclivities crowned to their very summit by villages or simple hamlets, whose white stone contrasts with the lively green of a healthy vegetation, covered at their feet with vines, orchards, and rich crops, and crowned by the blue tops of a chain of high mountains which fall back into the horizon, and mix with the evergreen ridges of the firs of the Black Forest; a forest whose name recalls to the memory a crowd of old chronicles, ancient traditions of forgotten melodramas, and popular songs.

This long and sombre chain of tall mountains runs parallel with the Rhine, from the frontiers of the north of Switzerland, as far as Ems, near Pforzheim, and encloses in its bosom a considerable number of beautiful valleys. It is in the sweetest of these charming valleys that the little town of Baden-Baden is situated, two leagues from Rastadt, and where the French plenipotentiaries were assassinated in 1793, and seven from Carlshrue, the capital of the domains of the Grand Duke of Baden.

You arrive at Baden-Baden by a well kept road, passing through the middle of a rich prairie, bordered on the right by fields covered with rich crops and magnificent vineyards, and the scattered villas of the richest inhabitants of the town; on the left by woods of fir trees, heavy masses of rock, and the picturesque ruins of the old Burg, the cradle of the ancient house of the margraves of Baden.

In the centre, at the end of this causeway, is situate the old Civitas Aurelia Aquensis, the battis of the Emperor Aurelian, at present Baden-Baden, a name given to it by the Germans towards the middle of the seventh century; and the chateau which the margraves (who up to that time the necessity of being constantly on guard against unforeseen attacks had compelled to reside at the Burg) built towards the commencement of the 13th century.

This chateau has been tried by severe and different fortunes. It was not completed until 1417. Rebuilt on a better plan, by the care of the Margrave Philip of Baden, and finished in 1579, it was, a short time afterwards, burnt and completely devastated by the French generals, forced to obey the orders they had received from the imperious Louvois. But it was soon re-established in the state it exists at present.

A wide and commodious road, constructed by the efforts of the reigning Grand Duke, conducts to the chateau, which, except from its position, (and that a magnificent one, from its overlooking the distant country,) and the vaults which it conceals, offers nothing remarkable.

It is in these subterranean chambers that, according to some savans, were held the sittings of a tribunal of free judges, similar to those which existed, at the same period, in Westphalia and many other parts of Germany.

These chambers are composed of a suite of vaults, which are entered from the tower of the right angle of the chateau, after descending a spiral staircase, and passing close to an ancient swimming bath in the Roman style, and two blocks of stone fixed one upon the other in the wall at the entrance of the vaults. After descending again two steps, you enter an arched but narrow passage, seven feet high and six in length, which leads to a vestibule about sixteen feet in diameter; after this vestibule, you traverse various other passages of different lengths, in one of which you remark in the walls, on the left, two parallel lines of holes, and on the right six seats of stone; this passage leads to a chamber or vault, to which tradition has preserved the name of the *chamber of question*, by reason, no doubt, of the many rings of iron still remaining in the wall; after the *chamber of question* comes a narrow passage, closed by a trap door. This is where existed the famous dungeon of the *Virgin's kiss;* if we are to believe traditional report, when a prisoner approached the fatal trap, it suddenly opened, and he fell into the arms, furnished with sharp blades, of a moving statue of the Virgin. Some years ago, they discovered in this dungeon, the remains of garments, dried bones, fragments of wheels garnished with sharp blades, and many other objects which had no doubt belonged to the unfortunate victims of the Weimique tribunal.

At the present day, the dungeon of the *Virgin's kiss* is completely filled up; it is not, however, without feeling a strong sentiment of mysterious fear, that the country people approach the place where it formerly existed.

One part of the town of Baden-Baden, which is protected from the east by the mountains called Grosse-Stauffenberg-Mercurius, and by the Little Stauffenberg, on the west by the Fremersberg, and on the north by the chain of mountains, the highest of which are situated in this direction—lies at the back of the hill, which rises in terraces placed one above the other. The other part covers the hill, and is overtopped by the chateau of which we have spoken.

The Grosse-Stauffenberg-Mercurius, the Little Stauffenberg, and the Fremersberg, which form a natural barrier round the town, are covered with extensive forests, which form the riches of the Swiss confederacy; but the most advanced of these hills nourish those substances indigenous to temperate climates, the beech, the oak, the elm, which are mixed with copses of chesnuts, the picturesque birch, the ever green holly, and the juniper branches, whose blue berries are intertwined in the underwood.

The old walls of the town of Baden-Baden, which, in the last sixteen years, has been considerably improved, have been pulled down; the moats of the old fortifications have been filled up, and converted into Boulevards, along the sides of which are the handsome houses of the bourgeois and brilliant shops; the ancient Stadt-Graben exists no longer. Still Baden-Baden, like all the towns situated on the borders of the Rhine, has preserved that rustic appearance peculiar to the cities of the middle age, that appearance which so much pleases the imaginations of the pensive and the amateurs of old chronicles. It is still irregular in its shape, and its ancient constructions, flanked by little towers, are in general so deeply buried in the uneven ground, that in many you may easily pass from the granary to the garden.

A covered rivulet crosses and cleanses the lower part of the town, which comprises, with its faubourgs, an assemblage of about four hundred houses, over which the steeples of three churches rear their heads, the most remarkable of which is the one whose foundation is attributed to the monks of Wissembourg.

Alte-Schlos, the old burg of Baden, is situated at half a league north of the town, at the back of the mountain.

The ruins of this chateau give a grand idea of its importance and its early rise. Time has only spared the remains of a square tower, still accessible to visitors, who can reach its summit by a staircase which recent reparations have rendered practicable; arrived there, you find yourself at such an elevation that you are almost seized with vertigo. And yet, what remains of this tower, only rises, it is said, to a moiety of the original height.

'Tis from the platform of the square tower of the old burg, that we must admire the landscape offered by the *ensemble* of the different places we have endeavoured to sketch, and the most favourable moment for the *coup d'œil* is when the sun sets, when the thousand rivulets, which glide through the surrounding meadows, murmur softly in the confused vapours of the twilight, and the windows of the neighbouring villas are silvered by the last rays of the day star. At such a time a golden dew sparkles on the foliage of the clustering orchards, which half conceal the hamlets of Schevern, Nascheurn, and Dolle; a mild breeze assists the poor invalid, who advances at slow steps towards the healthy sources which are to restore him his health, to breathe more freely; and the heart is more sensible to the kindly impressions to which the view of a magnificent landscape necessarily gives birth.

Roman had arrived at Baden-Baden neither to take the baths, nor to admire the sites, the valleys, the fine woods, or the old monuments which surround the town; he was tormented simply with one desire, that of play. So after engaging a lodging at the Hotel de la Cour de Darmstadt, and having made an excellent repast at Chabert's, he repaired, as soon as the evening approached, to the gambling room. He had no reason to complain of his first sittings, he followed to the letter the rule he had laid down for himself; he was prudent when losing, bold when winning, and at the end of each sitting he realised a profit of several thousand francs. They began to admire the *sang froid* and profound science of the skilful player; and Roman, who had placed aside his winnings, which had risen to a considerable sum, promised himself faithfully not to touch what he had brought with him.

"If I do not break the bank, as I had hoped," he said to himself often, "I shall at least quintuple my capital; but, whatever happens, I shall not break in upon my reserve until next year, what I have already won ought to suffice to finish the season. Baden-Baden is a charming lounge, I should like to come here often."

"Alas! man proposes, and providence disposes," says an old proverb.

Roman, when he found himself a winner of sixty thousand francs, divided this sum into twelve parts of five thousand francs each; he took one every evening either to lose or win, and whichever of these hypothesis was the result, he ceased to play, and gave himself up to pleasure; but, as he won oftener than he lost, each day his treasure assumed a more respectable *en bon point.*

A passion augments with the facility of satisfying it. Roman, imagining one day that if he doubled the stakes of his martingal he would much sooner attain the object of his desires, the divisions of five thousand francs were increased to ten. A series of red zeros carried off, with the rapidity of lightning, the first which he risked.

"Tron de l'air!" he said to himself, "these devils of red zeros left me no time to look about me; but I must not count upon this as a trial, and I can well for once, simply for to-day, risk a second mass."

This was a fatal resolution.

It is certainly impossible to submit to calculation, or to rules, that which of all others is the most variable, chance; still we cannot deny that, if some men follow, from the practice of games of chance, an industry which procures them the means of living, and living well even, it is surely because they have adopted a rational plan, which they never quit, whatever may be the sensations of gain, or the emotions from a heavy loss. But these men are rare; they are easily recognised by their bald heads, their dull eyes, which never quit the card covered with red and black hieroglyphics, and constantly in their hand, except to follow the capricious revolutions of the ivory ball which is to decide their fate; and we may say of them, as of the majority of those who wander from the straight road opened to every man, that they waste, perhaps, more energy and more efforts, in the exercise of their pitiable profession, than would be necessary to create an honourable position in the world.

Roman's second mass followed the fate of the first, with this difference, that this time it was in struggling against a series of black double zeros that occasioned his loss.

Superstitious, like most gamblers, who, although probably very intelligent in all the ordinary relations of life, have their heads constantly filled with a thousand chimeras, Roman satisfied himself that he ought to cease playing for some days, in order to allow his vein of ill luck the time to exhaust itself.

After the painful emotions of gambling, Baden-Baden offers a thousand other distractions; the literary circles, concerts, balls, theatrical representations, and a company composed of very different elements, but in the end brilliant, varied, and in which admission is easily obtained, provided we can pay a little with our person, and are not forced to interrogate our purse every hour in the day. Roman, who knew, when necessary, how to assume the manners of good society, and whose joviality of character, and the almost candid expression of his physiognomy, made him to be sought after by all he met, was soon admitted to the reunions and parties which assembled together almost every day.

He could thus agreeably pass a few days, during which he abstained from play.

He was walking, one morning, in front of the Conversation House, a magnificent edifice, built upon a large plot of ground situated on the south side of the town, between Oldbach and the foot of the Friesenberg, when, by chance, his sight was attracted by an equipage which had stopped for some minutes before the principal entrance of the Conversation House.

"My faith!" said he aloud, at the moment that the carriage, drawn by two stout horses, disappeared from before him, leaving nothing behind but a cloud of dust; "but that's a little vehicle, rather smart; spotted gray horses, light green livery, groom costumé, in the latest fashion. Peste! from the freshness of all this, I would bet that it is the property of some flaneur, some confidential intimate of the telegraph."

"What is your soliloquy?" demanded a charitable passenger, who had heard the preceding exclamation; "you haven't seen, then, the person seated in the interior of the carriage?"

This passenger was the illustrious but neglected poet, whom we have seen figuring at the dinner given at Lemardelays, and who had arrived at Baden-Baden for the purpose of offering to the Grand Duke Leopold the dedication of an epic poem of some thousand verses.

"Why, not too well," replied Roman, after the usual polite introduction; "all, thus, has been to me as fugitive as a synthesis, the analysis has escaped me; have I committed such a gross blunder as merits my being called to order?"

"Not precisely," replied the poet, "but what you have taken for a lynx is nothing more than an animal of a much less dimension, an animal much in vogue in our days, although one of the ruminating and omnivorous family. In a word, it is a *rat*—others even call it a *raton*.*

"I understand you. Old as I am, the vocabulary of the *lions* is as familiar to me as that which the new literature has brought into fashion; but, as you have kindly pointed out my error, you ought also to make me acquainted with the biography of this *rat*."

"The biography? Peste! how fast you get on; you will hear an entertaining one; and, besides, who could ever relate all the details of such an existence? the amiable little *rat* herself would be very much embarrassed if she was charged with such an enterprise; if you wish it, however, and since we are here both of us as idlers, I will recount a trait of her character passably eccentric."

"Willingly; come, begin."

"One moment. But what is it I see? 'tis as though done on purpose!"

"Of whom are you speaking then? I am waiting for the history of the *rat*, which I expect from your politeness."

"Certainly, but be easy; what occupies me is no stranger to my subject.

"Look at that little old man, bent, broken, with a sanctified look, and an odd dress, who walks as though all his joints were loose, and carries under his arm a modest wallet, which he exerts all his dexterity to conceal. If you are a physiognomist, I leave you to guess what may be his profession."

"My faith, it is not necessary to have grown pale by studying the Lavaters, Galls, Spurzheims, *et altri doctores ejusdem farinæ*, to perceive at once that he is an old decoy; but to tell you at this moment his profession, if he does not present the holy water brush at one of the three churches of this town, I'll forfeit my character for divination."

"You are wrong, my friend, 'tis an artist."

"An artist! oh! you wish to have a laugh at me! I have never seen one cut after such a model."

"Let us understand each other, my dear sir; there is more than one description of artist, as there is more than one species of rogue; and this little man is an artist of the humblest class, although we have to thank his skill that our floors enjoy a certain éclat."

"The devil! he must be a procureur du roi! My faith, we may well exclaim with the poet:

'Le vrai peut quelquefois n'etre pas vraisemblable.' "†

"But I do not tell you a bit the more, whether it is true or even credible; this old man is quite simply an *artiste frotteur*,‡ who is charged, with many more of his partners, to give a lustre to the floors of the Conversation House."

"Well, what is there in common between this old frotteur and the *rat* respecting whom you have promised me an anecdote?"

"What is there in common? a thousand things. But allow me, before I enter into detail, to quote a few pretty lines from one of our old poets."

"Quote away, then; I am all attention."

* The name of rat and raton were given to the ladies of the corps de ballet of the Royal Academy of Music.
† "The truth may, sometimes, not be probable."
‡ One who paints or chalks floors.

LIFE IN PARIS.

THE FIGHT IN THE CAVERN OF SANS REFUS.

"........' Auteurs qui ne medisent,
N'ont les rieurs souvent de leur coté;
Voila le siecle et le train qu'il vent suivre.
Dit-on du mal, c'est jubilition ;
Dit-on du bien, des mains tombe le livre,
Qui vous endort comme bel opium.'*

" These lines belong to Séneca.

" Let me intrench myself once more behind some powerful authority, to justify my incursion into the private life of these two personages. And first, and to commence with the one who seems to inspire you with the most interest, I shall say to you, with Demosthenes, that the Greeks had three sorts of women: the first for their pleasures, these were the courtesans; the second to attend to their persons, these were the concubines; the third, the wives, were destined to perpetuate the family, and govern with wisdom the interior of the house.

" I am too polished to tell you, in its proper terms, to which of these three lists belongs the charming person of whom we are speaking; I can only affirm that she does not belong to the last.

" If you will now permit me to continue my investigations through the depths of history, I shall inform you, if you are not already aware of it, that among the Greeks, the women of the first class became the companions of statesmen, poets, and philosophers; that they lived and conversed with those who obtained immortality; that thus, and whilst the honest mother of the family fell into oblivion, those others figured in history; that the epoch of their birth was a subject of inquiry; that they recounted with minute detail their adventures; that their bon mots and their sallies were scrupulously treasured up; and that, having frequently worn a diadem during their existence, were at length buried in a tomb whose magnificence might create a belief, in those who were strangers to the Athenian morals, that it was a monument consecrated to the greatest hero, philosopher, or magistrate of Greece."

" Bon Dieu! kind poet, how fruitful you are in oratorical precautions! Have I, by chance, the honour of conversing with a professor of history, or a member of the academy of titles and belles-lettres?"

" Pardon my pedantry, dear sir; I am not, in fact, the text book, but merely circulate certain morceaux which recall the manners of another age. I may well, as the political leaders of the day express themselves, rest my case on the precedents. Thus, to the question you have asked me—what is there in common between the old frotteur and the raton who has just passed us? I may now reply—

" That one is the cause, and the other the effect.

" Or, if you like it better, that one is the tree, the other the bud.

" Or, if I were more gallant, that one is the rose-tree, and the other the rose.

" Or still further, that one is the cocoa-tree, and the other the cocoa-nut.

" Have you understood me?

" I must add, that it is the old man who is entitled to the credit of developing the intelligence of the young person. Before she was two years old, she perfectly comprehended that celebrated phrase, ' Ring the bell, if you please.' "

" How! is he the father of the young and brilliant dame who we saw pass in that dashing equipage? and is she the daughter of a porter turned frotteur? She must have had a numerous list of admirers, to leave her father at this distance?"

" Not as yet quite so many as the daughter of that king of Egypt, who only demanded a stone from each who entered the lists with her, and yet amassed sufficient to erect the most celebrated of the Pyramids. But patience, she will soon be able to give her points."

" The devil! the devil! She must indeed be outrageously beautiful, to place so many slaves in chains. She has great talents then?"

" Beautiful! this is a question it is difficult to answer. Do you know that it requires an aggregate of thirty items to constitute a woman beautiful. Witness these lines of one of our old poets—

' Celle qui vent paroir des femmes la plus belle,
C'est dix fois trois beautés, trois longs, trois courts, trois blancs,
Trois rouges, et trois noirs—trois petits, et trois grands,
Trois etroits et trois gros—trois menus soient en elle.'*

" Perhaps you would be curious to ascertain all these by their names; but I cannot name them except in a dead language, for as Boileau says:

' Le latin dans les mots brave l'honnetete.'

" This then is the description of an accomplished belle, such as I find her in a very rare and very ancient poem."

And hereupon the poet leaned towards Roman, and for some minutes said something to him in a whisper.

" Now," he continued, " I see by your anxious eye, that you wish to know if this portrait is applicable in all points to the person in question. Not absolutely. Thus, wherever the author has placed nigra, we must substitute flava, and where there is a stricta, ampla; for the rest, they say she is the finest made woman it is possible to behold, and that the costume which best becomes her is that which the Queen Pomare formerly wore, and which was only composed, as it is said, of a collar or necklace of red beads.

" As to her talents, they are summed up in two words; to seduce and please; so you see her fate is not a very miserable one.

" I return to my history; for I hope you have no more questions to put to me."

" I do not renounce them, but for the present a truce to digressions."

" I told you then that Josephine, or rather Maxime, (for the first of these names, which is her proper one, appearing too common, she chose the second,) is gifted with a heart the most expansive, the most loving; she even finds it necessary, in order to diminish the superabundance of her sensibility, to place it on a perfect equality with that of her admirers. To accomplish this, and also to turn to some account the overplus of sensibility, she some time ago bestowed a great affection on a spaniel bitch, of an immense size and great strength, called Miss. Maxime and her dear Miss were inseparable; it was enough to make Saint Roch burst with spite. In the carriage, at the theatre, at table, in bed, at the promenade, there was Miss—everywhere. When Maxime was seen leading this enormous beast in a leash, it involuntarily recalled the question of Cicero to his son-in-law, who, being little, had the affectation to carry a large sword: ' Mon Dieu, son-in-law, who has fastened you to your sword?' In the same way we might say to

---

* " Authors who despise,
Have not often laughers on their side ;
This is the age and fashion we must follow.
Do they speak a libel, 'tis jubilation ;
Do they speak a truth, down drops the book,
That induces sleep like opium."

* " If a woman would appear as the handsomest belle,
Thirty things she must have—three long, three short, and three white,
Three red and three black, three small and three great,
Three straight and three large—and three little as well."

Maxime: 'Who then has condemned you to be tied to the chain of this villainous beast?'

"To be brief, it might well be supposed that so extraordinary a passion for an animal would cause more than one ridiculous scene between Maxime and those of her admirers who wished to reign alone in her heart. It is no part of my subject to narrate such scenes; but, to cut short, I shall tell you that those who displeased *Miss* were promptly *dismissed*.

"'Tis really a problem which I could never solve, that a woman who worships no other divinity than *inconstancy*, should place all her affections on the emblem of *fidelity*.

"However this may be, as I am a faithful historian of the catastrophe which put an end to the days of the unfortunate Miss, I may as well tell you that the precautions and cares which her mistress took to preserve an existence so precious, brought about her death long before the hour marked by her fatal destiny. Gorged with bonbons, biscuits, macarons, champagne, coffee, and punch, at the termination of a little supper of three, enjoyed in company of her mistress and a person who, from discretion, I will not name, the unfortunate Miss was struck with apoplexy, and soon breathed her last sigh. Ah! that awful night, in which was suddenly heard, like a clap of thunder, the dreadful words: 'Miss is dying! Miss is dead!!!'

"Oh Gresset! that I had the pen with which you traced the death of *Vert-Vert!* or rather, Muse of the Epic Poem, repeat to me the griefs, the tears, and the cries of the unhappy Maxime! No, Andromache never shed so many tears for her Hector; no, the sensitive Dido regretted not half so much the son of Anchises.

"Alas! this object of so much love, so many tears, is nothing more at the present moment than a cold and insensible corpse! The voice, the caresses of the inconsolable Maxime, will rest henceforth without an echo in that heart frozen by death.

"A moody sadness took possession of her. She wished that public and ostensible tokens should bear witness to the regrets she experienced for so cruel a loss. During three days! yes, for three mortal days, she shunned every masculine regard, she plunged into the deepest mourning; and that no one might be ignorant of it, *ô-infandum*, she attached the funereal crape to her garter! At this sight, the Loves, scared, fled with their swiftest wings.

"But what is the unfortunate Maxime to do? What interment is she to give her dear Miss? She who reigned all powerful in her heart, now a pitiable object, shall she, like the lowborn beings of her species, be abandoned to those barbarians who love not their dogs but preserve their skin?

"No! a thousand times, no!

"A new mausoleum, the tomb of her favourite spaniel, must be an eternal monument to her grief and her tears! She prepares, therefore, whilst still sobbing, to regulate the funeral obsequies of the interment. A box of heart of oak is ordered; it is lined with wadding, perfumed with fine essences; they then proceed to make the last toilette of Miss; she is washed and combed, they place in her mouth a handkerchief of fine batiste, impregnated with eau de Cologne and patchouli; her body is first enveloped in one of the richest robes of her mistress, afterwards follows a chemise, sheets, serviettes, tablecloths; at length the box is closed upon these sad relics by means of silver screws.

"Here was a fresh embarrassment for Maxime! What ground would be worthy to receive the mortal remains of Miss, of the celebrated Miss?

"In this perplexity, Maxime ordered Lapie's Atlas to be brought to her; she inspects every sheet, but in the midst of her grief, is it possible she can make her choice! Suddenly, however, a gleam of hope rises through the profound darkness in which her mind is plunged. Miss, the faithful Miss, can only be interred in a worthy and suitable manner in the classic ground of *fidelity!* Picardy, then, is fixed upon to obtain the glory of preserving her remains.

"The servant of Maxime is called, to her is confided the sorrowful mission of conducting the last ceremonies.

"Poetry and eloquence shower in profusion their flowers on the tomb of Miss. *Consummatum est!*"

"Dieu de Dieu!" exclaimed Roman, "I am almost in the vein to weep.

"'Excusez ma douleur, cette image cruelle
Sera pour moi, de pleurs une source eternelle!'"

"What a kind heart! what sensibility! what a good character! This Maxime is really the pearl of women; I love her, I am mad for her. Eh! but this poor old man, who is you say her father, you have not mentioned him again? I hope that his daughter bestows upon him those cares and attentions which prove that, in her estimation, the *father* is infinitely above the brute?"

"Before I reply to this question," said the unappreciated poet, "examine, I beg of you, the woman who descends from the carriage, the door of which is about to be opened by a sort of commissionaire, whose tottering limbs and stupid looks sufficiently proclaim that he has imbibed a more than reasonable quantity of *little goes*.

"The equipage is at least as elegant as that of the little *rat* of whom I have just spoken to you; and yet the female who is descending from it is not so attracting as the charming Maxime, in addition she employs very different means to support the luxury by which she is surrounded; what the former demands from the charms of her person, the latter procures from the finesse of her wit.

"This woman has bidden adieu to her tenth lustre; she has not, however, renounced the hope of still appearing young; but her childish manners, her little affectations, accord but ill with an exterior which has nothing distinguishing; her height is below the usual standard; her size, of an evident amplitude, reminds one of the Hottentot Venus; and if her highly coloured features are not marked with purple streaks, the certain index of a sanguine temperament, they have to thank the oft-repeated use of the cucumber pommade.

"If I were obliged to enumerate to you all the tricks and the swindlings she has committed, and you were obliged to listen to me, we should be under the necessity of remaining here until to-morrow morning; so that I think you will be satisfied in knowing that she hesitates at nothing, that every means by which she can procure money are in her opinion legitimate; she knows how to assume all disguises; every ruse is familiar to her. She even found means to plunder, of every thing she possessed, an old lady who thought herself her equal in finesse, and who named herself, I know not for what reason, the Queen of Hungary."

"In truth, my dear poet, you are a singular narrator: for more than an hour you have kept my beak in the water; will you tell me at length what affinity there is between Maxime and the old frotteur—between the woman you have last mentioned and the half drunken commissionaire?"

"Forgive my grief, this cruel spectacle
Will, for my tears, be a source eternal!"

" ' Repondez-donc enfin, on bien je me retire ;
Ah, de grace ! un moment souffrez que je respire.'*

" Maxime and the Baroness —— (I shall not mention her name, but simply apprise you that it is the same as that of a man who occupies the highest station in the directorial hierarchy of the theatres) roll in bank notes and gold ; both of them have sumptuous apartments, expensive wardrobes, and, as you see, equipages and liveries to be envied by a duchess. Maxime, without reckoning the son of a peer of France, has already ruined a number of young men of family ; the Baroness —— has swindled the whole universe. We might, however, find some excuses for their conduct, if they had preserved some of those natural sentiments which exist in the heart of nearly every woman, but Maxime allows her old father to die of starvation ; and the commissionaire is the only son of the baroness, who leaves him in the most atrocious misery. You see, my dear sir, that it is possible to encounter at Baden-Baden some of the *mysteries of Paris.*

" *Tron de l'air!* I think you are right."

" Is this the first time you have visited Baden-Baden?"

" Yes, my dear poet ; but I shall return again, for I am much amused here."

" In fact, it is difficult to feel dull, for we meet here the noblest, the richest, and the most distinguished in all Europe ; and the *lions* of every country, who are at least as ridiculous and amusing as our *lions* of the capital. Here the republican, the Carlist, and the *milieu juste* live together in the greatest harmony—each, on entering the town, leaves his political opinions at the gate, as a useless incumbrance ; they have really many better affairs in hand, and many more important ones to discuss! Do they not vie in eccentricity one against the other ; that the luxury of one may outshine that of their neighbour? And, then, the balls, the reunions, the princely dinners given by the proprietor of the gambling tables to the aristocracy of bathers, and especially the play, which so well occupies every moment of the visitors of Baden-Baden, who appear, men and women, young and old, to apply every faculty they possess to the study of the hazardous combinations of *rouge et noir.*

" Among these noble and rich foreigners you listen to the buzzing of a swarm of parasites and knaves, who only attend the watering places to fish for fresh dupes."

" Really! there are parasites and rogues here?" said Roman to the poet, who had so kindly become his cicerone ; " I should not believe it, if I did not hear it from you."

" As many as at the dinner where we met for the first time ; and it is not saying a little, we are indeed in a veritable forest of Bondy."

At this mention of the forest of Bondy, which reminded him of the crime of which Alexis de Pourrieres had been the victim, Roman could not control a convulsive movement, and became so dreadfully pale that his companion remarked the alteration in his features.

" What's the matter then?" he said, " you are as pale as one of the miserable workmen at the white lead manufactory of Clichy."

Roman had a hundred times recalled to his accomplice the crime they had committed together, without feeling the slightest remorse, yet this time the name alone of a place contiguous to that where the victim had rendered his last sigh, had aroused the voice of conscience. It must be admitted, and 'tis a consoling truth, conscience is never *dumb.*

" But, cheer up," continued the poet! " we are not, it is true, in the forest of Bondy, but we are near neighbours of the Black Forest, and its reputation is no better than the former. But, courage, the bandits you will meet with at the Conversation House, at the Ursprung,* at the abbey of Lichtental, at Geroldsane, at the Angle Vert, at Fremersberg, and at Alte-Schlos, will steal neither your purse nor your watch ; and among them there are many honest persons in every acceptation of the word, who show in all their relations an extreme delicacy, but who nevertheless become rogues the moment they sit down to the gaming table.

" These individuals are for the most part known to the frequenters of the baths ; but those who have been their tributaries guard themselves well against making them known to the new comers ; they are, on the contrary, delighted to see the latter fall into the gripe of these individuals, who play every game to perfection. Add to this science their address, marked cards, and the consequences of this, and you may easily guess what happens to the new arrival.

" What takes place at Baden-Baden, passes also at every place where there is gaming ; the high classes of society have founded clubs in which they assemble for the pleasures of conversation, to swallow the best wines, make good cheer, and play when the occasion offers. To become a member of these sort of establishments, the candidate must be presented by several *godfathers,* and consent for his name to be posted up during a certain lapse of time, in the principal saloon of the club, in order that if there should be any opposed to his admission, they might make known to the committee the objections they have to allege against him. This measure is a prudent one, and if it was rigorously enforced, the clubs would be very agreeable reunions ; unfortunately they are not so. As we each flatter ourselves that we are strong enough to fear nothing, and are not in general disposed to make enemies without some object ; if the reputation of the candidate is only doubtful, they are content to vote as others do ; if it is decidedly bad, they abstain in toto. If the candidate is rich, if he bears an aristocratic name, if he is a *bon vivant,* and especially a player, he is received with acclamation. From what I have told you of the mode in which the admissions are obtained, you may conclude that the *exploiteurs* find easy means of introducing themselves among the frequenters of the most famous clubs, in which we should expect to meet the most estimable persons ; by this we may conclude, without fear of being contradicted, that we shall find among them all, at whatever time we may be introduced, individuals always ready to aim at your purse. We must, however, admit, that it is not in this way they commit themselves ; there are too many experienced eyes watching their operations ; but when a débutant arrives, in the career of dandyism and fashionable manners, they immediately throw their net over him, and sooner or later he is taken. They will find a thousand modes of circumventing him : one proposes a well bred horse to be admired, or a dog of pure race ; another will vaunt the charms of such a *rat* à la mode ; and the result of all these advances is usually an invitation to a dinner lost in a bet, an invitation which he cannot avoid accepting.

* " Answer me, then, or really I retire -
Ah ! for mercy ! a moment let me respire."

* The principal spring of Baden.

"After the repast, when the fumes of champagne have sufficiently warmed the temper of the victim, the games are arranged, and whatever might be the play chosen, whether bouillote, ecarté, creps, or roulette, (these gentry have roulette tables manufactured in England, the squares of which are so adroitly arranged, that the slightest movement made apropos, renders those which are favourable to the *ponte*, inaccessible to the ball,) he loses every stake he places on the board.

"When I mentioned just now that very honest men in all the relations of ordinary life were rogues at play, you shook your head with an air of doubt. Because you are honest, my dear sir, and are not conversant with all the ruses of a Parisian life, you cannot believe that the man who presses your hand with a friendly grasp, would pillage you without scruple if you sat before him at a gaming table. This incredulity does you credit; but if you will believe me, stake your money at no other establishments than such as these, or what is much wiser, play not at all, it will be much more prudent.

"Two individuals opposed to each other, with cards or dice in their hands, to contend for a stake more or less heavy, are, as long as the game continues, two enemies who each seek to be the vanquisher. Well! admit for a moment, that the most honest man in the world has the power of changing the cards at the moment he is about to lose the game, do you suppose he would not make use of it?"

"Eh! eh!"

"'Tis the history of the mandarin mentioned by Rousseau in some work. Many men, who, when they have attained their knowledge of play, are satisfied at first at fancying themselves beyond the reach of the tricks of these *fripons*, have eventually become the most dangerous and the most intrepid *exploiteurs*; and this is quite natural, if you place arms in the hands of an individual, he will make use of them when he finds it necessary to defend himself.

"Thus, men who stand high in the social hierarchy, the grand seigneurs, faithful in the performance of their word, devout notaries, patriotic counsellors, negotiants, to whom the exchange accords a certain consideration, find in play valuable resources, an amount of profit often more important than what they procure by the exercise of their profession.

"These are the men who are generally looked for to arrange the dinners, the parties, the soirées, at the finish of which the dupes are to be plucked.

"In addition, if they do not wish to play themselves, they will introduce with their friends one or two *grecs*, who manage with so much dexterity, that no one thinks of suspecting these new comers, presented sometimes by friends of twenty years growth.

"To operate with more chance of success, the *grecs* are always provided with several packs of marked cards, which they dexterously substitute for those which have been placed on the table, and contrive to make the latter disappear by transporting them to a certain place. Full of security, the victims play without distrust; they lose considerable sums, and accuse the fates, who have nothing whatever to do with it.

"The number of men who swindle, or make others swindle, at play, is much more considerable than is generally imagined; and if I dared name those whom I know, how many masks you would see dropped, and how many men would be surprised, if not grieved, at having been so long the friends of Monsieur the Marquis of ——, of Monsieur the Count of ——, of Monsieur the Viscount ——."

"Are you not a misanthrope, dear poet? and is it not because your verses have not met with the reception which they merit, that you treat society so unkindly?"

"Oh! mon Dieu, no. We have nothing to do until the opening of the saloons, and we prattle to pass away the time; that's all."

"It's true! and since we have arrived at the dinner hour without noticing it, we will visit Chabert together."

A brilliant society was assembled in the magnificent saloon, embellished with paintings and splendid mirrors, of the Very of Baden-Baden, when Roman and his companion entered; they took their seats, and the first moments were consecrated to the satisfying the vigorous appetite obtained by their long promenade.

After the desert, Roman, who had listened with pleasure to the histories and long dissertations of the poet Chevelu, asked him if he had not preserved among the treasures of his memory, some anecdotes concerning the parties who at this moment were assembled in the saloon de Chabert?

"I only know," said the poet, after taking a survey of the company, "among the persons who are here, that man and the two pretty women."

"And you can, no doubt, recount me the histories of which they are the heroes?"

"Oh! certainly, if you can find any amusement in it. Which shall I commence with?"

"Let us first get rid of the man, who must be an undoubted scamp, if there is any truth in Lavater."

"We can see at the first glimpse that this man, who carries his head high, and his nose to the wind, who endeavours, without success, to imitate the airs, the tone, and the manners of the distinguished persons with whom he is now conversing, is of the lowest extraction. Examine with a little attention his short and thick stature, the shoulders of a street porter, his black and thick hair, his little eyes of the same colour, which only look obliquely, his red and rough hands, which have resisted all the almond paste toilette soaps imaginable, and the feet of immense size. Do you believe that all this can belong to an aristocratic nature? And yet this individual calls himself the Count de Bon ——, de Bon ——"

"Well?" said Roman.

"His name escapes me," replied the poet.

"It is but a short time since, that, of his own authority, he has decorated himself with a title of nobility, for if we refer to the year 1830, we find him in the principal town of our departments of the west, preaching liberty, equality, and fraternity. As he seasoned his harangues with an infinity of dangerous sentiments, his auditors, at this period, surnamed him the *cuirassier* or the *tanneur*. The devil! I cannot recall his real name, nor his assumed one; for the rest, if you are desirous of knowing it, consult the *Gazette des Tribunaux*. This personage was for some time the political enemy of the procureur du roi, he has had some troubles to contend with before the court of assize.

"After a very dirty bankruptcy consummated in 1833, this contraband count fled into Belgium; but the merchants whom he had swindled, complained, and the *extradition* of the Count and Countess de —— (our man had taken with him his **chaste partner**, to whom we will give, if you will permit it, the name of Marguerite) was demanded and **obtained**.

"From Brussels to the court of assize of the department where the count had established his residence, is a long journey, and the count found means to escape on the way, leaving his wife as an hostage. Luckily for her, the jurors were not quite satisfied in their consciences with the evidence against her, and she was acquitted; but the count was condemned for contumacy to ten years of hard labour.

"The count, who, in 1830, was, as I have told you, the Corypheus of the republican party of his native town, became suddenly a fervent royalist. Arriving by some means in London, he engaged himself in the foreign legion at that time forming by Don Carlos to recover his kingdom, and in which corps he obtained, I know not how, the rank of a captain.

"The count, despite the ungracious exterior he has received from dame nature, ingratiated himself into the confidence of the Spanish prince, who, in a short time, made him the depositary of all his secrets. The count desired nothing more. So having learned all he wished to know, he quitted the royalist army, without drum or trumpet, and hastened to Paris; paid a visit to the ambassador of her Majesty Maria Christina, to whom he sold all the secrets of Don Carlos.

"The ambassador, willing to recompense meritoriously the services of Count de ——, put him in report with a certain high personage, thanks to whose cares he was incorporated in the thousand secret services which spring up and oppose one another at Paris.

"The Count de —— was immediately charged by the chief of one of these police, to repair to Bourges, to surveil his ancient master, Don Carlos; but in consequence of a mistake between the party from whom he received his mission and the authorities at Bourges, he was *brûlé*,* and compelled to return to Paris, Gros-Jean, as before.

"At this period, the Duke de Bourdeaux having visited Italy, the Count de ——, in his quality of ancient officer of the army of Don Carlos, was charged to go and present his respects to him.

"Arrived at Rome, he was at first well received; they kindly remembered a preceding voyage he had made to Goritz, in order to prove his attachment and devotedness to the princes of the elder branch. But, alas! every thing in this world has an end! The Duke de Levis, who accompanied every where the young hope of the partisans of the decayed dynasty, requested one day Monsieur le Comte de —— to enter his cabinet.

"'Monsieur,' he said to him, 'we know you, and we know also the character you are come to play amongst us. The wisest plan you can adopt is, to quit Rome much quicker than you entered it, unless, indeed, you have a desire to be made conspicuous.'

"The count thought it best to follow to the letter the charitable advice he had received. In fact, he was looked upon as one more than suspected. He took flight.

"But what a shock! On arriving at Paris, he found the Countess Marguerite and her own nephew in one of those positions in which an outraged husband seeks the aid of the commissary of police, in order that he may testify to the very fact.

"And so did the Count de ——.

"And, now, what shall I tell you? Why, that from 1835 to 1840, Monsieur the Count de —— has gained wherewith to pay those whom he had *flounced* in 1833; that he has purged his contumacy;

* Recognised as a spy.

that he still exercises his profession of a spy, and is paid liberally for so doing; 'tis the history of many others. For the rest, this political cameleon, who deserves to be placed in the pillory of public opinion, would sell to-morrow the men whom he serves to-day, if the secret service money chest was not at their disposition."*

"And is the company here aware that this man is a *mouchard?*"†

"It's probable; however, they tolerate him, for, if they forced him to decamp, those by whom he is paid would replace him by some other individual of the same stamp, who, less known, would perhaps be more dangerous."

"Let us waste no more time about this personage, but tell me, I beg, something about these two pretty women."

"Ah! the transgressions of these ladies are delicate ones; but I do not know if I ought."

"Speak without any fear, my dear poet, not a soul shall know a syllable of what you are about to amuse me with."

"You are not married?"

"'Femme souvent varie.
Bien folle est qui s'y fie.'‡

"'Tis because these two lines of the good king Francis the First, have never deserted my memory, that I have been unwilling to choose a manager."

"Since you are a bachelor, I can, without the fear of hurting you, recount what relates to these two ladies. I commence : The —— husband deceived, beaten, and ——."

"Content," exclaimed Roman.

"Not at all, discontented," replied the poet Chevelu; "my history has no resemblance to the tale of la Fontaine.

"For some time there had been remarked at all the promenades, and public places habitually frequented by the fashionables of Paris, at the Tuileries, at the midday mass at the assumption, at the balcony of the Italian opera, a little woman, whose slight and graceful figure seemed modelled by the hand of the Loves; she possesses, as you may see, a physiognomy which reminds one, by the regularity of its features, the perfect harmony of its outlines, and the freshness of its hue, of the *chefs-d'œuvre* of Mignard. This pretty face is encircled by hair blacker than the darkest ebony, whose long and glossy curls caress a neck whiter than the alabaster.

"This graceful creature is the wife of a foreign count, somewhat savage, despotic, and jealous.

"The lions of the Boulevard Italien, who had long admired this precious pearl, which a miser kept hidden in the ground, came to a resolution to carry her off. This determination once taken, they drew a lottery as to who should have the honour of attempting to soften the heart of this belle; the chance fell upon a gentleman from Lorraine, a faithful attendant at the Café Anglais and the Jockey Club, who possesses an agreeable countenance, an advantageous height, and whose upper lip is ornamented with a neat black moustache, carefully arranged, who possesses, in a word, every thing requisite to succeed in the career of love.

"After paying a long court, this gentleman at length obtained the sweet reward of his sufferings. He had been made happy for some time, when the husband, whose attention had been awakened by some indiscreet words, watched his inconstant spouse, and finished by discovering the rendez-

* Historical. † Spy.
‡ "A woman often varied
Is scarcely to be trusted."

vous of the two lovers. But, whether he failed in address, or fate was against him, all his endeavours to surprise them together, in a conversation technically called criminal, remained without result. Wearied, at length, of champing his bit in silence, he harassed and menaced his poor little wife so much and so well, that she avowed her fault; but when he demanded the name of her accomplice, this woman, who had not the strength to defend *herself*, regained her energy, in order to shield from danger the man she loved, and opposed an obstinate resistance to the prayers, the menaces, and the promises of pardon, which her husband made to her; the latter was furious, he was determined upon washing out, in the blood of his wife's paramour, the blot on his escutcheon, but all the efforts he made to discover him were useless. They say that love is blind, but I am rather of opinion that he places a bandage before the eyes of some who would disturb the pleasures of those whom he favours.

"The husband was the more furious, from the knowledge that his misfortune was the common conversation of all the frequenters of the fashionable cafés of the Boulevard Italien; and that every time he entered one of these establishments, his arrival was greeted by the malicious smiles which husbands themselves never spare towards those amongst them who are unfortunate.

"The poor husband then had been unfortunate for nearly two months, when one day, or rather one evening, after a good dinner, having entered, to procure some distraction, one of those houses opened to the amateurs of easy pleasures, the divinity to whom he had thrown his handkerchief recounted to him his own history, accompanying it with some commentaries sufficiently provoking, and not omitting the names of the parties.

"The poor man was in purgatory; and when Aurora, with her rosy fingers, opened the doors of the east, he rose without noise, and, having furnished himself with a pair of pistols, repaired to the residence of the gentleman of Lorraine.

"The valet de chambre of the latter guessed directly what was the matter; and not willing to awaken his master for the purpose of announcing unpleasant news, he replied to the husband, that his master, who had retired to bed very late, would not be visible till two o'clock in the afternoon, and placed himself before the door of his sleeping-room, in the attitude of a man determined to defend the entrance against all the world.

"'At two o'clock!' exclaimed the husband; 'at two o'clock! Why, it is hardly nine as yet, and I cannot wait five hours for the pleasure of shooting this miserable.'

"The valet de chambre, delighted at the opportunity of resisting a superior, made the same reply to the continued observations of the poor count:

"'Monsieur is wrong to insist. I have received from my master directions not to disturb him until two o'clock, and I must obey him; besides, it is not very polite to awaken gentlemen for the purpose of shooting them.'

"The husband was compelled to resign himself.

"At length two o'clock struck, he was then introduced into the apartment of the gentleman of Lorraine, who received him with a yawn.

"The explanation was a warm one; the lover denied the charge; in such a case it is the duty of a gallant knight; the husband asserted; it was at length agreed that they should meet to settle the affair with weapons in their hands.

"When the friends of the husband presented themselves to the lover to regulate the conditions of the combat, the latter observed that, having been provoked without any cause, he had the right to choose the weapons; there were no means for the husband to explain his position; he could not, without covering himself with ridicule, invoke the evidence of his wife, who knew it but too well; he was consequently forced to submit to the terms of his adversary, who chose the sword, a weapon he was perfectly acquainted with.

"Ah! deign to spare me the rest.

"The good cause succumbed.*

"And now for the history of the second husband.

"He is a duke of the old stamp, who has preserved the manners of the regency, and who loves especially to laugh at husbands—unfortunate.

"This noble duke is very fond of his wife, he is jealous, very jealous even, of her; but which does not prevent his having for a mistress the sister of a celebrated tragedienne, who lost the good graces of the greatest captain of the age by an unlucky ring of a bell.

"Some slight circumstances, which would be unimportant except to the eyes of the jealous, having attracted the attention of the duke, he took a fancy to assure himself whether or not his suspicions were well founded; he directed one of his old domestics to follow his wife, and render him an account of her wanderings. This servant, babbling and indiscreet, like most of the gentry of his kind, confided the object of his mission to his wife, the latter to a milliner, who mentioned it to the femme de chambre of the duchess, who apprised her mistress: thus forewarned, the duchess was more prudent, and did not again meet her lover (for she also had a lover), until she had taken all possible precautions to prevent a surprise. The husband thought he was in the wrong; but, some indiscreet words giving fresh fuel to his jealousy, the surveillance was redoubled; but the domestic, despite all his zeal and dexterity, was deceived in a very adroit manner, as follows:

"The femme de chambre, who was nearly of the same height as her mistress, repaired, on the days of rendezvous, to a baroness, a friend of the duchess; arrived there, she dressed herself in a costume exactly similar to that of her mistress, (it must be kept in mind that the latter had mentioned to her husband the visits she intended making,) who, on her arrival, sent out her substitute, who, completely hidden under a thick veil, entered the carriage, and the coachman, whose route had been previously laid down, continued his course, and pulled up at all the houses indicated. The femme de chambre, who played the duchess admirably well, gave the visiting cards to the chasseur, who left them with the porter, and, whilst all this was passing, the clever duchess left the house of her complaisant friend, and repaired to a small house where the happy possessor of her charms awaited her.

"The husband, on the other hand, dreading the surveillance of his wife, who, by way of exchange, had attempted some flights of jealousy, profited by the time she employed in rendering her visits, the duration of which he had no wish to curtail, to pay his respects to his mistress.

"As it often happens, the lover of the wife was precisely the most intimate friend of the husband, who did not conceal from him the means he had resorted to for entrapping his wife, at the same time assuring him of his confidence in her virtue.

"He imagined himself at length the happiest of husbands, so much so that one day a jester, whom

* Historical.

No. 14.

LIFE IN PARIS.

THE RENDEZVOUS OF THE TWO LOVERS.

the lover had placed in his confidence, and in whose presence the duke was felicitating himself upon his happiness, could not refrain from saying to him: ' Vrai Dieu! dear duke, I think you were born *coëffe*.' This pleasantry caused the noble personage to frown; but the facetious fellow, remarking the febrile movement of his features, immediately added: ' When I say that you were born *coëffe*, be assured that it is in the honest acceptation of the word.' Husbands are always disposed to believe they make the exception to the general rule; still, despite the slight satisfaction given to his self-love, there remained on the physiognomy, and in the imagination of the duke, a cloud which, malgré all his efforts, and the daily reports of his *escogriffe*, which attested the exemplary conduct of his wife, he could never shake off.

CHAPTER XV.

BADEN-BADEN.

" HOWEVER, at the end of a month or two, the duke, having learned nothing fresh, became again tranquil, and at length slept in peace; when his mistress, whom his little conjugal disturbances had not caused him to forget, manifested a desire to visit Baden-Baden. The duke, who wished to accompany her, complained of a violent nervous affection, and induced his physician to order him the baths. The wife, who was informed by her lover of all that took place, determined to justify, by her conduct, the good opinion of her husband, and informed him that she could not suffer, for the three months he had to remain in a strange town, that the care of watching over him should be confided to strangers; she would, she said, be his nurse; could he find another more devoted? The husband was compelled to accept this proof of her attachment.

" To have them both with him in a place like Baden-Baden, where, having nothing to do, one half like to occupy themselves with the affairs of the rest, was really a thing impossible. The excellent husband, however, found means to conciliate all parties; he requested his intimate friend to come with him to Baden-Baden; and as the latter, to keep up the farce, refused, he told him it would be rendering him a real service, that we ought, in the ordinary relations of life, to oblige our friends, if in our turn we should apply to them; at length he made use of such arguments, that the handsome young man was willing to sacrifice himself.

" They departed both within a few days of each other. The lover of the duchess accompanied the mistress of the duke. I cannot inform you of what took place between this couple during the journey; I shall only remark to you that the young man, who detailed to his mistress whatever was done by her husband, never mentioned a word of the dramatic artiste in question, which might lead us to suppose that the noble duke was at one and the same time betrayed by friendship, love, and hymen.

" The arrival at Baden-Baden of these four individuals produced a general sensation, for at least two-thirds of the lions and lionesses who come here from Paris are perfectly cognisant of what I am telling you; the noble duke, nevertheless, sleeps happily on his two pillows; so we may conclude, that it pleases providence to drop a thick veil before the eyes of husbands who are generally deaf and blind."

" And the conclusion of all this?" said Roman, when the poet Chevelu had finished the preceding narration.

" The conclusion? 'Tis this, that at Baden-Baden, as well as at Paris, we often meet with knaves, fools, and rogues;

" Observers by taste and by profession;

" Artists, who have no other merit than what they assume to themselves;

" Men of letters, who have no other wit than what they pilfer;

" Magistrates crippled by debts;

" Deputés whose consciences are for sale;

" Lawyers, barristers, and bailiffs, flaying their clients;

" Bankers who are usurers;

" Soldiers, heroes of the anti-chamber, who have seen no other fire than that in the kitchen;

" Pickpockets, covered with ribands of every colour;

" Amiable and elegant young men, whose whole fortune is staked upon a pigeon match, marked cards, and loaded dice;

" False devotees, inhuman philanthropists, millionaires without hearts; false and ungrateful friends; merchants without honesty; women, coquettes, jealous and unfaithful, and so on."

When Roman and the poet rose from table it was night, and the melodious sounds of an orchestra announced that the saloons were already opened. Our two heroes followed the eager crowd of gamblers and amateurs of the dance, and then separated, to follow the amusement which each of them preferred. The poet mixed in the groups of young elegants and pretty women, who waited with impatience the moment for commencing the dance; Roman took his usual place at the gaming table.

Fortune was decidedly weary of favouring him; he lost his first mass, then a second, afterwards a third; the little prudence he had as yet preserved now entirely abandoned him; the blood mounted to his head, his arteries beat with violence, the veins of his neck swelled; he took, without reckoning them, the gold pieces and bank notes, and placed them on the fatal *tapis vert*, and thus continued, until he discovered he had not a gold piece left.

He had lost, in less than an hour, all he had won since his arrival at Baden-Baden.

He left, that he might breathe more free.

" 'Tis well done," he muttered, when he attained the magnificent terrace in front of the Conversation House; " 'tis well done; I ought, as I promised myself, to have waited a week without playing!"

Roman recovered his *sang froid* in the balmy and reviving air; and as, after all, he had only lost what he had previously won, and the sum he had brought from Paris being still untouched, he soon regained his cheerfulness.

The results of the sittings which followed this last were in his favour; he regained, in less than a week, an amount nearly equivalent to what he had lately lost; then came the alternations of gains and losses, which were at length followed by a general break up, which, in a few sittings, carried away from Roman the whole of his ready money.

" 'Tis pleasant," he muttered, tapping his note case, which was no longer bursting with bank notes, and striking his pockets, which returned no longer that metallic sound so agreeable to the ears; " 'tis pleasant! it appears that my martingal was not infallible. But was it possible to foresee a series of twelve reds, followed by three double black zeros? Well, 'tis a decided affair, I shall play no more!"

All that remained to Roman was his wardrobe,

which, however, was in a tolerably good condition, a few bijoux, and the postchaise which had brought him to Baden-Baden. One of those brokers whom we are sure to encounter at every place in which there are gambling houses, purchased, for two thousand francs, objects which were at least worth double; and Roman, who had just vowed to play no more, hastened to carry to the fatal table his last pieces of gold.

Having nothing more to do at Baden-Baden, which appeared to him a very tiresome residence, now that he had no longer the hope of ruining the gaming administration, he determined to retake the road to Paris; and, to procure the small sum required for the expenses of his journey, he was compelled to make a fresh visit to the broker, and to get rid of a heap of objects which had escaped him at the first sale.

Roman's first step, on arriving at Paris, was to see his friend, who guessed, from his sad looks and his paltry equipage, that he had been deceived in his hopes.

"Well!" he said to him ; "you are not returned a millionaire, as it seems?"

"They are empty, my dear Salvador," replied Roman, striking his pockets. "I am returned very similar to the philosopher Bias; that is, I carry about me my whole fortune."

"You see I was not wrong when I foretold that this last attempt would not be a happier one than those preceding."

"You were right; I will not deny it," replied Roman, after comfortably seating himself in a fauteuil á la Voltaire ; "but if you will permit it, we will talk a little about some trifling affairs. Give directions that we may not be disturbed."

Salvador rung the bell.

"I am at home to no one," he said to the domestic who presented himself.

"Monsieur le Marquis has no doubt forgotten," replied the servant, "that Madame the Marchioness of Roselly has sent word that she will come at one o'clock, to take Monsieur le Marquis to accompany her to the wood of ———."

"Monsieur the Marquis is at home to no one." said Roman, "not even to Madame la Marquise de Roselly."

Salvador nodded as a sign that he approved of what his intendant had said.

The domestic made an inclination, and retired.

"Now I can listen to you," said Salvador, when they were alone.

"Among the many old proverbs which have traversed the world for ages," replied Roman, "there is one, the truth of which has never been doubted."

"And what says this proverb?"

"It says that we are always ready to see the mote in our neighbour's eye, but that we can never perceive the beam which is in our own. You tell me I did wrong to play, that it is probable that if I continue I shall lose a good part of what we possess."

"Well, and is it true?"

"I do not say no, but when you preach morality to me, it is useless, for I have for some time preached to myself exactly in the same words; but do you think yourself reasonable enough to have the right of reprimanding me?"

"If I had lost at play 250,000 francs in two years, I think I should hang myself directly."

"You do not reply to my question; I ask you if you think you act with sufficient prudence yourself, to claim the right of reprimanding me?"

"Certainly I am not a Cato, but I do not think myself so great a fool as you are."

"Proverbs are always right, I think."

"Eh! you will kill me with your proverbs. Come, let me know the burden of all this?"

"To prove to you that you are as great a fool as myself, to say the least."

"I am listening."

"The Marquis de Pourrieres in dying left us about 60,000 francs a-year, am I right? It was a very handsome legacy, and we could both of us lead a very agreeable life in spending each of us 30,000 francs per annum."

"No doubt."

"But I have gambled, and I have made in this fortune a breach ———"

"Too considerable, morbleu! 250,000 francs in two years."

"I did wrong; I know it, but since my account is squared, let us examine yours a moment.

"The reparations and furnishing of the old manor of Pourrieres have cost, if I do not mistake, 40,000 francs; the organising and music of the national guard 10,000 francs. I only speak from memory of these two items. 'Twas quite necessary to repair and furnish conveniently our residence, and I am not sorry to see that red rag shine at your button-hole. The fêtes, fireworks, and what followed, 25,000 francs; your house, horses and carriages, 150,000 francs; the house at the Champs-Elysées, the horses, equipages, the plum-coloured gold-laced habits of monsieur; the waistcoats and breeches of red plush for the livery of Madame la Marquise de Roselly, at least to the same amount; all this makes nearly 365,000 francs. Am I exact?"

"But too much so, unfortunately."

"We have then, besides our revenue which has been absorbed by a crowd of trifling expenses, dissipated more than 600,000 francs, and at the present moment there remains to us but 30,000 francs a-year, 15,000 francs each; it is but a trifle, isn't it?"

"We must, however, determine to make ourselves content with that."

"And the sooner the better; for my part, I make a solemn oath never will I again place a gold piece on a *tapis vert*."

"You do right, my friend, you do right!"

"We will, in addition, return to Pourrieres, you must renounce your dreams of ambition, and the elegance you are surrounded with; you must make your mistress comprehend that two lovers, so fondly attached, can be amply satisfied with a thatched cottage, refreshing glades, a clear rivulet, fruits, and milk."

"Come then, Roman, I really think you are laughing at me?"

"You are wrong then, I assure you; what has recently happened to me has caused some very serious reflections, and I am now of opinion that there is not a more agreeable life than that of a country gentleman."

Roman rose up and walked about the room we have mentioned in the early part of this history, humming the refrain of a romance become popular:

" Quand on est toujours vertueux*
On aime a voir lever l'Aurore."

"Are you turned mad?" exclaimed Salvador, rising in his turn.

"And so, my poor friend," replied Roman, "you have no ambition to bury yourself again at Pourrieres, where we remained just long enough to allow those who knew us to forget us; and you

† " Whilst yet virtuous we remain,
To view Aurora rise, is still our aim."

fancy your mistress will not willingly quit her pretty little house in the Champs-Elysées, her carriages, and so on; as to what regards myself, I am afraid that the oath I have just made will resemble all the rest I have made."

"But what will become of us in that case?"

"Listen: we are each of us governed by a different passion, although the results may be the same, and all the efforts we might make to escape our destiny, will, I fear, be entirely useless; for this reason, I think the wisest plan we can adopt is, that each should follow the impulse of nature, and wait for the denoument with patience and resignation."

"Oh! we shall have no occasion to wait long, the denoument is much nearer than you think perhaps. To procure ready money, I have been obliged to pledge a good part of the lands of Pourrieres; and at the present moment 'tis doubtful if I possess 10,000 francs; and unless I mean to fail, I must, at the end of the month, pay what I am indebted to my furnishers and those of Silvia."

"This Marchioness of Roselly, then, has no fortune?"

"Eh! when I made her acquaintance, she had already dissipated all she possessed."

Roman and Salvador were at this point of their conversation, when the servant, whom the latter had directed to admit no one, entered the cabinet, preceding Silvia.

"Monsieur le Marquis is a witness that madame has forced my consigne."

"Very well," replied Salvador; "you may retire."

"You are not gallant, Monsieur le Marquis," said Silvia; "you promised yesterday to accompany me to the wood to-day, and when I come to remind you of your promise, you leave directions that you are absent; this is not kind."

"Be assured, madame."

"Oh! I excuse you; but 'tis because I find you with Monsieur Lebrun, whom I am delighted to meet here."

"Madame la Marquise is infinitely too good," replied Roman, bowing with all the humility of an intendant of a marquis.

"Well! 'tis decided," muttered Silvia; "I shall discover nothing to-day again: come, let us go," she said to Salvador.

"I am at your service, madame," replied Salvador, rising.

Silvia put on her bonnet, which she had taken off on entering, and had placed on her shoulders the light and silken scarf in which she usually enveloped her fine and pliant waist.

"Apropos," she said, addressing Salvador, "as Monsieur your Intendant is here, have the extreme kindness to request him to bring me to-morrow 10,000 francs; I have promised some money to my milliners, linen drapers, &c., and I should be greatly annoyed to fail in my word. I will reimburse you this bagatelle the first opportunity."

An expression of evident discontent overspread the features of Salvador at this unexpected demand; he was about to reply by a promise, but Roman, to whom he had just detailed the precarious state of his finances, did not leave him the time.

"I fear, madame, that it will not be possible for the marquis to render you the trifling service you have requested. When you entered, I had just completed my accounts; and as he has been forced to pay recently some very heavy sums, my chest at this moment is nearly empty."

"Is it true?" said Silvia, addressing Salvador.

"But too true, alas!" replied the latter, heaving a deep sigh.

"Shall you be ruined?" cried Silvia.

"Oh! not quite," replied Roman, smiling; "but perhaps it may be necessary for the marquis to sell a part of his estates."

Silvia was seated, and Salvador, who had also resumed his seat at the bureau, seemed buried in deep and painful reflections.

"You must not trouble about it," said his mistress; "'tis but a moment's uneasiness; you must diminish the establishment of your house, decrease the number of your carriages, and of mine," she added in a low tone.

Salvador was touched in the most sensitive place.

"Diminish my household train!" he exclaimed, "cut down the number of my equipages! that is impossible! What shall I be thought of in society? they will think I am ruined, and the minister will not bestow on me the place I have solicited."

"It is certain, Monsieur le Marquis, that if you are seen to fail in the first act of your appearance in the world, your hopes in that world are gone for ever."

"I must, however, extricate myself from this dreadful labyrinth."

"Ah! if you had but the value of what I have just seen, you would be clear of your embarrassment at once."

"Eh! what have you seen then, Madame la Marquise?" said Roman, more for the purpose of continuing the conversation, than out of curiosity.

"The finest collection of precious stones it is possible to conceive; diamonds, emeralds, sapphires, rubies, amethysts, topazes, magnificent opals, and admirable pearls."

"In fact, all the treasures of Golconda and Visapour," said Salvador. "And who was the happy possessor of all these riches?"

"A countryman of Monsieur de Roselly," replied Silvia, "whom I met yesterday at the house of Madame the Duchess of Beautrellis, and who called this morning to pay his respects to me."

"And these pearls were really very handsome?" continued Roman, as the conversation seemed to interest him.

"Admirable. I fancy I now see before me, in all their brilliancy, the scarlet gorgeousness of the topazes, the pale crimson of the rubies, the golden reflections of the opals, the mysterious violet of the amethysts, the blue of the sapphires, and the deep green of the emeralds, which resembles the pure sky in a beautiful summer's day, and the sombre foliage of the forests."

"The compatriot of Monsieur the Marquis of Roselly is at least the richest merchant jeweller of the noble city of Venice?" said Roman.

"You are in error, it is no merchant who possesses this rich collection of precious stones, but a gentleman of good family. The name of Coloredo has been inscribed for many years on the golden book of the Venetian nobility."

"And no doubt he wishes to dispose of these jewels?"

"He has arrived in Paris expressly for that purpose, and it was after leaving the house of Halphen, whom he wishes to charge with the commission relative to this sale, that he came to visit me."

"I hope sincerely that this stranger may not ruin himself at Paris; but if he furnishes his house as elegantly as Monsieur le Marquis has done his, it is likely that after selling his jewels, he will also dispose of his domains."

"Oh! there is no danger of that, the Count Coloredo is the most avaricious of mortals. He contents himself with one of the smallest apartments in the Hotel de Castiglione, and dines at a table d'hôte at five francs a head; besides, he has no intention of remaining at Paris. But we amuse ourselves in talking about indifferent matters, and forget that the hour for the promenade will soon be passed; let us go, Monsieur le Marquis."

"I am at your service, madame."

At the moment Salvador was going. Roman took him aside to request of him a note for a thousand francs, and as Salvador was about excusing himself:

"Be tranquil," said his friend, "this time it is not to play that I demand this sum; go and amuse yourself, and don't be uneasy about the future; in a few days I shall probably have some good news to announce to you."

Roman went immediately to the Hotel des Princes, to collect such things as he had left there prior to his departure for Baden-Baden; he sent the whole of it, which still constituted a very respectable wardrobe, to his friend's hotel; and when this was done, he left, taking a cabriolet at the door, which conducted him to the station of the railroad to Orleans.

He departed by the first train, and descended at Orleans at the hotel of the Golden Ball, from whence he wrote to Salvador to send him, by the quickest mode, his trunk and baggage.

"What I request of you may perhaps seem extraordinary," he said, in terminating his letter, "and you will no doubt be surprised that I have assumed a name which at present does not belong to me; but let not this prevent your doing what I have requested of you, I hope to succeed in proving to you, that if I lose money, I know also how to regain it."

After receiving what he waited for, Roman returned to Paris by the same means he had arrived at Orleans; and, from the railroad station, was driven to the Hotel de Castiglione, where he arrived in the evening, enveloped in a large cloak, his head covered by a black silk cap, and holding his handkerchief to his mouth, as though suffering from a violent toothache.

Before engaging an apartment, he observed to the people of the hotel, that he was desirous of knowing, in consequence of his state of health, who were the persons he would have as neighbours, and whether they were noisy. They replied to his remarks, which appeared quite natural, that the apartment numbered 11, was the one of all others the most likely to suit him; number 12 being occupied by an Italian nobleman, who seldom returned before bed time, and occupied himself, when by chance he remained at home, in reading and writing; number 13, by an old deaf lady, who received no one, but went out to dine, and returned at 11 o'clock, or later; and the one beyond, by the book-keeper of the premises.

Roman engaged number 11.

When, the next morning, he left his chamber, Salvador himself in passing would not have recognised him; from a brown, he was become a fair man, moustaches and a thick beard covered his face, which, instead of being as usual round and florid, was become thin and pale, his eyes were in addition concealed by green spectacles of more than ordinary size; in fact, he appeared so suffering, so sickly, so broken up in constitution, that the proprietors of the hotel, on seeing him support himself on the arm of the domestic to reach the carriage he had ordered, could not help pitying him, and remarked to each other that the unhappy stranger would leave his bones in France.

Roman, however, had no intention of dying; the dexterous questions he had put to the servants of the hotel, when choosing his apartment, had satisfied him as to the one occupied by the Count Coloredo; this information once obtained, he found no difficulty in seizing upon a favourable moment to take the impression of the lock, and he left, for the purpose of obtaining the instruments necessary to work with at the proper occasion.

Roman, who had already *traded* in Paris, was aware that he could procure at the Temple, and at every locksmith's in the street de Lappe, keys of every shape and every size; he purchased two small bunches, one to serve for the exterior door, and the other for the furniture; three gimlets, a small chisel, and a file. He was in hopes, however, of not being forced to make use of these latter instruments, for he had already remarked that the locks of the doors and of the furniture of the Hotel de Castiglione, were, like most of the furnished hotels, but slightly made, which might be easily opened by almost any key.

He had no difficulty in procuring what he wanted, and when he found himself alone in his apartment, he said to himself, rubbing his hands, and throwing his peruke and false beard on the floor, that the most difficult part of the project he meditated was accomplished, and that it now only required patience; fortune, in addition, favoured him more than he had expected.

He had been only five days at the hotel, when one morning he heard in the apartment of his neighbour an unusual noise; they opened and shut several pieces of furniture, removed boxes; this bustle seemed to indicate the preparations for an approaching journey. Roman's heart beat with violence. For more than an hour, each movement he heard increased the painful anxiety to which he was a prey, when a domestic pronounced these fatal words: "Go instantly for a carriage. Monsieur de Coloredo wishes to go out directly." No further doubt, the treasure upon which he reckoned was about to escape him. The sound of a fresh voice now struck his ear; it was that of the stranger, who desired the waiter of the hotel to choose for him the best carriage he could find, and to engage him by the hour. "On second thoughts," he added, "desire the driver to come up, I will engage with him myself." Roman, his ear applied to the partition which separated his apartment from that of the stranger, held his breath that he might not lose a syllable.

The coachman arrived.

"I shall take you by the hour," said the stranger; "you will conduct me first to Boivins, the noted glover of the Rue de la Paix, afterwards to the Austrian embassy, where you will wait for me until four o'clock. What is your charge for all this?"

The driver demanded twenty francs. The noble Italian, who was in reality as niggardly as Silvia had represented, refused to give more than fifteen, and he maintained his interests with so much tenacity, that the coachman was compelled to yield. Ten minutes after, Roman, from his window, saw his neighbour mount the numbered vehicle, which was to conduct him to the Rue de Grenelle-Saint-Germain.

"A pleasant journey!" he said: "go dance with Madame d'Appony;* for my part, I go to make dance your precious jewels."

* Some years ago the dancing morning of Madame d'Appony had obtained great celebrity.

After the lapse of an hour, Roman left his apartment, and casting, from the top of the staircase to the bottom, a glance to guard against surprise, he introduced himself, by means of the keys he had procured, into that of the unfortunate proprietor of the precious jewels which Silvia had so brilliantly described in his presence.

He was in possession of the apartment, and the count would be absent several hours; he had thus before him more time than he required, to visit, without fear of being disturbed, all the furniture in the chamber. He locked the door on the inside; he put his weapons in order, for he was determined not to be taken alive, if by chance he should be surprised; and placing on his feet socks of plaited hair, in order that the noise of his steps might not be heard by the lodgers on the floor beneath, he commenced a minute visit to all the furniture. He had already searched all the drawers of the commode, of the secretaire, of the cupboards, which he had opened with the greatest facility with his bunch of keys, and he almost despaired of the success of his enterprise, when he perceived in a corner a sort of small chiffonier, which he had not at first remarked.

"The *magot* is in there, or 'tis no where," he said to himself.

And the drawers of the chiffonier went through the same ordeal as the other pieces of furniture. Roman was not disappointed; in one of the drawers of this piece, he found a small box of chagrine, in which were all the jewels which Silvia had mentioned; he wasted no time by examining them.

After replacing the furniture in its proper state, he left the apartment of the count as favourably as he had entered it.

His first care, on entering his own room, was to make a slight toilette; he then rang, and ordered the servant who presented himself to obtain a carriage for him.

Roman, with his precious capture concealed in his bosom, and leaning as usual on the arm of a domestic, reached his carriage; and when his driver, who had vigorously applied the whip to his two Rozinantes, had left far behind him the street and the Hotel de Castiglione, an "Ouf!" considerably prolonged, escaped his pent up chest.

At the moment Roman had mounted his vehicle, another carriage, numbered, had stopped before the door of this hotel, and a lady, who in his preoccupation he had not remarked, descended from it, and demanded of the concierge if the Count Coloredo was at home. The lady retired, after receiving a reply in the negative, when she perceived our hero.

"'Tis singular," she said to herself, "this man who appears so ill, greatly resembles, despite his beard, his moustaches, and green spectacles, which hide his face, the intendant of Monsieur le Marquis de Pourrieres."

"Coachman," she said, addressing her automaton, "follow that coach, but at a distance, and so that you may not be observed; twenty francs for you, if you acquit yourself of this mission with dexterity."

The driver of a public vehicle will attempt any thing for a person seemingly in a position to fulfil his promise, who offers him a napoleon, so that the coachman of Silvia (our reader has already guessed that the lady he conducted was no other than the Marchioness de Roselly) employed all his efforts to show himself worthy the magnificent recompense he hoped to obtain.

Roman was driven to the Barrier de l'Etoile, where he left his vehicle.

"Follow the man," said Silvia to her coachman, "but at a distance, and so that he may not observe you."

Roman entered the wood of Boulogne by the Maillot gate.

"Quick, quick," said Silvia, "he is entering the copse, we shall lose him."

The coachman lashed his horses, who quitted, to their great regret probably, their easy pace; but when they arrived at the Maillot gate, the ill-natured old man, who had walked so quietly all the way from Neuilly, had disappeared.

"This old man is very nimble," said Silvia; "I am evidently on the traces of the secret I wish to penetrate; but how to find him again! Well, 'tis an opportunity lost; but please God——"

Silvia was about to direct her driver to return, but, by one of those sudden inspirations which we obey without seeking to find the cause for the sentiment which has produced it, she told him to follow the path they were in, which led to the round point. Arrived at this part of the wood of Boulogne, Silvia beheld, leaving a cross path, and entering the one which leads to the gate at Passy, the intendant of the Marquis de Pourrieres, dressed in a redingote which buttoned up close to his body, and despoiled of his moustaches, his beard, and his spectacles, which but a few minutes before had completely disguised his features.

"At length!" said Silvia.

She stopped her vehicle, gave the coachman the promised recompense, and left, after desiring him to wait for her at the Maillot gate.

Roman walked with such rapidity that Silvia had much difficulty to keep pace with him; but her eagerness to succeed, inspired her every moment with new forces. Roman frequently turned back, but Silvia, who was enveloped in her shawl and had lowered her veil, followed him at a distance; and it was not probable that the sight of an elegant woman, if indeed he even remarked her, would cause him any inquietude. At length he arrived at the stand of the barrier des Bons Hommes, where he took a cabriolet. It was time. Silvia, whom the long course she had made had almost exhausted, could hardly sustain herself; she entered a coach and followed that of Roman, who stopped at the door of the hotel of the Marquis de Pourrieres.

Roman entered; Silvia waited some moments before she followed him; and when she supposed he was installed in the cabinet of the marquis, she entered, and, despite the efforts of the servant, who attempted to dispute her passing, she arrived in the room in which were the two friends. The jewels stolen from the Count Coloredo were displayed on the bureau of Salvador.

"Le voila donc connu ce secret plein d'horreur,"* said Silvia, raising a journal which Roman had thrown over the precious stones, at the moment she had entered the apartment.

"What do you mean?" exclaimed Salvador; "and what signifies this habit you have taken, of forcing the orders of my servants, when I desire to be alone?"

"You will permit me, no doubt, to sit down?" replied Silvia, who had taken off her bonnet and shawl, and seated herself in a chair, which she placed near that of her lover. "These precious stones belong to the Count Coloredo, and they have been stolen by your intendant Monsieur Lebrun."

* "Now for the knowledge of this horrible secret."

"Madame la Marquise will allow me to observe that, without doubt, she has lost her senses," replied Roman.

"Put aside, if you please, our respective titles, and let us explain ourselves simply, and without the forms of politeness; but first, my dear M. Lebrun, permit me to prove to you that I have not lost my senses. When you left the Hotel de Castiglione, you were enveloped in a riding coat of brown cloth, you had a light peruke, moustaches, and a beard of the same colour; you mounted a vehicle on four wheels, bearing the number 266, which conducted you to the barrier de l'Etoile, where you left it; you afterwards followed the route of Neuilly; you then entered one of the copses of the *Allée des Voleurs*,* which you left, habited in the costume you wear at present, after leaving, no doubt, in the brushwood your riding coat, your peruke, your beard and moustaches; you afterwards took another vehicle, which has brought you here. Well! have I lost my senses?"

Roman, whilst Sivia was speaking, and without her perceiving it, drew from the side pocket of his redingote a poniard with a short triangular blade; he rose suddenly, placed one of his hands on her shoulder, and threw her back on the seat she occupied; he raised his arm to strike, but Salvador, who had observed his movements, jumped forward to restrain him.

"Are you mad?" he exclaimed.

Silvia was not aware of the danger she had ran until it was past; her features were then overspread with a mortal paleness, but she retained the use of her senses.

"You are not very prudent, my good Monsieur Lebrun," she said to Roman, who perceived the error he had committed, and had replaced in his pocket the shining poniard.

"Recover yourself," said Salvador, "you have now nothing to fear."

"Oh! I am quite myself again," replied Silvia, "and perfectly in a state to listen, if by chance you have any thing to say to me."

"I have in fact many things to communicate to you. You have known for some time that a secret existed between me and Lebrun, and that he was only my intendant by form. Well, we are not only friends, but accomplices, and the crime we have committed to-day is not the first; you know what you have to do. As to denouncing the robbery committed by Lebrun upon the Count Coloredo, you will do nothing of the sort, as we can accuse you as an accomplice. Now, shall we be three to march in the same steps, in the same career, or shall we only remain as two?"

"We will remain three," replied Silvia, offering a hand to Salvador and Roman; "I claim to have my share of the precious stones of this worthy Count Coloredo."

"And you shall have it handsomely, I'll answer for it," exclaimed Roman. "I see that I was wrong in distrusting you, and that my friend was not mistaken in telling me that you were a resolute woman, and upon whom we might reckon in need."

"Monsieur le Marquis de Pourrieres knows that I am quite devoted to him," replied Silvia, resting her pretty head on the breast of Salvador, who deposited a kiss on her fair forehead.

If, by the assistance of the invisible crutch of an obliging Asmodeus, it was permitted for a

* There is, in fact, in the wood of Boulogne, an alley which bears this name, (the alley of thieves,) a notice indicates it to the *promeneurs*.

modern Don Cleophas to witness what was taking place in the cabinet of the little hotel in the faubourg Saint-Honorè, a ravishing picture would be presented to his sight; and if his cicerone had requested of him an account of his impressions, it is probable he would have replied nearly as follows: "I see in an apartment, in which every species of luxury and comfort has been invited by the hand of taste, two young and handsome beings who regard each other lovingly, and are prodigal in their caresses. A man with full and florid features, and whose black hair is just commencing to turn gray, is smiling at their pastime. He is no doubt a kind father, happy in the happiness of his children; 'tis very touching, and quite patriarchal." And if the devil, after giving vent to that sardonic sneer which they say is so familiar to him, had informed him who were the individuals before him, the poor Don Cleophas would no doubt accuse Asmodeus of calumniating humanity. And that would have been natural. Crime is habitually represented as covered with rags, and inhabiting places whose aspect is sombre and desolate; we can hardly believe that persons whose physiognomy offers nothing remarkable, who are habited like the rest of the world, and who reside in sumptuous dwellings, recoil not before the most frightful crimes, when determined to satisfy the passion which governs them.

The conversation continued between Salvador, Silvia, and Roman. The latter had finished the recital of the means he had employed to possess himself of the jewels of the Count Coloredo, and his two auditors were greatly amused at the expense of the victim.

"And so," said Silvia, "the idea of appropriating these jewels entered your head the moment I mentioned them to you."

"Oh! mon Dieu! yes," replied Roman; "I plan promptly—and execute in the same way."

"And you are a noble friend," said Salvador; "to give me my part of an affair in which I have not participated! 'tis a good trait."

"And now you will let me play a trifle without scolding me too much?"

"Certainly, my friend; and the moiety of what may be realised by the sale of these admirable pebbles shall be handed to you in good and handsome bank notes."

"There is no hurry for that; at present I am not in the vein."

"An idea!" exclaimed Silvia, laughing aloud, "the Count Coloredo has not lost every thing, since you have left your portmanteau at the Hotel de Castiglione."

"Ah! charming! but the boxes are absolutely empty; a rag left inside would perhaps have put the police on my traces."

"You see, however, my dear Roman, how the smallest event might annul the cleverest combinations; if Silvia, instead of being a woman after my own heart, had been an ordinary creature, we should have been lost."

"My dear comrade, you know not what you say; an ordinary woman would not have recognised me. Isn't it true, belle marquise?"

"I think you are right."

"Well, well, all is for the best in the best world possible, and I think that we three can effect some grand affairs."

"When our purse is empty," said Silvia, "I shall talk to you about a little affair, whose results, I hope, will be as agreeable as those just obtained by Monsieur Lebrun."

LIFE IN PARIS.

THE DINNER AT SANS REFUS.

"I shall remind you of your promise at the fitting time, Madame le Marquise."

The conversation was prolonged for some time on the same topics; at length the question of ascertaining to whom the jewels should be sold was proposed. Salvador, Roman, and Silvia, who had lived more in the provinces than at Paris, were not acquainted as yet with all the resources of the capital.

"We could ourselves lay out these jewels and place them on paper; but to whom sell them, or even pledge them? this is the question to which we need an answer," said Salvador.

"'Tis, in fact, very embarrassing."

"Oh! I have it," added Salvador, striking his forehead, "I have the affair. Do you remember that *original* whom we met at Lemardelay's, who brought with him an old woman, with a figure so grotesque, and whom every one overwhelmed with compliments and salutations."

"Monsieur Justè?"

"Justè; I think this man is the one we stand in need of."

"And do you know where to find him?"

"Not precisely, but I know where to find the Count Paladin of the Holy Roman Empire. You know the man of the portfolio? and it is probable that this noble personage can indicate to me the lurking hole of Monsieur Justè."

"It is not necessary to recommend you to be prudent, to make no overtures to these gentry of a nature to awaken suspicion."

"The recommendation is certainly useless."

"The reason is, that I do not place much confidence in this Count Paladin, who so rascally cheated his friend in the affair of the note-case."

"Be easy, I tell you, I have not forgotten that the Parisian *workmen* have no honesty."

"It would not be very agreeable to get shipwrecked at the port, and especially as this affair will probably be the last we shall conduct: for if the promises I have received are realised, I shall obtain in a short time a lucrative employ."

"If you will allow me to see the minister, and solicit for you," said Silvia to Salvador, after significantly glancing at Roman, "I am quite sure you would not wait long."

"Au fait! 'tis an idea," replied Roman.

"Let us not talk about it, I beg of you; I should not like to be indebted to the fascinating eyes of my mistress for the employment I have solicited."

"Well! 'tis agreed, I shall know to-morrow where Monsieur Justè resides, and Madame le Marquise shall be charged to manage the affair we wish to have with him."

CHAPTER XVI.

A USURER.

ROMAN knew that the Count Paladin of the Holy Roman Empire was one of the most constant frequenters of the establishment of the limonadier with the gray moustaches, and that in order to meet this noble personage, it was only necessary to pass a few hours of the afternoon in this house, which he visited every day.

Roman did so. He had not been there an hour when the person he waited for entered; he called to him, and the count came at once and took a seat near him. After the compliments usual amongst persons of good company, the count demanded of Roman if the results of his journey to Baden-Baden had been satisfactory.

"Alas! no," replied the latter, "and at the present moment I would pay for an excellent dinner with the greatest pleasure to any one, who would indicate to me an honest possessor of cash disposed to discount, at a reasonable rate, some paper covered with excellent signatures."

"Why don't you address yourself to the proprietor of the establishment?"

"I have not too much confidence in this man; I heard related at the dinner where I had the pleasure of meeting you for the first time, a certain history."

"That of the lingot?"

"Precisely; you will agree with me?"

"I respect your scruples; but if you like, I will take you to a toy merchant, who will conclude your affair."

"He will give me polchinellos and rocking horses, instead of good crowns."

"If it is crowns you want, there is but Monsieur Justè who can manage your business."

"Monsieur Justè, you say? but that name is not unknown to me; I have heard it mentioned somewhere; but where?"

"Eh! parbleu, at the dinner in question; Monsieur Justè was there."

"That man suits me, and if you will give me his address, I will visit him to-morrow on your recommendation."

The count gave the address required, reserving to himself *in petto* the intention of seeing the usurer the same evening, in order to stipulate with him as to the commission he would have a right to claim."

Roman, as he had promised, paid for an excellent dinner to the count.

He employed the evening which followed in collecting information concerning Monsieur Justè, and what he learnt convinced him that he would not be averse to any proposals relating to affairs, however ambiguous; and his discretion was, they said, undoubted towards all who procured him the means of obtaining money. When, however, he reported to Salvador and Silvia all he had collected, he recommended to the latter to act with extreme prudence, and to make, if she thought it convenient, but half overtures to the usurer upon her first visit.

"Don't trouble yourself," replied Silvia; "I shall see this monsieur to-morrow, and I promise you, you will be satisfied with what I do."

The next morning, as it had been agreed, Silvia left her hotel to visit Monsieur Justè.

She ordered herself to be driven opposite the principal gate of the garden of the Luxembourg, where she left her carriage, and after directing her chasseur not to follow her, she enveloped herself in her shawl, drew over her face the laced veil which ornamented her bonnet, and entered the garden, which she completely crossed, in order to leave by the gate of the street d'Enfer.

Arrived in the Rue Saint-Dominique d'Enfer, she rang at the door of a house of a very mean appearance, and waited patiently some minutes before any one came to open it. The barking of a dog, whose deep-toned notes pronounced him to be of a formidable size, was the first reply to the jingling of the bell. Silvia was not afraid, but rang again; the baying of the dog was redoubled; a small wicket cut in the door, and defended by some strong rods of iron, was opened, and she then discovered a face, yellow as parchment, enlivened by two small sea green eyes, and surmounted by a cap, whose original colour was lost under a thick coat of grease.

'Twas the face of Monsieur Justè.

"What is your demand?" he said.

"To see Monsieur Justè," replied Silvia, "but shorten, if you please, the formalities which ought to precede my admission into this place," she added, raising her veil sufficiently to allow Monsieur Justè to catch a glimpse of her pretty face.

"Yes, yes," said the worthy usurer, who was perhaps a little softened by the sight of such a seducing little creature; "I will open it for you; just give me time to fasten up my dog."

The door was at length opened, and Silvia, in passing into a small court, which it was necessary to cross, in order to arrive at the building inhabited by Monsieur Justè, could not fail to remark the companion of the usurer, a Newfoundland dog of the strongest breed, who growled in his kennel.

"Eh! eh!" said Justè, "what do you say to the companion of my solitude? Do you think that, with a guardian of such a size, and as incorruptible as he is, I ought to fear messieurs the thieves of the good city of Paris?"

A gap, closed by a strong door of oak, provided with a safety lock and several bolts, gave entrance to the dwelling-house, in which every window was furnished with enormous bars of iron; and before arriving at the cabinet in which Justè had introduced Silvia, it was necessary to cross several chambers, the doors of which, at night, were carefully secured.

These rooms, which served as a magazine for Monsieur Justè, were filled with a miscellaneous collection of objects brought from every country in the world, and belonging to every age, arranged without order, some hung to the ceiling or against the walls, others thrown pell-mell on the ground: objects of natural history, stuffed boas and birds, two cases, one filled with insects, the other with butterflies; specimens and minerals in a box of white wood; shells of every shape and every colour; a complete collection of Michael Angelo, Poussin, Salvator Rosa, Murillo, Paul Potter, Mignard, Teniers, and of Rubens, somewhat apocryphal, in the midst of which, however, we might discover a few undoubted works, quite disconsolate at being forced to remain in such bad company; mouse-traps and clocks from Nuremburg; all the works of a modern library, and some good old books, brought into this Capernaum we know not how; arms defensive and offensive, antique, modern, and of the middle age; morions, bucklers, head pieces, cuirasses, halberds, partisans, two-handed swords, arquebuses, matchlocks, pistols, Scotch claymores, Malayan jacks, Tyrolean carbines, guns for the chase and for war: porcelains from Saxe, from China, and Japan, old Sèvres and China from Bernard de Palissy; Etruscan vases and lacrymatory urns; a death's head, crowned with a garland of artificial roses; the calumet of the red skins of North America, the chibouque of the Turks, and the narguillè of the Italians; bottles of champagne with brilliant labels, pets of the pomade du lion; cups of bronze and silver, chased by Benvenuto Cellini, and siphoid inkstands; a fœtus and some lizards preserved in bottles filled with spirits of wine; scapularies, an Egyptian mummy, an Agnus and Dei, a reliquary containing a model of the true cross; musical instruments, and kitchen utensils; Roman medals: packets of wax lights and boxes of German chemical matches: a head perfectly tat-

tooed, of a chief of a South Sea colony; Sardinian boots, old epaulettes, the sword of honour, and a peer's mantle of a marshal of France; all the spoils of the rich and the poor, of the man of the world, the artist, and the servant, and the whole covered with dust and cobwebs.

A few straw chairs, a small table of black wood, in front of which was placed a cane fauteuil, a washhand basin, and a water jug placed upon the chimney piece, and surmounted by a miserable engraving nailed to the wall, composed the whole furniture of the cabinet in which Justè had introduced Silvia. The windows of this cabinet, similar to all the other rooms, were secured by strong bars, sufficiently near each other to prevent any but a pale and doubtful light to penetrate into the apartment.

The walls were vulgarly stencilled with white flowers on a blue ground, and broken in several places; the chimney was furnished simply with two small andirons of brass, and, by their neat and shining appearance, it may be guessed that, even in the most rigorous days of winter, Monsieur Justè remained without fire.

He offered Silvia one of the straw chairs, and placed himself in the fauteuil.

"You will permit me," he said, after drawing round him the old redingote of black stuff, covered with stains and out at the elbows, in which he was habited, "you will permit me to finish my repast; I was at breakfast when you rang at my door."

"Don't disturb yourself," replied Silvia.

A cup of milk and a morsel of brown bread composed the breakfast of Justè.

"Will you explain to me," he said, soaking a slice of bread in his cup of milk," what procures me the honour of your visit?"

Silvia made an attempt to *take a cross road*, in order to arrive at the object she wished to attain.

"You possess some very curious and very rare objects, which you will be no doubt very glad to rid yourself of," she replied; "and, as it is possible that I may purchase some, I am come to see them."

"You are quite deceived then," said Justè, anxiously regarding Silvia; "the articles which fill my magazines are not for sale. I sometimes make them a present to those whose paper I discount, but I repurchase them as soon as they are sold; if, however, you wish to have a sight of my curiosities, I am at your service."

Silvia expressing a wish to examine attentively this collection, of which she had only obtained a glimpse, Monsieur Justè, who had expedited the last mouthful of his modest breakfast, rose, and preceded Silvia into the rooms in which were assembled the heterogeneous mass.

"There" he said, "you behold some magnificent paintings, due to the pencils of the most celebrated masters of the schools of France, Italy, Holland, and Spain; the best works of the most distinguished writers of the day—the *Vierge de Meudon* of Monsieur Groult de Tourlaville; the *Christiede*, a *Blonde; le Mousse*, of Madame Augusta Kernock; the *Code des Honestes Gens*, and a multitude of other *codes;* and many other *chefs d'œuvre* of the Elzevirs, Etiennes, the Aldes, and of Manuces. In this glass jar is preserved the asp of Queen Cleopatra; and there you see the vin de champagne of Moet and Company of Epernay; the fly-box of Madame de Pompadour; the stiletto used by Dibutade, when she traced on the wall the profile of her lover; the palette of Apelles, the chisel of Phidias; an autograph of Molière; the riband with which Androcles led his lion through the streets of Rome."

Monsieur Justè, in order to sum up the enumeration of all his riches, had assumed the tone of a charlatan, who boasts to the gaping crowd about him of the marvellous properties of his balms.

"Have you, among all your curiosities, the ring of Gyges, and the seal of the great Solomon?" said Silvia, smiling.

"Have you a wish to purchase those two articles?" replied Monsieur Justè, fixing on Silvia his little sea-green eyes.

"If they were for sale—Gyges' ring, especially, would please me infinitely; it is often necessary to enter places in which we do not wish to be seen."

"With the usurer Justè, for example?"

"As you say, my master," replied Silvia.

"And may I know, madame, the motive which has led you to a place in which you do not wish to be recognised?"

"You are discreet, Monsieur Justè."

"Very discreet, belle dame, especially when I find any account in it."

"If you are willing, we can manage together an affair of which you will not have to complain."

"And what is this affair?"

"You are very hasty."

"Excuse my impatience, it is quite natural; the affair you wish to propose to me is, you say, very advantageous?"

"You shall judge; but let us proceed in order. You do not know me, and as I live in a society in which you are not admitted, it is not probable you will again see me when once I have left your house; I can, then, without compromising myself, inform you what has brought me here."

"Quite true, madame."

"If you were offered, for a hundred thousand francs, some precious stones which are worth at least one hundred and fifty thousand, would you accept the proposition?"

Monsieur Justè fixed his keen eyes on Silvia for some minutes before replying to her, he then approached, and whispered these few words in her ears:

"If the jewels are really worth one hundred and fifty thousand francs, I will count you down the sum you demand, if even the jewels are those which were stolen, two days ago, from the Count Coloredo."

"I see that you are a reasonable man, and that there are means to make one's self understood by you; but, if I bring you, in a few hours, the precious stones in question, shall you be in a position to hand me immediately the sum in bank notes?"

"Immediately; in bank notes or in gold, at your choice."

"In that case, my master, open your chest, I have brought the jewels with me."

"I was sure of it; and they are those of the Count Coloredo?"

"What difference is that to you, if they are really worth one hundred and fifty thousand francs?"

"You are right, but will you allow me to examine these stones?"

"Nothing more reasonable; I have no desire to sell you a pig in a sack."

Silvia put her hand to the chaplet attached to her waist, to draw from it the little packet which contained the jewels, and old Justè wiped the glasses of his spectacles, when a strong ring at the bell, accompanied by the formidable baying of the yard dog, suddenly startled them. Silvia turned pale, and her eyes, fixed upon those of the usurer, seemed

to ask of him the explanation of this unexpected visit. Justè placed on her arm one of his bony hands.

"Don't be uneasy," he said to her, "you have nothing to fear here; I'll go and see who it is has rang the bell with such violence; no doubt, 'tis some client come to demand money of me after a night spent at the gambling table."

Justè left upon this, after placing in his pocket the key of his bureau.

Silvia, when she found herself alone in the bazaar of Monsieur Justè, said to herself, that, although treason on the part of Monsieur Justè was not probable, yet still it was not unlikely that the police were in search of the authors of the robbery committed at the Hotel de Castiglione; that, perhaps, she might have been followed, and that, in such a case, she ought to dispossess herself of the jewels which she carried about her person. This resolution once taken, she thought about the execution of it; she observed, in a corner, a soi-disant vase antique, with a very narrow neck, which was half-concealed under a heap of old armour of every kind, and covered with a venerable dust; she introduced into this vase the whole of the jewels, which she easily effected, by drawing them from the paper in which they were enveloped; she had finished this operation when Monsieur Justè re-entered; the most complete satisfaction was visible in his countenance, he almost smiled!

"Have no fear, madame," he said, "'tis nothing; 'tis a general, a friend of mine, who is come, after leaving his club, to request I will lend him fifty thousand francs, which I am going to do. I have begged him to wait for me a few moments in an adjoining room, that you may have time to conceal yourself, if, as I suppose, you do not wish to be seen."

Justè conducted Silvia behind a partition of trellis-work, furnished with small curtains of green linen, and which divided the cabinet into two equal parts; he brought her a chair, and, after again assuring her that he would not keep her long in waiting, he introduced the general into his cabinet.

Silvia, from the place she occupied, could hear all that was said by the general and the usurer, and the texture of the small green curtains which covered the trellis-work was so thin, that she could almost distinguish their features.

The general, hardly forty years of age, was a handsome man in every acceptation of the word; his graceful form, and the flattering tone of his voice, announced a man of the best society.

"Really, my dear Justè," he said, on entering the apartment of the usurer, "from the difficulty we have to contend with before arriving at your sanctum sanctorum, we might be almost tempted to believe that you were in luck's way."

"Eh! eh!" replied Justè, "why shouldn't I be allowed to seek some distractions in the goddess?"

"Oh! I know that you are rich enough to purchase the good graces of the handsomest women."

"Purchase! purchase! why, general, do you think that I am indebted for my good fortunes only to my money?"

And the little monster caressed his chin, and proudly admired himself in a small toilette-glass nailed to the sash of the window.

"Pardon me, my dear Justè, you have misunderstood me; I simply mean that the handsomest men are sometimes obliged to make sacrifices to satisfy the little caprices of an amiable and pretty woman."

"It's possible; but to the present hour I have

been lucky enough to escape the snares of co-quettes."

"That is easy, when we are, like you, firm in our resolutions; but, alas! I am not endowed with a similar strength of character and the fifty thousand francs that you are about to lend me are, as you know, intended for my mistress."

"General, you are *un cornichon!* such a sum for a woman who laughs at you!"

"You would not say so, if you knew this adorable creature, whom every one overwhelms with homages, and is only in love with me."

"And your bank notes!"

"You are wrong; you do not render to Coralie the justice she is entitled to."

"It's possible; but I am of opinion that it is not behind the scenes of the opera that we shall discover disinterested women."

"Allow me to differ from you in opinion; it is only since I have been beloved by Coralie that I have known any real happiness."

"In that case I congratulate you; but let us return to our own affairs."

Silvia, who was not aware that Justè had withdrawn, and placed in safety the key which served to secure the door of the partition, trembled lest the general should feel disposed to assure himself if his suspicions with reference to the amorous flights of the money lender had any foundation; but Justè left her no time to make herself uneasy on that score.

"You wish me to lend you fifty thousand francs?" he said to the general; "I am, as usual, disposed to oblige you."

"Very well, my friend; but this time I give you notice, 'tis cash I want; I will have no more of your merchandise, which only leave your magazines to return there."

"Cash! cash!" exclaimed Justè; "but where the devil do you think I am to procure such a sum as you have requested of me?"

"You will take this sum from your strong box, my master, and I shall merely give you in exchange some slips of paper."

The general drew from his note case several sheets of printed paper, which he handed to the usurer.

"You see," he said, when Justè, after reading one of the pieces, placed it on the small table, "the act is perfectly in order, it only remains to add the name of the lender."

"Oh! the moment that madame the duchess engages herself wholly with you, it totally alters the face of things and I am ready to count you the sum in question."

"Well, then, the affair is settled."

"You will take from me, however, only ten thousand francs worth of curiosities and objects of vertu."

"I shall not take even the very simplest article. 5,000 francs premium, and 10 per cent. in interest, is, I think, reasonable enough on my part."

"Well, well, I'll go and get the sum, but you promise me not to have any more dealings with my confrère Josuè?"

"I promise you not to deal with the Jew, except for the affairs which you refuse."

"Very well! very well!" exclaimed Justè, rubbing his hands, "if he takes an affair refused by me, he will lose money, and that will be cleverly done."

"You sincerely detest this Messieur Josuè then?"

"I hate every Jew; but let us talk no more about this heathen, whose name I cannot hear pronounced without getting into a rage. Let us terminate our business."

"I am waiting for you."

Justè again took the act, which he read a second time with the most scrupulous attention, pausing at the end of every phrase, and mentally commenting on the terms; quite convinced that it was perfect in form, he told the general to fill up the blanks expressly reserved, with the names and surnames, and he reminded him that besides this act, he must hand him bills of exchange at 3, 4, and 6 months, invested with his wife's surety.

"Here are the bills of exchange, my dear Justè," said the general; "a thing promised is a thing due."

The usurer left, after examining the bills of exchange with the same attention with which he had examined the act.

After a short absence, he re-entered the cabinet, carrying under his arm an old portfolio of green morocco, from which he drew one after the other 50 bank notes, which he handed to his client.

The general, delighted at being in possession of the sum he wanted, left, after affectionately pressing the hand of the usurer, who accompanied him to the street door.

When he opened the door of the partition to Silvia, he pointed at the green portfolio. There still remains in that note case, he said, gently tapping it, enough to satisfy you, and if you will allow me to examine these jewels of which the journals have made such a pompous parade, we shall soon finish the business.

Silvia took the vase antique, and emptied on the ledge of frame work which surrounded the small table of the usurer, the whole of its contents.

"Ah! madame," exclaimed Justè in a voice greatly softened, and his eyes full of tears, "you are a most estimable person, such a precaution at the moment you appeared so troubled; you remind me by your features and presence of mind of my poor late wife."

"I feel greatly flattered at my resemblance to the late Madame Justè," replied Silvia, smiling.

Justè heard no more; the fixed regard with which he examined the jewels of the Count Coloredo consumed all his faculties. His little eyes sparkled beneath the glass of his spectacles, and he expressed his admiration by short inarticulate exclamations: "What rare diamonds!" he said, "what magnificent emeralds! all these are worth at least 200,000 francs," he muttered at length, yielding, without caution, to the joy he felt in the certainty of acquiring, at half their value, the riches displayed before him.

"Ah! ah!" said Silvia to him, "they are worth 200,000 francs, eh? In that case, my master, you can well afford to give me 150,000 francs for them."

This unexpected observation restored to the usurer, the *sang froid* which his ardent admiration of the jewels had caused him for a moment to lose.

"I shall give you," he said, "the sum agreed upon, and not a liard more. These jewels are those of the Count Coloredo, and to make them available, I must send them to England or Holland, and must charge with the sale of them one of my fraternity, to whom I shall be obliged to allow a very heavy commission, by which my profits will be much less considerable than you suppose."

"Very well! let us hold to what has been agreed upon then."

Justè handed to Silvia ninety-nine notes of 1,000 francs.

"Here is one missing," said Silvia, after counting them.

"I know it well," said the usurer, "but as you have no doubt a library, I thought you would probably purchase a few books of me."

"You are jesting, my dear! what do you think I can do with your old rubbish?"

"Old rubbish! *Une blonde, la Vierge de Meudon,* and *the Code des honestes gens!* Ah! madame, you do not appreciate at their just value the most remarkable works of distinguished litterateurs."

"It's possible, but I like better my note of 1,000 francs; come, give it me, or none at all."

"Here it is, you see that I am straightforward in business; so that if another occasion presents itself, I hope it will be to me that you will address yourself."

"Without doubt."

"And especially never think of dealing with my confrère Josuè, he is a miserable, without faith, who flays his clients."

"You seem as though you cordially detested this man."

"Why has he quitted Marseilles to establish himself at Paris, and entice away a good part of my clients?"

"Ah! Messire Josuè of Marseilles is now at Paris!" said Silvia to herself.

"You know him?"

"Not personally, but a lady, a friend of mine, has had some transactions with him."

"Send this lady to me, I am much more reasonable, and I have much more money than Josuè."

"More money than Josuè! that seems doubtful to me; I have been assured that this Jew is three or four times a millionaire."

"I am richer than he is," said Justè, accompanying his words with a smile of proud satisfaction."

"Oh! oh!"

"If you do not believe it, speak of me to the general whom you meet, you say, in society, and you will be edified."

"I believe you, but tell me, dear Monsieur Justè; I often meet this general in society, and I should be very glad to learn something about him; can you not give me some little information about him?"

"You are Mademoiselle Coralie!" exclaimed Justè.

Silvia burst into a loud laugh.

"You never attend the opera then?" she said.

"Never; it is a pleasure which costs too dear."

"Then that explains your error, but let us talk of the general."

"Ah! I do not know if I ought: a client—"

"Monsieur Justè, you must place some confidence in me, if you wish for the future that I should not address myself to your confrère Josuè. I really want to learn all that concerns this general, and by means of your relations with him, you must know his affairs as well as himself. Speak. I am all attention."

"I must do as you desire. We cannot apply to the sons of the great men of the imperial age the well known proverb, like father, like son. In fact, with some rare exceptions, the sons of the favourites of the great emperor collect the mud from the kennels wherewith to soil their new escutcheon.

"The general who has just left, is the only son of one of the bravest generals of the empire; a degenerate scion of a noble stock, my client inherited none of the qualities of his father but his noble carriage, and his manly and expressive physiognomy. In this I am not telling you much that you do not know already, since, as you have told me you meet him often in society.

"The intrepid chief of the most valorous demi-brigade of the republic and the empire, left his son a considerable fortune, which allowed him to hold a distinguished rank in the world.

"My client, young, rich, and the possessor of a name to which were attached so many and such glorious remembrances, was very well received on his first entrance into society. The moment, it is true, was favourable; it was a short time after the events of July 1830, and at this epoch, all those who bore an illustrious name during the splendor of the imperial dynasty, beheld every avenue which led to fortune opened before them.

"At this period, the passion for the national guard turned every head; the bourgeois, the most debonnaires, learnt the charge in no time, and allowed their moustaches to grow; the women dressed their children *en voltigeurs* of the citizen militia; it was, in a word, a universal mania, and I believe that if you were to search well, you would find among the other contents of my wardrobe an old uniform of a citizen soldier, though covered with dust.

"My client, thanks to the influential persons who protected him, (we are never in want of patrons when we do not stand in need of them,) obtained the post, which he still occupies, of a general of one of the brigades of the Parisian national guard."

"I see, said Silvia, that I have strangely deceived myself, I fancied that this general was one of the heroes of our young African army, a rival of Chaugarnier and Lamoricière."

"You are indeed strangely deceived: my client, general as he is, and despite the decorations which glitter at his breast, possesses not one of the excellent qualities of his father, whose probity, bravery, and devotedness were the order of the day amongst the armies of the republic and the empire, and whose name has continued pure in the midst of the impurities of our period.

"Become general, the saloons of the highest were opened to him, he was even received at court; but that did not continue long. The great rate at which this honourable personage lived, the dinners of Lucullus which he bestowed on the superior officers of the citizen brigade, placed under his orders, the pretty women he kept, his equipages, which rivalled, if they did not excel, those of the princes, all this cost him every year a sum at least treble his income, so that one fine morning he found he had bidden adieu to his last note of 1,000 francs. His position was embarrassing.

"The devil, the devil! soliloquised the general, after a slight reflection, the chest is empty, I cannot however do without money, I must have some for my servants and my mistresses; but how to procure it?"

"'Monsieur le Comte seems embarrassed,' said his valet de chambre to him, a true Frontin of comedy, and who had heard the monologue of his master. This unexpected question did not offend the general, who was too well aware of the aptness of character of his valet, not to guess immediately that if he permitted himself to address his master at a moment in which the latter seemed so much annoyed, it was because he was enabled, as it had often before occurred, to give him some useful advice; so instead of treating him harshly, he engaged him to explain himself without fear, and the following is nearly what the valet said to him, after demanding pardon for the liberty he was taking.

"'Monsieur le Comte is young, the position he occupies in the world is very honourable, and although the whole property of Monsieur le Comte may be burdened by heavy loans, he would easily find, if he were inclined to marry, a woman who would bring him a considerable dowry.'

"'And have you a woman to propose to me, Monsieur Frederic?' replied my client smiling, who, for the first time in his life, faced, without trembling, the necessity of getting married.

"'Monsieur le Comte smiles,' replied the Frontin, 'but he knows well whom I mean.'

"In fact, the general did know the person to whom his valet had alluded. One of the superior officers of his brigade was the father of a young girl, whom all the beaux of the staff overwhelmed with homages and little attentions. Were they seduced by the sprightly eyes of the damsel, or by the no less tempting one's of the casket of papa? We cannot reply in a positive manner to this question, all that we can tell you is that the young girl was ravishing, and that the purse of papa, according to the *on dit*, was respectable. At all events, this young lady, similar in this to most other women, disdained the whole crowd of her admirers, and was quite disposed to receive with great indulgence the only man who seemed willing to contest the powerful influence of her charms.

"This man, I have no occasion to tell you, was no other than the general in question, so when, in his turn, he placed himself in the ranks, those who, until this moment, had been suffered as a matter of course, were successively dismissed; from henceforth it became his duty to carry the bouquet and the fan of Mademoiselle, when they were at the ball together, and I have no doubt, he acquitted himself with much grace of the functions of a cavalier.

"The father of the young lady, the most ill-shaped post 'tis possible to conceive, remarked with much pleasure the assiduous court paid by the general to his daughter; the elevated position of my client flattered his pride, and although he knew something of the doubtful state of his affairs, his name, his golden epaulettes, and his tri-coloured scarf, ornamented with silver fringe, excused in the eyes of the post in question, the peccadilloes of the past.

"The marriage was concluded.

"Alas! alas! why are the days of the honey-moon so short lived? why run so fast?

"The general, who, during the first months of his marriage, had seemed delighted, enchanted with his wife; who praised her charms, her wit, and her graces to such as would listen to him, insensibly grew cold. At length monsieur and madame, who every night had hitherto retired to the same chamber, had each their separate apartment; next, madame was obliged to make her visits and drive in the wood without being accompanied by monsieur; at last monsieur wearied, as it seems, of listening to the reproaches of madame, who had not accepted, without complaining, the position in which she was placed, and which she certainly did not deserve, for she was young, pretty, sprituel, and, what is more rare, she loved her husband; monsieur, I say, returned suddenly to his unrestrained habits of a bachelor.

"His debts had been paid at the time of his marriage, he contracted fresh ones. I have often had the pleasure of lending him money."

"And taking your securities," said Silvia.

"Of course, that is understood," said Justé. "When he could borrow no more money, he bought merchandises of all sorts, and resold them at a great loss. To tell you all he bought would be too long a history; it will suffice for you to know that he owes in the neighbourhood at least 1,600,000 francs."

"As much as that!"

"Quite as much; and it is probable he would owe a great deal more, if many of those whom he attempted to take in, had not discovered from the head of a certain establishment, which may heaven confound, some information which deranged a good part of his combinations.

"He found means, however, of purchasing from a wine merchant in the environs of Paris, 150,000 francs worth of Bourdeaux wine; the success of this operation induced him to try a second; he said to himself that since he had the wine, he ought to buy some bottles and the corks, and for this purpose he addressed himself to an honest merchant of these two articles; but the latter, better advised than the wine merchant, was not to be dazzled by the high rank, the decorations, and the polished manners of the individual; he reasoned that it would not be prudent to deliver, without taking certain precautions, 32,000 francs worth of bottles and corks; so he went in his turn to demand some information to the establishment in question, and that which he obtained was of such a nature, that he retained, and luckily for him, his bottles and his corks.

"The wine was sold by the efforts of one of those agents of doubtful affairs, at a loss of fifty-five per cent.

"The merchant who had sold it to the general, not being paid at the expiration of the bills of exchange, and not being enabled to place his debtor at Clichy, the only means of compelling him to do so; (my client, I forgot to mention that, was a depute, and, thanks to his legislative functions, he laughed at messieurs the gardes du commerce and his creditors so long as the session lasted;) the merchant was thus compelled to put up with his misfortune, and bear his loss with patience.

"This affair, and several others which would be too long to narrate, provoked some slight rumours in the honourable society in which my client was received; some punctilious parties, who would not absolutely make to our age those concessions which it demanded, went about declaring to those who chose to listen to them, that a rogue, though well dressed, was still a rogue. The general at first kept his head to the storm; he treated as a calumny and vile insinuations the reports which were spread about him, so much so, that many persons observing him so calm in the midst of the tempest, could not refrain from repeating:

'Rien ne l'emuet, rien ne l'etonne.'

"But when every door was shut against him, when men, who till then had appeared to seek him, turned their heads on passing him, in order to avoid the necessity of returning his salute, he was at length forced to look about him.

"To-day, it is only by the signature of his wife that he can obtain money, and you have seen that he does not hesitate to make use of it, and to satisfy the most frivolous caprices."

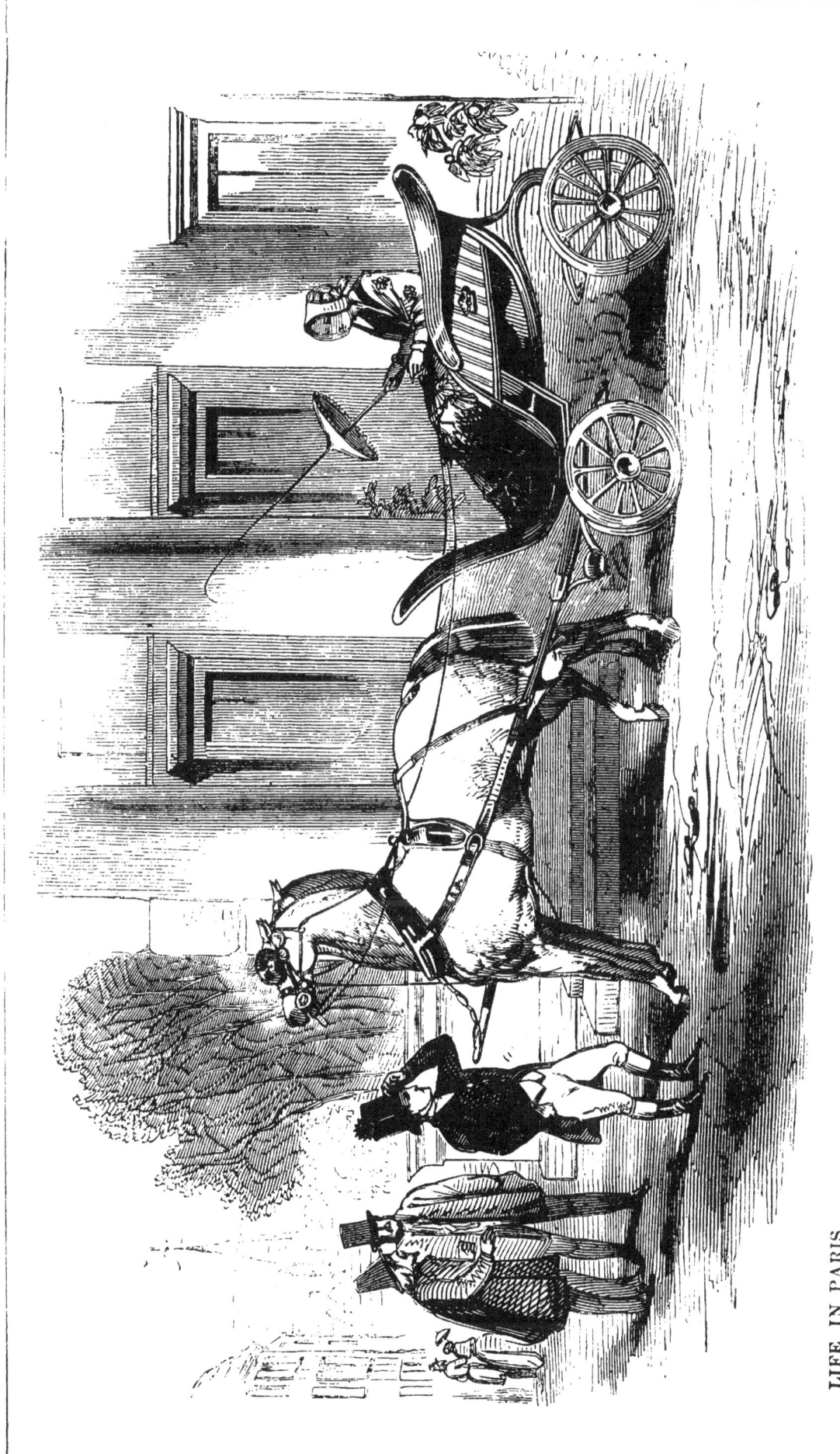

LIFE IN PARIS.

BADEN-BADEN.—THE CONVERSATION-HOUSE.

"And does he really mean to give to Coralie the 50,000 francs that you have lent him?"

"Without doubt. Coralie, as I am assured, is a woman who bestows her sweet charms upon those only who pay ready money, and she also knows how to make a handsome profit from those she has seduced; so that it is more than certain that the bank notes extorted from the wife, will serve to purchase the favours of the mistress."

"And for this reason," said Silvia, who had listened with the most serious attention to all that Justè had told her, "you probably think that the recommendation of this general would not be of much utility to any one who might solicit employment of a certain importance."

"On the contrary, I think, madame, that it would only injure him; for I tell it you in confidence, my client is now a star in its decline; and, if my foresight does not deceive me, he will in a short time be obliged to resign his commission of a general. It is said, indeed, that he intends to fix himself at Rome, to solicit from the Holy Father the rank of generalissimo of the Papal troops."

When Justè had finished recounting to her all he knew respecting the general, Silvia left the house, eager to join Salvador and Roman, who waited for her, no doubt, with the greatest impatience. She was delighted at having it in her power to prove to them, that they were not wrong in confiding to her the negotiation of an affair so delicate as the one she had just terminated, with so much intelligence and benefit; and that she was worthy of making a third in the association they had formed. She was, besides, very much relieved that chance had enabled her to enlighten her lover on the score of the general; for Salvador, upon his arrival at Paris, was the bearer of a letter of recommendation, addressed to the general by a noble personage of his department, who, no doubt, was not aware of the real character of the latter; and he relied greatly on the promises which had been made to him by this noble personage.

If the reader will permit us, we will allow Silvia to rejoin those whom we may now term her accomplices, and will remain a few minutes longer with Justè, with whom we shall meet some fresh personages, who, as well as himself, will play certain parts in the course of this work, and furnish us with the occasion to initiate our readers into some more of the mysteries of the Parisian life.

There is carried on at Paris, and in the face of day, a number of trades and industries, which, quite honest in appearance, are in reality nothing but *blinds* for every artifice and swindling transaction.

In the midst of the finest quarter of the capital, in the most conspicuous part of a brilliant street, we are often astonished at observing a hole, black and ill lighted, left by chance at the foot of an elegant mansion, whose renting value, however, it increases by a few hundreds of francs. This hole, despised for some time by all the little industriels, ceases one day to be uninhabited; its humid and saltpetred walls are garnished with shelves purchased at Chapon-street; a counter of oak wood, and some chairs, complete the furnishing of the hole in question; and a sign hoisted above the door, is charged to indicate to the passers, that Monsieur Such-a-one has established himself as a slopseller, and that he redeems objects from the Mont-de-Pietè, in order to effect their sale.

A certain quantity of men's clothes, purchased at the sales of the Mont-de-Pietè, some uniforms, and two or three pair of old epaulettes, such, in general, is the merchandise displayed before the eyes of the public, by the proprietors of these sombre bazaars—bottomless gulfs, in which every thing that enters is swallowed up.

A person in want of a small sum, comes to these shops, and sells a part, or the whole of his wardrobe, which will be afterwards purchased by some one who wishes, at a modicum of expense, to procure the equipment of a fashionable. This is, in fact, the known branch of the commerce of messieurs the fripiers; it is likewise the one which produces the least profit, and we may believe that they exercise it only to give a countenance, and to screen from over curious eyes, the secret division of their affairs.

Let us suppose a moment, that a person who reads the foregoing, and who wishes to have the explanation of what appears to him at present an enigma, enters a cab, and orders it to stop at the corner of a street facing the Boulevard, which serves as an habitual promenade to the inhabitants of our good city, he will remark the entrance, into a small shop of insignificant appearance, of individuals arrived, some on foot, others in coaches, who will leave, some minutes after, covered with a rich and new costume, gold chains, bijoux, and so on.

And here is the explanation:

An individual who is in want of money, comes to the fripier, to whom he sells his trunk and the whole of its contents, his watch, his bijoux, even his cane.

But not wishing or not being satisfied to remain constantly habited in the same garments, it is agreed upon beforehand with the fripier usurer, that every time he may wish to change his costume, he shall do it with facility, paying a premium of five, ten, or twenty francs, and the previous deposit of the old suit and a certain sum to make up the difference.

We meet in the gallery of the opera, on the Boulevard Italien, at the divan, at the estaminet of the Grand Balcon, and elsewhere, a crowd of dandies, fashionables, yellow gloves, lions, or whatever they are named, who have never changed their costume, except with the fripier in question, who has given to his clients the soubriquet of *lezards*.

The shop of the father of the *lezards* is constantly filled with a crowd of these would-be-somethings; some sell, the others buy, some hire, but all live on good terms with their father; a father, in addition, full of indulgence, and who could no more do without his children, than they could manage without him.

One day a very elegant cabriolet, behind which was perched a negro dressed in a handsome livery, gold-laced hat, a redingote of fine cloth with metal buttons bearing a crest, doeskin breeches, top boots, and white gloves, pulled up before the door of the father of the *lezards*, and from this splendid vehicle descended a handsome young man, a viscount *by trade*, who enters without ceremony into the shop, draws forth a chemise from his hat, and demands five francs from his father, to whom he offers, as security, the said chemise. The pledge was, perhaps, rather small, but the father of the *lezards* is very accommodating; he is aware that the very slightest operation, frequently repeated, produces some benefit, and that several small rivulets united form in the aggregate a large river. The five-franc piece was bestowed with a grace quite aristocratic; and the noble viscount, delighted probably at the result of this important negotiation, remounted his hired cabriolet, and started at a gallop.

There exist also for the ladies, houses similar to those of the father of the *lezards*. We shall find occasion, perhaps, to speak of them in the sequel of this history.

Silvia had just left Monsieur Justè, and the old usurer was calculating the probable benefits of the affair he had just concluded with her, when the ringing of the bell, and the barking of the dog, announced a fresh visit to him; he rose and went to the entrance of his habitation.

After examining, according to his custom, the person who demanded admission into his castle, he opened the door; he recognised the countenance of a friend, or rather of a person from whom he had nothing to fear; for Monsieur Justè, like most of his profession, had neither friends nor relations.

"Ah, ah! 'tis you, Rigobert!" he said to the new comer, when he had introduced him into his cabinet. "How goes business, and what lucky wind blows you here?"

"Business proceeds badly, Monsieur Justè, and the wind which wafts me here does not blow from a good quarter," replied the visitor; "I come to ask you for money."

"What you say astonishes me. How is it that, being at the head of a commerce in which the profits are very considerable, you find yourself compelled to-day to have recourse to me for money?"

"Eh! bon Dieu!" exclaimed Rigobert; "days run on, but resemble not each other; if at present I am a little behindhand, it is because I wished to follow in your wake."

"*Ambition destroys mankind*, my dear pupil! I commenced like you; but it was not until I found myself the possessor of a good sum that I increased the circle of my operations. But I will not follow the example of the schoolmaster who preached discipline to the boy while he was drowning; you want money, how much is necessary?"

"I want ten thousand francs; lend me this sum and I am saved!"

"Really! Well, my friend, bring me to-morrow a part of your merchandise equivalent in value to the sum you stand in need of, and the money shall be counted down on the instant."

Rigobert, (the reader has no doubt guessed that this individual was no other than the father of the lezards,) usurer as he was, was still not so much a one as to expect that Monsieur Justè would treat him as he would treat the first individual who might address him.

"Eh! eh!" said the latter, who had observed his astonishment; "do you suppose I shall lend you the money, without taking any security? You have deceived yourself, my dear child. Let what has happened to-day, serve you as a lesson; and remind you for the future, that when it is a question of business, and especially of money affairs, we must forget the ties which link us to the person who addresses us. If you had always kept your *lezards* at a distance, you would not be compelled to-day, to supplicate father Justè to come to your assistance."

"Well, Monsieur Justè, what is done, is done; but, as you observe, what has happened to me to-day will serve me for a lesson; if you will have the kindness to call, you may choose in my magazines the merchandise you require as security. At what rate will you lend me these 10,000 francs?"

"Six per cent."

"Very well!" exclaimed Rigobert, delighted at meeting with such an honest money-lender;"I am saved! six per cent. per annum; 'tis very reasonable."

"But I did not say that," replied Justè; "I will willingly lend you 10,000 francs on security, but at the rate of six per cent. *per month; it is the* general return of my capital."

"The devil!" muttered Rigobert; "I was wrong, it seems, to fancy that this old miser would remember the services I have rendered him." And as he remained silent:

"Once, twice, does it suit you?" said Justè.

"You are hard, father Justè," he replied; "but we must needs submit to him who holds the purse strings."

"Come, come, my dear pupil; you will make it up by raising the small shot a little to your *lezards*."

"I must do so. 'Tis agreed; you will come to-morrow to my house."

However hard were the conditions imposed upon him, Rigobert, who had a pressing need of money, thought himself but too happy in accepting them; for in reality, this money, which was to cost him 72 per cent., was to render him a very great service. The resources of the trade he carried on are incalculable; and the Almighty alone, and the usurer who lends, can know how much a piece of five francs, lent upon a pledge to a *lezard*, is capable of producing. Let us hasten to say, in order that our readers may not accuse us of inconsistency, that if Monsieur Rigobert found himself momentarily pressed, the causes of this pressure were quite personal, and that he did not accuse his trade of it, which, on the contrary, had never been so flourishing.

Justè, after promising again to visit him the next day, accompanied Rigobert to the door of his house, which he only half opened, to allow him to make his exit, as was his usual custom.

When Rigobert had turned his back upon him, he attempted to shut the door, but was prevented by a very tall man with an agreeable physiognomy, whose elegant morning negligé announced him as moving in the best society, who passed his arm between the door and the sill, and closed the door quickly, when he had entered the small court.

Justè, who was ignorant of the object of the intruder, trembled in every limb, and dared not pronounce a single word. He was quite ready to suppose the entrance of this individual connected with some criminal intentions, when the Viscount de Lussan (for it was no other) reassured him a little by saying to him, at the same time laughing outright:

"You see, Monsieur Justè, that all your precautions may be set at nought; here, you are at my discretion."

The usurer, who seemed petrified with astonishment, and who still trembled a little, made an attempt, however, to persuade his unexpected visitor that he had not felt the slightest fear from the moment he had recognised him.

"The sudden entrance of an individual, whom I thought a stranger," he said, "did, it is true, a little disturb me; but now that I know I have the honour of speaking to an estimable gentleman, I have recovered all my *sang froid*, and I am perfectly at ease."

"Despite your assertions," replied the Viscount de Lussan, regarding the usurer, who still appeared uncomfortable, "I am persuaded that you have still some suspicions, since you do not show me to your cabinet; do you know, Monsieur Justè, that it is not very polite to receive me in the vestibule?"

"I must confess to Monsieur le Viscount, that the rather brutal manner in which he introduced himself here, has caused me a certain fright, and with much more reason, that Monsieur de Lussan is generally very polite and excessively reserved; but at this moment I am, I repeat, perfectly tranquillised."

De Lussan, who was excited to a little mirth by a good breakfast, observing that the usurer, in spite of his efforts, could not conquer the fear which still lurked in him, took a pleasure in adding to his fright.

"You must directly introduce me into your cabinet; I will enter by fair means or foul; but deign to believe, my dear Justè, that I have not taken the respectful liberty of disturbing you in your important occupations, without being forced to it by a powerful motive."

Justè would willingly have dispensed with doing what the viscount demanded, for he remembered that his green morocco portfolio, which still contained, after the two strong bleedings it had already submitted to, a very round sum in bank notes and other securities, rested on the chimney piece of his cabinet, and he feared, beyond every thing, that it might attract the observation of his noble visitor; he attempted, by an insidious discourse, to retain him in one of the entrance-rooms, in which, whilst conversing, they had entered.

The viscount regarded for some minutes the miserable usurer, whose piteous expression was really a comedy. He then burst out in a loud laugh.

"Monsieur Justè," he said, when his hilarity had passed, "you are an old imbecile! Am I a stranger to you, then? I think I have given you sufficient proofs of my loyalty to merit your confidence."

"Monsieur le Viscount is right; I have always been more than satisfied with his proceedings; but he will allow me to observe that I am alone, that I inhabit a quarter nearly deserted, that every day we hear of robberies and assassinations, and consequently I may be permitted to take some little caution. I should also add, that your language and manners seem to me to-day so little in harmony with your principles and habits, that I might well fear a moment for my life and my fortune."

"Your frankness, my dear, obliges me to tell the whole truth. Before coming here, I had breakfasted at Desmares with the deputés of my province; we had fêted Bacchus with all honour; and when I arrived at your door, the fumes of champagne and chambertin were still rising in my brain. I came to seek you that we may talk of various affairs; and I can assure you, I had no intention of frightening you; but the occasion of proving to you that the most careful men may sometimes be at fault, presented itself, and, my faith, I did not let it escape. I wished to be sportive for a moment, nothing more. You have been frightened, I continued in order to increase your fright; it seems I succeeded beyond my expectations. And now, I give you my word as a noble Breton, that I had no intention of injuring either your purse or your person."

"You give me your word, as a gentleman, that I have nothing to fear?"

The Viscount de Lussan replied in the affirmative to this question of the usurer. Justè, who seemed quite himself since the viscount had given him his word as a gentleman that his person and his property would be respected, introduced him at length into his cabinet. He forgot not, however, on entering, to throw his handkerchief over the portfolio; and this movement, according to all ap-

pearance, having escaped his companion, he felt himself relieved from a great weight.

He offered a seat to the viscount, and placed himself in his old cane fauteuil.

"You can boast of having caused me a mighty fright, Monsieur le Vicomte," said Justè, as soon as he found himself intrenched behind the railings, which formed a kind of rampart round the small table which served him as a bureau.

We must now explain to our readers, what were the means employed by Justè to place himself beyond the reach of the attempts of those of his clients whom he thought capable of injuring him.

The Newfoundland dog, an animal which he had brought up and trained himself with the greatest care, was certainly a formidable guardian, and very capable of devouring a man at a sign from his master; and he was always at liberty. Father Justè, who relied upon his vigilance and incorruptibility, qualities which he had often put to the proof, and which had never deceived him, was thus perfectly at ease.

If any one rang, he did not open his door until he had examined, through the small wicket we have mentioned, the person who solicited admission. When admitted, he showed him into his cabinet, and retired himself into a species of fort, the door of which was secured on the inside, and could not be opened except by a cord placed at the right hand of the usurer. If any one attempted to force the railing, he could retire into the court to his faithful guardian, who would then defend him to the death. The room he called his cabinet was formerly a bed room, the treillis work and little green curtains of which still remained. It was in this alcove that Silvia had been concealed during the time the general had been closeted with Justè.

From what precedes, we may naturally conclude, that Justè could, to a certain point, receive into his house, without fearing any thing from them, the suspicious gentry with whom he was in regular correspondence; in fact, in his court he had his guardian at his disposition, and, in default of that, he could demand succour from his neighbours, whose windows looked into the court; besides, it was not probable that any one would dare to attempt a crime against his person.

Lussan conversed some time with the usurer, and had not broached the subject of his visit, the fumes which still obscured his brain had not quite subsided.

"You do not render me justice," he repeated; "do you think that a gentleman of such a good family as your humble servant, has ever failed in his word?"

In finishing this sentence, he lifted with the end of his cane the handkerchief, with little blue squares, which concealed the valuable portfolio, and immediately took possession of it.

The physiognomy of Justè, upon seeing his treasure at the mercy of de Lussan, assumed suddenly an expression of painful anxiety, which it would be impossible to describe; some heavy groans were the only evidence of his terror, as they escaped his bosom, and it was with much trouble he could collect sufficient strength to articulate these few words:

"Monsieur le Vicomte!—my portfolio—your word—return me my portfolio!"

The viscount had opened the portfolio, and examined with much attention its contents.

"The devil!" he said at length, without seeming to remark the profound consternation painted on the features of Justè ; "bank notes, orders upon receivers general, bills at sight ! there is a whole fortune in this musty portfolio !"

"Monsieur le Vicomte," repeated still the poor Justè, "you have given me your word as a gentleman. I am not in the least fear."

De Lussan, whom the mortal agony of the unhappy usurer singularly amused, appeared not at all inclined to hear him.

"I was saying then," he continued, "that there is in this portfolio quite a fortune ; and if I wished, I could leave, and carry it with me without your attempting to oppose my passage ; it is even probable that you would not so much as put the police in the confidence of what had happened to you."

"It's true," said Justè, "I love you too much to have the courage to denounce you ; but I am ruined—dead—"

"You are neither dead nor ruined : but you are, and always will be, an old imbecile, a pinch penny, an old Jew, Christian as you are ; you deserve beyond doubt a severe lesson, but I do not forget that I have given you my word."

"And the Viscount de Lussan handed to Justè, through the wicket made in the rails, the old portfolio, together with the whole of its contents."

There are no words in our language sufficiently expressive to describe faithfully the change which was suddenly effected on the visage of the usurer at this unexpected restitution ; the most brilliant colours replaced at once the frightful paleness which had overspread his countenance ; in fact, it needs at the same time to be usurer and miser, to be enabled to depict the evident satisfaction he felt.

"I merely wished to continue the joke," said the viscount in tendering the note case, "but I believe that you are now a little corrected, and that you will not again be tempted to distrust a man like myself."

"Ah ! Monsieur le Vicomte, what gratitude," exclaimed Justè, after burying the treasure in one of the vast pockets of his old houppelande : "if ever you stand in need of a few notes for a thousand francs, I will lend them to you, for good and valuable security, and a reasonable interest," he hastened to add, from the fear that the latter might immediately put his benevolent intentions to the proof.

"Let us drop all these fooleries, and speak about the object which has brought me here," said the viscount ; "you are now, I suppose, in a fit state to hear me ?"

"Yes, Monsieur de Lussan."

"Some time ago I met at the house of a noble dame de charité, the jeweller with whom she has dealt these ten years ; I conversed with this man, who made, as usual in such cases, his offers of services, and at once begged me to pay him a visit if by chance I had any acquisitions to make. You have already imagined, worthy father Justè, that a few days after this rencontre, I took a whim of purchasing a few bijoux, and repaired to the jeweller in question, where I spent a few hundred francs.

"At the time of my first visit, which I rendered as long as possible, I found occasion to address a few words to the amiable wife and daughter of my man, who are, besides, two very pretty women.

"I returned several times to make some fresh purchases with the honest merchant. Thanks to my extreme politeness, to the compliments which I paid unceasingly to the two ladies, who are a little disposed, like all women, to bestow a confidence upon those who flatter them : and to a few flowers offered apropos, I had not much trouble to become the most intimate friend of the family : by which means I easily took the impression of three patent locks, which secure the door of the apartment, and which the jeweller thought invulnerable."

"'Tis a magnificent affair ! is it ripe ?"

"Not yet quite ; but I want two men whom I could put my hand on at a convenient time, two expert and determined men to execute it ; can you procure me such ?"

"But why don't you take Lion the Taffeur and Maladetta, or Robert, or Cadet Vincent ?"

"Lion and Maladetta are special men not suited to this affair ; and as you are aware, I do not wish to be in direct relation with the two others, whose manners and expressions are of a nature to compromise the most honest man in the world."

"Ah ! the devil ! to whom then can we confide the execution of this affair ?"

"Look you, make inquiries of Sans Refus, there ought to be amongst the frequenters of her establishment, some one whom it may be possible to speak with, without compromising one's reputation."

"Will you have Delicat, Coco-Desbraises, Robert le Mauvais Gueux, Charles la belle Cravate, le Grand-Louis, Vernier les bas Bleus ; I will speak, through Mother Sans Refus, to such amongst them as would suit you."

"You are a fool, Justè ! I must personally give the necessary instructions, and I really cannot compromise myself with any of the miserables you have named to me."

"But if you know them, they are as ignorant of you as they are of myself, and you can, without inconvenience, meet the two most proper ones, Charles la belle Cravate and Vernier les bas Bleus, for example."

The Viscount de Lussan reflected for some moments.

"Decidedly," he said, "I will have neither of these miserables ; all these gentry have such atrocious slang, such piteous costumes, and such disgusting manners, that they make my heart sick. Look about you, father Justè, you ought to have amongst your acquaintance what would suit me ; the two that you procured me for the affair of the paper merchant for example."

"Ah ! you mean Fanfan la Grenouille and Poil aux Levres ; these two honest boys have been arrested by means of information : they are in gaol."

"I am sorry for it. But you can no doubt find others : I will wait, it is not pressing."

"If there is no danger in delay, I will engage for you. I think if you leave me a little time, I shall be enabled to procure you persons with whom you can easily come to an understanding."

Justè, when he made this promise to the Viscount de Lussan, was thinking of the woman from whom he had, some hours before, purchased the jewels of the Count Coloredo : he supposed, and our readers are aware, that his suppositions were well founded : that this woman was no more than an emissary of the individuals who had committed the robberies, individuals who would not probably stop there, and whom sooner or later he would finish by knowing.

"Now that we have come to a perfect understanding, I must make you comprehend that all the precautions with which you surround yourself would be useless, if an individual like me, for instance, wished to assassinate you, in order to rob you afterwards. In the first place, your Cerberus could be easily poisoned."

And as the usurer shook his head and made a negative grimace,

"There are such savoury balls," resumed the viscount, "that they tempt the most elevated and most sober dogs. Besides, if on that side your animal is invulnerable, are there not a thousand known means of *charming* dogs, and of rendering as harmless as a lamb the most ferocious of these companions. And then you live alone, and since the death of Madame Justè, you go out but rarely, so that you might be dead a long while before there was any disturbance about you."

"Yes, all this is possible; but when I should be dead who would indicate to the assassins the hole which preserves my treasure, my gold, my note case? for it is an extraordinary chance that I have carried it about me; 'tis an imprudence I have committed to-day for the first time, and which will not be repeated, I can assure you. It is true I had only to treat with a woman, and a general, one of my friends, and I had nothing to fear from these two personages."

"And thus, then, you are persuaded that it would be impossible to discover your treasure vault?"

"Yes, Monsieur le Vicomte."

"How much you are in error, my dear Justè! it *will* be discovered, and so be careful not to doubt it. But tranquillise yourself; not one of those with whom you are in relation would dream of doing you the slightest injury; for, admitting for a moment that they carried off a few hundred thousand francs, which, divided among three or four persons, would be soon dissipated, where would they find a man like you afterwards? for you are really our providence! whatever may be the affair, you pay down; whilst your confrères only dole it out in parcels; you know so well how to convey away the items you purchase, that once with you, there is nothing more heard of them. With you it is settled immediately; it is true you give the least possible, but that's your affair. You see we have the greatest interest in preserving you. What would become of us without you? You are necessary to us, indispensable; so be easy as to your fate, you have nothing to fear; we are always careful of the man we stand in need of; and besides, have I not proved the truth of what I am saying, by returning your portfolio, which I could have kept with impunity?"

"'Tis true, but all my clients are not noble gentlemen of Brittany. If this note case had fallen into the hands of Coco-Desbraises or Delicat, they would have kept it."

"I must confess, my dear Justè, that you made a most pitiful grimace both painful and laughable; whilst it was in my possession, death was painted on your very lips. You are very fond of money then, Monsieur Justè?"

"Oh! yes, I love it! gold and God, you see, are the two objects of my worship! Money! why, what can we do in this world without money! is it not with this metal, with this vile metal, as say those who possess none of it, that we can procure all the pleasures and enjoyments of this world, and the blessings of the next?"

"I know," replied de Lussan, "that when we possess plenty of money, it becomes easy to obtain honours, places, and pensions: that to have superb horses, magnificent equipages, and pretty mis-

tresses, in fact every pleasure, it requires a **great** deal; but for you, father Justè, who live like **an** anchorite, who are always ill dressed, and never breakfast at the Café Anglais, of what use, tell me, is all that you possess, since you know not how to enjoy it?"

"I know not how to enjoy it! Monsieur de Lussan, I know not how to enjoy it! what an error you have made! I enjoy it much more than yourself; I relish all the delights, all the enjoyments of which you make such a case; I *intoxicate* myself from the cup which *your* lips scarcely touch, and my enjoyments are much keener and more delicious, as they do not drag after them the regrets and misfortunes of ordinary life. I have, like you, mistresses, horses, and equipages; mistresses, prettier and better dressed, horses of a nobler breed, equipages more brilliant than yours, Monsieur de Lussan!"

"You astonish me, dear Justè! I confess I had not the least suspicion that you possessed so many and such delightful luxuries. But where are they then? I am really desirous of seeing all these marvels."

Justè drew from the pocket of his houppelande the old portfolio of green morocco; he then took out the bank notes, mandates, and bills of all descriptions, and displayed them on the small table of black wood, and exclaimed with enthusiasm:

"Here are all my gilded saloons, my perfumed boudoirs, my baths of jasper and porphyry, my fashionable equipages, my English horses, my dogs, and my valets bedecked in golden liveries! These are my mistresses! gifted with every charm my imagination can lend them! brown and fair, haughty or unaffected, gay or melancholy, faithful even if I please; for with money, you observe, we can purchase every thing, even fidelity, a merchandise the most rare."

The Viscount de Lussan listened to the usurer with an air of profound astonishment; he had no expectation of finding, under such an ignoble envelope, the almost poetical ideas which had been expressed by old father Justè.

"Continue," he said; "I listen to you with much attention, and I confess that, until the present moment, I could not conceive that father Justè, that old man whom I have often seen shivering in a room without fire in the coldest days of winter, and blowing on his fingers to prevent their freezing, was susceptible of relishing such superlative enjoyments."

"Enjoyments! but are there any more keen, more real, than that of plunging into a bath of gold, to press against your heart many millions in bank notes, and of being enabled to say, ' When I please, I can satisfy every fantasy, every caprice? Women! I can possess them of every country and of every condition; opera singers and opera dancers, peasants, beauties, and bayaderes, if it suits me; I have the means of paying them the price at which they sell themselves; when I but say the word, the breast of the old usurer of the Rue Saint Dominique d'Enfer will be covered with ribands of every colour and the cross of every order, I shall be no longer father Justè,but Monsieur de Saint Justè!"

"But, Monsieur Justè, as you understand so well the joys of life, why the devil, since you have the means, are you contented with the shadow, when you could procure yourself the substance?"

The usurer, a prey to an over-excitement almost febrile, had forgotten all prudence; for some instants he fixed his little sea-green eyes, which sparkled like two carbuncles, on the Viscount de Lussan, and then burst into an eclât of laughter.

"Ah! ah!" he said, "you are but half poets, you gentry of the world; you tell me I am wrong to content myself with the shadow, when I can procure myself the substance; you are short-sighted, Monsieur le Vicomte de Lussan. You do not know, then, that every day my treasure becomes more considerable, and that, in proportion to its increase, the desires I can satisfy increase also—there exists a pleasure, which includes the whole; and that I possess, in having gold, money—much more than you can imagine, if I were to tell you the sum to which my riches amount, much more than is possessed by those who think themselves considerably richer than myself; and this gold is neither in the state chests nor in those of a banker—it is here. I can, each day, if it so pleases me, lie down on a bed of gold and bank notes, and this bed would be softer to me than the bed of rose leaves of Lucullus; I can take up a handful and say, without the fear of being contradicted, ' With this I am superior to all men, whom I can at my pleasure render supple and servile; with this, I hold in my hand the honour of the married and the single; of fathers and of husbands; I can have every door opened to me, and make every conscience bow before me; I can, in fact, obtain the worship which is only due to God !"

The physiognomy of the old usurer, during the whole time he had employed to utter this long tirade, had expressed, by turns, the most fanatical joy and the most delirious satisfaction. His complexion, usually so pale and so earthy, alternated to the most lively colours.

" Faith, my dear Justè," said the Viscount de Lussan, "you are so eloquent, and so far persuasive, that I am compelled to agree with you in opinion, and to believe that real happiness is that which you know so well how to describe; I would wish, for the future, to walk in your steps; but, to taste the joys of which you so much vaunt, I stand in need of the principal elements. Father Loisseau will furnish me, I hope, with the foundation stones of the edifice I wish to build."

"We must hope so, Monsieur le Vicomte," replied Justè, tendering, through the wicket of his railing, his meagre hand to the viscount, "we must hope so."

The viscount left.

CHAPTER XVIII.

THE VISCOUNT DE LUSSAN.

As we have observed, in the commencement of this history, Mother Sans Refus was the natural daughter of an assassin broken alive in 1787, in one of the courts of Bicêtre, and of a girl, Marianne Lempave, condemned for theft to several years in prison.

After the execution of her father, at which, in consequence of circumstances which we shall report at the proper time, she was compelled to assist, Marie-Madeleine-Colette-Comtois, or rather Mother Sans Refus (we shall preserve to this woman the name under which she is known to our readers up to the present time,) who, till then, had carried on, in the Rue Grenier-sur-l'Eau, a commerce which has received no baptism in good society, took, on her own account, the ancient establishment of the street de la Tannerie, into which we have several times introduced our readers.

It is not without reason we have said the *ancient establishment*, for certain houses, certain streets even, seem fatally destined to be inhabited by the most vicious and miserable of the population. Notwithstanding the changes wrought in our morals and our habitudes by civilisation, all the streets assigned by the old ordinances of our kings to the infamous commerce of prostitution, which have not been completely demolished, are still at the present day inhabited by prostitutes, or by those who live by their commerce; and to produce but one example, amongst many, which would serve to prove the truth of what we advance, we shall cite simply that in which Marie-Madeleine-Colette-Comtois commenced business, the street Grenier-sur-l'Eau.

This street has been entirely demolished, elegant constructions have replaced the sombre and unhealthy ruins which formerly served as an asylum to individuals of a more hideous aspect than the places they inhabit; there is now fresh air and sunshine in the street Grenier-sur-l'Eau. Well, one of the ancient ruins of this street, situated at the corner of the street Geoffroy-l'Asnier, has not suffered the fate of its companions; it has escaped, by chance, the general demolition which has been made. You think, perhaps, that, forced to appear in open day, the old barefaced hussey has changed her morals; that she endeavours, at least, to cause the faults of the past to be forgotten; not in the least; she is to-day the same she was thirty years ago, fifty years ago, and perhaps longer still; she is the same as she will be for fifty years to come, if she then remains above ground.

The establishment of Mother Sans Refus was at first frequented by all the malefactors who had known her father and mother; but, as years rolled on, their ranks thinned more and more, and there remained soon, none but a few whose heads had become blanched, and whose bodies were bent with age, too old, in a word, to continue their trade, but still very capable, as they said, and the sequel will show that they told the truth, to train up some excellent pupils.

These miserable remnants of a struggle formerly engaged in against society, remained the only faithful adherents, it is true, but very little capable of making the fortune of a similar establishment, by reason of the reserve imposed upon them by the inaction in which they were compelled to live; on this account Mother Sans Refus seemed disconsolate every hour in the day, and her lamentations found an echo in the heart of these faithful followers.

"Listen, my child," said one of these to her one day, an old man of eighty-four, who had passed two-thirds at least of this long existence in the prisons or houses of correction,* "your *boccart*† will come to nothing if you will not join a new branch to your commerce. The *fanandels*‡ spend their *auber*‖ where they can dispose of their merchandise."

* The personages we describe are not all fictitious ; and if some among them appear too eccentric, the author is not to be accused for it.   Thus, for example, the old man of whom we are now speaking is a real personage, whom those of our readers who have visited the poor at Bicêtre have no doubt remarked ; he is, in reality, eighty-four years of age ; he has, as we have observed, passed two-thirds of this long existence in the prisons and houses of correction ; and yet, at the present day, he still possesses all his faculties, and he is more vigorous than many men younger than himself, who have passed their lives in all the comforts of life.
The name we have given him is not his own ; it belonged to a man who rendered some services to the police, after exercising for a long time the profession of a thief.   To be a thief, and name one's self *Cadet Viloux*, we must confess the games of chance are sometimes singularly combined !
 † House.   ‡ Comrades.   § Money.

LIFE IN PARIS.

SILVIA DISCOVERING THE STOLEN JEWELS OF THE COURT.

Mother Sans Refus, whom the terrible death of her father, and the unhappy end of her mother, who at this period had died in prison, had inspired with a salutary terror, feared she might have to suffer sooner or later the consequences of the trade of a receiver; but the old man lectured her so well and so frequently, that he finished by overcoming, not her scruples—the daughter of Comtois and Marianne Lempave had been too well brought up to retain any of them—but her fears, which, until then, had prevented her from crossing the extreme limit which separates those gentry who, without being honest, escape, however, the consequences of the law, from those whom it has the right of punishing.

It was thus agreed that Mother Sans Refus should make known, to those whom the news might interest, that she was ready to give a reasonable price for all merchandises which should be offered to her.

This resolution, once taken, the old friend of Mother Sans Refus—this Nestor in crime, who was gifted with an eloquence so persuasive that we might say of him, as of the king of Pylos, that, when he spoke, his words were sweeter than the honey of Mount Hymetus—undertook to see the new generation of malefactors, who had replaced those who had known Mother Sans Refus, at the time of her début in the street Grenier-sur-l'eau.

His steps were at first crowned with success. He was received in all the *tapis* which he visited with the respect and attentions which they thought due to a *brave garçon,** proved by a long residence at the galley and in the prisons; and the overtures he made to the frequenters of the miserable places which still infest the streets Aubry-le-boucher, of Bondy, Bievre, Plâtre Saint Jacques, of the Marmousets, the Place Maubert, the Boulevard of the Temple, were received with the greatest delight; and they all promised him, (when he had favourably stated the reasons which militated in favour of Mother Sans Refus,) that they would never, until after they had proposed to her, pay a visit to the *Tete-de-Mort,*† the *Pomme-Rouge,*‡ or to the *Fouille-du-Pot.*||

They showed themselves faithful observers of the word they had given their elder, and the establishment of Mother Sans Refus, almost deserted a few days previously, became suddenly the most flourishing of any of the same nature.

Similar to those birds of passage, who quit without regret our climate at the commencement of bad weather, her odalisques had all successively abandoned her harem, for want of meeting with a sultan; they returned in a crowd with the fine weather.

Mother Sans Refus had soon purchased, of those of her frequenters whom the reader is already acquainted with, so considerable a quantity of jewels and plate, that she found it necessary to dispose of

---

* He who, in the exercise of his profession of thief, has never betrayed his comrades. This is the best eulogy that a robber can make of a comrade.

† A noted receiver, who resided some years ago in the street de Grenelle Saint Honoré, and who continued the trade for a very considerable time without being caught in the act. Her physiognomy, which had some resemblance to a *death's head*, had procured for her the surname under which she was generally known.

‡ A clothes dealer and receiver, who inhabited, at the same period, the quarter of the Sorbonne. He was named Lesage, and the thieves, I am ignorant for what reason, had named him the *Red Apple*. He died at the galley.

|| A well-known receiver of the Market Saint-Martin. He obtained his surname from his constant habit of taking from a cup, or measure, the money with which he paid for his purchases. The thieves, who respect nothing, took possession, one fine day, of the cup and its contents. The unfortunate receiver could not support such a dreadful misfortune. He died from despair.

it, in order to realise a sum for the purpose of continuing her operations.

Cadet Filoux, such was the name of the old man of whom we are speaking, was again the providence of Mother Sans Refus. Habited in a costume which he owed to the munificence of the tavernière, and which gave a relief to his respectable physiognomy, and his venerable white hair, he put himself on the search, and, after numerous visitations, he finished by discovering the honest Monsieur Justè.

This personage was already in correspondence with all that the capital encircles of titled and decorated rogues, when Cadet Filoux paid him a visit, and it happened to him oftener than it suited, to buy either from one or the other, a rich bracelet, a broach of great value carried off by her cavalier from a pretty duchess, or from some coquettish financière, in the midst of the delights of a waltz, a gallopade, or a polka; these objects, as soon as they were purchased, were immediately forwarded secretly to England or Holland—countries in which Father Justè had engaged some intelligent correspondents, whom he served in the capital with a zeal equal to that which they employed for him upon every occasion which presented itself.

When Cadet Filoux, after employing the usual precautions which are not to be neglected in such affairs, had informed Monsieur Justè of the object of his visit, the latter did not at first show himself very ambitious of establishing with Mother Sans Refus the relations proposed by the Nestor of the galley; but Cadet made him such a well-turned discourse, that he determined at length to see his protegée; and the place, day, and hour were fixed upon for the first interview.

Justè and Mother Sans Refus easily came to an understanding together. It was agreed that Justè should purchase and pay in cash, but only at two-thirds of their real value, every article of gold or silver which should be offered him by the tavernière, who should treat at her own risk and peril, with the last possessors, to whom he was never to be made known.

All the clauses of this contract, which both parties had an equal interest in respecting, were scrupulously observed; only that Mother Sans Refus, a little more communicative than Father Justè, made him successively acquainted with those whom she called her *workmen*, which explains how Father Justè could, when occasion required, place in report with men of execution the Viscount de Lussan, a young Breton gentleman, who, after being successively chevalier d'industrie, *grec*, was become in trading terms, a *donneur d'affaires.**

From a recital of the preceding facts, our readers have naturally concluded, that at the period at which we are arrived, there existed in the capital all the elements of an association of malefactors, and that from these events, the moment they should be united and directed by one or more clever hands, there must result a *society in society*, a hundred times more dangerous than all the associations, the records of whose crimes we have seen unfolded before the court of assize of the Seine.

In fact, the former could be numerous, composed of resolute individuals of all classes, and directed by men, to whom their name and the position they occupied in society, would, in a manner, give the certainty of impunity. But would all these men, some of whom lived in the smoky atmosphere of

---

* The individual who plans the robbery, but takes no part in it.

the kennels in the street de la Tannerie, whilst the others set the tone in the most aristocratic saloons of our good city; would these unite and march together in the same path towards a common end? Alas! yes.

Take a certain quantity of mercury and throw it with force on the floor, the metal will divide itself at first into several millions of imperceptible molecules, then by degrees, and insensibly, these molecules will rejoin one after another, and soon all these scattered particles will have formed a whole, perfectly homogeneous; it is nearly the same with malefactors of all classes, they meet without seeking each other, without knowing each other, they understand each other, without even speaking; can we say that in thus approaching each other, they obey a fatal law of their organization. No, thank God! but the truth is, that the habit of living continually on their defence against all the world, (and such is the law of existence of malefactors,) gives to the body certain movements which are imperceptible to the vulgar, but which are easily perceptible to the initiated.

A fresh crime, committed by Salvador, Silvia, and Roman, was destined to unite amongst themselves the scattered link of that long chain which stretched from the noblest dwellings, to the infected den of Mother Sans Refus.

The wicked instincts of the pretty Silvia, had not waited to develop itself, for the epoch at which we have arrived; the events of her life which we have already reported, proved that this woman was capable of committing every or any crime, when either of her passions were to be satisfied; that in a word, she concealed, under a most gracious envelope, a soul quite worthy of belonging to the last branch of the miserable scelerats to whom she owed her birth.

Continually in contact with two men so little scrupulous as Salvador and Roman, whose audacity she appreciated, and for one of whom she felt a strong affection; pride, which as we have seen, was one of her ruling passions, inspired her with the ambition of showing herself worthy of them, of surpassing them, even, if the occasion presented itself.

At the moment almost when Silvia, by the discovery of the jewels stolen from the Count Coloredo, acquired, respecting her lover and the man who passed himself off as his intendant, the certainty of a fact which the conversation she had heard in the park of the chateau of Pourrieres had only allowed her to surmise; she had conceived the idea of a crime, of which the Jew Josué was to become the victim. And during her conversation with the usurer Justè, she said to herself that the latter one ought neither to be forgotten, and that it would be a coup de maitre to despoil at the same time the Christian and the Israelite.

Having learnt from this conversation that Josué was at Paris whilst she had supposed him at Marseilles, she had adroitly questioned Justè, in order to discover his residence; but this usurer, who feared she had some motive in finding his worthy confrére, constantly held himself in reserve; so that she found it impossible, despite all her address and insidious questions, to arrive at the object of her wishes.

After rendering an account to Salvador and Roman of the more than satisfactory results of the mission she had accomplished; and having received, with a proud satisfaction, the praises which she merited by her audacity and intelligence, she communicated to them, without giving herself the trouble of making any precautionary introduction by way of remark, the projects she had conceived.

"But to operate in this manner, it will be absolutely necessary to get rid of these two men, who are continually on their guard," exclaimed Salvador, when Silvia had finished the exposure of her plan.

Silvia made no reply to this observation, which seemed to imply a blame.

The countenance of Roman was embarrassed, he feared that the proposition of Silvia, whose extreme malice he knew how to appreciate, was but a touchstone intended to enlighten her as to the real sentiments of her two companions.

"It seems that these two operations do not suit you?" said Silvia, whom the boldness of her lover, and the good Monsieur Lebrun, as she usually called Roman, singularly astonished.

The latter, however, determined at length to break the ice, but avoided, however, giving a reply in a positive manner.

"We can at any time," he said, " procure the address of the Jew Josué, examine the place he inhabits, and obtain some information respecting him; these steps will not engage us to any thing at present, and their results may serve us for the future."

"The future, the future!" said Silvia, "the one we have before us is not very brilliant, the hundred notes of a thousand francs which I have brought you, will not carry us far."

"It's true," replied Roman, " we must absolutely bleed the strong box of Messieur Josué; what do you say to it?" he continued, addressing Salvador.

"I am of your opinion, but if we could arrive at our object without being forced to——"

"Impossible!" exclaimed Silvia, in a tone which did not allow her good faith to be doubted; "and besides, it would be rendering society a veritable service to rid the earth of such a miserable."

"Well, well," replied Roman, " now that we are very near coming to an understanding, it only remains to discover the residence of Messire Josué, and I shall attend to that myself, and immediately."

Roman, in fact, put himself at once en route, but as he was obliged to act with great caution, it was not until he had employed several days in his search, that he discovered the dwelling of Josué.

This Jew inhabited, in the Rue Saint-Gervais, No. 4, at the corner of that of the Roi-Dorè, a house surrounded on all sides by a strong iron railing let into a wall, breast high, of edged stones, and surmounted by a cheveaux de frise. All the windows of the habitation, situated at the end of a garden, planted with little stunted trees and some withered flowers, were furnished in the interior with strong oaken shutters, lined with sheet-iron, and defended on the outside by Venetian window-blinds also of iron. Josué kept himself continually in a large cabinet situated on the ground floor of his house, and from whence he could see all who presented themselves at the railing, so that he only opened it to the persons he wished to receive; his bedroom was placed immediately over his cabinet, and it was thought to be in this chamber—into which he allowed no one to enter, and which was secured by a heavy door, furnished with several strong bolts, resembling the door of a prison more than that of a bedroom—that he preserved his treasure. This is not all: the Jew Josué, as the good women of the neighbourhood asserted, slept very light; and at the least noise, at the slightest movement which seemed unusual to him, he rose to take a survey, either by a *Judas* of about fifteen inches, which he had cut in the floor of his bedroom, or by the openings neatly made in the shutters and door. It was also asserted, that every night brass wire, which corresponded with a large bell placed at the head of his bed, was stretched by every means in all the apartments.

A very old woman, whom they called his sister, and a young Israelite, to whom he taught the first elements of the trade of a usurer, and who served him both as a clerk and servant, inhabited with him the house in the Rue Saint-Gervais, which never remained empty. In addition, Josué only bestowed on his messmates the confidence he received from the solidity of his coffer, and the numerous precautions with which he had surrounded himself.

Roman, who at first fancied it should be at his own house he ought to attack the old Jew, discovered, when he knew all that we have informed our readers of, that this would be no easy matter, not to say impossible; and that the plan proposed by Silvia, offered greater chances of success; this they adopted then, after submitting it to some slight modifications after an animated discussion.

As it was necessary beyond every thing to have a personal interview with Josué, but still impolitic either to visit him or write to him, seeing that after a visit they might be recognised, and that a letter might, if any unforeseen circumstances took place, compromise the three associates, Silvia was charged to intercept the victim on his road.

Silvia was aware that the Jew, like all the people of his religion in general, and particularly those who exercise an illicit industry, whether Jews or Christians, was excessively devout, at least in appearance, so that he repaired every Saturday, if not every morning, to the synagogue. One Saturday morning then, at the suitable hour, she engaged a public vehicle, at the Rue du Temple, at the corner of the street Notre-Dame-de-Nazareth, where the Jews' synagogue is situated. Her expectation was not deceived; ten o'clock sounded, when she saw at a distance, and advancing towards the place in which she was waiting, the person whom she expected. She now told her coachman to move on, and at the moment her coach passed in front of the Jew, she tapped at the window; Josué turned his head, and having at once recognised the pretty cantatrice of the Grand Theatre of Marseilles, he stopped, and seeing her in such a brilliant toilette, he made her a multitude of reverences. The back of the worthy child of Abraham was at least as flexible as that of a place hunter admitted into the cabinet of a minister, or of a candidate to the deputation, whilst paying a visit to the electors of his department.

"Ah! there you are, my good Josué," exclaimed Silvia, who had ordered her coachman to open the door of the vehicle, and remount his seat; "I am really delighted to meet you; but you have quitted Marseilles, then, to come and fix yourself at Paris?"

"Yes, madame, I have quitted Marseilles, but only a few months ago."

"Take a seat by me, I want to talk to you."

"I am sorry I cannot accept your kind invitation, but to-day is Saturday, and we are not allowed to enter a carriage on the sabbath day."

"You are devout, Monsieur Josué, 'tis right, and I will keep you no longer from your religious duties; but come and see me to-morrow, between one and two o'clock, I wish to propose an excellent affair to you."

Silvia handed her card to the Jew.

"When you present yourself at my house," she added, "you will give this card, without saying a single word, to my femme de chambre, who will hand it to me, and you shall be immediately introduced. Have you understood me?"

"Perfectly, madame, perfectly; I will be with you to-morrow at the appointed hour," replied Josué, who did not retire without again commencing a fresh series of salutations.

The old Jew had been informed of the marriage of Silvia with the Marquis of Roselly, whom he had always supposed very rich; consequently he was very much surprised to meet his ancient acquaintance in a fiacre. "Has she ruined herself," he muttered, whilst retiring; "at all events I shall keep on my guard; as we appreciate the saints, so we adore them."

The few words which precede had been exhanged in a low tone between Silvia and the Jew, and the driver had profited by taking a nap during the tête-a-tête, of twenty-five minutes; indeed it was not without some trouble that Silvia contrived to awaken him.

"Drive me," she said, allowing him time to rub his eyes, "to the street Notre-Dame de Lorette, No. 4."

Arrived at the place she had indicated, she paid the driver, and entered the house to which she had been driven. After demanding of the porter the first name that came into her head, she left, and engaged at the place of the Rue Flechier another vehicle, which conducted her to the faubourg du Roule at the corner of the street d'Angoulême, where she quitted it; she wished to enter her own house on foot, as she had left it some hours before.

Her first care was to give an account to her two associates of the results she had obtained; they appeared delighted with them, Roman, especially, who said her success had surpassed his expectations.

"You were the only woman worthy of Monsieur le Marquis de Pourrieres," he said to her.

"It's true," replied Salvador; "and we may say, without the fear of being contradicted:

" ' Nos pareils à deux fois ne se sont pas connaitre,
Et pour leurs coups d'essais veulent des coups de maitre.' "*

"It's quite true, Monsieur le Marquis," added Roman; "it's very true."

This qualification of the marquis produced a smile on the lips of Silvia, who could not reconcile the position of her noble protector with the profession, somewhat equivocal, which he exercised in concert with the man who passed himself as his intendant; she was persuaded that she had as yet only raised a corner of the veil which concealed the former life of these two men; and as none of the attempts she had made to obtain the secret had been successful, she left to chance the care of satisfying her curiosity.

It was at length agreed that the direction of this affair should be left to the Marchioness de Roselly; the confidence placed in her by two men so expert in these matters as Salvador and Roman, singularly flattered her, and, to prove that she was quite worthy of it, she spoke to them again about the good Monsieur Justé.

They had no expectation that this usurer, who knew the three associates, would permit himself, like Josué, (respecting whom they were in a favourable position for the success of their project,) to be the victim of a snare; it was necessary, therefore, if they wished to bring it about, to get an entrance to his house. This was no easy matter, it

* " Our equals have not twice been seen :
Our master strokes are strong and keen "

is true; the Newfoundland dog was a serious obstacle, which it would be absolutely necessary to rid themselves of; but how? And admitting that they found means natural enough to escape the suspicions of the usurer, was it quite certain that, once admitted into his house, they would be enabled to discover the place in which he preserved his treasure? After a long discussion, the associates, with a common accord, decided that an enterprise against Justé did not offer sufficient chances of success to be immediately attempted; it was then agreed to be deferred, and that they should occupy themselves exclusively with the Jew Josué.

The next day, at the hour indicated, the Jew presented himself at Silvia's, who, as we have said, inhabited at the Champs Elysées (Avenue Chateaubriand, No. 22) a charming little hotel. Following the instructions given to him the day before, he gave the card he had received from the marchioness to the femme de chambre, who introduced him at once into the boudoir of her mistress.

This small chamber was fitted up with every luxury and elegance imaginable: it was lighted by an arched window with stained glass of different colours, in order to soften the strong rays of the sun, and which only allowed to penetrate a sort of half daylight quite voluptuous. The curtains and hangings were of white merino, with tassels and ornaments of the same colour; and no doubt for the purpose of producing a contrast, the screen intended to hide the entrance door, which rolled on a thyrse of gilded wood, was composed of a magnificent curtain of red silk, brocaded with gold; the floor was covered by a thick carpet with large flowers, a chef d'œuvre of the manufactures of Aubisson. A greenhouse embellished with the rarest flowers, some stages on which were grouped with taste a crowd of Chinese curiosities; statues, and oddities, a tripod of bronze which supported a perfume pan, and some chairs after the fashion of the middle age, composed the ensemble of this boudoir, lighted in the evenings by a silver lamp suspended from the ceiling by a chain of the same metal; and this was the sanctum sanctorum of the pretty marchioness.

When the Jew entered, Silvia, in the most seducing negligé possible, was, according to her custom, reclining on an ottoman. She almost raised herself on his entrance, and gave him the most coquettish inclination of the head, and the most charming smile imaginable; she knew, the infernal creature, that although armed at all points, there does not exist the organization masculine upon whom the charms of a pretty woman do not produce a favourable impression.

Josué, after glancing upon the objects which composed the furniture of this charming little boudoir with the interrogating eye of an expert appraiser, advanced towards the mistress of the house, whom he saluted down to the ground. Silvia requested him to take a fauteuil, and be seated.

"I know too well what is due to you, Madame le Marquise," replied Josué, who placed himself on the corner of a chair, his feet brought close to each other, and squeezing between his knees a hat once black, but at the present moment of a yellow colour and greasy, to bring one's heart up.

At the moment Silvia spoke to him, he rose, in order to assume a more respectful attitude; but the movement was so sudden, that he fell backwards, whilst his old feutre and his wig rolled each in an opposite direction, showing a cranium as naked as any in the four quarters of the world.

Roars of laughter, which Silvia could not repress, saluted the fall of the poor Josué, who made vain efforts to raise himself, all the time begging the marchioness to excuse his mal-adresse; at length the excess of hilarity to which Silvia had given way, having moderated a little, she extended her hand to the unfortunate child of Israel. Josué's first care, when on his feet, was to run after his wig, which resembled a piece of dried grass; he picked it up, and, in his hurry, placed it the wrong side uppermost on his head. Thus accoutred, he made such a ludicrous appearance, a physiognomy so grotesque, that Silvia again commenced laughing outright. The unhappy Jew, in order to please madame, attempted to imitate her. Is it possible to conceive a baseness which a Jew, both usurer and miser, will not commit when desirous of pleasing a person by whom he hopes to gain a profit?

After amusing herself for some instants at the expense of Messire Josué, Silvia, who at this moment resembled a cat playing with a mouse before consigning it to death, took him by the two shoulders, and forced him to seat himself in a long chair, similar to her own.

The conversation then commenced.

Silvia wished to know why Monsieur Josué had left Marseilles, what were his reasons for establishing himself at Paris, if he had been long in this city, if business prospered with him, and a thousand other things; she then referred to the friendship which had formerly existed between them, when residing in the good city of Marseilles, which, she said, ought to induce him to place confidence in her, and not conceal anything.

The worthy Josué commenced the recital of his short history, which might serve as a companion to that of the life of Cartouche.

"You know, madame," he said, "how I like to oblige my fellow-creatures; I never can see a man in a distressed position without instantly flying to assist him; you know that, Madame le Marquise. Well, the persons to whom I had frequently rendered a service, had the infamy to lay a complaint against me before the procureur du roi, and the justices had the weakness to take this complaint into consideration. Alas! Madame le Marquise, when a Christian, in speaking of any one of the religion of Moses, says, 'Kill him,' the others immediately reply, 'Yes, kill him!' For this reason no doubt it was, that one morning the king's servants seized at my house all that I possessed; when I say all, 'tis a manner of speaking: they found seventy-one francs and seventy-five centimes, and a little book of expenses; the rest was, luckily, concealed. The ill success of their research did not prevent them continuing their pursuits; witnesses were examined, but I had the precaution to make them work through the Rabbin, (that cost me dear, Madame le Marquise,) so they all declared they had never been treated usuriously by me; that certainly I had often lent them money, but that I was always content with a reasonable interest; that was true. However, they were not listened to, and I was forced to pay a fine of 30,000 francs, besides the expenses of the process. This crying injustice made me take in aversion the city of Marseilles: I collected all I possessed, and I came and established myself at Paris. I have been in the capital about eight months. I live with my sister and my nephew, in the Rue Saint Gervais, 4, at the corner of that of the Roi-Doré, a house which I have bought, so that I might arrange it at my pleasure. I have done a very good business, and, if you stand in need of me, I am entirely at your service."

"I thank you, good Josué," replied Silvia, who had listened very seriously to the lamentable recital of the misfortunes of the Jew, "I thank you kindly; I am not, at present, in want of your services; my reason for requesting you to call upon me was, to speak to you respecting a friend of mine, who wishes to contract a loan. This person is a man who occupies an eminent position in society, and who possesses, at least, a million and a half in property."

"You are aware, madame, that I know no greater pleasure than that of obliging. By giving me the address of the person in question, and whom I will see on your part, you will render me a real service."

"I would willingly do what you appear to wish, good Josué; but you see I cannot, until I know it would be convenient to him, refer you to Monsieur the Marquis de Pourrieres."

"The Marquis Alexis de Pourrieres!" exclaimed the old Judas, on hearing his name pronounced; "the Marquis Alexis de Pourrieres! why, I know him, particularly; he is an excellent young man, with whom I have already done some considerable affairs, almost without interest."

"How, you know Monsieur the Marquis de Pourrieres? but how long ago, then?"

"For more than fifteen years. I lent him nearly 300,000 francs, at different times; he paid me well; he is a very honest man. It was his intendant who came to me at Marseilles, to arrange the matter. He approved my account, both in capital and interest, and without making me a single observation. This intendant is also a very excellent man."

"How! you know, also, the good Monsieur Lebrun?"

"I only saw him once, but I shall remember him always; he is an honest man, and round in affairs. He is quite worthy to serve so good a master."

"You will not be sorry, then, to have another affair with Monsieur the Marquis de Pourrieres?"

"On the contrary, I shall be quite delighted. But how is it, then, that Monsieur Alexis is in want of money? He possesses, if I am not wrong, more than a thousand crowns of revenue."

"He has, in fact, more than 60,000 francs a year; but his places, and his name, oblige him to keep up a considerable establishment; and besides, he wishes to be named deputé of his arrondissement, which will be an easy matter, for he is already auditor to the council of state, commandant of the National Guard of his district, and member of the general council of his department; all these require great expenses; he must have splendid equipages; receive and return excellent dinners; and, I mention it between ourselves, my fortune is not very considerable, and Monsieur the Marquis de Pourrieres has sometimes very kindly obliged me."

"I understand you, I understand you, exactly," said Josué, to whom the last words of Silvia had sufficiently explained the momentary embarrassments of the Marquis de Pourrieres. "Well! let Monsieur the Marquis give me notice, and I shall hold at his disposition 200,000 francs; and even more——"

"I will convey to Monsieur de Pourrieres your good intentions, and I am persuaded that you will come to an understanding together."

"That dear Monsieur Alexis! I assure you I shall feel very great pleasure in seeing him again. He must be much changed within the last fifteen years. Is he still old garçon? He was a handsome brown, with well-marked eye-brows, and eyes——"

"Blue, fendus en amande," interrupted Silvia; "with an agreeable physiognomy, and the rest suitable."

"You say that his eyes are blue?" replied the Jew; "I think, on the contrary, that they were handsome black ones."

"'Tis strange," said Silvia to herself, whom the observation of Josué had surprised; "'tis very strange!"

"My memory is doubtless unfaithful," continued the Jew, who had not remarked the pre-occupation of the marchioness; "it is so long since I have seen Monsieur the Marquis de Pourrieres; at all events, whether he has black eyes or blue ones, it will make no difference as to the affair in hand."

"You are right; but I ought to tell you at once, that he will not feel disposed to give you the same interest as formerly. You cannot expect that a man like him would like to borrow money, at twenty-five per cent. for six months. If you wish to have this affair, you must be a little less a Jew than in general."

"Very well, Madame la Marquise, very well, we shall finish by a good understanding, be assured; especially if you would be good enough to speak favourably of me to Monsieur Alexis."

Silvia and Josué were at this part of their conversation, when the femme de chambre who had introduced the Jew into the boudoir, announced the Marquis de Pourrieres.

"Request Monsieur le Marquis to walk into the garden, where I will rejoin him in a few moments," said Silvia; "place yourself near this window," she added, addressing Josué, "you will see if you recognise your client."

At this moment, Salvador entered the garden, and advanced in his promenade towards the window behind which Josué had placed himself.

"Well!" said Silvia, "do you recognise him!"

"Perfectly," replied the Jew; "the same beautiful black hair, and slight waist; but I cannot distinguish at this distance the colour of his eyes, which you say are blue."

"But do you recognise him?" again demanded Silvia, who could not explain in a satisfactory manner, the change which seemed to have taken place in the colour of her lover's eyes; "is it really the Marquis de Pourrieres whom you recognise?"

"Yes, Madame la Marquise, 'tis certainly him whom I know."

"In that case, go and see him, he will speak to you probably of the loan in question."

Silvia conducted Josué to the garden.

"Ah! 'tis you, Josué," said Salvador, who at once recognised the Jew from the description he had received of him.

"'Tis surely M. Alexis de Pourrieres," said Josué in a whisper to Silvia, "he has recognised me at once."

"Old imbecile!" muttered Silvia, "he thinks it quite natural that black eyes should become blue!"

"I am delighted," continued Salvador, "at the chance that has brought us together again. I have just at this moment, need of 200,000 francs; if you can dispose of this sum for six months, we can arrange a fresh affair together, but you must be contented with a reasonable interest: I am no longer a young man, my dear Monsieur Josué."

"I shall be contented with twenty per cent., Monsieur le Marquis, with fifteen, even, to oblige you."

" 'Tis a little dear; but we will discuss the clauses of our treaty when we sign it."

" If M. le Marquis approves of it, I will call upon him to-morrow, after his breakfast, or later if that will suit him better."

" To-morrow! impossible; I have many visits to make in the day, and I pass the evening at the Spanish Ambassador's. Come here the day after to-morrow, at half-past seven in the evening; bring the amount in bank notes, and the printed paper, in order that we may terminate at once."

" Yes, M. le Marquis."

" Well, 'tis understood, let us talk of other matters."

Salvador, who knew all that had happened to Alexis de Pourrieres during his stay at Marseilles, and who wished to captivate the confidence of the Jew, spoke to him about Jazetta, of father Louiset, the maitre d'armes, of the old Genoese, and of different events of his youth.

Silvia listened to him with much attention.

" 'Tis singular," she said to herself, attentively regarding her lover, " this man never had black eyes; there is in all this a mystery which I must penetrate; but how?"

After nearly an hour's conversation, Salvador dismissed the Jew, who retired after making his usual display of salutations, and promised to be exact at the rendezvous.

On the next day but one, as agreed upon, Josué arrived at Silvia's at half-past seven in the evening. He conversed with the Marquise de Roselly for an hour, when a servant of Salvador's came and announced that his master having been suddenly sent for to the Minister's of the Interior, could not attend upon him, and that he must defer till to-morrow the conclusion of the affair. This delay, which seemed to indicate that the marquis was not much pressed for the money; this delay, we say, short as it was, only increased the ardent thirst for gain which incessantly tormented the unhappy Jew.

" Do you think M. le Marquis has changed his intention?" he said to Silvia, who appeared vexed.

" I do not think so," she replied, " since he requests you to return, but I know that yesterday he was spoken to about a certain Monsieur Justè."

" God of Israel!" exclaimed Josué. " endeavour, Madame le Marquise, that this good M. de Pourrieres may not fall into the gripe of this miserable; he is, although a Christian, a hundred times more of a Jew than I am."

" You astonish me, Monsieur Josué; I am assured, however, that this M. Justè is an honest man, and very strait in affairs."

" May the God of Abraham and of Jacob preserve you from falling into his hands!" replied Josué, heaving a deep sigh.

It was not without design, that Silvia had spoken to Josué of the usurer Justè; she thought that if she allowed the Jew to imagine it possible that the Marquis de Pourrieres might seek from another speculator the sum he wished to borrow, he would show himself more eager for the prey; and that the desire of withdrawing from his confrère an affair which he might consider very advantageous, would induce him to neglect many little precautions.

Silvia, who had studied her part with much care, endeavoured at first to calm the fears of the old Jew; after almost succeeding, by telling him it appeared certain that the Marquis de Pourrieres would not address himself to Justè, unless he could not arrange with him, she changed the conversation, and recounted to him the events which had produced and followed her marriage with the Marquis of Roselly. At length, after a thousand circumlocutions, she found means to bring back the conversation to the sum which the child of Judah was to lend her lover.

" Really, my dear Josué," she said to the poor Jew, " if I carried about me a sum so considerable, I should not be as tranquil as you are; I should be afraid of losing it, or of being robbed of it."

" I never lose any thing," exclaimed Josué.

" But the thieves?"

" Thieves!" he said in a low tone, " they could not, after killing me, find the two hundred notes of one thousand francs. I have sewn them into my scapulary;" and he drew from under his waistcoat a sort of dirty rag, of a very doubtful colour, which all Jews carry in their bosom; the notes were in fact sewn into it. " They certainly would not think of finding any thing in this dirty rag, and besides, I have more the appearance of a poor old beggar, than that of a man who carries a whole fortune about him."

" You are endowed with a rare presence of mind," replied Silvia, who had learnt all she was desirous of knowing; " none but a man like yourself would have such ideas. But it is already late, and I feel a want of repose; adieu! my dear Josué, until to-morrow."

Salvador, Roman, and Silvia, employed the best part of the next day, to place themselves in a position to succeed; it was agreed that Silvia should make use of all her address and imagination to retain the Jew until half-past eleven at night, and indeed to invite him to sup with her if it became necessary.

All passed off well. Josué, who feared above all that the Marquis de Pourrieres would address himself to Justè, arrived some minutes before the appointed time; he waited patiently till the moment when the domestic who had presented himself the evening before, came to announce that his master begged Madame la Marquise de Roselly to make his excuses to the person whom he had to meet, and to request him to return the next day.

" No more doubt," said Josué, in a doleful voice, when Silvia had informed him of the message she had received, " no more doubt he means to avail himself of Monsieur Justè."

" Fear nothing," replied Silvia, " I promise you that Monsieur le Marquis *shall take your* 200,000 *francs;* but as I do not wish you to have so long a walk for nothing, you shall do me the pleasure of taking supper with me."

Josué in vain endeavoured to excuse himself, protesting that he was not worthy of such an honour, but Silvia insisted so politely, that he was forced to admit, that, according to the laws of Moses, he could neither eat nor drink with a Christian.

" Accept simply a biscuit, and a glass of Tokay wine," Silvia said to him; who had no idea that the law of Moses would place any obstacles in the way of her projects.

" Alas! Madame la Marquise," replied the unfortunate Jew, pushed to his last extremity, " we must abstain from wines and food which are not prepared by the children of Israel, even the milk of which we make use ought to be collected by our co-religionists."

" Well, my dear Josué, your laws are absurd, and I wish that, for to-day, you would disobey them; I promise you, in addition, that you shall not be served with impure viands."

Silvia procured for Josué a most agreeable sup-

LIFE IN PARIS.

SALAD, BRANDY, AND A WOMAN DRAGGING BEPPO INTO THE HOUSE OF SANS REPUS.

per; a slice of paté de foie gras, quails en caisse, some sweetmeats of Bar, and some fine fruits. The worthy Josué was not accustomed to such good things. Obeying at the same time his desire of making, without any expense to himself, an excellent repast; and also, from the fear of disobliging the marquise, who had renewed her invitations, he placed himself at table, and once there gave himself up to the enjoyment; he swallowed, without making many grimaces, the numerous bumpers of generous wines which his perfidious Hebè helped him to. At length he was quite gay, when he left her at nearly midnight.

Salvador and Roman, habited in a costume which rendered them not recognisable, waited at the corner of the Avenue Fortuné, from whence they could easily perceive the Jew leave the house of Silvia.

He passed near them to reach the Champs-Elysèes, his old hat was cocked on one side, and he chanted, in marching, the air of an old German ballad.

"I think, vrai Dieu!" said Roman in a low tone to his companion, "that he is half drunk."

"He is quite so, parbleu," replied Salvador, in the same tone; it rains in torrents, and he doesn't even think of using the umbrella which he carries under his arm."

"Madame la Marquise de Roselly is really a valuable woman," continued Roman; "if you were not my friend, and if I were a little younger, I should try to carry her away from you."

Roman and Salvador had exchanged the few words which precede, in walking at a distance in the track of Josué, who had followed the grand avenue of the Champs-Elysèes, and crossed the Place de la Concorde to reach the quay of the Tuilleries.

"Attention!" said Roman, when Josué had passed a few metres beyond the Bridge de la Concorde; "attention!" he then threw himself upon the Jew, fixed round his neck a handkerchief twisted into a sort of cord, and turning himself quickly round, the poor Jew was suspended from his shoulders, and half strangled, before he had the power of making the slightest effort to defend himself. Whilst Roman advanced towards the parapet, Salvador snatched the scapulary, secured round the neck of the victim, and the crumpling of the silk paper told him that he was in possession of his object.

"'Tis done," he said to his companion, "leave there the poor wretch, who is not perhaps quite dead, and who certainly has not recognised us."

"My dear friend," replied Roman, "the dead alone are silent;" and, without waiting the reply of Salvador, finding himself at this moment, at the corner of one of the descents which led to the river, he threw over the parapet the body of the unfortunate Josué.

"Oh! 'twas a useless murder," said Salvador, when he heard the noise made by the body in falling into the water.

The miserable Jew had not uttered a single cry, nor made the slightest movement.

"Come, come," said Roman, "let us make haste, we have no time to lose in idle discourse."

Roman and Salvador hastily quitted the blouses and large pantaloons which they wore over their usual costume; their caps were replaced by a mechanical hat, concealed in their bosom, under their waistcoat. Of these casts-off, they made a bundle, in which they placed several heavy stones, and also threw into the river; they then left, and regained the faubourg Saint Honoré.

An individual, whom caprice or some other motive had attracted to the edge of the river, and who remounted the quay by the towing path which leads to the river, had been a spectator of all that took place.

As we have said, when the Jew left Silvia's, it rained in torrents, and the sky was overcast; but during the time he had taken to clear the distance which separates the Avenue Chateau-briand from the Tuilleries, the rain had ceased by degrees, and at the moment that Roman had thrown the Jew over the bridge, the wind had chased away the clouds which until then had hidden the night stars. By which means, the man we have mentioned, whose attention had been attracted by the splash caused by the falling of the body into the water, had easily noticed all the turns of the lugubrious drama which had been played.

Whether from fear or some other sentiment, this man during the whole time Salvador and Roman had employed to rid themselves of their disguises, had concealed himself behind a large heap of planks, from whence he could easily see, without the fear of being discovered, all that took place. When the two assassins put themselves en route, he followed them at a distance, to their hotel, which they entered at half-past one in the morning.

The man who had followed them did not retire until he had remained for more than an hour in front of their door.

The next morning, Silvia paid a visit to her two accomplices, who informed her of what had taken place in the night; she was delighted at learning that they were in possession of the precious scapulary, which they threw in the fire, after taking out the bank notes.

After examining the notes, which were in good preservation, an examination seasoned with many a joyous proposal at the expense of the unfortunate Josué, the three scelerats placed themselves at table and breakfasted with a good appetite.

Why is it, that such monsters do not carry a mark in front, that they may be recognised when boldly mixing with other men? Why is their appearance similar to our own? or rather, why is it that the Almighty has willed that the existence of such organizations should be even possible?

Silvia, who had some visits to make, had retired at the moment they were about serving the coffee and liqueurs; it was then half-past eleven in the morning.

Salvador and Roman, far from supposing they had been discovered, and that their heads were at the mercy of a man whom chance had made a witness of the crime they had committed, were discoursing gaily together, each smoking a cigar, when a servant brought them the card of a monsieur who begged to be introduced to them.

"Do you know that?" demanded Salvador, handing to his friend a card of the finest workmanship, upon which was written, in almost imperceptible characters, the following name, surmounted by a coronet with three points:

"The Viscount de Lussan."

"The Viscount de Lussan!" replied Roman, after some moments of reflection; "eh! yes, my faith, I ought to know it; this name belongs to that tall and handsome young man who gave us the history of the lingot at the famous banquet. 'Tis singular! it seems we are to meet, one after the other, all the parties who assisted at this fête. I have already encountered the Count Paladin of the Holy Roman Empire, his inseparable friend, and the poet Chevelu; we are almost in relations with the usurer

Justè; and behold, to-day the Viscount de Lussan presents himself; 'tis singular!"

"What can he want with us?" added Salvador.

"We shall know that after speaking with him."

"Request him to enter," said Salvador, to the servant, who, whilst waiting for the orders of his master, had discreetly retired near the door of the apartment.

The Viscount was immediately introduced.

"I have the honour of speaking to M. le Marquis de Pourrieres," he said to Salvador, after saluting him with a perfect grace and elegance. And as Roman, assuming his character of intendant, was about to retire : "Remain, sir," he added, "the motive of my visit is as interesting to you as to M. the Marquis; and besides, it is not the first time I have had the honour of being in your society, messieurs; I was, if I am not mistaken, one of the guests at a banquet in which you also assisted."

"You are quite right, sir," replied Salvador; "but take a seat, and let me know, I beg of you, the motive which procures me the honour of receiving you."

The Vieount de Lussan seated himself, without ceremony, in the fauteuil which Salvador had offered him.

"My visit astonishes you, it disturbs you, perhaps; there are days on which the most simple events have the privilege of causing us trouble, of inducing a certain inquietude;" said the viscount, regarding the two friends with looks which strangely surprised them.

"Will you explain, sir," exclaimed Salvador, rising from his seat, "what this tone and language signify."

"Let us first hear what M. the Viscount has to communicate to us," said Roman to Salvador; "we will get angry afterwards, if there is any occasion."

"Perfectly well reasoned, my dear sir," replied the Viscount de Lussan, "perfectly well reasoned. Chance, gentlemen, has often accomplished wonders ; it has tarnished many a reputation, changed positions, destroyed many a future; chance elevates to-day to the summit a man whom to-morrow she will precipitate into an abyss; thanks to chance, many a crime lies buried in obscurity, and it is almost always chance which causes the discovery of these same crimes; chance——"

"For pity's sake, sir. leave alone all these chances, and hasten to let us know the motive which has procured M. the Marquis de Pourrieres the honour of your visit."

"It's precisely what I was about doing myself the honour of communicating to you when you interrupted me. Yesterday evening, by chance, I paid a visit to a pretty danseuse, to whom, I know not by what chance, I am infinitely attached, but who I never visited except of a morning ; I was not admitted. Some charitable friends whom I met by chance at the club, and to whom I confided my troubles, gave me a piece of information which all the world, except myself, had known for some time; namely, that one of the generals of brigade of the citizen militia had purchased, for 50,000 francs, the good graces of my danseuse; and that it was probable, that at that very moment he was receiving the merchandise of which he had made the acquisition. We do not hear of such events without being a little vexed; I played, in order to distract myself, and I lost a considerable sum. Betrayed both by love and fortune, I took it into my head to end my life, and braving the wind and rain, I put myself en route, on foot, to seek my home. I live in the Rue de Varennes. On pass-

ing in front of the river, the foolish ideas which some moments before had crossed my mind, again agitated me, though more effectively, and I descended to the edge of the water."

Salvador and Roman exchanged with each other a rapid glance, they had pretty nearly guessed the motive which had procured them the visit of the Viscount de Lussan. The latter drew back his fauteuil and continued thus:

"At this moment the wind chased to a distance the clouds which shaded the silvered disk of the night star, and I could see that the surges of the river were yellow and muddy; this sight cured me of my intention to terminate my life.

"I regained the quay by the towing path ; it was then nearly midnight ; when, at the extremity of the road, I saw two men, habited in blouses of blue linen, throw into the water, from above the parapet, another man, small and weakly, after wresting from him an object which I could not exactly distinguish, but which he carried in his bosom. The man thrown into the water had probably been previously strangled, for he made not the slightest movement. The two men in question rid themselves of their blouses and linen pantaloons, of which they made a packet, and sent into the river to keep company with the man they had previously thrown into it. Whilst these events were passing, I had concealed myself behind a heap of planks, placed by *chance* on the towing path; not from fear, I can assure you, I fear nothing, but because I remembered at this moment the old proverb, which says: *that there is always something to fish for in troubled waters.*"

Salvador and Roman were struck nearly senseless, they saw clearly the end at which the Viscount de Lussan was driving; but they feared that his pretensions were not exaggerated.

"Now, gentlemen," continued the viscount, who had hesitated a few moments, in order, no doubt, to leave his auditors the time to make some observations; "I think that if I tell you that I followed these two men in question when they retired, and that by these means I have discovered that these two individuals are no others than yourselves, I shall inform you of nothing that you do not already know. You see clearly, gentlemen, that *chance* is a strange divinity; if it had not pleased a general of the citizen militia to become amorous of an opera dancer, the Viscount de Lussan would not have come this morning to beg you to bestow upon him a small share of your booty."

"Sir," said Salvador, "does not your proceeding, admitting that our position may be such as you are pleased to tell us, authorize us to profit by the *chance* which places you at our discretion?"

"Not a doubt of it, and if you could, without being compromised, rid yourselves of me, and were to do so, I can assure you, I should say it would be quite natural, but I am not at your discretion; you have not supposed, I hope, that the Viscount de Lussan has thrown himself into the lion's mouth, (excuse the comparison,) without having previously taken every measure for his leaving it; I am, I think, tall enough to defend myself, I have sufficient courage, and faithful weapons."

The viscount drew from the side-pocket of his coat a pistol richly damasquined, and which he handled in a manner to show his perfect acquaintance with it.

"There are a pair of them," he said, "and I give you my word as a gentleman, that at need they will not play me false, they are real kukenreitters. This is not all; I have left at your door, in my tilbury, a young Parisian gentleman, one of my friends, M. de Preval, who, if he finds that I do not return, will undoubtedly demand from you some explanation; you see, therefore, that I am prepared at all points; what is your intention?"

"To request that you will dine with me to-day," said Salvador, extending to the Viscount de Lussan a hand, which the other affectionately pressed in his own.

"I am really sorry that I cannot accept your kind invitation; for I have passed my word to a venerable ecclesiastic, with whom I must dine to-day."

"The one who was at the banquet in question?" said Roman.

"The same; do you remember him?"

"Very well; he was one of the gayest of the convives."

"Chut!" said the viscount, "you must not speak so, he has been appointed bishop."

"Ah! bah."

"'Tis as I have the honour of telling you. I am, I repeat it, very sorry, Monsieur le Marquis, that I cannot, to-day at least, accept your kind invitation; I shall retire, then—"

"Wait a few moments longer, I pray," said Salvador; "we have something to remit you."

"Ah! it's true; on my honour I did not think of it."

"Let us see," added Roman, "how much do you expect?"

"Oh! I am reasonable; hand me simply the eighth of what the affair has brought you; I leave the rest to your honesty."

Salvador made a sign to Roman, who left the apartment; he returned in a few minutes, holding in his hand twenty-five bank notes for a thousand francs each, which he handed to the Viscount de Lussan.

The latter placed them in his note-case, after having counted them.

"This comes in time to repair the breaches made in my chest by *bouillotte*, and I am really delighted at having made your acquaintance; but since you have acted with such a good grace, I wish to be the means of your regaining, and with interest, the small *forced* loan you have made me."

The Viscount de Lussan then recounted to those, whom he already considered as new friends, all that the reader has heard him narrate to the usurer Justè, respecting the robbery he intended to commit at Loiseau's, the jeweller. He then spoke to them of Mother Sans Refus, of the men who assembled at her house, of the possibility of making use of them; afterwards, of the usurer Justè. Roman having demanded of him if it was not possible to clip the wings of this old Arab?

"We might, no doubt," replied the viscount, "pluck a few handsome feathers from this old bird of prey, but I think it would be impolitic; it would, in fact, be difficult to find another man always ready, as he is, to purchase at once, and pay cash for all that is offered to him; if you will listen to me, we will preserve Father Justè, who, if my expectations are realised, will be very useful to us."

Salvador and Roman had listened to the Viscount de Lussan with much attention, and gave him the assurance that he might reckon upon them for the *affair* Loiseau, (this was the term they made use of,) when the moment should

arrive; at length, they parted, in perfect intelligence, after a mutual promise to meet again.

"Well!" said Roman, to his friend, when they found themselves alone.

"Eh, eh!" replied Salvador, "do you know that we might effect some good things, if we had at our disposition the men who frequent the establishment of the mother of my mistress; I have a great mind to attempt giving a useful direction to all these scattered elements."

"And so you are not sorry at having made the acquaintance of the Viscount de Lussan?"

"Since we have decided upon retaking to our ancient trade, I do not see why we should stop, in such a good road, and I think this man will be very useful to us."

"I think so, too; but he's a galliard who does not seem to me disposed to stand upon trifles; and, for the rest, I shall not regret the 25,000 francs which his acquaintance has cost us, if the affair of the jeweller Loiseau succeeds."

"I believe you well; 50,000, at least, in jewels, and the Viscount de Lussan only demands 10,000 for his share."

A few days after the events we have narrated, the journals announced to their readers that there had been found, at the bridge of Neuilly, entangled in the long weeds which grow on the islands of the Roi, the body of an old man, who, no doubt, had voluntarily thrown himself in the river, since his watch, and seventeen francs, were found on the corpse.

"Oh! Providence!" exclaimed Roman, after reading the article relating to this event.

CHAPTER XVIII.

BEPPO.

THE reader may not have forgotten that, at the moment when Silvia broke off her connection with Servigny, a man, habited in the costume of the provincial fishermen, had introduced himself into the boudoir of the cantatrice, of whom he had demanded if she wished him to murder the man who had just quitted her.

We must now turn our attention to this man, who was attached to Silvia by ties which will be sufficiently explained by the events which follow; and who plays a conspicuous part in the sequel of this history.

Beppo (thus was he named) quitted Marseilles, where he usually dwelt, immediately after the marriage of Silvia with the Marquis of Roselly, in order to reach Frejus, and dispose of some property left to him by his father.

When, after terminating these affairs, which had retained him at Frejus much longer than he expected, he returned to Marseilles, the Marquis of Roselly was dead, and Silvia had taken her departure, no one knew whither. Our readers are aware that she was then at Venice, where she had gone to collect what had fallen to her on the death of her husband.

The disappearance of the cantatrice so strangely upset the projects of Beppo, that he immediately resolved to travel through Italy and France to rejoin her. He had already visited, without obtaining any results, the greatest part of the cities of Italy, when he arrived at the capital of the Lombard-Venetian kingdom, and learnt, without difficulty, in that city, that the person he was seeking had remained there some time, and that she had left with the intention of visiting Lyons.

Beppo, whose savage affection (our readers have already guessed, probably, that this was the sentiment which drew him in the track of Silvia) seemed to increase with the obstacles he encountered, was no ways discouraged; he put himself immediately *en route*; but when he arrived in the latter city, Silvia had just left with Salvador, and no one could inform him to what place they had retired.

Beppo, who knew the adventurous spirit and insatiable pride of the woman he loved, was convinced that, as all the efforts which he had made in France and Italy had been useless, it was only at Paris he could recover her, he resolved at once, then, to visit the capital.

The mother of Beppo, like most of the provincials, conceived of Paris a monstrous idea; she feared some misfortune would happen to her son, in this immense city; she begged him to renounce his project, but her remonstrances, her prayers, her tears even, were thrown away. Convinced, at length, that she could not induce him to change his resolution, the good woman, who felt towards her son one of those attachments without limit, which are only known to rustic natures, told him that since he had resolved to go, she would accompany him; this news was gladly received by Beppo, who, on his part, was fondly devoted to his mother.

Beppo's mother was but fifty-two years of age; she was of the middling height, but stoutly built; her features were regular, but strongly pronounced; black hair, in which a few silvery threads began to show themselves; teeth white, and well set; a complexion somewhat browned, from the habit of living much in the open air, composed an ensemble which an artist would have loved to reproduce, but which, however, might appear a little rough at the first aspect. The mother of Beppo was one of those perfect types of that race of men known at Marseilles under the name of Castilians, who, although born in France, of fathers born in France, have preserved the language, the manners, and the costume of another country, which, for ages, exercise the same industry, and only form connections amongst themselves.

It is some time since it was first said, that there is no rule without an exception; it was to prove this exception, no doubt, that the mother of Beppo determined to espouse a man who, although not a Castilian, was still handsome; and this man, who, in order to obtain the hand of the woman he loved, had been forced to adopt the manners of his new family, had still required that his son should learn to read and write; which, however, appeared to the learned of the quarter of the Castilians a monstrous anomaly; and by which, although Beppo was not quite civilised, he was a little less savage than the people amongst whom he had been brought up.

The journey once resolved upon, Beppo and his mother put themselves *en route* for Paris; they took with them a small vehicle, to which a mule was harnessed, intended to carry the baggage, and into which the mother entered when fatigued; as to Beppo, he was endowed with such a robust constitution, that fatigue made no impression on his muscles of iron.

The first care of Beppo, on arriving at Paris, was to lodge his mother conveniently; he then informed her he should be absent several days.

He went himself immediately in quest, but it was in vain that he visited all the music shops, and addressed himself to the conservatoire, and all the theatres.

One day, while lounging in the environs of the opera, and looking to chance for the consummation of his desires, a man touched him on the shoulders and said to him:

"'Tis you, Beppo?"

Beppo turned round, and, in the person who had accosted him, recognised one of his compatriots, who had filled a subaltern situation at the theatre of Marseilles, at the time of Silvia's being engaged there.

After shaking him by the hand, Beppo inquired of him the news respecting the cantatrice.

"I well recollect that woman," replied his friend, "and I think she is at this moment in Paris."

"Where is she?" exclaimed Beppo; "show me her house."

And he addressed to his compatriot a multitude of questions, which succeeded one another with the rapidity of lightning.

When Beppo had finished interrogating him, the man replied that he could not satisfy him; "all that I can tell you," he added, "is that this lady is actually at Paris; that I have met her two or three times in a superb equipage, accompanied by a young man, handsome and decorated, who seems to be her husband."

"Married! married a second time!" exclaimed Beppo, after listening to his compatriot.

And by turn the expressions of rage, resentment, and the desire of vengeance, were painted in his physiognomy. After recovering himself a little, he made some fresh inquiries of his new friend, whom he could not resolve to quit, and who could give him no other information than what he had already told him; he added, merely, that it was on the Boulevards, and at the wood of Boulogne that he had met Silvia; and that if he wished to encounter her in his turn, he must frequent these latitudes.

This information was a ray of light to Beppo, who immediately resolved to attend the places mentioned, until such time as he had encountered Silvia; the next day, therefore, after having in the morning run over all the streets of the Chaussée d'Antin, (for it was, in his opinion, in this quarter that he hoped to find her,) he posted himself at the Boulevard des Italiens, towards the hour when the carriages commence entering the wood.

He had been there nearly an hour, when he remarked that he was become the focus of the regards of every one; he knew not to what to attribute the importunity of these persons who pressed around him, when he was accosted by a man of a respectable age and physiognomy, who spoke to him in the provincial patois.

Beppo, who spoke French, it is true, but with a Marseillais accent very pronounced, was delighted to meet with a person to whom he could use his paternal idiom. After exchanging with the stranger the compliments preliminary to all conversation between persons who meet for the first time, Beppo inquired of him why all the idlers of the Boulevard regarded him with such attention.

"It is because your costume is not similar to that worn by themselves; there is no need of any thing more to attract the observation of the lions and lorettes who promenade here," replied the old Provençal.

Until this moment Beppo had never fancied that his costume was ridiculous, and if he had had no object to attain, he would probably have braved the regards of the curious, and retained his fisherman's costume; which appeared to him, at least, as graceful as the scanty equipments of those whom he encountered; but he foresaw that, to succeed, his person must not be remarkable, and he begged his new friend to indicate to him a place where he could purchase some fashionable garments. The latter sent him to the market Saint Jacques, whereby, the next morning, the Castilian fisherman—who had quitted his large linen pantaloons, his bonnet of brown wool, and his *caban* of the same stuff and the same colour, to equip himself in a nice blouse of blue linen, ornamented with embroidery of every colour, pantaloons of ribbed velvet, which, in his simplicity, he considered superb, and to cover his head with a cloth cap, with a large front—had all the appearance of a lighterman in his Sunday's best, and was enabled to traverse, without the fear of being remarked, the places where he still hoped to find Silvia; and, these were the line of the Boulevards, the great avenue of the Champs Elysées, and the fashionable drive of the wood of Boulogne.

One morning, leaving at the break of day the auberge of the White Horse, market Lenoir, faubourg Saint Antoine, where he lodged with his mother since his arrival at Paris, he turned his steps, contrary to his habit, towards the barrier du Trône.

He had taken the resolution to follow the exterior Boulevards as far as the barrier de l'Etoile, from whence he wished to return in crossing Paris. Arrived at the extremity he had assigned to himself, he discovered that his morning walk had produced an appetite; and as at the moment he found himself exactly in front of the culinary temple, opened by Graziano to the amateurs of maccaroni à l'Italienne, and veal cutlets à la Milanaise, he entered, and ordered a good breakfast, which he quickly despatched; and was just relishing a cup of coffee, accompanied with a small glass of cognac, when the noise of an equipage which came from Neuilly, and was hastening towards Paris, caused him mechanically to turn his head.

It was a blue open calèche, lined inside with white satin, a veritable chef d'œuvre of Thomas Baptiste, and to which were harnessed four beautiful spotted gray horses. Silvia, magnificently attired, was seated alone in the interior of the carriage.

The carriage had passed before the windows of Graziano with the rapidity of lightning, and Beppo had only been enabled to obtain a passing glimpse of it; but this glance had been quite sufficient for him to recognise the woman he loved.

He had placed himself for breakfasting before one of the windows of the first floor, which had remained open. He saw at once, that if he took the time to descend and pay his host what was due to him, he risked the chance of not seeing again a carriage drawn by four vigorous horses.

He was endowed with sufficient resolution, and was too determined, not to let so favourable an occasion escape, to hesitate long as to the part he had to take. The floor, which separated him from the ground was not very high; he jumped from the window, and commenced running the length of the avenue de Neuilly, in order to overtake the equipage, which fled before him, and which at this moment was entering Paris by the barrier de l'Etoile.

Graziano, however, and his waiters had remarked the flight of Beppo, and started in pursuit, waving their serviettes, and crying with all the strength of their lungs; "A thief! a thief! stop, thief!" but Beppo ran with such agility, that it is likely they would not have caught him, if some workmen engaged near the triumphal arch had not opposed his passage.

Beppo, as long as he kept in view the carriage which contained the woman he loved, employed all his strength, all his courage, to escape from the hands of those who held him; but when it became an imperceptible point in the horizon, and she at length disappeared behind a cloud of dust, he ceased the struggle, and allowed them to conduct him, without offering the slightest resistance, to the guard-house of the barrier.

A few minutes after, he was taken before the commissary of police of the commune of Neuilly.

Beppo found, that, by his imprudence, he had placed himself in a serious position, from which he would not escape without a little presence of mind; he informed the commissary of police, that, being at Marseilles, he had known a woman connected with the grand theatre, in the quality of premier chanteuse, to whom he had lent all his savings; that this woman had quitted Marseilles by stealth, carrying away the money of several persons, and from him alone more than four thousand francs; and that it was from seeing her pass in a brilliant equipage, and endeavouring to follow her, in order to discover her residence, that he had left the house of Graziano, and omitting to pay for his breakfast. In support of what he advanced, he exhibited his papers de sûreté, which were perfectly regular; his purse, which contained at least a dozen Napoleons, thus doing away with the supposition that he had any intention of evading the amount of a bill of less than five francs; and letters from the notary of Frejus, who had been charged with the commission of selling his property, and which, in consequence, justified the legitimate possession of the sum he had exhibited.

"These colours are not healthy ones," said one of the waiters of Graziano, who wished to play the advocate; "I have known this worthy for more than these ten years, and, to my knowledge, he has played the same trick, and told the same history at least twenty times."

Beppo burst into a rage, and it is probable that if he had been alone with the waiter of the restaurant, who seemed quite satisfied at the short speech he had invented, he would have made him pass rather an unpleasant quarter of an hour. However, he calmed himself.

"Sir," he said to the commissary of police, "this waiter is either a fool or a slanderer. I have not been at Paris more than fifteen days; I am lodging at the Lenoir market, with my mother, and it will be easy to convince yourself of what I say by questioning her."

The firmness of Beppo's replies, had convinced the commissary of police that it was only in consequence of a mistake that he had been brought before him; he was satisfied, by ordering him to pay what he owed to Graziano, and allowed him to depart.

Beppo handed two five franc pieces to the restaurateur, and told him to divide amongst the waiters what remained after paying himself, in order to recompense them for their trouble.

The two five franc pieces put Graziano and his understrappers in good humour, who made all imaginable excuses to Beppo, when leaving together the office of the magistrate. The idea then struck Beppo that the restaurateur might give him some information which would prove useful to him in his researches; he described minutely the woman and the equipage to which he had been giving chase when arrested, and demanded if he knew one or the other.

"The carriage, which you have so exactly described to me," replied Graziano, "passes often enough before my door to repair to the wood; but it is but very rarely that the woman you speak of is alone; her husband is generally with her. He is a handsome man, decorated."

"Eh? how do you know that this man is her husband?" exclaimed Beppo, who could not fancy for a moment that Silvia was again married.

"I presume it," replied Graziano; "at least if he is not her beloved, or her brother, or a friend; but all that I can tell you is, that I do not think the lady you have described is the one who has deceived you; she has too handsome equipages, and too rich a livery not to be honest."

"No, no, I am not mistaken, I am quite sure it is her; and as you tell me she passes very often before your house, from to-day I will become your pensionnaire, and, to avoid suspicions, I will place every morning in your hands a sum sufficient to cover the expenses for the day, for I wish to be at liberty to go out and come in when it suits me; do you agree to this?"

"A merchant never refuses to sell," replied Graziano, "but I think you will lose your time and your youth; the rest is your affair, not mine."

Beppo installed himself the next day with Graziano, where he remained until eight o'clock in the evening.

The next morning he arrived at seven o'clock, and remained till the night had approached.

More than twelve days had passed, and neither the woman nor the carriage he waited for had appeared in the horizon. The frequenters of the house of Graziano, who knew the motive for these long sittings, were quite disposed to consider him mad; it was, in fact, rather an odd proceeding, to pass whole days waiting for the appearance of a carriage before a door. Beppo, however, was not tired; and as he appeared not to be of too easy a temper, and of sufficient size to impose on any one inclined to make him a jest, those who at first had shown an inclination to laugh at him, left him in the end perfectly tranquil.

The cat, which constantly watches for the mouse in its path, finishes by putting her paw upon it. The constancy of Beppo, who had at least shown as much patience as the most cunning water rat, was at length rewarded. One evening, towards eight o'clock, Graziano and his waiters, who began to interest themselves about him, saw him rise precipitately and crying, " There she is."

In fact, the blue calèche, with its four mottled gray horses, in which were Silvia and two elegant messieurs, passed at a slow trot before the shop of the Italian restaurateur.

Beppo followed it without difficulty; it passed the barrier; he then saw it enter No. 22, of the avenue Chateaubriand. " It's there she lives, then," he said; he then posted himself at the avenue Fortané, at the same place where a few days before Salvador and Roman had remained to intercept, in his passage, the unfortunate Josué. He was determined to know how long the two individuals who had entered with Silvia would remain; they left together, and much sooner than he expected. Beppo, like all men, was quite disposed to believe what he hoped for; and concluded, quite naturally, that Silvia belonged to neither one nor the other.

As he intended to present himself the next morning to Silvia, it was necessary to discover by what name he was to ask for her. He questioned, with more address than generally belongs to a child of nature, a servant who was passing by, and the latter having informed him that the hotel he pointed to was occupied by the Marchioness of Roselly, Beppo began jumping like a young deer, exclaiming: "What joy! what joy! she has not remarried."

Beppo had not yet attained his thirtieth year; he was tall, strong, and elegantly built; his black hair was slightly curled; his eyes were blue, and ornamented with long lashes; his mouth was, perhaps, rather large, but, in return, his teeth were white, and perfectly even; the result of all this was, a very good-looking man; but who risked, however, a great chance of not being admitted to the Marchioness of Roselly, if he presented himself habited in a blouse and a cap. Beppo knew enough of Parisian life, by this time, to comprehend these things; he put, therefore, a good sum in his pocket, and as he had heard it said in his youth, that, with money, he could procure whatever he needed at the Palais Royal, he turned his steps that way; it was rather more than nine o'clock in the morning.

"Can you tell me," he inquired of a respectable old man, with white hair, who waited, with watch in hand, the discharge of the cannon at twelve o'clock, "where I can purchase some well-made and fashionable garments?"

"My friend," replied the old man, "'tis no longer with the tailors of the Palais Royal that you will find what you want. If you wish to be well fitted out, you must attend, near here, at the Gallery Vivienne, Nos. 18 and 20, at Bonnard's; 'tis a creditable house, and to a certainty you will obtain there every thing you wish."

Beppo followed the advice of the obliging lounger; he went to Bonnard's, and, in less than twenty minutes, he had made the acquisition of a complete costume of a man of fashion; he found, at the Gallery Vivienne. every thing necessary to complete his costume—linen, polished boots, cravats, hat, gloves, cane, &c. He determined to be habited as elegantly as the two individuals who had accompanied the pretty Silvia, the evening before. These acquisitions he had transported to a carriage, and after confiding his person to the capillary artiste, Thiberge, who dressed his hair and beard to suit his physiognomy, he was driven to his own house, in order to change his costume.

He had remarked on the counter of the merchant tailor, several cards; one, among the rest, bearing the coronet of a count, had particularly struck him, by its extreme elegance; he took it, to examine it more closely, and mechanically placed it in his pocket. Whilst his vehicle followed the great avenue of the Champs Elysées, he asked himself by what name he should get himself admitted to Silvia? he could find no answer to this question—so true is it, that often the most simple affair gives us the greatest embarrassment.

"My faith," he said to himself, at length, "I will give this card, which, by chance, I have kept. and it will indeed be the devil if M. the Count de Badimont be not admitted without difficulty."

Arrived at the door of Silvia's hotel, he rang. He was on the point, at last, of seeing her whom he had looked for so long, he should speak to her, and this interview was to decide his future fate. His heart, consequently, beat furiously, and it was

LIFE IN PARIS.

DE MATHE) ANNOUNCED TO LUCIE AND LAURA.

No. 19.

with great trouble he could restrain himself. He demanded of the Swiss, (Silvia had a Swiss,) Madame le Marquise de Roselly.

"Madame le Marquise is not yet visible," replied a femme de chambre, who happened, *by chance*, to be in the lodge of the liveried Cerberus.

Beppo, who had never had the leisure to learn the uses and customs of Parisian life, during the time he had exercised, in the Isles of Hyerés, the profession of a fisherman, could not perfectly comprehend the meaning of the femme de chambre; so, fearing she had not understood him, he renewed his inquiry.

"I have already had the honour of telling monsieur," replied the official, "that madame is not visible at this time of day; and that she receives no one except from twelve till four o'clock; if, however, monsieur would leave his name—"

Beppo now understood the meaning of the domestic, whom he had at first supposed a young lady of good family. After telling her he would return, he left, to take a walk, and wait for the appointed hour.

When he returned, Madame la Marquise was at length visible. After giving his card to the official, and waiting some minutes, in a saloon fitted up with every comfort and elegance, he was introduced into the boudoir we have already described. Fearing that his sudden appearance might occasion Silvia to utter a cry of surprise, he had, in order to salute her, placed the forefinger of his left hand on his lips; a precaution, it is true, quite useless, for the costume he wore had so changed his appearance, that Silvia did not, at first, recognise him; it was only when, in reply to the question she made to him, to inform her of the motive of his visit, he pronounced some few words, that, recognising his voice, she exclaimed:

"Heavens! Beppo!"

"At length, Silvia," said the latter, "I have found you once more."

"Eh! what do you want? What do you wish of me?" replied the marchioness; who, since she had lost sight of Beppo, had acquired a dose of audacity, which she did not possess at the time we encountered the fisherman for the first time. She had, at once, comprehended that the man, who, to be introduced to her, had adopted the costume of the fashionables, had already mixed in society, and that he was much less to be feared than when he simply wore, as a rude child of the ocean, a cap of brown wool, an old fisherman's cloak, and walked with naked feet on the strands of the Mediterranean.

"What will you do?" she repeated, "I have already told you, I do not wish to follow you, and the time is past when you inspired me with terror."

"Heaven is my witness," said Beppo, "that neither is it this sentiment with which I wish to inspire you; sometimes, perhaps, I have allowed myself to be carried too far by the violence of my character; but tell me, Silvia, have not my excesses been sufficiently justified by your want of faith?"

"If you are come here to talk to me of what has formerly passed between us," replied Silvia, "you can retire; nothing fatigues me more than the recital of old histories, and I have neither the wish, nor the leisure, to listen to you any longer."

Silvia was about to pull the cord of a bell, to summon her domestics.

Beppo seized her by the arm, and repulsed her so roughly, that she fell into the long chair she had just quitted.

"You shall hear me," he said to her, "you must—I wish it!"

And as Silvia made a negative sign of the head;

"Listen," he added, "and do not force me to commit a fresh crime; the one I have committed has already brought sufficient remorse. I swear to you, by Notre Dame de la Garde, that if you utter a cry, if you make a gesture, I will plunge this poniard into your heart, even to the very handle."

Silvia turned slightly pale; the past had taught her that the fisherman was incapable of failing in an oath similar to the one he had just uttered.

"Speak then," she said, with some expression of disdain, which did not escape the penetrating eyes of Beppo; "speak then, I will listen to you, as I can do no otherwise."

"It's quite time there was an end to all this," said Beppo, speaking to himself in a low tone.

He was seated near to a small table, on which, a few days before, Silvia had supped with the old Jew; he held his head between his two hands, and seemed buried in sad and deep reflections.

"I am ready to hear you," said Silvia.

"You told me, but now, that you loved not old histories; you must, however, listen to one, of which you already know all the details.

"A young woman, who concealed, under the physiognomy of an angel, the soul of a demon, came one day, to seek in his cabin, a poor fisherman, who had never as much as spoken to her.

"She knew, however, that this fisherman loved her with all his strength of affection; that he revered her as the equal of a Madonna; that she became his thought by day, his dream by night; for she had observed that he followed her steps every where; and she read in his looks, which he hardly dared to fix upon such a great lady, the violent passion she had inspired. This young woman, then, came to seek the fisherman.

"She did not wait for the avowal of his passion; she told him she had discovered it, and that he was not forbidden to hope; then, after she had intoxicated him with her words, fascinated him with her regards, she placed a poniard in his hand, and required him to murder a man, who, at a certain hour, would pass a spot she indicated to him. As he hesitated, she recounted a history which would have justified a crime, if a crime could be justified; a history which she invented at the moment, and which, however, drew tears from him who listened to it. She said to him, to this man who was mad, that she had loved him from the day on which, for the first time, she had seen him; and that it was only from this day, that the tyranny of him it was necessary to strike, was become insupportable to her; she told him that this man was the only obstacle opposed to their happiness; that when no longer in existence, she should be free, and that she should consider herself happy in dividing with him the modest future it would be in her power to offer him. The miserable promised to do all that the enchantress required; and, as she appeared to doubt his word, he swore to her, by Notre Dame de la Garde, to accomplish her design. Must he tell you the rest? He hid himself at the corner of a street; he waited in ambush for a man who never dreamt of defending himself, and he plunged into his heart the poniard which you see.

"Are all the details of the history I have narrated to you exact, Madame la Marquise?"

"I have nothing to say to the contrary," replied Silvia, with an air of the most perfect indifference. "Have you finished?"

Beppo felt his blood boiling in his veins, and, with his right hand, which he had mechanically passed into his bosom, tore his flesh; he had, however, sufficient force of mind to restrain himself.

"No, I have not finished," he added; "but there remains little more to tell you.

"When the murderer, still covered with the blood of his victim, demanded from his accomplice the wages of his crime, he could not find her; and, it was not until some time he discovered her; then, as now, and at every time it was possible to meet her, she reproached him in outrageous terms, and showed him the utmost contempt. Is this also true, madame?"

Beppo, in pronouncing the last words, rose from the seat he occupied, and, drawing himself up to his full height, stood over Silvia, who was half reclining on her long chair, and playing negligently with the tassels of the girdle which encircled her waist.

She made no reply.

"I have asked you, if what I have told you is true?" repeated Beppo.

"Listen to me," replied Silvia, who saw it would not be prudent to push Beppo to extremities, whose increasing irritation began to make her uneasy; "I will not attempt to deny it; you may justly reproach me; but why refer without cessation to these *faits accomplis*. We have each obeyed our destiny, and I think that the wisest part we can take, is to forget the past, and not engage in a struggle, the results of which must necessarily be fatal to you or me."

"And thus," continued Beppo, "you would make the same use of me as of an instrument, which you can break when no longer serviceable. It shall not end thus, madame."

"What do you require then? For in fact it is time there was an end to all this; I am really wearied of these continual harassings."

"I require that you fulfil the promise you have given me; you have disinherited me of my place in paradise; it is but just, I think, that I obtain here below as much happiness as I have any claim to, and it is only with you I can be happy."

"You are mad: to follow you, my poor Beppo, I must renounce those things which I cannot live without, the luxury with which I am surrounded."

"Certainly, I would much rather that you were poor; I should be more at my ease in reclaiming the execution of your promise. But when you made me this promise you were still poorer than myself; and if since, your position is changed, it is only by a want of faith on your part. I can then, without giving you a right to lend me thoughts which do not belong to me, tell you every where, and at all times, that, be you rich or poor, cantatrice or marquise, Silvia, you have given me a promise, you must keep it."

"And so you wish that I should renounce the pleasures and ease of a life of elegance; that I should quit the world in which I have hitherto lived; that I bid adieu to all my friends, to bury myself with you in some unknown solitude. You are mad, my dear; it is only from heroines that such sacrifices are required; and, thank God, I am neither a Clarissa Harlowe or a Pamela."

Beppo, who for some instants had been seemingly reflecting, made no reply.

Silvia thought it a favourable moment to strike a grand blow.

"And besides," she added, "I owe you a confession, which will determine you, perhaps, to change your resolution. When I said I loved you, I rendered myself, perhaps, no account of my sentiments; but the avowal had hardly escaped my lips, when I discovered that I had deceived you in deceiving myself; I would gladly have recalled you, and told you that I released you from the oath you had made me, but it was too late. Thus, not knowing what defence to make, when you should come to claim the execution of the promise I had given you, I seized with eagerness an opportunity for escaping, which presented itself by chance. But, I swear to you, I no more loved the man with whom I fled, than I loved you, that I loved not those whom chance afterwards threw in my way, nor even the man whose name I at present bear. My hour was not yet come."

Beppo's ideas, since he had lived at Paris, and mixed in a civilised world, had become singularly modified, and at the present moment he felt that the character he was playing towards Silvia was perfectly ridiculous; he was thus very glad that Silvia, by endeavouring to justify herself, spared him the pain of recurring to violence. He would not, however, renounce his projects; he believed himself to possess rights over this woman, for whom he had committed a crime, and these rights he would have respected; but, perceiving that violence would not serve him, he had recourse to stratagem.

"And now?" he said, without raising his voice.

Silvia examined him a few minutes, before determining a reply.

The expression of his physiognomy was sad, though calm.

"Now," she added, "my hour is come; I will not attempt to conceal it from you; and be assured, it is not because I hold my person at a price above the devotion you have proved to me, that I will not fulfil the promise I have made you, 'tis simply because I cannot bestow on you a heart, which to-day belongs to another."

"'Tis well," replied Beppo; "'tis well, I now know what remains to be done."

"Return to Provençe, Beppo, you will still find some happy days under the beautiful sky of your own country. If really you love me, if you love me for myself, you ought to desire my happiness, and I cannot be happy with you; the image of him you have killed, for my sake, would for ever be a barrier between you and me. But, be assured, I shall forget you never; the recollection of the attachment you have shown me, will be always present to my memory; and, who knows, perhaps we shall be permitted to meet again, when many years have passed over our heads."

Silvia, whilst entertaining Beppo with the preceding, had employed the most caressing inflections of her voice, and as the latter had listened to her with much calmness, she was willing to believe that her words had produced the effect she had hoped. She wished, however, to hear him speak a few words, to prove to her that she was not mistaken.

Finding that he made no reply, she thought to strike a last blow, a decisive one, and which, in her own opinion, would give her the certainty of what she had to hope or fear. She continued, therefore, in these terms:

"But, if I cannot, my dear Beppo, recompense you, for the present, in the manner you seem to wish, you will allow me, I hope, to divide with you a part of what I possess. I am rich, very rich, indeed; I can then, without distressing myself, beg of you to accept this slight proof of the friendship I feel towards you."

In finishing these words, Silvia placed on the small table, near which Beppo was seated, a large packet of bank notes.

Beppo reasoned with himself in substance as follows:

"If I accept the sum she is offering me, she will think I accept, with it, the position she wishes to place me in, and she will no longer distrust me; if, on the contrary, I refuse, she will suppose that I have not yet renounced my projects, and she will be constantly on her guard."

"I accept this sum," he said to Silvia, taking up the bank notes, which he placed in his pocket, after counting them; "as you observed, just now, the wisest part I can take is not to engage with you in a struggle, which must be fatal to one of us; I think I shall do well to return to Provençe, and endeavour to forget you; it is what I shall do, and this very day."

"Really?" said Silvia, fixing on Beppo a regard which seemed to doubt his words.

"I have never given you, I believe, any reason to doubt my word; I quit you, madame, and I hope, very sincerely, that you will be happy."

Beppo retired, after respectfully saluting the Marchioness of Roselly.

Within a week from this interview, Silvia, to her sorrow, was in the power of Beppo.

The latter, scarcely out of the hotel of the Marchioness of Roselly, had rejoined his mother, whom he found at the door of the Auberge of the White Horse, waiting his return with impatience, and who demanded of him, at once, if he was satisfied with the result of his undertaking? Beppo, whose heart was raging, since Silvia had avowed to him that she loved another, begged his mother to allow him to collect himself a moment, and retired to his own chamber. After remaining there some hours, he left it in a much calmer mood than he had entered it. His resolution had been taken, and it only remained to execute it.

His mother, it is unnecessary to state, was ignorant of the ties which attached him to Silvia, she did not know even what was the position of this woman; she was simply aware that he had met, at the Isles of Hyerés, a woman gifted with a marvellous beauty, and of whom he became desperately enamoured; that he had long sought after this lady without being enabled to find her, and that it was to discover her that he had come to Paris. The good woman had only learnt in the morning, that his efforts had been crowned with success, and that it was to meet the woman he loved that he had gone out in such a brilliant toilette. The Castilian had not doubted, for an instant, that her son would succeed in the steps he had taken; it appeared to her impossible that a woman would be insensible to the praises bestowed upon him.

She was greatly surprised, then, when Beppo, without giving her more details than he wished her to be acquainted with, informed her of the ill success of his last effort; she made fresh importunities to induce him to renounce a woman who seemed to treat him with such disdain; but she reasoned with a deaf man, the obstacles had only increased the blind passion to which the unhappy Beppo was a prey; he had conceived a plan, of which he himself did not attempt to conceal the absurdity, but which he was resolved to execute, at any hazard. We may add, that it was not simply love which drove him to act at present, but that, to this sentiment was added those of jealousy, wounded pride, and perhaps, also, a desire of revenging himself for the contempt shown to him by a woman, whom he loved without the power of stifling it, at the same time appreciating, at its just value, her atrocious character.

As his mother (after a long discourse, composed of arguments which he did not attempt to refute, seeing the impossibility,) inquired of him if they should soon return to Provençe, he replied, that he had determined to fix himself at Paris, where it would be easy to obtain a trade that would enable him to live, and live well, without intruding on his small capital, which he intended to place at a banker's. The good woman, who was perfectly satisfied to remain with her son, opposed herself but little to the project, hoping that the distractions of a large city would drive from the thoughts of her son, the passion which rendered him so unhappy; so that when Beppo had assured her, that, for the present, at least, he had no wish to think about her, she found herself more tranquil; and the only question between them was, respecting a convenient lodging, to fix themselves definitively.

Beppo, whose constant walks had familiarised with the noise and tumult of the capital, undertook this charge, and the next morning put himself *en route*.

For several days he sought in vain for what he desired, and this is not surprising; he wished for apartments in a house situated in an isolated quarter, and very little inhabited; and, also, that the lodging itself should be far from any habitation, and so disposed, that, if by chance those who inhabited it were inclined to make themselves heard, such cries would not reach any officious neighbours. This was not very easy to discover, especially in a city like Paris, where the value of every inch of ground is well understood, the consequence of which is, that the habitations approach each other as close as the cells of a bee-hive; he found, however, in the Rue Contrescarpe, Saint Marcel, No. 21, all that he desired.

This house, double in depth, consisted, next the street, of a ground floor and five stages, which constitutes a very considerable height; but the proprietor having, as it seemed, remarked that his house was sufficiently solid in foundation to support a supplementary building, had constructed, on the roof, a sort of square pavilion, composed of two large rooms, placed one above the other, which increased, by about two hundred francs, the renting value of his house.

From the windows of this crow's nest, perched on a house situated in the most elevated part of Paris, you overlooked the capital and the surrounding country, and were so near the sky, that the thousand noises of the city only strike the ear as a vague murmur. Thus the pavilion of the house, situate in the Rue Contrescarpe, Saint Marcel, was usually inhabited by poets, anxious to approach, as near as possible, the stars to whom they address their invocations. But, however, it was uninhabited at the period Beppo was looking for a lodging for himself and his mother; and as it seemed to unite all the conditions he required, he hastened to engage it and establish himself in it, after furnishing it with all the objects necessary for living.

It was of importance that Beppo, after establishing his mother in this sort of pigeon-house, should induce her to lend him assistance in case of necessity; this was not difficult.

When he mentioned to her his conviction that, if he had in his power, only for a few days, the woman he loved, he was sure she would change her resolution; that in case of refusal, she could do no otherwise than yield to the foreign influences around her; and that, it was only to submit her to these influences that he wished to carry her off; the good woman, who desired nothing beyond the happiness of her son, whom she thought incapable of committing a bad action, and was also ignorant of the condition of the person he spoke of, promised to do every thing he wished.

Beppo had now obtained the aid of an auxiliary, as devoted as possible; the cage was prepared, and pretty enough, it is true, and provided with every thing which could render existence supportable to a woman accustomed to all the appliances of luxury and comfort; it now only remained to entrap the bird, for which it was to serve as a prison. This was the most difficult. But Beppo, however, did not despair of succeeding; he knew, by experience, that with patience and resolution we can accomplish much, and the carrying off a woman, appeared to him much less difficult, than to discover her address in a city like Paris. It must be added, that he reckoned a little upon chance, and said to himself, "that, as she had once before come to his aid, it was not impossible that she might favour him a second time."

He had no settled plan, then; he limited himself simply to wandering, without cessation, in the neighbourhood of Silvia's house, waiting the chance of a favourable moment, which he promised himself faithfully not to let escape.

Silvia was nearly as superstitious as her lover; it is a fatal law, which is obeyed by all who have not a very clear conscience; like him, she believed in dreams, omens, and the influence of days; and, frequently of a morning, she might be seen taking a walk to consult a celebrated divineress, very expert in phrenology, physiognomy, the use of cards, æromancy, palmistry, astrology, magnetism, and other juggleries, who lived in the Rue des Vignes, at Chaillot.

Having no wish to put her people in the confidence of this weakness—and the domicile of the fortune-teller not being far from her hotel, as, in order to reach it, it was only necessary to cross the Champs Elysées—she went there on foot, and very simply attired. Beppo, who, as we have said, was constantly in the proximity of her hotel, habited in one manner to-day, and in a different one on the morrow, would infallibly finish by encountering her.

It is exactly what happened, one sombre and rainy morning, which Silvia had unluckily chosen, that she might not be observed, and at the very moment when Beppo, quite persuaded that the person he waited for would not leave her house on such a miserable morning, was about to retire.

When Silvia stepped into the street, there fell only a small rain, from which she could easily shelter herself with the umbrella she had borrowed from her femme de chambre; but, she had scarcely arrived at the end of the avenue Chateaubriand, when all the cataracts of the heavens opened at once, and torrents of rain drove to a distance those, who, like her, had up to this moment braved the storm.

She was at an equal distance from her own hotel, and the domicile of the fortune-teller. Should she return home, or proceed to the card-drawer? She continued her route bravely, despite the wind and rain, when she was suddenly seized upon by Beppo, whom she certainly had no expectation of encountering."

The unexpected apparition of this man, whom she supposed to have been long since returned to Provence, caused her such a sensation, that she had not the strength to cry for help.

"If you utter a cry, if you make a gesture, a single movement which might attract attention," said Beppo, "you die. I wish to do you no violence, but I must speak with you; do not attempt to deceive me; make me no promises, which you have no more the intention of keeping, than I have of listening to them, it would be taking useless trouble; you have heard me, you know what I am capable of; follow me then, for you must."

Whilst speaking, Beppo had hurried Silvia towards the barrier de l'Etoile, where he hoped to find a vehicle. His expectation was not deceived; by one of those rare chances on a rainy day, a fiacre had remained on the place; he made Silvia enter it, who seemed overcome by the surprise she had received; he then spoke a few words in the ear of the coachman, who, desirous, no doubt, to obtain the magnificent recompense promised him, vigorously applied the whip to the two meagre Rosinantes attached to his vehicle, who, being for once willing to second the intentions of their master, started at a gallop.

CHAPTER XIX.

CHOISY-LE-ROI.

DAYS, weeks, months, passed without Silvia reappearing at her hotel, and without any news being received of her; Salvador and Roman knew not to what they could attribute this sudden disappearance, which nothing had provoked, nothing had justified; and which appeared to them still more inexplicable, when the law officers, coming to place seals to the domicile of the Marchioness of Roselly, it was stated that she had taken away nothing which belonged to her, neither habiliments, nor jewels, nor money.

Salvador, who really loved Silvia, appeared for a considerable time greatly afflicted at the disappearance of his mistress; and when Roman, or the Viscount de Lussan, who was become his most intimate friend, attempted to console him, he repulsed them rudely; he took no interest in any thing, neither solicited the advancement he had hoped for, nor the magnificent affairs which the viscount constantly proposed to him; and the latter began to fear that his new friends would not prove as useful to him as he had at first imagined.

But time will calm the most poignant grief. Salvador, after employing a whole month in regretting Silvia, and doing nothing but seeking her, said to himself at length, "that if she was lost to him, it was un fait accompli, which he could not remedy, and of which he must make the best." Still, not wishing that his mistress, if he chanced to refind her, should reproach him with having neglected any means which might serve to put him in her trace, he visited the police, in order that they might search every where for the Marchioness of Roselly, who had vanished from her residence in so singular and unexplicable a manner.

His title, his position in society, and perhaps also the magnificent recompense he promised to the subalterns employed, procured him a favourable reception. They promised to do all that was humanly possible to recover the noble lady; but they did not conceal from him that it was almost certain they should not succeed.

"It is probable that some accident has happened to this lady," said the one he addressed. "For some time past, the capital has been infested by a gang of fellows, who, every day, commit fresh crimes; there are some rovers about the barriers, to whom nothing is sacred, who assassinate a man to rob him of two five-franc pieces; and it is not at all improbable that the lady you speak of, has fallen into the hands of some among them."

And as Salvador observed to this functionary, that his conjectures were not well founded, as it was proved that the Marchioness of Roselly had left her hotel in the day time, and that the gentry he spoke of were only to be feared at night:

"It's true, it's true," replied the functionary, "there is, in this event, something mysterious, which confounds me; but let us hope, M. le Marquis, the eye of the police is constantly open, and nothing which takes place in the capital escapes its sight; if Madame the Marchioness of Roselly is still in this world, we shall discover the place in which she conceals herself, or rather where she is concealed; we have certainly discovered the assassins of the Jew Josué."

"Ah! you have discovered the assassins of the Jew Josué," said Salvador, who could not restrain, without trouble, a slight movement of fear.

"When I say that we have discovered these assassins, I am going a little too far, perhaps; but we have, at the present, under lock and key, two of these rovers of the barriers, who, certainly might be the authors of the death of this unhappy man, and which had been attributed at first to suicide."

"I wish very sincerely that you may not be deceived, sir," said Salvador; "it would really be deplorable, if the authors of this frightful crime escaped the just vengeance of society; for my part, I should be much grieved at it. I was well acquainted with Josué, with whom I had some affairs when I lived at Marseilles, and I can say that he was a very honest man."

"They will not escape, Monsieur le Marquis; nor even those miserables who have for some time terrified the capital by their numerous depredations."

"Indeed," added Salvador, "we hear nothing spoken of but robberies committed with an audacity and address unheard of; we might really be tempted to belive, that the men who commit them, are directed by some clever hand, and that they receive indications from persons well placed in society. Are you not of my opinion?"

"Not at all, M. le Marquis, not at all; the robbers act alone; and there are not in society, I mean by society, that in which you mix, persons who give them any information. But, however it may be, we have declared a rude war against them, and if to-day they march with impunity, to-morrow it may be our turn."

The presumption of the functionary greatly amused Salvador, and despite the heavy grief he felt, when he quitted him, recommending him not to neglect the mission he had confided to him; he could hardly refrain from laughing in his face, for he knew better than the functionary, how to account for the numerous crimes which for some time had laid waste the capital.

In fact, during his somnolence, Roman and the Viscount de Lussan had not lost their time; thanks to the latter, the companion of Salvador had been put in report with father Justè, who had encouraged him in the pursuit of the enterprise he meditated; and also assured him, that however great was the value of the objects presented to him, he would purchase them without an observation. The usurer had afterwards introduced him to Mother Sans Refus, to whom he had recommended him as a man upon whom she could faithfully reckon, and very capable of rendering important services to the society.

Roman, habited in a costume appropriate to the game he intended to play, had, several times, visited the house of Madame Sans Refus; he had at first spoken to those frequenters who seemed to merit the most confidence; these overtures had been received with the greatest eagerness, and it was not long before he acquired over these men, for the most part illiterate and vulgar, the authority which the notorious audacity he was endowed with, and the education he had received, was likely to procure for him; for criminals are, perhaps, of all men, the most disposed to acknowledge with facility, the influence of men who appear superior to themselves, either from their personal qualities, or their education; it is remembered, no doubt, that the accomplices of Lacenaire, never addressed him otherwise than as Monsieur Lacenaire, and that this infamous criminal only considered them, he said, as his domestics.

Salvador, when he awoke from the state of torpor in which he had been plunged for some time, had, at first, blamed the proceedings of his companion; but the thing was done, and Salvador was a man of the world, who knew well how to accept the logic of *facts accomplished*, so that he soon turned his attention to the best means of obtaining the most advantageous results from what his friend had done; and, in a short time, he found himself at the head of a band of criminals, ready to attempt any thing, provided they found themselves gainers by it; all of whom he knew, but by whom he was not known in return.

Here then is the point to which things had arrived a short time before the period at which we have commenced this history.

Salvador and Roman were the recognised chiefs of all the bandits to whom the den of Mother Sans Refus served as a place of rendezvous; they never acted until they had received orders from one or the other; and the produce of each robbery was sold to Mother Sans Refus, who paid for it nearly on her own terms, on condition to resell it at a higher price to Father Justè, and to remit to Roman, Salvador, and the Viscount de Lussan, a certain sum, which was divided between them; the first produce, in which the three associates always had a share, belonged, without dispute, to those who committed the robbery. Mother Sans Refus bought, on her own account, all that did not consist of gold, silver, or jewellery; such objects being considered as valueless by the triumvirate; as to coin or bank-notes, they remained the property of those into whose hands they had fallen, for despite their promises, they were not such fools as to bring them into the general mass. There existed, therefore, between the three friends, Justè, and Mother Sans Refus, a real commercial society, *en participation*, whose operations consisted in purchasing from the malefactors, on the best terms possible, the fruits of their depredations, and to divide the difference.

It must also be observed, that when a good affair presented itself, Roman and Salvador executed it alone, and retained the profit, after remitting, in cash or bank-notes, to the Viscount de Lussan, the sum to which the information he had furnished had given him a right; for it was generally as a mere *donneur d'affaires*, that the latter was known in these matters. If, by chance, they wanted a few men of execution to give them a helping hand, they were always careful to appropriate to themselves the lion's share.

It was at this period, that, finding the necessity of having at their disposition a place in which they could deliberate, and also conceal, if requisite, those objects which they were not in a hurry to get rid of, Salvador and Roman engaged the isolated pavilion of Choisy-le-Roi, into which we have introduced the reader in the first chapter of this work.

A few days after the house had been thus far furnished, Roman returned to the pavilion, accompanied by four domestics, who conducted a travelling waggon, drawn by two stout Flemish horses, which were unharnessed, and led to the stable.

The waggon was loaded with such articles as they had not been enabled to bring at the first journey, the kitchen requisites, some large pieces of furniture, hampers of fine wines, and several other objects. When the waggon was unloaded, and the articles put in their places, Roman took the railroad to return to Paris, and the kitchen not being yet *organized*, such of the domestics as remained at the pavilion, to complete the arrangement of the furniture, were obliged to sup at the auberge, in which may be seen the old engraving representing the chateau in its day of splendor, of which we have spoken in the first chapter of this work.

After the repast, they emptied a few bottles of the ordinary wine of the country, and the conversation becoming general, the chateau was introduced, and each was desirous of knowing how it happened that the Pavilion of the Guards had been respected, whilst a great part of the principal edifice had been destroyed. An old man, whose round and hearty physiognomy, and respectable rotundity, bespoke perfect health, took up the subject in his turn, and expressed himself as follows:

"I am, perhaps, the only man who can at the present moment satisfy your curiosity. I am now nearly eighty years of age. I was born at the chateau, and I left it only in 1792, so that I know many things of which the country is ignorant; and it is one of these events which I am going to narrate to you."

Every one drew near to the old man, who took a glass of wine, which he emptied at one gulp, and continued thus:

"My father, Pierrot Coquardon, was the gardener of the chateau; he was a tall and handsome youth, and loved by all the girls of the neighbourhood; and many a time did the pretty marchionesses honour him by a familiar touch on the cheek with their ivory fans, which did not prevent his dying when I was but seven years old.

"My poor mother soon followed him to the tomb.

"Left alone in the world, I was about to be conducted to the hospital for the Enfants trouvès, when Father Kerval, an old Breton, who was the Swiss of the chateau for a long time, received me, and brought me up with as much care as though I had been his own child.

"When he died, I was a young and handsome galliard, of five feet eight inches, and stout in proportion, so that I had not much trouble in succeeding to his place.

"You should have seen how I looked in grand uniform, laced hat, royal blue habit, covered with gold lace, red plush breeches, silk stockings of the same colour, shoes with silver buckles, and all the et ceteras; and what handsome epaulettes, my

children! they would have shamed those of a lieutenant-general of the king's armies! So, the young girls and the pretty women of the canton called me the handsome Swiss! the amiable Swiss! Alas! it is some time since then, and I am much changed, besides you cannot see it."

And the old man, in finishing this little exordium, rose up to show to his auditors how much he had preserved of his noble carriage, and his former graces.

"At the period of which I am speaking," he continued, passing his hand under his chin, "there happened on a sudden, to our beautiful France, a total overthrow, in comparison with which the revolution which took place a few years ago, is really nothing at all. So that, a short time after the taking of the Bastile, a superb fortress, situated at the entrance of the fabourg Saint-Antoine, all our masters took flight to rejoin, among strangers, our good princes, who had previously left; and as the greatest part of them were accompanied by their domestics, I remained alone in the chateau, with a young man named Louis Tristan, called the '*Bit of Love*,' who had been a fifer in the French Guards.

"The authors of the overthrow I have mentioned, were Messieurs the *Sans-Culottes*. They came here to organise what they called a '*popular society*,' and they recommended me to take great care of every thing in the chateau; this, my children, was truly a useless piece of advice, for there remained nothing at this time in the poor chateau: the Messieurs Sans-Culottes of the country and villages in the neighbourhood, had visited it before those from Paris; they had carried off every thing which seemed to them worth the taking, and had afterwards burned the remainder, drank the wine, and broke the windows and doors.

"Messieurs the Sans-Culottes from Paris, who, no doubt, had come here to do that which their comrades of the country had already achieved, appeared not greatly satisfied to find the work finished, and it was, no doubt, to revenge themselves, that they undertook to change every thing here as they had done at Paris.

"I must tell you that these messieurs would allow nothing to remain as it had existed before their time; the white cockade was replaced by the tricolour. It was no longer permitted to wear powder, nor to sport the royal bird. One of them, who was called, I think, Fabre d'Eglantine, a very droll name for a Sans-Culotte, changed the whole calendar; there were years and months after the fashion of the republic, with the decades in the place of the holy sabbath, and the complimentary days at the end of the year; the brumaire, the nivose, fructidor, and pracrial, to replace the months, so that it was totally impossible to recognise any thing at all. They even replaced in the almanac the names of the saints by the names of fruits, vegetables, and instruments of husbandry; *Saint Onion* took the place of *Saint Louis*; *Saint Girkin* usurped that of *Saint Joseph*; *Sainte Madeline* was very ungallantly turned out by *Saint Pruning Knife*, and so on. It was neither permitted any one to be named Peter, Boniface, or Nicholas; it was required to give one's children the names of the ancient Roman Sans-Culottes, and call them Brutus, Horatius-Cocles, or Mutius Scevola; they even went so far as to remove from Paradise the good and Holy Virgin, Mother of God, to put in her place the goddess of liberty, a certain Theroigne de Mirecourt, who, it was asserted, was no virgin at all.

LIFE IN PARIS.

EDMUND DE BOURGREL PROTECTING EUGENIE DE MABEL FROM THE COUNT DE D——

"The churches were transformed into temples of reason, in which the priests, after the fashion of the republic, said masses, of which nothing was understood; after which, they danced the sarabands, minuets, and country dances, before the holy altar, to the tunes of the *Carmagnole* and *Ca ira!* Very droll tunes, my children, which spoke of nothing but killing and cutting the throats of every one, and of suspending the aristocrats to the lanterns.

"When I say that Messieurs the Sans-Culottes had changed every thing, both great and small, I am not imposing on you; they had even changed the games of the cards, so that, when you played at piquet with a friend, you no longer said fifth to an ace, or sixteenth to the lady; but fifth to the *law*, or sixteenth to *liberty*. 'Twas required for every one to say thee and thou: there was no longer masters or valets, those were become officious citizens. It had arrived at such a point, that, if by chance, Madame de Pompadour, the Marchioness de Pompadour! had returned to the chateau, I should have been compelled to address her with thee and thou, as I might to a cow-keeper; at length they wished to make a new sun from the moon, and dethrone Almighty God, as they had dethroned the good king, Louis the Sixteenth, and his august wife."

Arrived at this part of his recital, the good Father Coquardon, from respect, took off the large cap of brown wool which covered his long white hair, a movement which was followed instinctively by all his listeners.

"Messieurs the Sans-Culottes, who had made such great changes," continued Father Coquardon, after a short pause, "could not, however, manage to change the march of time, which crept on the same, so that it often rained, when they wished to see the sun shine to celebrate the *Feast of Reason*, of *Liberty*, or any other fête à la mode republic; so that, not being enabled to transform either God or his saints, who were too distant and too high to be reached by them, they exhausted their rage on their images, which they burned and dragged in the mire.

"One might really say, that all these messieurs of the republic were turned madmen. Furious at not being enabled to dethrone the Almighty from his Paradise, they threw themselves upon the nobles and the priests; they guillotined all those they could entrap; they hoped, by thus acting, to destroy religion, and render every man as wicked as themselves, in order to deliver them afterwards to Satan, with whom, they said, they had made a compact. But the Almighty, and the Holy Virgin, prevented these grand crimes, and Messieurs the Sans-Culottes have been nearly all guillotined in their turn; even their chief, M. de Robespierre, the most wicked of the band, although he was always very suitably dressed; a dark blue habit, canary-coloured breeches, and white waistcoat, powdered and *coiffé* with the royal bird, and the rest consistently

"These men, who had plundered all the property of honest men, sold it for vile *assignats* to persons who had no objection to enrich themselves at the expense of others. The chateau of Choisy, like many others, was purchased by some unknown individuals, who travelled over the whole of France, buying the chateaus which they demolished, in order to sell the materials. At this period, I was no longer Swiss, they called me in the country nothing more than the *citizen concierge*, which, you may well believe, vexed me not a little, for we do

not easily renounce the *honours and dignities* we have once enjoyed.

"These individuals made a regular hash of the chateau. In the first place, they carried off the lead and iron, and sold a part of it for at least double the price they had given for the whole. At length came the turn of the Pavilion of the Guards, which they had preserved till the last moment, in order to lodge themselves during the demolition.

"The first blows of the axes were directed towards the demolishing a grating which defended the entrance on the side of the chateau, and the four workmen charged with this work, made a hole, in order to remove a post which prevented them raising a large stone. After some laborious efforts, the post yielded to the united strength of these men, and discovered a trap door, covered with a thick bed of rust. Hoping to find a treasure in it, they concerted amongst themselves, and it was agreed that, for the present, they should occupy themselves with something else; that they should mention to no one their precious discovery; and that they should not return to their hole, except at night, in order to explore, at their ease, and without the fear of being disturbed; they took care to cover the trap with earth and gravel, and then adjourned to the cabaret, to celebrate, by anticipation, their happy discovery.

"Each made his own supposition, and built castles in the air; they saw themselves already possessors of immense treasures, and their only fear was, that the commissioners of the nation would despoil them of it; and they adopted, in their wisdom, some sagacious line of conduct, so as not to awaken suspicions, and to transport to their domiciles the chests which were to contain the treasure they already possessed in imagination. They drank for a considerable time, and the fumes of the wine already began to mistify their brains, when the twelfth hour of the night sounded; 'We must go,' said one of them, 'it is time;' they then armed themselves with tools and pickaxes, which they thought necessary for their midnight expedition, and started bravely for their destination.

"Arrived at the ground, and lighted simply by the feeble light of a candle, they commenced, by ridding the place of the gravel and earth which they had heaped upon it. They then endeavoured to raise the trap, but their first efforts were in vain. It was not until after great exertion that it yielded, and discovered a second trap; the latter was secured on the exterior by an enormous bolt. It was no trifling affair to draw this bolt, the rust had so fixed it into the staple, that it seemed impossible to move it; so that it was only from the heavy blows of a hammer, that three of the workmen, whom the fourth lighted by the candle held in his hand, contrived to make it slide on the metal. At length the trap was opened. At the same moment, a bluish flame rushed from the yawning gulf, and the four unfortunate workmen fell dead, as though they had been struck by lightning!

"The next morning, other workmen, charged, like those whose unfortunate end I have mentioned, to take away the lead and iron, found the bodies of their four comrades in the hole, which the latter had dug the evening before; they were not wounded; there was simply remarked on the features and on their hands, traces nearly similar to those left by electricity; this extraordinary death threw a consternation over the whole country; it was immediately said that these workmen had been struck by fire from Heaven, who was angered at the demolition of the noble dwellings of France. It is as well to add, that whenever the blow of a pickaxe is given on this side, there are heard heavy moanings, which seem to come from the cave where the four workmen found their death, in place of the treasure they expected; all the inhabitants of the country, that is, all who believed in God and venerated the saints, heard these groans, so much so, that from this day, no one has attempted to demolish the pavilion. The new proprietors of the chateau had kindly permitted me to occupy a small chamber situate above the old lodging of the Swiss, and I had often found occasion to render them some slight services. As much to oblige me, as to please the gentry of the country, who did not regard them with a very friendly eye, and who were attached to the pavilion, simply for this—that some spirits returned there, who would have wandered about the country, if they had been deprived of the retreat they had chosen for their dwelling—they determined not to bring from Paris persons who would willingly have done that which the country people would not do, and to leave the pavilion to its peaceful existence.

"You see, messieurs, how it is that the Pavilion of the Guards has not been demolished; this miracle has been attributed to the powerful intercession of an almoner of Madame de Pompadour, who died in the odour of sanctity, and who was, it is said, interred in the cave, under the pavilion; it is this holy almoner, then, who has preserved the pavilion, and who has killed the four men who attempted to disturb his ashes."

Servants, for the most part, are not very religious; but, in revenge, they are nearly as superstitious as criminals; those of Salvador, submitted to the customary law, so that the recital which Father Coquardon had made them, had produced a certain impression on their spirits; one of them, however, who wished to show his bravery and his boasting, pretended that he had no more fear of devils than of holy almoners, and that if either the one sort or the other had the least power, they had only to show it to him; that he waited for them with a firm heart; and similar fanfarronades.

After squeezing the hand, however, of the old Coquardon, and drinking the stirrup-glass, it being necessary to quit the cabaret to return to the pavilion, this brave worthy would not retire to sleep alone, and repaired to the stable to find the coachman.

The next morning Roman came to examine if the instructions, given by him the evening before, had been executed, and if every thing was in complete order; he congratulated the domestics he had brought to the pavilion, and retired, quite satisfied, after seeing that the apartments were in a state to receive a gay and numerous company.

In fact, whilst the fine weather lasted, Salvador gave fêtes, and received, at his country house, all the elite of Parisian society; but the moment the winter appeared, he made but rare visits, and only in the evening, and to bring the produce of some robbery, which he did not wish to get rid of immediately. It is thus that, in the first chapter of this work, we have seen him bring there, in company with Roman, the jewels and bijouterie stolen from the unfortunate jeweller, Loiseau, who had at length been stripped by the triumvirate, after having been long kept in play.

The reader, no doubt, remembers, that the Viscount de Lussan would not receive more than 10,000 francs, as his share of the robbery, the value of which was nearly 50,000 francs; such, in fact, was the ordinary mode of acting of this extraordinary personage; the viscount was contented with a share much less considerable than his accomplices, but this part he wished, as we have already said, to receive at once, and in silver or bank notes.

Now that we are returned to our point of departure, we will take it up, where we left our recital, which shall meet with no more interruptions, except to inform our readers of what happened to Servigny, from the moment he quitted Salvador and Roman, after the combat with the gendarmes of the brigade of Beausset, until the time at which we shall again meet with him.

A personage (Ronquetti, called the Duke of Modena) whose name we have already several times mentioned, and whom we have not yet brought forward, will be charged to inform our readers of the events, which, from the Isles of Hyerès, where Silvia made the acquaintance of Beppo, conducted her to the Grand Theatre of Marseilles.

If the reader is now willing to follow us, we shall take him to the Rue Saint Lazare, near that of Saint George's, and we shall request him to enter the hotel of the Count de Neuville, where we shall again find the Countess Lucie de Neuville, and Laura de Beaumont, who, no doubt, have not been forgotten.

CHAPTER XX.

MATHEO.

As we have observed, the Countess Lucie de Neuville could learn nothing from the domestic whom Salvador had charged to deliver the little packet, containing the case she had lost at Sans Refus's, and the small note which accompanied it.

The return of this case proved to the countess that her conjectures were partly right. By this it was certain that the man, who at first had caused her so much fear, was a man of the world, and that she would probably meet him, at an early day, if she were to believe the contents of the note she had received.

Laura, who up to this moment had endeavoured, by all the means possible, to calm the fears of her friend, began to share them; but, from a wish not to increase the anxiety of the countess, who for some instants appeared buried in profound and painful reflections, she did not wish it to appear.

"There is, really, in all this, something inexplicable," said Lucie, at length, who had several times already commented on the terms of the note she held in her hand; "if this note, as every thing seems to prove, has been written by a man of good society, why has he not signed it? Why was this man in such a place, dressed in a costume which is not that of his class? Why did he address me in unqualified language, before knowing to whom he was speaking?"

Laura, who had listened to the countess with much attention, rose suddenly from the seat she occupied, and striking her hands against each other:

"But what tells you," she exclaimed, "that this man, who has so frightened you, is really the same who has sent you the case? May not this case have fallen into the hands of some other person? for example, into those of one of the persons whom your cries attracted to the cavern, at the moment we escaped?"

"You are mistaken, my dear Laura," replied the countess, "this note, which I have read more than ten times, has certainly been written by the man I speak of; the terms in which it is couched, also proves it."

And Lucie read, to her friend, the note in question, accompanying each line with remarks, which proved that she was not mistaken.

Laura was at length compelled to believe such evidence.

"In fact," she said, "I now believe that this note is written by this man; but, after all, what have you to fear? nothing obliges you to conceal the circumstances which took you to this house; so, even supposing that this man might have some evil design, I do not see that you have any great cause to fear him."

Lucie was about replying to her friend, when Paolo announced Doctor Matheo. The countess gave directions that he should be shown into the saloon.

The doctor appeared much older than he really was; he was but thirty-five years of age, and yet his head was nearly bald, and the few black hairs which still remained at its posterior portion, were mixed with some silvery threads. Troubles, remorse, or study, had lined with deep furrows a face, which seemed also covered with a dark cloud. In the total, however, Doctor Matheo was not a man of an ungraceful aspect; he expressed himself with elegance and facility; and, thanks to his profound intelligence, and the austerity of his manners, during the five years he had fixed himself at Paris, where he had established himself after quitting the naval service, in which he had been long employed, and in which he had commenced his career, he had acquired a practice, composed of the most recherché families, and by whom he was much beloved.

After taking off the dressings he had applied the evening before to the wound of the countess, which was a very slight one, and in a healthy state, he was about to retire, after exchanging with Lucie the ordinary chit-chat, when the countess, who still held in her hand the little note she had received, inquired if he knew the name of the person to whom the coat of arms, impressed upon the seal, belonged?

"I cannot, at this moment, satisfy you," replied the doctor, after attentively examining the seal; "but if, as the appearance of these arms indicate, they belong to an ancient family, it will not be difficult to find his name, and if it will do you the slightest pleasure, Madame la Comtesse, I will willingly undertake to discover it."

Lucie, driven by a curiosity which she could not explain to herself, was determined to ascertain what she was at present ignorant of; and she replied to the doctor that he would be rendering her an important service if he could manage to discover the name of the person to whom the seal belonged, which she tore from the letter and handed to the doctor. She even added that if, after discovering it, he would obtain some information as to the person, his position in the world, indeed any thing which might enable her to form some opinion of him, he would greatly oblige her.

"What you require of me will not be very difficult," added Matheo; "I shall infallibly discover the name of the person in question, by consulting either the *Armorial de France*, the *Tresor des Chartres*, or the Herald's College; the rest will

follow, and I shall be delighted to have found this occasion of being useful to you."

The countess, now that she was assured that the doctor would endeavour to pierce the sort of mystery which enveloped the circumstance which had happened to her, became much calmer; she now inquired of him some news respecting the poor Eugenie de Mirbel, to whom, from the directions she had given him, at his first visit to dress her wound, he ought already to have visited. Matheo informed her that the young person had passed a very good night, and that he could assure her that she would recover her health; he even thought that she might now be removed to a maison de santé.

Lucie had at first intended to place her friend in one of these establishments, but, as she remarked, since she was about to do a good action, she might as well make it complete, and that she would do much better to engage a small lodging, and furnish it, into which her friend could be removed at once, and where, with great attention, she would recover much quicker. Afterwards, assisted by friends, who would not be wanting, (for she was too well aware of the noble heart of her husband, to doubt that he would approve what she might do,) Eugenie could wait, until she had, by the use of the numerous talents she possessed, obtained a creditable and independent position.

"I regret, very much, that I cannot go out," she said, after informing the doctor of her intentions, who approved of them, without reserve; "I would undertake this affair at once, for my poor friend cannot remain longer in the miserable attic she has at present; and I do not wish to charge with it any of the persons whom I know, who are all moving in the same society in which Mademoiselle de Mirbel has lived, and are mostly known to her."

"If you think me worthy of your confidence, I will readily take charge of these proceedings, which you could not yourself do, for some days," replied the doctor. "I have not the honour of knowing Mademoiselle de Mirbel, but I think she is quite deserving of your efforts for her, and I shall be most glad to associate myself, as far as you will allow me, in such a good action."

"I recognise yourself there, doctor," said the countess, "you are neither sparing of your time, nor, as I am assured, of your purse, when it concerns the being useful to any one."

"I do what lies in my power to obtain a pardon of God for the faults I have committed," replied the doctor, whose visage was covered by a passing cloud, when the Countess de Neuville had addressed the few words to him we have reported.

"Do you know, M. Matheo," added Laura, who had recovered all the amiable gaiety of her character, since her friend had appeared more tranquil; "do you know that to see you sometimes so sad, you, who are esteemed and beloved by every one, and have no complaint to make against fortune, who treats you, as I am assured, like a spoiled child; one might be led to suppose that you have committed some great faults, and that you are tormented by remorse."

The words of Laura had, without any intention on her part, created a violent storm in the heart of Doctor Matheo, and an expression of bitter discouragement passed rapidly over his features.

"To God, alone," he said, "belongs the right of teaching me, whether some of the actions of my life are, or not, great crimes. But we are wandering very far from the subject which ought to occupy us," he added, making an effort to smile.

"Without doubt," continued Laura, laughing cheerfully; "but be assured, Monsieur the Doctor, I have not supposed you were a great criminal, I only wished to make a sort of war against you; because I do not like to see you always so sorrowful, and that I am sorry you neglect us for other patients."

Laura, in finishing this sentence, had glanced at her friend with a look of intelligence.

"Laura is right," added the countess, "you neglect us, M. the Doctor."

"I do not really understand you, madame."

"I mean to say, that as you consecrate your whole time to the poor patients, there remains none for your clients who have the misfortune to be rich."

"I will find some, madame, you may be assured, to do whatever may be agreeable to you."

And Doctor Matheo left, after promising the two ladies that he would go at once, and busily occupy himself about the missions he had been charged with.

The next morning he returned to the countess, who waited for him with the greatest impatience.

"Well!" she said to him, the moment he was introduced into the small saloon.

"Your friend, Madame la Comtesse," replied Doctor Matheo, "is now in a small lodging, but healthy and commodious; and I have left with her, to give her such attentions as are necessary, a nurse upon whom I can rely: for she seems to have a great affection for Mademoiselle de Mirbel, who is also much attached to her, as she would not be separated from her: 'tis the same old woman, she told me, who brought here the letter which informed you of her unhappy situation. I mentioned to Mademoiselle de Mirbel the reason of your not seeing her, she seemed greatly afflicted at the accident which happened to you; but as I assured her that there was nothing serious in it, and that in a few days you would be enabled to go out, without inconvenience, she became calmer. For the rest, I am now convinced that Mademoiselle de Mirbel requires nothing to complete her recovery, but quietness and care, which, thanks to you, madame, will not be wanting to her."

"And so this poor Eugenie," said Laura, "is no longer in that villainous little room, so naked, and so dilapidated."

"She wants nothing?" continued Lucie; "you have provided her lodging with every thing necessary?"

And as the doctor replied, that, to arrange the affair comfortably, he had had nothing to do, but follow, to the letter, the instructions of his patient, the countess.

"Oh! there are many things, necessary to a woman, but which a man never thinks of, and so I'll wager that you have not thought of a cradle for her little girl."

"You are mistaken, Madame la Comtesse: at the present moment, the little daughter of your friend sleeps very quietly in as pretty a cot as you would wish to see."

"That's right, doctor, that's right," added Laura, extending her neat little hand to Doctor Matheo, who took it in his own, his eyes, at the same time, moistening with the tears he could not restrain.

"Why," said Lucie, "do you seek to hide the tear, which is a proof of the sensibility of your heart? are men thus made, that when they feel a virtuous sentiment, they fear to let it appear in it?"

The doctor took no notice of this observation of the countess; as it often happened, he remained several instants buried in profound sadness.

"Come, Lucie," said Laura, "are you not again wounding this good doctor, who has taken so much trouble to oblige us?"

"Ah! I hope not," said the countess, "but I am so happy in knowing that our poor friend is now quite out of danger, and that she wants for nothing, that I know not what I say."

"I wish I was married," said Laura suddenly, and in a deliberate tone.

"Eh! and why? Grand Dieu!" exclaimed the countess, "are you not happy with me, that you are in such a hurry to quit me?"

"I do not say that, but if I were married I could go and come, without its appearing strange; and, as I am not wounded, I could easily find a moment to go and see the poor Eugenie de Mirble."

The countess gently clasped the head of her friend, and kissed her on the forehead.

"Listen," she said, after this sweet pressure, "the doctor assures me that, in two or three days, I shall be enabled to go out, and you may be certain that my first visit shall be to our friend; well! and I promise you that you shall accompany me."

"Quite true!" exclaimed Laura. "Ah! but you are kind, my dear Lucie;" and the young girl returned, with usury, the caresses she had received.

Neither Laura nor the countess spoke to the doctor respecting the second commission with which he had been charged; the two charming women were happy in the good they had effected, and the pleasure they felt caused them to forget the object, which, two days before, had so strongly excited their curiosity.

"Do you think, by chance, that I have neglected one of the two missions you confided to me, since you do not speak to me about it?" said the doctor, drawing the seal from his pocket.

"It's true, doctor," replied the countess, "but I am happy in knowing that my poor friend is out of danger, and not quite so unhappy, and forget my own troubles; well, are you aware to what family belong the arms of this seal?"

"These arms are those of a very noble and very ancient family of Provence, that of de Pourrieres; and it is certain that this seal has been impressed by M. the Marquis Alexis de Pourrieres, the only member who exists at the present day."

"'Tis singular!" said, at the same time, Laura and the countess, and they exchanged a look of intelligence, which was a faithful translation of their thoughts.

"And is it known what sort of a man is this Marquis de Pourrieres?"

"The Marquis de Pourrieres, if we may believe many of my patrons, whose word I have no reason to doubt, is a gentleman as noble of heart as of family; he came to reside at Paris about two years ago, and immediately, thanks to the recommendations he brought from his province, he was received into the first saloons; when he quitted Provence he was Commandant of the National Guard of his district, Knight of the Legion of Honour, and has been appointed Auditor to the Council of State; he is rich, still young, and he might, they say, pretend to any thing. For some time he has been much troubled at the loss of a lady he was about to marry; according to report, this lady, who is named the Marchioness de Roselly, has disappeared, without its being known what has become of her: the efforts which the marquis has made, and has caused to be made, and the endeavours of the police, have been in vain. As I have had the honour of telling you, the marquis, for a long period, has been much afflicted, but at present he is, if not quite consoled, at least nearly so; it is said that he intends being married, which will not be a matter of difficulty, for there is not a father who would not be glad to bestow the hand of his child upon such a gallant man."

All that the doctor had said, had plunged Lucie and Laura into the greatest astonishment; this man, so noble in race and character, so rich, so well placed in society, the countess had encountered in one of the most infamous places of the capital; he appeared quite at his ease, and he was habited in a costume in perfect keeping with the tone, the manners, and the language, which he had assumed for a certain period; this was a strange mystery, a mystery in which Lucie was mixed up, and which it was her interest (at least she thought so) to penetrate. Laura, on her side, although she did not attach so much importance to the event as her friend, would not have been displeased to see this singular marquis, who walked the streets of Paris dressed in a costume, which, in her opinion, must render him frightfully ugly.

The two women, both governed by the same sentiment, curiosity, (and where is the daughter of Eve, who, whatever may be the virtues she possesses, is not somewhat curious?) regarded each other in silence.

Laura was the first to break silence.

"I guess," she said to her friend, "that which you are afraid to say to me; you have a mind to ask me if we must confide to our good doctor the circumstance of the street de la Tannerie?"

Lucie made an affirmative sign.

"Eh! bon Dieu! I see nothing to the contrary; this event might have happened to any one, and there is nothing in all this which you ought to conceal. You will do wisely, after all, to take the advice of a man who has a sufficient interest in us to render us a service, if necessary; and who is quite experienced enough to say if you do right to trouble yourself, or whether you are not making a monster of a mere chimera."

The Countess de Neuville felt that her friend was right; it was not, however, until she had hesitated for some time, that she determined to narrate to Doctor Matheo what had happened to her, two days before, in the cabaret of la Sans Refus, in consequence of the wound she had received on leaving the house of Eugenie de Mirbel.

The doctor, who had listened to the countess with much attention, replied to her, that, in fact, she ought not to fear the consequences of this event; and added, that it was not probable that the man, who for some moments she had to complain of, and the Marquis de Pourrieres, were one and the same individual.

"You have mentioned," he said, "that at the moment when, accompanied by your friend, you had escaped from this receptacle, your cries had attracted several persons; is it not possible that the Marquis de Pourrieres was among them, and that it was he who picked up your case, and who has sent it to you?"

And as the countess, having to defend her opinion against the doctor and her friend, who had ranged herself on the side of the latter, persisted in maintaining that the man in the costume of a sailor and the Marquis de Pourrieres were the same individual, since it was the latter who had sent her the card-case, the doctor added:

"Listen, Madame la Comtesse, if it is really the Marquis de Pourrieres whom you have encountered in this cabaret, and you appear so convinced of it, that I have no longer the right to doubt it, there is certainly, in this event, something of the mysterious, and which it will be as well to clear up; since you have been so much struck with this man, you ought to remember his features, endeavour to describe them to me, I will visit the Marquis de Pourrieres, upon some pretext—for your name must not be mentioned in all this, and I will soon inform you whether your conjectures have any foundation."

"And you think," replied the countess, "that you can, without any disagreeable result, either to yourself or me, pay a visit, without motive, to the Marquis de Pourrieres?"

"I repeat, madame, that your name shall not be pronounced, so that you have really nothing to fear; as to what regards myself, be under no uneasiness, we doctors have the privilege of introducing ourselves everywhere, without exciting suspicions."

The countess described to the doctor the man whom she believed to be the Marquis de Pourrieres; and, in the portrait she drew of him, confined herself to the regularity and beauty of his features, the winning tone of his voice, and the perfect elegance of his manners, when he had changed his tone and language.

The doctor listened attentively to the Countess de Neuville, who, without being aware of it, had used expressions, which seemed to imply, that this encounter would not have so strangely preoccupied her, if the man she was speaking of had not made a lively impression on her imagination.

Women are for the most part thus organized; endowed with an imagination richer, and more active than that of men, they are readily attracted by any circumstance which travels beyond the ordinary limits; and it is not rare to find them extending towards men placed considerably beneath them in society, a morbid feeling of sympathy, which soon transforms itself into a more tender sentiment, and of a more determined nature, when unforeseen events do not intervene, and provide fresh nourishment to the incessant activity of the imagination.

Doctor Matheo only left the Countess de Neuville to repair to the Marquis de Pourrieres, whose address he easily procured.

When he was announced, Salvador and Roman were together, in the cabinet we have already described. This name—Doctor Matheo, pronounced by the domestic charged to announce persons desirous of being admitted, caused Salvador and Roman to start in their seats, and they regarded each other for some instants, without speaking. Salvador was the first to break silence.

"Doctor Matheo!" said he; "what do you think of this visit? is it, by chance, the Matheo whom we know?"

"'Tis probable; this name is not a common one."

"You think, then, that we are discovered?"

"I fear so; but after all we have nothing to dread; if Matheo knows a part of our secrets, we are acquainted with the whole of his."

"Request him to enter," said Salvador to the domestic; "we shall know directly," he continued, addressing Roman, "if we are to fear the results of this visit."

Matheo, on being introduced into the cabinet, recognised at once Roman, whom he knew more intimately, and for a much longer period than Salvador, whom he had never seen, except during the short stay at the prison of Toulon. He was immediately seized with such a surprise, that, for some moments, he had not the strength to utter a word. From Roman his regards wandered towards Salvador, whom he examined attentively, and whom he soon recognised, despite the change which time had made in his physiognomy, and the colour of his hair, which, as the reader knows, was now black, whereas it was formerly fair.

The astonishment manifested at first by the doctor, had not escaped the two friends; they naturally concluded that when he visited the Marquis de Pourrieres he had no expectation of seeing the two forçats, whose evasion he had facilitated some years before; but now they were recognised, they could no longer doubt of it, the disguise was no longer useful. Let us add, that they feared but little the results of this discovery, seeing that Matheo, admitting it to be his intention, could not ruin them without ruining himself. They thought it best, therefore, to meet the question, and it was Roman who, after consulting Salvador by a look, first began the conversation with Doctor Matheo.

"Well, my old friend," he said, "when you were announced to M. the Marquis de Pourrieres, you did not expect to meet with this noble gentleman such ancient acquaintances?"

"It is true," replied the doctor, who was not quite recovered from the surprise he had received; "it is true;" and yielding to a movement of despair he could not restrain, the doctor buried his head in his two hands.

"Is he turned virtuous, by chance?" said Roman, in a whisper, pointing to Doctor Matheo, who seemed completely overwhelmed.

"We must find out," replied Salvador.

"Well, Matheo," replied Roman, "you say nothing to us, one might really believe that you are sorry at having met us again?"

"'Tis true," replied the unhappy doctor, "I say nothing to you, but I confess that I was so astonished at seeing you here, that surprise at first deprived me of speech; and then, this new name, under which Salvador is known at present——"

"That name is my own," exclaimed Salvador.

"Oh! I do not deny it," replied the doctor, "I think, however, that I cannot say to him, whom I have known under the name of Salvador, that which was destined for the Marquis de Pourrieres. There remains nothing for me but to retire; Roman is aware of secrets which might ruin me, and no doubt he has confided them to you. You are then the only man in the world whom I have to fear; but, if my life is in your hands, your liberty is at my disposition; we have no occasion, therefore, to make mutual promises, the interest we have to conduct ourselves cautiously, will be a security for each of us. We have, both of us, by means which have appeared to us the most convenient, acquired an elevated position in the world, let us each, then, depart our own way, without attempting to meet again, and may God conduct us all in the path we have chosen."

And, finishing these words, Matheo rose to depart.

"I think you are right," said Salvador to Roman, while the doctor approched the door; "he is become virtuous, very virtuous, indeed! but leave me alone with him; I must absolutely know the motive which brought him here. Stay," he said, raising his voice, and addressing Matheo, who had not heard what was said between him and Roman, "I wish to speak with you;" and at a sign, Roman retired.

"Listen, Matheo," said Salvador, when he found himself alone with the doctor, "I should not like you to quit me with the idea that the lessons of the past have been lost upon me; you know what were the faults which led me to the prison, at Toulon; and how, thanks to your assistance, which you lent to Roman, rather than to me, I contrived to escape. Actively pursued, after the event of Beausset, we were forced to take refuge in the forest of Cujes, and associate with the band commanded by the brothers Bisson.

" 'Twas not until after numerous accidents, that I contrived to leave France. After passing two years out of the kingdom, having heard of the death of my father, who had remained ignorant of the faults, or rather the crimes I had committed; for it was luckily under a feigned name that I had been condemned, I hastened to take possession of my estates, and when I had put all my affairs in order, I came and fixed myself in Paris, and by my exemplary conduct, I am bold enough to say, I have endeavoured to blot from my memory the crimes of my past life; when I met with Roman, whom I had quitted after the singular death of all the men who composed the band of the brothers Bisson." Arrived at this point of his recital, Salvador hesitated a few moments, and steadily regarded Matheo, whose face was covered with a profuse perspiration, and who was visibly in deep trouble.

"Roman was miserable," continued Salvador, without appearing to notice the trouble of his listener; "I had reason to fear him, and he promised me to conduct himself well for the future; his arguments induced me to receive him into my house, and give him the place of the major-domo, whom I had lost; but I ought to add, since he has lived with me, I have been quite satisfied with his services. You see, then, my dear Matheo, by my example, by that of Roman, by your own even," added Salvador, lowering his voice, "that after committing great faults, it is still possible to follow the right path."

"I do not know," replied Matheo, "what may be the motive which has induced you to make me this confidence; however, I believe you, I wish to believe you; but since you seem desirous of convincing me; tell me what you did, three days ago, dressed in a costume which is not your own, in one of the most infamous kennels of the capital?"

This question, which was unexpected, greatly astonished Salvador. Was Matheo aware of the circumstances of his new existence, and ought he to continue his disguise? He took the latter part, 'twas the surest, and he could at any time abandon it, if that became necessary.

"I know not how you have been made aware," he said, "that three days ago, habited, as you say, in a costume which does not belong to me, I was found in a disreputable house, in the Place de la Tannerie; but, however, I will not deny it. A few days ago, then, I went out alone on foot, by chance, and I was accosted by a man who was at the same time as myself at the prison of Toulon, in the cell No. 3. This man had recognised me, despite all the precautions I had taken to render my features unknown. I feared that he would follow me, in order to find my address, and hold me at his discretion. He did nothing of the sort; he accosted me, on the contrary, humbly; he told me

LIFE IN PARIS.

EUGENIE DISHONOURED.

he was very miserable; that as yet he had not robbed, but that he was pushed to the last extremity, and that the same evening, assisted by several individuals whom he was to meet in a place which he described, he was to commit a robbery. I wished to save this miserable from the dreadful fate which awaited him, if he committed this fresh crime, and as I had not about me a sum sufficient to place him beyond want, until such time as his work had procured him the means of an honest existence, I gave him a rendezvous to remit him the sum I intended. Such is the simple explanation of my presence in the establishment of the Rue de la Tannerie, and of my disguise."

Matheo was a little more tranquil, since he had listened to Salvador; the explanations which the latter had given him, were not destitute of probability.

Salvador, however, knew not as yet what were the motives which had brought the doctor to the Marquis de Pourrieres, and this was the object which interested him the most.

"And now, my dear Matheo," he said, "you will tell me, no doubt, what has induced you to visit me."

Matheo, driven into a corner, knew not how to act; he could no longer, after the confidence Salvador had shown him, refuse to satisfy him; and grieved him to speak of Madame de Neuville to a man against whom he could not help feeling some prejudice; but, from the interest he felt towards the countess, it was necessary to ascertain what was the motive of Salvador in writing the little note which he had sent to Madame de Neuville, a note certainly useless, if he had merely wished to send her the object she had lost; and if he had had no intention of entering into a more particular relation with her. He determined to speak of this lady with Salvador.

We think the moment is now arrived, in which we ought to make known to our readers the events of the life of Doctor Matheo, which have any connection with our history.

Matheo had scarcely attained his sixteenth year, when his father, who exercised at the town of La Vallette, in the island of Malta, the profession of a physician, committed a crime, from the effects of which he was compelled to quit the town, to escape the pursuits which were directed against him. This man was the most infamous scelerat it is possible to imagine, and the crime he had committed had been accompanied with circumstances so revolting, that the English government demanded his being given up, in whatever place he might be discovered, a demand which was willingly granted.

He had arrived in the neighbourhood of Aix, with much trouble, and by travelling on foot only, for he had not had time to furnish himself with passports, and he feared every instant to fall into the hands of the gendarmerie. However, he did not fancy himself in security in this part of France; he was desirous of gaining one of the small ports of the Mediterranean, where he should find means to embark, which he thought possible, as he was not without money, when himself and his son, whom he had brought with him, fell into the hands of two of the bandits who infested at this period the forest of Cujes, who robbed them of every thing they possessed, and conducted them to their chiefs, the brothers *Bisson*, rich cultivators of the Department of the Bouches-du-Rhone, who united the two professions of agriculturists and highway robbers.

He was indebted for his life to his son, who

several times threw himself before the knives directed against the bosom of his father, and whose courage and extreme youth had so interested the two bandits, that, being undecided as to assassinating a child, they carried him to their chiefs, that they might decide his fate. The father had profited by the sort of respite granted to the son, and a few minutes after, they were both before the brothers *Bisson* of Tretz.

Two bandits were to be arbitrators of the fate of a third bandit. Between men of the same stamp, it is easy to arrange matters. The Maltese perceived at once, that there was but one way by which he could escape a sudden fate, and that was to propose to the brothers Bisson to enrol himself in the band which they commanded; he did not hesitate; and to give them a proof that he was worthy to be one of their number, he confided to them the nature of the crime he had committed, a crime so horrible, that the brothers Bisson, whose hands had many a time already been dipped in human blood, were almost terrified at its narration. However, they could not refuse a fellow-labourer, in whom the events of his past life permitted them to place an unlimited confidence, and whose profession (Matheo had taken care to inform his future chiefs that he was a physician) might render important services to the troop, he was, therefore, unanimously accepted.

Matheo's son, too young as yet to comprehend all the infamy of the trade which his father had adopted, who had made him believe that he had quitted Malta in consequence of the part he had taken in a conspiracy which had been discovered, followed the fortune of the author of his being, and during a considerable period, took part in the expeditions of the band of the brothers Bisson.

But the young man, however, was not born for the infamous trade he exercised. As long as he had been very young, he followed, without attempting to account for the events of his life, the impulse which had been given him, not wishing to see any evil in the acts of his father, for whom he had preserved a profound respect. The brothers Bisson, desirous, in addition, not to wound the susceptibilities of the young man, had only employed him in enterprises of little importance, so that he had never been a witness of the shedding of blood. But time brought experience, and he very soon perceived that he was, in reality, neither more nor less than an infamous bandit.

His father was the man who, in the simplicity of youth, the young Matheo took as the confidant of his thoughts; he laughed at him and observed, that he had supposed up to the present moment that his son long since had got rid of the prejudices of his infancy; that he saw with pain that it was not so, but that he could do nothing in it; that if the life he led did not suit him, he could leave it. Matheo wished his father to leave with him; but the latter replied, laughing, "that he found himself very well where he was, and that it was not very amiable to endeavour to disgust persons with the position which pleased them."

The young Matheo then perceived, that, in order to leave the circle in which he found himself engaged, he must depend upon himself alone. He was not, however, discouraged, the present life of disorder was insupportable to him; he therefore took the resolution to seize the first favourable opportunity of making his escape.

But the brothers Bisson and the principals of the band, had remarked, that, for some time, he had been gloomy, preoccupied, and that he seized every pretext for not taking part in the expeditions. This conduct necessarily led to suspicions; they questioned the father, who, scelerat as he was, began to repent having led his child into the gulf into which he had thrown himself, and would say nothing as to the intentions of his son.

The latter, thus became, to the whole troop, an object of distrust and apprehension, when, one evening, the look-outs brought intelligence, that the diligence from Paris, which, for some time, the authorities of the country had provided with an escort, would soon pass, and that, contrary to all expectation, it was alone. The brothers Bisson, determined to profit by this lucky occasion, gave the order to the whole troop to arm themselves, and keep in ambuscade. Matheo would have employed the same means which had often hitherto succeeded with him, to pretend an indisposition, in order to excuse himself from taking any part in the expedition; but the brothers Bisson intimated to him, in a tone which admitted of no reply, the order to take his carbine and follow them; and his father, who, at the same moment passed before them, whispered him to obey without making any observations, as his comrades might otherwise be hasty with him.

Matheo was thus compelled to obey, and, a few minutes after, he was in ambush with the brothers Bisson, and the other bandits of the troop.

The diligence slowly advanced, impeded by the snow which had fallen for several days, and which, had clogged up the roads; it entered a part of the route bordered on each side with tall tufts of broom, behind which the whole band had concealed themselves, when the brothers Bisson, who expected to seize an easy prey, rushed to the horses' heads, whilst Matheo, the father, Roman, (who at this period composed one of the band,) and some others opened the doors, and intimated to the travellers an order to descend. They certainly did not expect the warm reception they met with; the diligence was filled with gendarmes in disguise, who saluted the bandits with an instantaneous discharge, and ran in pursuit of those who had not been wounded.

Matheo, who had, from the commencement of the action, kept himself as much in the background as possible, was struck by a spent ball, and fell upon the snow, dangerously wounded in the head, and quite deprived of his senses. He was the only man wounded, the balls had spared such as had not been killed. Favoured by their perfect knowledge of the country, and the obscurity of the night, the other bandits found it easy to escape the pursuit of those who had given them such a rough reception.

The gendarmes, quite convinced that all their efforts would be useless, rejoined the diligence, when one of them struck his foot against the wounded Matheo; he knelt down, and discovered that he still breathed. This was a precious capture; they might hope, if he recovered, to obtain some information from him, of a nature to put them in the track of the individuals who composed the band of the forest of Cujes; he was raised with the greatest care, his wounds were dressed by a gendarme a little more expert than the others, and carried with precaution to the coup of the diligence, which he did not quit, until he entered the prison at Aix.

He was literally between life and death; but, thanks to the attention bestowed upon him, (none are more carefully waited upon than those who are destined for the scaffold,) and perhaps also to his youth, and the vigour of his constitution, he recovered his health. Then commenced for him a long series of interrogatories, which, in the end, would have led him to the scaffold, and which he could not have escaped, except by giving information: a determination which he would have taken, perhaps, if the fear of compromising his father, who, according to all appearance, had remained with the brothers Bisson, had not prevented him.

As soon, therefore, as he recovered his strength, his first and only care was to seek the means of escaping from prison. It is no part of our plan to say how he contrived to succeed, and what were the events of his life up to the moment we find him as assistant-surgeon in the navy, and attached in this capacity to the hospital of the prison of Toulon; we shall merely say that this period of his life was visited with long and painful trials, and it was only from his strength of constancy, energy, and efforts almost supernatural, that he at length overcame his destiny, and surmounted obstacles before which an organization less vigorous than his, would have broken itself twenty times.

Time, and the troubles he had undergone, had so changed his features, that he might hope he should not be recognised by such of the band of the brothers Bisson, who, from chance or special grace, should be brought to the prison at Toulon; so that, when, after obtaining his nomination, he saw that all his efforts to obtain a change of residence were in vain, he resigned himself to the post which had been offered him. This modest employ was to him a port after continual storms, and we must say, the miserable man had spent nearly all his strength, in the terrible struggle he had maintained. His back was bent, his hair had turned nearly white, although it had been formerly black. "Heaven," he said to himself, "has no desire to subject me to fresh trials; have I not, great God! cruelly expiated the faults I have committed?" He deceived himself; he had not occupied his post many months, and already his zeal, his assiduity, the profound skill he had acquired, had obtained for him the esteem of his superiors, when Roman, who had left the band of the forest of Cujes to travel through life with Salvador, was brought to the prison with the latter.

Roman recognised at once his ancient companion, and directly perceived the use he might make of him. He seized upon the first occasion which presented itself, to converse with him alone, and after informing him that the band of the brothers Bisson, despite the numerous losses on the field of battle, was still flourishing, and that his father had been killed, with arms in his hands, a short time after the arrest of Matheo; he gave him to understand that he had no intention of remaining long in prison, and that he counted upon him to favour his evasion.

Matheo was obliged, at the risk of compromising himself, and losing a position painfully acquired, to do all that Roman demanded, who held suspended over his head the sword of Damocles. We have seen how Roman, Salvador, and Servigny, escaped, assisted by him, from the prison of Toulon, and how the two former rejoined, in the forest of Cujes, the band of the brothers Bisson.

Roman, like all who are too far advanced in the career of crime even to turn a look behind, could not behold, without a strong feeling of hatred, one of those, whom he had seen for an instant follow a path which he might continue all his life, endeavour to reconquer a position in society.

We are told by the Evangelist, that "There is more joy in heaven over one sinner that repenteth, than for ten just men who die in the faith." We may also be allowed to believe, although the Evangelist says nothing about it, that, in hell, there is more weeping and gnashing of teeth for one guilty person, who is saved, than for ten just ones who are condemned. It is the same in this world. The demons who cannot, whatever may be the efforts of their blind rage, clear the immense space which separates them from the kingdom of the elect, no doubt use all their endeavours to increase the population of their dismal abode; in the same way, there exist men—demons endowed with a human physiognomy, and Roman was one of them—who seek by all possible means to replunge into the abyss, those who attempt to leave it.

Roman, therefore, did not keep faith with the unfortunate Matheo; his first care, after rejoining the band of the forest of Cujes, was to inform the brothers Bisson what was become of their ancient companion. It was not long before Matheo felt the effects of this indiscretion; he was at first compelled to exercise his skill upon one of the miserables, who had been wounded in an encounter; he was then required to procure for a forçat all that was necessary to effect his escape. At length the demands of these desperadoes, increased with the facility of satisfying them, they desired that he would furnish them with such information as was necessary to enable them to commit a robbery in a chateau, in the neighbourhood of Toulon, in which he was received. The cup of misery was full to overflowing. The unhappy Matheo could no longer live under such a cruel restraint; he must either become openly the accomplice of these miserables, or, renouncing suddenly the position he had acquired, shamefully take flight, if he would not carry his head to the scaffold. The brothers Bisson had not concealed from him that they would denounce him, the first time he objected to obey their orders, and he knew well they were men who would keep their word. It was then, that he determined they should all perish; we have seen how he succeeded, and in what manner Roman and Salvador only escaped, by chance, this wholesale execution.

Let us hasten to add that Matheo, when he rendered himself guilty of this action, which may well be called a crime, had nearly lost his reason; for it was in this manner he argued, in order to justify it.

"The crimes of the author of my being, the encounter of the two bandits at the corner of the wood, circumstances, completely independent of my will, have brought me, still very young, into the midst of a band of scelerats; I have been almost trained up among them; I have been forced to listen to their discourse; to be the spectator, and sometimes the accomplice of their crimes; and yet, at an age at which we have not yet acquired proper notions of right and wrong, which would serve to regulate the conduct of a man formed to live in society, I have been enabled, partly, to resist the contagion of the example; I have never, voluntarily, taken my share in the depredations of my companions; my hands are free from the stain of my fellow-creatures' blood; and if, sometimes, it has been shed in my presence, I had not the power of preventing it. I have committed many faults, I will not deny it, but are these faults really my own? Ought they not rather to be imputed to the fatality which has not ceased pursuing me from my birth? Arrested in consequence of an affair in which I only acted the part of a spectator, and simply because I had been compelled to it, I have not betrayed my infamous companions. I have acquitted myself, then, of any obligations to them, and I have not demanded at their hands, (to escape from a dreadful fate, which, thanks to them, was reserved for me,) either assistance, succour, or protection.

"It was not until I had passed through every extreme of a most cruel existence; after having supported trials, before which the most intrepid man would have recoiled; that I have attained a position, less than modest, but which suffices for my desires. Well! this position they would deprive me of, by forcing me to renew with them the connection which has been broken by the irresistible force of events; but it is not simply my position, I have to defend; 'tis my honour, my life, which they now attack, and which I must defend. I am, then, at war with them, but it is not I that have declared this war; from which it follows, that my position is absolutely similar to that of a people, who, attacked by others, ten times more powerful than themselves, are compelled to employ, in order to preserve their nationality, those extreme measures, which the most cruel necessity will alone excuse or justify, I am, then, opposed to them, in a state of legitimate defence.

"If I were opposed to a single man, in a similar position to that in which I am at this moment with regard to several, what ought I to do? It is not difficult to find an answer to this question; this is what I should do: go and find this man, tell him what I have a right to say to him, provoke him, fight him; and if, assisted by the Almighty, I became the vanquisher, no one, I am convinced, would think of blaming me. But I cannot, in my position, do that which I might effect if I had but a single enemy to deal with; in fact, I cannot, without being mad, attack singly at least a dozen individuals—and yet these twelve individuals are my enemies; they have attacked me at the very moment I sought to forget them; and, if they do not perish, I must either commit crimes against which my conscience revolts, or resolve, not only to lose that which I have acquired by painful efforts and irreproachable conduct, but, also, submit to a cruel and ignominious death.

"The science I have acquired has placed at my disposal terrible weapons, not very courteous ones, to a certainty; but they are the only ones I can make use of, and those against whom I would employ them are infamous desperadoes, whose heads have long been the property of the executioner, and who will never make an effort to escape the fate with which they are menaced. I am but advancing their fatal hour a few days—perhaps a few months. But, may I usurp a right which only appertains to the Almighty; and, next to Him, to society, which is represented by the magistrates charged to apply the laws which regulate this right? No, certainly not; to God alone the right belongs to withdraw that which He alone has given; to society, that of punishing, humanly speaking, the crimes, committed by any of its members. But I do not pretend to play the game of Providence in this world, nor to set myself up as the avenger of outraged society; I only wish to do one thing—defend myself; and the right of self-defence is the most sacred, the most incontestible, of all rights. And besides, in ridding the world of such miserables, I save the lives of a number of fellow-beings."

Such were the pitiable sophisms by which Matheo attempted to justify the crime he had committed; but a crime committed, as we have said, at a moment when misfortune had deprived him of the free use of his faculties, and the remorse for which, even at the period at which we are now arrived, he still carried in his heart.

We have observed that Matheo had determined to speak to Salvador, respecting what had occurred between the latter and Madame de Neuville.

"A lady," he said to him, "who has kindly honoured me with her confidence, was conducted, in consequence of an accident which might have happened to any one, to the house in which, by chance, you happened to be; you permitted yourself, with regard to this lady—"

"Liberties which I deplore," replied Salvador, "but we were both buried in obscurity; I was not enabled to see the person with whom I spoke; I supposed, for an instant, that I was addressing one of the inhabitants of the house, and I was forced, in order not to excite suspicions, to assume the tone and manners of one of the individuals usually met with there; besides, this lady no doubt informed you, that, the moment I discovered my error, I hastened to excuse myself."

"It's true. It was you, then, who forwarded to this lady the small card-case, containing some cards, and two notes of a thousand francs, and who wrote the letter which accompanied this packet?"

"It was me."

"The terms of this note seem to indicate that you preserve some hope of again meeting this lady in society; is this, in fact, your intention?"

"You subject me, my dear Matheo, to an interrogatory, the disagreeable nature of which I willingly excuse in favour of the motive under which you are no doubt acting. I can assure you I have not the slightest intention respecting the Countess de Neuville; I sent her the card-case because I did not think it right to appropriate it, and the note which accompanied it was but a mere form of politeness. It is probable I shall not again see this lady, unless I meet her in society, which is doubtful; but I shall for ever preserve the remembrance of her gracious physiognomy, and a very sincere regret for having caused her so great a terror."

"A terror, in fact, very painful," replied Matheo, "and which the sight of a corpse, concealed under a sort of counter, near which she was sitting, greatly increased."

"You can, in order that she may be tranquillized, give her the assurance, that this corpse was not that of a man assassinated. The amphitheatre, although well provided, does not constantly furnish to the laborious students, and to some of our medical celebrities, a sufficient quantity of subjects; so, in order to procure them, they have adopted the plan of addressing themselves to some industriels, who steal, during the night, from the cemeteries, such bodies as may suit their patrons. Some of these industriels assemble in the establishment in question; and it was, no doubt, one of the objects of their commerce which they had disposed of there for a short time, not finding a more immediate place, which has so greatly frightened Madame the Countess de Neuville."*

Salvador had just finished this short recital, when Roman entered the cabinet, without being announced.

"I must ask your pardon," he said, "for interrupting your conversation, but what I have to say to Salvador admits of no delay. You will permit me?" he said, addressing Matheo.

"Don't be uneasy on my account," replied the latter. "I will retire."

"No, remain; I wish to speak to you," said Roman.

Matheo retired to the embrasure of a window, and left the two friends an opportunity of conversing freely.

"It seems that this is to be the day of events," said Roman to Salvador.

"What has happened now, then?" demanded the latter.

"Delicat, Coco-Desbraises, and Rolet le Mauvais Gueux, know who we are."

"Not possible!" exclaimed Salvador.

"'Tis as possible as it is true."

"But what unlucky hazard has so well informed them?"

"I'll tell you."

"Since the event by which Madame de Neuville was thrown down by Vernier les bas Bleus, as he escaped from Mother Sans Refus's, this man has not reappeared in the den of the rue de la Tannerie. As he had no desire to associate himself with the intentions which the other bandits were plotting against Salvador and Roman, he feared they might deal summarily with him; by reason of which, he had not encountered either one or the other of the two friends, to whom he intended to denounce the plot formed against them. It was only a few minutes before the entry of Roman into the cabinet, that Vernier les bas Bleus had met him, and informed him in what manner Delicat and Coco-Desbraises had introduced themselves into the pavilion of Choisy-le-Roi; and afterwards, by following them, how they had procured their address and their names, and the nature of the project which they had formed against them, a project to which all the other bandits had agreed; 'but,' added Vernier les bas Bleus, 'Rolet le Mauvais Gueux is the only one to whom they have confided their whole plan; he is the only one, with them, who knows who you are; for they have come to the decision that their three selves might easily murder and rob you. They have, however, promised to the others, to give them a share of the pie, and to inform them of your names, &c. If they do not succeed, they intend to *manger le morceau.*"†

"The devil! the devil!" said Salvador, after listening to Roman with great attention; "this is serious. Does Vernier les bas Bleus also know who we are?"

"Vernier knows nothing; at present, there are only the three individuals I have named to you, who are to be feared."

* Long before the names of Robert Burk and the resurrectionists of Edinburgh were known, in France, criminals, whose names are often cited in the annals of the police, such as *Nifflet, Casque, Filou*, *Postillon, Lorgnebr, Lasonde*, *Brasseur*, and *Barbaro*, were in the constant habit of stealing bodies, recently interred, for the purpose of selling them to the surgeons and students; but often, during the night, in taking up the bodies from the church-yards, or *cemeteries*, they brought away an old man for a young one, a male subject for a female one; on such occasions, their employers refused to pay them the price agreed upon; an unfortunate miscalculation for the body-snatchers, who received two or three five-franc pieces, instead of a much larger sum. On this account, and to prevent such mistakes, they determined, in order to serve their patrons to their wishes, to strangle the first person (being such as was desired) whom they might encounter in the streets at night. It was at this period that the *charriage à la mecanique* was invented. They had a double chance; first, they robbed the victim; secondly, they sold his body.

† Denounce.

"They must absolutely be so no longer. To-day they are three; to-morrow they will perhaps be four, and so on. There is no reason why it should finish there. But is it quite certain that Vernier les bas Bleus does not deceive us?"

"What interest has he?"

"'Tis true. Be............. .... on the features of the men whom I have met at the *plakue*,* yesterday, and the day before, an air of constraint which promises no good."

"Well?"

"In a few days the fête of Mother Sans Refus, takes place; she gives, it is said, on this day, a grand dinner to her intimate friends; we shall assist at this dinner, and we shall see what we have to do; and if we must have a bout, we shall be three there, and equal to many of them."

"Who have you then, besides ourselves?"

"Eh! parbleu! the Viscount de Lussan. Since we have brought him to give the signal to our men, do you think he will refuse to lend us a hand under circumstances which interest him, as well as ourselves?"

"Certainly not; we can reckon besides, in case of necessity, on Vernier les bas Bleus."

"Well! 'tis settled. But we must prevent the three individuals in question speaking together, and to effect this, we must give them so much to do, until then, that they find no time to pronounce an indiscreet word."

"How shall we manage it?"

"You know where to find Vernier les bas Bleus again?"

"No doubt. I met him at the Champs-Elysées, where I sauntered to breathe some fresh air, while you conversed with that cursed doctor. I took him to a small café in Bourgoyne street, where I told him to wait for me, and I ran here to recount the affair to you."

"Very well! we must, for the present, do this: take some money, and go to Vernier; you will give him two notes of a thousand francs, you will tell him to keep one for himself, and spend the other with Delicat, Coco-Desbraises, and Rolet le Mauvais Gueux, with whom it will be easy for him to get reconciled; he will tell them he has just committed a robbery, and that he is willing to spend his money with them as much as they like. The principal thing he must do, will be to persuade these individuals to eat and drink, drink especially, so that they may not have a moment to reason; if he brings them drunk to the banquet of Sans Refus, he shall receive another note for a thousand francs."

"Well! very well! I will go and find Vernier."

"Finish first with Matheo."

"Ah! Matheo! well, what do you think of him?"

"I think that, as we said just now, he is become virtuous, but I confess, that after hearing him, I can explain with difficulty what you told me of him in prison, that he was selfish, and a coward."

"My dear, I told you that to give you confidence; but to speak candidly, I think he is no more a coward than you or me. But I must not give Vernier time to get impatient. I will leave with Matheo, for I must really know why he sent into the other world, our old friends of the forest of Cujes."

Roman, in fact, left with the doctor; but in spite of all his efforts, he could not induce Matheo to enter on the subject he desired, and they parted quite discontented with each other.

* Secret meeting place.

CHAPTER XXI.

A DIGRESSION.

It is certainly not without a sentiment strongly allied to fear, that we have determined to write the few pages which follow. The subject which we are now about to take in hand, has been so often treated of, it has so frequently attracted the attention of men of the greatest merit, that we shall be thought, perhaps, somewhat presumptuous, in attempting to speak after them, and expose ourselves to a comparison, which, we are aware, would be disadvantageous to us; but, like many others, we wished to bring our stone to the edifice which is at present building; we are also of opinion, that we owe to humanity some account of the impressions which a long experience among criminals of every degree, has left upon our minds; we have, in fact, imagined, that where science has advanced all its arguments, developed all its theories, and accredited every system, that practical experience might still raise its voice, and proclaim its convictions.

And in order that ours might remain intact, we have read none of the works written on the subject, and this is a homage we have rendered to the authors of such works, for it is simply because we have feared to subject ourselves to the influence acquired by their celebrity and their talents, that we have objected to read them. We were aware, that after having perused them, we should appear in their own character, and that it would be no longer our own individuality that we should bring to the discussion of practical ideas. We have sought for no inspiration but from our own feelings, and from continued and conscientious observation.

For a long time past, but especially during the last few years, philanthropists have endeavoured to discover some means of ameliorating the destiny and moral condition of prisoners; but whether it is that they have not understood the question, or that their different systems were not ready to receive an immediate application, it is certain, that if they have done something towards the *physical* well-being of those confined, there still remains much to do, if not every thing, for their *moral well-being;* and we think we can thus explain the nullity of the results, and of the innovations recently attempted. Some only see in the condemned, the victims of an ill-organized social state, and from this, they have presented, as applicable to all, certain theories which could only receive a partial application; others, on the contrary, have not taken into account the weakness of human nature, and those circumstances which might exercise a certain influence upon the destiny of man; they have dug, if we may use the expression, an abyss between the innocent and the guilty, and would for ever banish from society those who have once sinned, and who, from that alone, according to their notion, must for ever remain a scourge to it. The too great indulgence of those who seek to explain every crime by the actual organization of society, has prevented their attaining the end they had proposed; and the severity of the others has compelled them to travel beyond it.

If we accepted the system of the former, repressive laws would be no longer necessary: if, on the contrary, we listened to the latter, the same punishment should be adjudged to every criminal, Death!

It has been often observed, that in order rightly to appreciate the just bearing of our repressive laws, it would be desirable that the interior of the establishments destined for those who have violated them, should be well studied by living in the midst of the prisoners, who should have no suspicion of this voluntary captivity; this would be, in fact, the only means of appreciating, at its just value, the efficacy of the punishments decreed by our codes. But it is very easy to perceive the impossibility of such an experience, as it would be necessary that the stay which the philanthropist should determine to make at the galleys and prisons, should be of sufficient duration to render complete the examination of the important questions connected with our criminal legislation.

The events of his life have afforded to the author of this work, the painful advantage of having been enabled to study, on the very spot, the morals of prisoners. He believes that it is in his power to submit to enlightened and impartial judges, some results of his observations; and he will esteem himself happy if he can obtain the interest of real philanthropists, towards men who are sometimes more deserving of it than is supposed.

The first question to ask ourselves before proposing any penitentiary reform, is this: is the object of society, by inflicting punishment on the guilty, that of *merely punishing*, without troubling itself as to their future destiny; or would she *correct* them, in order to recal them to her bosom?

In the first hypothesis, (so monstrous a one, that it would revolt every enlightened mind,) society would have nothing to do but enforce the preventive laws; all its efforts would be limited to so moralizing the classes, as to diminish the number of criminals. As to our repressive laws, they would all have to be repealed, and our prisons and penitentiaries suppressed, as objects of useless expense. From the moment, in fact, that we should despair of the guilty, they would all be annihilated without mercy, and the code of Draco, which condemned to death for the slightest crime, ought to be exhumed, and placed again in vigour; it would at least guarantee society, at present so governed by a sentiment of egotism. It has no other object in punishing the guilty, but that of obtaining security, without troubling itself about their amelioration.

If we glance at our code of laws, we observe that they have classed the punishments; that they have endeavoured to proportion them to the crimes and misdemeanours; that they have, besides, left to the magistrates appointed to carry them out, the power of still further mitigating them, according as the criminal may seem to them to merit, either by a repentance, or from his past life, more or less indulgence; we conclude from this, that the legislature has supposed that the man who had merited a temporary punishment, might correct himself, and resume in society the position he had momentarily lost.

This conviction of the legislature, is not, and we are thankful for it, all illusion; a very great number of those condemned, would, in fact, become corrected partially, if not entirely, if the authorities would but take measures to arrive at this result. But to attain this object, they must be well persuaded that the prisoner is still a member of society, and that this society has only empowered them to punish him, that he might be rendered more deserving of remaining as a member of the family

When an unfortunate, who no longer possesses the sound exercise of his intellectual faculties, commits any act of a nature to compromise the public security, the authorities charged to watch over the preservation of every interest, are not satisfied with placing him beyond the possibility of doing an injury; they appoint skilful physicians to attend upon

him, until such time as he shall have recovered his reason; why do they not act in the same way towards those unfortunates against whom they find themselves under the necessity of awarding punishments?

Generally speaking, men, at least we hope so, are born honest; we ought, therefore, to consider as attacked by a moral disease, those who are driven to crime by their fearful passions; they ought, like persons who have lost their reason, to be placed beyond the possibility of injuring; yet, in order to effect this, they are rejected from the bosom of society, and banished for a certain period to places destined to such purposes, and where they are no longer to be feared! But we do not see why the individual who is nothing more, in fact, than an unhappy creature in whom some moral qualities are wanting, or whose organs may be vitiated, should be abandoned, more than the other patients. We can with difficulty comprehend, in fact, why they should not attempt to recover him also, or rather to restore to him, if we may thus express ourselves, the moral health which he has lost; in other terms, to replace him in the path he should never have quitted, that of integrity and honour.

Let us be well convinced of this, that the number of incorrigibles is considerably less than is generally supposed, and they are not idle theories which we here advance; we have made numberless experiments, and they are experiments which authorize us to make this assertion, not under a doubtful form, and as a belief which the result might disprove, but as a reality of which we have made the proof, and which we may loudly proclaim, since, in the end, it can but do honour to the human species.

During twenty years and more which the author of this work passed at the head of the police de sureté, he almost constantly employed none but *liberated forçats*, often even *escaped convicts*, whom the authorities tolerated, in consideration of the services they had rendered; he chose, from preference, even such as had obtained a certain notoriety from their former criminal deeds; well! he has often confided to these men the most delicate missions; they have frequently had in their possession considerable sums of money, to carry to the police and registers; they have taken part in operations, from which they might easily have drawn large resources, and not one of them has forfeited his honour. And, what is remarkable, if, by chance, the administration has been compelled to punish agents guilty of fraudulent subtractions, it has been constantly against such as were called *" the pure,"* or, in other words, against those who had never been visited by a condemnation.

After his leaving the police, when the administration refused to employ these same men, who, during all the time they had been placed under his orders, had given so many proofs of a sincere contrition, many of them, suddenly deprived of the means of existence, and unwilling to resume their ancient trade, went to work at the manufactory of white lead, at Clichy, not allowing themselves to be terrified at the certainty of painful diseases—a consequence, alas! foreseen, from the nature of the work—diseases always followed by a cruel death, which many suffered in preference to committing fresh crimes.

The manufacture of white lead and some others equally poisonous and fatal in their results, are nearly the only trades which the returned convicts can exercise. These trades, which destroy the workmen employed at them, and which produce

LIFE IN PARIS.

THE COUNTESS DE NEUVILLE AND LAURA ENTERING THE MARCHIONESS DE VILLERBONNE'S SALOON.

but a moderate salary, do not, however, remain dormant; and the men whom they employ are mostly returned convicts, sufficiently experienced, expert, and audacious, to exercise with a certain impunity the trade of robbing; these men are, therefore, sincerely corrected.

The author could, in addition, cite a thousand examples of conversion, which are publicly known, or, at least, which most persons could verify.

When retired from the police de sureté, he established, at Saint Maudè, a pasteboard manufactory, and was desirous of continuing the experiments he had already made respecting the returned convicts, and to seek for means to be still useful to this class of *Parias*—too much neglected up to the present moment, or, rather, about whom the government occupies itself no further than to place them beyond the possibility of honestly gaining a livelihood—he had principally in view, the procuring, for the greatest number possible, an easy occupation, and sufficiently remunerating, to prevent their seeking in crime the means of existence. He employed, therefore, in his workrooms, none but individuals, of both sexes, whom the surveillance of the police, and the prejudices of society which usually follow them, had reduced to inaction, misery, and despair. The same efforts reproduced the effects he had before remarked. Many of these beings, whom a long practice of vice, and a residence more or less prolonged in the galleys and prisons, had almost entirely degraded, amended themselves, and became honest, sober, and industrious labourers; and he has much regretted that the government did not think proper to encourage his work, (which he has no fear in saying was really philanthropic,) and place him, by some small sacrifice, in a situation to defray the expenses which are required in the commencement of every establishment. He would have been followed, no doubt, by numerous imitators, and the results obtained would, before long, have settled in the minds of others as well as his own, the most important of all the questions which are now undergoing consideration.

If from general facts we pass to particular ones, examples in support of our opinion will not be wanting. Among a number which present themselves to our memory, we shall choose but two, which appear to us the most striking.

A young student was refused at his first examination; he pretended he had not been fairly used; his anger was excited, and he went directly to the professor, to whom, right or wrong, he attributed his disgrace, and directed against him the pistol with which he had armed himself. The professor was lucky enough to escape the death intended for him. A few days after this attempt at assassination, the young man was arrested, and immediately brought before the court of assize for the Seine. He did not attempt to deny the criminal act, for which the public vengeance demanded a reparation, but he maintained that he was unable to explain to himself, how, with the character he was endowed with, he had brought himself to the determination of committing such an action.

The advocate of the young man endeavoured to establish the insanity of his client, and that he did not enjoy the free exercise of his faculties when he attempted the life of his professor. He cited facts to prove that he possessed a character which rendered inexplicable, in some measure, the crime he had attempted to commit; facts, which, in addition, were confirmed by the declarations of many estimable witnesses.

This ground of defence was well received. The following question was put to the jury:—"Was the accused in possession of the free exercise of his faculties when he committed the crime which has resulted in this accusation?" A negative reply was the acquittal of the young man. The magistrates who had proposed this question, and the twelve citizens who had replied to it, in a sense favourable to the accused, necessarily admitted the possibility of the fact which it declares. An opinion, shared by the magistrates of the royal court, by twelve honourable citizens, and by a crowd of lawyers, physicians, and learned men, ought not, we think, to astonish any one. Moreover, in the end, the result has shown that the magistrates and jury acted wisely, for the young student of that day is now the father of a family honourably placed in society.

Two assassins, named Blanchet and Henry, condemned to die on the wheel, by the court of justice of Paris, were detained at the Bicêtre, when the events of the first revolution broke forth; thanks to these events, they were forgotten, and they soon regained their liberty, by escaping at the period of the massacre of the prisoners, in September, 1793, and they preserved it for several years. They were not again placed in confinement until justice had resumed her regular course; but so much time had elapsed since the sentence had been pronounced, that the authorities could not resolve to execute it, so that they were merely detained in prison. For a period of nearly thirty years, they gave the authorities not the slightest subject of complaint; their conduct, on the contrary, might have been cited as an example for the other *detinus* to follow. At length it was determined they should be set at liberty. Both of them still live; the one is a master perruquier, and the other a compiler of geographical charts; and they enjoy the esteem and consideration of all who know them. They are both proofs, that men may become corrected after committing the most enormous crimes, and that what Boileau has somewhere observed, is, perhaps, wrong:

"L'honneur est comme une ile escarpée et sans bords,
On n'y peut plus rentrer, des qu'on est dehors."*

We have sufficiently demonstrated, and that by facts, that even the greatest criminals may be recovered from their desperate course of life.

We have also, in the preceding pages, sketched the principal traits in the character and morals of the men whom we think capable of being amended; we shall, therefore, not return to this subject, as we think we have said enough to make them known; but our work would not be complete, if, after having described men, as they are, we said nothing as to the causes which produce similar effects, and if we did not shortly indicate the means which appear to us requisite to avoid them.

A great number of writers, *soi-disant* philanthropists, have taken up their pen and written FOR the people, and *in the interest* of the people, who have never read them, books, which we are quite willing to believe, are full of excellent ideas. They have gained, at this trade, large territories, decorations, and inscriptions, in the great register of the public debt; but, 'tis in vain that we look

* " Honour is like an isle rugged and torn;
When once outside it, there is no return."

round us, we do not see what the *people* have profited; and we may be allowed to wonder that they have not gathered the fruits, which the labour of men who fancy they so well understand its welfare and its misery, ought to produce.

We have no intention here, of attacking that small band of conscientious men, whom a real sentiment of humanity has drawn into the arena, and whose names are venerated by the public gratitude; but *their efforts* have been stifled by the declamations of those would-be philanthropists, who sleep away the forenoon, and, whilst sipping their wine, display their pity for those unfortunates who *fast*, and whom they have undertaken to assist; these latter, and the number is such, that we might say with reason, "It is the same with philanthropy as with wit, it runs about the streets;" the latter, we say, have only complicated the question, by multiplying its theories and difficulties.

In fine, what great measures have been taken, what objects of importance accomplished, which might serve to ameliorate the condition of the lower classes? None, that we are aware of. Much has been written, no doubt, but nothing has been attempted, at least nothing worthy an observation.

In order to be convinced of this truth, we must, without any fear, observe, as through a magnifying glass, all the wounds which are destroying the social order; and, afterwards, dissect the body of our penal code, to seek the remedy applicable to the healing of these same wounds.

"We are born poets, we are born masons," says an old proverb; we may also say, by giving this proverb a little extension—we are born thieves; and may add, that the law has not the right to punish a man, simply because his organization is vicious; but experience has long since proved, and phrenologists themselves (if their science is a true one) have acknowledged, that education will correct the faults of nature; it follows, from this, that if a well-regulated society has the right to punish those who violate its laws, the exercise of this right should be subordinate to the observance of certain conditions. Before punishing for crime, every thing should be done to prevent it; and, in inflicting the punishment, the principal aim should be, to *correct* the author of the crime; it ceases to be just when it is severe, without having previously made every exertion to remove the causes, which generally induce one of its members to commit a first crime.

The family of thieves, we must admit, is much more numerous than is generally supposed; and we only mean to speak here of those who openly violate the penal laws of the country; there are, also, causes to which they may be referred; these, also, are so numerous, that their elucidation would fill a volume; we shall only speak here, of the principal one:

The want of education!

Nearly all thieves by profession issue from the ranks of the people. Why? It is not difficult to find an answer to this question.

The mass of the *people*, with some rare exceptions, quit their dwellings in the morning to repair to their labour, and only return at night to sup and retire to rest; those amongst them who have children, leave them to run about the streets the whole day, and remain ignorant of what they do, or what they learn; but if they act in this way, it is not from indifference, for these same *people* are fond of their children, but they think it

better for their health, to allow them to run about than to keep them confined; they are, besides, alarmed at the accidents which happen to those whom they are imprudent enough to leave in a room, and for this reason it is, perhaps, difficult to blame them.

Thus left to themselves, without other guide than their own free will, these children envy the lot of their comrades, a little older, and already perverted, who can play at pitch-and-toss, or buy a few dainties; and to do as these latter, they steal some object of trifling value from the stall of a shop; from this they get inured to minor crimes, and finish by becoming audacious and dexterous thieves. And let it not be thought that we draw too grave a consequence from a fact, in itself insignificant; experience has demonstrated to the writer, the truth of what is here advanced. The majority of the children he has remarked wandering, without any object, in the public streets, have become, after having commenced by some peccadilloes, shameless thieves, who have, in the end, fallen into his hands.

But, we shall be told, all the children of the people are not thus trained up—there are school-rooms, asylums; agreed. But the asylums, institutions eminently useful, are not sufficiently numerous for all the children to obtain admission; they are opened *too late*, and closed *too early*, (the same reproach attaches to the different schools consecrated to the children of the poor,) to allow the workman, without losing a portion of the time devoted to labour, to take their children there and bring them back.

But in these asylums, in these primary schools, the number of which is evidently too small for all to profit by them, and even in schools of a more elevated character—do they teach the children of the poor to respect the laws? no; this essential part of all education is completely neglected. We must admit, therefore, that, to a certain point, he who commits his first crime, only errs through ignorance. Since every Frenchman is expected to know the law, teach the law to every Frenchman.

Ignorance is to morality, what the small-pox is to the body; both leave ineffaceable marks; and it is certain that those which scourge the mind, are ten times worse than those which disfigure the body. Every possible care has been taken to spread among the people the benefits of the discovery of Jenner; premiums are offered, by way of encouragement, to mothers who have their children vaccinated, and certain privileges are afforded to the latter; thus, these alone are admitted into the government-schools: they also impose on nurses the obligation of having their nurselings vaccinated; and as soon as they arrive in the regiment of our armies, the young recruits are subjected to this operation. Why do they not do something similar to spread the no less precious benefits of education? Why should the instruction of children for ever remain a charge upon the poor parents? Why, in those of our schools which *are called* gratuitous, are the latter left to defray the expense of books and paper? and why are they compelled to furnish their children with any particular costume? We would willingly admit that these books, this paper, and this compulsory costume, require but very small sacrifices; but, small as they are, they are frequently too considerable for the unfortunates, who sometimes rise from their bed without knowing how to procure food for the day. Until you cease to make it a question of misery or avarice with the parents, in sending their children to the schools, which should be sufficiently numerous to satisfy the exigencies of the population; and until you can bring them to consider this duty as an obligation, you will not have accomplished enough.

But, this done, is it admitted there is nothing more to do? no, certainly not; we must take cognizance of all ages as well as all classes; and we ask, are there in France any establishments in which adults may, while learning a trade, complete the education, which, in a civilized country, every man ought to possess, and at the same time contract habits of sobriety and industry? No! This is a reply we regret to be compelled to make to this question; the foresight of the administration has not yet reached to this point.

One man is vicious because they have neglected to develop the germ of the good qualities with which nature has endowed him; another dies of hunger, because they have disdained to teach him a trade; or that he finds no opportunity of exercising the one he has learnt by chance.

From this state of things to a robbery, which will speedily be followed by many others, there is but a step; and the man who is only an occasional thief, or one from necessity, will soon become a thief by profession.

But we are told there is work for every one. Those, however, who inscribed upon their banners, "*Let us have work, or die fighting!*" had no work; and yet, every day the courts condemn individuals, who have neither home nor means of existence, although they are not yet become thieves. It is assuredly allowed us to believe that if these men had found an occasion of utilizing their faculties, they would not have failed to seize it; for their misery itself is a presumption in their favour. And yet, as we have said, individuals seek a cruel death in the pestilential work-rooms of the manufactory at Clichy! undoubtedly from the want of work in establishments less life-destroying.

It is from a determination to remain ignorant of the real cause of the deep distress which overwhelms so many unfortunates, that there have been written in our codes those monstrous laws against vagabonds—laws, which have given birth to more crimes than it is possible to imagine.

The article 269, of the penal code, declares that vagabondage is a crime.

The article 270, thus gives the definition of the word:—*Vagabonds, or persons without confession, are those who have no certain home, nor the means of subsisting, and who do not exercise constantly either a trade or profession.*

Such are the laws written in the code of a nation which esteems itself as more enlightened than any other! No one elevates his voice to complain of you, but misfortune has constantly followed you, you are therefore guilty; the rags which cover you, are your accusers. Simply from your being unfortunate, you have no longer the right of breathing the pure air; and the lowest constable in the police may capture you, as a wild beast, and which he does not fail to do. *You are worth a small crown;* you are seized, thrown into a dark and unhealthy prison, and after some days of detention, the gendarmes drag you before the magistrates charged to render you justice; your conscience is pure, and you fancy that at the voice of your judges the doors of the gaol will be opened to you. Poor victim that you are! the law dictates to the magistrates, who sigh while condemning you, unpitying decrees. Whatever you may have to say in your defence, you will be condemned to three or six months in prison, and after having suffered your punishment, *you will be placed at the disposition of government, during such time as it may determine upon.*

If they thus treat with severity the individual whose only crime is often that of having been born, and still being, miserable; they exhibit, in return, an extreme indulgence for the criminal of noble race. Thus, whilst they sacrifice to example the son of a poor workman, they shield the accused of good family. Where then is justice? Does the honour of a family favoured by fortune, appear to them more worthy of preservation than that of the family of a proletaire? We do not think so; but still such is the fact.

In our opinion, the man who appears before a court, after receiving a liberal education, is, the crimes being equal, evidently more guilty than he who has always lived in ignorance. It is not necessary, at least we presume so, to deduce any reasons in support of this opinion; we should only exhaust ourselves in superfluous efforts to prove it by evidence. Why then is the *well educated* man almost always treated with much indulgence, whilst severity is meted out to those whose greatest crime is *ignorance?* Why? we cannot reply to the question. But we may be allowed to think that this mode of acting, deeply wounds that instinct of justice and injustice, which exists in the nature of every man, and which determines many a one to rebel against society.

Our legislation respecting mendicants is neither more moral nor less fatal in results, than that which applies to vagabonds; if the former are twin brothers of the latter, if they are both born of the same parents, we must acknowledge that our laws treat them with the same severity, and that under this head, they are at least impartial, if they are not often unjust.

To obtain a right to blame mendicity, and to punish mendicants, we should place within the power of the necessitous, the possibility of living by the aid of work; for there is a right which predominates over all things, and which belongs to every man—that of living, (by work be it understood.) If we show that we are severe, before acquitting ourselves of this duty, we run the risk of punishing the man who has preferred begging to thieving, and this is precisely what happens every day.

The agents of authority fail not to arrest all the needy they find in their path, and such as are thus arrested are condemned to two or three days of imprisonment; they are afterwards placed at the disposition of the administration, who cause them to be confined, and only restore them their liberty when they have acquired a capital of thirty or forty francs, which consumes a whole year in amassing; afterwards turned adrift, what can a mendicant accomplish with such a trifling sum? He dissipates it, seeking, or in not seeking, for work; and quickly finds himself in the same miserable situation as before his arrest. This would not happen, if, instead of a prison, these unfortunates had found an establishment for their industry, with work fairly remunerated.

Has the administration performed its duty towards these mendicants, that it should act with such severity against them? We have, it is true, depôts of mendicity, and we might wonder why the needy are not more eager to repair to them; but our wonder ceases, when, after an examination, we rest convinced that these depôts are no better than prisons. Eh! what! do you imagine that a poor fellow will yield up his liberty, the only blessing which remains to him, for a morsel of brown bread and a basin of miscalled soup? this is neither just nor reasonable! what inconvenience would you find, then, in leaving him the shadow of this liberty, and allowing him the privilege of going out at least once a week?

The labour of these poor in the depôts of mendicity, might also be more liberally rewarded; nearly all the poor might be usefully employed by an intelligent administration; this is so true, that the majority of those who are *honest poor* at the Bicêtre are always at work; they know how to find employment for themselves, suited to their strength and capacity, and thus, make very good days; this is an incontrovertible proof that the administration shows itself parsimonious towards those detained in the depôts; or that it is ignorant how to make the best use of their labour. And whichever it may be, we can easily conceive that a man whose labour only produces him five or six centimes a-day, is soon disgusted with it.

Among the number of mendicants, there are several who implore the public charity on no other account, than because their real infirmities place them beyond the power of working; if any deserve indulgence, assuredly these are the persons, for they suffer doubly, both from their physical infirmities, and the moral violence which they are subject to; and yet the greatest severities are reserved for these, whilst the administration leaves the privileged beggars quietly to pursue their industry.

When such mendicants as are found in the streets are arrested, and conducted to the depôts of mendicity, why is it that others are allowed the privilege of begging at the church doors; is it, by chance, that beggary is less repulsive at the door of a church, than at the corner of a street?

The produce of the public charity destined to the relief of the poor, cannot be worse distributed than it is; they inscribe on the registers of the benefit offices all such as present themselves with some recommendations; and repulse, without pity, such as have nothing but their misery to speak for them, and who cannot bring the name of any one to their support; so that there are in Paris, individuals who receive assistance at the same time, in five or six different arrondisements, whilst the most necessitous are not relieved at one.

Those who contrive to get inscribed at an office of charity, are always assisted, no matter what changes take place in their positions; on the other hand, those whom unfortunate circumstances plunge for a time in distress, cannot, whatever may be their recommendations, procure themselves to be inscribed and assisted, until long after the necessities of the moment have ceased, and have produced their irreparable effects.

Thus, if an industrious workman falls sick, his family, deprived of the daily wages which procure their living, finds itself soon reduced to the most frightful misery, and in the impossibility of procuring some little nourishment for him who only waits his return to health to be again their support. A very little would often quicken his recovery so desirable, but he not unfrequently dies before he is enabled to obtain relief from the offices of charity: or, if he recovers, it is but to listen to the cries of his children for bread, without his being enabled to satisfy them, and to find himself a prey to that sullen despair, the inseparable companion of mi-

sery; and it is scarcely necessary to observe, as all the world knows it, that despair and misery are very bad counsellors.

The funds destined for the poor are insufficient; and it would, perhaps, be just to tax those who are in possession of riches for this purpose, in proportion to their means. Those who possess fifty or a hundred thousand francs a-year, give merely a few hundreds towards the relief of the poor, and yet they think they accomplish much; they despise the poor; it is, however, among the latter class that they find every thing they want, workmen, servants, substitutes who would, if necessary, shed their blood for their sons, and sometimes even young and handsome women to gratify their passions.

Workmen, it is said, are nearly all drunkards and brutal; servants rob; this, perhaps, is but too true, but whose fault is it, if not yours, messieurs who are rich? If your gifts were proportioned to your fortunes, and to the necessities of *the poor*, the children of *the poor* would receive a better education, they would learn the history and laws of their country, and there would soon remain not the slightest trace of the defects, the vices even, of which you reproach those whom providence has placed in the lowest scale of the social edifice.

So long as we are contented, in order to assist the poor, with sending them a lady richly attired, and sparkling with diamonds, as the bearer of such gifts as a loaf of bread and a basin of soup; so long as we confine ourselves to the imprisoning those who implore public charity, the result of the present state of things will be to be feared.

We shall not enlarge upon this subject, which would be interminable, if we chose to describe all the abuse, and indicate all the remedies which it might be possible to propose for it; it is sufficient to have shown that society has much to do for the mendicants, to prevent their embracing a profession much more dangerous to it, that of becoming thieves.

The honourable M. de Belleyne, who was not enabled, during his short administration, to accomplish all the good he meditated, found time, however, to form an establishment which might serve as a refuge to every individual of the poorer classes, and in which they might find the means of usefully employing their abilities; the happy effects which this attempt soon produced, might well have encouraged the friends of humanity, but the institution of M. de Belleyne was unfortunately received with that indifference which but too often accompanies the labours of the real philanthropist.

Drunkenness is, of all the vices, that which most degrades the man; it is also one which often produces in him a disposition to commit crime, and even murder. Who has not felt his heart rise in disgust at meeting in the bye-streets, and sometimes in the most frequented parts of the capital, men stupified by drink, dragging themselves from corner to corner, and running the risk of being killed at every step they take? Who has not, besides, shuddered with horror at reading in the journals, the details of crimes, of which drunkenness alone has been the primary cause? And yet the authorities have taken no measures to suppress the sad effects of this inconceivable passion, and our legislation remains without arms to combat with it; and yet this passion is a thousand times more dangerous than vagabondage; a thousand times more degrading than mendicity, which it punishes with a severity often inconsiderate.

If we endeavour to explain this indulgence for drunkards, we shall be lost in conjectures, and we shall arrive at this conclusion: drunkards consume the products from which the administration receives immense sums; is this the reason of such indulgence? Really, we should be tempted to believe so, when we observe the prodigious number of half-hidden establishments which infest the capital and barriers, those dens of perdition, which are only frequented by malefactors and prostitutes of the lowest class, and drunkards, attracted to them by the cheapness of the liquors retailed there. Every populous quarter of Paris possesses one or several houses of this nature, and without speaking of Paul Niquet, whom every one knows, we might cite, only comprising in our enumeration the most notorious; the *Chapeau Rouge*, Rue de la Vannerie; the *Auvergnat*, Rue Planche Mibray; the *Abbatoir*, quarter of the arsenal; the Cassis in the Rue Plâte Saint-Jacques; the *Petet Bal Chicard*, Rue Saint-Jacques; the *Drapeau Tricolore*, Rue Galande; the *Maison Muraille*, Rue de Marmousets; the *Hotel de la Modestie*, Rue de la Tacherie; and lastly, the *Grand Saint Michel*, or the *Grand Bal Chicard*, Rue de Bievre.* At these kennels are retailed brandy, cassis, and other spirituous liquors, at eighty centimes the quart; these liquors, adulterated with unwholesome matter, are as disagreeable to the taste, as they are pernicious to the health; but they produce the effects which the unfortunates who swallow them hope for; they make them drunk; they procure the delights of intoxication, and dispose their blood for orgies and saturnalias, which constantly follow a few copious libations. The masters of these establishments, to increase the powerful attraction, take good care to assemble women, the refuse of their sex, who sell their favours for a few sous, or a few glasses of wretched eau de vie; but allow no occasion to escape of robbing those they have been able to captivate, when drunkenness has arrived at such a point as to stupify their whole being.

Legislators! who have never thought it your duty to combat with drunkenness; administrators! who encourage it in a manner, because it augments the budget of receipts, step for a moment into such sinks as the *Grande Lutêce*, where debauchery has made her dwelling place, where the walls *sweat* with orgies! listen to the language of the individuals you will meet there; behold them getting drunk, fighting, squabbling, men and women, in mad and furious struggles, and then yielding to that leaden sleep which has the insensibility of death, without its calmness! and you will then be enabled to judge of the powerful source of demoralization you allow to subsist in the heart of your metropolis.

But, without descending to these dens of corruption, have you not been sufficiently struck with the inseparable effects of intoxication, at meeting, on the Boulevards, young men of family, in whom drunkenness inspires indecencies which cause a scandal to your wives and daughters; at elbowing, at every step you take in the streets, workmen, who have spent at the barriers the fruits of their labour for a week; who stun you with their obscene songs, and know not on the morrow how to procure their wives and children a morsel of bread; lastly, have you not been frightened at those combats, so numerous, and often so fatal, in which drunkenness alone aims the blow? Count the victims of this ignoble passion, and you will find that cupidity has

* Notices respecting these establishments will be found at the end of the work.

not shed so much blood, or piled up such a hecatomb of martyrs, as drunkenness; and you will remain convinced that your indulgence to the present moment has been a culpable weakness.

Thieves, for the most part, only make attempts against the property of others; drunkards, constantly threaten the lives of their fellow-creatures; this, perhaps, is the only distinction we might draw between them. And yet, not only is the vice of the latter *not* ranked under the head of crimes and delinquencies, but in the eyes of our laws, it often serves as an excuse for the crimes it commits, by which it happens that both the immorality of the cause, and the criminality of the effects, go unpunished. Every day, in fact, we hear the unfortunates brought before the correctional police, or the court of assize, invoke no other means of defence but that of drunkenness: "they were drunk!" such is their justification, and the magistrates generally, taking into consideration this state, which excludes premeditation, adjudge the minimum of punishment, when they do not altogether discharge the culprit; intoxication is become a brevet of impunity.

In our opinion, it is time to put an end to such a state of things; it is time to find some punishment for the cause of so many crimes and delinquencies, or to repress with the greatest vigour its deplorable excess. For ourselves, we see no very great inconvenience in attacking the cause itself, and placing drunkenness, drunkenness of itself, apart from its effects, among the number of offences; arrest and prosecute every individual, of whatever class he may be, whom you find in a state of intoxication, either in the streets, or the public places; prosecute equally, as their accomplices, the heads of those establishments who, excited by the most infamous cupidity, make no scruple of serving with drink men who are already deprived of reason, and you will powerfully contribute to improve society; you will prevent many a crime.

Let us not be told that drunkenness by itself prejudices no one, or ought not to be ranged under the head of offences; it ought not to be permitted to a member of society to degrade humanity in his own person, so far as to deprive it of that distinctive character which separates the man from the brute; it is a moral suicide which our laws ought not to tolerate; besides, intoxication is a scandal, an outrage to public decency, which the authorities might easily suppress, without being accused of an attempt against individual liberty. You have suppressed the gambling houses; you prosecute the proprietors of establishments who allow gaming at their houses; why do you not treat with the same severity drunkards, and those who tolerate them, and induce them to drink? Why do you not also close the establishments which retail spirituous liquors at prices which permit the consumers to swallow nothing but poison? Drunkenness ruins as many individuals as gambling; it leaves as many children without bread, as many mothers of a family in the most complete deprivation; it exposes them, in addition, more frequently to the ill-treatment and brutalities of their parents and husbands, of those who ought to afford them protection and assistance; considered in this point of view, drunkenness is, of the two passions, the most fatal, and sends a number of recruits to increase the ranks of malefactors. Let it be well understood, however, that we wish to make no exception in favour of the passion for gambling, which is more in vogue among the inferior classes than is supposed; for there is not the smallest cabaret which is not provided with its billiard room, and which, like many other bad passions, is a powerful cause of demoralization; we simply maintain, that drunkenness is a vice still more fatal in its results than gaming.

No one, we think, will attempt to place in doubt, either the necessity of applying to the evils we have noticed, suitable remedies; or, what is even still more important, of creating in favour of the lower classes, establishments in which they could always find education, work, and bread. These establishments, if they should ever exist, ought to be regulated and administered by enlightened, though honorary philanthropists.

If we would wish to diminish the number of malefactors, we must do that which is not impossible, render better and a little happier those who belong to the lower classes of society, a starting point we must never lose sight of.

To this end, when you have destroyed the causes which produce evil, interest the man to do some good; interest, you are aware, is the prime mover of all our actions.

Ancient governments knew how to punish crime, but they knew also how to reward virtue; a crown of oak leaves, a palm branch, were bestowed on those who had rendered the country any eminent service, or who had uniformly well performed their duties. Modern governments, which the experience of ages ought however to have instructed, have, it is true, judges to apply the law, gaolers, galley serjeants, and executioners to carry them out; but they have not, like the ancients, magistrates to dispense the public rewards bestowed for meritorious actions. By the side of the law which punishes the assassin with death, should there not be also one to recompense the courageous citizen who, at the peril of his own life, saves that of his fellow-creature? If the law punishes him who violates one of the articles of the social compact, why not also recompense him who religiously observes them all. Men, like children, require attraction, this is a truth, unfortunately too well proved, 'tis a truth among all people, and especially among Frenchmen.

Look at our armies; to a certainty they are naturally courageous; but will it be denied, that the presentations, the swords of honour, the crosses especially, have not greatly contributed to the prodigies they have achieved? We may judge from this, how little it costs to induce emulation among Frenchmen; words are often sufficient, provided they have some signification; and when Napoleon exclaimed to the battalions which he commanded: " *From the heights of these Pyramids forty ages behold you,*" he turned his soldiers into so many heroes.

The same causes will produce the same effects in the civil career; hold out to every man, that he may well conduct himself, the same stimulants which have rendered our soldiers immortal, and you will not want citizens who will immortalize themselves by their private virtues.

After thus glancing at our social system, we find ourselves compelled to admit, that the realization of our wishes appears to us still at a distance; from a certain class every thing is expected, and yet nothing is done for its welfare; what sort of a future then is reserved for it. Can a man for ever resist those pernicious influences which will not fail to assail him on his entrance in the world? Can he steer, without a guide, through the numerous shoals which he will probably find in his voyage, without getting shipwrecked? We fear the contrary, so long as we do nothing to prevent it.

The strong man, that is, he who has never fallen, because he has, perhaps, never felt necessity, or has only had to struggle against a feeble enemy, expects that another should resist his passions, bad examples, and even the most severe privations; and yet the former takes no opportunity of performing the office of guide to the feeble man; he gives him no means of resisting, of combating with advantage the necessities of humanity, and the imperious wants which soon overwhelm him, and which may lead him to crime; and yet we are astonished, after this, that the man succumbs, and increases the population, already so numerous, of the galleys and prisons! this is throwing a man into an arena, in the midst of wild beasts, without even placing arms in his hands, and to wonder that he suffers himself to be devoured by them.

From the moment that an institution offends at its base, all that attaches to it, or issues from it, will be vitiated, we must, in consequence, take man, such as he is, from the circumstances which surround him, and not require him to show himself such as he might have been probably, if the social organization had not corrupted him, and caused him to lose his natural purity.

Finally, when there shall exist schools in which the children of the people may receive an education proportioned to their capabilities; when professors shall be appointed to teach them to understand and respect the laws of their country, and induce them by their advice, and especially by their example, to cherish virtue; when, after leaving these schools, they are enabled to enter an establishment, to learn a trade, and contract habits of order and sobriety; when a man, deprived of resources, may, without the fear of losing that last and most precious of his blessings, liberty, seek the commissaire of police of his district, and require that which he will then obtain, work and food; when we shall have met and overcome that shameful passion which assimilates the man to the brute, by depriving him of the distinctive character, reason; when, at length, some laws *preventive* shall be placed by the side of the laws *repressive* of our code, and rewards shall be accorded to the virtuous man, then, and not till then, we may be allowed to be severe, without ceasing to be just; for no one will then be enabled to throw in the face of the magistrate, who, sitting on the bench, represents society as a whole, words like these: "I have robbed in order to live, I would willingly acquit myself of the task imposed upon me; but I am a man, I have a right to live, and society, whose representative you are, society, which has suffered me to remain in ignorance, has not the right to let me die of hunger;" or some such truisms, which, if they are not an apology for crime, at least explain them, and might, to a certain point, make them appear more excusable.

In the present state, we must admire those who remain virtuous; pity those who fall, and offer them a hand, when, after having expiated their faults, they are willing to rise up and seek with earnestness the means of preventing a relapse.

We have attempted to prove that if thieves are corrupted, they are not incorrigible; and that, with some exceptions, it would be possible to reclaim them if we took the pains; and to enumerate the principal causes which increase without cessation the ranks of the malefactors. This long preamble, we think, was necessary to understand what fol-

No. 23.

LIFE IN PARIS.

SALVADOR DECLARING HIS LOVE TO LUCIE.

lows; it is right, when the author places in view personages who, at the first sight, might appear somewhat eccentric, real as they are, that the reader should know what these personages are, where they come from, and where they go; what follows then, is no more than a sort of commentary on the preceding observations, but still let him guard himself against taking for an opinion of the ideas of the author, the discourse which he puts in the mouth of these personages; he has simply made them converse as they converse in general; the reader will do wrong to accord to what they say a bearing which the author himself is very far from wishing to attach to it.

CHAPTER XXI.

THE FETE OF MOTHER SANS REFUS.

THERE was a time, say the nestors of the galleys and prisons, when, in the yard or in the fire-room in which they had assembled, they drew around them a crowd of auditors, greedy to listen to their lessons in the expectation of following their example; there was a time when thieves were brave and discreet, this was the good time. Old men are always fond of praising the past at the expense of the present; then a *rousse à l'arnache** or a *cuisinier*,† unless sure of not being recognised, would certainly not have been incautious enough to introduce himself in places where the *grinches*‡ were in the habit of assembling; he was too well aware that at the slightest indication of a nature to discover a *macaron*,§ he would have been sacrificed to the general security. This has happened frequently, even in prison, and the guardians have been contented, when the macaron was despatched, to drag his body by the leg to rid the yard of it, saying, " 'Tis well done; if he was a spy, why didn't he keep himself aloof ?"‖

In these times the thieves, when taken, never denounced their comrades, those who had worked with them could sleep without fear; often, indeed, he might see his *camarade d'affaires*¶ gloriously terminate his career on the *place publique* rather than denounce his comrades; in these times they possessed honesty and courage!

At present things are changed, the spies *drop in* openly, and when a thief is taken in the fact, he denounces his comrades, there is no longer *de vrais tapis*;** so that a *bon garçon* when he leaves the prison or the galleys, knows not where to direct his steps.

What is here said by the nestors of the prisons, to preserve the name we have given them, is only true to a certain point. Without doubt there are now fewer characteristic types than formerly; there has been such a fusion in our morals that many are effaced; unfortunately this proves nothing in our favour; yet there still exist in the forgotten corners of our old Lutèce, some places where the old traditions are yet preserved intact. The house of Marie-Madeleine Comtois, called Sans Refus, was one of these rendezvous. For a long time it had been known as nothing else than a receptacle for thieves. The police made frequent descents upon it, but these visits were constantly without results, and if sometimes they effected captures, they were those of novices who were not as yet initiated into the mysteries of the place, and whom it was thought necessary to consign for a few years to the *college** to complete their education. The sacred words, *enter the cave*, were not pronounced except upon grand occasions, and in favour of those elect, few in number, who had given to the association proofs of their zeal, of their capability, and their discretion.

We have already described with as much exactness as lay in our power, the exterior of the house of Sans Refus; a house which still exists at the place we have indicated, and in the same state it was in at the period in which the events of this history took place. We must now perform for the interior of this house what we have done for the exterior.

The shop, as we have already observed, was divided into two equal parts, by a partition formerly glazed, the absent glass having been replaced by oiled paper. In the one part were assembled the odalisques attached to the establishment, and the lower class of customers. The other formed a kind of sanctuary in which the adepts alone were entitled to admission.

A door had been framed in the wall at the bottom of this division of the shop. This small door, low and garnished with strong iron-work, gave entrance to a little square court, surrounded with high walls, from which one could only catch a glimpse at the sky. The cheerful rays of the sun never descended into this court, in which we should find it chilly in the warmest days of summer, the paving was uneven and rugged, always miserable and dirty, and the walls, on which grew the poisonous toadstools, had attained that almost green tint which is evidence of the humid and unhealthy nature of the place.

A second door had been formed in the partition wall on the right, contiguous to the small street of the Teinturiers. After passing this door, you arrived in a few paces on the bank of the river, the tide of which, at this moment, had attained a tolerable height; but this door was but rarely opened.

At the opposite extremity of this court there existed a pump, under the spout of which was placed a trough, narrow and not large, formed of a single rough stone. This trough, generally full of dirt and muddy water, could easily be raised from the place it occupied by means of a strong broom-handle passed through two holes formed at its opposite extremities. When this was removed, might be seen a hole dug in the ground, enlarged in the base, where, by means of strong cramps and iron pins, they had adapted a straight ladder. The trough could be as easily replaced as taken off, so that when once replaced and replenished with water, it became impossible, at least to those uninitiated in the mysteries of the secret, to discover the retreat of which it concealed the entrance.

After descending the twenty steps of the ladder you entered a large square cavern formed from the cellars of the house, divided into three equal parts, of which this cavern was one, by strong walls, to

---

* A police agent who does not receive a regular salary, but simply a remuneration proportioned to the importance or utility of the information he obtains, or the captures which he effects.

† An avowed and recognised agent of police.

‡ Thieves.

§ Informer or denouncer.

‖ A man named Clarembourg was assassinated at the *Bal des Negres*, a small public house, notoriously bad, of the Champs-Elysées, for having prevented a girl named Louison, surnamed la Blagueuse, with whom he lived, carrying assistance to her lover, named *Lartifaille*, condemned to 24 years in chains.

¶ Accomplice.

** Places where a thief may find an asylum and resources in case of necessity.

* Prison.

which they had taken the pains of giving, although of a modern construction, the appearance of antiquity, and the venerable blackness of old buildings.

This cave might also be deserted, if occasion required, by a low arched door which gave entrance to the vaults which, before the buildings of the quay lately constructed, extended the whole length of the Quay de Gevres.

A table, formed of some planks seven or eight feet long placed upon tressels, round which twenty-five or thirty persons might find room without being too much incommoded, had been laid out in the cave into which we have introduced our readers.

The planks were covered, by way of table-cloths, with sheets of coarse unbleached linen, taken from the virginal beds of the pensionaires of Mother Sans Refus, but perfectly white and clean, and on which were displayed a number of plates of common delft ware, of every shape and colour, similar to that of the convives who were to take part in the feast. A monstrous turkey, properly stuffed with mince-meat and large chestnuts, two geese, and an Italian cheese, dishes of sausages, some others filled to the brim with butter, radishes, mustard, sprats, and gherkins; such was the substantial fare, and the outworks which were to accompany it. The turkey, in addition, was flanked by two (equivocal) rabbit pies, and two salads of endive garnished with beetroot; two enormous *bonnets de Turc* or savoy biscuits, each surmounted by a large group of immortels, and of the image in crusted sugar of the saint whose fête they were about to celebrate, embellished the two extremities of the table, which was lighted by a dozen candles stuck in candlesticks of copper and plated metal, venerable representatives of every past age, brushed up for this solemn occasion, and surmounted by paper sockets of different colours; the dish-covers of silver, *de conseiller,** upon which might still be seen the remains of ancient coats-of-arms, roughly effaced, like the candlesticks, belonged to every epoch; a *petit pere noir,*† full to the brim of that excellent *blue* wine only consumed at Paris, stood sentinel at each dish; no knives were to be seen, the individuals belonging to the class of persons who were to take a part in this banquet being in the habit of carrying one constantly in their pocket.

Upon an old chest, covered, like the table, with a sheet, abstracted from the bed of one of the ladies, and whitened with lie, was disposed the dessert, which consisted of two cheeses, one from Brie, the other from Gerard-mer, vulgarly called Geromée; walnuts and filberts, a salad bowl full of prunes, spice-bread and Reims biscuits; the whole accompanied by several bottles, labelled, on which we might decipher these signs: *cent cept ans, vanillé, parfait-amour, cognac,* the names of liqueurs cherished by the children of Mercury.

The old fauteuil of Mother Sans Refus, also enveloped in a white sheet, in order that the gala habits of the heroine of the fête might not run the risk of absorbing any of the thick bed of grease with which it was covered, had been transported into the cavern, and placed at the upper end of the table. Upon this seat was already throned the taverniere, who, to do honour to her guests, had completed a toilette really extraordinary, and had decked herself in her most gaudy attire. Her face, usually black and filthy, had been polished with

* The produce of plunder, and unmarked.
† A jug of brown ware, containing one or two litres of wine.

jasmin pommade; but in spite of this precaution, it was still furrowed with small black streaks, and as the serviette impregnated with the precious cosmetic had not reached these furrows, it detached itself in white patches upon the dark ground of the under parts, very similar to a half-cleaned window; a robe of merino, of the deepest scarlet, trimmed and edged with green cord; an apron of green silk, somewhat lighter in shade than the trimmings of the robe, and embellished with black lace; a waistband of velvet of the same colour, attached in front by a buckle enriched with roses and fine pearls; a cap trimmed with ribbons *d'Aurores;* a flaxen front of hair, its corkscrew locks rolling over her hollow cheeks, and a neckerchief of fine lace, composed the *ensemble de toilette* which could only belong to Mother Sans Refus, or a woman of her species.

But if the attire of la Sans Refus was in the very worst taste, it was, in revenge, of an extreme richness; the scraggy neck of the old shrew was enclosed with diamonds of considerable size and rare beauty; her meagre and bony fingers were bedecked with rings of different shapes; in fact, her whole person nearly resembled one of those show dolls on which the jewellers, who attend the fairs, display the riches of their magazine.

The two seats placed on the right and left of Mother Sans Refus, were occupied, one by Cadet Filoux, the oldest of the *grinches** and *escarpes,*† the other by Cadet l'Artesien, a handsome old man of seventy-two, still fresh and gay, who had passed forty-five years of his life at the galleys at Brest, from whence he had several times effected his escape. These two venerable remains of an age gone by, who had been the friends of *Comtois* and of *Marianne Lempare,* and who, on this account, had obtained the places of honour, had preserved the costume they wore when young and vigorous; they were the privileged sultans of the Venuses Callipiges, inhabitants of the dens, which at this period infested the streets de la Vieille Lanterne, de la Vieille place aux Veaux, de la Mortellerie, and others; a large three-cornered hat, cravat of immense amplitude, very short waistcoat, wide pantaloons, stockings with clocks of the colour and fashion which were known as issuing from the magazines of the successor of Mother Rousselle.‡

Another old reynard, Coco Lardouche, was placed near Cadet Filoux; these three messieurs conversed with Mother Sans Refus, whilst waiting the arrival of the other guests.

The latter arrived one after another, and when, upon descending the twenty steps of the ladder they made their entrance into the cavern, the superb disposition of the banquet, drew from them exclamations of admiration. The Grand Louis, Charles la belle Cravate, Robert, Cadet Vincent, and several others, had already arrived, there only remained Delicat, Coco Desbraises, Rolet le Mauvais Gueux, Rupin, le Provençal, and the Grand Richard, with Vernier les Bas Bleus, upon whom, however they did not reckon.

"Must I come down?" cried Cornet-tape-dur, who had remained above to introduce the convives as they arrived.

* Thieves.
† Assassins.
‡ Mother Rousselle, a shoemaker, in the street la Vannerie, formerly patronised by the thieving fraternity. The shoes which left the magazines of Mother Rousselle were easily recognisable, and the moral value of the customers of this shoemaker was so well appreciated, that one of the interrogating judges, attached to the Lower Court, was in the constant habit of sending at once to prison, such as were brought before him, wearing the shoes of Mother Rousselle.

" Not yet, my boy," replied Mother Sans Refus; " Rupin, le Provençal, and the Grand Richard, have not arrived."

"Ay, ay, 'tis right, mother," replied Cornet-tapedur, " 'tis all the same to me to wait; but, however, don't let me starve any how."

" Eh! why should we wait for the Rupins?" added Charles la belle Cravate, who still bore in mind a certain correction which Salvador and Roman had administered to him; a correction to which Delicat and his two comrades, who endeavoured by every possible means to irritate all the bandits against their enemies, had alluded on various occasions. " Why should we wait for them? are they such grand seigneurs that they cannot arrive at the same hour as the comrades?"

" Will you finish shaking your red rag so, miserable," exclaimed Mother Sans Refus. " Am I not free to have who I like to eat my supper? and it pleases *me* to wait for these Rupins."

" There, there, don't get angry, mother," said le Grand Louis, " we will wait for the Rupins, since it pleases you; but I must confess, however, that you love them like your own bowels, and if by chance the police should discover the *planke*,* you'd be very likely to hide them under your petticoats."

" Well! yes, I do love them, they are men who bring order, management, and courage to their work, by which one might pick up a poor livelihood, and they are always *flambants ;†* but such idlers as you, only work when you haven't a rag to your back; you are always nearly as naked as a swimmer, with wretched clothes, and such shoes on your feet, that you might pare your toe nails without taking off your shoes and stockings."

"Ay, ay, laugh at our misery; but the last will always laugh the best; and your supper looks well without even as much as a small ham, doesn't it?"

" Ah! you think I have not done things well, you miserable *pègre à marteau.‡* Well, don't eat any of it then, that's all; the wine, bread, and the meat will pass under your nose."

" Hey! come then, you below," cried Cornettape-dur, through the hole, " don't chaff so much, the *Rupins* are coming."

In fact Salvador, Roman, and the Viscount de Lussan, habited in costumes suitable to the occasion and the place, although in good trim, descended the steps of the ladder, and entered the cavern.

The three late arrivals, after having slightly saluted those who were already assembled, went to occupy the places reserved for them near Mother Sans Refus, and the respectable triumvirate, consisting, as we know, of Cadet Filoux, Coco Lardouche, and Cadet l'Artesien.

" Heim! how they carry their heads," said the Grand Louis to Charles la belle Cravate, " they didn't even say good morning to the friends."

" Patience, 'twill not last long; when Delicat, Coco Desbraises, and Rolet le Mauvais Gueux arrive, they must change their note."

" Come, come, good-for-nothings," said la Sans Refus, in a tone intended to be agreeable, " take your places."

" At table, at table!" exclaimed nearly all the convives.

" And why then should we take our places before Delicat and his friends are arrived, since we have waited for the Rupins?"

" You will see whether I mean to wait for these

* Hiding place.
† Well dressed.
‡ One who thieves articles of small importance.

idlers," replied Mother Sans Refus; " since they are so well off where they are, let them remain."

" Had we not better wait for them?" said Salvador; " as our friends have had the politeness not to seat themselves without us, it is but right that we should wait in our turn; at all events give them the quarter of an hour's grace."

" Well, then, for a quarter of an hour," continued Sans Refus.

" If they do not come, said the Viscount de Lussan," addressing Salvador, " it will be very disagreeable, I shall be quite disconsolate to have come for nothing into this atrocious cavern."

" There is no fear of it," replied Roman; " Vernier les bas Bleus, who has not quitted them for three days, sent me word this morning, to the small café of the street de Bourgoyne, that he would bring them."

" Here are the rest of our friends," cried Cornettape-dur.

Delicat, Coco Desbraises, and Rolet, in a state of inebriety, which announced that Vernier les bas Bleus had faithfully acquitted himself of his mission, descended the ladder, followed by Vernier, who, the moment he had put his foot to the ground, approached Roman, and said to him:

" There they are: for three days that I have been their pilot, they have spoken to no one. You see that I have faithfully performed my task."

" And you see that I keep my promise," replied Roman, handing him a note for a thousand francs; " a thing promised is a thing due."

" Thank you; if there should be a row, you may depend upon me."

" Cornet, shut the shop, and come to the table, my boy," cried Sans Refus to the bandit who had remained above.

It was not necessary to repeat the order; he had soon finished what was to be done in the shop, and in his turn made his entrance in the cave, but diligent as he was, he did not arrive soon enough to choose a place; he was obliged to content himself with a stool placed at the end of the table.

The repast commenced as peaceably as might be expected from a reunion composed of elements similar to those assembled in the cave of Mother Sans Refus. The bandits were at first desirous of satisfying the craving appetites which most of them had the happiness of possessing. It is useless to observe that Salvador and his two companions, accustomed to cheer much more delicate than that which, for the moment, was at their disposition, hardly tasted the dishes, except by way of keeping countenance, and only moistened their lips from the large brimmers which the hideous Hebe of this banquet of infernal gods filled up for them with a gracious liberality.

At the dessert, the guests, who washed down every mouthful they swallowed with a copious bumper of blue wine, became sufficiently animated to commence a certain confusion, a precursory diagnostic of the orgie about to follow.

Mother Sans Refus, overcome by the very *sensitive* wine, shed some sentimental tears in recalling to the old men near her, the sorrowful end of her father, condemned to perish on the wheel, and who died without an exclamation. All the bandits, with the exception of Salvador and his two companions, who remained mere observers, and of Vernier, who followed the example of his patrons, drank heartily one with the other, spoke all at a time, or sung a chorus in which the crudity of the idea disputed the cynism of the expression.

The old men, to whom the company had continued to offer the attentions and regard due to their age and former life, began to get animated; their eyes sparkled with more vivacity than usual, and the movement of their heads announced that they were about to speak.

All the bandits became silent in order to listen to them.

The oldest, Cadet Filoux, filled his glass with wine which he elevated above his head, the two others, Coco Lardouche and Cadet l'Artesien followed his example.

"To the memory of the old *Pègre!*" they exclaimed in chorus.

"To the memory," continued Cadet Filoux, "of those who, like us, have known how to suffer without denouncing our comrades."

Every one hastened to do justice to this toast, and the conversation was approaching subjects where it was not likely to languish.

"Ah! 'tis a good trade all the same, that of a *pègre*,"* said Cornet-tape-dur, who was struggling with the drumstick of a fowl.

"Yes, yes, you find the trade a good one when it concerns the filling your belly," replied the Grand Louis, "but when there is any work to be done, 'tis not to your taste, poltroon."

"It is not such a very good trade with the perspective we have before us," added Vernier les bas Bleus, who had not yet spoken, "the prison, the galleys, or the guillotine."

"'Tis your own fault," said Coco Lardouche, "if the moment one of you are taken you did not split, the police, the judges and the attorney-general would not have so good a game."

"Come then, old one!" exclaimed Charles la belle Cravate, "are there any among us who have turned traitors?"

"That's not what Coco Lardouche means; he knows as well as I do that you are all good boys incapable of betraying a comrade; but he knows also that the *jeune pègre* dishonours himself."

Cadet Filoux filled his glass with wine, and emptied it at a draught.

"Listen to me, my children," he said, after collecting himself a few instants. "I began very young. I have seen the great and the little châtelet; at thirteen years of age I was whipped under the *custode;*† and if I had not been so young, it is probable that with the whip I should also have had the mark. Years have whitened my hair, (the old scelerat showed with a certain pride the magnificent white hair whose locks descended upon his shoulders;) my best years have rolled away at the *pré,*‖ and in almost every prison of our lovely France; the *baton* of the galley serjeants has fallen on my shoulders; I have been the companion of the great men who have illustrated our profession; the Comtois, Josas, of the Marquis called the Golden Hand, of Mabou called the Apothecary, of Molin the hatter, of Jallier called Bombance, of the Nazels, Cornu, and many others whom it would be too long to name.§ I can then give you some useful advice, and I should think that my words would have a certain authority among you."

"Has this old droll the intention of making us a sermon?" said the viscount to Salvador.

"Let us wait until we find an occasion to bring things to a point," replied the latter.

"All the *grinches*," continued Cadet Filoux,

"whatever species they belong to, whether *l'escarpe*.* or *la tire*,ᵃ *la carre*,ᵇ or *la detourne*,ᶜ *le chantage*,ᵈ or *le charriage*,ᵉ† whether they are *cambriolleurs, roulottiers, bonjonrriers, ramastiques, soulasses, romanichels, vanterniers*, or *neps* ;‡ ought to consider themselves as children of the same family, lend one another aid and assistance in case of need, in a word, cherish each other as brothers; unfortunately, this is not the case, you have all forgotten that if you choose you might form *a society within society*, and one which they could with difficulty, if ever, destroy, if the members had always before them this maxim: where several small states are domineered over by a large one, *Union produces strength*. But no, those among you who are not so lucky or less expert than such or such a one, become jealous of him and employ every means they can devise to destroy him.

"There are in the world, my children, men who cram themselves every day with truffles and champagne wine; who sleep on eider-down; who are drawn in sumptuous equipages, and who pass their evenings in leering at the legs of the opera-dancers, and employ the moments they know not how otherwise to dispose of, in writing fine treatises, in which they recommend those who drink no wine but that at six sous the litre, even if they drink any—who sleep on a miserable palliass, when they sleep not under the canopy of heaven, and who, to a certainty, never catch a glimpse of the *à la mode* tibias of Mlles. Fanny Elssler and Cerito—these they recommend to live and die without ever wandering from the path of honour; these men, my children, are called philanthropists.

"Among these philanthropists are some who tell the people to eat dainties, when they cannot even procure bread ; these are the philanthropists who, when a cruel plague devastates the population of the capital, recommend the miserables who have nothing to cover their wasted limbs but a piece of sacking, to keep themselves *very* warm, to nourish themselves with wholesome viands, and to drink none but generous Bourdeaux wine.

"To live, suffer and die, without once leaving the path of virtue! these are fine words, no doubt, but he who has no roof to shelter his head, no clothes to cover himself with, or food to appease the craving hunger which torments him, the poor devil who is not enabled to find work, who has been turned out of doors by his landlord because he has not paid his modest lodging, who has not dined, and who is condemned because he is asleep and fasting under the porch of a church or in a brick kiln, says to himself at length, that the philanthropists are mere distributers of nonsense, and the following is pretty nearly the extent of his reasoning:

"'The penal code, which the favourites of the period have manufactured for their own private use, is nothing more than an arsenal in which they find, always ready, weapons to strike those who cast a look of envy at their magnificent hotels, their brilliant equipages, and their sumptuous tables. If I had wrested from these happy mortals a small part of their superfluity, my physiognomy at the present moment would not be livid and earthy, my garments would not fall in rags! Who has told them that I have endeavoured, without

---

* Thief.
† This punishment was inflicted on the patient between the two gates of the prison, considered as a place of liberty.
‡ Galleys.
§ All names of celebrated thieves.

* Assassination.
† The explanation of these terms are given at the end of the volume.
‡ The name of a certain class of Jewish thieves, who know how to sell at a good price a cross of some order, set with false stones.

success, to utilize what I possess of strength and faculty? Since no voice is raised to pity me, why, instead of giving me what every man in a well-organized state ought to obtain, work and bread, do they condemn me to pass some months of my life in prison, and place me for a certain time at the disposition of the government? is it that misfortune has deprived me of the right of breathing the fresh air?'

" When a man says all this to himself, (and those who do not say it, think so, which is absolutely the same,) he is very near becoming a *grinche*: so that, thanks to a decree dictated by unpitying laws, to the magistrates who, I well believe, sigh whilst pronouncing it, when, after passing some of his dearest years in prison, he shall be restored to liberty; that which he had no intention of doing before being sent there, he will infallibly accomplish after leaving it, he will become a thief."

" Yes, it's quite true," said Cornet-tape-dur, "we find in prison, friends who make us *free of it*, who give us good lessons; and, my faith! as we have already seen that it serves no good to be honest, we do as they do."

" And you do well," continued Cadet Filoux; " if they knew the past life of those condemned to hard labour for life, or to death, perhaps they might pity them a little more than they do; and as they generally relieve those whom they pity, it is certain there would be many less thieves than there are, it is probable even that many *pègres*, and good ones, would quit the trade to go to work."

" Quite true," said Cadet Vincent, " I am certainly not one of the most maladroit caroubleurs, I have always money in my pocket, gold watch, chains, rings, and fine clothes, well! that does not prevent my wishing in preference, to work hard from morning till night, and earn fifty sous a day, rather than rob, but there are no means. Let us suppose! I have been for one year, two years, more or less, in a workshop where I labour at my trade of an ebonist: I work like a slave, I never get drunk, I am esteemed by the master and loved by the comrades; this is just as it should be; but all at once they find I have been *la bas*:* and, good servant as I am, they show me the door; and 'tis always the same history; my faith! one gets wearied at last, and the moment they are sure that we have appeared but once at the assizes and been condemned, we must die of hunger, if we wish to die an honest man; we turn thief again, 'tis more sure, and less deceitful."

" 'Tis more sure and less deceitful." said Robert, the *comrade d'affaires* of Cadet Vincent, " that's doubtful; for my part, I think there is no trade which is less certain and more deceiving than that of a grinche."

" And why so, if you please ?" replied Coco Lardonche.

" Why so? why so? I cannot well explain myself, for I do not speak as well as some of you; but I simply recollect that my mother, a poor though honest woman who died of grief because I did not follow her good counsels, always told me that wealth dishonestly acquired would never prove a benefit."

" Oh! what a farce!" exclaimed Charles la belle Cravate, " you mean to say then, that if to-day I were to commit a *chopin*† of some hundred thousand francs, and place them with a *beurrier*,‖ that he may pay me the interest, I could not live peaceably on my revenue, like a good bourgeois, and become a juror and churchwarden in my parish?"

" But where then are the *grinches* who live quietly after making their fortunes?" continued Robert, "look at the *birbe** who has made some good hits, much better ones than any we can accomplish; well! at this very day, if his children, who are honest, did not give him a small revenue, and if the *recleuse*‖ and Rupin did not sometimes put some gold pieces in his pocket, he would be forced to die of hunger; and yet he is one of the luckiest; how many *pègres de la haute* are there who, after rolling in gold and silver, and getting embarrassed, have gone to die *la bas*. Look you, there is one fact, and 'tis this, that that which is earned by vice will be squandered in vice."

" Well! what matter," added Coco Deshraises, " if we die misérable, we have always the consolation of saying on our death-bed, that we have joyously passed our lives."

"A pleasant life certainly, to have continually the fear of soldiers, gendarmes, informers, and judges before your eyes! not to know in the morning whether we shall sleep at night in our beds; when every tap at the door makes our heart beat quicker; and besides, this is not all; for you see, if there is still a little left here," and Robert in saying this struck his bosom with some force, "we often think it is not right to wrest from the poor devils what they have earned by working like devils."

" But since the trade of a *grinche* seems so poor a one, and you pity the honest men on whom we levy contributions, why don't you become an honest man yourself ?"

" Oh! why, why! d'ye think I can tell?"

" Well then, I will tell you," said Cadet l'Artesien, " 'tis the surveillance.

" Many very estimable persons, whose good intentions are not to be doubted, consider the surveillance as a measure eminently useful. It appears to them just and natural that society should have its eyes constantly fixed on those of its members who have violated its laws, and who, from the simple fact of this violation, have voluntarily placed themselves in a state of legitimate suspicion.

" Unfortunately, it is easier to refute by facts than reasoning, the arguments which these persons bring forward to support their opinion.

" The surveillance would be a useful measure, if we were all exempt from prejudices; but we are far from having arrived at this elevated state of civilization.

"Although we are honoured by being cited as the most enlightened people in the world, we are yet governed by prejudices; and of all the prejudices with which we are imbued, the most fatal in its consequences, the one which produces the greatest number of crimes, the most anti-social in fact, is that which repulses those who are discharged from confinement.

" When a debtor has discharged his liabilities, no one thinks of reproaching him for the delay in acquitting them; and ninety times out of a hundred, on the contrary, those who were his creditors extend to him a helping hand, lend him their assistance, and continue to him their credit. The position of the liberé, is, in my opinion, quite similar to that of the debtor in arrear, who at length frees himself; he owed to society an example, some reparation, he has paid his debt by submitting to the punishment inflicted upon him; why then do they not treat him as they do the former? Why reproach him constantly with the

---

* In Gaol.   † Robbery.   ‖ Banker.   ʳ Old man.   ‖ Receiver.

fault or the crime he has committed? Why drive him away without mercy? From what law, human or divine, have they borrowed these principles of an eternal reprobation?

"No one, I think, will be inclined to doubt the force of those prejudices which repulse the liberated convict.

"Men who occupy in the world very high positions have suffered condemnations more or less heavy; but very luckily for them, they are not known; for although these men merit the esteem which they inspire, if their life was known, those who now squeeze their hand, and admit them to their table, would run from them as from a plague or a leprosy.

"I have often seen those who have been discharged, contrive, by concealing their position, to get admitted into a workroom, conduct themselves well for several years, and yet be ignominiously driven away when such position became known.

"The consequences of a condemnation thus becomes more terrible than the condemnation itself, to those who, at the expiration of their punishment, are subjected to the surveillance of the police, who never allow them for any length of time the possibility of concealing their position of liberés; and I have no fear in saying, that the liberés who are without resources, have no other choice but that of dying of hunger."

"Die of hunger! thank you," said Cornet-tapedur, "I'm in no hurry for that."

"Or become what they were before," continued Cadet l'Artesian.

"To die; all men have not sufficient courage for that, therefore the liberé, repulsed continually by that society which he formerly offended, but to which however he does not owe the sacrifice of his life, resumes his ancient habits; he again seeks his comrades of former times, who give him what he stands in need of, an asylum and food, and he soon returns, in spite of himself, to that which he was formerly. Who is wrong then? Society and prejudices. Why not listen to the man who returns to a proper conduct, the man whom a circumstance, often independent of his will, a bad education, a vice which has not been subdued, has induced to commit a fault, sometimes involuntary, and often excusable? Why show ourselves inhuman for the mere pleasure of being so? Of what use is a code which proportions the punishment to the offence, if the guilty is marked for ever with the stamp of reprobation? *An unjust prejudice produces a relapse;* this is a truth which every legislator and philanthropist ought to meditate upon.

"Let them not suppose that the liberé succumbs in every case without a struggle."

"Ah; that's true," said Charles la belle Cravate, "when I was *affranchi à la rebiffe** by the comrades, I had eaten nothing for two days."

"Well! if you, who were at that period honest, and who could, without blushing, present yourself any where, have been reduced to such an extremity! judge of what might happen to an unfortunate liberé who is repulsed by every one like a scurvy dog!

"With such results before us, one of two things must be done, either destroy the prejudices which induce society to repulse the liberated and refuse him work; or modify, if not suppress, the surveillance in such a manner, as to leave the individual subject to it the possibility of concealing his position; it is, perhaps, less in fact against the surveillance itself, than against the manner in which it

* Having committed a first offence, and being induced to commit a second.

is exercised, that we must complain. Upon his leaving prison, the liberé is told—you cannot inhabit Paris or the large towns, you cannot reside at the sea-ports, nor in places which are fortified; where will you reside? This is to retain in one hand what is offered with the other; 'tis a mockery. Where do you wish that this man should reside and labour, since every place which is the centre of activity and industry, by which alone the workmen are reclaimed, is shut against him?

"The privileged liberés who obtain permission to reside in the large towns are compelled to present themselves, at certain periods, at the police office, so that if they contrive to conceal their true position, they are soon suspected of being informers, and they gain little by the error, for by one of the caprices of our national character, liberés and informers are subjected to the same reprobation; the former are continually feared, and the latter are needed as a security, and yet both are equally despised; this is an anomaly in our prejudices.

"As to the liberés confined by a surveillance in the rural districts, they are subject to the arbitrary will of the lowest *garde champêtre,* and those among them who cultivate any ground, cannot quit their district to sell their vegetables at the market of the neighbouring town, without breaking their ban and exposing themselves to a correctional punishment; for them the surveillance is a captivity following a captivity.

"The best arguments which we can oppose to the surveillance, are, without contradiction, some extracts from the passport delivered to the forçat who is subjected to it. At the head, and in large characters, are these words: "*Congé de forçat.*" And then follow the principal clauses of the decree of the 17th July, 1807, and especially the articles 5, 10, 11, and 12, thus conceived:•

"'Art. 5. No liberated forçat, except by the special authority of the director-general of the police, can fix his residence in the cities of Paris, Versailles, Fontainbleu, and other places in which there exist royal palaces, in the ports where prisons are established, in depots, nor within at least three miriameters of the frontier of the coasts.

"'Art. 10. No liberated forçat can quit the place of his residence without the authority of the inspector of the department.

"'Art. 11. Throughout the whole route to be followed by the forçat liberé, the public officer of the place to whom he shall be required to present himself, shall examine his papers, and mark down the sum he shall give the liberated forçat to proceed to the night's lodging indicated to him.

"'Art. 12. Arrived at his destination, the liberated forçat shall present himself to the commissaire of police, or to the mayor of the place, who will deliver to him his passport in exchange for his feuille de route.'

"I have shown the inconveniences which result from the disposition of the articles 5 and 10, but I have said nothing to you about the articles which follow; throughout his whole route and upon arriving at his destination, the liberated forçat is required to present himself to the public officer of the district; but are the authorities certain as to the discretion of the latter? To observe what passes, we cannot doubt that the question must be answered in the negative; in certain places, in nearly all even, the arrival of a forçat is an *event,* and the public officer who receives him has nothing more pressing than to inform his neighbours of it; the forçat instantly becomes an object of the public curiosity, the talk of the whole neighbourhood;

No. 24.

LIFE IN PARIS.

SALVADOR DISCOVERING THE ROBBERY.

each repeats the news, every one runs in his way; 'tis a real exposition which continues from the moment he departs till the moment he arrives at his destination; nay more, it continues beyond this term, for in the place he has chosen for a residence, the curiosity is not satisfied when they have seen him arrive, it lasts until they find fresh excitement in other events.

"With so many precautions which prevent the liberé from hiding, for a moment, his position in a country where prejudice rises so strongly against him, what do you wish him to do? What do you wish him to become? How do you think he can find work?

"To drive an individual into this position is to place him over a precipice on a swing-board, and order him to move on; presently the equilibrium gives way, the plank drops, and the man tumbles into the abyss.

"Legislators and philanthropists! have you ever reflected upon the *empire* of necessity? You, who are patrons of the surveillance, have you calculated what *want* can do? what hunger can produce upon those tormented by it? For my part, I am convinced that Virtue herself if she were personified to inhabit this earth, would succumb, if she were placed under surveillance.

"Let me not be accused of exaggeration, in what I have said, facts speak louder than words; and I could cite you facts to satiety in proof of what I advance.

"An individual named Carré, scarcely thirteen years of age, was condemned to sixteen years of hard labour, for stealing two rabbits, at night, with an accomplice and by means of *effraction;** but on account of his age, the punishment he had incurred was *commuted* to *sixteen* years in prison. Carré conducted himself well during his captivity, and learnt the trade of a polisher of buttons; he was lucky enough upon his liberation to obtain work, and for several years gave not the slightest reason for complaint; but the trade he exercised having failed, he found himself suddenly in the most abject misery; for some time he attended every two or three days a charitable person, who gave him upon each visit two or three francs; but fearing that this person would weary of assisting him, he visited him no longer, and stole from a kitchen two saucepans, which might have been worth ten francs at the most; he was arrested for this deed, and condemned to hard labour for life, and to be marked.

"At the departure of the gang, the person in question came to see Carré, and as he was ignorant of the circumstances which had induced him to commit a fresh crime, he thought it his duty to make him some reproaches; 'Eh! sir,' replied Carré to him, 'I could find no work any where, I was repulsed by every one, I have only robbed to be sent to the galleys; there, at least, I shall have food every day.'

"Shall I recount to you the history of a liberated forçat, whom many of you might have known at the prison at Toulon, that of *Aubert?*† This man was condemned, on the 2nd of August, 1826, for a forgery, committed under circumstances which rendered it almost excusable, to five years of hard labour; he underwent his punishment at the prison at Toulon, and was liberated the 2nd of August, 1831. He repaired, legally, to Caen, where he rejoined his wife and daughter, whom prejudice, and misery which is the inevitable consequence of it, soon forced to quit for their own

* Breaking open.
† This is religiously true.

interest, and that they might not share the reprobation he was subjected to; he then went to Bourdeaux, he addressed himself to one of the authorities of the town, who, touched at his misfortunes, assisted him liberally from his purse, and obtained him a passport, not stigmatised, which allowed him to seek an employment. He contrived to get himself received as a preceptor in a family in the neighbourhood of Bourdeaux; he merited the confidence placed in him; but a fatal circumstance unveiled the mystery he was enshrouded in, and although they could do no otherwise than praise his conduct and his labours, he was dismissed.

"He then enrolled himself in the armies of Don Pedro, was promoted, and passed three years in Portugal, he then remained five years in Belgium, at first as a workman in an iron manufactory, afterwards as the head of a school for young children, but the reprobation followed him there, and he was driven away; he then contrived to get himself received as an inspector on the railroad, in the section of Gouy, of the workmen at Charleroi; but the works being completed, he found himself again without employment, and unable to obtain any, because his real position was known; he passed into Prussia, where he was arrested and brought back to the French frontier; in France he was also arrested, and after a detention of twenty-three days, he was condemned to twenty-four hours in prison for breaking his ban. The certificates he possessed pleaded in his favour, and in condeming him, the president of the tribunal deplored the severity of the law, but it dictated his sentence, he could only employ the power it left in him to inflict the minimum of punishment.

"After suffering this condemnation, the liberated forçat repaired to Metz, where the prefect of the Moselle sent him to Remelfding, in the colony of M. Appert; he remained there eight months, and left it because it was impossible for this generous philanthropist to continue longer his charitable work. The liberé then wished to go to Couvron, near Vitry, where the work for the railroad was in full activity; he requested an authority for that purpose, it was refused him by the caprice of a secretary of the mayor; and it is in consequence of such an inexplicable refusal that this unfortunate, the bearer of excellent certificates, and of a letter of recommendation, very honourable, of the under prefect of Toul, found himself reduced to solicit charity, throughout the whole route he travelled to reach Dreux, when I encountered him.

"This victim of prejudice, and the rigours of surveillance, twenty-three years after the expiration of his punishment, shed bitter tears in telling me that he knew well he was but a coward for enduring so long such tortures and humiliations, without having the courage to destroy himself."

"Why didn't he rob?" said Coco Desbraises.

"He had his notions," said Cadet l'Artesien.

"The notions of a fool," added Cadet Filoux. "But if this man, returning to himself and society, which he finds inexorable twenty-three years after the perpetration of a crime, almost excusable, again rebels against her, and becomes criminal, who ought to be accused, eh?"

"Certainly not him," replied the Grand Louis to this question of old Cadet Filoux.

"At all events," continued Cadet l'Artesien, "Aubert is not the only *fagot* whose history I could recount to you; but as I do not wish to keep you here till morning, I will only mention one other, which is Blanchet:

"Blanchet had been condemned to prison for a

robbery of minor importance, committed in a moment of drunkenness; at the expiration of his punishment he was placed under surveillance, and sent to a small locality of the province, where he had neither friends or relations, and obtained no work. Accustomed for twenty years to a Parisian life, the only city in which he could earn a living, (he was *marchand des quatre saisons*,)* he returned there, but was soon arrested for breaking his ban, and condemned. Again sent to the province, necessity once more compelled him to seek the capital; but this time, taught by experience, he concealed himself. The means of earning a living thus became more difficult, and he relapsed. This man, however, had no taste for the trade, his sentiments were honest and straightforward. He remained some time at the Conciergerie, and gained the esteem of the other detenus and of the guardians. His conduct was always exemplary, and it is said he obtained the confidence of the director of the prison; this confidence was entire, and he never abused it. It is asserted that the director would affirm, if required, that Blanchet had none but honest sentiments—yet the surveillance has made him a robber like ourselves.

" When a punishment, or rather that which is but an accessory of the punishment, produces such effects, this punishment, or this accessory, which ever it is called, is judged; it should disappear from our code, or submit, in its application, to some considerable changes; society has undoubtedly a right to punish, but it cannot possess the right of depraving.

" It seems, in fact, that our legislators themselves have acknowledged the slight moral value of our laws respecting surveillance; for during a long time, they allowed the libéré the privilege of freeing himself by the deposit of a sum of money, the amount of which varied, but which never exceeded a few hundred francs; a noble guarantee, truly, for society !

" They discovered at length that it was monstrous to accord to the libérés the privilege of redeeming a punishment, of turning a chastisement, as it were, into a venal merchandize, and at present every libéré remains subject to the surveillance; they would have done wiser to enfranchise the whole, if they refused to remedy the evils they produced.

" These evils are real, they are widely spread, and produce their effects every moment; observe the statistical tables, the relapses increase progressively; they have generalized the surveillance, it thus strikes a far greater number of individuals, and those who have relapsed are more numerous; it could not be otherwise, it is a *forced* consequence; and if they would establish a rule of proportion, they would find, I have no doubt, that the affinity between the relapses and the number of libérés, surrounded by the surveillance, has constantly been the same.

" Let them not seek then elsewhere the cause of this *manufactory* of crimes which terrify society, but endeavour to combat or destroy this cause; and let them not hope for a remedy in a new penitentiary system, which, should it even produce the good effects they might expect from it, will do nothing for the security of society, if previously they do not destroy the prejudices which still ride over it."

" Cadet Vincent, my children, has told you," resumed Cadet Filoux, " what happened to the grinche who was fool enough to turn an honest

man; I return to the point at which he interrupted me; I told you just now that many *garçons* would, if in their power, quit the trade, to labour honestly; we have no occasion, therefore, to dwell on this point."

" The old scelerat is decidedly preaching," said the Viscount de Lussan to his two companions, " I have a mind to send to the devil both the preacher and his congregation."

" No; do not attempt it, dear viscount," replied Salvador; " we must not be the aggressors, unless we wish to have the whole of this vile canaille upon us at once."

These few words spoken in an under tone, had not interrupted Cadet Filoux, who continued as follows: " If the crimes of some amongst us affright society, if our depredations unsettle the equilibrium of the social machine, may we not accuse the organization, the laws, the morals, of this same society, as well as ourselves?

" To justify the rigour of the laws which govern the lower classes of society, it is asserted that nearly all the grinches issue from the ranks of the proletoriat. This is true, or nearly so, but what does it prove, but the truth of the old proverb, which says, ' *that a hungry belly has no ears ?*'

" Let us admit, then, that all the grinches by profession issue from the ranks of the people. I will not speak to you about the grand criminals, who, with some exceptions, belong to the higher classes."

" My faith, the old fox is right," said Roman to the Viscount de Lussan, " 'tis oftener from the saloons than the garrets that assassins and forgers are let loose."

" And why not, M. l'Intendant?" replied the latter; " the lower orders have not an intelligence sufficiently developed to mature any grand affairs."

" This admitted," continued the speaker, " I ask you if there are in France any establishments in which this multitude of children of the people, who wander about the streets and boulevards, may be conducted, in order to learn a trade, and receive, in contracting habits of industry and sobriety, the education which, in a country that esteems itself at the head of civilization, every man ought to possess? No.

" And why? Because in order to establish them, money is wanted—but the money fails—a very dignified reply truly! Money is not wanting when journals, or theatres are to be purchased, at which the people never attend; or for paying the opera-dancers, who never dance for them; or erecting palaces in which they are not allowed to enter. Money therefore is not wanting, and you will all agree with me, that it is desirable that some of it was employed to found some philanthropic establishments similar to those which I have mentioned.

" However, there exist none, and the children to whom they would be useful, pass their time at the Quatre Billard,* or some similar rendezvous, where they become young thieves (des pegriots).

* The house known under the name of des Quatre Billards, or the Cave, is situate on the Boulevard du Temple. Apprentices who have left their masters, after robbing them sometimes of considerable sums; servants dismissed from their situations; workmen who, whilst *appearing* to seek work, pray to heaven they may find none; thieves by profession, and prostitutes of the lowest class; in a word, all the elements composing the most hideous debauchery, are the usual frequenters of this establishment, the existence of which is only tolerated for the purpose of affording the police an opportunity of making some important captures there; woe to the provincial who, by chance, enters this den, if ever so good a player, he will, on leaving, find himself stripped of his last piece of money, and lucky if he does not also leave his watch and redingote; and let him not be advised to com-

* The sale of flowers.

"The *pegriot*, my children, occupies the lower steps of the ladder, at the summit of which, are placed the *pègres de la haute*;* men like Rupin, the Provençal, Richard, like Cadet l'Artesein, Coco Lardouche, and myself formerly, and of which you occupy the intermediate steps. Want, guides the hand of the *pegriot*, when he commits his first crime, and perhaps if some one were to give him bread in exchange for his labour, and assist him with advice, he would abandon a trade, the commencement of which must appear to him rather rough. The *pegriot* is timid, and it is not until driven to his last extremity that he attempts to draw from the pocket of an individual within his reach, a handkerchief, which the receiver purchases of him at a quarter of its value; the *pegriot* is always dirty, and ill clad, he never breakfasts, and dines but seldom; if in possession of a few sous, he takes a lodging at one of the *night hotels* of the city; when his *purse* (?) is empty, he promenades the whole night, if the first patrol he meets does not carry him to the guard-house, which he will not leave except to appear before a *quart-d-œil*,† who will consign him *à la cigogne*.‡

"This is the way a man becomes a thief. If poor, he falls into vagabondage, and is sent to the *Force*, and leaves it a thief. The ignorant and abandoned child turns a *pegriot*, he is sent to prison, he leaves it a confirmed thief; 'tis continually the same story with different variations; once arrived at this point, do you know what you must do?"

"Well, what must we do?" said Delicat.

"Take time as it flies, the soup as it is, and follow your trade like a *bon garçon*," replied Cadet Filoux.

"Ah! do you mean it, old one?" said Charles la belle Cravate, "when once you have put your hand in the dish are there no means of withdrawing it?"

"None, my boy, none; and to prove that I am not imposing upon you, I will recount to you in a few words the history of a grinche, who endeavoured to become an honest man. Tell us then, Cadet Vincent, did you know, *la bas*, in the cell No. 3, a man named Etienne Lardenois?"

"I believe you; a handsome brown fellow; strong as a bull, and as daring as a lion, twenty-five or thirty years of age; but I say, Coco Desbraises, you knew him also, Etienne Lardenois, for I recollect one day his giving you a regular mauling."

"Yes, yes, I know him," replied Coco Desbraises, in a sulky tone.

"Well, this is what happened to him," continued Cadet Filoux:

"Etienne Lardenois was condemned to five years of hard labour, for a burglary in an inhabited house. Twenty years and upwards of hard labour is killing work; ten years is endurable; five years is a mere bagatelle, this you know; thus Etienne Lardenois, who was a lively comrade, did not fret much about his condemnation, and when he arrived at the prison at Toulon he was as merry as a cricket. In the course of a few days the case was altered, Etienne Lardenois could not reconcile to himself the smarting blows from the rattan of

messieurs the galley serjeants, so he pulled through his five years as well as possible, and when he received his papers as a *fagot affranchi*, he promised himself faithfully never to revisit Toulon—poor simpleton! He had no idea of the thousand obstacles he would have to surmount if he determined upon keeping the promise he had made to himself; as he had been condemned at a time when it was allowed to redeem the surveillance."

"Ah! that was the good old time," exclaimed such of the company who were aware that in a similar case at the present time, the privilege of which Cadet Filoux had spoken, would be withheld; "that was the good old time."

"He had not too much to complain of; he was permitted to reside at Paris."

"I say, old one, do you know that it's a queer law, that of the surveillance, now suppose that I, who was a jeweller by trade before I turned grinche, happened to be condemned, and afterwards, under surveillance, they would send me to some hole of a town or village in Normandy?"

"As you say, my cove."

"Well, in that case I could not turn honest man, as they do not manufacture jewels except at Paris; I should be compelled to steal to keep from starvation."

"It is just what you would do, and you would do right, my boy; but to return to Etienne Lardenois, I said that he was allowed to remain at Paris. E. Lardenois was a chaser by trade, he was an excellent workman, almost an artist, he was thus soon admitted into a factory without difficulty, where for some time he earned five francs a-day."

"'Twas handsome, he could enjoy himself with that," said Cadet Vincent.

"Unfortunately for E. Lardenois," continued Cadet Filoux, "a grinche with whom he had had some dispute in prison, and who hated him for having received from him a sound thrashing, happened to meet him, and contrived to discover where he worked; he wrote to the master of E. Lardenois and informed him that the man he employed was a *fagot affranchi*."*

"And so Etienne Lardenois was dismissed from the factory, I suppose," said Cadet Vincent.

Cadet Filoux burst into a loud laugh.

"You do not know," he continued, when his hilarity had passed, "you do not know what rogues *honest* men are. The master of E. Lardenois did not dismiss him; but being well aware that his workman could not, if he left him, find work elsewhere, he lowered his wages by a moiety, and paid him two and a-half francs in lieu of five francs; the poor fellow was compelled to be satisfied with it."

"But this employer was as great a villain as either one of us," said Rolet le Mauvais Gueux.

"I do not deny it; however, Etienne Lardenois, who had the simplicity to believe that his master merely wished to put to the proof the sincerity of his return to honesty, worked as hard and as well as for the five francs. This did not satisfy the grinche who had betrayed him; seeing that after the denunciation he had made to the master of Etienne Lardenois, his enemy was not ignominiously driven from the factory, he fancied he should be more successful if he addressed himself to the comrades of the latter, and in consequence he accosted them at a cabaret, one day when E. Lardenois was not with them, for he was too cowardly to attack his enemy in person."

"Which is as much as to say—" exclaimed Coco Desbraises.

plain, the frequenters of this house, who are not over patient, would soon come to a reckoning with him, and the neighbours whose assistance he claimed, would reply that he deserved what had happened to him, and that he who has no desire to be devoured by wolves should abstain from entering their dens.

* Thieves of the higher classes.
† Commissary of police.
‡ To the *Force*—Gaol.

* Liberated convict.

"Do you know the enemy of Etienne Lardenois?" demanded Cadet Filoux.

"No," replied the miserable, delighted to find that the old man had no intention of naming him.

"In that case hold your tongue, and let me finish my history. As the traitor who denounced Etienne Lardenois had anticipated, so it happened, the workmen would not consent to work with a *forçat libéré*, and the master was compelled, against his own wishes, to dismiss him; you may suppose that the position of Etienne Lardenois was soon known to all the men in his trade, and that in consequence he had to give it up; what could he do?"

"Parbleu! thieve," said Cornet-tape-dur.

"He did not choose to. But this is what he did: after having exhausted every resource, pledged or sold every thing he possessed, and invoked heaven and earth to send him work without succeeding.

"There exists at Clichy an establishment in which they manufacture white lead——"

"Well!" said Robert, "I have frequently heard this manufactory spoken of as something terrible; what is it then?"

"You wish to know what is this manufactory of white lead at Clichy," replied the Viscount de Lussau, who up to this moment had taken no part in the conversation, "I will tell you."

"Well, you will do us a very great favour," said Cadet Vincent.

"We reward with crosses and wreaths of laurel, those who have carried themselves bravely on the field of battle," continued the viscount; "we have crowns of oak, and medals of every size and of every composition, for those who have had the happiness to save one or several of their fellow-creatures from the consequences of a fire or an inundation; this is just, certainly, every good action should be recompensed, eh?"

"No doubt," said Robert; "if thieves, we are still Frenchmen; and when we see the cross of honour sparkling at the breast of a brave trooper, who has earned it on the field of battle; when we see a handsome silver medal suspended by a tricoloured ribbon upon the jacket of a sailor, who has saved from drowning some dozen of beings, we cannot help being pleased."

"Well! my friend, there are men still braver, and more virtuous than those to whom they grant such recompenses, and for such, they have nothing but rebuffs, contempt, and repulsion."

"Bah!" said Cornet-tape-dur, whose staring eyes announced the greatest astonishment, "and who then are these men?"

"Who are they! why, they are the workmen of the manufactory of white lead at Clichy! These unhappy creatures have certainly great virtue, and unshaken courage; whom misery or the rigours of a surveillance, badly understood, oblige to seek, at the manufactory at Clichy, the means of existence for themselves and their families; and who prefer a cruel death, which they are well aware they cannot escape, to the necessity of committing a second crime or a fresh relapse; in fact, the manufacture of white lead is so pernicious, the emanations which escape from the compounding of the substances which are employed in it, amongst which substances the oxide of lead greatly predominates, are so destructive, that before determining to work at Clichy, it is requisite to have made the sacrifice of one's life; a man of ordinary strength is sent to his last account in six weeks, or two months at the most, a healthy and vigorous constitution resists for three or four months, and those who last six months must be related to Hercules.

"If good wages allowed these miserables the hope of leaving behind them a morsel of bread for those who are dear to them; if, at least, their last days, which they pass in the practice of a rare virtue, self denial, were not filled with bitterness, there would not be quite so much to complain of against the white lead manufactories; but it is not thus, these men earn from one and a-half to two francs a-day; and the lepers of the middle age did not inspire more horror, than is at present shown towards the workmen at Clichy; these unfortunates are regarded by the people of the country as men infected by the plague, cursed by God and man, and carrying about with them contagion and death; and this is so true, that there is not in all Clichy, a girl who (knowing him) would dance with one of these men; these moving or living corpses, (oh! the force of the French character,) dance to drive away their care. A pinch of snuff is refused from their box, and no one would offer them a pinch from their own; in many cabarets they are not received, and those into which they are admitted, are only frequented by themselves; if there are any customers already there when they arrive, they immediately leave; and if, by chance, a countryman is seen to drink unknowingly with one of these men, they have a password to apprise him of it: *au plomb*, and at this warning he quits the workman, who drops from his temporary enjoyment into the most complete solitude.

"When you have nothing better to do, take a stroll in the neighbourhood of Clichy, and you will remark, wandering about the environs of the manufactory, miserable women dragging along rickety and sickly children, to whom the men, still paler and more diseased than themselves, remit a small sum destined to defray the expenses of the morrow's subsistence; you will see these unhappy women depart, with death at their heart, after reading in the eyes of the father of their infants the announcement of an approaching dissolution.

"Such is the fate which society reserves for those among you who, urged by the desire of becoming honest men, may hereafter seek the means of existence at the white lead manufactory at Clichy."

"Ah, well! I'm in no hurry for it," said Charles la belle Cravate, "but how comes it that they suffer establishments to exist where men may poison themselves at the rate of two francs a-day."

"Because trade requires colours which are fine and durable," said the Grand Louis, "and they pay more attention to that than to the existence of a heap of machines like us."

"Richard told you just now," continued Cadet Filoux, "that to support life for six months at the white lead factory, you must be a Hercules; the Hercules are rare, but there are a few, and Etienne Lardenois was one of them. I encountered him one day, when by chance I took a short morning walk, it was him who accosted me, for I did not recognise the poor fellow. The most frightful paleness had usurped the healthy complexion of his countenance; his eyes were sunken and dull, and the white portion of them veined and blood-shot, and hardly able to endure the light of day; his hair had nearly all fallen off, his lips had received that violet colour which reminds one of the marbling remarked on bodies which have remained for some time under water, his teeth were all destroyed and gone, he was thin, and more bent at thirty years than I am at eighty-four.

"'Well! *birbe*,* he said to me, in a tone nearly inaudible, 'you do not recognise me then?'

"'My faith!' I replied, 'you are so changed, that if you had not told me your name, I should have doubted if it were you. You must change your trade, my boy.'

"'It is too late, *rioque*,† it is too late! my account is settled—I shall last another month, I shall then have been six months here; 'tis a long while, and I must not complain. Come, let us drink a glass of wine together.'

"We entered the nearest wine-shop, and whilst disposing of a bottle, which he would absolutely pay for, he recounted to me what had happened to him. The poor fellow had no ill-feeling towards the man who had caused him the loss of his place, he merely observed, on leaving me, that God would punish him sooner or later. Probably he had some thoughts about religion when he saw death so near."

"He was not so very wrong either in believing there is a God," said Cadet l'Artesien, "for after all, there must be one. Neither you or me have created what we behold around us; and it is more than probable that we have not been sent upon the earth to live like dogs."

"That's the argument of a devotè, who is afraid he is going to hell, where the devil will turn him round and roast him. Because he is close to his grave, he wishes _ come the good apostle over us," said Coco Lardouche, in his hollow and trembling voice.

"I have done my utmost, my children, to prove to you that circumstances contribute to produce more thieves than the desire or the wish of those who exercise the profession; and from what I have told you of Etienne Lardenois, you can see, that unless you are resigned to follow his example, there are no means of returning to the strait road, when once you have wandered from it. I can only then repeat to you in other terms what I said in the commencement. 'Since you are thieves, remain thieves; but do not give those who are at war with you, weapons to be used against yourselves.' Instead of hating one another, let the *pegriot* serve, without pride, the *pègre de la haute*, whilst waiting for his own turn to arrive. 'Paris,' says an old proverb, 'was not built in a day.' Submit without complaining to the consequences of the life you lead; not a single battle takes place without costing the lives of more or less soldiers; your liberty, sometimes even your life, is the stake of the game which you play against society; a game which sooner or later you *must* lose. This is a truth which you would do wrong to attempt to hide from yourselves; you ought then, if you are reasonable, to endeavour to make it last as long as possible."

"The old one's malicious," said Charles la belle Cravate, "but what he has told us is true, for all that."

The venerable Cadet Filoux, whom the praises of his auditory, vulgar as they were, seemed greatly to flatter, would have been in no haste to conclude, if Salvador had not leant towards him, and told him to pass at once to the peroration of his sermon. He could not continue after Salvador had intimated to him an order to be silent; for he had an interest in not doing any thing which could displease the latter, who often slid into his hand a few gold pieces, which, with what he received from Mother Sans Refus, who considered herself bound in honour not to leave in misery an ancient camarade d'affaires

of the author of her being, added to the small revenue he possessed, enabled him to pass his life in ease and comfort.

"In order that this game may endure," he continued, after fixing upon Salvador a look which indicated that he had arrived at the conclusion of his address, "let the comrade at liberty never abandon the comrade in trouble; and the latter especially must never encourage the thought of bettering his condition at the expense of his comrades at liberty; in a word, you must each give the other a hand, and be as affectionate one towards the other as brothers; this is my earnest wish towards you, and I now give you my blessing. Amen."

"Bravo! bravo!" exclaimed all the bandits, laying hands upon the *petits peres noirs* placed before them. "To the health of the old boy."

Their heads were already tolerably inflamed, when the decanters of parfait amour, of cent sept ans, and of cognac, which for some moments the guests of Mother Sans Refus had been ogling with the corners of their eyes, were placed upon the table.

The liquors finished what the *blue* wine had so well commenced, when Mother Sans Refus, willing to allow her guests every possible liberty, and fearing no doubt that the presence of one of the sex would impose upon them a disagreeable reserve, did as the English ladies who quit the table in order to allow their husbands the privilege of drinking at their ease, shortly after the dessert has appeared.

The three venerables, Cadet Filoux, Cadet l'Artesien, and Coco Lardouche, on whom their great age imposed a sobriety and habits of regularity which the other individuals of the company were not forced to observe, followed the example of the mistress of the fête.

Mother Sans Refus before leaving her convives favoured them with a grimace which they were satisfied to receive as a smile, and recommended them to amuse themselves well, and not spare the wine of which there still remained three pieces in one of the corners of the cave.

"No! we will not spare your wine," said Delicat to his two accolytes, when Mother Sans Refus had retired. "Have you remarked the old woman? She's worse than the stall of a jeweller; and only fancy that all she has is our sweat, our blood! what harm would there be in taking by force from her all that the old receiver has robbed us of?"

Delicat, Coco Desbraises, and Rolet le Mauvais Gueux occupied at table the opposite end to that at which were seated Salvador, Roman, and the Viscount de Lussan.

Vernier les bas Bleus who, on entering, had placed himself at the centre of the table between Cornet-tape-dur and Cadet Vincent, quitted without any affectation, his place, and approached Roman who had signed to him to come and speak with him.

"Listen," said Roman, who had been charged with the negotiation; "you have guessed no doubt that Rupin, Richard, and myself, have the greatest interest that the secret discovered by Coco Desbraises and Delicat, a secret which they have already made known to Rolet, should not be divulged further."

"Pardine!"

"And do you think there are any means of forcing these men to be silent?"

"I know but one; and if you will employ it, you may reckon upon me," said Vernier, regarding Roman significantly, "I have not forgotten that they had a mind to *quiet* me."

---

* Old boy.   † Old boy.

"Let us consider a moment," said the Viscount de Lussan, "there are fourteen here; if a combat takes place, who are those who will be against us, and upon whom can we reckon to remain neuter?"

"You will have against you, besides the three in question, le Grand Louis and Charles la belle Cravate, and perhaps one or two others; Robert, Cadet Vincent, and the others will not mix themselves up in it."

"Eh! but the game is a much better one than I expected," continued the Viscount de Lussan, "it only remains to commence it."

"That will not be difficult," replied Vernier les bas Bleus, "if you will allow me to manage it."

"Take a carte blanche, my dear," replied Roman to him, who said to his two friends, when Vernier had quitted them in order to place himself near Delicat and his two supporters; "this man, during the three days he has passed with these individuals, has probably learnt a great deal too much. When he has helped to rid us of them, we will balance his account."

"Again!" said Salvador.

"Monsieur Roman is perfectly right," said the Viscount de Lussan.

Whilst the *Rupins*, if we may be allowed to preserve to these three personages the name which they were known by in the place they were in at present, exchanged in an under tone the few words which precede, Vernier, on his side had lost no time with Delicat and his two friends.

"I have been talking with the *Rupins*," he said to them.

"Well; what did they say to you?" demanded Delicat, his countenance inflamed by wine and rage.

"That they laugh at you and your friends," replied Vernier les bas Bleus.

"Oh; they said that, did they?" exclaimed Coco Desbraises, "they shall smart for it."

"We must murder them," added Rolet le Mauvais Gueux.

"Well, it's your own fault," continued Vernier, "after acknowledging that it was impossible to enter their house, where, as you said, there were a lot of servants of the devil, you charged me to tell them that if they did not hand you over ten bank notes of a thousand francs each, you would denounce them, and you told me nothing about the secret you had discovered, so that I looked very much like a fool."

"Well then, bas Bleus," replied Coco Desbraises, "it's my opinion that you are not quite such a fool as you may have the appearance of, and that it is not without an intention that you have marched us about the country for three blessed days, and I think you go halves with the Rupins to deceive us."

"If I were certain of that," added Delicat, drawing from the pocket of his redingote a long dagger-knife, "I would plunge my knife in your heart up to the handle."

Delicat had risen his voice in pronouncing these words; his eyes, which were nearly out of their orbits, sparkled like fire, and small spirts of froth issued from between his lips.

"What's the matter, what's the matter?" exclaimed at once the other bandits.

Vernier les bas Bleus had quickly dropped astern, when he saw Delicat arm himself with his dagger-knife.

"The matter is," he said, pointing to Delicat, "that this villain wishes to murder me, because I won't help him to assassinate the *Rupins*."

"Oh! you betray us, *lezard!*" exclaimed Coco

Desbraises, "well! you shall know nothing, and we *will* murder you."

"It seems that Vernier knows nothing," said Salvador to Roman.

"Without doubt, Coco Desbraises has saved his life," replied the latter. "Well, viscount, I think it is time to open the ball; are you prepared?"

"Quite ready, my dear," replied the viscount, rising with the utmost sang froid; "which do you think I had best commence with?"

"Stay a moment," said Salvador, "as they have no fire-arms, we must let them attack us."

Vernier le bas Bleus, profiting by the tumult, had approached the *Rupins;* Delicat was haranguing in the midst of a group composed of his two intimates, of le Grand Louis, Charles la belle Cravate, and some others, and vomiting forth at the top of his voice, the most foul abuse against Salvador and his friends.

"Will you be silent there," said Salvador, at length, in a voice of thunder, "it has lasted quite long enough, and if you do not instantly cease, you will force me to administer a correction to the whole of you."

"What does he say? correct us," exclaimed Rolet le Mauvais Gueux; and nearly the whole of the bandits advanced towards the Rupins; Robert, Cadet Vincent, Cornet-tape-dur, and some others, foreseeing a struggle in which they were unwilling to take a part, made haste to mount to the uppermost steps of the ladder, from whence they could be spectators of what was about to take place without the fear of receiving any misdirected blows.

The Rupins and Vernier les bas Bleus placed themselves against the length of the wall in order to prevent being surrounded.

"*Arma presto, subito!*" said Roman; they then each placed a hand on the pistols which they had taken care to be provided with. They had to overcome nine resolute bandits, whom wine and the brandy they had swallowed, had transformed into so many wild beasts.

"Let us murder the Rupins first," cried Delicat, Coco Desbraises, and Rolet le Mauvais Gueux; "to the slaughter! we will *stiffen* the old receiver after, and rummage the house; there's plenty to grab in the crib."

"Down with your knives, you heap of miserables," cried Salvador, in a voice which was heard above the tumult; "down with the knives, or I'll scorch you."

"Death to the Rupins! death!" and the bandits, each armed with a long dagger-knife, and like a torrent which has burst its dykes, flung themselves with fury against the small group of their enemies; Vernier le bas Bleus was the first to suffer, by receiving a severe cut from a knife on the left arm.

"Ah! that's it, is it?" said the Viscount de Lussan, on seeing the blood flowing from the arm of Vernier; "the blood be on your own heads then;" and discharging one of his pistols at Rolet le Mauvais Gueux, who had wounded Vernier, he shot the miserable man through the head, and his brains were scattered against the walls of the cavern.

Two of the bandits being frightened, had retired behind, the Rupins had now in front of them only Delicat, Coco Desbraises, le Grand Louis, Charles la belle Cravate, and two others. "To you! Marquis of Evil!" exclaimed Delicat, rushing upon Salvador with all the agility of a tiger cat; "to you!" and he aimed at the heart of Salvador a

No. 25.

LIFE IN PARIS.

EDMUND DE BOURQUET AND EUGENIE.

furious blow with his dagger; unfortunately for him. the blade slid on one side, and caused only a slight wound.

This sudden attack had surprised Salvador, but did not discourage him; he seized Delicat with one hand, and holding him at arm's length, in order to prevent his attempting to renew his attack, he sent two balls through his body. Delicat made one turn round, and fell with his face on the ground.

"Give the secret to the others," he said, in a voice struggling with agony, to Coco-Desbraises, who was wrestling with Vernier, whilst Roman and the Viscount de Lussan kept in respect the other bandits whose ardour began to cool; "give the secret to the others; they must murder the whole of them or dance——"

These were his last words.

The chairs, table, and every article placed upon it, had been upset, crushed, and broken in a thousand pieces; the smoke produced by the discharge of the two pistols, not finding any issue for escaping, formed itself into a thick cloud in the cave, lighted merely by the pale and doubtful light of a candle, which Cadet Vincent had furnished himself with, at the moment he had taken refuge on the steps of the ladder.

The words pronounced by Delicat, before rendering his last sigh, had been heard by Roman; leaving for a moment, to the Viscount de Lussan and Salvador, the care of making head against those of the assailants who still remained, he seized a strong bar of iron, forgotten by chance in the cave, and which he found within reach, and gliding in the shade behind Coco-Desbraises, he dealt him so determined a blow on his head, that it stretched him on the floor before he had time to utter a word to encourage his friends.

"That settles the third!" he said, brandishing above his head the formidable bar of iron which he had just used, whilst his friends kept at a distance, by means of their fire-arms, the four assailants, who were not yet *hors de combat*. "Who'll be the next? Come, speak, and you shall be served."

"Come, put up your knives, and surrender yourselves at discretion," said the Viscount de Lussan, "unless you wish me to charge again."

"Surrender yourselves, then," cried those who were upon the ladder; "you see plain enough that you have no longer any chance."

Le Grand Louis and Charles la belle Cravate, seeing that they were but faintly supported by some, and that the others kept the most perfect neutrality, wished for nothing better than to do as they were advised; but they feared that the *Rupins* would take some revenge; the latter, who had no longer any interest to prolong the struggle, since those who knew their secret were not among the living, having again offered them quarter, they eagerly embraced it.

Vernier les bas Bleus was the one who had most suffered; it was against him that those who had lost their lives were more particularly enraged, the wound which Rolet le Mauvais Gueux had given him in the arm, caused him great agony, and Coco-Desbraises had very roughly handled him in the struggle they had engaged in; the wound of Salvador was but a scratch.

CHAPTER XXIII.

BEPPO AND SILVIA.

As it often happens that men pass from one extreme to the other, so, when once peace was concluded between Salvador, his friends, and those who had taken part in the intended plot by Delicat and Coco-Desbraises, the bandits were the first to accuse of all that had taken place, those who were no longer there to defend themselves; and to promise an unlimited submission, and a blind obedience, to Salvador, as well as to his friends.

"It's very well," said Salvador to them, after listening with much patience to their protestations of regret and devotedness, "but this does not concern the present moment, it is time to depart, and we cannot leave these three bodies there, we must get rid of them."

"If, before dying, they had given us the address of the doctor, to whom they would have sold themselves, we might have disposed of them," said Charles la belle Cravate, striking with his foot the corpses as they lay stretched on the floor.

"But you have not this address," replied Roman, "you must therefore renounce the speculation, and contrive to rid us of these *charognes;* but how to manage?"

"Indeed it is rather embarrassing," said the Viscount de Lussan.

"Let me manage it," said le Grand Louis, formerly a butcher's assistant, and of most athletic form; after tucking up to the elbow, the sleeves of his shirt, "let me manage it, I have an idea; we must first disfigure these galliards, so that they may not be recognised, and I'll undertake it." And without waiting for a reply, he commenced cutting, with the aid of his dagger-knife, the faces of the defunct, and every part of their body, in which there existed any marks. There was something so horrible in this monstrous profanation, accomplished with as much sang froid and nonchalance, as if it were one of the simplest and most natural actions in the world, that Salvador, Roman, the Viscount de Lussan, and the other bandits, inured as they were to sights of horror, could not help shuddering, and turning their heads from this disgusting scene; they said nothing however, what the Grand Louis did was necessary to their safety.

"'Tis done!" said le Grand Louis, when he had finished the task he had undertaken, "and I defy the cleverest *mouchard* to give a name to either of these worthies; we must stave in the casks of wine, and stow away in them our three comrades, whom we will shove into the water, after making some holes in the tubs to prevent their floating."

"And neither seen or known," said Charles la belle Cravate.

"Go above and see if all is quiet, and bring the wherry," said Salvador to Cornet-tape-dur.

"'Tis all quiet," cried the latter through the hole, a few minutes after leaving the cave; "it rains in torrents, the night is quite dark, the women are not returned home, the mother is asleep at the bar, now is the moment; there is'nt a man in the street; there's a cord."

The casks in which, not without some trouble, they had enclosed the three bodies, were, by means of the cord, drawn up into the small court by Cornet-tape-dur and Cadet Vincent, who had mounted in order to lend him a hand, and were then carried into Salvador's boat, through the small street of the Teinturiers.

Salvador had just taken possession of the oars, when suddenly some confused rumours, and especially the cries of a woman, approached from the bridge of Notre Dame, and were quickly followed by a long cry of agony, and exclamations, "Murder ! arrest the assassin !" struck his ears.

"Throw over the tubs quickly, and return," cried Roman to him, who had remained on the bank, "the crowd approaches this side."

Salvador hastened to obey his friend. He had got rid of the last of the three casks, when a man, probably the one who was pursued by the public clamour, flung himself from the bridge of Arcole into the river, and commenced swimming vigorously in the wake caused by the boat, which he soon passed. This man landed opposite the street of the Teinturiers, through which he resolutely took his way, and where he was followed by Salvador who had just disembarked, and also by Roman, who had waited on the bank for the return of his friend. The man in question, having probably remarked that the night was so dark and the atmosphere so charged with mist, that those who pursued him must necessarily have lost his traces, stopped to take breath, but hearing some confused cries almost above his head, he took to flight, and found himself, after a few paces, in the midst of the habitués, of the house of Mother Sans Refus, who had all quitted the cavern, and after replacing the trough which concealed the entrance to every one, were retiring.

He naturally supposed they were a part of those who pursued him, and that they had placed themselves in ambush in this obscure street, merely to intercept him in his passage. Determined to sell his life dearly, he brandished his knife above his head, and rushed upon those in front of him.

"Let me pass, or I'll be the death of you !" he exclaimed.

From his very apparent provincial accent, Salvador and Roman recognised a compatriot, and as they were behind him, they seized him by the two shoulders, and made him quickly enter the little court, the door of which, upon a sign, had been opened by the Viscount de Lussan.

The crowd coming from the two parallel quays of the city, and the Hotel de Ville, began to spread themselves in the street de la Tannerie ; the bandits not caring to mix themselves in it, after what had taken place, quietly entered their rendezvous.

It was time, the street de la Tannerie was invaded by the crowd ; and from their place of concealment, the bandits, and the man whom Salvador and Roman had saved, could hear their clamours.

This man, when he found himself suddenly seized, and introduced almost by force into the small court, had remained for some moments with haggard eyes, a heaving bosom, and almost deprived of the use of his faculties.

"Who are you ? What do you want with me ? In Heaven's name let me go !" he exclaimed, when he had recovered his senses.

"Hold your tongue, brawler !" said Charles la belle Cravate, placing his hand on his mouth ; "don't you hear that they are searching for you ?"

In fact, they heard again the confused cries of the crowd who were passing in front of the house of Mother Sans Refus, to reach, no doubt, the place of the Hotel de Ville.

When every thing became quiet in the neighbourhood, the bandits entered the room behind the shop, and one of them awoke the mistress, who, thanks to the numerous bumpers she had swallowed since she had quitted the cavern, had continued in a profound sleep.

"Well! my children, has all gone off well?" she said, bringing with her a candle and a bottle of brandy.

"Perfectly, mother; perfectly," replied Salvador. "You sleep soundly, it seems?"

"Oh! yes, I sleep well. Ah! mon Dieu!" she exclaimed, examining herself hastily; but finding at her side her chain garnished with keys, her countenance returned to its serenity, she then for the first time observed the new comer.

"Who is this person?" she said to Charles la belle Cravate.

"An assassin," he replied, "whom the *Rupins* have saved."

"Poor young man !" continued Sans Refus, approaching the unknown with some interest, to whom she offered a glass of cogniac ; "the boy is not bad looking."

The stranger trembled in every limb, a frightful paleness covered his face ; he tottered for a few moments like a drunken man, and then fell heavily on the floor.

"Good! you see at present he is ill," said la Sans Refus.

"He must be carried to the room of one of the women," said Roman ; "who will lend me a hand?"

Cadet Vincent took the feet of the stranger, whilst Roman was at the head, and preceded by Sans Refus, who held the candle, the two bandits carried him into one of the chambers of the first floor, and placed him in a tolerably good bed.

The unknown was a prey to a burning fever.

"He is not yet accustomed to the work," said Roman to the Viscount de Lussan.

"He will come to it," replied the latter, " 'tis only the first step which is *expensive*."

A woman, who entered at this moment, undertook to pass the night in attendance on the stranger, in order to give him such necessaries as he might require.

What sentiment had Salvador and Roman obeyed when they saved this man?

What sentiment did the woman we speak of obey, when she proposed to pass the night with this man, whom she had never seen, in order to bestow upon him the attention he required?

What sentiment, in a word, was obeyed by these bandits, who seemed delighted that this man had escaped the pursuit of which he had been the object.

A sentiment of pity, which is naturally felt for every man who is unfortunate, whatever may be the fault he has committed ? a sentiment of humanity. Neither, bon Dieu!

A much less ennobling sentiment explains the interest which Roman and Salvador at first, and the others afterwards, had just shown ; it was attributable to that desire of baffling justice, which predominates among those who have been taken in her net, or who know that at some future time, more or less distant, they will have to render to her an account of their actions. Among these gentry, (and our readers are aware that all those who appeared interested in the stranger were of this number,) to perplex the operations of justice, to render its investigations next to impossible, in a word, to *destroy* it by every means in their power, this is a pleasure, a species of anticipated vengeance, which they never refuse when the opportunity of satisfying it presents itself.

Our readers have, no doubt, divined that the stranger with the provincial accent, to whom the bandits, assembled at the Tavernieres of the street de la Tannerie, bestowed such attentions, was no other than Beppo. We shall inform them of the events which accompanied the carrying off of Silvia, and those which followed it, up to the moment when the ex-fisherman Castilian, after committing a terrible crime, threw himself from the bridge of Arcole into the Seine, to escape the pursuit of those who were seeking for him.

It has not been forgotten, probably, that Silvia, frightened in a manner by the sudden apparition of this man, whom she expected never to see again, had allowed herself to be conducted to a carriage, without offering the slightest resistance. She believed at first that Beppo had no other intentions than to profit by a favourable occasion for which he was indebted to chance, and to renew those entreaties which he had already made; and she would rather have given way to this necessity than provoke, by resistance, a scandal before which she knew well that the half-savage nature of Beppo would not recoil.

She had fallen, rather than sat down, in one of the corners of the vehicle, and she waited, not without a certain impatience, that Beppo might say something to her, when the carriage stopped. She raised her head and looked about her, in order to ascertain to what place she had been transported. The sombre and desolate aspect of the neighbourhood in which the house occupied by Beppo was situated, completely overcame her.

"Where am I?" she exclaimed, "where are you leading me?"

Beppo had paid the driver, who, conforming to the instructions he had received, had disappeared with all the haste which the two Rosinantes under his orders could accomplish.

"Be good enough to follow me, Madame la Marquise," said Beppo to Silvia, whose arm he had seized the moment they had descended from the vehicle.

The slight expression of irony with which he accompanied these words, an irony which did not escape the attention of Silvia, so much increased the anxiety to which she had been a prey from the moment she had observed the disconsolate aspect of the habitation to which she was about to be introduced, that she fainted, and Beppo was compelled to take her in his arms and carry her into the house. His mother, who was expecting every moment the mistress of her son, was ready to receive her. Beppo placed her on a good bed, though furnished with coarse sheets, and left her alone with his mother for a considerable time. All the attentions bestowed upon her produced no results for some hours. Her fainting was accompanied by a suffocation brought on by a long restrained and violent rage, but to which she gave vent when at last she recovered the use of her faculties.

"Where am I? who are you? and who has placed me here?" she exclaimed.

To all these questions, which succeeded each other with the rapidity of lightning, Beppo's mother, quite embarrassed in the character she had to play, could not or would not make but one reply: "I do not know."

Silvia, quite recovered, told her imperatively that she would see Beppo, that without doubt he had no intention of keeping her a prisoner in the chamber she was in, and that if he did not hasten to render her at liberty, she knew well how to do justice to herself, and cause him to repent his conduct towards her. At length she determined to rise from the bed in which they had placed her during her fainting; but she was forced to renounce her design, for her clothes had been taken away.

Believing herself abandoned for the moment to the care of the old woman who was near her, she raised her voice several times in succession, in the hope that her cries would bring some one to her succour; but this hope failing, she rose up despite the efforts of Beppo's mother, who continued to beg of her to be calm, and to have patience at least until the arrival of her son, who, to a certainty, would not refuse to give her her liberty; and the good woman, when she made this promise, did so in good faith, for she could not believe that her son would be mad enough to retain at his house, against her inclination, a woman who, far from loving him, appeared (at least to judge from her discourse) to entertain the most violent hatred towards him.

But Silvia, who, from the exasperation to which she was a prey, had forgotten all discretion, jumped out of bed and opened the small door of the landing, determined to demand protection from the first person she might encounter on the staircase. Unfortunately for her, Beppo, who had only quitted the room from propriety, was upon the landing; she was thus compelled to return, which she did without pronouncing a word.

She had exerted, in this last effort, all the energy which the emotions of the day had left her; and her will, imperious as it was, was forced to submit to a power stronger than itself.

A few minutes after, and whilst she was still under the effects of a sort of febrile agitation, produced by the rage at finding herself powerless, and the regrets she felt at having allowed herself so easily to be led into a snare which she could not escape, Beppo entered.

After making a sign to his mother to retire, he approached the bed in which lay Silvia.

"Listen, Madame la Marquise," he said in a low tone, "to the resolution I have taken, a resolution which will not be changed either by your menaces, or your tears, nor even, if you compel me to it, the necessity of committing a fresh crime; you forced me to shed the blood of your lover upon condition that you would be entirely mine; blinded by the foolish passion I felt towards you, which I have kept under restraint, probably, by your seductions, I struck the blow, I religiously acquitted myself of my infamous mandate. Now however, I will not force you to fulfil your promises. I know, and you know it as well as myself, that there are certain favours which are valueless, unless the person from whom we desire to receive them, bestows them with a good grace; you have therefore no violence to fear; but since you will not, or you cannot, accord me a love upon which I had a right to depend, I shall guard you here, in order that the man you at present love, may not possess that which belongs to me."

Silvia, we may believe, did not expect such a declaration; she had not supposed that the rude fisherman of the Isles of Hyeres would have so much delicacy, and she began to comprehend, in spite of all the esprit she possessed, that her conduct towards him had not been justifiable. The nature of this woman was so corrupted, that she supposed this man was only actuated by a sensual desire to possess her, and at the moment even in which he expressed to her his sentiments regarding her, she thought to herself she should be quit of him by paying for her liberty by some complaisances. The discovery she had made destroyed her last hope, she hazarded however a few observations of a nature to induce Beppo to change his resolution.

"It is useless to endeavour to deceive me, madame," replied Beppo; "why tell me to-day the contrary of what you asserted the last time I had an occasion of seeing you? do you believe, then, that I am ignorant that if you tell me now, that if I had acted otherwise, you might have finished by loving me, it is because you are in my power that you hold this language? No, madame, no; you have never loved me, you do not love me, and you never will love me; do not then allow to escape your mouth words against which your heart revolts. I have read your indifference, your hatred even, in your every action; I read it at the present moment in every movement of your body, which despite your efforts recoils within itself at my approach, as though I were a reptile or beast of prey; and but now, when you attempted to bestow upon me a smile similar to those which once fascinated me, I saw it *burst* in your eyes. And for myself, do I love you still? I do not believe it. But it is you who have filled my life with remorse; it is owing to you that my poor mother, who grieves to witness the sufferings of her only son, is so unhappy. Well! I am determined that your happiness shall not insult my sufferings; I do not choose you should have it in your power to say that you have made use of me, as of an instrument which you can destroy when you have no longer any occasion for it, I wish to avenge myself; for this reason I have carried you off from the man you love; for this reason I shall force you to live by the side of a man whom you detest, and in order that you may not escape from the fate I have reserved for you, I shall guard you with as much care as the miser guards his treasure."

"And how long, Beppo, do you reckon upon making me support this life?"

"I do not know, when indifference shall have replaced the love or the hatred I feel towards you, (I scarcely know how to describe the sentiment with which you inspire me,) I will then set you at liberty."

"But, miserable!" exclaimed Silvia, who then made an attempt to terrify Beppo, "by what right will you imprison me here?"

"By the strongest, since that is the only one you have left at my disposition."

"But I can make my voice heard, they will come to my succour, and I shall have it in my power to punish you severely."

"You can scream out, no doubt," said Beppo, smiling bitterly, "but did you possess even the voice of a stentor, you would be heard by no one; take the trouble to cast a look through the windows, and you will be convinced that the solitude of this house is such that all your cries for help will be quite useless. Yes, yes, I have well taken every precaution. For the rest, the wisest plan you can adopt is that of resigning yourself, for I am resolved to guard you in spite of every one, and not to quit you, if it must be, until I have plunged a dagger in your heart."

The preceding words had been exchanged in an under tone; so that Beppo's mother, who had retired into the embrasure of a window, had been unable to hear a word that passed.

"Mother," said Beppo to her, "come here and listen to me."

The poor woman who had remarked that for some time her son had conversed quietly with the female, who was so violent and enraged but a few minutes preceding, believed, at first, that the two young persons had come to a perfect understanding and she approached her son quite gaily.

"You see this lady," said Beppo to her, and pointing to Silvia, "it is only by means of a ruse and some little violence that I have brought her here, where I intend to guard her against her will."

"You have acted thus, oh! my son," replied the old Castilian; "but this lady, you have told me, loved you, and that it was with her own consent, and to withdraw her from foreign influence, that you should bring her to our dwelling, where I have only consented to receive her, because you gave me the assurance that a marriage should consecrate the love you felt for her; I see now that you have deceived me."

"Yes, my mother, I have deceived you; but what is done, is done——"

"You are right, and I will not make you any useless reproaches; but since this lady does not love you, allow her to depart, and endeavour to forget her; I have no doubt but she will cease to remember your wrongs and your violence."

"Oh! yes, madame," exclaimed Silvia, employing the mildest inflections of her voice, and assuming the softest expression of countenance; "allow me to go, and I promise you that not a person shall become acquainted with what has happened to me to-day."

"I am determined that madame shall not quit this house," cried Beppo; "and as I foresee that I shall be obliged to absent myself occasionally, you must consent, mother, to replace me during my absence; for, I repeat to you, madame shall remain here."

"You do not expect, my son, certainly, that I can consent to do what you require of me?"

Silvia, whom the opposition of Beppo's mother had inspired with fresh hope, and who was aware that the latter could not guard her if his mother did not consent to aid him, could not prevent herself from regarding Beppo with a look of triumph and cold irony.

"Mother! mother!" exclaimed the ex-fisherman, who started under this glance, as though struck by a spark of electricity; "I swear to you by Notre-Dame de Bon-Secours, and you know whether I have ever failed to keep such an oath, that if she quits this place I will kill her. And now do just as you like, and may it happen just as it pleases God."

Upon hearing the last words, the mother of Beppo became deadly pale; she threw herself in sobs on Silvia's bed. Beppo had left the room, and Silvia, who was all attention, had distinctly heard him descend the staircase; she determined to profit by the profound stupor in which Beppo's mother was plunged, and endeavoured to rise.

"Oh! stop, I entreat you, madame," cried the Castilian, "stay I beseech you, both for your own sake and that of my unfortunate son; for, as certain as there is a God in heaven, he will do what he has sworn. Beppo has never failed in an oath made to our holy patroness, Notre-Dame de Bon-Secours."

Silvia knew that the old lady was not imposing upon her, and felt satisfied that the despair of the Castilian, who ought to know the character of her son, was not a comedy played expressly to induce her to have patience; she dropped her head upon the pillow, she had acquired the certitude that the individual, who a few moments before had so strongly pleaded for her liberty, was suddenly become, in order to spare her son a crime, an incorruptible gaoler. The haughty Marchioness of Roselly was a second time vanquished.

Several days passed in this manner.

Silvia at length became convinced, that in order to escape from the hands of her ravisher, it would be necessary to dissimulate; to this last resource she devoted herself, and before a month had elapsed she appeared, if not resigned, at least much less afflicted than a short time previously. Without, however, allowing the secret motive of her change of conduct to be suspected, she continued to supplicate her gaoler to give her her liberty, or at least to allow her to take the air; she employed, to gain his confidence, every means which her sprightly imagination suggested to her, prayers, tears, caresses, menaces, but Beppo was invulnerable; he discovered the trap concealed under the manœuvres of the syren.

Six months thus passed. Silvia, who possessed that tenacity which only belongs to such as have accepted as a *fait accompli*, a position from which, however, they hope to escape, seemed almost satisfied with her lot; at times even she attempted a laugh, or hummed some short airs. Thanks to a perfect knowledge of the provincial idiom, which she had acquired during her stay at Marseilles, she had completely gained the confidence of Beppo's mother; and this kind woman, who could scarcely fancy it possible that any one could see her son, for any length of time, without loving him, was not far from thinking that she might soon leave the cage open without the bird attempting to take flight. Beppo himself believed his captive resigned, and although he relaxed in nothing the incessant surveillance, of which she was the object, it sometimes occurred to him that this proud woman had at length accepted all the consequences of the position in which the crime she had caused him to commit had placed her; and that, perhaps at no distant period, he might receive the reward of his firmness, and of a love, which, in spite of all his efforts, had not ceased to reign in his heart.

But this resignation was but apparent; Silvia had frequently asked herself, whether, during one of the short absences of Beppo, she might not attempt to employ violence, to escape from the sort of prison in which she was confined; but after remarking the strong build of her Castilian gaoler, which announced a strength much superior to her own, she renounced this project, and resolved to have recourse to a ruse, and to wait a favourable occasion for her escape.

Several reasons, which will be known in the sequel, concurred to prevent Silvia having recourse to violent means to recover her liberty.

The kind of pavilion she inhabited, in company with her gaolers, was divided into two stages; the upper one, which was composed of a single room, was occupied by Silvia; the under one, much more considerable, served as a habitation for Beppo and his mother, and as a place of reunion for the little colony.

Beppo's mother acted as a gaoler to Silvia against her inclination; for as she was ignorant, *not* of the preceding connection which had existed between her son and Silvia, but of the cause which had given birth to this liason, she did not seek to hide from herself the injustice of withdrawing a young woman from her affections and her habitudes, in order to keep her sequestered from the world and its pleasures, at an age when air and exercise is so much required; but still, as her son's firmness of character convinced her that he would realize the oath he had sworn, whilst acquitting herself conscientiously of her charge, she studied to render the captivity of Silvia as mild as possible; and upon every occasion in which she found herself alone with her, she gave her to suppose, that it only required a little patience for some short time further; that Beppo would soon tire of the life, which the constraint he kept her in, compelled him to lead; and that if she served him as an accomplice, it was but to spare her (Silvia) a misfortune, and a crime to the son she loved, although she could not justify his conduct.

To all this discourse, Silvia generally replied, "That she had taken her part, that she knew well she should not be kept eternally in prison, that she almost excused a fault, in favour of which must be considered the motive which had caused him to commit it; and that besides, she acknowledged sufficiently the difficult position of her companion to prevent her having any feeling of ill nature on account of her conduct towards her."

From the moment she took the resolution of being constantly on the watch to seize, at the moment, the first favourable opportunity of escaping, Silvia, who during the first days of her captivity had remained constantly in her room, (where, we may observe, every necessary of life had been conveyed,) mixed herself somewhat more with her companions; she wished, indeed, to take a part in their occupations.

During the first few days after his arrival in Paris, Beppo, passing by chance the Quay of the Megisserie, had stopped to examine the articles for shooting and fishing, which are displayed in the shop of the Sieur Kretz, the best provided merchant of the capital: Beppo regarded the nets with such attention, and his inspection so completely indicated that he was quite capable of appreciating the good workmanship of these articles, that the Sieur Kretz asked him if he would purchase some, and whether he was an amateur at the sport? Beppo replied negatively to the first question, but he added, in replying to the second, that he was more than an amateur, that before visiting Paris, he exercised at Marseilles, his country, the profession of a fisherman, and that he was very expert in the art of making good nets. "If that's the case," replied Kretz, "let me see your work, and if you wish for employment, and are as expert as you tell me, it will be in my power to occupy you as long as you like."

Beppo, delighted at finding, at the very moment he least expected it, the possibility of employing his leisure hours, and in so profitable a manner, procured what was necessary, and commenced his work; he then showed to Kretz the first net he had finished, and the merchant, neglecting for a moment his commercial habits, could not help exclaiming, "The work is perfect in every part! how much a foot will you take for it?"

Beppo, who had already discovered that everything at Paris fetched better prices than at Marseilles, demanded a third more than he would have asked in his own town, promising to himself, *in petto*, to diminish his pretensions if they appeared too exorbitant; but, to his great surprise, the merchant accepted the price eagerly, and at once gave him an order sufficient to employ him for several months; this was the occupation in which Silvia wished to take a part, and, as she was very quick, she became, after a few lessons, as expert at it as her professors, and could weave the pretty little nets of different colours, intended for ladies of fashion.

Thanks to the prodigious height of their habitation, the recluses breathed a fresh and pure atmosphere; and a view of the magnificent panorama which displayed itself from the windows, in some manner proved a substitute for the daily promenade;

thus the sedentary life which our prisoners led, had in no way injured their health. Silvia had a piano in her room, music, and every requisite for drawing; so that when weary of her work, she could retire to her chamber, and draw, or sing a few morceaux, which Beppo and his mother, impressionable like all southern natures, listened to with a new pleasure; they were thus in appearance satisfied with one another.

Beppo, who at first had only gone out at long intervals, and but for a few moments, now absented himself more frequently, and sometimes remained several hours away; but still he never neglected to recommend his mother not to relax in her surveillance, and it was very prudent, for had he not taken this precaution, the good woman, who knew not the meaning of dissimulation, observing the serenity which appeared on the countenance of Silvia, would have thrown open the doors to her, provided the latter had given her a promise to return.

Beppo said one day that he was going out for a longer time than usual, as he had to leave with Kretz the work he had finished, and purchase some further materials for the new nets; all this might detain him five or six hours, and as it was now nearly two o'clock, it would probably be seven or eight before he returned.

Silvia, who had retired to her room at the moment of his departure, under the pretext of taking some repose, hearing him say to his mother what we have reported above, and recommending her strictly not to take her eyes off her for a moment, said to herself, that she might probably wait a long while before so favourable an occasion would again present itself, and that she ought to endeavour to profit by it. This resolution once taken, she descended to the Castilian, fully determined to risk every thing to recover her liberty.

She had fixed upon no plan, but still she bestowed a thousand caresses on the old lady, in order to withdraw her attention, and adroitly seized a cravat and the red woollen cap of Beppo's, which she concealed under her blouse. (We have omitted to say, that Beppo, in order no doubt to place a greater obstacle to the flight of his captive, had removed her female attire, and had replaced it by a complete costume of a Parisian school-boy, viz: large pantaloons of rich velvet, a waistcoat of the same stuff, and over this a blouse of blue linen.)

Silvia had observed that the old Castilian generally carried in the pocket of her apron, the key of the door which opened upon the landing of the staircase; she waited consequently, with a certain degree of impatience that the old lady might commence her work, for she hoped to be enabled, whilst the latter was engaged in the fabrication of her nets, to seize the key, and be active enough to open the door, secure it, and save herself, before the old woman could offer any resistance, but seeing that the latter remained idle, she pretended herself to wish to be engaged.

"But we have absolutely nothing to do," replied the old lady, "all the nets were finished yesterday evening, and we have no materials to begin fresh ones;" and as Silvia appeared rather vexed at being obliged to remain unemployed, her companion tapped her on the shoulder, exclaiming:

"Do you know how to cut out a robe?"

Although they were yet in the month of March, the weather was superb, a cheerful sun glared upon the tops of the neighbouring houses, and, to take advantage of such a fine day, the inhabitants of the pavilion had opened all the windows; a flash suddenly illuminated the mind of Silvia, she had conceived a plan of escape, the success of which seemed to her all but certain.

"Certainly I do," she replied, "I know perfectly well how to cut out a dress, and if you have one to be made, give it to me, I shall be glad to be occupied, I cannot remain a moment idle without feeling my nerves unhinged."

The old lady took from a wardrobe a remnant of silk stuff, brought from Provence, and manufactured, to all appearance, long before the first revolution; she handed it to Silvia.

The latter did not fail greatly to admire this specimen of antiquity, which was nothing more than a *pekin chiné*, in the worst taste; and in order to exhibit the joy she felt at the precious garment being confided to her for the purpose of turning it into a dress, she commenced singing a romance, displaying all the resources of her voice. The Castilian was delighted at thus finding her in such a good humour.

"Ah!" she said to her, sighing, "if I had but the pleasure of calling you my child."

This was the first time she had permitted herself to allude to the position of her son and her captive.

Silvia looked at her, and smiled.

"Really!" she replied, "well! we will talk of that another time; at present, assist me to carry this table near the window."

The old woman hastened to do as she was requested, and Silvia, after taking very leisurely the dimensions of the dress she was about to commence, laid out the silk. The table was not sufficiently large to contain the remnant when displayed, so that she was compelled to allow a good moiety to hang outside the window. Whilst leisurely applying upon the silk, the patterns which she had previously cut, she conversed with her companion upon different matters of gossip, in such a way, that, at the moment when the latter was seeking from her brain a reply to some perfectly absurd question which Silvia had addressed to her, (she had asked the good woman, whose knowledge of music was limited to the tambourine and the little flute of the merry children of Provence, "Whether she preferred German or Italian music,") she let fall from the window a large piece of the magnificent and flaming dress.

"My robe, my poor robe!" exclaimed the old lady.

"It is not lost," said Silvia, who had quickly removed the table, and placed herself at the window, "the piece is resting on the roof, which is quite dry, and from the window of the stage below, it will be very easy to reach it with the help of a pole. Run down quickly, I will watch that they do not take it away."

Beppo's mother hastened to do as Silvia had requested, she left the apartment armed with a long broom handle, but did not forget, however, to secure the door by drawing a couple of bolts.

The moment she was outside, Silvia left the window, and ran to a cupboard, from which she took a glass, and filled it with vinegar, she then placed herself against the door, and when the Castilian dame opened it to re-enter, she threw with violence into her face, the liquid contained in the glass.

The surprise and agony drew from the poor woman fearful exclamations.

"I am blinded! I am dead!" she said.

And she fell upon the first step of the lower stage, still rubbing her eyes; Silvia, without troubling herself any further as to what might happen to the old lady, took advantage of the moment to

LIFE IN PARIS.

FATHER WILLIAM DISCOVERS THE BODY.

escape; and descended the hundred and ten steps which led to the street, with the nimbleness of a fawn.

Once outside her prison, Silvia found herself rather embarrassed; her first care was to take refuge in a passage, in order to place round her neck the long cravat, and to put on her head the thick woollen cap, of which she had possessed herself; this completed, she wandered for some time in the sombre labyrinth formed by the narrow and crooked streets of the quarter of Saint-Marcel, and frequently, to her great terror, found herself in front of the house she had lately quitted; she was ignorant of the neighbourhood, and she dared not take a vehicle, or demand her way, from the fear that the persons she addressed might discover her sex. The night soon approached, it was dark, and some drops of rain already announced the storm, which, in a few minutes, would descend with violence. After making several marches and countermarches, which, to her infinite despair, invariably brought her to the same point, she found herself close to the Barrier Saint-Jacques; she now determined to engage a carriage, and be driven to her hotel, at the risk of whatever might be the consequence; but, following their praiseworthy custom, the drivers of the fiacres and cabriolets had left the station, on the first signs of rain which they had observed.

Silvia now resolved to accost a man and woman of a respectable appearance, sheltered under an immense green umbrella, who at the moment were entering Paris, in order to ascertain from them some information as to the place in which she found herself, and the road she ought to follow to reach her home at the Barrier de l'Etoile.

"You are," replied the man, "at the Barrier of Saint-Jacques, my boy; but how is it that you are, at nearly nine o'clock at night, and in such weather, in a neighbourhood so distant from your home?"

A tradesman of Paris never makes a direct reply to a question, however simple it may be; he must first know why he is asked the question, and all that may concern it.

Silvia thought she ought not to take for a confidant, the honest resident of the quarter Saint-Marcel, and confined herself to a renewal of the question.

"I have lost my way," she said, "I wish to reach the Avenue Chateaubriand, near the Barrier de l'Etoile, and I really do not know which road I ought to follow."

"Well! my boy, you have not arrived at the end of your journey, the Barrier de l'Etoile is some distance from hence, at least two good leagues; but that you may not again miss your route, you must follow this street in a straight line, as far as the second bridge, which you will cross; you will turn to the left on the quay, to the Champs-Elysées, from whence you will see the Barrier de l'Etoile, the end of your long journey; you understand, always quite straight, without making a turn; there go, my Jesus! and may Providence accompany you!"

The woman had not spoken a word; she had remained in a sort of trance, her mouth open, her eyes winking, the effects, no doubt, of the inferior wine of Argenteuil she had been swallowing, and which the people so justly entitle *du-casse-poitrine*.

The good man was still speaking, though Silvia had made some progress on her road.

As she had been walking for more than three hours, she was soaked with the rain, and her legs began to tremble under her; but still she took courage. Whilst following the street Saint-Jacques, she questioned herself in what manner she could escape from the unlucky position in which she found herself; ought she to go to her hotel? It was probable she might find no one there; should she go to the hotel of Salvador? but during her long absence some unforeseen accident might have deranged the position of the marquis; she must, however, determine to repair to his hotel, and take the risk of the consequences.

She was still buried in these difficult and painful reflections, when upon arriving at the corner of the quay *aux Fleurs*, she felt herself seized roughly by the arm.

She turned round quickly, and recognised Beppo. The countenance of the fisherman was as pale as a winding sheet; she uttered an exclamation of terror.

"Follow me," said Beppo to her, in a trembling voice, placing his hand on her mouth; "follow me."

"I would rather die!" replied Silvia. A vigorous struggle released her from the nervous grasp of the fisherman, and she attempted to take to flight.

In three bounds Beppo was at her side.

"Spare me a second crime," he said to her.

Instead of replying to him, Silvia uttered the most piercing cries; several persons who had observed the violent gestures of the two individuals, hastily approached, and Silvia implored their assistance, when Beppo, enraged at the idea that she would infallibly escape him, drew from his pocket a long poniard, and plunged it in her bosom.

She fell upon the pavement before she could pronounce a word.

Beppo, terrified at the action he had been guilty of, remained motionless before the body of his victim.

Those who had been witnesses of this crime, frightened, no doubt, by the knife which he still held in his hand, dared not approach.

This state of indecision lasted but a few minutes; Beppo, recalled to himself by the tumult of the crowd, broke through the circle which surrounded him, and fled in the direction of the bridge of Arcole; arrived at this bridge he found himself on the point of being captured; the throng of persons who pursued him, had divided itself into two bands, one of which followed the quay de Givres, and the other that of la Cité, would consequently meet on the bridge of Arcole; so that if he escaped the one, he would infallibly be taken by the other; it was to escape this imminent peril that he threw himself into the river, and, thanks to the obscurity, they lost sight of him.

We have seen how he was received at Mother Sans Refus's, at the moment when the bandits (after the scene in which Delicat, Relet le Mauvais Gueux, and Coco-Desbraises, had lost their lives) were about to separate. It is here we shall refind him, a prey to a devouring fever, and attended by one of the odalisques of the house, who, from his tall figure, his striking physiognomy, his magnificent black hair, and more than all this, perhaps, the position in which he was encountered, and the crime he had committed, became much interested in his favour.

Nearly all the places where the events of this authentic history took place exist at the present day, and we could invite our readers to visit them, which would spare us the trouble of a description; but as we wish to believe that all our readers are persons of the best society, and that they would not be flattered at being forced to pass some moments in a place where they might encounter individuals nearly similar to those we have traced in the preceding chapter, we shall—to satisfy as much as possible the very natural desire of becoming acquainted with the strange scenes in which we place our heroes, and the repugnance, not less natural, which they would feel were they obliged to accompany them—attempt to describe the room in which Beppo was carried, and to sketch the physiognomy of the woman who watched at his bed-side.

There is nothing more sad or gloomy, in our opinion, than a room in a furnished hotel; and this is occasioned, at least we think so, from there being not the slightest effort at harmony in the furnishing of these sort of establishments; in fact, we perceive at the first glance, that this furniture which belongs to every age, and is in every condition, collected without taste and without choice, in the asylum offered to the traveller by the avaricious hospitality of the hotel-keepers, has been purchased at auction after a death, a bankruptcy, or a removal; and we feel ill at ease in the midst of these remains of death, misery, and absence; well, there exists between the rooms of a furnished hotel and those of places similar to that in which Beppo was confined, a strange similarity; let the reader judge for himself.

As we have observed, the Castilian fisherman had been carried, in a fainting fit, into one of the rooms of the first floor of the house in la Tannerie street.

It was a large square piece with two windows à *guillotine*, fronting the street, secured by padlocks, and embellished with wide curtains of red calico. Like those in the shop, the glass of these windows had been daubed with whiting, which only allowed a pale and doubtful light to penetrate into the bed-chamber.

A mahogany bedstead—manufactured during the reign of the Directory, at an epoch when the ebénistes offered to the amateurs of the renewed fashions of the Greeks and Romans antique furniture of the latest taste—was placed in an alcove, formed at the end of the room opposite the windows; upon this bed lay Beppo, who had not yet spoken a word. He was enveloped in sheets of coarse calico, and covered by one of those counterpanes composed of a thousand pieces of stuff of different colours sewed together, and his own clothes, which they had taken the precaution to dry.

A commode of different sorts of wood, ornamented with mountings of copper, formerly gilded; two fauteuils, covered with yellow Utrecht velvet; (the curtains of the windows and bed were red,) a few chairs, unmatched and torn; an old toilette table, on its last legs; and, enclosed in some old gilt frames, a few infamous engravings, whose authors deserved hanging, completed the furniture of this piece; the best in the house, next to that of madame, a *sanctum sanctorum*, into which no one had the right to enter.

Some logs burned, or rather smoked, in the chimney, bewidowed of every species of necessary, unless we give that name to two large and long bricks, which served the office of hand-irons, and surmounted simply with a tolerably preserved Venetian mirror, astonished at finding itself in such unworthy society; and two vases of porcelain filled with artificial flowers at a shilling the box.

The woman who had been charged with the care of Beppo, in spite of the visible traces of its passage which debauchery had left upon her countenance, was still a handsome girl. She was tall and well made; her hair, which, to judge from the amplitude behind the head, must have been long and thick, was of the richest black; her large eyes, of the same colour, were bordered with long and silky lashes; her features were perfectly regular, her figure long and slender, her feet small and well shaped; but by the side of all these attractions, which formed an ensemble nearly faultless, there was an acquired imperfection; thus, the movements of her body were sudden and unsteady; she had none of that graceful pliancy, the envied appanage of the Parisian females; her hair was totally neglected, and its irregular curls descended over cheeks slightly marbled; her eyes were surrounded with violet-coloured circles, which gave them almost a sinister expression, and her nails were tipped with black lines.

For some time she had been regarding Beppo, who trembled in every limb, although enveloped in a thick and heavy covering, and his eyes were fixed upon her, without his appearing to observe her.

"What a strange illness!" she said, "he has not yet opened his mouth; he looks at me, but does not see me; and yet, although suffering from a violent fever which consumes him, he has no fit; I cannot comprehend it."

She drew the counterpane over the bosom of the patient.

"He is cold," she said. "What a pity, that such a handsome fellow should be no better worth than the wretches who frequent this house. Ah! bah! I will not think of it."

She drew from the pocket of her dress a small bottle of eau-de-vie, and swallowed two or three mouthfuls; she then raked together the scattered logs in the fire-place, and attempted to make them blaze.

"To the devil!" she said, throwing into the middle of the room the miserable bellows she had been using.

Beppo made a movement; she quickly approached the bed, and raised the head of her patient.

"Drink!" said the sufferer, in a feeble voice.

"At length!" said the girl.

She handed Beppo a glass of water, into which she had dropped a morsel of sugar, and which the latter drank with avidity; she then gently laid his head upon the pillow, and he slept soundly.

At this moment, some one knocked at the door, which the girl opened, and Mother Sans Refus entered the room.

"Well! my child," she said, "how does this *escarpe** get on?"

"He has just requested some drink, and after satisfying his thirst, fell into a deep sleep."

"We must hope that his sleep will be of use to him, and that he will be able to leave at night."

"How! you mean to turn him out, weak as he is?" exclaimed the girl; "why, the poor fellow will not take three steps before he'll drop in the street."

"Well! but do you suppose then that I am going to keep him for ever in my house; and besides, it would look well, if, by chance, the police pay me a visit."

"Well! perhaps you are right," said the girl, in a tone of evident ill-humour, "let him sleep; and as he can now speak, and seems to understand what is said to him, when he wakes up, I will tell him that he must leave; and at night, I will take him to an auberge, where they will give him a room, and take care of him until he is recovered."

"As you like, I know you have a good heart;

* Assassin.

and I am quite at ease, on his account, since you will take charge of him."

"Sure enough, I've a good heart; a much better one than yours, old sorceress," said the girl, when Mother Sans Refus had left the room.

Left alone with Beppo, she lighted a candle; for although scarcely four o'clock, the room was already dark; she then seated herself at the head of the bed, and waited patiently until the sufferer awoke.

She did not wait long; the sleep of Beppo became too agitated to endure for any length of time.

He cast looks of surprise at every thing about him; and observing an unknown female sitting near his bed—

"Where am I?" he said to her, "and what has happened to me?"

"Have you so soon forgotten?" replied the girl; "do you not remember that, no later than yesterday, you assassinated a woman; that you threw yourself into the river to escape your pursuers; and that some men made you enter this house, at the moment you were nearly taken."

"In fact, I do remember it," said Beppo, after resting some minutes, with his head concealed in his two hands. "I recollect!" he continued in a gloomy voice, "I have committed a second crime; but what has taken place since yesterday?"

"This is what has happened, at least, so madame has told me, for I was not here at the moment you were brought in; you were below in the back room about five minutes, and had not spoken a word, when you swooned; they carried you into this room, and when I came in, they begged me to take charge of you; 'tis what I have done, and with a good heart."

Beppo regarded, with an air of the profoundest astonishment, this girl, who spoke to him of what had taken place the evening before, as an affair of the most natural and every-day occurrence.

"But since you are not ignorant of the crime I have committed," he said to her, "how is it that I do not inspire you with horror?"

"Are you not aware of what I am, and in what place you are?" she replied

"No."

"I thought so! it was not to rob her, was it, that you attempted to assassinate this female?"

"To rob her!" exclaimed Beppo, who, weak as he was, had sat up in bed to reply to this question. "To rob her! Oh! you do not believe it."

"No, I do not believe it; and now, I guess that this woman is a mistress who has betrayed you; and that it is from jealousy you attempted her death."

"It is nearly so."

"I was sure of it," replied the girl. "You love this woman then, much?" she added after a few moments of silence

"I do not know, I do not know," said Beppo. "I was mad."

And his head dropped on the pillow, he would perhaps have relapsed into that state of prostration he had just recovered from, if the girl had not quickly restored him, by holding some strong essence in a small flask to his nose.

"You must not get so dispirited," she said, when he had recovered his senses; "what is done, is done; and besides, your mistress is not dead; the wound you have given her, although dangerous, is not mortal, as I am assured; and as the surgeons of the Hotel-Dieu, where she has been carried, are skilful, it is most probable she will recover from its effects."

"Ah! so much the better," replied Beppo.

As he stretched out his hand to take the glass of eau sucrée, placed upon the night-table, his dagger-knife, which the bandit had carefully replaced in the side pocket of his caban, escaped from it, and rolled upon his bosom; he seized it, and threw it with violence into the fire-place.

The girl, upon seeing him take this formidable weapon, had mechanically retired a few paces.

"Fear nothing," said Beppo, to her; "I have, true enough, committed a crime, but I am no assassin; on throwing aside this knife, I break with my past life; and, if the justice of man does not demand from me, at once, an expiation for my crimes, my future life shall be consecrated to satisfy the justice of God."

"I do not well understand you; but if it is that you fear being arrested, I think that, for the present, you are wrong; your victim has not yet been enabled to speak, you can, therefore, return home; but if that is impossible, I can take you to an auberge, where, indeed, you will be more in safety than in this house."

"But where am I, then? and what are the generous people who have saved me, and placed you to watch over me?"

"Really! you do not know them?"

"I believe I have already had the honour of replying to you, no."

"What are those, who, when a robber or an assassin is pursued by the public clamour, saves him, instead of opposing his flight?"

"So that those who have saved me, are—"

"Robbers and assassins!" said the girl, lowering her voice so much that Beppo could hardly collect the sense of her words; "and it is in a house which they habitually frequent, that you are at this moment."

"But you," exclaimed Beppo, "you, so kind, who have attended me with such a touching solicitude?"

"What are the women found among thieves and assassins? Those miserable creatures who no longer possess anything of their sex but the name."

"Saved by thieves and assassins, who have received me as one of themselves!" murmured Beppo.

"The expiation commences!"

"And, attended by a prostitute, who believed she was rendering a service to one of the men with whom she habitually lives," said the girl, fixing her regards upon Beppo. "Why did you not express your thought entire?"

Tears were mixed with the voice of the girl, when she pronounced these words; Beppo, without positively knowing why, felt himself deeply moved; he took the hand of his nurse, and pressed it affectionately in his own.

"I am persuaded," he said to her, "that here, you are not in your place."

"Thanks, for your good opinion," she replied; "but, since you are now aware of the place, and the occupation of the inhabitants, you must see that you cannot leave too soon. Are you strong enough to get up, and engage at the quay, which is not two steps distant, a vehicle, which will conduct you to one of your friends, if you fear entering your own house?"

"I am weak," replied Beppo, "but courage will replace the strength that is wanting. I will return home, for I wish to do nothing, either to ruin or to save myself; the crimes I have committed must be punished, either in this world or the next;

and I must leave to the will of God the care of deciding upon my destiny."

The girl having retired to the extremity of the chamber, Beppo rose, and dressed himself, with more ease than he had expected, after the terrible crisis he had gone through. He found, in one of the pockets of his *caban*, the bag which contained the sum, pretty round, which he had received the previous evening, from Kretz; he drew it out, and placed it on the chimney-piece.

"Those who have saved me," he said, "have not wished to make me pay for the service they have rendered me."

"Ah!" replied the young girl to him, "if they have saved you, it is because they supposed you of the same metal as themselves, and thieves do not prey upon each other."

Beppo had finished dressing himself, and as the night had quite set in, he was on the point of leaving.

"What is your name?" he said to the girl.

"Georgette," she replied.

"Well, Georgette," he continued, "you know that, at the day of judgment, the Almighty will weigh in the same scales, our good and our bad actions, and in proportion as the weight of good will exceed that of the bad, so shall we be recompensed or punished; I have already committed many faults, and some crimes; will you not allow me to do an action, which may be counted in deduction of my iniquities?"

"If I can be of any use to you, dispose of me," replied Georgette; "I will do whatever you wish."

"Since that is the case, accept this small sum; if you remain here, as I hope and believe, simply because you cannot do otherwise, it will assist you to leave; and I shall carry with me, in quitting you, the consolation of having, at least, effected one good action."

The girl would not accept the money offered to her by Beppo.

"I have done nothing more for you than I would have done for another," she said to him. "If the gift you would make me to-day, had been offered a little sooner, I would have accepted it with gratitude; but, it is now too late! the stuff has received its folds, and I must, you see, remain where I am. Go, then, and trouble yourself no more about me. I am not so unhappy as you suppose."

Beppo took a few steps, in order to leave the room, and as he did not appear very steady on his legs:

"Would you wish me to accompany you," said the girl, "as far as the nearest coach station?"

"It is not worth while," replied the fisherman; "the fresh air will revive me; and besides, I have but a short way to go."

"Go, then; and may Providence be your guide!"

Beppo left the room, and descended the staircase, upon which he encountered no one; Georgette, who preceded him, opened to him the door of the passage.

"Adieu!" she said to him.

And reascended to her chamber.

She took from her pocket the small phial of cogniac, to which she had already paid so many visits, and emptied it of its contents.

"I am very glad," she said, "that he has left; I think I begin to love this man."

Beppo had presumed too much upon his strength. After following the Street de la Tanniere, by supporting himself along the walls, to prevent his falling, he was compelled, when he had reached the place of the Hotel de Ville, to sit down on a stone; his limbs refused to carry him further. After resting a few minutes, he requested a workman who passed, to support him as far as the quay, where he could engage a vehicle. The honest workman, who would not have refused a beggar the slight service demanded of him, having remarked the frightful paleness which covered the visage of the man who claimed his assistance, would do more than was required; he counselled Beppo not to stir from the place, and hastened to the nearest station and engaged a fiacre, which he brought back, and assisted him into it.

Let us now leave Beppo, rolling towards the Street Contrescarpe-Saint-Marcel, and return to the Countess Lucie de Neuville's hotel, where we shall again find Dr. Matheo.

CHAPTER XXIV.

EUGENIE DE MIRBEL.

A CHEERFUL fire blazed in the chimney of the boudoir, or rather in the cabinet, of Lucie de Neuville, and enlivened the apartment, furnished and decorated with such a rare elegance.

The countess and Laura de Beaumont were differently occupied. Lucie was embroidering a superb altar-piece, destined for the chapel of the Chateau de Villerbanne, an ancient and magnificent signorial manor, which would one day belong to her husband; Laura painted, upon a screen, a group of rare flowers, and the porcelain vase which contained them.

The boudoir of the Countess de Neuville was not that of a fashionable woman.

It is long since it was said for the first time, that "the appearance alone of the place, indicated the character of those who inhabited it;" and this is true; a grocer, retired from his commerce, will not choose for himself a cottage, with green window shutters, situated on the decline of a pretty hill, and whose façade will be ornamented simply with a branching vine tree and a few straggling wallflowers; the poet will not lodge himself, if he can contrive otherwise, in the most populous street of the modern Babylon; a sailor will not inhabit the fallow grounds of la Beauce. The grocer fixes upon a house, in a small provincial town, in imitation of those in Paris, and, if his means allow him, he will place a couple of statues, in plaster, under his vestibule; the poet will accept with delight the retreat disdained by the grocer; the sailor enjoys his *otium cum dignitate* with a view of the sea from his sleeping-room.

And all, whatever may be in other respects their characters, their manners, and their habits, who have a fashionable existence, retain for themselves in the most secluded corner of their habitation, a sort of nook or retreat in which they love to retire, and which the ladies name a boudoir, and the men a cabinet, into which they admit none but their intimate friends, or at least those to whom they would kindly accord this title; well, those of our readers who have had an opportunity of visiting any of these private retreats of the privileged orders of the present age, have no doubt remarked that the boudoir of the *danseuse*, whether named Fanny Essler or Cerito, resembles in nothing that of the devotee; that the boudoir of the wife of a rich banker, even were she Madame James Rothschild, has no resemblance to that of a noble duchess of the Faubourg Saint-Germain; that nothing less resembles the cabinet of one of these Lionnes (as they are named) who have preserved, at the nineteenth century, the dissolute manners of the regency, than that of a noble descendant of a Montmorency or a la Tremsuille. In fact, we shall find, in the boudoir of the danseuse, by the side of the small statue in bronze of the Divinity of the Temple, if she has obtained this species of celebrity, (and her merit must indeed be small if it be not thus,) the armorial cards of the adorator of the quarter, the crowns and bouquets bestowed the previous evening by an idolizing public on the new sylphide, and perhaps even the keys of some cities of the new world. Some mystical engravings, some books of the day, from the magazin of Curmer, and the protrait of the preacher à la mode, will be found in the boudoir of the devotee, lighted by a sort of half daylight, more fitted to inspire voluptuous thoughts than Christian meditations. In the boudoir of the wife of the millionaire, gold on the wainscotings, gold on the panels, gold above, gold below, gold every where; so that, in short, the apartment of madame is nothing less than a reflection of the chest of monsieur her husband.

The cabinet of the roué (why not preserve to these messieurs a name which they deserve in every respect?) will be ornamented with the portraits of the unfortunate women, whether blondes, brunettes, or chestnuts, whom he has betrayed or would have betrayed; Manilla cigars in elegant boxes of satin-wood; and although the roué may not be very expert in the art of a Bertrand or a Daressy, it may yet happen that an amorous epistle, written by the last loved woman, may be hung up, richly framed, in the most conspicuous part of this same cabinet; and the same with others. There is always, in each of them, the signet of the individuality of the persons to whom they belong; but we sincerely believe that although those we have cited may not be irreproachable, there are others of an opposite character, both with respect to elegance, duration, and an agreeable choice of the articles destined to embellish them, and for this simple reason, we intend to essay a description of the one occupied by the Countess de Neuville.

As we have before remarked, the boudoir of the Countess de Neuville resembles in nothing that of the coquette. It is hung with silk tapestry, on a clear lilac ground, interspersed with flowers and fantastic birds, relieved on each panel by wreaths of green silk encircling very small rosettes of silver plate. The thick draperies have not yet been drawn before the windows of this apartment for the purpose of introducing the half daylight so loved by the coquettes, no doubt because it dispenses with blushing, (which would be almost impossible to the majority of these ladies,) and increases the audacity of those who may venture to attack their virtue. The light, to penetrate to the boudoir of Lucie de Neuville, is not compelled to traverse a triple compact of gauze, muslin, and silk, there is absolutely nothing before the windows of her apartment, each composed of one magnificent pane; only that when the rays of the sun are a little too strong, she can lower the blinds upon which she has painted two of the most enchanting landscapes it is possible to imagine.

Hence we observe, that the boudoir of Lucie de Neuville has some resemblance to the glass-house of Socrates, every thing which took place in it might easily be seen from the immense garden

which it overlooked; but what did this matter to Lucie, it was neither to write billetsdoux, nor to receive the numerous adorers whom her irreproachable beauty, her modest graces, and the charms of her wit, constantly attracted to her, that she retired there.

In addition, it was easy to perceive on entering it, that the boudoir of Lucie was a temple consecrated to the arts; thus the most remarkable pieces of furniture were a magnificent piano of Errards, a harp, an easel, and every thing requisite for painting, some bronzes by Barry, and some small statues after the antique, disposed with taste upon a stage; and ranged with care in an elegant library of citron wood, the best works of ancient and modern literature.

Among all these objects connected with the arts, it was pleasing to remark a pretty work-table, and a frame for embroidering; these two little bits of furniture seemed placed in the situations they occupied to indicate that the mistress of the sanctuary had not renounced the habitual occupations of her sex, and that she cultivated the arts and sciences as an amusement, and not as the sole employment of her time.

Since the departure of M. de Neuville for Algiers, Lucie, who went out but rarely and in order to receive but few visits, passed in this cabinet, where her friend Laura de Beaumont kept her company the greatest part of her time; and we can assure those of our fair readers who may feel disposed to think the existence she lead somewhat monotonous, that it was but very seldom that she felt ennui.

Is it, in fact, possible to feel ennui, when we can seek, by occupation which may be rendered attractive by varying without end, those distractions which we are not disposed to search for in society, and have, besides, near us, a person to whom we feel attached by a similarity of character and imagination.

For nearly an hour, in which they had been both employed, the countess and Laura de Beaumont, contrary to their usual habit, had exchanged nothing but monosyllables; since the adventure of the street de la Tannerie, Lucie had been gloomy, and Laura, who had several times in vain, endeavoured to convince her that she fought against a chimera, and that her fears were absolutely without foundation, had made up her mind to speak no more upon the subject, as any reference to it appeared to be so disagreeable to her companion.

Laura had risen to judge of the effect of what she had painted, and she was so satisfied with her progress, that she struck her hands together and exclaimed with a naiveté which was a part of her happy nature:

"Oh! but it is pretty, and how well I have traced that beautiful rhododendrum, and the brilliant colours of that magnificent Vulcan; but look then, Lucie," she added, placing under the eyes of her friend the screen she had painted, "'tis almost as perfect as an *aquarelle* of Madame Jacolet."

Lucie raised her head to admire the chef d'œuvre of her friend, the latter observed the expression of deep sadness impressed on the features of the countess.

"Really, Lucie," she exclaimed, "I do not understand you, I am certain that you are still thinking of what happened to us the other evening."

"What would you have? my dear Laura; a presentiment, which I cannot conquer, tells me that the encounter I made in that house will be fatal to me, and it is not in vain, you know, that God has permitted us to have presentiments."

"I believe so with you; and, no doubt, it is for the purpose of putting us on our guard, that he places in us these inward emotions, which apprise us of the approach of danger; but if this is true, what have you to fear, a danger foreseen is much less formidable than one we are ignorant of, for it is at least possible to lessen its effects, if not to escape it altogether?"

"You are really much more reasonable than your poor friend, my dear Laura, and yet you are much younger than she is; but you must excuse me, for you see, I am so vexed that this confounded doctor is not yet come to inform me how that poor Eugenie de Mirbel gets on, that I am positively out of humour with myself."

"But you forget, no doubt, that you have requested the doctor to effect a commission for you, which, perhaps, has taken some time, and probably the necessities of his patients may have retarded him. You are aware, besides, that it is in his service they have placed the woman habited as a man, whose assassination was attempted on the bridge of Notre Dame."

Lucie and Laura were at this point of their conversation, when Paolo announced to his mistress that Doctor Matheo requested to be introduced to them.

"Let him be shown up at once," said Lucie.

The doctor was paler than usual, and appeared still more gloomy than was usual with him.

"At length, doctor, you are come," said Lucie, when Matheo had seated himself on the chair, which, at a sign from his mistress, Paolo had presented to him; "we have been expecting you with the greatest impatience."

"To such a point," added Laura, "that when you were announced we were speaking of you, and I was saying to Lucie that if you had neglected us so long, we must not accuse your indifference, but your numerous occupations."

"I thank you sincerely, mademoiselle, for your kindness in defending me; I have, in fact, been so much occupied, that I have found it impossible, until the present moment, to obtain an instant to pay you a visit."

"You could not probably quit that poor young woman so cowardly assassinated."

"It is true, mademoiselle, the wound they have given her is serious, very serious, and I was unwilling to leave to any one the care of removing the first dressings."

"Tell me, doctor, is this woman as handsome as we are informed by the journals, which have given us the account of what has happened?"

"Yes, mademoiselle; this woman is really endowed with an extraordinary beauty; there is between her physiognomy and that of Madame la Countess de Neuville some points of resemblance."

"You flatter me, doctor," said Lucie, smiling.

"Not at all, madame," replied Matheo, "this woman, who is exceedingly beautiful, resembles you a little; there is nothing extraordinary in that."

"And they have not yet discovered," continued Laura, "either the name of the person who struck her, or the reason of her being habited in the costume of a man?"

"Alas! no, mademoiselle; there is really something mysterious in this event. The journals have informed you the mode in which the assassin contrived to escape by precipitating himself into the river. It is not known whether he managed to save himself, or has perished; the night was so dark, and the atmosphere so charged with mist, at the moment the crime was perpetrated, that he escaped the observation of every one; and by an unlucky hazard, the shock, or some other cause, has taken from the victim, who is still too weak to write, the use of her speech. But I am talking of matters which can but little interest you, and am forgetting to render an account to Madame la Countess of the mission she was good enough to charge me with."

The doctor took from his note-case the armorial seal of the note written by Salvador to the Countess de Neuville, and handed it to the latter.

"I have visited," he said, "the person who addressed the letter to you, to which this seal was attached."

"Well! doctor," replied the countess, "this man no doubt is an honourable one, and his features, which announce a noble mind, are not a deceitful mirror; is it not so? Well, but answer me," she added after a pause of some moments, impatient at Matheo still keeping silence.

The doctor fixed upon Lucie de Neuville a regard full of the deepest pity; a profound sigh then escaped from his bosom.

"But what's the matter then, doctor?" said Laura, who had remarked the expression of regard he had fixed upon the countess; "one would think you had really some calamity to announce to us."

"Come, doctor," added Lucie, "who is this Marquis de Pourrieres? I confess I am anxious to know how such a noble personage found himself in a place such as that in which I encountered him."

The countess without, perhaps, being enabled to account to herself for the sentiment she obeyed, assumed an air of the most profound indifference, whilst putting a question, the answer to which she awaited with the most anxious impatience; Matheo was not the dupe of this little feminine ruse.

"The family of de Pourrieres," replied Matheo, "is, as I have already informed you, one of the most ancient and most considerable of Provence; the person who has written to you, is, as I am assured, the last branch of this ancient house; for the rest, his position in society appears fixed; he is, as you know, auditor to the council of state, and a knight of the legion of honour."

The information which the doctor had given, caused an evident pleasure to the countess and her friend, the expression of which appeared on their charming features.

Lucie was satisfied that the man in whom she was interested, without knowing why, was, by his birth and his position, of the same class as that in which she moved; she did not, *perhaps*, wish to see him again, but she thought to herself that if by *chance* she met him in any of the circles she frequented, and that he should speak to her, she could reply to him without the fear of compromising herself; she was very glad, in a word, that the Marquis de Pourrieres was a person with whom she might be permitted to be acquainted.

Laura, on her part, was rejoiced to acquire the certitude that the man whom her friend had encountered, frequented good society, for the very simple reason, that she was persuaded that Lucie, once certain that she had nothing to fear from M. the Marquis de Pourrieres, the vague terrors she had continued to manifest, and the sudden fits of humour which followed them, would disappear for ever.

LIFE IN PARIS.

SERVIGNY PROMOTING SIR EDWARD IN INDIA.

"I hope," she said to her friend, "now that you are certain that this man whom your imagination had turned into a sort of hobgoblin, is almost a grand seigneur, that you will no longer retain your foolish terrors which render you so unhappy."

"I was indeed foolish," replied the countess, smiling, "I was really foolish. I was there myself, in that detestable cabaret, it is not extraordinary therefore that he was there also."

Matheo listened to the two ladies but said not a word.

"Well done!" exclaimed Laura, "only see how you pass from one extremity to the other; you were, it is true, in this cabaret, but it was an accident which led you there; you did not disguise yourself to go there, whilst this marquis (who, as it seems, was quite at his ease there) was, you have told us, habited in a costume which it is not customary to wear in the saloons."

"Mon Dieu, 'tis true," replied the countess, "'tis true. But tell me another thing, doctor; did you see this man? what did he say to you?"

"I have seen, certainly, M. le Marquis de Pourrieres, and if we are to credit what he said to me, his presence in the place you encountered him, and his disguise, may be perfectly justified. But nothing attests the truth of his words."

"But tell me, what did he say to you?"

"Oh! mon Dieu! madame, things which we find in our imagination when we justify an equivocal action, supposing that it is an action of this nature that we seek to justify."

"And therefore, doctor, you think this marquis is a man whom we ought to distrust."

"It is always best, Madame the Countess, not to accord one's confidence to parties whom we are not perfectly acquainted with. But I am giving you a useless recommendation, you have too much sense not to know what you have to do."

"Do you know," said Laura, "that you are neither one nor the other very amusing. Eh! what is it to us after all, what this marquis is, or what he is not? We know that he is neither a thief nor an assassin; that ought to be sufficient; is it not true?"

"I am of your opinion, mademoiselle."

This reply of the doctor put an end to the conversation, of which, up to the present moment, the Marquis de Pourrieres had been the subject; and the countess, who, on the previous evening, had received a letter from Eugenie de Mirbel, thanking her for what she had done for her, and begging her to come and see her, demanded of the doctor the news as to her friend. The latter informed her, that the young lady, thanks to the attention he had been enabled to bestow upon her, was, if not recovered, at least completely out of danger; and that her strongest desire was to see the friend to whom she was indebted for the comforts she at present enjoyed. The countess no longer suffered from the wound she had received some days before, and the sky announced a fine day. Lucie proposed to Laura to accompany her to pay a visit to Eugenie de Mirbel.

Laura eagerly accepted the proposition; she considered it as a fête to see once more her, who, during the short period they had passed together at school, where both of them had been educated, was one of her most cherished friends. Lucie rang, and ordered Paolo to prepare the carriage.

The doctor took leave of the ladies, to allow them time to proceed with their toilette, and left, after promising the Countess de Neuville to pay her a visit on the morrow.

In less than half an hour after his departure, Lucie and Laura again met in the salon, dressed and ready to start. The countess and her friend were not, as we may see, of that class of women who pass at their toilette the best part of the day, who, in fact, dress in the morning, chatter all the day, and undress at night; and yet, my fair readers, they were not less beautiful, nor less tastefully attired than the prettiest and showiest amongst you; for it is neither the luxury of her toilette, nor the time she employs at it, which add to the attractions which a pretty woman already possesses; indeed, had she the carriage of the huntress Diana, and the expression of the goddess of beauty, she would still remain but a very ordinary creature, if she knew not how to dispose her attire with some taste, and was not in possession of that graceful coquetry, an innate appanage of the amiable Parisiennes, a coquetry which allows itself to be understood, but not seen.

Matheo had engaged for Eugenie de Mirbel, in a neat little house of a tradesman of the Rue Ribouttè, a small apartment which he had directed to be furnished quite plain, but if he thought it unnecessary to surround the poor girl with the thousand recherché luxuries of an elegant life, he had endeavoured, conforming to the intentions of the Countess de Neuville, that nothing should be wanting which might serve to induce her to forget the cruel vicissitudes she had supported; thus Eugenie de Mirbel, reposing, after she left the garret in which he found her, on a good bed, furnished with fine and white sheets, and warm coverings, and placed in an apartment, warmed by a cheerful fire, had experienced a sensation of comfort she could not express; and this sensation, more perhaps than the prescriptions recommended by the doctor, had contributed to the recovery of her health and strength.

When Lucie and Laura arrived in her apartment, she was sitting in a comfortable fauteuil à la Voltaire, which she had drawn near the fire, and the good old woman, from whom she would not be separated, was scolding her for having determined to leave her bed.

It was no longer the same woman whom she had seen in the garret of the street de la Tannerie that Lucie had now before her eyes; it was true that Eugenie was usually very pale, but her handsome black hair was arranged with neatness, her eyes had recovered their transparency, and the black circles which then surrounded them had begun to disappear.

"You act like a providence," said Eugenie de Mirbel to the Countess de Neuville; "you do good and are not seen."

She attempted to rise to embrace her friend, Lucie forced her to keep her seat, and after kissing her several times, and preparing her for the visit she was to receive, she signed to Laura to advance, who, until this moment, had remained in the entrance room.

Eugenie at once recognised Laura, whom, however, she had not seen since her departure from school.

"I am quite delighted," she said, "to meet at the same time my two dearest friends."

"We are more delighted than you, my dear Eugenie," replied the countess, "since it is to us that heaven has furnished an occasion for doing a slight benefit to a person that we both cherish from our very heart."

"My dear friends!" said Eugenie de Mirbel, pressing in her warmth against her bosom both

Lucie and Laura, who had thrown themselves into her arms, and for some minutes the three charming women joined their tears and their embraces.

The cries of an infant drew them from this sweet pressure; Eugenie ran to the cradle of her child, which was placed at the head of her bed; she took the infant in her arms, and with blushes on her cheeks, brought it to Lucie de Neuville.

"She owes her life to you," she said, "will you not kiss her?"

Lucie took the child and covered it with kisses, whilst Laura, who had lifted the lappels of the lace cap which almost hid its little head, could not cease from regarding it.

Some innocent exclamations betrayed at every instant her lively admiration.

"How happy you are in having such a sweet little infant," she said at length.

"Let us sit down and chat," said the countess, who wished to prevent Eugenie the necessity of replying to the innocent remark of Laura, "it is so long a time since we have seen each other, that we ought to have much to talk about."

Lucie handed to the old woman, to replace it in its cradle, the little cherub, who had dropped asleep in her arms, and the three friends seated themselves before the cheerful fire which blazed in the chimney.

Lucie was desirous of knowing, in order to remedy them, if that were possible, the events which had precipitated her friend into the abyss from which she had saved her; but she would not demand of her a confidence which the latter, from gratitude, perhaps, might think herself bound to make; she thought the best way to obtain this confidence was by bestowing her own. She narrated then to Eugenie the events, very ordinary, of her life since her leaving school, the death of her father, followed soon after by her marriage with the Colonel Count de Neuville, although he was much older than herself, and the recent departure of the latter for Algiers.

"I have nothing to recount to you," said Laura, when Lucie had finished her recital; "my life, still less interesting than that of Lucie, really will not furnish the subject of a narration:

"I passed my first years at Lagny, a pretty little town of Brie, celebrated for its fountain, and the not very courteous manners of its inhabitants, who throw into the said fountain any one who may demand of them the price of barley, without putting their hand in the sack. I only quitted this town to enter school, at the moment you were leaving it, my dear Eugenie. My education finished, I went, with the permission of an uncle, whom I sincerely love, although I have never seen him, to live with Lucie. I pass my time in reading, drawing, and music; I go to the ball; in a word, I am as happy as it is possible to be, for I am never dull except when Lucie is unhappy, which for some days has happened much oftener than I like.

Eugenie had taken the hands of her two friends, which she pressed affectionately in her own.

"I must," she said, "recount to you what has happened to me since I saw you at school; mine is a very sad history, of which you already know the denouement," she continued addressing herself to Lucie de Neuville.

The latter tenderly embraced Eugenie, who, after a few moments' silence, continued in these terms:

"I was not yet twelve years old when I lost my father, who had been the most intimate friend of yours, my dear Lucie, and also my mother, who soon followed him to the tomb. My parents, in consequence of ruinous commercial speculations, and the bankruptcy of parties to whom they had confided considerable sums, had lost their fortune at the period of their decease, so that death appeared in time to spare them those torments, the inseparable companions of poverty. I know not what would have become of me, if an elder sister of my mother, who had always lived in the country, had not hastened to Paris at the news of the painful misfortune which had fallen upon me, and taken charge of me.

"I brought with me into the house of this estimable woman, the trouble which, to date from this period, has never ceased to pursue me.

"My aunt, wishing to give me an education worthy of my birth, placed me, about two years after, in the school in which we were educated. I know not whether you remember the character I had at that time."

"You were gifted," said Lucie, "with the happiest temper it is possible to imagine; you laughed without cessation, and if one of us chanced to be dull, it was always you who found means to cheer us up; but this did not last long, a short time after your arrival at school, your character changed all at once."

"You remember, no doubt," continued Eugenie de Mirbel, "one of our under mistresses, rather a handsome person, whose fine blue eyes, and rich black hair, we all admired, although sometimes quizzing her melancholy and pensive manners."

"Madame Delaunay?" said Laura.

"Precisely. This woman, who, as they said, had experienced great misfortunes, and who had lost her husband shortly after her marriage, had been admitted into our school upon the recommendation of an English lady, with whom she had remained some time, in order to commence the education of a young girl whom they had sent to India to rejoin her father. I was, as you may remember, the first, for a considerable time, to laugh at the languishing airs of Madame Delaunay, who never opened her mouth unless to utter deep sighs, and who was constantly telling us, that her birth had allowed her to expect a better lot than was hers at this moment; but in the end, the unalterable mildness of Madame Delaunay, who made no other opposition to all our innocent railleries of thoughtless young girls, but silence, and that inconceivable dulness before which the sharpest points become blunted, disarmed me, and I became, young as I was, her most intimate friend.

"Madame Delaunay employed the whole time she could dispose of in reading romances, which she easily procured, and which, by infinite address, she knew how to conceal from our good mistress, who, as you are aware, was a declared enemy of these sort of works. You can easily guess what happened; she lent me some of them, which I read with avidity; then others, and again more.

"Unfortunately, I have received from nature a very susceptible imagination; so that these readings were not long in producing their usual results. I lost one by one those qualities which made me beloved by my companions. No more mad sallies, no more gay repartees, which caused a laugh among you all; I was no longer willing to take part in your games; I was become, in fact, a reflection of Madame Delaunay; I lived in a world created by my own imagination, and peopled with the heroes and heroines of the books I read. At this hour, I would willingly laugh at the foolish ideas which at that period crossed my imagination without cessation, if the consequences had not taught me that the ideas of our early years are destined to exercise over the first events of our life, an important influence, either salutary or fatal.

" My aunt possessed, at the time she took charge of me, a fortune, which, without being considerable, permitted her to live honourably; but wishing to see me occupy one day a brilliant position in society, a position which I could only acquire by a rich marriage, my kind aunt resolved to increase her fortune, in order to be enabled to give me a large dowry, when I had attained an age for marrying.

" It happened with her, as it must of necessity happen to any woman without experience in affairs, who launches suddenly into the absorbing vortex of speculation. Men, in whom she had placed her confidence, deceived her, without feeling the least scruple; some induced her to purchase, at a dear rate, shares of companies which were not even quoted at the exchange; others induced her to lend money to grand personages, who are only peers of France, or deputés, to prevent them the trouble of paying their debts; and this to such an extent, that one day the poor woman, who fancied that at least she had doubled her fortune, and who, on my account, built the most magnificent *chateaux en Espagne*,* and slept tranquilly on a pyramid of scrip of every size and every colour, awoke to find herself ruined, or nearly so; there remained for her about two thousand francs a-year.

" Her means did not allow her any longer to pay the somewhat heavy charge for my schooling. She was compelled to let me quit it before my education was completed. It was with pleasure that you witnessed my departure, my dear friends, for I led you to believe that I left in order to espouse, I don't know what grand personage of whom I had traced to you a portrait, which more resembled some fantastic hero of the last romance I had read, than a real personage.

" Was it from pride, or simply to deceive, that I invented such a tale? It was neither for the one lustre nor the other; but romances produce in those who read many of them, before experience has ripened their faculties, so false an idea of the world and those who inhabit it, that they can with difficulty determine themselves to believe in the friendship of those who surround them, when this friendship does not prove itself by ridiculous transports and exaggerated demonstrations. I did not believe then, in your friendship, which, however, and the result has proved it, was as genuine as it was calm; it was for this reason I did not inform you of the frightful misfortune which had fallen on my good aunt.

" I did not separate without pain from Madame Delaunay, upon whom I had bestowed the confidence which I had refused to you, and it was not until after she had made me a promise to come and see me often, that I withdrew from her embrace to follow my aunt, who waited for me in the apartment of our mistress.

" My aunt received, without complaining, the terrible change in her circumstances, and at once resigned herself to the more than modest existence which for the future was to be our lot. Hence, it was not to the almost sumptuous apartment which she had hitherto occupied, that she conducted me, but into a secluded retreat in one of the most

* Castles in the air.

populous quarters of the capital, (if we wish to be forgotten, we must plunge into the crowd,) a retreat excessively simple, and quite in accordance with the precarious state of our fortune; but in which, however, nothing that could contribute to make the life we were to lead less monotonous to me, had been neglected My aunt, who, to augment the small capital which remained to her, had disposed of several objects of some value which embellished the apartments she formerly occupied, had faithfully preserved every thing which personally belonged to me; thus, I found in our modest hermitage, and arranged with care, in a small room absolutely similar to the one I had once pompously dignified with the title of boudoir, every object I loved; my books, my easel, my palette, and my brushes, my albums, my music, and a magnificent piano of Errard's, as good as it was handsome, and for the fate of which I had not ceased to tremble.

" My good aunt enjoyed my surprise, and tears of delight rolled down her venerable cheeks.

" ' You see, my child,' she said to me, ' we can, although we may be poor, still procure a few moments of happiness.'

" I threw myself into her arms, which were opened to receive me, and for some minutes we held each other in a warm embrace.

" ' Listen, my child,' said my aunt, when we had resumed our calmness, ' it was because I wished to make you rich, that to-day we are both in poverty; you must not then blame me; there remains to me, my dear Eugenie, two thousand francs revenue; 'tis very little! still, if we are economical, a thousand or twelve hundred francs will suffice us for each year, by which, in about ten years, we shall find ourselves at the head of a small capital, which shall be your dowry; you are handsome, you have talents, and you have received a good education; you will always be prudent, I have no doubt; well! we must not despair as to the future; you will infallibly meet with, if you preserve these valuable qualities, an honest man who would possess all this, who will render you happy, and whose happiness you will ensure; and let not the retirement in which we are about to live, cause you uneasiness; however deeply the violet may be hidden, its perfume betrays it, and leads to its discovery. It is the same with women, those only are neglected who are not worth the trouble of seeking.'

" My good aunt spoke to me thus, no doubt to give me courage and hope; I quite agreed with her in opinion; but that which she expected from time, a uniform and prudent conduct, and perhaps simply from the goodness of the Almighty, I looked for either from chance, or my own personal merit; the books I had perused had turned my head to such a degree; my imagination was so full of kings who had espoused shepherdesses; grand seigneurs who had solicited on their knees, the hand of peasant girls who worked for their bread; and I valued my own little person at such a high price, that it seemed to me impossible that the world would forget me in my retreat.

" Yet days flew on, and as I had neither the time nor opportunity to spoil at once both my heart and my imagination, my character soon resumed its wonted stamp; I became again as gay as on my arrival at school, and with my gaiety, I recovered the brilliant colours of a young girl, which, as you may remember, I began to lose when I left you; I occupied myself with the cares of our little ménage; I painted, I practised music, and in the evenings I read to my worthy aunt some passages from our best authors. My life, you see, had not many incidents; my aunt, whose great age rendered infirm, could go out but rarely, so that, when she found herself a little stronger than usual, and fine weather permitted us to pass a few hours either at the Tuilleries or the Luxembourg, these gardens were situate at nearly an equal distance from our domicile, I was as happy as a bride who discovers in her *corbeille*, a chatenure or a casket she did not expect. At any rate I was not unhappy, so true is it that a serenity of mind, and a calmness of conscience, can compensate for all the comforts we may be deprived of.

"Six months had nearly elapsed since I had quitted school, and I had not yet heard a word of Madame Delaunay, who, as I learnt soon afterwards, had been dismissed from it a short time after my quitting, no doubt because our worthy mistress had at length discovered that she was not endowed with a character equal to the mission which was confided to her.

"I was at first cruelly disappointed at the abandonment of this woman, but as in the end I did not feel towards her that attachment which persons really worthy alone know how to inspire you, I had completely forgotten her, when one morning she presented herself at our house.

"A visit, of whatever nature, was for my aunt whom misfortune had not rendered a misanthrope, and for myself whom it distracted for a few minutes, a happy event, an event very rare in our existence; for since we had become poor, no one seemed inclined to visit us; hence we received Madame Delaunay with the most lively satisfaction. She excused herself for not coming to see me before, by saying that shortly after her leaving the school, which she had only quitted, she said, because her health did not permit her longer to support the fatigues of the profession of an instructress, fatigues, however, which were very light, she had fallen ill and had been compelled to keep her bed for a considerable time.

"We chatted for a long while. Madame Delaunay informed us of all that had happened to her since the death of her parents, whom she had lost whilst yet a child. It was a very long and very lamentable history, which resembled a little all that I had read, and I verily believe now that Madame Delaunay appropriated to herself the adventures of the heroine of one of the romances in 12mo., printed upon scented paper, formerly edited by the famous Pigoreau, and which are not met with at the present day, except on the top shelves of one of those antique cabinets of corrupt reading in the chief towns of a canton. This history, however, full of extraordinary events, of mysterious complications, unforeseen recognitions, and whose denouement was yet a mystery, interested me considerably, and magnified so much, in the eyes of my aunt, the person who recounted it, (and who, as you may well think, had contrived a scene which should produce a grand idea of her character,) that the poor woman who could not believe there existed persons who found an unworthy pleasure in lying, overwhelmed Madame Delaunay with the strongest entreaties to prevail upon her to pay us a visit as often as it might be in her power.

"Madame Delaunay revisited us several times, and she was soon our most faithful messmate; my aunt received her visits with the greatest pleasure. Madame Delaunay, despite the inequalities of her character, possessed a cultivated imagination, and conversed very agreeably; and besides, as I have already mentioned, my aunt being infirm, could go out but seldom, so that I was also forced to remain confined to the house, at an age when it is so requisite to take some little exercise, and breathe the pure air. Madame Delaunay, by the position she had occupied, and her previous relations with me, inspired sufficient confidence in my aunt to permit me sometimes to accompany her for a walk, and which I gladly took advantage of.

"I thus frequently accompanied her in a promenade either in the Tuilleries or the Luxembourg, or in the king's garden, but oftener in the Tuilleries than elsewhere; for my companion, despite her romantic ideas, loved the world, and the places in which it predominated, whilst I preferred the silent retreats and umbrageous bowers.

"When the day was fine, we took with us some light female work, and seated ourselves under the magnificent chestnuts of the Tuilleries, where we frequently remained for several hours before thinking of returning. Sometimes I remarked passing in front of me, covered with rich attire, leaning on the arm of the man they had accepted as a husband, and followed by a valet, some of my school companions, but not one of them bethought herself of recognising the young girl, plainly attired, who worked with such activity, not one bestowed upon her a friendly inclination of the head; they supposed me, no doubt, much poorer than I was in reality.

"One day Madame Delaunay entered our apartment very richly dressed, she wore a bonnet of the newest fashion of the most fashionable artiste, and was enveloped in a handsome cachemere shawl; her robe composed of rich stuff of magnificently watered silk. We complimented her on the subject of her brilliant toilette, which appeared to us so unusual, for we knew that the pecuniary means of this woman were very limited. I know not whether she guessed our thoughts, for her first care was to inform us of the source from whence all these riches sprung. She told us that one of her brothers, who had acquired a very considerable fortune in India, had arrived in Paris, and that he wished her to share with him all he possessed; she then eulogized the noble character of this brother, and, in support of what she advanced, showed us several bank notes."

"Nothing authorized us to doubt her word; my aunt was requested to allow me to walk out with her; she wished, she said, to make several purchases, and it would be some distraction for me to visit the different magazins at which she intended to call."

"We put ourselves *en route*. Not wishing to make a contrast, I contrived with the remains of my ancient splendor to complete a toilette, more simple perhaps, but assuredly in much better taste than that of my friend. We visited, as had been agreed upon, several shops; my friend purchased a few trifling objects, and forced me to receive a few *bagatelles*, which I accepted with pleasure, for I saw, not without experiencing a grateful sensation, that fortune had not changed the heart of my friend."

"It was not yet two o'clock when we had completed all our purchases, and although the cold was very sharp, the day was magnificent, and cheered by a noble winter's sun. Madame Delaunay said that if I would accompany her, we would take a turn in the Tuilleries. I had no reason to oppose her desire: but I merely observed that our carriage was full of the purchases we had made, and that we must absolutely get rid of them. 'Don't let that be any hindrance,' she replied, 'I will send it all to your house by our driver, who will carry at the same time a short note to your aunt, that she may not be surprised at our long absence, and we will go on foot as far as the Tuilleries.' This plan was agreed upon, and we discharged the carriage.

" We had arrived at the extremity of the passage of the Tuilleries, which runs along the Terrace des Feuillants, and were returning by the same walk, when we were accosted by a monsieur already aged, and decorated with several orders.

" 'My faith! my dear Clelie,' he said, addressing Madame Delaunay, after saluting me perfectly in accordance with the customs of good society, 'I did not expect the pleasure of meeting you here, and in such charming company.' He made me another salute, which I returned by a slight inclination of the head.

" ''Tis my brother,' said Madame Delaunay to me, 'Is he not handsome?'

" I did not remark the singularity of this question, but, however, I was not of my friend's opinion.

" I do not know if you think with me, but nothing in the world appears so ridiculous, and so afflicting at the same time, as to see an old man affect the tone and manners of a young one; I think, that respectable white hair, and the deep furrows which time produces in a venerable visage, are the only ornaments which suit old age. The man, therefore, who accosted us, merely from his personal appearance, inspired me with an invincible repugnance.

" He had evidently passed his tenth lustre; and yet he was as rigorously busked, gloved, and spurred, as the most ferocious lion of the *loge infernal*. A white camelia, of a fabulous dimension, ornamented the button hole of his coat, and he flourished, with a juvenile gaiety, a superb cane surmounted with an immense golden apple, and beautifully chased.

" Fancy for a moment, a diminutive figure in a *journal des modes*, to which you will give an old visage, which neither the skill of the dentist, nor the immoderate use of every liniment and every cosmetic imaginable has succeeded in making look young, and you will have before your eyes the portrait exact of the brother of Madame Delaunay.

" After a rather long walk, during which, he continued to praise my beauty and my esprit, although my sulky mien, and the almost complete silence which I preserved, must have given him a very poor idea both of one and the other, he proposed to take us to dine at a restaurateur's, a proposition which was made in very respectful terms.

" 'It is so long,' he said to me, 'since I have seen my sister, that I must naturally seize every occasion which presents itself, to pass a few minutes in her society, and you will render me a real service, by not preventing her from accepting my proposition.'

" And from politeness, and quite certain beforehand, that Madame Delaunay would not accept this invitation, I left to the latter the care of replying to him.

" 'I do not see,' she said to me, 'why we should not accept the kind invitation of my brother, we will make a little haste, so that your aunt may not have time to get uneasy.'

" I was taken in a snare I had myself set; still I hesitated, but my friend joined her entreaties to those of her brother; I was in a manner forced to accept; in short, the affair passed off tolerably well: we hurried ourselves a little, and our Am-

phytrion, who seemed aware that I must be impatient to retire, did not attempt to retain us; I was pleased with his discretion and his extreme politeness, and at the finish of the repast, he appeared to me a little less ridiculous than when we placed ourselves at table.

" At the time I am alluding to, it was the Carnival. Some young men, seated at a table near us, were conversing among themselves of the last bal masqué at which they had been present.

" 'You have never been at a bal masqué?' said Madame Delaunay.

" 'Never,' I replied, ' and it is not probable that I shall very soon go to one I am sorry for it,' I continued, without attaching to my words more importance than they deserved; 'I am very sorry for it, really; I have frequently heard it said, that nothing is more amusing than a bal masqué.'

" 'It is quite true,' replied Madame Delaunay; 'I have been there occasionally with my husband, and I have been much pleased with them.'

" And she commenced describing to me a picture of a bal masqué, quite capable of turning the head of a young girl, and gave me a description of an opera saloon, on a ball night, which resembled a palace of the Hundred-and-One Nights. To listen to her, it was nothing but gorgeous chandeliers, and clusters of lights, whose rays were reflected in immense pier glasses, and in the gilded panels and wainscotings; they promenaded on the most magnificent carpets; and every step of the staircases, and each vestibule, were decorated with elegant boxes, enclosing the rarest and most odoriferous flowers. And then, it was the immense orchestra of several hundred distinguished musicians, who obeyed, as but a single man, the baton of the Napoleon of quadrilles, the illustrious Muzard; this was the orchestra to be listened to! That of the Conservatoire was nothing in comparison to it. And then, it was the immense variety of rich and brilliant costumes, borrowed of every age and every known country, which must be seen; the noble lady of the fourteenth century, leaning on the arm of a French guardsman of the reign of Louis the Fifteenth; the chevalier of the time of the Crusades, courting a *Merveilleuse* of the Directory; and close to a soldier of the Republic, who conversed in a corner with a Dominican; whilst the dominoes, white, black, rose, blue, every colour, mysterious phantoms, glided through the different groups, and took a part in all the excitements of the ball, without being recognised by an individual.

" The brother of Madame Delaunay thought proper to add a few touches to the picture, already so brilliant, which his sister had just painted.

" 'The holy alliance of the people,' he said, 'really exist nowhere but at a bal masqué. French and English, Italians and Austrians, Poles and Russians, Belgians and Dutch, Greeks and Turks, live together on the best terms in the saloon of the opera; hence, when all these men, habited in costumes so picturesque, and of such different forms, assemble for the final galope, and pass, rapid as a torrent which has burst its dykes, before the dominoes, who have taken refuge in the stalls of the rez-de-chaussée, we fancy we see reconciled Europe, hastening towards a happier futurity.'

" You have remarked, my dear friends, that Madame Delaunay and her brother, constantly took care to place in one of the corners of the picture which they offered to my view, several dominoes, a sort of mysterious personages, who could see and hear all without being remarked. They intended, no doubt, by showing me the possibility of my presence at the opera ball, to produce in me a wish to be present; if such, in fact, was their intention, their success was complete.

"'Next Thursday, the last ball for the season will take place,' said Madame Delaunay, 'and it is said, it will be more brilliant than those which have preceded it. I should very much wish to go.'

"'And so should I,' I said in my turn.

"I ought to observe, that when I expressed myself thus strongly, I did not think the accomplishment of my desire was possible.

"The brother of my friend undertook to prove to me that I was not wrong.

"'But, since both of you wish to be present at this ball, nothing prevents you, as it seems to me, procuring yourselves this pleasure, and I shall very willingly be the cavalier of my good sister, and also of her charming companion.'

"'Well?' said Madame Delaunay, who regarded me with an expression, the intention of which I perfectly understood.

"'My aunt would never permit me to pass a night at a ball,' I replied.

"And, despite the efforts made to restrain it, a deep sigh escaped from me.

"'It's true,' said my friend, 'your aunt would not allow you to assist at the ball where we should be so much amused.'

"I replied to my friend, that not being compelled to make her will depend upon that of another, nothing prevented her going to the ball, as she desired it, and her brother would serve as her cavalier.

"'You will relate to me,' I said, 'all that you may see, and it will be the same as though I had absolutely been there myself.'

"Madame Delaunay replied, that she loved me too well to determine to take a pleasure by herself, a pleasure, which, besides, would be none to her, if I did not share it.

"I was greatly moved at the affection and strong friendship which my friend showed; but, to the regret I felt at thinking I could not behold the marvellous scenes of which they had made me such ravishing pictures, were added those much stronger ones, I assure you, which crept over me at the resolution she had taken not to attend, without me, the bal masqué.

"The conversation I have reported to you, took place in a carriage we had engaged at the door of the traiteur with whom we had dined, and when near the residence of my aunt, the brother of my friend quitted us, and Madame Delaunay begged me not to mention him to my aunt, she feared, she said, that the latter would blame us for having accepted his invitation to dinner. I attempted at first, to overcome her scruples, which appeared to me exaggerated, but finding, at length, that I could not succeed, and that I ought to refuse nothing to a person who professed so much friendship for me, I promised all that she desired, so that when we arrived at my aunt's, I was forced to confirm the history she invented to justify our long absence, a history, moreover, which succeeded completely; my good aunt was so far from believing me capable of telling an untruth, that she would have implicitly believed me, if I had told her at midnight that the sun was shining in all its splendor.

"When Madame Delaunay quitted us, after promising to renew her visit in the morning, I read to my aunt her daily portion, which was prolonged till nearly ten o'clock, when we parted to take our necessary repose, my aunt, as was her regular custom, kissed me on the forehead, and wished me a good night; I had on my conscience the lie I had told her, and I was on the point of confessing it to her; I know not what demon retained within my lips the admission ready to escape from it; no doubt, my evil counsellor, who, to recompense me for having obeyed him, sent the most bewitching dreams to accompany my slumbers. I dreamt that I was at the ball of the opera, in that magnificent hall, of which my friend and her brother had made me so pompous a description, and from the formidable orchestra, directed by the illustrious Muzard, escaped torrents of harmony, which set in movement the variegated crowd of lightermen, paysannes, and postilions of Longjumeau.

"The next morning Madame Delaunay came to breakfast with us; the weather was too unsettled to think of going out, and it was arranged that she should pass the entire day with us. About one o'clock, my aunt, who felt rather unwell, retired, and left me alone with my friend.

"'Well!' she said to me, 'have you thought of the bal masqué, for Thursday? As for me, I have dreamt of it the whole night.'

"'It has been the same with me,' I replied.

"'If you like,' she added, 'we can go to this ball.'

"'But how?'

"'Listen, my dear friend; I love you too much, you know, to give you bad advice, so that I am persuaded you will not interpret unfavourably what I am going to say. Our old relations, to whom their age has given a necessity of repose, will not understand that, when we are young, we stand in need of excitement, of change of air, that we are anxious to see every thing and to know every thing. We must not blame them; they submit to a natural law, which we shall submit to in our turn; but shall we be very culpable, I ask you, if, without infringing any received usages, without offending in any manner their prejudices—which, moreover, spring from the tenderness they have towards us, since it is only to shield us from the dangers which they themselves have experienced, that they wish to interdict us from a series of innocent pleasures—shall we be very culpable, I repeat, if we make some little use of our own free will?'

"I have admitted to you that I had, thanks to Madame Delaunay, read a collection of romances, some of which were certainly not the expression of a very pure morality; still, I did not absolutely comprehend a word of the formal preface of the mystifying discourse she had commenced. Of the books I had read, the facts alone had made any impression upon me; my imagination, thank God! was not yet sufficiently subtle, to deduce any consequences from them.

"'I do not understand you,' I said to Madame Delaunay.

"She regarded me with the deepest astonishment; she could not believe, I suppose, that the seeds planted in my imagination had produced so little fruit.

"'My poor friend!' she said to me.

"The air of profound pity with which she pronounced these words, wounded me more than you can imagine. I had the vanity of supposing that I was endowed with an imagination, at least equal to that of my former under-mistress, and she it was who spoke to me in such a tone of disdainful superiority; it was, therefore, in a somewhat angry

No. 28.

LIFE IN PARIS.

THE ROBBER SURPRISED AT THE ESCAPE OF SERVIGNY.

manner that I requested her to explain herself categorically.

"'Well! I like that better,' she said; 'would you go to the ball, at the opera?'

"'I should like it, exceedingly; but I cannot, my aunt would not allow me.'

"'Well, then, come without the permission of your aunt.'

"'But how?'

"When I put the question, I can fearlessly assert, I had not the intention it seemed to indicate. I obeyed, simply, a defect to which we are all more or less subject—curiosity; I merely wished to know what were the means which Madame Delaunay intended to employ, to get me to the ball without my aunt being aware of it.

"Madame Delaunay replied, as follows, to my question, 'But how?'

"'The door of the house you inhabit is never closed until after midnight, and opened in the morning by day-break, and the number of lodgers residing in it is so considerable, that the porter never troubles himself as to who goes in, or who goes out. I will request your aunt to allow me to take you to the theatre, a permission which I am certain she will not refuse me; we will go to my residence, where you will find a costume or a domino, at your choice; my brother will conduct us to the ball, and after we have passed the night there we will return to my house, you shall change your costume, and you can return home on foot, where you will arrive, and be fast asleep, before your aunt rises, and she will know nothing, as she invariably retires to bed at ten o'clock, at the latest, and, as you have frequently told me yourself, that she sleeps so soundly that nothing awakes her until her usual hour.'

"The affair could, in fact, be managed in this way, and I confess, to my shame, that when once I was well persuaded that it was possible for me to attend the ball, without the knowledge of my aunt, I promised my friend everything she required of me.

"I will not recount to you the thousand arguments she made use of, during the few days which preceded the Thursday, the arrival of which I anticipated with a certain uneasiness, in order to justify the fault I was about to commit. I was on a fatal precipice, I felt it, but could not restrain myself; I obeyed an unknown influence, which drove me to commit an action which I blamed, at the very moment I was preparing to complete it; and when I left with Madame Delaunay, after my aunt had given me permission to accompany her to the theatre, I thought of the poor little birds, whose eyes have met those of the basilisk, and who advance with panting breasts and trailing wings, obeying some indescribable but fascinating power, to throw themselves into the throat of the monster who is waiting to devour them.

"I had lost half my senses when I arrived at Madame Delaunay's, who occupied a very neat little apartment, in the Rue Notre-Dame-de-Lorette; and instead of enveloping myself in a domino, as I had intended, I put on an elegant costume of a Milanese peasant girl, without well knowing what I was about. My friend had made choice of a man's costume; this appeared to me a serious imprudence; I told her so: she replied to me, laughing, 'that everything was allowed at Carnival time, that a man's costume was much less inconvenient than a woman's, and that, besides, she had only adopted the one I saw her in, that I might be enabled to dance.'

"'How!' I said to her, 'do you mean to dance?'

"'Most certainly,' she replied. 'Do you fancy then that I go to a ball to sit cross-legged?'

"I was much astonished; in quitting the garments of her sex, she had totally changed her tone and manners, and she commenced a step, which, as she assured me, would proclaim her the queen of the ball; when the bell, violently rung, announced a visit.

"When our conscience is not quite at ease, the least sound which suddenly surprises us, disagreeably agitates our nerves; I started from the seat I occupied.

"'Who is that ringing?' I exclaimed.

"'Eh! parbleu! 'tis our cavaliers,' replied Madame Delaunay; 'my brother, and one of his friends.'

"She opened the door, and her brother entered, accompanied by another individual, whose figure displeased me at once; my friend seized her brother by his waist, and, despite the efforts he made to disengage himself, he was compelled to resign himself, and make, in a galopade, the tour of the apartment twice over; his friend laughed till he was nearly black in the face.

"'Charming! 'tis charming!' he exclaimed; whilst the other repaired, before a glass, the disorder of his toilette. 'You are still an excellent cavalier, and I am persuaded that, if you will dance, you will seduce the prettiest women at the ball.'

"'You think so, M. le Chevalier de Saint Firmin,' said the brother of my friend, who was evidently in a very bad humour; 'I am then, in your opinion, quite capable of making an impression?'

"'On my honour! I am persuaded of it.'

"'Well, then, you see how the most precious qualities, are often quite useless.'

"'Useless?'

"'Undoubtedly! what occasion have I to make love, since I have in my service men, who undertake to procure it for me ready made?'

"I only mention these words, which I then listened to without comprehending, to give you an idea of the character of the persons into whose hands I had fallen.

"'Cease, I beg of you, gentlemen,' said Madame Delaunay; 'I am sorry my brother, for having made you galop! come, don't be out of temper, but offer your arm to my friend, and let us go; it is quite time.'

"The brother of my friend approached me, and after addressing to me a few words of politeness, offered me his arm, and we left.

"A few minutes afterwards, we were at the ball of the opera.

"I looked more like a victim on the way to execution, than a young girl whose most ardent wish was about to be realized; I trembled in every limb, cold perspiration ran down my body, and my mask seemed burning into my face. Before we had made three paces in the saloon I was compelled to stop.

"'What is the matter with you?' said my cavalier.

"'Nothing, nothing,' I replied; but I felt myself turn pale under my mask, and it was only by the greatest efforts I could prevent myself from fainting.

"Madame Delaunay approached me.

"'I am suffering,' I said to her, 'I would rather leave the ball.'

"'It will be nothing; the sudden change from

the cold to so great a heat, causes this slight indisposition; we will place you in a stall, where we will remain until you are familiarised with the noise and the tumult which seems to reign here.'

"The chevalier conducted us to a stall in the first circle, which had been retained for us.

"The dizziness which obscured my sight vanished by degrees, and I was enabled to take a glimpse at the objects which surrounded me; the saloon presented really an enchanting *coup d'œil*, and the reality exceeded the greatest stretch of my imagination. I followed with curiosity the undulations of this crowd, variegated with a thousand brilliant colours, which, at one moment grouped into one of the corners of the saloon, left around it a vast and empty space; at another moment, dispersing without order, resembled a hive of bees commencing its flight; and when the long chain of the galop, which terminated every country-dance, passed rapidly before my eyes, I felt a restless desire to take an active part in the amusements of the party, whose features appeared animated by an expression of the liveliest gaiety; and I involuntarily called to mind those ancient dances, mentioned in chronicles, in which it becomes a necessity to join, when by chance we are spectators.

"Madame Delaunay danced nearly into my stall, and every minute she demanded if I found myself better?

"When at length I replied in the affirmative, a prolonged 'ouf!' escaped from her.

"'In that case, come and dance, then,' she said.

"I avow, with shame, that I made no other resistance than what was necessary to induce her to believe that I did not obey with pleasure; and it was not until I was bruised, broken, and exhausted, more perhaps from the different emotions I had experienced, than from actual fatigue, that I quitted the ball. My costume, so fresh, so coquettish, when I entered the saloon, was torn, and covered with dust; my dishevelled locks fell in long irregular meshes over my pale cheeks, marbled with fine red streaks: a pier glass, before which I had placed myself to wipe the dust from my face, revealed to me this frightful state of my person. I turned, with disgust, from the contemplation.

"It was then a little after three o'clock.

"'My aunt will see that I have been to the ball,' I said.

"'What a child you are,' said Madame Delaunay; 'when you have bathed your face in some fresh water, and slept for an hour or two, nothing will remain of these slight traces of fatigue. But, however, let us go to supper, I am dying with hunger—and you?'

"I replied to my friend, 'that I had no wish for anything, that it would be much better to retire at once.' She observed, by way of vanquishing my scruples, 'that I could not return to my residence—at least without being remarked, until eight o'clock in the morning; that to refuse, would disoblige her brother, who was very susceptible, and that it was her interest to please him.' In fact, she talked to me so much, and so well, that I consented to accompany her to the Café Anglais.

"The most *recherché* supper was served to us, in one of the cabinets of this establishment; I merely tasted some soup; Madame Delaunay, on the contrary, helped herself from every dish that was placed before us; as to the men, they emptied with such rapidity the decanters of choice wine, that I was frightened without knowing at what.

"Madame Delaunay was placed at table near the chevalier, and by my side I had the brother of my friend.

"The wine these men had drank put them in good humour, and for some moments they had exchanged between themselves, whilst regarding me, looks of intelligence, whose expression began to make me tremble; the chevalier had lighted a cigar, and although the odour of the tobacco really annoyed me, I dared not complain. My friend's brother drew his chair towards mine, he praised my beauty and my graces, he then took my hand, pressed it in his own, and then covered it with kisses. I turned red, then pale, I was in torments; and Madame Delaunay, whom I implored by a look, laughed outright, and told me that everything was allowed on a Carnival night!

"'And here's a proof of it,' said the chevalier, who deposed a hearty kiss on the lips of my friend.

"I concluded that Madame Delaunay would manifest, in a striking manner, the displeasure I supposed she must feel, and that, at length, we should be enabled to leave; this hope was soon destroyed, for, on the contrary, she invited her brother to follow the example which the chevalier had set him.

"I can find no terms strong enough to describe the indignation I felt, when the wrinkled and painted face of this old caricature approached mine; I guessed, at once, that this man was not the brother of her who called herself my friend, and what were the intentions of these three ignoble companions; it crossed my brain, like a flash of lightning! it was a revelation from above, which would not permit their triumph! I rose so suddenly, that the chair I occupied was upset; my face was burning, and my eyes, I felt, flashed as though on fire.

"'You are an infamous set!' I exclaimed, in a voice trembling from rage and emotion, and profiting, with address, by the stupor of the persons I had so naturally apostrophised, I descended rapidly a small staircase I saw before me, and which conducted me on the boulevard.

"I knew not where I was, my only desire was to escape Madame Delaunay and her accomplices; and I had scarcely arrived in the street, when I began to run forward, without troubling myself as to where I should arrive; but I had not made ten steps on the boulevard, when I heard, behind me, the voice of the chevalier, who cried out to me to stop. I know not what foolish terror seized hold of me, but I threw myself into the arms of a young man, whom I saw before me, exclaiming, 'Sir, sir, protect me, I entreat of you!'

"The young man threw away the cigar he was smoking when I appealed to him.

"'Fear nothing, mademoiselle,' he said to me, 'fear nothing; whoever may be the miserables pursuing you, they shall not injure you, to a certainty, as long as I have strength to defend you.'

"At this moment the chevalier arrived near us.

"'Are you mad?' he said to me, whilst I clung to the person who had promised to protect me; 'are you mad, to quit us so hastily and abuse us, because the brother of your friend allowed himself an innocent jest?'

"'Be silent!' I replied, to this man, who displeased me more, perhaps, than the pretended brother of Madame Delaunay; 'and no longer name, as my friend, the woman who has so unworthily deceived me.'

"The chevalier commenced laughing outright.

"'I understand,' he exclaimed, when his mirth had ceased; he wished, no doubt, to place me, in the opinion of my protector, in a light which would induce him to abandon me: 'I understand, perfectly! Monsieur has a better talent in pleasing you than we have, and you wish to remain with him; but it shall not be thus, I give you my word of honour; it was by your own desire that you came with us; and, morbleu! you shall stay with us.'

"My protector had not, as yet, spoken a word, and his silence began to make me uneasy. Had the chevalier attained the end he had in view, and was I to fall again into the hands of my persecutors? The approach of danger gave me renewed strength; I would not have it said that I fell without defending myself.

"'Sir, sir!' I cried, pressing with force the arm of the young man, 'do not believe it;' and without giving him time to reply, I informed him, in a few words, how I had been induced to visit the ball at the opera, and why I had sought his protection.

"'It's all nonsense,' exclaimed the knight of Saint Firmin, 'sheer nonsense; come, sweet odalisque, we have ordered some punch, come and take your share;' and he extended his hand to seize me.

"I uttered some piercing shrieks.

"'Away, sir!' said my protector, in a voice of thunder, 'away!' And as the weak and sickly chevalier had placed himself before us, and seemed disposed to dispute our passage, he repulsed him so roughly, that he sent him rolling some distance in our front.

"The latter rose up, completely *hors de combat!* 'Sir! you shall render me satisfaction for this insult,' he said, in a piteous tone.

"'Go, go, monsieur the spurious limonadier! I recognised you in spite of your lunettes,' said the young man, with the utmost contempt; 'return to your kennel, resume your own costume, and your gray moustaches, and prepare for your pigmy actors the refreshments they must stand in need of, after dancing the polka. You know well that men who respect themselves do not cross weapons with you; but as, from the portrait which mademoiselle has sketched to me, I imagine that your companion in all this is no other than M. the Count de D——, of whom you are the proxy in ordinary, you may say to him, from me, that I am quite at his service. Vrai Dieu! it would be doing a meritorious action, to rid society of this old representative of the dissolute manners of the regency.'

"I trembled in every limb, for I perceived among the many persons who were assembled round us, the individual of whom my protector spoke in such disdainful terms.

"'Will you repeat, before the person to whom you allude, what you have now uttered?' said the Count de D——.

"'Beyond a doubt,' replied the young man; 'not only what I have uttered, but much in addition: for example, that old men—old men, do you understand, M. le Count—who dye their hair, and paint their face to appear as young men, should be treated as though they were so in reality; that whatever may be the position we occupy in society, the title we may have received from our ancestors, or the decorations we may be enabled to dress ourselves with, we only merit the contempt of honest men, when we use these privileges to carry trouble and dishonour into a family.'

"'Monsieur! monsieur! are you aware that I am the Count de D——,' said the individual so strikingly apostrophized, and turning pale, even under the rouge.

"'Eh! do you fancy for a moment that I did not know it,' replied my protector. 'Go, go, worthy scion of the roués of the regency, and the handsome sons of the directory; go wash your face, and wipe off the blemishes which stain your escutcheon, leave to the remnant of your hair the time to take to its natural colour; you may afterwards call upon me to demand reparation, if you think it advisable; go, M. le Count de D——, although you use your utmost skill to pass for a young man, I pity your great age.'

"'You will give me your name, sir; you shall give it to me.'

"'Well! be it so; there's my card, since you require it, to-morrow morning I shall be at your disposition.'

"'To-day—this very day,' roared the Count de D——, who attempted to oppose our passage.

"'No, not to-day,' replied my protector, 'I have need of the hours which yet remain, to repair the mischief you have caused. Gentlemen,' he continued, addressing those who surrounded us, 'restrain, I beg of you, this old madman; I shall be really sorry to visit him with the same treatment I have inflicted upon his worthy companion.'

"The multitude has generous instincts, to which an appeal is never made in vain; that which surrounded us was principally composed of young men who had passed some part of the night at the ball, and who, from the different establishments where they had supped, had been attracted to the boulevard by my cries, and the discordant voice of the chevalier; *debardeurs,* French guards, pirates, and postilions joined hands, and danced around the unfortunate Count de D——, of whom we still heard the cries of rage, and imprecations of his wrath, long after losing sight of him.

"'Mon Dieu! monsieur,' I said to my protector, when we found ourselves alone on the boulevard, 'you will now be forced to fight with this man, and all through me. Oh! I am sure I shall not survive it.'

"'Cheer up, mademoiselle, I assure you I do not fear the results of a meeting with this M. le Count de D——; but let us attend to yourself. Where do you wish me to conduct you?'

"This very simple and natural question recalled to me the whole horror of my position, which I had for a moment forgotten, in thinking of the dangers which, on my account, was threatening my protector. I should be compelled to return home to my aunt's, habited in a costume which felt heavier to me than a mantle of lead. The poor woman, I was sure, would pardon the fault I had committed: but what would those persons think who should see me enter alone, and so strangely accoutred; my reputation would be ruined—it was the only treasure I possessed in the world, and still the fault I had committed was in some measure excusable.

"I said all this to the young man; he listened to me with much attention. He seemed to comprehend the unfortunate position I was in; and as I had mentioned to him the plan I had arranged with Madame Delaunay, to return home without being perceived, he said it was the only reasonable one, and that I ought not to abandon it.

"'But,' I replied, 'my own dress remains at Madame Delaunay's, and I cannot, after what has taken place, go there to obtain them.'

"'Why not? Now that the character of this woman is known to you, you need no longer fear her; besides, I will accompany you to her house, where she ought now to be returned, and nothing will happen to you, I will answer for it, even should we meet there M. le Count de D——, and his worthy associate.'

"The plan proposed by the young man was the most reasonable. I knew it well, still I needed the greatest efforts before determining to adopt it, and it was not without feeling a strong repugnance that I resolved to follow my generous protector to the house of Madame Delaunay.

"I walked, with the assistance of the young man, who, to preserve me from the cold, which was very sharp, had wrapped me in his cloak. My flight from the Café Anglais had been so sudden, that I had forgotten my pelisse. It was only at long intervals that we exchanged a few monosyllables. I reflected on the sad position in which I was placed, in consequence of an imprudence, and I resolved that what had happened should serve me as a warning for the future; I knew not, alas! that, at this very moment, I was incurring a much greater danger than any I had escaped from; each time I raised my eyes I encountered those of the young man, and then quickly bent down my head; he, on his part, said nothing, but he guided my steps with a touching solicitude, and drew round me the folds of his cloak, which the morning breeze had removed.

"The distance from the place we were now in to Madame Delaunay's was not considerable, and we were not long in reaching the domicile of the latter.

"'Madame is within, she has this moment returned,' said the porter to us. 'No doubt mademoiselle has missed her at the ball, that she did not return with her; and that is the reason madame appeared so disturbed when she entered, and has forgotten to favour me with the douceur which it is usual to pay the concierge when parties return after midnight.'

"The commentaries made by this Cerberus upon an event quite natural, and the conjectures he seemed determined to draw from it, gave me some idea of what I had to expect on my own account, if I could not contrive to enter without my escapade being observed. So that I blessed inwardly, a hundred times, the person who had induced me to obtain my own dress from the place I had left them in.

"My protector slipped a five-franc piece into the hand of the concierge, who entered his lodge as a dog to whom we chuck a bone. We ascended.

"Madame Delaunay had not exchanged her costume, when she opened the door to us; she turned somewhat pale when she saw the person who accompanied me, and nearly let the candle she held in her hand fall on the floor; however, when we had entered, she attempted to justify herself.

"'Do not waste time in idle words,' said my protector to her; 'I know you, Madame Delaunay, you are well aware of it; and that you may not be enabled to reinstate yourself in the good opinion of mademoiselle, I shall make it my business to narrate to her what I know of your character.'

"'At your pleasure, my dear, at your pleasure, recount to her just what you like; but I recommend you to pass over some few facts; or, at least, to draw a light veil over them, if you do not wish to compel the chaste ears of that modest creature to listen to some singular adventures.'

"The effrontery of this shameless woman, made **my heart turn sick.**

"'I would I were far from here,' I said to the young man, in an under tone.

"'I can well understand the disgust you must feel,' he replied to me, without even taking the trouble to lower his voice; 'but reassure yourself, we will not remain here long; pass, if you wish it, into the next room, Madame Delaunay would rather rest here to keep me company.'

"'You are a simpleton, my dear; I really thought you were going to act as her femme de chambre.'

"This outrage, which I so little deserved, although addressed to me by a person I despised, caused me to shed some bitter tears.

"'Enough, madame,' exclaimed my protector, advancing towards Madame Delaunay, with a violence which made me tremble for the latter; 'enough. Go, mademoiselle,' he continued, addressing me; 'quit this costume, and do not let the miserable jests of this creature afflict you; we can well allow her to exhaust the rage which chokes her, since she has been unmasked.'

"It took me considerably longer to change my costume than I had expected; I had every moment to break the cords and laces, which took me an infinite time to adjust afterwards; but for all the world I would not have called Madame Delaunay to my assistance. I think, that if I had been compelled to choose, I would rather have had recourse to the young man who had afforded me such a generous protection.

"The day began to appear, when, at length, I was ready; and although it was some distance from the domicile of Madame Delaunay, to that of my aunt, I had yet more time before me than was necessary to arrive at the appointed hour; we left, however, at once; I wished rather to be in the street, than in her apartment, and I verily believe that, on his own account, my companion felt the same desire.

"He had, on entering Madame Delaunay's, taken off his cloak, and, as he replaced it on his shoulders at the moment we were leaving, I saw, at the button-hole of his coat, the red ribbon of the legion of honour. This gave me pleasure; such a sign, I thought, could only belong to a man who deserved to wear it; and when I made this reflection, I no longer remembered that the breast of the Count de D—— (and I knew the opinion entertained of the individual) was covered with decorations. I was thus disposed, when we had put ourselves en route, to accord my entire confidence to my young protector, so that, when we had arrived at the place at which he was to quit me, he knew everything that had happened to me since my departure from school to that day.

"In return, he had favoured me with his confidence; he informed me his name was Edmond de Bourgerel, that he was captain in the first regiment of African chasseurs, and that it was only by chance he happened to be in Paris, where he had come to pass a leave of absence for six months, on account of a severe wound he had lately received.

"'Promise me,' I said to him, at the moment we were separating; 'promise me not to engage with the Count de D——.'

"'I cannot,' he said to me, 'make you a promise on this subject; but I will undertake to do all that depends upon myself to avoid this unfortunate affair; and, in doing so, I shall obey as much my own wishes as your request. I confess to you, I would sooner charge a troop of Arabs, at the head of my squadron, than cross weapons with this old rake, who will absolutely pass for a young man.'

"This last remark caused me a reflection, which I should have made much sooner, if my mind more tranquil, had allowed me to catch the sense of some words spoken near me.

"'But you know then,' I said to my protector, 'the three persons in whose company I have been to-night?'

"'For some time, mademoiselle; but I hope I shall again have the happiness of seeing you, and I will then inform you of all I am in possession of respecting these three individuals. Adieu, mademoiselle.'

"And as I opened my mouth to thank him.

"'Say not a word,' he continued, 'I have experienced so much pleasure in obliging you, that you are in no ways indebted to me.'

"Not a person at this moment was passing the street, the young man seized my hand, which he carried to his lips, he then quitted me.

"I entered my apartment without being remarked, and a few minutes after I was in bed and fast asleep; and you need not be surprised at it, the laws of nature, you know, are imperious; and it is only in the romances of the celebrated Anne Radcliffe, that we meet with heroines who never seat themselves at table, and who pass their nights in romancing about subterranean caverns, which lead from the north to the south, without any need of reposing by day.

"It was my worthy aunt who awoke me.

"'It is nearly mid-day,' she said to me, when my eyes were opened; 'and finding that you had not risen, I thought, for a moment, that you were indisposed, but I am glad to see it is not so; you are going to rise, are you not? the breakfast is waiting.'

"The same day we received a letter from Madame Delaunay, which informed us, that, intending to take a voyage with her brother, she should not for some time have the pleasure of seeing us. I guessed, at once, that it was my protector who had advised or compelled this woman to write such a letter, in order that the sudden cessation of her visits might not appear extraordinary to my aunt; I was pleased at it, as it proved to me that he had neglected nothing which might ensure my tranquillity, and it gave me an assurance that he was interested about me.

"Many days—many weeks passed away, and it is probable I should have forgotten the events I have recounted to you, if the image of my protector had not constantly presented itself before me to recal them; for I must tell you, this man, whom I had only seen but once, I loved—I loved him with all my strength of passion, and even now, I cannot restrain the tears which the remembrance of him draws from me."

In fact, the eyes of the poor Eugenie de Mirbel were bathed in tears.

"My poor friend," said the Countess de Neuville to her, who had taken one of her hands in her own, "we must not despair as to the future; if heaven has permitted so many sufferings to follow you, it has no doubt some happy years in store."

"Eh! no doubt," added Laura, "fine weather soon appears after a storm; the Almighty has no desire that you should become an exception to this general rule.

"If love has abandoned you," continued Laura, "you have still friendship, and we may rely upon this sentiment, when it is felt towards each other by individuals like ourselves."

"I know it, my best friends, I know it, and believe me, if ever it should please the Almighty that either of you may require the assistance of Eugenie de Mirbel, (but which I trust may never be the case,) you will not need, when you come to claim her services, to remind her, in order to obtain them, of what you have done for her."

After a silence of some minutes, Eugenie de Mirbel, who had dried her eyes, continued in these terms:

"I loved then this young man, which ought not to astonish you; he was young; without being what the world calls handsome, he was gifted with a physiognomy full of distinction which pleases at the first sight, no doubt because a sort of intuition tells us that it announces a good heart. He had appeared to me under circumstances the most likely to make a strong impression upon an organization such as mine; this was enough, was it not? to captivate at once the heart and the imagination of a solitary young girl to whom no one paid any attention, whose heart enclosed treasures of affection which only demanded to pour themselves out, and whose mind had been altogether disorganized by having read a heap of romances.

"You have not forgotten probably, that in quitting me, Monsieur Edmond de Bourgerel said he would see me again; and placing a reliance on this promise, I was quite sure that at some future time more or less distant, I should again see him; I was only impatient that he did not make more haste, and yet, when I did see him again, the emotion I experienced was so great, that my trouble, and the frequent blushes which mounted to my cheeks, would infallibly have unveiled the secret state of my heart to any eyes a little clearer than those of my good aunt.

"To understand the events which follow, I must describe to you in a few words the situation of our apartments.

"There exist in Paris a large number of buildings very similar to the hives of bees, and which enclose in their bosom a population at least as considerable as the chief village of a canton, if not of an arrondissement; a population composed absolutely of the same elements as those of a town; aristocracy, middle classes, and plebian; societies which live, increase, and die, under the same roof, without ever mixing together, who meet one another without speaking, who are insensible to the sufferings of each other, who fear each other, and have also their individual jealousies. The house which I inhabited at this period, with my aunt, is one of these singular constructions; it is situated in the Faubourg Saint-Denis, No. 56. This house, which is composed of five buildings, each with the same number of floors or stages, and a court, encloses a specimen of all the species of which the Parisian population is composed; a nobility much less reputable than that which it has not contrived to replace; but, in revenge, much more roguish, and much less spirituel; the arts, sciences, commerce, and trade, have each sent their representatives to this colony, who live there side by side in peace and tranquillity, without troubling themselves the least in the world about the miseries, the virtues, or the cries which swarm above their heads in the mansardes of the upper stages.

"I conclude, that the proprietor of this immense ark, having awoke one morning with his imagination a little more lucid than ordinary, questioned himself, after reading his journal, the *Journal des Debats* probably, as to what means he could employ to increase by some hundreds of francs the renting value of his property, that after studying some time, he called to mind that there are upon the ridges of the lofty mountains of Switzerland, habitations which are called chalets,(cheese-houses) and that at this auspicious moment he ordered a carpenter to be sent for, and said to him, pointing out the largest of his five courts: 'Build me here, opposite each other, two Swiss chalets, and let them be in want of nothing.'

"The carpenter, who knew no more what a chalet meant than his employer who commanded two, set about the work however in earnest, and a few days after (nothing makes a Parisian contractor work faster than the certainty of being paid on the nail) he brought to the proprietor the keys of two little wooden houses, which as much resembled chalets as they did any thing else. The proprietor, I farther imagine, after having examined them attentively, had declared that he was perfectly satisfied, and that he gave orders to his concierge to suspend above the porte cochere of the property a notice bearing these four words : *Chalets à louer presentement.**

"Do you understand? *chalets à louer!* Thus without quitting Paris, it was possible to inhabit a house similar to those of which romance writers and tourists have given us so picturesque a description. The speculation of the proprietor ought infallibly to succeed, and it did succeed. The notice which announced to the good Parisians that there were, in the centre of the most populous quarter of their city, chalets, and that these chalets were to be let, had at the moment it had been exposed, attracted the eyes of my aunt, who sought for a lodging consistent with her limited means; she entered out of mere curiosity, and as, after all, these habitations, intended for a single family, were neither more nor less inconvenient than the others, she engaged the one which was exposed to the cheerful sun.

"As I have already told you, several months had elapsed, and I had not heard a word of Monsieur Edmond de Bourgerel, who, however, I was always expecting; every effort I had made to drive his image from my mind, had only engraved it deeper in my thoughts. I had thus at length accepted the love I felt for him as a *fait accompli*, and I hoped, what ? I could not answer the question : I hoped—I can say no more.

"The fine weather had returned, the young vine which our proprietor had planted before our habitation, in order to give it a rustic appearance, commenced spreading its large green leaves, and I was enabled to cultivate the few flowers of a small parterre, which I had contrived in front of the only window of my maiden apartment.

"I was occupied one morning in pruning the branches of a Bengal rose-tree, when a window of the chalet opposite the one we inhabited, and parallel to that in front of which I was placed, was softly opened ; I mechanically raised my head, Monsieur Edmond de Bourgerel was at this window.

"The surprise, the emotion caused me to utter a sudden cry. Monsieur Edmond placed his finger on his lips, no doubt to recommend me to be silent, and retired behind the curtains of his apartment ; it was time, my good aunt ran quite bewildered, and demanded what had provoked the scream she had heard.

"'Oh! nothing,' I said, 'only an enormous spider.'

"'Child,' she replied to me laughing, 'arn't you afraid it will devour you?'

* Chalets to let immediately.

"And after kissing me she left me to attend to the affairs of our little household ; I had a mind to follow her, but an irresistible force retained me in the place.

"As soon as my aunt was gone, Monsieur de Bourgerel reappeared at his window, he was extremely pale, and he carried his right arm in a sling ; these signs made me perfectly comprehend that it was on account of his having been wounded, that I had not seen him sooner, and as no doubt he read by my looks that I shared his sufferings, he quickly withdrew his arm from the handkerchief which supported it, and waved it about, as a sign that he was perfectly recovered ; he then placed himself at his piano, and played, with an expression which brought the tears to my eyes, the sweet air of Marie Malibran, *Bonheur de se revoir apres dix ans d'absence.*

"'The chalet opposite to us,' said my aunt, at the dinner hour, 'is occupied by a good musician ; really he performed this morning the air of that pretty romance which you sing so often, you know, *Bonheur de se revoir,* did you hear him?'

"I felt myself turn red and white successively, and it was not until I had hesitated for some time that I stammered out this reply, 'I do not know, I think I did not hear him.'

"If my aunt had lifted her eyes towards me, which at this moment were fixed upon the work she held in her hands, my trouble, to a certainty, would have informed her that something extraordinary was passing.

"'Play me a short air,' she said to me, after a few minutes' silence, for she had not even dreamt of noticing the strange reply I had made her. The request of my aunt annoyed me exceedingly, our neighbour would think, no doubt, that I wished to correspond with him, and yet I neither could nor wished to refuse my aunt, but to prove to M. de Bourgerel that I only played as an amusement, and that I did not think entirely of him. I attacked the first notes of the most lively country dance I could think of; but without intending it, I softened by degrees the notes, and from transition to transition, I finished by the air he had executed in the morning : *Bonheur de se revoir.*

"''Tis charming,' said my aunt, kissing me, 'what you have played deserves from our neighbour a reply, as he will no doubt attempt to prove that he is as good a musician as yourself.'

"In fact, the first notes of the air from the Reine de chypre, *Pour tant d'amour ne soyez pas ingrate,* struck upon our ears.

"This was a declaration; I understood it perfectly, and I was not sorry for it; I had more than once, during the day which had passed, interrogated my heart, and it had always made me the same reply: I loved M. de Bourgerel; I loved him as women ought to love but once. I was not then sorry that he loved me in return. The next morning when I opened my window to attend to the flowers of my little parterre, he was already at his; after making me a respectful salute, to which I replied by a slight inclination of the head, he showed me a letter, and his signs made me comprehend that it was intended for me; I made a negative sign, he seemed disappointed, but did not insist.

"The following morning he placed himself at the lower end of his apartment, and unrolled before my eyes a long sheet of paper, upon which he had written these words in characters sufficiently large to be easily read:

"'I beg of you, accept the letter, it encloses the

LIFE IN PARIS.

THE MARRIAGE OF SALVADOR

information which I promised you, respecting the persons in question.'

"I then recollected that M. de Bourgerel had said he would inform me what, in reality, were Madame Delaunay and the two individuals with whom I went to the opera ball; I might then, without giving my protector the right of thinking ill of me, accept the letter he offered, and which, I was quite sure, contained something in addition to what he announced to me; I gave him an affirmative nod of the head, he then made me comprehend that the same evening I should find the letter among the thick branches of my Bengal rose, he then retired.

"It is scarcely necessary to say that I waited with the most anxious impatience for the coming evening; as it had been arranged, I found the letter in the place indicated, and you may guess, that my first care, when I found myself alone in my room, was to unseal and read it.

"This letter is here:" arrived at this point of her narrative, Eugenie took from her pocket a small note-case, from which she drew a letter, worn in its folds, from having been frequently read, and handed it to Lucie de Neuville.

The following are the contents of the letter, which the countess read aloud, whilst Eugenie de Mirbel, who seemed absorbed in deep and painful reflections, kept her face concealed in her two hands.

"'Mademoiselle, you have, no doubt, not forgotten, that at the moment I quitted you, I promised you some information as to the persons you were in company with, at the time I was fortunate enough to render you a slight service; I should long since have acquitted myself of this promise, if it had been possible; but wounded slightly in consequence of a meeting, I was carried to my house, which I hoped to have been soon enabled to leave; unfortunately it was not so, I was attacked with locked-jaw, and for more than three months was between life and death, totally deprived of sense; and it was only from the assiduous attentions of the good doctor Matheo, for whom I shall preserve an eternal gratitude, that I recovered life and health; it is only within the last week I have been re-established, and now I acquit myself of the promise I made you.

"'I do not think you have again seen Madame Delaunay. This woman, to whom I returned immediately after quitting you, and whom I compelled to write to your aunt a letter she has no doubt received, feared that I should realize the menace I gave her, to put the authorities in possession of her conduct, if she attempted to revisit you. Nevertheless it is right you should know what she is; it is our duty, when we encounter similar beings, to withdraw the mask which conceals their features; once unmasked, they are no longer to be feared.'"

Here Edmond de Bourgerel informed Eugenie de Mirbel, what the reader has probably by this time guessed, viz. that Madame Delaunay was no other than an *intrigante* of the vilest nature, who had only got herself admitted in the school, from which she had been ignominiously driven as soon as she was known, by the aid of false recommendations; that she was the purveyor in ordinary to several rich *libertins*, and that the Count de D——, as one of them, had given her a considerable sum to betray to him Eugenie de Mirbel, and which she had endeavoured to accomplish without being enabled to succeed; that the Chevalier Saint-Firmin was the worthy lover of this woman, and

that he assisted her as much as possible, because he shared, no doubt, the premium of her infamous commerce.

"'And now,' (continued Edmond de Bourgerel, after the paragraph of which we have given the substance to our readers,) 'I ought to stop and close this letter, by telling you, you might, under every event of your life, reckon upon the affection and attachment which your graces and happy character merit; but I cannot do so.

"'Since I have seen you, mademoiselle, before and after the illness I have suffered, and even during the short intervals of respite which my most cruel sufferings allowed me, I have very frequently interrogated my heart, and each time it replied to me, that I loved you, and that a love, deep as that with which you have inspired me, ought to end only with my life. Will you receive this confession favourably? I dare not believe it; it would prove for me a greater blessing than man is permitted to hope for; and still, do not suppose I have views which I do not entertain, for I have only resolved, upon writing this letter, to beg an indulgence you would not refuse, perhaps, to him who renders the most complete justice to your eminent virtues, the permission to present myself to your aunt, from whom it is my intention to solicit your hand.

"'I will give her, mademoiselle, as to my family and position in the world, every detail she can require, and these details will be of such a nature, that I am bold enough to believe, that if your wish should not place an obstacle to it, nothing will oppose the realization of my warmest desire; but you will perceive that I cannot, without allowing your aunt to suppose that I already know you, present myself to her at once; she must, at least I think so, before I risk this step, the success of which I would not compromise, have time to remark me, and I must advance in her good graces; in fact, the relations of one neighbour to another, must precede the request I wish to address to her. You will decide, mademoiselle, as to how I should proceed; and whatever may be the commands you may think it desirable to give me, they shall be executed to the letter, and upon this I pledge my honour; but, I entreat of you, do not withdraw from me a hope without which I cannot live, and permit me, until I am allowed to converse with you, to feast on your regards, and that sometimes your voice may mix itself with the melodious sounds you can draw from your piano.

"'Give me a reply, mademoiselle; tell me whether I am to hope or despair; to-morrow morning, by daybreak, I will search for a letter under the branches of your Bengal rose, shall I find one there?'

"This, I think, has been written by an honest man," said Lucie, after finishing the reading of the letter of Edmond de Bourgerel; "no twisted phrases, no declamation, no sentimental pathos.

"Isn't it," replied Eugenie; "but how is it then.—But let us not anticipate events. I have but little more to add.

"The perusal of this letter, I must confess, caused me a lively pleasure; we feel a secret and intense satisfaction in acquiring the certainty that we are loved by one that is dear to us, I ought, no doubt, to have carried it to my aunt, and confided to her the events which had preceded its receipt, and regulate my conduct by her counsel and experience; but do we always follow the rule of right? especially when we act under the impression of a sentiment in which all our faculties are included, and when, like myself, our head is so full of marvellous adventures, that nothing more has the privilege of astonishing us?

"Listen to what I replied to Edmond de Bourgerel:

"'I much regret, sir, that I have been the cause of the misfortunes which have overtaken you. I easily comprehend, although you have said not a word about it, that it was with the Count de D—— that the meeting took place, in consequence of which you received the wound which was followed by an attack of tetanus, which has produced you so much suffering; deign to believe, sir, that the remembrance of what you have done for me will never be effaced from my memory.

"'I sincerely believe all you tell me, your conduct has given me no right to doubt your word; and thus I have no hesitation in avowing to you, that in addressing my aunt, you will not displease me; I think, with you, that to spare the feelings of this amiable woman, we ought to conceal the fault I have committed; you must, in fact, wait a short time before making your request; for the rest, sir, you know better than myself how it is requisite to proceed.'

"And I signed.

"Scarcely had the day commenced its journey, when M. Edmond de Bourgerel mysteriously left his room, quietly cleared the space which separated our two chalets, and approached to take the letter I had deposited for him in the place indicated; he carried it to his lips, and kissed it several times; had he guessed that I was behind the curtains, and were the kisses imprinted on the letter intended for her who had written it? I think so.

"I had not said to M. Edmond de Bourgerel, that, as he had requested me, I would sing to him some of the romances of my collection; but I seized the first moment which the cares of our little arrangements left me, (the small extent of our revenue prevented us keeping a domestic,) to place myself at the piano; but what should I sing, I really could not determine; I took the album of Loïsa Puget, resolved to sing the first romance that met my eyes, after opening it, at hazard; chance has sometimes very strange caprices; the album opened, I was obliged, if I remained faithful to the promise I had made myself, it was necessary, I repeat, to sing the romance which commences thus:

'Le nom de celui que j'aime!'

"I hesitated a few moments, should I sing this romance? Certainly not, replied my reason; sing, sing, said my heart; he will be very happy to hear it. Alas! where reason and the heart are at war, reason does not always remain mistress of the field of battle.

"The last words of the romance of Loïsa Puget had scarcely left my mouth, when the sounds of the piano of M. Edmond de Bourgerel announced that he was about to reply to me; a few joyous preludes, intended, no doubt, to prove to me the satisfaction he enjoyed, preceded the morceau he sang; it was borrowed from an opera comique of an old collection, of which the title escapes me, and commences thus:

'Oh! bonheur extrême,
Enfin elle m'aime.'

"We understood each other perfectly.

"The history of our loves resembles that of most others; long hours passed side by side, during which we say nothing, although we have a thousand things to communicate, when the moment arrives to separate; furtive regards exchanged in the dusk, a soft pressure of a hand which we think we encounter by chance, and which is generally left in the place in which it is found, because we know well it will be sought for; vows of an eternal affection, often broken, alas! as soon as they have been uttered. Let me then hasten at once to the period when Edmond de Bourgerel, whom my aunt had at first received as a neighbour with whom she might keep up an agreeable society, made, through a distant relation, the only one remaining to him, a formal demand of my hand, which was acceded to, the information which had been obtained regarding him, having given my aunt the certainty that he possessed all the qualities which would secure the happiness of a wife.

"Our banns were about to be published, when my aunt received from a notary of Peronne, whom she had commissioned to procure the sale of a small property she possessed in the environs of that town, the price of which was to form a part of my dowry, (my worthy aunt, in spite of all that Edmond de Bourgerel could say to the contrary, had resolved to impoverish herself in my favour,) a letter which informed her that if she would herself visit the place, he would put her in relation with a person who desired to purchase the property, the sale of which had not yet been publicly announced, and that it was probable she would obtain, by treating with this person, a few thousand francs more; but the notary added, that her presence was absolutely necessary, seeing that the conclusion of this bargain was subordinate to certain conditions which she would not understand unless he explained them to her personally. If it had only concerned her own interests, my aunt would certainly not have disturbed herself; but I was in the question, and for me there was nothing which this kind parent was not ready to perform; besides, she said to me, when, fearing the journey might injure her health, always weak and changeable, I endeavoured to persuade her not to incommode herself, 'Peronne is not so far from Paris that I cannot easily return, and, at the most, I shall not be absent more than a week.' The journey was thus decided upon.

"M. Edmond de Bourgerel accompanied me and my aunt to the diligence.

"'I go satisfied,' she said to me, mounting the vehicle, and pointing to my future husband, who had retired a few steps, in order that we might converse at our ease, 'I am certain that your conduct will be worthy the name you bear, and that you will not forget what nobility requires.' This was the first time my aunt had spoken to me of the nobility of our family, and I was as much surprised as deeply moved at the solemn accent in which she knew how to invest these simple words: nobility requires!—'Certainly, my good aunt, nobility has its obligations,' I replied, 'be not uneasy, I will not forget it.' 'I am sure of it, my child,' she continued, after kissing me a last time, 'and besides, you will not have to defend yourself, he also is noble, noble in name and in heart, he will show himself worthy of the confidence I willingly place in him.'

"My aunt saluted Edmond de Bourgerel with her hand, he returned it respectfully, and the coach started on its journey.

"Fatal confidence, unfortunate error of a generous heart. Alas! alas! my poor aunt, you were not again to look upon your niece, but as branded and dishonoured!

"Can I say that M. de Bourgerel proved himself totally unworthy of the confidence which had been placed in him, that he employed to seduce me, that ignoble science practised by the roués of our times? no! I cannot, to excuse, in your sight, the fault I have committed, accuse him of vices he does not possess; do not think me, however, more guilty than I am; I should, indeed, have shown more strength than I did; I ought to have defended myself, and the defence, I am still convinced of it at the present moment, would have been easy; but is it my fault if I am feeble, is it always possible to defend one's self, when we love the one who attacks us? Listen, and judge me.

"My aunt had been gone two days; eight o'clock was near striking, when an old lady, a friend of my aunt, came to pay her a visit: this lady knew that I was to espouse M. de Bourgerel, whom she had frequently seen at our house; the latter seeing her enter, from the window of his chalet, requested permission to come and perform a little music with me, not being alone. I thought I could not refuse him. He came accordingly, and I placed myself at the piano, but I had hardly commenced, when the old lady rose up suddenly from the seat she occupied, and pointing to the sky, which was charged with thick and black clouds, said to us: 'that wishing to be at home before the storm which was gathering burst, she should leave us at once;' all our efforts to retain her being useless, we were forced to permit her to leave, so that I remained alone with Edmond; I ought to have dismissed him at once, but I saw that he was so happy in my society, that I said to myself, I might, without there being any great harm in it, allow him to remain a few moments longer; I was on the point, however, of requesting him to retire, when suddenly, gusts of wind which carried away every flower that embellished my window, and the distant roaring of the thunder, announced to us that the storm we had some time expected, was at length about to break.

"I have always had an extreme fear of a storm; you remember, no doubt, my foolish terrors of former days, when the thunder groaned in the distance, and the lightning flashed in streams through the clouds? You may recollect, that in these moments, my senses left me almost, that I ran here and there, that there was no obscure corner in which I did not attempt to conceal myself; at the period I am speaking of, age had rendered me a little more reasonable, but still, if my fears no longer exploded in such exaggerated demonstrations, to be restrained, they were not less violent: besides, you remember, no doubt, the storm I allude to, was quite capable of inspiring in persons more resolute than myself, the liveliest terrors. At first, this storm was announced by a violent whirlwind, which in its rapid course threw down, broke, and whirled about in its vortex, every thing which opposed its passage; my poor flowers were blown from the box which contained them; their remnants were strewed about the court, and at every moment we heard the noise produced by the falling on the ground of slates and panes of glass. The sky was black, not cloudy, but black; and, at every instant, the pale rays of sheet lightning pierced the sombre mantle which covered the atmosphere, and gave a fearful tint to every object that surrounded me. Then followed the thunder, now heavy and distant, at another time bursting and roaring over head like a park of artillery; and then the rain which, falling in complete waves, had turned our court into a sort of lake; I trembled and turned pale at every flash,

and in spite of the efforts made by M. de Bourgerel to calm me, and whom I did not then dream of dismissing, (I verily believe I should have died with fright, if I had been obliged to remain alone in such weather,) every time that the bursting roar of the thunder struck my ear, I bounded from my chair, and buried my face in my hands. M. de Bourgerel had insensibly drawn his seat near mine, we were plunged in the deepest obscurity, the storm had surprised us at the fall of day, and I felt too much terror to seek in another room for a candle to light the one we were in; the rain continued to fall; the thunder groaned at less distant intervals, and the flashes of lightning rapidly succeeded each other, but paler and more frequent; but whilst I was near M. de Bourgerel, I felt somewhat less timid. I know not what secret voice whispered me that in his society I had nothing to fear. Suddenly, the rain poured down in fresh torrents; the sky seemed to open in order to give passage to a flash of lightning more blinding than any that had preceded it; and a gust of wind (if not the thunder) threw down the upper part of a chimney, which fell in the court with a deafening noise; I uttered a loud scream, and threw myself into the arms of M. de Bourgerel. He passed his arm around my waist, and pressed me closely to his bosom; his face approached mine; his lips touched mine; I know not what came over me, but fright had nearly snatched from me the use of all my faculties. It was at this moment, I think, that I lost my senses, for 'tis in vain that I task my memory. I remember nothing! nothing; but when, by the exertions of M. de Bourgerel, who had obtained from his room a bottle of scented vinegar, which he made me inhale, I came to myself, the rain had ceased; the black clouds, which a few moments before had hid the sky from us, had disappeared, and the azure vault was sprinkled with pure and brilliant stars, but I—I—I was lost and dishonoured!

"I was pale, my hair dishevelled, my eyes wandered without sight; I heard, without comprehending, the words M. de Bourgerel addressed to me; but, when the devouring fever, which made my teeth chatter against each other, allowed me a few instants of respite, a flash, as clear and lucid as the lightning, traversed my mind, and discovered to me the depth of the abyss into which I had plunged. My lover was obliged to unlace me and carry me to bed. I allowed him to act without making the least resistance, or arresting him in any thing; I had lost the consciousness of my being in existence; I was no longer a woman; I was a machine that suffered, and to this machine there remained not even the strength to complain.

"Alas! why had I not died? Was I then fatally doomed to drain to the very dregs the cup of bitterness from which I had just wetted my lips?

"I was in so pitiable a state, that M. de Bourgerel was compelled to pass the night by my side, and it was not until late the next morning, that I was in a fit state to listen calmly to his endeavours at consoling me. He renewed his protestations of an eternal love; we were guilty, no doubt; but, after all, was the fault we had committed, the consequences of which I had no right to fear, as we were intended for each other; was it as grave as I imagined it, and had we done more than glide down the descent which drew us towards each other? In fact, all the sophisms which men find in their imaginations when they wish to justify a fault they have committed, or those they have caused others to commit.

"We are easily disposed to believe what we hope; the words of my lover calmed by degrees the torrents of my mind and of my heart, and two days after the fatal evening I have alluded to, I was not tranquil—that we never are when we cannot, without distrusting the reply it will make us, interrogate our conscience—but reassured, in fact, I had no reason to doubt the word of my lover.

"When my aunt returned, she at first remarked the extreme palor of my features, which I placed to the account of the fright caused by the memorable storm which had broken loose upon Paris a few days previously. My aunt, who was in high spirits from the happy results of the journey she had made, jested me a little as to what she called my foolish terrors, and there was no further question about it.

"M. de Bourgerel, who required, in order to be married, the permission of the minister of war, at length obtained it, as well as a prolongation of his leave of absence which he had requested at the same time. He ran overjoyed to announce to us this piece of news, and as we had at our disposal for some time the other necessary papers, the next morning our first banns were published. My betrothed, obeying the impulse I had given him, or his own wishes, (I cannot, after what has passed, explain to myself the nature of the sentiment which guided him,) and whose impatience seemed quite natural, had manifested to my aunt an intention of shortening, as much as possible, the formal preliminaries of our marriage; but the worthy woman, who liked matters to proceed regularly, would not consent. 'Eh! bon Dieu!' she replied to his supplications, to which, as you may well fancy, I would have given the world to be allowed to join mine, 'have you not, young as you are, time to wait a little? I am not impatient, although much older than you, and quite as anxious to see you happy, as you are to become so; but there are, you know, usages which we cannot brave without sooner or later repenting it; I myself do not wish the world to believe that I am in a hurry to marry my niece.'

"We were compelled to resign ourselves.

"The days, however, ran on, and as we approached the goal in which were centred my earthly wishes, my security became greater; the eagerness of my lover did not belie itself for a moment, and when, by chance, he perceived a dark cloud pass rapidly across my brow, he contrived to find an occasion to speak to me in secret, and reassured me by words of eloquence, which proceeded from his heart.

"I counted the days as they rolled on, and I do not think it necessary to say how extremely long they appeared to me. At length, on a fine day in the month of June, they brought me a pretty *corbeille* of white satin, which contained the thousand gewgaws given to the young maiden, but which is to be used by the wife; each object was the proxy of some delicate thought, or some gracious attention; my lover had anticipated all my wishes; the dresses were those I should have chosen, the shawl was my favourite colour; I passed several hours, the most delicious of my life, in examining one after another, these objects which I handled with a sort of veneration, and yet there was in my *corbeille*, neither the cachemere of India, nor sparkling jewels; the modest fortune of M. de Bourgerel did not permit him to purchase such costly superfluities; a handsome French shawl, a

plain suite of pearls, were the most precious objects of my *corbeille;* but the purest taste, the most perfect perception of what is consistent, had presided at the choice of all these articles, which, besides, appeared to me a hundred times preferable to the richest treasures of Golconda and Visapour.

"The night came, and on retiring, I could say to myself, ''twill be to-morrow.'

"And yet, my heart had been grievously full all the evening, and, when alone in my chamber, a few tears, which I did not attempt to restrain, forced a passage, and trickled slowly down my palid cheeks; the cause of this was, that my intended had not appeared, as was his custom, to give us an account in the evening of his engagements during the day, and that I could not explain, except by some misfortune of which he was the victim, this absence, on the eve of a day like the one the sun was to shine upon on the morrow.

"I resolved to wait his return, seated near my window.

"One hour, two hours passed, and he came not. I was overcome with fatigue, and began to think that if I did not take some repose, I should appear with a strange physiognomy for the ceremony of to-morrow; this reflection determined me to seek my bed, but despite all my efforts, and the arguments I conjured up to find a reason that would explain the absence of my lover, I could not contrive to fall asleep till the break of day. Thus, as it often happens after all our strength is exhausted in an unequal struggle, I fell into a leaden sleep, and did not awake until the rays of as brilliant a sun as it is possible to conceive, approached to caress my pillow; I hastened out of bed and ran to my window; alas! I was assured from the appearance of that of my lover, which I had remarked the evening before, even to the minutest folds of the drapery, that he had not returned home.

"The day passed without his appearing; the parties who were to be present at our union, those whom my aunt had invited, as well as those invited by himself, arrived in succession; no one could give us any news of him, and to every one it was necessary to repeat what had happened. What a day, followed by others still more painful!

"Our efforts to ascertain what had become of M. de Bourgerel, remained without results; it was in vain that we addressed ourselves to different persons who knew him, to the minister of war, to the relation who had requested from my aunt the favour of my hand, not a soul knew more than ourselves; his disappearance, not only to us, but to every one, was mystery, an enigma without an answer.

"I fell ill, and for a month I was between life and death; my kind aunt attended me with the same devotion she had always shown me; and thanks to her care, and perhaps also to the strength of my constitution and my extreme youth, I recovered my health; but it was only to acquire the certitude of a misfortune still more terrible than any I had yet suffered; I discovered, from signs that left me not the slightest doubt, that I should ere long become a mother.

"As long as I could hide my position from the eyes, not very clear seeing, of my aunt, I was tranquil enough; the very excess of my misfortune augmented my courage. It is not the Almighty's will, I said to myself, that I should die so young; for I shall die to a certainty, if I am compelled to put my aunt in the confidence of the fault I have committed; and this thought, and the habit I insensibly assumed, of considering death as a last and certain refuge against the results of my position, permitted hope, that beneficent divinity who watches constantly at our side, to glide into my heart; and every night on retiring to bed, and after remarking the rapid progress of my pregnancy, I said to myself; 'He will return to-morrow.'

"But alas! he did not return!

"At length the moment arrived when it was no longer possible to conceal my state. The restraint that I had already been obliged to impose upon myself, put me in tortures, and I had more than once observed that the eyes of my aunt were fixed upon me with a curious attention; I was mad, I heard not the questions that were put to me, or if I heard them, I replied in a contrary way. My aunt, who was greatly alarmed about me, spoke of calling in the skilful physician who had attended me for the illness I had suffered a short time previously. This was what I wished to escape at all hazards; the physician would infallibly discover my state, and then what would become of me? How should I support the angry looks of my aunt? I repeat to you, I was become mad Instead of throwing myself at the feet of my aunt, and avowing to her my fault; instead of weeping on her bosom, where I am satisfied I should have found a refuge and a solace, I took the resolution of flying, and this resolution I executed a few days after I had determined upon it.

"I collected a few bijoux, some clothes, and one morning, whilst my aunt still slept, I fled from that house in which I had been so happy, and yet so miserable. I knew not where to turn my steps, but I walked, I walked; I had but one object, one desire, to conceal my shame from every one.

"I know not what road I followed to arrive at the corner of the street Saint-Lazare, and that of the Chaussée d'Antin, where, exhausted by the rapidity of my walk, I was compelled to stop to take breath.

"I had been leaning against a post for some minutes, when I saw coming towards me your husband, my dear Lucie, who no doubt had just left his house; he remarked, I think, the position I was in; I had not, in the hurry of the moment, taken the usual precautions before leaving; the small packet I carried under my arm, my extreme palor, my trouble, my precipitate flight at the moment he advanced towards me, probably to question me; all these circumstances united, completely opened his eyes; for a short time after, when I presented myself at your house to implore assistance, I found it impossible to see you."

"Continue, my dear Eugenie," said Lucie de Neuville, at this point. "I will tell you, when you have finished your narrative, what reasons determined M. de Neuville to forbid my receiving you, you were slandered in his hearing, my poor friend."

"By whom, then, grand Dieu!" exclaimed Eugenie de Mirbel, "I have never injured any one."

"That is no security. There exist, unhappily, men who bear us a hatred for the sole reason that they have not succeeded in doing us all the injury they intended; but continue, I will give you immediately an explanation of what I have advanced."

"I have but little more to add," continued Eugenie de Mirbel; "I took a lodging at a modest hotel, where I waited, trying to obtain work, without succeeding, the period of my delivery which was not distant. At length I gave birth to the innocent creature who reposes in that cradle, but I could not yet rise from the bed of misery to which I had been long confined, when I discovered that my feeble resources were exhausted, and that I had nothing left in the world, nothing! and the mistress of the hotel informed me every day that if I could not pay her, she should be compelled to turn me out; it was then that an honest woman, whom I had taken on the recommendation of my hostess to attend me during my illness, touched at my extreme misery, pitying my youth and my frightful despair, had me carried, although nearly as poor as myself, to her house; and her devotedness since, has not relaxed a moment. I was ill, she attended me; I required medicines, she sold, to procure them, the few objects of value she possessed; and when I attempted to place limits to her extreme kindness, 'Let me alone, let me alone, mademoiselle, God has created us to assist one another, and to love one another as brothers and sisters; what I do for you to-day, you will return me another time, and if it is never in your power, which may Providence avert, well, it will be accounted to me above.'

"But at length the moment arrived when the resources of this estimable woman were exhausted, as were mine; it was then I determined to write you, and it was her who undertook to carry you the letter in which I begged you to come to my assistance; you know the rest, and I think it is useless to renew my proofs of gratitude, of which you ought to be assured. Explain to me now what you promised."

"Monsieur de Neuville is endowed with the best and noblest heart, hence it was not without motives that he resolved to take the extreme measure which has so much afflicted you; but listen to what happened; as you have said, he was approaching to speak to you, when you took to flight; grieved at this sudden disappearance he continued his walk; by a fatal hazard it happened that this very day, contrary to his usual habit, being very warm, he entered a café at the back of a theatre of phantasmagoria and young comedians, situate in a passage near the Boulevard, to take a lemonade; several persons, among whom was the master of the establishment, who no doubt can be no other than that Chevalier de Saint Firmin so roughly handled by M. de Bourgerel, occupied a table near the one at which he had placed himself, and your name having caught his ear, he listened to their conversation. The proprietor of the café narrated the duel which had taken place between the Count de D—— and M. de Bourgerel, and he expressed himself respecting you in terms which no doubt had been inspired by his worthy mistress, Madame Delaunay; this conversation, heard so soon after the encounter he had met with some hours before, gave M. de Neuville, as you may well suppose, a strange opinion of you, and it was under the excitement of this impression that he forbid our servants to allow you to see me, if by chance you called at our hotel."

"My God, my God!" exclaimed Eugenie, burying her face in her hands, "am I thus miserable; but what have I done then to this man, that he fears not to drag my name in this manner through the mud."

"Take courage, my dear Eugenie, all this will soon end, please God; I have already written to M. de Neuville, and I am certain beforehand that he will render you justice when he knows, that, after all, you are more to be pitied than blamed!"

"May it be so; for if I am to be a subject of trouble between you and your husband, if he should blame you for what you have done for me, I shall die with despair."

"Fear nothing, something tells me that your troubles are passed; but that they may not return, there remains much for us to do. Eugenie, you must again see your aunt."

"Oh! never! never! at least not until M. de Bourgerel leads me to her feet."

"M. de Bourgerel, if he is not dead, will return, for nothing in his conduct towards you indicates that his intention was to abandon you; but have you well considered, my dear Eugenie, of the cruel torments, the anxiety and uneasiness, suffered by the estimable woman who so loves you, for nearly a twelvemonth during which she has been ignorant of what has become of you?"

"She thinks me dead, no doubt, and I would rather she had this idea, than to know me dishonoured."

"Be reasonable, my friend, there is always in the heart of those who love us, treasures of indulgences, and they are always ready to throw a veil over the faults we have been led to commit; for the rest, I will previously see your aunt, and will not take you to her until I have disposed her to receive you with open arms, for all our acquaintance must be kept ignorant of what has happened to you; you shall therefore remain here, where, thanks to the talents you possess, you can easily establish an independent position."

It was not until after continued entreaties that Lucie and Laura, who had joined her prayers to those of her friend, could induce Eugenie to see her aunt again; the poor girl could not resolve to appear before her after the fault she had committed: but at length, moved by the touching exhortations of her two friends, she left them free to pursue, for her tranquillity, (we cannot say her happiness, she no longer expected days of happiness since she had lost the hope of again seeing M. de Bourgerel,) any plan they might think reasonable; and after tenderly embracing her, and again inspiring her with a hope of serener days, Lucie and Laura, who wished to dine with the Marchioness of Villerbanne, bid her adieu and left.

The old Marquise de Villerbanne scolded her niece for remaining so long without visiting her; Lucie excused herself as well as possible, and the marquise, when she had received their promise to attend her next soirée, recovered her usual good humour.

"We shall have," she said, "some fresh faces, especially a gentleman, whose father I knew well during the emigration, and whom they say is a gallant cavalier; we shall see whether he will add another to the number of those who already make their court to you."

Lucie, impelled by an indefinable sentiment of curiosity, was on the point of asking the name of this cavalier of whom she had just heard so pompous a eulogy; but a servant entering to announce to the company assembled in the saloon, that the dinner was served, she was compelled to give her hand to one of her admirers, and to defer the question to a more opportune moment.

After the dinner, the arrivals succeeded each other in such rapidity that Lucie could not find an instant to converse in private with the Marchioness de Villerbanne, so that, her curiosity not being satisfied—and what more cruel punishment

could a child of Eve experience?—she was not in the best of humours on her return home.

Her femme de chambre handed her a letter, which had been brought by a porter who was unknown, and which he had not left without an express injunction to deliver it to the countess herself. Lucie broke the seal of this letter, which was from Dr. Matheo, and contained, as follows:

"Madame la Comtesse,—The events of my life are such (and yet, believe me, I am, in reality, more unfortunate than guilty) that, in consequence of the encounter I have made with the man, who bears the name of the Marquis de Pourrieres, I am forced to quit France, never to return. My fortune—which, in the possibility of an event which is realized to-day, I have always kept disposable—is moderate, but it suffices for my wants; and I seek, in a retreat, known to God alone, to forget mankind, the injuries they have inflicted on me, and endeavour to be forgotten myself. When you receive this letter, I shall be already far from you, and the immensity of the ocean will soon place, between France and myself, a barrier that will be difficult to overcome. But I wish, as you are the only person in the world in whom I am interested, to give you some advice, which I entreat of you, on my bended knees, to take into serious consideration.

"I know not whether I am wrong, (I pray to heaven it may be so,) but I think I have perceived that the Marquis de Pourrieres, who, however, you have seen but once, inspires you with that interest, the ordinary forerunner of a more tender sentiment; excuse me, madame, if I express myself with so little ceremony, but I have no time to study my phrases, and I think the circumstance is sufficiently serious to justify me.

"You will, probably, meet M. the Marquis de Pourrieres in society, this is infallible; for, if the occasion does not present itself, this man, although he has given me an assurance to the contrary, this man, I repeat, will bring about one. Well! Madame la Comtesse, if I do not deceive myself, and I think I am not deceived, in the name of all you hold most dear in this world, for your tranquillity and future happiness, shun his regards, avoid speaking to him; fly, fly from those places, in which you may by chance meet him; stifle at its birth a sentiment, which, if you are not careful, will make your whole life one of bitterness and misery. Avoid the Marquis de Pourrieres! this man, whom I know well, (for the misfortunes of my life have afforded me the sad privilege of being enabled to judge mankind,) this man, is more dangerous than you can suppose him.

"To explain the reasons which induce me to speak thus to you, would require from me the whole history of my life, and for that I have not the time; the post-chaise which is to carry me out of the kingdom of France, waits for me in the court of my house. When I shall have arrived at the end of the long voyage I am about to undertake, this history, which I cannot give you to-day, I will send you; and if, at the present moment, this letter should seem to you uncalled for, when you know the life of the unhappy Doctor Matheo, and the character played by the individual who, right or wrong, calls himself the Marquis de Pourrieres, you will admit, I am quite sure, that, in writing it, I have only acquitted myself of a duty imposed upon me by the lively interest I take in your welfare.

"Adieu, Madame la Comtesse: I leave you forewarned, and defended by your virtues, which

LIFE IN PARIS.

THE FIREMAN RESCUING SILVIA.

will not desert you, if, contrary to the sincere wishes for your happiness, which will be the continued prayer of him who knows how to render justice to your eminent qualities, you find yourself in danger.

"I hope to arrive, within three months, at the end of my voyage, and my first care shall be to address to you a letter, which shall explain the present one, and which you will find at Paris, poste restante, with the initials, C. D. N."

Lucie, after reading this letter, rang violently for her femme de chambre, who entered the bedroom of her mistress, quite bewildered. The poor girl, who was not accustomed to such sudden appeals, believed some accident had happened to the countess, or, at least, that the hotel was on fire.

"Request Mademoiselle de Beaumont to come to me," said Lucie, in a hasty tone.

"Mademoiselle is in bed and asleep, long since," replied the femme de chambre; "however, if Madame la Comtesse wishes it. I will go and wake her."

"No, 'tis useless."

And, as the femme de chambre waited for her mistress to give her any further directions:

"You may retire," said Lucie to her suddenly; "I want nothing more."

"To a certainty madame has received some very bad news," said the femme de chambre, after retiring.

Lucie read and re-read the letter of Doctor Matheo several times, before she thought of her bed; her sleep was agitated, and full of strange dreams, in the midst of which constantly appeared to her the features of the Marquis de Pourrieres, sometimes cheerful and graceful, at others sombre and terrifying.

The first streaks of morning had scarcely appeared on the horizon, when, wearied of invoking the refreshing sleep, which seemed resolved to keep aloof from her, she rose from her bed, dressed herself hastily in a robe of white muslin, and ascended to her friend, who still slept profoundly.

CHAPTER XXV.

A FRESH CONSPIRACY OF GRECS.

As we have observed, Laura still slept tranquilly. Her regular breathing, her rosy lips, which seemed half opened for a smile, and which discovered a double row of little pearls of dazzling whiteness, announced that sleep, so calm and so refreshing, which only accompanies those amongst us whose soul has not yet scorched its wings with the devouring breath of the passions, and whose mind is only disturbed by dreams which issue from the port of ivory—the dreams of childhood, where all is *couleur de rose!* and which leave in the memory none but agreeable remembrances, and induce us to regret our slumbers.

Lucie had stopped a few paces from the bed of her friend, whom she could not determine to awaken. "Why," she asked herself, "is not my slumber as calm as the sleep of this innocent child? Why has the image of this man, whom I have seen but once, followed me through the night, and placed itself constantly before my eyes? Is Doctor Matheo by any chance right? and is it true that the sentiment of curiosity, with which this man at first inspired me, is the precursory index of a more tender sentiment? Oh! no, that is impossible. I am the wife of a man whom I love as much as I respect; I will not, I ought not, to think of another in the world!"

After remaining for some minutes absorbed in these sad and painful reflections, the countess seemed resolved to drive away the bitter thoughts which weighed upon her spirits; she advanced softly towards Laura's bed, and dropped a kiss on the pure and delicate forehead of the young beauty; the latter, awakened by the caress, at first rubbed her eyes, and, when she recognised her friend, passed her two arms round her neck, and drawing her towards her, returned, with usury, the sweet kiss she had just received.

The two females thus entwined, the one a brunette, the other a blonde, but both young and pretty, forming as delicious a group as it is possible to conceive, reminded one of Mina and Brenda, the two charming sisters of the German ballet; and to paint them, the most exacting artist would leave them where they are, in a fresh and cheerful maiden's chamber, lighted by the bright rays of a morning sun, and filled with rare flowers, and the hundred *nothings*, which make us dream, when we are permitted to behold them; because we perceive, from the brilliancy of their colours, the delicacy of their *shapes*, from a multitude of signs—which are felt though they cannot be expressed—that they belong to a pretty woman.

"How! already up?" said Laura, after regarding the pendulum of white marble, placed on the chimney-piece, between two cups of agate, intended to receive her bijoux.

"Yes, for I have much to tell you, my dear Laura," replied Lucie.

"I'll engage that you still wish to speak to me about that tiresome Marquis de Pourrieres; Lucie! Lucie! I am disposed to think it is not simply curiosity which induces you to take an interest in this man."

"You are mad!" exclaimed the countess, who felt the blood mount to her cheeks, when she heard her friend telling her nearly the same that Doctor Matheo had written her; she repeated, however, "you are mad!"

"Not so mad," continued Laura; "and the proof is, that you blush upon hearing the truth."

Laura was far from attaching to her words the importance which she appeared willing to give to them; she merely wished to laugh a moment, at the expense of her friend. She was, therefore, strangely astonished, when the latter threw herself into her arms, weeping bitterly, and heard her exclaiming, in a voice half choked by her sobs:

"My God! my God! is it true?"

"Lucie! what ails you, then?" exclaimed Laura, greatly alarmed; "I assure you I would not afflict you; calm yourself, I entreat of you."

And the young girl endeavoured, by her caresses, to restore to her friend the calmness she seemed to have lost.

"Come, tell me what disturbs your mind; you have not come into my room so early for nothing; speak, my dear Lucie, for I am all attention."

The countess had by degrees recovered her composure.

"I was greatly annoyed to find your ideas so similar to those contained in this letter, and I was hurt," she said, giving to Laura the letter of Doctor Matheo; "but my vexation has disappeared as quickly as it came," she continued, attempting to smile.

"This is much more serious than I imagined," replied Laura, after attentively reading the letter;

"and I see that you were right in considering the encounter of this Marquis de Pourrieres as an unfortunate circumstance. How! our good doctor obliged to quit France because he has fallen in with this man? Lucie, Lucie, Doctor Matheo is a man of honour, you must follow the advice he gives you; if he has written you such a letter, he had his reasons for it."

"But still, this precipitate flight indicates, that, if either of these men have anything to fear, it is not the Marquis de Pourrieres—"

"It's true; however, I repeat, the letter of Doctor Matheo seems to have been written for your interest; follow, then, the advice it gives you. In my turn, Lucie, I shall believe in presentiments; shun the Marquis de Pourrieres—fly from the places in which you might by possibility meet him."

"But can I? this man has a large acquaintance, and I must necessarily meet him, sooner or later, in one of the saloons in which we are admitted."

"You forget, no doubt, that since the departure of your husband for Algiers, you only visit the Marchioness de Villerbanne, and it is not probable that you will meet him there."

"You are mistaken; you remember that my aunt informed us that, at her next soirée, they were to present to her a cavalier, whose father she had known well during the emigration?"

"Well!"

"I am certain that this cavalier, whose name I could not ascertain, is no other than the Marquis de Pourrieres."

"What an idea!"

"You will see whether I am deceived."

"But, admitting it were so, you can, it seems to me, decline speaking to him, unless you are actually compelled to, and can receive him with that coolness, which will prevent his having the temerity to make any approaches to you; besides, nothing induces us to suppose that he will be very eager to converse with you."

"I wish it may be so, and very sincerely."

"For the rest, my dear Lucie, you do not require to be told the line of conduct you ought to pursue, even admitting, which I neither can nor will do, that Doctor Matheo is deceived. The remembrance of the happiness you owe to the affection, so pure, of M. de Neuville, of a desire for the preservation of the irreproachable name you bear, will be a sufficient defence for you."

Lucie pressed her friend closely to her bosom.

"You are more reasonable than I am," she said to her, after tenderly embracing her, "and yet you are much younger."

"Oh! very much younger," replied Laura; "it amuses you to say that, three or four years at the most, I believe, what an immense difference! But let us leave these follies, I only see in all this, one thing, which ought to grieve you—the departure of that good Doctor Matheo, who, for my part, I regret exceedingly."

"We shall know, in a short time, what are the reasons, which have forced him to quit France so suddenly, and the brilliant position he has established for himself."

"I hope, sincerely, they are not of a nature to interdict all hopes of his return."

After conversing a few minutes longer on the subject which occupied them, Lucie and Laura recollected, at the same time, that on this day they were to pay a visit to the aunt of Eugenie de Mirbel, whom they wished to reconcile to her niece. They separated, to proceed to their toilette,

and after breakfast they entered the carriage, and were conducted to the Rue Faubourg Saint Denis, 56.

Madame de Saint Preuil, the aunt of Eugenie, since the sudden flight of her niece, whose motive for so acting she did not discover for some time, had witnessed an increase of the trials which afflicted her; hence, the weakness of her mental and corporeal faculties was such, that it was with much trouble that the Countess de Neuville and Laura de Beaumont, who had had several opportunities of seeing her before the catastrophe which had deprived her of the best part of her fortune, managed to get themselves recognised.

"I remember," said Lucie to her, after the usual compliments of persons who meet after a long absence, "that my father had the honour of being among your friends, and I wish you to accept the sincere homage of his daughter; be assured, madame, I should long since have acquitted myself of this duty, but it was only yesterday that a person, whom I am surprised at not seeing with you, and whom I met by hazard, informed me of your residence."

The countess anticipated, and it was to bring about this question that she thus expressed herself, that Madame de Saint Preuil would demand of her the name of the person to whom she alluded. In fact, it happened as she had expected.

"And who is this person?" said Madame de Saint Preuil.

"Why Eugenie, my school friend; do you not know it?" replied Madame de Neuville, who endeavoured to guess, from the features of the good old lady, the effect which the name she had pronounced might have upon her.

Madame de Saint Preuil was seized with such surprise, that she remained some instants without the ability of uttering a word; but a gleam of joy illuminated the countenance, withered from excess of grief, and she exclaimed:

"My niece! you have seen my poor niece? Oh! I beseech you, Madame la Comtesse, lead me to this ungrateful child; until I have pressed her to my bosom, I shall not scold her, for choosing rather to fly, than to confide her troubles to a second mother."

Eugenie was pardoned; the countess, therefore, had no further occasion to dissemble. She then narrated, to Madame de Saint Preuil, all that had happened to her friend, from the time she had quitted the house of her aunt up to the present moment.

"Poor Eugenie! she must have suffered much," said the old lady, after listening attentively to the narration; "and how much I thank you, Madame la Comtesse, for all that you have so kindly done for her; but let us go at once, I am burning with a desire to embrace her, I feel that the joy has restored me all my strength, and besides, I have good news to carry to her, to this dear child."

The countess neither could, nor wished to resist these touching entreaties; assisted by Laura, she supported to the carriage Madame de Saint Preuil, who would not allow herself time to change her toilette, and ordered the coachman to conduct them to the apartment of Eugenie de Mirbel.

During the short distance which separates the Faubourg Saint Denis from the Street Riboute, where Eugenie resided, Madame de Saint Preuil recounted, in a few words, to her companions, the events which had followed the flight of Eugenie.

The destiny of the latter would have been very different, if she had remained with her aunt but one day more; in fact, during the evening of the day following that which she had chosen for her flight, Edmond de Bourgerel who, (as the reader has probably guessed,) had never an intention of abandoning her, arrived at Madame de Saint Preuil's at the moment when the latter, who, as we have observed, knew not to what motive to attribute the disappearance of her niece, was plunged in the deepest despair.

We will now state what had happened to Edmond de Bourgerel.

We have heard Madame de Neuville say to Eugenie de Mirbel, that there existed unfortunately persons who swear an implacable hatred to those to whom they have not succeeded in doing as much injury as they contemplated. The charming countess told the truth, in support of which she might have cited, if she had known them, the events which happened to Edmond de Bourgerel.

The Count de D—— was a man of the stamp of those to whom we have alluded; hence this old debauché, furious at the interference of the young man, by which the success of his enterprise against the honour of Eugenie de Mirbel was totally frustrated—and at his having received in exchange for a scratch, the painful consequences of which he was ignorant, a serious wound—had sworn that sooner or later Edmond should pay for the affronts he had given him; but what could he do to this young man who, as he had experienced, was well able to protect himself; and what means should he adopt to injure him? The Count de D—— could think of no means, but was not discouraged.

The Count de D——, although the last scion of a very ancient and noble family, was himself nothing more than the secret head of one of those thousand hidden police who are charged to watch over the health of the state car, (the style of the old Constitutionel,) but which does not prevent the said car from being sometimes in a pretty considerable "fix." Alas! yes, the last and only descendant of a family whose nobility dated from the time of Charlemagne, of him whose ancestors had fought in Palestine, "foraged" with both his hands in the *secret-service chest,* and unfortunately he was not the only one; we know more than one gentleman of noble origin, more than one amiable countess of the Faubourg Saint-Germain, who exact a handsome payment by the police, for the services they afford it.

The Count de D——, reasoning much in the same way as the other *mouchards** past, present, and to come, said to himself, when the idea of injuring Edmond de Bourgerel occurred to him, "that if we look well into the private life of any man, it is possible to discover at least one action, which, if not a culpable one, might, by being presented either in a certain light, or accompanied by some facts real or supposed, have the appearances of criminality;" having thus reasoned, the Count de D—— called before him one of his "men of all work," and, after promising him the most magnificent rewards, he charged him to "*enlighten,*" (the professional word) all the actions of M. de Bourgerel, and bring him an account of his movements every evening.

The estafier departed full of ardour to accomplish the mission confided to him. Unluckily for him, Dame Nature, who is not always prodigal of her favours, had bestowed upon him a countenance which could only belong to a man of his profession, and would never be forgotten after being

once seen; so that towards the evening of the first day, Edmond, who observed in his track at the moment he was entering his house, the same ignoble face which he had remarked in the morning when he left, advanced at once to the possessor, and demanded his business: to this formal question, which demanded a categorical reply, the estafier (spy) knew not what to reply, and M. de Bourgerel who, as we have seen, was not gifted with the patience of Job, taking him for one of those half-starved *industriels* who cultivate with great success an acquaintance with your watch or your handkerchief, thought proper to exercise his cane across the man's shoulders.

The Count de D——, after reproaching his estafier for his stupidity and maladress, sent for the most cunning of his satellites, to confide to him the commission left unaccomplished by the former; the latter was not a whit *less ugly* than his associate; but he was so diminutive and so puny; he knew so well how to slide, without being perceived, through the smallest opening, that his colleagues, rendering justice to his talents, had surnamed him *Passe-partout.**

"Listen, Passe-partout," said to him the Count de D——, after explaining to this worthy personage what was required of him; "I charge you with a very delicate mission; but you will show yourself worthy of it, as well as of the magnificent recompense which will be given you if you manage to escape an accident like the one which happened to your colleague; go, and remember, it *is a guilty one* I require."

Passe-partout, from this moment attached himself to the movements of Edmond de Bourgerel; wherever he went, he followed him; and every evening gave an account to his noble patron of the daily actions of the young man; after reading it, the count placed each report in a portfolio made expressly for this occasion; and the next morning, a man fitted both by nature and costume for the game he had to play, was charged to find the answer to the enigma of which Passe-partout had the evening before proposed the solution.

The first results of these mysterious explorers, only apprised the count of matters perfectly insignificant, and from which, despite his eagerness, it was impossible to derive any good. Thus, Edmond, who at this time only thought of his marriage, employed himself in nothing else but furnishing his house, and his business was confined to cabinet-makers, upholsterers, and other individuals of this sort, and as early as possible he returned home, where, to the great satisfaction of Passe-partout, who had established his observatory in the shop of a wine-dealer, situate opposite the coach door of the house he inhabited, he passed away the greatest part of his time.

The count, weary of seeking, without finding, an occasion to destroy his enemy, was about to direct his spies to cease their occupations, when one of them handed him a report, which drew from him an exclamation which expressed both his surprise and satisfaction.

The count presented to the agent who had given him this report, a gratification proportioned to the rank he held in the hierarchy of police; and as this rank was not very elevated, the reward was very slender. The spy, however, appeared satisfied; he hastened to the nearest wine shop, where he absorbed so much of the liquid, and committed so many amiable follies, that he was indebted to his position of an employé of the government, for

_____
* Spies.   * Latch-key.

the favour of not passing the night at the station-house of Saint-Martin.

The count, on the other hand, habited in a costume which seemed to have borrowed something of the serious from the grave nature of the circumstance, and furnished with the famous report which he had, after correcting and considerably augmenting, transcribed in his best manuscript, on a sheet of *tellière* paper, of the purest whiteness, ordered his horses to be attached to his carriage, and was driven to the house of an Excellence, whom he disturbed from the delightful transports of a private tête-à-tête with a charming *sollici-teuse*.

This excellency was in no very good humour when he entered the saloon in which the Count de D—— was waiting, and he had some reason for it; if it is really a crime unpardonable to derange an honest man at his dinner, it is a much more serious one to come, as an unlooked for visitor, and withdraw from his grave meditations the statesman who, in the seclusion of his cabinet, regulates the health of the empire.

His excellency, we repeat, was in a very bad humour, and the reception he gave the Count de D—— was a slight proof of it.

"Ah! you are here, M. le Comte de D——," he said to him; "really you arrive at a very unlucky moment; I was engaged when they told me you were here, and that you had something to communicate to me which did not admit of any delay. Come, what does it concern? And be brief, I am in haste to return to my bureau."

"Monseigneur," replied the Count de D——, (if our readers observe to us that we commit here a *lapsus linguæ*, seeing that for several years the monseigneur belongs, in France, to none but princes of the reigning family, we will reply to them that an *excellency* is never angry at being monseigneurized,) bending as low as the corset in which he had imprisoned his bust permitted him, "I am aware that your whole time is dedicated to the services of the king, and that you occupy yourself constantly with the welfare of France, it is for this reason I have taken the respectful liberty of insisting upon your being disturbed; for, however important may be the subject upon which you are occupied, it is less so, I have no fear of asserting, than the one which brings me here."

"This solemn debut announces something to me, indeed," replied his excellency, who determined with a sigh to listen to the end Count de D——. "Have the goodness, M. le Comte to take a seat, and I will attend to you."

His excellence was seated in a vast fauteuil, the Count de D—— took a more modest seat, and, when the usher in waiting, on a sign from his master, had retired from the saloon, commenced thus:

"Monseigneur, we are resting on a volcano."

"I have known that for some time," replied his excellency.

"You know also, that the worst passions are making, every day, breaches in all our institutions, and that the very highest position is daily made the object of their attack."

"Proceed, proceed, I beg of you, I am also aware of what you remark; neither I nor my colleagues are sheltered from the attacks of libellers of different parties who make war against us; but thank God, their broadsides, their pigmy wounds, and their caricatures, do not prevent my sleeping."

"The dangerous position, very dangerous, in which we are placed, makes it a duty upon every honest man to save, by every means in his power, an administration which understands, as well as the one at the head of which you are placed, the wants of the country; it is simply on this account, monseigneur, that I have determined to offer you my assistance."

"Which you did not refuse to my predecessor, and which probably you will afford to my successor, if he will pay the price. But let us proceed, M. le Comte, you have, you tell me, something very important to communicate, and as yet you have only entertained me with enigmas."

"These preambles were necessary, for it is my sincere desire that you may be convinced that it is not the love of vile metal which induces a man like myself to render you some service."

"We know, M. le Comte, that you are the most perfect model of disinterestedness; but let me hear, I beg of you once more, the subject of all this introduction."

"Well, monseigneur, the life of the king is menaced."

His excellence, who until now had paid but very slight attention to the discourse of the Count de D——, at mention of the last words pronounced, rose hastily from his seat.

"This is very serious, M. le Comte; but are you quite certain of what you advance?"

"Quite sure, monseigneur, and it is not without pain, I can assure you, that I find myself compelled to inform your excellency that the chief of the plot of which our monarch would infallibly have been the victim if we had not discovered it, is a young officer of our brave army in Africa, at present in Paris on leave for convalescence."

"And what is the name of this officer?"

"Edmond de Bourgerel."

"But this is the name of one of the bravest officers of our African army, and I cannot believe—"

"If monseigneur will be good enough to glance at this report, his doubts will be removed."

His excellency took the report which the Count de D—— presented to him. The following are the terms in which this piece was conceived, which, despite the corrections, interpolations, suppressions, and augmentations of the Count de D——, had still preserved some remains of its pot-house origin; we might, after giving it an attentive perusal, be satisfied that it was written with a turkey quill, nearly "used up," on the most ricketty table of some hole and corner cabaret, between an eightpenny litrè of wine, and the well picked bones of a pound of pork cutlets à la sauce piquante.*

"I was this morning with Passe-partout."

"Who is this Passe-partout?" demanded his excellency, after looking at the last page of the report, which was signed Bon-Œil; "and from whom did you receive this?"

"Passe-partout is a charming young man, who has dissipated the fortune left to him by his father. His name is one of the most illustrious of the imperial dynasty. Bon-Œil is the only son of a gentleman of Lower Normandy, who was compromised by the last events of La Vendée. These

---

* We think this note unnecessary, but still we place it here, for we do not wish our friends to amuse themselves in seeking among our writings what they will not discover, like many others, we make use of a dramatic anecdote, reported by the brothers Parfaict in their " *History of the French Theatre,*" and of which the Abbé Pellegrin, a dramatic author, now forgotten, is the hero, we simply dress it in a fashionable style, *voila tout.*

two men serve faithfully, but they are very expensive.

"I was with Passe-partout this morning, at the place and hour indicated, in order to observe the individual described, (M. Edmond de Bourgerel, captain in the first regiment of African chasseurs,) leave his house. We did not wait long. Towards ten o'clock he left. After being again with the three merchants who were described to you in the previous reports, he repaired to the Boulevard des Italiens, and for nearly an hour he promenaded in front of the passage of the opera, smoking a cigar. We conjectured that he was waiting for some one; and in fact we were not mistaken, for at the moment when, no doubt, tired of waiting, he was about retiring, he was accosted by an individual whose physiognomy and costume at once announced to us an enemy of the government; he wore, in fact, a gray hat, his hair was extremely long, and his beard very thick, and descending nearly to his bosom.

"After conversing for a few minutes on the boulevard, they separated, after shaking hands, and each took a separate direction. Following the instructions I had received, I quitted Passepartout, and followed the steps of the individual whose revolutionary aspect I have described.

"He repaired at first to a house in the street Lepellatier, where he remained some minutes, and which he left, accompanied by an individual who had somewhat less the appearance of a conspirator, but who, however, ought not to be an enemy of government, for he wore a red œyelet at his coat button-hole. From Lepelatier street, these two individuals went to the street Chaussée d'Antin, and stopped at the café which makes the corner of the Rue Neuve-des-Mathurins, where they picked up a third conspirator, who was waiting for them. (It is not without reason that I say conspirator, as the sequel of the report will prove to you.)

"From the street of la Chaussée d'Antin to that of Fontaine Saint Georges is not far; it did not require much time therefore to arrive before the house which bears in this street the number 20, and into which they all three entered. After waiting nearly an hour in front of this house, and which I saw entered by the man of the Faubourg Saint-Denis, and several mean-looking individuals, seeing no person leave it, and not doubting but that this was the seat of the conspiracy, Passepartout, who had followed the steps of the man of the Faubourg Saint-Denis, said we should do well to introduce ourselves, if we could contrive it, into the house in question, and that perhaps we might hear something worth knowing. As there is no concierge in this house, he determined, at the risk of passing for what we are not, to enter it; and after following a long passage, which led us to a sort of garden, we arrived close to a small side building, in which, to all appearance, the conspirators were assembled.

"We were not deceived; they were, in fact, in a room of the ground floor in this building, and as the windows were open, (no doubt on account of the intense heat,) we could hear a great part of their conversation.

"W. placed ourselves in the best situation for listening, and the following is nearly what we heard.

"'And so you will not change your plan,' said one of them.

"'No,' replied the one who was addressed, and who, from his voice, we recognised as the man

from the Faubourg Saint-Denis; 'my plan is prudent, it is well conceived.'

"'But consider, to have the king killed in the midst of his guards, it is placing the chief of the conspiracy in a danger, which it will be thought extraordinary if he contrives to extricate himself from.'

"'But why?' said another, 'when he strikes the tyrant, he will be dressed in his uniform, and there will necessarily be a moment of hesitation among the soldiers, who will not dare upon the instant, to lay hands on one of their officers, which will give time to the other conspirators to act.'

"''Tis no matter; to strike the king in the midst of his escort is difficult.'

"'Let it remain then. The proclamation, which is full of fine words, will rouse the people; and besides, if I change that, I must also change many things besides, and my faith, I have not the time; so let us leave things as they are.

"'Well! let it go as it is; for the rest, you may rely upon it, that we will give you, at the moment of danger, a famous coup de main.'"

The two agents of the count, after explaining to their noble patron how they had been forced to quit precipitately the place they were in, to escape being discovered by the conspirators who were strolling about the garden, finished their report, by soliciting the recompense to which they were entitled for the wonderful discovery they had made.

"Well! monseigneur," said the Count de D—— when his excellency had finished reading the preceding report.

"This is indeed a serious affair, and I do not think we can act too soon; we must this very day procure the arrest of all the conspirators."

"But we have not the means; one alone is known to us, the Sieur Edmond de Bourgerel. It results from the information I have obtained, that the house in which the reunion took place, and where the conspirators agreed in their plan of acting, is occupied by an artist who for more than six months has been voyaging in Switzerland, and who appears to be a perfect stranger to the conspiracy. He has confided the keeping of his rooms to one of his friends, who has lent it to the revolutionists, and unfortunately we do not know the name of this man."

"But what are we to do then?" exclaimed his excellence, striking his forehead in despair.

"I think," replied the Count de D——, "that the most prudent way is to procure the secret arrest of Captain Edmond de Bourgerel, and keep him in the most rigorous confinement until he has made known his accomplices."

"I am of your opinion, Monsieur le Comte, and I shall immediately give the necessary directions."

His excellency at once placed himself at his bureau and wrote a despatch, which he immediately sent off, and also an order for a good round sum, which the Comte de D—— hastened to get cashed.

The next morning, poor Edmond de Bourgerel, who did indeed conspire, but merely against the poetry of Aristotle, was waylaid by a party of bludgeon-men, commanded by the illustrious Passepartout, thrown into a fiacre, conducted to the prefecture of police, and *deposited* in a dark cell, where he was left several days before being examined.

The unfortunate young man knew not to whom, or to what he could attribute his arrest; he was far from supposing that it was because he had assembled a few of his friends, in order to read to them a drama which, in his own opinion, was to excel every thing that had lately appeared.

He was at length permitted to defend himself. When the motives which had induced his arrest were made known to him, which they were forced to do, for the very simple reason, that, knowing nothing about it, he had not a word to say; the hearty laugh, which he could not restrain, despite the vexation he felt at having been so long detained for so futile a motive, somewhat disconcerted his interrogator, whose astonishment was carried to its height, when Edmond de Bourgerel informed him of the object for the reunion of the Street Fontaine-Saint-Georges.

It was not without some hesitation that they determined to let slip the threads, at the end of which they had hoped to fasten a nice little conspiracy, capable of furnishing the materials necessary for the concoction of a reasonable number of reports, acts of accusation, suits, and other pieces of eloquence; so that, before he obtained his freedom, Edmond de Bourgerel found it necessary to produce as witnesses the whole of his pretended accomplices.

When it had been proved, demonstrated, and sworn to, that he had only been guilty of a drama, in five acts and eleven scenes, they politely showed him the door, demanding pardon for the great liberty; at the same time observing to him, that if instead of attempting to march in the steps of Hugo and Dumas, he had contented himself with studying the theory of service abroad, and the treatise, by Vauban, on fortifications, the misfortune which had fallen upon him would not have happened.

This was informing him, in polite terms, that he might think himself very lucky in getting off so cheap. Edmond perfectly understood this, and although he had passed more than two months in prison, of which six weeks were in solitary confinement, he said nothing; and acted wisely in so doing.

His first business, on leaving his prison, was to search for Eugenie, for he knew the motive which had determined the unhappy girl to leave her aunt's house; but all his exertions, as well as those of Madame de Saint Preuil, to whom he thought it his duty to confide (taking upon his own shoulders a fault, which our elders are always disposed to pardon when we offer to repair them,) what had taken place during her journey to Peronne; all his exertions, we repeat, had been in vain. Madame de Saint Preuil and Edmond de Bourgerel no longer expected—but from the kindness of Providence—the return of her, whom they both loved, though in different degrees ; when the young officer received from the minister of war an order to rejoin his regiment.

On his departure, he earnestly requested Madame de Saint Preuil to write to him the moment she might, by chance, discover Eugenie; promising her that he would immediately return to Paris, if he should be obliged even to resign his commission.

All that we have succinctly narrated to our readers, Madame de Saint Preuil, who had already so far informed Madame de Neuville, repeated to her niece, with considerable details.

We shall not attempt to describe the joy of Eugenie de Mirbel when her aunt, after fully bestowing her pardon, assured her that she might yet hope for some happy years. We shall simply remark that the Countess de Neuville and Laura de Beaumont were equally as happy as their friend, who continued embracing them, and only left them to return to her aunt, to whom the reconcilement seemed to have brought renewed health, and who took into her arms her little niece and poured on her the most touching caresses.

Lucie and Laura thought that the worthy Madame de Saint Preuil and Eugenie de Mirbel must have much to converse about; they retired, happy at having produced a reconciliation, the result of which would be the happiness of their friend.

CHAPTER XXVI.

AN ENCOUNTER.

THE salon of the Marchioness de Villerbanne, as we have before observed, was a neutral ground, upon which were often assembled the most distinguished representatives of opinions, whether religious, political, or literary, which divide the world; but here they were forced to live on good terms, and to remember, without fail, that before being of such a communion, such an opinion, or of such a school, they must become men of the world; and that they must not, to the great displeasure of the ladies, and of those whom a profession of faith, a dissertation on the last project of law, and a renewed literary quarrel of Vadius and Trissotin, but indifferently seduce, transform into an arena, the saloon of a woman, who, above all, wished her guests to be amused.

But let it not be supposed that the society of Madame de Villerbanne occupied themselves with frivolities ; this lady, although aged, was too much identified with the period for it to be thus. She permitted argument, provided it was carried on with calmness, and of a nature to interest those who took no part in it; she allowed even skirmishing, when the combatants made use of courteous weapons, and the spectators, or rather the auditors, escaped without wounds. Thus, the saloon of Madame de Villerbanne was quite recherché; for such assemblies are rare, and when they exist, every one renders justice to them, although few persons show themselves worthy of being for a long time admitted to them.

These last words require an explanation, which we hasten to give our readers; that those amongst them, to whom their fortune will allow it, may use, if it pleases them, the receipt employed by Madame de Villerbanne to obtain agreeable society.

It was not difficult to be admitted at the Marchioness de Villerbanne's; this lady received, with that grace and affability which belongs but to a privileged few, all those who were presented to her, and it is unnecessary to observe that those only were presented, whose name and position in society rendered worthy of the honour. But the marchioness had adopted a rule, from which she only departed in favour of her intimate friends; which was, that a presentation to her did not bestow on the individual who obtained it, the right of a second appearance, unless a letter of invitation was previously addressed to him. Every one was aware of this rule, and every one submitted to it; the elect affirming it as very prudent, and those who were not favoured by it, alone complaining.

If, as usual with us, we now attempt to give our readers some idea of the saloon of the Marchioness de Villerbanne, we shall describe it as one of those

LIFE IN PARIS.

THE MURDER OF ROMAN BY SALVADOR.

vast halls which are at present nowhere seen, except in the hotels of the Faubourg Saint Germain and of the Place Royale, in which we can breathe with freedom; that it was ornamented with wooden panels of sculptured oak, which, in our humble opinion, is infinitely superior to all the gilt and pasteboard moulding recently brought into fashion; large and handsome glasses, real chef d'œuvres of the royal manufactories, surmounted, as well as the doors, with medallions, enclosed with garlands of gilt wood, upon which a pupil of Boucher had painted the most charming pastorals it is possible to conceive. The chimney-piece, of sea-green marble, was of sufficient size to permit ten or a dozen persons to seat themselves in front of it without inconvenience, and on this chimney-piece was placed a magnificent pendulum, of Boull, which, old as it was, equalled the modern chefs d'œuvres of Thomire and Deniére.

We know that Madame de Villerbanne, after taking Lucie to task for remaining so long without paying her a visit, had made her promise to assist at the fête she was about to give to all the persons usually admitted to her society.

This fête was to be very splendid; for the Marchioness, whose saloon had this year remained open somewhat later than the preceding ones, wished to close the winter season in a brilliant style, and produce in those who were to be present a desire to appéar often at similar ones; for this reason she had neglected nothing which could add anything to the attractions already so great of her gay assemblies. She was desirous that the most distinguished artists should adorn it with their talents, and those to whom she had addressed herself had all promised their assistance with readiness; for they all knew that, although they should receive from the Marchioness de Villerbanne the just tribute which people of fortune ought to pay to those who endeavour to amuse them a few moments, this noble dame, like most others of the class to which she belonged, was sensible of the regards due under every circumstance to eminent talents, often possessed by men of the noblest character, and that, with her, they would be treated with the most perfect equality.

Our readers must allow us here a slight observation. Many of them, no doubt, have remarked, that persons who can boast of the highest birth, do not, in the ordinary relations of life, generally carry themselves with haughty and insolent pride; but that a confidant of the *telegraph*, a prince of the bank, a lynx, or however named, are often very impertinent, (we may remark that there are no rules without exception,) whilst a noble descendant of the Montmorencies or the Rohans, is, on the contrary, an example of polite manners. This difference must singularly astonish those who, brought up at the school of old liberalism, have been nourished with the perusal of the ancient *constitutionel;* which, among other curious things, should have informed them, that such as bore a noble name were powdered vieillards, and coiffés with the royal bird, and dowagers wearing patches and fardingales, always ready to turn up their noses at those who, not having the luck to be of noble race, deserved, in their opinion, the epithets of clowns and *malotrus!*

Lucie de Neuville would willingly have dispensed with being present at the fête of Madame de Villerbanne; for, as we have observed, she was persuaded that the person of whom her aunt had spoken, without seeming to attach to it any great importance, was no other than the Marquis de Pour-

rieres; and what she feared, above all, was to find herself face to face with the man whom she had dreaded, before she had received the letter from Doctor Matheo; but in whom, however, by one of those singular traits of the human heart, which escape analyzation, she could not prevent herself being interested.

But all her little efforts to avoid being present, were attempted in vain, against the wish of her aunt and the entreaties of Laura, who, reasonable as she was, could not contemplate, without a feeling of vexation, the idea of being deprived of the pleasure she promised herself at the last ball of the season.

And now, let us enter the saloon of the Hotel de Neuville, where we shall find Lucie and Laura, who have just completed their toilette, and are waiting the announcement of their carriage.

The two friends are dressed nearly alike; they have each a robe of white crape, and one beneath of satin, of the same colour: but whilst Laura has simply ornamented her head with some flowers, which, fresh as they are, seem less so than herself, and graced her neck with a plain pearl necklace, Lucie, whose position as a married woman allows a greater luxury, appears with a complete set of most magnificent diamonds.

"One would really think that we were two sisters," said Laura, who had drawn Lucie before the large mirror placed over the mantle-piece.

"And are we not?" replied the countess.

"It's true, we love each other as though we were of the same blood, and, for my part, I am quite certain that it will always continue so."

"Dear Laura!"

"But can you conceive the reason of this?" added Laura, who had glanced at the pendulum; "it is past ten, and this idle Paolo has not yet announced the carriage."

And as she extended her hand towards the bell, Lucie stopped her, and said:

"You are very desirous, then, of going to this ball?"

"Certainly!" replied Laura; "'tis the last of the season, and they say it will be very brilliant. But are not you delighted in having an opportunity of distracting yourself a little?"

"I must confess that if it were not for the fear of displeasing my good aunt, and I could have resolved to deprive you of a pleasure you seem to anticipate, I should have remained at home to-day; for I still fear that this man spoken of by my aunt may be the Marquis de Pourrieres."

"Lucie, Lucie!" said Laura, "you know that it was agreed between us, that you would not again speak of this individual, about whom you occupy yourself too much."

"You are right; but still, if the event proves that my presentiments are well-founded, what must I do?"

"Eh! mon Dieu! not speak to this marquis, unless you are actually obliged to; and, in that case, you are not ignorant that there is a certain mode of showing persons that they are disagreeable to us, without any necessity of appearing destitute of good breeding."

"I will follow your advice, my dear Laura."

The conversation of the two friends was here interrupted by Paolo, who came to announce that the carriage was ready.

"But why have we waited so long?" said Laura to the old domestic, who begged his mistress to excuse the servants, for having kept them waiting.

Paolo replied, that at the moment of putting to,

they had discovered that one of the screws was missing from the axle-tree of the carriage, and that it had required a short delay to replace it.

"Perhaps it is a presage," said Lucie smiling; "who knows?"

"Ah, bah!" said Laura, impatient to be off; "I remember reading, that Cæsar, in spite of an omen, which was considered as having an evil tendency, passed the Rubicon, and gained the battle. Will you show yourself less courageous than this hero of ancient Rome?"

"Let us pass the Rubicon then," replied Lucie de Neuville, throwing over her shoulders a handsome cachemere shawl; "I will lead the way."

Laura took her gloves, her bouquet, and her fan, and followed Lucie, who had already left the saloon.

The entrance of the Countess de Neuville, and her friend, into the saloon of the Marchioness de Villerbanne occasioned a little excitement; they were both so pretty, and so well dressed. When, therefore, they had paid their homage to the mistress of the house, and had placed themselves in the midst of a group of young and handsome women, a charming parterre, in which they shone as the sweetest flowers, they found themselves immediately surrounded by a court eager to render justice to their amiable qualities—a court, certainly, very well composed; and amongst those who made part of it, might be remarked more than one stern republican, who played the courtier in equal perfection with the rest; so true is it, that beauty and the graces constitute a power which has but one enemy to dread—time; which, alas! respects nothing.

Lucie, on entering the saloon, had thrown a rapid glance upon those assembled in it; and this glance had sufficed to assure her, that the person she so dreaded to meet was not amongst them. Laura had replied to a sign she had made to her, by a slight movement of the shoulders, which we might thus translate: "You see plainly, my dear friend, that presentiments are often deceitful;" she then accepted the invitation of a young diplomate, who advanced to escort her from the place she occupied, between her friend and a very pretty little woman, who was also quickly engaged; so that Lucie remained, when the first notes of the orchestra commenced, encircled by a levy of men who forgot, whilst in her presence, both the dance and the tables for bouillote.

She replied, with her usual grace, and presence of mind, to the numerous compliments paid her; but still, it was not what was said to her that she listened to; it was the voice of the valet charged to announce the names of those invited, in the order they presented themselves, and which arrived clear and distinctly to her ears, despite the confused murmurs of the orchestra, with the noise of the steps of the dancers, as they glided over the floor, and the ceaseless conversation of scattered groups.

"M. the Viscount de Lussan," said the valet. "M. the Marquis de Pourrieres!"

CHAPTER XXVII.

THE THREE PACHAS.

THE countess rose hastily from her seat to satisfy herself, that the man who was just announced, was really the one she had before met; her presentiments were not deceived—it was him! The Viscount de Lussan, whom she had often before seen at her aunt's, preceded him, and they both crossed the saloon to approach Madame de Villerbanne.

The viscount presented the Marquis de Pourrieres, who was graciously received; and who, after remaining a few minutes with the marchioness, retired to mix himself amongst the different groups which surrounded the dancers.

Lucie became so dreadfully pale, that one of the gentlemen who surrounded her, considered himself called upon to ask her if she felt indisposed.

"No," she replied, with hesitation, for she perceived they had noticed the sudden movement she had made, when the marquis had entered the saloon, and she feared they might conjecture the cause which had provoked it.

"Madame became so suddenly pale, that I was afraid, for a moment, that the great heat here——"

"Indeed, I do not know how I feel," added Lucie, who, in spite of her efforts, could not recover her sang froid; "but I shall not be sorry to breathe the fresh air for a few moments."

The cavalier to whom she spoke, hastened to offer her his arm, which she accepted, and he conducted her to the apartment of Madame de Villerbanne, where she wished to remain for a short time to recover herself.

Laura, who we must observe, was a great lover of dancing, had not remarked the absence of her friend; she listened to the compliments offered her by the young German diplomate, her partner, whose long and fair hair, and sentimental regards, caused her much enjoyment.

Salvador and the Viscount de Lussan, to converse the more at their ease, had retired to the embrasure of a window.

"You see, dear marquis," said the Viscount de Lussan, "that I have faithfully acquitted myself of the promise I made you."

"And I thank you for it, viscount; but I do not see the lady of my thoughts has she not arrived yet, I wonder?"

"The charming Countess de Neuville has just entered the apartment of Madame de Villerbanne, no doubt she will return soon. Do you know, marquis, that I must have a very great friendship for you, thus to sacrifice my hopes of making so desirable a conquest."

"Be assured that I shall not forget it; but the young friend of the countess, you have told me, is charming; why do you not make an attempt? Do you know, it would be delightful if——"

"I am not happy enough to please Mademoiselle de Beaumont; I have already danced with her several times, and I discovered, at once, that I only lost my time with her."

"That is very extraordinary."

"Is it not? but the world is full of extraordinary things; is it not one, to see you and I in the most virtuous saloon in Paris?"

"Why? do we not possess all that is requisite to be admitted here—talents, fortune, and birth?"

"Oh! as for birth, I am, it is true, the last scion of an ancient house of Brittany; but is your nobility so well authenticated, marquis?"

"How! what is your meaning?"

"Stay, I must open to you my whole mind; promise me, however, not to get angry."

"In the relations we stand to each other, we can, I think, have confidence in one another."

"Well! I have an idea, that your history greatly resembles that of the false Martinguerre. Eh! don't get into a passion, marquis," added the

Viscount de Lussan, observing the blood mounting to the face of his friend; "I can assure you, I have no intention of offending you; I merely wish to remark to you, that I perceive you are now become a brown, whereas, at the time I first saw you, you were decidedly a blonde."

A general movement which took place in the saloon, prevented Salvador replying to the Viscount de Lussan. The country dance was finished, and the company approached the piano, to which an old knight of St. Louis had led a young and handsome woman.

The eyes and cheeks of this lady, of more than middling height, and elegantly shaped, were so striking and so fresh, her complexion was so transparent and rosy, her forehead so pure and lofty, and her features so soft and sweet, that her appearance drew forth a general burst of admiration.

"Dieu! how handsome," exclaimed Salvador.

"Do you not recognise her?" said the Viscount de Lussan.

"Certainly," replied Salvador, "she's an artiste of the greatest merit; but I have never seen her except on the stage, and I confess she gains infinitely, on a nearer view."

The deepest silence reigned in the saloon, when the cantatrice commenced the first notes of the grand air of *la reine de chypre*. The extent and purity of her voice were really remarkable; and when she had finished, she was rewarded by a triple round of applause.

"Really," said Salvador, "if the Countess de Neuville did not reign as an absolute sovereign in my heart, I think I should increase the number of admirers of this charming woman."

"Ah! there, there, my dear; don't get into a flame, I beg of you; the citadel is taken, and well guarded."

"Well! upon my honour, I am sorry for it!"

"Come, I see, that to prevent your compromising yourself, I must recount to you in a few words, the history of this admirable chanteuse."

"I am listening, my dear viscount, I am listening to you."

"As there is no good history without a title, I shall bestow upon the one I am about to narrate to you, that of the ' *Chanteur et Chanteuse.*' "

"Ah! very good," said Salvador, who remarked that the viscount had dwelt upon the word chanteur, in a peculiar manner.

"There were three brothers," continued the Viscount de Lussan, "a species of noxious trinity, which for a long time chose the Faubourg Saint-Germain, for the theatre of its exploits.

"I shall not give you their real names, let it suffice for you to know, that they were vulgarly called the three *pachas*.

"After the fatigues of the day—the laborious fatigues of the *cadet*,* and the *caroublet*†—they winged their flight, similar to three vultures, towards the Palais Royal, and took refuge more particularly in the street Jeannisson, which was then called the street des Boucheries, and only inhabited by the priestesses of the cloacine Venus.

"It was the good time of the Reppins, the Chevelots, Molieres, Alexandre Leblords, and other individuals of the same species, who are become what it has pleased the Almighty to make of them.

"The three pachas had, as it often happens, a mother as honourable as they were the contrary, and a sister, a sickly child, whose precocious genius for music was already celebrated.

* An instrument with which thieves force doors.
† False keys.

"One day, the indicated hour at the prefecture of police, sounded for two of these devourers, whom the court of assize, at Paris, sent to increase the number of messmates at *Brest*.

"There remained one, less redoubtable than the two others; he soon quitted the too hazardous industry of false keys, to return to his old trade of a mason; this was a great step. It was in the exercise of his functions, that his messmates bestowed upon him by common accord, and on the completion of placing the roof on a building, the glorious surname of P. Vinaigre.

"P. Vinaigre, then, masoned away as peaceably as possible, living with his old mother; and what is remarkable and worthy of praise, receiving lessons in music from his sister, whose improvement increased with her age.

"But alas! we must believe, that by hearing her sing, he felt in himself a desire to *make others sing*, and he placed himself in the formidable brigade of *chanteurs*, in renown at the period, S—— called Lagrille, C—— named Pistolet, T—— called C'Arnache, L—— called la Bete-a-chagrin, and A—— named Monfâme.

"One fine day, not long since, P. Vinaigre was directed towards Poissy, to display his voice there for two years.

"Since then, his life has been a continual song, sometimes in the upper notes, and sometimes in the lower ones.

"His sister had prospered. A noble artiste, whom Duprez, with his immense talent, could not make us forget, took her by the hand; and by his assistance and lessons, she acquired a share of the qualities which she possesses at present.

"At length she made her debut in one of our first lyrical scenes, on the same day that, by way of parenthesis, her brother was conducted to the prefecture of police.

"She succeeded.

"At present, of the *three pachas*, one is dead, another still at the prison at Brest; Philip Vinaigre, condemned to two years of surveillance, mixes mortar at Vernon, in Normandy; and his sister, who receives every day the orations and frenzied applause of an idolizing public, is no other than the charming person of whom you would infallibly have become amorous, if I had not recounted to you this history."

"But what conclusion do you draw from this history?"

"What conclusion would you wish me to draw but this: that in the arts, as in every other profession or trade, there are no obstacles we cannot surmount, when we have the talent, and do not fail in perseverance."

At this moment the sounds of the orchestra announced a fresh country dance. Laura, who had been reconducted to her place by the young German diplomate, glanced round the saloon, and appeared astonished at not recognising her friend.

"I leave you, dear marquis," said the Viscount de Lussan to his friend; "I am going to invite Mademoiselle de Beaumont; perhaps I may find it possible to dispel the prejudices she seems to have against me."

"Go, viscount, go, I shall offer up my wishes for your success; but, for my part, I am very vexed at not seeing Madame de Neuville."

At the moment Salvador uttered these words, Lucie, completely restored, entered the saloon, conducted by the Marchioness de Villerbanne, who had been to search for her in her room; not seeing Laura in her place, (the latter was dancing with the Viscount de Lussan,) she seated herself near her aunt and the old chevalier of Saint Louis, who had acted as cavalier to the cantatrice, in leading her to the piano.

This venerable knight of Saint Louis was one of the oldest and most intimate friends of the Marchioness de Villerbanne, who was in the habit of consulting him on any important undertaking; and she considered as such the according to any fresh personage the entrée of her saloon; when she left to seek for her niece, she was speaking of the Marquis de Pourrieres, she resumed the same subject of conversation as soon as she returned to her place.

"So that I can, with all confidence," she said, "again invite this Marquis de Pourrieres; he's a gallant man, of irreproachable manners, amiable, spirituel, a man of the world in fact."

"I have already had the honour of telling you, madame, that he is the living portrait of his father, whom I knew well during the emigration."

"Since it is so," replied the marchioness, "he shall become, if he desires it, a frequenter of my private circle. I also knew, at the same period, the late Marquis de Pourrieres, and as his son resembles him,—"

"He has committed, however, a serious fault, and one which, most certainly, the old marquis would never have forgiven him," observed the chevalier.

Lucie was all attention.

"And what faults? mon Dieu!" said the marchioness.

"He has rallied!"

"Chevalier! chevalier! don't let us talk politics, you are exclusive, and I am not."

Lucie was pleased at hearing persons in whom she had the utmost confidence, thus express themselves respecting the Marquis de Pourrieres, and in terms so favourable. At this moment Laura was led towards her by the Viscount de Lussan.

"Well! my own dear Laura," said the countess to her friend, when the viscount, after exchanging a few words with them, turned away to rejoin Salvador who had beckoned to him, "my presentiments are realized, he is here."

"Really?"

"He has been presented to my aunt by the Viscount de Lussan."

"And has he spoken to you?"

"Not yet; I do not think even that he is aware I am here."

"Is it not him who is now conversing with the Viscount de Lussan, and regarding us?"

Lucie turned her eyes, and made an affirmative sign to Laura.

"How do you like him?" she said, after some moments of silence.

"Not much," replied Laura; "he possesses a distinguished physiognomy, his toilette is irreproachable, and his movements and manners announce a man of good society; but there is in his regard an expression of harshness and extreme artifice; in fact, he displeases me more even than the Viscount de Lussan."

Lucie was so visibly disappointed at the words of her friend, that Laura remarked upon her features an expression of great discontent.

"Mon Dieu! Lucie," she said, "you must not be angry at what I have said."

Lucie was about replying, when she was accosted by the Marquis de Pourrieres, who solicited her for the next country dance.

Lucie had refused him, alleging as an excuse a slight indisposition; but Laura making her a sign to accept him, and the marquis saying to her in an under tone that he was indebted to her an explanation of his presence in the house in which he had met her for the first time, she resigned herself, and with some trembling accepted the hand of the marquis.

Laura, already fatigued, remained in her place, where the young German diplomate returned to keep her company.

As faithful historians of the acts and deeds of our heroes, we must observe, that the Countess de Neuville, in spite of her determination to shun every contact with a man whom a letter written by a person in whom she placed confidence, had denounced as a dangerous being, had awaited with a certain impatience the invitation just made to her; she said to herself, that the marquis meeting her after what had passed between them in a saloon in which he was just presented, it was from her he ought to solicit permission to remain; she was, besides, curious to ascertain what had induced him to visit the ignoble cabaret of the Rue de la Tannerie, either because, although she refused to acknowledge it to herself, she felt interested about him, or simply that the fact was so extraordinary, as to excite strongly her curiosity. So that it is very probable she would have accepted the invitation, had her friend even attempted to persuade her to decline it.

We shall report the conversation of Salvador and the Countess de Neuville; a conversation held in an under tone, and frequently interrupted by the change of places which the different figures of the country dance required.

It was Salvador who commenced:

"I thank heaven, madame," he said, "that my anticipations are so soon realized, and that I have an opportunity to-day of humbly suing for a pardon."

"But I have nothing to pardon you for, monsieur," replied the Countess de Neuville; "it was not to me that you addressed yourself, and you could not suppose that any thing but an accident had led a woman of any respect to the house in which you encountered her."

"It's true, madame, and 'tis a pleasing reflection to know that my presence in the midst of the troop of bandits, gave me an opportunity of rendering you a slight service."

The countess raised her eyes towards Salvador; she was deeply astonished to find him approach the question in so frank a manner. He spoke of his presence in this horrible place in the midst of a troop of bandits, in so unconcerned a tone, and as so natural an affair, that she no longer knew what to think, and fancied herself called upon even to return him her thanks; for after all, the offence, as she had said, was not meant to her, and it was certainly her whom he had prevented from being robbed, and to whom he had forwarded the carnet, and the two bank notes for a thousand francs.

She concluded, therefore, that she ought to thank him.

"I am ready to acknowledge, sir," she said, "that it was you who prevented one of the bandits amongst whom you were present, robbing me of my necklace, and I thank you for having forwarded me the card-case which by chance fell into your hands."

It was not without intention that Lucie made this reply, which included an indirect threat of not concealing the encounter she had made; "if he fears any thing," she said to herself, "if he does not beg me to preserve a silence, I shall, at least, observe upon its features the traces of some sort of emotion."

Lucie's intention had not escaped Salvador; and consequently, he allowed not the slightest symptom of emotion to appear upon his countenance.

"If I did not remember how much you were terrified," he said, "I should really be tempted to laugh at the singular aspect I must have exhibited, attired in the costume I then wore."

Lucie suspected that the marquis made the preceding observation, merely to introduce the explanation of his presence in the place alluded to; at length, then, she was arrived at the point she wished, her curiosity was about to be satisfied; well! at this moment she could not resolve to listen to the marquis, it was almost a confidence he was making her, ought she to hear it?

Salvador left her no time to continue her reflections; if he had not sooner frankly broached the subject, it was because he had been inventing, since his entrance into the saloon of the Marchioness de Villerbanne, the fable he should narrate, to justify to the countess his presence in the house of Sans Refus, and his costume of a sailor. This fable he had just matured.

"I owe you, Madame la Comtesse," he said, giving to his features and his voice an expression of seriousness, which announced that he considered what he was about to say of some importance; "I owe you the explanation of an event, very simple of itself, but which, however, might be interpreted unfavourably towards me. As it is probable that I shall frequently have the pleasure of meeting you in society," he said, smiling, "I cannot allow you to suppose me one of those men, the habitual frequenters of the den of the Rue de la Tannerie."

"Ah, monsieur!" said Lucie, who, since she had spoken to the Marquis de Pourrieres, was become quite reassured, and was also astonished that she could dread, for a single moment, a man so well placed in society, and who expressed himself with such distinction.

"The individual who called upon me," said the marquis, "has, no doubt, informed you of my position there?"

"He did so, monsieur," replied Lucie, trembling and hesitating, for this question had put her in mind of the letter of Doctor Matheo, which she had completely forgotten.

This emotion did not escape the penetrating eyes of Salvador.

"Has the doctor spoken?" he said to himself. "No! he could not, without compromising himself; and, in that case, this woman would not, at this moment, be dancing with me."

Salvador then recounted to Lucie a well-invented history, and which completely justified his presence at Sans Refus's. Our readers shall hear this history when we pay another visit to Madame de Neuville, whom we must now quit for a short time, in order to look after Servigny, whom we have lost sight of for a considerable period.

CHAPTER XXVIII.

SERVIGNY.

At the end of the chapter entitled "The Escape," we told our readers that we would shortly inform them of what happened to Servigny; and the moment is now arrived to keep our promise.

Servigny, then, whom we have seen the passive spectator of the combat engaged in between Salvador and Roman and the gendarmes of Beausset, profited by the confusion of the scene to escape from those of the gendarmes who might have been tempted to pursue him. He threw himself at once into a field of olives, which bordered the road, and this without knowing, or even caring, as to the direction he was taking. Stimulated by the dread of again being arrested and conducted to prison, and afterwards, by that, not much less, of encountering his two comrades of the evasion, and being forced to become their accomplice, or, at least, to be considered as such, wherever he might accompany them; these different considerations had augmented his courage and vigour tenfold.

The rain still continued to pour down, the night was dark, not a sound which could disturb him was to be heard; every thing seemed united to favour the projects of Servigny. Anxious to remove himself as far as possible from the scene in which a crime had been just committed, he ran with such precipitation, that having struck against a stone with his foot, he fell, with such violence, that he was precipitated at some distance into a rivulet, the bed of which was covered with pebbles and the roots of trees. The shock was so rough that he immediately lost his senses, and remained some time in this state. But the freshness of the little stream of the rivulet soon brought him to a state of consciousness. His first care was, to assure himself that his limbs had received no fractures; after stretching out his legs and arms, he had the satisfaction of finding himself in a sound condition; but he suffered horribly in his head, in his breast, and at his elbows, parts of the body which had been placed so violently in contact with the fragments of rock and roots upon which he had fallen. The blood ran from him in streams, principally from the head, in which there was a large and serious rent; the other wounds were not so dangerous, but the pain was not less intense, especially at the elbows, the extreme sensibility of which is well known. Extricated, at length, from this unfortunate chasm, and not knowing what means to employ for staunching the wounds, which still continued to bleed freely, he determined to tear up his shirt, make bandages of it, and apply them to his wounds. These means having partly succeeded, he no longer delayed continuing his route, as well as possible, though still without any certain direction.

Nothing could be more miserable than the position of Servigny at this moment. Alone, wounded, without money, wandering at a venture in a country absolutely unknown to him, covered with the infamous livery of the prison—which would cause him to be recognised and arrested by the first individual that met him, and who would be tempted, by the reward of a hundred francs, awarded for the capture of a forçat—these reflections added to his fears and his despair. The blood he had lost diminished his strength, lowered his courage; he was compelled to rest himself on one of the blocks of stone, or rock, so frequently met with in these countries; but this repose, by tranquillizing his spirits—excited to the greatest paroxysm in consequence of the different events we have narrated—only discovered to him, more distinctly, all the horror of his position.

He hastily rose up. "Where is the use of struggling against a fatal destiny?" he exclaimed; "all my precautions are useless; no human prudence prevent my being arrested and reconducted to prison; I shall be condemned to three years of additional punishment, placed in the cell of the suspected, confounded with the scum of malefactors who people this sojourn of crime. What a cruel perspective! To be for ever lost, without having to reproach myself with a single action which can justify the rigours of which I am the object. Wretched fate! all is lost for me; honour, prospects—ah! sooner death, than be again conducted to that hell! none but a coward and a villain would accept of such ignominy.

"I must finish it; God will pardon me!"

Servigny fell upon his knees, and prayed with sincerity. After finishing his prayer, he rose with firmness, collected the remains of his shirt, and made a cord, for the purpose of putting an end to his sufferings. He laboured with such activity, and at the same time with such sang froid, in these dreadful preparations, that those who might have regarded him at this moment, would never have supposed that he was preparing the instrument of his own execution. At length, every thing is ready; he searches a place fit for the execution of his fatal project, but none of the trees near him—young and fragile olives—present the necessary strength and height This circumstance in no ways disconcerted him; his determination was irrevocably taken; he would find, at a short distance, what he could not meet with here. The hope of speedily terminating all his troubles, renders him greater energy. After walking for nearly an hour, without discovering what he searched for, he perceived, at last, a small wood, whose branching trees gave him some hopes of their fatal assistance, but he was separated from it by a torrent, which the last night's rain had considerably increased. Determined not to yield to any obstacle, he attempts to overcome this one. Upon a closer examination, he finds that the current is more rapid than deep; he descends to the bed of the torrent, clinging by the angular pieces of rock which border the sides; he ascends the opposite side, by taking the same precautions. At length, he attains his object; he steps, in his imagination, into the promised land! his sufferings are near their end! the tree is chosen—all is prepared—the cord is attached! But, at the supreme moment, he thinks it his duty to address a last prayer to the all-powerful and eternal Being, from whom he hopes for pardon!

Suddenly, a reflection suggests itself; and this is to rid himself of his garments. "If I remain covered with the livery of crime," he says to himself, "I shall inspire no compassion in those who may find my body; none will pity the unhappy galerien, whom they will think a great criminal. If, on the contrary, I am naked, and they observe the wounds with which I am covered, my body will be shown some respect; they will, probably, suppose that, after being despoiled, the brigands resolved, by a refinement of cruelty, to make me undergo this sort of death, to induce the belief of suicide. By dying in this state, I shall, at least, have the consolation that my position will be unknown, and, who knows? perhaps some charitable soul will give me a decent funeral!" Saying these words, he drew off the infamous garments which remained to him, and pitched them into the torrent, which soon carried them away in its rapid course.

Nothing now prevented the execution of his fatal purpose; he was just about placing the cord round his neck, when the sound of a clock, at a short distance, fell upon his ear. He listens; it tells him it is midnight. Struck with these sounds, which recal to him at once the religious souvenirs, the virtues, the happiness of former times, alas! so fugitive for him! a fresh order of ideas takes hold of his spirits. He fancies that the voice of the clock is a warning from above, which recals him to the sacred duties which religion imposes on its faithful followers. His feelings are suddenly tranquillized; the dreadful truth appears to him in all its horrors; he acknowledges and detests the crime he was about to commit by attempting his own life. "Oh! my God!" he exclaimed, "my chain is heavy, but I shall have strength to bear it until the moment that your infinite goodness may see fit to lighten the burden!" Having thus accepted a renewed compact with life and its sufferings, he tears away the cord and throws it into the same torrent which had already carried to a distance the rest of his garments.

The sudden resolution to which Servigny had come, by restoring to him his serenity of mind, could not lessen, in a great degree, the severe troubles to which he was a prey. Exhausted by hunger, cold, and fatigue; his blood wasted in abundance; the fever which had overtaken him, and which so many causes had produced in his brain; all contributed to extinguish, in this youth, lately so courageous and so proud, every grand and generous idea, and leave him to the sole and vile instincts of material preservation.

He resolved to direct his steps towards the church, which he knew was not far distant. The rain had now ceased; the sky, less clouded, permitted him to distinguish the church spire, feebly, but sufficient to serve as a direction for his hitherto uncertain and tottering steps. After walking a few minutes, he found himself in front of a house, which the feeble and unsteady light of the moon allowed him to remark. A cross—a sign always venerated by unfortunate Christians—surmounted the door, and every thing indicated that it was the presbytery. He hesitated; he is uncertain whether he ought to knock and implore assistance. His complete state of nudity, the wounds which cover him, all this causes him to imagine he might frighten the respectable man whose repose he is about to interrupt, and be repulsed. Besides, how is he to avoid suspicion? and, if he escapes these, how avoid exciting the suspicion of the mayor and authorities, always ready to prey upon misfortune? How invent a tale that may interest them in his position, obtain their compassion? How reply to that multitude of questions that each will put to him? His anxiety is at its height; he finds himself giving way under these different impressions.

But by a mechanical instinct he seizes the knocker, and decides upon knocking.

"The die is cast! may God protect me!" he said.

Two minutes had scarcely elapsed, when the voice of a man, from the interior, is heard, and demands of him, in a provincial patois, through a small grating in the door:

"Who knocks, at this advanced hour of the night, and what do they seek here?"

"Ah! Monsieur le Curé, pardon! I am completely naked, wounded, dying of hunger, cold, and fatigue," replied Servigny; "I implore your succour."

"Wait, my friend," said the worthy curate; "I see your pitiable state; wait two minutes, and I will open the door to you."

He soon returned, with the key and a lantern in his hand; he opens the door and hastens to throw

LIFE IN PARIS.

SALVADOR DE LUSAN AT THE INN.

a cloak over the shoulders of Servigny; then, regarding him attentively:

"God of heaven!" he exclaimed, "you are, no doubt, one of the victims of the brigands who infest the forest of Cujes?"

Then, without waiting for the reply of Servigny:

"Follow me," he said to him; "there is not an instant to lose!"

He led him into a small dining-room, where order and neatness reigned entire. He rang for attendance, and in the twinkling of an eye, a man and woman, Sylvain and Marguerité, both already aged, but with an exterior which inspired confidence, quickly hastened to the summons of their respected master; he desires the medicine chest, which was constantly kept well furnished, to be brought to him; he orders warm water and linen. They lead the wounded man towards the sparkling fire which the domestics had lighted. The venerable pastor undertakes to examine and dress the wounds of Servigny. Those at the elbows, although serious were not dangerous; but those of the head were likely to be followed by unpleasant consequences; they were all dressed by the respectable curate with the skill of an expert surgeon. These preliminary attentions accomplished, he gave the patient some soup, and when this had well warmed him, he ordered them to place a night-shirt over him, and put him in bed. Servigny was placed in the same room as the domestic, Sylvain; before separating from the kind curate, he wished to recount to him the long series of his misfortunes, and especially the manner in which he had been so ill-treated, a few hours before; but the worthy curate prevented him, recommending him to observe the most rigorous silence, that he may not aggravate the fever to which he was a prey.

This prescription was far from being to the taste of the honest Sylvain; who, besides having the best title to pass for the greatest babbler in France and Navarre, was "curiosity personified!" With these excitements, he burned with impatience to listen to the marvellous circumstances which, according to him, had reduced a robust young man to the necessity of taking refuge at night, entirely naked, in the presbytery of his master. He quietly approaches the bed of his guest, and in a voice which he renders as engaging as possible:

"Ah! my good sir," he says to him, "what infamous scelerats! how they have treated you. Do recount to me the different circumstances of this event; I wish that the moment day breaks the whole village should hear it, and that each should become your avenger. We will arm ourselves with pitchforks and scythes, we will search the whole country, and, by the Death! if we find the miserables, we will drag them away bound hand and foot. I am so incensed, you inspire me with so much compassion, that I shall put some cord in my pockets, and, by the Death! I'll be the man to throttle them! How many were there, the rascals? Were they armed? Were their countenances very ferocious—savage-like? So much the better! by the Death! they will find that old Sylvain has still a strong arm; yes, Sylvain, who has for forty-two years carried the halbert, with honour and glory, in the church of the good and brave Saint Marsault!* by the Death! I have made many a one tremble!"

* Saint Marsault enjoyed a high reputation in the southern provinces. Among other prayers addressed to him, is the following, from the rustic masons:—"Monsieur Marsault,

"Worthy Sylvain," replied the unfortunate Servigny, overcome at this long tirade, "I thank you for so warmly espousing my cause; but it is impossible for me to satisfy you at this moment. In addition to its being a serious wrong to disobey your excellent master, my strength will not allow me to afford you the information; be good enough, therefore, to excuse me, and permit me to take some little repose."

"Right, right, my good friend, I see that you are suffering; I will leave you to sleep at your ease. But still, on reflection, I think that if you were to narrate the events in a low tone, it would not much fatigue you; I swear to you that I will not speak of them, to-morrow morning, except to the school-master, to the *grand Guillaume*, the garde champêtre, the wife of the head churchwarden, and also of the grocer, at the corner. They are all my friends, and I can rely upon their discretion like my own. They will come and see you to-morrow morning; yes, indeed! and I hope the churchwarden's wife will bring you some fresh eggs, when you are convalescent, which, I trust, may not be distant; for, thank God! I know myself. What you have to say may be reduced to a little; and listen—I am sure, that as soon as you have unburthened yourself to me, you will find yourself relieved."

"Once more, my good Sylvain, it is impossible, absolutely impossible, to-night. Allow me to repose."

"Devil of a man!" grumbled Sylvain between his teeth; "there's plenty of trouble to make him speak; it has an air of suspicion about it—exceedingly suspicious These sulky and silent ones have, to a certainty, something on their conscience; for I have always remarked that the honest man is generally liberal, and abounding in words. But, however, it is very vexing to me, and I can truly say that this is the first time anything extraordinary has happened in the country and that I go to sleep ignorant of it. Cursed sulker! go! you may rely upon it the hens of the Margeuilliere won't lay for you; and as for her milk, it won't turn your stomach! Go, I detest you; and to prove it, I swear I'll tell you nothing more."

Sylvain, having finished his soliloquy, and finding his patient was asleep, again sought his bed; but susceptible, like most of the curious whose sensible fibre has been violently agitated, he had some trouble to coax himself into a slumber. Besides, he had lain down with his head so full of scenes of brigands, that he soon fell into a state of hallucination, which was betrayed by the agitation of the bed-clothes.

At this moment, and by a coincidence which the position of Servigny sufficiently explains, disordered as he was by the raging of a burning fever, he asks for drink; he calls:

"Sylvain! Sylvain!"

Sylvain, still a prey to the same hallucination, frightened at hearing so near him a strange voice, imagines he has a whole legion of brigands at his heels.

"Ah! my God!" he exclaims, "assistance! confiteor Deo; the guard, the guard; in nomine Patris, et Filei; mea culpâ, me maximâ culpâ. M. le Curé; Marguerité; Grand Guillaume; help! in

our good founder, pray for us, to our Seigneur, that he will preserve our *raba*, nostra castagna, nostra fama, alleline!"

N.B.—The "raba," is a species of turnip radish, much relished by the peasants, and which they eat without taking the trouble to cook them.

manus tuas domine, they are murdering me. Ah! *gentlemen !* don't kill me, I am a poor man—grace, grace!"

To be brief, Sylvain made such an uproar, and such exertions, that, exhausted, he tumbled out of bed and rolled on to the floor.

M. le Curé, justly alarmed at the cries of his domestic, hastens to his room, and finds the poor Sylvain more dead than alive. The curé questions Servigny, who gives him, in a few words, an account of the matter; the worthy curate then returns to Sylvain; calls him—"Sylvain, Sylvain, are you wounded, or dead? come, speak; don't you recognise me?"

Sylvain at length opens his eyes. "Are they gone?" he said; "ah! M. le Curé, what brigands; what countenances. There were more than a dozen—but 'twas especially the big crippled one, that caused me the greatest fright. Dieu de Dieu! what a sword, and what moustaches! never mind, I well remarked him, the villain! but patience, I shall have my revenge."

"My good friend," said the curate, with mildness, "you are, at present, a victim of the wanderings of your brain. See, every thing is quiet here but yourself; every door and every window is closed: how do you think the brigands could enter your room—where there is nothing to carry off—without your neighbour seeing them as well as yourself? Recover from your illusion, calm your spirits, and go to bed. I will take my pistols, and guard the door; you can sleep undisturbed for the rest of the night. This is quite enough of it for once."

This short, but serious allocution of the worthy curé, produced its effects upon the weak and superstitious Sylvain, who, accustomed besides to great docility towards so good a master, received every one of his words as oracles. All resumed its quietness, and the curé finished the rest of the night in his apartment.

Towards seven o'clock, the worthy curate entering to obtain the news as to his patient; Sylvain, who was awake, answered that he slept still.

"No, my father, I do not sleep," said Servigny, "indeed I find myself much better since you received me in your holy mansion, and I am become the object of your skilful attention. I know not how to prove to you my gratitude, except by begging you to listen to me in confession."

Touched as well as surprised at the religious sentiments of the stranger, the curé hastened to acquiesce in his desire. Upon a sign from him, the domestic retired, and when they were alone, Servigny glided out of bed, and threw himself at the feet of the venerable ecclesiastic, who, restraining him, requested him to keep his bed; but Servigny insisted.

"No, father," he said, "'tis at your feet so great a sinner ought to remain; deign to listen to me."

For more than an hour the unhappy Servigny remained kneeling before the venerable curé, without the latter once interrupting him. When he had at length finished the recital of all that we have read, the curate ordered him to bed, and listen to him:

"All that you have just confided to me, my dear child,' he said, "excites in me the greatest interest. If, as I wish to believe, you have told me the truth, I promise you aid and protection. If, on the contrary, you have deceived me, I shall follow that which charity prescribes to me with regard to you; I shall restore you to health, and

soon after dismiss you. You can hope for **nothing** beyond that."

"I have not deceived you, I am incapable of **it**, my father! you may be assured of it; all that I have told you is the truth, the exact truth."

"That is sufficient; be tranquil, and rely upon me," replied the worthy curate.

Leaving the chamber of Servigny, he called Sylvain and Marguerite.

"My children," he said to them, "no one must be informed of what has passed here to-night. It is necessary to repair, at the same time, a great misfortune and a great injustice, in which you will become accomplices if you permit yourselves an unworthy indiscretion. Promise me then, by our holy patron, that you will preserve an inviolable secrecy."

"I swear it by Saint Marsault," said Marguerite.

"And I also," said Sylvain, with an eagerness that surprised the curé, for he knew that discretion was not the ruling virtue of his domestic. But, however, never was a promise better kept, so much did the honest Sylvain dread the pleasantries which he must have submitted to on the subject of the apparition of the big cripple, whom he had so well recognised in the course of this same night.

The secret was thus religiously kept on both sides, and from this moment, Sylvain not only addressed no more questions to Servigny, but redoubled his attentions, and seemed to have conceived a sort of respect for him.

Servigny, surrounded with comforts, and the consolations of the curate, and in his absence, of Sylvain and Marguerite, who attended upon him constantly, soon recovered his health. The curate, who was desirous of ascertaining the truth of the revelations of his protégé, wrote to every place from whence he might obtain any information; the answers were all in favour of Servigny; he was enchanted at it. At length, when he had received the letter of the procureur-general of Aix, he called Servigny into his cabinet, and thus addressed him:

"You have told me the truth; I am convinced that you are only guilty of great imprudence. I have promised to save you, and I wish to keep my word. Here is a passport, by means of which you can pass to the East Indies; your passage is paid. Favour me by accepting these two hundred francs, to assist you on arriving there, and trust in Providence. You will find in this trunk some clothes, some books, and nearly all that is requisite for a young man in your position."

Servigny was so sensible of this noble conduct, that he could only thank his benefactor by a torrent of tears. "Yes," repeated the kind curate, "I have found means of passing you to the East Indies; I have recommended you to a man of wealth, the captain of a vessel which will transport you to these rich countries. Make yourself useful on board; I am certain that by your good conduct, and your education, you will be enabled to obtain a place there, and procure a comfortable existence."

We shall not follow Servigny in his voyage; all that it is necessary to know is, that he arrived safe.

Neither does it enter into our plan to imitate certain inventors of romance, whose borrowed information consists of maps and collections of voyages to compose their descriptions of countries, and productions which they have never seen. At the same time, that we may not be taxed with inability on this point, and also to identify our readers with the different fortunes which attended our hero in these distant realms, we shall rapidly sketch, with the assistance of our memory, the principal features which distinguish them from our own.

Of all the quarters of the globe, Asia is the most remarkable for its extent, the number of its inhabitants, and the importance of its historical reminiscences. It would require whole volumes to describe the superb regions which develop themselves to the south of the Himalaya, of those rendered so celebrated by ancient traditions, and which lie along the rivers Euphrates, the Tigris, and the Jordan, and the Mediterranean; as also of the regions, still more extensive, which lie to the south and east of the great level of Central Asia. These magnificent regions have been, from the commencement of history, the object of expeditions of all the great conquerors, and it is by these means that we have partly received our religions, our sciences, and our civilization.

The intellectual state of these people presents a phenomenon which is perhaps reserved for phrenology alone to explain in a lucid manner. In fact, we may reckon in this part of the world nearly thirty different dialects written and spoken, and yet they do not possess a literature. If, as it is asserted, the size of the brain indicates a corresponding intellectual capacity, must we not conclude from it, that the absence of literature is a consequence of the slight development of the brain of these people, their heads being generally one-third less in size than those of Europeans.

The religious systems are not less numerous than the languages, and we may safely assert that Asia is the domain of fables, of useless dreams, and flighty imaginations. Thus, what extraordinary variations, what a deplorable diversity is observed in the manner in which human reason, deprived of guides, and left to its own inspirations, has satisfied this first want of ancient societies, religion! If Judaism and Christianity were born in Asia, if there are but few truths that have been taught in this part of the world, it may be asserted in return, that there are but few extravagances which are not honoured, or have not sprung up there. The superstition of the Sabeans, the worship of fire and other elements, Islamism, the polytheism of the Brahmins, that of the Boudhists, and the followers of the great Lama, the worship of the sky, and of ancestors, of spirits and demons; and so many secondary, or but little known sects, outvie each other in mad and even atrocious dogmas, give but a feeble idea of the astonishing variety presented by the religious beliefs of the people of Asia. And remember, that we do not bring into the account the different sects which the English have imported there, in order that we may not surcharge the picture by a religious Babel to which no other country in the world presents a parallel.

It is hardly necessary to remark, that this multitude of sects, joined to the manners, the ancient customs, fixed ideas, and errors, are, with regard to power, so many shackles, more embarrassing than written stipulations, and from which they cannot free themselves, without being exposed to perish by violence. In all the rest, despotism is so much the more intolerable, that if the prince ceases to raise his arm, if he cannot annihilate, on the very instant, those who exercise the highest functions, and frequently substitute their own ty-

ranny for his, all is lost; for the support of government, which is fear, no longer existing, the people have no other guarantee, there is nothing but oppressors. In fine, we cannot speak without shuddering of the monstrous governments of this part of the world.

As to the morals, nothing is more effeminate, more corrupt; and no doubt owing to the climate, for it is remarked that the native of Europe soon loses here the hereditary courage of his parents. On the other side, the women pass their time in supineness, idleness, and luxury; being occupied the whole day either in having their bodies rubbed by young slaves, which is one of their chief delights, or in smoking the tobacco of the country, which is so mild, that they can consume it from morning till night. The least vicious apply themselves to needle work, which they perfect admirably. Adultery is there punished with death, which, however, does not prevent the women, in certain countries, on meeting a man, having him seized, and threatening to denounce him to their husband, if he treats them with disdain. They steal into a man's bed, and if he refuses them, threaten to allow themselves to be surprised in the fact, which leaves no other alternative but the accomplishment of their desires, or a frightful and inevitable death.

And although polygamy is pushed to its utmost limits, we shall add, that the men, to extend the circle of their sensual enjoyments, do not hesitate to outrage nature!

The subject we are treating of, induces us to give a short notice of the city of Benares, for which Servigny had taken his passage, after which we shall continue our history without interruption.

Benares, built on the borders of the river Ganges, and which may be regarded as the ecclesiastical metropolis, or the Rome of India, is very large and populous, there being nearly 650,000 inhabitants. It has been from time immemorial the principal seat of the Brahminical literature, and has a reputation for holiness *par excellence*. The houses are very lofty, none have less than two floors; the majority have three, and others in great numbers, five and six, and in general richly decorated. The temples are very numerous; most of them very small, disposed like niches in the angles of the walls, and under the wing of some grand mansion. Many are completely covered with flowers, animals, palm branches, sculptured with elegance, and admirably finished. The inhabitants ornament the fronts of their houses with cameos, painted with the liveliest colours, representing men, women, bulls, elephants, gods, goddesses, with their different shapes and attributes. Bulls of all ages, consecrated to Siva, as tame and familiar as the domestic dog, circulate freely in the streets, whilst troops of monkeys, sacred to Hanoumân, climb over the roofs of the houses and temples, or steal with impunity from the shops of the fruiterers and confectioners. The high reputation for sanctity enjoyed by this city, attracts to it, from all parts of India, an immense number of pilgrims and beggars.

We have said that it was to Benares that Servigny had taken his passage. Arrived in a country so new to him, and to which he had no recommendation, he endeavoured at first to make use of his talents; but there, as elsewhere, it is difficult to inspire confidence in those who dispose of fortune. The inhabitants are generally hostile to strangers, whom they consider as so many parasites come to enrich themselves at their expense; or as criminals who have fled their country, in order to escape from the hands of justice. They have, besides, been so frequently taken in by adventurers, whom they have received and provided with good situations; they have so often witnessed the violation of hospitality, their women seduced, their daughters and treasures carried off, that a legitimate sentiment of repulsion was but too well deserved.

These acts of ingratitude, unfortunately too often renewed, had thus shut every door against Europeans, who, like Servigny, sought their existence in the career of labour or employments; it was even very difficult, not to say impossible, to procure admission into any house, under any circumstances, even for the most menial employment. The money given him by the charitable curate was all that Servigny possessed, and this could not carry him very far; as an additional misfortune he fell ill, and in a very short time he found himself absolutely destitute of resources. In this extremity he was forced to work as a mere journeyman, nor did he obtain constant employ in this way, from his being so weak and little accustomed to this sort of labour. What he earned was barely sufficient to procure him the common necessaries indispensable for the preservation of life.

At length, after a sojourn of three or four months, and by perseverance and exertion of all kinds, he contrived to make himself useful. An under steward, by whom he had been often employed, had remarked him, and interested himself about him; and commissioned him to take an account of the work executed in a shawl manufactory which belonged to a rich English nabob, in whose service he was. Servigny acquitted himself with talent and promptitude in his situation, and his superior was satisfied with him; but his evil destiny would not allow him to remain long in a position where, at least, he was sheltered from want. A workman, a native of the country, and whom Servigny had replaced in the confidence of the steward, had conceived against him a sentiment of jealousy so strong, that in concert with some of his comrades, he resolved upon the destruction of the young man. To contrive it more surely, they worked secretly upon the nabob, who, not being able to see through it, failed not to receive these false reports. In addition, the train had been so skilfully laid, the proofs seemed so evident, so well combined one with the other, that both were dismissed without being heard. The intendant of the nabob, who could not endure strangers, and especially Frenchmen, because a traveller from this nation had recently carried off his wife, whom he worshipped, and at the same time the greatest part of his treasures, contributed not a little to the fatal decision which again plunged Servigny into misery.

In consequence of this dismissal, Servigny found himself worse off than ever, for his enemies hastened to publish it, and to add to it all the wicked inventions to which their preceding conduct was only the prelude.

The steward soon quitted the country. As to the unfortunate Servigny, every heart and every door was shut against him, so strongly did prejudice work against him. And what more convinced them of his being culpable, was the fact, that the nabob, under whom he had been employed, was generally known as a kind man, sensible, generous, and fond of pardoning. The offence was much less excused, as the person offended did not deserve it. But although Servigny was in the greatest distress, so much so, that he often went two or three days without the necessary means of existence, he could not resolve to seek public charity; rather than fall so low, he preferred living by the precarious means of the commission intrusted to him of carrying letters and packets. How many times did Servigny regret a prison life! there, at least, he found amongst his companions a few compassionate hearts to soften his misfortune, whilst here, free, he was an object of contempt to every one. Was not this the utmost limit of opprobrium?

In order, therefore, to escape so many humiliations, he was in the habit, when in his power, of penetrating the vast forests in the neighbourhood of Benares. There, forgotten by all, and isolating himself from the rest of the world, the productions of nature, so luxurious, so magnificent in this privileged land, by giving a different current to his thoughts, became for him the subjects of profound meditations. Indeed, who can contemplate, cold and unmoved, the immense *basbab*, the giant of the forest, a true vegetable colossus, the trunk of which attains twenty-five feet in diameter! it is said that it requires several thousand years for this tree to attain to this monstrous size. This immense trunk, crowned by numerous branches extending horizontally, remarkable for their denseness, and still more for their length, which is from 50 to 60 feet, is not less so for its roots, which intersect the ground to a distance of 150 or 160 feet. Next we view the catalpa, whose trunk is less graceful, but whose ample foliage and handsome flowers of white and spotted with purple, produces so beautiful an effect; the nopal, the date-tree, the grave and noble chesnut-tree, at present so cultivated in Europe; the daphné indica, whose sweet odour perfumes the atmosphere; the manguer, the guayava-tree, the darien, and especially the mang, the fruit of which is so delicious; in a word, this vegetation which displays the luxury and majesty usually presented in the tropical climates, when seconded by the most powerful agents, as the nature of the soil and moisture of the atmosphere.

Servigny left with reluctance the bosom of these vast forests, where, according to the ancient expression, he was never less alone than when in solitude. He only returned to Benares as seldom as the necessity of renewing his provisions obliged him; but the moment he had satisfied this imperious law of existence, he returned to his cherished solitudes.

He had discovered a place to which he principally attached himself, and gave himself up to his enchanting reveries, it was a small rock, steep and difficult of access, one of those abrupt contrivances of a soil so fruitful in pleasing contrasts. A bouquet of odoriferous shrubs crowned the head of this little pyramid, and there, he could not only meditate without dreading the teeth of ferocious animals, but it seemed to him he could also brave another deluge. He had found it very difficult to climb this steep rock, but having explored it in every way, he discovered a small spring, whose fresh and limpid waters had given birth to some climbing plants, which he had made use of on his first ascension, and by which he continued to assist himself, every time he renewed his visit.

At first sight, nothing could be more wild than this insulated spot. Still, upon regarding it with attention, a certain arrangement in the fragments of rock which carpeted the bed of the spring we have mentioned, the remains of posts planted here and there, induced him to believe, that habitations had existed there at some former period. This supposition encouraged him to make a further search, and to consider these vestiges as marks which had been placed there with a design which he could not yet clearly explain to himself. After passing from one obstacle to another, foraging and sounding every where the intestines of a thick turf which covered the top of the rock, the traces of an ancient path, partly concealed by briars and bushes, confirmed him in the opinion that this small level had formerly been inhabited, but that the buildings had been consumed by fire. He was in the transports of a discovery which for many ages, perhaps, had escaped all who had visited this distant part of the forest. From the summit of this rock he looked over an immense country; a thousand different thoughts assailed him by turns; perhaps, as a modern Robinson Crusoe, it was reserved for him to give life to these remains of a civilization destroyed by the scythe of Time, or by the fury of parties; but to commence as a Robinson, he wanted a Friday, and where could he discover so faithful a companion in a country that treated him as a veritable Paria.

At length he retired, taking every precaution possible for marking the spot. Returned to the city, to the old woman who gave him an asylum for a small contribution, he fell asleep, cradled in the dreams which had reference to the project he had for a while conceived, of establishing himself on the summit of this rock; he contemplated himself surrounded with every necessary, and even the comforts of life. Unluckily, he awoke too soon to the painful reality.

Still, although he could not positively decide as to the result of his discovery, he continued to occupy himself with it. But to erect buildings without tools, impossible! Defend himself without arms, also impossible! He commences then to put by a few savings, by means of which he can instal himself with some provisions, and thereby assist his enterprise. After succeeding in this project, he borrows from his hostess all the tools she can dispense with: a hatchet, spade, a hoe, a pickaxe, and an old spear half broken. He determines to commence, by exploring the soil to a certain depth; afterwards, according to circumstances, he intends giving his labours a larger field.

Departed with these instruments, which he transports to the spot at different journeys, as well as his provisions, he makes no delay in commencing work. The creeping-plants once removed from the soil, he obtains a proof that the cabins had been burnt; he discovers even human bones, half consumed, as well as fragments of animals, which his knowledge in paleontology informed him belonged to the oviparous and viviparous races. But his enthusiasm was at its height, when, after sounding the excavations, he discovered a fossil, which, in its character, resembled the megathorium, a vertebrated animal reconstructed by the celebrated Cuvier, the race of which has disappeared from our globe since its last revolution. It required nothing further to persuade Servigny that this rock, so long disdained, forgotten, had been the theatre of scenes equally worthy the study of the naturalist and geologist. Eager to arrive at results more immediately necessary, he reserved for another time the sequel

of his scientific investigations. For the present, he confined himself to erecting a shelter from the inclemency of the seasons, and which also secured him against the attack of wild beasts, so formidable in these countries.

He had already laboured some time in the execution of his project, when one day, and at a moment when he least expected it, his attention was suddenly excited by the sound of hasty steps; it was a man—pale, exhausted, covered with blood—endeavouring to escape the pursuit of a tiger of great size, which was close upon him. The unfortunate man had nothing to defend himself with against his redoubtable adversary, but the barrel of his gun, the stock having disappeared in the struggle which had just taken place between them; he had also lost his couteau de chasse, the belt and sheath only remaining. The tiger was wounded, and foaming with rage, and would inevitably seize his prey, and immolate him! Servigny, himself frightened, rose suddenly, seized his spear, and put himself on the defensive. The stranger, surprised, arrests himself at this unexpected sight—the tiger itself seemed to hesitate; but the time was precious; and although the costume of Servigny gave but little confidence to the stranger, he did not hesitate to unite himself with him, to give battle to the horrible monster.

"Fear nothing," exclaimed Servigny, who perceived his hesitation; "although poor, I am honest, and I know the duties your position imposes upon me!"

During this short time, the animal had regained its strength, and appeared to be deciding, with its eyes, upon which of his adversaries he should first rush; but our two combatants had intrenched themselves in the entrance of a cavity, which, by protecting their retreat, rendered their defence more easy, and at the same time more formidable.

All at once, the fury of the tiger knew no bounds, and he threw himself with the rapidity of lightning upon his enemies; he attacks them by turn—upsets them—presses them; but in consequence of his savage instinct, 'tis the stranger whom he pursues with the most fury. They both, in vain, increase their blows; he escapes them with a bound, or by a feint, which exhausts them in useless efforts. Servigny preserves his sang froid, and also makes a good use of his strength and address. The stranger, on the contrary, is soon exhausted from the blood he had lost since the commencement of the combat. He is seized and thrown down by the infuriated animal; Servigny himself is wounded in the thigh, in an effort to disengage the stranger. A struggle now ensues between Servigny and the tiger. In vain did Servigny, by a first blow, wound him in the flank; the animal retires, and then rushes madly at his adversary. The latter, his lance in rest, attends him with a firm foot, and with another blow aimed at the head, destroys an eye; but the more wounds he receives, the greater his rage becomes.

This diversion had allowed the stranger to recover his feet; he armed himself with the hatchet, which was luckily within reach, and determined once more, by engaging in the struggle, to share the danger of his companion; but his blows failed from weakness, and did but little good. At length—stunned, exhausted—the animal drops upon the ground, which he colours with his black and smoking blood. Our two heroes believe his death certain; but, at the moment they run to finish him, with one impetuous bound he springs up, and flies at the stranger with redoubled fury. There would have been an end of him, if the danger had not exalted the courage of Servigny to its highest pitch. Uniting every effort, and adding dexterity to strength, he plunges his spear into the breast of the animal, and buries it nearly in his body.

The weakened animal still retains some strength and fury; he attempts with his mouth to draw forth the instrument of his torture—vain efforts! He then turns upon himself; he rolls, he writhes, and in his blind fury, throws himself upon the stones imbedded in the arena, which he bites, and reddens with his ensanguined mouth.

His dying hour had sounded; but he still continued his loud roaring, which the echoes of the forest repeated a hundred-fold; but they lessened, as his strength became exhausted by the loss of blood; a horrible rattling in his throat soon followed; and at last, he yields his last breath.

Our two combatants can hardly believe their eyes; 'tis not till after they have turned over the monster, now motionless, that they are quite convinced of their victory. After a moment's repose and silence, to calm their feelings, the stranger rises, throws himself into the arms of Servigny, presses him with great emotion, and proclaims him his liberator.

"I am indebted to you for my life," he said, "whoever you are, rely upon the proofs of my gratitude."

Servigny hastens to thank him, and observing that he is very weak, and suffering from the effects of the combat, he makes him swallow a few drops of tafia. The cordial restores him a little strength, and allows him to assist Servigny, who forgot his own wounds to attend to those of his companion.

Servigny had also felt the effects of the formidable teeth of their enemy; but he was less dangerously wounded than the stranger. The latter had received several deep and severe bites, which occasioned him great suffering, and prevented him almost from moving. Servigny, after partly undressing him, bathed his wounds with a few drops of tafia, which, for a moment, redoubled his agony; but he soon experienced a sensible relief. The kind and respectful manner in which Servigny attended the stranger, produced in the latter a desire of knowing this man, sent from heaven to extricate him from the greatest danger he had ever ran; but it was neither the time nor the place to put any questions to him.

The stranger, supported by Servigny, had much difficulty in descending from the platform of the rock, in which the least inclined places presented serious obstacles even to the most active men. Having reached the bottom without accident, they directed their steps slowly towards the town through the forest, but the strength of the stranger soon failed him; he fainted! All the efforts of Servigny to arouse him were in vain. What was to be done in such a case? it was already late, and the night had long since closed in. Fatigued and wounded himself, would he find strength to carry the individual whose life he had saved, and whom he must serve a second time to complete his noble devotion? His anxiety was at its height! He dreaded every moment to see his unfortunate companion expire in his arms; but could he abandon him in this state, to seek assistance in the town, which, alas! was still more than a league distant? His resolution, his courage, rose with the danger; he dexterously raised the body of the stranger, placed it on his shoulders, and, despite the severe sufferings from his wounds, he threaded his way towards the town with a firm and steady step, glorying in his precious burden.

He had arrived within a few hundred yards, when he found himself suddenly surrounded by a small squadron of armed men, composed of sepoys on night-duty. He is arrested, taken for a robber, and on the point of being ill-treated, but upon a remark of the chief of the patrol, they carry him before the magistrate appointed for the Safety Service. There Servigny deposits his burden; but scarcely had these men examined it, than they exclaimed: "'tis the Honourable Sir Edward Lambton, who left this morning to hunt in the forest. What has happened to him then?" Servigny then narrated succinctly the different circumstances we have reported, and each congratulated him for his noble conduct. They hastily procured a litter, placed the wounded man upon it, and carried him with all possible care to Beauchamps, a country house he possessed at a short distance. Physicians are soon at hand, and our two patients, by turns, carefully attended to, and their wounds healed. Sir Edward still remaining in a swoon, was bled to some extent; at length he opens his eyes, and shows unequivocal signs that he has recovered his senses. Yet, and before he can pronounce a word, his looks seem to indicate that he is in search for some one. At length he recovers his speech, and the first use he makes of it, is to inquire for the stranger, "where is his preserver?" They reply, that "he is in an adjoining apartment;" but on a sign he makes, a bed is arranged by the side of his own, and Servigny is carried there. Sir Edward takes his hands, covers them with kisses, bestows upon him his sincere and heartfelt thanks, and informs him that he must remain with him for that he will not allow of a separation. Tears of gratitude flow in abundance; and to him it appears, that this gratitude is the memory of the heart.

The recovery of Servigny made such rapid progress, that at the end of a week, he could sit up for an hour or two every day; but Sir Edward's was of longer duration. Two physicians were constantly at his side, to observe the progress of his malady, which at length yielded to skilful efforts; and at the end of a month, he was completely out of danger, and Servigny perfectly re-established. It was then that, pressed by questions, the latter recounted to Sir Edward all his adventures (except his condemnation.) When he arrived at the circumstance of his entrance into the shawl manufactory, and of his having been dismissed under the suspicion, in consort with the steward, of having robbed the chief of the establishment.

"Heavens!" exclaimed Sir Edward; "'tis you, brave and generous youth, that they have thus treated; and 'tis I that have been cruel enough to subject you to such indignity! No, you were not guilty, I have been grossly deceived. A thief is incapable of such noble sentiments!"

Servigny could not recover his surprise; but, when he remembered that he had known but the steward and intendant of the shawl manufactory in which he had been employed; that he had neither seen nor heard mention the proprietor of the establishment; all that at first appeare obscure in the exclamation of Sir Edward, wa explained to him; he found in him a kind and generous master, and to increase his happiness he had saved his life.

"All is for the best in the best of all possible worlds," said Sir Edward one day to Servigny; "for

SALVADOR IN THE CELL.

in fact, if enlightened as to the manœuvres which produced your dismissal from my establishment, I had punished the cowardly authors of them, it is certain I should not have encountered you so apropos, to save me from the teeth and the gripe of that devil of a tiger, whose remembrance still makes my hair stand on end with horror!"

"'Tis, however, true," replied Servigny; "and it is another proof of my capricious destiny, to be indebted to this ferocious animal, for an occasion to justify myself in my past conduct; and to obtain, at length, the assurance of a protection, which my long and faithful services would never, perhaps, have acquired for me."

CHAPTER XXIX.

THE ROBBER'S MANSION.

ON the road to Normandy, between Neuilly and Nanterre, there exists a house of rather mean appearance, bearing the number 2.

This house is the first from the village of Nanterre, from which it is distant but a few hundred yards.

Above the entrance-door of this house is exposed a sign, upon which an imitator of the Charlets and Bellangers has painted a cuirassier, a hussar, and a lancer, of the imperial army, with these words: "The Three Brothers."

Some of our readers may probably have remarked a similar indice, or above the door of a wine merchant, whose establishment is situated in Paris, at the entrance of the street Beauregard, near the gate of Saint-Denis; the reason of this is simply, that the house we have mentioned belongs to Sieur Favre, one of the ancients who serves Bacchus, after having served Mars with honour and glory, and is nothing more than a country edition of the house in Paris.

If, wishing to visit the house in question, you request an inhabitant of the neighbourhood to indicate to you the cabaret of the *Three Brothers*, it is possible he will not know how to reply to you; but if you ask him for the *Maison des Voleurs*, he will inform you at once of the shortest road to arrive at it.

Do not fancy, however, that the cabaret of the Three Brothers, or rather the Robber's Mansion, since it is under this title that the establishment is generally known, is one of those places we must pass without visiting; the Robber's Mansion is an honest cabaret, kept by a very honest host, and frequented solely by honest drunkards; from whence then comes the name somewhat inauspicious by which we know it?

It is that not long ago this house—which served as a retreat to the famous Capahut, chief of the band of chauffeurs and assassins which desolated, in the years three and four of the republic, the neighbourhood of Paris*—was still, within a few years, inhabited by a notorious assassin and his family, of whom the author of this work has spoken

in his memoirs; this man, who has received at the place publique of Rouen, the just punishment for his crimes, had converted the house at present kept by the Sieur Favre into a worthy appendage of the auberge of Peyrabeillo, of notorious memory; woe to the traveller who, at that time, entered the auberge of Bienvenu—he left it a corpse, if his exterior promised to the band of assassins directed by Cornu, called *la pere tranquille*, a considerable booty.

The manner of proceeding of these assassins was very simple, and invariably succeeded, especially with individuals who suspected nothing.

All the rooms of the auberge of Bienvenu, furnished very simply, contained beds very neat, and quite good enough to produce in the travellers a quick repose, which the fatigues of the day had rendered necessary. At the head of, and above these beds was a movable panel, which opened from without, and fell inwards; and which might easily escape the observations of travellers, as it was half-concealed by the curtains of the bed. When the traveller was asleep, this panel was mysteriously opened by the assassins, who dropped it upon their victim, in such a way that he found himself stifled without the ability to utter a single cry, or oppose the least resistance; the corpse, despoiled of everything which might cause it to be recognised, was carried to a distance by the head of the family, who had a car especially made for this purpose, and whose frequent journeys did not appear suspicious, as he exercised, actually, the profession of a hawker.

At the period in which the principal events of this history took place, the assassin proprietors of the auberge of Bienvenu enjoyed the best reputation in the country. They vaunted everywhere the honesty and goodness of the father—rare qualities in a hawker—the devotion of the mother, the industry of the two daughters, the activity of the son; and thus it continued, till the day when the police, at length placed in the track of this nest of assassins, by a crime committed in the neighbourhood of Versailles, appeared one fine morning, to the great astonishment of the inhabitants of Neuilly, Nanterre, and the adjacent villages, and seized the whole brood of these scelerats, who, as we have observed, expiated their numerous crimes in the market place of Versailles.

From the period of that event, the name of the Maison des Voleurs has attached to the property in which the Sieur Favre honourably exercises his commerce.*

It is into this house, at the time it was still occupied by the individuals we are speaking of, that we are about to introduce the reader.

In the lower room of one of these small houses used as cabarets and auberges, so frequently met with, as if by accident, on the roads in the neighbourhood of the capital, and which serve as a caravansary to the tribe of travellers, three women, by the doubtful light of a lamp of a secular form, were occupied in preparing the evening repast. The room they were in served both as a kitchen and dining-room; everything was neat, and in the most perfect order; the stoves, upon which were some saucepans, the emanations from which agreeably tickled the organ olfactory, were polished with a lustre which had not a little contributed to bring the hotel of Bienvenu into reputation among the postilions, cattle-dealers, waggoners, mountebanks, and other individuals of the same

---

* Capahut and his accomplices terminated their execrable career on the Place de Grève, in the fourth year of the republic. We shall here mention to our readers a fact, the reason for which escapes us; and this is, that the dens which existed more than fifty years ago, are at this day what they then were, viz., places of reunion of malefactors; there seems to exist in these spots an attraction which invites fresh generations to this gaping Vesuvius, which has ingulfed their predecessors. To the band of Father Cornu, in the Maison des Voleurs, succeeded that of Blaise *le petit Christ*, called Sans Pitie, whose crimes terrified for a long time the department of the Seine and the Seine et Orse.

* Historical.

stamp, all of them great natural consumers, and great boasters by profession.

The three women in question were seated round a small low table, placed in a distant corner of the room, the neatness of which yielded in nothing to the brightest and best ordered kitchen in Holland. The eldest might be about forty or forty-two years of age; she was tall and strongly built, with a fresh and regular countenance; her eyes were blue, and adorned with long black and silky lashes; her nose slightly turned up; her mouth small, and improved by thin and rosy lips; her waist was round, fine, and well turned; a large bosom, whose apparent contours agreeably excited the visual organ, without in the least intruding upon decency, completed an ensemble of a very agreeable woman. Her dress was that of an aubergiste of the environs of Rouen, or rather of Lower Normandy, though her head-dress seemed to indicate the country of Caux.

Near the latter, on the right, was a girl of twenty-two years, of a strong constitution, although thin; her regular figure, vermilion mouth, which showed to advantage thirty-two pearls of admirable purity; her brown complexion; her black eyes, surmounted by two thick arches of the same colour; her ebony hair; all this indicated an energy which is not the habitual share of her sex.

At last the third, who was on the left, appeared about eighteen years of age; she had fiery red hair, a long thin face, upon which the remains of the small-pox appeared in all their eclat Her eyes were, in truth, large, handsome, and lively; but in revenge, the mouth, which was horribly extensive, was absolutely destitute of teeth. Her angular and scraggy shape, her large and deformed feet, her strong and bony hands, the whole ensemble of her person reminded one involuntarily of the witches of Macbeth; or rather that of Teniers, in his extraordinary picture of the temptation of Saint Anthony.

This female trio worked with much industry and in silence, which is not often the habit of the sex; but the violent storm, which had just burst forth, had suspended their gossip, and introduced fear into every heart. This silence was suddenly interrupted by the cuckoo of the wooden pendulum placed in a corner of the room.

"Already half-past nine," said the mother, "and no one yet! Providence, no doubt, will not permit us to-night to make choublanc. This is six days we have touched nothing."

"Indeed it is very strange," said the brunette; "all the men who have slept here were poor; 'tis downright ill luck."

"I think," said red hair, "that you missed the chance the other night."

"What, the old fellow that appeared like a beggar at chateaus and farms ?"

"Yes, he had a belt round his waist; it was not empty; I ogled it well."

"Why did'nt you tell father?"

At this moment a flash of lightning entered the darkest part of the room. "Stop, the storm is not over," said the mother. Immediately a violent clap of thunder was heard.

"What weather," said red hair; "it's not likely to bring us trade."

"Who knows," said the eldest ? Do you remember the goldsmith who travelled on foot to save his purse, and who came here and supped and slept? the chicken was fat, heim ?"

' Amen!'

A second clap of thunder nearly shook the house. "Holy mother of God," said the mother, making the sign of the cross, "have pity upon us! Notre Dame de bon Secours, protect us!" Saying this she opened a cupboard, took out a bottle, and a small branch of consecrated box-tree; she then sprinkled the room, and also her daughters, repeating in a loud voice the litany of the Holy Virgin.

The storm having at length somewhat abated, the three women placed themselves again at the small table, and the conversation resumed its course.

"If we have been idle at home," said the mother, "we must hope that the work at the church of Colombe will be finished without interruption; the weather has favoured our governor, and by this time the church is sacked."

"I do not know why," replied the brunette; "but I have not the same idea, daronne; last night I dreamt of cats, 'tis a sign of danger."

"Do you believe in dreams, you ?" said the youngest. "What can dreams do? Nothing."

"Listen," said the mother; "I hear a cry."

"Stay, it's true, 'tis a man's voice."

"I'll go and see, and tell you the reason of it," said the masculine brunette.

"Take the vingt-deux* in case of accidents," said the mother.

The brunette soon returned to announce that a man, a horse, and a cabriolet had fallen into one of the reservoirs in the road-side; and that the traveller was buried in such a manner, under the head of the cabriolet, that he could not extricate himself.

"'Tis Providence who sends him to us!" exclaimed the mother. "A lantern quick, let us hasten to assist the poor man."

"Yes," said the youngest, "let us go to the assistance of this honest man, and try to bring him to the Hotel de Bienvenu to stop the night."

They all three started, and arriving at the place where the accident had happened, they soon disengaged the horse, who got on his legs with some trouble; it was then easy to uncase the traveller, and extricate him from the cabriolet. He was bruised and covered with contusions in every part of his body, but principally his head. At length he was brought to the house; a fire was quickly prepared to dry his garments, which were soaked with water, blood, and mud, and also to warm him, for he was shivering with cold.

"God be praised," said the mother, "you are safe. Marguerité, run quickly and get the Sunday clothes of your father, and we will let this brave monsieur change, for he is as wet as a sop. As we have been in time to recover him, we must not leave our good work incomplete."

"Yes, madame," replied the traveller, "without you I should have been stifled to death under the capote of my cabriolet. I owe you my life; but I trust you will believe that I shall acknowledge your praiseworthy conduct." And, as if struck by some remembrance, he exclaimed: "Ah! my God! my good woman, I have forgotten to take from my cabriolet, a small box, which was under my feet, and which encloses some valuable things."

"Gold, perhaps?" inquired the mother.

"No, not gold, but equivalent; bank cheques, payable to bearer."

Marguerité, who at this moment brought some garments of her father, undertook the mission with

* Knife.

her sister. During the absence of the two girls, Servigny, (the unlucky traveller who had entered the auberge of Bienvenu was no other than our hero,) changed his clothes, and his own were placed before the large fire to dry.

The two sisters soon returned, carrying the small box, which, in comparison with its size, was very heavy. Servigny appeared satisfied at seeing it again in his possession; he placed it near him, took a glass of cogniac which they offered him; and after his wounds had been washed and bathed with eau de Boule de Nancy, he felt somewhat relieved; he then inquired for his horse and cabriolet, and was told that Jean Louis, the stable-boy, had contrived to bring them both to the house; that the horse had broken both knees, that the shafts of the cabriolet were broken, the head damaged; but that all this was nothing, and could be easily repaired.

Servigny remained in the clothes of the proprietor of the house whilst his own were drying; and the better to show how sensible he was of the kind attentions shown him by his hostesses, he became communicative beyond all prudent limits. Amongst other things, Servigny told them he had arrived from India to purchase a large mansion at Paris, and a country-house in the environs. At this moment the clock struck eleven; the hostess, observing that our traveller seemed to have forgotten the events of the evening and recovered his spirits, proposed to him to take some soup, and eat one of the chickens in the pan, from which the odour mounted so agreeably to the nose, when Jean Louis entered, to receive the orders of Servigny; the latter asked him if he could not conveniently obtain the assistance of a veterinary surgeon, to attend to his horse, and the wheelwright to repair his cabriolet.

.. "Send for both of them," said Servigny; "I shall depend upon you, but there is no immediate hurry."

Jean Louis, who was no other than the son of the aubergiste, Bienvenu, retired; but returned directly, under the pretext of obtaining a candle for his lantern. He turned his face towards his mother's ear, and thinking he was not understood, he said, in a half whisper, but loud enough to be heard by Servigny:

"There has been some danger; the affair at the church has failed; father is returned."

Servigny, who had perfectly understood the slang terms in which this was uttered, had some difficulty to repress a sudden movement of surprise and dread.

"Alone and unarmed, what defence can I oppose," he said to himself, "to the expert villains in whose den I have fallen? This, then, is doomed to be my last night."

At the same time, he allowed none of the emotions he felt to be perceived, and soon regained his usual sang froid. He inquired, with the greatest coolness, of the mistress of the auberge, if she had supped? Upon her replying in the negative, he requested her to do him the *honour* of supping with him, as well as the *young ladies*. He acted thus, from a fear that if he supped alone, they might place some narcotic in his drink, without his perceiving it. The mother and daughters, after a few airs, could not refuse, and they placed themselves at table. Servigny did the honours, with that grace and affability which distinguishes the man of the world, and which, in his circumstances, were more particularly necessary, in order to observe the designs of his companions. But

all passed off well, and he remarked nothing to trouble his tranquillity in the least.

About midnight, the supper having finished, the mother directed her daughters to prepare the bed for the traveller, and to warm it with *pounded sugar* in the warming-pan, which was punctually executed. During these preparations, the mistress of the hotel of Bienvenu conversed with Servigny, in that motherly tone so likely to inspire confidence and negligence; the word "religion," was frequently repeated; in fact, the whole of her conversation was of a nature to produce in our traveller a feeling of the greatest security; and he said to himself:

"It is asserted that 'the eyes are the mirror of the soul;' if this rule be true, that of the aubergiste must be excellent, for her features, respectable and even handsome, command confidence."

He was not far, at this moment, from bestowing upon her his own, despite the slang terms which had awakened his suspicion; when he distinctly heard *l'arcon** made, and these words pronounced: " *Du maigre !* † there is a *messiere !* "‡

There was no longer any doubt, he was in a den of thieves! There was a moment of hesitation, as to the plan he should adopt, but as he was a man of resolution, he prepared for the consequences, good or ill.

"If it is impossible for me to escape the poniard of these brigands, I will make them purchase my life dearly."

He dissembled his emotions with address, being well satisfied that upon the first suspicion, it would be all over with him. At length, he was conducted to his chamber by the mother, who indicated to him the place in which he would find such things as he might have occasion for. She wished him a good night, and a pleasant repose, with an air of kindness capable of turning the suspicions of the most distrustful man.

She had scarcely disappeared, however, when Servigny listened; he heard them talking in a low tone, but could distinguish nothing. He took a turn round the room, and remarked its neatness. A commode, a leather-covered trunk, a curtained bed—furnished with sheets scattering an odour of lessive perfumed with the iris, a crucifix in plaster on the chimney-piece, a few sacred prints, a *benitier* at the head of the bed; every thing invited confidence and repose. At the same time he could not at all comprehend what he had seen and heard; in fact, how reconcile so much piety with the language of crime? He was lost in conjectures. The chamber into which he had ascended, by an upright staircase, was only lighted by a window, *à tabatiere*, at some height; but he could reach it by placing a chair on the commode, surmounted by the drawers. When this scaffolding was established under the window, it was easy to open it and attain the roof; but how descend? he found himself more than thirty feet from the ground. It is necessary to observe that after hearing the slang terms which had alarmed him, he had taken from the corner of the chimney, and without being observed, a strong pruning-knife, with which he hoped to defend himself in case of being attacked, as was but too probable. After sufficiently exploring the whereabouts, he resolved to attempt every thing to escape from such a position. With the sheets of the bed he made a rope, with which he could reach to the ground; and from a fear of being observed through

---

* Signal. † Prudence. ‡ A man worth robbing.

any opening, he extinguished his lamp, being enabled to finish his preparations by the moonlight which entered through the window in question. Whilst he worked for his deliverance, let us see what was passing in the salle in which we left the other personages of our history.

Round the large table are seated five individuals, whose different figures it is as well to describe. The first, who is the husband of the hostess of Bienvenu, has an air of remarkable superiority over the others; his manner is serious, his costume is that of the hawkers of Lower Normandy, and he is fifty years of age. His great height, his corpulence, his large and strong hands, indicate a man, endowed with unusual vigour. He expresses himself slowly, like the majority of the inhabitants of his province, and with that accent which is the peculiar signet of it. He appears to preside at the council which they are holding; his wife is near him, and his two daughters at the other extremity of the table.

On the left of Father Blaise, (le petit Christ, as he was called by the country people, and the frequenters of the house,) was his son, Jean Louis; whose eyes, figure, gestures, and movements of the body, revealed the atrocity of his character. This chameleon, seen out of his usual occupations, or the game he has to play, had the manner of an idiot, who has no other instinct but that of satisfying the wants of the brute; but, to the eyes of an observer, crime and blood sweat through every pore of his body.

Near him sits a man, thirty-six years of age, large and strongly built, habited as an herb or salad dealer; his accent, of Lower Normandy, indicates his origin. He has a smile stereotyped upon his lips, and the complete tone and manner of a pleasant fellow; in fact, to look at him, he seemed one, as they vulgarly express it, to whom they could give le bon Dieu, without confession.

On the other side is a man, short and thick-set, with hair black, crispy, and greasy; his dress is that of a strolling tinker. From his mouth, constantly filled with a large quid of tobacco, trickles an infectious liquid, which has no name in any language, and the odours he exhales renders his neighbourhood anything but agreeable. He has one eye damaged, and his face is horribly marked with the small-pox; in a word, he is the most repulsive being it is possible to imagine.

And last, at the side of this monster is a young man, of eighteen or twenty years of age, still beardless, dressed as a miller's boy; his open expression, which crime has not yet blemished, forms a striking contrast to that of his neighbour. One is astonished to observe so much candour and mildness apparent in such a reunion; it is like the appearance of an angel amidst the imps of Lucifer!

Blaise le petit Christ opens the subject of their meeting; he laments that a casual circumstance obliged him to bring two men to sleep at the house. They were two men whom he had met on the Colombe road, and whom he knew as truqueurs,* but who knew him as nothing more than an honest hawker.

"You know, my good friends," he said, "that we must work with caution, and proceed in such order that we may not become malade. An extraordinary occasion presents itself; you have heard my wife and my two momignardes† inform

you that the negriot* was fat, that it weighed well; we must pounce upon this maurecand; and, in my opinion, this is not the easiest thing in the world. The two truqueurs will hear us, if we murder the man; if, on the other hand, we purchase their silence, we shall expose ourselves to a serious inconvenience. In such a case, what's to be done?"

"Silence the whole!" exclaimed, at the same time, the mother and the beardless youth; "'tis the only means of making them safe. You know that witnesses are dangerous."

"Murder is the expedient we make use of, generally," said Blaise le petit Christ, "but does not conscience whisper to you that it is an atrocious crime to murder one's neighbour, and especially when he doesn't possess a sou. These are poor devils who will plague us as much, and more so, than if they were productive. I assure you it is repugnant to me to shed the blood of these two truqueurs."

The red-haired daughter, who was named Pacifique, speaking in her turn, said to her father:

"We can easily see that you are come from church, for you assume the devoté! What's the use of all this argument? I would murder ten truqueurs to get hold of the box in question."

"My sister is right," said the elder; "we must settle the whole, and seize all."

The whole band at length agreed to assassinate the three unfortunate guests; they sent Marguerite, surnamed la Vierge Noire, to listen.

In a few moments she descended, and informed them that the two truqueurs were still conversing, but that she could not hear the least sound in the traveller's room.

"A little patience," she added; "'tis not yet two o'clock."

They commenced drinking to pass away the time, and when the moment arrived, the parts were distributed; the father, la Vierge Noire, and the miller, took charge of the stranger; the others were ordered to despatch the two truqueurs.

At length, two o'clock sounded. When they had ascertained, by another visit, that the two unfortunate strollers slept soundly, and that, probably, the traveller had followed their example, the brigands repaired, without noise, to the different positions in which they were to operate. Pacifique mounted a tree, which still exists, and which bears at the present day, as formerly, the number 93, which overlooked the house, to act as a watch, and at her sign the brigands were to strike; but, hearing a noise, she thought it prudent to wait a moment. The brigands, however, were at their post; their eagerness, the thirst for murder and gold, rendered their sight horrible! A sign—and the doors placed at the head of each bed were opened, the movable panels were lowered, and thus ended, as was supposed, the lives of the three unfortunates, who, from the sleep of the living, passed into the sleep of the dead. But Pacifique, whose ear was as sure as her eyes, again heard the same noise; it was a man who glided along the garden wall, the obscurity had prevented her from observing him with more precision. Alarmed, she descends from her observatory, and hastens to give an account of what she had seen to her accomplices.

Jean Louis lights his lantern, and hastens out to ascertain, from the exterior, the occasion of the alarm; when arrived at the left wall of the garden,

---

* Men who exercise any or every unlawful trade.
† Girls.

* Coffer.

he observes the rope manufactured by Servigny. At first, he cannot comprehend the meaning of it, but his father, who follows him, guesses at once that the man and the coffer have disappeared. The better to make sure, he ascends to the room he had occupied; he attempts to open the door, but it is barricaded. He calls his accomplices; these assist him to force an entrance, and to push away the furniture by which the traveller had intrenched himself; but it was tenantless, the bird had taken wing.

"This is a very extraordinary flight," they exclaimed; "what motives, or rather, what suspicions could he have, to adopt such a plan, at the risk of breaking his neck?"

The bandits made a thousand conjectures, each advanced a different opinion.

"Ah, bah!" said Blaise le petit Christ, "probably he is a *piquet*,* who has conceived the project of observing with his own eyes what is taking place here, in which case, 'tis a lost game. But, however," he added, "we have no time to lose; take away the *gré*† *le pot*,‡ and the *frusquins* § of the man who has escaped with mine; the rest is my affair."

He untied the rope and burned it, and then speaking a few words in his wife's ear:

"Go, you others; I will give you a rendezvous at the Vert-Galant, near Livry, where I will follow you. By changing the route we shall see what events take place."

Upon this they departed. The three women remained in their establishment to wait the solution of this enigma.

CHAPTER XXX.

A MISFORTUNE COMPLETE.

In spite of the entreaties of Madame de Villerbanne, Lucie, as soon as Salvador had led her to her place, wished to retire; her carriage was ordered, and in a few minutes she was in her bedroom, where Laura, who was anxious to know what had taken place between her and the Marquis de Pourrieres, had followed her.

Lucie was sorrowful, preoccupied, and when her femme de chambre had retired, after undressing her, instead of imparting to her friend, as was her custom, her impressions of the evening, she preserved a mournful silence. Laura, who, after what had passed, fancied she should find her friend quite reassured, knew not to what she could attribute this state of half prostration: it was not, therefore, until she had hesitated some moments, that she determined to demand of her the cause of the dejection in which she found her.

"But I have nothing, I assure you," replied Lucie, after a hesitation of some minutes; "I am merely a little indisposed."

"Is that all?" continued Laura, who suspected that Lucie, for the first time in her life, wished to conceal something from her.

"Beyond a doubt."

"You do not tell me what was the result of your long conversation with the Marquis de Pourrieres?"

"What do you wish me to tell you? Although, as you observe, we conversed for some time, we really talked of nothing but insignificant affairs."

* Police agent.   † Horse.   ‡ Cabriolet.
§ Garments.

"What! he didn't give you any reason for his being seen, habited as a workman in the docks, in that house of la Tannerie Street? To me, that appears astonishing."

"Yes, he did; and if we had had a little more thought, we could at once have explained a circumstance, which will no longer appear extraordinary to you; we are in carnival, my dear Laura."

"Well?"

"How! you cannot comprehend that the marquis, who was disguised to appear at a subscription ball, given every year by a leather merchant, of whom all the journals speak, under the name of *Chicard*, determined to profit by this unique opportunity, to visit all the public establishments of Paris, which offer to the observer some curious physiognomies."

"Ah!" replied Laura, with an air of profound astonishment.

The excuse alleged by the Marquis de Pourrieres, and which Lucie never dreamt to place in doubt, appeared to her somewhat unlikely; she would not, however, impart this idea to her friend. Lucie was tranquil; she appeared to have no further dread; and Laura, who could divine what was passing in the heart of the countess, questioned no further; she retired, after tenderly embracing her companion, to whom she wished a happy night's repose, accompanied with agreeable dreams.

Left alone, Lucie took from an elegant little box of satin-wood, and richly inlaid, several letters in one packet, and placed herself to read them before the cheerful fire, which, by the attentive solicitude of her femme de chambre, blazed in the hearth. These were the letters addressed to her by her husband since he had been in Algiers.

Lucie finished not the perusal of the first, which fell from her hands; it was in vain she attempted to drive away the subject which clouded her spirits; she could give no meaning to the characters traced upon the sheet of paper before her eyes, her thoughts were elsewhere; she placed the packet of letters on the mantel-piece.

"My God! my God!" she exclaimed, with an accent of the most painful anxiety, why have you willed that I should again meet this man?"

This exclamation of the unhappy Countess de Neuville revealed the state of her heart.

It was but too true, she loved Salvador, and we need not be astonished at it. As we have already observed, this man possessed every quality which constituted an individual of the best society; features of a perfect distinction, a flattering tone, and an elegant figure. There was, besides, in the manner he had appeared to her, something uncommon, which had seduced her. His physiognomy was, in the eyes of Lucie, surrounded with a certain mysterious shadow, which necessarily interested a woman gifted with such a lively imagination, and whose heart had not yet spoken—we cannot give the name of love, to the affection, mingled with respect, with which the colonel had inspired his wife; and we all know that from interest to love, the distance is not far.

"Alas! alas!" continued Lucie, "it is true then, I love this man! what shall I become if I cannot stifle this fatal passion? But I will stifle it, by the help of God; the remembrance of the happiness I owe to the estimable man whose name I bear, will come to my assistance in the painful struggle I shall have to sustain against myself, and from which I hope to retire victorious."

From the moment Lucie became satisfied with the exact state of her heart, she found herself much more tranquil; she again took the letters of her husband, which she could now read without being distracted by thoughts foreign to the subject which occupied her.

"Yes, certainly," she said to herself, when a phrase, a word, or some feeling expressions of the strong attachment felt towards her by Monsieur de Neuville, presented itself; "yes, I shall know how to fulfil the duties imposed upon me! I will not show myself ungrateful for the proofs of affection thus addressed to me!"

Lucie, we perceive, had no similarity with the novel species of shadowy and unmeaning women brought into fashion by the modern romances; who, the moment they fancy they have a passion of the heart, carry it, accompanied by him who has inspired them with the same passion, to wander by moonlight on the banks of blue lakes; and who find in their imagination, when they have fallen without making a struggle, a heap of diatribes, more or less eloquent, against the social vices which in their idea have induced their fall. She knew that she must wrestle with all her strength against a sentiment which, unperceived, had stolen into her heart; that she must preserve pure and without blemish the name she had received from her husband; she had measured the extent of her duties, and from the moment she said she would know how to accomplish them, she had become more tranquil. Decidedly, the Countess de Neuville, although we have described her as young, amiable, spirituel, and pretty, was a very prosaic woman, and will appear, we fear, but little interesting to those of our readers who have a *penchant* for more liberal passions, and women of the same feelings.

We shall permit several weeks to pass, during which nothing of interest happened to those of our heroes in whom we are at present occupied.

Fine weather had succeeded to the wintry days and their sombre cortége of rain, snow, and frost; and M. de Neuville, whom Lucie expected to arrive at the commencement of spring, had written to her on the contrary, that it was probable he should remain at least another year in Africa. He could not, he said in his letter, quit the post which had been confided to him, when the war, which it was supposed had nearly terminated, had recommenced with fresh energy; and at the moment when, to recompense the services he had rendered during the last campaign, the king had just named him a field-marshal. Lucie therefore had a prospect of a very unhappy summer, unless she could prevail upon her aunt to pass the charming season at the Chateau de Villerbanne.

It was with much difficulty that the old marchioness determined to quit Paris, a residence in which, even during the summer, she preferred to that of the finest country in the world.

"At Paris," replied the marchioness to those of her friends who were astonished at meeting her still in the capital when all the frequenters of her society had taken their flight into the field; "at Paris there is always something fresh to be seen, whilst in the country, it is for ever the same trees, the same rivulets constantly before one's eyes; the fresh and mysterious labyrinths, the purling streams, the song of the nightingale in a soft summer's night, all this makes one dream, and at my age, dreams are not good for the health, they remind us that there are but a few steps between us and the tomb."

It is not that we are of the same opinion as Madame de Villerbanne, that we report her replies to such of her friends who invited her to visit them at their country quarters. We would merely prove that it was not without trouble that Lucie determined her to leave a residence she loved, to go and bury herself (this was her expression) in an old manor house which had existed from the time of the first crusade.

And now let us say, why Lucie, who, under any other circumstance, would have considered it a law as well as a pleasure to conform to the wishes of her kind old parent, had in some measure forced her to do as she desired.

In order to follow up the resolution she had taken, Lucie must avoid every occasion of meeting the Marquis de Pourrieres, and this it was difficult to manage, unless she resigned herself as a prisoner in her own house, for the marquis was much sought after; she had frequently met him in different saloons, and whenever she repaired to the promenade, there was the marquis, accompanied by the Viscount de Lussan, who paid assiduous court to Laura, (which considerably displeased the artless young girl,) caracoling at the door of her carriage.

If Salvador had made a confession to Madame de Neuville of the sentiments she appeared to have inspired in him, no doubt she would have shown her displeasure in a manner which would have destroyed the hope of witnessing the success of his attempts; but it was not so. The marquis was ready, gallant, without ever ceasing to be perfectly consistent; he left it to his eyes to express what his lips dared not utter, in such a way that the usages of good society imposed upon Lucie the obligation of accepting attentions which she could not refuse, without appearing to suspect their real character.

Hence it was only to avoid Salvador that the Countess de Neuville had determined, the moment she became certain that the absence of her husband would be prolonged, to pass the summer at the country-house of Madame de Villerbanne; she did not reflect, alas! that the meadows, shaded by the old oaks, and purling rivulets flowing with soft murmurs between two flowery banks, are not the resorts in which we may expect to find a remedy for the troubles we experience in endeavouring to chase from the heart a passion which has once taken root there.

Chateaus similar to that of the family of Villerbanne will not long be seen in France. The hammer of the speculators finishes every day the work commenced by the demolishers of the first revolution, and 'tis really a great pity; for the sickly buildings of the present age will not induce us to forget these vast and magnificent halls, which seem to us to have been built by, and for the use of giants; and when our wanderings lead us before one of these manor houses, to which we might apply this line of Delille—

"La masse indestructible a fatigué le temps,"*

we experience an intense pleasure in finding ourselves in front of this old representative of ages, which, we may add, were at least equal to our own.

Let us salute, then, the old Chateau de Villerbanne, of which we just observe the high gray walls, pierced with arched windows, and the two towers surmounted with noisy weathercocks, at the end of that long avenue of venerable oaks.

* Its indestructible mass has wearied time.

No. 34.

LIFE IN PARIS.

BEPPO FOLLOWING THE CARRIAGE OF SILVIA.

After admiring this splendid edifice, which is situated on the banks of the Seine, between Montereau-Faut l'Yonne and Sens, and which overlooks the most picturesque and animated landscape it is possible to conceive, we shall scarcely comprehend how the marchioness could prefer the residence at her hotel, to that of the antique dwelling of her ancestors; but if we reflect a few moments, the antipathy of the old lady will appear to us perfectly natural; the chateau is no longer what it was when she was obliged to quit France; the moats have been filled up, an iron grating has superseded the drawbridge, raised in former times every evening when the night had commenced; it has been necessary to replace the old painted windows of the chapel; the books of the library, and the family portraits which embellished the large gallery and the armoury, have helped to feed an immense funeral pile round which danced the stupid peasants; so that the sight of her chateau always brought to her mind painful remembrances, and it required all the attachment she had for her niece to determine her once more to shut herself up in it for several months.

Lucie and Laura both loved the country; hence it was with the greatest pleasure they had put themselves en route for the Chateau de Villerbanne, which they had inhabited for nearly a month, when the marchioness, who sought every means of making herself agreeable to her two companions, inquired of them, one morning after breakfast, if the life of recluses they were leading, did not begin to weary them a little.

"No, my dear aunt," replied Lucie; "have we not every thing here which can amuse us; delightful shady walks, books, music, all that we require for painting, and charming landscapes for study?"

"Ah! plenty of amusement, all this, no doubt; but don't you find it very tiresome to perform music simply for the echoes of the neighbourhood, and to have no person to whom you can show the pretty sketches you have drawn?"

"No doubt," said Laura, sighing; "but what we cannot obtain, we must learn to do without; this chateau is so far from Paris, that it is not likely we shall receive any visits."

"Come, come, don't despair," said the marchioness, gently patting the rosy cheeks of Laura, "don't despair, I intend you a surprise which will not displease you."

The marchioness, despite the entreaties of Lucie and Laura, whose curiosity was excited by what she had said, would not explain herself more clearly. She left the two friends, beseeching them to have a little patience.

"What is this surprise then that my aunt is catering for us?" said Lucie, when she was alone with Laura.

"Why, can't you guess?" replied the latter, "Madame de Villerbanne, notwithstanding her affection for us, is tired of being alone, and this is not surprising; she cannot, like us, go out or come in, race through the fields, in the park, visit the farm; so that, I'll wager, she intends to give some brilliant fêtes here, in order to attract her society from Paris."

"Do you think so?" exclaimed Lucie, in a tone which betrayed her alarm.

Laura could not help smiling.

"Eh! bon Dieu!" she said, "you are really in the wrong to get alarmed; it is certain that neither M. the Marquis de Pourrieres, nor M. the Viscomte de Lussan will be invited; in the country they receive only the most intimate friends and neighbours, and these messieurs, thank God, are only simple acquaintances of your aunt."

"I cannot endure that Marquis de Pourrieres, and if I were sure of meeting him here, I would immediately leave for Paris."

Lucie, we see, had not confided to her friend the real state of her heart, she had, on the contrary, by affecting an aversion which she was far from possessing, and which Laura thought quite natural, endeavoured to destroy the suspicions which the letter of Matheo, and the conduct of Salvador, during and after the soirée of Madame de Villerbanne, had aroused.

"'Tis the same with me," replied Laura, "I detest this marquis above every one."

"It seems then," said Lucie, making an effort to smile, (for 'twas not without feeling much hurt that she found her dearest friend manifesting such an aversion towards the man she loved,) "it seems that M. the Vicomte de Lussan has at length obtained your good graces?"

"I forgot him," exclaimed Laura; "I detest him equally with his friend, and if he is to visit here, I shall be the first to request you to leave; but there is no danger of that."

The two friends had exchanged the preceding dialogue whilst continuing their walk in the most shady part of the park, to which they had repaired after leaving Madame de Villerbanne. As they passed on their return to the chateau, in front of a small door which opened on the road from Montereau to Sens, they encountered Paolo, whom the countess had brought with her to Villerbanne, and who was at this moment entering the chateau.

An expression of the greatest delight sparkled in the countenance of the faithful serviteur, who respectfully drew aside to allow the two ladies to pass.

"You appear highly delighted, Paolo," said Lucie, who was much attached to this devoted attendant, who, as we have observed, had served her father for many years with the same zeal he showed towards his present mistress; "is it possible to ascertain what causes you so much satisfaction."

"I feel very grateful for the interest Madame la Comtesse takes in me," replied Paolo, "and her extreme kindness emboldens me to solicit a favour."

"Ah! you have some request to make me, Paolo? Well, speak, my friend, and if I can satisfy you, be assured I shall not refuse it."

"Madame la Comtesse is really too kind; but I dare not——"

"Come, fear nothing, Paolo; speak, I am waiting to hear you."

"Madame la Comtesse inquires why I am so joyful? To reply to the question of madame, I shall mention, that in strolling about the environs of the chateau, I met with a compatriot, who served in the same regiment as myself, and whom I have not seen for many years, and is at present in the service of the proprietor of one of the neighbouring chateaus; he has proposed to me to engage with his master, who is just in want of a servant. Madame la Comtesse may be assured that at first I refused this offer; we can never quit with a free will such a good master as I have the honour to serve; but he observed, that he made me this proposition because matters of business called his master to Savoy, where he will remain about a twelvemonth; and that it would be for me a rare opportunity to revisit my country; so I said to myself that if Madame la Comtesse would kindly favour me with a year's leave of absence."

"You would be delighted to revisit your mountains and sweet valleys?"

"Well! yes, Madame la Comtesse, I shall enjoy this journey with the greatest pleasure, if I may be only provisionally replaced in your service; but if matters cannot be thus arranged, I shall defer to another time the visit to my mountains and my family."

"Well, my good Paolo, I grant you the favour you solicit, and I promise that you shall be received with a welcome on your return to the hotel. Go then and find your friend, and arrange at your ease the preparations for your departure."

"Ah! thank you, Madame la Comtesse," exclaimed Paolo, whose eyes were moistened with tears of joy; "thank you, thank you, how kind you are."

And without waiting for a reply to these exclamations, the worthy servant left by the small door by which he had entered, and commenced running along the road to Sens.

"I am delighted at being enabled to do something for this honest man," said Lucie, who had followed with her eyes the faithful domestic. "I am quite certain I have not obliged an ingrate."

"I am of your opinion," replied Laura, "Paolo is one of those rare domestics who do honour to the livery they wear."

The distant sound of the clock announcing the dinner hour, reminded the two friends that they must hasten their return to the chateau, unless they meant to allow Madame de Villerbanne the time to get impatient.

"You are arrived then!" said the good lady when they entered the saloon; "I really feared for a moment that we should be obliged to sit down without you."

Madame de Villerbanne was not alone; an elderly man, but whose age had not yet bent his tall figure, was seated near her; he rose up to meet the two young friends, and seizing Lucie by the waist, he deposited a smart kiss on her forehead.

The old gentleman was endowed with one of those frank and kind military faces which at once inspires confidence; so that Lucie, although a little surprised at the sudden attack, never dreamt of being angry;, she merely complained that the moustaches of this gallant cavalier had used her rather roughly.

"They are in fact rather tough," replied the old gentleman; "but be assured, Madame la Comtesse, that the next time, I will not press you so hard."

"The next time!" said Lucie, who fancied she ought to know the person before her, but whose features had escaped her remembrance; "you intend, then, monsieur, to kiss me again?"

"Not a doubt of it, and I trust you will not be more cruel than formerly, and that you will return me my kisses."

"Well, I'm surprised," exclaimed Lucie, regarding her aunt, who seemed greatly amused at her perplexity.

"How, Lucie," said Madame de Villerbanne at length, "you do not recognise Monsieur ——."

"Wait, my dear aunt, wait a moment—Monsieur the General, Comte de Morengy!"

"I was quite certain she would remember me," cried the old general. "Madame la Comtesse you have a better memory than I have; for I do not think I should have recognised you, if Madame la

Marquise had not given me your portrait; but I must add, that you were but an infant when I came to take my leave of your father, before commencing my journey. The woman has fulfilled the promise of the young girl," continued the general, addressing Madame de Villerbanne.

"Has she not, general?" replied the marquise; "well! she is as good as she is handsome," she added, after kissing Lucie, who was rendered quite confused by these praises.

Monsieur de Morengy addressed a few gracious words to Laura, and the company passed into the dining-room, where, thanks to the talents of the valet of Madame de Villerbanne, the most elegant dinner had been served.

The General Count de Morengy was, notwithstanding his great age, a gay and witty convive; so that the dinner passed off with more gaiety than usual.

"I am really delighted, dear general," said Madame de Villerbanne when, after dinner, the company found themselves assembled to take their coffee, "that chance has made us near neighbours whilst in the country."

"You are really too good, Madame la Marquise," replied M. de Morengy, "the pleasure is all upon my side; and I sincerely regret that important business obliges me to undertake a journey to Savoy, which will keep me away from you for at least a year."

"'Tis you, then, general, who carries off my most faithful attendant," said the Countess de Neuville.

"How, madame, has this domestic resolved to leave your service. I did not wish him to do so, and if I had not sent him forward to prepare relays for me, I would not take him with me to Savoy."

"That would be depriving yourself, general, during your voyage, of the devoted attentions of a good and loyal serviteur."

"I shall do as you tell me, and I am fully persuaded I shall find myself in the right."

The evening was already advanced, when the Count de Morengy quitted the Chateau de Villerbanne, after promising the old marchioness and her two charming companions, that he would pay them a daily visit until his departure for Savoy.

The general and Madame de Villerbanne, on quitting each other, had exchanged a smile, and looks of intelligence which were remarked by Lucie, and the explanation of which she requested of her aunt.

"Ah! there now," replied Madame de Villerbanne, who had some trouble to resist the entreaties of Lucie, who was resolved to ascertain what had given rise to the looks of intelligence exchanged between her aunt and the Count Morengy. They may well say there is nothing in the world so curious as a daughter of Eve; "know then, my dear niece, since you will not allow me the pleasure of surprising you, that, thanks to the general, who has assembled at his chateau a numerous society, I shall be enabled to afford you here some fêtes as brilliant as though we were still in Paris."

"I guessed as much!" exclaimed Laura, jumping up; "and we shall dance too, shall we not, Madame la Marquise?"

"Yes, my child, we shall have some dancing."

The next morning, in fact, an army of workmen, directed by the Count de Morengy, who had readily accepted the post of master of the ceremonies of the fête about to be given, and who acquitted himself of his functions with all the ardour of a younger man, invaded the Chateau de Villerbanne. They had soon changed the old manor house into a sort of enchanted palace.

"Well, ladies," said the old general in the evening, "are you satisfied with me?"

"More than satisfied, M. le Comte," replied the marquise. "And 'tis for the day after to-morrow."

"Yes, madame, the day after to-morrow; and here is my programme, which I submit to your judgment; first, a dinner in the armoury of the chateau, transformed for this occasion into a banquetting hall, a general illumination of the garden and park; ascent of a balloon; a dance; fireworks; and the departure, at the break of day, of your humble servant, whom a post-chaise will call for at the chateau."

"It is then quite decided you leave?"

"I cannot defer my journey; but my absence will not be eternal, and I intend on my return, to purchase an hotel in the neighbourhood of your own."

And yet, neither Lucie nor Laura were to receive from this fête, given expressly on their account, the pleasure they promised themselves.

If our readers will be good enough to follow us to the most distant spot in the park of the chateau, and accompany for a few minutes the Countess de Neuville and her friend, they will learn the causes which has produced the clouds which hang over their charming features.

"Well, Laura," said the countess, when the sounds of the orchestra only reached their ears like a distant echo, confounding itself with the murmur of the breeze, which gently ruffled the foliage of the old trees, "well, what do you say to all this?"

"Why, that it is a fatality!" replied Laura; "am I condemned then to meet in every place that odious Viscount de Lussan?"

"Who has constantly in his train the Marquis de Pourrieres, whom I never behold without immediately calling to mind that frightful cabaret of la Tannerie."

"But if it is so," exclaimed Laura, "why do you then converse with this marquis, with the affability you do?"

There was in the accent of Laura, when she addressed this question to her friend, a meaning which did not escape the countess; for the world's treasures, Lucie would not have allowed her to guess the secret of her heart.

"But can I act otherwise?" she hastened to reply; "my aunt greatly esteems this Marquis de Pourrieres; she is delighted that he is included in the society assembled here by M. de Morengy; and I really believe, if I did not meet him with a good grace, I should draw upon me the censure of Madame de Villerbanne."

"So that it is simply the dread of disobliging Madame de Villerbanne, which induces you to listen to this man, as you have just done, for hours together; to smile upon him when he regards you; to dance with none but him, for to-night you have danced with none other?"

"Oh! Laura, I danced also with M. Winkelman."

"The German diplomatist, who pays his court to me, and who resembles one of the ballads of Goëthe, he counts for nothing."

"But if, as you imagine, I show so great an interest towards M. de Pourrieres, it is not without a motive; and since you seem disposed to doubt what I advance, what are the motives you suppose me to be led by?"

"Is it possible for me to know? I am only certain that you do not feel towards the Marquis de Pourrieres a hatred similar to that I have vowed against the Viscount de Lussan."

"Good God! Laura," exclaimed Lucie, almost alarmed, so much energy had Laura used in pronouncing these last words, "I have never heard you speak thus; we have known the viscount for a length of time, and you have to-day, for the first time, expressed with such violence the hatred he inspires you with, really this is extraordinary."

"It's true," replied Laura, "I am astonished myself at feeling so great an aversion towards these two men; for, before I had seen them, I believed it impossible for me to hate any one, even those who might have injured me; but it is impossible for me to prevent it; when I behold them, I experience the same emotion that I should do on meeting a loathsome animal, although I may be certain that I have nothing to fear."

"Thus," thought Lucie, who had listened to Laura, whose countenance, usually pale, was flushed with the deepest colours, "I shall lose the affection of my most cherished friend, if she discovers that I love the man she detests the worst of the two. My God! my God! am I so unfortunate?"

At this moment Laura, who walked before the countess, like a pigeon scared at the sight of a bird of prey, approached her, and said in a low tone:

"They are coming this way, we shall meet them at the turn of this path, if we continue to follow it; let us turn back, I entreat you!"

"But can we do so? It will appear as though we feared them; and, besides, it will be offering them an insult which nothing justifies."

"They may think of me just what they please," replied Laura to these prudent remarks of her friend.

And before the latter could oppose her intention, she bounded away in an instant, and soon disappeared amongst the immense trees of the park.

Lucie was accosted by Salvador at the moment that she was probably on the point of imitating her friend. The marquis was alone, the Viscount de Lussan, who had observed the flight of Laura, had quitted his friend, in order to procure for him a tête-à-tête with the Countess de Neuville.

Lucie, upon every occasion of meeting the Marquis de Pourrieres, was for some moments subject to a painful impression, arising from the remembrance of the circumstance which had made her acquainted with him; but this passed as the lightning; scarcely had she exchanged a few words with him, than she allowed herself to be captivated by the harmonious flattery of his voice, and the charms of an imagination she was quite capable of appreciating.

These casual shades had not escaped Salvador, who was endowed with that penetration possessed by nearly all those upon whom a constant practice of crime renders it an obligation to observe all that passes around them; he discovered, from the thousand indications which have no meaning for those who have not a quick penetration, but which are easily seized upon by an attentive observer, that the Countess de Neuville loved him, and that the efforts she made to wrest from her heart the sentiment which had taken root there unknowingly, would be useless. He had not, however, as yet, made a confession of his own feeling towards her, the dread of losing, by alarming her, the ground he had taken such pains to acquire, restrained him; but at the time we have now arrived, he considered his power seated on a sufficiently firm basis to preclude the chance of a defeat, if he chose to commence hostilities. He had therefore accosted the countess, determined to profit by the occasion which presented itself of conversing without witnesses, an occasion he had long waited for in vain.

But his expectations were deceived. After employing the introductory phrases which commonly precede a declaration of love addressed to a woman, whose position in society, her talents, and character, do not allow her to be treated cavalierly, his lips gave free utterance to the confession which hung suspended between them, and he found himself much farther from his object than before.

"I would readily believe, M. the Marquis," replied Lucie, "it is because you have forgotten that you are speaking to the Countess de Neuville, that you have addressed me in such a manner; I trust, therefore, that you will not recommence a similar attempt; if you do, I shall be compelled to apprise Madame de Villerbanne, and I confess that it would be with considerable pain I should find myself compelled to take such a step."

Saying this, Lucie quitted Salvador, to rejoin Laura, whom she found walking with de Morengy.

Salvador, who, we may be sure, expected a very different reception, was so confounded, that he made not the slightest reply to Madame de Neuville.

He was aroused from this species of torpor by loud bursts of laughter; 'twas the Viscount de Lussan, who, concealed behind the trunk of a large oak, had listened to the declaration of Salvador and the reply which was made to it.

"Touch it, marquis," he exclaimed, presenting his hand to Salvador; "we can shake hands, I think; you have not been better treated by the Countess de Neuville than I have by her young friend. Repulsed with loss, my vassal, we must, unless we would imitate those preux chevaliers who sighed away a quarter of a century before they could obtain permission to kiss the tips of their beloved, carry our homages elsewhere."

"It is easy for you to say so; you make court to Mademoiselle de Beaumont merely as a distraction, and from a spirit of imitation; but with me it is very different; I love Madame de Neuville, I really am in love with her."

"Really, marquis?"

"'Tis as I have the honour of telling you."

"How! you have still these weaknesses? In truth, you astonish me exceedingly."

"Oh! but I will succeed," exclaimed Salvador: "I will not leave this woman the privilege of laughing at me."

"Bravo, morbleu, bravo! they are but cowards who permit themselves to be discouraged by the obstacles they meet with. I like to see this noble resolution in you, and I am ready to acknowledge that you are a worthy gentleman; and besides, my dear, this woman loves you! and it is only to acquit her conscience, that she has treated you so rudely."

"Do you think so?"

"I am sure of it. Ah! you are happier than I am. 'Tis not simply because she is virtuous, that Mademoiselle de Beaumont endeavours, by every possible means, to shun my presence: that young girl detests me."

"I pity you, my dear friend."

"I thank you, for saying so; I must, however, confess, that the contempt of Mademoiselle de Beaumont afflicts me much less than the infidelities of Coralie."

"You have not, then, yet left that danseuse?"

"Alas! no; I am accustomed to her. But let us leave this, and rejoin the company, a longer absence may be remarked."

Salvador in vain looked for Lucie, that he might make her some excuse for his conduct; the countess, pretending a sudden indisposition, had retired to her apartment, accompanied by her friend, after bidding adieu to the Count de Morengy, who, as we have said, was to put himself en route, at the break of day.

Salvador, the Viscount de Lussan, the Marchioness de Villerbanne, and several other persons, accompanied the general to his travelling carriage.

"I leave you," he said to the marchioness, and presenting his two friends to her, "two charming cavaliers to enliven your solitude. These gentlemen, if you will kindly receive them, will bless, I am certain, the chance, which forces me to quit you so suddenly, after inviting them to pass the whole season with me."

The marchioness, as much to please her old friend as to increase the society of her chateau, joining her request to that of the general, it was arranged that the Marquis de Pourrieres and the Viscount de Lussan, whom the departure of M. de Morengy left, as they said laughing, without an asylum, should install themselves at the chateau, and pass a fortnight there.

Salvador determined to profit during this period, in which it would be possible to encounter Lucie frequently alone; but his hopes were again doomed to be disappointed, for the moment the countess heard of this arrangement, she determined to quit the Chateau de Villerbanne and return to Paris.

It required some pretext to justify this hasty departure; Lucie found one, by informing her aunt, that she feared the indisposition of which she had complained the evening before, would proceed to a serious illness, and that the advice of her usual physician was absolutely necessary to her. The marchioness, who was aware of the confidence placed by Lucie in Doctor Matheo, and who was yet ignorant of the flight of the latter, thought her desire quite natural, and was the first to advise her not to defer her departure.

Salvador was not the dupe of this comedy, but he was compelled to champ his bit, and resign himself, as well as the Viscount de Lussan, to the company of the Marquise de Villerbanne. His punishment, however, did not continue long; it was only out of compliment to him that the old lady had remained at the chateau after the departure of her niece. As soon, therefore, as her guests manifested a desire to return to Paris, she said she should also wish to be again in the capital; so that, within a few days after the events we have narrated, she was reinstated in her hotel of the Place Royale, which she promised herself faithfully not to quit the following year.

Her first visit, on the morning after her return to Paris, was destined for her niece, whom she had not apprised of her arrival, and to whom she wished to cause an agreeable surprise. She did not anticipate, alas! the sad news she was to hear at the Hotel de Neuville.

"Madame has given orders for no one to be announced to her," said the femme de chambre of Lucie, to whom she had addressed herself to be introduced to her niece; "but this order can have no reference to Madame la Marquise, whom madame supposed to be still in the country, and to whom she wrote this morning, begging her to rejoin her at once; so that I will go and announce you. Ah! my poor mistress sadly wants consolation," exclaimed the poor girl, on leaving the saloon, and crying bitterly.

"Ah! come, my kind aunt, come and weep with me," exclaimed Lucie, throwing herself into the arms of Madame de Villerbanne.

The countess was frightfully pale, her hair was in disorder, her eyes were red and swollen, and tears had traced some deep furrows along her checks; she was habited in mourning. The most intense grief was painted on the features of Laura, who had entered the saloon, following her friend.

"He is dead!" said the Marquise de Villerbanne, and dropping on a divan.

Lucie presented to her a letter, as her only reply.

The following were the contents:

"Madame,—It is with a feeling of the deepest grief, that I find myself compelled to announce to you, that your husband, M. le Marechal du Camp, Comte de Neuville, has died gloriously for his country.

"The reports of the lieutenant-general, commanding the army of occupation in Africa, which will shortly be made public, will inform you of the details of this unhappy event.

"You have lost, madame, a husband who is dear to you; the country, and the king, lose a faithful and courageous servant. The grief which such sentiments must inspire, is so natural, that I will not attempt to offer you consolation.

"Accept, &c.

"For the Marshal,
"MINISTER OF WAR."

The Marchioness de Villerbanne read this letter in a loud voice. When she had finished, she buried her face in one of the cushions of the divan. Lucie and Laura, who had placed themselves near her, wept in silence. It was easy to perceive that the eldest of the three women was the one who suffered most, and that she was not destined to support the heavy blow she had just received. In fact, the Count de Neuville, the son of a sister who had perished on the scaffold in 1793, was the only relation that remained to Madame de Villerbanne, who had never been happy enough to become a mother, and who had seen perish, under the revolutionary axe, and the field of battle, under the Empire, all who had been dear to her; and he was lost to her, at the moment when she reckoned upon him to close her eyes, and with him descended to the darkness of the tomb one of the most illustrious names of the old French monarchy. This last trial, then, filled the measure; the Marchioness de Villerbanne experienced the fate of those old oaks, who yield at last, after supporting the shock of many storms.

When, after remaining some time in the same position, she at length raised her head, there rested on her pale features such a poignant expression of profound despair and bitter grief, her jet black hair disordered, and her eyes, which had not shed one small tear, announced such a vacant hopelessness, that the two young women forgot, for a moment, their own troubles, to offer her some consolation.

The marchioness repulsed them mildly.

"Weep, my children," she said, "weep; the tears, which cannot flow, fall back upon the heart, and consume it."

"My good aunt" exclaimed Lucie, sobbing, and who had guessed the painful thoughts of the old lady, "you must not die."

"I would live, my child, I would live for you, poor angel, who now remain alone upon this land of griefs; but that will not be possible; at my age we cannot support such blows." The marchioness, in finishing these words, rose up, and after embracing Lucie and Laura, quitted the saloon.

The next morning she was a corpse.

We shall not attempt to describe the grief of the Countess de Neuville when she received this sad news; we shall merely observe that it was deep and sincere; and that it was to the affectionate attentions paid her by Laura and Eugenie de Mirbel, who had hastened to her on the first news of her misfortunes, that she was mainly indebted for her recovery.

A short time after the death of M. de Neuville and Madame de Villerbanne, Lucie, who, in spite of the entreaties of Laura, had not put her foot outside the hotel, and had refused to receive such as had presented themselves to offer their respects of condolence, was informed, by Laura, that one of the aides-de-camp of her husband, who had arrived from Algiers, requested the favour of being presented to her. "'Twas in his arms," he said, "that M. de Neuville had rendered his last sigh; and he came, fulfilling the order he had received from his general, to render an account to his widow, of his last moments."

Lucie retained Laura, and gave orders to introduce the officer.

"It requires, madame," he said, after saluting her with every mark of respect, "the powerful motive by which I am urged, to excuse the boldness of disturbing a grief so legitimate as yours."

"Speak to me of my husband," said Lucie, in a voice interrupted by her sobs; "'twas in your arms that he breathed his last. What did he say to you, sir? Speak, speak, I beg of you."

"Alas! madame, death left him no time to write to you, as was his intention; he was only enabled to charge me to repeat to you his last words, and my first anxiety, on arriving at Paris, has been that of acquitting myself of the painful and melancholy mission with which he intrusted me."

"Speak, sir."

"They are the last words of your husband, which I am about to repeat to you, Madame la Comtesse; I add nothing to them, I give you my word."

And as the officer observed the astonishment created in Madame de Neuville, by the preamble with which he thought it his duty to introduce what he had to say, he added:

"It is not without reason, madame, that I thus express myself; and you will acknowledge it when I have repeated to you the words of my general.

"'Monsieur de Bourgerel,' he said to me—"

"Monsieur de Bourgerel," exclaimed at the same time Lucie and Laura; "your name is M. de Bourgerel?"

"Yes, ladies," replied the officer, who seemed greatly astonished. "You know my name?"

"Continue, sir; I must, before I reply to the question you have addressed to me, learn the last words of M. de Neuville."

"I obey you, Madame la Comtesse. This then is what the general said to me, when, by the assistance of the other ordnance officers, I had him carried to the military hospital:

"'Monsieur de Bourgerel, I wished to have written to my wife, for I have much to say to her;

but death will not allow me time. Listen to me, then, and promise me that as soon as you arrive in Paris, you will repeat to her what I am about to say to you.'

"My general knew that, as I had resigned my commission, I was to leave in a few days; I gave him the promise he required, and he continued in these terms:

" ' You will say to my dear Lucie, that I die full of gratitude for the happiness I have enjoyed since I become her husband ; and that if it is permitted those in the other world to occupy themselves about those who still remain in this one, I shall pray without ceasing to the Sovereign Ruler of our destinies, to secure her happiness; and I approve, beforehand, all that she will think it her duty to do to be happy. You will say to her besides, that I have chosen you to carry to her my last words, because I wished to associate myself, as much as I have it in my power, with the good action she wishes to accomplish, in assuring your happiness.'

"The general could say no more, Madame la Comtesse; death, unrelenting death, seized upon his prey, and I am thus compelled to seek from you the explanation of the few last words."

The preceding facts, that they may not appear strange to our readers, require to be explained, which shall be done as succinctly as possible.

Lucie, as soon as she had met with Eugenie de Mirbel, had written to her husband, to inform him of what she had done for her friend ; but she was unable to give him, at first, the name of the child's father, which she had not learned until Eugenie had narrated her history. It was not until after she had effected the reconciliation of her friend with her aunt, that she wrote again to her husband, in which letter, after giving him the details it was necessary for him to know, she begged him to seek the officer, whose name she mentioned to him, and to employ the influence of his station and character, to induce him to repair the injury he had caused.

This letter M. de Neuville had not received until the evening before the battle in which he lost his life. The officer, mentioned by his wife, was then his aid-de-camp ; but he had charged him, two hours previously, with a mission which would keep him at a distance until the next morning ; so that the general was forced to defer till after the battle, the preparations for which were making when he arrived, the conversation he proposed to have with him.

Death prevented the accomplishment of his intention; he had only the time, as we have seen, to charge Edmond de Bourgerel to seek his wife, leaving to the latter the care of completing the work she had so worthily commenced.

If to this we add, that the letters written to M. de Bourgerel a few days later, by Eugenie de Mirbel and Madame de Saint Preuil, arrived in Africa when Edmond arrived in Paris, where his first visit had been to Madame de Neuville, we shall not be astonished that the words of the general had appeared to him somewhat extraordinary.

It was Lucie de Neuville then, who informed this young man of all that had happened to the one he loved, since she had quitted the house of her aunt, to spare herself the pain of acknowledging to the worthy woman the fault she had committed.

Edmond could not finish thanking the friendly countess ; he pressed her hands, and those of Laura in his own. Lucie had not allowed him

to remain ignorant of the part her friend had taken in the kind action for which he was congratulating her.

"Ah! ladies," he said to the two friends; "how much I thank you, and how happy I am that death, which I have so often sought on the field of battle, has refused me. Believe me, the image of Eugenie has never ceased to accompany me; in the midst of the unceasing dangers of the fatal campaign we have just made, I had but one desire, one thought—to discover her; and it was because I wished to seek her myself that I have given my resignation, and have come to Paris as soon as I was enabled."

The visit of Edmond de Bourgerel was a fortunate circumstance for the Countess de Neuville: for, by forcing her to occupy herself about her friend, it withdrew her, for a few moments at least, from the heavy grief which bowed her down. Laura understood this, and saw it was necessary to chase away the painful thoughts which haunted her.

"You will, no doubt," said the kind girl, "hasten at once to Eugenie, for you must be impatient to make her forget all the trouble she has suffered."

And as Edmond replied in the affirmative to her:

"But don't you fear," she added, "that the surprise and joy may induce a revolution which might end fatally with her ?"

"You are right, mademoiselle, I will first see Madame de Saint Preuil."

"But this good dame requires as much, if not more management than Eugenie."

"How shall we arrange then ? I have but one relation to whom I could confide the mission of preparing these ladies to receive my visit, and I know that at present he is absent from Paris."

"If Lucie was not, at this moment, absorbed in her grief," said Laura, lowering her voice, but high enough, however, to be heard by her friend, "I would propose to her to go with me to Eugenie, it would be a convenient remedy ; but she would not consent to it."

"And why not, my friend?" said Lucie, moved by the deep sigh which escaped from M. de Bourgerel. "Why not? grief has not rendered me selfish ; and I do not think I can better honour the memory of those who are no more, than by endeavouring to do some little good to those who remain. I shall accompany M. de Bourgerel to our friend."

She rang the bell, and ordered the servant to have the carriage prepared.

"Ah! madame," said Edmond, who had seized her hand, and covered it with kisses, "you are an angel from heaven. The Almighty, I trust, will recompense you."

A melancholy smile rested, for a moment, on the lips of Lucie, she doubted not of the goodness of the Creator; but Hope—that welcome divinity we find constantly at our side, to console us under our sufferings—had spread her wings and sailed away from her. Would she return? The future must answer this question.

Lucie did not require much time to repair the disorder of her toilette ; she thought no longer, alas! about her dress ; and when she descended again to the saloon where Edmond and Laura had remained, the valet de chambre had not yet announced that the carriage was ready. She then took an active part in the conversation, which, during her short absence, had been established

LIFE IN PARIS.

SALVADOR ROBBING HIS WIFE OF HER JEWELS.

between Edmond and Laura. The latter had requested the young officer to inform her of all the circumstances which had accompanied the death of M. de Neuville. Edmond confirmed what the bulletins of the French army in Africa had already apprised Lucie. M. de Neuville had died gloriously in the breach; and it was in the attempt to make a rampart for him, with his body, that Edmond had received the slight wound which obliged him to carry one of his arms in a sling. Lucie paid a fresh tribute of tears to the memory of her husband; and the horses being ready, they departed.

Lucie and Laura first ascended to Eugenie's room, and found her occupied in painting flowers on a screen; the young woman had found no difficulty in procuring means to establish an industry capable of procuring her an honourable existence; for, as we believe we have already observed, she possessed a remarkable talent for flower painting, and her pretty figure, her modest and touching graces, had interested those to whom she had addressed herself, and each had shown a readiness to afford her employment. But we may as well add, in order that our readers may not accuse us of keeping back the truth, that the worthy dealers in these brilliant specimens, in whose service she had placed her ready talent, soon perceived her inexperience, and had neglected no opportunity of procuring the works of the artist, at a price usually given for coloured prints; commerce above all.

When Lucie and Laura entered her modest apartment, Eugenie threw away her palette and brushes, and ran to her two friends, and pressed them to her bosom by turns.

"Thank you for coming to see me," she said; "thank you. The sincere grief you feel, my dear Lucie, has not made you forget that you have here an affectionate friend who pities you, and who is, herself, also unhappy."

"Alas! my dear Eugenie, if I did not know that you will soon be as happy as you are now the contrary, I should believe that we have only been sent on earth to suffer, for my griefs, alas! are irreparable."

"I have no further hope," replied Eugenie, in a melancholy voice; "he has not answered the letters we have addressed to him; he is either dead or has forgotten me. Oh! if the innocent creature to whom I have given life, did not link me to the world, I would willingly descend to the tomb."

"Eugenie! Eugenie! you must not despair," said Laura; "we have this morning seen an officer of the African army, who has announced to us the approaching arrival of M. de Bourgerel in Paris; he only preceded him, he said, a few posts, so that it is possible that to-morrow, to-day perhaps, you may see him; for we know that he has not forgotten you, and that his first visit is intended for you."

"Laura, in the name of heaven! you do not deceive me, eh? Oh! that would be more than cruel. But who then has told you all this? It is not likely that Edmond has confided to a stranger secrets——"

"We have brought with us the person of whom Laura has spoken," replied Lucie; "he is below in our carriage? Would you wish us to request him to ascend?"

"Oh! yes, a friend of Edmond; no doubt charged to announce to me his return! as you have brought him with you, I shall receive him with pleasure."

Eugenie was about giving orders to her servant to descend. Laura prevented her:

"Eugenie," she said to her, "prepare yourself for the interview; you will require all your strength to receive this visitor—you know him!"

"Eugenie," added the countess, who observed that her friend, having a suspicion that the person of whom they spoke, was no other than Edmond de Bourgerel, had become dreadfully pale; "my good Eugenie, be as calm in being made happy, as I am after the painful losses I have suffered."

"Ah! let him come, let him come!" exclaimed Eugenie, her eyes filled with tears; "there is no longer any danger, I weep."

The good old dame, whom our readers already know, had not waited, to descend, for the order of her mistress; and a few minutes after, Edmond pressed to his bosom the faithful fond one, whom a series of untoward circumstances had kept so long at a distance from him.

Edmond could not finish embracing by turns the mother and the child, which Eugenie had placed in his arms.

Lucie and Laura waited patiently for the first transports of the two tender lovers to pass, and found time to address a few words to them; the spectacle of their happiness was useful to them; the thought of having contributed to it was a refreshing balm, which helped to cicatrise the wounds of Lucie's heart.

Edmond, stronger in nerve than Eugenie, was the first to approach the Countess de Neuville.

"Be assured, madame," he said, "that I shall be for ever grateful for what you have done for her; I shall always remember that you forgot your own heavy griefs, to occupy yourself for us. Ah! madame, madame! you are indeed the worthy wife of my brave general."

"Do not thank me," replied Lucie, "now that I have the certainty, that the troubles of my dear Eugenie have arrived at their term, I feel somewhat less unhappy; but do not forget, M. de Bourgerel, that there is another person who awaits your return with the most anxious impatience, and to whom I would also conduct you."

"The kind Madame de Saint Preuil. Ah! I regret to have forgotten her so long," said Edmond de Bourgerel; "but is it not excusable?" he added, regarding Eugenie with looks full of tenderness.

The latter, who had thrown a shawl over her shoulders, was ready to depart, and a few moments after, they all arrived at the house of Madame de Saint Preuil.

"I do not come, madame," said Edmond de Bourgerel, kneeling before the old lady, who had been previously apprised of his coming, "to solicit a pardon, which you have already had the goodness to bestow upon me; I come simply to beg of you to embrace the husband of your niece, and to give you an assurance that my whole life shall be devoted to the endeavour of making you forget the trouble I have already caused you."

A scene nearly similar to the one with Eugenie de Mirbel now took place, and Lucie and Laura left M. de Bourgerel at the house of Madame de Saint Preuil.

We may here inform our readers that Edmond de Bourgerel, after arranging his affairs as a retired officer, married Eugenie. The peculiar position of the two young persons, imposed upon them the necessity of giving to their union the least publicity possible; they were married then without parade, merely accompanied by indispensable witnesses, and a small party of friends, from whom they had no fear of listening to ungracious commentaries or malicious epigrammes. After the religious ceremony, the married pair approached Lucie and Laura.

"We mean to retire," said Edmond de Bourgerel, "to a small property I possess at St. Leonard, a pretty little village in the neighbourhood of Senlis; our fortune will not allow us to live consistently in Paris; and Madame de Saint Preuil, that she may follow us, has consented to quit the Swiss chalet she inhabits. May we hope, ladies, that you will sometimes pay a visit to our modest hermitage? You will certainly not find there the luxury and comfort to which you are accustomed, but you will always meet with frank and devoted hearts."

"And that is worth all the rest," replied Lucie, offering her hand to Edmond, who pressed it affectionately in his own, after kissing it several times. "I do not refuse the invitation you have made me, M. de Bourgerel; as soon as I am able I will visit, and I shall remain some time with you, be assured; a view of the happiness you are about to enjoy, will sometimes cause me to forget my troubles."

Edmond, before his marriage, had arranged all his affairs which might keep him at Paris; a travelling carriage, therefore, waited at the church-door, for Madame de Saint Preuil and the young couple. Madame de Neuville remained to see them depart.

"May you be happy," she said to them, as the horses moved away; "may you be happy; and think, sometimes, of the friends you leave at Paris."

"For ever! for ever," replied Eugenie de Bourgerel, waving her handkerchief. "Adieu, Lucie, adieu, Laura; or rather, till we meet again."

The carriage disappeared in the cloud of dust which it raised behind it.

"Ah! my dear Laura," said Lucie, who threw herself into the arms of her friend as soon as they had entered their carriage, "now that all who loved me are dead or gone, what will become of me if you quit me?"

CHAPTER XXXI.

A FATAL AMOUR.

THE Countess de Neuville, on reaching her hotel, found a letter for her, bearing the arms of the Marquis de Pourrieres; she showed it to Laura.

"What can this man have to say to me?" she said, unsealing the letter. "Can he have the audacity to speak to me of love, at such a moment?"

"I do not think so," replied Laura; "I cannot deny to the Marquis de Pourrieres the quality of being a man of good society, and I do not think he would dare to talk of love to a widow, before the remains of her husband are yet cold."

"Read," said Lucie, after glancing at the short missive of Salvador, which was written in these terms:

"Madame,—The journals have apprised me of the painful misfortune with which you have been visited; believe that I take a very sincere part in the profound grief you must feel, and deign to accept, with an assurance of the most disinterested devotedness, that of the very great respect with which I have the honour of subscribing myself,

"Madame la Comtesse," &c.

"It is merely a letter of condolence, similar to all the others you have received, and which you have not taken the trouble of opening," said Laura, after reading it.

"I feel thankful to him for writing me nothing more," replied Lucie.

With the letter of the Marquis de Pourrieres, several others had been handed to the countess, as well as the daily list of persons who had subscribed their names since the death of her husband.

Whilst the countess read the letters, which were nearly all similar to Salvador's, Laura ran over the lists; a name, among those of the previous evening, suddenly struck her.

"Do you know that?" she said.

"Paul Feval," replied the countess, after reflecting a few moments; "this name is quite unknown to me; no doubt 'tis the name of some one we have met in society."

"It's singular! I have a vague recollection that I have heard this name pronounced somewhere. Ah! I have it; 'tis the name of an old lady who inhabited, at Lagny, the house next to ours. Can it be her son who has called upon us? I must ascertain this."

Laura rang, and ordered the concierge to ascend to the drawing-room.

"Do you remember," she said to him, showing the list, upon which was written the name which had so strongly attracted her attention, "the person who wrote this?"

"Yes, mademoiselle," replied the concierge, after collecting himself; "I remember, even, that you were the person this gentleman inquired for, and it was merely because he learnt our recent misfortunes from some other individuals who were at the same time in my lodge, that he inscribed his name on the list; you will find, among the correspondence, his card, which he charged me to deliver to you, with a request that you would receive him to-morrow. 'He has,' he said to me, 'something important to communicate to you, from a person you hold dear.'"

"I am now sure," said Laura to Lucie, after making a sign to the concierge that he might retire, "that this gentleman is the son or the nephew, I know not which, of our old neighbour of Lagny, and that he has something to tell me from my uncle; for my uncle and yourself are the only persons in the world who are dear to me, and are interested in me."

"This visit, which seems to give you so much delight, grieves me, I know not why," replied the countess; "something tells me that we shall be forced to separate."

"No, no, my uncle has several times already announced, that I should soon have the pleasure of seeing him, and his promises have never been realized. For my part, I think I am destined never to be married, but to grow old in your society."

The next morning, the individual whom Laura waited for with some impatience, presented himself at the Hotel de Neuville. In consequence of previous orders, he was introduced at once to the two ladies, who received him in the salon.

He was a man a little beyond thirty years of age, tall, and well made, and had an interesting and agreeable physiognomy, although somewhat serious; his dress, at once simple and elegant, announced the man of good society.

After saluting the two ladies with the greatest respect, he handed a letter to Laura.

"'Tis from my uncle," said the young girl,

after reading the address; and she hastily opened it.

The young man, whilst she read it, could not take his eyes off her; in fact, the charming person now before him recalled to his remembrance a graceful child, and he now sought to collect from his memory her different features, to compose an ensemble.

"My poor friend," said Laura, after finishing the perusal of the letter, which she handed to Lucie, "your presentiments have not deceived you, we shall soon be obliged to separate; but do not despair," she added immediately, for she observed the tears trickling down the cheeks of her friend, "I do not quit Paris. We shall see one another often, every day even."

"Sir Edward Lambton mentions you in such honourable terms," said Lucie, who, in her turn, had read the letter brought by Paul Feval, (who was no other, as our readers have no doubt already suspected, than Servigny,) "that we know not how we can better convince him of the affection we have for him than by offering you a share. We therefore hope, sir, that you will accept a residence at our hotel until the arrival of Sir Edward at Paris."

Paul Feval (we shall preserve for the present to our hero this name, which was that of his mother) replied in respectful terms to the warm reception of the Countess de Neuville, whose kind invitation however he did not accept; to justify his refusal, he alleged the frequent absences he would be obliged to make, Sir Edward having charged him at once to engage and furnish his house in Paris, where he intended to fix himself, and also to purchase for him a property situated in the neighbourhood of the capital.

"But although I must refuse, that I may not render myself troublesome, the kind offer you have made me," continued Paul Feval, addressing the countess, "I shall, madame, more than once have occasion to put your good nature to the proof; Sir Edward having expressly charged me to do nothing without the advice and approval of his dear niece; I hope you will sometimes serve me as a guide, for I must not conceal it from you, the long residence I have made in India has rendered me somewhat of a stranger to the customs of the Parisian fashion."

"I will do every thing for my dear Laura," replied the countess, "whatever may be agreeable to her; but you will have a dull companion in your excursions."

"Indeed, madame, upon my arrival in Paris, I was informed of the death of M. le General Count de Neuville. The death of such a brave officer is a real calamity; but the thought that all who love their country share your grief, must be to you a strong source of consolation."

"I accept with resignation the cross which the Creator has seen fit to place upon me, but it is nevertheless heavy to support; for I lose, almost at the same time, a husband I loved, the only relation who remained to me, and my dearest friend."

"Why, Lucie, you cannot mean it, one would really think I was going to reside at the antipodes. You do not perceive then that my uncle intends to fix himself in Paris."

"I think, indeed, Madame la Comtesse, that you are wrong to be alarmed. Sir Edward, although he only knows you by reputation, loves you, madame, almost equal to his niece, and when you are acquainted with this worthy man, you will not find it possible to refuse him your friendship. It is, therefore, a friend that heaven sends, to enable you to support the loss of those who are no longer on earth."

"May the will of God be done! Whatever may be His decrees, I shall accept them with gratitude."

During the whole time that the three persons assembled in the saloon of the Hotel de Neuville had occupied in the preceding conversation, Paul Feval, upon every occasion that presented itself, had attentively examined Laura, who, on her side, whilst he conversed with Madame de Neuville had several times regarded him with interest. These attentions had not escaped Lucie's observation.

Most women possess the wonderful faculty of comprehending each other, without the necessity of speaking; a gesture, a sign almost imperceptible, rapidly exchanged between themselves, inform them sometimes of what we men could not express without the aid of a long discourse. Thus, a simple wink of the eye, to which she had replied by a slight shrug of the shoulders, told Lucie that her friend thought she recognised in the young man before them, the individual of whom they had spoken on the previous evening, that she wished to ascertain if she were deceived, but that she dared not question him.

Lucie could refuse Laura nothing.

"Your name, monsieur," she said to Paul Feval, "is not unknown to us; and yesterday, when we observed it on the list of persons who had inscribed their names, we expected to receive to-day the visit of an individual already known to my friend."

"Mon Dieu! madame, if it is a hazard it is a very singular one; for the name of mademoiselle recals to me that of a companion of my younger days, who must now have the same age and the graceful features of mademoiselle."

"No more doubt!" exclaimed Laura, after hearing the reply of Paul Feval; "you are from Lagny?"

"Yes, mademoiselle."

"I thought so; in that village I passed a good part of my infancy. Your mother's house was next to the one I lived in with my aunt; 'twas you who promenaded me in the garden of your house, and also made me cocoa-nut boxes and the droll figures that moved their eyes and tongue in so comical a manner that they nearly made me die with laughing. I was very little then, but I have a good memory you see."

"And you have attained all that you promised at that period."

"It's true," replied Laura, whom the pleasure she experienced in recalling the scenes of her days of childhood had prevented perceiving that she was paying herself a compliment. "Do you remember how gay and foolish I was, and how delighted when you made me a present of a nest of goldfinches or linnets, which, at the risk of breaking your neck, you went to seek for me in the top of one of the old trees which border the Marne?"

"You remind me, mademoiselle, of the happiest period of my life. Why, alas! has it been succeeded by so many painful days?"

"As my uncle has charged you to purchase a property which no doubt we shall often visit, you must choose it at Lagny or the neighbourhood; I shall be really delighted to behold once more the spot where I passed my childhood."

Paul Feval, who had listened with intense pleasure to the innocent reminiscences of the young girl, replied, "that in pursuing any plan most agreeable to her, he should only be fulfilling the orders he had received from Sir Edward; that she may be assured that the next morning he would put himself *en route* for the country, to explore the neighbourhood of Lagny; and that if he found in the environs a suitable mansion and grounds, he would, before concluding the purchase, give her an invitation to visit it;" he then added, "that Sir Edward having also charged him to purchase an hotel in Paris, he should be very glad to learn what quarter she wished to reside in."

"I should like, if that were possible, that from my windows, I could look upon those of my kind Lucie," replied Laura.

"Had I but the lamp of Aladdin, mademoiselle, your wishes should be granted as soon as formed; but I possess, as a substitute for this wonderful lamp, two talismen, by the aid of which we may surmount many obstacles."

"And what then are these pair of talismen?"

"Plenty of good-will, and plenty of cash."

"Ah ça! my uncle is very rich then."

"Much richer than you may suppose; but a splendid fortune was never placed in worthier hands. Sir Edward Lambton makes the best use of his; he is aware that in his possession it is but a deposit of which the unfortunate deserve their share; thus, every day he dries some fresh tears, every hour of his life is marked by a good action. Ah! mademoiselle, you are happy in belonging to him; if all the favoured ones of the land resembled your uncle, no one assuredly would complain of being poor."

There was so much emotion in the voice of Paul Feval in pronouncing the preceding words, it was so readily perceived that what he said was the sincere expression of his conviction, that the two women could not help being deeply affected.

"'Tis well, monsieur, 'tis well," said Lucie to him, and offering her hand, "heaven recompenses Sir Edward Lambton for all the good he does, since it has bestowed upon him a friend who knows so well how to appreciate the eminent qualities he possesses."

We must conclude that some choice minds obtain a perfect understanding at a first interview, since Paul Feval, although somewhat of a misanthrope, from the misfortunes he had experienced, found himself quite at his ease in the company of the two amiable women who had received him with so much affability; their conversation appeared to him so interesting, that it seemed as though he had been long acquainted with them, and he no more thought of taking his leave than they did of dismissing him. It was, therefore, with considerable surprise that he heard the valet de chambre enter the saloon, and announce that dinner was ready; he had been more than three hours at the Countess de Neuville's.

He rose at once to take leave.

"Time passes imperceptibly in your company, ladies," he said, "and I therefore trust you will be indulgent, and pardon me for the immoderate length of my first visit."

"Why leave us so soon?" replied Lucie, "dine with us, if you have no other engagement; you are here the representative of Sir Edward, and I am persuaded he would not refuse me if I made him the same request I now do to you."

"Remain, M. Feval," added Laura, "we will talk about Lagny and the souvenirs of past times, will you not?"

Paul Feval could not resist such friendly entreaties; he accepted, happy at being enabled to pass a few more hours in the society of Laura, towards whom he felt himself attracted by a sentiment of a very different nature from that which he had formerly felt towards Silvia.

For some days following, Paul Feval employed himself in exploring the environs of Paris, for the purpose of choosing a residence which would be to the taste of her he already loved; this was not difficult; for as he had observed in conversation, he could dispose of a talisman nearly as powerful as that of Aladdin—plenty of gold.

Laura experienced a lively joy at her being at length about to see a relation whom she had never yet known, except from the benefits he had bestowed upon her; but this joy was lessened by the pain which the separation from her friend caused her, and which was the more intense, as she observed that Lucie's sadness increased in proportion as the arrival of Sir Edward in Paris approached.

Lucie was no doubt afflicted at her friend being obliged to quit her; but the moody sadness to which she was a prey, was induced by other causes. The reader has probably not forgotten, that in the letter he had written her, Doctor Matheo had made her a promise to send her in a short time a detailed explanation of the motives which had engaged him to address his first epistle to her, several months had elapsed, and Lucie, who had frequently sent to the post office, had not yet received the letter which she expected, and which would, at least she thought so, put an end to the cruel perplexity to which she was a prey; this was the principal cause of her sadness, and this unhappiness will appear quite natural, when we have stated the motives which induced her to wait with such anxiety for the promised letter of Doctor Matheo.

Salvador, after hearing of the death of the General Count de Neuville, and also of the Marquise de Villerbanne, thought to himself that to marry the countess, would be a master stroke, and would secure at once his position in the world, and his fortune, broken by the rude assaults which the daily prodigalities and continual losses of Roman had made upon it; thus, what at first was but a caprice, which might have passed away from inability to satisfy it, had become a project, to the success of which he had taken the resolution of consecrating all the ability and perseverance he possessed, and the letter of condolence which we have placed before our readers, was the first scene of the comedy he intended to play, to attain the object at which he aimed.

Lucie had not replied to this letter, which was imprudent; she might have received it as a simple acknowledgment of the interest which her position would necessarily inspire those who knew her, and have made him one of those commonplace replies, which actually signify nothing, but which are no less exacted by the laws which regulate good society: not to reply to the Marquis de Pourrieres after what had passed between them, was to bestow upon the letter he had written her, an importance it did not possess; it was in some measure giving him the right to suppose that she dreaded him too much, to allow her to have the least relation with him; thus at least thought Salvador, and he acted in consequence.

Other letters followed, much longer ones, but in which, however, he only spoke of herself, and of the share he took in the grief in which she was absorbed. These letters were written with such a touching sensibility, the Marquis de Pourrieres mentioned the good Marchioness de Villerbanne with so much veneration, "who," he said, "had been the most cherished friend of his father," it was so plainly perceptible, although he did not express it, that he loved the person to whom he addressed them, that Lucie—predisposed, perhaps, by a thought of the solitude with which she was menaced, to receive with a certain indulgence those who showed themselves attached to her—replied to him in a few affectionate words.

Any one less skilful than Salvador would have been in haste, after obtaining such a result, to solicit the favour of being admitted to the Hotel de Neuville; he was not guilty of such maladresse; he considered the countess as a wild bird, which he must grow familiar with by degrees before making an attempt to seize it, and he acted in consequence.

He replied to the first letter of the countess—that, obliged to visit his estates, he should be compelled to deprive himself of the pleasure of corresponding with her for some days; it was a sort of treaty that he concluded with her, something of an engagement he made her enter into unknowingly; this rather astonished the countess, but as the terms of Salvador's note were perfectly respectful, she bestowed upon this view of her relations with the marquis but very little attention.

The absence of Salvador—who, that he might not run the risk of being surprised *en flagrant délit* of a falsehood, had gone to hunt with one of his friends—was prolonged for several weeks, and more than once, during this time, Lucie—disposed by the complete loneliness in which she had lived since the death of her husband, to receive favourably anything that might help to break the habitual monotony of her existence—was desirous of receiving a letter from the Marquis de Pourrieres; at length there came one. Salvador gave her an account of the results of his travels; he spoke of his estates, their situation, the improvements he intended to make in the cultivation of his land, of the revenue they produced him; then, returning to himself, he told her he was taking steps to obtain a general payment, and that he hoped they would be crowned with success.

This letter, the object of which, as Salvador had hoped, escaped Lucie, much amused the Countess de Neuville, and brought the reply upon which the marquis had reckoned when writing it. Lucie's reply said, that, no doubt, he supposed he was writing to his lawyer or his agent; and that she could not conceive why, unless his letter was the result of an error or inexplicable preoccupation, he sent her so exact an account of his revenues. She finished by congratulating him that his fortune was so brilliant and so firmly secured, and her wishes for the success of his projects.

The following is the reply of Salvador to the last letter of the Countess de Neuville:

"Madame la Comtesse,—It was under the expectation that it would bring the reply you have just made me, that I determined to write the letter which has so greatly astonished you. May you receive this with the same indulgence you have granted to those which have preceded it.

"You tell me, Madame la Comtesse, in terminating the letter I have now received, that you wish I may succeed in *all* my projects; if, after reading this, you do not retract these amiable sentiments, I shall, without contradiction, be the happiest of men; I confess to you I have but little hope of it; but, however, as upon yourself depends the accomplishment of my dearest wish, I have determined, at the risk of what may be the consequences, to write you this letter, which, perhaps, you will throw aside without perusing farther, when you cast your eyes upon the following paragraph:

"I love you, Madame la Comtesse! Before I had met you I felt somewhat disposed to doubt the maxim of Labruyère—'*L'amour naît a la première vue!*'* but I am compelled to acknowledge, to-day, that the celebrated moralist was not deceived when he wrote this; for the love you have inspired in me, and which, I feel assured, will only end with my life, took its date from the day on which we encountered each other for the first time.

"This love, the avowal of which I was] bold enough to make you at Madame de Villerbanne's, an avowal which you repulsed as became you at that time, and which, perhaps, will raise to-day between us an insurmountable barrier, (for I cannot attempt to excuse a fault which I can only attribute to the violence of the sentiment with which you inspired me, and such an excuse I am sure you would not accept;) this love, I repeat, I have vainly endeavoured to tear from my heart; superfluous attempts! useless trouble! 'Tis in vain I seek distractions in society, 'tis in vain I ask from study for a remedy to my disease. In the midst of the most brilliant circle and the liveliest scenes, as in the silence of the cabinet, a graceful image was for ever in my sight. It was yours, madame! I am therefore compelled, after exhausting all my energies in the struggle, to resign myself to suffer in silence, if you do not condescend to bestow upon me one look of pity.

"The death of M. le Comte de Neuville, which, be persuaded, I deeply deplore—and that of the Marchioness de Villerbanne, leaves you, Madame la Comtesse, isolated in the midst of the world; I am aware that you have had the misfortune to lose all your relations. It is a very miserable situation, that of a being, whatever may be her fortune and position in society, who has no devoted arm upon which she may lean whilst following the tortuous path of life. I may speak to you in this manner, Madame la Comtesse, for my position is identically similar to your own; like you, unpitying death has carried off all those who were dear to me; like you, I am alone in the world! I have friends, without doubt, who has not? but is it quite prudent to reckon upon the affection of mere friends—and is it not natural that they should abandon us, when the ties of blood, or love, call them to a distance from us?"

Salvador knew the strong friendship which united Lucie and Laura, and it was not without intention he inserted this phrase; he wished, by showing her the possibility of a separation between herself and her friend, to alarm her still more as to the loneliness which, in such an event, would surround her, and, in his opinion, dispose her not to refuse, without an examination, the request he had made her. His anticipations, as the sequel will prove, were not deceived. Chance, also, favoured him—that strange divinity, which appears sometimes, by favouring the most foolish and even criminal enterprises, to aim at proving that the poets were not wrong in telling us she was blind—for it was but a short time after the arrival in Paris of Paul Feval, and his first visit at the Hotel de Neuville, that the countess received

* "Love springs at first sight.'

the letter, of which we will now give the remainder to our readers.

"You would not, Madame la Comtesse, bury yourself in an obscure retreat, when you possess all the amiable and brilliant qualities which would be the ornament of your society? It would, besides, be neglecting the mission imposed upon you, since the Almighty, in calling to himself the estimable man you have lost, did not will that you should end your days with him—it was, that in his justice he reserved to another the happiness of possessing you!

"You have guessed, Madame la Comtesse, that I solicit on both knees the honour of becoming your husband. I have certainly no pretension to replace the one you have lost; I cannot offer you a name made illustrious in every battle field of the Empire! (We shall observe to our readers in passing, that these praises, so generously accorded to M. de Neuville, and so flattering to the countess, were intended to remind her of the husband she had lost, who was much older than herself, and to draw a comparison, which could not be otherwise than advantageous to him who offered himself.) But, such as it is, my name is honourable—that of one of the most ancient families in the south of France; and I feel that the desire of pleasing you, if you are ambitious, would render me capable of making it as illustrious as formerly.

"I shall say nothing as to my fortune; the letter, which this one is intended to explain, has informed you upon this subject of all it is necessary you should know, and you have been enabled to judge that, without being colossal, it is at least reasonable. Pardon me, Madame la Comtesse, if I trespass on a ground which I would not willingly approach, but we live in a society so strangely organized, that it is as well sometimes to observe that the feelings of our heart are not always regulated by interested motives. I should wish that you were poor, that I might have the pleasure of enriching you; but since it is not thus, I am happy that heaven has kindly granted me sufficient wealth to place beyond a possibility the supposition that I wish to obtain aught but that which I solicit—your hand! to which, if you bestow it upon me, you will soon join the gift of your heart; for you will then be enabled to appreciate the real affection and devoted tenderness which echoes in my own!

"Do not reply to me hastily, Madame la Comtesse; take time to reflect. Whatever may be your decree, whether favourable or not, it will in no way change the sentiments of affection of him, who subscribes himself, &c. &c."

This letter, every sentence in which Salvador had scrupulously weighed, and which was received at a favourable moment, made a great impression on the mind of the Countess de Neuville. After reading it with the most serious attention, she questioned herself whether she ought to refuse, without consideration, the offer made to her in such respectful terms by the Marquis de Pourrieres.

After glancing at the future that awaited her, she imagined herself descending to the tomb without leaving a regret behind her, after an old age passed in sadness and solitude. Laura loved her, beyond a doubt; her friendship was dear to her—but Laura, young, handsome, rich, must necessarily, and at no distant period, marry; she would then have children, a family to which she would be forced to devote herself. But she herself, also, possessed every quality that promised to her friend

so happy a destiny! Ought she, then, as a modern Artemisia, to be disinherited of all her joys, because she had lost a husband, whom she had no doubt loved, and who was worthy of being so; but for whom, notwithstanding, she had never felt that exclusive passion, which prevented another object occupying the place of him who was no longer here? No! without doubt.

A man, possessing an honourable name, a fortune at least equal to her own, of whom every one spoke in terms of praise, and who seemed to have vowed a real affection for her, presents himself, and says to her:

"Like you, I am alone in the world; let us accept the hand of each other, and each support the other in traversing the rough path of life." And this man she loved! 'twas in vain she endeavoured to conceal it—she loved him with all her strength, with all her soul! Ought she to refuse him?

The conclusion of the preceding reasonings is not difficult to guess. The unhappy Countess de Neuville sent to the Marquis de Pourrieres a letter, which, although it did not enclose a complete acquiescence in his wishes, still allowed him to hope that they would soon be realized.

After receiving this letter, Salvador requested permission to pay his respects, occasionally, to the Countess de Neuville.

Lucie had not confided to her friend the events which were passing; and this is not strange. Laura, every time the name of the marquis was pronounced in her presence, accompanied it with some cruel epigrammes, too certain signs of the hatred which, without knowing why, she had vowed to this individual, as well as his friend the Viscount de Lussan; so that Lucie, too timid to defend the man she loved when attacked without reason in her presence, would not, for all the world, that it were known to what a point her relations with him had arrived; and she sometimes surprised herself in wishing for the arrival of Sir Edward, who, by separating her from Laura, would leave her at liberty to act at her pleasure. She replied to Salvador, then, that for the present she could not grant him the favour he solicited; that she wished, before receiving him, to allow a short time yet to elapse; but that he may rest assured that the moment her saloon should open, the name of the Marquis de Pourrieres should figure among the list of invitations.

She had given this last letter to the servant to be carried to its address, and was searching in a small desk, in which she kept her correspondence, for another, received some time back, and to which she now intended to reply, when the letter written to her by Doctor Matheo, and which she had entirely forgotten, came to hand.

A sudden revolution took place in the ideas of Lucie, at the sight of this letter.

"My God! my God!" she exclaimed, "if the revelations he wishes to make me should render this union impossible! Ah! this would be a dreadful misfortune, and which I certainly could not survive."

And as the doctor had now been absent some time, and, however distant might be the spot he had chosen for his residence, the letter he had promised had had sufficient time to arrive, Lucie sent immediately to the post, to inquire if a letter remained there, bearing as an address, the initials "C. D. N."

The domestic returned with a reply in the negative. Lucie sent again, at intervals, but the reply was always the same. This letter, to which she

No. 36.

LIFE IN PARIS.

THE MASK OF ROMAN SHOWN TO SALVADOR.

attached a great importance, precisely for the reason that she was ignorant of what it might contain—this letter, which was to give her the character of the man she had almost chosen for a husband—this letter did not arrive. Was the doctor dead? Had he forgotten her, or had his letter been written simply to induce her to shun a man she felt disposed to love? Of the three suppositions, the last was the one Lucie admitted the most willingly, although the serious character of the doctor rendered it little probable; but she loved the Marquis de Pourrieres—and it is a long while since it was said for the first time, and with truth, that "when we love, we do not reason."

The purchase of an estate near the small village of Lagny, which Lucie and Laura had visited, and which appeared charming to the latter; and, also, of an hotel, next to that occupied by the Countess de Neuville, had taken up much time, and Paul Feval therefore, to his great regret, had appeared but seldom at the Countess de Neuville's; but he consoled himself with the thought that he should shortly live under the same roof as Laura, and that he could then see her and speak to her at every hour in the day. Must we say that he already loved this young girl, and dreamt of being loved in return? Of a truth, no. He merely obeyed that sentiment, so natural, which is not already love, but which much resembles it; and though without an object, without hope, makes us desirous of being in the company of an amiable and pretty woman; the position of Paul Feval with Sir Edward, and his fatal antecedents, prevented him even thinking of her whom he had loved while she was but a child.

Paul Feval, who endeavoured to acquit himself conscientiously of the different missions confided to him by Sir Edward, had displayed so much zeal, and so usefully employed his time, that the hotel was furnished, the domestics at their posts, the horses in the stable, and the carriages in their houses, when he received from his generous protector a letter, inviting him to meet him at Vernon, where he had rested with one of his old retainers; "Seeing," he said, "that he would not make his entrance into Paris without the society of his faithful friend."

Paul Feval, after carrying to Laura a letter enclosed in his own, put himself en route at once. He took with him a considerable sum in gold, which Sir Edward had requested him to obtain from his banker and bring him; and to travel more expeditiously, he had harnessed the best horse in the stable to a light cabriolet, which he drove himself, not wishing to encumber himself with a servant for a journey he intended to accomplish in one stage.

His visit to the Hotel de Neuville where he had been invited to dinner, had retained him some time; so that it was already late when he started. However he arrived at a good port, and much sooner than he expected, although accompanied with a heavy rain.

It was not without a feeling of considerable emotion that he passed in front of the auberge of Bienvenu, where his life, a few days previously, had escaped so great danger.

The small house, feebly lighted in the interior, was tranquil and silent.

"Who knows," said Paul to himself, "if, at this moment, they may not be assassinating some unlucky traveller, for the purpose of robbing him?"

"The miserable weather has not prevented your starting," said Sir Edward, when he saw Paul Feval enter the humble apartment he occupied in the house of his retainer, at Vernon; "it's right! I like people to be punctual, morbleu! But have you brought me what I requested?"

"I have enclosed, as you ordered me, five hundred napoleons, quite new, in an elegant box, which I have brought you."

Sir Edward opened the little chest which Paul had handed him, and in which the napoleons were enclosed in a secret drawer and covered by a lady's work-box, furnished with every necessary. "Yes, this is quite right," he said, after satisfying himself that Paul Feval had rigorously conformed to his instructions; "it is quite right. I wished to stop here a few days," he added, "before fixing myself in Paris, as I knew there resided here a man who found an occasion some time ago to render me an important service, and I am verily arrived àpropos; this worthy man, who has not been lucky enough to make his fortune, gives his daughter in marriage, but cannot bestow a dowry upon her. I wish to give her one myself; it is one mode among others of acknowledging the services rendered to me by the father, who, poor as he is, is as proud as a Spanish hidalgo, and would never accept anything; but he will be well trapped! I shall, in his presence, and only a few moments before entering the carriage, give my little box to mademoiselle, who will be delighted at receiving such a handsome dressing-case; when they discover the secret drawer, I shall be far away, and if they come to speak to me respecting it, I shall reply that I know nothing about it!"

Sir Edward, it is perceived, was one of those rare men, who do good simply for the pleasure they feel in so doing, and who trouble themselves but very little about the thanks or praises their benefits may be worth; let us add, however, that we may not be accused of having *mis en scene* one of those *enrichi* of the modern world, and met with in a number of vaudevilles and melo-dramas, that Sir Edward was not in the habit of flinging his purse at the head of every one he met, and that if he presented ten thousand francs to the daughter of his host as a dowry, he felt satisfied that the service which the father had rendered him justified his generosity. If we should now be told that there is no great merit in acknowledging a service, and that many others, in the place of Sir Edward, would have acted in a similar manner, we shall reply, that it is possible, but that we do not think so; gratitude, in our opinion, being a virtue of the rarest kind. Besides, we would not here enumerate all the qualities of Sir Edward, which the events that are to follow will sufficiently distinguish; and also, remarking that the present which he destined for the daughter of his host was accepted, as one of those pleasing bagatelles it is the custom to present to a newly-made bride. We shall place ourselves by his side in the seat of the cabriolet which conducts him to Paris, and after listening to his conversation with Paul Feval, shall repeat it to our readers.

"Well! my friend," he said, when the cabriolet had passed the retiring houses of Vernon, and was rolling along the beautiful road of Normandy, "you have seen my dear little niece! is she really as pretty as this poor Count de Neuville has often written me?"

"However M. le Comte de Neuville may have exalted the charms of Mademoiselle de Beaumont," replied Paul Feval, "he has, I am sure, kept below the truth; it is impossible to picture a more charming creature!"

"The devil! the devil!" replied Sir Edward laughing; "you alarm me, my dear Feval; we shall require a very handsome cage to guard such a beautiful bird! Are those which you have chosen quite suitable?"

"I have conformed to your orders; I have done nothing without previously consulting Mademoiselle de Beaumont, and as she is, as well as her friend—who has kindly assisted me with her advice—endowed with an unerring taste and most delicate perception, I think you will be satisfied."

"And so our hotel at Paris——"

"Is charmingly and tastefully furnished."

"Our house in the country——"

"Is a sweet little chateau, situated a few leagues from Paris, quite close to Lagny—a pretty little village in the department of Seine-et-Marne—where Mademoiselle de Beaumont was brought up."

"But, if I do not deceive myself, you are also from Lagny?"

"It is true, and chance has ordained that I should find in Mademoiselle de Beaumont a young lady whom I knew when she was but a child, and myself but a very young man."

"Really, and you recognised each other at once?"

"The house inhabited by Mademoiselle de Beaumont at Lagny, was next to that of my mother, and her name fixed itself in my memory; it was this remembrance which enabled me to recognise your niece, for time has changed the graceful child into such an admirable young woman."

"That I foresee, I must make up my mind to be soon separated from her," replied Sir Edward, attentively regarding Paul Feval; "admirers will present themselves in crowds at the hotel; and as I have no intention to condemn my niece to remain a vestal, I must bestow her hand on some one."

Paul Feval could not listen to these words without feeling some emotion; he replied, however, in the most natural tone in the world, that he was quite certain Mademoiselle de Beaumont would make a choice worthy of herself, and that would secure her happiness.

Sir Edward, as the reader may have already guessed, cherished a project which he would not easily have renounced, and did not expect so insipid a reply as the one he had received; we ought rather to say, that he had hoped to see some dark clouds lowering on the brows of Paul Feval. These hopes being destroyed, by the firmness of the unhappy young man, he continued for some minutes in somewhat of a bad humour, and it was quite suddenly that he said to his travelling companion, from a wish to renew the conversation:

"You will not be sorry then to dance at the wedding of my niece?"

The intention which had dictated this question would have been perceived by an intelligence much inferior to that possessed by the individual to whom it was addressed; it did not therefore escape Paul Feval. His blood rushed to his heart, when he saw to what a brilliant future he might aspire; the hand of a young female, amiable, lovely, and rich, was in a manner offered to him, to him a poor Paria, who possessed nothing in the world; and this woman he loved, he became certain of it at this moment; the words of Sir Edward had revealed to him the state of his heart; it was too much happiness, or rather, it was too great a misfortune; for after taking a review of the events of his past life, he said to himself, that this woman whom he loved, and by whom he was sure he could make himself beloved; that this woman whose hand his protector had so generously permitted him to hope for, could not be his, for he could not even present to her the offering of the poorest individual, a name pure and without blemish. Ought he, as a reward for the generosity of Sir Edward, to associate to a destiny so uncertain as his, whose course may be interrupted by the most trifling event, that of a young and innocent girl, before whom opened the most brilliant prospects, and whose days should be spun of silk and gold? Oh! no, honour imposed upon him a duty he knew how to fulfil; but how beat down to the bottom of his heart the sentiments which had grown up there.

Are there not moments in every man's life during which he is not master of his will? And ought not he to dread these moments, whom destiny beckoned to live with Laura! how should he act then? Depart, quit his benefactor, abandon the position he had acquired near Sir Edward Lambton, at the risk even of passing as an ingrate. The sacrifice was great without doubt; but the Almighty who had given him strength to support the cruel sufferings of his past life, would still enable him to accomplish this bitter task.

Such were the thoughts of our hero, whilst Sir Edward, delighted at having found the means of placing him as we may say at the foot of the ladder, waited impatiently for a reply, and employing himself in caressing his chin, but astonished at length by the silence of his companion:

"You do not reply to me, Feval?" he said to him. "I asked you if you would be very glad to dance at the wedding of my niece."

The resolution of Paul Feval was settled, when for the second time Sir Edward addressed this question to him.

"I believe that I shall not enjoy this pleasure," he replied; "I have well reflected since my arrival in Paris; I have said to myself that repose is not intended for a man at my age; so that I have determined to request your permission to allow me to return to India."

"You have not the least consistency in your ideas, my dear Feval," replied Sir Edward; "I wished, as you may remember, to give up one of my plantations to you; you however refused this offer for the purpose of following me to Paris."

"I could not resolve to abandon you."

"And can you do that to-day without regret, which nothing could induce you to do a few months back. Oh! the men! the men!"

"Sir Edward," exclaimed Paul Feval, who was greatly afflicted at the doubt which the exclamation of the former seemed to imply, "you do not think me capable of such ingratitude."

"I believe nothing," replied Sir Edward; "but as I cannot attribute any reasonable motive for this sudden desire of revisiting the country you have just left, I have the honour of informing you that if you have any wish of preserving my friendship, you will remain with me as agreed upon."

Was Paul Feval really sorry that Sir Edward had so unanswerably refused the request he had appeared to make? We do not think so; at all events he did not insist.

"You know, Sir Edward, that your slightest wish is an order for me," he said.

"Very good, my young friend, very good, and to recompense you your desire of acceding to my wishes, I promise you that when my niece is married, we will all three visit Switzerland and Italy, two beautiful countries, and far preferable to India, which is only visited to make a fortune."

Sir Edward, we perceive, would not relinquish the project he had formed.

"My God! my God!" exclaimed Paul to himself, "inspire me—how ought I to act to show myself worthy of the kindness of this excellent man?"

"Advise me," said Sir Edward, "shall we drive to our hotel, or go at once to Madame de Neuville's? I am inclined for the latter plan, I confess, and 'tis that I shall adopt, if you see no inconvenience in it. I think the countess will excuse the modesty of our travelling costume, in favour of an impatience which I presume will appear natural to her."

"Madame la Comtesse is a charming woman; she is neither coquettish nor affected, and she will consider it quite natural that you should be impatient to embrace your niece."

"In that case, let us go to her hotel."

A few minutes after, the cabriolet entered the court of the Hotel de Neuville, at the same moment that an elegant tilbury, driven by a good-looking cavalier, who wore at his button-hole the ribbon of the legion of honour, left it.

The eyes of Paul Feval rested for a moment, and by chance, on this individual, at the moment he stooped to give some orders to his groom.

"It's singular," our hero said to himself, "it seems to me I have seen this individual somewhere."

And a dark cloud lowered upon his visage.

The noise had attracted Lucie and Laura to the windows, which looked upon the court.

"'Tis my uncle," exclaimed Laura, who had at once recognised Paul Feval, despite a cap, whose visière shaded his eyes; "'tis my uncle, I shall go and meet him."

And the young girl commenced running. Lucie followed her friend, so that the two ladies were under the peristyle when Sir Edward and Paul Feval descended from the cabriolet.

Sir Edward would probably have been much embarrassed to guess which of the two charming creatures was his niece, if the mourning costume of Lucie had not rendered any mistake impossible. He took the hand of the countess and pressed it affectionately in his own, and then opened his arms to Laura, who threw herself upon his bosom.

"I return you my sincere thanks, Madame la Comtesse," he said to Lucie in an affecting voice; "I thank you sincerely for the kind attentions and friendship you have bestowed upon the child of my poor sister, who, without you, would have been compelled to pass the best days of her youth at a dull school; and I trust that when you know him, you will reckon Edward Lambton among the number of your friends."

"I know you already, Sir Edward," graciously replied Lucie; "one of our best writers has said that the style betokened the man, and I have read with the liveliest pleasure, all the letters you have written to my friend; so that you have acquired my friendship for some time back; but do not restrain yourself; embrace your niece, Sir Edward, repair the lost time."

"I will profit by your permission, Madame la Comtesse."

"She resembles my poor sister," he said, after keeping Laura folded in his arms for some time: "there are the same traits, the same smile; but I hope she will be happier," he added, addressing Paul with one of those looks which we may interpret thus: "You are the one I commission to secure her happiness."

Laura, who had followed the regards of her uncle, encountered those of Paul, and blushed prodigiously. Had she guessed his thoughts? 'tis probable, there are things which young ladies can unriddle, without the necessity of much information.

The ladies had conducted Sir Edward and Paul into the salon, and the conversation was continued for some time; and it was late when the friends thought of retiring.

"I am going to carry off my niece from you," said Sir Edward to the countess; "I should wish to receive a visit from you to-morrow, and I must have some one to do the honours of my hotel."

The desire of Sir Edward was so natural, that the Countess de Neuville, notwithstanding the pain she felt at the necessity of separating from her friend, offered not the slightest objection. Laura, for her part, could place no obstacle to the first wish of a relation to whom she owed every thing.

"We do not separate," she said to Lucie, before leaving her, "for the distance between us is so short, that we must count it as nothing; and so good bye, my dear Lucie, until to-morrow."

"Good bye. To-morrow!" repeated the countess, who could scarcely restrain the tears which filled her eyelids, and allowed them a free passage, when she found herself alone in her bed-room, "to-morrow!"

Several hours passed before she even thought of her bed. "Alone! alone!" she murmured every time that any distant noise aroused her from the kind of stupor into which she seemed plunged. "Alone! Ah! they are quite right in saying that riches by themselves cannot constitute happiness." Suddenly she rose up, opened her secretaire, from which she took the materials for writing.

At the moment of taking a step upon which would depend the fate of her future life, she hesitated, but only for a few minutes.

"The die is cast," she said, after a little reflection; "let my destiny be accomplished. I have never done an injury to any one: God, who has placed this passion in my heart, will not allow me to be unhappy from it."

Lucie hastily wrote a few lines, which she sealed, and then retired to bed; but it was daybreak before she could induce the god of sleep to visit her.

The letter she had written, and which she ordered her femme de chambre to send at once to its address, was intended for Salvador, and the following are the contents:

"M. le Marquis,—Come at once, I wish to speak with you, and if you can reply in a satisfactory manner to the questions I must address to you, I do not forbid you to hope. I shall expect you at ten o'clock.

"LUCIE DE NEUVILLE."

"At length!" said Salvador, after reading these few words; "though it is not without pain that she has decided; but what are the questions she wishes to put to me, and to which I must reply in a satisfactory manner, as a permission to hope favourably? The devil take me if I know; but what matter? We will try, sweet countess, to satisfy you."

At the appointed hour, Salvador was announced at the Countess de Neuville's, and at once introduced into the salon where Lucie awaited him.

"I have hastened," he said, after saluting her with every mark of respect, "to obey your request."

"I thank you, M. le Marquis," replied the countess; "have the goodness to be seated, and pray listen to me with the most serious attention."

"It seems to me we are about to enter upon a very important affair," thought Salvador, greatly astonished at the almost solemn manner of the Countess de Neuville. "Attention; and, whatever may happen, let not a muscle of my countenance betray the emotions I may feel."

"I am about, M. le Marquis," continued Lucie, after collecting herself a few moments, "I am about to speak to you with extreme frankness; may I hope, and will you promise me, to follow the example I mean to show you?"

Salvador gave Lucie the promise she demanded, a promise which he accompanied with all imaginable protestations.

"I have no wish," said the countess, "to recal to you the event from which our acquaintance sprung. I ought to believe, after meeting you at the Marchioness de Villerbanne's, in the explanation you have given me of your presence in the tavern of la Tannerie Street, which I should have denounced to the police, if I had not dreaded the being forced to justify my own presence there. I had no other reasons for not listening to the avowal you made me of your sentiments, (an avowal which I must believe sincere, since you now renew it joined with a request for my hand,) than those which were dictated by the duties imposed upon me. What I am now saying, M. le Marquis, allows you to suppose that I am not far from granting you that which you appear to consider as a favour."

"Ah! Madame la Countess," exclaimed Salvador, (and at this moment, villain that he was, he played no comedy; for there are moments during which even the most perverted natures are softened,) "what gifts, of which I am not worthy! and by what proofs of affection and gratitude shall I acknowledge the signal favour you are granting me?"

"I require no other proof than that which you have promised me."

"In that case it will be easy for me to satisfy you."

"I desire it, M. le Marquis, I desire it very sincerely. You remember, no doubt, that, anxious to ascertain the person who had returned my cardcase, which I had lost in la Tannerie Street, I sent to you—"

Salvador, guessing at once that he had been damaged in the mind of Lucie by Doctor Matheo, did not allow her time to finish the sentence she had commenced.

"Doctor Matheo," he said; "I remember perfectly this circumstance; I was even astonished that you had confided to such a man so delicate a mission."

Lucie regarded Salvador; his features were calm; he seemed in no way to dread the results of a conversation the commencement of which might well alarm him, if he had any thing to fear. She continued:

"Some days after the visit he made you, to oblige me, the doctor quitted France, abandoning a good practice, and the position, almost brilliant, which he had acquired, and here is the letter he wrote me before putting himself en route."

Lucie handed Salvador the letter of Doctor Matheo, which the reader is already aware of, and she invited him to read it.

He did as the countess requested him, and although she examined his countenance attentively,

she observed not the slightest trace of emotion on his still tranquil visage.

"I should never have spoken to you of this letter," said Lucie, when Salvador had finished its perusal, "if Doctor Matheo had addressed to me the one he promised when writing this, and which would probably have informed me of some precise facts, if any such there are; but it has not been so; I therefore feel myself, to-day, (unless I determine to break with you,) forced to demand from you an explanation, which you will be, if I am not mistaken, impatient to give."

"You are not mistaken, Madame la Countess; I ought not, neither do I wish, when I solicit the supreme happiness of calling you my wife, and you permit me to hope that my prayers may be favourably received, to allow the faintest shadow to subsist in your mind. I will, then, give you an explanation of this letter, which, I think, will leave you nothing to desire."

"Speak, M. le Marquis, I wish sincerely it may be so, and I am ready to listen to you with the most serious attention."

"I will not attempt to conceal it from you," said Salvador, after collecting himself a few moments, "I have long known Doctor Matheo, and I am not surprised that he has addressed to you such a letter as this; but there is one fact, Madame la Countess, which will not fail to strike you, if you will only take the trouble to reflect a moment."

"And which?"

"The precipitate flight of the doctor, the moment that, in consequence of an event he could not foresee, I was made aware of his sojourn at Paris. Ought not this fact alone to prove to you that this man had reasons to dread me, and that it was his interest to destroy me in your opinion; and from this reflection to a conviction that we ought not to place much reliance upon interested calumnies, is not a great distance."

After this short preamble, which made some impression on the mind of Lucie, Salvador observed to her, that the doctor was so well convinced beforehand of the little reliance they would place upon his allegations, that he had thought it necessary to promise her, to give them more weight, a letter, which was to corroborate them—a letter which she had not received, and which she certainly never would receive, for the very simple reason, that the doctor knew very well that he (the Marquis de Pourrieres) could easily reduce to nothing all the calumnies he chose to invent, and that he liked better to leave him under the weight of vague imputations, which allowed his imagination to lend it every imaginable crime; and then recounted to her a history in which he played, himself, the character of the hero, and presented Doctor Matheo under the most odious colours. Chance, he said, had made him the witness of a crime committed by the latter on a foreigner, some years before, and for which he ought to have received a punishment; but the doctor had contrived to escape, by flight, the chastisement which had been reserved for him, and he had never heard him spoken of until the moment he presented himself at his hotel, charged with the mission confided to him by the countess. "I ought to mention to you," added Salvador, "that, at the period which I am speaking, desirous of concealing from my family some youthful follies, which I have cruelly expiated, since my poor father closed his eyes without my being with him to receive his last embrace, (here Salvador, to give greater force to his lament, made a short pause, during which he carried his handkerchief to his eyes,) the different places I resided at, I travelled under a name which did not belong to me. Without this you would not easily comprehend how the doctor presented himself at the hotel of the Marquis de Pourrieres, knowing it was myself he was about to meet.

"When this man, who did not recognise me at first, had acquainted me with the object of his visit, I was, as I have informed you, greatly astonished at his appearing to possess the entire confidence of a woman of whom every one spoke in the highest terms; but my astonishment ceased when I remembered that the greatest villains knew best how to assume all the appearances of the most austere virtue. Then, madame, I confess, I trembled for you; and as you had already inspired in me the most lively interest, I made myself known to Matheo, who, thanks to the obscurity of the room in which I had received him, or some other cause, had not yet recognised me, and I told him that, unless he ceased upon the instant all intimacy with you, if he did not even quit France promptly, I should make him known to the authorities. The wretch then told me he had expiated, by his remorse, the crime he had committed, and supplicated me, on his knees, not to ruin him. I was weak enough to promise him to say nothing, and I should have kept this promise, if to-day I had not found myself compelled to break the silence in order to defend myself.

"Doctor Matheo, no doubt judging others by himself, believes that I shall fail in my word to him, and to this fear we must attribute his flight, which somewhat resembles that of the Parthians, for 'tis in retreating that he has endeavoured to give his enemy a wound, which, thank God, is not very dangerous."

Salvador had uttered the preceding in a tone so natural, in a voice so calm, he knew so well how to give a semblance of truth to the history he had invented to justify his anterior relations with the doctor, and besides, we are all so disposed, men and women to believe the words which issue from the lips of those we love, that after listening to him, there remained not a doubt on the mind of the countess, who had given him the most kind attention; she was only grieved that she had so long bestowed her confidence upon a man so little worthy of it as Doctor Matheo.

"Eh! my God! Madame la Comtesse," replied Salvador, to whom she had imparted her thoughts, after giving him an assurance that every prejudice against him had been dissipated, "I have already told you, and I repeat it, no one understands better than the greatest villains how to preserve all the appearances of virtue; he whose conscience is pure, seldom calculates the bearing of his actions; he does not believe, which however sometimes happens, that it may be possible to put an unfavourable interpretation even on the most innocent movements; do you suppose that if I had suspected the unhappy doubts which the desire of satisfying a vain curiosity might give rise to, you would have encountered me in the infamous den of la Tannerie Street."

"Ah! do not speak to me of that," said Lucie, "I entreat you; I fancy I still see you covered with that infamous costume, which, I assure you, becomes you not so well as the one you are accustomed to wear; I still fancy I hear those frightful words you pronounced when you approached me."

"That day, the remembrance of which you would efface from your memory, will, nevertheless,

Madame la Comtesse, be the happiest day of my life, if you will not tear from me the hope you have permitted me to entertain."

"I will promise you nothing," said Lucie, accompanying the words with her most gracious smile, "but if it will give you any pleasure, I will repeat what I had this morning the honour of writing you; I do not forbid you to hope."

In finishing this sentence, she extended to Salvador her neat little hand, which the bandit raised to his lips.

"I will not, Madame la Comtesse," he said, "by prolonging indefinitely this visit, abuse the favour you have kindly granted me, and will retire, but may I not be allowed to appear sometimes, and present my homage to you?"

"M. le Marquis, you are now acting the diplomatist; and really that is not right."

"I *do not* comprehend you, Madame la Comtesse."

"Say that *you will* not comprehend me, and I shall believe you; have you not come to-day to make me a visit, which I have received with infinite pleasure."

Salvador kissed, with more ardour than he had yet done, the hand of Lucie, for the reply she had made him was equivalent to an express authority to present himself when he judged it convenient at the Hotel de Neuville.

CHAPTER XXXII.

A WORTHY PRIEST.

WHEN Salvador entered his hotel, he found there the Viscount de Lussan, who had engaged with Roman in a discussion which, without being stormy, appeared however very animated.

"You arrive very àpropos," said the viscount to him, "to grant me what your worthy friend absolutely refuses me, whom I did not think capable of such an act towards me."

"But what is it then," replied Salvador, who fancied he remarked on the countenance of Roman the traces of a certain embarrassment, of which he was very glad to have an explanation.

"This is the fact, dear marquis," added de Lussan, "I am absolutely in want of five thousand francs, and as my chest is unfortunately bewidowed of my last crown, I am very naturally come to request you to lend me this bagatelle; not finding you, I addressed myself to your friend; well! would you believe it? he has refused me."

"But I tell you, morbleu! that I have no money," exclaimed Roman.

"Am I to understand," said Salvador, "that you have really so soon lost all that our late affairs produced you?"

"Eh! what is there so astonishing in that? Monsieur de Lussan, who has touched nearly as much as I have, finds himself to-day without a sou; his horses, his dogs, and his danseuse, have swallowed up a sum at least equal to that which I have lost, thanks to the frequency of *trente et un,* and the black and red zeros; each takes his pleasure where he finds it."

"A wretched pleasure!" said Salvador, "which does not leave to the madman, who seeks it at all hazards, the satisfaction of obliging a friend; but be not disturbed. Monsieur le Viscomte, I will hand you the small sum you stand in need of."

Roman, who for some moments had walked about

the room, whistling the popular air: *Tu n'auras pas ma rose*, left the apartment.

Salvador took from his pocket a small key, and opened the drawer of a bureau, in which he was in the habit of keeping his money.

The drawer was empty.

We shall not attempt to describe the stupefaction painted on his physiognomy.

"Robbed!" he said, "robbed! I!"

The viscount, seeing the marquis resting motionless before the drawer, the depth of which he seemed to be mechanically measuring with his eyes, approached him:

"Why, what's the matter then, dear marquis?" he said, for the exclamation of Salvador had not reached him.

No one feels a robbery more keenly than a thief; we have seen them more than once brave the danger of getting themselves arrested, in order to procure themselves the sweet revenge of punishing judicially such of their accomplices as had rendered themselves guilty towards them of a fraudulent subtraction; we beg our readers therefore not to be astonished at the indignation to which the unfortunate Salvador yielded himself.

"I am robbed!" he replied to the question of the Viscount de Lussan; "robbed, as though in a forest! I had in this drawer seventeen thousand francs, in bank-notes, and fifty double napoleons; well! they have left me nothing, the brigands!"

"And you may add that the robbery has been committed by men who are well acquainted with the spot," exclaimed the Viscount de Lussan, who had taken off the lock and examined it with the practised eye of a connoisseur. "The false keys they have used have been manufactured by the hand of a master, for the traces they have left in the wards are hardly visible."

"Why, it's an infamy!" exclaimed Salvador, when he at length roused himself from the surprise in which he had been plunged on the discovery of the robbery he had been the victim of; "it is a scandalous infamy! But I will at once make my complaint to the commissaire of police of my quarter, and, if it pleases God! the audacious authors of this crime shall be punished as they deserve."

"But who will you accuse, my dear?" said the Viscount de Lussan, who was singularly amused at the disaster of Salvador.

"Why, if I knew who I ought to accuse, do you think, by chance, I should be obliged, in order to punish the criminal, to put the police in the confidence of my affairs?"

"But do you really intend to make your complaint?"

"Beyond a doubt."

"Well, then, you are mad, dear marquis!"

"I am mad! I am mad! because I will not allow myself to be robbed without complaining."

"But, dear marquis, it only happens to you to-day, thanks to yourself, as it has frequently happened to others."

"Oh! it is very different."

"I was not aware of that; but since you are quite decided to get the criminal arrested, I will at once go and urge Roman to make his escape."

"How! what do you mean? Do you suppose that Roman——"

"Without doubt! 'tis he and no other who has made the '*coup!*' Did you not observe his embarrassed manner, and his sudden disappearance when you declared yourself willing to lend me the sum I wanted?"

"The miserable! You see, dear viscount, how a passion so imperious as that of gambling, can lead us on to the commission of crime—to rob a comrade!"

"An accomplice! 'tis really abominable; but as the deed is done, you must put up with it."

"Oh! I will never pardon him for this. Rob a friend!"

"An accomplice. Can *we*, who exercise the profession we do, say we have friends? But let us finish this, and talk about other things. How proceeds your affair with Madame de Neuville?"

This question drove from the mind of Salvador the misfortune which had happened to him.

"Au fait," he said to himself, "I can well support without complaining, a loss, which in reality is nothing to me, since I am certain of marrying a woman I love, and whose fortune is considerable."

But remembering the question of the Viscount de Lussan, he replied, "that he had not succeeded better with Madame de Neuville, than the viscount had with Mademoiselle de Beaumont."

"Oh!" replied the viscount in the most indifferent manner, "I merely asked you the question because I saw you, yesterday, leave the hotel of this lady."

"It seems," thought Salvador, "that this devil of a man is everywhere; but what matter, it does not lie in his power to prevent the success of my plans; and besides, he has no interest in injuring me."

"I will go and request some money from Father Justè," said the viscount; "this old Arab must consent to oblige me. Will you accompany me, marquis?"

"Willingly; if you can get this old usurer to lend me a few thousand francs, you would render me a real service. I will write to my agent, at Pourrieres, to forward me some cash; but I must wait for its arrival, and I am literally without a sou; this miserable Roman has carried off my last five-franc piece!"

"You possess noble and valuable estates; you have, as they say, 'roots in the ground.' Ah! you are much happier than I am; I have nothing but a bundle of old parchments, and what I obtain by an industry which rarely gives me an occasion to profit by it."

"Shall I order the horses?" said Salvador.

"No," replied the viscount; "the weather is splendid, we will, if you like, go there on foot, and will afterwards dine at the Café Anglais. Your misfortune, I presume, has not taken away your appetite?"

"No, certainly; on the contrary, I feel disposed to do honour to an excellent repast."

Salvador and the viscount left together; as they crossed the Place de la Concorde to reach the Quay, they found themselves in front of Roman, who was conversing, near the railing of the obelisk, with an individual, whose features they could not observe, his back being turned towards them. The viscount simply remarked that he was nearly as tall as himself, and possessed a breadth of shoulders which announced more than usual strength.

"That's a galliard solidly built," he said to Salvador, pointing out the companion of Roman, who at this moment quitted the other, who remained motionless in the same place, like the wife of Lot, when changed into a statue of salt.

"Ah! double traitor," exclaimed Salvador, who had quitted the arm of the viscount to arrive at Roman the quicker; "if you do not return **my** money it will fare badly with you."

LIFE IN PARIS.

SALVADOR RECOGNIZED BY FATHER COQUARDON.

"Come, come," replied Roman, without seeming to be much alarmed at the anger of Salvador, "just calm yourself, my friend; you will retain these seventeen thousand francs when we touch our revenue."

Salvador made a grimace; the necessity of sharing with Roman the revenues of the estates of Pourrieres commenced being burdensome to him; but he said no more.

"Get rid of the Viscount de Lussan," continued Roman; "I must speak to you about the rencontre I made with the man you saw me conversing with just now."

"Is it important?"

"Very important."

Salvador returned to the viscount, who, out of discretion, had retired a few steps.

"Roman," he said, "has explained to me in the most satisfactory manner the disappearance of my seventeen thousand francs, and which he will instantly remit to me. Go, then, without me, to Father Justè, you will find me at the Café Anglais; if you do not succeed with the usurer, I will lend you, this evening, the sum you want."

The viscount continued his way alone, and Salvador returned to Roman, who was still near the railing of the obelisk.

"Is it your intention to take root in this place?" said Salvador.

"I am so astonished that I have nearly lost the use of my legs."

"Well! what does it concern? What is the cause of this prodigious astonishment?"

"You did not recognise the man I was conversing with just now?"

"Why, blockhead! I did not see his face, as he turned his back to me; I merely observed that he was pretty stoutly built."

"Well! that man is the one who gave old Lartifaille such a famous *warming*, while we were at the prison at Toulon."

"You speak to me of a fact of which I have not the slightest recollection."

"Well, then, the one who drubbed old Lartifaille is no other than the companion of our escape."

"Servigny?"

"Himself! we came plump upon one another in crossing the Place de la Concorde."

"How the devil did he manage to get out of the scrape? If I remember rightly, we left him on the journey, only a few leagues from Toulon, without a sou, and in the dress of a forçat."

"He has not given me any light upon that subject."

"He has done right, parbleu! Would you have recounted to him, if he had asked you, the events which have made us what we are at present?"

"Undoubtedly not; but I should not have received him with the same harshness he did me."

"Well! to come to the point, have we any reason to fear the results of this rencontre?"

"Really, I cannot tell; for the rest, this is what occurred: as I have told you, we found ourselves face to face in crossing this place, and I think we each recognised the other simultaneously; however, I was the first to wish him the *bon jour*, calling him by his name."

"You were wrong; it would have been more prudent, as he did not speak to you, to continue your way."

"No doubt; but I remembered that this *fagot* was only a *man of letters!* and as these gents are not celebrated for courage, I wished to have a moment's gaiety; I thought that, on finding himself recognised, he would show the white feather; well, not a bit of it! I will repeat to you, word for word, the short discourse he addressed to me:— 'Bonjour, Monsieur Duchemin,' he said to me; 'I am glad to find you have not returned *la bas*,* and I trust that, like myself, you are become an honest man. If you were in poverty, I would readily offer you assistance; but the elegance of your costume, the bijoux which adorn you, and, above all, the air of perfect content which is painted on your countenance, tell me that you want for nothing. I wish it were possible for me to see you often; you are—I have not forgotten it—a man of very good society, and you have an infinity of wit; but you perceive that your presence would recal a period which I would for ever banish from my memory. Thus, therefore, in whatever places we may happen to meet, for the future, we must not recognise one another. Your name will never escape my lips; endeavour, equally, never to pronounce mine. If I were speaking to a man less reasonable than yourself, I should tell him that I am determined to risk every thing to preserve the position I have attained; and that I have, thank God! hands and arms to defend myself; but it is useless to make use of such language to you! Adieu, then, Monsieur Duchemin, I wish you every sort of prosperity.'

"And finishing this little sermon, which, I must confess, I did not expect, he left me, without waiting for a reply, or even as much as saluting me."

"This Servigny appears to me a resolute man, and whom we shall do well to respect, if we meet him in society. He required nothing from you but what was reasonable."

"And you think, then, we have nothing to fear?"

"I think so."

"He spoke to me so calmly, he seemed so certain of himself, that for a moment I thought he belonged to *the shop*" (police).

"My poor Roman, I observe, with more pain than you can imagine, that your faculties are considerably impaired. For some time past you have seen agents of police everywhere; you dream of nothing but gendarmes, arrests, condemnations, and executions; and when you are a prey to these hallucinations, your countenance, formerly so joyful and so placid, would of itself indicate, to the least practised observer, that you have on your conscience more than one heavy sin: you must look to this, my friend."

"Why, you are dreaming, I think."

"No, I do not dream, unfortunately."

"And so you think that I, Roman, am a prey to remorse?"

"I do not say that; but this is the fact: when you have lost—and you lose, I am sorry to say, oftener than you win—you ascend to your apartment with a bottle of rum, the whole of which you swallow, to stupify yourself; we can never with impunity give way to such excesses, and you suffer at present from the consequences of your conduct."

"It's true, by all the devils, it's true; but what's to be done?"

"You must play no more, and abstain from drink; but that is no longer possible, the cloth has received its folds."

"Listen, Salvador, decidedly I wish to correct myself. If I had no money, I should never play; and I only drink, as you observe, to drown my thoughts. Well, when you receive our revenues, give me nothing."

* To the galleys.

"But, miserable, if I do not give you money, you will rob me. Ah! what a thorn, what a thorn is a man like you! Roman, we must absolutely separate."

"Never! We have lived together; together we have committed those crimes which have made us what we are; we will die together, unless, however, one of us should be carried off by a lucky illness before the other."

"May the devil send you one, to rid me of you!" thought Salvador, who replied rather angrily to his friend that they must nevertheless separate, if he would not correct himself.

Roman and Salvador, whilst conversing, had arrived at the Boulevard. The latter, who wished, in case the Viscount de Lussan should not obtain from the usurer, Justé, the loan he was gone to borrow, to be in a condition to hand him the sum he had promised him, entered the shop of a toy merchant, who had joined to the trade of German tops and dolls, the professions much more lucrative, of discounter and usurer. Of this merchant, the following anecdote is reported:

The worthy tradesman had lent a thousand francs to a young man of family, who was not to return it for two years; he had shown himself very reasonable; that is to say, he had contented himself with the interest he received from his best customers, twenty-five per cent. per annum; and had very kindly refrained, in this instance, from forcing the young man to purchase some dozen of dolls and punchinellos.

He had just handed to his customer, who had left, delighted at having met with so honest a man, five handsome piles of crowns, each comprising twenty bran new five-franc pieces, when his wife, who had witnessed the negotiation he had completed, said to him in her sweetest voice:

"You have just arranged, I think, a pretty good affair?"

"Why yes, yes," replied the toy merchant, "the young man is honest; unfortunately the bill will be paid when it is due, so that there will be nothing to be gained from expenses; but never mind, the money is well placed."

"It seems to me, however," continued the wife, "that if you had insisted, this affair might have been more advantageous to you. For by lending these thousand francs for four years, instead of two, as you retain the interest, you would have had nothing to hand him."

The toy merchant took his wife in his arms, and pressed her to his bosom.

A touching union of two hearts made to comprehend each other.

Salvador obtained, without difficulty, what he desired of this virtuous tradesman, who was well aware that the Marquis de Pourrières was one of the richest proprietors of the department of Var; and that it was merely because he would not trouble himself to seek elsewhere for what he needed, that he applied to him. Let us hasten to add, to render justice to his honesty, that he granted to this noble client, conditions quite special—he lent to him at six per cent. only, for three months!

When Salvador left the toy merchant, he looked about the Boulevard for Roman in vain; the latter, who had discovered in his waistcoat pocket a few pieces of gold which he supposed he had lost on the previous evening, had followed into a *tripot* the Count Paladin of the Holy Roman Empire, whom he had encountered by chance.

"May he never come back," murmured Salva-dor, crossing the Boulevard to repair to the Café Anglais, "I must absolutely find a means of ridding myself of this man, who will ruin me, if I do not take care; I must absolutely do so."

If our readers will allow us, we will leave Salvador and the Viscount de Lussan féting themselves at the Café Anglais, with the dainties of red partridges, accompanied with truffles, moistened with excellent Chambertin wine, and we will rejoin Paul Feval, or rather Servigny, who is promenading in the darkest alley of the Garden of the Tuilleries.

The encounter he had made no doubt deeply impressed him, for his countenance is sorrowful; he walks with hasty strides; bitter exclamations escape his bosom, and he frequently stops and appears to be in a profound reflection.

"What am I to do, great God!" he said to himself; "and how emerge from this cloud in which I am enveloped; ought I to leave my generous protector ignorant of the events of my past life, and unite to my fate a woman whose attractions and fortune call her to the highest destiny. Oh! no. The encounter I have made is a warning from heaven, to prove to me that the lightest puff of wind can upset a building raised upon sand." He then resumes his walk, still hasty, and again stops to reflect afresh. On a sudden, he strikes his forehead, and the clouds which lower upon him disappear.

"Ah! 'tis heaven that inspires me," he says almost in a loud voice, "I will go and seek the generous man who stretched out his hand to me when I was plunged in an abyss from which I could not hope to rise again; the worthy pastor who so well practises the maxims of his Divine Master; he will direct me how to act; and the advice he may give me, I will follow; whatever sacrifices he may impose upon me, I will accomplish them, and may God be my witness."

This resolution once taken, Servigny, much more calm than a few moments previously, left the garden of the Tuilleries, and rapidly cleared the distance which separated the palace of our king's from the Rue de la Sourdière, where he entered a modest house, but of honest appearance.

These are the circumstances which brought Servigny to the venerable ecclesiastic who inhabited this humble dwelling.

After employing all the morning of this day in visiting in detail his new habitation, and when Laura had left to visit Madame de Neuville, (if our readers will remember that Sir Edward was an Englishman, and that the manners of his country leave the young ladies at liberty to go out alone, and when it suits them; they will not be astonished that the worthy gentleman, who besides allowed his niece every thing she desired, had not waited for an invitation from her friend, that she may ask his permission,) Sir Edward had invited Servigny to follow him to his cabinet, he had something very important to speak to him about.

Servigny took a seat, and disposed himself to listen to his protector, who, after collecting his thoughts for a moment, commenced thus:

"You have rendered me, my dear Feval, many services; after saving my life at the risk of your own, you have devoted to me many of the best years of your youth, during which, thanks to your activity, your intelligence, and above all, to your honesty, my fortune has considerably increased; no doubt you would answer me, for I know how disinterested you are, that I have generously paid you, and that consequently I owe you nothing; you would be in error; there are things which all the treasures of India would not purchase; first, because their value is beyond a price; and, secondly, because they are given but not sold; these are friendship and devotion, and you have given me proofs of one and the other, since you have refused, in order to follow me, the establishment I wished to give you, which of itself constituted a fortune already considerable, which it would be easy for you to increase in a short time.

"I wish, however, to make you some recompense. What can I do for you?"

"You owe me no recompense, Sir Edward," replied Servigny; "and nothing, I assure you, is wanting to complete my happiness. I have attained an honourable position under you, and one which is equal to my desires; and my sole wish is to show myself worthy of it, and to preserve it."

"But that cannot be; whatever regard I may retain for you, the world, in which I shall now be compelled to enter, for I have no wish to condemn my niece to the life of a recluse, would not for ever see in you merely my secretary; and besides, it cannot and ought not to satisfy me; the man who has saved my life; who, by his industry, has augmented my fortune, ought, in the eyes of the world, as well as my own, to be my equal, my friend."

"You exaggerate too much, Sir Edward, the value of the services I have been happy enough to render you; in saving your life, when, at the most, mine was equally exposed with your own, and in fighting for you, I was merely fighting for myself I did no more than you would have done in my place; if I have, during the time I was placed at the head of your establishments, been enabled to contribute to their prosperity, I have done nothing more than acquit myself of a duty imposed upon me, by the nature of the contract which bound me to you; you took me without having any knowledge of me, at a moment when my state of extreme misery might have inspired you with suspicions, for which no one would have dreamt of blaming you, not even myself, who would have been the victim of them; for it is unfortunately in a life of such positions that we must traverse to conceive them. I endeavoured, then, as much out of gratitude as from a wish not to disgust you with the desire of conferring obligations, so to apply myself that I might prove that you were right in your judgment of me."

"Feval, you are a noble young man, and what you have now said to me, proves that I am right in wishing to attach you to me by indissoluble ties."

"Ah! Sir Edward," exclaimed Servigny, in a voice broken with emotion, "do not let me dream of a happiness to which I cannot pretend; in devoting to you all my friendship, in serving you with zeal and fidelity, I have only performed my duty, you owe me nothing, absolutely nothing; leave me then as I am, or rather let me depart."

"You are mad, my dear friend," replied Sir Edward, smiling, for he imagined that Servigny manifested a wish to return to India, simply to acquire a fortune which would permit him, on his return, to aspire to the hand of Laura; "you are mad, a fortune equal to your ambition at this moment, is not acquired in a few years; but we can very well do without it, when an honest gentleman, like myself, says to you on shaking your hand, you pretend to have done no more than your duty; very well, so be it; but men who acquit themselves like you of the duties imposed upon them, are so rare in the times in which we live at

present, it is but justice, that whilst waiting for the reward in reserve for them by Heaven, they should taste a little happiness whilst on earth. In order that it may be so, I have a niece, young, amiable, pretty, and quite rich enough to dispense with your being so, whom you love, I am sure; whom you will render happy, for you possess every quality requisite for it; and by whom, if I am not deceived, it will not be difficult to make yourself beloved; well, I offer you the hand of this amiable girl."

Sir Edward stopped, in order to hear the reply of Servigny; the latter was so troubled that he knew not at first how to reply to his generous protector; a cloud seemed to envelop his eyes; his heart beat as though it would burst; he contrived however, to collect his ideas.

"Sir Edward," he said, after raising to his lips the hand of the worthy gentleman, "my generous protector, I will not attempt to deceive you; I love Mademoiselle de Beaumont, but ought I to accept a proposition which is inspired in you by a sentiment of exalted gratitude. Mademoiselle de Beaumont is rich, I am poor; I possess nothing in the world but the friendship you retain for me; she is noble, I can only offer her an obscure name."

"My dear Feval, the establishment I offered you, and which you refused for the purpose of following me, is worth twelve thousand pounds sterling; you will at once, unless you wish me to believe that you are governed by pride, accept this sum in good notes of the Bank of France; a man who possesses somewhat more than ten thousand francs a year, is rich enough to pretend to the hand of a Russian princess, or the daughter of a nabob; behold, then, your objections on the score of fortune, removed; as to what regards nobility, you possess a nobleness of heart and sentiments, which is quite as valuable as the other."

And as Servigny, not knowing how to reply to the concise arguments of Sir Edward, remained silent, Sir Edward rose and added, after shaking him by the hand:

"I leave you, my dear Feval; remember that in confiding to me that you loved my niece, and I should not have believed you if you had told me the contrary, you have removed the only reasonable motive you could allege to avoid doing what I desire; you will give me a reply to-morrow morning; and we will busy ourselves at once about the necessary steps; I like things to be set about and finished as soon as they are decided upon."

Servigny found himself in a singular position; he must either accept the proposition of Sir Edward, for, by confessing the love he felt for Mademoiselle Laura he had removed, as was well remarked by Sir Edward, the only reasonable motive for refusing her hand; or consent to make the avowal of his position as an escaped convict, and this confession, it is easily imagined, would cause him considerable pain; probably lose him the estimation of Sir Edward. And Laura, Laura, what would she think of him? He would willingly, that he might not associate this happy young girl to his own destiny, which might be altogether changed by the slightest event, renounce the hope of possessing her; he would willingly fly from her, but he could not reconcile to himself the idea of becoming in her estimation an object of contempt and disgust; and would he be less than this when she learnt that he had been the bed and board companion of such hideous beings? whom she would imagine to be even more degraded than they are in reality; that he had been chained to one of these ignoble beings; would she believe that he had not been soiled by their contact, that he had not imbibed some of their vices?

To escape the cruel perplexity to which he was a prey, he had left the hotel of Sir Edward to walk in the alley of the garden of the Tuilleries where we last saw him.

As he crossed the Place de la Concorde, he had met Roman (whom he only knew under the name of Duchemin). The reader is aware how he received his former chain companion; he would have shown himself perhaps somewhat less severe towards a man whose past life he was unacquainted with, and to whom, after all, perhaps he owed a debt of gratitude; for it was to Roman, it may be remembered, he was indebted for his liberty, if he had encountered him at any other moment; but every thing which recalled this fatal period of his life so grievously vexed him, that we need not be much astonished at the cavalier style in which he addressed Salvador's companion.

An old domestic had opened the door of the humble dwelling which we have seen him enter, and had introduced him into a small room on the ground floor which served both as an ante-room and dining-room.

This chamber, more than plainly furnished, was only remarkable for its extreme neatness.

"And so," said Servigny, after accepting the seat offered him by the old servant, "you are certain that M. l'Abbé Reuzet will return in a few minutes?"

"Quite certain, monsieur; M. l'Abbé never dines in town, and five o'clock is close at hand."

"In that case I will wait; it is absolutely necessary that I should speak with your master, whom I have known for some time, but have not yet had the happiness of meeting since I have been in Paris, although I have called several times."

"We have been spending a few days in the country, in consequence of a serious illness of M. l'Abbé; and no doubt 'twas during our absence you have called?"

"It's very probable, my worthy Sylvain, but M. l'Abbé Reuzet, I hope, is at present completely recovered?"

"Oh! yes, monsieur," replied the domestic with astonishment, "my master is now quite recovered; but I think monsieur has just pronounced my name?"

"Well! does that astonish you?"

"Why no doubt, monsieur, it does astonish me very much; you know me, whilst I have not the slightest knowledge of your honour."

"Ah! my honest Sylvain, you do not possess a very excellent memory."

"Pardon me, monsieur, I possess an excellent memory; but 'tis in vain I endeavour to remember your features."

"How! Sylvain, you have forgotten the unfortunate traveller who, a few years ago, came wounded, dying from hunger, and knocked, in a stormy night, at the door of the presbytery of Saint-Marsault, and to whom your respectable master bestowed the kindest attentions, attentions to which you added your own, and which the traveller has not forgotten."

Servigny placed in the hands of Sylvain a dozen napoleons; the worthy domestic, who had never even dared to dream of possessing so considerable a sum, knew not in what terms to return his gratitude.

"Oh! monsieur!" he said, "it is too much, it is indeed too much; I do not know if I ought, without obtaining the permission of Monsieur l'Abbé, to accept so large a sum."

"Fear nothing, worthy Sylvain, accept this small present, I will speak to your master, if that will please you; for I do not mean to limit the profits of my gratitude to such a bagatelle as this."

"You are too good, monsieur, and I am very glad to see you at present, as happy as you were unhappy when you sought our house for the first time. But 'tis my master who will be delighted to see you; he has not forgotten you, no; every time you forwarded him a sum for the poor, he read to us, to the good Madeleine (she is no longer among us, poor woman) and me, some passages of your letters, which came from a great distance, as it seemed, for he had to pay nearly five francs before he received them; and he told us that we ought never to miss an opportunity of assisting our fellow-creatures, seeing that a good action is never thrown away."

The tingling of the bell, placed at the entrance-door, prevented the old domestic from saying more.

"That is Monsieur l'Abbé," he exclaimed, and hastened to open it.

It was in fact the Abbé Reuzet.

This worthy priest was still young, but study and meditation had whitened nearly all his hair; the austerity of his features, otherwise remarkably handsome, indicated a man who had come off victorious from the battles he had engaged in with his passions, but not without having received some wounds; but from the placidity of the regards which seemed to caress those upon whom they rested, one might be certain it was a pure and golden heart which beat in his bosom, and that he would know, in such an event happening, how to find words to calm every suffering, courage to support the weak, a leaning staff to sustain the tottering steps of those who were on the brink of falling.

He recognised Servigny at once, and tendered to him a hand which Servigny pressed affectionately in his own.

"I am delighted at again seeing you," he said to him; "your letters have informed me that the Almighty had favourably received the prayers I have not ceased to make for your happiness; accept then my congratulations, and at the same time my thanks, for the frequent donations you have forwarded me; they have served, as was your intention, to assuage unmerited misfortunes."

"Thanks, thanks," replied Servigny; "my first anxiety on arriving at Paris, was to present myself at your house, but you were absent."

"The Almighty, to prove his follower, had visited him with a cruel malady; but I am now quite recovered. I even think I am going to do honour, which has not been the case for some time, to a modest repast, which the worthy Sylvain is about to serve at once, if you will share it with me."

Servigny, who wished to have a long conversation with the Abbé Reuzet, hastened to accept the kind invitation offered to him.

After the repast, which, although simple, was not, however, that of a father of the desert, or a trappist; for the worthy Abbé Reuzet believed, and we are quite disposed to agree with him, that if God has covered the earth with wholesome and agreeable food, it is that his followers may make use of it, and that the putting in practice the moral of his Divine Son, is infinitely more agreeable to him, than prolonged fasts and mortifications. The abbé and his guest adjourned to a small saloon, furnished in the same simple fashion, but quite as neat as the dining-room, and there enjoyed their coffee.

The Abbé Reuzet, who, from a few words spoken to him at dinner by Servigny, had guessed that his companion wished to have some private conversation, dismissed Sylvain.

"The letters you have received," said Servigny to the abbé, "have informed you of all that happened to me up to the moment when Sir Edward, completely healed of his wounds received in struggling with the ferocious animal, which had placed both his life and mine in danger, confided to me a post which enabled me to be useful to him, and to prove that I was worthy of his estimation. If services impose duties of obligation upon those who receive them, they also exact delicacy among those who have rendered them; I endeavoured, therefore, to acquit myself of every duty imposed upon me in a manner that would not cause Sir Edward to regret the confidence he had placed in me; and I must believe that I completely succeeded, since, very shortly after, he charged me with the direction of his principal establishment, one of the most considerable of these rich countries."

The following is in substance what Servigny narrated to the abbé, who listened to him with the utmost attention:

After an administration of some time, Sir Edward remarked that considerable savings had been made, and that, by means of quicker methods introduced by Servigny, the productions of the manufactory were more abundant and better attended to. On the other hand, the workmen, better guided in the employment of their time, had experienced a great improvement in their position, as much by the increase of wages, as by the affectionate and really fatherly attentions Servigny bestowed upon them.

He had comprehended from the first, that good masters make good workmen, and without any other system, he had obtained the happiest results. In a word, he knew how to conciliate the friendship and good-will of all; he was thus endeared to the master who reposed every thing in him, and looked upon him as a counterpart of himself.

The return of Servigny to a better fortune, had not made him forget the old woman who had given him an asylum in his days of adversity; he often went to see her, and never failed to carry her consolation and assistance. She was an unfortunate Irishwoman, whose husband had been robbed and massacred in an expedition of the English troops against the Affghans. Left alone, without money, without support, she lived by the feeble produce of her labour, of which a strict economy enabled her to devote a part to the wants of the unfortunate; a pious work in which Servigny assisted her with his purse, without wounding her delicacy.

This state of things continued some time, when Sir Edward took the resolution of quitting India for France, to live happy in the midst of a people whom he had never ceased to love, and whose glory, although travestied by English hatred, had often caused his heart to beat!

Under these circumstances, he decided upon selling his property; but before he acted upon this decision, he proposed to Servigny to leave him to settle his affairs. Touched even to tears at so generous an offer, Servigny thanked him in these terms:

"I was grievously unhappy. A circumstance which I will not recal, induced you to favour me with your confidence; since which you have loaded me with benefits. What more could I wish for than to remain all my life near you, unless indeed you have some motive for deciding otherwise! if not, permit me to continue to devote to you what remains to me of youth and strength, that I may acquit myself of the gratitude I owe you, and which will endure as long as I have life."

Sir Edward could not resist this last proof of attachment, he threw himself into the arms of Servigny, pressed him a long time against his heart, and from this moment it was agreed they should not separate, and that the return to France should not divide the two friends.

Servigny would not leave the country without seeing once more the good old woman we have mentioned, and whom he had found so charitable at a former period; he wished to leave with her another pledge of remembrance and gratitude.

One morning upon visiting her with this design, he found her fatigued and sorrowful; he demanded the cause, but instead of replying, she placed her finger mysteriously on her lips, at the same time indicating to him her sleeping-room.

"What is it you mean?" he said to her in a low tone.

"A woman, a French woman, still young and handsome," replied the old woman, "is now sleeping in that apartment. Silence!"

Then leading him outside the house, and having invited him to take a seat on a bench near the door, she narrated to him in these words the circumstances which had brought the unknown to her house.

"The day before yesterday, towards the dusk," she said, "I was returning from the house of the old Englishman whom you know. I was crossing the little wood which overlooks the mountain. When arrived at the extremity nearest the town, I fancied I heard groanings issue from amongst the thick brushwood. I stop, listen, the most absolute silence reigned all round me. I thought at first I had deceived myself; but scarcely had I advanced a few steps, when the same noise again struck my ears. Stopping a second time, a plaintive voice reached me distinctly from a short distance. I approach; 'Whoever you may be,' I said in a loud voice, 'indicate to me where you are, and I will bring you assistance.' No reply. I renew my warning, and listen, and acquire the certainty that a human creature is lying close to me, and that the state of suffering she is in, was the sole cause of her uttering the groans I had heard.

"The night became very dark. In spite of this, I search, I call. I receive no reply, not the slightest movement indicates to me the direction I ought to follow, to arrive at the unfortunate who had already inspired great interest in me. To increase my torment, the sky, covered with black clouds, the absorbing heat of the atmosphere, menaced a violent storm. Hearing nothing more, I was about to abandon my search, and continue my road, when suddenly the lightning furrows up the clouds, the thunder groans heavily, the rain descends in torrents. I again stop, in the hope of being enabled to assist the unfortunate being who was lying not far from me; but I can hear nothing, absolutely nothing. Compelled now by the dreadful weather, and perhaps also by some little fear, I quit this scene of horror to return home. It was midnight when I arrived there, fatigued, harrassed, wet to the skin. I threw myself hastily on my bed; but I found it impossible to close my eyes, so greatly was I agitated! I fancied I still heard the plaintive accents of the voice vibrating with difficulty through the foliage, the wind, and rain. What reproaches I addressed to myself for my pusillanimity, and want of perseverance! I should have saved her, I exclaimed! if I remain, 'tis all over with her, I shall be the cause of her death!

"The storm had now ceased; but the day did not approach quick enough to satisfy my impatience. At length exhausted with fatigue, imperious nature gains her sway, and I yield to sleep. But a frightful dream soon awakens me on a sudden, palpitating, and covered with perspiration. I saw in this dream, enormous serpents devouring a human body, whose agonising screams made my very soul quiver! I rose in haste, resolved to return to the spot, hoping this time, if not yet too late, to save the individual whom I blamed myself for having so cowardly abandoned.

"But, that I might not fail in the object of this fresh excursion, I thought it better to wake my neighbour, Father William, begging him to accompany me to the spot where lay the unhappy victim whom I wished at all risks to assist. He willingly agreed to. Arrived at the copse, we commenced our search, which lasted some time, when suddenly Father William exclaimed in an agitated voice:

"'This way, come, come quickly!'

"I ran towards him; what a horrid spectacle presented itself to my sight! a woman, still young, with a good figure, but pale as death, lay motionless in the bottom of a deep hole or pit.

"'She is dead!' I exclaimed.

"'I am afraid so indeed,' replied Father William; 'but we cannot by ourselves extricate her from this. I will seek some one and return.'

"A quarter of an hour had scarcely elapsed, when William returned with some willing men who had hastened to assist in so good a work; others were gone to seek a surgeon, who soon arrived at the place.

"They descend into the pit, and with great care and attention bring out the unfortunate young woman, who appeared to be still alive. They place her on a litter of the branches of trees, hastily put together; the doctor examines with the most scrupulous attention; she is frozen. He orders a fire to be made, that she may be warmed; but she still remained in the same state. A few tardy and low pulsations scarcely distinguish her from a corpse! the doctor even appears to think that all assistance is in vain. But I beg of him to redouble his care and attention; it seems to me that her lower extremities are less rigid, and not so cold; he soon becomes of my opinion. He then orders them to carry her to my house, where she was placed in my bed, warmed by degrees, and then bled. This having been attended to, he administered to her two tea-spoonfuls of a potion which seemed to revive her. At length she opened her eyes; but too weak to support the light, she suddenly closed them. The doctor then ordered her to be kept warm, and the cordial which had already produced such good effects, to be redoubled; he then retired, promising to see her again during the day.

"She passed the day and night in my bed. During this time, the doctor visited her five or six times. At his last visit, he gave me some hopes of saving her; but up to the present she has neither opened her eyes, or uttered the least complaint; she is completely motionless. However, a mild perspiration pervades her body; her blood has resumed its circulation; at length, material life is restored to her, and every thing announces that the doctor's expectations will be realized. These are her clothes; I have dried them, and although in a sad condition, the fineness of the texture, as of her linen, seem to announce a person who has known happier days."

When the old woman had finished her narration, in which she appeared to lessen all that concerned herself, Servigny expressed his congratulations on her praiseworthy conduct; he took a purse filled with guineas, offered it to the old woman, and compelled her to accept it, to defray the expenses which her generous sensibility had imposed upon her. After which he retired, promising not to leave without again seeing her, and giving her a last adieu.

Returned to Sir Edward's, he continued to regulate and close up the business; and when at length every thing was ready for the voyage to France, he repaired to the house of the old woman as he had promised her a fortnight before. He found her occupied in some domestic affairs; near her was seated a young woman of an extreme paleness, which more strikingly set off her long black hair, and her handsome eyes of the same colour. She seemed to have once possessed beauty in a remarkable degree; but she was so weak, so bowed down, that she could scarcely support herself on the seat she occupied, contrary to the orders of the doctor, who had ordered her to repose herself on a long chair. After saluting her, Servigny continued his conversation with the old Irishwoman, to whom he was also indebted for his life. The latter questioned him as to the country he was about to inhabit. He replied, that the vessel in which he was to embark with Sir Edward and his suite would take them to France, and disembark them at Havre; that from Havre he should go to Marseilles.

"Marseilles," exclaimed the patient, "Marseilles, it is my country!" she then fell back in her chair quite overpowered.

When she recovered the use of her senses, she exclaimed afresh:

"Marseilles! Marseilles! 'tis my own country! it is in that town my family should now be, if they still exist, malgré the torments I have caused them; for my sake, monsieur, if you visit the city which gave me birth, be kind enough to see my family, and inform them of the position I am in at this moment, namely, a prey to remorse, and one foot in the grave! I shall die happy if you promise me to see my parents, and remit this ring to the Marquis de Pourrieres, whose address my family will give you. Attend! here is something which is still more precious."

She then drew from her bosom a small box of tortoise-shell and gold, saying:

"This is all that remains of my former prosperity! this box contains the registry of the birth of my son. Alas! I have shamefully abandoned him, as also his unfortunate father!"

At this moment a torrent of tears rushed over her face; she could not continue from the emotion caused by her sad remembrances.

Servigny and the old woman seeing her on the point of swooning, hastened to give her those attentions which would revive and calm her. Servigny assured her he would see her family, as also her son, and the father of the child; that she might rely upon him as to what she had charged him with. She appeared to be somewhat recovered, and thanked her two benefactors for the kind interest they took in her. She added, that being too fatigued at this moment, she begged Serviguy

LIFE IN PARIS.

SALVADOR AND DE LUSAN AT OLD TURK HOUSE AFTER THEIR ESCAPE.

to return soon, that she would prepare by the day for his departure, the letters she intended for him.

In a few days Servigny again visited the unhappy girl; he found her somewhat improved. She handed him all the notes he might require in making the researches she requested of him, and entreated him to inform her instantly of all he might learn of any interest to her.

"I shall find strength to live," she added, "until I know whether I have still my parents and friends, and especially if my son yet exists. This certainty will make me forget all my misfortunes, all my sufferings."

Servigny again assured her that she might rely upon him, and at the risk of being thought indiscreet, he questioned her as to her life, and the circumstances which had reduced her to the state of destitution she was in at present.

These questions brought forth a fresh torrent of tears.

"Alas!" she said to Servigny, "when you hear my adventures, I shall be an object of your contempt, as well as of that good dame, whose generous devotion has saved my life. But there is nothing I can refuse you."

She then recounted what we already know of her history; her flight with the Englishman, who, in his turn, had abandoned her almost without resources, after taking her to India.

"Since then," she added, "I have opened my eyes to my position, to my faults, my infamous conduct. How I repent at this moment having quitted the man who loved me, who had loaded me with benefits; and whom I repaid with the blackest ingratitude! and my son, what remorse I feel at having left him in the hands of strangers, without ever troubling myself as to his fate! all this had inspired me with a complete disgust for life; it seemed to me that a strong and inward voice cried to me without cessation: 'You are a wicked mother!' in consequence of these different circumstances, accompanied with frightful presentiments, my courage abandoned me. I became ill; all that I possessed, money, effects, jewels, all was sacrificed to re-establish my health. Scarcely convalescent, the persons who had received me, knowing that my resources were exhausted, intimated to me to choose another asylum; in two days more, they would unmercifully turn me out of doors.

"A prey to the most violent despair, I had wandered about at hazard, resolved to walk until the moment when, failing in strength, I should drop from sheer weakness. This was not long in taking place. I walked so far, that I lost myself in the small wood which is near the town. I did not stop until the night closed in, and at length seating myself at the foot of a tree, I fell asleep. My slumber was tranquil enough until the next morning, and when I awoke, the sun was far advanced in his journey; but although I had passed the whole night in a repose I had not enjoyed for some time, I was not the less a prey to the most horrible torments. My weakness, the absence of nourishing food, contributed to plunge me into the most sombre ideas. I fancied myself followed by those midnight spirits created by a delirious imagination. In a word, the whole contributed to make me persist in the resolution to end my life.

"And yet, the thought of death, the idea of putting a term to the anguish of the heart, to that pyramid of wounds and griefs; to that mass of flesh we are composed of, makes cowards of us all: all hesitate and change colour before the feeble shadow of this thought. I rose up then, and found myself renewed in strength; but quite decided to die of hunger. If I once more faced life, it was to rejoice at the end of my misery. At length, arrived at the last point of weakness and delirium, I felt, I saw the night approach; but indifferent to every thing, what was the night to me, when I no longer breathed, suddenly my eyelids became heavy, closed, and I fell exhausted on the turf!

"If I may judge from the agitation of my sleep, I remained a long while in this state, for I was assailed by a crowd of singular and terrible dreams which haunt a nervous brain. At one time I seemed to be falling from dangerous precipices, and rolling in the bosom of black and infected water, which dragged me to the bowels of the earth; and then, hideous serpents tore me in pieces with their venomous teeth!

"At length, what shall I say? from this moment to the time I found myself at the house of the good old Irishwoman, I have no other recollection of my existence, than a feeling of all the torments of hell! 'tis to God and you, my worthy and respectable host, that I owe my life; may the future be made a better use of than the past!

"Stop," she said to Servigny; "here are the papers which will enable you to obtain some information of my unfortunate son. Promise me once more to occupy yourself about him when you arrive in France, and to inform me of the result of your proceedings."

"You may rely upon me," replied Servigny; "I swear to you I will see the father and the son."

"The father I have so shamefully betrayed," said the woman, "has probably abandoned the child to avenge himself for the perfidy of the mother."

"That is not probable," replied Servigny; "a man like the Marquis de Pourrieres could not commit such an injustice."

"Alexis was so young, he loved me so," said the woman, "that my flight must have brought him to despair, he will have cursed the mother and the child!"

"For pity's sake, calm yourself, madame; he who truly repents is farther from evil than he who never knew it. For the rest, I have a better opinion of the Marquis de Pourrieres; I undertake to see him, and to revive in his heart the feelings of a father, if, contrary to all expectation he has for a time forgotten them."

"What obligations I shall owe to you, monsieur; if I still desire to live, it is that I may have time to bless you."

The moment for separating having arrived, Servigny embraced the two women and quitted them, promising to write to them. Never was a separation more touching; the young woman shed tears in abundance; as to the old Irish dame, it seemed as though she was losing a dear and cherished son, so inconsolable was she at parting, in Servigny, with a friend and a protector as generous as he was delicate. At length, they must part.

A few days after, Servigny learned that the poor girl died—blessing him!

CHAPTER XXXIII.

THE DEPARTURE.

Sir Edward, the possessor of considerable riches, honourably acquired, embarked with Servigny.

During the voyage, which was an agreeable one, he spoke frequently of his niece, whom he had not seen since her infancy. The letters he had received from this young girl had engaged all his affections; he burned with impatience to see her. He read, again and again, her correspondence, with a renewed satisfaction, and he read it to Servigny, who also found it charming. The *naïveté* of the style, the purity of the sentiments expressed in them, was all impressed with the seal which indicates a rare mind. At length, after a voyage of ten weeks, interrupted by no accident, they disembarked safely at Havre.

Sir Edward, who had business of importance to settle at this port, and afterwards at that of Marseilles, requested Servigny to get forward to Paris, to prepare every thing necessary for his installation. He gave him a carte blanche for the purchase of an hotel, in an elegant yet quiet neighbourhood, as well as for a pretty little country-house in the environs. He wished, on his arrival in Paris, to find every thing in readiness, and depended entirely upon the faithful and intelligent Servigny, whom he regarded, and rightly, as his best friend.

After receiving the orders and different commissions of Sir Edward, and furnished with letters of credit upon the first bankers in the capital for considerable sums, the departure of Servigny was fixed for the next day; but before visiting Paris he requested from his protector permission to go and see an old aunt, who resided at Mantes; she was the only relation who remained to him.

"Do just as you like," said Sir Edward; "provided that, in two months from the present time, I find every thing ready for my reception, I shall be perfectly satisfied."

Matters being thus arranged, Servigny turned his steps towards Saint Marsault, to throw himself at the feet of the worthy curate who had so generously saved him and fitted him out for India. There he found that this good ecclesiastic had been for some time at Paris, vicar of one of the parishes of the city. He paid a visit to the successor of the man of God, and, without confiding to him any of the facts we are acquainted with, commissioned him to say a few masses, and to distribute liberal charities to the poor of the village. He was happy at being enabled to do some little good in a place where he had been so miserable; he then put himself en route for Paris.

Arrived at Sens, and lodged at the Hotel de l'Ecu, he purchased an excellent cabriolet and a very good horse, sold under some law process; he took advantage of this opportunity, knowing that he should soon be in want of them to perform his rambles through Paris and its environs.

On his arrival at Mantes, he descended at the Hotel de Cheval Blanc, and at once inquired for his aunt. He learned that she had died, only a few months previously, after making a will in favour of a distant relation. Servigny had no wish to disturb the last will of his good aunt; he quitted Mantes the next morning, at day-break, to arrive at Paris, being anxious to behold again his preserver, the former curé of Saint Marsault. The morning was wet; but towards mid-day it cleared up, so that he accomplished this route agreeably after dining at Poissy. In passing through Saint Germain, he stopped a few minutes in order to obtain from a notary some information as to the properties for sale in the neighbourhood. Several were pointed out to him, but, on inspection, they did not suit; he then directed his steps to Nanterre, and it was almost night when he arrived there; but

from thence to Paris the distance is not great, and he fancied he might take his time. He refreshed his horse, then, at Gillet's, and after giving a few sous to the blind musician who entertains the travellers with a tune upon his flute, and who, it is said, has amassed something considerable at this trade, he jumped into his cabriolet, proposing to ascend leisurely the hill which takes us out of this part of the country; when suddenly he observed that the sky was clouded, and that the lightnings flashed through the heavens at long intervals. He continued his road, hoping the storm would pass over; but at this moment the thunder groaned heavily, the flashes of lightning crossed each other and formed a thousand *gerbes* in the air; the loud detonations, multiplied and repeated by the echoes of the valley, became deafening and fearful; in spite of all this, Servigny continued bravely his route; he had even arrived half way between Nanterre and Neuilly, when a flash of lightning, succeeded by a heavy clap of thunder, made his horse start and rear up. He fell, as though struck with the thunder; gets on his legs again, but alarmed at the terror which surrounds him, he backed, and precipitates both himself and the cabriolet into a deep cistern on the side of the road, from which he could not extricate himself.

The shafts were broken, the horse under the cabriolet; and Servigny, buried under the flattened head of the cabriolet, made useless efforts to leave his unenviable position.

The reader has been made acquainted with the events which happened to our hero during and after his introduction into the auberge of Bienvenu.

"Such," said Servigny, when he had finished the recital of the foregoing circumstances, "are the events of my life which I have not as yet communicated to you; I have passed over in silence but one circumstance, of which I will speak to you when you have told me how I ought to act, as to the unfortunate woman whose history I have mentioned. I shall acquit myself of the mission she has confided to me, and for that purpose I only wait for chance to furnish me the opportunity. I shall write to Geneva, to ascertain where the young Fortuné is at present, and the moment I know the place of his residence I will carry to him the last words of his unhappy mother and the lock of hair she gave me for him."

"Very good, my son, very good," replied the Abbé Reuzet; "I expected nothing less from you; you ought, indeed, to discharge the mission confided to you by this unhappy woman; in fulfilling the last wish of a sinner who has repented in her dying moments—of a mother, who sincerely regrets the not having performed her duties, you render yourself acceptable to God! for the good we accomplish, without any hope of reward, is seen by Him, and will be remembered at the day of judgment, when our faults and our virtues will be weighed in the balance."

Servigny, after again assuring the Abbé Reuzet that he should faithfully discharge the mission confided to him by Jazetta, inquired of him what he ought to do, relative to what had happened to him at the isolated auberge of Bienvenu?

"I should wish to make known to the authorities," he said, "what takes place in this infamous house, and what the persons are who keep it; but can I, without compromising myself? One of the men I saw—and who would undoubtedly be arrested after being denounced—was, at the same time as myself, at the prison at Toulon, and he would not fail to denounce me; and you can judge what would be the consequences of such a denunciation?"

"You cannot, however, my friend, suffer such a nest of assassins to exist; it is not without design that Providence, who conducted you there, has permitted you to escape from it. Justice must absolutely be made acquainted with it, and at once; for each day's delay may probably cost the life of some unfortunate traveller. But, however, we must avoid making you the victim of the good action you are about to accomplish."

"But what means can be employed to secure this? I should necessarily be brought into the presence of all the individuals who frequent the auberge of Bienvenu; well, is it not possible that among them may be found some who have been my companions during my imprisonment at Toulon, and that my features may be engraven in their memories?"

"It appears to me," said the Abbé Reuzet, after reflecting a few minutes, "that an anonymous denunciation, well detailed, addressed to the prefecture of police, will effectually accomplish your design; for it will necessarily cause a visit to this auberge, in which it is impossible for them not to discover something to fix their doubts. But no! we cannot even employ this mode; your cabriolet and horse, which remained at the auberge of Bienvenu, would serve to make you known if they fell into the hands of the police."

"Oh! I have no fears on that score; the cabriolet is not of French make, and the horse was purchased with several others; these objects, therefore, cannot leave any traces of me; so that I shall at once follow your advice, and forward a denunciation to the authorities, in which I will furnish them with such precise details, that they must place some faith in it.

"And now," added Servigny, "you must serve me as a guide in a serious affair, and upon which the happiness of my life depends! These are the facts."

Servigny then narrated to the Abbé Reuzet all that had passed between him and Sir Edward, and the offer which the latter had made of the hand of his niece.

"And undoubtedly," said the good priest, "you love this young girl?"

"Oh! yes," replied Servigny; "I love her! and this love, I assure you, has no resemblance to the passion inspired in me by the cantatrice of the theatre of Marseilles, of whom I have spoken to you, a passion which led me to such fatal results. I have vowed to Mademoiselle de Beaumont an affection as pure as it is disinterested; I feel that I can render her happy if she becomes my wife; but still, if you tell me I ought not to unite my fate to the life, so pure, of this amiable girl, I shall find strength enough to renounce the happy future which is offered me, and which I have merited. I have no fear in saying this, my worthy friend, for you know my whole life; you know what efforts it has cost me to attain the position I possess at this moment."

"Listen, my friend," said the Abbé Reuzet; "you are quite determined, are you not, to continue in the road you have chosen? You wish, at all risks, to preserve the esteem of the generous man who would confide to your care the happiness of his niece?"

Servigny gave an affirmative sign, and the abbé continued in these words:

"Well! my friend, you must acquaint him with all the events of your life that you have concealed from him to the present; if, after you have made him this confidence, he does not renounce his intentions, and this is not unlikely, for if the punishment which mankind inflicted upon you was severe, the fault you committed was no more in reality than youthful heedlessness; you may then accept, without fear, the hand of the woman you love; after, be it remembered, you have made the same confidence to her, as to her uncle."

"To her! my friend; must I tell her that I have worn the infamous livery of the galleys?"

"You must! Believe me, if you are to become the husband of this young girl, do not leave to chance, which probably may not present itself, but which however is possible, the care of acquainting her with a fact, which will appear to her much less enormous, if she learns it from your own mouth."

"Ah! never, never could I resolve to give Laura the right of despising me; I would rather fly without saying a word, and leave her ignorant, as well as Sir Edward, of what might become of me."

"You ought not to do anything of the sort, and you will not do it; for you must remember that Sir Edward is attached to you, and that your flight by afflicting him, would permit him to look upon you as an ingrate."

Servigny justly conceived that in his singular position, he had no other part to take, but that indicated by the Abbé Reuzet; he could not, however, determine to adopt it; he would willingly, as we have said, renounce Laura, fly far from her; if necessary, he would frankly make a confidant of Sir Edward, not simply that something told him he should find in his protector a merciful and indulgent judge, but that honour made this duty a necessity; but this was all he felt himself capable of undertaking, unless with superhuman efforts. He said as much to the Abbé Reuzet.

"Well!" said the priest, "these superhuman efforts must be made, and believe me, you will be rewarded for them; something is always gained by doing our duty. What could you say to your wife if, by chance, made acquainted with a fact you had concealed from her, she reproached you with having deceived her? Would you have any right to complain if, following your example, she deceived you in turn? Tell me, would not your happiness be much the greater if, after listening to the confidence you are about to place in her, Laura tenders you her hand, and says, that in spite of your misfortunes, she consents to become your wife?"

"Oh! certainly, for that would be a real proof of love and devotion which I should return by making her as happy as it is possible to be on earth; but this cannot happen, this innocent young girl will never consent to unite her destiny to that of an escaped convict."

"Women, when they love, are capable of every sacrifice. Do not despair, therefore, of your destiny; God, who to the present moment has so manifestly protected you, will not abandon you so long as you continue to walk in the right path. *Do your duty*, whatever may be the consequence; you ought, my friend, since you would forget the fault you have committed, have this maxim constantly in your memory."

"I will do as you advise me," said Servigny, after reflecting a few moments.

"I was sure," exclaimed the abbé, "that you possessed all the qualities of a gallant man; but as you are now quite decided, I will endeavour to render less severe than you suppose the task imposed upon you. There are confessions, I know, which are painful to make, and what you have to say to Sir Edward is of this nature; I think that the indulgence of this excellent man, will render them as easy as possible; I do not wish, however, that you should be a witness of the astonishment he will naturally exhibit when he is informed of that which till the present he has been ignorant of. Your plan will, therefore, be as follows; to-morrow morning, Sir Edward, who seems to me rather impatient, will not fail to demand your reply; to which you will answer, that the offer he has made you crowns your happiness, but that you cannot accept it until he has seen me; and you will request him to visit me at once; if, as I presume, what I acquaint him with does not change his resolution, I shall solicit from him permission to see Mademoiselle de Beaumont, who, I am convinced, will preserve her esteem for you, should she even withdraw her love, after listening to me. Do you think, my friend, we can do better? and will you commission me to be your interpreter?"

Servigny took the hand of the abbé, and pressed it affectionately.

"You are a worthy servant of the Almighty," he said to him, "I approve beforehand what you do, and if I must renounce the friendship of Sir Edward and the love of Laura, it will be with you, my dear friend, that I shall seek those consolations which I am sure you will not refuse me."

The conversation between the Abbé Renzet and Servigny would probably have continued for some time, if old Sylvain, after discreetly knocking at the door, had not entered to announce to his master that the Viscount de Lassan wished to speak to him.

"I am obliged," said the abbé, "to leave you to receive this gentleman. An revoir, my dear Servigny; keep up your spirits, I repeat to you, the Almighty never abandons those who walk in his steps."

"May his will be done," replied Servigny. "accept this for your poor," he added, sliding a bank-note into the hands of the abbé, "I much regret I cannot do more at present, but the amount I have just forwarded to the procureur du Roi at Aix, to indemnify the Jew Josué, for the money I involuntarily caused him to lose, has nearly dried me up, another time I shall be more generous."

"Thanks, my friend, thanks for myself, to whom you procure the pleasure of doing a little good, and thanks for my poor, whose prayers will bring you happiness."

"Apropos, I have given your honest Sylvain a slight proof of my remembrance, which he would not accept without having your permission to retain it."

The Abbé Renzet gave the old domestic a harmless box on the cheek, as he was waiting at the door of the saloon for an order to introduce the Viscount de Lassan.

"You see, my friend," he said to him, "a kindness is never thrown away, as you receive to-day a reward for the attentions you bestowed, long ago, on a poor wounded individual; keep the money, and make a good use of it. And now introduce M. the Viscount de Lassan."

Sylvain hastened to obey.

"Will you take a seat, M. le Comte," said the abbé, who conducted Servigny to the door of his modest apartment; "I shall be at your service in a moment."

"Do not hurry yourself, M. l'Abbé," replied the viscount; "do not hurry yourself, I can wait your leisure.

"What the devil can he have to do here," he said to himself when alone in the saloon; "this is the same man I saw this morning, conversing with the worthy intendant of my noble friend, the Marquis de Pourrieres."

CHAPTER XXXIV.

TWO MARRIAGES.

If our readers are not tired of following us, we will request them to enter with us into the small church of Guermantes: a neat village of the depart-ment of Seine et Maine, situated a few hundred paces from Lagny, and only remarkable for the beautiful country houses, the gardens of which have mostly been designed by Lenôtre.

It is not yet eight o'clock in the morning; the feeble rays of a winter's sun have not collected sufficient strength to pierce the thick clouds, with which the atmosphere is closed; it is a keen frost, the snow still covers the neighbouring fields and the naked branches of some old trees planted in front of the church door, which is however open, and ornamented as for a fête day. We shall dis-cover, by listening to the words exchanged between the few peasants assembled before the grand altar, for what ceremony the little church of Guermantes displays at so unusual an hour all the riches of its sacristy.

"Well! it's a droll idea," says to her neighbour, a fat countrywoman with a jovial countenance, who had risen at daybreak in order to arrive first at the church; "to choose for being married in, a paltry village church, when they might, without any trouble, have the high altar of the church at Paris, which I went to see with my man, a superb church, my dear, all yellow and gilt, with pictures nearly as handsome as those of the Turkish garden, and besides it smells good all over."

"'Tis a new fashion, the bourgeois coming to be married in the village churches, saying 'tis to avoid publicity, but I don't think that's the reason, not I; 'tis much more likely that they find it cheaper, the rich are so stingy."

The sharp nose, thin lips, and sleepy-looking eyes of the woman who had thus expressed herself, announced one of those beings, so unfortunately constituted, that their greatest pleasure consists in slandering their neighbour. Those of our readers who are simple enough to believe that the country people are such as are painted by the honest captain of dragoons, named M. de Florian, when we have informed them, that the parties who had chosen the little church of the village of Guermantes to be married in, had forwarded to the mayor of the said village a pretty round sum for the poor of the parish, will think perhaps that the malicious jests of the woman with the bat-looking eyes, were dis-approved of by her auditors; if so, they are in error! and a very great error; they were on the contrary received with a murmur of approbation, which en-couraged her not to stop in so good a work; and yet the most slanderous among them will be the first to arrive at the porch when the married pair leave the church, in order to salute them and catch an offering, namely, a piece of money. It is as well to apprise our readers, that the country people, sometimes in easy circumstances, receive without scruple, the alms which are kindly given them.

As we have said therefore, the auditory of the woman with her half-open eyes, was disposed to receive with eagerness all the jests she chose to utter.

"Now," she continued delighted at the considerate attention bestowed upon her by her listeners, "you will tell me, that sometimes there are reasons for not wishing to be married in the sight and with the knowledge of our equals; for instance, when a damsel has met with a misfortune, and the husband only marries her for her dowry."

"Ah! Mother Pitroux is witty as usual," said a fat buxom fellow, the cock of the village, and laughing coarsely, "she knows all that passes, let me tell you."

"Ah! ah! I know enough, and if I choose to speak, I could tell you plenty about the pretty bride, of her husband, and this red-pated Englishman who calls himself her uncle; but I shall hold my tongue. I have not forgotten that at his last sermon, M. le Curé told us we ought not to slander our neighbour."

The old sorceress was only silent because she actually knew nothing, and that her instinct of female maliciousness told her she had said quite enough to cause matter for conjectures.

"It's my opinion," said the jolly farmer, "that the Englishman is no more her uncle than I am the nephew of M. le Curé, and that 'tis to rid himself of her, that he passes her with a handsome dowry to the young man who is going to marry her."

"A good-looking man all the same," replied the woman who had first spoken, and who, compared to the other villagers, was an excellent woman; "and he's going to marry a handsome bit of a girl! you may say of them what you like, but it won't prevent their making a pretty couple."

"That is to say," replied the jolly farmer, much vexed no doubt that any woman allowed herself to think well of any other than himself, "the man is not so very handsome either, besides he is too tall."

"You say that because you are so short, my boy."

"We are as we are, Mother Catois, that does not prevent our not wishing to change figures with every parvenu from Paris, who only come to our villages to humble us."

"You make me sweat with your slanders," exclaimed the good Madame Catois; "stop, since I must tell you, you have no more gratitude than crocodiles. When there is no one at the château, you say every day, ah! 'twould be a good thing for the village if the property was inhabited by some rich people. Well! the rich are come, and kind ones, who have done good to all the poor in the parish, and now, on the occasion of their marriage, have handed to the mayor a pretty round sum for our poor; well! because they like to be married here, you set to and tear them in pieces just as though they owed you something; fie, fie! you ought to be ashamed."

We ought, as faithful historians, to inform our readers that the sharp rebuke of Madame Catois was much less kindly received than the slanders of Mother Pitroux, and that she would probably have been obliged to change her place to escape some blows, if the entrance into the church of the married couple and their friends, had not arrived to distract the general attention.

"Am I wrong," said Pitroux, "isn't it a secret marriage, since they have invited no one to the ceremony, and have only with them their witnesses, the two Englishmen who come from we know not where, Father Robertin, the notary from Lagny, and his son-in-law the bailiff, who seems proud enough that the English redpate has chosen him to answer for his niece; and this curé of Paris, who is to officiate in the place of our worthy pastor whom probably they do not think good enough for them."

The marriage which set in movement every wicked tongue in Guermantes, was, as our readers have probably guessed, that of our hero Servigny, who espoused the charming Laura de Beaumont. After the ceremony, which the good Abbé Reuzet wished to perform himself, the happy pair, accompanied by Sir Edward, entered a travelling carriage which waited for them at the church door, and started for Florence, where under the beautiful sky of the Grand Duchy of Tuscany, they were to pass the remainder of the winter before fixing themselves definitively at Paris.

"Adieu, my children," said the abbé to Servigny and Laura, the moment they had seated themselves in the carriage, "adieu! you will be happy, for you have both done your duty; but if any unforeseen misfortunes happen to you, if the Almighty still wishes to prove you, pray with confidence to our Divine Redeemer, you will receive from prayer, strength to surmount the obstacles, and resignation to support the evils you cannot avoid."

Whilst the abbé thus conversed with the young couple, who paid him all the attention his noble character deserved, Sir Edward, surrounded by a dense circle, emptied his purse into the hands of the beadle, the sacristan, the choristers, and the parish poor. When he had nothing more to give, the almsseekers dispersed themselves, and he rejoined Servigny and Laura who were waiting for him in the carriage.

"We shall meet again, monsieur," he said to the abbé, shaking him by the hand in a manner which drew a slight grimace from the countenance of the good priest; "I am not of your religion, but this, as you may have seen, does not prevent my being a tolerably good sinner, and I am quite ready to admit, that the religion which is preached by such ministers as yourself, is a very excellent one. Adieu, Monsieur l'Abbé, come often to our hotel when we have returned to Paris, we shall all be gainers by it, ourselves first, and the poor afterwards, for upon each of your visits I will hand you the wherewith to continue the work so generously commenced by this worthy boy."

In saying these last words Sir Edward tapped Servigny on the shoulders, which brought a blush on the face of our hero.

"Ah! ah! my dear friend," said Sir Edward, who remarked the embarrassed air and the blushes which covered the visage of Servigny, "is it by chance you say that Monsieur l'Abbé has placed me in the confidence of your secrets; that would not be right, now that we are of the same family, we ought to have nothing to conceal from one another."

"A secret!" said Laura, "I should like to know it."

"Your husband will no doubt inform you of it," said the abbé.

"Yes, my child," added Sir Edward, "you shall know this secret, and you will well scold your husband for having concealed it from us so long."

After a few respectful and obliging words addressed to the curate of Guermantes, who had joined the Abbé Reuzet, Sir Edward, Laura, and Servigny departed, carrying with them the blessings of the two venerable pastors, to which were joined the acclamations of those among whom Sir Edward had emptied his purse.

"They are good people, however," said the potbellied farmer to Mother Pitroux; "they have behaved handsome to our poor."

"Very handsome certainly," replied the old woman. "to give a few crowns when they are as rich as both be; 'tis one mode of throwing a little dust in our eyes, that we may not observe how they run away the moment they are married."

"Eh! come then, Pitroux." said a gossip, tapping the shoulder of the bat-eyed woman, "are you going to the town hall? they say that the mayor is about to divide what has been given by the bourgeois who have been married, and which will amount at least to twenty francs for each needy one."

"I'm off at once, my child," said la Pitroux, "I'm off at once."

And the old sorceress left the church.

"Well, Claude, what do you say to that?" said Mother Catois to the jolly peasant, "do you call it honest to take the money of persons they have just been defaming?"

"Well! if they have given this money, I suppose it suited them; to have the right of taking our share, must we deprive ourselves of the pleasure of laughing a little bit at the expense of these rich ones?"

Ah! the pure morals of the fields! amiable village candour; how seducing you are in the ideals, the romances of M. de Florian, and the operas comique!

About three months after the marriage of Servigny and Laura, a similar ceremony drew together in the gilded church of Notre Dame de Lorette, a company much more numerous than the one we left at the little village church of Guermantes. This assembly, habited in silk and velvet, perfumed with patchouli and eau de Portugal, expressed themselves in much more elegant terms than those we have lately listened to. Must we conclude that they were better? Really we cannot say. The villagers of Guermantes knocked down without argument those whom they busied themselves with; the fashionable coterie assembled in the church of Notre Dame de Lorette, to make use of an expression borrowed from the lively curate of Macedon, "tenderly cut the throats of people with genteel little pocket knives." We shall leave to our readers the trouble of deciding which of the two is the best mode of killing a man *or woman;* we shall simply entreat them to observe that the gentry *comme il faut* defame *one another,* whilst the villagers only calumniate those whom the chance of birth or fortune has placed above them; which tends to prove that the former only slander for the purpose of killing time; whilst the latter, real wolves who do not eat one another, calumniate because they are vulgar, envious, and malicious.

The Reverend Father Lemoine, of the society of Jesuits, who has written a small treatise,* intended to render the exercise of all the ceremonies of religion easy to people of fashion, if he returned on earth and was conducted into the church of Notre Dame de Lorette, might easily believe, on beholding such a temple, that the maxims in his work were generally adopted. For our part we have never entered one of these stately edifices without feeling ourselves disposed to raise our minds to our Creator; we do not remain cold in one of the modest temples of our villages, but when we find ourselves at Notre Dame de Lorette, which happens upon every occasion that Alexis Dupont kindly leaves the Royal Academy of Music, that his beautiful voice may be heard by the faithful, we listen willingly to the preacher in vogue; we warmly applaud the distinguished artiste who sings so sweetly the sacred hymns; but we may well beat our sides to kindle in our hearts a few sparks of

* "Devotion made easy."

religious fervour, it is quite impossible; the fact is, that the church of Notre Dame de Lorette, has a greater resemblance to the boudoir of the charming singers who inhabit the quarter in which it is situate, than a temple devoted to the worship of Him who died on the cross, that we may be redeemed. Nothing is better painted than this pretty sweetmeat box; but nothing assuredly has less of grandeur, less of mystery, and speaks less to the heart and the imagination of the greatness and merits of the Creator.

It was no doubt for this reason, that the different personages whom the ceremony about to take place had attracted there, accosted and saluted each other, and conversed with as much ease and negligence as though they had met in a saloon.

"Ah! good day then, my dear de Lussan, I am really delighted to meet you."

"Believe me, my dear de Preval, that it gives me infinite pleasure to see you."

And the viscount affectionately pressed the neatly-gloved hand which de Preval offered him.

"I willingly believe you, dear viscount; but allow me to observe that you have become excessively scarce."

"And what do you wish, I have sown my wild oats, and have a great desire to make a finish, to imitate my friend de Pourrieres; to get married, in fact."

"Really! why yes! if you found as he has, a peg to hang your hat on, you would not perhaps be wrong."

"I had fixed my eyes upon the amiable friend of the pretty Countess de Neuville, and it is probable I should have contrived to make myself acceptable, if her uncle had not brought with him, from the East Indies, some adventurer who has cut the grass from under my very feet."

"That *is* unfortunate."

"Ah! I assure you I am perfectly consoled; an opportunity lost may be easily recovered."

"Especially, when, like you, we possess so many amiable qualities, a large fortune, and an illustrious name."

"Flatterer, you know well that I possess, like yourself, but one thing, the name which my ancestors have transmitted to me."

"And that's not much."

"What blasphemy, M. de Preval; but if you prize so lightly the nobility, why have you affixed to yours a *particle nobiliaire.*"

"Eh! how do I know; to throw dust in the eyes of fools."

"Let us finish, I beg of you."

"You do not think, dear viscount, that I meant to offend you."

The viscount, evidently annoyed, made a few steps in the church before replying to de Preval. who kept at his side, and seemed disconsolate at having displeased the man whom he had been in the habit of considering as his master.

"The married couple keep us waiting," timidly said Preval, to give a turn to the conversation.

The viscount, touched at the repentance visible in the countenance of Preval, replied:

"It shows good breeding," he said. "'tis only kings and water-carriers who arrive to the minute."

"It seems that M. the Marquis de Pourrieres has entirely forgotten the charming Marquise de Roselly?"

"I do not answer for that; Silvia is a woman who is not easily forgotten; is it not true, Monsieur de Preval?"

"I give you my word, I have only to think of

LIFE IN PARIS.

ROMAN AND SALVADOR.

her, in order to remember that she is a very dangerous woman."

"I believe you. It seems that the galliard she made choice of to rid herself of you, made a good use of his hands; I recounted that history to the Marquis de Pourrieres; it caused him a hearty laugh."

"I am glad I have been of some use to this noble personage; I do not wish, however, that he again finds *Celeste Comtois.*"

"Eh! why so?"

"Because I am persuaded that this woman would be fatal to any one who became connected with her."

"You may well be right; Father Justè gave me a certain history, of which I presume that she is the heroine!"

"What is this history then?"

"You are much too curious, my dear; if you wish to know it, go and ask Father Justè to narrate it, perhaps he will be kind enough to do you so great a pleasure."

The viscount and de Preval were at this moment accosted by an ugly old man, who wore at his button-hole the ribbon of the legion of honour.

"Eh! good morning, M. de Preval," he said to the companion of the viscount, "you can inform me, as you are here, whose marriage they are about to celebrate."

"Who is this monsieur?" said the viscount to de Preval in a whisper.

"Monsieur la Chevalier Fontaine, the nominal father of the handsome Marchioness of Roselly," replied his friend.

And as the Chevalier Fontaine waited for a reply to the question he had asked:

"Don't you know," he said, "that M. the Marquis de Pourrieres espouses the widow of the General Count de Neuville?"

"A union well assorted," replied the chevalier, "they are both rich."

The parties invited to the ceremony arrived one after another, so that when the married couple and their friends arrived in their turn, the church was already filled. The old chevalier of Saint-Louis, whom we have seen at Madame de Villerbanne's, gave his arm to Lucie.

The features of Salvador were resplendent with pride; he gave the Viscount de Lussan, as he passed in front of him, a slight protecting nod of the head, which we might thus translate—"You see, my dear friend, that I know how to surmount every obstacle, and that what I wish for, I obtain."

"Hey-day!" said the viscount to himself, "do you forget by chance that it is almost to me, my excellent friend, that you are indebted for what you receive to-day! we shall see, morbleu! we shall see."

Lucie was not sad; and yet we might notice a certain apprehension on her sweet face. But when she fixed her regards on her husband, she fancied she read so much love in his eyes, that the light clouds which gathered on her features were at once driven away.

We shall not report here all the details of the ceremony which consecrated before God a union already contracted before man. There was the usual mass for marriage; we shall merely add that as the Marquis de Pourrieres had forwarded a large sum for its use, the church was decked in its gayest attire; by daybreak all the treasures of its sacristy had been displayed; the velvet cushions, fringed with gold; the satin canopy, with silver fringe; the heaviest and best chased chandeliers;

the choristers habited in their handsomest copes; the Swiss, in his gayest uniform, washes his singing boys and invites his best organist.

After the ceremony, the friends of Lucie and the Marquis de Pourrieres, amongst whom might be observed a crowd of distinguished personages, offered their congratulations to the married pair, and begged them to accept the prayers they made for their happiness, prayers alas! which were barren, and not to be received with favour.

Salvador, conforming himself to the English fashion at present adopted by most people in good society, had expressed to his wife a wish to depart immediately after the marriage and pass the honeymoon at his chateau. Lucie had nothing to oppose to a desire which appeared so natural; and it was therefore arranged that immediately after the religious ceremony was performed, they should leave for the Chateau de Pourrieres.

This ceremony was now terminated, and the newly-married couple were soon to quit the sacristy, when a woman of extraordinary beauty, but frightfully pale and miserably clad, entered the church; she took her place in the front rank, taking care to keep herself amongst the persons who waited, in a double line along the two sides of the nave, for the exit of the married couple, whom they wished to see enter their carriage. When Salvador, who had Lucie under his arm, passed triumphantly close to her, she uttered a slight exclamation, which caused him to turn his head on one side, in such a manner that her eyes, which sparkled with a latent fire, were met by his.

The features of Salvador, when he beheld this woman, were covered with a mortal paleness, and truly there was some reason for it; she appeared to him like Banquo's ghost at the feast of Macbeth; and his trouble was so evident that Lucie remarked it, and inquired what was the matter? He attributed his emotion and paleness to a sudden indisposition caused by the heat, and that the fresh air would dissipate it; and he hastened to reach his carriage, scarcely replying to the compliments and felicitations of the numerous friends who pressed round him; but when the Viscount de Lussan approached him, he said a few words to him in an under tone.

The viscount appeared greatly astonished, he saluted the countess, and re-entered the church.

He had scarcely made a few steps, when he was accosted by de Preval.

"Guess who I have encountered here?" he said to his friend.

"Eh! how can I tell," replied the viscount.

"Well! I have just been face to face with the handsome Marchioness of Roselly, Silvia, Celeste Comtois, whichever you like to call her. Oh! I easily recognised her, despite the extreme pallor of her features, which seems to indicate that she has supported a long illness, and the poor garments with which she is covered."

"Where is she?" said the viscount, "I must speak with her, I must absolutely see her."

"Faith, my dear friend, I cannot satisfy you; I slid away the moment I saw her. I surmised that she came here merely to serve some one a bad turn, and that this some one may be myself as well as any other, my faith! I can assure you, however, that she is still in the church."

The Viscount de Lussan, disgusted at the cowardice of his friend de Preval, quitted him without making a reply, and commenced searching every corner of the church. The temple of Notre Dame de Lorette is not very large, and the eye can easily encompass every part; and he had not much trouble to find the individual he was in search of.

"As I did not care to expose myself to be recognised by any one in these miserable rags," said Silvia to him, "I remained in this corner, where I knew well you would discover me."

"But by what misfortune, Madame la Marquise, are you in so pitiable a state, and what has become of you for more than a twelvemonth past."

"Oh! it's quite a history, and will be much too long to recount to you here; he has, no doubt, requested you to occupy yourself a little about me."

"Without a doubt; ah! would that you had come a few days sooner."

"I came as soon as I was enabled; and so the Marquis de Pourrieres is married?"

"He supposed you dead, Madame la Marquise."

"And he was impatient to console himself; very good,'tis really very considerate; and is the woman he has married decidedly very handsome?"

"Ah! madame, if you had been there, it is probable he would have refused Venus in person."

"Do you think so?"

"I am persuaded of it; but you know the old proverb; 'the absent are wrong.' "

"The proverb says true, but the absent sometimes return, and they are right."

"I do not understand you, but I am at your orders, are you coming?"

"We will wait, if you will allow it, a few moments; I can still observe in the church many persons whom I know."

The dry and cutting tone of Silvia had slightly vexed the Viscount de Lussan; however he obeyed and remained with her, braving the looks of the curious, who could not imagine that such an elegant personage, could converse in public with a woman so meanly clad; he yielded, without suspecting it, to the influence which this singular woman exercised over every one who became acquainted with her, still he spoke not a word to her.

"You tell me nothing, M. le Vicomte," said Silvia, after a silence of a few moments, which seemed to weary her excessively.

"I have nothing to tell you, madame," replied the viscount, "unless it is that the church is now nearly deserted, and that we should do well to profit by the moment and retire."

"Let us go then, M. le Vicomte, I am ready to follow you."

Silvia passed her arm through that of the viscount, who blushed up to his eyes, but dared not refuse her. He then handed her into his cabriolet, placed himself at her side, and applied his whip to the horse, impatient to escape from the observation of some curious loiterers, assembled at the entrance of the church.

We shall profit by the time which is to be passed at Florence by Servigny, Laura, and Sir Edward, and at Pourrieres, by Salvador and Lucie, to whom we regret, it is not permitted us to give the name of the Countess de Neuville, to acquaint our readers with the events which had preceded the two unions which they have just witnessed.

Servigny after quitting the Abbé Reuzet, entered the hotel of Sir Edward much calmer than when he left it, the resolution he had come to had put an end to the cruel perplexity to which he was a prey; and being endowed, as we may conclude from a recital of the preceding events, with an extraordinary strength of character, he waited the result with tranquillity, quite determined to accept it, be it what it might.

The next morning after breakfast, Sir Edward, as he expected, requested him to follow him into his cabinet, and when they were alone, asked him for an answer to the proposition he had made him the day before.

"You may well suppose, my generous protector," replied Servigny after reflecting a moment, "that if I did not accept at once, and with a sincere and deep gratitude, so honourable a proposition as the one you have so kindly made me, my hesitation was induced by very powerful motives; for I did not attempt to conceal from you that I loved your niece with all the devotion I am master of, and I trust I have given you sufficient proofs of the attachment I have felt towards yourself, to place beyond any doubt, the very great value I should place upon an alliance with you."

"But these motives, my dear Feval, you ought, if you have any confidence in me, to make me acquainted with."

"I know it, Sir Edward, but I thought you would kindly spare me the sad necessity of making you a confession which will cost me perhaps, if not your friendship, at least your esteem. A venerable ecclesiastic attached to the church of Saint Roch, M. l'Abbé Reuzet, knows every secret of my life; seek him, my kind protector, he will tell you all, which I regret I have not strength to tell you myself; and if, which I dare not hope for, after hearing him, you consent to retain me in your service, I shall yet esteem myself too happy."

"I will see this ecclesiastic," replied Sir Edward, visibly affected at the deep emotion of Servigny; "I know not what he has to tell me, perhaps you attach too much importance to an event in reality insignificant. Is the secret he is about to confide in me then, of a nature to prevent the completion of a project to which I attach such an infinite price? Whatever it be, my dear Feval, be persuaded that I shall never forget the important services you have rendered me."

"I am sure of it, Sir Edward, I am sure of it," said Servigny, "but seek at once the Abbé Reuzet, I am now impatient that you should be informed of every thing that respects me."

Sir Edward pressed the hand of Servigny without replying to him, and started on foot for the residence of the abbé, which had been indicated to him by our hero.

The Abbé Reuzet, as he had promised Servigny the day before, expected the visit of the English gentleman who was at once introduced to him.

Sir Edward remarked at first the extreme simplicity and neatness of the furniture of the apartment occupied by the abbé; this prepossessed him in his favour and disposed him to listen favourably to him. He said to himself, if this priest who possessed, he knew, a reasonable fortune to which he could add the emoluments arising from his functions, and the produce of several works of celebrity of which he was the author, could be content with such a modest dwelling; it followed that he experienced a greater pleasure in shedding his benefits upon those of his fellow creatures, who, when under misfortunes, addressed themselves to him, than in surrounding himself with the thousand objects of luxury and comfort.

The Abbé Reuzet dismissed Sylvain who had introduced Sir Edward into his cabinet, and after placing a seat for the worthy gentleman, thus spoke to him:

"I am aware, sir, of the motive which brings you here; you wish to know the reasons which have induced M. Paul Feval to refuse, in some manner, an offer which would have overwhelmed him with joy, had he been permitted to accept it. These reasons, sir, are of such a nature, that this young man rather than acquaint you with them, wished to fly; however I must add, that you may not be left any longer under the weight of a wrong impression, that in my soul and conscience, my friend (I am proud of being enabled to give this title to M. Paul Feval) is in reality more unfortunate than guilty."

"Continue, M. l'Abbé, continue, I beg of you," exclaimed Sir Edward; "I am more delighted than you can imagine to hear you speak thus. I am not, as you are, clothed in a character which obliges me to be indulgent; but I think that your heart and mine are not unworthy of each other."

And Sir Edward, with the frankness of an Englishman, seized the hand of the abbé which he pressed warmly in his own.

"The person of whom we are speaking," continued the abbé, "is not named Feval, his right name is Servigny; but he might, without injuring any one, assume the one under which you have known him till to-day, for the name of Feval is that of his mother, who has been dead some time.

"The name of Servigny, Sir Edward, has been branded before man; but I do not hesitate to say, that it has long since reconquered before God its former purity!"

The abbé, after a moment's hesitation, then recounted to Sir Edward all the events of the life of Servigny, which our readers are already aware of.

When he had finished, Sir Edward, who had listened to him with the most serious attention, and without once interrupting him, again shook him by the hand, and said to him in a voice which showed his emotion:

"If the facts are such as you have narrated to me, and of which I have no doubt, as you are the guarantee for them, Servigny is truly more unfortunate than guilty; but in my sight he has acted very wrong in not making me a confidence to which I was entitled; but I willingly pardon him, and what you have made me acquainted with will in no way change my intentions."

"It's right, sir, it's right!" replied the abbé to the worthy gentleman; "I expected nothing less from your noble character, but I ought, as much to complete the mission with which I am charged, as to acquit myself of the duties which my station imposes upon me; make a few observations which I trust you will receive with indulgence."

"Speak, Monsieur l'Abbé, speak, I am ready to listen to you."

"You ought not to hide from yourself, Sir Edward, the position of Servigny; he is, after all, but an escaped convict from the prison of Toulon, which an event the most insignificant in appearance might betray, whose destiny may be destroyed in a moment. Will you associate the existence of your niece to a position so precarious? and if such in fact, is your intention, do you not think it your duty to acquaint her with the events of the past life of him you have fixed upon as her husband?"

Sir Edward, after reflecting a few moments, replied thus:

"I appreciate, M. l'Abbé, the motive which induces you to make me these observations, to which I will endeavour to reply; Servigny was only sent to prison in consequence of one solitary event in his life; he entered it without any antecedent faults, and he remained there but a short time, he is therefore not known by men whose trade it is to seek out those who are in similar positions; you tell me he might be recognised by some of his companions of misfortune, but it is not probable he will encounter any in the society in which we shall move. I can easily, thanks to the great influence it is in my power to move in his favour, obtain his pardon if anything unfortunate should happen; but until then, I think we should do well to remain as we are, are you not of my opinion?"

"Beyond a doubt, if your intentions are still the same; it is better to avoid furnishing the world, which is not as you are, exempt from prejudice, with an occasion of judging from facts, which assuredly it will not appreciate at their just value."

"I think with you, that my niece ought to know all that regards the man who is to be her husband, and I shall charge you, M. l'Abbé, to inform her of it. Tell her that I shall with pleasure see her united to Servigny, because I am convinced that the young man is quite capable of making her happy; but that nevertheless I leave her entirely free in her choice."

"I will this very day see Ma'mselle de Beaumont," said the abbé; "and now, sir, that you are informed of nearly every thing which regards my friend, I do not fear to tell you, that I sincerely hope your niece will not be opposed to the union you contemplate, a union which I trust will be as happy as possible."

"Yes, Monsieur l'Abbé, this union will be a happy one, and being persuaded of this, I desire its accomplishment."

The conversation between Sir Edward and the abbé continued for some time. The former listened with much interest to all the worthy priest said to him, who on his part felt a sincere pleasure in proving by facts, that he to whom he had extended a hand when abandoned by the world, had shown himself worthy of his benefits; and that by his virtue and his courage he had been enabled to regain his place in society.

"Yes, Sir Edward," he said to the worthy baronet, "yes, Servigny, or rather Paul Feval, for we will preserve, if you will permit it, this name to our friend, is every way worthy what you are doing for him; and to give you a fresh proof, I will acquaint you with a secret which his modesty has no doubt concealed from you. Since he has been attached to your person you have liberally remunerated him for the services he has been enabled to render you. Well, do you know in what he has employed the greatest part of the magnificent appointments you bestowed upon him?"

Sir Edward having made a sign in the negative, the Abbé Reuzet opened a drawer of the bureau before which he was seated, and took out a packet of letters, he picked out a few and handed them to Sir Edward.

It was not without experiencing a very strong emotion that the worthy baronet finished the perusal.

"Good young man!" he said, "and sometimes I asked myself, remarking that he took no part in the speculations which so often present themselves in that country, and by means of which so many contrive to enrich themselves in a short time, what became of his money."

"Yes, Sir Edward, this is what he did and what he still does. 'Whatever motives I may have to serve me as an excuse,' he said to me in the first letter you have read, 'I cannot accuse mankind, of having unjustly condemned me; I ought then, as much to be enabled to prove to them that I am not quite unworthy of indulgence, as to thank the Almighty for the benevolent protection he has bestowed upon me, to devote to a good work the best part of what I possess. Who knows what I should have become, to what miserable extremes despair and misery would have driven me, if you had not extended to me a helping hand; furnished the means of passing to India, and if afterwards I had not met with the generous Sir Edward! Employ then, my worthy friend, the sum which I send you and such others as I may hope still to forward you, in assisting unfortunates like myself; what you have done for me, is a sure guarantee that you will understand my intentions, and that I have no occasion to explain myself farther.'

"I have faithfully acquitted myself, I think," said the abbé, "of the mission which my friend charged me with. I have not always waited, to make use of it, that the unfortunates he wished to assist, addressed themselves to me; I have often sought them, and at present if he does not possess this world's goods, he is rich in good deeds of which, whatever may happen, the Almighty will keep a just account. Thanks to him, unfortunate creatures whom misery had driven to despair, have arrested their steps on the road which led to their destruction, bitter tears which the injustice or the errors of mankind have made them shed, have been dried up. Ah! Sir Edward, notwithstanding the observations I made you but a moment since, you did not think it your duty to renounce your projects; 'tis God, no doubt, who moved at the prayers which are daily addressed to him by so many sufferers in favour of an unknown benefactor, has strengthened you in your resolution."

"I desire, Monsieur l'Abbé, to associate myself in the good works of our friend; which is saying that he will always be in my family."

Sir Edward rose, and after recommending the abbé to see his niece the same day as agreed upon, took leave of the worthy priest whom he already looked upon as a friend, although he had known him for so short a time; but before leaving, he observed Sylvain who walked before him in order to open the door. "This is no doubt," he said to the abbé, "the honest attendant of whom you have spoken to me, and to whom our friend Feval caused so great a fright when he presented himself in so pitiable a state." The abbé making a sign in the affirmative; "allow me," he added, "to offer him a slight gratification which he will no doubt accept." And without waiting a reply, Sir Edward slipped into the hands of the honest domestic, several pieces of gold, with an injunction to drink his health.

The Abbé Reuzet, faithful to the promise he had given Sir Edward, presented himself after dinner on the same day, at the hotel of the rich English baronet, and inquired for Mademoiselle de Beaumont to whom he wished to speak in private. The young girl was alone with her uncle when this visit was announced to her.

"I do not know this ecclesiastic," said Laura to him, "and I doubt if I ought."

"I think you may receive this worthy priest." replied Sir Edward; "for the rest, I will leave you a clear field, I have some letters to write. If after the conversation you are about to hold with M. l'Abbé Reuzet, you wish to speak to me, you will find me in my cabinet."

Sir Edward quitted the saloon, and a few moments after, the abbé entered.

We shall not report here the conversation of Laura de Beaumont and the Abbé Reuzet, which was nearly similar to the one which had taken place a few hours before, at the house of the worthy follower of God, whose noble character our readers can appreciate.

The abbé recounted to the young girl all that he had narrated to Sir Edward, he withheld from her however, the motive which had induced Servigny to commit the fault so severely punished, he thought it was at least useless that the young girl should learn, that the heart of him who would perhaps become her husband, had once beat for another woman; no one, we imagine, would think of blaming the good abbé for this restriction, which was made with a good intention, and from a knowledge, little expert as he was in these matters, that women, when they love, are jealous, even of the past life of him to whom they have given their heart.

"Monsieur l'Abbé," said Laura when the priest had finished the narration he had to make her, "I must inform my uncle of all that you have told me."

And without waiting a reply, she left the saloon to seek Sir Edward, who, as he had promised, waited for her in his cabinet.

She threw herself into his arms, and her tears, which she had with much difficulty restrained during the recital she had just listened to, opened a passage and flowed abundantly.

"Calm yourself," said Sir Edward, "calm yourself, my dear child, I have no wish believe me, to force you to marry my protegé."

The abbé, in order to leave the young girl entirely free, had not informed her that the visit he had made was authorized by Sir Edward. Laura regarded the latter with astonishment, and a smile, like the rays of the sun, which sometimes break forth in the midst of a storm, shone forth on her features.

"But, my uncle," she replied, "I only wept because I was afraid, that after what I had learned from the abbé, my marriage with M. Paul Feval would be impossible."

"God be thanked, there is no harm done," exclaimed Sir Edward, who embraced his niece affectionately; "Servigny, despite the misfortunes of his life is worthy of me, and worthy of you; you shall marry him since you do not fear to associate your life with his, and as the Almighty is just, we shall all be happy, for we shall all have done our duty. Now dry up your tears, and again join in the saloon the Abbé Reuzet, whom you have quitted, I think, somewhat suddenly."

Whilst Laura was in the cabinet of her uncle, Servigny, absent since the morning, had entered the saloon; upon finding his friend there, he at once surmised that his fate at this moment was being decided. The anxious manner of the good abbé, rather astonished at the hasty disappearance of Laura, augured nothing in his favour.

"Well?" he said to his friend.

"They know all," replied the abbé. "Sir Edward has received as well as it was possible to hope for, the confidence I have made him."

"And Laura," exclaimed Servigny, "you do not mention Laura?"

"My friend, collect all your courage, I think, without however being at all sure of it, that you will stand in need of it."

A fearful paleness suddenly covered the face of Servigny, but he replied in a calm voice:

"It must be so, she will refuse me. Ah! I hope the one who is to be her husband, will render her as happy as I would have done."

The entrance into the saloon of Sir Edward and his niece prevented his saying more; the baronet approached him and took his hand.

"I know all," he said to him, "Servigny, embrace your wife, my niece willingly bestows her hand upon you."

Servigny believed himself in a dream; before he could determine to kiss the fresh and rosy cheeks of the girl he loved, Sir Edward found it necessary to give him a gentle push towards her.

He was then about to throw himself at the feet of his generous protector and his niece, whom he now considered as his betrothed ; but Sir Edward left him no time.

" Upon my heart ! upon my heart !" he said to him.

And as Servigny commenced speaking in order to show his gratitude :

" The past is a dream which we must all forget," he continued, "and the wisest plan we can adopt for this purpose, is never to mention it, do you hear, M. Paul Feval ?"

Sir Edward, as we have seen, wished his projects to be executed as soon as decided upon ; so that from the day upon which these events occurred, it was necessary that Servigny busied himself, in procuring the papers without which he could not be married, this was not a very difficult affair, notwithstanding the extreme caution with which his position obliged him to act.

Information previously obtained at Lagny by a clever man, and upon whose fidelity he could rely, having apprised him that the report of his condemnation, notwithstanding the singular circumstances attending it, had not reached his native town; he put his courage to the proof, and started for Lagny, and after getting himself recognised, obtained without difficulty the papers which were necessary, namely the registry of his birth, with those of his father and mother, &c.

When Servigny had procured these different proofs, Sir Edward, himself, and Laura went to ——, where they were to remain until the completion of the marriage.

Sir Edward wished the ceremony to take place in the country quickly and secretly, in order to avoid the commentaries of Parisian society, and without apprising any one; and it was only after repeated entreaties, that Laura obtained permission to inform her friend the countess, who replied that she offered up the sincerest prayers for her happiness, and that she hoped, on her part, to impart to her in a short time, some news which would greatly astonish her.

Laura suspected what the news would consist of, which she was so soon to receive from her friend; she had often met at her house the Marquis de Pourrieres, and it was already whispered in society, that the Countess de Neuville waited with some impatience for the completion of the consecrated year. Eager as she was, to tie once more Hymen's fetters, it astonished no one; it was thought quite natural that Lucie, married very young to a man much older than herself, and to whom she had not been enabled to bestow an affection more than filial, should espouse, since fate had decided that she should again be free, a man whom she could love as a woman, and who, besides, appeared to every one, quite worthy of possessing her.

Laura was the only one who did not share in the general opinion; she had not been enabled to overcome the antipathy with which the Marquis de Pourrieres inspired her; it was in vain she said to herself that this man, in addition to his being a handsome cavalier, possessed in reality every quality which could ensure the happiness of the woman he chose for a wife: she could not reflect, without experiencing much sorrow, upon the determination of her friend to bestow her hand upon him; she felt herself constrained, disturbed, ill at

case, when in his presence, and she visited Lucie much seldomer than she would have done, if she had not had the fear of meeting him there.

No events worthy of notice preceded the marriage of Laura and Servigny, which as we have seen was celebrated at——, and consecrated by the Abbé Renzet, who wished to give the young couple this proof of his friendship for them. No one had been invited to the religious ceremony, letters conveying the information, being forwarded instead.

Three months later, the marriage of Lucie de Neuville and the Marquis de Pourrieres was, as we have seen, performed with pomp at the church of Notre Dame de Lorette. All the elite of the Parisian society had been invited to the ceremony. Lucie, who much regretted that her friend, at this moment at Florence, was not with her upon this solemn occasion, was conducted to the altar by the old chevalier of Saint Louis, the worthy man, who during the emigration had been the intimate friend of the old Marquis de Pourrieres, witnessed with pleasure the marriage of his son with a woman to whom, appreciating as he did the brilliant qualities of her head and heart, had vowed towards her an affection quite paternal.

CHAPTER XXXV.

A RETROSPECTIVE GLANCE.

" WHERE are you conducting me?" said Silvia, when the horse had advanced a few steps.

" Oh! parbleu, to my own house," replied the Viscount de Lussan, "where you shall remain until I can find you a convenient residence."

Silvia did not reply at once, but, after reflecting a few moments, she said to the viscount that she preferred being taken to a furnished hotel.

" But you can present yourself no where, habited as you now are," exclaimed de Lussan.

" I know it well," said Silvia, " but there are means of arranging it; if you will, at first, conduct me to a modest furnished hotel, where you will engage and pay for a small chamber for me, even a cabinet, for that will be more consistent with the present state of my toilette; you will afterwards purchase for me every thing necessary, and when I am suitably dressed, you shall take me either to the London Hotel or to that of the Princes, where I shall remain until my house is refurnished."

The Viscount de Lussan conformed to the desires of Silvia; and as at Paris it is easy to procure every thing when the cash is not spared, in a few days the Marchioness de Roselly, completely equipped, was installed in one of the most luxurious apartments of the Hotel des Princes, and received the homages of the Russian princes, English lords, and German barons, the usual locataires of this hotel.

The next morning the viscount paid a visit to the Marchioness of Roselly ; Silvia begged the friend of Salvador to breakfast with her, but she appeared not to understand the side questions of the viscount, who, we may assert, would have been very glad to know what had happened to her since her disappearance, but was forced, however, to retire as ignorant as he came.

A few lines will suffice to acquaint our readers with the events which happened to Silvia, from the moment she was stabbed by Beppo on the Pont au Change, to the present time.

The wound he had given her was a very serious one, and, after examining it, the surgeons, under whose hands she had been placed, declared it to be mortal, and that nothing could save her; but Doctor Matheo, principal physician in the institution, who examined it in his turn the next morning, was not of this opinion, and had no fear in asserting that it was yet possible to recover her; he prescribed, in consequence, what he considered necessary; and as those who were placed under his orders respected his science as much as his character, his prescriptions were so punctually followed, that in the course of a few days, the state of the patient was visibly improved, and at length it was notorious to every one that her life would be saved.

But if Silvia was not to lose her life, she was threatened with an infirmity which would render it, for the rest of her days, a cruel pilgrimage. The fright she had experienced at the moment she encountered Beppo, the suffering to which she had been a victim, the painful uncertainty in which she was plunged—these causes united had acted so strongly upon her nervous system, so disturbed her constitution, that she had lost the use of her speech.

Similar phenomena, however extraordinary they might appear, are much less rare than is generally supposed in such cases; and, unfortunately, science is yet compelled to a mere notice of it, unable as it is to discover a remedy; it has been merely observed that causes having some analogy with those which had produced them, could make them disappear.

Silvia then had lost the use of her speech, and the physicians, whom she could only question by signs, and who were interested in her from her remarkable beauty, could only persuade her to resignation.

She had been for three months between life and death, in a state of complete prostration—in a word, quite unable to reply to the numerous questions addressed to her. Seeing it was impossible to obtain from her any information of a nature to procure traces of her assassin, who, to the present time, had contrived to escape detection; the police, forced to obey the doctors, had consented, at first, to leave her to repose, but when she was convalescent, they returned to her bedside, and again commenced their investigations.

The physician had apprised the police that the individual they wished to interrogate was dumb; but that did not discourage Madame Justice, who demanded of Silvia if she could write.

The latter, who had resolved upon a rule of conduct from which she would not depart, replied by a sign that she did not comprehend him.

"You do not understand French?" said the species of magistrate who was sent to question her. "Of what country are you?"

Silvia looked at the person who spoke thus, and then turned her back to him.

She much regretted, at this moment, the not being enabled to inform the honest functionary that she requested him to bring an interpreter, seeing that she was dumb, and only understood Italian, which he would probably have done without suspecting malice.

The irreverence of Silvia shocked him, though he knew not what to attribute it to; however, after scratching his head for a moment, he said to himself, it was perhaps because she did not understand French that she had not replied to him, and, as he was the greatest linguist in Jerusalem Street, he addressed her in German.

Silvia made not the slightest movement.

In English.

In Spanish.

In the Flemish patois.

The same silence.

The poor man was at the end of his thread, but, happily, remembering a few Italian words, he hastened to pronounce them.

Silvia turned round and made him understand, by signs, that she perfectly understood him.

"She speaks Italian!" exclaimed the honest man enthusiastically, "she speaks Italian! I was quite certain we should finish by understanding each other," he continued, addressing those who surrounded the bed of the convalescent.

"You say she understands Italian," observed one of his clerks. "You have, no doubt, not forgotten that she is dumb?"

"It's true, she is dumb; I had forgotten it; but never mind, there are still means of being understood. Can you write?" he said to Silvia.

The patient made a sign in the negative.

"She cannot write; it's very disagreeable. Do you know the man who struck you?"

Another sign in the negative.

"Ah!"

"An Italian signora?"

Affirmative sign.

"From Rome?"

Negative sign.

"From Firenze?"

Negative sign.

"From Livorno?"

Affirmative sign.

"Can you read?"

Negative sign.

"She can neither read nor write, and she is dumb!" exclaimed the magistrate, in a tone both of despair and discouragement. "We can never discover either her name, or the motive which has brought her to France, or the reason of her being dressed as a man. 'Tis a complete puzzle."

The magistrate would probably have prolonged the interrogatory from which he could learn nothing he wished to know; but the physician observing to him that the patient seemed much fatigued, he good-naturedly retired.

Scenes similar to the one we have described were renewed at different intervals. Silvia continued to affirm that she was from Livorno, that she did not know the man who had struck her. This was the whole that could be drawn from her respecting the motives of her journey to France, and her disguise as a man; she confined her replies to signs in the negative, which drove her interrogators to despair.

The reasons which had induced her to act thus are not difficult to be surmised.

She would gladly have had it in her power to be revenged on Beppo; but could she, without compromising herself, denounce the ex-fisherman? Would she not have to fear that this man, whose savage energy she had just received an example of, once arrested, would endeavour to drag her with him into the abyss? This would not be difficult, if he resolved to recount to the magistrate what he knew of her life; and Dame Justice, excessively curious in her nature, once putting her nose into her affairs, it was quite certain she would discover secrets she wished to keep the world ignorant of: for instance, they might discover that the noble Marchioness of Roselly, ex-première chanteuse of the Grand Theatre of Marseilles, was no other than Desirée Celeste Comtois, educated under a false name, at the Institution of the Legion of Honour; she must then bid adieu (and this was the least

LIFE IN PARIS.

SERVIGNY AND THE ABBE.

misfortune she had to dread) to the position she had occupied in society, and which she still hoped to reconquer. They might discover that she was well acquainted, while at Marseilles, with the Jew Josué so miserably assassinated at Paris; and, from conjecture to conjecture, from one investigation to another, obtain evidence that it was shortly after leaving her house that he was murdered; and from this discovery to that of the truth was no great distance; whilst in the system she had adopted there was absolutely nothing to fear. When, after interrogating her on every point, they were at length convinced that it was impossible to pierce the mystery in which chance, and not her will, seemed to have enveloped her destiny—as they had nothing besides to reproach her with, as they could not convert into a crime the blow of a poniard which she had received—it was probable they would leave her free to direct her steps where she might choose. It only required patience, then, and Silvia was one of those creatures who, well persuaded that time is a grand master, knew when to say to herself, that all ends well to him who can wait and who acts in consequence.

What we have above stated will dispense with our explaining to our readers the reasons, nearly similar, which prevented her writing to Salvador an account of what had happened to her.

When Silvia was perfectly recovered, the authorities, who had not yet given up all hope of obtaining some curious revelations, had her taken from the hospital in which she had been placed, and conducted to a prison. As she was aware that the last means of interesting those upon whom her fate depended was to submit, without murmuring, to their orders, she restrained herself, when they announced this news to her, and merely crossed her hands over her bosom, and raised her eyes to heaven as a sign of resignation.

During nearly five months which she passed in prison, before she was placed at liberty, she did not belie herself a single moment; she worked with continued industry, and her mildness was unalterable. At length she manœuvred so well, that she interested the almoner of the prison, who took active measures for the purpose of obtaining her liberty.

These measures were on the point of being crowned with success, and Silvia expected every day an order to receive her liberty, when a lucky event happened to her, although it prolonged her captivity some days, and placed her life in danger.

She was at the same time so handsome and so mild, there was so much distinction in her manners, that the director of the prison had determined that she should not be mixed with the other female prisoners. For this purpose, he had assigned her a distant cell, which formed part of a small building in which they locked up the wood consumed in the prison. Every night she was shut up in this cell, which was opened in the morning to allow her the privilege of walking about the house so long as the day lasted.

Silvia had, in the morning, received the visit of the worthy clergyman who had interested himself about her, and she had retired to sleep, happy in knowing that she would soon be set at liberty, when, towards the middle of the night, she was awakened by the cries of her companions in captivity, and the exclamations of the warders of the prison, who were running across the courts and corridors; a dense smoke filled her cell, and through the bars of her windows she could observe the flames devouring that part of the building in which the wood was secured.

A few minutes more and the flames would reach her, and no one came to her assistance. The guardians, occupied in securing the prisoners whom they had been compelled to remove form their dormitories, and who were uttering frightful screams, although out of the reach of danger, seemed totally to have forgotten poor Silvia. Her fright was so painful, that a sudden revolution took place in her entire being, and she could utter piercing cries, followed shortly by this exclamation: "Assistance! assistance!"

She had recovered her speech!

The exclamations of Silvia, luckily for her, were not heard by the employés of the prison, who were in the court; but they attracted a fireman, who, standing up, with a hatchet in his hand, on a burning rafter, laboured zealously to arrest the fire. The brave soldier, without thinking of the many dangers he would have to confront, threw himself on the roof of the building of which the cell occupied by Silvia, formed a part. The flames, the smoke, nothing stopped him; he arrives near the cell; Silvia, nearly stifled by the smoke, had fallen, in a swoon, on her modest couch. The brave fireman, who sees behind him the fire making rapid progress, does not hesitate; he hammers with renewed strength against the bars which secure the window of the cell; he dislodges one, then two; at length he contrives to enter the cell of the unfortunate prisoner, takes her in his arms, and, despite the flames and smoke, which have redoubled in intensity during the last few minutes, returns by the way he entered; and, with the aid of a ladder raised by his comrades, at length arrives in the court, where he deposits the woman he had saved, at the moment that the roof of the flaming building sinks and falls with a loud crash.

This scene occupied less time than we have taken to describe it. The fireman had deposited Silvia in a distant corner of the court, and hastily returned where his duty called him, without farther troubling himself about her, so that she was alone when she recovered the use of her senses.

We shall leave it to our readers to appreciate the extent of the joy she experienced when she had come to herself. She had escaped a horrible danger, a most cruel death, and she had recovered her speech!

But what was she to do with this precious gift? Ought she to use it, or conceal it with caution? After reflecting a few minutes, she adopted the latter plan; and, indeed, it was the wisest. They had given up the hope of obtaining any information, since they had all but decided upon giving her her liberty; and whatever confidence she might have in the finesse of her talents, she was not quite certain of replying in a satisfactory manner to the additional questions they would not fail to put to her, if they arrived at the knowledge that she was not dumb.

But suddenly she remembered that, before falling in a fainting state on the bed, she had uttered some piercing cries, and demanded assistance; either, these cries had been heard, since she had been snatched from death, or she was indebted to chance for her delivery, by one of the employés recollecting that in the distant cell there was an unfortunate prisoner whom he must not allow to perish. In the first case, she ought to speak before they even dreamed of interrogating her, that she might not be suspected of having any thing to conceal; in the second, her own interest required that she should maintain her silence. Her perplexity was great; she knew not how to determine, but accident assisted her.

The fireman, assisted by the employés of the prison, had at length contrived to make themselves masters of the fire, which they had completely arrested, and they commenced playing the pumps in order to extinguish the smouldering embers. The fireman who had saved Silvia came by chance into the corner of the court in which he had deposited her, and from which she had not moved. By the pale light of the still burning rafters, he remarked the extreme beauty of the woman who owed to him her life.

He was secretly flattered at having saved so handsome a creature; he stopped near her.

"You owe a famous candle to the good saint who allowed your cries to reach me. If I had not by chance been within a few paces of the window of your dungeon, at this moment you would be in the other world; for the devil if those who were in the court would have heard you."

Silvia looked around her, and resolved not to reply to her liberator until she had ascertained that no one could hear her, and that they were all too much occupied to observe her.

"How," she said to him, "you were the only one who heard me? my cries only reached you?"

"Ah! mon Dieu, yes," replied the fireman, "and I am now very glad of it; I am delighted, in reality, that I had no need of any one to save so pretty a woman as you are."

"I regret it is not in my power to prove my gratitude to you otherwise than by thanks."

"But that's all that's wanted," exclaimed the courageous fireman; "to save a person from being burned is one of the obligations of the state."

"A noble state, certainly, which obliges those who exercise it to sacrifice every moment their own lives, to save those of their fellow-creatures."

There was so much dignity in the voice and features of Silvia, in pronouncing these few words, that the worthy fireman stood quite amazed in front of her.

"Excuse, madame," he said at length, "excuse; I didn't know.—But I stop here talking with you, and the work is not finished."

"Go," replied Silvia, "go where duty calls you; I shall not forget you."

The soldier joined his companions. Silvia, from the corner in which she was crouched, saw him manœuvre a pump with great activity, and retire with his comrades, when the fire was completely extinguished.

He had spoken to none of the employés of the prison, no one, then, knew what had happened to her.

It required plenty of courage to play the game she had resolved upon, and this courage she possessed. Constantly on her guard, she had never allowed it to be suspected for a moment that she could now reply, if she chose, to the questions which were sometimes put to her.

Her perseverance was at length rewarded; the endeavours of the worthy ecclesiastic were crowned with success, and, one fine morning, the doors of her prison were thrown open to Silvia. The good priest had given her a small sum he had collected for her among several charitable individuals, and which was destined to defray the expenses of the long journey she had to undertake; for she had stated that it was her intention to return to Livorno, and the director of the prison, wishing to contribute to the kind action of the almoner, had made her a present of the humble costume which she wore when she made her appearance in the church of Notre Dame de Lorette.

She might, if she had chosen it, have procured a better costume; for the sum given her by the worthy almoner of the prison, although not considerable, was sufficient; but she had preferred keeping the one which rendered her the least recognisable.

She went straight from the prison to the Avenue Chateaubriand, in which was situate the small hotel she inhabited at the time she was carried off by Beppo. She was in hopes of obtaining, from the information of the neighbours, some intelligence as to what was become of her house and servants. She had no fear of being recognised, for, during the time of her prosperity, she seldom went out on foot, and the physical and moral sufferings she had lately gone through had greatly changed her features.

The persons to whom she addressed herself, under the pretext of obtaining the address of the Marchioness of Roselly, acquainted her with what our readers already know, that, after waiting several days, her servants had apprised the police of her strange disappearance—that they had actively searched for her, but that all their efforts had been in vain—seals had been placed upon all that she possessed—and that, after a certain time, her furniture, horses, and equipages had been sold, under the orders of the administration—and that the produce of the sale had been deposited in the treasury of deposits, to be returned to her, in the event, somewhat problematical, of her appearing to claim it. For the rest, it was generally believed that she had been assassinated; and it was not known what had become of her servants, who had dispersed a short time after her disappearance.

"I have nothing to fear on this head," said Silvia to herself, after quitting the loquacious groceress who had given her this information, and which she had accompanied by a few commentaries not very welcome to the Marchioness of Roselly, whom she detested, for the simple reason, that it was not at her shop that the lady furnished herself with these articles; "I have actually nothing to fear. Let us now go to the Marquis de Pourrieres."

The residence of Salvador was not far from the hotel lately inhabited by Silvia, so that, notwithstanding her weakness, it took her but a short time to reach it; it was then about eleven o'clock in the morning.

The folding doors of the hotel were wide open, and the court thronged with brilliant equipages. Silvia, holding a handkerchief to her face, from a fear of being recognised by some of the servants of the marquis, entered the court. She then observed, before the peristyle, a carriage, quite new, and harnessed to it were two superb white horses. The arms which ornamented the panels of the equipage informed her that it belonged to the Marquis de Pourrieres; the coachman, the chasseur, and the lackeys wore dashing new liveries; they had white gloves and enormous bouquets at their fronts.

"It's strange," said Silvia; "is it, by chance, that he is going to be married?"

She remained a few moments buried in deep and sorrowful reflections, which ended thus: "How must I act, and what means employ, to prevent this marriage?"

She was aroused from these reflections by cries of, "Make way," twenty times repeated, and she was obliged to fall back precipitately against the wall, to prevent being upset by the carriage of the Marquis de Pourrieres, which passed rapidly in front of her, followed by those which, two minutes before, had filled the court of the hotel.

Silvia, after wiping her forehead, from which fell large drops of perspiration, approached the Swiss of the hotel, a new attendant, whom she did not know, engaged at this moment in closing the folding doors.

"Your master is going to be married, then?" she said, in her sweetest voice, for she dreaded lest this important personage, proud of his livery, quite new, and resplendent in gold, might not condescend to converse a few moments with a woman, certainly pretty, but, in truth, more than poorly clad.

The new Swiss of the Marquis de Pourrieres, either from his being a little less brutal than his confrères, or that he allowed himself to be softened by the bright eyes of the woman who spoke to him, replied to her kindly:

"Oh! the marriage has already taken place," he said in almost a mild voice. "M. the mayor, to do honour to the married couple, was good enough to inconvenience himself a little on their account."

A cloud passed before the eyes of Silvia.

"What is the use of afflicting one's self?" she said, after a moment's silence; "the deed is completed; but I will be revenged."

"Why, one would really think," said the Swiss, with a very marked provincial accent, who had observed the sudden affliction of Silvia, "that you were sorry at what you have heard!"

"Me!" replied Silvia, who had recovered her self-possession; "on the contrary, I am delighted that the Marquis de Pourrieres, who, it is said, is a very charitable man, is married to-day to such an amiable and handsome woman as—stay, I forget the name of his wife."

"Madame la Comtesse de Neuville, the widow of the famous general; nothing but that," said the Swiss, rubbing his hands with an air of profound satisfaction.

"And do you know where the religious ceremony is to take place?"

"At Notre Dame de Lorette. Ah! it will be superb; and if I were not obliged to take care of the hotel, in which there is no one, I would go and see it."

"Well; I am going to Notre Dame de Lorette, and if you will promise me to give to M. Lebrun, as soon as he returns, a letter which I shall write after the ceremony, I will come and recount to you all that takes place at the church."

"I shall see you return with infinite pleasure, my pretty dame; but I cannot, in spite of my wish to be agreeable to you, render you the slight service you require. M. Lebrun has departed more than a week ago for the chateau of M. the Marquis, where the newly-married couple are to pass the season; they will start immediately after the ceremony, without even returning to the hotel—an English fashion."

Silvia, having obtained all she desired from the Swiss, quitted him after a promise to return. The worthy man entered his lodge rubbing his hands, imagining that the display of his livery had seduced the pretty woman with whom he had been conversing.

A few paces from the Hotel de Pourrieres, Silvia mounted a cabriolet which conducted her to the church of Notre Dame de Lorette.

"I will try," she said to herself, more than once during the time it occupied, "to turn their honeymoon into a red moon; and, please the devil, I shall succeed."

Our readers know what took place at the church.

CHAPTER XXXVI.
THE CHATEAU DE POURRIERES.

THE sun was just commencing his toilette, the dew still sparkled like watery pearls on the branches of the old trees of the Parc de Pourrieres; Roman promenaded, whistling, along the natural barrier to the park of the Chateau de Pourrieres, by the ravine in which the unhappy Ambroise had met his death.

Roman no longer possesses the round and florid complexion which we formerly noticed. The once pure lines in his face, appear as in a tempest; his flabby cheeks are pale; numerous wrinkles invade his forehead; 'tis not remorse which has caused such ravages—no, 'tis gaming and drunkenness; for his eyes still preserve their usual expression of thoughtlessness, and his lips, which are slightly turned up at each corner, have lost none of their sardonic contempt.

Roman walked for some moments alone, when he saw Salvador approaching.

Their conversation will inform us of the motive which brought them together at such an early hour and at this distant part of the park.

Roman advanced a few paces to meet his friend, he presented his hand, which Salvador refused to accept.

"As you like," he said, "as you like."

And he recommenced his promenade.

The fine blue eyes of Salvador shot forth lightnings, his step was short and hesitating; it was quite evident he was a prey to a violent rage, which had been long compressed, but which was now about to burst forth.

"Well," said Roman, "is it simply that I should assist at the rising of Aurora—a spectacle cherished by all virtuous men, if we are to believe the song of the late M. Bonilly—that you have requested me to attend this morning in this isolated spot in the park?"

"The moment is ill chosen for jesting," replied Salvador; "so, oblige me by putting an end to your foolish citations, which I am in no humour to listen to."

"Ah! the devil! Well, since it is so, let us speak seriously. What do you desire of me?"

"I wish you to give me an explanation of the scandalous scene which took place here during my absence."

"And what do you expect me to tell you? I had drunk, it must be confessed, a few glasses of jurançon too many; I laughed in the saloon with one of the women of your noble wife, who entered at this moment, and ordered me to leave the room, in a tone to which I have not been accustomed since I have been in the service of the Marquis de Pourrieres." In pronouncing these words, Roman gave to his voice a sardonic inflection, which did not escape Salvador. "I got into a passion, and sent Madame la Marquise to her promenade, in a manner rather less polished, perhaps, than I ought to have done—that's the whole of it."

"That's all! that's all! Really, I admire you. And do you know what are the results of your conduct? My wife insists, and I shall be obliged to obey her, that I dismiss you on the very instant."

"You will say to your wife, that what she insists upon is impossible; she will make a little noise, perhaps, but when she is quite convinced that her attempts are useless, she will take her part and think no more about it."

Salvador made no reply to this little discourse, which his friend had pronounced in the most sprightly and free and easy tone it is possible to conceive; he continued his walk at a quick pace.

Roman, whose obesity prevented his following him, seated himself on the trunk of a tree, and waited patiently for his return.

"It must be," said Salvador to himself, continuing his walk at a great pace; "it must absolutely be so; for now he will not alter; but what means employ?"

He returned to Roman:

"Listen," he said to him, " you must be aware, that, after what has passed, you must absolutely quit the chateau."

"But I wish for nothing better," replied Roman. "Give me a little money, and I will leave even to-day for Paris, where you will find me, I promise you, completely corrected."

"I wish it may be so, but I do not reckon upon it," replied Salvador, who took from his note-case three notes of a thousand francs, and handed them to his friend. "Do not gamble with them," he added; "for I give you my word, I shall forward you no more for three months from to-day. You have now dissipated more than the moiety of what fell to us; you have nothing more to demand."

"Very good, very good, lecturer; I know you are an excellent boy, incapable of leaving in embarrassment your dearest friend, if he tumbles into it by chance. I will this moment rid you of my presence, which, I see, annoys you just at present. You are still under the influence of the honeymoon, but that will pass away, my most dear, that will pass off."

Roman, after shaking the hand of Salvador, directed his steps towards the avenue of the park which led to the chateau, whistling the air of the Tartars' March, which, to all appearance, he seemed to have a great affection for.

We are almost certain that our readers have already surmised what were the ideas which germinated in the head of Salvador, whom Roman had left alone near the ravine in the park, who still continued the fatiguing exercise to which he had given way so long.

They have surmised that this man, who had attained, by crimes and the success which had attended all his enterprises, an honourable name amongst the most honourable, an elevated position, a considerable fortune; that this man, who had married a woman whom the richest and the noblest envied him, wished to preserve all this; and that, as he had discovered, to allow to live with him a man whose faculties were nearly destroyed by drunkenness and gambling, it would be impossible for him to do so; he had come to a resolution of ridding himself of his accomplice.

But how could he rid himself of a man attached to him by so many mysterious links? Would he consent to expatriate himself? and, even supposing this, would his absence ensure his tranquillity? could he not, at a distance, as well as near him, impose laws to which he would be compelled to submit?

Roman was less to be feared at home than at a distance, for there was a frightful link that bound them; upon the safety of one depended that of the other; but distance broke this link, the sole guarantee among villains.

Roman, then, must not be far off; and yet Salvador, well convinced that the vices of his friend, or rather his accomplice, would only increase with age, was fully determined to support the consequences no longer.

Salvador had said all this to himself, when his wife narrated to him the odious scene which had produced the interview in the park, at which we have been present.

Then, and not till then, did Salvador look boldly at the necessary conclusion of the reflections, of which we have just analysed the substance.

He said to himself, in positive terms, that the death of Roman could alone secure his happiness and his tranquillity; and the death of Roman was instantly resolved upon.

He had only remained in the solitary spot in the park, in which he had been left by him whose death he had just sworn, that he might the more easily decide upon the means of taking his life, without running the risk of compromising himself.

Thus, this man who, for more than twenty years, had been his constant companion; this man, whose hand he had just pressed; this man, in a word, who had given him, and to whom, in his turn, he had given so many proofs of attachment, he was about to murder, without feeling more pity than he would for a venomous serpent which he is forced to crush under his foot. Our readers must not be astonished at this. Salvador disposed himself to act in the same manner as any other individual, placed under the same circumstances, would have acted, or, at least, would wish to act; even as Roman himself would have acted, had he been in his place; so true is it that sentiments of attachment are not real, have neither value nor duration, when not based upon the mutual esteem of those who experience them.

We are well aware that this opinion, which we advance as a positive fact, may be opposed by a great number of examples, and that it would be easy for those of our readers who have compiled the annals of crime, to cite a number of criminals, who have given to their accomplices many proofs of friendship, who have even sacrificed their own lives for another; but numerous as may be the facts, they are much less so, happily, (we say happily, with design,) than those on the other side. And besides, if we would take the trouble to examine, with attention, the character of the individuals who have furnished, or who may furnish for the future, these examples, we shall be soon convinced that, instead of disproving the opinion we have advanced, the facts to which we allude only serve to give it additional strength.

Indeed, we have often seen criminals sacrifice every thing, their liberty, their life even, in favour of an accomplice, for whom they appear to feel a sincere friendship; but we are enabled, at the same time, to remark, that the individuals who gave these proofs of devotion, were mostly men entirely deprived of intelligence, having nothing of the human creature but the envelope; whilst, on the contrary, those in favour of whom they sacrifice themselves, are remarkable either for their finesse, or the cultivation of their imagination.

If our readers will remember that we have already mentioned, that criminals allow themselves to be easily governed by those among them who possess a certain amount of intelligence, they will probably not accord the name of friendship to that sentiment which acts upon the individuals we have spoken of—a sentiment without reflection, nearly similar to that shown by dogs to their masters, by wild beasts for those who have managed to tame them.

A community of interests might easily, for a certain lapse of time, more or less attach to each other individuals endowed, as were Salvador and Roman, with an intelligence nearly equal; but when these interests cease to be similar, there is an immediate struggle, and this struggle is generally terminated by the total destruction of one of the two, sometimes even by both at the same time.

In the struggle which was commencing between Salvador and Roman, the latter, entirely swayed by his passion for gambling, blinded by the usual carelessness of his character, and to whom age, and the strong liquors of which, as a consolation for his daily losses, he made an immoderate use, must necessarily be the one to give way.

Salvador had no arranged plan when he engaged his accomplice to return to Paris; he merely wished to keep at a distance from the chateau the victim whom he was fully determined to sacrifice to his tranquillity; he thought, and with reason, that he should find there, with less trouble than elsewhere, an opportunity of committing, with security, and of hiding under a thick veil, the additional crime he meditated.

We certainly would not justify Salvador, whose odious character is too well known to our readers; we must, however, say, that it was not until after many a struggle and long hesitation, that he determined to sacrifice his accomplice; we shall even add, (for this proves that when once the career of crime has passed certain limits, there is no possibility of arresting it,) that he did not resolve to commit this fresh crime, until he had acquired the certitude that, so long as his accomplice was near him, he should be compelled to continue in the path he had followed till the present, and which he had resolved to quit.

Besides this, the marriage he had effected had increased his pride; and the free and easy manners of Roman, whom he had accustomed himself to look upon as merely the head of his servants, sensibly wounded him.

The motive of Roman for so hastily accepting the proposition of quitting the chateau, was, that the life he led there grew tiresome to him; for, annoyed, more than he allowed it to appear, at the disdain and haughty manners of his accomplice, he would not have made this concession to him, if his doing so had in the least crossed his desires; but, however, he started the same day, as he had promised; and, thanks to the marvellous celerity of the coaches of the government department, five days after the conversation we have reported, he was installed at the Hotel de Pourrieres.

On the same day that Roman arrived in Paris, Salvador received, at the Chateau de Pourrieres, the following letter:

"M. le Marquis de Pourrieres,—'If ever I deceive you,' you said to me one day, at the finish of a violent quarrel, in which I had manifested a wish to quit you, but to which you thought right to oppose yourself, 'if ever I deceive you, you will have acquired the right of avenging yourself.' I know not as yet whether you have deceived me, but I know very well that you have married Madame la Comtesse de Neuville, to whom, as I am assured, you are greatly attached—that you have married this woman to give to your position in the world an additional relief, that her dowry may augment your fortune, this I can easily believe, and I have no intention of complaining of it; but that you loved her when I am here, before I have ceased to love you, when it is, in some measure, on your account that I have supported, for more than a twelvemonth, sufferings under whose weight a woman with less strength than I have would have been crushed a hundred times—this is what I will not suffer—this is what I look upon as a deception—'tis this, believe me truly, that I will avenge myself of. I am perfectly aware that your destruction will ensure my own, but I think you have sufficient foresight, and consequently, know my character too well, to believe that this consideration would make me hesitate for a single moment.

"I desire, then, (you understand, I desire,) that you will explain to me the reasons which determined you to espouse the Countess of Neuville; I desire that you give me an assurance that I have not lost the place I ought to occupy in your heart eternally ; I desire that your actions should prove to me the sincerity of your words.

"I am aware that I owe you the narration of what has happened to me since we have been separated; this recital I will give you when you have replied to this letter, and it will prove to you, I hope, that I have the right of speaking to you as I now do.

"Reply to me at once, at the Hotel des Princes, where I am now residing, thanks to your friend, the Viscount de Lussan, with whom I am perfectly satisfied; at once, understand, for I have very little patience, you know, and sometimes impatience drives us to commit a heap of imprudences, of which we repent when it is too late to repair them.
"Wholly yours,
                      "SILVIA."

Salvador expected to receive from Silvia a letter somewhat similar to the one we have placed under the eyes of our readers; this one did not surprise him, then; but, as he knew his mistress to be quite capable of putting in execution the threats she had boldly made to him, he thought it best to write her at once, and in a manner to satisfy her; he therefore, replied to her as follows:

"Your letter has much astonished me. How! is it you that offer me threats? is it you who demand of me an account of my actions? However, as I wish to believe that the narration you promise me, will prove that you have the right of speaking to me as you do, I will willingly reply to you.

"Roman, who is now at Paris, will acquaint you with the reasons which determined me to take as a wife the Countess de Neuville, whom I have married, believing you dead, or, at least, unfaithful, (and could I believe otherwise?) in order to give a relief to my position in the world and to increase my fortune by her dowry. I will not say, that, if you had not returned, I might not have been seduced by the amiable qualities she possesses; you would not believe me, and you would be right; but there exists a woman who will, in my eyes, be always preferable to every being of her sex—and that woman is yourself, you know it well.

"But I desire (understand, I *desire*) that you give me an account of the events which have kept you from me for more than a year; and, before I acknowledge the rights you arrogate to yourself, perhaps a little prematurely, the explanations you owe me must be sufficiently clear and succinct to prevent any doubt remaining in my mind.

"I think, Silvia, you have sufficient judgment to know well my character, and that, consequently, you will not suppose that the menaces you advance can terrify me. I am, as you are aware, a man of the world, who accepts, with all resignation, *les faits accomplis;* I shall, therefore, recommend to you neither patience nor prudence; you are perfectly free to act in any manner that may appear to you the most suitable.—Wholly yours,
                      "A. DE POURRIERES."

Salvador did not forward this letter to Silvia, until he had addressed another to Roman, in which he traced out for him the conduct he should pursue regarding his mistress. He knew that his accomplice, as interested as himself in not displeasing the Marchioness of Roselly, whom he feared, in spite of the confident tone he affected in his letter, would serve him faithfully, notwithstanding the germs of discontent which existed between them.

As we have no wish to take our readers a journey from Paris, where, at this moment, we should find Silvia and Roman, to the chateau of de Pourrieres, where we have left Lucie and Salvador, and from thence conduct them to the capital of the Grand Duchy of Tuscany, where Laura and Servigny, accompanied by Sir Edward, repaired immediately after the marriage of the former; we shall place before our readers their correspondence, which will inform them of all the events which took place until the period when we shall again find them assembled at Paris.

If it is true, as asserted by Buffon, that the style reveals the man, this correspondence, which has this very moment been placed in our hands, and which will form the substance of the following chapter, will show the character of the principal personages of this history.

We repeat, before proceeding farther, what we have frequently hitherto announced, this history is true, true in its whole, and in its details; all the personages who play any part in it are real, many even exist at the present time; we have merely changed the names of some amongst them; (it was useless to take this precaution respecting those whose names were in some measure become historical, and Salvador and Roman were of the number;) and, in order to be convinced of the truth of what we here advance, it only requires the sceptical to consult the annals of the prefecture of police and the criminal courts.

We merely insist upon this fact, because we are aware that readers are generally little disposed to believe authors, when they affirm the truth of the facts they recount; and we, therefore, hope to enjoy the only merit which this work may probably possess, that of being true.

CHAPTER XXXVII.

CORRESPONDENCE.

"*Lucie de Pourrieres to Madame Feval.*

"Chateau de Pourrieres.

"I have married, my dear Laura, the man whom at first I looked upon as a sort of hobgoblin, and whom you yourself, much more reasonable than myself, (I feel a pleasure in acknowledging it,) could not endure. This will be no news to you. You have received, no doubt, at Florence, (where, I believe, you mean to fix yourself, as you make no mention of returning to France,) the letter I wrote you, announcing the resolution I had come to, after consulting all my friends, and especially M. de Kerandec, the kind Chevalier of Saint Louis, whom you often met at Madame de Villerbanne's. They all spoke highly to me of the Marquis de Pourrieres; they have all told me I could not make a better choice; and, my faith, I decided.

"Well, my dear Laura, I am, at present, very well satisfied that I did not impose a silence on the *penchant* which drew me towards the man who is now my husband. M. de Pourrieres is gifted with the best of hearts, and the noblest character it is possible to imagine. His love for me is equal to mine for him; he thinks of nothing but me, and

allows no occasion to escape of giving me fresh proofs of the affection he has sworn to me.

"He has lately sacrificed, without hesitating a moment, an old family intendant, who had failed in respect to me. I wished to intercede in favour of the unfortunate man, whose fault was the consequence of his being drunk, but my husband would not permit me to do so. 'If Lebrun had shown his want of respect to myself?' he replied to me, when I requested the pardon of this man, 'I would have overlooked it, perhaps, in favour of his ancient and faithful services; but I cannot tolerate an offence offered to you. Our people must learn that I am in no humour to allow them to be wanting, for a moment, in the respect to which you are entitled from them. All that I can do in favour of Lebrun, is to keep him in my service; but he will reside at Paris when we are here, and he will return to Pourrieres when we visit Paris; for the rest, he is an honest servant, and will be as useful for the future as he has been to the present.'

"I had no reason for troubling myself more about this foolish business, and, the same evening, the intendant of M. de Pourrieres, well reprimanded, I suppose, left for Paris, where he will remain until we return there.

"I only mention this little circumstance, my dear Laura, to show the extent of the regard M. de Pourrieres has for me, and the attentions with which he surrounds me; and to prove to you, at the same time, that he is quite worthy of the friendship you will accord to him, if you are not ungrateful; for, although he hardly knows you, he loves you infinitely, and every time I speak to him about you, he manifests a desire to see you soon returned to France. He wishes, he says, to make your husband his most intimate friend; this will be, as he asserts, the best means of having you often with us. Is he mistaken?

"Answer me, my dear Laura, and tell me every thing; what interests you will interest me; our new positions must not be the cause of our forgetting the friendship we had for each other. There is in my heart a place for friendship as well as love. Are you like me? If I did not fear to afflict you I should reply, No; for you have not yet given me a reply to the first letter I wrote you.

"I have received news of Eugenie de Mirbel, or rather Madame de Bourgerel; her husband has also a noble heart; her daughter grows prettier every day; Madame de Saint Preuil is well and happy.

"My husband, whom I would not allow to read this letter, does not insist upon it, but he will absolutely add something; I do not think I can oppose his wish.

"Adieu, my good Laura, or rather, to a speedy meeting, believe in the constant friendship of

"LUCIE DE POURRIERES."

At the end of the last page of this letter, Salvador wrote as follows:

"I have but rarely, madame, had the honour of seeing you; I have, however, forgotten neither your graces nor your talents. I cannot dare to solicit from you a small share of the friendship which you have entirely devoted to my wife, but I have a hope that you will kindly allow me to accompany her when she may visit you. I am impatient to know M. Feval, persuaded, as I am, that the man upon whom you have bestowed your hand, is fully deserving of the friendship of every worthy person. Have the kindness, I entreat you, to present to him my homages. Deign to accept, madame, the assurance of the profound respect

LIFE IN PARIS.

SALVADOR INRODUCED TO SERVIGNY BY SIR EDWARD.

with which I subscribe myself,—Your very humble and very obedient servant.

"A. DE POURRIERES."

"*Silvia to the Marquis de Pourrieres.*

"Paris.

"I have seen Lebrun," (our readers are aware that Silvia thus called Roman; the Viscount de Lussan, having heard him named at the banquet given at Lemardelay's by Alexis de Pourrieres, was the only one among the friends of Salvador who knew his real name,) "and I am almost satisfied with what he has told me; you were, he tells me, very much afflicted at my loss, and that it was not until you had long sought me, and had me searched for, that you determined to marry the Countess de Neuville.

"I repeat to you, it is not your marriage (which, I easily believe, could alone repair the breaches made in your fortune by the misconduct of your intendant) that I shall complain of, if it does not destroy your affection for me.

"Can you not rid yourself of the worthy M. Lebrun? Is it absolutely necessary that you retain in your service this man, who, if I am to believe what M. le Vicomte tells me, loses daily, at the gaming table, considerable sums, which he must take from your coffers?

"I am well aware that he knows many secrets, and that it is probably on that account you allow him to do almost as he likes; but it seems to me that there exist remedies to heal all wounds, and that, in the position you are now in, the employment even of the most energetic ought not to frighten you.

"In case you have any intention of curing the evil, you can reckon upon me; I shall be happy in finding an opportunity of giving you a fresh proof of my devotion.

"The Viscount de Lussan informed me that you left with the intention of passing the season at the Chateau de Pourrieres. As you have, no doubt, announced this design to your wife; and as a sudden change of resolution might appear strange to her, and induce her to believe that her charms had lost the power of retaining you near her, change none of your projects. I shall wait, to serve you, until you return to Paris. You see that my composition is a very accommodating one. I hope, therefore, that you will take into account, at a future time, my extreme gentleness.

"Now that peace is nearly established between us, I ought to recount to you all that has happened to me. You will peruse a very singular history, and, perhaps, you would not believe it, if it had not become, so to speak, of public notoriety."*

Silvia here narrated to Salvador the events which our readers already know—namely, what happened to her since her abduction by Beppo, at the moment she left her house to visit the fortune-teller of the Street des Vignes, at Chaillot, up to the time she appeared to him at the church of Notre Dame de Lorette.

"If now," she continued, after finishing the recital, "you ask me who this Beppo is, who so audaciously carried me off in open day, two steps from my residence, I shall reply to you, that he is the same man I charged to punish the presumption of M. de Preval. This, perhaps, requires an explanation, which I will give you when we meet.

"The narration I have given you has proved, I

hope, that I had absolutely nothing to reproach myself for, and that I had the right of speaking to you in the manner I did in my last letter.

"Adieu, my friend; write to me often; your letters will console me for your absence.

"Wholly yours,   SILVIA."

"P.S.—You have already perceived that my purse is in the most pitiable state it is possible to imagine; have the kindness, therefore, to send me a few bank notes for a thousand francs. I shall remain at the Hotel des Princes until you arrive at Paris. We will not think of refurnishing my house, until you have returned here."

"*The Marquis de Pourrieres to the Marchioness of Roselly.*

"Chateau de Pourrieres.

"I have just received your letter, my dear Silvia, and the eagerness with which I reply to it will prove to you how much pleasure it has occasioned me.

"I am as satisfied as it is possible to be with the explanations you have so willingly given me; and I acknowledge, at once, that you had nothing to reproach yourself with, and that you had the right of speaking to me as you did.

"I shall remain, since you will permit me, until the end of summer, at the Chateau de Pourrieres.

"When I return to Paris, we will talk about the *good* M. Lebrun. What you tell me of this excellent serviteur proves to me that we understand each other perfectly, without the necessity of making long discourses, and that the sufferings you have lately experienced have not caused you the loss of one of your brilliant qualities.

"I send you ten thousand francs, in an order upon M. Mathieu Durant, banker, at Paris. Do not spare the cash; I can, thank God, without inconveniencing myself, supply your wants liberally; and, if I can find a remedy for the malady with which I am attacked, I think it will continue so.

"Your house shall be refurnished when I return to Paris, and more luxuriously than before. You are aware, no doubt, that a considerable sum, the produce of the sale of the things belonging to you, which comprised the furniture of your Hotel of the Avenue Chateaubriand, is deposited in the treasury of consignations. It is, perhaps, possible to recover this sum ; we will consult about it.

"Are there no means of ridding ourselves of this Beppo who appears to me a very dangerous man?

"Adieu, my dear Silvia, rely faithfully upon the affection and entire devotedness of your faithful lover,   "A. DE POURRIERES."

"Thus," said Salvador to himself, when he had sealed the letter, "I must, when I have rid myself of Roman, satisfy all the caprices of this woman, which, at present, I scarcely know how to do. It shall not be thus, Madame la Marquise de Roselly ; I will make use of you, since you offer me your assistance; and, my faith, afterwards—But how many victims will compose the bloody hecatomb I must sacrifice to my safety ?"

Salvador remained for some moments with his head buried in his hands; he then rang and ordered the domestic who presented himself, to take to the post the letter he had written.

"*Laura Feral to the Marchioness de Pourrieres.*

"Florence.

"Your two letters, my dear Lucie, were handed to me at the same time. They arrived at Florence before us, for we stopped at several towns in Italy,

* Our readers will remember that the abduction of Silvia was noticed at the time by all the journals.

at Genoa, at Milan, at Venice, before arriving at Florence, but as we had written, at the last town, to secure a residence, they kept them until my arrival.

"I have a little neglected you, I own; I am certain, however, that you did not think for a moment that I had forgotten you.

"So, you are married; you have espoused the man who caused you so much fear. I was not wrong, then, when I told you that he occupied too much of your thought to be indifferent to you.

"I am delighted to hear that you are happy; this, indeed, does not surprise me: you are so pretty, so good, so amiable, that should the Marquis de Pourrieres not possess even one of the qualities which every one grants him, it would be impossible for him not to love you; and I think it is impossible to render unhappy the person we love. I have often heard it said, it is true, that there exist individuals so unhappily organized, that they can love no one; but I do not believe it, and, were it even so, M. the Marquis de Pourrieres is not one of them.

"I am likewise as happy as yourself, my dear Lucie; every day I bless the Almighty for having associated my destiny with that of the estimable man who is now my husband. He has been very unfortunate, my dear Lucie. One day, perhaps, I may be allowed to narrate his history to you; and I am fully persuaded you will tell me, that my constant study should be to endeavour to make him forget the anguish of his former days.

"You are wrong to remind me of what I formerly said to you respecting M. de Pourrieres; they were the follies of a young girl, which nothing justified, and to which you have the good sense to attach no more importance than they merited. I shall readily accord to the man who ensures the happiness of my dearest friend, a large share of my esteem and friendship; but if, by chance, he should change his conduct, oh! then, there will spring up between us a serious war; and I shall be brave, if you need a defender.

"I shall not speak to you of the towns of Italy which we have already visited. The works of our tourists have given you grander descriptions than I am capable of writing you; and, besides, although I found all that we have yet seen very interesting, all this, you see, is not worth our good old France, which we regret the moment it is out of our sight, and which we again behold with pleasure. If any adventures, however, should happen to us, before our return to Paris, I shall not forget to furnish you with them.

"We shall visit Rome and its neighbourhood, Savoy, and Switzerland; we shall stop a few days at Geneva, and then return to France. This route will not occupy us more than two months, so that we shall be at Paris towards the end of the summer. We shall remain there till towards the middle of autumn, and I hope sincerely you will come and see us.

"My good uncle charges me to deposit two weighty kisses on each of your cheeks, and I acquit myself of the commission, without demanding the permission of M. le Marquis de Pourrieres, who, I trust, will not trouble himself to be jealous about it.

"My husband writes, by the same courier, to the marquis; no doubt, to thank him for the amiable things he has addressed to him.

"I have written to Madame de Bourgerel; there is no occasion for my telling you that I am as delighted as yourself to know that she is happy.

"Farewell, my dear Lucie, I am impatient to press you to my heart.

"Your friend,
                    "LAURA FEVAL."

"*M. Paul Feval to M. the Marquis de Pourrieres.*
                    "Florence.

"M. le Marquis,—My wife has shown me the few lines you have addressed to her. I am, you may believe, extremely sensible of your great politeness, and also delighted that chance has furnished me with an opportunity of proving my wish of serving you."

Servigny here narrated the meeting with Jazetta in India, and the circumstances which accompanied the death of that unfortunate woman.

"I send you, M. le Marquis, the objects she confided to me at the moment of rendering up her soul to God, for the purpose of being placed in your hands, if by chance I encountered you. You will receive, I am convinced, with a melancholy satisfaction these objects, which will remind you of a woman of whom you had much to complain, but whose long sufferings redeemed her faults, and who died full of repentance and resignation.

"This unhappy woman, M. le Marquis, died with the fear that her faults had determined you to abandon her son. She deceived herself, no doubt; and I am persuaded that you have been, hitherto, for the young Fortunè, an indulgent and tender father.

"If you will permit me, M. le Marquis, and, in case your son is still in the same town, I will, on passing through Geneva, see this child, who must now be almost a man. I promised his dying mother to carry him her last words, and I should wish to be allowed to accomplish this last desire of a woman, guilty, it is true, but very unhappy.

"The links which attach you to the best friend of my wife, give me a hope, M. le Marquis, that you will accord me at first your esteem, and afterwards your friendship; I shall endeavour, for the rest, to show myself worthy of both.

"Accept, M. le Marquis, the assurance of the perfect consideration with which I have the honour to remain, your very humble servant,
                    "PAUL FEVAL."

"My situation gets complicated," said Salvador to himself, after reading this letter. "The devil, if I remember ever to have heard of this Jazetta and her unfortunate son; however, it is very lucky for me that the mother is dead, and that the son, who is perhaps still alive, is ignorant of the name he has the right to bear.* Let me show myself, at the same time, since it will cost me nothing, and cannot compromise me, a sensible man and an excellent father.

"I really believe that this M. Paul Feval, who appears to me a very worthy man, would have brought to Paris the poor Jazetta, if she had not died so apropos."

After this short monologue, Salvador wrote the following letter, which he sent at once to Servigny:

"*The Marquis de Pourrieres to M. Paul Feval.*
                    "Chateau de Pourrieres.

"Monsieur,—I have received your kind letter, and the precious reliques which accompanied it, I have bathed with my tears the medallion and lock of brown hair which have recalled to me a

* It may be remembered that the woman Moulin, to whom the young Fortunè had been confided, in order to appropriate to herself the sums forwarded to her by Alexis de Pourrieres, had kept the child in ignorance of his right name, having passed him off as the child of a sister who had died in poverty.

woman I so much loved, and whom I should, perhaps, still regret, notwithstanding her ingratitude, if the angel who has bestowed her hand upon me had not made me forget her.

"What I have here said will abundantly prove to you, monsieur, that I have no place in my heart except for the pity which should be inspired, in every feeling mind, by such great misfortunes as those which have fallen upon the unhappy Jazetta, whether merited or not.

"You tell me that Jazetta died with a fear that the wrongs I had to reproach her with might have determined me to abandon our child. This surprises me, monsieur, and I must believe, since, after all, it is so, that the misfortunes she experienced before her death, had produced in her mind a very degrading opinion of men in general, to believe me capable for a moment, knowing me as she did, of such unworthy conduct.

"If Providence had allowed it, monsieur, I should never have ceased being towards the unhappy Fortunè a most tender and devoted father ; unfortunately, it has not been so."

Salvador here informed Servigny of all that our readers already know of the adventures of the young Fortunè, and he finished his recital by observing, that even had he wished to abandon this child, it would not be possible for him, seeing that he had given him his name, which, sooner or later, he hoped, a decree of Providence would restore to him.

"I would have permitted you, with a thankful heart, to go and embrace my son," he continued, after the above passage in his letter, "however, since you intend to pass through Geneva before entering France, I will beg of you to see at this town all the persons who might give you any information of a nature to put you upon the traces of my unfortunate son; but I am quite convinced that all the steps you may take will be useless; for I have already done every thing in my power, under such circumstances; but the Almighty is so good, and the chances are so great.

"I hope, M. Feval, that, upon your return to France, you will honour with your presence the old manor of Pourrieres; my wife and self will endeavour to render your sojourn at it agreeable. We have a charming society here, splendid landscapes, fine ruins, and, if your are fond of sport, I can promise you an ample harvest of game.

"Remember me, I beg of you, to Madame Feval, and induce Sir Edward to accompany you to Pourrieres.

"Accept, monsieur, the assurance of the affectionate sentiments with which I am,

"Your very humble and very obedient servant,
"A. DE POURRIERES."

"*Roman to Salvador.*
"Paris.

"My dear Friend,—Misfortune is not weary of pursuing me: I have lost the three one thousand franc notes which you gave me when I left Pourrieres, and some others that I have borrowed from the kind Viscount de Lussan, who, I am certain, has just completed an excellent affair, for he has renewed his furniture, changed his horses and his equipages.

"I am absolutely, then, without a sou. You will comprehend that I cannot continue in such penury, and I am convinced that you will at once send me a good little sum.

"Your friend,
"ROMAN."

"*Salvador to Roman.*
"Chateau de Pourrieres.

"You are grossly deceived, my dear friend; I shall *not* send you the good little sum you demand from me; and this for the very simple reason, that I am absolutely in the same position as yourself— namely, without money; and, to send you some, I must borrow, which I cannot do at this moment.

"The passion for gambling and drunkenness must have rendered you stupid, since, in writing to ask me for money, which you will carry to the green cloth of some private hell, the moment you have received it, you do not seize the opportunity of mentioning many things which interest me exceedingly, as you know. You have seen the Marchioness of Roselly, what is she doing? What does she say? Have you seen the men of *la-bas?* Have you any thing in view? You must absolutely find means of some sort to replenish our strong box, since you know so well how to empty it. I think I have just effected a pretty good affair. Signalize yourself in your turn. I have now the right of returning you the reproaches you made me, when the vexation, caused by the disappearance of Silvia, had rendered me quite incapable of working. But be prudent, however, very prudent, excessively prudent; do nothing, especially, without consulting me; do not forget that, in consequence of the two fatal passions which govern you, you have not, at present, the practised eye and that rare intrepidity which formerly made you so valuable a man.

"And now let us talk reasonably. As I do not wish to leave you absolutely unprovided with money, I send you five hundred francs. At the end of every month I will remit you, or hand you a similar sum. Six thousand francs a year is, I think, a very respectable revenue, especially for a man who has committed the folly of losing at play more than four hundred thousand francs in a few years; and I think that if you will recollect that you have lost more than what belonged to you from the fortune of Alexis, and of what has fallen to us from the different affairs we have made, you will be reasonable enough to exact no more.

"Adieu, my dear Roman, be reasonable; this is the sincere wish of your friend,
"SALVADOR."

Every word composing this letter was traced between the lines of an insignificant letter, with sympathetic ink, and would not appear until held before the fire. Salvador and Roman, from a fear that their letters might be mislaid at the post, or otherwise lost, never neglected this precaution, common enough amongst gentry of their metal.

"*Roman to Salvador.*
"Paris.

"Monsieur le Marquis,—I have just lost the five hundred francs you so kindly sent me, and I have been so confused, so annoyed at having committed this fresh fault, that I immediately returned home, that I might hide from every eye my sorrowful countenance; and, to console myself, I swallowed, at one sitting, a whole bottle of your excellent rum.

"The divine liquor of Jamaica produced such a revolution in my spirits, that I do not think myself, at this moment, as guilty as I appeared just now. What is it I say? I look upon myself as even so innocent, that I am almost astonished that you have not sent me, in lieu of a sermon, which I care for but little, the white robe, symbol of innocence, which the young Levites assumed, before proceeding to the sacrifices.

"Ah, ça! my dear friend, I think, really, that you laugh at me. I have lost, you say, all that belongs to me of the heritage of Alexis de Pourrieres, and my share of the different affairs we have effected. Perhaps you are right; I have not taken the trouble to calculate; but you are, I believe, the possessor of a fortune somewhat considerable, and of this fortune the moiety belongs to me; probably you have not thought of this.

"Have the extreme kindness, therefore, to forward me cash every time I ask for it, if you wish me to continue,

"Your best friend.
"ROMAN."

"Salvador to Roman.
"Chateau de Pourrieres.

"The fortune to which you have alluded is that of my wife, and not mine; I neither can nor will make a sacrifice of it, to enable you to satisfy your mad passion.

"I send you five hundred francs, and no more.
"SALVADOR."

"Roman to Salvador.
"Paris.

"As you like; keep your money, since you will not sacrifice a part of it to oblige your friend, and, besides I have no necessity for it. I have found means of procuring myself plenty without being compromised, so much the worse for him at whose expense the affair will be arranged.

"Wholly yours,   "ROMAN."

"The Marchioness Roselly to the Marquis de Pourrieres.
"Paris.

"My dear Alexis.—Do you know that the good M. Lebrun is at this moment playing the devil's own game, and that he loses daily enormous sums? The Viscount de Lussan told me, but an instant ago, that yesterday he lost at least fifty thousand francs!

"If the good M. Leburn had *alone* effected an affair which had procured him such considerable sums as those he disposes of at present, we should know it, for the journals, which have for some time been desperately monotonous, would have given us information of it. The money that he stakes and loses, therefore, must be yours. Perhaps you have confided it to him for some object. Perhaps he has robbed you of it. However, as you are now apprised of it, you can act as you think advisable. I am very desirous of seeing you once more, my dear Alexis; therefore, hasten your return to Paris.

"SILVIA."

"The Marquis de Pourrieres to the Marchioness of Roselly.
"Chateau de Pourrieres.

"I thank you sincerely, my dear Silvia, for the advice you have given me, although it is perfectly useless to me. The money which M. Lebrun stakes and loses at present does not belong to me; he has procured it, I know not how; but it is not from my chest he has taken it.

"Amuse yourself well, and believe me, that if you are impatient to see me again, I am not less so to be enabled to press you in my arms; but conjugal duties——

"I shall leave Pourrieres at the end of the ensuing month, perhaps before.

"A. DE POURRIERES."

"M. Paul Feval to the Marquis de Pourrieres.
"Geneva.

"M. le Marquis,—Immediately upon our arrival at Geneva, I employed myself in finding the persons who were in a condition to give me any information by which we could trace your unfortunate son. I have seen the successor of the worthy Father Humbert, at the Crown Hotel, Messieurs Faz Pasteur and Piachund, as well as the old burgomaster of the town, and the different members of the courts before which the poor Fortuné, falsely accused of having assassinated the man who had taken care of his early days, was compelled to appear; and to-day I have the grief of announcing to you, that all my steps have been in vain, not one of these persons have informed me of any thing I was not before acquainted with.

"Excited by the desire of being useful to you, and anxious to acquit myself worthily of the mission confided to me by the unfortunate Jazetta, I have had it published throughout the town that I would give a handsome reward to any one who could procure me any information respecting the young Fortuné. As the crime with which this unhappy young man was accused had made a great stir, I was in hopes that, in all probability, some persons might have encountered him as he left the town, never to return there, and that, allured by the hope of obtaining the promised recompense, they would come and inform me in what direction he had directed his steps.

"This expectation has not failed. A few days after the publication of the notice I had had inserted in the journals, a peasant of the neighbourhood came and informed me that the young Fortuné had been received, at the time of his departure from Geneva, by a family of mountebanks, whose chief was named Riberpré. This man, whose curiosity had induced him to be present at the trial of your son, perfectly recognised him; and it was from himself he learned that, not knowing what to do, since all the inhabitants of the town in which he had been brought up repulsed him harshly, notwithstanding his innocence, he had determined to travel with these mountebanks.

"The measures I took after this information has proved to me, that the facts advanced by this man were true; there was, indeed, at Geneva, at the trial of Fortune, a family of mountebanks, whose chief was named Riberpré. We are in possession, therefore, M. le Marquis, of the first thread, and, probably, if we can contrive to find out the family of Riberpré, which does not appear to me impossible, it might be easy to discover what has become of your son, in case he should not still be with them.

"I would willingly have continued my researches, but the unhappy Fortuné, of whom all the inhabitants of Geneva who remember him (now that his innocence has been demonstrated in a striking manner,) speak in praise, both of his extreme mildness and intelligence, has a father, from whom I would not usurp the satisfaction of attempting himself every thing that is humanly possible, for restoring him to his tenderness.

"I sincerely hope, M. le Marquis, that the steps you are about to take may be crowned with success: it will be pleasing to me to hear that an unfortunate young man, for whom I have interested myself, notwithstanding I am unknown to him, has at length recovered the name and position which belong to him.

"I cannot accept the gracious offer you make me, of passing some time at the Chateau de Pourrieres; when we quitted France, Sir Edward invited two of his countrymen to pass the remainder of the season at his seat, and he must be there, as also my wife, at the appointed time, to receive them as they would expect. As to myself, different affairs of interest will oblige me to make a voyage to England before returning to France, where, in all probability, I shall not arrive until the commencement of winter; but, be assured, M. le Marquis, that I do not renounce the privilege of a more friendly connection with you. Winter will find us again in Paris, and I hope to have the pleasure of meeting you frequently.

"My wife charges me to say to you a thousand amiable things for her, and it is with the greatest eagerness that I acquit myself of the commission. I have the honour of being, M. le Marquis, your very devoted servant,

"PAUL FEVAL."

"*Laura Feval to Lucie de Pourrieres.*

"Geneva.

"An adventure has happened to me, my dear Lucie, which I cannot resist narrating to you, for I am persuaded it will interest you.

"The environs of Genoa (the writings of our modern tourists must have informed you of this) are the most picturesque in the world, the richest in superb views and natural curiosities. Amongst these curiosities, there is one, especially, which all travellers hasten to visit—as much, perhaps, because a very old and singular chronicle is connected with the subject, as that it is really remarkable. It is a grotto, or rather, a hermitage, composed of several chambers, one of which serves as a chapel, entirely cut out of the living rock; this hermitage, it is said, is the work of one man, who employed more than thirty years of his life in completing it; if what they say is true, and I am not far from believing it, (for a work like that of the hermitage could only be the result of religious enthusiasm or an unaccountable caprice,) the strength and perseverance of the man must be beyond imagination —for you do not suppose, I hope, that I believe in the chronicle I mentioned above, which narrates that the *builder* (?) of the hermitage, seeing that he could not finish his work alone, from despair of his capabilities, entered into a compact with the Devil to assist him in it!

"To give you an idea of this hermitage, my dear Lucie, you must figure to yourself an immense block of granite—in which they may cut out your hotel of the Rue Saint-Lazare, for example—(I exaggerate a little, perhaps; the hermitage of the environs of Geneva is much smaller than your house:) commencing by the door-way, which is the only part visible from the outside, and following in such a manner that the edifice, notwithstanding the perfection of its interior form, is nothing more than a cave, or hole, ingeniously designed.

"Curious as I am, I could not resist the desire of visiting so singular a spot, and my good uncle, who refuses me nothing, the moment I expressed a wish to see it, ordered horses and a guide, to conduct us to the hermitage in question. I do not mention my husband, who has been sent to England by my uncle to sell some property which Sir Edward possesses in the county of Sussex; a property he does not mean to retain, seeing that he has no intention of quitting France.

"The road approaching the hermitage is extremely narrow, and winds through an interminable suite of ravines and precipices; so that the curious.

when they near this retreat, are in the habit of dismounting from their horses, and finishing the rest of the way on foot.

"According to custom, I was about quitting my horse, when suddenly the confounded beast, driven by I know not what devil, carried me away with the rapidity of lightning towards that part of the road which, as I have told you, is bounded by precipices; I must infallibly have perished, as well as my uncle who had followed in my wake at a triple gallop in order to arrest my runaway, when a man rushed in a moment from a tuft of trees which bordered the road, and sprung to the head of my horse, which, after several efforts, he managed to subdue; my uncle, master of his horse, had pulled up the moment he was certain I was no longer in danger.

"The fright, my dear Lucie, which I experienced at the sight of the precipices, from which I must have been dashed at the slightest deviation of my horse, caused me to faint when I found myself almost out of danger. When I recovered the use of my senses I was in the hermitage, where I had been carried by my uncle and our guide, and my preserver bestowed upon me the kindest attentions.

"My preserver, my dear Lucie, was no other, (you will be greatly surprised) than our good Doctor Matheo; judge of my delight, I should simply have thanked him as I should a stranger; I could not refrain from clinging to his neck, and kissing several times the man who had just saved my life, and as my uncle seemed astonished at this excess of gratitude:

"'Monsieur,' I said to him, pointing to my preserver, 'is not a stranger to me;' and I informed him that I had known Doctor Matheo for a length of time, during which he had practised with skill at Paris.

"My uncle, you know, is very demonstrative. He shook heartily the hand of the doctor, and insisted that he should breakfast with us. The doctor, malgré his habitual reserve, could not refuse to accept this invitation.

"After visiting the hermitage in all its details, we displayed on the turf the provisions with which we had taken care to provide our guide, and we enjoyed the most agreeable repast it is possible to conceive.

"The heat was extreme, and my uncle, who contracted in India a habit of taking the *siesta* after the morning's repast, fell asleep under one of the old trees planted before the entrance of the hermitage. I profited by this moment of liberty to inquire of the doctor what were the motives which had induced him to quit so precipitately our good city of Paris.

"'Madame the Countess of Neuville, who has no secrets for you,' he replied, 'has no doubt shown you the letter I have had the honour of writing her, that letter, and the one which followed it, would have informed you of what you desire to know.'

"'Lucie has certainly shown me the first letter you wrote her,' I replied; 'as to the one which was to have followed it, and which you assure me was addressed to her, she has waited for it in vain.'

"'That letter then has been mislaid at the post,' added the doctor, 'I shall make amends by writing a second to Madame la Comtesse de Neuville.'

"'Say, to Madame la Marquise de Pourrieres; my friend has determined to marry the man of whom you spoke in terms so unfavourable, probably because you did not know him.'

"'Is it really possible,' exclaimed the doctor, hiding his face in his hands, 'is it really possible!'

"One of your letters which I had in my pocket by accident, served to convince the doctor of the truth of what I had said to him.

"'There will be no necessity for your writing to Lucie,' I said to him, after giving him time to read your letter, 'tell me what you wish to acquaint her with, and I will repeat it to her.'

"'The information I should have given to the Countess de Neuville, must not be made known to the Marchioness de Pourrieres; say merely to your friend, that in the silent retreat in which I shall bury myself, I shall not cease to pray to God for her.'

"And the doctor retired after bidding me adieu, and without permitting me to awaken my uncle; so that I neither know what he wished to inform you of, nor where it will be possible to find him again.

"I am a little disposed to believe that the head of our good doctor is somewhat deranged.

"I have only reported this little event, my dear Lucie, that I might put an end to hope, which I am sure you had not abandoned; and if you are reasonable, you will see that I have rendered you an important service. You are happy; do you wish to know more? Happiness is a thing so rare in this world, that I think we should accept it with gratitude in whatever shape it comes, and that it would be folly to demand from ourselves the causes which procure it for us, and those which may be the means of our losing it.

"I shall soon, my dear Lucie, have the pleasure of pressing you to my heart. Geneva is the last town in which we are to rest before entering France, and it is probable that in a fortnight we shall be in Paris, where you will come and see us I hope.

"Au revoir, and wholly yours,
            "Your friend,
                "LAURA FEVAL."

On the morning of the day succeeding that on which Lucie received the letter, Salvador received from Paris the one which follows:

"*Justè, banker, at Paris, to Monsieur le Marquis de Pourrieres.*

                    "Paris.

"Monsieur le Marquis,—I should not take the liberty of writing you, if I was not certain of the friendship you feel towards your intendant, M. Lebrun; for I know very well that I have no right to make the least claim upon you; but some estimable persons who know the extreme kindness of your heart, and especially M. le Viscount de Lussan, having given me an assurance that you would do every thing in your power to extricate M. Lebrun from the serious position to which he has fallen by his own fault, I have resolved upon addressing to you this letter.

"I have the honour, therefore, M. le Marquis, to apprise you, that if within ten days from this date, (I leave you, you observe, sufficient time to arrive in Paris,) I do not receive a visit from you, I shall find myself compelled to deposit with M. le Procureur du Roi, an accusation of forgery against M. Lebrun; to which charge will be added four bills of exchange, amounting in the whole to the sum of one hundred thousand francs, which I only discounted, as they bore a signature, falsely attributed by M. Lebrun, to M. le Marquis de Pourrieres.

"I am in hopes you will spare your intendant the fatal results of an accusation of forgery, and take into consideration the position of an unfortunate capitalist, who now finds himself a victim, for believing that he could place every confidence in a man upon whom you have bestowed your own.

"I have the honour to be, with the greatest respect, M. le Marquis,

    "Your very obedient and very humble servant,
                        "JUSTE."

"The die is cast," exclaimed Salvador, after crumpling in his hands the letter of Justè, "all this must be finished, and at once; this miserable Roman has already lived too long."

Salvador, after giving orders to harness the horses to the carriage which was to take him as far as Aix, where he intended to meet the post, went to seek his wife to announce to her his departure.

Lucie, who had just finished perusing the letter of Laura, which we have before inserted, was somewhat sorrowful. She rose, however, from the long couch upon which she was seated, in order to meet her husband.

Salvador kissed her forehead.

"I have received," he said to her, "a letter which informs me that I am in danger of losing a considerable sum; my presence at the spot where my interests are menaced, may perhaps prevent the misfortune which threatens me; I am come, therefore, to beg of you, to allow me to leave you alone here for a few days."

"Go," replied Lucie to him, "I shall pray the Almighty to favour your enterprise."

"I am certain to succeed, since such is your prayer," replied Salvador. "The prayers of an angel like you cannot fail being granted."

A few hours after, the stout horses of the administration des postes, hurried Salvador on the road to Paris.

CHAPTER XXXVIII.

CRIME PUNISHED BY CRIME.

WE owe our readers a recital of the events which preceded the sending by Justè to Salvador of the last letter we have placed before them.

Roman, well convinced after reading the last letter from Salvador, that his friend would send him no more money at present, sought for means to procure it himself; the miserable man, like all who allow themselves to be governed by the fatal passion for gambling, was ill every day, when he had no hope of passing the evening before a green cloth which he could cover with gold.

After long and useless endeavours, he one day, whilst sauntering on the Boulevards des Italiens, heard pronounced near him the name of Justè, by two young men who complained of having been robbed by the usurer.

"This old Arab has plenty of gold," murmured Roman, "heaps of bank-notes, loads of jewels, is it impossible then to carry off the whole, or at least a good part of his riches?"

And he continued his way reflecting; suddenly he stopped, and striking his forehead, uttered an exclamation of joy.

"Parbleu! I am a great fool," he exclaimed, "for not thinking of this before; ah! ah! Sir Salvador, you will not give me with a willing hand a few miserable bank-notes; well, my dear friend, you shall give me by force a good number, and these, I think, will cost you dear; that's it, morbleu! that's it, it is twenty to one that I succeed; besides,

LIFE IN PARIS.

BEPPO AT THE BEDSIDE OF GEORGETTE.

"nothing venture, nothing have; and, as I wish to have something, I must risk much."

After saying this to himself, Roman entered a hired cabriolet, and was driven to the Rue Saint Dominique d'Enfer.

Nothing was changed either in the exterior or interior of the dwelling of the old usurer. The Newfoundland dog was still in the court of the building, as vigorous and as morose as formerly, seemingly only waiting for a sign from his master, to spring upon such as the usurer wished to have devoured.

Justè introduced Roman into the room which served him as a cabinet, and after inviting him to be seated, and intrenching himself in his fort, he continued, without any ceremony, to finish the remainder of his breakfast, composed, as usual, of a cup of milk and a morsel of brown bread.

"You do not recognise me," said Roman, who did not know in what manner he should commence the conversation.

"I ask your pardon, monsieur," he replied, without even lifting his small sea-green eyes, "I perfectly recognise you; you were, as well as myself, one of the guests at the banquet given at Lemardelay's by M. de Courtivon."

"You are, M. Justè, it seems to me, endowed with a most excellent memory."

"They say so; but pardon, you are no doubt come to me to propose an affair?"

"As you say, I am come to propose to you an affair, an excellent affair."

"Really! well, if it is so, we shall easily understand each other. I seize with eagerness every occasion which presents itself to me of gaining a few sous; speak, monsieur, I am ready to pay you all the attention I am capable of."

"You know the Marchioness de Roselly?"

Justè took from one of the shelves of the small bureau of black wood before which he was seated, a very thick register, covered with parchment, every leaf of which was blackened with hieroglyphics, classed in alphabetical order. He turned to the letter R.

"I do not know the lady of whom you speak," he said, after running through several leaves.

"That's strange: you have, however, purchased from her a very large quantity of jewels, which belonged to the Count Coloredo."

Justè regarded Roman; he was anxious to read in his countenance the object of the questions he addressed to him. The features of Roman were immovable.

"I do not know this lady," he repeated.

"Do you know, then, M. the Marquis de Pourrieres?"

"M. le Marquis de Pourrieres," he said, after opening the parchment-covered register at the letter P.; "I know him well by reputation; he has done some business with one of my confrères, who keeps a toy shop on the Boulevard; my confrère was perfectly satisfied with him; besides, M. le Marquis de Pourrieres is very rich himself, and his fortune is increased since his marriage; one might, without compromising one's self, discount for him two or three hundred thousand francs."

"So that you would give two hundred thousand francs against the bills of exchange of the marquis?"

"If M. le Marquis offered me a reasonable interest, and a first mortgage on his property, we might come to an understanding; but is it an ordinary affair that you wish to propose to me?"

"No," replied Roman, "on the contrary, 'tis a very extraordinary affair."

"Explain yourself, my dear sir, I do not dislike extraordinary affairs."

"You are discreet."

"A useless question, you would not have come, if you were not previously persuaded of my extreme discretion."

"This is the affair then; I am the intendant, the friend, or rather the accomplice of M. le Marquis de Pourrieres. I know so many secrets, that I am convinced that my master, my friend, my accomplice, as you choose to call him, would give his whole fortune, without hesitation, rather than see me appear before a court of assize; for he knows that no one babbles like an accused. Well, if you will count me simply sixty-three thousand francs, I will sign to you, in the name of the Marquis de Pourrieres, one hundred thousand francs by bills of exchange; do you agree to it?"

Justè reflected a few moments.

"I cannot give you a positive answer to-day," he said; "call upon me to-morrow morning, we will talk of it, and I think the affair may be arranged."

Roman quitted Justè much happier than he had entered the kennel of the usurer; besides the pleasure he felt in thinking that the next day he would be enabled to satisfy his favourite passion, he was delighted at stealing a march on Salvador.

The next morning the usurer Justè equipped himself in the garment we have described, placed his classical *tricorne* on his head, and after letting loose his Newfoundland in the court of his habitation, the door of which he carefully secured, he repaired to the Viscount de Lussan's.

"What lucky wind brings you here," said the noble gentleman of Brittany, "are you come to breakfast with me?"

"We will breakfast, since you are kind enough to invite me," replied Justè, "and you shall afterwards give me some advice, for which I will pay you five thousand francs, if it is of any use to me."

The Viscount de Lussan rang, and ordered his valet de chambre to bring into his bed-room every thing requisite for breakfasting comfortably.

"I am ready to listen, M. Justè," he said to the usurer, when they were both seated at a small mahogany table, on which was placed a poularde from Mons, a pasty de Chartres, some magnificent fruits, and several bottles of excellent wine.

Justè recounted to the viscount what had taken place the evening before, and inquired of him if he ought to accept the proposition of Lebrun?

"If you had not promised me five thousand francs, I should advise you not to accept this affair, of which, in the end, my friend de Pourrieres will be the only victim; but as you have shown yourself generous, I will be true to you: you may, without fear, if the solvency of the Marquis de Pourrieres appears to you sufficient, discount the bills of exchange proposed to you by Lebrun."

The viscount, in order to prove to the usurer that he might with safety follow the advice he had given him, and no doubt, also, to obtain the promised five thousand francs, narrated to him all that he knew of Salvador and Roman.

"'Tis charming," exclaimed the worthy M. Justè, "'tis charming; how! these are the messieurs who have sent into the other world my confrère, Josue? The death of this Jew has been so advantageous to me, that I will readily oblige one of those to whom I am indebted for it. Adieu, M. le Viscount, you shall have the five thousand francs I promised you."

After taking leave of the viscount, Justè returned home immediately; he had scarcely entered, when Roman rang the bell.

In order to introduce him to his cabinet, the usurer, who had been informed by the viscount of what he was capable, took still greater precautions than on the previous evening.

"I will readily do what you have demanded of me," he said to him, "but as the operation you have proposed to me is purely contingent, I shall only give you fifty thousand francs; does that suit you?"

"Fifty thousand francs?" said Roman, "'tis very little."

"My chances of loss are equal—if not beyond—my chances of gain."

"I accept the fifty thousand francs, M. Justè."

"Be good enough, in that case, to sign the bills of exchange."

Roman eagerly complied with this request; the usurer took the bills of exchange and left the cabinet; after an absence of a few minutes he returned, and handed Roman the fifty thousand francs, which the latter was waiting for with the greatest impatience.

"Do not forget," the usurer said to his client, when the latter was on the point of putting his foot into the street, "that these bills of exchange will be deposited with M. le Procureur du Roi, if they are not paid when due; you have two months before you."

"I shall endeavour to employ well these two months," replied Roman; "perhaps they may be the last two that remain to me."

The same evening, Roman, anxious, as he had said, to make a good use of his time, was seated before a gaming-table, and luck—no doubt to make his approaching ruin appear more cruel to him—so befriended him, that he won a considerable sum.

The letters which form the subject of the last chapter have informed us, that fortune soon ceased to favour him. After alternatives of loss and gain, there followed a succession of ill-luck, which was crowned, towards the period of the expiration of the bills of exchange, by a loss of thirty thousand francs, announced to Salvador by Silvia.

After this, Roman returned to the Hotel de Pourrieres. He was almost mad. His eyes, which were streaked in the white by small sanguinious threads, half protruded from their orbits; the expression of his features, imprinted with a cadaverous pallor, was such, that the Swiss, who had taken a lamp to open the door for him, started back terrified, and inquired if he felt himself ill, and if he needed anything?

"I want nothing, imbecile!" replied Roman, who retired to his chamber; where, following his custom, he had a bottle of rum brought him, which he finished before he retired.

The next morning he was so feeble that he was compelled to remain in bed.

Salvador, before arriving in Paris, rested at Melun, at the Hotel de la Galère, where he left the post-chaise, and, in order to reach Paris, took the coach which leaves this town at four o'clock. At the expiration of two days the usurer Justè would realize the menace he had given him, and these two days Salvador determined to employ well.

"What must I do?" he said to himself, when alone in the streets of the capital; "Roman once dead—and he shall die!" he muttered, grinding his teeth, and fondling the sharp point of a *tire-point*, concealed in the pocket of his coat—"I cannot be compelled to pay the bills of exchange given to Justè by this miserable. But what assures me that, to induce this infamous usurer to give him money, Roman, stupified by the immoderate use of strong liquors, blinded by his infernal passion, has not made him some confidences which he might turn against me? what assures me that I shall not be questioned respecting the death of Roman, if I refuse to pay this usurer—who will move heaven and earth to find the means of compromising me? What a labyrinth! and how extricate myself?

"I will pay—I must!" continued Salvador, after reflecting a few minutes; "glad, very glad, to be quit of it at so cheap a rate."

When night had completely set in, Salvador threw over his shoulders the large cloak which he had till now carried on his arm; he drew over his eyes the large brim of the hat he wore, and directed his steps towards the Rue de Courcelle.

The atmosphere was oppressive, and the sky hidden beneath dark clouds. Salvador posted himself at a few paces from his residence. Concealed under the door of a court-yard, he could see, without being seen, every one who entered or left the hotel.

He had been for nearly an hour at the post he had chosen, when Roman left the hotel; the miserable gambler was unsteady in his walk. He was drunk. He passed close to Salvador without observing him. The latter allowed him to advance a few steps; he then followed him. Roman, whose drunkenness seemed to have increased in the open air, staggered more and more, and rolled against every passenger; however, he marched somewhat rapidly, and at length arrived in the Rue Richelieu, and entered a respectable-looking house near the Boulevard.

Roman, as our readers will rightly imagine, had taken with him all the money he had remaining, and despite his extreme weakness, he entered the private hell in which he passed his evenings, to tempt fortune for a last time.

Salvador had not lost sight of him. Enveloped in his cloak, and half his face concealed by his large brimmed hat, he sauntered on the pavement, opposite the house which Roman had entered; the shopkeepers of the pavement and the seducing *butterflies* who promenade there every evening, remarked him at first, but when one and the other took it for granted that this mysterious man waited, no doubt, for the arrival of his *belle*, they paid no more attention to him.

It was past one o'clock in the morning when Roman left the house, in front of which his accomplice still waited. The light thrown from the gas-lamp placed above the porte cochere, allowed Salvador to remark that his countenance was greatly inflamed.

He took a few steps on the Boulevard, now nearly deserted.

"Want a cab, monsieur?" said the driver of a cabriolet, near which he stopped.

Salvador trembled.

"He is saved if he enters a cab," he muttered.

Roman hesitated a few moments; he then continued his road, without replying to the coachman.

"At length," again muttered Salvador; "God be praised!"

He fastened his cloak by the clasp, and threw it back over his shoulders, that he might leave his arms at liberty to act in a moment, and drew his tire-point from the side pocket of his coat.

The blade was well tempered, strong, and the point sharpened to a nicety.

Salvador crossed the Boulevard; he would not strike his accomplice until he had arrived in one of the deserted streets in the neighbourhood of the Hotel de Pourrieres.

Roman's walk was hasty and uncertain; he frequently stopped, making use of angry exclamations and worse blasphemies. At the top of the Rue Caumartin he broke his cane against one of the posts of the Boulevard.

Salvador followed all his movements with attention.

The Rue de Courcelle, in which the Hotel de Pourrieres is situate, was not, at the period of the events we have narrated, lighted by the gas of the English company; and the lamps which, as is their custom, had reckoned upon the fair Phœbe, (who had fixed upon this very night to pay a visit to Endymion,) had all been long since burned out when Roman entered it, so that it was in complete darkness.

Salvador allowed his accomplice the time to take a few steps only. Like a panther that springs, quick as lightning, into the midst of a herd of buffaloes, seizes his prey, in the flanks of which he buries his iron talons, and clings to it until stretched lifeless on the sand—he threw himself on Roman, whom he seized by the neck that he might deprive him of all chance of calling for assistance.

The abuse of strong liquors had so enfeebled the miserable man, that he retained none of his former strength; he made, however, a few efforts to defend himself, but Salvador held him too safely, and plunged his tire-point three times into his heart.

When Salvador relinquished his hold he fell heavily on the pavement.

He was dead!

"There's an end of one," said Salvador, after depriving him of his jewels and note-case; "they will believe that thieves have been guilty of this murder. Who could say," he continued in a deep tone, "that it is the Marquis de Pourrieres who killed this man?"

"I!" said a woman's voice above the assassin.

Salvador raised his head, and at the window of an apartment on the landing of a small house, in front of which his accomplice had fallen, he observed, as though sketched in the darkness, the form of a woman.

"Silence," she said to him in a low tone; "I will descend and open the door."

Salvador recognised the voice of Silvia.

A few minutes after she mysteriously opened the door of the house, into which she introduced Salvador.

The daughter of Sans Refus was simply dressed in an elegant peignoir of white muslin bordered with lace; her small and delicate feet were incased in rose satin mules, or slippers, worthy of imprisoning those of Cinderella; her long curls of black hair fell over her face, now somewhat pale.

Silvia and Salvador entered the room, from which the ex-cantatrice had observed what had taken place in the street.

"By what accident are you here?" said Salvador, "I supposed you at the Hotel des Princes."

Silvia before replying to her lover, closed the shutters of the window and rang the bell.

At this appeal a tall stout girl presented herself at the door of the chamber.

"Marie," said Silvia to her, "M. the Marquis de Pourrieres will pass the rest of the night here; you will therefore retire to your room, my child, and not leave it until I call you to-morrow morning—not until I call you—do you hear, Marie?"

"Yes, madame," replied the servant; "I shall not leave my room until you call me. I perfectly understand."

"'Tis well, my child."

The servant retired.

"We must provide against every thing," said Silvia smiling, when alone with Salvador; "if by any chance you should get in the humour to treat me in the same manner as this poor M. Lebrun—this girl will remain after me."

"Ah! what an idea," exclaimed Salvador biting his lips.

"Can you assert," replied Silvia, regarding him fixedly, "that the idea of ridding yourself of me, has never presented itself to your mind? However, I will not blame you," she continued, after a few moments' silence; "the same thought would have possessed me, perhaps, were I in your place; you cannot read my heart—you cannot know all the devotion and affectionate sentiments it feels towards you!"

There was in the voice of Silvia, when she pronounced these words, such an accent of tenderness, that Salvador, who had just assassinated the man who for nearly twenty years he had been accustomed to call his friend, was almost affected.

"If I am in your way," added Silvia, "if one of us must perish, fear not to say so; speak but a word—a single word! I have sufficient courage to die—provided it is not your hand that cuts the thread of my life."

"But I do not wish that you should die," exclaimed Salvador; "you are the only woman in the world that I can love!"

"Is it not so?" replied Silvia, throwing herself into the arms of her lover, who pressed her warmly to his bosom.

The artful creature had regained the empire she had so long exercised over Salvador.

The sound of the measured paces of the patrol recalled to the two assassins (Silvia—an unmoved spectator of the murder which her lover had committed—ought she not to be considered an accomplice?) what had taken place. They both approached the window. The soldiers who composed the patrol had stopped close to the body; the words they pronounced arrived clear and distinct to the ears of Salvador and his mistress.

"He is dead," said one of the soldiers.

"Quite dead," replied another.

"As dead as a withered branch," added a third.

"The result proves that you struck with a steady arm," said Silvia.

Salvador smiled, and squeezed the hand of his mistress.

"Listen," he said to her.

"What must we do?" said one of the soldiers.

"Conscript," replied the corporal in a hasty tone, "you must go and seek the commissaire of police."

"They are going to raise up the body," said Salvador.

"As they like," replied Silvia.

The two assassins quitted the place they occupied at the window, and seated themselves side by side on a divan.

"You have not replied to the question I asked you when I entered here," said Salvador, after taking the two hands of Silvia in his own.

"You inquired, I think, why I had left the Hotel des Princes to inhabit this house?"

Salvador made a sign in the affirmative.

Silvia, after collecting herself a moment, informed her lover that a few words exchanged between her and the man who had just been sacrificed, words which she had heard by accident, had proved to her that the worthy M. Lebrun, who without ceremony helped himself to his master's cash, was not an ordinary intendant; that the Viscount de Lussan having informed her some time since, that Lebrun staked and lost considerable sums, she was anxious to apprise the Marquis de Pourrieres, but that the reply she had received to the letter she had addressed to him had not satisfied her, and that quite certain that the money lost by Lebrun with such coolness, was not the produce of an *affair*, she was desirous of knowing what he did, in order to write to her lover, if any new facts presented themselves. To arrive at the point she wished to attain, she had found no better means than that of residing near the Hotel de Pourrieres; she had not however given up her apartments at the Hotel des Princes, which she still occupied; her lodgement of the Rue de Courcelle, was but an observatory. Coming to install herself as was her daily custom, she had recognised Salvador, notwithstanding the care he had taken to disguise himself, she had at once surmised that he thus kept himself concealed, because he had in his head some projects, of which the worthy M. Lebrun was to be the victim. Delighted to see her lover at length take so energetic a resolution, she had placed herself in a joyful mood at her window, from which she had seen, without being remarked, all that had passed, concealed as she was by the half-opened shutters.

The Marquis de Pourrieres knew the rest.

"You are," said Salvador, when Silvia had concluded the narration of which we have given the substance to our readers, "a very artful creature, and I am now persuaded, that it is much more advantageous to have you for than against one."

"I am glad to find you think so," replied Silvia; "'tis giving me a certainty that we shall never separate from each other."

A noise in the street again attracted their attention; anxious to see what was taking place, they extinguished the light and approached the window.

The commissaire of police had arrived.

This worthy functionary appeared much annoyed at having his first nap disturbed so very suddenly, and much more inclined to return to his bed and his wife than to hold a discourse.

He stooped over the body of Roman, however, and examined it by the light of a falot or lantern, carried by one of the soldiers of the patrol.

"This man, who seems to belong to the higher classes of society, has been robbed of his money and his jewels," he said; "the assassins have not left upon him a single paper that might serve to make him known; you must carry him to the morgue."

The soldiers made a sort of litter with their carbines, upon which they placed the body of the miserable Roman, and followed the commissaire of police.

The regular sound of their steps was soon lost in the distance.

"A pleasant voyage, M. Lebrun!" said Silvia; "I have no wish to see you again, not even in the other world," she added; "for I wish to believe that our death is the last act of a drama, which has no epilogue."

"It's possible," replied Salvador, "very possible, dear friend; but the contrary is also possible, and if such is the case, you and I, when we appear before our Judge, will have a famous account to render him; but I am falling asleep."

He then stretched himself at full length upon the divan.

CHAPTER XXXIX.

COMPLICATIONS.

THE next morning about ten o'clock, the servant of Silvia left her chamber at the call of her mistress, and went out to procure a coach in which Salvador, disencumbered of his large cloak, entered, accompanied by Silvia, whom he conducted to the Hotel des Princes, he was then driven to the station of the Orleans railroad, which took him to Corbeil, from which he easily reached Melun by means of the diligence.

At the latter town, he resumed the post-chaise he had left at the Hotel de la Galère, and immediately returned to Paris.

His servants were already aware that during the night, the body of a murdered man had been discovered in the Rue de Courcelle, but none of them suspected it to be the body of their master's intendant.

"Is M. Lebrun here," inquired Salvador of the one who had accompanied him to his bed-room.

Taken thus unawares, the domestic hesitated a few moments.

"Will you answer me?" added Salvador.

"M. Lebrun left yesterday evening about ten o'clock, and he has not yet returned to the hotel," replied the domestic.

"Very well, you may retire; desire the coachman to put the horses to the landau."

Left alone, Salvador changed his dress, and when he supposed the order he had given was executed, he descended, and was driven to the Rue d'Enfer-Saint-Dominique.

He entered the habitation of Justè.

The usurer loaded the Marquis de Pourrieres with every sort of politeness.

"I was quite sure," he said, "that M. le Marquis, would not see me a victim of the confidence I placed in his intendant."

Salvador cut short these extravagant demonstrations of which he was not the dupe.

"I am come here," he said to the usurer, "to endeavour to arrive at an understanding with you, respecting the payment of these miserable bills of exchange, and not to listen to your complaints, let us talk of business, therefore, if it so please you."

"Let your will be done, M. le Marquis."

"You have discounted for Lebrun one hundred thousand francs of false bills of exchange, how much must I pay you to receive possession of these valuable pieces of paper?"

"Why, no more than one hundred thousand francs."

"You are jesting, I should imagine?"

"I never jest when it concerns money, besides I have taken from M. Lebrun but a very slight interest, I cannot therefore, however anxious I may feel to serve you, make the smallest sacrifice."

"In that case you risk losing the whole; I shall leave Lebrun to suffer the consequences of his fault."

"You are his master, M. le Marquis, you are his master."

"Come, M. Justè, show yourself worthy the name you bear: sixty thousand francs?"

"Impossible!"

" Seventy ?"

" Impossible !"

" Eighty ?"

" Impossible ! I will allow you ten thousand francs only, but I do not consent to this concession, but under the condition, that you give me a promise to address yourself to none but me, when you desire to dispose of any objects of great value."

Salvador was treating with a man as tenacious as himself, and he was in some measure dependant upon him, he was therefore compelled to resign himself.

" I must consent," he said to Justè, " but as you ought to know, that however considerable a fortune one may possess, it is not always possible to find ninety thousand francs at one's disposition, I hope therefore you will allow me a short time to collect this sum ?"

" As much time as you like, M. le Marquis, as much time as you like, a fortnight, a month even; you will sign bills of exchange for the same amount however, and give me a mortgage on your property."

" I shall do all that you wish, M. Justè."

" I am delighted, M. le Marquis, to find that you are reasonable, I will send to your notary's to-morrow the bills of exchange signed by your intendant."

" Agreed, to-morrow at ten o'clock, at Maitre Chardon's, notary."

Justè reconducted the marquis to the door of his habitation.

When Salvador was in the street, and the door closed upon him, Justè opened the grated wicket cut in one of the pannels, drew his wrinkled and parchment face close to the bars.

" M. de Pourrieres, M. le Marquis," he cried out.

Salvador, whose foot was on the step of the coach, turned round.

" Do not forget, I beg of you," said the old usurer to him, " to present my respects to Madame la Marquise de Roselly."

Salvador would have demanded of the usurer the explanation of these last words, but Justè, without more ceremony, shut the wicket in his face.

" I was not wrong," said Salvador to himself, " this miserable usurer has given the money to Roman in return for some confidences the latter made him, the two wretches have conspired to defraud me."

At the turn of the Rue Saint-Dominique d'Enfer, the tilbury of the Viscount de Lussan crossed the landau of Salvador; the noble gentleman who had dictated to Justè the letter which the latter had addressed to Salvador, being well persuaded that his friend would allow no one to outrage the memory of the unfortunate intendant, was on his road to receive the five thousand francs which had been promised him.

" Will you wait for me a few minutes," he said to Salvador; " I am going to borrow some money from the old Arab who lives in this street. As I have some good pledges to leave in his hands, he will hand me at once what I want. We will send back our carriages, and take a turn in the Luxembourg garden before breakfasting; I have news to tell you that will much astonish you."

" Go," replied Salvador, " you will find me in the west alley."

Salvador sent away his carriage, and went to the spot indicated to wait for his friend; the latter, as he had promised, was but a few minutes absent.

" You are returned to Paris then," he said to his friend, " I am really overjoyed at it, your absence was beginning to inconvenience me; you do not return to Pourrieres, I hope?"

" I shall remain in Paris, since I am here; I shall to-day write to my wife to rejoin me here."

" My dear marquis, believe me, I am rejoiced at your happiness."

Salvador, after replying as they deserved to these proofs of friendship, reminded the viscount that he had promised to inform him of some news that would much astonish him.

" That poor Roman !" said the viscount in a tone of affliction which belied the sardonical expression of his features, " what a sad end !"

" What has happened to Roman then?" replied Salvador; " I only arrived this morning, and I have not yet seen him. He did not pass the night at the hotel."

" Have not you heard that a man was assassinated last night in the Rue de Courcelle?"

" Certainly; but what connection is there, I beg of you, between the man assassinated and Roman. Has Roman, by any accident——"

" Oh! no, luckily; on the contrary, Roman is the man assassinated."

" You are jesting?"

" Not at all. Having read this morning in one of my papers the account of this event, and the description of the victim, and the details having excited my curiosity, I went at once to the morgue, and I perfectly recognised the body of poor Roman."

" I shall make my declaration to the police then, and give orders that the body of my poor friend may be reclaimed, and funeral honours bestowed upon it."

" Right, my friend, you are quite right."

" Let us breakfast," said Salvador; " the promenade I have made has given me an appetite, and I do not believe we can bring back Roman to life, by condemning ourselves to starvation."

" Perfectly well reasoned, dear marquis, you are indeed a philosopher."

Salvador and the viscount repaired to Desmares, where they were served with an excellent breakfast.

" Should you like me," said the viscount at the dessert, " to speak candidly to you?"

" You will oblige me by so doing," replied Salvador.

" Well, I think you knew before I did, of the death of Roman."

" What do you mean?"

" You perfectly understand me; and if what I believe should be true, I give you credit for it, you ought long ago to have rid yourself of a man whose detestable habits would sooner or later have compromised you, and who made use of your fortune as though it was his own."

" Ah! dear viscount, you are always ready with a joke," said Salvador, quitting the table.

The two friends separated on leaving Desmares, and Salvador immediately returned home.

He shut himself in his cabinet, and took a seat before a bureau, upon which he placed several bundles of paper, which he examined successively with much attention; this affair occupied him several hours.

" There will only remain to me, when I have paid the usurer Justè," he said, when he had finished them, " but ten thousand francs a-year, and the property of my wife, which might produce about twenty-five thousand francs; thirty-five thousand francs a-year, 'tis very little.

"Decidedly I cannot," he continued, after reflecting a few moments, "be contented with so small a revenue; the establishment of the Viscount de Lussan, who does not even possess the old ruined tower which served as an habitation to his noble ancestors, is nearly as considerable as mine. I cannot therefore give up *work*; I have claims upon me, heavy and numerous claims; my house to support, that of Silvia to refurnish; I cannot, without compromising the honour of the name I bear, retrench the least item of my train."

The monologue of Salvador informs us that this man, very far from renouncing his criminal industry, meditated, on the contrary, fresh crimes; and so it must be. The impunity he had constantly enjoyed, had hardened him to such a point, that he could not believe the day would arrive when society would demand of him a severe account of every crime he had committed.

He replaced himself at his bureau, which he had quitted to take a few turns in his cabinet, and wrote the following letter to Lucie.

"*The Marquis de Pourrieres to the Marchioness de Pourrieres.*

"Paris.

"My dear Lucie,—I have terminated as happily as I could have expected, the unfortunate affair which obliged me to quit Pourrieres long before the time we had mutually fixed upon; but this is not all, other affairs have arisen unawares, so that it is impossible I return to you directly; I cannot, however, support your absence any longer, and as I know you to be as kind as you are pretty, I am in hopes that as soon as you receive this, (which I trust will find you very dull,) you will put yourself *en route* for Paris, where I am awaiting you with the greatest impatience.

"I beg you to observe, my dear Lucie, that it is not an order but a prayer that I address to you; if the country has such charms for you that you cannot resolve to quit it as yet, I leave you entirely free to act as you like.

"A thousand kisses, and believe in the eternal love of your happy husband,

"A. DE POURRIERES."

———

"*Laura Feval to Lucie de Pourrieres.*

"Guermantes, near Lagny.

"We have finished, my dear Lucie, our perigrinations through Italy and Switzerland, and I am at the present moment, installed with my uncle in the pretty little chateau we possess at Guermantes, near Lagny.

"I hasten to announce this good news.

"My husband is still in England, he writes us that the affairs which required his presence in that country, will retain him there at least another month, will you not come and offer a little consolation to a poor widow? My good uncle charges me to tell you that he will go and seek you if you do not quickly make your appearance, and as he is very capable of doing what he says, I hope you will spare him the trouble of taking a journey of more than two hundred leagues.

"We shall be highly flattered, I need not tell you, to receive with you M. the Marquis de Pourrieres.

"Adieu, for the present, my dear Lucie, for the present is it not? Do not even take the time to answer me, but hasten, I am anxious to fold against my heart the oldest and best friend I have.

"LAURA FEVAL."

The last letter was handed to Lucie at the same time as the preceding one. The pretty Marchioness de Pourrieres, quite certain that her husband would not refuse her permission to pass the rest of the season with her friend, whom she was impatient to see once more, determined without much regret, to quit the Chateau de Pourrieres; she therefore wrote to her husband, that in conformity with his wish, she should start at once for Paris and that she would probably be there as soon as her letter.

Salvador, in order to receive her, had completely renewed his furniture and equipages, and had his hotel decorated in greater style than formerly.

"Does the house you are to reside in appear convenient?" he said to his wife, after making her admire the thousand luxurious objects assembled in the hotel.

Lucie did not thank her husband, but she dropped her pretty head on his shoulder, and affectionately pressed him by the hand.

Salvador bestowed a kiss on his wife's forehead.

"He will not refuse me what I wish him to allow me," she said to herself.

They were at this moment in the sleeping-room intended for Lucie, near a small door in front of which Salvador had stopped designedly.

"I have contrived a last surprise for you," he said.

"What is it then?" replied Lucie smiling; "I cannot, after what I have just admired, be astonished at anything."

Salvador drew from his pocket a key with which he opened the mysterious small door, and introduced Lucie into a room, in every way similar to the one which served her as a boudoir at the Hotel de Neuville; there was the same ..... lilac ground, studded with flowers and .... ls, the same green fringe attached b........... l, the same blinds adapted to the win........... in the same manner, the same pieces ...., nothing was wanting.

"Ah! 'tis charming," said Lucie.

"Do not attach greater value to it than it merits, 'tis a slight souvenir; be assured that I am happy at being enabled to do any thing that pleases you."

Salvador devoted the first few days which followed Lucie's arrival in Paris, in visiting the persons who had assisted at his marriage, who were still in the capital, he afterwards accompanied his wife to the wood, to the concerts which had just commenced, every where, in fact, where her extreme beauty, the perfect grace of her manners, would be remarked. Perhaps he did not love Lucie, but the numerous compliments addressed to her flattered his pride; it was glorious to be enabled to say to himself, "This woman so handsome, so gracious, so innocent, this woman whom you overload with homage, of whom you beg a smile, a look, she is mine, she belongs to me, whom you would deliver to the executioner if you knew the events of my life; she loves me, does this woman, whilst I am only attracted towards her because she is handsome."

Salvador wholly engrossed with the pleasure which his gratified pride procured him, had almost forgotten Silvia when he received the following letter;

"*The Marchioness of Roselly to the Marquis de Pourrieres.*

"Paris.

"Dear Marquis,—I will not order you to render your wife miserable, I will not request you even to love her less than you do, this perhaps would be to demand an impossibility of you. Madame de Pourrieres, whom I have had the honour of meeting several times at the wood, is very handsome, hand-

LIFE IN PARIS.

THE DEAD BODY OF ROMAN.

somer than myself, and I conceive it would be difficult not to render her attractions the justice they are entitled to; but for the present, I will limit my desires to the occupation of the second place in your heart; you would be, dear marquis, the most unjust of men, if you did not sometimes visit me to prove that I am not entirely banished from your memory.

"If you knew, my dear Alexis, how much I am ennuied, how unhappy I am, as several days have passed without the pleasure of seeing you, you would pity the wretched Silvia, and would not neglect her as you do. Have you forgotten that there is in a corner of this Paris through which you are driving every day, accompanied by your happy wife, another woman who loves you, to whom your neglect causes most horrible sufferings, and who will soon die if you do not come to console her?

"I cannot believe it.

"Come, my dear Alexis, come; leave me no longer a prey to the gloomy despair which agitates me, and which will drive me perhaps to take an extreme part.

"I hope, dear Alexis, that I shall receive a visit from you, either to-day or to-morrow at the latest; for this reason I sign myself, your devoted and faithful friend,

"SILVIA."

"Silvia laughs at me," said Salvador to himself after reading this letter, the style of which more resembled that of a simple and innocent young girl, than that usually employed by the Marchioness of Roselly, "she is laughing at me to a certainty; but the last paragraphs of her letter intimate a threat she might be foolish enough to put in execution; let us go to her, since I cannot do otherwise. Ah! would I were rid of this woman!"

Our readers need not be astonished at these last words of Salvador, the presence of Lucie had somewhat shaken the foundation of an empire, of which the artful Silvia might easily reconquer the sceptre.

Silvia seated at her piano, accompanied herself by singing a bravura air borrowed from the last Italian opera, when Salvador entered; she squandered on the winds the most fictitious gamuts, the most marvellous *fioritures*, without seeming to pay more respect to them, than to the squeaking notes escaping from the clarionet of a blind musician.

She had recovered the brilliant colours of her features, and the toilette she had chosen gave such a relief to her attractions, that Winklemann himself would have been puzzled, if he had been forced to decide whether Lucie or Silvia was the prettiest.

"There is still a fortune in this throat," she said, placing her finger on her neck admirably modelled, and whiter than alabaster.

"Why then do you not resume your profession at the theatre?" replied Salvador.

"Would you wish me to?" exclaimed Silvia, launching at her lover the look of a viper, "do you wish me to? Indeed, I think it is the wisest plan I can adopt; I shall easily find, if I again mount the boards, men who will love me better than you do, and will not leave me in a furnished hotel, if their fortune permitted them to give me another habitation."

What the ex-cantatrice had said, conveyed to Salvador the possibility of losing a woman he loved, not simply because she was as pretty as it is possible to be, but also because she knew it, and in her presence he was not compelled to constrain himself. A few minutes before he had complained that he could not get rid of her, and if at this moment, any one had wished to carry her off from him, he would

not have yielded if in his power to do otherwise. Human nature is full of singular contradictions. The fates of Salvador and Silvia were united by indissoluble ties; Salvador might, it is true, one day murder his mistress, but he was certain he should regret it the next. Silvia gifted with a rare perception, knew this, and it was perhaps on this account, that she preserved a lover, against whom she was, in some degree, forced to defend her life.

"You are mad, Silvia," exclaimed Salvador, "you are mad, on my word of honour!"

"No, I am not mad," replied Silvia, "I am simply very glad to tell you, that I will no longer be your dupe."

"But how is this? and what subject has brought on this anger, have I refused you any thing, tell me, what do you want? You are well aware that if it is possible for me to satisfy you, I will not refuse you."

"Eh! I trouble myself very little as to what you can give me; do you believe, by any chance, that if I wished it, I could not obtain to-morrow, all that I want at this moment?"

"Eh! bon Dieu! I am persuaded of it; I have never doubted your capacity; but you have not told me the cause of this temper, and what has provoked the ridiculous letter I have just received."

"You ask me!" exclaimed Silvia, a prey to an exaltation which increased every instant, "you ask me! But have you supposed for a moment that I would consent to be neglected for another woman? No, M. le Marquis de Pourrieres, it shall not be thus, and I call Heaven to witness it."

It was with some difficulty, that Salvador contrived to make his mistress comprehend that his position in the world confined him to certain rules, which he could not neglect without exposing himself to be pointed at. The sight of Lucie, perhaps, as she had said, prettier than she was herself, for there was in her features an expression of serenity, springing from a pure conscience, to which the other was a stranger, had sown in her heart a sentiment she had never yet known—jealousy.

"For the future, I shall do whatever you require of me," said Silvia, after listening to the discourse, somewhat lengthy, with which Salvador had favoured her; "but I wish previously, that for a fortnight you conduct me about Paris; that you take me to the wood, to the concerts, in fact to every place that you have taken your wife to; I am wearied, at last, of leading the life of a recluse; I have not left one prison to enter into another, and this apartment, which I seldom leave, is it anything else?"

"But what you demand of me is impossible," said Salvador, "what will the world say, to whom the relation which formerly existed between us is no mystery, what will my wife say?"

"I care very little about the world or your wife either; the world pays great respect to those who dazzle their sight: as to your wife, you can send her from whence she came."

"Be reasonable, Silvia, do not demand of me what I cannot accord you."

"But really I do not see how you can refuse me the favour I ask; we will request M. the Viscount de Lussan to accompany us, his presence will save appearances. For the rest, whether you find my wish unreasonable or not, or even absurd, you must absolutely submit to it."

"But have you forgotten," exclaimed Salvador, hurried forward by an anger that for some moments he had restrained with difficulty, "have you forgotten that I can crush you like a wine glass!"

"Well! rid yourself of me, if such is your will; I would prefer death to the thought of your neglecting me for another woman; but I give you this caution, your death would soon follow mine. I can see a long way, M. le Marquis, and consequently I have taken the precaution to deposit with a notary a will, which if opened, might easily compromise you."

"You have done this?"

"And why not, what can it matter to you if you really love me as much as I do you."

"Your love, you infernal creature, is that of a wild beast."

"Is it not one that suits you, and would you wish then, that we should seek together, crook in hand, the umbrageous shade, and there tranquilly adore one another."

The idea of seeing himself, as well as his mistress, accoutred like the shepherds of M. de Florian, and saying "soft nothings," under the old trees of a green forest, appeared to Salvador so comical, that he could not help bursting into laughter.

Silvia imitated him.

"Come," she said, when this excess of merriment had passed, "be reasonable; you may well, after the proofs of attachment I have given you, grant me in your turn what I request of you."

"I will do all that you wish," replied Salvador, "and let it turn out as the devil pleases."

"That's like a man!" exclaimed Silvia; "I was quite sure that after making a grand fuss you would finish by doing just as I please; but since I have gained the victory, I will show myself a generous conqueror. I know, my dear Alexis, that you must consult the proper susceptibilities of the world in which you live, and that you cannot do that which I only required of you just now, to assure myself that I had still some little empire over you; I now only ask one thing of you, come and see me often, devote to me as much time as you give to your wife, and I shall be satisfied; I have never wished, believe me, to force you to put the public in the confidence of our loves."

Salvador so little expected to see Silvia make a sacrifice of the least of her desires to the exigences of the world, that he fancied at first she was not in earnest, and that this condescension concealed a snare he could not perceive; to persuade him that she had spoken sincerely, she was obliged to repeat several times what she had just said.

Salvador and Silvia did not separate until they had sworn, that nothing that might happen should make them forget what they owed to themselves, and in appearance and in reality enchanted with each other.

The countenance of Salvador was radiant when he entered his hotel; Lucie, who hoped to obtain from him a favour on which she was much bent, was delighted at seeing him in such a good humour.

Whilst Salvador had been with his mistress, Lucie had received a letter from her friend; Laura wrote that she had heard of her return to Paris, and that she was very angry she had not been to see her. "You must not permit love," she said in finishing her letter, "to make you entirely forget friendship; come, I entreat you, and pass a few days in the society of a friend whom you neglect more than you ought, and who would not submit to it if she did not love you in an equal degree."

Lucie was touched at the just reproaches of her friend, and it was the permission to pass a few days with her, that she intended to solicit from her husband.

"Like the ancient seigneurial ladies," she said to him, "I am going to beg you to bestow upon me a donation."

"And whatever it may be, noble dame," replied Salvador, "it is accorded you beforehand."

Lucie placed in the hands of Salvador the letter she had just received.

"Do you know, noble lady, that if you had not obtained from me my word, I should perhaps refuse what you have demanded of me; it will cause me some pain to consent to separate myself from you."

"You can," added Lucie timidly, "if your affairs do not retain you in Paris, accompany me to my friend; she has often said to me, that her uncle Sir Edward, a very worthy gentleman, would receive you with the greatest pleasure."

"Your wish is a very natural one, I think, and I am too courteous a cavalier to oppose myself to its accomplishment. Go then, my dear Lucie, visit your friend, remain with her as long as you like, I shall be happy, if you are so, and if friendship does not make you forget my love for you; I much regret that affairs prevent my accompanying you, but you will excuse me with Sir Edward, say to him that I shall trespass upon my occupations and often visit you all."

"Since you are kind enough to let me visit my friend, I shall leave to-morrow morning if you think it convenient."

"Your will is mine, my dear Lucie."

Salvador, as our readers may imagine, was delighted that his wife, at the moment he was seeking the means of getting her out of the way for the few days which he intended to devote to Silvia, had asked him for permission to absent herself; Lucie, on her part, was pleased at the manner in which her husband had consented to part with her, and she employed herself gaily in collecting a thousand little objects scattered about the saloon, which she intended to take with her into the country, when the Viscount de Lussan was announced.

"I leave you with M. the Viscount," she said to her husband, after addressing to the Breton gentleman a most gracious reverence; "you know that to-day I shall be very busy."

"Don't disturb yourself, my dear," replied Salvador after kissing her forehead, "M. le Vicomte will, I am sure, excuse you."

Lucie quitted the saloon, and left Salvador and the viscount alone.

The latter himself closed every door of the saloon, he then took a fauteuil, and placed himself close to Salvador, who was seated on a divan.

"Are you in want of money, dear marquis?"

"We are always in want of money, dear viscount, and I do not hesitate to say that at this moment, I am horribly inconvenienced for the want of it."

"Will you join with me in an affair, which would, if it succeeded, bring to each of us nearly a hundred thousand francs."

"Such affairs are never refused, in what does it consist?"

"To carry off from a chateau, occupied simply by an old man, a young girl, and some servants, a reasonable quantity of gold lingots, which Justè will purchase of us for two hundred thousand francs."

"The risks?"

"Very few."

"What matter! nothing venture nothing have."

"I like to hear you talk thus, and I am so fully persuaded of the truth of what you say, that this time, as I wish to receive all my share of the cake, I shall not confine myself to the rôle of an indicator; I shall take an active part in the expedition."

"So much the better; but what are to be the means of execution? who will give us the necessary intimation? and by whom shall we be assisted?"

"If you accept, I will inform you on the road, of all that is necessary you should know; for the rest, I may as well tell you, that persuaded you would consent to be with us, I have already arranged everything."

"Very well! reckon upon me; when do we start for the country?"

"This very moment; go and kiss your wife."

"How? this moment?"

"It is absolutely necessary, this very day we must be at least eight leagues from Paris."

"Be it so."

Salvador went to seek his wife in her boudoir; Lucie assisted by one of her women whom she intended to take with her, was packing with care into bandboxes and large trunks, the different articles for the toilet which were to accompany her.

"I am delighted," said Salvador to her, "that you start to-morrow morning for the country, for I should have been obliged to leave you alone; the Viscount de Lussan has imparted to me some news, which will force me to be absent some days."

"'Tis not at least bad news which requires this prompt departure?"

"'Tis not at least bad enough to prevent your diverting yourself, if you find an opportunity; I have some capital engaged in different enterprises, many of these enterprises are good, some are bad, and I am engaged at present in withdrawing such of the capital, as I do not consider well placed, that's all."

It was merely that he wished to present to his wife some possible losses, that Salvador gave to the journey he was about to take, the motive he had announced; but as this was but the first stake planted on the route he intended to pursue, in order to attain the object he had in view, he did not quit Lucie until he had tranquillized her.

He found in the saloon the Viscount de Lussan, and left with him.

CHAPTER XL.

A CATASTROPHE.

At a few hundred paces distance from Lagny, on the road which leads from this town to Guermantes, there exists an isolated auberge, frequented only by waggoners and such travellers whose purse is not sufficiently well lined to permit them to seek the hospitality of the proprietor of the Bear, the best hotel (probably because it is the only one) in Lagny.

We shall find in the principal room of this auberge, a large piece which serves at once as a kitchen, parlour, and dining-room, an individual to whom our readers have been already introduced, Vernier les bas Bleus.

It is almost night, and despite the extreme warmth of the season, the vine stalks and ends of faggots blaze in the large chimney, under the mantle of which Vernier les bas Bleus has taken his seat.

The bandit is habited in the complete costume of a waggoner, his new blouse of blue linen is adorned with a triple row of embroidery of different colours, his legs are incased in long leather gaiters, and his glazed hat is ornamented with a profusion of ribbons of all colours, rose, green, yellow, &c.

A fat servant, with round and coloured features, and formidable attractions, is brightening in a corner the plates of pewter and brass, the brilliant ornaments of a vast dresser placed opposite the chimney; this servant and Vernier les bas Bleus are alone in the room, the other inhabitants of the auberge are seated on the two benches of stone placed in front of the door, and enjoying the cool breeze of the evening.

When the fat servant, in order to take breath, ceases for a moment to rub vigorously the dishes and saucepans she has undertaken to make resplendent, she casts looks of interest towards Vernier, who then approaches the fire and allows some long and heavy groans to escape his bosom.

We have not yet informed our readers, that Vernier is a very good looking man, that he has a full and jovial countenance, and a magnificent pair of black whiskers, very capable of turning the head of a servant at an auberge.

A groan, stronger and more accented than those which had preceded it, made the stout girl suddenly turn her head; she let fall on the ground the rag covered with sand, and the pewter dish she held in her hands.

"It does not get any bettter, then?" she said to Vernier les bas Bleus.

"It gets worse, on the contrary, my kind miss," replied the bandit.

"Will you have anything?" replied the servant, inwardly flattered at being called miss.

"I thank you, but it's getting easier."

"Why did you get up? when we are ill we ought to remain in bed."

"I was cold, and I thought the warmth of the fire would do me good."

"I must admit that you have not much chance, all the same, to be forced like this to stop on your way, returning from your first journey; the ribbons you have put in your hat have not brought you luck."

"Ah, bah! the misfortune is not very great, since I have carried my merchandise to a good port, and am at this moment empty. And besides, you may believe me if you like," continued Vernier, tenderly regarding the armful before him, "truth, I ain't sorry to be suddenly taken ill in your auberge, since it has procured me the pleasure of making your acquaintance."

"You are very honest into the bargain, monsieur; what is your name then?"

"Jerôme Carré, at your service, if I were capable, my pretty miss."

"Ah! now you are playing the gallant; a sure sign that you are better."

"Much better, the fire has done me a sight of good, and I think I could pursue my road to-night, or to-morrow morning."

"Perhaps it would not be prudent."

"Ah, bah! for a small luck, I've no wish to rest a bachelor, and to get married I must collect the halfpence. Am I wrong there?"

"I do not say so, Monsieur Jerôme, but before all, you must preserve your health."

"You are a good girl, Miss Madeline, and if you like—"

"We will talk of that another time, coaxer," said the fat servant, purple with delight.

The arrival before the door of the auberge of a cabriolet, from which descended two elegant personages, who were quickly surrounded by all the inhabitants of the auberge, put an end to the conversation between Vernier les bas Bleus and the servant.

The two fresh arrivals exchanged a rapid glance

with Vernier, who resumed his place near the chimney, which he had quitted, to get a little nearer the servant.

Our readers have surmised, and they are not wrong, that the new personages just arrived at the auberge are no other than Salvador and the Viscount de Lussan, and that it is not chance which has brought together the three bandits.

"Give the horse some water, and also a feed of oats," said Salvador.

The aubergiste and his stable-boy left.

"I am as thirsty as the devil," said the viscount to the mistress of the auberge; "will you, madame, have the extreme kindness to serve us with a bottle of your best wine."

The aubergiste's wife lighted a candle and descended to the cellar.

There now only remained in the kitchen the fat servant, who had resumed her work, but could not cease regarding the new comers. The poor girl had never seen such handsome messieurs at her master's house.

"Mademoiselle Madeline," said Vernier les bas Bleus, in a piteous voice, "will you have the kindness to take from the pocket of my waistcoat, which you will find on my bed, a small parcel, and bring it to me."

The buxom girl, delighted at the occasion of doing any thing for Monsieur Jerôme Carré, instantly left her work, and climbed as nimbly as the rotundity of her person enabled her, the few steps of a straight ladder which led to the upper floor.

"'Tis well," said the viscount to Vernier, when they were alone in the room, "you are at your post."

"And I can remain here without giving birth to the slightest suspicion until to-morrow night, if necessary, but try, however, to get through the affair to-night."

"It must not be thought of, but it shall be to-morrow."

"As you like, I shall get another day's warming by it, that's all; I fear nothing, my papers are all right. The brigadier of the gendarmerie who has examined them, is to bring me this evening the receipt for a remedy which will cure the fever I have given myself, and I pay my court to the servant, who would hide me under her petticoats, if any thing disagreeable was likely to happen to me."

"Very well, 'tis agreed then, you will be at the place appointed with your cart to-morrow night, precisely at two hours after midnight."

"That's agreed; I will be punctual."

"And on our side, we will be punctual in paying you what we have promised; ten thousand francs if we succeed, one thousand francs in case of our failure."

"Thank you, you may rely upon me."

"To-morrow, two o'clock in the morning!"

"To-morrow, two o'clock in the morning."

The aubergiste, his wife, the ostler, and Madeline, entered together the kitchen.

"There's the wine, messieurs," said the aubergiste's wife, "and I flatter myself it's good."

"We have no doubt of it, madame," replied the viscount, "but we shall be much better judges when we have tasted it."

And without more ceremony, he placed himself with Salvador, at one of the corners of the large table, the principal furniture in the room.

The servant had not been able to find in the pocket of Vernier les bas Bleus, the small parcel he had sent her for.

"Ah! well, I have probably mislaid it," said the bandit, to put an end to his grievances.

When the horse which had drawn the cabriolet of Salvador and de Lussan was sufficiently refreshed, the two friends took leave, after exchanging with Vernier, unperceived, a rapid glance. Salvador drew from his pocket two five-franc pieces, which he threw on the table.

"If there is any over, it belongs to this jolly mother here," he said, softly smacking the red and buxom face of Madeline.

"Those masters are very dangerous," said Vernier les bas Bleus, when Salvador and the viscount were gone.

"They are so rich," said the aubergiste.

The viscount and Salvador, seated behind a good horse, soon stepped over the distance which separated Lagny from the auberge in which we have left Vernier; arrived at this town, they descended at the Bear Hotel.

Leaving Paris suddenly, and not having rested on the road, except to say a few words to Vernier, no wonder that they were as hungry as Tartars, so that their first care was to get themselves served with a good repast.

"Will you explain to me, dear viscount," said Salvador when the first course was despatched, "the affair we are about to execute, and in what manner we are to proceed."

"I can tell you no more, my friend, than you know already," replied the viscount, "but here is some one who will completely satisfy you," he added, turning to an individual who at this moment entered the room in which they were supping.

This new comer was an old man, dressed in a nut-brown coat, black ratteen breeches, white waistcoat; he had blue cotton stockings, thick shoes, with large silver buckles, and a three-cornered hat on his head.

"M. Justè," exclaimed Salvador.

"Himself," replied the viscount, "'tis to the brave and worthy M. Justè that we are indebted for the good fortune which will fall to us to-day."

The usurer, on entering the apartment, had saluted the two friends as though he had been unknown to them, and had placed himself near them to be served with dinner, or rather a supper.

Our readers are aware, perhaps, that in the dining-room of most of the inns of Provence, there is but one large table, which serves for every body; it is also notorious, that no where can we converse more at our ease, than in the dining-room of an hotel, in a small town, when the time for the arrival and departure of the public coaches is past.

"You arrive àpropos, M. Justè," said the viscount; "M. the Marquis de Pourrieres has been tormenting me for the last hour, to inform him of things which, as far as the present, you alone have a knowledge of."

"I shall have the honour of satisfying the legitimate curiosity of M. the Marquis."

"These are the facts, it is right that you should not be ignorant of them, so that you may act in consequence.

"No one more than myself likes to oblige his friends. M. the Viscount de Lussan, to whom I have been enabled to render some slight services, is there to contradict me, if what I say is not true. I could claim, in addition, the evidence of the unfortunate M. Lebrun, if the blade of an assassin had not prematurely ended his days."

"Pass on, M. Justè, pass on; I know that you are a very gallant fellow, and my friend de Pourrieres will readily take my word. Is it not true, marquis?"

Salvador made a sign in the affirmative.

"I was telling you then," continued Justè, "that no one more than myself wishes to oblige his friends; you may imagine, therefore, that I seize with eagerness every occasion which presents itself of being useful to them.

"A few days ago, a rich English gentleman, who has resided in France but a short time, came to me and said that he had received from his correspondent at Amsterdam, a letter, which informed him that the greatest part of a freight of gold and silver lingots, which had been forwarded to me by the said correspondent, who is also mine, was intended for him; he begged me to send him these lingots, as soon as they should arrive, to his country house, situate near here; I promised to do as he desired, and as the value of the objects I had to send him was very considerable, I told him it was my wish, in order to place my responsibility out of danger, to bring them myself to the place appointed, in order to have my discharge; I already thought of you, M le Vicomte.

"The Englishman, a very worthy gentleman, my faith! greatly admired my prudence, and said he would receive me with pleasure at his country house.

"The lingots arrived to me two days ago, and I immediately placed in a vehicle those which did not belong to me, and after apprising M. le Vicomte de Lussan of what he had to do I hastened to carry them myself to their legitimate proprietor.

"It now remains to appropriate to ourselves adroitly these lingots, for which I engage to pay you two hundred thousand francs."

"But you do not tell us," exclaimed Salvador, "what means we are to employ for this."

"Patience, a little, patience, I beg of you, every thing comes to a point if you have patience; you have guessed that my motive for taking charge of the lingots myself, was merely to ascertain in what place they would be deposited, and to examine the approaches; it only remains for me to impart to you my observations.

"The lingots have been deposited in a little cabinet contiguous to a bed-room, which is part of a pavilion that forms a wing of the house; this piece, as well as the rest of the pavilion, is at present uninhabited; the lingots, enclosed in several small chests, are placed near a commode, and are covered with an old carpet; you can easily introduce yourselves with the help of a scaling ladder into the chamber of the pavilion, the windows of which open on the high road; if the door of the cabinet is secured, which is probable, it will be easy to force it by means of the wonderful instruments with which you have no doubt furnished yourselves.

"There is no dog in the house. The people whom you are going to *visit*, should not reside in the country without such a faithful servant. The man you have seen, and for whom M. the Viscount has procured a complete equipage of a carrier, will transport the camelotte* to the pavilion of Choisy le Roi, belonging to M. de Pourrieres; 'tis there I shall take possession of it; the rest is my affair."

"The success of this job does not appear to me impossible," said Salvador, after attentively listening to Justè; "but we must look a little beyond; and first, is it quite certain that Vernier, when in possession of the said lingots, will not endeavour

* Plunder.

to deprive us of the whole, or even a part of what would belong to us?"

"Vernier not knowing the value of the booty, as the lingots are in chests, will be satisfied with the pretty round sum we intend to allow him; we can then, to a certain point, rely upon him; besides, nothing prevents our following him at a distance, until his arrival at Choisy.

"As to the rest, we must proceed in this manner," added the viscount; "we will pass the morning of to-morrow in visiting the environs of the town, under the pretext of finding a property for sale; our presence here will therefore be justified, without the necessity of publishing our names; we will quit the auberge at ten o'clock at night, and will saunter about until the moment of acting is arrived; we will leave with M. Justè, whom we shall find at the hour named, near the house in question, our cabriolet, which he will conduct slowly on the road to Paris. The affair once completed, it will be easy to overtake it, and if it pleases God, we will enter our good city at the break of day, a little richer than we are at present.

"And look you, dear marquis, that unless taken in flagrante delicto, (in which event I think you know as well as myself what we have to do,) we risk absolutely nothing; the gendarmes, when they meet men like us, rich individuals and well standing in society, and a capitalist who has gold enough to fill the tomb of the Danaides, content themselves with making a profound salutation."

"You are right," said Salvador, "and if the plan is executed as cleverly as it has been well conceived, the success is infallible."

"And now," replied the viscount, "let us talk no more about this affair."

Justè, Salvador, and the viscount, after the preceding conversation, quietly finished their supper, and each retired to the apartment prepared for him.

The viscount and Salvador had ordered a double-bedded room.

"Do you know, dear viscount," said Salvador, when he found himself alone with his friend, that this M. Justè is really a valuable man."

"Very precious, marquis, for this reason I should be sorry if any misfortune happened to him."

"He is very rich; eh?"

"Very rich, extremely rich, indeed. But I am persuaded he would allow himself to be hacked in pieces, or sawn between two boards, rather than confess in what part of his house he has concealed his immense treasures; and supposing we were rid of him and his Newfoundland dog, upon which, I may remark, he seems to place too much reliance, it would be necessary to demolish his house from top to bottom, in order to discover the chest which holds his treasures."

"Good night, viscount; I am so fatigued that I shall sleep, I think, the sleep of the righteous."

"Good night, marquis, don't dream of poor Roman."

"Ah, bah!" exclaimed Salvador, striving in vain to compress a wearied yawn.

Salvador and the viscount, as they had agreed, passed the next morning in visiting the neighbourhood of the little town of Lagny-sur-Marne, under the pretext of looking for a property that would suit them.

The host of the Bear, dazzled by the elegance of their costume, and their aristocratic manners, had volunteered his services as a guide; and the viscount could not refuse the offers of service so graciously made. Through the host, therefore, Salvador and the viscount were introduced among the proprietors of the environs of Lagny, and thanks to his inexhaustible information, they were enabled to collect a volume of *statistics*, which they promised themselves to make use of when an occasion offered; it is certain, that when the evening had arrived, they had not found what they appeared to have been seeking; they had, however, visited several properties, but some were too extensive, others not sufficiently so.

They returned to the hotel of the Bear as night commenced, and after doing honour to an excellent repast, of which they obliged the host to take a share, they had the horse put to the cabriolet and left.

The hour of two sounded from the church clock of the little village of Guermantes, when they arrived near the house they intended to plunder. The night was calm and silent, except that at distant intervals was heard the deep baying of some watch-dog in a neighbouring farm. Vernier, dressed in his costume of a carrier, and conducting a cart drawn by two active Normandy horses, which he had pulled up a few paces from the house, waited, sitting on the edge of a ditch, the arrival of his accomplices. Salvador and the viscount passed in front of him, after giving him a sign of recognition, and followed the high road until they encountered Justè, who was quietly walking; they gave him the cabriolet, after taking from the box what they required, two blue blouses, in which they immediately enveloped themselves, weapons, false keys, and a rope ladder, most skilfully put together; they then returned, after directing the usurer to proceed slowly, that they might soon overtake him.

The house in which they were to find the treasures they coveted, was as quiet and as much in repose as the country in the midst of which it is situated; no light appeared in the interior; the moment for acting was favourable.

"Ah, ça! let us lose no time," said the viscount, "don't let the day find us at work."

"It would be very awkward," replied Salvador.

"Which of us two shall first attempt the enterprise?"

"Eh! parbleu, it shall be me: I am more accustomed than you to these sort of expeditions."

"Come then, and may heaven help you."

Salvador very expertly threw the rope ladder on the balcony of the window through which he intended to introduce himself into the house, and when he had made sure that it was firmly fixed, he commenced with the agility of a squirrel, his perilous ascent.

The viscount was at the foot of the wall, ready to raise himself in the air as soon as Salvador had entered the house.

Vernier had quitted the place he had occupied, and sauntered on the road smoking his pipe.

Salvador, after attaining the balcony, rested against it as a support, and with the help of a diamond, enclosed in a hair ring he wore on his finger, he removed without noise the best part of a square of glass; he then passed his arm through the aperture he had made, and easily opened the window.

He threw himself into the apartment.

As he supposed it uninhabited, he walked fearlessly towards the door, which, if the indications given by the usurer Justè were exact, led to the cabinet in which the lingots should be deposited.

The creaking of his boots on the floor, and the flickering of the lucifer match by which he lighted a candle he had taken care to furnish himself with, awoke two females who were sleeping in two beds on a parallel in an alcove, which faced the window through which he had obtained an introduction.

The two women, terrified at seeing in their room a man habited in a costume by no means encouraging (our readers will remember that Salvador had placed a blouse over his dress,) uttered piercing cries, and yielding to a mechanical movement, threw themselves on the outside of their beds.

"Be silent, on your lives!" exclaimed Salvador, "be silent, or you die!" and as the two women, in a feverish agitation which deprived them of the free use of their faculties did not cease crying out, he drew from his coat pocket the poniard he had made use of against Roman, and rushed forwards to strike them.

"God! my husband!"

"My wife!"

"The Marquis de Pourrieres!"

The three exclamations were uttered at the same time. The two women against whom Salvador had just raised the assassin's knife, were no others, in fact, than the poor Lucie and her friend Laura.

"Monsieur, monsieur," exclaimed Lucie, "do not murder us, we will not mention a word, I give you my promise."

The poor woman was paler than a corpse, and could not turn her eyes from her husband, whose singular accoutrement announced but too plainly his criminal design.

Laura had taken refuge behind her bed, and trembled in every limb; she spoke not a word.

The foregoing scene had occupied less time than we have taken to describe it.

Salvador ran to the window, the Viscount de Lussan had heard the cries uttered by the two women; imagining they might be heard by the other occupiers of the house, and draw them to the scene of action, and resolving that his friend should not alone support the chances of an unequal struggle, he climbed the steps of the rope ladder, assisted himself by the use of one hand, in the other he grasped his two magnificent Kukenreitters.

"Save yourselves," said Salvador to his two accomplices, "the game's up. I will rejoin you in a few minutes."

Without waiting for further explanation, the viscount descended the ladder. Vernier placed himself at the head of his horses, who put themselves en route the moment they heard the repeated clanging of his whip.

Salvador returned to the two women who had remained in the same place, petrified with astonishment, and not having courage to exchange a single word.

"I will not attempt, madame," he said, addressing his wife, "to conceal from you the motive which has brought me into this house, where, indeed, I did not expect to meet you; it would be useless; the disguise in which I am hidden, the unusual mode in which I have entered this apartment, have already informed you what was my design; I am both grieved and satisfied at what has happened; I am sorry at having caused you a fright, which I am sadly afraid, will be fatal to your health, and at having lost at the same time your esteem and your friendship, to which I must acknowledge I have no further claim. On the other hand, I am thankful that your presence has arrested me on the

LUCIE AND LAURA.

brink of a precipice, into which fatal advice was alluring me headlong. When you know the reasons for my conduct, I shall, no doubt, appear to you much less guilty than I do at this moment, I have therefore a hope that yourself, as also your friend, will mention to no one what has taken place.

"To-morrow, I shall have the honour of presenting myself to Sir Edward."

Salvador left no time to the two women, stupified with astonishment, to make a reply. The moment he had finished his short discourse, he left by the window through which he had entered.

He rejoined the usurer Justè, and the viscount, who was quietly conducting the cab on the road to Paris.

Vernier drove his cart, and had taken a different direction.

We will leave our three bandits for an instant, to return to Lucie and Laura.

Salvador had only taken a glance at the letter his wife had given him to read when asking permission to pass a few days with her friend, and the viscount entering suddenly, as we have seen, to take him with him, he had never thought of inquiring of his wife where the house of Sir Edward was situated; we have seen that the usurer and the viscount, either from design or chance, had avoided pronouncing the name of the person who was to be plundered, so that nothing had arisen to give Salvador a suspicion; his apparition in the chamber occupied by his wife and Laura ought not therefore to appear surprising.

Lucie, as it had been arranged, had left the morning after the departure of her husband with the viscount, and had arrived in good time at the country seat of Sir Edward; the good gentleman had received her with much kindness; and as much perhaps to satisfy his pride as a proprietor and wealthy man, as to make the day pass off agreeably, he had obliged her to admire all the wonders assembled, at a vast expense, in and about his country house; so that Lucie and Laura, who had a thousand things to communicate to each other, little secrets which women in general, and more particularly newly-married ones, never drop into ears profane, had not found, during the whole day, a moment to speak in confidence, the constant presence of Sir Edward, who, in reality, did every thing in his power to be agreeable, had at first somewhat annoyed the two friends; but they soon took it in good part, and promised to repay themselves amply when the hour of retreat sounded, and for this purpose Laura ordered a bed to be arranged for her in the pavilion chamber, which had been set apart for Lucie.

CHAPTER XLI.
MISFORTUNE.—CONTINUATION.

LUCIE and Laura retired early, they had so much to say to each other. Lucie especially was impatient to apprise her friend of a fact she had only that morning become aware of, and which she accepted as joyful news to communicate to her husband upon his first visit to the worthy Sir Edward. Lucie was in the way to become a mother.

After a long chat, the two friends, overcome by fatigue, dropped off to sleep, happy at being so near each other. Our readers are aware under what circumstances they were awakened.

When left alone, they remained some time without speaking.

Lucie, her head sunk in her two hands, her lovely black hair scattered over her alabaster shoulders, wept ready to break her heart.

Laura, seated in a chair, at a few paces from her friend, regarded her in silence, the tears trickling down her pallid cheeks. The indistinct light of the daybreak was their only companion during this unhappy scene.

Laura, in deep distress, rose from her seat, and approached her weeping friend, who seemed to have preserved the little strength still left to her for her sufferings; she kissed her forehead.

"Poor, poor friend!" she said.

Lucie fixed upon Laura her eyes bathed in tears. "I do not inspire you with horror, then?" she said to her friend.

"And why should you inspire me with horror?" replied Laura, who took Lucie in her arms and pressed her to her bosom. "Ought *you* to be punished for a fault which is not your own? and is the friendship between us so brittle that it can be broken at the first slight shock?"

"Oh no!" replied Lucie, "I do not wish you to cease loving me; your friendship is now the only blessing that remains to me."

"And it shall not desert you—that I can promise."

The assurances of Laura somewhat calmed Lucie. The unhappy woman felt herself a degree less miserable, in knowing she could rely upon the devoted and disinterested friendship of the companion of her youthful days.

The ice once broken, Laura exerted her utmost to console her friend under her heavy misfortune. Despite the secret repugnance she felt towards the Marquis de Pourrieres, she believed he had spoken the truth upon finding himself discovered, she therefore remarked to Lucie, that, however serious the crime of her husband, she must not despair of the future.

"Who knows," she continued, "if, one day, you may not have to bless Providence for what has just happened? Your husband has told you, and I think he was serious, that your presence had saved him from the abyss into which he was about to throw himself. Well, he loves you; you will talk to him; and we may hope that when he hears of your being likely to become a mother, he will endeavour to preserve in purity, for his infant, the name he has received from his ancestors."

"'Tis my ardent wish, my dear Laura, that your hopes may be realized; but I despair of it. My husband, you see, is not what he pretends to be; there is, in the life of this man, I am certain, some fatal secret which I shall learn sooner or later. Ah! why did I not follow the advice of Doctor Matheo?"

"You have acted, my dear Lucie, as you ought to have acted; you had no right to put faith in a letter which stated no positive facts, and especially when the writer, by his flight, left the accusations to prove themselves."

Lucie listened attentively, but her tears still left their traces on her careworn cheeks.

"Laura! my kind Laura!" she exclaimed at length, "how grateful I feel for the efforts you make to console me! but they are useless. United for ever to a burglar!—an assassin, perhaps! Oh! I shall never survive it."

"Lucie, Lucie," said Laura, in a solemn voice, "have you forgotten you will soon be a mother?"

"'Tis true, indeed," replied Lucie, "'tis true; and who, if I die, will take charge of the innocent creature I carry within me?"

" Be assured, my friend," replied Laura, " that the Almighty has no intention of making you for ever miserable."

When she pronounced these simple words, Laura appeared so convinced of what she advanced, her voice was so energetic, the expression of her eyes, raised towards heaven, gave evidence of so much confidence, that poor Lucie felt herself somewhat relieved.

" I believe you," she said to her friend, " I have need to believe you."

" What has transpired to-night must be kept as a secret of our own ; and, to prevent the paleness of our cheeks giving rise to questions from my uncle, to which we may find it difficult to reply, we must resolve to take a few minutes' repose. Come, Lucie, to bed ; I shall take upon myself to efface the marks of the entrance of M. de Pourrieres."

Laura broke off the remaining pieces of glass from the window by which Salvador had introduced himself into the chamber, and drew in the rope ladder which had remained hooked to the balcony ; she then carried poor Lucie to her couch, upon which she placed her as she would an infant, so utterly prostrated had she become.

As it frequently happens to such as experience any sudden or violent grief, a heavy sleep soon closed the eyelids of the two friends, who did not awake till the morning was far advanced.

" If you had known what awaited you here," said Sir Edward to his niece, after affectionately saluting Lucie, " you would not have lain so late in bed."

Laura excused her unusual tardiness by a slight indisposition, upon which her uncle jocosely rallied her. The worthy man remarked the extreme paleness and traces of fatigue observable in the countenances of the two companions.

" Why, you are both of you ill !" he exclaimed ; " I shall immediately send for a physician."

" It will be of no service, my dear uncle," replied Laura, " I assure you it will be useless ; tell us, instead, who is the person that is to join us at breakfast?"

These few words were exchanged in the dining-room, and Laura observed to her uncle that there were five covers laid on the breakfast-table.

" You cannot guess, then?" inquired Sir Edward.

" My husband !" exclaimed Laura, and a ray of joy lit up her charming features.

" Himself !" said Servigny, who, in compliance with a wish of Sir Edward to give his niece an agreeable surprise, had until this moment concealed himself in a small ante-room adjoining the dining-hall.

Servigny pressed his wife in his arms, before giving a thought about saluting the Marchioness de Pourrieres.

" Happy Laura !" softly whispered Lucie to the wife of the young man.

" Yes, I am happy," replied Laura ; " and yet, the apprehension of some possible calamity embitters my days, and haunts me when asleep. Alas ! my poor friend, we have both, unhappy creatures as we are, a heavy burthen to carry."

" You also, my kind Laura, is your husband—?"

" Paul is a perfect model of every noble quality, and yet—I will disclose to you a secret that I have kept from you to this hour, because I did not wish to afflict you ; and you will then admit you are not the only one deserving of pity."

The two friends could say no more ; Sir Edward and Servigny, who had retired into the recess of a window, for the purpose of conversing, approached, and invited them to take their seats at the table.

The breakfast was not a dull one. The happiest results had crowned the voyage to England, which Servigny had just accomplished ; so that Sir Edward was well satisfied, and, in consequence, made every effort imaginable to enliven the two friends, who, on their part, not wishing it to be supposed there existed a secret between them which they wished to conceal, endeavoured, as much as possible, to hide the grief to which they were a prey.

A few days after the arrival of Servigny, Lucie received a letter from her husband, which informed her that, on the next morning, he should present himself to Sir Edward.

" I have thought it right," he said, " to announce to you this visit, (which I should not make, if my neglect might not seem extraordinary to Sir Edward,) in order to allow you time to apprise your friend, and that my presence, which, I admit, must, after what has passed, appear in an unfavourable light to you, may not take you unawares."

Lucie's first care, after reading the letter, was to communicate the contents to her friend, and solicit her advice how she should act under the circumstances.

" You must not show yourself too severe," replied Laura ; " the letter he has written you proves that he comprehends the whole enormity of his crime, since he does not attempt to excuse it ; and the man who is humble, is not far from repentance, if he does not repent already."

" I shall do as you advise me, my dear Laura ; I shall talk to him, and I trust the Almighty may bestow upon me the gift of persuasion."

The next morning, as he had announced to his wife, Salvador presented himself to Sir Edward. Servigny was absent, having been called away to Lagny, on important affairs.

Sir Edward received Salvador with evident delight and cordiality, and endeavoured to exact from him a promise to pass at least two or three days at his seat.

Salvador found himself in a very embarrassing position ; he knew not what reasons to allege as an excuse to Sir Edward ; and the fear of incurring the displeasure of Laura, whom his presence, after what had transpired but a few days previously, would inspire with horror, prevented his accepting at once the hospitable invitation of the worthy baronet.

" You do not afford me any good reasons, M. le Marquis," said Sir Edward, at length, visibly annoyed at the continued refusal of his guest ; " you shall remain, unless you wish me to consider that my company is not fortunate enough to please you."

Salvador threw a supplicating glance at Lucie and Laura.

The two fair judges took pity on him.

" Remain, M. le Marquis," said Laura, after pressing in her own, the hands of her friend, " remain ; do not refuse my uncle a favour upon which he seems to place so much value."

" I know my debt to you too well, not to obey you, madame," replied Salvador, after making a respectful inclination of the head.

" How fortunate you are !" joyously exclaimed Sir Edward, addressing the two ladies, " how fortunate you are, to be not only women, but pretty ones ; you are refused nothing."

Sir Edward, anxious to entertain in style the husband of the dearest friend of his neice, and also to give the Marquis de Pourrieres a splendid sample of British hospitality, left the two ladies and Salvador alone for a few minutes, whilst he gave the necessary directions to the domestics.

Salvador turned to account this momentary liberty.

"Ah! ladies," he said, giving to his voice a penetrating tone, "ah! ladies, how great is your kindness, and how can I enable you to forget—?"

Laura allowed him no time to finish the sentence he had commenced.

"Do not allude to what is past," she said to him with dignity; "it is not the Marquis de Pourrieres who raised the weapon of an assassin to our heads; that affair was with a miserable madman, who, we fain hope, has recovered his reason."

"M. le Marquis de Pourrieres," said Sir Edward, entering the room at this moment, followed by Servigny, who had just arrived at the chateau, "I have the honour of presenting to you my nephew."

Salvador hastily quitted the seat he occupied, and bowed to Servigny, who returned his salutation.

When they found themselves face to face, the two men started backwards simultaneously; they had recognised each other.

The sudden movement of Salvador and Servigny had not escaped the observation either of the two ladies or Sir Edward. The females said nothing, but Sir Edward, who had not the same reasons for being silent, inquired of them if they were acquainted.

A moment had been sufficient to recover themselves. Salvador replied first, with the utmost sang froid:

"I see to-day, the first time, M. Paul Feval, but I confess that your nephew so much resembles an Italian gentleman I met with during a stay I made in Venice, some years ago, that I could not, at the moment, restrain a momentary feeling of surprise, very natural in itself, for the gentleman in question has been dead a long while."

This explanation, which Servigny thought it prudent not to contradict, appeared quite natural to Sir Edward, who, in fact, had attached no importance to the question he had demanded.

It was not the same with the females.

"They know each other! my poor friend," said Lucie, squeezing the hand of Laura, "they know each other! Oh! I am still more miserable than I believed!"

Laura, in order to encourage her to support her sad position, had apprised her friend of the past life of her husband, and Lucie now guessed in what place her husband and that of her friend had become acquainted.

Servigny, distressed beyond imagination at encountering in the house of his wife's uncle, a man whose morals and character he was able to appreciate, became impatient to have some conversation with him, which might initiate him as to what he had to fear from him; he therefore requested his wife, from whom he concealed nothing which interested himself, to arrange so that he might remain alone with the Marquis de Pourrieres.

"I will give you, this evening," he said, "the reasons which induce me to request this favour from you."

"I can guess them," replied Laura, after shaking hands with him, "and I will obey you."

"My kind uncle," she said to Sir Edward, after the company had sipped their coffee, out of the beautiful little silver chased cups, "if you are willing, you shall take my friend and myself for a walk in the country. It is said, and with reason, that in the country there is no ceremony; and these gentlemen who, if they do not feel disposed to stir out, have an excellent billiard-room at their disposal, will cheerfully permit us to leave them alone for a few minutes."

"But," objected Sir Edward, who comprehended nothing of the whim manifested by his niece, "it seems to me, that if you are anxious for an excursion, we could have the carriage, and all go together."

"No, no, my good little uncle, we will go on foot, if you please, and we will leave these messieurs here, for I do not wish them to be in the secret of what we propose doing."

Sir Edward, accustomed to comply with the slightest wish of his niece, whom he treated like the "spoiled child," took his cane and hat, and, after begging the marquis to accept his excuses, he accompanied the two ladies for a promenade.

Salvador and Servigny were nearly equally embarrassed, more especially the former, who guessed that the motive of Laura in being accompanied only by her uncle and Lucie, was simply to afford her husband an opportunity of conversing alone with him; however he himself began the tête-à-tête.

"I think, sir, it is useless to dissemble any longer," he said to Servigny; "we have recognised each other."

"It is true, sir," replied the latter, "and, I confess, I was somewhat unprepared to meet you here."

"My astonishment has not been less than your own; is it really you?—you, whom we abandoned in so piteous a state, after the combat we were forced to submit to with the gendarmes of the brigade of Beausset, and whom I find, to-day, the husband of a charming woman, and as rich, by all accounts, as she is handsome."

"Allow me to observe to you, in my turn, that I do not feel less surprise than yourself at encountering you here, the bearer of a name which probably is not your own, and the possessor of riches obtained possibly from no legitimate source."

"These doubts are offensive to me," said Salvador, in a vexed tone, "and I think they would sound better from any lips than yours. I can, M. Servigny, prove to you, by authentic documents, that my name and my riches are the inheritance of my ancestors. M. Feval might not probably find it so easy a matter to establish the genealogy of the Fevals."

"The somewhat inconsistent tone you assume, in replying to observations which ought to appear quite natural to you, might induce me, so be aware, to take an extreme part, which I must apprise you, would ingulf us both in a bottomless pit; but you may be certain I shall not recoil before that which I should regard as the accomplishment of a duty."

"Menaces and threats are usually the weapons of a coward," said Salvador.

"Sir!" exclaimed Servigny.

"Allow me to conclude," continued Salvador, "you can, it is true, do me some injury; but, as I have just told you, a threat is the weapon of a coward, and I think I know you sufficiently, to be convinced that you have no wish to make use of it. You would infallibly be the victim, if we engaged in a struggle; for it would be easy for me to establish an incontestible alibi from the day of my birth to the present hour: whereas, upon a word of mine to the worthy Sir Edward, you would, despite the connection which attaches you to this estimable gentleman, be indignantly driven from his house."

"You are in error. Sir Edward and my wife are perfectly aware, thank God, who I am. I am, indeed, thankful that I have not been induced to deceive my generous benefactor. They know that Paul Feval is no other than the unhappy Servigny; they know the circumstances that drove me into an abyss from which I was enabled to extricate myself by courage and perseverance."

This information of Servigny, we may well imagine, caused a profound astonishment to Salvador. He found himself entirely at the discretion of Laura's husband. He might hope, it is true, that Laura, yielding to the entreaties which would, undoubtedly, be urged by her friend, would not place her husband in possession of the circumstances which had passed a few days previously. He thought it prudent, therefore, in order to avoid, as far as possible, the danger which menaced him, to change at once both his tone and language.

"Your sentiments," he said to Servigny, after taking several turns in the apartment, "are those of a man of honour—of a man who deplores the errors of his youth, who wishes, by every possible means, to force the world to forget, and to forget himself, that he once wore the livery of a criminal. I highly approve your conduct, and I would willingly believe you have the purest intentions, the noblest sentiments; but if it is so, if you have really been purified in the school of misfortune, you will not be unjust enough to believe that you are the only individual capable of returning to a virtuous life, after a youth of errors and disorders."

"May heaven forgive me, if ever such a thought occurred to me; but a presentiment which I cannot conquer, the sadness of Madame de Pourrieres, which seems to announce that she is not so happy as she deserves to be—all this induces me to think that Salvador and Duchemin, whom I met in Paris, some time since, are incorrigible, or nearly so."

"Duchemin is dead," replied his companion; "and as to Salvador, as he is anxious to divest your mind of any unfavourable impression, he is desirous of narrating to you the events of his past life; and he hopes that the recital he is about to make will give you a less unfavourable opinion of him. Are you disposed to listen to him?"

Servigny, anxious to ascertain the motives Salvador would allege in justification of the faults, or rather the crimes, of his former life, replied in the affirmative.

Salvador assumed an air of repentance, and, after collecting himself for a moment, he recounted to Servigny, a history nearly similar to the one he had fabricated to Doctor Matheo; a history probable enough, if our readers have not forgotten it; and which Servigny, above any individual, might easily believe, and which concluded in the following words: "You see, M. Servigny, by my example, by your own even, that, after committing some great faults, it is still possible to enter into the right path."

The frank and kind nature of Servigny rendered him incapable to imagine it possible for a human being to forge, with so much ability and boldness as did Salvador, sentiments which did not belong to him; so that, after listening attentively to the Marquis de Pourrieres, he offered him his hand and said: "I believe you, M. de Pourrieres, (from henceforth this is the only name you will hear from my lips,) I wish to believe you. The happiness of my wife is as necessary to mine as the air I breathe, and I am convinced she would be miserable if her friend were so."

"Believe me, M. Feval, I shall do every thing that depends upon myself to ensure the happiness of Madame de Pourrieres, and, as a consequence, that of your amiable wife; but let us drop, for a moment, the subject of a conversation which recals to both of us days of bitter sadness; and tell me what you have done at Geneva; may I, in fact, preserve a hope of discovering any traces of my unfortunate son ?"

Servigny reported to Salvador, with considerable detail, the information contained in the letter we have placed before the reader. "I think," he said in concluding, "that you will find considerable difficulty in attaining the end you are anxious for; but still the realization of your hopes is not impossible. The troop of Riberprè, if you can discover it, will, no doubt, be enabled to inform you what direction he took after quitting it, and, advancing from one indication to another, you will arrive, by the blessing of God, at the place in which he at present resides."

"May your prayers be listened to. Believe me, 'tis the dearest wish of my heart," replied Salvador. "It is not necessary for me to recommend silence to you," he added, "I do not wish Madame de Pourrieres should be informed of the existence of my son, until I have succeeded in discovering him."

The desire manifested by Salvador was so natural, that Servigny acquiesced, and gave the promise required.

The conversation between the two men was here interrupted by the return of the ladies and Sir Edward.

The countenance of the worthy squire was beaming with delight.

"It appears you have enjoyed a most delightful walk," said Salvador.

"We have indeed," replied Sir Edward, "and I am now sorry at having made so much ceremony in taking it. It was to join in a benevolent action that my niece determined that Madame de Pourrieres and myself should accompany her; and it arose from the desire to carry assistance to an unfortunate family, ruined by a fire, the father of the same family being at this moment very seriously ill."

The fact announced by Sir Edward was true in every word. Some peasants had appealed to the unlimited charity of Laura, in consequence of the misfortune narrated by Sir Edward, and Laura had seized upon the occasion to attract her uncle and her friend to the house of the poor sufferers, reduced to misery by fire and disease, and she had retained them there a sufficient time for her husband and the Marquis de Pourrieres, to hold their tête-à-tête. This was not very difficult; Sir Edward and Lucie were equally disposed to every charitable action, and they never allowed to escape an opportunity of assisting the unfortunate, when their case appeared worthy of commiseration.

"I trust, Madame Feval will permit us to add our mite in favour of her protegés," said Salvador.

Sir Edward did not allow his niece, who was astonished that her husband seemed to accept, by his silence, of some sort of community with the Marquis de Pourrieres, to reply.

"You arrived too late, sir," he said; "the honest people we have assisted, have at this moment nearly all that is necessary; their humble dwelling will be rebuilt, their stock will be replaced, and they can, without fear, wait till the head of the family is again enabled to undertake the rough labour which earns their daily bread; to do more, would only induce them not to rely upon themselves, if, by chance, fresh troubles should fall upon them, and withdraw from other individuals that which legitimately belongs to them. We must act with discretion, while in this world, even in charity; good frequently results from misfortunes, my friends, and to go beyond the mark is not the way to overcome them."

These prudent sentiments admitted of no reply, and no one answered them. As the hour for retiring had not arrived, Salvador proposed to Sir Edward to play a game at billiards.

"It will enable us to pass the time," he said, "but which will not appear long, if these ladies will condescend to be judges of the combat."

Sir Edward, like most of his countrymen, was passionately fond of every game of dexterity, and eagerly accepted the proposition of the Marquis de Pourrieres.

Salvador was a first-rate performer at billiards, so that he easily vanquished his worthy antagonist, although the latter was any thing but a novice at it.

Sir Edward was not in the habit of finding himself thus *cushioned*, and being naturally of a quick temper, the ill humour which had been latterly collecting itself, at length burst forth.

"Gamblers, whatever may be their virtues or their vices, are all the same," said Salvador to himself, "it is not so much the loss of their money, as the wound which such loss inflicts upon their pride, and which destroys their reason, when they deliver themselves over to the demon of play. Here is a man, amiable and virtuous in every sense of the word, from whom I could win, if I wished, a considerable sum.

"Why should I not?" he again soliloquized, after a magnificent coup.

Sir Edward, transported with rage, threw his cue with such violence on the floor, that it broke into several pieces.

Salvador softly placed his on the billiard table.

"I think," he said to his adversary, "you are not at this moment quite master of yourself; perhaps we had better finish where we are?"

"Not at all, not at all!" exclaimed Sir Edward. "If you do not continue the game, I shall fancy you are vexed at the slight movement of anger I have just allowed myself."

"Ah! I have an idea," said Salvador to himself, again taking up his cue, "by bestowing upon myself the only fault I do not possess, I shall obtain the best excuse I could find."

Servigny and the two ladies had retired some time, so that Salvador, Sir Edward, and a servant to mark the points, were left to themselves in the billiard-room.

"Let us play for something," said Salvador; "you will preserve a little more coolness, perhaps, when you have to defend your purse."

"Be it so," said Sir Edward. "What shall the stakes be?"

"Only a trifle; suppose we say five hundred francs a side—thirty points up—for a beginning."

"I accept, for five hundred francs."

Sir Edward took from the rack a fresh cue, which he carefully tipped with chalk, and the party again commenced.

The short interruption which had taken place had dissipated the ill humour of Sir Edward, so that he now played with much greater caution than in the former games, and found more than one occasion of exhibiting his address by some admirable *coups*.

Salvador, who wished to lose something considerable, (of which intention our readers are probably aware,) so managed his play, that his adversary should profit by the position in which he took care to place the balls; but still contrived to play his game with sufficient address to prevent Sir Edward from perceiving that, if he did lose, it was with his own consent. The victory, zealously disputed, appeared not the less agreeable to the worthy baronet, who, overjoyed at his success, and delighted at vanquishing, in his turn, the opponent who had so lately punished him, overwhelmed the marquis with his raillery.

In a short time, Salvador lost the sum of three thousand francs.

"You are decidedly in greater force than I am," he said, taking from his note-case three banknotes, which he handed to Sir Edward; "it is useless to struggle longer against you. I confess myself vanquished."

"In that case, let us conclude the game and go to bed, the victory I have gained is really the most glorious it is possible to conceive."

The two champions separated, mutually charmed at having attained the object sought for by each. Sir Edward wished to triumph, simply because his vanity (the wisest men have some few weaknesses) acknowledged with pain that it was possible for any one to play better than himself at billiards: and Salvador was anxious to lose, from an idea he had conceived, which will be known by what follows.

Lucie, certain that her husband would pay her a visit before retiring to the apartment prepared for him, had not retired to bed, but sat reading till the billiard-room should be deserted.

"I expected you, sir," she said to him, as he entered the room; "will you take a seat?"

Salvador obeyed without replying.

"Are you disposed, sir, to listen to me, and to favour me with your attention?" continued Lucie, after a few moments' silence.

"I am come, madame," replied Salvador, "not to justify myself, I know that that is impossible; but to communicate to you the events which have allured me to the brink of that precipice from which I should undoubtedly have fallen, if your presence had not preserved me at the moment I was about to render myself guilty of a first crime; but, since you have something to say to me, I shall reserve my explanation until you have finished."

"Listen to me, sir," said Lucie, in a tender, yet solemn tone: "I can, by a threat of divulging what has transpired, force you to consent to a separation; you are fully convinced of that, are you not?"

"Undoubtedly, madame," replied Salvador. The power which these words seemed to imply evidently alarmed him.

"Reassure yourself, sir," resumed Lucie, "such is not my intention. My destiny, before God and before men, is linked with yours, and I do not think it right to dissever the ties consecrated by our holy religion; I shall therefore remain your wife, whatever be the consequence; and if I am fated to suffer further trials, if your future conduct does not induce me to forget that which is past, I shall be consoled by the assurance, that the trials I have submitted to on earth will be some passport to a greater happiness above."

"Ah! madame," exclaimed Salvador, "banish from your mind these gloomy ideas. I have, by yielding to perfidious advice, forgotten that I am the Marquis de Pourrieres, and that I have the honour of being your husband; but, believe me, my heart is not so degraded as to be incapable of appreciating your noble character."

"If such is the case, sir, we may still hope to enjoy some happy hours. I am forgetful of injury, sir; never shall a word from me recal to your remembrance that which took place in this chamber but a few days since; but, in the name of heaven, in the name of every thing you hold most dear on this earth, should you (which may heaven prevent) find yourself tempted a second time by those who have once seduced you, remember that you have raised the weapon of an assassin against a woman who loves you, against a woman who will shortly render you happy as the father of her first born."

These last words were uttered in a tone so melting, that, despite the triple armour in which his heart was cased, Salvador felt himself *almost* affected.

"This is what I wished to say to you, sir," continued his wife; "you will shortly be a father; you have no longer merely your own honour to protect; you are, from this moment, the depository of that of the infant which heaven sends you, and to whom you are bound to transmit a name, pure and without reproach; you will not forget this, I hope."

"No, madame, no; I shall not forget it."

We must hope that Salvador was sincere when he made this promise, and which he would probably have kept, had not a fatal influence intervened and caused him to forget it. There rests in the heart of man, however corrupted it may have become, some chords which respond, when invoked by one of those noble sentiments which seem to have been placed in every heart to remind it of its celestial origin.

Salvador rose from his seat, and, for some moments, paced the room. He found it necessary to collect his scattered thoughts, somewhat disturbed by the revelation just made to him by Lucie.

"There remains for me, madame, one duty to fulfil," he said at length, "and I shall now acquit myself of it. I received from nature some good qualities, I do not hesitate to say so; but education has developed in me the germ of one vice, which long remained buried, and this vice tarnished the lustre of every virtuous sentiment I may have possessed. In one word, madame, I am a gambler. I blush in making this avowal. There is no passion the influence of which is so fatal as that of play. The gambler, in the ordinary relations of life, is often an excellent husband, a fond father, a faithful friend; but the moment that finds him seated before the green cloth, with the cards in his hands, he forgets wife, child, and friend, that he may think of nothing but the uncertain combinations of chance. Tell him that his mother is dying—that his family is a prey to the most frightful misery—that his best friend has been arrested or killed—he will not listen to you; but speak to him of a martingale capable of breaking the bank—of the most advantageous mode of marking the *coups*, or of neutralizing the fatal odds of red and black zeros, and the dreaded *apres* of *trente et un*—and he will be all attention. But this is not all; when the means of gratifying his unhappy passion have failed him, he will risk every thing to procure them—his own life, that of his nearest and dearest—aye, even his honour. This has been my case. Unfortunate speculations deprived me of a portion of my fortune, but what remained was more than amply sufficient to allow me to occupy in society the position to which the name I received from my ancestors gave me a right, when chance led me into one of those infamous saloons, constantly open, in spite of the active campaign carried on against them by the police.

"Gold and bank-notes were spread in all directions before my wondering eyes. A voice—that of my evil genius—whispered in my ear, that I might, by risking a trifling sum, recover, in a short time, what I had lately lost. I listened to the infernal whisper; I played! The execrable demon who presides over our destinies, not willing that the victim should be enlightened in his road, and arrested on the edge of a precipice, allowed me to be a winner. I was lost, lost beyond redemption. After some lucky sittings, followed others of alternate loss and gain. Then came the unlucky ones, during which I tore my hair, and even my very flesh, without knowing it. In a word, I passed, in a short time, through every degree of joy, hope, and despair."

Salvador stopped a moment to take breath. This man was so perfect an actor, that the expression of his countenance lent its aid to complete the hideous picture he had unrolled before the view of his unhappy wife. His eyes were haggard, his cheeks pale, his hair, blacker than ebony, bristled on his head.

Lucie sobbed in silence.

Salvador, after striking his forehead several times, continued as follows:

"One day, when about to take some gold, for the purpose of once more tempting fortune, my coffer was empty. It was at this time that a man, whose acquaintance I had made in one of the houses I have mentioned, came and proposed to me to aid him in the execution of a project he meditated. There is no occasion for my naming to you what this project was. This individual was gifted with a fatal eloquence. I allowed myself to be seduced—you know the rest.

"And now, will you believe me, if I tell you that the fear of being forced to diminish somewhat of the luxury I felt a pleasure in surrounding you with, contributed as much, perhaps, as the fatal passion to which I was a prey, to make me face, without horror, a crime, the consequences of which I now so deeply lament? Will you believe me if I tell you that it is because I love you to distraction—because I could not resolve to make you the confidant of my sad position, that I became guilty?

"After the scene which took place in this room, I rejoined my accomplice, and compelled him to quit the neighbourhood of this mansion into which he seemed determined to enter, and accomplish his purpose alone. Arrived at my hotel, the false courage which had till then supported me, suddenly abandoned me; for several days I remained in a state of complete prostration, a state from which I emerged, to view with horror the dreadful position in which I had placed myself by my own fault.

"I then made a solemn vow never again to put my foot inside a gambling house—never to approach the green cloth—never to touch a card—in fact, never to play again—and yet, this oath, madame, I have broken this very evening!"

Salvador then recounted to Lucie all that had taken place between himself and Sir Edward, placing much greater importance in the facts than they required.

"But should my hair grow white upon my head—should I live until my hands become but dry skin and bone—what has happened shall never be renewed."

"I have listened to you with the most serious attention," said Lucie, when Salvador stopped, and I have no hesitation in telling you, that your words were uttered with such an appearance of truth, that I give entire faith to them. I believe you have only yielded to the struggles of an irresistible passion,

THE ESCAPE.

and to evil advice; I believe, since you have told me so, that it was partly on my account that you have rendered yourself guilty; I believe, also, that you will keep the vow you have made me; but, that you may do so, it is necessary to adopt energetic measures, and, whatever they may be, I trust that you will not refuse to employ them."

"Speak, madame," replied Salvador, "speak; I am ready to obey you. What must I do?"

"You are, if I have rightly understood you, completely ruined?"

"No, madame, thank God, I am not reduced to poverty, although a portion of my revenue is engaged, nearly all my land burdened with mortgages; but I can yet make some arrangement with my creditors, and, by a few years of economy, repair the inroads on my fortune."

"Well, this must be done. I can rely upon the discretion of my friend. There is no need to add, on my part, that I shall never make you a reproach. From this moment, therefore, throw a veil over what has passed, and that veil shall never be raised, for it is with sincerity, and without any reservation, that I pardon you."

Salvador took one of the hands of Lucie and pressed it affectionately in his own, and raising his eyes toward heaven—

"Dear angel!" he said, in a voice quite penetrating.

Lucie, touched at the deep repentance manifested by her husband, returned, probably without knowing it, the soft pressure of his hand.

"There is, says the evangelist," continued Lucie, "more joy in heaven over one sinner that repenteth, than for ten just men who have never sinned; and it is on this account, no doubt, that the Almighty opens so wide a path to repentance. You will renounce, therefore, the habits of your past life; this, perhaps, will be much less difficult than you imagine. You will do it, in the first place, for me, to whom you have made the promise, and, secondly, because you will remember, that, sooner or later, wicked actions are punished, and that those which escape, by any chance, the justice of man, elude not that of God.

"You will remember, that, with an honourable name, you must transmit intact, to your infant, the fortune your parents have left you; and, to effect this, you will do every thing which prudence and experience may suggest to you. Whatever resolutions you may decide upon, as I have no doubt they will be honourable, you may reckon upon a willing and disinterested approval on my part; and, in order that you may not doubt, for a single moment, the sincerity of my words, from to-day I place at your disposition—so that you may free your income, disengage your estates, and pay your creditors—all that I possess. Indeed, I think this is the most pressing at the present, for we must not allow usurious interest the possibility of swallowing up the savings we can make in our incomes, by living retired and without luxury in the country. I presume, that, like myself, you will be glad to pass a few years, either at the Chateau de Pourrieres or elsewhere; I leave you perfectly free to choose the place which must serve as our retreat."

"All that you have prescribed to me, madame, shall be executed to the letter; and to-morrow, if you are agreeable, we will return to Pourrieres, which I regret to have quitted for Paris, if it were not that in this city I had the happiness of meeting the best and most indulgent of women."

"We will depart to-morrow, if it is your wish, sir: it was my intention, however, to have passed a few days more with my friend."

"But, madame, it was only to prove to you that I am ready to fulfil your wishes, that I proposed to start to-morrow; remain here some days, if such is your desire."

Salvador, after exchanging a few more words with his wife, quitted her, that she might seek some repose. We shall follow him to the apartment prepared for him, and shall report to our readers the discourse he addressed to himself, when he found himself alone.

His first care, on arriving in his room, was to take off his coat, which he threw on a chair, complaining of heat; this done, he lighted a cigar, and drew towards the open window a fauteuil à la Voltaire, in which he seated himself.

The clear blue sky was sparkling with a thousand brilliant stars. The silence of the night was only interrupted by the rustling of the foliage of the magnificent trees which surrounded the property of Sir Edward, gently agitated by the soft breath of the zephyrs. The warm and perfumed breeze caressed, with an agreeable sensation, the olfactory nerves of Salvador.

"My faith," he said, at the same time sending into the air the capricious clouds which escaped from his cigar, "a lounge in the country is very agreeable. I love the brilliant stars which sparkle in the canopy of heaven; I love this nature, calm and silent, the grand trees, with their green foliage—the song of the nightingale, who balances himself on the flexible branch—the cry of the landrail, who hides himself in the long grass—the gentle buzzing of the demoiselle, with the elongated waist, and extended blue wings, who timidly skims the silvery surface of a quiet lake—I love all these mysterious harmonies, which seem to chant the praises of their Creator in an unknown language.

"Eh! eh!" exclaimed Salvador, after venting the preceding tirade in an emphatic tone, "were I told, at the present moment, that reading the romances of the age was more noxious than useful, I should well receive the clown who held such a language to me. All this rodomontade is borrowed, or nearly so, from the last work of one of our most celebrated *bas-bleus*, and I am certain it would cause soft tears to trickle from the pale cheeks of my most virtuous wife.

"I ought, perhaps, to follow her advice—bid adieu to all the enjoyments of a Parisian life, and seek with her the retirement of the country; her example would, no doubt, lead me to delight in virtue. The Almighty, she told me, offers a wide path to repentance. What then? It is too late. Love virtue? I! Salvador! 'tis impossible. Live in the country, far from excitement, luxury! oh, no, no! I must lead a life of activity, of gaiety, and one that will not leave me time to dwell upon the events of my past life."

It was late, or, rather, it was morning, for the first streaks of daylight began to gild the horizon, when Salvador, after finishing his cigar, threw himself on his bed to take a few hours' repose.

Servigny and Laura had retired to their apartment, leaving Salvador and Sir Edward wholly occupied in the game of billiards, of which we have reported the different turns of fortune.

We have already observed that Servigny kept no secrets from his wife, so that his first care, on finding they were alone, was to inform her that he had only begged her to carry off Sir Edward and the Marquise de Pourrieres, because he wished to remain alone a few minutes with the Marquis de

34

Pourrieres, whom he had known at the *bagne* of Toulon, under the name of Salvador.

Servigny then informed his wife of all that had passed between him and Salvador, during the time they had been left alone.

"I should probably have given faith to the history he recounted to me, to justify his new position, except for a circumstance which has but just occurred to me. I perfectly remember that the *payot* Salvador, who was at the *bagne* at the same time as myself, with whom I made my escape, had the most beautiful fair hair it is possible to conceive, and now his hair is as black as ebony. This change conceals, most assuredly, some mysterious iniquity, which, perhaps, at the risk of what might happen to me, I ought to endeavour to penetrate."

Laura, we can easily believe, felt the greatest astonishment and deepest distress, when her husband made this revelation to her. The former life of Salvador explained to her, at once—giving to them a sombre tint—a heap of facts, which, up to the present moment, had appeared to her almost insignificant: the presence of the Marquis de Pourrieres in the den of the Rue de la Tannerie, the letter of Doctor Matheo, and, lastly, the attempt at robbery committed, a few days previously, at the house of Sir Edward, just at the moment the lingots had been brought there. This attempt no longer appeared as an isolated event, which, although not excusable, might be pardoned, from the sincere repentance manifested by the man who had been guilty of it; it appeared to her as the last crime of a man who had probably committed a number of others.

The amiable and gentle Lucie—that friend whom she cherished as a sister, and reverenced as a mother—was she, then, become the prey of a noted scelerat? Laura could not believe that heaven would permit so monstrous a union; but it was in vain that her heart repulsed such an idea, her reason told her that she must adopt the sad anomaly which her heart refused. What ought she to do, then? Apprise her friend? But would Lucie, endowed, or, rather afflicted, with sensations of extreme delicacy, and already broken in spirit, have strength enough to support so frightful a blow? And, should it even be so, Laura was sufficiently acquainted with the character of her friend, to be persuaded beforehand, that, in making known to her the past life of her husband, she would break her heart, without, however, inducing her to adopt the only part which, in her position, it was necessary to take. She foresaw the reply that Lucie would make her, if, after such information, she entreated her to abandon her husband.

"Since the Almighty has permitted my union with this man, it is probable that it is in accordance with the views of his divine wisdom, before which I ought, whatever may be the consequence, to bow in silence; death alone ought, in this world, to dissever the ties of which he has taken note in heaven."

"Poor Lucie! poor Lucie!" said Laura. "You, so pure, so good—were you, then, destined to be so unhappy? What *ought* I to do, great God, to prevent the misfortunes which threaten you?" And the large tear-drops chased each other down the cheeks of the young wife.

Laura, after recovering a little calmness, imparted to her husband the reflections she had made. She thought she ought not to leave him in ignorance of the attempt at robbery committed at Sir Edward's.

"I think," replied Servigny, "that if such in-

deed is the character of your friend, we ought, for the present, to keep her in ignorance of what has come to our knowledge by accident. To inform her of it, would be, as you observe, to place her life in danger, and, if she did not fall a victim, would render her life more miserable than it is at present.

"The Marquis de Pourrieres, or rather, Salvador—for I cannot think this man is the last scion of the noble family whose name he bears—is, beyond contradiction, a very dangerous man, probably covered with crimes; but, if my fate is, in some measure, in his hands, I have also the disposal of his; and as, thank God, I have strength to defend myself, and he knows it, I have nothing to fear from him.

"This, then, if I do not mistake, is the wisest plan we can adopt:—We will use our utmost exertions to prevent our friend returning to her husband. So pure a mind as hers must not be blemished by the contact of such a man as Salvador; and I do not think it will be difficult to persuade her to remain with us. We will guard both her person and her fortune, which I do not think she would permit her husband to dissipate, for she would wish, no doubt, to preserve it intact for her child.

"The Marquis de Pourrieres is, to a certainty, the chief, or, at least, one of the chiefs, of the band of malefactors who, for some time, have infested and laid waste the capital and its neighbourhood. Sooner or later, he will receive the just punishment for his crimes. The unhappy Lucie must not be shipwrecked in the storm which will ingulf both his person and his fortune. This is the end we must endeavour, by God's assistance, to attain."

Laura pressed her husband in her arms, when he finished. She was happy at seeing the husband she loved, so warmly espouse the interests of her friend.

CHAPTER XLII.

HOW AN ENGLISH COACHMAN CAN USE HIS WHIP.

SILVIA, it must not be forgotten, still inhabited the Prince's Hotel; Salvador amply furnished her with funds, but the proud creature having encountered—in her daily excursions in places where the Parisian fashionables assembled—some of those whom she had previously met in society, and these individuals inquiring of her if she intended shortly to furnish her house—that she was regretted by all, as they assured her; Silvia said to herself that she would no longer remain in the apartments of an hotel, whilst her rival (she had the audacity thus to name the unhappy widow of the Count de Neuville) resided in a magnificent hotel, and lived surrounded by every species of luxury and comfort.

Her resolution once taken, Silvia never delayed the execution of it; she therefore at once wrote to her lover, and sent the letter by an express. She informed him that the life she led was become insupportable to her, so much so, that she would endure it no longer; that sensible people would laugh at her, if, young and handsome as she was, she contented herself with the more than modest style of living he wished her to enjoy; that if he was unwilling to make some sacrifices on her account—viz., place things upon the former footing—she would be compelled to accept the brilliant offers made her at this moment by a rich stranger;

and that, as she feared he would forget her if he remained too long with his wife, she was fully determined to seek him herself, at the country-house of Sir Edward, if he did not return with the messenger who delivered him the letter

Salvador had not been enabled to inform his mistress—as at the moment of his wife's departure he was ignorant of it himself—in what direction the country-seat of Sir Edward was situated; but Silvia could easily procure this information, by questioning adroitly the domestics of the Hotel de Pourrieres and those of Sir Edward.

Salvador, being either well convinced that his mistress was quite capable of carrying out her threat, or glad of having a pretext for abandoning the position, somewhat embarrassing, which held him between Lucie and Laura, soon made up his mind, and announced his departure to Sir Edward; but perceiving that he should be obliged to comply with the demands of Silvia, and for that, as well as to pay the usurer Justè, he should require money, he determined upon seeking it from his wife.

He therefore ascended to her room before breakfast was served.

Lucie was in somewhat better spirits than on the previous evening; she had just finished her toilet, and was preparing to descend, when Salvador, who had previously requested permission to enter, (a permission readily granted, as a sort of reconciliation had, a few hours before, taken place between them,) entered her room.

Of all the passions that excite and dishonour the human species, that of gambling—of which we have seen Salvador draw so frightful a picture—is, without contradiction, the most horrible, the most frightful in its fatal results; for we have continually the strength to play—we have it not in drinking, or in following the flowery paths of Venus. The gambler is by nature like a polypus—he has no heart within him. He knows neither home nor country; he would give, were it in his power, the entire universe, and all that it encloses, to play another and a last *coup!* In the every-day relations of life, he is generally cold and monotonous; he feels no excitement until he is seated before the green cloth, and looks with covetous eyes upon the piles of bank-notes and heaps of gold which shine before him, when the nasal voice of the "dealer" shoots into his ear these sacred words: "*Monsieur, faites votre jeu, le jeu est fait, rien ne va plus.*"

Then, struck as with an electric shock, his cheeks inflame, his eyes sparkle; he follows with a beating heart the capricious evolutions of the ivory ball which is to decide his fate; he waits, with open mouth, the red or black card, which tells him whether he wins or loses. If fortune is favourable to him, hideous smiles—like those which animate the visage of demons when receiving a condemned soul into their gloomy empire—will unite his lips; if, on the contrary, he has lost, he reddens or becomes pale, according to his cold or sanguine temperament, every colour in the rainbow passes successively over his excited features.

Such, in a few words, is a gambler; the portrait is not very flattering, but it is exact. Well! by one of those inconsistencies of the human heart, which it is almost impossible to account for, the gambler is, of all men, the one most easily governed by an evil passion, and the one soonest pardoned by women.

Lucie, in her misfortune, felt herself still happy in the conviction, that the crime attempted by her husband had been occasioned by the temporary embarrassment of her husband, owing to an insur-

mountable passion; she was happy in the thought that the Marquis de Pourrieres was not a burglar; and if we add that she believed the protestations of repentance he had made her, we shall not be much surprised at her conduct towards him.

Salvador, after saluting his wife with every mark of the highest respect, informed her he was fully determined to follow to the letter the counsel she had given him; he therefore came to request her to authorize him to dispose of a sum of three hundred thousand francs, deposited with her notary, and which belonged to her individually. This sum, he said, was nearly sufficient to free his estates, redeem a portion of his revenue, and pay his most pressing creditors, whom he was determined to satisfy before retiring to the country; for he felt unwilling to leave behind him the reputation of a debtor who has escaped, by flight, the just demands of his creditors.

This susceptibility pleased Lucie, whose noble character understood these delicate annoyances.

"You would not deceive me, I hope?" she said, casting on her husband a look, which the latter sustained with an unmoved countenance.

"Ah! madame," exclaimed Salvador, "could you really believe me capable of such an infamy? But I have no right to complain," he added, after a short silence.

He gave to his voice, whilst pronouncing these words, an intonation so touching, that Lucie was convinced.

She made no reply, but approached a small table upon which was disposed the materials for writing, and rapidly traced the following note and handed it to Salvador.

"M. Chardon,—Be good enough to remit to my husband, M. the Marquis de Pourrieres, all the funds you hold at my disposal, for which this shall be your discharge, &c."

"M. Chardon, who knows you," she said to him, "will hand you, without hesitation, all the funds he has of mine; you will make a good use of them, I feel assured, if you will but remember that it concerns the fortune of your infant."

"Ah! madame," exclaimed Salvador, "if I do not prove myself worthy of the confidence you place in me, I shall be the most miserable of men."

He took the hand of Lucie, which he kissed several times, and descended with her to the breakfast-room.

After breakfast, Salvador announced to Sir Edward, that he must leave for Paris directly. Sir Edward endeavoured to retain him, but the Marquis de Pourrieres, alleging that business of importance required his presence in the capital, he insisted no longer, especially when Salvador observed to him, that his wife had determined to spend the remainder of the season with him and his family.

The carriage which had brought him to Sir Edward's, now carried him to Paris.

His first visit was to Silvia. He found the brilliant marchioness surrounded by a numerous circle of admirers, among whom was conspicuous, by the strangeness of his costume and the profusion of jewellery with which he was decorated, a man, still young, whose complexion—as fair as that of a woman, his large blue eyes, and long hair, of dubious flaxen, was easily recognised as a subject of the northern emperor.

Salvador, who perceived at once that this stranger, who professed himself the most devoted of the crowd which at this time surrounded his mistress, was no other than the person to whom she had alluded, could not restrain some slight indications of ill-humour, to which Silvia, at first, did not condescend to pay the slightest attention; however, after enjoying, with a voluptuousness quite feminine, the trifling vengeance which chance had thrown in her way, Silvia dismissed, one after another, all her admirers, and remained alone with her lover.

"At length!" exclaimed Salvador; "they have done well to leave, I should have burst if they had remained much longer."

Salvador joined to his other defects that of being jealous of the artful creature to whose influence he submitted.

"And why, if you please, should you have burst?" replied Silvia; "you will not, I suppose, contest my right to receive a few visits, to assist me in supporting your absence?"

"But I imagine that this ridiculous Tartar is no other than the stranger of whom you spoke in your letter to me; is it astonishing, therefore, that his presence in your house, at the moment I arrive to tell you that it is at length possible for me to accomplish your wishes, should seem disagreeable to me?"

"You are mad," said Silvia, after favouring Salvador with one of the most winning smiles it is possible to conceive, "you are mad! you must not believe all that women say, or even write. I shall accept with pleasure what you are willing to do for me, for the life I lead here is positively not endurable; but, believe me, I shall exact nothing, if your fortune does not permit you to be generous; were you even poor, I would be as faithful to you and as devoted as I have been until now."

"You are a sorceress—a downright fairy!"

Salvador and Silvia employed this, the first day, in seeking an hotel fit for the residence of the Marchioness de Roselly; those which followed were consumed in providing the mansion fixed upon with every thing necessary to make it agreeable; this cost a heavy outlay, but did not prevent Salvador from devoting nearly the whole of the three hundred thousand francs, which he had received from the notary of his wife, to pay his debts, and the different sums he had borrowed on the domains of the house of de Pourrieres. Our readers have probably surmised that the fruits of fresh depredations, committed in company with the Viscount de Lussan, defrayed the expenses of Silvia's hotel, of her furniture, of her horses, and equipages.

Let us make the reader acquainted with the state of the fortune of which Salvador could dispose, at the time at which we are now arrived.

The property of the house of de Pourrieres, as we have already had occasion to observe, produced, one year with another, somewhat more than thirty thousand francs; the funds belonging to Lucie having served to discharge all the debts, Salvador could dispose of this revenue; there only remained for him to pay ninety thousand francs, the sum equal to the total of the bills of exchange signed in favour of the usurer Justè. His financial position—despite the enormous losses sustained at play by Roman, and the heavy expenses he had incurred—was still sufficiently ample to allow him to lead a life of pleasure, without seeking resources from crime. It was not the same with that of Lucie; the three hundred thousand francs which she had so readily confided to her husband, formed at least the moiety of her fortune; the large property of the Count de Neuville and the Mar-

chioness de Villerbanne, who had both died intestate, having descended to distant and collateral relations.

Salvador, since his marriage, and the last visit he had made at Pourrieres, had not put his foot in the house of Sans Refus; relieved of Roman, he was anxious to cease all relations with the associates of the lowest degree who frequented this infamous den, and by whom he would, sooner or later, be compromised; but he had not on this account, as we have said, abandoned a profession which he exercised with such extraordinary address, that he had arrived at the conviction that he was all but invulnerable; he had come to an understanding with the Viscount de Lussan, whom he easily made comprehend, that two men, expert, resolute, and received with readiness in the best society, could effect as much, if not more, by themselves, than the whole band of thieves put together.

Their success had justified the predictions of Salvador. The two associates had successively robbed a peer of France, who had just taken his seventy-ninth oath of allegiance; a deputy, who had just pronounced a magnificent discourse in favour of the concession of the lines of railway to companies; a rich banker, who was to start the next morning for England; an opera-dancer, who had received the previous evening a first visit from a Russian prince. These "affairs," it is unnecessary to say, had produced as satisfactory results as they could hope for; the peer was a very efficient placeman, the deputy was eloquent, the banker prudent, and the ballet-dancer pretty.

As soon as Salvador had possessed himself of the different vouchers, to prove that he had satisfied his creditors, he set off for Sir Edward's, to show his wife that he had made a good use of the funds committed to his hands.

Sir Edward received him with his usual affability. Lucie, to whom he at once protested that she would be satisfied with him, and that he brought her the proofs that he was amended—since, having a considerable sum at his disposition, he had not entered a house of play—pressed his hand as a sign of contentment; but Servigny and Laura gave him such a chilly, almost frozen reception, that he saw at once that the husband and wife had exchanged confidences, which had not resulted in anything to his advantage.

Salvador, after a long conversation with his wife, returned to Paris, refusing even an invitation to dinner from Sir Edward; who, observing that his presence was agreeable neither to his niece or Servigny, made no great efforts to retain him.

In the evening, whilst Sir Edward and Servigny were playing at billiards, (the worthy squire would much have preferred for an adversary the Marquis de Pourrieres, who made him pay dearly for his victories, whilst he was compelled to give points to his nephew,) Lucie and Laura, seated close to each other in the recess of an open window overlooking the garden, conversed together in an under tone.

Laura had just inquired of her friend, what use her husband had made of the funds she had confided to him?

"An excellent use, thank God!" replied Lucie; "this time, the gloomy presentiments to which your remarks had given birth, have not been realized; he has shown me incontestible evidence that now all his creditors are satisfied. But still, I acknowledge that I have been imprudent; I ought, myself, to protect the fortune of my child."

"Yes, my friend; you ought, indeed, to watch over the fortune of your child. Your husband, I would willingly believe, is somewhat corrected, but you have a right to demand, for the present, every proper guarantee, and this right you must not yet abandon; could he not again be led away by treacherous advisers?"

"Ah! Laura, Laura, why do you still continue to terrify me by the possibility of evils still greater than those I have lately gone through?"

"Because I should wish you fortitude, in case—which may Heaven avert—you may be tried by fresh sufferings; because I would that the moment of danger, if it arrives, found you with sufficient strength to face, without trembling, the depth of the precipice under your feet; because I would, at any price, preserve my friend! Our life, my poor friend, is a vast ocean strewn with shoals, we must expect at every moment to be shipwrecked."

"Laura, you know something which you are unwilling to tell me?"

"I know nothing."

"Has your husband informed you of nothing?"

"Paul does not know M. de Pourrieres, whom he has seen here for the first time."

"Oh! thank you, thank you," exclaimed Lucie, raising her hands to heaven; 'I should have died if what I had suspected had been true!"

We shall leave Lucie to spend tranquilly the remainder of the season, at the seat of Sir Edward, and shall follow Salvador to Paris, where important events are to take place.

As it frequently happens, on the eve of grand catastrophes, fortune seemed to take especial delight in favouring all the enterprises of Salvador and the Viscount de Lussan; so that these individuals rolled in gold and bank-notes.

The viscount, not knowing what to do with his capital, had renewed the furniture and carriages of Coralie, the dancer, whom he had pardoned for her liason with the general, encountered by Silvia at the house of the usurer Justè.

Salvador, malgré the enormous expenses of his house and that of Silvia, had discharged the bills of exchange, given to provide against the last fault of Roman, and paid the remainder of his debts to a few creditors.

He took care to write frequently to Lucie, as he said, to put her in possession of his endeavours to place his affairs in order; and as the information he transmitted her was satisfactory, poor Lucie, who, in the retired life she led, was ignorant of what took place at Paris, by degrees recovered her peace of mind, the most precious of all blessings! Her letters, however, often inquired of Salvador, if he should soon prepare to take her to Pourrieres, for she could not but tremble when she reflected that in a city like Paris, her husband would, at every step he took, find a fresh opportunity of yielding to the fatal passion which had led him to the brink of a precipice; but Salvador only returned evasive replies; when she recalled to him the promise he had given her, he could not, he said, quit Paris at this moment; he wished, before burying himself in privacy, to regain the three hundred thousand francs she had lent him; but this would be sooner than she expected, it only required a little patience.

Salvador devoted to Silvia all the time he could spare from the company of the Viscount de Lussan, being resolved to prevent the Russian prince, who was become excessively enamoured of the ex-cantatrice, the opportunity of being near her.

Silvia knew well how to excite the jealousy of her lover when she wished him to grant her any favour; she threatened him, although without the least intention of realizing her menace, to listen to the Calmuc—thus she denominated the subject of the autocrat of all the Russias—whose immense riches and brilliant qualities she would place in relief before him; and Salvador thought himself happy in obeying her.

Salvador and Silvia, often accompanied by the Viscount de Lussan, went most days, seated in a magnificent equipage belonging to the latter, to the drive in the different alleys of the wood of Boulogne, which are regularly frequented by the Parisian fashionables.

Salvador was vain at being accompanied everywhere by the proud beauty at his side, who excited universal admiration, and Silvia was not the least unwilling to exhibit to the eyes of all, the luxury she was surrounded with.

On one of these occasions she observed to her lover, that the dusty rides of the Bois de Boulogne were becoming monotonous to her, and that she should not be sorry to vary in some manner her daily promenades.

"Why, nothing is easier," said Salvador; "our good city, thank goodness, is surrounded with drives, much more agreeable than the wood of Boulogne, which fashion, I know not why, has taken under its protection; if it is agreeable, we will, to-day, take a turn in the wood of Vincennes."

"Well, let us do so then," replied Silvia; "if I do not find it agreeable, we will visit the others afterwards."

Silvia, Salvador, and the viscount, seated themselves in the calèche, and were driven away. The sky was magnificent, and a number of pedestrians were sauntering through the sombre alleys of the wood.

"This is charming!" said Silvia frequently to her two companions; "this is charming, really! there is, at least, here, both trees and shade; we will come here again."

At the turn of one of the most retired drives, which he entered at the request of his mistress, Silvia's coachman was obliged to pull up, to avoid running over a man who walked quietly before the horses, and seemed buried in deep reflection.

The repeated warnings of the coachman at length aroused the man from his abstraction; he hastily stepped on one side, and his eyes were, by chance, directed to the individuals in the calèche, for which he had made way.

"Silvia!" he muttered, loud enough to be heard by the marchioness and her two companions, "Silvia!"

"Who is he? what does the man want? do you know him?" inquired Salvador in the same breath.

"Drive on," said Silvia to her coachman, before replying to Salvador, "drive on, as swift as possible."

The marchioness had recognised Beppo.

The coachman, anxious to obey his mistress, applied the whip smartly to his horses, and the calèche rolled, as rapid as the lightning, the length of one of the large avenues of the wood.

Salvador and the viscount knew not to what to attribute the evident terror and singular conduct of their companion; she enlightened them in a few words.

Salvador turned his head, and observed, running behind the carriage, the man whom Silvia appeared so strongly to dread; he was about twenty paces distant; his manner sufficiently indicated what was his intention; he wished to follow the carriage, in order to discover the name and residence of those he had encountered.

The viscount had followed the movement of Salvador.

"Why, I know that man," he said to his companion in an under tone.

"Likely enough, parbleu!" replied Salvador; "he is the man we made enter into the house of Sans Refus, after assassinating the marchioness."

"The devil! the devil! this man, who seems a very resolute fellow, must not know who we are."

The carriage continued its rapid advance, but the man who ran behind followed it without any difficulty; he kept always at the same distance.

"The drôle has muscles of iron," said the Viscount de Lussan.

"Will you not rid me of this man?" exclaimed Silvia, giving way to a most violent rage. "Ah! if I possessed as much strength as I do courage!"

"We would willingly do what you so anxiously desire," replied the marquis, "but the place is not propitious, and your coachman is an inconvenient witness.

"There are means. You are expert?" he continued, addressing the coachman.

"Very expert, M. le Marquis," replied the Jehu.

"You know how to use your whip?"

"As well as you do your sword."

"Well! here are five and twenty napoleons for you, on condition that you use it in such a manner as to sicken him of the whim of following our carriage any longer. You know what you have to do?"

"Perfectly, M. the Marquis; you shall soon be convinced of it."

"What the devil does he mean to do?" said the viscount to Salvador.

"Something clever, I am certain," replied the latter; "a whip, in the hands of an English coachman, is a formidable weapon."

The coachman slackened, imperceptibly, the pace of his horses, so that he soon brought Beppo within his reach. The ex-fisherman spoke not a word to those in the carriage, but continued to run by the side of the calèche, regulating his pace by that of the horses, and launching at Silvia glances of undisguised jealousy.

The coachman seized a favourable moment, and expertly whirling round his whip, like a lasso, inflicted on the face of Beppo such a severe cut, that the wheal was traceable by its red and blue streaks.

Beppo, maddened into fury, attempted to throw himself at the head of the horses and seize them by the bits, so as to force them to stop; but the coachman allowed him no time to accomplish his design; he redoubled his blows, the last of which, deprived the unfortunate fisherman of one of his eyes.

Vanquished by the pain, Beppo fell howling to the ground.

"Shall I drive over him?" inquired the coachman.

"No, it is useless," replied Salvador.

The cries of Beppo had brought several of the promenaders round him, and Salvador was impatient to escape the attention, which, from the wounded, would be certain to be transferred to the cause of the wound.

Goaded by the repeated application of the whip, the horses flew with the calèche, which disappeared behind a cloud of dust, at the moment in which those who had at first attended to Beppo, prepared to pursue it.

The latter, who was suffering dreadfully, was at once carried into a neighbouring cabaret, and when the surgeon from Vincennes had applied to the numerous wounds which disfigured his face, the necessary dressings, he found himself strong enough to be taken to his lodgings in the Street Contrescarpe Saint Marcel, which he still occupied with his mother.

"I will be revenged!" he said to himself, as the coach which had taken him to the cabaret, to have his wounds dressed, passed the spot where he had been flogged so unmercifully, in its way to his lodgings. "I will be revenged, and my vengeance shall be complete! I here take a solemn oath of it!"

CHAPTER XLIII.

THE HOUSE OF MOTHER SANS REFUS.

When Beppo was brought home, his poor mother gave way to the most violent grief at the appearance of her son—his face disfigured with frightful wounds, his clothes in disorder, and covered with blood and dust.

"What has happened to you, my dear child," she said to him, in the provincial dialect, for her maternal instinct satisfied her that the piteous condition of her son was the result of some mysterious cause.

"I will tell you, by and by," replied Beppo. "For the present, I have more need of repose than to hold a conversation."

His mother generously rewarded those who had assisted her son to mount the seven stages which led to his apartment, and having helped him into bed, left him alone in his room, and sought her own to weep over her misfortunes.

Attended by a skilful physician, Beppo soon recovered his health, and in less than a fortnight after the event we have narrated, his wounds were completely healed, and he found himself in a state to go out. He had to regret the loss of one eye, which the whip of the English coachman had completely forced from its socket.

He had not informed his mother of his having encountered the Marchioness de Roselly, and that his present condition was the result of that encounter, but placed it to the account of a squabble he had engaged in against his inclination.

"Let us quit Paris," said the worthy woman, "let us return to our happy Provence; I shall not be happy until we once more see our modest dwelling on the sea-shore."

"We will soon go," replied Beppo; "just give me time to terminate some affairs, and your wish shall be satisfied."

The devoted mother, overjoyed at her son's renewing a promise so often made to her, embraced him, and became more tranquil.

One morning, Beppo took the clothes he had purchased at Bonnard's, and which he had only worn on the occasion of visiting Silvia, and after putting them on, requested his mother to obtain a coach for him.

"Where are you going?" inquired the Catalonian, greatly astonished at this unusual toilette; "still to this marchioness, perhaps?"

"No, mother, no," he replied; "I am going to take a step, after which, I hope, we shall prepare to return to Provence."

LIFE IN PARIS.

SLAVIGNY STOPS AT THE ROBBER'S MANSION.

"**You** do not speak very clearly to me, you cruel child, but I believe you; you surely would not deceive your mother—a mother who is doatingly fond of you?"

"Poor woman!" said Beppo, casting a pitying look on his mother, who left the apartment to do as he requested.

" *Tooth for tooth! Eye for eye!*" he said, regarding himself in the glass which hung over the chimney-piece; when his mother entered, to say that the coach was waiting for him in the street.

He embraced the good woman and left.

He ordered the coachman to drive him to the prefecture of police.

Before we introduce our readers to the interview between Beppo and the police, we will fill up the hiatus in the life of the fisherman, from the moment we left him, in the apartment of one of the pensionnaires of Mother Sans Refus, until we find him in the wood of Vincennes, encountering the calèche of Silvia.

We must recollect that it was with difficulty he could support himself when he quitted the chamber of Georgette, so that his first care, on arriving at home, was to seek his bed, where he remained for several days, nearly deprived of feeling, and attended only by his mother, whose attention relaxed not for a moment.

When his condition was somewhat improved, his mother anxiously questioned her son; and Beppo, unwilling to inform her that he had rendered himself guilty of a crime, told her that, at the moment he was leaving the house of Kretz, he had seen the Marchioness of Roselly in a brilliant equipage, still habited in the garments of a man; that enraged at the escape of this woman, without whom he could not live, he had directly thrown himself in the river, so fully determined to end his days, that he had fastened his arms to the waistband of his trowsers; but that the instinct of preservation being stronger than his will, he had with much difficulty gained the shore, by swimming, and making use of his legs only; that he was afterwards taken care of, by some charitable persons who found him—which explained his two days' absence—and that his illness was only attributable to the violent excitement he had undergone, and which he still felt, and perhaps, a little, to the sudden revolution produced in his constitution by the intense cold of the water.

His mother was satisfied with this explanation, unlikely as it was.

Beppo, although a prey to the deepest remorse —for the nature of this man, notwithstanding the two crimes he had committed, was not entirely corrupted—was faithful to the resolution he had taken. As soon as he had recovered the use of his reason, he made no attempt to escape any pursuit he might be the object of. "I will submit to my fate," was his constant assertion, " I have no wish to avoid the punishment I deserve. The eye of God sees every crime, unnoticed by man, and if he allows them to go unpunished in this world, he reserves a more terrible judgment for them in the next; let His will be done! I shall not attempt to struggle against it."

Beppo's illness was a lengthened one; but thanks to the vigour of his constitution, and the affectionate attentions of his mother, he recovered his health, and could at last resume his usual occupations.

He had resolved to forget Silvia, and had sufficient energy not to attempt to ascertain what was become of her; (it will be remembered that he had learned, through Georgette, that the wound he had inflicted was not mortal, and that the surgeon had hopes of saving her.) But this resolution was beyond his power; the gracious features of the Marchioness Roselly troubled him in his dreams, and often (although to chase away the gloomy thoughts which followed him, he worked with ardour at the nets for ladies, which he made for Kretz) they appeared before him, at one time all smiles and good nature, at another, gloomy and forbidding.

Beppo would then throw away his work, and seek diversion in the country; the sight of the trees, the streams, the flowers, the merry chaunt of the birds, mitigated his sufferings, and after a long walk he would return home, not cheerful, but, at least, less miserable than before.

His mother, observing this, when she saw the cloud darkening the features of her son, invited him to take his walk; so that, what was simply undertaken at first as a diversion, became at length his daily custom.

The wood of Vincennes was his most usual selection, it was much less frequented than the other walks in the neighbourhood of Paris, and here he could find what was absent from the others, the shade, and the possibility of communing.

The appearance of Silvia, resplendent with beauty and dress, changed in an instant all his resolutions, and he had followed the carriage in order to know where he might find her when necessary. The loss of an eye, and several wounds, the marks of which he would carry to his grave, was the result of this foolish enterprise.

Beppo left the coach at the entrance of one of the narrow and obscure streets which adjoin the prefecture of police. After threading his way through a number of small streets, he found himself on the Quay de l'Horloge. One of the doors of the place he was seeking was before him. He entered a court enclosed with high walls; on the left, a building of sinister aspect, and windows garnished with strong iron bars, which pronounced it a prison into which the sunshine never penetrated; he followed this court and arrived at another, in which were several individuals, among whom could be remarked a few bearing figures which are commonly seen on the shoulders of spies, gaolers, and porters; he inquired of one of these to whom he must address himself, to make a revelation; the man pointed with his finger to the entrance of an office placed under one of the gloomy vaults. As he directed his steps to this office, he heard several voices repeat; *he's an informer.* He entered and asked to speak to the chief; after a few words he was introduced into a large ill-lighted room, furnished simply with a few benches covered with greasy leather, upon which were seated several individuals of doubtful appearance, a small table surrounded by a desk, before which sat a man somewhat aged. The walls of this room were furnished with shelves, upon which reposed a number of boxes full of cards, upon each of which was written the name of some individual who had had some account to settle with justice.

Beppo was in the ante-room of that mysterious power, named the police, the goddess of a hundred eyes, a hundred arms, who must see all, hear all, foresee all, prevent all; who must at all hours of the day and night enter the vilest dens, penetrate the filthiest slums; who must listen to everything she is told, and must only believe that which is true; who renders services to every one, but of whom every one complains, and to whom, notwithstanding, are accorded but few thanks, when it **conscientiously** acquits itself of a moiety of the task which is confided to it.

After waiting a few minutes, Beppo was introduced into the cabinet of the man who, at the period when the events we have narrated took place, was charged with the direction of this important branch of the Parisian *edilité*.

"You wish to render a service to the administration," he said to the fisherman, "and you promise to put us on the traces of the chiefs of the band of malefactors, who for such a length of time, have plundered the capital and its neighbourhood?"

Beppo replied in the affirmative.

"What is your name, your age, birth-place, profession, and residence?"

Beppo replied to these different questions, and placed in the hands of his interrogator the papers which he had taken care to furnish himself with, and which established beyond any doubt the truth of his replies.

"What is the motive which induces you to act thus?" said the chief of police, after attentively examining the papers.

"Revenge!"

"You have no doubt taken part in the robberies of these bandits, and because you now fancy you have reason to complain of them, you wish to deliver them up."

"You are mistaken. I have committed many faults, possibly, but I am an honest man."

The chief rang the bell, and spoke a few words in a whisper to the man who answered the summons. The latter left directly, and shortly afterwards brought to his superior one of the small boxes placed on the shelves of the ante-room.

The chief in vain searched, in alphabetical order, for a card on which the name of Beppo was inscribed.

"What proof have I, that in case your offer is accepted, you will faithfully serve us?" demanded the officer of police.

"If you cannot trust me, you can put me under surveillance; besides which, I have no interest in deceiving you, since I offer you my services gratuitously. If I succeed I shall be amply recompensed by the satisfaction of rendering an important service to society, whilst pursuing my own revenge."

"Well!" said the chief to himself, after paying considerable attention to the words of Beppo, "this is indeed an informer we do not meet with every day."

"'Tis well!" he continued aloud; "I accept the offers you have made me. If you wish it, should you serve us faithfully, you will be handsomely rewarded, but if your proceeding should be only a snare, look to it, for it will be fatal to yourself alone."

"I have no fears, and the result I hope will convince you that you can put faith in Beppo when he has once passed his word."

"Go then, and may Heaven favour your enterprise; it is right, whatever they say, to place beyond the power of doing injury, those who make it their game to brave every law that regulates society."

Beppo left the cabinet of the head of the police, after giving him a promise to call frequently and render him an account of the result of his progress. At the corner of the street he rejoined the cabriolet which had brought him, and was driven home.

A man habited in a long blue redingote, buttoned up to the chin, the neck imprisoned in a stock of black leather, a hat with large rims which concealed his eyes, and armed with a leaded bludgeon which he frequently hooked to one of the buttons of his redingote, followed every step of Beppo; the latter observed him, but felt not the least alarm; he had no intention of concealing anything from those he wished to serve.

Arrived at home, he quitted the elegant attire he had lately appeared in, and commenced his work as usual after his walks, and continued at it zealously until the moment of dinner, which was prepared by his mother at the customary hour.

"Mother," he said to the Catalonian, at the finish of this modest repast, "of all the proverbs which prevail with us, which is the one a good Catalonian ought never to forget?"

"Why, I do not know," replied the poor woman, who trembled at its remembrance.

"I will bring it to your memory," continued Beppo, at the same time showing his mother the blue seams which furrowed his visage, and the square piece of black silk which hid the bloody hole now tenantless of its eye: "*Tooth for tooth, eye for eye.*"

"You seek vengeance, unhappy boy!" exclaimed his poor mother. "Ah! my son is lost!"

"Yes, I will have revenge," said Beppo in a moody tone, "it is decided upon; those who gave the order to their lackey to treat me like a dog, shall perish like dogs, their blood shed upon the scaffold shall wipe out the cruel injury they have inflicted upon me; but tranquillize yourself, my dear mother, for the present I run no risk, I can march without fear towards the object I wish to attain; let me pursue my plan, do not oppose my constantly coming and going, unless you wish me to determine upon quitting you."

And Beppo, without waiting his mother's reply who, knowing as she did the untameable nature of her son, and terrified at the threat of his leaving her, was not disposed to hazard the slightest objection, took his brown woolly cap and cloak, and left the apartment.

He rapidly descended the Street Saint Jacques, crossed the two bridges which lead to the right bank of the river Seine, and entered the labyrinth formed by the little dirty streets which surround the Hotel de Ville.

The man with the blue redingote and large brimmed hat still walked behind him.

With some trouble Beppo found the house he wished to enter; it was not until he had made the tour of the streets Jean-Pain, Mollet, Vannerie, and several others, that he arrived in the Street la Tannerie, and stopped before the house occupied by Mother Sans Refus.

It was not yet night, one of the odalisques of this infamous harem exhibited her eye through the circular space left clear upon one of the windows covered with whitening, which garnished the sash of the shop.

She looked at Beppo with a most inviting glance. He entered.

Mother Sans Refus was asleep in the old arm-chair placed behind the counter; her lodgers, in different groups, drank, smoked, or played cards; one of them, alone at a table, her head leaning back, was supported by the wall, her mouth half-open.

This was the one Beppo sought, he placed himself near the table, and requested a woman who had quitted her companions as he entered, to bring him two glasses of brandy.

"Two drops of brandy for monsieur; there they are," replied the girl, secretly vexed that it was not herself to whom the stranger, more decently dressed than those who usually frequented the establishment of Mother Sans Refus, had thrown the handkerchief.

She brought the two glasses of brandy, however, and returned directly to her companions.

"Georgette?" said Beppo, gently elbowing the girl, near whom he had seated himself, and whom he thought asleep, "Georgette?"

She only replied by a nasal grunt, similar to that of the animal whose flesh is forbidden to the followers of the alkoran, and the movement occasioned by it having deranged her comb, her long black hair fell in dishevelled order over her neck and shoulders.

The unfortunate girl was dead drunk.

"She is *not at home*, my chicken," said one of the others, laughing outright.

"I will wait till she returns," replied Beppo.

He approached Mother Sans Refus, who was awakened by roars of laughter among her pupils, and placed two five-franc pieces in her hand, after whispering a few words in her ear.

The sound of the money roused the old beldame from the state of torpor in which she seemed plunged; she rose precipitately from her chair, after directing to Beppo a grimace which the latter was at liberty to accept as a smile, and gave directions for Georgette to be conveyed to her chamber.

"You do not mean to rejoin her?" she said, when the order she had given had been complied with.

"I shall remain here a few minutes, if you will allow me," replied the fisherman.

"Most certainly. We shall consider it a great honour."

"You do not recognise me?" said Beppo to Mother Sans Refus, after a short silence.

"When we have met once more, it will make twice," replied the tavernière.

"It will make three times, if you please."

"Impossible, my jewel, I never forget a portrait I have once looked at."

"It appears that this bit of black silk and the seams that meander over my visage, render me unrecognisable; so much the better, my faith, as I can pass the informers and gendarmes without fear."

"Ah! why, who are you then?"

"How! you do not remember a poor devil whom some honest people made enter here, about a twelvemonth ago, at the moment he was about being taken by those who were in pursuit of him, who fell ill, to whom Georgette paid such kind attentions?"

"And who had just murdered *une largue camon-flee en chène*,* on the Exchange bridge?"

Beppo, who was not initiated into the mysteries of the jargon made use of by Mother Sans Refus, was compelled to admit that he did not comprehend her.

"Ah! you don't speak our language; so much the worse, for in that case you will not be able to converse agreeably with the friends. Well then, I told you that the young man who was attended by Georgette at the period you mention, had just killed, on the Pont au Change, a woman disguised as a man."

"It was myself."

"Is it possible? It seems you have made some progress the last year and a half; Georgette has never ceased reminding me that at the moment of assassination, you were an honest man."

Beppo regarded with a smile the hideous Sans Refus.

"I was a fool," he said to her in an under tone.

* A woman disguised as a man.

"Green; say you were rather green!"

"Green, if you like."

"And at present?"

"Ah! at present I am much changed; I quitted Paris after the affair in question, and met in the provinces with some honest people, to whom I was very useful, and through whom I earned a deal of money;" Beppo in concluding these words, struck his pockets and produced a metallic sound which delighted the ears of Sans Refus. "But I was forced to quit these poor people," continued Beppo with a melancholy expression, "they met with trouble!"

"I understand, nabbed."

"You mean?"

"Arrested."

Beppo nodded in the affirmative.

"But how comes it, that you do not *hit the hammer*, that you do not understand the *argot?*"

"How should I, I have only lived as yet with honest country people, but I have a great wish to learn it."

"I do not doubt it, my son, I do not doubt it: but tell me, what do you intend doing in Paris?"

"When my companions were—what do you call that word?"

"*Nabbed.*"

"*Nabbed*, I said to myself, that as my face was not recognisable, in consequence of an event I will narrate to you another time, I could without fear return to Paris, where I might find it easy to make some useful acquaintances; and as I had often thought of your house——"

"You are right, my son, you are right, you should never forget those who have rendered you any service; you will find here, to a certainty, every thing you can desire."

In order to ingratiate himself with Mother Sans Refus, Beppo offered her as well as her pensionnaires a small glass of brandy each, which was readily accepted.

During the long conversation we have recounted, several individuals, already known to us, Charles la belle Cravate, le Grand Louis, Cornet Tape-dur, and many others, had entered the den of Sans Refus, and after exchanging a few words in an under tone with the mistress, and giving a suspicious glance at Beppo, they retired to the room beyond.

"Should you like me to present you to our friends," said Sans Refus, "you will be let off for a few litres of brandy?"

"You will be doing me a favour, and I will cheerfully pay for all," replied Beppo, who began to understand the usual language of the place he was in.

Mother Sans Refus took the hand of Beppo, and led him into the back room we have already described.

"Who is that fellow again," said le Grand Louis, "some spy?"

"Have you finished, miserable?" replied Sans Refus, "'tis I, is it? I, Marie-Madeline-Colette Comtois, who is capable of introducing traitors among you?"

"I suppose we may laugh a bit," continued le Grand Louis.

"You had much better work a little more, and laugh a little less; but it's all the same, you can now drink as much as you like; this cove, who owes you all a flaring candle, will pay for four *doublets* of eau-de-vie."

After this exordium, which disposed the bandits to receive favourably the person she presented to them, Sans Refus recalled to the habitués of her kennel, the event which had brought Beppo amongst them the first time, and narrated to them in a few words, the history fabricated by the fisherman to ensure her confidence.

When the bandits knew that the man before them had been guilty of an assassination, and that he had only come to Paris because the band with whom he had *exploited* the country, had been dispersed, they pressed round him, each was jealous to shake him by the hand; and the four litres of brandy being brought in by Sans Refus and Cornet-tape-dur, who had preserved at the tavern his functions of Master Jacques, enthusiasm soon attained its summit, and Beppo was proclaimed, with one voice, a member of the association which assembled at the rendezvous of Marie Madeline Colette Comtois, called Sans Refus.

The night was far advanced when he quitted his new made friends to rejoin Georgette; the noxious fumes which, a few hours before, had obscured the brains of the miserable girl, had left her, so that she had considerably improved her appearance in order to receive him. The ex-fisherman placed his candlestick on the chimney-piece, took from his pocket a cigar, lit it, and seated himself in an old arm-chair, placed at the head of the bed in which was Georgette. This rather strange conduct, greatly astonished the girl, but she dared not say any thing.

Beppo, to make himself recognised, was obliged to recal to Georgette the circumstances which had accompanied the first interview he had held with her.

"And so," said Georgette (when she was quite convinced that the man before her was really the same she attended upon eighteen months since,) "you are compelled to-day to seek a refuge in this house? It does not surprise me, when you have made one step in the path of crime, you must follow it to the end."

"Do you think so?" inquired Beppo.

"Alas!" added Georgette, "I am myself an evident proof of the truth of what I say."

"You deceive yourself, perhaps; on the contrary I believe it is never too late to return, and 'tis as much to furnish you with the means of emerging from the frightful position in which you are placed, as to accomplish a design I will communicate to you if you will promise not to betray me, that I am come here."

Beppo spoke the truth; at the moment he entered the house, he remembered the woman who had lavished upon him such attention, both affectionate and disinterested, and he had at once determined to wrest her, if that were possible, from the ignominious life she was leading.

Georgette, as we know, felt a lively interest in Beppo; she made, therefore, every promise he required, she even offered to serve him.

In order to put her willingness to the test, Beppo charged her to watch all that took place in the house of Sans Refus, during his absence, and to render him an account of it; "he wished," he said, "to ascertain what his new comrades thought of him."

"It is useless to attempt to deceive me," replied Georgette, "I guess what your motive is, you wish to deliver over to the police all who frequent this house?"

Beppo now regretted that he had spoken with so little prudence, as to allow the girl to divine his project, but Georgette did not leave him long in uncertainty.

"If such, in fact, is your intention," she continued, her eyes sparkling with excitement, "oh! I will aid you with all my powers. I shall be rejoiced to repay these men, whom I have been obliged to submit to, a little of the evil they have done me."

There was, in the voice of Georgette, as she pronounced these words, such an accent of truth, that Beppo was convinced that from this moment he could rely upon her as a devoted auxiliary.

It is time we should inform our readers how it came to pass that Beppo sought, at the house of Mother Sans Refus, for the means of revenging himself upon the two men who were in the calèche of the Marchioness Roselly, at the moment he had been so frightfully disfigured.

It may not be forgotten, perhaps, that Salvador accompanied Silvia, when Beppo, who had established himself with the restaurateur Graziana, that he might intercept her carriage, had succeded in discovering her former residence. At the time of his encounter in the wood of Vincennes, he at once recognised this man, whose physiognomy, besides, was so remarkable as to remain engraven on a memory less faithful than Beppo's.

Carried to his lodgings, after this event, he remained, as we have observed, for more than a fortnight nailed to his bed, and a prey to sufferings so intense that he could not obtain an hour's sleep. Whilst this want of rest continued, the image of one of the two men who accompanied the marchioness in the Bois de Vincennes was constantly before him; his imagination represented it to him, not such as he had seen him in the calèche of the ex-cantatrice, pimping, frisèd, spurred, musked, and decorated, but habited in a costume, and speaking a language, which indicated the habits of men not of the best society. Beppo in vain tried to banish this image, it reappeared without cessation, with the same shape and the same colours. His memory, at length, made a grand effort, and a light broke upon his spirit; he remembered that the two cavaliers who accompanied Silvia were no other than two of the men who had made him enter a den at the moment he was about to be seized by the crowd which pursued him, and whose features he had been enabled to observe before his senses left him.

From this to the conclusion, that these two men were the chiefs of the band of depredators, who, as Georgette had informed him, assembled at the house of Sans Refus, did not require any great stretch of probability.

The project of Beppo, when he offered his services to the police, was this:—

He had judged, that, to acquire the confidence of the bandits, he had only to remind them of the crime he had committed, and the services they had rendered him; and, as he supposed that many of these bandits, if not all, knew who were their chiefs, he hoped that one of them would shortly make them known to him. The ruin of two men, to whom Beppo, excited by jealousy and the thirst for vengeance, had sworn an equal hatred, (he was ignorant which of the two was Silvia's lover, and he attributed to both an equal share in his late misadventure,) would follow the revelations which would not fail to be made by such of the bandits as might be previously arrested

Such was the plan conceived by the ex-fisherman, communicated by him to the chief of police, and approved by the latter. This plan might only succeed in part. Chance, a greater master than all human foresight, was to furnish Beppo with the means of attaining the object he had in view.

However, he conducted his bark with so much

prudence and address, that, a few days after his introduction among the daily attendants at Mother Sans Refus's, he became the oracle of all the scelerats among whom he lived. These wretches put him into the secret of every crime they meditated, and, oftener than once, proposed to him to take a part in such of their perilous expeditions as would turn out the most profitable; but Beppo managed to refuse without arousing their suspicions. He told them he should not commence *working*, (he now used their slang as fluently as the smartest among them,) until he had spent all his money—that he wished, before risking his neck, to enjoy a few of the pleasures of a Parisian life. The bandits looked upon this desire as the more natural, as, for some time past, they had not been fortunate in their enterprises. Many of them had been arrested in *flagrante delicto*, and at the very moment they fancied themselves completely out of danger.

We need hardly observe that it was to the information forwarded by Beppo (powerfully supported by Georgette, who served him with unflinching fidelity) to the police, that they were indebted for their arrest.

"You are quite right in not desiring to have a finger in the pie," said, one day, le Grand Louis to the ex-fisherman; "we are unfortunate at present."

"In fact, I begin to think the trade is not worth continuing."

"Don't talk to me about it; the most brilliant affairs slide from under our very hands. And this is not all. Our best comrades are constantly being *taken at work*. I am sure there's a traitor amongst us."

"We must silence him."

"If we knew him, it would be already done," exclaimed le Grand Louis, grinding his teeth; "but the brigand won't come and say to us, 'Tis I who get you all arrested.'"

"Who knows? strange things sometimes happen."

"There, shut up, do; the spies, agents of police, informers, traitors, are all cowards."

Beppo was at this moment alone with le Grand Louis, for the conversation above narrated took place in the small court of the house of Sans Refus, (we will presently state the motive for which le Grand Louis had brought Beppo into this place.) He felt much inclined to prove to the bandit, at this moment, that he was deceived, and that it was quite possible to be both an agent of police and also courageous, but he restrained himself.

"Business went on much better when le Grand Richard, Rupin, and the Provençal attended here; they were men; but we complained of them, because they kept the greatest part in all the affairs they procured us. 'Twas just, however; but we are never content; 'tis only when we have lost what we had in our hands, that we regret it."

This was not the first time that Beppo had heard pronounced the names of Grand Richard, of Rupin, and of the Provençal, and something told him that two of these names belonged to the men he sought to be revenged on. He was unwilling, however, from a fear of rousing the suspicions of his companions, to speak to them of these two men; and Georgette, to whom, as well as the rest of her pensionnaires, Mother Sans Refus allowed nothing to be known that might compromise her, had been unable to discover any thing. The Grand Louis, therefore, had now furnished him with an opportunity which he was determined should not escape him.

"But, as these men were so useful to you," he

replied to le Grand Louis, "why do you not go and beg them to return among you? you would be enabled to remedy your wrongs, if you have any."

"It is much easier to say than to do; not one amongst us knows where to find the Rupins."

"Bah!"

"'Tis as I tell you. Oh! they are cunning as foxes; they look upon us as their slaves; but still they enabled us to do a good day's work."

What le Grand Louis had told Beppo, proved to him beyond a doubt, that the two individuals he wished to destroy, had ceased to be in relation with the habitués of the house of Sans Refus, and that, consequently, it would be very difficult to attain the object he had in view; for it was not sufficient for him to say to those he served, that these men were the accomplices of those whose arrest he had already procured; it was necessary for him to prove it; but he did not despair of succeeding.

"Listen," said le Grand Louis to him, after some minutes' silence. "You are a brave fellow, are you not?"

"I do not fancy I have given you any right to think otherwise of me."

"Well, if you like, you, Charles la belle Cravate, and myself, will manage a splendid affair, and which will pay us well, without running the slightest risk."

"What is it?"

"Listen. The mother is a rich *fence*; there is enough here to make a magnificent booty. Well, I have thought to myself that it would be like holy bread, if we could ease her of a part of her *auber*."*

"No doubt; but how arrange it? Sans Refus is constantly on her guard."

"I have considered every thing."

Le Grand Louis approached the trough, placed at the extremity of the small court, and, aided by Beppo, he displaced it, after explaining to his companion the use of the cave, the existence of which was revealed to him. He told him that he and Charles la belle Cravate, furnished with the requisite instruments, would conceal themselves the next day but one, as soon as it was night, (le Grand Louis retarded, by two days, the execution of his project, being aware that on that day there would be brought to Mother Sans Refus a large quantity of stolen plate and jewels, which he was anxious to secure along with the rest;) and that, when the other habitués of the house had retired, he, Beppo, who could remain in the house without exciting the suspicions of Sans Refus, since he was in the habit of passing most nights in the company of Georgette, could come and assist them to get out, after fastening the women in their rooms. The three being then masters of the house, it would be an easy matter to put a heavy hand on the gold and jewels of Mother Sans Refus, who, finding herself caught in a trap, would not dream of opposing the least resistance, and would esteem herself very fortunate, if they made her a present of her life.

Beppo could not refuse taking part in an expedition, the success of which appeared certain; he, therefore, accepted the proposition made to him by Louis le Grand.

After quitting the bandit, who then left, in order to apprise Charles la belle Cravate, Beppo ascended to Georgette's room. He requested the girl, in whom he was much interested, and whose devotion he wished to recompense, to dress herself and **wait**

* Money.

for him at his lodgings, where he promised to join her in two or three days.

The girl was already accustomed to comply with his slightest command, without making a single observation; she obeyed, therefore.

As soon as Georgette had left, Beppo quitted the house of Sans Refus, and entered a cabriolet on the Quay de Gévres, and was driven to the domicile of the chief of police.

" 'Tis very well," said the latter to him. " I am satisfied with you. The measures you indicate shall be taken, and if they succeed, as I doubt not, we shall take, with one sweep of the net, all that remain of the band. But the chiefs! the chiefs! this Grand Richard, this Rupin, this Provençal, who roll, as you say, their equipages about Paris, these are the ones we must lay hold of."

" I will discover them, depend upon it," replied Beppo; " I will discover them, or lose my reputation."

" I hope so; but I fear it will be difficult, if fortune does not favour you. Oh! they are cunning blades; those we have already wish for nothing better than to make revelations; but they do not know what you have already informed us of."

" Let us first take all the soldiers, we will then have a turn at the officers. I promise you, that when once I have hit upon their track, it will not be long before they tumble into our nets."

Beppo could, without fear, make such a promise, for he was persuaded that when once he had procured the new address of the Marchioness of Roselly, which would not be very difficult, it would be easy to discover those of the two individuals, he had sworn to destroy.

In the course of the next night, whilst the hour of one sounded from the clock of the Hotel de Ville, the street of la Tannerie, for some time past gloomy and silent, was suddenly invaded by several detachments of police agents, town serjeants, and municipal guards. Sentinels, to whom they had recommended the greatest vigilance, were placed at every egress, without exception, of the house of Sans Refus. These precautions taken, a man, whose tricoloured scarf denoted him as a commissary of police, approached the door, and, after knocking loud enough to awaken every sleeper in the street, he articulated these words, which those who have not a very clear conscience never hear pronounced without a certain trembling:

" In the name of the law, open!"

The house of Sans Refus remained sombre and silent. It was not until after a second summons, accompanied, this time, with a threat of breaking open the door, that the bolts were heard to creak.

The door was opened, Mother Sans Refus, in her night attire, holding in her hand a *brass* candlestick surmounted by a *tin* shade, appeared on the threshold.

" Is it possible!" exclaimed the old sinner, "awaking in this manner honest people out of their first nap; you ought, however, to be well aware, considering the many times you have favoured us with your nightly visits, that the house of Colette Comtois is not a suspected place."

" Take charge of this woman," said the commissary of police; and, without deigning to reply to the tavern-keeper, he crossed the shop and entered the back room, followed by his *under graduates.*

Two municipal guards alone remained in the street.

" Well, mother," said the agent in charge of her, " you had no expectation of this? Netted at last! 'tis rather hard."

At the sound of this voice, which was not unknown to her, Sans Refus hastily seized the candle she had placed on her counter, and brought the light to the visage of the agent of police.

" How, is it you, Fanfan la Grenouille; you are in the *shop*, then, now?"

" What can you expect? we must do something to earn a poor living; I am only sorry that you should be the first person I am forced to tie."

" Listen, Fanfan; before you can gain ten thousand francs, you must put more than one *pègre* in the shade."

" That's true."

" Well, just let me walk, and I'll pay them down on the nail in good bank-notes."

" You're joking."

" Look at them."

Sans Refus drew from her bosom a small packet of bank-notes, which she placed in the hands of the police agent.

" Well?" she said.

The temptation was too strong. Fanfan la Grenouille put the bank-notes in his pocket, after having counted and well examined them.

" 'Tis a bargain," he replied.

Sans Refus threw over her shoulders an old pelisse, resting by chance on her arm-chair. Fanfan la Grenouille quietly opened the shop-door, before which strutted the two municipal guards; but, to obtain permission to leave with Sans Refus, he had only to show them the triangular card, ornamented by an eye surrounded with rays—a distinctive mark of his functions.

Fanfan and Sans Refus ran for some way together; but, when they supposed themselves at a sufficient distance from la Tannerie Street to be out of danger, they stopped to take breath, and separated, after mutually exchanging wishes for all sorts of prosperity.

Whilst this was passing, the commissary of police, followed by his troop, had entered the back room, in which, as he had expected, he found no one; he crossed it, and, arriving at the small court, ordered two of his men to displace the trough.

" Come out!" he cried, when the opening of the cave was visible to every one. " Ascend! unless you wish to be smoked like hams."

The bandits who had taken refuge in this retreat, until then impenetrable, the moment they heard the first summons at the door, were taken in a trap, all resistance was in vain, they had nothing to do but resign themselves. As sheepish as so many foxes snared by a troop of chickens, they scrambled one after another up the straight ladder. As each arrived in the little court, he was bound, and handed over to a strong detachment of municipal guards, who were stationed in the narrow street des Tenturiers.

" Robert, Cadet Vincent, le Grand Louis, Cornettape-dur, Charles la belle Cravate," said the commissary of police, when the agent he had sent to examine the cave reported there was no one left in it; " the capture is not a bad one. Who is that one?" he added, pointing out Beppo to one of his agents.

" That one," exclaimed le Grand Louis, who was not yet bound, " that one is a traitor, I am sure of it."

And, quick as lightning, he threw himself on the ex-fisherman, and dealt him, between the shoulders, a heavy blow with his sword-knife.

Beppo fell to the ground; the blood burst in

THE INTRODUCTION INTO THE BEDROOM.

largo gushes from the deep wound inflicted by Louis le Grand.

"Bravo! Grand Louis, bravo!" cried all the bandits. "Death to the traitors!"

A few cuffs with the ends of the muskets imposed silence on these miserables.

The commissary of police had Beppo conveyed to one of the bed-rooms, and sent an agent to procure a surgeon.

It was not until after this event that they discovered the flight of Fanfan la Grenouille and Mother Sans Refus. Despite the absence of the receiver of stolen goods, a minute search was made into every corner of the house, which resulted in the discovery of a large quantity of stolen articles, which were seized to serve as evidence to convict.

The pensionnaires of Sans Refus, whose conduct the police wished to examine at their leisure, were directed to the hostelry which the administration keeps constantly open for all who resemble them— 117, in the street of the Faubourg Saint Denis; and there only remained in the house of the street la Tannerie, Beppo and two agents, charged with his safe custody and also to attend to his wants.

The surgeon sent for by the commissary of police certified that his wound, although not dangerous, would prevent him, for the present, from being removed.

CHAPTER XLIV.

THE CONCIERGERIE.

THE exterior appearance of the conciergerie, the prison of the department of the Seine, is nearly similar to most others, and consists of high walls, formed of enormous hewn stones, to which time has given a mouldy and sombre cast; small windows, defended by strong iron bars; doors, low and arched, garnished with all sorts of iron-work, and secured by heavy bolts and massive locks.

The principal entry, opening into a small court, in which are placed the ignoble vehicles, to which they have given the name of *salad baskets*,* is defended by an oaken door bound with iron, and a strong grating. Between this door and the grating is a sentinel constantly in attendance, who permits no entrance of visitors, until he has attentively examined the permission of which they must be the bearers, and which they deposit at the register, and again receive it on leaving. In spite of these minute precautions, of the imperious necessity of which there can be no doubt, prisoners sometimes contrive to elude them and obtain their liberty. No one has forgotten the extraordinary escape of M. de la Valette, who, thanks to the noble devotion of his courageous wife, succeeded in quitting his cell on the very eve of the day fixed for his execution.

After descending a dozen steps, we enter a vast octagonal room, arched and vaulted, and of prodigious height, in which remain the keepers whose services are not required in the interior of the building.

Notwithstanding the excellent fire which these gentlemen keep up, in all seasons, in an enormous stove, (the sole piece of furniture, besides the few oaken benches upon which are seated the privileged

prisoners, who have obtained the unique favour of conversing freely with their relations and friends in the vast room,) a penetrating cold, like a heavy mantle of ice, settles on the back of the visitor, the moment he puts his foot in this spacious hall.

Out of this leads a long and dismal corridor, the sinister aspect of which is sufficient to create a disagreeable impression upon such as are the least susceptible of those vague terrors with which we are sometimes seized without being enabled to account for the cause.

This corridor, (as well as many other parts of the conciergerie,) constructed nearly fifteen feet below the ground, leads to an intermediate wicket; on the right, another corridor, rather better lighted than the former, conducts to the large yard of the men; on the left, an iron gate bars the entrance to the women's quarter.

The surveillance of this portion is confided to the ladies Painparé and Yvose; and it would be desirable, if every person occupied in similar employments, understood as well the duties they imposed.

For the rest, the very numerous *personel* of the conciergerie is as satisfactory as the arrangement of a prison can be, and this is not astonishing; it feels the influence, it models itself after the man who is placed at its head. M. the director of the conciergerie, joins to every amiable quality of a man of the world, a kindness of heart, appreciated by all who know him, and done justice to by those even against whom he is sometimes obliged to be severe.

The women's court forms a long square, in the middle of which is a parterre, cultivated with much care, and enlivened with shrubs and flowers. These unfortunate plants, despite the continual attention of which they are the object, allow their blossoms to fall negligently over their stems. It would seem to be from regret alone that they thus resolve to blossom in this vast pandemonium of every misery and every crime—that they regret the cheerful rays of their warm sun, which only arrive in patches, and broken by the elevated buildings which surround the conciergerie on all sides.

To the left of this court is a room in which the prisoners work, under the continual inspection of a guardian; then, a gloomy vaulted piece, forming an arcade, under which they can promenade in rainy weather; damp and melancholy cells, but which are not inhabited, except when the prison is full, have their so-called windows under these arcades.

On the right, at the bottom of the court, is situated the chapel, which offers nothing very remarkable to our notice, before which, however, one cannot pass without feeling a very strong emotion, for remembrances of the most unpleasant nature attach to it. The sacristy of this chapel formerly served as the bed-chamber of the unfortunate Marie Antoinette. It was afterwards inhabited by the widow of General Beauharnais; but the latter was more fortunate than her predecessor; she quitted her prison to espouse the great captain who seated her on the first throne in the world.

Near the chapel is the bathing-room; this piece, which forms a part of the last apartment granted to the unfortunate queen of France by the blood-hounds of 1793, served her as well for an ante-chamber as a dining-room.

The first stage of the building looking into the women's yard, which is ascended by a stone staircase, lighted simply by the pale and flickering light

---

* The first carriage that received this name was made at Lyons, to conduct to Paris a notorious burglar named *Josas*. This carriage, as well as those constructed upon the same model, was of osier, from which resulted the name of *panier à salade*.

of a smoky lamp, and which seems to have been cut from the rock, comprises, on the right, several rooms destined for the privileged prisoners. These rooms are tolerably commodious; some of them have been decorated by their hosts with much taste. One of them has been tenanted by Prince Louis Napoleon. On the left are the dormitories for the community of martyrs. These rooms, furnished, some with three, others with four beds, are constantly kept in a state of propriety; the bedding is composed of a palliasse of common straw, a good mattress, pillow, two warm and good blankets, and linen sheets of good quality, changed every month. This bedding is the same throughout all the houses of correction of the department of the Seine, the prefecture of police excepted, in which it cannot be obtained, unless at exorbitant prices. It is said that the prisoners of the department of the Seine are indebted to the Duchesse de Berri for this amelioration in their condition, and which is refused to such of the other prisons of the department whose tenants have not the means of purchasing it.

The day is fine; the dormitories have just been opened; the women detained at the conciergerie are all assembled in the court we have attempted to describe; some old, and almost infirm, are seated on a wooden bench which they have placed in front of the covered way under which they take their exercise when the weather is bad; they are willing to profit by a few rays of the sun, which is now visiting their prison; others, a little more active, are slowly enjoying their walk, consoling themselves with a few pinches of snuff—that consolation to the prisoner, which our modern philanthropists, enthusiastic promoters of systems borrowed from the English and Americans, would suppress, with what motive we are ignorant; others, still young, some pretty, are playing at what it is agreed upon to call "innocent games," such as hot cockles, blindman's buff, reading romances, working, or enjoying the pleasures of conversation. Were it not for the motley description of costumes, nearly all sordid and even in rags, the wan and earthy features upon which vice has set its degraded seal, we might fancy ourselves in the play-ground of some school, when the youthful pupils give way, under the steady guidance of their guardians, to the pleasures and distractions which suit their age; for, as we have observed, the largest portion of the prisoners are young, and many join to youth an irreproachable or a gracious gentleness; but, to continue this fancy, we must stop our ears, that we may not listen to the words that leave the mouths of these women, who have all of them, young and old, to reproach themselves with some crime.

We say crimes designedly; our readers are probably aware that the conciergerie is the *ante-room* of the court of assize alone; the houses of correction appertaining to the police offices are situated elsewhere.

We shall give no specimen of the discourse of these unfortunate women; equally unpleasant pictures have passed before our readers; and we can say, without hesitation, that we cannot determine to write any thing which might deprive the sex of a single flower of the garland with which, whether grand dame or grisette, we choose to adorn her. And moreover, have we the right of crying as loud as we do against crimes which nearly always may be attributed to ourselves?—against vices with which the poor feeble creatures who compose a moiety of the human race, would not be afflicted, if we accorded to them the disinterested protection to which they are entitled, and if our social organi-

zation did not compel the child of the poor man to prostitute herself for a living—if, in fact, many among us were not insensibly habituated to regard as things set apart, from the beginning, to serve our pleasures, and which may be destroyed without remorse when wearied of, those among whom we count our mothers and our sisters.

The stentorian voice of the keeper, placed as guard at the intermediate wicket, comes suddenly to interrupt the conversation and the games of the prisoners assembled in the court-yard of the conciergerie:

"Adelaide Moulin, for examination!"

At the sound of this name, a woman decently attired, whom illness, more than age, had rendered feeble and sickly, rose from the bench on which she was seated, and advanced with difficulty, by supporting herself against the wall, towards the outlet of the yard which leads directly to the intermediate wicket.

One of her young companions of misfortune, moved at the efforts she was obliged to make, ran to her and supported her till she had left the yard.

Youth is generally commiserating.

The gate-keeper delivered Adelaide Moulin to a gendarme, who made her traverse the many underground passages which unite together the conciergerie, the prefecture of police, and the Palace of Justice, to conduct her to the ante-room of a judge of instruction.

Another gendarme had taken, at the same moment, from one of the *mousetraps* of the Palace of Justice, a young man, hardly twenty years of age, whom he had brought into the room in which the female Adelaide Moulin had been conducted.

This young man, endowed with an interesting physiognomy and features, with a remarkable expression of mildness, was extremely pale; his thick black hair, still handsome, though neglected, the brown circle which surrounded his eyes, of a similar colour to his hair, his emaciated limbs and discoloured lips, betokened a victim of that excessive misery of large cities, which claims the children of the poor at their exit from the cradle, and retains possession of them till they descend to the grave.

This young man and Adelaide Moulin were placed by chance on the same bench next to each other.

The woman, whom misery and illness had considerably worn, and who endeavoured to guess the questions about to be addressed to her by the magistrate, that she might prepare replies of a nature to make her appear less culpable than she was, did not at first remark her young companion in misfortune, but her attention was at last attracted by a short dry cough which escaped from the chest of the young man, and which was followed by a slight spitting of blood.

"You are suffering," she said to him.

"Ah! it's nothing," replied the young man; "a slight irritation of the chest; I am subject to it."

The weather was damp, and the young man, clothed simply in the woollen garment allowed to necessitous prisoners by the administrative generosity, trembled in every limb.

"You are cold?" added the old woman.

"Indeed," replied the young man, "my clothing is rather slight for the present weather, and the chamber in which I passed more than three hours before being brought here, is spacious and damp; but what can I do? We may as well endure patiently what we cannot prevent; and, besides, I am used to every suffering."

A fresh fit of coughing prevented his saying more.

The efforts he had made to repress the cough had slightly coloured his pale cheeks; this transitory blush produced on his features a novel expression. The old woman, who, for some moments, had been attentively examining him, uttered a deep exclamation.

"I am not deceived," she said, "'tis surely him! Ah! God be thanked, that he has furn'shed me to-day with an opportunity of repairing the wrong I once committed."

"What is the matter, madame?" inquired the young man in his turn, to whom the faded physiognomy of his neighbour confusedly recalled that of a person whom he had formerly well known.

"Your name is Fortunè, is it not?" continued the old woman.

"Yes, madame."

"You were brought up at Geneva?"

"'Tis true; but why these questions?"

"How, you do not recognise me?"

"Yes! yes!" exclaimed the young man, who had, at length, collected his ideas, "you are Madame Moulin, 'tis you that took care of my youth, you are my aunt."

The poor youth, who knew not the just reproaches he had the right of addressing to the woman Adelaide Moulin, allowed her no time to reply, but took her in his arms and kept her some time pressed to his bosom.

We must now inform our readers what happened to Fortunè, from the moment when, although his innocence had been recognised by a solemn judgment, he was repulsed by every one, he quitted Geneva, almost naked, and dying of hunger, until that wherein we find him in the ante-room of the judge of instruction, or magistrate.

Once outside the town, he took the first route that lay in his way. He walked for nearly a quarter of an hour, and the buildings of the city in which he had passed his young life, and which he quitted to wander he knew not where, were disappearing from the horizon, when he encountered a troop of mountebanks, whose turn-out was so comical, that, despite the profound gloominess to which he was a prey, he could not withhold from laughing.

This procession of ambulating artistes was composed of a carriage, or rather a small cart, covered with a cloth, whose texture was so worn that it resembled a net stretched over the two halves of a hoop. On each side of the species of vault formed by this old covering, a rival of Davignon* had written these words in black and red letters, at least a foot long: "*The incomparable Riberprè and his family, premier rope-dancers to the sovereigns of the four quarters of the world, known and unknown.*"

This cart, in which were seated M. de Riberprè, his wife, his two youthful daughters, and the whole troop he directed, consisting of sixteen actors and actresses, was drawn by a Jerusalem pony, a modest and patient animal, but so slender, so bald, so old especially, that he might well be a cotemporary of that of Balaam. He had as auxiliaries a mastiff and a Danish dog, who, like the coursers of Hyppolytus, jogged on with closed eyes and drooping heads.

M. de Riberprè, his family, and troop, who had been giving some representations at Geneva, were returning to France, where they hoped to gather an ample harvest of laurels and penny-pieces.

Fortunè mechanically followed, for nearly an hour, this grotesque cortège, when M. de Riberprè

* A celebrated *letter* painter.

descended from his vehicle, which he had drawn up on the extremity of a fine level, skirted with old and branching trees; he presented his hand to his gracious wife and his two daughters; the male and female artistes who composed his troop had no need of the assistance of any one, to follow the movement, they leaped quietly to the ground, and after modestly scattering themselves, returned and seated themselves in a circle round their director, who, after giving to the donkey and his two companions their daily allowance, served them with an humble repast, which appetite, that seasoning which gave a flavour to the black sauce of the Lacedemonians, made them swallow as delicious.

This duty accomplished, and leaving his troop to wander at liberty over the plain, M. de Riberprè, his wife and two daughters, seated themselves on a small hillock; Madame de Riberprè spread an old cloth on the green turf, and one of the damsels drew from a bag some provisions and two bottles, which was to serve as breakfast for the family.

Fortunè, whose stomach, since the previous evening, had been sorely tried, very much resembled at this moment a penniless gastronome; his eyes followed the morsels, and as he watched them disappear, a sigh escaped his bosom involuntarily.

M. de Riberprè at length observed the poor devil, whose ragged attire and piteous mien sufficiently indicated his state of complete indigence.

He ordered one of his damsels to go and invite him to partake of the family meal.

The young girl advanced towards poor Fortunè, not with a timid and mincing step, but boldly and majestically.

This gracious creature was, as well as her sister, dressed in a robe of apricot silk, trimmed and ornamented with red galloon, and *crowned* with a turban of green gauze.

"Will you," she said, "breakfast with us? 'Tis with a free heart we make you the offer; if it does not displease you, accept it without making any ceremony."

Fortunè, after thanking the young girl, placed himself near Madame Riberprè who gave him an enormous piece of bread, upon which she had spread a sort of hash, which he found delicious. A few nuts and two glasses of wine completed the repast, after which he found himself a little less sad than he was while fasting.

M. de Riberprè was a man about fifty years of age; but his diminutive figure made him appear stouter than he really was, for his height did not exceed four feet six inches. His hair and moustaches, blacker than ebony, shone like a polished boot, every colour in the rainbow had a representative in his features; but their expression, notwithstanding, was not disagreeable, for it denoted one of those frank and merry creatures who live from hand to mouth, and say to themselves, when a day of misfortune arrives, "*A hundred crowns of tears do not pay six francs of debt.*" He was attired in a green coat with large skirts, a waistcoat and breeches of scarlet cloth, covered with stains of different colours; his stockings, once white, were ornamented with yellow clocks; his shoes had large buckles; he had no other head-gear than a counsellor's wig, hung up for the moment to one of the pegs of the cart.

The physiognomy and costume of his worthy spouse was neither less original nor less grand. If M. de Riberprè, short and thick, resembled a leather bottle, Madame de Riberprè, in revenge, resembled the handle of a broom. The hair of this lady was the brightest red imaginable; her skin, *perhaps*, had once been of a dazzling whiteness, but at this time, the numerous gray spots with which it was interspersed gave it a tint very similar to coffee and milk, which annoyed the worthy Madame de Riberprè; for the rest, every turn of her physiognomy, as well as those of her body, were sharp and angular; her head-dress was an old hat à la Henri Quatre, surmounted by two feathers, one white, the other red, and she was habited in a robe of sky-blue, ornamented by well-silvered galloon.

We shall say nothing of the two damsels whose costume we have already described, except that they were as pretty as young ladies could be, who passed nearly all their life on the high road, whether fine weather or foul, and were totally ignorant of the use of *l'huile antique*, cold cream, la bandoline, almond paste, and all the other cosmetics of which the fashionable Parisians make so prodigious a consumption.

When Fortunè had appeased his appetite, he recounted his sad history to M. de Riberprè.

The worthy rope-dancer listened to him with much attention, and the whole family shed tears at the recital of his misfortunes.

"And what do you think of doing at present?" he said to the poor devil, after giving an inquiring look at his wife and two daughters, who nodded affirmatively.

"I really do not know," replied Fortunè; "I hope to find work at some farm."

"Listen, my young friend; you are, I suppose, an honest and industrious youth, and I am sure you are as unfortunate as 'tis possible to be. Since you know not where to sup or where to sleep to-night, why, remain with us; you shall be my controller, my director of the scenes, and register general of my troop; you shall announce the exhibition, &c., &c., as for the rest, what is enough for twenty-three is enough for twenty-four."

M. de Riberprè, we find, did not resemble the majority of theatrical directors; he did not separate his own interest from that of his artistes; he placed upon the same footing his wife, his two daughters, the donkey, and the two mastiffs which drew his cart, and the sixteen learned dogs which composed the *personel* of his troop.

Fortunè knew better than to refuse so advantageous a proposition; he replied that he felt excessively flattered at the confidence about to be placed in him, and that M. the director might reckon upon his zeal and endeavours to serve him.

"Very well, young man," said the worthy director, with much majesty, "very well; you are, from this moment, one of the members of my numerous family; when we have good cheer, you will partake of it, and when we are obliged to dance before the cupboard, which sometimes happens to us, we must not be down-hearted, for a good storm generally makes way for sunshine."

In concluding these words, M. de Riberprè took from his little waggon, a long bottle, incased in a chemise of osier twigs.

"We will empty this old pilot," he continued, "to celebrate your admission amongst us."

He gave the bottle a most paternal embrace, and then handed it to his wife, who followed his example; it went the circuit and at length arrived at Fortunè, but almost empty.

The brandy it contained having put the convives in good humour, the father, the mother, and the two girls sang together the following refrain from one of Beranger's prettiest songs:—

" Les gueux, les gueux,
Sont des gents heureux,
Ils s'aiment entre eux;
Vivent les gueux!" *

Fortunè, whose gaiety had returned since his excellent repast and the few mouthfuls of eau de vie, joined in the chorus.

After a few minutes devoted to mirth, M. de Riberprè, after observing to his family that it was time to be en route, if they intended to reach before night the place at which they intended to rest, each rose, and, at a signal from the director, the scattered performers returned from the prairie, and jumping into the waggon, one after another, the cortège put itself in motion.

Fortunè remained sometime with M. de Riberprè, who treated him as one of the family.

The young man acquitted himself with credit in his functions of controller, scene director, and registrar general. He bestowed on the artistes who composed the troop such affectionate care that they all gave him proofs of their attachment.

The family of M. de Riberprè visited Dauphine and nearly every town in the south of France; it had even remained several days at Pourrieres, to give some representations at the chateau, inhabited at the very moment by Salvador and Roman, (the unhappy son of Alexis de Pourrieres was far from supposing that it was before the door of the dwelling of his ancestors that he followed the profession of a mountebank,) and were preparing to quit Provençe to enter Lyons, when death, which spares no one, suddenly carried off its worthy chief. Madame Riberprè, who, although ugly, old, and original, was an excellent woman, and was strongly attached to the man with whom she had wandered about for so many years, was taken ill, and died at the hospital of Montelimart.

Deprived of their guides, Fortunè and the two young girls were compelled to separate; the cart, the old donkey, and the two mastiffs were disposed of, for ten crowns, to a peasant of Provençe; and, after fraternally dividing this little sum, and giving the male and female artistes the liberty of seeking a new engagement, the three friends, who had found employment, separated after mutual wishes for prosperity.

Malaga, the eldest and prettiest of the two girls, and the one who had shown towards Fortunè the most lively friendship, engaged herself in the quality of tight-rope dancer in the troop of the Bonthers, travelling emulators of the brothers Franconi.

An old dealer in Agnus Dei and holy images, took charge of Brigantine, the youngest.

Fortunè, less fortunate than his two companions, was forced to enter the service of the proprietor of a menagerie of wild beasts.

This man had taken the character of the beasts he exhibited for money; he was, besides, bigger than most of his brethren in that profession; brutal, because he knew himself endowed with a prodigious physical strength. When drunk, and that was daily, he struck indifferently his beasts and his servants; and he used the same instrument in the correction of both, an iron rod somewhat thicker than the little finger, and terminating in a point.

Fortunè, who, notwithstanding his adventurous life and the rags he had on, had preserved a figure and exterior above the common cast, particularly displeased this man—perceiving, no doubt, by his

* " Beggars, beggars,
Are happy fellows,
They love each other;
Long live the beggars!"

vulgar instinct, that his valet belonged to a station superior to his own. He therefore eagerly seized upon every occasion to ill-treat him; he paid him no wages, and only gave him sufficient nourishment to prevent his starving.

Thus ill-treated every day, and compelled, almost, to dispute his meagre pittance with lions, tigers, and boa constrictors, he remained for nearly a year in the service of the proprietor of the menagerie; but, wearied at length of suffering, he signified to his master that he intended to leave him, and demanded his wages.

There was due to him rather more than sixty francs, and he had resolved that the moment he touched this small sum, he would procure a costume better suited to his mind, and visit Paris, and hoped he might find, in so vast a city, the means of employing his abilities and industry.

His master, by way of reply to these demands, seized the iron rod and struck him so furious a blow between the shoulders that he sent him rolling to a distance.

When the cup is too full, it runs over; the best tempered dog, if too long tormented, turns and seizes his persecutor. It is the same with certain men gifted with unchangeable mildness; for a certain time they may be made the victims of every imaginable injury with impunity, but a moment will necessarily arrive, when, tired of suffering unjustly, they revolt, and then woe betide their persecutors, their rage will be dangerous.

Fortunè, quick as lightning, regained his feet; he took a large knife which was used to carve the viands intended for the wild beasts, he then seized his master by the throat, and held to his breast the unsightly weapon he had in his hand.

"Pay me," he said in a voice struggling with rage, "pay me instantly, unless you wish me to run this knife into your heart."

The black eyes of the youth flashed like sparks of fire, and his countenance was as pale as a corpse.

The exhibitor of wild beasts was as cowardly as he was cruel; he trembled in every limb; and did not even attempt to escape from the furious grasp of his young domestic.

"I will pay you, my boy," he stammered at length, "I will pay you."

"Instantly, instantly; I will wait no longer."

The proprietor took fourteen five-franc pieces, which he handed to Fortunè.

"Is that your demand?" he said.

"I do not require any more of you," said the youth. He put the five-franc pieces in his pocket, and hastily left the show-yard in which this scene had passed.

A fortnight after quitting the showman, Fortunè, who had procured at Lyons a proper costume, entered Paris by the Barrier d'Italie, rich in the possession of three five-franc pieces, and full of hopes.

He lodged himself in the most humbly furnished hotel in the quarter Saint Marcel, and, after devoting one day to repose, (he had journeyed on foot a distance of nearly two hundred leagues,) he commenced seeking for employment.

This was, to make use of a popular expression, looking for a needle in a bundle of hay. Who would employ a young man, whose slight limbs gave no indication of strength, who knew nothing, or almost nothing, and had no one to recommend him? It was, therefore, in vain that the poor boy went from door to door, offering to give the whole of his time in exchange for the most humble salary; he had been repulsed at Geneva, because he was not known.

Fortunè observed, with despair, the evident diminution of his small store; what was he to do when nothing remained? Should he thieve? should he solicit charity? Both these alternatives inspired him with equal disgust.

One of the lodgers in the miserable hotel in which he lived, to whom he had made known his sad position, advised him to become a soldier; Fortunè started to find out the recruiting captain of the Seine.

M. Gibassier was obliged to refuse him; the surgeon considered him much too weak in constitution, and, in addition, he was not furnished with the necessary papers; but the good-natured officer, touched at his extreme misery and destitution, gave him a five-franc piece.

"There are some good souls on earth," thought Fortunè, after receiving this charity, which arrived very apropos, (he had spent his last sou the previous evening;) "let us not lose courage; the Almighty has determined that I shall not die of hunger."

He again commenced his search after occupation.

A cutler agreed to employ him three days a week, at the rate of two francs a day, to turn the wheel of his grinding machine. He remanied for nearly six months with the cutler, who for want of work, was at length obliged to dismiss him.

Fortunè, during the six months which had expired, had acquired a certain experience. His patron had informed him, that, in a city like Paris, an intelligent man, who is content with a little, might find a thousand honest means of gaining his living: pick up in the streets the old corks, and sell them to the makers of the small oil lamps; follow the *lions* in their walks, and collect the cigars they throw away but half consumed, to make *cigarettes* which are sold to *lions* of an inferior order; open the coach-doors at the entrance of theatres and balls; place, in rainy weather, a plank across the gutters; wash and comb dogs; sell lucifer matches; copy books at two sous a piece; small trading, the profits of which are certainly not considerable, but which give a livelihood to those who exercise them.

Fortunè, no doubt, would have determined to adopt one or other of these industries, if a few days after his leaving the cutler, he had not fallen ill.

The proprietor of the boarding-house in which he lodged had him conveyed to the Hotel Dieu.

His illness continued some time, but at length he recovered, and, one cold and gloomy morning in autumn, he was dismissed from the hospital. The physician who, on the previous evening, had signed his discharge note, had recommended him to clothe himself warmly, during his convalescence, to drink a little Bordeaux wine, and to eat wholesome and nourishing food. Fortunè had, in fact, much need of all this; the thousand privations he had supported so long had so weakened him, that in order to walk, he found it necessary to lean for assistance against the walls.

He consumed more than two hours in clearing the short distance which separates the Hotel Dieu from the modest hotel he inhabited before his entrance into the hospital. He imagined, simple boy, that his landlord would not refuse to receive him; he was deceived.

"Your room is let, my boy," replied the host, after patiently listening to his humble supplication, "and there is not one left at this moment of which I could dispose. Go, my friend, go, and may God bless you."

Fortunè left more dead than alive. After walking for some time at random, faint with want and fatigue, he sank on the pavement.

Some city serjeants who passed, directed him to be conducted to the nearest guard-house.

The soldiers divided their meagre pittance with him, and covered him with the night cloak of the sentinel.

The next morning, Fortunè was taken before the commissary of police, to whom he recounted his history.

The commissary listened patiently to him, and the result of what he heard proving that the poor wretch exercised habitually neither trade nor profession, that he had neither a home nor the means of paying for one, nor any certain resources of existence; and that, consequently, section 270 of the penal code, viz., " Vagabonds, or persons without confession, are those who have neither a certain residence, nor the means of subsistence, and who do not exercise habitually either trade or profession," might be applied to him, he directed two soldiers to conduct him to the prefecture of police.   He was for two hours in this prison, confounded with the infamous band of the habitués of the depôt, when he encountered the female Adelaide Moulin in the ante-chamber of a magistrate. We have seen how he embraced her and pressed her to his bosom.

"You are not angry with me, then?" she said to him.

"Eh! and why should I be angry with you? You only abandoned me because you were forced to quit Geneva to avoid being sent to prison; and perhaps you were not more guilty than I was, when they imprisoned me for the first time—than I am now, even."

Fortunè then recounted to the female all that had happened to him, from the moment he was received by Father Hubert, of whom he could not speak without shedding tears, until the present time.

"Poor child!" said the old woman, after listening to him, " you have suffered much, and I was the original cause of all your misfortunes.   But I will endeavour to repair the injury I have done you, and I shall succeed, I hope; it will not be in vain that God has permitted us to meet."

A gendarme, who came to seek Fortunè to carry him before the magistrate, interrupted this conversation.

"Take this," said the woman, putting two double-franc pieces into his hand, " get some good soup, a little wine, take care of yourself, and hope."

"Adieu, adieu, my kind aunt," replied Fortunè, who did not comprehend much of the discourse of Adelaide Moulin; " alas! perhaps I shall not be allowed to see you again."

"Hope," repeated Adelaide.

Fortunè was obliged to follow the gendarme into the sombre passage which leads to the cabinets of Messieurs the Judges of Instruction.

Shortly after, another gendarme came for Adelaide, who was also conducted into the cabinet of a magistrate.

CHAPTER XLV.

A CORNER OF THE VEIL IS DRAWN ASIDE.

SALVADOR had just finished his toilette, and was leaving his house to visit Silvia, when his valet de chambre brought him a letter which had been delivered to the porter of the hotel, who was re-

quested to deliver it immediately to M. the Marquis de Pourrieres.

As the letter was impressed with the seal of one of the magistrates of the Seine, Salvador quickly opened it, and read as follows:

" My Lord Marquis,—Will you take the trouble to call immediately at my cabinet; I have a communication to make you, which, I think, will overwhelm you with joy.

"I have the honour," &c.

"This," said Salvador, after reading it, " does not seem to be an order to appear; I think I might, without compromising myself, accept the invitation of this estimable judge; the communication will fill me with joy, perhaps.   I cannot understand it—if it should turn out to be a trap?——'tis not probable; and, after all, there must be an end."

Salvador rang.

"The carriage!" he said to the valet who presented himself.

"The horses are harnessed," replied the domestic.

Salvador descended, and ordered the English coachman, whom he had taken into his service since his adventure in the wood of Vincennes, to drive him to the Palace of Justice.

He was immediately introduced into the cabinet of the magistrate who had written to him; this functionary rose upon his entrance and offered him a chair.

"Decidedly," said Salvador to himself, after replying as he ought to the civility of the magistrate, " decidedly I have nothing to fear."

In the office, besides the judge and Salvador, there was an old woman, seated on an humble straw chair, and a tall robust gendarme in charge of her.

"Do you know this gentleman?" said the judge to the old woman, when Salvador was seated.

"I have never seen him," replied the female, " I cannot, therefore, have the honour of knowing him."

The judge, evidently, did not expect this reply which seemed to occasion him much astonishment.

"And you, sir," he said to Salvador, " do you know this woman?"

Salvador attentively regarded the old woman, who seemed as much surprised as the judge himself.

"I have never seen her," he replied.

" 'Tis singular," said the judge, rubbing his forehead.   " Monsieur is the Marquis Alexis de Pourrieres," he continued, addressing the woman.

Adelaide Moulin rose from her chair with such precipitation, that the gendarme, thinking, no doubt, she intended to escape, placed himself before the door.

She approached Salvador, whom she examined with much attention.

"This gentleman is not the Marquis Alexis de Pourrieres," she said, when her examination had finished.   " There is, between the features of monsieur and those of the Marquis Alexis de Pourrieres, some little similarity, which might deceive at first sight; but that is all; monsieur is stouter and more strongly built, his eyes are blue, those of the marquis are black."

These concluding words of Adelaide Moulin caused a slight pallor on Salvador's countenance, which the judge might have remarked.   Salvador, who considered the position in which he found himself much more perilous than it really was, wished to attribute it to rage.

"What means this ridiculous comedy?" he exclaimed, addressing the judge, " and what has this woman to do with me?   I neither know her, nor have I any wish to know her."

LIFE IN PARIS

AN IMPORTANT INTERVIEW.

"Calm yourself, M. le Marquis," replied the magistrate, "calm yourself, I beg of you. I will explain to you what has taken place. Will you favour me with replies to a few questions I shall have the honour of addressing to you?"

"I am ready to obey you."

"You confided to a female, named Adelaide Moulin, of Geneva, to be brought up and educated, a natural son, recognised by you, and whom you had by the female *Jazetta Louiset*, born at Marseilles, and the daughter of a master of arms of that city?"

Salvador had heard quite sufficient to comprehend that the old woman, who had refused to recognise him, was no other than the female Moulin, of Geneva, and that it was because they had discovered the young Fortunè, that the magistrate had sent for him; the terms of the letter he had written him left him no doubt on this head.

"Ah! if I had known," he thought to himself, "I would directly have recognised this woman; I would have pressed to my bosom the young Fortunè, who waits, no doubt, in an adjoining room, the moment to enter on the scene, and all would have been right; but I have advanced too far to recede.

"It is true, sir," he said to the judge, "when I returned to France, after long travels, I learned that the woman in whom I had placed my confidence had shown herself unworthy of it—that she had not given to my son the education he ought to have received—that, contrary to my orders, she had kept him in ignorance of the name he would one day bear—and that, at length, being forced to quit Geneva, to avoid the just pursuit of the magistrate, she had abandoned my unfortunate son. I learned what I now inform you of from the municipal magistrate of Geneva. You are aware, probably, of the rest—how my son, having been unjustly accused of the murder of a benevolent man who had taken care of his youth, was compelled to quit Geneva."

The judge made an affirmative sign.

"I have not ceased," continued Salvador, "my efforts to discover the trace of my unhappy son. One of my friends was lately at Geneva, and I begged him to take further measures, and this is his reply."

Salvador had, fortunately, about him one of the letters which Servigny wrote to him from Geneva; it was the one in which he informed him that Fortunè, on his leaving Geneva, had joined the troop of mountebanks and learned dogs of M. de Riberprè; he handed it to the magistrate, who perused it with much attention.

"'Tis singular," said the worthy man. "If we were to place any reliance on the words of this female, I should believe that the young man who, from what she has said to him, pretends to be your son, is so in reality; for they both appear to be perfectly instructed in the particulars which concern the female Moulin, of Geneva, and the young Fortunè."

"Monsieur is not the Marquis Alexis de Pourrieres," repeated the woman.

"Hold your tongue, woman," exclaimed the judge. "Do not add to your injuries by maintaining such an absurdity. Recollect that a severe punishment——"

"Monsieur! monsieur!" continued Adelaide, "do not condemn me without a hearing. The whole of this is clouded in a mystery, which you will be enabled to dispel with the aid of Providence. There is a letter of the Marquis de Pourrieres, which I have preserved by chance; 'tis already the commencement of proof."

The judge took the letter, and, after reading it, placed it in the hands of Salvador.

"'Tis, in fact, myself who wrote that letter," said the latter.

"Well, sir," exclaimed Adelaide Moulin, "write a few lines and submit them to the magistrate; he will see whether I am imposing upon him in maintaining that you are not the Marquis Alexis de Pourrieres."

Salvador, without waiting for an order from the judge, took a pen and paper, and transcribed the first few lines and the signature of the letter they had shown him.

There was between the writing and signature of the two pieces such an identity, that those who knew not that Salvador was, as we have already observed, a most skilful forger, and that he had applied himself to counterfeit the writing of Alexis de Pourrieres, would undoubtedly suppose them to be traced by the same hand.

"Take back this woman," said the judge to the gendarme, after examining the copy.

"Sir," said the unfortunate woman, "you have not done all that is yet necessary; I know that in this affair it does not concern me alone, but the future life of a young man who has already suffered much."

"Very well, madame, very well," replied the judge. "I know what my duties are."

Adelaide Moulin, forced to follow her conductor, quitted the office, and left Salvador and the judge alone.

"What has just taken place astonishes me to the last degree, what can be the motive of this woman in endeavouring to pass for a person whose name by a singular chance is similar to her own."

"That of extorting a recompense by passing off an impostor as the son I have never ceased to regret."

"Undeceive yourself, Monsieur le Marquis, the young man, I am sure, is no impostor. I have questioned him; all his replies have an expression of truth."

"Ah, sir! if the hopes your words inspire are realized, I shall be the happiest of men."

"They will be realized, Monsieur le Marquis, something tells me that you have found the son you regret so deeply."

"Neglect nothing, sir, spare neither trouble or expense, if money is necessary."

"Be easy, Monsieur le Marquis, I am aware of the task imposed upon me, and I shall know how to prove myself worthy of it; I shall write to Geneva; I shall even, if necessary, summon to Paris persons who are acquainted with the young Fortunè, and the female Adelaide Moulin, and I am persuaded that the result of the investigation which I shall undertake, will be what we both so much desire: you can then, with certainty, press in your arms the son whom, until to-day, you have supposed lost for ever; and the woman you have seen, and whose conduct I confess is to me inexplicable, shall be either justified or exposed."

"I trust sincerely your expectations may not be deceived."

"They will be fulfilled, Sir Marquis, they will be fulfilled; do not doubt it."

"As this is the case, sir, allow me to deposit in your hands this trifling sum;" Salvador took from his note-case a note for five hundred francs, which he placed on the desk of the magistrate. "I request that the young man of whom you speak, and who is probably my son, may want for nothing."

"Your desire is too natural not to be granted; I shall give the necessary directions."

"It will be rendering me an important service; but you have not told me what was the fault for which the unhappy boy was detained in prison; has he rendered himself unworthy the name he will, to all appearance, succeed to."

"Be under no alarm, my lord, this young man, whoever he is, is quite worthy of belonging to you."

"Oh! you give me new life. I confess I was fearful I might have to regret finding the son I have so long deplored as lost."

After exchanging a few more words with the magistrate, Salvador left his office. His carriage waited for him at the entrance of the grand staircase of the palace.

The coachman was absent; he had transferred the care of the horses to the chasseur, so that Salvador was compelled to wait for him some minutes. He saw him come hastily out of a cabaret in the place of the Palace of Justice, opposite the staircase which leads to the chamber of the Pas-Perdus, or fatal step.

"What means this!" he said to the coachman, who seemed to have swallowed the contents of more than one bottle; "you have obliged me to wait for you."

"Do not scold me, Monsieur le Marquis," replied the coachman, in a tone which implied that he felt sure of himself, "I have just rendered you a famous service unawares."

"Oh! that's true, added the chasseur," anxious to come in aid of his comrade, whom he had, no doubt, upon different occasions, replaced at the cabaret.

"Very well, sirs," said Salvador, whom this little event, after what had just transpired, greatly annoyed, "you will give me an explanation of your conduct when we arrive at the hotel."

We shall state what took place in the court of the Palace of Justice, during the time that Salvador was engaged in the cabinet of the magistrate.

The English coachman had dismounted from his seat, and was walking with his comrade, the chasseur, near the carriage, when he was accosted by a man, decently dressed, whose right eye was concealed under a shade of black silk; this man seized him by the arm, and the pressure was so strong, that the coachman, although a sturdy one, did not coincide with this somewhat cavalier mode of accosting people; he plainly perceived that he had to do with a galliard who was quite his match.

"You do not recognise me?" said the man to coachee.

"I do not know you," replied the automaton of the Marquis de Pourrieres.

He told a lie. He had perfectly recognised the man who accosted him, for it was the one whom, a few months before, and to obtain a premium of twenty-five louis, he had deprived of an eye by the use of his whip.

"It's possible," said Beppo, "you will, however, follow me to a commissary of police."

The wound of Beppo, whom we left under the charge of two police agents in the house of Mother Sans Refus, after the escape of this woman, and the arrest of the bandits who frequented this den, being found much less dangerous than was at first supposed, he was enabled, in a few days, to be transferred to an hospital, not wishing to be taken home on his mother's account; he had written to the devoted woman that he had commenced a journey which would detain him from Paris for some months; he recommended her, at the same time, to take the greatest care of Georgette, in whom he felt a very great interest.

The good woman felt a greater willingness to comply with his wishes relative to this girl, as her goodness of heart naturally drew her to acts of benevolence; but she also supposed (though wrongly) that her son felt towards the girl an attachment that would drive from him that inspired by the Marchioness de Roselly.

Through the skill of the physicians at the hospital, he recovered in less time than he expected. The knife of the Grand Louis had glided over the dorsal spine, and had only inflicted a deep stab in one of the two shoulder blades.

When he had recovered his health, he was conducted before his patron, to whom he thought proper to complain of the sort of arrest he had been obliged to submit to. The latter observed, that it was for his interest, and that he might not be taken for what he was, that they had acted as they had done; and inquired whether, considering what had passed, he still preserved the hope of placing in the hands of justice, the chiefs of the band of malefactors, which, through him, they had been enabled to arrest. Beppo replied, that he would accomplish the task he had undertaken, and his patron, after bestowing upon him the praises which zeal and devotedness merited, and offering a recompense, which he declined, allowed him to depart.

His first step, after his liberation, was to visit his mother; the good woman, from the letter he had written her, had not suffered much during his absence, which had not been as long as he had announced; she lavished the most tender caresses upon him, and presented to him Georgette, of whom Beppo, to her great astonishment, had not spoken.

Two months had not elapsed since this girl had quitted the infected atmosphere in which she had till then lived, and yet she was no longer the same whom we formerly looked upon, stupified with brandy, in the tapis franc of the Street la Tannerie.

She was simply, but properly dressed; her handsome black hair arranged with neatness; her eyes, no longer surrounded with the black circle, certain index of a depraved life, had lost some of their hardy expression; her cheeks, formerly pale, began to freshen.

Beppo embraced her on the forehead.

"I thank you," he said in a low tone, "for all the services you have rendered me, and especially for having been discreet. 'Tis all well," he continued, elevating his voice, "'tis well, I am satisfied with you, remain always with my mother, my dear Georgette; you are young, futurity has in reserve for you, I hope, some happy days; and if I die before her," turning to his mother, "which after all is possible, you will console her, will you not?"

"What an idea!" exclaimed the Catalonian; "you die? you do not think so, you are young, you are strong."

Georgette, who guessed what were the ideas passing in the mind of Beppo at this moment, said nothing. It was with some difficulty she restrained the tears which filled her eyes.

"We must be prepared for all, my poor mother," replied Beppo, "for singular events happen in this world."

"Beppo! my dear child! you conceal something from me; you have not yet made me acquainted with the reasons for absenting yourself so often."

"Do not be alarmed, mother," said Beppo, after passing his hand across his forehead, "do not alarm yourself I shall soon, I hope, have accomplished the duty I have undertaken, and we will then return to Provençe; I cannot at present say more, avoid questioning me therefore; for to save myself the pain of replying to your questions, I shall feel myself compelled to remain away until I am disposed to tell you all."

"Alas! my God!" exclaimed the poor woman, raising her two hands towards heaven, "protect my unhappy child, if he still merits your divine mercy."

"Ah! you can pray for me, mother, my object is a right and honest one."

"You are not deceiving me."

"No, mother, no. I give you my assurance."

"If so, my son, let God's will be done, come here as often as possible, I promise never to question you."

Beppo again embraced his mother and Georgette, whom he left, after promising to pay them another visit soon. It was on leaving his house that he encountered the coachman of Salvador, whom he resolved to conduct before a commissary of police.

"Come," said Beppo, "leave your comrade to take care of the carriage, and follow me quietly; you ought to be convinced that I am strong enough to force you, if you do not obey me."

The miserable wight began to tremble in every limb at hearing this menace; he knew that once in the hands of justice, his master would abandon him, if the crime he had committed was proved, and he could not help admitting he deserved a rigorous punishment.

"Come," he replied, for he was determined to get out of the scrape somehow or other, "come, let us see if there are no means of arranging the matter; you seem to me an honest young fellow, you do not wish the death of a sinner; let us enter a wine shop, we will talk it over, and if we do not come to terms, why, I'll follow you wherever you like."

"Just so," thought Beppo, "I have no malice against this poor devil, who has only obeyed the orders of his master."

He then entered the cabaret, from which we have seen coachee make his exit.

He had no other object than to learn the name of the person to whom the coachman belonged who had so roughly treated him, and who was no other, he felt persuaded, than one of the three men, whom he had so often heard mentioned at Sans Refus's, under the names of the Grand Richard, Rupin, and the Provençal. It may be said that Beppo, who knew Silvia's name, might easily have discovered her residence, and consequently, that of the individuals of whom he wished to be revenged. To this just observation we shall reply, that the residence of Silvia, newly installed at Paris, being neither known at the post nor elsewhere, every effort made by Beppo, until the present moment, had been in vain. He might, no doubt, by calling in the assistance of the harpies of the police, which would readily have been placed at his disposition, have certainly attained his object; but this was precisely what he wished to avoid, and it is unnecessary to say for what reasons.

"What have you to say to me?" he asked of the coachman when they were both installed in a private box, with a bottle of wine between them, which had been ordered by the latter. The coachman was a cunning and cautious blade, who sur-

mised at once that it was not simply to prevent a man running after his carriage that his master had ordered him to get rid of Beppo at any price, and at the risk of what might happen.

"Listen," he said to Beppo, "I may as well, since we are alone, admit to you that it was I who inflicted, unintentionally, the wound which deprived you of an eye."

"Whether you admit it or not, matters little to me! I took care to secure the address of persons who were by chance witnesses of the event, and these persons, I am certain, will recognise you."

"It's very possible; but that is not the concern at present; you may well suppose it was not of my own accord that I treated you so roughly. If I had been the master, you may have ran behind the carriage till you were tired of the pastime; but it was not so, I only struck you to obey the orders of my master, and, between ourselves, to earn twenty-five napoleons, which he handsomely counted down to me when we reached the hotel."

"Miserable!" exclaimed Beppo, disgusted at so much impudence.

"Why! my faith, I was not so guilty as you imagine," replied the coachman, "we servants of great houses must do as our masters bid, if we wish to keep our places.

"You ought to know, if there are any, the reasons which induced my master to act as he has done; and in any case, I think it will be more advantageous to address yourself to him than to me; see him, demand from him a sum proportioned to the injury he has caused; he will not refuse it you, for I am certain he will not be very anxious to see this affair come before the tribunals, to whom, in order to disculpate myself, I shall be forced to tell the whole truth."

"Do you really think your master is in a condition to give me a good sum? Is he rich?"

"Is he rich! do you say? Why, he rolls in silver and gold."

"Ah! ah!"

"Believe me, follow the advice I give you, you will find it good. If by chance you are not satisfied with him, you can afterwards do what you wish to do at present."

"But supposing I let you go, how shall I be able to find you another time; you may quit the service of your master, even France."

This objection, which he might have expected, however, somewhat embarrassed the coachman, he could find nothing but entreaties to help him.

"Do not ruin me," he said to Beppo, "I am certain, I tell you, that you will have nothing to complain of in the generosity of my master; come, let me go, and I will hand you the five hundred francs I have received."

"Listen," replied Beppo, "I will set you at liberty and your money with you, if you promise to answer faithfully the questions I am about to put to you."

The coachman, as we may suppose, gave the necessary promise.

"What is the name of your master?" demanded Beppo.

"De Pourrieres," replied the coachman, and to prove that he was speaking the truth, he exhibited his book.

"Where does he reside?"

"Rue de Courcelle, Faubourg Saint-Honoré."

"Who were the persons with him in the carriage the day of the accident?"

"Madame the Marchioness de Roselly, and M. the Viscount de Lussan."

"Where does the marchioness reside?"

"Allée des Veuves, Champs-Elysées."

"And the Viscount de Lussan?"

"Rue de Varennes."

Beppo had obtained nearly all the information he desired.

"I shall not retain you," he said to the coachman, "but remember, if what I require is not accorded me, I shall know where to find you again."

"I do not doubt it," he replied, "but I have no fear, M. the Marquis is extremely rich, and very generous."

Beppo should have recommended the coachman, who would probably have obeyed him, not to mention to his master either their meeting, or what had passed between them; but he did not take this precaution; (we do not think of every thing;) this negligence, added to some other circumstances, one of which is already known to the reader, delayed the success of his project.

CHAPTER XLVI.

THE FLIGHT.

The carriage of Salvador rolled rapidly along the grand avenue of the Champs-Elysées, and to follow it only at a distance, the driver of a hired cab was forced to apply the lash vigorously to his Rozinante, although a good one, which he the more skilfully performed, desirous as he was of earning the reward promised by the individual seated within.

It is almost useless to say that the cab had been hired by Beppo, who had determined to make sure that the information he had acquired was true.

Salvador, stretched on the voluptuous cushions of his calèche, was smoking a cigar, the smoke from which ascended in blue and curling wreaths over the head of the carriage.

"My edifice trembles at its base," he muttered to himself, "it would perhaps be wise to place between myself and those who seem determined to occupy themselves about my affairs, a distance somewhat difficult to be cleared."

The calèche stopped before an elegant mansion in the Allée des Veuves. Beppo, now satisfied that the coachman had not deceived him, directed the driver to conduct him to the prefecture of police.

The whole house of Silvia (where Salvador was driven, that he might forget for a few moments the vexation he had experienced during his visit to the magistrate,) was upside down; the porter had abandoned his lodge, the other domestics were running here and there, like persons bereft of their senses.

"Oh! sir," said a femme de chambre to Salvador, when she saw him enter the hall, "what a frightful misfortune! Madame la Marquise——"

"What has happened to the marchioness then?" exclaimed Salvador.

"Enter, M. le Marquis," replied the girl, "madame will be very glad to see you; she has already sent twice to your hotel."

The girl preceded Salvador, who entered the chamber of Silvia.

The Marchioness of Roselly was stretched upon a long chair, her dress was in disorder, her hair, eyebrows, and lids were burned; the fire had traced on her face, her neck, and her arms deep and bloody furrows. When Salvador entered, a surgeon was occupied in applying bandages upon the numerous wounds.

"I have courage, sir," said Silvia to him in a short bluff tone; "I have courage, I tell you! answer me then with candour; is it not true that I shall remain horribly disfigured?"

"My utmost hope is to be enabled to prevent you losing your sight," replied the surgeon; "the marks of the cruel event of which you are the victim, will remain engraven on your features."

"Malediction!" exclaimed Silvia, who rose from her chair, malgré the efforts of the surgeon, and approached the mirror. "Malediction! no hair, no eyebrows, the face covered with abominable cicatrices; ah! I am horrible."

"What has happened then?" said Salvador to the surgeon.

"One of those events unfortunately too frequent," replied the latter; "Madame la Marquise, who had sealed a letter, left the taper she had used close to her, the windows were open, the wind blew near the candle one of the strings of the bonnet-de-tulle she had on, it caught fire, the flame spread, the marchioness lost her senses; you can surmise the rest. She would probably have lost her life, if her attendants, hearing her cries, had not come to her assistance."

Silvia, who in her trouble had not observed Salvador, had again seated herself in the long chair; she remained for some moments motionless, and only roused herself from this state of torpor to inquire if Salvador had arrived.

"I am here, Madame la Marquise," said Salvador.

"Why did you not say so?" exclaimed Silvia in a stifled voice, and which announced that a violent rage was smouldering in her bosom.

"Retire all of you, leave me alone with monsieur," she said, after a short silence.

The domestics and the surgeon hastened to obey the order. The latter left the apartment shrugging his shoulders; this woman, who found in her heart, at the moment of becoming the victim of a terrible misfortune, nothing but curses, inspired in him not the slightest commiseration.

"Well!" said Silvia, when she found herself alone with Salvador.

"This event is indeed a very great misfortune, but be sure it will not in any way change the sentiments you have inspired in me."

"I do not believe you, you would not drag after you every where a woman horribly disfigured, you only loved me because I was handsome."

"Grief renders you unjust, my dear Silvia, but I think the time is badly chosen to commence a quarrel; pressing affairs call me home, I will return to you when you are a little more tranquil."

"You would already be far from me, is it not so? Go, M. le Marquis, go, I will not detain you longer; when I wish to see you, I shall find the means of bringing you."

"Listen to me, Silvia, I am tired to death of never hearing you open your mouth, unless to utter a threat."

"Which I will perform, rely upon it, if you give me an occasion of complaining of you; I have nothing to lose now."

"I repeat to you, the moment is not wisely chosen for a quarrel; I leave you, therefore ; in a few days you will have less suffering, I hope, and it is probable you will be more reasonable; if you wish to see me, you can send for me."

Salvador waited not for the reply, but left her apartment.

"Behold," he said to himself when installed in his calèche, "a concurrence of disastrous circumstances, and this droll, who has, as he pretends, rendered me an important service. What can this be again?"

The calèche had arrived under the triumphal arch de l'Etoile; Salvador ordered his coachman to stop. "Dismount," he said to him, "and give me an explanation of what you told me in the court of the Palais de Justice, and especially be brief."

The coachman hastened to obey, he approached the door, and recounted to his master what had passed between him and Beppo.

"'Tis well," replied Salvador, after listening to him with much attention, "you have done well to promise this droll to pay him for his eye more than it's worth. I should not have believed," he said to himself, when the coachman had remounted his seat, "that this man would have been content with a trifle of money. I should think he had not recognised us."

After a few turns in the grand alley of the Champs-Elysées, he entered his house.

"Madame la Marquise has arrived from the country," said his valet de chambre, who had come to assist him out of the carriage, "and she begs monsieur to take the earliest opportunity of passing to her room."

"My dear wife arrives very malàpropos," thought Salvador; and preoccupied at all that had lately happened to him, he put into his pocket, without reading it, a letter, which his valet de chambre had delivered to him.

He passed at once to the apartment of Lucie.

"I did not expect," he said to her, "the honour I have received to-day. You have well remembered, madame, that your husband ought to feel some desire to see you."

The indirect reproach which these words seemed to infer, singularly astonished poor Lucie.

"I do not understand you," she replied; "I have, it is true, remained long enough with my friend, but that was merely to allow you full time and liberty to terminate the affairs which still retain you in Paris; if I had foreseen that you felt a desire to have me with you, I would have returned long ago."

"Pardon me, madame; I am so annoyed, that I am, perhaps, unjust."

"Ah! yes, very unjust; to remain a month, nearly, without writing me! I was alarmed; I might have fancied something had happened to you. But you told me you were greatly annoyed; what is it now?"

"Oh! nothing; or at all events, a trifle; some affairs which I cannot arrange as quickly as I could wish, so that we cannot leave for Pourrieres for some time."

"We must submit to what we cannot prevent; and besides, the delay you speak of is not one, at this moment; I could not, in the state I am in, support the fatigues of a long journey, for the one I have just accomplished has nearly upset me."

"It's true; my God! you are pale, you seem wearied, and yet I am detaining you; repose yourself, my dear Lucie; to-morrow, I hope, you will be much better, and I will then tell you how I have employed my time during your absence."

"I am fatigued, it is true, but not ill, and I can assure you I am in a fit state to hear you."

"No, no; I shall have to talk to you about figures, and a thousand dry subjects, which, at this moment, would drive you crazy; to-morrow. I will send your attendant to you."

Salvador, very glad to defer till the next morning, an explanation for which he was not prepared, hastily left the apartment of his wife.

"He is kind!" said Lucie to herself, who, seeing him walk on tiptoe in order to make no noise, was greatly moved at this instance of seeming affection; "he is kind!"

Poor abused victim!

When in his apartment, Salvador recollected the letter delivered to him by his valet upon his arrival; he drew it from his pocket; he then, for the first time, remarked the unusual form of the envelope, the coarseness of the paper it was written upon, and the bad penmanship and orthography of its superscription.

"I do not often receive such missives as this," he said, after breaking the seal; "does it announce good or bad news to me?"

The contents were as follows:

"My dear Rupin,—Father Justè, to whom I have given this letter, has promised me to deliver it to you. You have so often put money in my coffers, and behaved so handsomely towards me, that I cannot neglect the opportunity of rendering you an important service.

"You have, no doubt, learned that one fine night the police paid my house a visit, and that—as some traitor had split upon us, and discovered the secret of the cave—all the comrades were arrested. Thanks to the kindness of an old forçat, who had enlisted into the police to get his bread, and to whom I counted ten thousand francs down, I was able to save myself; and at this moment I am so well concealed, that I fear neither gendarmes, soldiers, spies, magistrates, nor judges.

"I wish that every *workman*, who has brought 'grist to the mill,' could say the same; unfortunately, 'tis not so; and I much fear that all who *amuse* themselves still in Paris, will soon be in quod; for it is probable that those who have been *pinched*, will babble, and denounce their comrades. The *pègres* of the present day have no honesty!

"You, however, my poor Rupin, have been the cause of all this. You shall learn how:

"You have not forgotten the assassin, who, after attempting the murder of a woman, on the Pont au Change, threw himself into the river, to escape the pursuit of the crowd, and that you made him enter my house at the moment he was about to be captured? Well! my boy, 'tis to this scapegrace we owe all our misfortunes. Some time ago, he came to my house, and gave me a long history, he said he had been *at work* in the country with some comrades who had got *into trouble;* that he had contrived to escape, and that he intended to follow his *profession* at Paris; he talked so fine that I gave him my confidence, I presented him to our *friends*, in fact, I treated him as if he were my child.

"Well! would you believe it? he was an informer!

"It was from a comrade of Fanfan la Grenouille, Poil aux Levres, an old *pègre*, who is in the police, that I learned all this; he even added, that it was said at the prefecture, that Beppo—the name of the traitor! had sworn he would never rest, until he had delivered over to the police the Grand Richard, le Provençal, and yourself.

"You will make what use you please of the advice I give you, my boy; if you are as secure as I am, you can remain at Paris, but if not, I advise you to *file*, at once; for it appears that this Beppo

—*mouchard* as he is—is not to be despised, and that it is more for the purpose of being revenged on **you**, than to gain a reward, that he has had all our friends arrested.

"Adieu, my dear Rupin; you will, probably, not hear me again spoken of, for I live quite alone, like an old wolf; and the better to conceal my game, I am turned *devotèe*! I go even to confession! Droll! is it not? Well! you will not believe me, and yet it is true; my confessor is such a worthy man, he speaks so well about the ends of religion, that I have sometimes a mind to take seriously all he tells me, and to make a real confession to him, that I might obtain full absolution. In fact, I'm turned honest! I have no ambition to finish my days at *the college!* which would be very likely to happen, if I allowed myself to be taken.

"Ah! if I only had with me my poor little Nichon!

"Adieu, once more, my dear Rupin; remember sometimes,

"Marie Madeleine Colette Comtois; called
"SANS REFUS."

"The old fool!" muttered Salvador, after reading the letter, which he tore in a thousand pieces, and flung to the winds; "the old fool! if I knew where to find you, I would send you the address of your darling; for in truth, at present, I should be very glad to get quit of her."

The perusal of this letter, produced some serious reflections in Salvador, the result of which has, no doubt, already been foreseen by our readers.

"If the Marquis de Pourrieres does not quit his hotel to-day," he soliloquised, "it is probable that to-morrow morning he will be arrested; he will then be confronted with those who are now in prison; and from these confrontations, and the thousand other circumstances which it is impossible to anticipate, it is almost certain that it will result in the proof, that the said marquis is neither more or less than a *pègre de la haute!* But, supposing for a moment that I escape this first danger, the affair of the young Fortunè! is there not a storm ready to break over it? Decidedly, I cannot face the torrent which threatens me; there only remains one course for me to take, that of flying, while it is yet time, and leave to those who remain behind to arrange matters as they like.

"But, Silvia! she is very ugly now! can I take charge of a woman, whose features, covered with horrible wounds, will attract to me the eyes of every one? Oh, no! I will warn her to be upon her guard; 'tis all I can do for her."

Salvador wrote the following note, which he sent at once to the Marchioness de Roselly.

"My dear Silvia,—A great danger threatens me, I am forced to fly; endeavour to do the same; we may, probably, meet shortly. Adieu!

"A. DE P."

"Oh, Fate! look at thy works! to quit such a noble hotel—such fruitful lands—such magnificent horses! 'Tis hard! but what can I do? France, after all, is not the only country in which it might be possible to live, and to procure all I am about to lose; when, like myself, we possess every thing necessary to succeed in the world—the exterior of a distinguished man; audacity; and a conscience, not over scrupulous."

Salvador was a man, who, the moment he had resolved upon a deed, executed it; a valuable quality, and one that, unfortunately, is possessed but by a few individuals. He rang; and his valet replied at once to the summons.

"You will, directly," he said, "take Cerberus to my pavilion, at Choisy-le-Roi; especially, do not tire him, as I wish him to be in a fit state, to-morrow morning, to take the road."

Salvador, after giving to each of his domestics, whose presence might incommode him, orders which would keep them from the hotel for a longer time than he required to execute his projects, took from his wardrobe a travelling portmanteau which had belonged to Roman, and in which he could stow away all the silver in the house and his jewels; this done, he repaired to the apartment of his wife.

Lucie, much fatigued from the short journey she had made, had gone to bed as soon as Salvador had retired. She slept profoundly. The lingering rays of the sun, softened by the curtains of purple silk which adorned her bedchamber, fell full upon her handsome face, enveloped in a triple cheveaux de frize of Brussels lace, a ravishing picture, upon which Salvador did not even condescend to drop a glance, eager as he was to accomplish the object which had drawn him to the apartment of his wife.

He crossed the bedchamber walking on tiptoe, and entered the small cabinet decorated and furnished similar to the one which formerly existed at the Hotel de Neuville, and which served Lucie as a boudoir and workroom.

He stopped before a bureau in which his unhappy wife was accustomed to secure the valuables she possessed, it was locked, but this trifling obstacle did not restrain Salvador, who had taken care to furnish himself with a small bunch of keys.

The bureau was opened, it contained all Lucie's jewels, a suite of rubies and opals, a present from Madame de Villerbanne, another of pearls, presented to her by M. de Neuville a short time before his departure for Algiers, a collar of fine diamonds which had belonged to her mother, some beautiful emeralds, a sapphire mounted as a brooch, two valuable antique cameos forming a bracelet, a small watch, an invaluable chef-d'œuvre of Breguet, encircled with precious stones of different colours.

These jewels were enclosed in several small morocco boxes. Salvador put them pell-mell into the pocket of his coat, he then replaced every box where he found it, and locked the bureau.

Lucie awoke as he was leaving the cabinet in which he had committed this robbery, the most infamous, perhaps, of any he had yet put his hand to.

"What!" she said to her husband, "you were in my room?"

"I came to inquire whether you found yourself a little better; but when I entered you slept so sweetly, that I had not the courage to wake you, so I strolled into your cabinet where I have been reading until now."

Lucie was far from imagining that her husband, at the moment he was lavishing upon her proofs of the tenderest affection, was preparing to abandon her, and that he had just committed a crime of which she was the victim; she thanked him, therefore, for his solicitude; and as it was already late, and she wished to dress for dinner, she begged him to leave her alone for a moment.

"I am sorry I cannot keep you company," replied Salvador; "but not knowing that I should have the happiness of seeing you to-day, I have made an engagement in which I cannot fail."

"This evening then, in that case," said Lucie, presenting her hand to her husband.

Salvador took the hand of the woman he had just despoiled of every jewel, and pressed it affectionately in his own.

"This evening," he said to Lucie, "this evening."

THE TRIALS.

SALVADOR AND ROMAN IN THE PARK.

Laura, we find, keeping to the resolution she had come to with her husband, had not informed her friend of what she knew respecting Salvador.

The latter, as soon as he had quitted the apartment of his wife, sent a servant for a hired cab, in which his portmanteau was placed. He discharged the cab in the street Saint Dominique d'Enfer, at the door of the usurer Justè, to whom he sold everything he had brought with him.

The old Arab, knowing that his client was forced to expatriate himself, showed himself a little more reasonable than was his custom; he contented himself with a profit of about twenty-five per cent. He therefore handed to Salvador a sum of thirty thousand francs in bank-notes, which, with the ready cash he had about him, made a total of nearly fifty thousand francs.

It was getting dark when Salvador left the house of the usurer; a street cab, which he engaged near the gate of the Luxembourg, conducted him to the station of the Paris and Orleans railway.

A few minutes brought him to Choisy-le-Roi, when he took refuge in the Pavilion des Gardes; he sent to the inn the domestic who had brought his horse, giving him directions to wait for him until the next day at noon; his intention being that he should not return to Paris, until he himself was far from Choisy-le-Roi.

Salvador in anticipation of any possible misfortune, had induced all his servants to place in his hands the different papers of which they were the bearers; he passed a portion of the night in preparing for his use those which would be necessary for him; he washed a passport, a certificate of birth, and also one of liberation, and afterwards filled up these acts of indication applicable to himself; we need not add, that these different operations were executed with such care and skill, that the forged documents would have supported triumphantly an examination by the most practised eye.

At the break of day, he packed in his portmanteau what linen and clothes he found at the pavilion; he saddled his horse, and slid into the holsters a pair of excellent pistols; he had shaved off his beard, his moustaches, and his whiskers, and dressed himself in a much more simple attire than his dress of the evening before.

He put himself en route.

"The Marquis de Pourrieres is no longer in existence," he said to himself, when he had left behind him the pavilion of Choisy-le-Roi, "the devil will doubtless protect Louis Rousseau, traveller for the house of Biot and Company, of Marseilles; he is well indebted that to one of his future guests."

CHAPTER XLVII.

SUDDEN TURN OF FORTUNE.

It is night, the sky is clouded, a thick mist envelopes the atmosphere, a fine and penetrating rain has fallen for several hours, the wind, already piercing, finds its way through the almost leafless branches of the giant trees of the wood of Bougeaux.

In a corner of this wood, close upon the highway, are assembled four individuals of suspicious appearance; they are sitting or lying on a heap of dry leaves, and perfectly sheltered from the rain, for the branches of the trees under which they are seated, interlaced one with the other, form above their heads, a sort of roof which they have rendered almost impenetrable, by spreading above several of the frocks worn by hawkers and waggoners.

Those of our readers who wish to ascertain the physiognomy and costume of these four individuals, may read once more the twenty-ninth chapter of this work. These individuals are, in fact, the male inhabitants of the *Robber's Mansion;* their conversation which, as a consequence of the happy privilege possessed by all romance writers, (we will not make an exception, even in favour of M. Emile Marco de Saint-Hilaire, who so well narrates to his readers, what Napoleon said when he was quite alone,) we were enabled to overhear, without running the slightest risk, will inform us of many circumstances it is necessary we should know.

"It begins to get cold," said Jean Louis, the son of Blaise le petit Christ, called Sans Pitie.

"'Tis true," replied the beardless youth, who wore the costume of a miller's boy, when we encountered him for the first time, in the *Robber's Mansion;* "if you like, we will cut it. We shall be better off, I am thinking, before a jolly fire, than in this pile of faggots, where it is darker than in the devil's den."

"Let us do as he says," added the great Bas-Normand, rising up.

"This is just like you all, a set of good for naughts," exclaimed the frightful ambulating tinker, "you have not even patience to wait a bit; you want the victuals ready cooked, I suppose?"

"If we had hopes of doing any thing," replied *beardless,* "we would wait without grumbling."

"We shall not even meet a pauper on the tramp," resumed the Bas-Normand. "And the weather is not fit to turn a dog out in."

Jean-Louis, whose hasty observation had provoked these remarks, had stretched himself on the mass of dry leaves which served him as a seat, and had comfortably fallen asleep.

"Follow Jean Louis," said the tinker, "take a snooze, if you are tired; but since the governor has ordered us to wait here, we ought to obey him."

"Well, well! we will obey him, there is an end of it, we shall see what that will bring us," replied the Bas-Normand.

"Perhaps more than you expect, my children," said a man, entering the copse which served as a retreat to the four bandits, and whose garments, streaming with water, and heated face, announced his having finished a long walk.

It was Blaise le petit Christ called Sans-Pitie.

"There will pass by here directly," he continued, "a travelling clerk, who journeys on horseback, we must not miss him. I was with him at dinner at the *tapis* de la Grange-la-Prevote, when the gendarmes came to demand his passports, and I remarked that his purse was full of bank-notes. I *filed* whilst he was having his horse shoed; he cannot be long."

"Well!" exclaimed the tinker with a triumphant air, "if the swag's good, to whom is it owing?"

"To you, parbleu!" replied Jean Louis, who was placing fresh caps on the pistols he had drawn from his pocket.

"Provided man and horse do not give us the slip," added the miller's boy.

"There is no danger of that," resumed Blaise le petit Christ, "he must positively arrive to-night at Melun, and to reach that town, there is no other road but this."

"Bravo! governor, bravo!" exclaimed the Bas-Normand, "let us settle his business, and go home, for I am dying of hunger, and in a hurry to look at a good fire."

"Alas! my poor children," replied Blaise le

petit Christ, in a tone of deep affliction, "when we have settled this affair and divided the swag, we must separate, perhaps for some time ; the mayor of Nautarre and a quart-d'œil,* followed by a troop of *cooks*, visited the house this morning; my poor wife, Pacifique, and la Vierge Noire, were pinched and taken to the prison of Versailles; a mousetrap† has been established at the tapis of Bienvenu; have you a mind to put your finger in?"

"No, parbleu!" exclaimed the four bandits together.

"There will be luck for us," added Jean-Louis, "if mother and sisters peach."

"There is no danger, my duck loves me too well, and my ducklings have been too well brought up, for us to suspect such an infamy ; however, we are not so compromised that we cannot return, they found nothing at the crib that can tell against us, and provided the witnesses do not bring additional evidence against them, my wife and girls will get out of this scrape."

"In that case they are safe, there will be no witnesses, as we exercised the praiseworthy habit of silencing those whom we plundered."

"We must not make too sure. I think we were denounced by the man who escaped from us with my clothes, and who left us his prad and his trap, which we had so much trouble to get rid of."

Blaise le petit Christ was not deceived, it was, in fact, Servigny who had procured the arrest of the wife and two daughters of this *scelerat*. A short time after the conversation he had had with the Abbé Reuzet, he forwarded to the police a detailed account of all that had happened to him in the auberge of Bienvenu; which he concluded by saying, "that although he had not signed it, they must not pay the less consideration to it, seeing that he only omitted this formality on account of his being on the point of taking a long journey which he could not defer; and also that a visit to this auberge would probably lead to the discovery of the horse and cab which he had been forced to abandon there, (and of which he gave a full description,) and which would prove that the facts he alleged were true. This denunciation was followed by an immediate visit of the police to the auberge of Bienvenu, but, as we have seen, the first care of Blaise le petit Christ, when he discovered that the person he had taken for an agent of police had contrived to escape, was to get rid of the horse and cab; they had found nothing in this auberge, announced as a rendezvous of malefactors of every description, which could compromise the inhabitants, who enjoyed in addition so good a reputation, that they did not dare to arrest them, having nothing against them but an anonymous declaration which might be attributed to the secret hatred of an enemy.

One fact, however, militated against the probability of this conjecture: the residents of the auberge of Bienvenu, might, it is true, have one or many enemies, (who has not?) but these enemies would, like themselves, belong to the popular class, and the denunciation which related to them was written

with so much care, and in such good terms, it was accompanied with considerations of an order so elevated, that it was evidently the production of a person who had received a good education; from this to the conclusion, that the writer belonged to the upper ranks was not far, and to this they came; and to forward the interest of all, it was decided that the auberge of Bienvenu should be kept under the best surveillance, and that they should not act, unless some new facts took place.

This determination was prudent; unluckily an accident which could not be foreseen, prevented at first the good results that might have been expected.

There are but very few honest men in France who determine to serve the police; (but in our opinion it is a creditable mission, when well executed, that of placing beyond the possibility of doing injury to their fellow-citizens, the men who openly brave the laws which regulate civilized society;) it is therefore compelled to place its confidence in men, who for the most part are little scrupulous, (it must be understood that we here speak only of individuals occupying the lowest steps of the social ladder,) these persons serve faithfully as long as they find their account in so doing; but as, thanks to the prejudices of the many, whom we obey without mistrust, their trade produces them neither consideration, or much profit, they are not much attached to it, and when the opportunity of making what they call a good job presents itself, they do not allow it to escape; so that transactions similar to that entered into by Fanfan la Grenouille and Mother Sans Refus, are much more frequent than is supposed; it is wrong, therefore, to accuse the police of ignorance or negligence; it would be much more just, perhaps, to say that it had been deceived by agents in whom it placed its confidence.

Blaise le petit Christ, traversing the village of Nanterre to reach his home, was accosted by an individual possessing a marked physiognomy, indicating at once to the eye of an observer, the profession of him to whom it belongs.

"You don't recollect me?" said the individual to petit Christ.

"Yes, I do," replied Blaise, who recognised a man with whom he had worked when he followed the trade of a contrabandist; "what are you seeking after in these parts?"

"You."

"Me?"

"Yourself. Listen Father Blaise, hand me fifty francs, and I'll give you some good advice."

"Give me the receipt first, and if it's good I'll pay you for it."

"None of that, Lisette, pay first. I know you, you are deep, but I'm deeper."

Petit Christ drew from under his blouse a leather bag, secured round his neck by a strong strip of the same material, from which he took ten five-franc pieces, and handed them to his companion.

"I am in the *cuisine*,"* said the man, after pocketing the fifty francs, and to give more weight to his assertion, he drew from his pocket a triangular cut card, upon which was impressed an eye, encircled with rays.

"Is that what you have to tell me? I knew it."

"It's very possible, but what you do not know, is that I am here with several of my comrades, for the purpose of observing all that may take place, for the next few days, at a certain auberge, with

---

* Commisaire of police.

† When it is supposed that a house serves as a retreat of malefactors, or belongs to a receiver of stolen goods, the police invest it with several agents charged to arrest every individual who presents himself, and whose appearance may justify such a measure, this is called "establishing a mousetrap." This ruse, which is known to every scelerat, nearly always succeeds; however, it rarely happens that he who *visits a friend*, or sells to a receiver any object he may have stolen, takes the precaution of obtaining previous information in the ......hood. Criminals are, thank God, the most improvi-

the sign of the *Bienvenu*, in which, as the police are informed, you carry on some droll manœuvres."

"There are such wicked people, my old friend."

"Whether you are slandered or not, I shut my eye; you are warned, I am paid, the rest is your concern. Adieu, Father Blaise."

"Adieu, my boy."

Petit Christ profited by the advice he had received; consequently for some time the auberge of *Bienvenu* was, of any in the country, the safest and best kept. We may safely infer that Blaise, for a few crowns, purchased every day from his ancient comrade, the information as to the reports relating to him, and that when the surveillance ceased, he was at once apprised of it.

He then recommenced his abominable practices.

Servigny, concluding that, in consequence of his information to the police, the assassins had been all arrested, troubled himself no more about the matter. It was only a few days before the events we have just narrated, that, passing by chance in a calèche in front of the *Robber's Mansion*, he recognised, seated before the principal entrance, the mother and her two daughters, Pacifique, and la Vierge Noire.

"Either my letter has not been received, or they have taken no notice of it, from its being anonymous, and perhaps these villains, encouraged by impunity, sacrifice daily fresh victims to their cupidity; such a state of things must absolutely be put an end to, and immediately."

He went to the Abbé Reuzet to ask his advice.

"I shall not be easy," he said to him, "until these *scelerats* are prevented committing further crimes; it seems to me I am an accomplice in every one they commit; and this is so true, that, if you can point out no other means, I am fully determined, at all risks, to present myself to the police, who will then be forced to act."

The priest who had listened to him attentively, shook him by the hand, and rose from the seat he had occupied.

"I have hit upon a method, an excellent method," he said, "indeed I am surprised I did not think of it before."

He said no more to Servigny, whom he left at once, to attend the prefecture of police.

The Abbé Reuzet was one of those worthy priests, the number of whom is much more considerable than is generally supposed, whose reputation is based upon a life so pure, and so many noble actions, that they are believed by the most incredulous, when they undertake to affirm a fact of any description.

Dame Police is not over credulous in her nature, and really she is fortunate in this, considering the strange tales and long histories that are so kindly told her. As soon, however, as the Abbé Reuzet had assured them that the denunciation it ought to have received a short time previously, the author of which, an escaped convict, could not make himself known, contained nothing but the truth, their eyes and ears were opened, and it was determined that the auberge of Bienvenu should be again put upon its trial.

It was necessary, to be at length satisfied as to the moral value of the inhabitants, male and female, of the auberge of Bienvenu—to ascertain from whence they came, what they did—to remark all that took place in their house, and to discover if any attempts were made upon the lives of the travellers who rested there. This difficult mission was confided to a man resolute and experienced,

to whom was promised a handsome reward, by way of inducing him to neglect nothing which might ensure the success of his undertaking.

This man, who had grown white in the service, somewhat resembled the honest rat of which La Fontaine somewhere speaks. We are not aware if he had lost any thing in battle, but we know that he had still in reserve more than one trick in his wallet. He chose some virtuous auxiliaries, and procured some costumes, half citizen, half peasant, and towards night he entered the auberge of *Bienvenu*, and, after depositing on the table his stout stick, ornamented with a leather holdfast, and a bag, whose jingling sound sensibly affected the auditory nerves of the wife and daughters of Blaise le petit Christ, he inquired whether they could serve him with a good supper and prepare him a bed. Madame Blaise, always affable and ready to oblige, replied that what the house contained was at his service.

"You render me an important service, my dear lady," resumed the police agent. "I was fearful I should have to proceed as far as Nanterre, which would have greatly annoyed me, for I have had a long walk to-day, and I assure you I am very tired."

"There are handsomer hostelries than ours in the country," replied Madame Blaise, "but there are none that are cleaner, and where travellers are in more safety or better treated."

"I don't doubt it, madame, and I shall, therefore, beg you to lock up for me this bag, which contains two thousand francs, that I have brought with me to pay a portion of the price of a small property which I have purchased in the neighbourhood."

Madame Blaise took the bag and deposited it at the bottom of a cupboard, and offered the key to the traveller.

"Keep the key, madame," he replied, "'tis as safe in your hands as in mine."

After this little incident, the traveller, desirous of retiring for a few minutes to the room prepared for him, Madame Blaise, who was occupied in the preparations for supper, directed one of her daughters to conduct him to it. The latter, after installing him, and saying she would call him when supper was ready, descended the straight ladder which served as a means of communication from the common hall of the auberge of Bienvenu to the bed-rooms of the travellers, and rejoined her mother and sister.

"I think we have him safe," she said to them. "The sack is full of tin; two thousand balls, it's not picked up every day under a horse's feet, is it?"

"Unluckily," replied the mother, "but we must return these two thousand balls."

"Return them!" added Pacifique, "eh! why so, if you please?"

"You forget, then, that the father, who is on the road with his comrades, will not return to-night, and that on leaving he recommended to us the greatest prudence; and besides, this cove seems to have pluck, and it is doubtful whether all three of us could settle his business."

"Never fear," said the Vierge Noire, "we will drug him at supper, and when he's sound asleep, we can do what we like with him."

"'Tis possible," replied the mother, "but the corpse?"

"Well, we'll keep it at home till father arrives. The old veteran will be pleased, if, on his return, we can put two thousand balls in his hand."

"Certainly," added Pacifique, "especially as we have lost much time, and that, since we have given up the *silencing* system, such a godsend hasn't fallen to our hands."

"Come, mother, try your luck," said the Vierge Noire, in an indolent tone; "'tis a good opportunity, and besides, you see, we mustn't throw at his feet the luck Providence has sent us."

"You must do as you like, my dwarfs," replied Madame Blaise. "Come, 'tis settled, we'll murder the fool; we must hope that the Holy Virgin will protect us; but the supper is ready, we must arrange the table, and request the old imbecile to descend."

Whilst the above conversation was being carried on in the dining-hall, the police agent, shut into his room, had not been idle; he had first examined the entrances by which assassins might introduce themselves into the room he occupied, the door and the two windows. The door, furnished with two good bolts, could be secured within; the windows, at some height from the ground, were both secured with strong bars.

"So far, I see nothing suspicious here," he said to himself; "the traveller reposing in this room might with reason think himself in perfect safety. They do not enter, however, through the keyhole; 'tis only in the Bible we find camels passing through the eye of a needle."

This judicious reflection induced the agent to pursue his search. He took a pistol from his pocket and made use of the handle to sound the walls.

He soon discovered the secret of the movable panel of the bed! All was then explained to him.

"Eh! eh!" he said, "but this appears to me ingenious, and, above all, philanthropical; the traveller, by the aid of this process, must pass without much suffering from sleep to death. Really the efforts of genius are apparent every day in some fresh improvement."

The agent had scarcely finished his examination, and replaced every thing as before, when Vierge Noire came to announce to him that supper was ready.

"I shall do credit to it then," he replied, "especially if you will do me the honour of sharing it with me."

The agent found in the dining-room a table covered with a cloth of pure white, on which was placed a dish, the smoke from which announced a delicious ragout.

"'Tis very charitable," thought the agent; "these honest people seem determined we shall not commence the grand journey without plenty of ballast. But we must not be coaxed by the delicacies of Capoue; and therefore, we will beg this worthy woman and her two amiable daughters to assist us in despatching this supper, of which I will take no part unless they will share it with me; we must be cautious."

The invitation of the agent was eagerly accepted, so that he eat and drank without the fear of having a soporific introduced into the viands he consumed.

During supper, the amiable hostesses of *Trotignon* (the name of the agent) filled him up bumpers of wine. He at once perceived their object; but, as he knew himself capable of taking a skinful, without being the worse for it, he had no need of showing much caution. Still, after doing honour to a few small glasses of excellent brandy, he thought it as well to simulate a sort of drunkenness; in fact, he played his game so well, that the three women, when he left the table, looked upon the affair as three parts cooked.

After supper, he lighted his pipe, which he smoked on the step of the door. Some individuals, perfectly well known to him, were walking up and down the road. He made some signs to them, which were replied to in a satisfactory manner. Being now certain of assistance at the moment of danger, the agent re-entered the auberge of Bienvenu, and expressed a wish of retiring to bed, a desire which was hastily complied with.

When in his room, he converted the sheets and a blanket into a mannequin, or figure of a man, which he put into bed in the position he would have occupied himself; he then took off his redingote and waistcoat, which he carefully placed on a chair, in such a manner as to be seen by the bandits, if they took it into their heads to peep through the key-hole, and retaining simply his pantaloons, and with a pistol in each hand, he placed himself at the side of the bed, and waited with his eyes fixed upon the movable panel, ready to fall upon him.

Madame Blaise, Pacifique, and the Vierge Noire, when they supposed the traveller sound asleep, took up their positions behind the movable panel of the bed, in which they believed him to have been long in full possession, for the snoring, like the sounds of a counter-bass, soon convinced them that their anticipations were right.

"He sleeps," said la Vierge Noire; "it is time."

Pacifique let go the spring retaining the movable panel, which instantaneously dropped upon the bed.

"He is ours!" exclaimed the Vierge Noire.

"Not yet! villains!" exclaimed the agent, who, not supposing that he was assailed simply by three women, discharged one of his pistols at the group, which the obscurity hindered him from more than half seeing.

The ball reached Pacifique, and broke her right arm. The unfortunate girl fell into the corridor, uttering the most piteous cries.

At the same moment, a noise was heard outside; the door yielded under the united efforts of several men, who invaded the house.

"They are agents!" exclaimed Madame Blaise, when the scene was enlightened by a torch which one of the agents had lighted; "we are served."

"As you say, my sweet ones; but where are the males?" he continued, astonished at finding only the three women before him.

"You havn't got them yet, mouchards," replied Pacifique, whom one of the agents had raised and placed on a chair.

The three women were secured, and the police commenced a search, which produced no result, for the simple reason, that Blaise and his four companions were at this moment in the country.

At daybreak, the commissaire of police of Nanterre, who had been apprised in the night, arrived at the auberge of Bienvenu, and ordered Madame Blaise and her two daughters to be conducted to the prison of Versailles.

The news of this arrest spread with the rapidity of lightning. Blaise le petit Christ heard of it in his turn, whilst at the auberge in which he had met the traveller whom he prepared to attack, at the moment we interrupted our recital to narrate the preceding facts; but as he was ignorant of the circumstances which accompanied the arrest of his wife and daughters, he was in hopes it would not turn out so serious an affair as it did.

Let us now return to Blaise and his companions.

The bandits, despite the continued rain, quitted the copse in which they were sheltered, and placed themselves in ambush on the edge of the road, which was lined by tall trees, behind which they concealed themselves.

"What weather! what soaking weather!" said the tinker, in a low tone; "the traveller won't come."

"He will come, I am certain," replied Blaise; "for, as I told you, when I quitted the *tapis*, he was finishing his supper, and had ordered his horse to be saddled; but silence; I think I hear something."

In fact, after listening a few moments, the assassins distinctly heard, at a distance, the sound of a horse's step.

"'Tis him," said Blaise; "'tis him! silence!"

Shortly after, a traveller passed before the bandits; he was enveloped in a large cloak with sleeves, which covered the croup of his horse; but he had so disposed it, that all his movements were free.

Blaise le petit Christ, who had not forgotten that he ought to set an example to his men, threw himself at the head of the horse; he was immediately followed by the rest.

"Your money or your life!" he said to the traveller.

"My friends," replied the latter, "if my companions had not remained behind, I should probably have made the same demand upon you; therefore, there is nothing to be done with me; I am a *workman*."

"Workman or not, deliver yourself with a good grace; you have gold, we want it."

"Cease, then, you highway robber, my purse shall pass before your nose."

"Ah! you speak the *argot*, to make us believe you are a *pegre*; that would do once," continued Blaise; "but now, it's no go. The wealthiest, since they have printed dictionaries of the slang, speak it like ourselves. Come, come, the purse and the note-case!"

The traveller had taken a pistol from the holster; he fired it at Blaise, who still held his horse by the bit; but a movement of the animal changed its direction, and the ball struck the tinker, who fell to the ground.

"Ah! is that it?" exclaimed Blaise; "death, then. Jean Louis," he said in a low tone to his son, who was near him, "hamstring his horse."

The traveller, who had stood several shots without being injured, had armed himself with another pistol; but the horse, held by the bit, continued rearing, so that he could not direct his aim; however, as he was determined to rid himself of his most dangerous enemy, he bent over the neck of his horse and discharged his pistol. Blaise made a sudden movement on one side, but the ball had struck his arm; he was forced to let go. At the same moment the horse fell, and his master shared his fate.

Jean Louis, to obey his father's orders, had slid behind the noble animal, and seizing a favourable opportunity, had, with the aid of a pruning knife, hamstrung him in both legs.

The traveller, disarmed, and nearly stifled under the weight of his horse, was unable to make the slightest resistance. The miller approached him and discharged two pistols at his breast, whilst Blaise, who was but slightly wounded, took from his pockets his note-case and all the money he found in them.

"'Tis fat, my children, tis fat," he said. "Come, *en route*, we'll divide at the nearest tapis."

"And the chaudronier, are we to leave him here?" observed the Bas-Normand.

Blaise approached the wounded man, stretched on the road by the side of the traveller.

"He is dead," he said, pushing him with his foot.

"No," said the miller, who had also approached the wretch, and had placed one of his hands in his bosom, "his *palpitant* still goes *tic tac*."

"He ought to be dead, then," added Blaise.

And he discharged one of his pistols, which he had found no opportunity of using, at the head of the unfortunate tinker.

"Ah! governor," exclaimed Jean Louis, whilst the two other assassins regarded him with consternation, not knowing what to think of the scene just enacted.

"Imbeciles!" said Blaise to them; "if he was not dead he was no better worth; could we take charge of him? and were we to leave him in the road? Don't you know that there are none so talkative as one of the trade, when on his last legs?"

"'Tis quite true," said le Bas-Normand. "I approve the deed."

"I believe it," replied Blaise, "I believe it; for the shares of each will be increased one-fifth."

"Ah! ah!" added the miller, "I had not thought of that."

"Come, boy, enough chattering; *en route*."

The four bandits drew on their smocks, which they had left in the copse, and dived into the thickest part of the wood, leaving in the road the bodies of the traveller and their comrade.

Some hours after, the patrolling gendarmes passed over the road where the preceding events had taken place; daylight was just appearing; they observed the two bodies, dismounted from their horses, and approached them.

The chaudronier was dead, but the traveller still breathed.

The appearance of the place, the costumes, so different, of the two men stretched before them, the numerous marks of steps impressed in the soil, the nature of the horse's wound, announced to the gendarmes what had taken place; they surmised at once that the man who still breathed was an unfortunate traveller, who had been attacked by bandits, and who had fallen after a vigorous defence, and putting *hors de combat* one of his adversaries. They raised him with care, and carried him to the first house they came to; arrived there, they borrowed a cart, and the traveller, stretched upon some trusses of hay, and covered with cloaks, was transported to their residence. The body of the chaudronier was placed crossways behind the cart, that he might not affect the sight of the traveller, if by chance the latter recovered his senses before arriving at their destination.

The entrance of this mournful cortége into Melun put the little village into a revolution. Every inhabitant before whom they were obliged to pass, in order to reach the barracks of the gendarmerie, questioned the gendarmes, who were obliged to repeat at least a hundred times the same story. The court of the barrack was invaded by the crowd of curiosity-mongers when the cart entered it, and it was with some trouble that the gendarmes (who, in the provinces, are much more polished, and infinitely less severe, than their confrères of the department of the Seine—we do not speak of messieurs the municipal guard) contrived, at length, to obtain a free space round the cart; the substitute of the procureur du roi and the commissary of police, apprised by the general clamour, was already at the barracks, accompanied by a doctor. The latter ordered the wounded man to be carried into one of the rooms of the barracks, where he had prepared every thing necessary for dressing his wounds.

"Holy mother of God!" exclaimed a patriarch with white hair, when the gendarmes who carried the body passed in front of him; "holy virgin! is it really possible?"

"What's the matter then, Father Coquardon," said a young girl; "do you know this unfortunate traveller?"

"Certainly I know him. Ah! what a terrible misfortune; so good a man!"

"But who is he, then?"

"A rich seigneur of Paris, who comes often during the summer to pass a few days in this part of the country."

"You know his name?" said the commissaire of police, who had overheard a good part of the exclamation drawn by surprise from Grandfather Coquardon.

"Yes, my procureur," replied the honest peasant, "'tis M. le Marquis de Pourrieres."

The commissaire invited Father Coquardon to enter the chamber of the wounded man. He required no repetition of the summons, delighted as he was to learn from the right quarter, and at once, by what unlucky hazard M. le Marquis de Pourrieres was brought to so deplorable a condition.

As soon as it was known that the wounded person was a man of wealth and station, the deputy gave orders in consequence; so that Salvador was conveyed to the best room in the house, that of the quarter-master, and placed in a bed furnished with the softest blankets and the finest sheets it was possible to procure.

Salvador's wounds were much less dangerous than their appearance indicated. By good luck, the balls, in lieu of passing through the chest, had glided along the sides, so that they were but superficial. The long swoon, resulting from the vast quantity of blood he had lost, would of necessity cease after a careful attendance, and so it happened.

When he recovered his senses, and found himself surrounded by several individuals, among whom were some habited in the costume of gendarmes, he felt, as we may well conceive, a very painful sensation; but he was soon himself again; and, after requesting something to drink, he waited patiently for the questions they would not fail to put to him.

The doctor immediately satisfied his thirst, and the commissaire of police, recognised by his tri-coloured scarf, had raised his head, in order to assist him; these attentions somewhat reassured Salvador.

"Come," he said to himself, "all is not lost; I think I shall get myself out of this awkward mess."

The substitute having inquired of him if he felt himself sufficiently strong to reply to a few questions, he gave an affirmative sign; they then informed him how he had been picked up on the high road, and brought to the place he was in, and they requested from him an account of what had previously taken place.

Salvador had no reasons for stating the facts otherwise than as they occurred, he therefore gave an exact and circumstantial account of what had happened to him. When he had finished, the substitute begged him to sign his declaration, which he did.

"Louis Rousseau!" exclaimed the substitute, stupified with astonishment.

"Yes, sir," replied Salvador, "there is nothing very extraordinary in that, I presume. Louis Rousseau, commission traveller of the house of Biot and Company, of Marseilles."

"'Tis singular," said the substitute; "approach, old man," he continued, addressing Father Coquardon, who had remained at the entrance of the room, with the other spectators of the scene, "approach."

Father Coquardon hastily complied with this invitation.

"You know this gentleman?" said the substitute to him.

"Do I know him? my procureur," replied Coquardon, "a worthy seigneur, as rich as the king," (here Father Coquardon, faithful to a habit of profound respect for royalty, took off the woollen cap which covered his white hairs,) "but makes the best use of his riches. Certainly I know him, and I am very much concerned at seeing him in this state, I assure you."

"I know not this man," said Salvador, who, in fact, had never remarked Father Coquardon.

"It's very possible, M. le Marquis; you grand seigneurs hàv'n't the time to pay any attention to little people like us; but that does not hinder me from saying to these gentlemen that you are really the kindest and most charitable of all the gentry of Choisy-le-Roi."

"Tell us the name of monsieur," exclaimed the substitute, who began to tire of the prosiness of Father Coquardon, "that will be much better."

"Eh! pardine, I have already told you, 'tis M. le Marquis de Pourrieres," replied the old man.

"'Tis strange," repeated the substitute.

"Very strange, indeed," added the commissaire.

"There is some mystery in all this, which it would be as well to penetrate," said the physician, in an under tone.

"I am at last in a regular fix," thought Salvador, who had heard the few words interchanged between the two functionaries and the doctor; "how am I to get out of it? The devil take this old scoundrel."

He turned himself in bed, and when the substitute approached to question him again, he told him he did not feel strong enough to reply to him, and that he would feel obliged by his giving directions for his being left alone a few hours. "To-morrow," he added, "I will explain what seems strange to you." He wanted time for reflection.

The substitute could not refuse to satisfy the request of the wounded man, which nothing, as yet, positively accused; and, besides, the Marquis de Pourrieres was not a man to be exposed to mistrust, except in good earnest.

He therefore retired, followed by the others who had followed him into the apartment.

We left Beppo on his way to the prefecture of police; we shall find him in the cabinet of his patron, to whom he was giving an account of the events that had happened.

"And so," said the chief of the police, after listening to him, "you are quite certain that the Marquis de Pourrieres and the Viscount de Lussan are no other than those to whom the revelations give the names of Rupin, the Grand Richard, or the Provençal?"

"As certain as it is possible to be."

"Consider, that you take the responsibility of a serious affair; the Marquis de Pourrieres and the Viscount de Lussan are persons of consideration, whom we cannot arrest without being sure that we are not deceived."

"I perfectly comprehend that; but I think there are means of convincing you."

"And what are these means?"

"Very simple, in truth. Let one of the informers, accompanied by a sufficient number of agents, to ensure his not escaping, wait in the neighbourhood of the residence, either of the marquis or the viscount, the ingress or egress of one of these two

LIFE IN PARIS

SALVADOR AND HIS WIFE.

individuals. If I am not deceived, as I feel assured of, they will both be infallibly recognised."

"Indeed I think this preliminary measure absolutely necessary, and I shall give directions that the Grand Louis be at your disposition for to-morrow morning."

"How! is the Grand Louis one of the informers?"

"Certainly he is. This man, who cried out so lustily against those whom persons of his sort called *macarons*,* was one of the first to turn informer. 'Tis always so. But you would probably not like to have him with you."

"I have pardoned, willingly, this miserable the wound he gave me; I will, therefore, go with him, if necessary."

The next morning, at daybreak, Beppo and the Grand Louis, accompanied by a number of agents, commanded by the chief of the police, who considered the affair of sufficient importance to take the direction himself, were at the door of the residence of the Viscount de Lussan. Their patience was tried for several hours. The noble personage they waited for was not in the habit of rising early. It was not until one o'clock struck that the viscount left his residence. As usual, his toilette was irreproachable; and the large white camelia, which blossomed at a button-hole of his coat, indicated his political opinions.

"'Tis the Grand Richard!" exclaimed Grand Louis. "Eh! what style! He has played us false, to be so flambant."

The chief of police turned towards Beppo.

"'Tis the Viscount de Lussan," said the latter, in an under tone.

The chief descended from the carriage, in which were Beppo, himself, and the Grand Louis. He left the latter in the custody of two stout agents, and, followed by the former, he advanced towards the Viscount de Lussan, who was humming a tune in his walk on the pavement of the Rue de Varennes. The agents followed at a distance, ready to lend a hand to their chief, if occasion required it.

The latter accosted the viscount with much politeness; he kept his hat in his hand, and his manner was humble.

"I have the honour of addressing the Viscount de Lussan?" he said.

"Yes, my friend," replied the viscount, rather surprised, "what can I do for you?"

"Follow me to the prefecture of police, M. le Vicomte. M. the procureur du roi has given an order for your appearance, which I am charged to execute. I trust you will not oblige me to use violence; you will follow with a good grace."

"How then?" replied the viscount; "in truth I am too happy in having it in my power to do any thing agreeable to you. Take me, as the procureur du roi desires it, to the prefecture of police."

The chief made a sign, and his agents, who had advanced by degrees, approached towards the viscount.

"Keep your distance, clowns!" he exclaimed, stepping backwards; "the first who makes one step towards me dies."

And he presented to the stupified agents the barrels of his kukenreitters, which he had drawn from his pocket.

The police dared not approach the viscount, who seemed fully determined to realize the threat he had made, and would probably have contrived to escape, if Beppo had not rushed upon him.

* Traitors.

"Take that, my dear fellow," said de Lussan coolly, "you have asked for it."

And he fired at Beppo, who held his left arm, and was calling in vain to the agents for assistance, the pistol he held in his right hand.

The unfortunate man fell to the pavement, his skull horribly fractured.

This frightful scene had collected an immense crowd in the Rue de Varennes. The agents, like a pack of dogs who hold at bay a ferocious wild boar, surrounded the viscount; but the sad end of Beppo had so terrified them, that they dared not advance a step.

The viscount kept them a few moments in awe of him, and, after giving a glance at the swelling circle which had insensibly formed around him—

"I might still despatch another," he said, "but that would serve no purpose. Come, my dear friends," he continued, after throwing on the ground the second pistol with which he was armed, "follow your trade; I only wished to show the world that a gentleman of Brittany never surrendered without fighting, that was all."

The agents threw themselves all at once on the viscount, who, in less time than we take in writing it, was bound and bundled into a coach, which conducted him to the prefecture of police.

The scene we have described had convinced the chief of police that the Marquis de Pourrieres was an individual of the same stamp as the one just arrested; he thought it his duty, therefore, to direct his steps at once to the hotel of the Rue de Courcelles. Public rumour might, in a few moments, acquaint the marquis with the arrest of his accomplice, and, if that happened, he would not fail to get out of the way; therefore, there was no time to lose.

The chief sent for a magistrate, and, thus accompanied, he went to the Hotel de Pourrieres.

"Madame la Marquise! Madame la Marquise!" exclaimed one of the femmes des chambre of Lucie, entering the bed-room of the unhappy woman, "the hotel is invaded by a crowd of agents and guards, headed by a commissary of police; they say they are come to arrest M. le Marquis."

"What is it you say?" exclaimed Lucie; "police agents! a commissary! What does it all mean, gracious God?"

And, without waiting the reply of her femme de chambre, she jumped out of bed. She had scarcely time to throw a large shawl over her shoulders, with the assistance of her attendant, when the commissaire of police, followed by several men, whose low-bred and rebarbative appearance caused her a mortal fright, entered her room.

The magistrate and commissary were men who knew how to blend the just severity which their painful duty often commands, with the regards due to weakness and misfortune. The commissaire knew that Lucie, when she married the Marquis de Pourrieres, was the widow of an esteemed general; and, besides, the reputation of this amiable woman was so well established in society, that the idea of rendering her amenable for the crimes imputed to her husband, would never have occurred, even to a savage; it was, therefore, only by employing every device possible, that he acquainted poor Lucie with the mission with which he was charged.

"Your servants, madame, inform me that M. le Marquis is at this moment absent from Paris. I regret exceedingly that it is so, for I am certain he would easily justify himself; but, notwithstanding his absence, I am compelled to make a rigorous search, in which you will be constrained to assist."

"Do your duty, sir," replied Lucie; "I have neither the right nor the wish to offer any opposition. Oh! my God! my God!" she continued, hiding her face in her hands, "am I destined to support so terrible a misfortune?"

"Calm yourself," madame, added the commissaire, who was much moved by the tears and extreme pallor of Lucie; "if M. le Marquis de Pourrieres is guilty, which God forbid, the widow of General the Count de Neuville will find in the world friends who will cause her to forget a husband unworthy of her."

The commissaire, gifted with a delicacy which was rightly appreciated by Lucie amidst her grief, searched her apartment but nominally; he seized, however, some papers, and after begging the poor woman to accept the expression of his regrets, he quitted her, recommending her femmes de chambre to watch her with the greatest care.

All the papers of the marquis, letters, receipts, and accounts, were seized, to be afterwards examined. This operation completed, the commissaire was retiring, when one of the agents brought into the saloon he was in, an individual who had just entered the hotel and requested to speak to the Marchioness de Pourrieres.

The individual was attired in a *costume de voyage*, and his dusty boots showed that he had been riding. The agents, presuming that he could give some news of the Marquis de Pourrieres, had determined to bring him before their chief.

"But I tell you," repeated the individual, "that I do not know the marquis, that I have never seen him, and that I only wish to speak to Madame la Marquise."

"Come, my friend," said the commissaire, "reply to my questions. What is your name?"

"Paolo."

"You are in the service of M. de Pourrieres?"

"I served for a long while the General Count de Neuville, and I left the service of his widow to enter that of M. le General Comte de Morengy, who has arrived in Paris, and has charged me to deliver a letter to the Marchioness de Pourrieres."

The commissaire, to interrogate Paolo, had seated himself before a small table, which the agents had drawn near the wall; above this table was a whole-length portrait of Salvador.

Paolo, while replying to the questions of the commissaire, could not withdraw his eyes from this portrait. The magistrate remarked this circumstance.

"Do you know the person of whom this is the portrait?" he said to Paolo.

"I think so, M. le commissaire," replied the old servant of poor Lucie; "this portrait, if I do not mistake, is that of M. the Viscount de Lestang."

"'Tis strange," said the commissaire to the chief of police, who made a sign that the circumstance appeared to him extraordinary.

"Tell us a little about the Viscount de Lestang," continued the commissaire, "and let it be true; you ought to conceal nothing from justice."

"I wish for nothing better than to tell you all I know relative to this personage," said Paolo, pointing to the portrait, "especially if it will contribute to his being hung."

Paolo then recounted, that whilst he was in the service of M. Carmagnola, a rich banker of Turin, an attempt at robbery had been committed in the house of his master, and, in his efforts to oppose

the flight of one of the robbers, who was no other than the Viscount de Lestang, a young seigneur from France, he had received a wound which placed his life in danger.

The commissaire made a note of the information of Paolo, and, as nothing more detained him at the hotel, he left, allowing the faithful domestic free liberty to present his homage to his ancient mistress.

The domestics of the hotel had heard the history of Paolo narrated to the commissaire, and as they knew very well that the portrait which had brought it on was that of their master, one of them had hurried to repeat it to one of the women who attended on Lucie; the latter did not fail to carry it to her mistress, so that the poor woman already knew that her husband was probably a robber and assassin, when Paolo was admitted to her.

Paolo was the bearer of a letter from the General Count Morengy, who, having heard upon his entering France, of the marriage of the widow of General de Neuville with the Marquis de Pourrieres, had, on the first day of his arrival, forwarded her his congratulations.

"Say to your master," said Lucie to Paolo, after reading the letter, "that I am sensible of the interest he feels towards me, and that I shall have the honour of replying to him;" and as she made a sign in order to dismiss the honest serviteur—

"Madame la Marquise has not forgotten," he said, "that she promised to retake me into her service?"

"My poor Paolo," replied Lucie, "I have no longer, alas! any occasion for attendants; I am poor now."

"That is nothing, madame; 'tis precisely when we are victims of misfortune, that we are in want of faithful attendants; and I dare say, Madame la Marquise will find none who are more so than I am."

"'Tis well, Paolo; 'tis well! it gives me some happiness in acquiring the certitude of a devotion, which I cannot, however, accept; return to your new master, my good Paolo; I can take no one into the exclusive retirement I shall seek, but rely upon it, that if the rule I am about to impose upon myself could admit of a single exception, it should be made in your favour."

Paolo retired, after kissing his mistress's hand.

When alone, Lucie entered her little cabinet, or work-room; she placed herself before the bureau, in which she was accustomed to secure her jewels, and wrote the three following letters:—

"*Lucie to the General Comte de Morengy.*
"Paris.

"Paolo has handed me a letter you have kindly addressed to me, my estimable friend; and it is with a heavy heart, and eyes filled with tears, that I hasten to reply to you. The journals will, probably, to-morrow morning, acquaint you with the cause of the deep grief to which I am a prey, and you will pity the poor Lucie, who deserved, perhaps, a better fate.

"I am fully sensible of the interest you feel towards me, and delighted that the results of the journey you have just completed, have been such as you hoped for.

"Adieu, my esteemed friend; you will, probably, not see poor Lucie again; but be assured that she will for ever preserve the remembrance of your kindness, and that she will not forget you in her prayers."

"Lucie to Laura Feval.

"Paris.

"I was this morning awakened by a commissary of police, who entered my bedroom, followed by several agents; he came to arrest my husband, who is accused of being one of the chiefs of a band of malefactors, which for a long time have levied their contributions on the public; he told me that the Viscount de Lussan had been just arrested, and taken to the prefecture of police; the same accusation rests upon him. The viscount did not allow himself to be taken, before he had shot one of the men engaged in his capture. They were prevented arresting my husband, who left the hotel yesterday evening, and who, as I have since learned from one of the domestics, passed the night at Choisy-le-Roi, in the Pavilion of the Guards, which he was to quit this very morning on a journey. I must suppose that some secret advice warned him of the danger hanging over him.

"This is not all: at the moment when the commissaire, who had seized the papers of M. de Pourrieres, was retiring, my old domestic, Paolo, presented himself at the hotel; he was charged with a letter for me, from his new master, the General Count de Morengy; the commissaire thought proper to question him—(Lucie here recounted to Laura, the circumstances to which the portrait of Salvador had given birth.)

"You see, my dear Laura, my cup of misery is full; but do not be alarmed, you will preserve your friend. I do not forget that I shall soon be a mother, and that I ought to live for the innocent creature I carry within me. My intention is to quit Paris; I cannot rest in a city in which the name I bear will, to-morrow, be publicly dishonoured. I shall hasten to our friend, Eugenie, I am certain that she and her husband will receive me with gladness; they have noble hearts!

"We shall meet again, my dear Laura; we shall meet again, rely upon it. I shall not die! I am much calmer, since I have been enabled to measure the extent of my misfortunes, than I was when I left you; I shall now endeavour to forget that my destiny is bound to that of a man who has, if report is to be believed, rendered himself guilty of every crime; I will try, I say, to forget that this man I have loved! alas! that, perhaps, I love him still!

"Adieu, my dear Laura; adieu, my good and faithful friend; I shall quit Paris to-morrow. I will write you again when I am installed with Eugenie. Adieu!

"Your friend,
"LUCIE."

———

"Lucie to Madame de Bourgerel.

"Paris.

"My dear Eugenie.—'If ever—which God forbid! either of you meet misfortunes, let her knock at my door; and, to find me ready to oblige her, she will have no need to recal what she has done for me to-day.' These, I think, if I have a good memory, were your words to Laura and me, when we had the happiness of coming to your aid. I did not expect, at that time, I should be so soon obliged to remind you of your promise. (Lucie here recounted her misfortunes, and thus continued:)

"Now that you know my troubles, I must tell you what is the nature of the service I claim from your friendship: I quit Paris, never to return to it; *I neither can, nor will, dwell in a city, in which the name I bear will, to-morrow, be publicly dishonoured!* and it is with you I have determined to fix myself.

I do not inquire whether you will receive me. I feel so sure of your reply, that my letter only precedes me a few hours.

"Adieu, my dear Eugenie. I add nothing for M. de Bourgerel, whom I shall see the day after to-morrow, and who, I am sure, will receive with joy an unfortunate woman, who has no other fault in his sight, than that of having quitted the name of his former general to take that of

"LUCIE DE POURRIERES."

Lucie, after writing the above letters, opened the secretaire, at which she was seated, and which contained the necessaries for sealing them; one of which, the seal, bore the initials of her own family, for the name of de Pourrieres inspired her with an insurmountable horror. The box, in which she expected to find this seal, and which in addition should have contained several other bijoux, was empty! She hurriedly examined several others; empty likewise! She surmised, at once, that it was her husband, who, anxious to save himself by flight, from the danger which threatened him, had carried off the whole of her jewels.

The blood mounted to her very forehead.

"This is infamous!" she exclaimed; "and he pressed my hand at the very moment he had committed so cowardly and base an action. Ah! God be praised!" she continued, after a moment's reflection, "now I despise this man; I will love him no longer."

She opened the letter intended for Laura, and added the following postscript:

"I am, my dear Laura, not quite so rich as I was yesterday; I have just discovered that my husband, before his flight, robbed me of all my jewels. I regret the loss, undoubtedly, of my bijoux, and, especially, a collar, belonging to my mother; but these regrets, lively as they are, do not prevent my thanking Providence for affording me the certitude, that my husband was a man still more despicable than most men resembling him, and that he played an infamous comedy, when he attempted to make me believe he loved me. You know we are always disposed to excuse the faults, even the crimes, of those who love us, whilst those whom we despise, can scarcely inspire us with pity."

After sealing the three letters, Lucie arranged several packages, which she sent to the coach, for Senlis; these boxes contained all that she required to take with her to the country: her dresses, her linen, her music, her books, and drawing materials —nor did she forget a magnificent piano, of Errard, a present from M. de Neuville, which she confided to a careful packer, who undertook the carriage of it. This done, she dismissed the domestics, whom she liberally paid. To fulfil this obligation, she was forced to send for money to her notary, Maitre Chardon, for Salvador had not left a single five-franc piece in the house. She only retained the youngest of her women, who was much attached to her, and gladly consented to follow her kind mistress into the isolated retreat she had chosen for a residence.

The next morning, Lucie, followed by her favourite femme de chambre, left the Hotel de Pourrieres, determined never to return there, to visit Maitre Chardon, to whom she gave a power of attorney, with a charge to defend her interests, which was accepted with pleasure by this estimable man; after this measure she mounted the coupé of the Senlis coach, and the same day, towards evening, she arrived at Saint Leonard, the village in which was situated the residence of Eugenie,

Madame de Saint Preuil, and Edmond de Bourgerel.

Eugenie and her husband had prepared for her reception the most agreeable apartment in the house; in this room, furnished with an elegant simplicity, Eugenie had arranged, with the most touching solicitude, most of the objects admired by Lucie; rare and handsome flowers, in magnificent Japan vases, some beautiful *aquarelles*, and Chinese curiosities.

Accompanied by Edmond, she conducted her friend into this charming retreat.

"You will not be badly off, here," she said; "and, besides, we have arranged every thing as well as it was possible to do."

"And in us, madame," added Edmond, "you will have kind and true friends, who will endeavour to find means of banishing from your mind, the thought, that misfortune has brought you amongst us."

"My good friends," said Lucie, taking the hands of Eugenie and Edmond, "my good friends, I am deeply moved at the proofs of friendship you bestow upon me, but that is not enough; you must add one more kindness to those I have hitherto received from you."

"Speak, my dear Lucie, speak," replied Eugenie, "be sure we are not disposed to refuse you anything."

Edmond joined his protestations to those of his wife.

"What has happened to me," resumed Lucie, "is a painful dream, which I should wish to forget; I would live, for the unfortunate victim I shall soon give birth to, and who, alas! will have no other protection on earth than its mother; but that will be impossible, if I recal without cessation that my destiny is linked to that of the man, whose name I am condemned to bear; this, then, is what I claim, more from the kindness of your heart than an obligation; Laura, her family, and my notary, Maitre Chardon, are the only persons in the world who are aware of the place I have chosen for my retreat; to them will be forwarded all letters addressed to me; M. Chardon has kindly undertaken to dispatch them here. Well! I am desirous that you should read these letters, before handing them to me, and that you will retain such as refer to any of the late events of my life, unless absolutely necessary to do otherwise; if fresh circumstances arise, I trust M. de Bourgerel will aid me with his advice."

Eugenie and Edmond de Bourgerel promised Lucie to do as she wished.

The night was far advanced when Lucie retired to her apartment. We need hardly say that her sleep was agitated, and troubled with painful dreams, which retraced to her imagination all the sad events that had taken place. It seemed to her that her husband was being dragged by a crowd of spirits towards a scaffold, the dim form of which was almost lost in the horizon; he made useless struggles to escape the furious grasp of these phantoms, which formed round him an impenetrable circle; and as he approached the scaffold, the unsightly aspect of the instrument became more distinct, and Lucie recognised, with a shudder, the horrible guillotine; all then disappeared, and she found herself in a saloon, where she met her friends and acquaintances; they spoke not to her, but as they passed, she was pointed out to those who were unknown to her, and sounds which resembled eclats of laughter, thundered into her ears: "'Tis the wife of the Marquis de Pourrieres!

she loved this man—a robber! an assassin by profession!"

"A robber! an assassin by profession!" exclaimed Lucie, waking up, "is it really possible? But, alas! the revelation made by Paolo forbids me to banish the belief of this last supposition. Oh! my God! grant that this man may soon become to me as indifferent as the unworthiest individual of his species."

Providence was pleased to listen favourably to the prayers of poor Lucie; for a while she preserved in her breast the germ of a grief, which would infallibly have carried her to the grave, if her friends, alarmed at seeing her continually gloomy and silent, had not reminded her that she belonged to those who loved her. But at length, and after long sufferings, and thanks to the unremitted attentions of Eugenie and Edmond, who for a long while withheld from her the knowledge of all the events which took place beyond the small circle in which she lived, she recovered somewhat of her former tranquillity.

Some time after her installation at Madame de Bourgerel's, Edmond, who rigorously conformed to the wish she had expressed, handed her, with the seal broken, a letter from Laura, who had already written to her several times. The letter was in the following terms:—

"*Laura Feval to Lucie.*
                    "Guermantes, near Lagny.

"My dear Lucie,—I have received a letter from Eugenie, and the information it conveys has filled me with joy; for I confess I had my fears that you would allow yourself to be bowed down by grief; I thank the Almighty who has given you strength to support with courage such cruel afflictions. My husband, and especially Sir Edward, who loves you as a child, and from whom it has been impossible to conceal the painful events that have happened, share my joy, and hope with me that if Divine Providence has thus so cruelly tried you, it has in reserve for you a future exemption from storms.

"I can imagine the motives which determined you to accord to Eugenie a preference, of which I have a mind to show myself jealous; but these motives, my dear Lucie, I appreciate, though I do not approve. I have not the courage, therefore, to make reproaches you would not merit, unless Eugenie and her husband did not render you as happy as you deserve; but of that there is no fear, M. and Madame de Bourgerel are persons whom we are happy to be enabled to reckon amongst our friends, and with such, deceit is not to be feared.

"I have expressed a wish to pass the winter at Guermantes, and as every thing which can please me is eagerly adopted by my husband and uncle, it was at once agreed that we should not quit our habitation until next year. Do not suppose, my kind Lucie, that it is simply because I passionately love the country, that I wish to remain at Guermantes; but I shall tell you no more at present, let it suffice you to know that I contemplate an agreeable surprise for you.

"There exist, unfortunately, individuals, who, when they suffer, would gladly see those around them suffer also; they pretend that the sight of another's woe, helps them to support their own. I do not know if I am wrong, but it seems to me that such persons are very badly organized; for on my part, I think that were I plunged in affliction, the best remedy they could employ to console me, would be to tell me of some happy event that had happened to one I loved. It is because I think you are like me, that I shall give you some news, which, I feel certain, will cause you an infinite deal of pleasure.

"My husband's most intimate friend, is a venerable ecclesiastic, attached to the parish of Saint Roch, whose talents and noble character you have, no doubt, heard praised more than once; for every one is pleased at rendering to M. l'Abbé Reuzet the justice due to him. Circumstances, which it would be too long to narrate here, discovered to this worthy priest the position my husband was placed in, and more than once he had to quiet my alarms, which, despite his efforts, frequently returned.

"The abbé, notwithstanding the efforts I made to conceal from those I love the griefs which preyed upon me, saw that I was unhappy; and, indeed, he was not deceived. Whilst my husband was away from me, I had no existence; when at home, every knock that sounded at the door, made me fancy that the summons announced the gendarmes come to arrest him. The abbé said nothing to me; he did not wish to create in me a hope, which might not, perhaps, be realized; but he visited every one who respected his talents and his character—and the number of these is considerable, and among them are many who are placed high in the social hierarchy—he wrested from their indifference the promise of warmly supporting a demand he intended addressing to the king. This man, who, probably, would not stir a step to obtain a cardinal's hat, trailed his cassock in the ante-chamber of all the ministers! at length, he succeeded; and yesterday, he ran, all joyfulness, to inform my husband that the king had granted him a full and entire pardon! To tell you how much patience and warmth this good priest exhibited, in order to obtain so great a favour as that he solicited, for a person whose name he would not make known until he had received a formal promise, would be impossible; the Abbé Reuzet, whose modesty is equal to his other virtues, would give us none of the details.

"At the present moment, my dear Lucie, my husband is free! I no longer suffer when I see him leave; if he is absent a few hours more than I expected, I await his return with patience; if by chance a stranger regards him, I am no more alarmed; I see him pass, without trembling, before the gendarmes of the neighbourhood. I am, in fact, as happy as it is possible to be, when we know that our best friend is suffering cruel torments.

"Adieu, my dear Lucie; forget not your faithful friend: moreover, forget not, that she intends you an agreeable surprise.

"LAURA FEVAL."

"Strange destinies!" said Lucie, after reading this letter; "my husband and that of my friend start together from the same place, and each, by following a different route, arrive at the same end; but he, who has always followed the straight path, preserves what he has acquired, whilst the other—what a frightful descent! Ah! I tremble to think of——God is just!"

The pregnancy of Lucie was already far advanced when she quitted Paris for the residence of Eugenie, consequently, a short time after her arrival at Saint Leonard, and whilst the events we shall report in the following chapters were taking place at Paris, she was taken with the first symptoms of labour.

The kindness of Eugenie and her husband to their unhappy friend, did not belie itself at this critical period; each vied with the other in unwearied attention. Lucie's accouchement was truly one of labour; the best physician of Senlis, whom they had sent for, was alarmed for her safety more than once, but she was at length delivered.

When she recovered her reason, she searched round her for the innocent creature, born under such gloomy prospects; astonished at not finding it, she cast her eyes upon the cradle, which, intentionally, had been placed near her bed—it was empty.

"My child!" she said, in a feeble voice, "give me my child! May I not be allowed to embrace it?"

Eugenie, who, seated at the head of her bed, leaned over and kissed her forehead, saying:

"Courage, my friend, courage!"

"My God!" exclaimed Lucie, "what has happened, then?"

"Your infant——"

"Well?"

"Courage, my poor friend, you will have need of it, alas!"

"He is dead?"

"It is true!"

Lucie replied not; her head fell back on her pillow, and bitter tears chased each other down her discoloured cheeks.

"I am very unfortunate," she said, after a short silence, whilst Eugenie endeavoured to console her. "Ah! my poor friend," she continued, in a faltering voice, "you cannot comprehend all the grief in the heart of a mother, who is forced to regard as a happy event, the death of her firstborn!"

CHAPTER XLVIII.

EXAMINATION.

SALVADOR had been two days at Melun; he cursed his unlucky stars for bringing near him the peasant who had recognised him, and as, despite all the efforts of his fertile imagination, he was not yet enabled to fabricate a history, of such a nature as to justify the position he found himself placed in; when the substitute came to him, he refused to reply to his questions, alleging that he was still much too feeble to support the fatigues of an examination.

The substitute, enveloped in a robe de chambre of flowered silk, his feet inserted in the embroidered slippers—for which he was indebted to the kindness of the wife of the sous prefect—endeavoured, whilst sipping a cup of chocolate, to guess the motive which could induce so noble a personage as M. le Marquis de Pourrieres to take a plebeian name and the quality of commission traveller, when his servant brought him his journal; the first article which met his sight, was entitled: "A band of robbers! arrest of a noble personage, who is supposed to be the chief: extraordinary circumstances!"

We shall here transcribe the entire article, which at the time of its appearance created such a sensation, that for the moment it superseded the weighty political affairs of the period; the following is a copy of the article:

"Such extraordinary things have happened since the commencement of the present age, that nothing which takes place now has the privilege of creating surprise; we believe, however, that the recital of the events we are about to narrate to our readers, will cause them to abandon for a moment their habitual indifference, and that after perusing us, they will not await, without a certain impatience, the process to which these events cannot fail to give birth.

"For a long time since, robberies, murders even, committed with an audacity and a skill inconceivable, have almost daily terrified the Parisian population; moreover, the circumstances which often accompanied the perpetration of these crimes, the quality of the persons who were the victims, made it conjectured that those who committed them were numerous, and that they had connections in the best society.

"The police, however, did not remain idle; it frequently visited the suspected places in the capital; the most expert agents were constantly in the country, but no results of any consequence were obtained; those whom it was anxious to encounter, unseizable Proteuses, knew how to avoid every research; every time the police believed it had hold of a thread of a nature to guide it, the thread gave way before it was possible to make use of it; thus, for example, the valuable jewels stolen from the Count Coloredo, and those abstracted from the jeweller Loiseau, were discovered; the first, at a Jew's at Amsterdam; the second, with one of the dealers in London, to whom the English have given the name of Lombards; but these individuals, against whom the French authorities are powerless, either cannot, or will not, make known the persons from whom they purchased them.

"They had almost lost the hope of putting their hands on these audacious malefactors, when lately an individual presented himself before the head of the police of safety, and offered him his services, promising, if they accepted them, to place shortly in the hands of justice, the chiefs and bandits who composed the band whose depredations desolated the capital; the offers of this man, who expressed himself favourably, and appeared both intelligent and resolute, and what is more extraordinary, named at once his place of residence and name, were readily accepted.

"A short time after, from the indication furnished by this man, they arrested, in a secret cave, situated at the extremity of a court belonging to a suspected house in the Rue de la Tannerie, several individuals known as robbers and assassins by profession, whom they had long been on the look-out for, although not successful. Some amongst them made confessions, from which it might be concluded, that for a considerable time the persons arrested had been directed by three men, whom they knew by no other names than Rupin, the Grand Richard, and the Provençal; that they were, as might be said, only the valets of these three mysterious individuals, who gave them in money a part of the value of the stolen articles, sold afterwards to a rich receiver, whom the informers could not discover, he being only known to Marie-Madeleine-Colette-Comtois, called Sans Refus, mistress of the house in which they had been arrested.

"This woman had escaped, owing to the guilty connivance of one of the agents who accompanied the commissaire of police charged with the arrest; the police therefore again lost the conducting link which might have put them in the track of these dangerous men, who they were resolved to discover.

"The individual to whom the arrest was due,

was grievously wounded by one of the bandits, enraged probably at having been made a dupe; when he recovered his health, he announced to the chief of police that he had at length discovered who were the individuals known by the name of Rupin, the Grand Richard, and the Provençal."

The journalist here narrated the different circumstances which had accompanied the arrest of the Viscount de Lussan, the death of Beppo, the visit to the hotel de Pourrieres, and the incident of the portrait, and then continued:

"Thus the declaration of this domestic, whose word could not be doubted, showed that the Marquis de Pourrieres had at one period, under the name of Viscount de Lestang, attempted to commit, at Turin, a robbery, and also to assassinate a person named Paolo, a servant of the banker Carmagnola; and weighing the fresh light brought to these affairs, we may suppose that this Rupin (not knowing what name to give this individual, we shall preserve the one under which he was known by his accomplices,) has no more right at present to the name of de Pourrieres, than he had formerly to possess himself of that of the Viscount de Lestang."

(Here followed an account of what had previously taken place respecting Fortunè, and the woman Adelaide Moulin.)

"The woman Adelaide Moulin, was not worthy of any great confidence; she has already suffered several correctional punishments, and is at this moment detained at the conciergerie, accused of forging bills, so that between her allegations and those of the Marquis de Pourrieres, there could be no hesitation; and it was simply from the lively interest he took in the young man whom the woman Adelaide pretends is the son of the Marquis Alexis de Pourrieres, that the judge of instruction, to whom she made some revelations concerning the young man, determined to write to Geneva in order to obtain from the municipal magistrates of that city, some information on the subject; but the late events have totally changed his opinions; he is now quite convinced that Adelaide Moulin is really the same woman to whom was confided the charge of taking care of the son of the Marquis Alexis de Pourrieres, and that the man who actually bears this name is nothing but an impostor, who has possessed himself, probably with the aid of crime, of a name and fortune which does not belong to him.

"We have no fear in saying we participate in the convictions of this worthy magistrate, and that we offer our sincere wishes that the efforts he will undoubtedly make to arrive at the truth, may be crowned with the happiest success.

"The papers seized at the hotel of the Marquis de Pourrieres, or rather of the man who bears the name, have been examined with the greatest care; this examination has revealed facts of the gravest nature, which we would make known to the reader, were we not afraid of throwing obstacles in the way of justice.

"The Viscount de Lussan (we cannot at least dispute the nobility of this man, who is in reality the last branch of one of the most illustrious families of Bretagne,) is very tranquil; he appears to have no fears for the result of the position he is in; he treats his keepers with a haughtiness quite aristocratic, and complains every moment that he is not paid that attention which is due to a man of his exalted sphere."

The deputy, after reading this article, wrote to Paris to apprise the authorities there, that accident having placed in his power the man calling himself

LIFE IN PARIS.

VERNIER, DE LUSSAN, AND SALVADOR.

the Marquis de Pourrieres, he held him at his disposition.

He immediately received an order to have him at once conveyed to Paris, under a good escort, if he was in a state to support the fatigues of the journey.

Salvador's wounds were, as we have observed, much less dangerous than was at first supposed; the surgeons, therefore, certified that he was quite *transportable*, if they would take some precautions.

"I am lost!" said Salvador to himself, when a bailiff, after handing to him the copy of a warrant for his removal, signed by one of the magistrates of the Seine, signified to him that the next morning he would be conducted to Paris. "I am lost, or nearly so. Ah! bah!" he continued, after reflecting a moment, "they can only accuse me of a few peccadilloes, which are yet far from being proved; come, come, if the Viscount de Lussan, and Silvia, who are probably arrested, show themselves as discreet as I shall be, I may perhaps, as well as they, escape this awkward step."

Orders had been given to the director of the conciergerie, that Salvador should be kept in the closest confinement; and he was in consequence deposited, on his arrival at Paris, in one of the cells of the women's side.

He passed nearly two months in this cell before his complete recovery. He had received no other visits during this space of time than from the guardians who brought him his daily pittance, and the surgeon who dressed his wounds; so that, when they came to conduct him before the examining magistrate, he experienced a feeling somewhat allied to pleasure.

We have neglected saying that the bandits commanded by Blaise le petit Christ, had contented themselves with carrying off his note-case and purse, which contained a tolerable sum in gold, and that they had left him his portmanteau, which contained, besides a reasonable quantity of linen and clothes, about five hundred francs in silver, intended to defray the first expenses on the road. As this portmanteau had not been seized, the contents of it were deposited with the greffier; he had wanted for nothing therefore while in prison. His toilette had been made with the most fastidious care, in which to appear before the magistrate, and he gaily followed the gendarme charged to conduct him.

The examination had been confided to the judge who had sent for him shortly before respecting Fortuné. The magistrate was one of those phlegmatic men who never allow to appear on their countenance the emotions they may feel, who seize at the first glance upon all the details of an affair, who allow nothing to escape, whose memory is prodigious, and who manage to derive something advantageous from circumstances in appearance the most indifferent; in a word, he was endowed with every quality requisite to be in possession of, to be enabled to cope with a man so *rusé* as Salvador.

We shall report somewhat lengthily the different *phases* of this examination, which will successively expose the catalogue of crimes committed by Salvador.

"Your name?" demanded the judge, when Salvador was seated.

"Alexis, Marquis de Pourrieres, born at the Chateau de Pourrieres, department of the Var, arrondissement of Brignoles."

"You are, as you assert, the Marquis Alexis de Pourrieres? I ought to inform you that you will be called upon to prove that this name and title,

which it is intended to dispute, actually belong to you; if you are not what you profess to be, a sincere avowal may perhaps dispose the law to treat you with an indulgence which, in that event, you would probably have great need of."

"I know not, sir, for what object you make this observation; but I am, thank God, in a condition to prove, when necessary, that I am rightly the only son of M. le Marquis Hector de Pourrieres, captain in the army of princes."

"That's enough. I felt bound to warn you as I have done. Reply now to the questions I am about to put to you.

"You were stopped in the wood Bougeaux by bandits, who robbed you of all you possessed, and left you for dead in the road?"

"It is true."

"You were found by a patrol of gendarmerie, and carried to Melun?"

"It is also true."

"When, thanks to the attentions paid you, you had recovered the use of your faculties, you were interrogated by M. le substitute of the procureur du roi of that town; you reported to that magistrate the different circumstances of the attempt of which you were the victim; circumstances, I ought to observe, which ulterior events have proved to be correct; and yet, when necessary to sign your declaration, you assumed the name of Louis Rousseau, travelling clerk of the house of Biot and Company, of Marseilles. Why so?"

"I was unwilling, from a fear of causing too great an alarm to my wife and my friends, that they should hear from any other than myself the event that had happened to me; it was my intention to have informed M. le substitute afterwards what was my real name."

"Was it not rather, that having been apprised that pursuit would be directed against you, you desired to conceal the name under which you were known, and therefore assumed that of Louis Rousseau?"

"It is permitted you, sir, to suppose that I had *any* intention agreeing with the accusation."

"But if such was not your intention, why were you the bearer of a passport in the name of Louis Rousseau?"

"I made no use of any passport in the name of Louis Rousseau!" said Salvador, who knew very well that the bandits who had robbed him had carried off his note-case and its contents.

"Here it is," replied the judge, and he showed Salvador the passport he had prepared at Choisy-le-Roi, the night preceding his departure. "Do you acknowledge it?"

Salvador refused to answer.

"You would do wrong to deny the evidence," resumed the judge. "This passport was seized on a man lately arrested at Compeigne, at the moment he was endeavouring to obtain an entrance into a church to steal the communion service plate. This man admitted that he made part of the band of Blaise, called le petit Christ, by whom you were attacked, and that it was from a traveller whose description he gave, and which applies exactly to your person, that he had stolen this passport. What have you to reply?"

"Nothing at present."

"Very well. You are aware, no doubt, of what crimes you are accused?"

"They might, sir, accuse me of being the author of a number of crimes; but as I do not remember having committed a single one, I am forced to confess my ignorance."

"I will acquaint you with them. For a long time a band of robbers have laid waste the capital, every day some fresh crime terrified the inhabitants. Well, it is said that the chiefs of this band were no other than you, the Viscount de Lussan, and a third individual only known by the name of the Provençal."

"Ah! they pretend that, do they? Well, sir, it must be proved, and I think that will be a matter of some difficulty."

"Less perhaps than you imagine. Do you know the Viscount de Lussan?"

"Intimately; M. de Lussan is one of my best friends."

"Do you know the person named Marie-Madeleine-Colette-Comtois, called Sans Refus?"

"I have never heard mention of this woman."

"You were never in a suspected house of the Street de la Tannerie, No. 31?"

"Never."

"And yet it was at this woman's house that the band of which you are accused of being one of the chiefs, assembled?"

"I know no more of the men who composed this band, than I do of the place in which they assembled."

"Do you know the name of the individual who passed under the name of the Provençal?"

"I know not to whom you allude."

"Was not this individual and M. Lebrun, your intendant, one and the same person?"

"I do not think so; I cannot, however, deny absolutely a fact of which I am ignorant, my intendant was master of nearly all his time; I know not how he employed it when not at the hotel; and after all, admitting it possible that he was connected with a band of robbers, am I responsible for his actions?"

"Had you any reason to complain of M. Lebrun?"

"No. M. Lebrun was an excellent servant."

"It will, however, be established, that this man, who was, as you assert, an excellent servant, was a gambler; that he passed every evening at a clandestine tripot of la Rue Richelieu?"

"You acquaint me with a fact I was ignorant of till this hour."

"Perhaps."

The judge selected from a voluminous collection of papers placed before him, a letter which Salvador directly recognised as one that Silvia had written him during the time he inhabited the Chateau de Pourrieres with his wife. It was usual for him to burn every letter he received, which might in any manner compromise him, but he had made an exception in favour of the one the judge held in his hand, which, in the event of his having to complain of Silvia, might be used against her.

"Are you intimate with the Marchioness de Roselly?"

"All Paris knows that for a long while I have been in the friendship of this lady."

"Here is a letter written by the marchioness, and addressed to you, and one which you received, since it was found at your hotel, and which abundantly proves that you were perfectly aware that Lebrun played, and lost frequently considerable sums."

"Eh! my God! sir, I could not suppose it necessary to inform you that the unfortunate man was in fact an outrageous gambler."

"This man was murdered in the night of the 10th and 11th of September last, as recorded by the proces verbal of the commissary of police, who discovered the body, and also your own declaration made the next morning before the same commissaire."

"Admitted."

"They say that it was you, who, to get rid of this man, (who, as I have observed to you, played and lost considerable sums, which he must have taken from your coffers,) assassinated him."

"To this fresh accusation I shall make the same reply that I have to those already put to me; they must prove it."

"And we will endeavour to do so; do you recognise these articles?"

The judge exhibited to Salvador a small card-case, inlaid with gold, which had belonged to Roman, and a snuff-box of platina. Salvador well remembered these two objects, but not knowing how they might make against him, he thought it best to feign ignorance.

"I have never seen them," he replied.

"These articles belonged to your intendant."

"Very possibly."

"They were seized at your hotel."

"And what does that prove?"

The judge opened the case, and drew from it one of those cards divided into horizontal columns, surmounted with letters of red and black, upon which the players mark, with the aid of a pin, the different phases of the game; this card, upon which was indicated a series of twenty-one blacks, followed by intermittants, and also several others in the case, bore, in the hand-writing of Roman, the date of the day he had used it, the 10th September.

"This case," continued the judge, "was, as well as the snuff-box, in the possession of the victim a few hours before his death; witnesses have so declared, and this date, written by the hand of Lebrun, gives much strength to their declarations. What have you to reply?"

"Nothing."

"But you forget, probably, that it was in your own apartment at your hotel that these articles were seized, and that they could only have been taken there by the assassin."

"It's possible, but I only arrived in Paris on the morning which followed the night in which the murder was committed; this will be attested, if necessary, by all my domestics."

"In my turn, I shall say, it is possible; but inquiries have been made, and this is the result: you quitted de Pourrieres to go to Paris, but instead of arriving there direct, you stopped at Melun, where you descended at the Hotel de la Galére; you quitted this town the 10th September, after a stay of some hours, and the next morning, the 11th, you returned there and took your post-chaise, which you had left at the hotel; it was undoubtedly in the morning of the 11th you arrived at your hotel; but there remains one night, that between the 10th and 11th, during which we know not what became of you, and it was precisely in this night that Lebrun was assassinated. These divers circumstances are serious."

"Very serious, indeed, but not enough, however, to allow it to be supposed that I was the author of a crime which I had no interest in committing."

"Why, on the contrary, you had an immense interest in committing this crime, if, as it is said, your intendant robbed you to procure the means of satisfying his fatal passion."

"In truth, sir, you draw from facts in themselves insignificant, very grave consequences. Could I not, if I had to complain of my intendant, dismiss him; hand him over to justice, even?"

"But if, as they pretend, this Lebrun was no other than the individual known under the name of the Provençal, you could not, since he was your accomplice, either dismiss him, or hand him over to justice."

"But it is no farther proved, I think, that this miserable was the one you designated under the name of the Provençal, than it is that I am not the Marquis de Pourrieres."

The judge touched the bell-rope placed near him, and whispered a few words to the clerk who presented himself; the man left, and shortly afterwards brought into the cabinet of the judge a small box of white wood, which he placed on the table; the gendarmes, at the same time, introduced two men, well known to Salvador, these were le Grand Louis and Charles la belle Cravate.

"Do you know these two men?" said the judge, when they were placed.

"I see them to-day for the first time," he replied.

"Ah! Rupin," exclaimed Grand Louis, "you disown your friends; that's not right."

"Didn't I say he'd show his pride till he got to the guillotine," added Charles.

"And so," said the judge, addressing Grand Louis, to whom he indicated Salvador, "you know this person?"

"Perfectly, sir; 'tis Rupin."

Charles la belle Cravate, questioned in his turn, made the same reply.

"You only know him under the name of Rupin?"

"Simply under that name, M. le Judge," replied Grand Louis; "but I know that Rupin is a great man, malicious, and rich. Ah! if he had not, with his two friends, Grand Richard and le Provençal, sent to the other world Delicat, Coco-Desbraises, and Rolet le Mauvais Gueux, they would have told you a pretty history; they had discovered the *rose-pot** of these messieurs, but it cost the poor devils their lives."

"We will talk about that affair by-and-by," said the judge, who ordered his greffier to open the wooden box lying on the table.

The greffier obeyed. He opened the box and drew from it a mask in wax, which he handed to the judge. The latter took off the silk paper, in which it was enveloped, and showed it to Salvador.

"Roman!" exclaimed Salvador, throwing back his head; the mask was so resembling, that for the moment he fancied it the head of his accomplice which they had placed before him; and the fright he experienced wrested from him an exclamation, of which he admitted to himself all the imprudence when he heard the judge say to his greffier:

"Write, that having shown to the accused the wax mask of the man assassinated in the Rue de Courcelles, in the night of the 10th and 11th September last, he exhibited a violent movement of surprise, and exclaimed, 'Roman!' which gives us reason to think that this is the name of the individual known at present under that of Lebrun."

The mask was afterwards shown to Grand Louis and Charles la belle Cravate.

"'Tis the portrait of the Provençal!" exclaimed both; "'tis his counterpart."

After this incident, the judge recommenced questioning Salvador.

"You see," he said "that these two individuals,

* Residence.

who are no less, on their own admission, than robbers by profession, recognise you perfectly."

"But I do not know them; and as the profession which they exercise, is not, I suppose, a title to confidence, I think that between their affirmation and my denial there cannot be a moment's hesitation."

"If really you are not him they call Rupin, if really you never entered the house of Sans Refus, to what motive do you attribute the formal recognition of these two men?"

"Eh! how do I know; to a desire of rendering themselves important, perhaps; if you will allow me to put a few questions to one or the other of these two wretches, I think it will be possible for me to prove that they are nothing but impostors."

Having obtained the permission requested, Salvador addressed Grand Louis.

"You know me?" he said to the bandit.

"Well," replied Grand Louis, "I was paid to do so, for I still feel on my shoulders the smart from the caning you gave me."

"I was with the Grand Richard, and the Provençal, one of the chiefs of the band which assembled at the house of this woman, whom you have named Sans Refus?"

"Why, certainly; and if you had not ceased coming amongst us, we should not perhaps be in the trouble we are now in."

"Therefore, I was one of your chiefs, and went at some period, more or less distant, to visit you in your den; I robbed with you?"

"Of course, 'tis proved; is it not, belle Cravate."

"'Tis proved," replied Charles; "Rupin must pay, and dearer than his bargains hitherto."

"As this is the case," resumed Salvador, "among the multitude of robberies of which you are accused, there must be at least one in which you can prove that I co-operated. When you have given this proof, I will confess that I am your accomplice; but until then," he continued, addressing the judge, "I may be allowed to feel some astonishment that the evidence of such wretches can reach a man like me."

To this sally, upon the effect of which Salvador greatly relied, the judge replied, that they could not as yet bring forward against him an accusation of robbery; that on this subject, presumption was the only grounds; but that, as it was proved in evidence that he had several times gone to the house of Sans Refus disguised, it was very allowable to suppose that he took an active part in the depredations committed by the bandits who accused him, either by assisting them personally, or by his advice, or by effecting a sale of the objects stolen, to Mother Sans Refus.

"But, sir," exclaimed Salvador, much annoyed that his sally had not produced the effect he anticipated, "when I affirm that I never entered this house, and that I have against me, only the evidence of wretches such as these, I ought to be believed!"

"Unfortunately for you, written proofs, which you will not dream of contesting, since they emanate from yourself, will be added to the evidence of *these wretches.*"

"I do not comprehend you, sir," replied Salvador.

The judge took from the packet of papers a letter, which he handed to Salvador, who turned pale on recognising it.

This letter was the one he had written to Lucie, on sending her the card-case she had lost at Mother Sans Refus's.

" Madame de Pourrieres has been interrogated," said the judge, " and notwithstanding the very natural desire she had not to compromise you, she was compelled to make known to justice the events which preceded her marriage with you; 'twas in the house of Sans Refus, which she had entered in consequence of an event, the details of which she has reported to us, that she encountered you for the first time; will you tell us, as you did this unfortunate woman, that you were in this house merely for the purpose of studying the eccentric manners of the capital?"

" Sir," replied Salvador, " the examination you have subjected me to has continued for a length of time; I am, and you must be, much fatigued; the weak state I am in, owing to my wounds, forces me to beg you will defer the continuance of this examination until to-morrow, or the day most convenient to yourself."

The judge could not refuse Salvador, who, in fact, appeared greatly fatigued; he gave orders therefore to the gendarmes to reconduct him to prison, after notifying to him to hold himself in readiness for the following morning but one, and also that his next examination would relate to the triple assassination he was accused of committing, in complicity with the Viscount de Lussan and the Provençal, on the persons of Delicat, Desbraises, called Coco, and Rolet, named the "*Mauvais Gueux*."

" I am much worse than I thought," said Salvador to himself, when alone in his cell at the conciergerie; and threw himself on the bed, where he remained for some time, his head buried in his two hands; in fact, he had as yet submitted but to one ordeal, and he could not dissemble from himself, that Justice held in her hands the thread which must lead to the discovery of all the crimes he had committed; it was already nearly proved that he was the author of the murder to which Roman fell a victim, and his presence at Mother Sans Refus's, which he could no longer attempt to deny, and could not explain, would add entire confidence to the declarations of the bandits, who pretended that he had joined in the misdeeds of which they had rendered themselves guilty.

" My head totters on my shoulders," he continued, rising, " will it fall? my faith, I cannot tell; but for the present I must defend it with courage and address. I shall not despair until I find myself in the fatal cart."

Salvador was at this part of his monologue, when the turnkey, who daily brought him the meagre pittance allotted to each prisoner, entered his cell.

" I am so satisfied with the result of my first examination," he said to him, " that I mean to celebrate it by a little fête; have the kindness, therefore, to bring me some delicate viands, a bottle of good wine, and some coffee, if that is possible; you will obtain the money from the greffier."

The guardian, upon whom the handsome features and elegant costume which Salvador retained in his prison, imposed, hastened to execute the order he had received; Salvador, delighted at varying a little the uniform nature of his ordinary, eat with an appetite the wing of a capon and some cutlets à la Soubise; he drank a bottle of old wine and a small cup of excellent coffee; and it being night, he went to bed and slept peacefully till the next morning.

On the following day he was again brought before the judge of instruction; le Grand Louis and Charles la belle Cravate were already in the cabinet of the magistrate.

" Your relations with the individuals who frequented the house of Marie Madeleine Colette Comtois, called Sans Refus," said the judge, after reading the formal heading of the proces verbal of examination, " are now fully established; not only by the evidence of Madame de Pourrieres, in whom we place the greatest confidence, but also by written proofs which you cannot call in question, *since they emanate from yourself.*"

Salvador replied affirmatively, of which the judge had a note taken.

" You admit, therefore, that upon several occasions you have entered this house disguised, and that you have taken part in the numerous robberies committed by these men?"

" Let us distinguish, sir. I admit, indeed, that I went several times, disguised, to the house of Sans Refus, but I deny positively having ever taken a part in the deeds of which these men are accused; motives, which I cannot at present make known, but perfectly honourable, imperatively required my presence in this house; but I repeat, I have taken no part in any robbery, I have committed no bad action, and I do not hesitate to say, it will be impossible to prove the contrary of what I assert."

" The declaration you have made will receive its proper weight. I ought, however, to observe to you, that in order to obtain belief, you must resolve to make known the motives, which, as you pretend, required your presence in the house of Sans Refus."

" What you demand of me is impossible."

The judge after this, questioned Salvador as to the facts which had preceded, accompanied, and followed the death of Delicat, Coco Desbraises, and Rolet le Mauvais Gueux. Our readers will remember that the bodies of these three miserables, after being disfigured by le Grand Louis, who had exercised the profession of a butcher before adopting that of a robber, had been put into empty casks which were thrown into the Seine; nor have they forgotten that Coco Desbraises and Delicat, finding nothing to steal in the pavilion at Choisy-le-Roi, which they had entered, the latter in opposition to the representations of his comrade, who observed to him that these articles would help to discover him, resolved to carry away a redingote and pantaloons, forgotten in a drawer. These garments belonged to a servant of Salvador, who not finding them in the place in which he had left them, made a declaration before the mayor of Choisy-le-Roi of the robbery committed to his prejudice; this theft was of too little importance to induce them to look for the authors, so that they merely took a note of the declaration.

Some time after, the casks, which contained the three bodies, were washed on shore; the sight of these bodies, covered with wounds and horribly mutilated, excited general horror, and the police made every exertion to ascertain who were the victims, and afterwards to discover the assassins.

The clothes of the victims were examined with the greatest minutiæ; it was ascertained that the garments in which two of the bodies were clothed, were ready-made articles sold by all fripiers, and of such similarity that it was almost impossible to guess the place they came from; they simply remarked the redingote and pantaloons on the body of the third; these garments, still in tolerable condition, were well made; and the buttons of the pantaloons bore the address of the tailor who had furnished them. They sent for this man, and showed him the garment, which he recognised at once, and mentioned the person to whom he had sold it; this person was the domestic of Salvador, who had shortly before made the declaration as to the robbery; as the redingote and pantaloons were much too large for Delicat, it was possible he had not purchased them; this led to the conclusion that the man whose body they had found was the author of the robbery at Choisy-le-Roi. This affair, putting aside the discovery which proved nothing that was necessary to be known, remained for the police an enigma which the revelations of Grand Louis and Charles la belle Cravate afterwards solved.

"That which I have now made known to you," said the judge to Salvador, after mentioning to him the facts we have stated above, "explains the interest you had to rid yourself of these three men; you could not permit to live, the individuals who had discovered the position you held in society, who wished to lay you under contribution, and who, if we are to believe the declarations of the informers loudly manifested their intention of discovering you to justice if you refused to satisfy their demands."

Salvador, to these precise interpolations of the judge, could only oppose a denial, which, he was perfectly aware, could not destroy presumptions so strong as those which appeared against him; he was terrified at the multitude of unforeseen circumstances which Providence seemed to have united for the purpose of his destruction.

"You have declared, in your former examination," continued the judge, after allowing Salvador, who had made the request, a few minutes to collect himself, "that you knew intimately the Marchioness de Roselly; you added, moreover, that all Paris was aware of your connection with this lady."

"What the deuce is he driving at?" thought Salvador; "has Silvia, by any chance, neglecting the advice I sent her, allowed herself to be caught; and, if so, is she fool enough to make any confession; or is it the Viscount de Lussan?—Ah! bah! neither Silvia nor de Lussan are capable of that."

"Reply to the question I am about to put to you," said the judge; "do you know the Marchioness de Roselly?"

"Yes, sir."

"At what period and in what place did you make the acquaintance of this lady?"

"I have known the Marchioness de Roselly for more than three years; it was at Lyons I saw her for the first time."

"Very well; Madame de Roselly, when she was *premiere chanteuse* at the theatre of Marseilles, frequently received at her house the visits of a Jew usurer, named Josué."

"It is unknown to me."

"It's possible; but you knew this Jew?"

"I did; I found myself, shortly after my quitting the paternal roof, in relation with the Jew Josué of Marseilles. This man lent me, at different times, sums which formed, in the whole, with the interest, a considerable amount. When I returned to France, after the death of my father, I paid him, and the affair was ended. In fact, I did not myself pay and adjust the accounts with the Jew Josué, I charged my intendant with it."

"M. Lebrun?"

"Himself; and I should observe, that I was fully satisfied with the manner in which he acquitted himself of it. As my papers have been seized, you ought to have in your possession the receipts of Josué."

"There they are. Have you seen Josué since your return to France?"

"No, sir."

"You have never met him at the Marchioness of Roselly's?"

"Never."

"Did you know, before I informed you of it, that this lady often received Josué at her house?"

"I was ignorant of it."

"You are quite sure of that."

"In truth, quite certain."

"You are, however, accused of having, in complicity with Catherine Fontaine, otherwise Silvia, widow of the Marquis de Roselly, ex-premiere chanteuse at the grand theatre of Marseilles, committed a murder, followed by robbery, on the person of this same Josué; what have you to reply?"

The previous questions had prepared Salvador for the accusation brought against him, so that he could reply, with some tranquillity, to the judge, who repeated the question:

"What reply have you to make?"

"That I am no more guilty of this crime than the others of which I am accused."

We owe to our readers a recital of the facts which led to the discovery of the assassins of the unfortunate Josué. In order that they may be easily understood, it is necessary to recal the principal circumstances which accompanied the perpetration of the crime.

When Josué quitted Silvia's hotel, half drunk, after supping with her, and had passed, by some metres, the Bridge de la Concorde, Roman sprang upon him, and threw over his neck, in order to strangle him, a handkerchief twisted into a cord. Salvador, in the mean time, seized the scapulaire suspended from the neck of the victim, which contained the bank-notes, the object of the murder. The victim dead and robbed, they threw the body into the Seine. They then made a packet of the blouses and large linen pantaloons, which they had worn over their usual dress, and threw them also into the river, after taking care to insert some stones to sink it; but so great was their haste, that the bundle became loosened before it touched the water, and the contents of it followed the course of the tide. One of the blouses—the one worn by Salvador—was stopped at the same time as the body of the unfortunate Josué, by one of the Islands du Roi, and chance so contrived that the blouse and the body became so entangled together, that the sailors who discovered it supposed it to belong to the victim. The questions addressed to Salvador will inform our readers of the results of this apparently insignificant event.

"The death of the Jew Josué," said the judge, after patiently listening to the protestations of innocence by Salvador, "was at first attributed to suicide; but, on examination of his body, they discovered round his neck evident marks of strangulation. Efforts were then made to find out the assassin; these efforts resulted in nothing. The body was given up to his friends, who had it buried, and the justice of man, powerless for the moment, transferred to Providence the care of bringing it to light. He has not failed them."

"I must confess, sir, I am curious to know what were the means employed by the justice of God to make me appear guilty of a crime I have not committed?"

"You shall know them."

The judge made a sign to the greffier, who spoke a few words in an under tone to the clerk, who, in a few minutes, brought a portmanteau into the office.

"Do you know this portmanteau ?" said the judge.

"Undoubtedly, 'tis my own," said Salvador.

"And all that it contains belongs to you?"

"Let me see," said Salvador to himself, "what have I put in this portmanteau? May I, without danger, admit all that it contains?"

The clerk had spread upon the table all the articles contained in the portmanteau, clothes, linen, and dressing-case.

"I may, without any fear, acknowledge all this," he said again to himself.

And as the judge repeated the question, he replied:

"Yes, sir, I recognise these articles; I can, if you require it, prove the legitimate possession of them."

"And of the handkerchiefs in particular?"

The judge showed Salvador several white cambric handkerchiefs, of English manufacture, marked with the letters A. P., surmounted with the coronet of a marquis, each bearing a number, and bordered with red and blue flowers.

"That will not be more difficult than for the rest," said Salvador, smiling. "I purchased them of Chapron, at the Sublime Porte, a short time after my first stay at Pourrieres; but I do not suppose they accuse me of having stolen them, that would indeed be too laughable."

"How many did you purchase?"

"A dozen."

"There are two wanting."

"There is one of them."

Salvador mechanically drew from his pocket the handkerchief; the clerk took it, and handed it to the judge.

"There is still wanting No. 7," said the latter; "what have you done with it?"

"How do I know?" exclaimed Salvador, impatient at not being able, despite every effort of his imagination, to surmise the object the magistrate had in view; "probably I have lost it."

"In what place? Reply to this question; it is, perhaps, much more important than you expect."

"I cannot, sir. If one of the handkerchiefs is missing, I must have lost it, or been robbed of it; I cannot tell you more."

The judge took from one of the drawers of his bureau a handkerchief, absolutely similar to the others, but soiled with mud.

"There," said he, "I think, is the one missing from your collection; you see the mark is the same, and it has the number 7. Well, do you know where it was found?—in the side pocket of the blouse, entangled with the body of the unhappy Jew, Josué, which induces the belief that it belonged to his assassin."

"Eh! good God, sir, that proves, at the farthest, that he who found or robbed me of this handkerchief, is, perhaps, the author of the crime of which I am now accused; and if they have no other proof against me——"

"Unfortunately for you, there do exist others. The journals have published your arrest, and also a category of the different crimes of which you are accused. One of these journals found its way to Metz, where the sister of Josué has retired, at the moment she was searching for information in one of the books used by her father to note down the appointments he had to keep; and in this book, which she has sent us, after having it identified by the authorities of the town, is the following memorandum: '13th May, at Madame de Roselly's, where I am to meet the Marquis de Pourrieres,

and take with me the 200,000 francs, which I am to lend him?" And on the 14th May, the body of the Jew was found in the Seine. Since the receipt of this registry, inquiries have been made; they have found two of the former domestics of the Marchioness de Roselly; and the result of their declarations is, that, on the 13th May, the Jew Josué did, in fact, visit this lady—that he took supper with her—and that he did not leave until half-past eleven at night. It was, therefore, upon his leaving her house that he was murdered. What have you to reply?"

"It is possible, sir, that the unfortunate Josué was assassinated upon his leaving the house of the Marchioness de Roselly—if, in fact, he visited this lady, who lived, at the period of this crime, in one of the most deserted quarters of the capital; but to accuse of so horrible a crime this woman, whose gentleness and amiability is acknowledged by every one—to accuse me of being her accomplice, and prop up an accusation merely upon presumptions, is, permit me to observe, to build a vast edifice upon a foundation of sand."

"You may not place any great value upon the presumptions united against you, but you will, nevertheless, have to render an account of the employment of your time during the night of the 13th to the 14th May."

The judge ordered the gendarmes to reconduct Salvador to prison. In one of the underground passages which lead from the Palace of Justice to the conciergerie, Salvador and his companions were met by the chief of the police, who accompanied a prisoner in the custody of two gendarmes, on his way to the office of a judge d'instruction.

The chief of police, endowed, as it seems, with an excellent coup d'œil, at once recognised Salvador. Our readers will remember that, upon the disappearance of Silvia, when carried off by Beppo, he had paid a visit to this functionary.

"Well, M. le Marquis de Pourrieres," said the chief to Salvador, "you see we have discovered the assassins of the Jew Josué; but I must say I had no idea, when you came to my office, that I had before me one of those I was exerting such means to discover."

"Alexis de Pourrieres, accused of murder!" exclaimed the prisoner who accompanied the chief; "it's not possible."

This exclamation aroused the chief of police, who ordered the gendarmes to allow the prisoner to approach Salvador.

"It is so far possible, that it is a fact," said the chief. "Present your respects to M. le Marquis de Pourrieres, since you know him."

The prisoner approached Salvador, whom he regarded attentively.

"I am not deceived," he exclaimed; "'tis Aymard—'tis the Viscount de Lestang—'tis Salvador."

"Bravo! Ronquetti," cried the chief of police, transported with joy; "bravo! worthy Duke of Modena, you have made a discovery that will be placed to your account in the proper time." He then continued his way, followed by the prisoner.

Salvador, gloomy and dispirited, entered his cell. The encounter he had stumbled upon, strangely abridged the task of those who endeavoured to prove that he was not the Marquis Alexis de Pourrieres. As he had been apprised that it was their intention to dispute this title, he had reserved all the resources of his fertile imagination for the moment of combat; and as he was minutely acquainted with every particular in the life of the man whose title he had assumed, after depriving him of life,

LIFE IN PARIS.

THE OLD LADY AND THE ABBÉ.

and as to every question put to him he could oppose this reply: "But who am I, then, if I am not the Marquis de Pourrieres?" as he imitated to perfection the writing of Alexis, he did not despair of coming off victorious in the struggle that would arise on this subject; but the encounter with Ronquetti, disposed, as he had given a proof, to make revelations—with Ronquetti, who had particularly known Alexis—whose companion he had been for a long while—who knew Silvia, and was once acquainted with Roman—was one of those unexpected events which we know not how to oppose, and which, like a thunderbolt, destroys the strongest building.

Salvador very soon experienced the effects of the encounter he had made. At first, he was not so often subjected to examination; he conjectured that, if it were so, it was that his judge required time to collect fresh elements against him, which the revelations of Ronquetti furnished him with; he was not mistaken as he soon proved.

When he was again sent for to the cabinet of the judge, he found a large assemblage there. Besides Ronquetti, there were two men, already aged and miserably clothed; an old woman, with swarthy physiognomy, habited in a costume adopted by the peasants of the western parts of France; two servants in livery, whom Salvador recognised as having been in the service of Silvia, at the time of Josué's murder; the chief of police and one of his agents; Paolo; the woman Adelaide Moulin; and several other individuals, whom the following pages will sufficiently make known.

The entrance into the cabinet of Salvador and the two gendarmes placed over him, was received with murmurs, which ceased on a sign from the judge, who then beckoned to the two men who accompanied the old swarthy woman.

These three individuals left the group in which they were mixed, and, upon the order of the judge, placed themselves before Salvador.

"Do you know monsieur?" said the judge, pointing out Salvador to the eldest of the two men, who made to this question a negative reply; it was then put to the other man and to the old woman, and a similar answer returned.

"It is evident," said Salvador to himself, "that if I am the Marquis Alexis de Pourrieres, I ought to know these three individuals; but who are they? I will neither say yes nor no; it is the best means of not compromising myself.

"The features of these honest people are not entirely unknown to me," he replied; "I do not think I see them now for the first time; but I neither remember their names nor in what place I have met them."

"If you are in fact the Marquis Alexis de Pourrieres, you ought not, neither could you forget these people, whom you must have well known. Come, recollect yourself."

"My recollections fail me, sir; I cannot name either these two men or this woman; still, I repeat to you, I think I remember them."

The questions were repeated to the three persons whom Salvador pretended to recognise, though he knew not their names; they again denied all knowledge of him.

"You affirm, then," said the judge, "that the man before you is not the Marquis Alexis de Pourrieres?"

"Yes, M. le Judge," replied the eldest of the two men and his two companions.

"Sign your declaration."

They all signed, and being told by the judge they might retire, they left the cabinet together.

"It is rather strange," said the judge to Salvador, when they had quitted, "that your memory does not recal to you the names of the father and aunt of the mother of the young Fortunè."

"Louiset?" exclaimed Salvador.

"Just so; 'tis Louiset and his sister who have just left;" and the judge showed to Salvador, at the bottom of the proces verbal, the signatures of these two individuals.

"Come," thought Salvador, "I have escaped tolerably well out of this awkward mess; I can now, without fear, recognise the grandfather of my son.

"You have brought me home," he continued, "and at present I perfectly recognise Louiset, the master of arms, who gave me my first lessons in fencing, and also his sister."

"In that case, you may also remember the man who was with them?"

Salvador could not make a satisfactory reply to this question; it was, indeed, rather difficult to remember a person whom he had never seen—whom he had never heard mentioned. The man of whom the magistrate spoke was no other than the provost of the hall of the master of arms, Louiset, who had well known Alexis de Pourrieres at the period when this unfortunate young man, to pay his court leisurely to Jazetta, was a frequent attendant at the hall of the father of this girl.

"It is at least singular," continued the judge, "that the parents of the mother of a child you have recognised, and with whom you lived for a considerable time could not or would not recognise you. To what motive can you attribute their ill will?"

"I know not; perhaps to the hatred inspired by my conduct towards their child, whom I abandoned, after having seduced."

"But I should observe to you that you accuse yourself of wrongs towards Jazetta Louiset, which you never committed. We know that it was not you who abandoned Jazetta, but that, on the contrary, she left you at Geneva, to follow an English officer to the East Indies; we will have a note made of your reply and observation. Adelaide Moulin, come forward. Your persist in maintaining that the man before you is not the same who called himself, at Geneva, the Count de Courtivon, and who confided to you, to bring up, a child of the male sex, whom he acknowledged, and to whom he gave the name of Fortunè de Pourrieres?"

"Yes, sir. There is, however, between the features of monsieur and those of the Marquis Alexis de Pourrieres, a certain resemblance, which might deceive at first sight; but, I repeat, the eyes of Fortunè's father were black, those of monsieur are blue; the former was less strongly built than the latter; the expression of his features was milder."

"You hear," said the judge to Salvador. "Do you persist in your assertion, that this woman is not the one to whom you confided your son?"

"Yes, sir, this woman is guided by some interest I am ignorant of; but it is certain she is imposing upon you."

"Ah! sir," exclaimed the woman, addressing the judge, and her eyes bathed in tears, "you know what is the motive that impels me, and whether my object is an interested one."

"Adelaide Moulin," replied the magistrate, "calm yourself; we know you are only guided at present by the desire of repairing a great fault, and you may rest assured your conduct will be recompensed. Undeniable witnesses," he continued, addressing Salvador, "have proved that this woman is really Adelaide Moulin, to whom a young child was confided by a French gentleman. Honourable persons, who lived at Geneva at the same time as herself, have positively declared that they knew her; these persons will be heard. What have you to reply?"

"Nothing, sir; I refer to my former replies."

"You still persist, then, in asserting that you are the Marquis Alexis de Pourrières?"

"Certainly; I cannot renounce a name and title which belong to me."

"It is precisely this name and title which are disputed; and I caution you, that you are accused of having, to possess yourself of them, murdered their legitimate possessor; and it is believed that proof can be obtained that you are really the author of this crime."

A livid pallor overspread the visage of Salvador, when he heard this fresh accusation made against him in so positive a manner. Notwithstanding the overwhelming charges which, since the commencement of the affair, had been daily collected against him, he had retained a feeble hope, not that impunity would crown his crimes, but that, at least, he would escape death; but if it were proved that he was the murderer of Alexis de Pourrières—if the horrible circumstances which had accompanied the crime were publicly known—he must renounce this hope; and it was this idea which had spread over his features the pallid colours of the shroud.

"You turn pale," said the judge to him.

This observation restored to him a good part of his sang froid. They might certainly prove that he was not the Marquis Alexis de Pourrières—they might even prove that he was no other than the forçat Salvador; but the assassin of Alexis, that was impossible, too many precautions had been taken in the commission of this crime.

"Yes, sir," he replied to the observation of the judge, "yes, sir, I am pale, but it is with indignation."

"Call forward the prisoner Ronquetti, surnamed the Duke of Modena," said the judge to the gendarme. "Do you know this man?" he continued, addressing Salvador.

"Perfectly. This man, I confess, to my shame, was my travelling companion for many years—my most intimate friend. We have visited, together, England, Switzerland, Italy, Holland, and many other parts."

"Well," said the judge to Ronquetti, "what have you to reply to these observations?"

"That they are true, and that they are not true," replied the soi-disant Duke of Modena. "This reply might at first seem extraordinary, and yet it is quite natural. The allegations of the accused would be true, if they came from the mouth of the Marquis Alexis de Pourrières, of whom, in fact, I was the friend and travelling companion for many years; but from him they are false in every point, and only prove one thing, that Salvador, Aymard, the Viscount de Lestang, as he is called, is very well instructed in all that concerns the poor Alexis."

That we may vary a little the nature of our tale, we shall place before our readers a letter, written by Ronquetti to the magistrate, the morning after the day on which he encountered Salvador in the underground passage. After reading this letter, our readers will presume the nature of the queries addressed to Salvador, and the replies thereto, and we shall consequently dispense with inserting them.

"*Ronquetti, called the Duke of Modena, to M. ——, Judge of Instruction.*

"Sir,—I yesterday encountered, in one of the passages of the prefecture," (here he narrated the circumstances of the meeting.) "More from a wish to render society an important service, than because the chief of police assured me they should feel greatly indebted to me for all I could do to assist the authorities in discovering the numerous crimes of this man, who assumes a name which does not belong to him—the result, probably, of some terrific crime—I have determined to write you this letter, and give you information which you might vainly seek for from any other than myself.

"I was very intimate with the Marquis Alexis de Pourrières, whose acquaintance I made, several years ago, at the baths of Baden-Baden. I was his most intimate friend—his travelling companion. We visited together the principal cities of Europe, so that, although I know not the man who has possessed himself of his name and fortune, I can affirm, without hesitation, that he is an impostor.

"If what I am told is true, the opinion of justice is already fixed as to his character. At all events, I hope that, after reading this letter, not a single doubt will remain in your mind, more especially if you will elicit the truth of the facts I shall have the honour of stating to you.

"I have committed many faults since I started in the world as an adventurer, but the one of all others with which I reproach myself with the greatest bitterness, is just the very one for which the justice of man has never demanded any account from me.

"The Marquis de Pourrières had received from a Jew of Marseilles, named Josué, with whom he had business, a considerable sum of money. As I had with him, on the evening of the day on which he received it, a serious altercation, I robbed him of it, and quitted him, leaving him at Brussels, almost without a sou. I came to Paris; but as I had, at this early period, reasons for avoiding the eyes of the police, I thought it as well so to disguise myself, that I should not be known. In consequence, I dyed my hair, my beard, and my whiskers. My features, which were naturally fair, I made swarthy. I changed all the habits of my body. In short, I so metamorphosed myself, that I was no longer recognisable. Tired of the adventurous life I had led for so many years, (I was by turns soldier, comedian, author, swindler, &c.,) and determined to utilise the tolerable sum I possessed, and which I owed to the robbery I had committed against my friend Alexis de Pourrières, I established, in one of the best quarters in Paris, a café, which I had decorated with all the luxuries required in these sort of establishments; and having provided my bar with a young and handsome woman, I waited for fortune.

"But fortune came not; but, in return, my establishment (I can't help thinking that the *fripons* are endowed with an attractive power equal to that of the magnet) became, in a short time, the rendezvous of all the *grecs*, the *faiseurs*, and *chevaliers d'industrie* in the capital; but I was so well disguised, that not one of those I had previously known, and they were many, recognised me. On one occasion, I saw enter my establishment the man I had so disgracefully plundered; it was, in fact, to myself he applied for what he wished served to him. 'Come, come,' I thought, when the beatings of my heart, which his appearance had produced, were somewhat abated, 'come, I am altogether unrecognisable, since this one has not discovered me.' This conviction gave me such confidence, that I was audacious enough to enter into conversation with Alexis de Pourrieres; and I think the unfortunate young man must have found me to his mind, for he returned several times, and made the acquaintance of most of the persons who frequented my establishment.

"One day——" here Ronquetti narrated how Salvador and Roman—whom he already knew, from having met them at the time when Salvador, under the name of Aymard, fleshed his sword at Valenciennes, where he robbed a young widow who fell in love with him—at Turin, where, under that of the Viscount de Lestang, he attempted to rob the banker Carmagnola—at Draguignan, where he robbed the receiver-general of the Var—made the acquaintance of Alexis de Pourrieres; he recalled the circumstances of the game between the latter and himself, and the banquet given at Lemarde-lay's, at which he was present, with most of the frequenters of his café; he then continued in these terms:

"As Alexis de Pourrieres, or rather the Count de Courtivon, (he had assumed this name to escape the inquiries of his family, after he had left Marseilles, taking with him Jazetta Louiset, and he had retained it from habit,) had announced to us his approaching departure, and that the banquet he had offered was a farewell dinner, we believed, not finding him reappear, that he had realized his project, and that he lived quietly on his estates, as he had oftentimes manifested the intention of doing. But now that I find a man whose character I have been enabled to appreciate more than once, in possession of his name and fortune, I am persuaded that Alexis de Pourrieres has been the victim of the confidence he placed in this man and his worthy companion—I am persuaded, in short, that he has been murdered by these two individuals.

"The results prove the interest they had to commit the crime of which I accuse them, and which it will be possible, perhaps, to prove, if the necessary investigations are carefully made. In addition, I will now give you some indications which may direct the police in its preliminary inquiries; and it is probable that these indications, as it generally happens, will lead to the discovery of others.

"Alexis de Pourrieres was somewhat shorter and not so stout as Salvador; his eyes were black, those of Salvador are blue. It is strange that this difference has not, as yet, been remarked by any one.* Alexis was brown, his hair was of the most glossy black you can imagine; that of Salvador, equally handsome, is naturally blond; if it is black now, it is so by being dyed; chemistry possesses means of elucidating this fact.

"Alexis de Pourrieres, when he made the acquaintance of Salvador and Roman, lodged Rue Joubert, 25. He occupied in this house a furnished apartment, which was let to him by an old woman who lived over him. It would be easy to find this woman, whose name I regret to be unable to state.

"If Salvador maintains that he is not the man I have described—that he is not himself, if I may so express myself—it will be an easy matter to confound him, by reminding him that he was born at Toulouse, where his parents were established as marchands de nouveautes, &c.—his sojourn at Valenciennes, at Turin, at Draguignan; then, at length, at the galleys at Toulon, where he was made a payot, and from whence he escaped, in company with Roman, who had been condemned under the name of Duchemin.

"The chief of police informs me that Salvador is accused of having committed a murder, followed by robbery, on the person of the Jew Josué, and that Catherine de Fontaine, Marchioness de Roselly, ex-premiere chanteuse of the grand theatre of Marseilles, was considered as his accomplice. I can give you no information relative to this crime; I can only observe that I shall not be astonished if the conjectures of the police turn out to be well founded.

"I well knew Catherine Fontaine, or, rather, the Marchioness de Roselly, since it is true that a Venetian nobleman was fool enough to marry her; and I must add, that this woman, despite all the charms of her person and mind, is capable of committing every crime.

"I met her for the first time at the Isles d'Hyères, she had just abandoned her first lover, a chevalier d'industrie, named Preval, who has added to his plebeian name a particle of nobility. Her extreme beauty, the original turn of her mind, seduced me, and I presented my homages to her, which were not repulsed. At this period I enacted the part of a grand seigneur, and I had sufficient gold in my purse to support in reality my surname of Duke of Modena.

"Catherine Fontaine was gifted with an admirable voice, a beauty without parallel, and a retentive memory. She had received an excellent education; it was not surprising, therefore, that she succeeded in the dramatic career. I proposed to her to enter the grand theatre of Marseilles, the director of which I knew well; she accepted this proposition with the greatest eagerness.

"I already considered myself the happy husband of a renowned cantatrice, a profession very agreeable and very recherché, of our young lions; no doubt because the only obligation of the husband who accepts it, and who can, with the magnificent revenues borrowed from the larynx of madame, lead a free and joyous life, is to know how to shut his eyes at the proper time; but my hopes were destroyed. Catherine Fontaine, when she had firmly placed her foot in the stirrup, forgot the numerous services I had rendered her, (I omitted to mention that, when I first met her, she was almost in poverty,) and dismissed me with as little ceremony as though I had been one of her servants.

"Do not, however, believe, sir, that her conduct towards myself has induced me to think her equal to any crime. I have no personal object; I have no other motive but that of assisting justice. In fine, send to Marseilles, where she has left some deplorable remembrances, a roving commission, and I am persuaded that all persons interrogated respecting her will express themselves in terms no less energetic than those I have made use of.

"I can tell you no more, sir. I sincerely desire that the information I have given you may assist in establishing the truth, and that it will induce those upon whom my fate depends to grant me an indulgence, which I shall show myself worthy of by my future life. I have the honour to be, with the most profound respect,

RONQUETTI, called Duke of Modena,

"At present detained at Saint Palagie, where he is suffering a condemnation of two years in prison, for simple bankruptcy."

This letter, as we have remarked, considerably abridged the task confided to the magistrate. Once ascertained what was the man who had taken the name and title of the Marquis de Pourrieres, it became easy to prove that he was only an impostor. Roving commissions were sent to Toulouse, Valen-

---

* Ronquetti was at this time ignorant that Adelaide Moulin had remarked the difference in the colour of his eyes.

ciennes, Turin, Draguignan, to the commissariat of the galleys at Toulon; and the information obtained, successively justified the allegations of the Duke of Modena.

As soon as it was established that the man they held in prison was no other than the escaped convict Salvador, a sequestration was placed on the property of the house of de Pourrieres, to be rendered, after judgment, to the young Fortunè, the sole heir, known, of the Marquis de Pourrieres; and they exerted themselves to discover by what means Salvador and his accomplice, Roman, had got rid of the victim whose place the former of these two scelerats had occupied.

As Ronquetti had observed, the circumstances he had mentioned led to the discovery of others, which at length brought the truth to light.

They first sought out the woman who had let to the Count de Courtivon the apartments in the Rue Joubert. This woman, who was found without trouble, remembered at once a lodger who had disappeared from her house. She had made no declaration to the police as to his disappearance, by reason of her not having been, at the period he lodged with her, licensed to let furnished rooms, and fearing, therefore, to be fined for so doing. To the reproaches made to her, she replied that she was an honest woman—that she had never had an idea of appropriating the effects left by the Count de Courtivon at his room, but had preserved them with the greatest care, and that she was enabled to produce them. She was ordered to bring these effects, which was done, and they underwent a rigorous search. In the pocket of a white waistcoat, soiled with several stains of wine—from which it was presumed to have been the one worn by Alexis de Pourrieres at the famous banquet at Lemardelay's, the details of which were furnished by Ronquetti—was found a visiting card of the Count de Courtivon, on the back of which was written these words: "Rue Notre Dame des Victoires, Hotel des Pays-Bas, Casimir de Feuillade, chambre numero 20." This card and the different effects which had belonged to the Marquis de Pourrieres, were seized as proofs in support of the accusation.

Leaving the Rue Joubert, they repaired to the street Notre Dame des Victoires, to the Hotel des Pays-Bas. From an inspection of the police-book of this hotel,* it appeared that, at the period which coincided with the disappearance of the Count de Courtivon, two individuals, who called themselves Messrs. Feuillade, had lodged there for more than a fortnight, and that they occupied together the room numbered 20.

The proprietor of this hotel, endowed, as it appears, with an excellent memory, gave a description of these two individuals, whom he had remarked from their being his countrymen, which applied exactly to Salvador and Roman.

He was shown the mask, in wax, of Roman; he instantly recognised it.

"The features from which this mask has been moulded," he said, "belonged to the eldest of the two Messieurs Feuillade."

Determined to render the proof more decisive, they sent for him to the Palace of Justice one day, when Salvador was brought with several other

prisoners; he recognised him among the individuals he was surrounded by; he merely observed, he could not comprehend how he had become so brown, having been a blond at the former period.

The proprietor of this hotel had proved a valuable witness for the accusation. They begged him to carry back his remembrances, and to give an account of all the facts regarding the two individuals who had lodged with him which he could recollect. At first he remembered nothing. The conduct of his two lodgers had been, during the short time they remained with him, nearly similar to that of most others; they left in the morning and returned at night. However, after considering some time, he remembered that, one morning, the eldest had ordered one of the waiters of the hotel to get him a cab, and that this cab, after receiving him at the hotel, had taken him to a colour merchant's.

This colour merchant, questioned in his turn, declared that he perfectly recollected that an individual, nearly similar in appearance to the one they described, had called upon him at the period in question, and that he had purchased of him several litres of spirits of turpentine, contained in one of those large jugs called *dame jeanne;* this jug and its contents were placed in the cab, and he left; the tradesman knew no more.

What occasion could a man, who appeared to be at Paris but temporarily, have for so large a quantity of spirits of turpentine as that purchased by Roman? This purchase concealed, probably, some mystery which it was the interest of justice to penetrate. It was resolved to be sure on this point, and the chief of police was charged to find the coachman who had driven Roman from the Hotel des Pays-Bas to the colour-shop. The coachman was found, and replied to the questions put to him, that he had driven the man who had purchased at a colour-shop, in the Rue de Notre Dame des Victoires, a large jug full of some liquid which he could not name, as far as the gate of the park of Raincy, that upon arriving there, this man had taken the jug and had quitted him, after liberally paying him.

This last declaration was, for the chief of police, to whom it was communicated, a precious ray of light; he remembered that, at about the same period as the disappearance of the Count de Courtivon, who was no other than the Marquis de Pourrieres, (the letters addressed to Alexis under this name, which had been seized at Salvador's, who had sacredly preserved them, for the simple reason that they would serve to prove his identity, if by chance it was disputed, left no doubt on this point), they had discovered, in the most secluded part of the park of Raincy, under a heap of dried leaves and branches, the shapeless remains of a body, the bones of which were completely calcined.

He obtained the reports which this singular discovery had given rise to. The scientific men who had been commissioned to report the state in which the body was found, after declaring that it was entirely unrecognisable, maintained that the fire had been fed either by spirits or other inflammable materials; and, indeed, the state of the place justified their report; the foliage of the neighbouring trees, half burnt, proved that the fire had been very considerable.

This discovery led to every inquiry being made, but to no effect; it was never ascertained whether a crime had been committed, or whether it was the consequence of a deplorable suicide, accompanied by extraordinary circumstances; however, under an impression that chance would one day furnish other evidence, they had, after the interment of the sad remains of the body, collected with care every object which had resisted the action of the fire. Among these objects which had been preserved, was found a small key, intended, to all appearance, to open a modern piece of furniture. The form of this key was so remarkable as to be easily recognised: it was bored with grooves; the head and stem were of steel; the ring, chased with neatness, was of copper.

They returned to the old woman of the Rue Joubert. They inquired whether the furniture in the room he had occupied was still the same; she replied in the affirmative. The key found among the human debris in the park of Raincy, was tried and found to open a commode, for which the old lady remembered she had been obliged to have another made, shortly after the disappearance of her lodger.

It was no longer doubted that Salvador and Roman, allied with the unfortunate Alexis de Pourrieres, had, under some pretext, enticed him into the park of Raincy, where they had murdered him; and that, afterwards, by the aid of his keys, which, no doubt, they had taken, as they were not to be found, introduced themselves into his lodgings, to carry off his papers, which they had been enabled to accomplish without being remarked, from the situation of the place. Our readers have not forgotten that the house in which Alexis had lodged was composed of two *corps de logis*, one looking into the street, the other into a garden which separated them—that the apartment of the marquis was situated on the third floor of the first, and the lodge of the porter on the landing-place of the second.

Before being reconducted to his cell, Salvador was confronted with the proprietor of the Hotel des Pays-Bas, who recognised him perfectly as the same individual who had lodged with him at the period mentioned in his police-book, under the name of Casimir de Feuillade, but simply remarked again that his hair was now black, though formerly it had been fair.

"In fact," observed the chief of police, "all the witnesses agree in asserting that the forçat Salvador had fair hair; and as, in our opinion, it is now established, that the man who persists in calling himself the Marquis Alexis de Pourrieres is no other than this individual, we think that the colour of the hair must be due to the recent prodigies in chemistry. Would it not be possible to ascertain this?"

"Quite so," replied the judge; "we have before us, for that purpose, a very skilful chemist. Approach, M. Arnault; examine the hair of the accused, and tell us whether it is indebted to art or nature for its colour."

The chemist approached Salvador. "There is no occasion," he said, "to examine the hair of the accused, to prove that it is dyed; you can perceive as well as myself that it is fair at the roots, owing, no doubt, to the accused being unable, since his confinement in prison, to continue an operation which requires to be renewed as frequently as the growth of the hair calls for it."

This fact was taken note of by a proces verbal.

The judge afterwards called forward Paolo. "Look well at the accused," he said, "figure to yourself that his hair is blond, instead of being black, and tell us if you would recognise him."

"Perfectly, sir," replied the servant; "I regret exceedingly to be compelled to accuse the husband of a good mistress, but I feel bound to speak the truth. Monsieur is certainly the person who was known at Turin by the name of the Viscount de Lestang. He it was who struck me with a poniard, the mark from which is still visible on my breast, because I endeavoured to arrest him at the moment he had made an attempt to commit a robbery at the house of M. Carmagnola, whose servant I then was. I ought to add, that he was accompanied by a man older than himself, who was understood to be his preceptor, and called himself M. Duchemin, and greatly resembled the mask in wax which was shown to the master of the Hotel des Pays-Bas, but as I have not seen the latter as often as M. le Vicomte de Lestang, I do not feel equally certain."

"You see," said the judge to Salvador, when Paolo had finished his deposition, "the accusation is abundantly supplied with proofs of your guilt; you ought not, therefore, to cling to the hope of escaping the justice of man. But do you not think that a sincere confession of all the crimes you have committed, one that will render more easy of accomplishment the duty imposed upon the magistrates, will prove the best means of appeasing the justice of God?"

"I appreciate, sir, the excellent intention which induces you to address me in such a way, and I thank you sincerely for your kind advice as to the care of my salvation, which, at the present moment, I have no anxiety about, for I do not think myself in such great danger as you may imagine. I am innocent, sir; and I hope that my judges, despite the many presumptions which have risen against me, will render me the justice I am entitled to. For the rest, I ought to apprise you, that, not finding with you the impartiality which should, on every occasion, characterize the seat of a magistrate, I have taken the resolution to reply to no further questions you may please to address to me."

The judge did not think it worth while to reply to the protest of Salvador, but took a note of it. This man, stained with a heavy list of crimes, all committed with the view of satisfying an insatiable cupidity, and accompanied by circumstances which disclosed the most disgusting cruelty, inspired him with too much horror and contempt to attach any importance to the accusation of partiality which he had brought against him. He ordered him to be taken again to his cell, delighted at having no more to do with him than to draw up the report to be submitted to the chamber *des mises en accusation*.

Shortly after this, Salvador and the Viscount de Lussan appeared before the court of assize for the Seine.

The indictment recited all the crimes committed by these wretches; first, those committed by Salvador and Roman together.

The attempt at robbery at Turin, at Carmagnola's, the banker, at the period when Salvador called himself the Viscount de Lestang, followed by an attempt at murder on the person of Paolo.

The murder of the brigadier of the gendarmerie of Beausset, after the escape from the galleys at Toulon.

The affiliation to the band of the brothers Bisson, at Tretz, whose depredations had laid waste the departments of the Var and Rhone, at a time corresponding to that during which they had composed a part of it.

The death of the Marquis Alexis de Pourrieres, to get possession of his name and fortune, in which they had succeeded.

Also the murder of the Jew Josué, followed by a robbery of the sum of 200,000 francs. Catherine

Fontaine, widow of the Marquis de Roselly, was accused of being an accomplice in this crime, having favoured the execution by inviting and retaining at her house the victim, until the auspicious moment for its commission.

Also the murder of Delicat, Rolet le Mauvais Gueux, and Desbraises, called Coco. The Viscount de Lussan, Grand Louis, Charles la belle Cravate, and Vernier les bas Bleus were accused of being parties to this crime.

De Lussan was accused with Salvador of having made part of an association of bandits, and of having been engaged, either by personally aiding their accomplices, affording them advice, or effecting a sale of the articles stolen to the woman Marie Madeleine Comtois, called Sans Refus, in an infinity of robberies.

The noble viscount had also to answer for the murder, with premeditation, of the person called Beppo.

Death spared the latter the shame of being compelled to sit on the bench of the court of assize, by the side of those he had caused to be arrested; for the revelations of the bandits taken at the house of Sans Refus had shown that he was guilty of an attempt to murder Preval, at Hyères, and the Marchioness de Roselly, and had given the police the solution of an enigma which had long perplexed them.

And, lastly, the act of accusation added to the list the murder on the person of Roman by Salvador and Silvia; and to the former, alone, of having fabricated a false passport, and of having made use of it.

Salvador, the Viscount de Lussan, le Grand Louis, Charles la belle Cravate and the other bandits arrested in the Rue de la Tannerie, appeared by themselves before their judges; they had in vain searched for the Marchioness de Roselly, Sans Refus, and Vernier les bas Bleus.

The debates were long and animated. The expectation of the fair sex who seek for emotions in the gloomy dramas that are acted before the court of assize, were not deceived; they found merely that the one in which Salvador and de Lussan played the principal characters failed in interest, owing to the weight of evidence. Indeed, the indictment had been drawn with such care, it had collected so many elements to support the accusation, that, from the first day, the result was foretold. When the jury, therefore, on leaving their room, brought in an affirmative reply to every question put to them, it astonished no one.

Salvador, the Viscount de Lussan, and the Marchioness de Roselly (the latter by contumacy) were condemned to the punishment of death.

Sans Refus and Vernier les bas Bleus, absent, le Grand Louis, and Charles la belle Cravate were condemned to hard labour for life.

The other bandits were punished more or less severely. Cornet-tape-dur, Robert and Cadet Vincent received the mildest punishment.

CHAPTER XLIX.

THE ESCAPE.

WHEN the president, after reading the articles of the penal code applicable to Salvador and the Viscount de Lussan, had pronounced the sentence of death against these two individuals, the latter arranged his shirt-frill and ruffles with as much grace and ease as though he were in the box of his dan-

scuse; he passed his right hand through the magnificent curls of his long black hair; and, after bowing to the tribunal, the jury, and the audience, he followed the gendarme. Salvador was somewhat less at ease than his accomplice, but met it with a good countenance.

"Well, my dear fellow," said de Lussan to Salvador, in descending the stairs which led from the court to the conciergerie, "what say you to this? A happy termination, and worthy of the exordium. Is it not so?"

"What would you have, viscount? We have lost the game. La Grève is the field of battle on which are concluded the exploits of men like us. We yield to the universal law; it would be bad grace in us, therefore, to complain."

"It is not the less true, however, that it is very disagreeable to die when, like us, we are still young and gifted with a constitution capable of defying the best physicians; but, as an honourable has very wisely observed, 'tis *un fait accompli.*"

"Let us say no more about it, then."

Salvador and de Lussan only remained a few minutes at the conciergerie; a carriole, or, rather, a salad basket (as these ignoble vehicles are nicknamed) waited to take them to Bicêtre.

The director of this prison received them with that politeness which is usually bestowed upon such as are condemned to death, and he directly gave orders for them to be placed in the corridor No. 1, back of the new building.

"Have the goodness, sir," said de Lussan, when the director had given this order, "if it is possible, to place us in the front, that we may amuse ourselves, and, especially, in an old building, for in a new one we shall be obliged to dry the walls, which, I am told, is very unhealthy; I have no wish to contract the pains of rheumatism, and I think my friend is of the same opinion.

"Don't be alarmed, M. le Vicomte," replied the director, who considered it rather strange to listen to such a remark from a man who had already one foot in the grave; "the new building was not finished yesterday, it has existed for more than seventy years; I can, therefore, assure you, that you will run no risk of contracting the pains of rheumatism."

"If that is the case," resumed the viscount, "allow us to be conducted to our apartments; I am somewhat fatigued."

"Your apartments are ready," said the gaoler, who had just arrived; "but before you are shown into them, you must *unrobe* for the visit; come, my man, make haste."

"I don't understand you; if you wish to have an answer, speak an intelligible language."

The greffier put an end to this dialogue, which would, perhaps, have become serious, by explaining to the noble viscount what was required of him.

"All who are in your position," he said, "must, on entering here, be rigorously searched; they must afterwards quit their usual dress, to put on that of the prison, and must also wear the camisole."

"I understand," replied the viscount, "and will readily submit to the general rule; but as I have not been condemned to support the insolence and familiarity of a clown like that," indicating the gaoler, "I have the honour of telling you that I shall not tolerate them if they are repeated."

When their prison toilette was completed, de Lussan and Salvador—who could not help smiling at the singular whims of his companion—descended nearly thirty stone steps, and after traversing several vaulted passages, lighted only by the pale

LIFE IN PARIS.

SALVADOR WITH CORELIA'S JEWELS.

and flickering rays of a few smoky lamps, they found themselves in the corridor of the cells named *cachots blancs*, no doubt from their being a little less obscure and rather more commodious than those called *de sureté*, which have not been used for some time.

They were placed in separate cells, but near enough to converse with facility; they had no dread of letting into the secret of their discourse the sentinels, parading in front of the little windows which introduced a small portion of daylight into their cells, for they were both well versed in the language of Tasso and Ariosto, but which they made no use of until they had ascertained by a timely question that it was *foreign* to their guardian.

"Well, M. le Marquis," said de Lussan, after examining the cell, which, from all appearance, was to be his last dwelling; "how do you find the lodging granted us?"

"It is not, I must confess, furnished with so much luxury as those we have lately inhabited; but such as it is, I would be contented with it, if this cursed *camisole* did not retain my hands captive."

"I must agree with you, this garment is really very inconvenient, it will become before long quite a punishment."

"Oh! my faith! we get used to every thing; after wearing it a fortnight, you will think nothing of it."

"A fortnight? you are mad, dear marquis."

"And why, then, if you please?"

"Because I fancy it is your intention to appeal *en cassation*?"

"Such, indeed, is my intention; is it not yours, also?"

"May God preserve me from committing so cowardly an action! The cork is drawn, we must drink the wine—the sooner the better."

"If so, we will swallow the nectar as soon as we can; but, at all events, we must expect to remain here, at least forty days; it frequently happens, that, in the expectation that ennui and solitude induce prisoners to make revelations, the procureur-general interposes an appeal."

"Why, certainly, my dear *ci-devant* ought to know this house and its usages; believe me, marquis, you have deceived me in a most unworthy manner; I have, for a long while, considered you a gentleman of good family; if I had known you were an escaped convict, I certainly would not have accepted the twenty-five thousand francs you handed me at our first interview; my connection with you has soiled my escutcheon!"

"Really, viscount, your strange susceptibilities make me burst with laughter; justice has recently proved to you that all men are equal in her sight: your many quarterings of nobility have not prevented the judges awarding you a similar fate to mine, and it is likely that they will not prevent Maitre Sanson from doing his duty; for the rest, my dear de Lussan, believe me, I shall die as nobly as yourself! I have rustled enough amongst nobility to catch some of its manners."

"It's true; and so, dear marquis, I shall pray the Almighty to guard you, and take a few minutes' repose, I am really quite fatigued."

"Good night, then, viscount."

"Good night, marquis."

The next morning, the Viscount de Lussan inquired for the almoner, the respectable Abbé Montés, whom he had seen frequently at the conciergerie, and whose conversation much pleased him. They were much astonished, no doubt, that a man like the viscount should appear so eager to fulfil his Christian duties; but at a period in which it was fashionable to join the movement of religious enthusiasm, which was manifested in so noisy a manner, he thought it as well to inscribe himself, with ostentation, among the most forward of the neo-Catholics; he might also, perhaps, in these matters, have shared the opinion of Montesquien, who says, somewhere: "That devotion finds, for committing bad actions, reasons which an honest man would never think of!"

The worthy almoner hastened to attend the invitation of the viscount, who, not having the slightest intention to appeal, thought it his duty to put himself in a state of grace. The almoner then apprised him that the procureur-general had interposed an appeal, and that, consequently, he must expect to live, at least forty days, yet; he added, that this delay might have a satisfactory result, that in such cases, the king examined the documents of the trial, and that, frequently, he allowed a commutation of punishment.

"A commutation of punishment!" exclaimed the viscount, "and by virtue of what law, can a king change the nature of a punishment? Send me to the galleys! me! the Viscount de Lussan! confound me with the miserable thieves, who belong, for the most part, to the dregs of the people! If such a favour were offered me, I would refuse it, of that be convinced. I am condemned; respect to the thing judged—let them execute me."

Salvador, who had obtained permission to assist at the interview between the viscount and the almoner, agreed with his accomplice; and the two scelerats entreated the priest, when he quitted them, to take steps that the judgment which hung over them was immediately executed.

It may be imagined that the recommendations of Salvador and the viscount were perfectly useless; the established usages could not be cast aside to please these miserable men.

They had been a week at the Bicêtre, when one morning Salvador awoke his companion to inform him that he had had a dream, which promised him a near and certain liberty.

The viscount could not help laughing at the expense of the superstition of him, whom he now called *Monsieur le Ci-devant!* since a solemn judgment had deprived him of his title and fortune.

"You need not laugh, M. le Vicomte," replied Salvador, "but believe; dreams, I cannot but think, are revelations of what is to happen to us. I assure you that if you will only undertake to reply by these words: *I will do all you wish!* we shall soon be free."

"*I will do all you wish!* dear ci-devant; it will be just one way of killing time."

"I may, then, reckon upon you?"

"I have already had the honour of telling you that *I will do all you wish!*"

"Very well, then."

The same day, Salvador, having requested the director to come to him, he asked him for writing materials; as soon as he was in possession of what he desired, he wrote a long letter to the procureur-general, which he would not allow his accomplice to read.

"Your part is merely passive," he said to him; "you must, according to our agreement, be content to execute my orders."

"It's true, dear ci-devant, it's true; *I will do all you wish!*"

Several days after forwarding the letter to the

procureur-general, Salvador was sent for to the *greffe;* when he returned to his companion, he informed him that he had procured the arrest, by the police, of at least a dozen individuals, covered with crimes, and that it was probable that, that very day, they would both be transferred to *la Force,* as he had had the address to get him implicated with himself, in some further affairs of magnitude.

"M. de Pourrieres has not fancied for a moment," said the viscount, with much dignity, "that I would turn informer to regain my liberty?"

"Eh! I have thought nothing at all about it," exclaimed Salvador, annoyed at length at the caprice of his accomplice; "our business is to get transferred to la Force, and I have employed the only means I had for that purpose; but allow me to manage, and trouble yourself about nothing; in all this, you have only to say: 'Amen!'"

"Very well, then; and, if there is need, reckon upon a stout arm, and a courage that will not shrink at the moment of danger!"

The expectation of Salvador was not deceived; on the approach of evening, the carriole came for the two accomplices; a peace officer, appointed over the transfers, occupied the seat in front of this carriage, and according to custom, two gendarmes galloped behind.

The travelling companions of Salvador and the viscount, gentry of the sack and cord, ready to risk every thing to gain their liberty, adopted with enthusiasm the project which was submitted to them, in a few words; and they quickly disencumbered the two friends of the shackles which prevented their acting.

Salvador had given an attendant, who made his bed and that of the viscount, (an old forçat who had preserved some good traditions,) a few pieces of gold, which, since he had been made aware of his fate, he had kept in reserve, to use in case of need. In exchange for these last remains of his former prosperity, this *garçon de service* had procured him an iron crow-bar, about eighteen inches long, and a strong gimlet, by the aid of which he could raise one of the planks, which formed the bottom of the *panier à salade.*

Salvador and de Lussan, in their quality of inventors of the plan of escape, had obtained from their companions the privilege of passing first through the opening that was to be effected;* when the plank was taken up they prepared to make use of it, but the opening was so narrow, that, to ensure their not being fixed in it, they were obliged to strip themselves almost naked, that is, to retain merely their shirt and trowsers. At length, they dropped themselves into the road, and commenced running towards the Seine, which they crossed, by swimming, near the Chateau de Bercy, whilst the gendarmes, who escorted the *panier à salade,* and knew not which way to turn, gallopped after the other prisoners, who had made a good use of the example set them.

They followed the course of the Seine, to reach the Barrier de Bercy. As it was quite dark when they entered Paris, the singularity of their costume was not remarked.

"Well, viscount," said Salvador to his companion, when the barrier was cleared.

"Well, marquis?"

"Behold us, free! but what is to become of us?"

* It is customary, when an escape is made in this mode, to allow those who are condemned to the heaviest punishment to pass first, and the rest in their order.

"Eh, parbleu! let us go to Father Justè; the old scelerat must furnish us with means to get out of the frightful position we are in."

"'Tis settled! let us visit Father Justè, and if he does not turn out accommodating——"

"Why, we will bring him to reason, dear marquis!"

Salvador and de Lussan were exhausted with fatigue, but they lost no time in clearing the distance which separates the Barrier de Bercy from la Rue Saint-Dominique d'Enfer.

They knocked and rang several times at the door of the mansion, inhabited by the old usurer; it remained sombre and silent.

"Father Justè, it seems, has got rid of his dog," said Salvador.

"I am rather of opinion," replied the viscount, "that Providence has rid the world of this old intriguer, for he never leaves of an evening; and, unless he were dead, he must hear the infernal noise, which, for more than an hour, we have been making at his door."

An old woman in the next house, tired of the noise made by Salvador and de Lussan, put her head out of the window, and called to the two friends.

"Who are you?" she said; "why are you knocking so late and so loud at the door of an uninhabited house?"

"Pardon us, madame," replied de Lussan; "we wish to speak to M. Justè, banker."

"M. Justè, the banker? you have chosen a strange hour, and a strange costume, to visit a banker!"

"We are neighbours," replied Salvador, "and we came out *en negligé.*"

"Your negligé is rather slight for the present weather; ten degrees of cold, and *en chemise!* Excuse me, but, since you are neighbours, how is it you are not aware that M. Justè has been dead for some time?"

"M. Justè dead!" exclaimed de Lussan; "we needed not this."

"Yes, he is dead! His dog, who was in the habit of flying at any one who entered the house, at last flew upon his master, and devoured him body and bones! They say he became mad, because his master was so miserly that he gave him nothing to eat."

"Oh! what a frightful disaster!"

"Disaster? on the contrary it is very lucky for this old beggarly Justè! if he were not dead, he would, at this moment, be in the cells, at Bicêtre, with his two friends—two noble rogues! count and marquis—chiefs of bandits! whom I am going to see executed on Saturday. But, good night, Messieurs I-don't-know-who! if you are of the clique of Father Justè, you can go and weep over his tomb; he is buried at *Mount Parnassus!*"

The old woman closed her window, leaving Salvador and de Lussan as much surprised as alarmed at the frightful death of the usurer Justè.

"There remains but one resource for us," said de Lussan, when they were at some distance from the house lately inhabited by the usurer; "we must make an attempt with Coralie."

"We should be wrong, I think, to rely much upon this woman, who has not even given you a sign of life, during the whole time we were in prison."

"Who knows? perhaps, on seeing us naked, and without food, she may be moved to give us a few pieces of gold."

"I rather think she will have you driven

away by her people, if she does not have us arrested."

"There is no danger of that; Coralie, although young, amiable, pretty, and rich, is extremely avaricious; she has in her service only one femme de chambre, whom we could easily bring to book, if she showed any evil intentions."

"Come, then, let us try our luck! we must do something."

It was some distance from the Street Saint-Dominique d'Enfer to that of Tronchet, where Coralie, the danseuse, lived; but Salvador and de Lussan, goaded by hunger, cold, and despair, courageously put themselves en route.

Eleven o'clock struck! the night was dark; the two adventurers, who endeavoured to avoid meeting the patrols, walked silently in the shade. Arrived at a small street, close to the Pont Saint Michael, a clamour, proceeding from a number of voices, suddenly reached their ears.

"Arrest—arrest! a thief! an assassin!"

And the street was invaded by several men, pursuing an individual, who, thanks to his heels, gained every instant a considerable way.

To avoid meeting the pursuers, among whom might very possibly be found some agents of Madame Police, Salvador and de Lussan suddenly darted into the Rue Poupée. They had not gone twenty steps in this street, when a man tumbled, we might almost say, into their arms.

"Let me pass," he said to them, "I am an unfortunate deserter."

Salvador and de Lussan at once recognised Vernier les bas Bleus. The many turns he had made had completely puzzled his followers, and he thought himself shipwrecked in port, when, in his turn, he recognised the two adventurers.

"Rupin! le Grand Richard!" he exclaimed; "it seems, then, that it will not be on Saturday?"

"We hope so, truly," said de Lussan, "especially if you will procure us something for supper, and an asylum for the night."

"I can take you to my room," replied Vernier; "the locality is not grand, but such as it is, you are welcome to it with all my heart. You put money in my pocket, when you were Rupins, it is quite just that I should do something for you, now."

When we are cold and hungry, and have not so much as a shelter for our heads, we seize, without hesitation, the first branch that presents itself. Salvador and de Lussan, therefore, quickly accepted the offer of Vernier; they had, besides, no reason to fear this man, whose position was no better than their own; for, condemned by contumacy to hard labour for life, he could take no steps for their arrest, without compromising his own liberty.

Vernier occupied, in a dilapidated house, without a porter, in the Rue de Tour Saint Hilaire, an attic, on the seventh floor, furnished with a bedstead, upon which was placed two thin blankets and an old counterpane; a ricketty table, the half of a buffet, two broken straw chairs, and lighted by a small sky-light, denominated a chassis à tabatière.

"This is the crib!" he said to his guests, when introducing them into this nauseous grenier; "it's not handsome, but it's safe!"

"'Tis all that we require for the present," replied de Lussan; "to-morrow, it will be daylight, and, please God! we will find means of procuring a better."

"Ah, bah! you, who have only tasted the soup à la Bicêtre, why you must be dying of hunger?"

"We would willingly eat a morsel," replied Salvador; "what say you, viscount?"

De Lussan, who had thrown himself upon the bed, made a sign in the affirmative.

"I will go, then," said Vernier, "and get two litres of wine, a loaf, and some ham; will that suit?"

"Go, my friend, buy what you like; if we live, we will find means of acknowledging, another time, what you are now doing for us; but if you wish your hospitality to be agreeable to me, speak no more of that vile slang. Where is the utility of using a base and vulgar language, which is now understood by every one?"

"You shall be obeyed; I have too much desire to go snacks——"

"Again!"

"Halves! I am hurried into it by the force of habit. I was saying, then, that I was too desirous to go shares in the 'affairs,' which, no doubt, you have already in view, to do anything which may be disagreeable to you."

The bread, ham, and wine, offered by Vernier, were dispatched in a few minutes.

"This is not equal to a hash de filets de perdreaux aux truffles, nor Chambertin wine," said de Lussan; "but it is eatable, and digests well when we are hungry."

"You are right," said Salvador; "'tis the want of them, which puts a price on things the most ordinary; therefore, as we are exhausted with fatigue, and are in great want of sleep, I am persuaded we shall find luxurious, the modest couch of our friend Vernier."

The three bandits slept together on this bed, which, luckily for them, was of an unusual size; and in a few minutes, the silence of the apartment of Vernier, was only broken by the calm and regular breathing of its occupants.

They awoke by daylight. Vernier, who had intended an agreeable surprise to his friends, placed on the ricketty table a pint of eau de vie, purchased the evening before, and the three accomplices, having each lighted a short pipe, charged with caporal, held a council.

Salvador, de Lussan, and Vernier, had not in their whole possession five francs a-piece, and yet, the two former required clothes, of some sort, and the means of disguising themselves, unless they resolved to remain confined in the attic of their host.

"I will write to Coralie," said the viscount; "our friend Vernier shall carry the letter."

"Do it, dear viscount. Ah! if I knew where to find my wife at this moment, we should have no occasion to address ourselves to this danseuse."

"But you do not know it, therefore 'tis useless to talk about it."

De Lussan wrote to Coralie a very pathetic letter, and very touching; which Vernier, as agreed, was commissioned to deliver.

He arrived at Coralie's before ten in the morning; madame had not yet risen; he was, consequently, obliged to leave the letter with the femme de chambre, who undertook, considering his earnest prayers, to deliver it directly to her mistress.

She returned to Vernier, who waited for her in the ante-room, at the end of a few minutes; from her affected air, and the haughty expression of her eye, the bandit surmised that she was not the ambassadress of good news. He was right.

"Madame," she said to him, "has no knowledge of the man who demands charity of her; she begs you to return him this letter, which she does not wish to preserve."

Vernier was forced to retire. When he left Coralie's, the Rue Tronchet was filled with a crowd of *Gazetteers*, who were bawling out: "*The exact and detailed account of the miraculous escape, after sentence of death, of two individuals, well known in Paris! A handsome reward for any one who will procure their arrest!*" Vernier purchased, for five centimes, this monstrous bill, which he showed to his guests on his return.

"It seems they are particularly anxious to shorten you by a head," said Vernier, when Salvador and de Lussan had finished reading the bill, "as they offer a handsome recompense to whoever will bring your neck under the knife; 'tis exceedingly flattering to you, I must say."

"Yes, and somewhat alarming," replied de Lussan, regarding steadily Vernier les bas Bleus; "the hope of obtaining this grand reward, might induce those to betray us, in whom we have placed our whole confidence."

"It is but too true," added Salvador.

"Hell! *Rupins!* 'tis not to me you say this, is it? I am a *grinche!* an *escarpe!* whatever you choose; I would butcher the holy father for a five-franc piece; but I'm an honourable man! Betray my friends? never!"

Salvador and de Lussan, inwardly delighted at hearing Vernier reject with such indignation the thought of an action, like the one they had momentarily supposed him capable of committing, soon became more tranquil.

"Listen, my friends," he said to them; "at present, alas! nearly all the *pègres* are infamous rogues; and for you—it is enough to forfeit your heads once! you cannot, therefore, take too many precautions. Well! if you like, during the whole time you remain here, I will not go out—I will not write; one of you shall wear my clothes, to go *on parade,** and the other shall remain with me: this will make you easy."

"You shall go out, you shall return, you shall write!" replied de Lussan to Vernier. "We trust in you, and are persuaded that our confidence is well placed; but we will visit your wardrobe, in which, perhaps, we shall find something we can dress in."

Vernier was richer than he fancied himself; the viscount discovered two pair of pantaloons, in tolerable condition, a new blouse, and a redingote, still wearable. He gave Salvador the redingote, and the best pair of pantaloons.

"'Tis because I intend you to play an important rôle, this evening, in a new comedy, that I allow you to dress yourself in this handsome manner," he said to his accomplice.

"I can guess your project; you mean to take from Coralie, by wholesale, what you have given her in detail?"

"You have it!"

"That's lucky! I have just taken the impression of the lock," said Vernier; and he showed to his two friends a card, upon which the wards of the lock of Coralie's house was minutely impressed.

"'Tis very well executed; but what means shall we adopt to succeed?"

"Let me act, all will go well; and this evening, I'll answer for it, we shall have gold—plenty of gold! and our friend Vernier, who will lend us a hand, shall have a good slice of it."

"Ah! these Rupins, they are clever!" exclaimed Vernier, who fancied himself already in possession

* To rob.

of the wealth, of which the viscount had promised him so ample a harvest.

The viscount was seated at the table, and drawing with much nicety, the fac-simile of a key.

"You are expert," he said to Salvador, "in the art of a locksmith, can you make a key absolutely similar to this on the card, I am quite sure there is every thing here that is requisite for it."

"Perfectly," replied Salvador.

"In that case, set to, I will explain my plan whilst you are at work."

Salvador, endowed with a marvellous dexterity, only required a few hours to produce a key, with which the viscount felt quite satisfied.

The three bandits now commenced a joyous discourse, and also to eat and drink, (Vernier had an account opened with the wine merchant, and pork-shop keeper,) for the rest of the morning.

When the evening arrived, each armed himself with a poniard, (they were all three fully determined, in case of a surprise, not to be taken alive,) and started for the Rue Tronchet.

Salvador and Vernier entered a wine shop, de Lussan took a post of observation opposite the porte cochère of the house occupied by Coralie.

He had been on the watch about half an hour, when he saw the danseuse leave. He followed her at a distance, and saw her enter the opera. Quite certain now that she would not return for the evening, he returned to his comrades.

"She is gone out," he said to them; "it only remains now to draw off the servant. Come, Vernier, remember that if you do not succeed, we shall be forced to employ stronger means, and I should be exceedingly sorry to do so, this servant is a very good and a very pretty girl."

Vernier, following the instructions he had previously received, took his way, and directed the coachman of a fiacre, which he took from the station nearest to the opera, to drive him to the domicile of Coralie, and deliver to the porter of the house a note, which the latter would give to the person for whom it was addressed.

There was no fear that the femme de chambre would observe that it was not written by her mistress, for Coralie, whose education had been somewhat neglected, constantly employed secretaries.

The coachman, generously paid in advance, acquitted himself of the mission confided to him; he handed the note to the concierge, and waited.

The porter, following the usual practice of his brethren, did not fail to read the letter, which, besides, was not sealed.

"Quick, quick, Mademoiselle Helène," he said to Coralie's femme de chambre, "Mademoiselle Desrivières has sprained her ancle entering the stage, she has sent for you and her orange shawl, there is a fiacre below to take you, and here is a note she has given the coachman for you."

"Thank you kindly, M. Fouchè," replied the femme de chambre, after reading the note, "I will go directly to my mistress;" and as the porter had ascended the stairs to speak to her, she descended one stage to light him.

Shortly afterwards, the servant carrying on her arm her mistress's orange shawl, entered the fiacre, which waited for her at the door.

"To go from hence to the opera, explain her coming to her mistress, then return," said de Lussan, "will occupy at least three quarters of an hour; it is more than we require. Come, marquis, there is a light at Dr. Delamarre's, who lives under Coralie, tell the porter you are going to him. Don't forget to give a glance at the two agate cups placed on the chimney piece of the bed-room. Coralie often leaves there some valuable jewels. The cash is in a glass cupboard in the same room, which is easily opened; you have the needful for that?"

"I have given Rupin my tools," said Vernier.

Salvador entered the house; he remained there longer than his companions expected.

"Probably something has happened to him," said Vernier to the viscount.

"It is not likely," replied the latter, "otherwise we should have heard a noise."

The arrival of Salvador put an end to the anxiety of his friends.

"Well!" said de Lussan.

"The affair is not bad," he replied, "but let us fly directly. I think I was observed by the porter."

The three accomplices quickly reached the Rue Four Saint-Hilaire. When safe in the loft of Vernier, Salvador placed on the table all that he had stolen from Coralie.

"Four thousand francs in gold, three thousand francs of jewels when sold to a fence," exclaimed Vernier, "we shall come out handsome after this."

"Have you a fence at your disposition?" asked de Lussan of him.

"I believe you, Louis l'Aventurier, who lives in the Sorbonne; he will buy any thing I choose to take him."

"Keep the jewels for your share then, and leave us the gold. Are you satisfied?"

"Quite so. You are more liberal than I expected."

"Let us sup then, and turn into bed. We will separate to-morrow morning."

The three bandits did honour to an excellent pullet, and some other eatables which they had purchased, Rue Dauphine, and went to bed.

The next morning, as agreed upon, they separated.

CHAPTER L.

THE LADY WITH THE GREEN VEIL.

THE history of the preceding facts has informed our readers that it was principally amongst his acquaintances that the Viscount de Lussan, whose name was a passport to the best society, chose his victims. We have seen that at first he confined himself to the giving Salvador and Roman instructions of a nature to facilitate the execution of the robberies which the two latter undertook to complete, and that it was not until a short time after the death of Roman, and when Salvador had determined to return no more to the house of Sans Refus, that he consented to pay in his person.

To understand what follows, we must beg our readers to take a few steps *en arrière*.

We said just now that the Viscount de Lussan had enrolled himself in the rank of the most forward new Catholics; it was not simply because *devotion finds, in order to commit bad actions, reasons which a plain honest man would never think of*, that he had taken this part; he was aware that the world is generally disposed to place great confidence in those who, although mixing in fashionable society, acquit themselves with regularity in their religious duties; and devotion was a mask he knew well how to wear, and which had expedited the opening of the salons of many a noble dowager,

who appeared to have forgotten, until a solemn judgment apprised every one that the Viscount de Lussan, despite the antiquity of his escutcheon, was nothing more than a notorious bandit, that we must not always trust to appearances.

However, the viscount had for a confessor, a venerable priest, attached to the church of Saint Roch, and he had the art of so well insinuating himself into his confidence, that very frequently the worthy ecclesiastic invited him to dinner.

When he was arrested, Rue de Varennes, a few steps from his lodgings, the viscount had left for the purpose of visiting the priest, as he often did.

The following facts will inform the reader what was the object of these visits.

One day, whilst the viscount and the good priest were at table tête-à-tête, they announced to M. l'Abbé the visit of an old woman, nearly blind, whose face was concealed by an ample green veil. She came to deposit with the priest a small sum of money for the saying of masses, and an anniversary for sins. The abbé rose to receive the pious woman in another room; but de Lussan told him not to incommode himself on his account, and indeed begged him to allow her to enter. The domestic having introduced her, she handed to the vicar a sum of twenty-four francs. De Lussan, a curious observer, and ready to turn every incident to account, remarked that this woman was very old, clad in sordid and even disgusting garments; she wore one of those balloon bonnets, of a shape quite unique, the colour formerly black, but now yellow and reddish, which, accompanied by an immense *eye shade* in green silk, produced that droll ensemble which characterizes the fortune tellers of the lowest scale. Lastly, the whole appearance of the old devotee, announced the greatest misery; and to complete the portrait, she walked with some trouble, apparently from her weak sight.

When she left, the viscount made these remarks to the vicar, and expressed his astonishment to see twenty-four francs given away by a woman whose costume betokened the most complete poverty. The latter replied that, "appearances were not always to be trusted to, and that far from this woman being in poverty, she was, on the contrary, rich, and very rich; that she did much good to the poor of the parish;" in short, he regretted that persons of her description were so seldom to be met with.

"In that case," said de Lussan, "you will agree, my dear abbé, that it may well be asked where does Fortune perch herself! for the good woman has a most repulsive aspect. For myself, I am of opinion that a love of God and our neighbour, devotion, even charity, does not preclude decency; and I frankly confess to you, I can hardly believe in the fortune of this woman, that appears to me inconsistent with the state of destitution she is in. I should rather imagine her to be only the instrument of pious individuals, who wish to remain unknown, and who, as a recompense for the little services she renders them, procure her the means of existence."

"You are in error, M. le Vicomte," replied the abbé; "she is rich, and when I say this, 'tis that I know it. I can even the better assure you of this, as I have seen, seen with my own eyes, all that composes her fortune, under the circumstances I will now relate to you:—

"It was not more than two months ago that this woman came to me for the first time, to request me to say some masses for the repose of the soul of her father and mother, deceased for a long time; she gave me, besides, forty francs for the poor, and the same for the church. Her visits were frequently renewed, and she always showed herself as generous. I could not conjecture from whence, nor how, she obtained the sums she disposed of, so much did her apparent misery contrast with her works of charity; but I was not long in the dark as to this species of mystery.

"About a fortnight since, she came to request me to call upon her to receive an important secret, a confidence, she said, which she could only make in her own apartment. I confess to you that this invitation appeared to me so extraordinary on her part, that for three or four days I hesitated to go there; but at length, after much reflection, I thought it my duty to satisfy her.

"Arrived at her dwelling, the ridiculous appearance of the concierge, his unusual questions, and afterwards the not less extraordinary ones of his wife, brought some strange ideas to my mind. However, after submitting to the customary interrogatory, I was conducted by the female Cerberus to the lady with the green veil. After knocking, in a certain manner, a wicket opened; I gave my name.

"'Ah! it's you, M. l'Abbé,' said the old woman, 'enter I beg of you.'

"She then undid two bolts, and the same number of locks; and when I was inside, secured the door with a precaution which much increased my curiosity, but without feeling the slightest alarm. She then introduced me to a ground floor, composed of several rooms in disorder, and as slovenly as the mistress of the house. The lady, after excusing herself on account of her great age and her infirmities, for receiving me so unfavourably, addressed me in these terms:—

"'M. le Vicaire, you are a man in whom I have the greatest confidence, and I shall immediately give you a proof of it; I am old and tolerably rich; I possess in gold, silver, bank-notes, and jewels, about two hundred thousand francs; I have besides a revenue of five thousand francs from the public funds. There is in the whole world, but one individual who is allied to me by the ties of blood, that is my daughter; but for a long while I have not heard her mentioned; I am absolutely ignorant of her fate. Her excepted, I have neither relations nor friends. The Almighty may at any moment call me to himself, and all my riches would be almost lost, if I happened to die without indicating the spot in which they are contained. I cannot do better than address myself to you, M. l'Abbé, to reveal a secret of this nature. I will, therefore, show you where these objects are hidden, and I authorize you, after my death, to dispose of them in the best way you can, with the exception I will presently name to you. There is a sealed writing which contains in this respect my formal will. Will you take upon yourself to be the depository, and not open until after my death.'

"Surprised at this language, and being always unwilling to busy myself in worldly affairs, which I understood but little, 1 wished to decline so rare a proof of confidence; the old lady would accept of no excuse; she begged, entreated with such earnestness, that at last I consented. She then invited me to pass into her bed-room, and after withdrawing her bed from the alcove, she raised some tapestry, and showed me a small door skilfully contrived in the wall. She opened it, and took out from this cachette, a pretty box in ebony, mounted in chased silver, bearing arms, and a ducal coronet. This box contained gold in large quantities, bank-notes, diamonds, and inscriptions on the funds. To be brief, I was convinced that it contained at least three hundred thousand francs in real value.

"'This is all I possess,' said the lady. 'If the person named in my testament still exists,' she continued, 'and by her conduct is worthy of my benefits, you will share my succession with her. In the contrary event, all is yours, to make a good use of. Such, most worthy and respectable minister of Christ, is my last will; and may that of God be done in all things.'

"Some observations I again offered, to dissuade her from her intention regarding me, she would not listen to; and after replacing the box in the cupboard built in the wall, she closed the door, and once more exacted from me a promise that I would punctually execute her intentions. In consideration of the good which might result to the poor, I thought it my duty to undertake it, not only without restriction, but also in a manner to merit the approbation of the world and my superiors. As to the rest, you know me well enough, M. le Vicomte, to be convinced that I shall acquit myself with zeal and accuracy of this important mission.

"Now, if I may be allowed to state my opinion of this woman, I think her intention is to repair, after her death, the faults of a life passed in disorder, and perhaps even in crime. What makes me think so, is, that her language, which is not very pure, is that of a woman of the people, that the want of education has made her not over choice as to the means of making a fortune.

"There is another reason which gives greater force to this opinion, and it is this:

"I believe the devotion of this woman is sincere, her good works are a sufficient proof of that; well! although she listens with much fervour to the religious exhortations I have thought it my duty to address to her, although she assists at all the offices, she has not yet confessed herself.

"'I am not yet ready,' has been her reply, when I have invited her to approach the tribunal of penitence; 'in a short time, Monsieur l'Abbé; I cannot yet reveal to you the numerous faults, the crimes even of my past life; but I am repenting, be assured.'

"I did not think it right to insist, and here the matter rests."

During this recital, the viscount was all eyes and ears, he could scarcely restrain the inward joy he felt, and already he was planning the means of getting possession of the treasure of the old lady. Certainly, the abbé had not indicated the address of the green veiled visitant, but in all the rest he had shown an indiscretion, which the name of the viscount, and his supposed sincere piety, could alone excuse. However, with men of the stamp of de Lussan, the absence of information of this nature was no great obstacle; he knew that the service demanded by the old lady was to take place the next morning, and that she would be present at it; that sufficed him. In fact, he repaired to Saint Roch, and was even in such a hurry to arrive there, that he was at the church an hour too soon. At length the lady for whom he was waiting with such impatience, arrived. Upon this occasion, she had not her inseparable green veil, but a very thick black one, which gave to her whole figure a most lugubrious complexion. She kneeled and prayed for some time with such fervour, that the service had been completed above an hour, ere, absorbed as she was in prayer, she

LIFE IN PARIS

SILVIA SINGING TO SALVADOR, DE LUSSAN, AND VERNIER.

thought of quitting the church. The viscount, who had intended following her on her retiring, in order to discover her residence, was enraged at being forced to imitate her, and simulate a devotion which was far from his heart; for heaven knows the vile projects he meditated at this moment. At length, after making several genufluctions and reverences before every chapel, the old lady touched the holy water and left. All this was still a work of time, from the difficulty she found in walking, and which caused her to stumble at every step amongst the chairs; but outside at last, and following the walls with precaution, she reached her house Rue Thérèse, No. 25.

De Lussan, expert and intelligent as we know him, made sure of its being her residence; he then retired, deferring to another day the investigations he would require to put his projects in execution. He slept not the whole night, so much had his anxiety, and the desire of getting possession of the treasures of the veiled lady, exalted his spirits. Scarcely was it daylight the next morning, when he commenced his investigations in the neighbourhood of the old lady; he learned that she was known by the name of the lady with the green veil, or the blind woman; further, they knew nothing about her; each told his history in his own manner; some said she *drew cards;* others that she was an old sinner, who, from her efforts at repentance, subjected herself to the taunts of the multitude. Some added, that if he wished to know more particularly this woman, who was an enigma to every one, he must address himself to Father Fleurus and his wife, who were the porters at No. 25, and appeared the only ones in the confidence of the stranger; that it was possible at the same time that the grocer opposite might also be of use to him.

The grocer, adroitly questioned by the viscount, replied "that the lady was not his customer, and that absolutely he knew nothing about her;" but he added, "that his neighbour, Mother Grignac, the fruiterer, could satisfy him; she is the most notorious gossip in Paris," he said; "it will not require great efforts to obtain from her all you wish to know." De Lussan thanked the grocer, and in two steps was with Mother Grignac.

He needed all his sang froid to prevent his laughing in the face of the enormous fruiterer! Imagine a mass of unshaped flesh, limbs as badly formed as they were ill connected, a height in proportion to the breadth; a countenance, jolly, square, variegated with red, white, and blue, &c., here and there covered with a thick layer of charcoal; a nose like a marmite's foot, viz., short, thick, pimpled, and a veritable *chapel of ease* to a storehouse for tobacco; eyes horribly squinting, chafed, and waxy; a mouth adorned with thirty-two teeth, incontestibly white, but belonging rather to the order of ruminating animals, than the human species; lips thick and turned up; in fact, a real caricature. But what completed this creature, an ideal of the grotesque and oddities of nature, was the clothing and common linen, shining in grease, the fashion of which coincided with the materials; her headdress was composed of a handkerchief of yellow orange, but so dirty, that the colour was become truly problematical. To sum up, she was a female Sancho Panza, whose ensemble was as repulsive as it was hideous.

De Lussan, with that exquisite politeness which he showed in every thing, principally with his inferiors, in order to impose more easily upon them, addressed himself, hat in hand, to the living wine barrel, of which we have sketched a faithful portrait.

"Is it to Madame de Grignac I have the honour of speaking?" he said to her.

"Yes, yes, *mossieu,*" she replied with a very strong cockney accent, whilst swallowing the last of her coffee, and wiping her mouth with the corner of a torn and dirty apron; "yes, *mossieu,* at your service."

"Pardon me, Madame de Grignac, if I am disturbing you for an object foreign to your business. I wish to obtain, but under the seal of confidence, some information respecting a neighbour of yours, and who is also, I believe, one of your customers."

"One of my customers, you say? Why, I have customers every where, and good ones too! Of which are you speaking, my good *mossieu?*"

"Before naming her, I should like to know if you will keep the secret?"

"The *shecret—fich'tra!* Mother Grignac is known throughout the neighbourhood as discretion itself; *fich'tra!* and there is not a soul in the world who can say I have a wilful tongue. Allez! me gossip, for what purpose, if you please? How would it serve me to tell you that the mercer is kept by the baker at the corner, who sells his bread by false weights, to give her silk gowns; and that, on her part, the mercer gives cravats and breeches to the son of old Gublin, concierge at No. 13. Or, that the cookshop-keeper is making himself bankrupt, because his banker, who has broken with madame his wife, will give him no more money. And then again, that the grocer opposite has nothing in his shop, that the sugar loaves are of pasteboard, as well as the packets of wax-lights and candles; that the boxes are empty; and the show-glasses filled with water of all colours, to dazzle the customers and passengers. Eh! Holy Father! what 'oud be the end of speaking about all this, is it my business or yours either? For my part, I detest scandal; allez, my bon *mossieu,* you ought to see that I am not one of the gossiping sort, and that I never meddle with the affairs of my neighbours."

Whilst the fruiterer uttered this infernal history, the viscount could scarcely contain himself; twenty times he felt inclined to send to the devil this old maggot, who, at the very time she was stating her dislike to meddle with the affairs of her neighbours, tore them to pieces without mercy; but his anxiety to obtain information as to the veiled lady, induced him to submit with patience.

"Now," resumed the imperturable fruiterer, "what was it you inquired of me just now? I have forgotten it already."

"I asked you, Madame de Grignac, if you know hereabouts, at No. 25, a respectable lady who usually wears a green veil, and who appears almost blind?"

"Ah! ah! I know, I know!" replied Grignac, "'tis that old sinner who shams blind, to cheat heaven and hell! Do I know her, I believe you. *Fich'tra!* she's an old *chorceress,* who has as many vices as she has crowns."

"Can you, my good Madame de Grignac, tell me her name, from whence she comes, what she does; in fact, give me any precise information as to her habits?"

"Her name! I don't know it, *nor nobody.* Where she comes from? most certainly she comes from a *witchery!* Where do you think such a loupgaron should come from?"

"Pardon, my good lady, but I'm told she is compassionate, charitable!"

"Yes, it's true they say all this, but nobody knows it for certain; 'tis my opinion, she's an old *chorchiere*, an old fortune-teller, who does nothing without consulting *Luchifer*, with whom she is shut up from morning till night; so that no one enters her room, 'tis worse than a prison. Allez, *mossieu*, there is something under all this, and quite certain that she has made a compact with the Wicked One, and has bargained away her soul to him, for one evening that I carried her a half-pint of beer, I saw the devil as plain as I see you."

"Really, my good Madame de Grignac, you are quite worthy of it, and I believe you. But try to put me in possession of the history of this old sorceress, I am more interested in it than you imagine."

"I will *chatisfy* you, but by all means don't repeat what I'm going to tell you, for she will cast a spell on me; and what would become of Mother Grignac, if she had a spell put on her; you will promise, won't you? Well, listen to me then:

"It is not more than three months since the old woman tumbled down here like a bomb, without any one knowing whether she came from heaven or hell. On arriving in the neighbourhood, she rented the apartment she is in, on the ground floor, all the windows were barred, but not content with that, she had the shutters lined with iron, as well as the principal door, in which she had a wicket cut; this door is secured with three or four *chafety* bolts, and she never opens it to any one. When she goes out to mass, or for exercise, Father Fleurus, her porter, keeps the door within eye-sight; our holy father, the pope himself, could not gain an entrance. Allez, *mossieu*, I am quite *chure* of what I say; she's an old *chorchiere*, who makes false money night times; there are some even who assert she has a black hen! But, mon doux Jesus, I tremble in telling you this; especially as she is not aware that I have spoken to you about her, for she is capable of changing me into a dog, or a she-goat, and who knows, perhaps, even into a hen turkey."

"Don't be alarmed, Madame de Grignac, I am a discreet man, and besides, as I have told you, I have more interest than yourself in being silent. Now, if I may be allowed to make an observation, I would remark that your fears seem to me much too exaggerated, and that so far from this woman having the power you suppose, on the contrary, she appears very unfortunate, and great difficulty in keeping herself alive."

"Trouble in living when she has a black hen, and has only to turn the sieve to have loads of money! It is quite clear you do not understand these things like me, *mossieu*; and besides, she has also des rentes *voyagères*."

"Yes, they say all this, but they know nothing about it," replied the viscount: "for my part, I think she is in poverty over head and ears."

"If she were so poor," resumed Mother Grignac, with dryness, "why does she take so many precautions to hinder people from going to her? Allez, *mossieu*, to a *chertainty* she has a treasure, and a famous one too! Father Fleurus and his wife know all that, but they are sly foxes, you may well question them, they will tell you nothing."

"And so you think, Madame Grignac, that she has money, and even plenty of it?"

"Come, now, is it so very difficult to have treasures, if you are *chorchiere?* I am *chure* she has *milards!*"

"From the details you have given me, my dear lady, I cannot think that this person is the one my family is in search of, and whose head is somewhat deranged. At all events, I will make some inquiries of Father Fleurus and his wife, whether this lady is the Countess of Gipavas, whose ideas have unfortunately been a long time at fault."

"Ah! ah! ah! a countess! thank you, a droll countess she must be, to go to a witch meeting every night with *Luchifer!*"

"Adieu, Madame Grignac, until next time," said de Lussan, pushing on the counter with affectation a piece of gold.

"Adieu, adieu, *mossieu*. But he does make me laugh, with his countess! 'tis the Countess *Proserpine*, no doubt, and her nobility is from the devil's manufactory! never mind, he is very *comme il faut*, this *mossieu*; I have not lost much by gossipping with him," she added, taking up the piece of gold; "voila un *petit chou*, as they say in my country."

Whilst Mother Grignac continued chattering to herself, de Lussan went straight to No. 25; he examined it with attention, but rapidly, on the outside, for the nearer he approached his object, the more circumspection he observed in his measures. He first entered the court, returned, and entered the lodge of the porter, situate on the left of the door, and where, by chance, he met with no one at the moment. It is as well to observe that the lodge door was surmounted with this inscription in letters six inches in length:—" Address yourself to monsieur le concierge, if you please;" and at the side might be read on a slate hung near the window, the following words, written in smaller characters: "Security. Discretion. The citizen Fleurus and madame his wife, do the work of the house only."

"The devil," said de Lussan, "here we have republicans not over liberal!" and being for a moment master of the lodge, he took a rapid glance at it, and made his own little remarks. He found it irreproachably clean, and tolerably furnished; a pendulum, with pillars of citron wood, with a pair of vases adorned with flowers; some prints, one of which represented the battle of Fontenoy, and for a companion, that of Fleurus, who had had the honour of giving his name to the intrepid guardian of the house; a pair of foils crossed, leather gloves, and a breastplate, the whole forming a trophy, indicating his worship of the games of Mars and Bellona. Beneath these instruments of death, is a small frame enclosing the discharge of Chrysostrome Gringilliard, native of Gaudiempré, in Artois, master of arms. At this moment the viscount was interrupted in his readings by the arrival of a man about sixty-eight years of age, and five feet eight inches in height, thin, but of an athletic constitution, wearing a police cap, ornamented with a grenade, and placed jauntily on the right ear; a military cravat; in the whole neat, and as spicy as a new-pin; but the brave old warrior, in consequence of a wound, had suffered the loss of his left hand by amputation. Upon seeing the viscount, he seized his police cap, raised it, extended his arm, and with a gesture graciously copied from that of the telegraph, he bowed three times with majestic gravity.

"Pardon and excuse, my *coronel*," he said to the viscount, "what do you desire?" Saying this, he replaced his cap with the same automaton movements as before.

"'Tis I, my worthy fellow," said the viscount, "who demand pardon for entering here in your absence. I am further delighted at meeting you, as I wish to speak with you."

"I am also enchanted," replied the intrepid janitor; "no doubt you have not the honour of knowing me, but never mind; an ancient *cuirassier* steady at his post, speak my *coronel!*"

"It concerns citizen Fleurus."

"Stay, you know my name then," interrupted the citizen? "How did you discover that my name was Fleurus?"

"You shall know presently," said the viscount. "At present, citizen Fleurus, I want you to render me a service; 'tis to give me some information about the lady who lives here, and almost constantly wears a green veil."

"Ah! you mean Madame *l'Alolyme*, Madame *l'Inconnito*, as she is called in the house; but if you will allow me to call Phillippine Craperel, or to speak plainer, my wife, Madame Fleurus, 'tis she that can satisfy you; she has a gilded tongue, and speaks like the aristocrats of *Colblance;* besides, she is a *philosophe!*"

"Do not disturb madame, I beg of you," said the viscount.

But without noticing this prayer, our man gave a whistle, and two minutes afterwards entered the lodge a woman of good height, straight and stiff as a hop-pole, from sixty to sixty-five years of age. Her dress which seemed to date from the end of the reign of Louis the XVth, was of an uncommon propriety; her head was encased in a coiffure of lace in folds, she wore a *caraco* with short sleeves and the back in plaits, the petticoat beneath was turned up gracefully through the pocket-holes and showed the one next in order, which was of good calico with large rays; green morocco slippers with high heels, and her leg, which improved the eclat of a fine and irreproachably white stocking, exhibited a contour which had charms of its own. In fact, the ensemble of her costume, and her carriage, had that sort of elegance which our grandfathers admired in the *soubrettes* of good family three parts of a century ago. For the rest, Madame Fleurus must have been handsome, for her features, although a little damaged by age, were still good.

Upon seeing the viscount in the lodge, she made him a profound and gracious reverence; and then, after begging him to excuse her for keeping him waiting, she offered him a chair, claiming his indulgence for her husband, who had been unpolite enough to allow him to stand.

"Your kindness overwhelms me, madame," said the viscount, "and I——"

"Madame," interrupted Maitre Gringilliard, "*mossieu* has a favour to ask you, a *confidence* to make you."

"M. Fleurus," said madame sharply, "it seems to me you ought not to interrupt this gentleman. Besides is it not possible for you to discontinue this mode of speaking, these *liasons dangereuses*, which are the rocks on which you split every moment? We may easily see, my friend, that you have served in the cuirassiers!"

"A little, my nephew, I flatter myself," quickly replied Fleurus, drawing himself up and standing before his wife. "I have served with honour and glory; I have been wounded in the service of the republic, the invisible and unexhaustible; and here is the proof," he added, showing the stump of his arm.

"It's true," said the viscount, "it does you honour, and I congratulate you with all my heart. You are a good Frenchman!"

"Sure enough a good Frenchman; but there is not so much to talk about, for simply doing one's duty! I had sworn to live free or die an honest republican, it is not my fault if the republic has perished before me!"

"Yes," replied Madame Fleurus, whose opinions did not coincide with those of her husband, "the republic has handsomely rewarded you; she has left you liberty—to pull the bell with one hand for the rest of your life."

"And you then, Madame la Ci-devant? what are you the richer for having been at *Colblance* with Pitt and Coburg, and your other aristocrats? You learned there how to make a curtsey, to speak French, which is a heap of nonsense, or I understand nothing; is that worth so much bother?"

"Hold your tongue, you old crust! know that I learned to live among people of fashion, and that I should not be out of place in a saloon; whilst you, you would be scouted for the vulgarity of your language and republican manners!"

"I am of the people! that is true; but of the *sovereign* people, Madame Fleurus! Endeavour for the future to speak with respect of the *sovereign* people, do you understand? A republican soldier has only to know the science of fighting; and I maintain that in her hands a bandy-leg is worth more than all your *grandmeres*, and all your *rhitouriques*, which are just a heap of so many *illusory* inventions. A sword, bread, and plenty of cartridges, this is enough to go to glory with! I speak without *illusions*. And where is the use of knowing how to get through a saloon, when your position forces you to remain at the door with your worthy husband?"

"Knowledge will always have its price," said Madame Fleurus, with her affected air, "and I see with pain, my dear husband, that you are not competent to solve the question. As to your republic, I hold it in horror, for all the evil it has done; it has destroyed all, religion, morals, legitimate royalty! Alas! let us pray to and fear God, for, good and merciful as he is, he will be wearied; and perhaps, the day is not far distant, when he will punish mankind for having raised a sacrilegious and parricidal hand against the throne and the altar!

"Pardon," continued Madame Fleurus, addressing the viscount, "pardon me for having carried so far this discussion in your presence; but my husband has well spoken, and well done; I shall never forget all that I owe to nobility."

"Let the opinion of each be respected, Madame Fleurus," said the viscount, "even that of your husband, although by the privilege of my birth, I ought to range myself on your side. In fact, and although I am not in the habit of boasting of what is a mere game of chance, I have much pleasure in informing you that I was born a gentleman."

"I conjectured as much, sir," said Madame Fleurus, assuming her most amiable tone; "I should have known it from your polished manners, which are the appendage of people of quality. And now," she added, "will you inform me how I can serve you?"

"This, madame, is the motive which brings me here:

"I was born in French Flanders; my family reside at Saint Sylvestre-Cappel, and my name is the Marquis de Woolbleck. At the period of the last revolution, my grandmother lost her reason, and, about a twelvemonth ago, she escaped from the chateau, carrying away a sum of four or five thousand francs. I am in search of her, and, from precise information recently furnished me, I have reason to believe that it is to this house she has retired, and where she is known by the description of the lady with the green veil."

"I regret to be compelled to destroy your hopes, M. le Marquis," said Madame Fleurus, "but the lady you speak of has lived here for two years; she cannot, therefore, be your relation."

Madame Fleurus told a lie, when she made the assertion above. De Lussan knew it well, but he could not allow her to see that he was well informed as to what he seemed desirous of knowing; and Madame Fleurus, probably, was only obeying the instructions she had received.

"If indeed," replied de Lussan, a little disconcerted, "it is true that this lady has been your lodger for two years, she cannot be the individual I am in search of. You will, therefore, excuse madame, a step which, as you see, was founded upon a very natural curiosity. At the same time, what has most contributed to my placing reliance in the information I have received, is, that the lady you have with you passes, in the neighbourhood, for a lunatic, which gives an air of some resemblance to my unhappy grandmother."

"Alas! M. le Marquis," replied Madame Fleurus, "the world is very censorious, very wicked. They treat this lady as mad, because she sees no one, and is partial to her church; but the truth is, she is not mad at all, I can attest it to you."

"Ah! bah!" said Maitre Fleurus, "if she is not mad, it's only by chance. What does she do, then, every day, from morning till night, with her fops of clergymen, if she is not mad?"

"M. Fleurus," replied his wife, "it appears to me you might speak with a little more politeness of a lady who gives you a living, and of a class of individuals who have a right to the respect of every one."

"Who keeps me alive? If I guard her *magot*, is it not just she should pay me? And as to all your church-goers, what are they to me? I only respect the curés of the republic, the *theophilon-en-troupe*."

"She has a fortune, then, this lady?" added de Lussan.

"On that point, I have no reply to make to M. le Marquis," said Madame Fleurus. "I have never taken the liberty of addressing to this lady the least question as to her position, because the affairs of our lodgers do not regard me, and M. le Marquis is too polished to provoke an indiscretion."

"You misunderstand me as to the object of my question," replied the viscount, a little piqued; "I have no reason for being curious in these sort of things, and if I inquired of you whether this lady had a fortune, it was quite mechanically, and certainly without any intention of inducing you to be wanting in your duty."

The viscount plainly saw he had nothing to hope for, either from this old caricature or her imbecile husband; besides, it was sufficient to look upon them for a moment, to be persuaded, that, had the lady been in her proper senses, she never would have chosen such a pair of confidants. He therefore allowed her to believe that he had experienced no annoyance at the manner by which the precious concierge had shut his mouth; and although little satisfied with the result of his inquiries, he knew enough, at least, to erect other batteries by which to bring about his designs. He retired, therefore, overwhelming the antiquated couple with politenesses and salutations.

We know too much of de Lussan as a man of resolution, to believe that he faltered in sight of obstacles, or held himself vanquished by the powerful dulness of the Fleuruses. He certainly felt some regrets at having so ill succeeded at first with these Cerberuses; but the hope of being more fortunate another time raised his courage. "Two hundred thousand francs in gold, silver, diamonds, and bank-notes, one hundred thousand francs of revenue in the funds, and payable to bearer! What a magnificent prey!" he said to himself. "Shall I allow it to escape, then? A real Tantalusian punishment: I touch it, and yet I cannot——but no, were I to perish in the attempt, I must absolutely bring it about."

We may well suppose, that the very day he had the conversation with the vicar of Saint Roch, and by which he had been made acquainted with all that regarded the lady with the green veil, de Lussan had not failed to give an account of it to his friend Salvador. Both had set their wits at work to invent some plan by which they could put the vigilance of the Fleuruses at fault; but the stupidity of the husband, more redoubtable than the wit and cunning of the wife, had disconcerted all their projects. In vain did they despatch emissaries upon emissaries; Father Fleurus, the docile slave of his wife, whom he regarded as an oracle, referred them to the latter, with the simple reply, "Address yourself to *Mame* Fleurus; I know nothing about the thing of *Mame l'Alolyme*." As to Madame Fleurus, brought up amongst her superiors, in the midst of a society quite *au fait* in lies—deceitful, painted, and dangerous—she possessed, in a supreme degree, the art of dissembling; and, after an hour's conversation with her, one became astonished that her fine-drawn phrases advanced not one step towards the question.

This affair, therefore, which promised such a brilliant result, must be renounced; but this neither de Lussan nor Salvador could resolve upon, and they were seeking the means of arriving at the object they had absolutely determined upon, when they were both arrested.

CHAPTER LI.

THE RESULTS OF THE PRECEDING.

WE are now compelled to conduct our readers to a place we will not name, but which the short description we shall endeavour to give of it will sufficiently proclaim.

The shop of a house situate in one of the small streets which open into the Boulevard Bonne-Nouvelle, has been turned into a little saloon, and the walls covered with a common red paper. This saloon—since saloon it is (?)—is merely furnished with a large round table, covered with a green cloth, a couch of yellow velvet d'Utrecht, and some cherry-wood chairs with horse-hair seats; some wretched lithographs, in gilt frames, are attached to the wall; an alabaster pendulum and two vases of gilt porcelain, in which are inserted two large tufts of artificial flowers, ornament the chimney.

There was a good fire on the hearth, which sent forth a grateful warmth over the saloon and appeared to comfort those who were its inmates.

And, first, six women, still young, and almost pretty, bare necked, habited simply (although the temperature was cold, and they were forced to leave the room nearly every quarter of an hour) in light silk frocks of clear colours; next, two men, whose physiognomy resembled most others, with the exception of being handsomer than the common run. One of these men wore a redingote and blue pantaloons; the other, pantaloons of striped velvet and a shooting blouse of gray linen, nearly new. We must add, however, that the man in the redingote wears green spectacles, which have a villainous effect, and that the other has the right eye covered with a band of black silk. Such as they were, however, these messieurs appeared to cause infinite pleasure to the inhabitants of the place, all of whom, with the exception of one pretty brunette, who was seated in the shade, and appeared to take no notice of what passed around her, lavished upon them a thousand little attentions and gracious smiles.

Our readers will comprehend the warmth and amiability of these ladies, when we tell them that these messieurs had ordered an enormous bowl of punch, which a servant placed, all in flames, on the table.

"Come, Flamant, help these ladies to some punch," said the man in spectacles to his companion.

"With pleasure, my dear Albert," replied Flamant, who, with a grace quite peculiar, took the gravy spoon, a worthy accompaniment to punch served in a salad bowl, and filled to the brims the glasses intended for the ladies.

"Well, Elizabeth," said one of the latter to the pretty brunette, "won't you come and drink a glass of punch?"

"I am not thirsty," replied Elizabeth, in a hasty tone.

"Come, stupid, 'tis good, and these messieurs say that when this is gone, we shall have more."

Elizabeth did not even take the trouble to raise her head towards the girl who addressed her.

"Leave her alone, then," said one of the women to the last speaker; "don't you know that when she has taken a whim into her head you cannot make her change it?"

"Ah! there are no means of making me change an idea!" exclaimed Elizabeth, rising suddenly from her seat. "Well, you are deceived in that, for I am going to drink punch, and more than yourself too;"and suiting the action to the words, Elizabeth took several glasses, one after another, and emptied them each at one draught.

"The unhappy girl is mad," said Flamant, in a low tone, to the girl next him.

"Rather so," she replied, "but never mind, she's a good comrade, and her fits don't last long."

"And they keep her here?"

"She is young, she is pretty, what more do you want?"

Whilst Flamant and the girl exchanged together these few words, Elizabeth, who had remained standing at the table, quietly approached Albert. She seated herself on his knee, and, after regarding him with the sweetest smile imaginable, she asked him for a small sum, which the latter quickly handed to her. When she had obtained what she desired, she ran out of the saloon.

The woman who conversed with Flamant had remarked what took place.

"You have given her money?" she said to Albert.

"Oh! a trifle," he replied; "but what is the meaning of all this?"

"Tell these messieurs the history of Elizabeth Neveux," said one of the women; "it will amuse them, 'tis droller than a comedy at the Gaieté."

"I wish for nothing better, if it will please them."

"Narrate, charmer," replied Flamant to this indirect question, "narrate; your voice is so sweet, that we shall listen to you with infinite delight; am I not right, Albert?"

The latter nodded his assent.

"I commence, then," said the girl, after swallowing a glass of punch.

"We are listening."

"Elizabeth Neveux belongs to a family of honest cultivators of Lorraine; she was born at Lacroix-Dieu, a pretty little village in the environs of Luneville. Elizabeth had so often heard talk of Paris —the people in her village whom chance had led to the grand city, spoke so gaily of the marvellous things they had seen there—that she was dying with anxiety to see it in her turn. When she had attained her eighteenth year, therefore, she begged her father to let her go; and the good man, who could refuse nothing to his daughter, escorted her one fine morning to the diligence, and saw her depart without disquietude, for he knew she would be received, on her alighting, by the eldest of the family, who had been some time in Paris, where he exercised the business of a working locksmith. Elizabeth, therefore, on arriving at Paris, went to lodge with her brother, and for some time her conduct was irreproachable. Every one praised her modesty and prudence, as well as her beauty. Unfortunately, her brother, who endeavoured to procure her every amusement that his fortune permitted, took her, one evening, to a little ball in the Rue Saint Antoine, which they call the *Bal des Acacias*. There she made the acquaintance of a handsome young fellow; this handsome young man made his court to her; and, my faith, it happened to her just as it had happened to many a pretty girl before her, she allowed herself to be seduced; and, one night, her brother waited supper for her in vain; she had deserted with the young man in question.

"Pierre Neveux, the brother of Elizabeth, searched a long while for his sister, without finding her; it was only by chance that he heard, some time afterwards, that she lived under the name of Lion——"

"Of Madame Lion?" said Flamant.

"Do you know Elizabeth's lover?" inquired the narrator; "he was a thief."

"I have no such acquaintances; but I partly know the rest of the history of your companion. Her brother presented himself, one day, at her lodging, Rue des Lions Saint Paul. She had just had a violent altercation with her lover, who had come home drunk, accompanied by one of his friends, named, I think, Maladetta. Pierre Neveux took the part of his sister, whom the two ruffians illtreated to his face. The latter also tried it on with himself; and, my faith, as he was endowed with Herculean strength, and held in his hand one of those heavy hammers constantly used by persons of his trade, he killed the two bandits, and afterwards escaped. The journals of the day informed me of what I am telling you; as to the rest, I am ignorant of it."

"This is what happened, then: Elizabeth was arrested. Many circumstances having led to the inference that she knew the assassin, they wished her to name him to the authorities. This she would not do. She could not determine to denounce her brother, who had only rendered himself guilty by his anxiety to defend her. She remained some time in prison, therefore: she was not set at liberty until they had contrived to get possession of Pierre Neveux. The unfortunate workman was brought before the court of assize, and condemned to ten years of hard labour. Elizabeth was so afflicted at being the cause of his condemnation, that she completely lost her reason. She was taken to Salpetriére. The most celebrated physicians attached to the establishment restored her nearly to her right mind in the course of a twelvemonth.

She was then turned into the street. It was cold, she was barely covered with a few miserable garments, and she was hungry. After what had happened, she could not endure the idea of returning to her family. What could she do? She entered here; but I suppose the trade did not agree with her, for lately her head has been again deranged. She is frequently out of spirits, she speaks to no one. Sometimes her spirits are lively, even to madness; she then drinks beyond measure, no doubt, to stupify herself. But, whatever may be the thoughts which agitate her, whether she is sad or lively, she never forgets that her unhappy brother is at the prison of Toulon, that he is suffering, and that she is the cause of his troubles. She puts aside all the money she can procure, and, when she has contrived to amass a small sum, she forwards it to Pierre Neveux, who is ignorant of what his sister is doing. As these little offerings are frequently renewed, it is probable that the poor boy, who, it is said, conducts himself very well, will find, on leaving the prison, a sum which will facilitate his means of establishing himself in business; but he will not find his sister. The doctors say she carries in her bosom the seeds of a mortal disease, and that two years is the longest limit they can place on her life, and it will be six years before Pierre is set at liberty."

The narration was interrupted by the entrance into the saloon of a man, whose brilliant costume drew from the women an exclamation of admiration. He was dressed in a superb light paletot, blue pantaloons, a gold chain took several turns round his black velvet waistcoat, his neck was imprisoned in a cravat of red satin, he wore a hat with a very long nap, his boots highly polished, and held in his hand a magnificent gold-headed cane; all this was new.

"You are very well amused, my galliards, whilst I am killing myself by running," he said to Flamant and Albert; "but, never mind, all is arranged for the best, and I shall have my turn soon. Some punch!" he exclaimed, striking the table several times with his fist, "some punch!"

The mistress of the place ran in frightened, and demanded, in a harsh voice, why they made such a noise in an honest house.

"Because we want some punch, and the best," replied the fashionable, throwing carelessly two gold pieces on the green cloth which covered the table.

The sight of gold suddenly calmed the old shrew; her features melted down a little.

"You shall be served, my chicken," she said, "you shall be served. A little patience. Talk with these ladies in the mean time."

The fop threw himself negligently on the couch.

"He is half drunk," said Albert to his companion.

"I am not surprised at it; the moment these miserables have a few pieces of gold at their disposition, this is the use they make of it."

"I shall not quarrel with him, if he has acquitted himself with intelligence of the missions we charged him with."

"This we must ascertain."

Flamant and Albert had retired to the extremity of the room to exchange the few preceding words; they signed to the would-be fashionable to join them.

The latter, who had previously inquired of the females if the smoke of tobacco would annoy them, and received a reply which accorded with his wishes, drew from his pocket a black clay pipe, which he lighted before joining his companions.

"Come, my dear Vernier," said Albert to him,

(our readers have probably conjectured by this time that this individual was no other than Salvador, and that the one we have hitherto called Flamant was the Viscount de Lussan,) "you are rather gay; but are you in a condition to listen and reply to us?"

"Death! why, I have drunk a few glasses of brandy, but my head is as clear as my body is sound, and that's not saying a little. The coffer's good; thunder!"

"Tell us what you have done, then, since the morning."

"Willingly, and you will see I have good legs and good eyes. On quitting you, I went to Louis l'Aventurier's; he gave me, as I expected, three thousand pippins for the jewels of the danseuse, and presented me with a complete rig-out in addition."

"Well?"

"Afterwards, knowing you would not find the time hang heavy at the house in which I requested you to meet me, I made a comfortable breakfast."

"What next?"

"I took a cabriolet and went again to Louis l'Aventurier, who waited for me at a wine-shop in Saint Martin's Court, and started on our pilgrimage at once. And after a long search, we at length found, in a secluded house, what you wanted, a floor containing two small rooms and a kitchen.

"The rooms have been engaged by Louis l'Aventurier, who has given his name and address, for two of his relations, who are to arrive this evening or to-morrow morning from the country. The place has been furnished; we have taken clothes and linen there; so that you may walk in with your two hands in your pockets, without creating the least suspicion. It is ready for you at this moment, and no doubt you will be in safety there. Here is the key of your rooms, and also of the street door. In order that you may not mistake, I have written on the door the name of Rupin."

"And Louis l'Aventurier is ignorant for whom he has engaged the rooms?"

"He only knows it is to be inhabited by two gaol birds, who have escaped from their cage; he gave the new names you have adopted, and all was finished. Louis l'Aventurier does all we wish, when he is well paid for it; but to-day he showed himself in style, he only took one thousand francs for the whole."

"We will repay them to you."

"There's no occasion; I have two thousand francs left; this is enough to last till a fresh coup, and to lead a joyous life besides."

"We shall make but one more in Paris, my dear Vernier, but that shall be a good one, I promise you."

"That of the lady with the green veil, of whom you spoke this morning with Rupin?"

"The same."

"She still lives Rue Thérèse, 25; I have made certain of it."

"Shall we succeed?" said Salvador, who, until now, had listened to, without taking a part in, the propositions exchanged between Vernier les bas Bleus and the Viscount de Lussan.

"We must, my dear Albert, should we even be obliged to pass through the key-hole to get into the old woman's treasury. With the miserable sum we are possessed of, we could not attempt to reach a foreign country."

"As you say, we will risk all for all, and if we fail, they shall not take us alive."

"That is a matter of course. For my part, I am not anxious to return to Bicêtre; that house I have

LIFE IN PARIS.

SILVIA ACCOSTING THE DUKE OF MODENA

a horrible dislike to; they treat a gentleman absolutely like a common clown."

"And I am to make one of you?" added Vernier.

"That's agreed. We will go to work as soon as our friend has completed the papers necessary to our quitting France."

The conversation of the three bandits was interrupted by the entrance into the saloon of a servant, who brought a bowl of much larger capacity than the one just finished, and full to the brim of flaming punch; she was followed by the mistress of the house, who placed upon the table two plates of porcelain, on which were placed some dozen biscuits.

The servant, who had not remarked the three men conversing at the bottom of the room, was retiring, after placing the punch on the table: she was prevented by one of the women.

"Remain with us, Celeste," said the woman, "you shall drink a glass of punch, and sing us one of your songs."

"I have no time," replied Celeste, "to-day is my turn for going out; it was merely because I had forgotten something, that I came in here; so I am going now."

"My good Celeste, I do beg of you, sing us something," resumed the woman.

"I will sing you nothing. You have plenty of soft words, when you can get anything by it, and you laugh at my ugliness; you call me la *mouchique*, when you have obtained what you wanted; I shall sing you nothing."

"Messieurs, messieurs, assist these ladies," said the mistress, "entreat Celeste to sing; you will not repent it; she sings enchantingly, and is equally *au fait* at music."

De Lussan, always excessively polite, thought himself called upon to address a few words to the woman whose musical talent was so praised.

Celeste regarded the viscount with such steadiness, that the latter was somewhat alarmed, and the frightful disfigurement of the woman caused him to take a step *en arrière*.

"I cannot refuse such gracious invitations," replied Celeste; and, without waiting, she commenced the first notes of the grand air of the *Reine de Chypre*.

"'Tis the Marchioness de Roselly," said de Lussan to Salvador, whilst she was singing.

"It is too true," replied the other, "and I think she has recognised us."

"What's to be done?"

"Wait, we run no risk; she has no reason to complain of us, and her position is no better than our own; we have, therefore, nothing to fear."

Salvador was not deceived, Silvia had recognised them. Whilst the other girls and Vernier les bas Bleus, all astonishment, applauded with ardour, she approached the two friends and whispered to them:

"Are the Marquis de Pourrieres and the Viscount de Lussan satisfied with the vocalist?"

"No imprudence, my dear Silvia," replied Salvador; "follow us when we leave this, but do not accost us until we arrive at our house."

"Very well; but do not hope to escape me, I shall have my eye upon you."

When midnight sounded, Salvador and de Lussan prepared to leave the amiable inhabitants of the somewhat suspicious place they were in; all entreaties to retain them were of no avail.

"We have disturbed you long enough already," they said to the mistress. "A sitting of twelve hours appears to us sufficient for a first visit: but we leave our friend to console you for our absence,

he's a jolly companion, with whom you will be quite content."

Vernier had, in fact, declared to his companions that he found himself in such good company, that he should not quit the place before the next morning.

Salvador and de Lussan arrived without delay at their new residence; Silvia, who, as agreed upon, had followed without speaking to them, entered with them.

Silvia did not feel justified in calling to account Salvador for having abandoned her at the moment fate had so cruelly visited her; she, therefore, made him no reproach, and appeared overjoyed at his having contrived to escape from the sad end that awaited him. She explained to him, how, after receiving the note he had sent her, at the moment he was about quitting Paris, she hastened to abandon her residence, carrying with her what she possessed in valuables. From her own house she was driven to a maison de santé, where she passed herself as an Italian lady, which was a matter of no difficulty, seeing she understood the language of the country, of which she called herself a native. She remained in this house some time, but her resources being nearly exhausted, she was compelled to leave it. At first, she had endeavoured to utilise her musical acquaintances, but that she found impossible, owing to her features being so disfigured, that she produced disgust in her young pupils; at last, falling from one step to another, and not knowing where to fly, she had, after in vain seeking her mother, dropped into the house he found her in.

Silvia, Salvador, and de Lussan were awoke the next morning by Vernier, who entered the house, followed by two hotel-waiters, carrying every thing necessary for providing a sumptuous breakfast. A few words explained the presence of Silvia.

"She's not handsome, certainly; but no matter, if the *becheur** has not lied, she's a knowing one, and I am very glad she is with us, especially if she pleases Rupin."

"She does not please me," replied Salvador; "but I support her, I must do so."

"Well then," continued Vernier, "why not get rid of her?" and ne gave a signicative sign, a faithful translation of his thought.

"For shame," cried de Lussan; "a companion of misfortune!"

"And who, after all, might be useful to us," added Salvador.

"At table!" said Silvia, who had finished laying out the breakfast, and had not heard the few words exchanged among the three accomplices; "at table!"

They quickly obeyed the invitation, and did honour to the rare wines and recherché viands brought there by Vernier les bas Bleus.

Several days thus rolled on. Thanks to the interested kindness of Louis l'Aventurier, and the skill in forgery of Salvador, the members of this society of bandits were all furnished with passports *en règle*. Nothing was wanting but money, to be in readiness to quit France, as they had intended The draft they had drawn upon the treasury of Coralie, the danseuse, began to dwindle; it was, therefore, time to think about the lady with the green veil.

Fresh measures were adopted; but the obstacles which had prevented the former ruses from succeeding still existed; how were they to be surmounted?

Salvador and de Lussan had frequently com-

* Public prosecutor.

plained, before Silvia, of the insurmountable difficulties which this enterprise presented, and of the necessity there would be of abandoning it; but she had always shown herself indifferent to their anxieties. But, at length, vanquished by their complaints, and finding that they had exhausted in vain all means, all resources, proud of showing her superiority, she reminded them of the part she had taken in the affair of Father Josué, and she swore to them she would execute the present one.

"Yes, messieurs," she added, with warmth, "I will succeed, if you promise to follow quietly my plan. You shall once more acknowledge that nothing withstands the genius or imagination of a woman endowed with a determined will." In saying these words, her eyes sparkled with unusual brilliancy; the satanic inspiration which had just aroused her rose to the surface.

Salvador and de Lussan, confiding in a promise that had never failed them, shared the enthusiasm of Silvia; they each pressed her by turns in their arms, and despite the horror which her features inspired, they proclaimed her the first woman in the world.

"To-morrow morning," she said, "I shall set to work; hold yourselves ready to second me."

This announcement raised their joy to its climax; they exhaust every adulating mode; the incense burns before the horrible divinity. But, at length, when their senses are a little calm, de Lussan, whose cautious and suspicious character slowly lent itself to confidence, would not blindly consign himself to the enterprises of the artful Silvia.

"For heaven's sake," he said to her, "I conjure you, tell us what means you intend to adopt in order to succeed; I burn with impatience to be initiated into this important secret."

"Listen to me," said Silvia, with emphasis, and with the air of a sybil who arouses a holy fanaticism; "the impotency of your conceptions, the assistance you are compelled to implore from a woman deprived of the advantages natural to her sex, all this announces to me that it is but the beginning of the end. Until now, you have lived in a brilliant position, thanks to a few lucky expeditions, in which I have acted conspicuously; but recollect well, a long suite of hazards is a fatal chain, whose length must necessarily produce misfortune. A catastrophe appears to me certain, inevitable, and you will succumb to it; for, in the career of crime, woe to him who hesitates, or casts a look behind! As to myself, I am more likely to escape adversity, as it is from my own misfortunes that I calculate upon the chances of success. In a word, 'tis upon my ugliness—yes, on these features, once so captivating, now so horrifying—that depends the success of this last enterprise. Formerly I owed my happiness to the regularity of my features; well, I will vanquish nature, and let my very ugliness serve me to overcome the obstacles before which you have yielded. I therefore thank my destiny, frightful as it is, since it has allowed me once more to guide you in the career."

"To-morrow the attack!"

The next morning, Silvia was punctual. She developed her plan, in all its details, to her accomplices. They found it so skilfully conceived, that they applauded it again and again.

"Be at Saint Roch," she said to them, "at nine o'clock; you shall judge for yourselves whether my disguise creates any suspicion, and, at the same time, of the effect that my presence will produce on the woman with the green veil."

At the hour appointed, the two bandits were at their post. The old lady soon arrived; she placed herself a few paces from the confessional, near the chapel de la Vierge. In a few minutes, they saw arrive another female, covered with garments in rags, the colours of which, faded and stained, nevertheless indicated, by their remains, that the wearer had once lived in affluence. It was Silvia; but, under this garb, she was not recognisable. Without looking about her, she took her station on the steps of the tribunal of penitence, and drew from a small bag she carried, a prayer-book, which, by the remains of its silver-gilt clasp, showed it had been richly ornamented, but, in other respects, a veritable *bouquin*, and as dirty as the remaining costume of the penitent. She opened it, and commenced praying, apparently with great fervour. The mass finished, she did not think of retiring, but, on the contrary, began another series of prayers, in which she seemed completely absorbed. The lady with the green veil had remained praying, on her chair, near her, her breviary in hand. Suddenly she let it drop, and stooped to pick it up, but the weakness of her sight caused her to feel right and left without finding it. Silvia, noticing her embarrassment, stooped, picked it up, and presented it to the old lady. The latter thanked her bountifully, and concluded by saying to her:

"God will bless you, my dear lady, for compassionating the sufferings of the afflicted."

"Many thanks for your wishes, venerable lady," replied Silvia, "I have great need of them, for I am very unfortunate."

"Persevere in the holy way you have chosen, my child; confide in the Almighty, he will not abandon you."

"'Tis what I would wish to do," replied Silvia, "and it is to obtain the strength to support the strokes of adversity, that I come to throw myself at the feet of the vicar of this parish, who, I am told, is a man as pious as he is charitable. I wish to make him a confession of my faults, and receive his counsels; for misfortune has persecuted me with such a hatred, that I have often dreamed of ending my days. I should already have done so, had I not been restrained by some remains of a religious sentiment which still lives in my heart."

"Oh! heaven! what are you saying?" replied the old lady; "God preserve you from such a thought; that will be seeking your eternal damnation. You will do well to see the worthy vicar, whose confessional is in this chapel; I rely much stronger on the efficacy of his consolations, as I have felt the power of them myself, since he has favoured me with them."

"I rely upon them as well, madame," said Silvia; "but when we are in want of every thing, and dying with hunger, what can we do?"

"What? reduced to this frightful necessity?" said the old lady; "here, take this trifle of money; there is also a small loaf I brought for myself, eat it."

Silvia threw herself on the dirty and emaciated hands of her benefactress, pressed them, bathed them with her tears, and, in the twinkling of an eye, swallowed the bread.

"God will reward you," she said to the old lady; "you have saved my life!"

"But," replied the latter, "you are still young, what prevents your working?"

"Alas!" said Silvia, "since I had the misfortune to have my face burned, I can obtain no work, so ugly am I considered. Stay, judge for yourself."

Saying these words, she raised an old veil which concealed her features. The old lady, who had approached close to her, on account of her bad sight, recoiled with surprise and horror upon seeing these horrible features.

At length, not to afflict her too much, she said to her coldly: " It is true you have been sadly ill-treated, but you have not ceased to be a member of the great family, and you must live. If you will come here every day, I will give you twelve sols to live upon, until better times. I repeat, place confidence in Providence, it will not abandon you."

" Oh! thank you, good and respectable lady, thanks for your unexpected succour; I accept them with joy, as well as your prudent counsels."

The lady *au voile vert* having retired at this moment, Salvador and de Lussan followed her.

In the meantime, Silvia remained in the church waiting for the vicar, to confess herself. He was not long in arriving, and, seeing her kneeling with this pious intention, he invited her by a sign to take a place in the confessional. Silvia approached, and having recited her *confiteor*, commenced the avowal of her faults, which she greatly extended; and then, assuming her blandest and most insinuating tone, she told so lamentable a history, and with such an accent of truth, that she caused the worthy and credulous ecclesiastic, who had listened to her attentively, to shed tears. In short, the perfidious creature had, in a few moments, contrived to render herself interesting, and convinced her confessor of her imaginable injuries. The worthy man was so moved at them, that he gave her some pieces of money, promising her his protection. At length she retired; but, observing Salvador and de Lussan, who, for some minutes, had again entered the church and witnessed her hypocritical manœuvres, she handed them an address, thus conceived:

" Mademoiselle Aimée Dufresne, Rue Maubuée, No. 13, chambre 37, au sixieme."

In the evening, Salvador and de Lussan, very modestly attired, repaired to this address; they found Silvia in a miserable attic! the plan and furniture of which, seems to have been sketched by Gresset, when he says, in his *chartreuse:*—

> " Une lucarne mal vitrée,
> Pres d'une gouttierre livrée
> A d'interminable sabbats,
> Ou l'université des chats,
> A minuit en robe fourrée
> Vient terur ses bruyants etats ;
> Une table mi-demembrée,
> Pres du plus humble des grabats ;
> Six brins de paille délabrée,
> Tressés sur de vieux échalas ;
> Voila les meubles delicats,
> Dont la chartreuse est décorée,
> Et que les freres de Borée,
> Bouleversent avec fracas !"*

Upon the arrival of her accomplices, Silvia placed upon a crippled table, an excellent fowl, and a bottle of old Bordeaux wine, which she kept at her side. She then rose to offer a broken chair to M. le Marquis, and a stool to M. le Vicomte, and took her own seat on the edge of the bedstead. "You

* " A window, awfully ill-lighted,
 Near a gutter oft benighted
 By the interminable sabbats
 Of a university of learned cats ;
 Who, nightly, in their furred robes,
 Come to chant their direful odes :
 A table, with only half its legs,
 Near an humble couch, on props—
 Six bits of straw, with rustic pegs,
 Nailed to so many sticks of mops.
 Such is the furniture supreme
 Which the chartreuse has within,
 And which—the brothers Boreas
 Upset with fury— by the mass !"

see, messieurs," she said, " that the ci-devant Marchioness de Roselly knows how to conform to circumstances ; she wishes to succeed—she will succeed! This morning has witnessed great progress," she added; " I am astonished at so much success. Can you believe that the green veiled lady already takes an interest in me? On the other side, my confessor, who appears to me an excellent man, a perfect Christian, has promised me his protection. You see that all goes well, and that I have some reason to say that the future is mine. Be tranquil, therefore, messieurs; if I have lost my charms, I have acquired much in intelligence, and besides, I have been at a good school."

" But where will all this lead us?" inquired Salvador; " for, in fact, we are in an intolerable position! It is enough to make one ill to see this disgusting hole. What will be the result of so many privations?"

" The result! can you doubt of it ? 'Tis the treasure of the old lady with the green veil."

" May heaven hear you," said de Lussan; " and ourselves—what have we to do?"

" You will receive daily a bulletin, which will inform you of the steps to take," she replied; " moreover, we shall meet again; but never here, where I am lodging with the five-franc piece given me by the vicar. It is probable he will make inquiries about me, if he has any real intention of befriending me; in which event, I must take certain precautions."

" You can rely upon his promise," said the viscount ; " the Abbé Reuzet is a most frank and candid man, the worthiest ecclesiastic I know; he has been my confessor for some time."

" Your confessor!" exclaimed Silvia; " he should have wide sleeves, then, or the power of absolving cases of reservation——"

" Eh! my God! what matter?" said de Lussan; " we are not going to discuss here a religious thesis. M. l'Abbé Reuzet is my confessor in ordinary, and simply to satisfy the fashion of the day— nothing more. He is a very worthy priest, who endeavours to do good, and never suspects evil. Moreover, it was at his house, and from himself, that I knew the lady au voile vert; so that I am well convinced he has not imposed upon me, in the details he gave me on this subject."

A fortnight passed in visits by Silvia to the vicar, and in assiduities of every species at the church. The veiled lady met there, every day, her protegée; she brought her the remains of her meals, and some money to assist in her other expenses. At length, Silvia, in her many relations with one and the other, played her part so well, that the vicar induced the old lady to take her home with her. " At your age," he said to her, " it is imprudent to live alone ; take this unfortunate with you, you will draw down upon yourself the benedictions of the Almighty!"

The old woman accepted the proposition, and the next morning the daughter of Sans Refus was installed at the house of the lady with the green veil.

The kindness and little attentions of Silvia, in a short time purchased the entire confidence of the old sinner. Every evening, she read to her; and sought in the fertility of her imagination every means of amusing her. At length, after a residence together of a fortnight, the old lady, whose interest in her protegée daily increased, requested her to give her an account of her past misfortunes; Silvia, who had expected this demand, had not neglected to compose a fable, which would not fail to instruct the old lady; this is shortly, then, what she recounted to her:—

"I was born at Orleans, of honest parents, but not very fortunate; my father was a master joiner. As I possessed some beauty, I became his idol, and he gave me a brilliant education, and one beyond his means and position. Far from limiting himself to the ordinary acquirements of the school of the celebrated Madame de Saint Prix, he engaged for me masters in drawing, declamation, music, riding, and dancing. I excelled, especially, on the piano, which I touched, I can say, to perfection.

"It did not require all this, to attract, in a provincial town, numerous admirers about me: and what contributed not a little to it was, that, unfortunately for me, we lived next to the hotel where most of the officers of the garrison resided. My beauty, which I can now speak of without vanity, the eclat of my voice, and the harmonious sounds I drew from my piano, soon occasioned me to be remarked by a young lieutenant of hussars, an accomplished model of graces and perfections. How shall I tell you? seduced, blinded by a passion, which the impetuosity of youth and the short-sightedness of my parents had not taught me to repress—seduced, further, by the fallacious promises of marriage he gave me—one fine night, I abandoned my home to follow the lieutenant Saint Denis.

"When I say fallacious, perhaps I accuse him wrongfully, for I really believe his intentions were honourable, and that he would have married me; but a frightful accident brought our liason to a different issue, and became an almost invincible obstacle to the realization of his projects as well as mine.

"One evening, at the finish of a supper, at the house of the lieutenant-colonel of the regiment, a monstrous bowl of punch was made. The vase which contained it was close to me, and lighted the whole of us with its brilliant flame; when, upon some occasion, I turned, and rapidly inclined my head towards one of the convives. By a fatality, quite inconceivable, one of my *anglaises,** which I then wore very long, got immersed in the flaming liquid; in a second, my hair, impregnated with perfume, became a volume of fire, to which I should myself have fallen a victim, if the same guest had not had the presence of mind suddenly to take off his redingote, and throw it over my head. By these means he contrived to extinguish the fire, but it was too late—I was disfigured for ever! I was taken to a maison de santé; but when, after a treatment of six weeks, my lover had acquired the certitude that the injury was irreparable, he abandoned me; and when, at length, I was in a condition to leave, I learned that his regiment had started for Paris.

"Judging him from myself, I went there to see him, but he obstinately refused any reconciliation with me. Convinced, but too late, of my misfortune, I took furnished lodgings; I sought for work, on all sides, and I failed not to praise beyond measure my abilities, but in vain; my excessive ugliness made me obnoxious everywhere. Driven to distraction, I was about ending my life, or dying of hunger, when Providence inspired me with the idea of going to Saint Roch, where I had the happiness of meeting with you; you know the rest. Without you, madame, I say it proudly, I should not be in existence! You have been to me a second Providence! I hope, now that you know

* Long curls.

me entirely, you will deign to continue your kindness, and be generous enough to keep me with you. I promise to give you, every day, fresh proofs of my devotedness and unbounded attachment; indeed, I shall love you, like a tender and venerated mother. Yes, madame, I feel that my heart is penetrated with love and gratitude towards you; you have been so kind, so compassionate towards me—an object of horror to all! that I ask from you no other favour than to remain near you —you shall do as you like for me, and with me. And if, in the ordinary course of things, you are called from this world before me, I will piously render you the last, though melancholy duties— each day I will refresh your tomb with my tears, and my mourning shall only end with my life!"

The crafty Silvia, seeing that her discourse made some impression on the old lady, continued for some time in the same tone, and concluded by introducing so much of the pathetic and the natural, that her benefactress, transported with delight, threw herself on her neck, shedding tears, and said to her: "Yes, you shall be my child! you shall replace the one that fate has deprived me of, or who, forgetful of her duties, has so long abandoned me to my miserable end. Since you assure me of your sincere and disinterested attachment, confide in me, I will never abandon you!"

"How sweet are these words to my heart," said Silvia, overjoyed; "it is now that I experience how heavy a debt is gratitude to a pure mind!"

This scene, and the discourse—prepared long previously by Silvia—put her altogether on a good footing in the house. From this day she had the care of the *ménage*, and took a more intimate part in the affairs of the old lady, without, however, being left for a moment, by the latter, alone in the house, or having one of the keys confided to her. At length, by her interesting and lively conversation, and her incessant attentions, Silvia had so captivated her mistress, that she could not do without her. The intimacy had attained such a point, that one evening Silvia sang her a romance, in that fresh and melodious voice, which had formerly attracted to her so many admirers.

"You sing admirably, my child," said the old lady, who had listened to Silvia with surprise.

"If I had a piano, it would be much more agreeable; one cannot sing well without an accompaniment."

"A harpsichord, you mean, my child; don't you?"

"Piano or harpsichord; but if you like this instrument," said Silvia, "I can satisfy you, without its costing you anything, for I have one at my poor father's. If you will allow me to write to him, and promise me to get a few words added to my letter, as a recommendation, by our excellent vicar, I am persuaded that my father will pardon me, and send my piano. Ah! how happy I shall then be with you, dear madame! you have already placed it in my power to delight your old age, by giving me the means of procuring you some agreeable distractions; it will be very sweet to me to think we shall never part!"

"I did not require this last proof of attachment," replied the old lady; "I am ready to do anything that will cause you a pleasure!"

Silvia, enchanted at finding her plan succeed to a marvel, wrote in the morning to her pretended father, a letter, in the following terms:—

"My dear and honoured father.—'Tis at your feet, and bathed in tears, that I throw myself— a guilty child! A blind and foolish passion drove me to forget my duty towards God, towards you, and towards society! Alas! why did I yield to the perfidious insinuations of a miserable seducer, who had sworn my ruin? Why did I abandon the best of fathers, to throw myself in the path of crime? Do not curse me, my father! Heaven has punished me enough—do not add to the burden of my miseries.

"Yes, my tender father, I have been very guilty; but I now detest my ingratitude. My repentance, and my tears, give me a hope, that you will regard with compassion your unfortunate child, and that you will deign to pardon her. She is no longer that child, who once was both the pride and the joy of your heart; that beauty, those graces, on which I prided myself, have been taken from me, by a frightful accident, which has rendered me a horror to all I approach. Plunged in misery, in consequence of this fatal catastrophe, abandoned by all my friends, and having no other resource but my labour to support me, will you believe that your miserable child has been repulsed by all as an object of fear and disgust? I should have died from despair and hunger, if Providence had not pitied me, and given me the idea of throwing myself at the feet of a worthy priest, who has extended to me the hand of charity. Without him—without M. l'Abbé Reuzet, I should certainly have died from hunger; but this man of God has placed me with an old and respectable lady, who has taken an affection to me, and promises to keep me with her, despite the horrible condition of my features. This lady, on account of her great age, has need of distractions, and derives much pleasure in hearing me sing; but, as she is no musician, she has no piano, and I am forced to sing unaccompanied. May I dare to beg you to send mine? It would give me extra means of pleasing my kind protectress, whose benevolence is beyond all praise. Do not, excellent and generous father, refuse my prayer, which I demand of you on my knees; do not treat me according to my deserts, but as a child, so much the dearer, from her offering herself to your eyes, purified by repentance and tears.

"I am, with the most profound respect,
"Your daughter,
"AIMEE DUFRESNE."

"P.S.—You will direct my piano, in a strong case, to M. Fleurus, Rue Thérèse, 25, à Paris."

At the end of this letter were the following words, from the Abbé Reuzet:—

"Sir,—If the recommendation of a man, devoted to the worship of God, and a friend to the unfortunate, can move you, I can assure you that your daughter is deserving, by her repentance, of all your indulgence, and all your affection. She is placed with a lady, as pious as she is respectable, and who will, probably, leave her sufficient to live upon, if not in luxury, at least in an honourable manner. Moreover, all that she writes you is correct. I therefore entreat you to send her piano, which is necessary to her, not in a worldly light, but to procure some distractions for her benefactress.

"I have the honour to be, sir, your very humble servant,

"L'ABBE REUZET."

A favourable reply from the father was not long in arriving; it was addressed to M. l'Abbé Reuzet, and in these terms:—

"Monsieur l'Abbé,—I have the honour of thanking you for the kindness you have shown in taking an interest in my daughter, and for withdrawing her from the unfortunate position she was in, in consequence of the fatal imprudence of her youth. Her letter has brought tears to my eyes, and bitter ones; but, leaning to the evidence of a good man, who preaches and practises the maxims of the Gospel, I cannot forget that I am a father, and—I pardon her.

"My child asks me for her piano, in order to procure some agreeable moments to her mistress; I cannot refuse it to her. Will you, therefore, be good enough, M. l'Abbé, to inform her, that she will receive it immediately, and well packed, at the address of M. Fleurus, Rue Thérèse.

"I trust, M. l'Abbé, you will not leave your good work incomplete; and that my child will always find in you that protection, and those good counsels, which have at length brought her into the path to heaven.

"Receive, M. l'Abbé, with the expression of my sincere gratitude, the respectful salutations of

"Your very humble servant,
"FRANCOIS DUFRESNE,
"Joiner, Rue Jeanne d'Arc, d'Orleans."

This letter was, of course, written by Salvador and de Lussan, who had, some days before, arrived at Orleans, by railway, where they had engaged lodgings in the name of Dufresne.

The Abbé Reuzet hastened to communicate this reply to Silvia; she was so overjoyed at it, that she clung round the neck of the old lady, and nearly stifled her with caresses. The latter was not less delighted; it seemed to her that a new era was opening for her, and that the magic sounds of the instrument, so anxiously wished for, would render her young again, and restore to her the beauty and graces of sixteen.

At length, in the course of a few days, the piano arrived.

At sight of the case, which contained it, the old lady exclaimed:

"Dieu! but your clavecin is grand."

"And heavy!" said the two lusty porters who had brought it.

"Oh! yes, it is heavy," said Silvia; "for 'tis an upright one, with six octaves, made by Pleyel—'tis the stoutest and most expensive one he has made."

"It appears that the man who packed it is a prudent one, too," said Father Fleurus; "for he has embalmed it in a case, jollily solid—and with two locks, as well!"

"Ah! it's true," said Silvia; "I can well recognise my father, from his extreme precautions."

The old lady seemed to examine all this with a peculiar satisfaction; but what embarrassed her, was, to find a place in which to put the enormous box, without disarranging every thing in her apartment. "Can we not take the clavecin out of the case," she said, "it will not occupy so much room, and we shall have less difficulty in bringing it in?"

"That's true," said the citizen Fleurus; "if there was a key, we could open it at once."

"Hold your tongue, Monsieur le Cuirassier," said Madame Fleurus; "you must be always insinuating your music everywhere:

"Le trop parler, monsieur, souvent nous est contraire;
Pour garder le silence, il faut savoir se taire!"*

"You are comical, Madame Fleurus! why I am quite au fait in the matter of instruments. Was I not trumpeter for three months, in the cuirassiers?

---

* "To say too much, sir, often spoils our fun,
And to keep silence, we should talk to no one."

Come, my friends, give me the keys· I'll show you how to uncase a *craversin!*"

"The keys—who has them?" said one of the porters to his comrade; "is it you, Fiston? where have you stowed away the keys?"

"Stay!" replied the other; "you know well that I gave them to Pierrot. It is possible he carried them to Father Moulard's, where he lodges, at Charonne."

One of these porters, it is almost needless to say, was no other than Vernier les bas Bleus, habited, as well as one of his comrades, (who, let it be understood, was not let into the secret, but had consented, for a consideration of two hundred francs, to play the part assigned him,) in the proper costume.

During the colloquy between the two commissionaires, Maitre Fleurus had brought a large hammer and a pair of pinchers, and had already commenced forcing the locks; but Silvia rushed to him, saying:

"What are you about, miserable Vandal! you will destroy my piano, injure it for ever, and perhaps put me to two hundred francs expense! For heaven's sake, madame," she continued, addressing the old woman, "order them to wait till to-morrow; this honest man, pointing to one of the commissionaires, shall bring the key. Besides, it requires an instrument maker to undo it without accident, and I do not think there will be the least inconvenience in leaving it till to-morrow in the first room. You must fix it there," she said, pointing to the place she wished to have it brought to.

The old lady making no objection, the case was placed as desired by Silvia, and all retired satisfied, except, however, the citizen Fleurus, who muttered between his teeth:

"There are more ways than one to kill a dog; it's just to get a second *pour boire* to-morrow, that these rascals have forgotten the keys."

It was nearly three o'clock in the afternoon when all this was concluded. A short time after, the old woman and Silvia sat down to dinner, and we may well suppose there was no further question about the piano.

"Dieu, but 'tis grand!" said the old lady, "I have never seen one so large." She then rose and turned frequently round the case, examining it in every sense, adding; "this box is well made, I have never seen one like it."

"My father made it express;" said Silvia; "he is a man who makes every thing solid."

The old lady again approached it; examined it afresh with attention, then tapped it with the end of her fingers.

"Stay," she said, "it seemed to me I heard something growl."

"'Tis nothing," said Silvia, "'tis the vibration which produces that effect."

"What's the vibration?" asked the old lady.

Silvia had some difficulty to make her comprehend the effect of the vibration she had heard, for, as we have seen, the intelligence of the old lady was rather obtuse, and the science of the Noels and Chapsals, and Bescherelles, was to her a sealed book. At length she was quieted by the demonstration made by Silvia, in striking a crystallized glass.

"We will now finish dinner, my kind mother," said Silvia, "and I will afterwards read you the second volume of the work we have commenced."

"If you have any other work to read to me, I should not be sorry," she replied, "for this one makes me dream of fearful things. The other night I dreamed that all the bandits of the Black

Forest had entered and concealed themselves in my room whilst I was praying to the Almighty at church, and that at night they had cut both our throats."

"Ah, bah! dreams are all lies, my dear mother; we must never believe in such nonsense."

"You are very right, dreams are but fables, as the proverb tells us."

"Stay," continued Silvia, "if you like, I will read you the Fables of Florian."

"Ah, yes! those fables are something like! let us see, they are fables which are not true, arn't they! Hush, I think I heard the case crack?"

"Yes you did, you are not deceived, dear mother, the case did crack; but it is the effect of change of *atmosphere* on the wood."

"There it is again, *l'arme aux spheres!* that makes the wood crack then? Ah, mon Dieu! listen, it cracks louder! 'tis just like my buffet, that cracks so loud at night, that it frequently awakens me."

"It's nothing, it's nothing," said Silvia, "all furniture is subject to it, when not perfectly balanced. We won't trouble ourselves about it; let us read Florian."

The old lady became all attention to the reading of Silvia, but from time to time made remarks which certainly would never have occurred to the mind of any commentator; their naïveté was laughable, and nothing but the serious preoccupation of Silvia prevented her from giving way to her mirth.

At length nine o'clock struck; the old lady prepared to retire, but when she wished to shut the door close, as was her habit, she found that the case was so placed as to prevent her so doing; she was therefore obliged to seek her bed, and leave things as they were; for they had not strength enough between them both to lift the case, or even to shift it. After kissing her, and wishing her a good night, Silvia retired to her room.

Let us now leave them a moment; we shall soon learn how they passed the night.

CHAPTER LII.

A DRAMA.

WE left the lady with the green veil and her companion, each retired to her apartment, to seek in refreshing sleep repose of the body, forgetfulness of the troubles of the day, and an illusion as to those which often wait us on the morrow! some hours have rolled away; let us penetrate into this interior, and glance at what is passing there.

The old lady is buried in the most profound sleep; Silvia, all attention, comes with stealthy pace and naked feet to assure herself of the fact. What then is the cause of all this solicitude? Is it the interest inspired by the woman who has received her with so much confidence and so much kindness? Does she fear that a sudden indisposition, a frightful nightmare, or some other cause, has interrupted her slumbers? No, none of these noble sentiments keep her awake; Silvia is incapable of them. The subject which thus excites her is the meditation of a crime, the thirst for gold; aye, and the thirst for blood! She has sworn the death of her benefactress, and she comes to assure herself that the moment for striking has arrived!

The room in which the old lady is reposing, is

LIFE IN PARIS.

CONCLUSION.

only lighted by the feeble rays of a night lamp; Silvia approaches, and casts an indescribable glance on her victim.

"She sleeps," she said; "she sleeps, but 'twill be the sleep of death!"

Then returning hastily into the adjoining room, she opens the case, from which two men make their exit, Salvador and de Lussan!

Enclosed for more than six hours in this species of tomb, they left it, bruised and almost stiffened; but by the aid of a glass of eau-de-vie, administered by Silvia, they soon recovered their natural state, and by it obtained the sanguinary and ferocious energy which the accomplishment of their murderous intentions demanded.

Ready to strike, they only waited the signal of their accomplice. The latter again approaches the old lady, who is still buried in the heaviest sleep.

Silva calls, and guides by a gesture the two assassins!

Rapid as thought, they throw themselves on the unfortunate old lady, and strangle her without her being enabled to utter a groan!

"'Tis done," said de Lussan.

"Yes," replied Salvador, "*this godmother will never meet me at the baptismal font.*"*

At the request of Salvador, Silvia brought a light; he wished to assure himself that his victim was quite dead; he held the light to her face.

"My God! my God!" he exclaimed, "'tis Mother Sans Refus!"

"My mother!" said Silvia; "what! I have murdered my mother!"

"How? Sans Refus, is it?" said de Lussan, in his turn; "this is a diabolical affair!"

Salvador and de Lussan regarded one another without speaking, their eyes fixed, and apparently petrified at the discovery.

"Ah, bah!" said Silvia, from whom so detestable a crime had not drawn forth a tear; "*c'est un fait accompli*, we must suffer the consequences. After all, 'tis only one means, among many others, of inheriting; sooner or later, the succession could not fail of falling to us."

"'Tis true," said Salvador, "Silvia is right."

And the three monsters upon this shook hands, in token of acquiescence and congratulation.

"We must not waste the time that is precious," said de Lussan; "let us proceed in the search for the hiding place indicated by my worthy confessor."

In an instant they discovered the cachette, so indiscreetly mentioned by the Abbé Reuzet, and took possession of every thing it contained.

Three o'clock struck as they finished this diabolical expedition; and to quit the scene without occasioning alarm required some address.

At a quarter past five, old Fleurus, like a vigilant man, arrived in the court to commence his daily service. Faithful to his ancient custom, and merry as a lark, he whistled the air of *la Carmagnole*, and the *Ça ira*, as in the happier days of '93. When the daylight had completely made its appearance, Silvia called from the little wicket, and begged him to run and buy her a little *fleurs d'orange* for her mistress, who, she said, was very unwell.

"Orange flower? where's the use of that? Much better make her take a nice drop of Paul Niquet, or of 107 *ans!*"†

"No, no, citizen Fleurus, she must have fleur

* This witness will never appear against me.
† Strong eau de vie, much over-proof.

d'orange. Go, quick; stay, here's the money; you may keep enough to get a glass of wine for your trouble."

"You are very good, ma'mzelle; but I cannot leave the house to take care of itself at this moment; we know not what may happen, the enemy is sometimes closer than we suppose; I shall therefore remain at my post, unless Mame Fleurus comes to relieve me; but it is not yet six o'clock, and it is generally nine before she rises and descends to the court. When she arrives I shall be entirely at your service."

"The old imbecile is capable of having us caught as though in a mousetrap," said de Lussan.

"If you could get him to enter," whispered Salvador to Silvia, "we would soon have the key of the fields."

"Excellent idea," said Silvia.

She returned to the wicket, called Father Fleurus, and told him that her mistress wished to speak with him, and requesting him to come in a moment.

"Ah, for that," said the crabbed concierge, "I am at your orders."

Silvia, who had all the keys, then opened the door to him; the two brigands concealing themselves behind. When Fleurus entered the first room, Silvia told him she wanted a kettle which was on a high shelf in the kitchen, and begged him to get it for her. The cuirassier, without mistrust, entered the kitchen, mounted a chair; but at the same moment the door was closed upon him and doubly locked; the three accomplices disappeared with the rapidity of lightning!

The worthy citizen, all amazed, was far from imagining the real motive for his imprisonment; it did not trouble him in the least, for he supposed it to be a wilful trick of Silvia's, in revenge for his refusal to go for the fleur d'orange. He laughed at it, therefore, with a good heart, but when he found it prolonged somewhat too long, he called out:

"Aimée, Aimée, let me out, do! I promise you another time I will be more polite. Come, open the door, quick, for *Mame* Fleurus will growl at me if my court is not in a proper state when she descends! Aimèe, Aimèe! What, no reply! Just wait a moment, you little deceiver, you shall pay me for this. I'll soon get the cage open!"

In fact, half laughing, half grumbling, in less than five minutes he had forced the lock; but although at liberty, he may well search, he saw no one.

"The devil! the devil!" he said, "this is no joke; what does it mean?"

He searched again, he called; no one replied. Seeing the room of the old lady open, he entered; what a spectacle!

All there was in the greatest disorder, the bed was in the middle of the apartment, and the body it contained was now a corpse!

"What a fate," he said, "this *is* a catastrophe, what will *Mame* Fleurus say? Mon Dieu, mon Dieu! all is lost; the devil is in the house!"

Saying this, he returned to the adjoining room, glanced at the open case, no piano. He merely remarked two places skilfully disposed and stuffed, and the recent impressions, the traces of which were still visible, pointed out the use they had been put to. There was no more doubt. The assassins had been introduced in this chest by Aimèe, and she had disappeared with them!

"Thieves! assassins!" bellowed the unfortunate porter. "Assistance."

* * * * *

The police used every exertion to clear up the mystery of this deed, but their efforts were all in vain, the fatal hour had not yet struck the knell of these scelerats!

On the day following the assassination of the miserable Sans Refus, Salvador awoke with the sun, and aroused de Lussan and Vernier from their sleep. (The latter had passed the night at their lodgings in the Rue de l'Ouest.) Silvia still slept tranquilly. Salvador led his two accomplices into the room adjoining the bed-chamber. "We have no time to lose," he said to them, "the police will send their emissaries every where, and as, unfortunately, the features of Silvia are more than remarkable, it is probable we shall be discovered if we remain here; we must therefore quit this lodging."

"Let us quit it then, and put ourselves en route," replied de Lussan; "we have money, the necessary passports."

"We cannot at this moment attempt to put ourselves en route. I think we had better allow some time to elapse, and confine ourselves to some secure retreat."

"We will act, dear marquis, just as you consider most convenient; you are, to-day, wisdom and prudence personified."

"I am very glad you render me this justice; for in that case you will not blame the cruel necessity which forces us to abandon our friend."

"How, abandon la marquise! her to whom we owe the success which has crowned our last enterprise? Ah, marquis!"

"Consider viscount, that the unfortunate Silvia is at present so ugly, so remarkable, that the first individual who sees her pass may well say: 'There's the woman who introduced the assassins into the house of the old lady of the Rue Thérèse.'"

"It's true." said Vernier, "I agree in opinion with Rupin."

"Let us leave la marquise then," added de Lussan, "a quarter of what we have."

"For what purpose," replied Salvador, "the fate of the unhappy woman is sealed; she will be taken ere three days have passed," he added, in a pitying tone; "is it necessary then that a part of what we have had so much trouble to obtain, should fall into the hands of justice?"

"Au fait," resumed Vernier les bas Bleus, "I do not see the necessity for it."

The result of the preceding conversation is easily guessed. The three bandits left, taking away with them the gold, the jewels, and bank-notes stolen from la Sans Refus; it was only on being pressed by the entreaties of de Lussan, that they determined to leave on the commode two bank-notes of one thousand francs.

"'Tis so much lost," said Salvador, whilst resolving to obey his accomplice; "she will be arrested when she wishes to change them."

We shall not attempt to describe the rage which engrossed Silvia, when she became convinced of her having been abandoned by her lover.

"I ought to have expected it," she exclaimed, giving way to the deadliest anger. "I ought to have expected it; he only loved me because I was handsome; but I will be avenged!"

Chance, or rather Providence, who had decreed that the crimes of the scelerats of whom she wished to be revenged, should be punished, came to her aid.

Several days had elapsed since the disappearance of de Lussan, Salvador, and Vernier les bas Bleus, and Silvia despaired of being able to discover them, when one evening she saw the latter directing his steps towards the cabriolets stationed at the Place des Victoires; his walk was unsteady, his face was flushed; in a word, he was drunk.

"Aux Batignolles, Rue des Dames, No. 13," he said to the coachman, whose vehicle he had engaged.

"At length!" said Silvia, who had heard these words; "I have him, I am sure; but that my vengeance may be complete, they must know that it is to me they owe their destruction."

Silvia, reflecting upon the means she should employ to gain her object, was seeking the retreat she had chosen, after having abandoned the lodging in the Rue de l'Ouest, when she found herself face to face with a man she had known for some time.

It was Ronquetti, called the Duke of Modena.

As she had anxiously perused every account in the journals, of the debates which had resulted in the condemnation of her lover and his accomplices, she was aware of the part played by this man; who, as a recompense for the revelations he had made, had obtained a remission of the rest of his punishment, and had entered the service of the police, in which he could render himself very useful.

She accosted him, resolutely.

"You are Ronquetti, Duke of Modena?" she said to him.

"At your service, if it is in my power, belle dame."

Silvia was elegantly dressed; a thick veil hid her face, and the gracefulness of her figure justified the further compliment paid to her by her ancient lover.

"You are mouchard," she added.

Ronquetti appeared angry.

"Do not put yourself in a rage," said Silvia; "we have no time to waste in idle words; confine yourself to answering my questions: you are mouchard?"

"I am mouchard, as you say."

"You do not recognise me?"

Silvia drew Ronquetti under a lamp, and lifted her veil.

Ronquetti recoiled with horror!

"I cannot claim that honour," he replied.

"I am Silvia, the cantatrice; or rather la Marquise de Roselly."

"Ah, bah! in that case, my dear friend, I arrest you, in the name of the law; you have a little account to settle with M. le Procureur de Roi."

"I am aware of it."

"You are, it seems, weary of your life? Au fait! I can believe it; your features——"

"Finish! I beg of you. I can put in your possession, Salvador, de Lussan, and Vernier."

"Ah! do that, my dear Silvia, and I promise that you shall have no reason to complain of me."

"I will do it, but upon one condition."

"Whatever it may be, it shall be granted you—provided it be possible."

"I wish to be present at the arrest of these three men."

"Is that all? granted—granted! I will guarantee it to you."

The next morning, early, a large posse of policemen surrounded the house, in the Rue des Dames, aux Batignolles, and entered an apartment, where they found the three bandits; whom, until then, they had in vain searched for.

Salvador, de Lussan, and Vernier, following up the determination they had taken, not to be arrested, alive, made a vigorous resistance; they killed two of the agents, in their attempt to secure them, (the police has its fields of battle,) but at length they were compelled to yield to numbers. Salvador, wounded in the arm; de Lussan, who had received a ball in the leg; Vernier, horribly maimed, could make no further resistance; they were at last secured, bound, and the affair was completed.

When they were beyond the possibility of doing injury, Silvia, who, until now, had kept in the back ground, approached them.

"It is to me you are indebted for your arrest," she said; "I am fully revenged! am I not?"

"Fury!" exclaimed Salvador; "rid me of your odious presence!"

"Do not get into a rage, dear marquis," said de Lussan; "we have nothing more than our deserts, we must acknowledge it; we ought not to have abandoned our friend."

"She will mount *la butte* with us," said Vernier; "that will be droll!"

"I shall escape the scaffold," said Silvia to Salvador. "Adieu! M. le Marquis de Pourrieres."

She raised to her lips a small vial, which contained prussic acid, and fell on the floor as though struck by lightning.

"She's gone to engage places for us above," said Vernier; "a pleasant voyage to her!"

Salvador endeavoured to get possession of the phial made use of by Silvia, but was prevented by the agents of police.

The three criminals were at once conveyed to the conciergerie, and orders were given that they should be constantly under sight. The fresh proceedings against them did not take long; their identity was the principal feature; and, moreover, they did not attempt to deny the further crime they had committed, since their escape.

At length, the sun—which was to shed its lustre on the day they were destined to receive the just recompense due to their crimes—rose in full brilliancy.

De Lussan had, early in the morning, had his hair cut as close as possible; he had himself torn off the collar of his shirt; his toilette was *then* complete.

"You see, maitre," he said to the executioner, when this functionary approached him, "I am ready for the ceremony; you will, therefore, have no occasion to put your hand upon me."

After completing his toilette, de Lussan, a true Catholic, as we have observed, confessed himself, and received the sacrament, with a dignity and collectedness very remarkable; after having performed these duties, he was as gay and witty as usual; and met his fate as became him—but without bravado.

Salvador, who, at first, had turned *sulky*, and had refused the consolations of religion, could not resist the exhortations of the venerable almoner of the prison, and the example of his accomplice, who succeeded in deciding him to finish as a Christian! and which he did.

The criminal confessed himself, with a fulness and sincerity of heart, which could not be doubted; he even made the avowal of a crime, an account of which had never been demanded of him—he confessed the murder committed on the person of the unhappy serviteur of the house of de Pourrieres, Ambrose; who, it will be remembered, met with a cruel death, in the ravines bordering the park of the old chateau; and, after receiving absolution, he resumed his natural gaiety, and from this moment until four o'clock, he conversed with the good priest and his accomplice, with a clearness and fluency truly remarkable.

Was the repentance manifested by these two men, who died with a calm courage, and without bravado, sincere? or was it but the last comedy played by them, as an amusement, at the expense of those who regretted to see terminate, on the scaffold, a career which would have been a brilliant one, if they had honourably employed the many advantages with which they were endowed? This is a secret between God and themselves!

To Him, alone, belongs the privilege of reading the heart of man!

CHAPTER LIII.

EPILOGUE.

AND now the reader may probably wish us to give him some information regarding such of the personages of this history as have not been mentioned in the last chapters he has perused. We will therefore, before taking leave of him, satisfy a desire so natural, and one we should have been sorry to find had not been manifested.

Within a few hundred yards of Senlis, some distance from the high road, in the midst of a beautiful prairie, interspersed with small plantations of trees, lies a pretty little village, called Saint Leonard. A few paces from this village is a noble and ancient chateau, which its new proprietors have just put into reparation, and in which is collected every thing which can contribute to enliven a country life—books, pictures, music. Not far from the chateau, at the entrance to the village of Saint Leonard, is a pretty *maison bourgeoise*, the façade of which is adorned with a young vine, some feet in height. The chateau is inhabited by Sir Edward Lambton, Laura, and her husband. The house serves as a retreat to Edmond de Bourgerel, his wife, and Lucie. The worthy Madame de Saint Preuil died in the midst of her family, happy in knowing that her niece was united to an estimable man.

Laura, who could not resolve to live at a distance from her friend, who, as we have seen, had only sought refuge with Eugenie, from a feeling that Sir Edward had no wish that she should consider that her fortune was no longer what it had been, persuaded her uncle to sell the estate at Guermantes, and fix himself at Saint Leonard; and as her wishes were as orders to him, Sir Edward and Servigny hastened to obey them.

The closest friendship united Servigny and Edmond de Bourgerel, both gifted with a noble character. Edmond, in addition, was an indefatigable billiard player, which caused much pleasure to Sir Edward, who passes his days tranquilly, surrounded with amiable beings and three handsome and merry infants, who will soon leave him no time to regret old England.

Two of these pledges belong to Laura and Servigny, the third is claimed by Edmond and Eugenie. There is every reason to believe they will not belie the old proverb "*Like father, like son.*" They appear gifted with the most amiable qualities of head and heart—qualities which, from the excellent education they receive, will, in time, be matured to solid virtues.

The good Abbé Reuzet often visits the little colony at Saint Leonard; he is sometimes accompanied with a young avocat, a relation, who has already acquired a certain reputation. The young man could not see without loving, the gentle Lucie, and we believe that a reciprocity of feeling is shown on the other side. If ever he should become the husband of Lucie, we are certain he will enable her to forget all the troubles she has supported.

Beppo's mother, after the death of her son, returned to Provence, taking with her Georgette. The honest woman beheld once more, with delight, her compatriots, the clear blue sky of delightful Provence, and the sandy shores of the Mediterranean; we think, however, she will not live long; but the affectionate attentions of Georgette, who has merged into a very honest girl, and will probably marry a fisherman, who will not demand too severe an account of her past life, will soften her last sigh.

Paolo is still in the service of the Count de Morengy, who resides in Savoy, in a pretty villa near the valley of Chamouny. The general has but for a moment passed before the eyes of our readers, we may, perhaps, shortly, give them the reasons which determined this brave officer to quit his country, although he loved it as fervently as we do our last mistress.

Matheo will end his days at the Abbey de la Meillerage. Brother Eugene (the religious name of Doctor Matheo) is, of all the Trappists, the one who imposes upon himself the heaviest punishment. The Almighty, we may hope, will deign to cast a look of pity upon this poor sinner, that he may find in a better world the repose he has not met with in this one.

The individuals we have so often encountered at Mother Sans Refus's, Charles la belle Cravate, Grand Louis, Cornet-tape-dur, Robert, Cadet-Vincent, Mimi, Lenain, Dejean la main d'Or, petit Crepine, Biscuit, Lasaline, and the others, have received the punishment due to their crimes; some are in the houses of correction, others in the galleys, where they will probably terminate their existence. Le Grand Louis and Charles la belle Cravate, as we are aware of, are among the latter; these two wretches have been condemned to hard labour for life.

Cadet Filoux, Coco-Lardouche, and Cadet l'Artesian, the three venerable representatives of the ancient *pègre*, died regretting the manners and customs of former times, which is to admit that they died in a state of unredeemed impenitence. Monsieur Satan ought, on their arrival in his kingdom of darkness, to favour them with a magnificent reception.

Fanfan la Grenouille, transformed from a thief to a police agent, could not make a good use of the ten thousand francs given him by Sans Refus for favouring her escape. After dissipating this sum in drunken orgies, Fanfan discovered himself, one fine morning, without resources, on the king's highway. Want compelled him to resume his former trade; but as he had nearly lost, from long idleness, the best part of his faculties, he allowed himself to be caught in the fact, and went to rejoin in prison those he had been the cause of sending there—a sad reverse of things in this world!

Vernier les bas Bleus, captured with Salvador and de Lussan, accompanied them to the scaffold. This miscreant did not follow the example of his accomplices, he died as he had lived.

De Preval, soon after these events, determined to live an honest man for the future. He collected the whole of his capital, which he converted into an annuity for life, and thus found himself in possession of a revenue of five thousand francs, more than he needed to lead a merry and easy life in a small provincial village; and such, in fact, was the intention of de Preval; but the devil, who has no desire to see his vassals transformed into honest men, reserved him for a turn after his own fashion. De Preval, entering his house at an advanced hour of the night which was to usher in the day of his departure from Paris, found himself, by chance, face to face with an unfortunate from whom he had won, at ecarté, a very considerable sum. This individual had, some hours before, purchased a pair of pistols, with which he had intended to destroy himself, they were both loaded, and he was repairing to the Champs-Elysées, in order to kill himself at his ease, when he encountered de Preval. The sight of the man whom he accused, not without reason, of causing his ruin, aroused him to a furious rage; and as, when we are quite decided to take away our own life; we have no fear of the consequences of any desperate action, he discharged one of the pistols at the breast of poor de Preval.

"You will never rob another," he said, when the unfortunate *grec* fell at his feet.

At daybreak, two bodies were discovered and taken away, one in the Rue Monsigny, behind *la salle Ventadour*, the other in the Champs-Elysées.

"We will recount you our history another time," spoke Mina and la Lorrette at the same time, before quitting the Marquis de Pourrieres and his two friends. These words, which terminated the eleventh chapter of this work, promised our readers the history of these two pretty women. These histories we have not given, for the simple reason. that, after hearing them, we found they so resembled that of Felicité Beaupertius that they would have formed but a duplicate of the former: young women, prudent and innocent, whom seduction drives into a path which is not a virtuous one; this is the end, the means alone differ. However, as, probably, some of our readers may wish to know what is actually the fate of Mina and la Lorrette, (we have traced a portrait of these two women which may well justify their curiosity,) we will satisfy them in a few words.

Mina is still handsome; a Wallachian prince is enamoured of her, and, as the courtesan, who is at this moment madly attached to a *mauvais sujet*, who beats her, will not listen to the tender discourse of the noble foreigner, it is presumable that, in a short time, she will be made a princess. As to the Lorrette, she has retired from the world; she has married a rich provincial merchant, in whom she has inspired a belief that she is very virtuous: she positively resides in a small village, whose inhabitants praise the dignity of her manners and the purity of her morals.

We have mentioned Felicité Beaupertius; this poor girl, more unfortunate than guilty, lately died at the Hospital de la Charitè. Her body was, according to custom, carried to the dissecting room. We were told that when the sheet which covered it was lifted, a former surgeon-major of the regiment, afterwards appointed chief of one of the departments of the Hospital de la Charitè, was taken ill and left the room, hiding his face in his hands, which caused some merriment amongst the students who remained.

These messieurs, it seems, not unfrequently encounter on the marble tables of the amphitheatre, the pitiable objects of their transient amours.

Coralie, the danseuse, malgré the robbery committed on her by de Lussan and his accomplices, is still the most fascinating creature imaginable. She ruins her admirers, 'tis true, but she does not deceive them; she promises to none a love she is incapable of feeling. "She vends her smiles, her glances, and her soft words;" and it is probably because she offers to return the money to those who do not find the merchandise of good quality, that she is never in want of purchasers. She tells those who chose to listen to her, that she will quit the stage when she possesses a revenue of fifty thousand francs, and that, if she does not marry a *diplomate*, she will turn devotee, and be so vigilant a guardian of good morals, that she will dismiss any of her people who may be unable to resist the tender proposals of the Lovelaces of the ante-chamber.

A frightful monkey occupies in the heart of Maxime the place formerly held by the unfortunate Miss. The *lions* of the *loge infernale*, begin to think the tastes of this young lady a little too eccentric, but Maxime takes no more notice of their discourse than a fish would of an apple; Maxime is so pretty, and there are always, at Paris, so many rich strangers.

The father of Maxime is still a *frotteur;* he often drinks a drop with the son of the famous baroness we have encountered at Baden-Baden.

The latter, whom an officious procureur du roi has contrived to have condemned to some years' confinement, will only leave it to make fresh dupes. She often says to those who visit her, that she shall again have a rich apartment, servants dressed in splendid liveries, fine horses, and magnificent carriages. We are of opinion that *la baronne* strangely deceives herself, and that her happy days are gone, never to return. "The mother of fools is not yet dead," you say, madame, and you are right; but we must allow these modern infants the time to grow big, before we can deceive them; and, thank God, you are now too old to wait.

Le poete Chevelu is no longer *un poete incompris;* he has published the epic poem he intended to dedicate to the Grand Duke of Baden. This poem, properly lauded by the great and little press, has obtained a towering success, so that its author has been decorated by every sovereign in Europe and *the other parts of the world.* The publishers wait at his door to solicit from him the favour of editing one of the works still buried in the depths of his brain. In the Academie he will be before Beranger, who will count as nothing, not even academician.

The noble duke and foreign count, whose conjugal misfortunes he narrated to Roman, during the short stay the latter made at Baden-Baden, are now what they were formerly, what they always will be—married and contented; but what matter, as the good La Fontaine has well observed, when speaking of unhappy husbands:

"Quand on le sait, c'est peu de chose,
Quand on l'ignore, ce n'est rien." *

Le Comte de —— still exercises the honourable profession we have before noticed; he serves under the orders of the noble personage to whom Edmond de Bourgerel was indebted for expiating by several months' captivity, the enormous crime of having written a bad drama. If you pass near him, beloved reader, (our portrait of him is so faithful that he will be easily known,) if, we say, you pass near him, call to mind the song of Beranger:

.........." Parlons bas,
Ici pres j'ai vu Judas."†

Passe-partout and his comrade (we must forget

* " When we know it, 'tis but little;
When we know it not, 'tis nothing."

† ...." Speak low, I mean;
Near here Judas I have seen."

none) still remain cunning and accomplished spies; they will go some lengths—if they do not happen to be hung.

Madame Delaunay is at the head of one of those establishments which is never called by its right name amongst honest people.

"Doctor Delamarre sells *aux femmes trompeès*, advice which sooner or later will conduct him to the court of assize." The prediction of the danseuse Coralie has been realised; the unfortunate doctor has been condemned to several years' imprisonment by the court of assize for the Seine. The husband of the young Agnes, whose history our readers may remember, the nominal father of his children, sends him assistance.

The general of the citizen militia, who made such handsome presents to Coralie, compelled to quit Paris to escape the pursuit of his numerous creditors, took refuge in the Territories of the Church. The name he bears, celebrated in Italy, has procured him a favourable reception. He is at present one of the best officers of the Papal Army. Our readers are probably aware that the soldiers of our most holy father no longer mount guard with an umbrella.

" Pulchra Laverna
Da mihi fallere, da justum sanctum que videri
Noctem peciatis et fraudibus objicere nubem."

Our readers are also aware, that the worthy ecclesiastic, who never recited any other prayer than this, is actually a bishop, but that which they do not know, and which we are happy in being enabled to inform them of, is that this holy individual is one of the most furious champions of ultramontanism, and that he often inveighs from the pulpit against the corruption and irreligious spirit of the age. They say his sermons and mandates much resemble the homilies of the Archbishop of Grenada; but those who allow such discourse are malicious, and for our parts, we will not believe them.

Spiteful tongues say many things besides; thus, for example, they assert, that, if the two honourables who assisted at the banquet given at Lemardelay's by Alexis de Pourrieres occupied themselves a little more with their own affairs, and entirely neglected those of the country, their creditors would be contented, and the country be no worse off. Must we believe them? Really, we know not what to say.

The *fools'-seed* of the Englishman and of the merchant of cotton caps no longer find purchasers, the grandiloquent announcements and magical prospectuses of the Wizard of *Societies* will no longer deceive the public.

M. Roulin is become an honest merchant: things quite as extraordinary do sometimes happen.

The father of the *lezards*, the unfortunate Rigobert, cheated by the majority of his numberless good-for-nothings, whom he nourished in his breast, was obliged to close his shop. What will become of the miserable reptiles who found with him the means of changing their skins at so little expense?

Let us not forget an avoué, who caused the condemnation of one of his former mistresses, guilty only of having too well remembered the lessons he had once given her; and an avocat, who taught a young thief that the gown does not always shelter irreproachable characters. The former is a knight of the Legion of Honour, director of the bureau de Charite of his arrondissement; he is eligible, and has the chance of arriving at the elective chamber. The second, by means of an inexhaustible perseverance, is become one of the stars of the modern bar; he will one day be rich and marry an heiress.

And the Count Paladin, of the holy Roman empire, and his inseparable friend? The first has left Paris, to avoid being sent where they have *forwarded* the second—namely, to one of the maritime towns of the south of France. It is said, even, that nets are extended at all the entrances into our good city, in order to take him as in a trap, should he attempt to revisit it.

The property of the house of de Pourrieres, into which Salvador has made a considerable breach, has been transferred to the son of the unfortunate Alexis; but it is probable that the young man will not long enjoy it. The troubles and privations, of every sort, which have assailed his young years have ruined his health. He does not deceive himself as to his fate; he has already made his will, in which the female, Moulin, (who has repaired, so far as lay in her power, the injury she had done him,) the two daughters of M. de Riberprè, Malaga and Brigantine, and the members of the family Louiset, have not been forgotten.

Fortunè has added to his will a codicil, which thus commences:

"An amiable woman has for some time borne the honourable name which, at my death, will be extinguished. Having no heirs of my blood, and being enabled, without injuring any one, and without trenching upon any acquired rights, to dispose of the fortune which has accrued to me, I appoint as my whole and sole legatee, subject to the pay-ment by her of the several legacies bequeathed by my will, the lady Lucie, born de Casteval, widow, by her first marriage, of M. le. General Comte de Neuville, &c., &c.

"In repairing, as far as in me lies, an injustice of fate towards a woman so amiable as the widow of the General Comte de Neuville, I consider I am doing an action approved of both by man and God."

And now, respected readers, that we are arrived at the conclusion of a somewhat lengthened career, we will remind you of what we said in a former part of this work, that when we had determined to write, we hoped to prove this: That faults of the lightest nature have nearly always deplorable consequences; that there is no crime, however well it may be planned, however thick the web in which it is enveloped, that escapes the punishment it deserves; that one crime is often punished by another; that the consequences of all liasons which are not founded on virtue, are always unhappy, if not fatal; that there is no fall from which we may not rise, if we have but courage to attempt it, &c.

If by the reception he may give our work, the reader proves to us, that, by a narrative of the adventures of Felicitè Beaupertius—of Elizabeth Neveux—of Salvador and Roman—of Silvia and Servigny—we have attained the object we proposed, we shall be satisfied, for we shall then have the conviction of having written a useful book. At all events, as the task we undertook was, perhaps, above our reach, we shall conclude with the words which close the comedies of the immortal Calderon: "Excuse the faults of the author."

NOTES.

However sombre may be the colours in which the artist who would paint the features of the localities in which are to be found samples of the eccentric population of the capital, may charge his palette—however vigorous the contours traced by him—and however extensive the power of his imagination—his pictures, unless copied from nature, will always fall short of the reality; and the reason for this is, that there exist things and men which must be seen, if their existence is to be believed.

The establishments we have mentioned are actually in existence; but we do not invite our readers to visit them, for, in our opinion, humanity is a sad spectacle, when it has lost the last trace of its celestial origin, and it is almost the only one they would encounter in these and many other places, the enumeration of which would of itself fill a volume. However, as, in the present age, we are generally curious to know every thing, we will endeavour to say a few words about them.

The *Grand Saint Michel*, surnamed the *Grand Bal Chicard*, Rue de Bievre, near la Place Maubert, is the most considerable of all the establishments, that, like the malignant scars which dishonour the features of the drunken and the debauched, boldly spread their allurements in the streets of Paris. Rag-pickers, ballad-mongers, organ-players, and match-sellers, thieves, and hideous prostitutes, always ready to yield themselves to these miserables for a few glasses of eau-de-vie or a wretched meal—these are the gentry usually met with at the Grand Saint Michel. But if a fine day has invited the good citizens of Paris to accept the pleasures of a walk, let them raise their eyes to the species of loft which overlooks the principal room of the establishment in question, and examine a little the individuals it contains. But they are properly attired; are they, then, persons of good society, attracted there by a desire to study the eccentricities of the manners of the *people*. Look again—and if your eyes are not sufficient, lend your ears—and endeavour to seize, *in transitu*, in the midst of the confusion which reigns here, a few specimens of the conversation of these men, so well dressed; but, in fact, the toilettes of the men, as well as the women, although rich, are in very bad taste. They drink eau-de-vie by the glass, and scraps of the most obscene ballads escape their lips. What, then, are these individuals? Eh! bon Dieu! no other than thieves and prostitutes, luckier or more expert than those they govern, who come here to display their riches, to excite the jealousy of their comrades, and to stimulate those amongst them who rest in idleness. They breathe an atmosphere they love, whilst attending the reverse of fortune which renders them a spectacle in their turn.

Eau-de-vie is sold at the Grand Saint Michel, at eightpence a quart, and the wine at fivepence only; but what wine! and, especially, what brandy! The wine, upon separating, leaves the blue traces of its origin; the brandy is a mixture of spirits of wine, sulphuric acid, (aye, sulphuric acid,) and burned sugar. The consumers, nevertheless, press round the immense tin counter where these infernal drugs are retailed—a retail so considerable, that, to spare the waiters the too frequent visits to the cellar, the directress of the establishment, Mademoiselle Victorine, has had constructed, from the cellar to the counter, a whole reserve of pumps, reservoirs, and pipes, as complicated as a steam-engine; so that, to fill the glasses of the drunkards, who are all required to pay beforehand, it is only necessary to turn the cock of an inexhaustible fountain.

Discord reigns supreme in the principal hall of the Grand Bal Chicard. Wretches, who have been compelled to tramp it all the night, for want of the two or three sous necessary to procure a lodging at Pageot's,* pass the day at the Grand Saint Michel. Their sole occupation is to *tirer des carottes*, (the slang of the place,) or to seek a quarrel with those who, luckier than themselves, can take their station before the counter—quarrels soon followed by combats more disgusting than those of the South Sea savages, in which the adversaries struggle to tear the eyes from their orbits, and devour the projecting points of the face. But do not fancy that, to separate the combatants, they will send for the armed police. If the struggle is getting too sanguinary—if it continues too long, the waiters of the house, whose efforts have been powerless, have recourse to Mademoiselle Victorine, who, without giving herself too much trouble, separates the combatants, whom she seizes by the shoulders, and ejects, without any ceremony, into the street, where they are free to set to again.

Woe to any who may fall asleep, after drinking, on one of the greasy benches of the Grand Saint Michel; they will profit by his sleep to rob him of all he possesses, and this in broad daylight, with as little fear as in the most natural action.

Business is also transacted at the Grand Bal Chicard; and what a commerce, grand Dieu! Like birds of prey who seek their food in a putrified carcase, brokers are always to be met with in this ignoble kennel, and always ready to purchase from wretches, tormented with an unappeasable thirst, the blouse, waistcoat, or shirt, with which they are covered; and the few sous received in exchange for these sordid rags are immediately carried to the counter; and it is something wonderful, if the venders reserve to themselves ten centimes to purchase the infamous pottage on which they exist.

Mademoiselle Victorine, the mistress of the place, is, without contradiction, the most singular individual amongst the motley group encountered at the Grand Saint Michel. This woman (who, be it remembered, is a part of that whole which forms the fairest moiety of the human race) appears perfectly at her ease in the midst of this ignoble troop which frequents her establishment; and what is

---

* Pageot is a lodging-house keeper, in the Faubourg du Temple, whose house is usually inhabited by *forcats liberés*, or those who have broken their ban, and even assassins. It was at his house were arrested Lacenaire, Avril, and several others.

more singular is, that this crowd holds her in infinite respect. Let us add, to render homage to truth, that it is not, probably, to her person that this respect is accorded, but to the Herculean strength with which she is endowed—a strength of which, as we have observed, the necessity of her position obliges her to give frequent proofs. And yet the exterior of this woman offers nothing extraordinary. She has not yet attained her sixth lustre; her physiognomy is not disagreeable; her voice is neither rank nor harsh; she can even look modest, when, by chance, an individual who is not one of her habitual customers regards her with too much attention; in a word, she more resembles an honest and coquettish countrywoman than the mistress of an ignoble tavern.

By what concurrence of circumstances has this woman found herself placed at the head of such an establishment? How has she managed to accustom her sight to the horrible spectacles so frequently before it—her ears to the frightful harmony of blasphemies and obscene words—her lungs to an atmosphere always impregnated with pestilential miasma? This is one of those impenetrable mysteries and unanswered enigmas, to which Œdipus himself would have failed in finding a solution.

It is asserted that the smallest star has its satellites; if it is so, the most considerable ones should not be without them; consequently, after the Grand Bal Chicard, of the Rue de Bievre, comes *le petit Bal Chicard*, of the Rue Saint Jacques. This is a miniature of the former one; the same individuals are encountered, equal in dirt and rags.

If we plunge into the sombre labyrinth of the old streets of the city, we shall find, at the commencement, under the porte cochère of a house of the Rue des Marmousets, opposite that of la Licome, *la Maison Muraille*. This house is the rendezvous of the low prostitutes who infest that quarter of the city, who find means of extorting a few sous from the miserables they meet there.

It was at the house of le Seur Muraille that the following circumstance took place, and which we narrate to give our readers an idea of the degree of abasement to which men, brutalized by the abuse of poisonous wine and strong liquors, can descend.

Two rag-pickers, each accompanied by his son, boys of 14 or 15 years of age, met in this house; they were all drunk, fathers and sons, yet they would have more drink. The wretches had not yet arrived at that point of drunkenness during which the man, transformed into a sluggish mass, preserves not even the consciousness of his existence; and it was this *ne plus ultra* of forgetfulness they wished to attain. But how is it to be done—what means can they employ to satisfy this desire?—they had not even a sou, or, rather, to make use of the language, somewhat ideal, of the place to which we have conducted our readers, *les toiles se touchaient*; but ah! the luminous idea! One of the two sons was dressed in a blouse; this blouse was nearly new, and the broker was there. It is true this blouse was the only garment of the miserable boy; but things can be arranged. The other son had also a blouse, old, to a certainty, but he had a waistcoat under it. The two fathers held a council, and it was decided that the one who had the waistcoat should give his ragged blouse to the other, and that the new garment should be sold, which was done. No sooner was the pocket replenished, than the two miserables placed themselves at the table, and were served a litre of eau-de-vie. A litre among four is not much, especially if, from a wish to suit the eloquence of the action to that of the words, they upset a

part of it in the attempt. It is just what happened. To secure the precious liquid spilled over the table, one of the old rag-merchants made use of his sleeve, and the damage was repaired without much loss.

A few minutes after, in attempting to light his pipe, this man, who began to lose the proper use of his legs, (a second litre had been absorbed, and the two children were already under the table,) let fall on his blouse, saturated with alcohol, the match he had just used; the fire seized his garments. Frightened, he approaches his comrade, to whom he communicates the destructive element. You may probably think the proprietor of the establishment brings assistance to the wretches—if so, you are grievously mistaken. He has really plenty of other fish to fry; he contents himself with ejecting them into the street, and, from the step of his door, observes them, with a laugh, rolling themselves like beasts in the gutter of the Rue des Marmousets, to extinguish the flames which threaten to destroy them.

Opposite to this is situated *la Maison Auguste*. This is the house to which the women of la Maison Muraille conduct, for the purpose of drinking wine, the poor devils with whom they have drunk brandy at Muraille's. The mixture of poisons stupifies them, and when they are totally deprived of sense, they . . . . . .

When these women find no customers in the places they usually frequent, they prowl about the bridges and the Quay aux Fleurs. Let those beware, who, seduced by the equivocal charms of these deceitful sirens, accompany them into the sombre cabarets of the Rue du Haut-Moulin; they will only leave, when despoiled of their finest feathers, the nest they have crept into.

The individuals who constantly frequent these infamous resorts, but *rarely dine*, and *never breakfast*. However, speculators discovered that it was possible to gain a few sous by selling them the meagre pittance with which they satisfy themselves; and the Sieurs André and François have opened for them—the first in the Rue du Haut-Moulin, the other in the Rue de la Tacherie—two culinary offices. The host with whom Gil Blas de Santillane made his first repast, after leaving the paternal roof, was a carnival compared to these two officiating ministers of Comus. What, in fact, are *fillets of mules* and an omelette aux craquelins, compared to the fantastic viands upon which the Parisian *people* exist? Listen: when the heats of summer are somewhat stronger than usual, the municipal administration visits the laboratories of messieurs the porkshop-keepers, butchers, poulterers, and fishmongers of Paris, and every article which does not appear to the examiners to be of a suitable freshness is seized, to be thrown during the night, at the flood-gates of Montfauçon and la Petite Villette. Well, despite every precaution of the police, these viands are fished out, and it is from these disgusting portions (we trust, however, they take the trouble to wash them) that the miserables who are besotted all day with the eau-de-vie, whose composition we have described, keep themselves alive. And let us not be accused of using too strong a colour; what we have written is true—unfortunately too true. Yes, we have seen men feed upon objects which the dogs have just refused; and this in the capital of the civilized world, a few paces distant from the Louvre, the prefecture of the Seine, and the prefecture of police!

The *Drapeau Tricolore* and *le Cassis* are principally frequented by mendicants, hawkers of baskets of the Place Maubert, bandbox-sellers, and prostitutes. After visiting these two establishments, we must rest a moment in the Rue des Noyers with Sifflet, distiller, before arriving at Paul Niquet's.

The name of Paul Niquet is a name celebrated among the celebrated; so that we have at Paris *le grand* and *le petit Paul Niquet*. In several towns of the departments, at Algiers even, they have founded establishments under the patronage of the name of Paul Niquet; but the original and veritable Paul Niquet is of the Rue aux Fers; and this is the one of whom we mean to say a few words.

This establishment is actually kept by the Sieur Feillieux. Paul Niquet, as we are assured, is at present a rich bourgeois, beloved and respected in the neighbourhood he inhabits—a martinet in morals, and disgusted at the sight of a drunkard. The ungrateful wretch! he has forgotten, then, that if to-day he is somebody, 'tis to the drunkards he is indebted for it. At any rate, the house of Paul Niquet has preserved its primitive physiognomy. A lantern, placed over the arch of a long and narrow alley, indicates to the passers the entrance of this establishment; and if you fancy that this alley leads to a cool room in summer and a warm one in winter, you are deceived. The counter, furnished in a similar mode to that of the grand Saint Michel, is very simply placed in one of the angles of a small court, which is covered in by a glazed window. There are neither chairs nor tables at the house of the successor of Paul Niquet; the customers must drink standing before the counter. It is useless to add that the quality of the eau-de-vie and liquors consumed there, is not superior to that of the other establishments.

By ten o'clock at night, men and women without an asylum, male and female thieves, but of the lowest grade, drunken workmen, keepers of girls, and prostitutes, amongst whom are mixed, at a later hour, a few honest inhabitants of the country in the neighbourhood of Paris, assemble at Paul Niquet's. Those who possess a few sous drink at once; those whose pockets are empty, like the herons who, perched on their long legs, wait on the brink of a river, to intercept a diminutive fish on its passage, attend, their back leaning against the wall opposite the counter, the coming of some one who procures them the means of refreshing themselves. This does not fail to happen. The house of Paul Niquet being the most known of any similar establishment in Paris, is accidentally frequented by every stranger who wishes to become acquainted with the manners of the Parisian populace—by such of the inhabitants of Paris as, after a late supper, choose to pass the rest of the night in a lounge—and by messieurs the students of law and medicine, in their first year, delighted, seemingly, to be enabled to pass a few hours in bad company. The poor devils of whom we speak, sneak among the aristocratic guests of Paul Niquet, to whom they act as benevolent cicerones; they recount the chronicles of the place, and the history of the most remarkable habitués; and work so cleverly that, at length, they squeeze a glass of brandy from one, a pipe of tobacco from another, a grand sou from a third; so industrious are they, that at last, when daylight appears, they are (oh! the supreme felicity!) as drunk, if not more so, than their richer comrades.

The arrival of the journeymen tailors at the house of Paul Niquet is saluted with exclamations of joy and friendship, and verily to some purpose; the whole society will be refreshed, without being put to any expense. These gents, who arrive about midnight, chanting scraps of patriotic songs, will order, after reckoning the number of persons in front of the counter, as many glasses of liquor as there may be individuals; they then jingle their glasses against those of the vagabonds and scamps, whom they take a pleasure in regaling. If, by chance any of the latter have been forgotten, they approach messieurs the tailors, whom they treat as citizens, and immediately they are admitted to take their share of this refreshing shower " of little goes"—a shower a hundred times more precious in their sight than was the manna of the desert in that of the Hebrews.

The reader may, perhaps, be aware, that the journeymen tailors are mostly outrageously ferocious republicans. Why are they republicans? They know no reason for it. The fact is, they are so, and it is at the successor's of Paul Niquet that they meet, to scatter their propagandism; 'tis among the infamous crowd we have described, that they recruit the future pillars of the republican edifice. Alas! alas! pardon their fault, they know not what they do.

When a man of honest appearance, but whose brain seems a little heated, arrives alone in this Eldorado of Parisian intemperance, and, to pay what he has ordered, throws upon the counter a five or double franc piece, the " little goes" arrive for a good part of the society, without any occasion for his giving the order, a few officious ones will save him the trouble, for the waiters can only take from those who have; where there is nothing, the king loses his rights. This old proverb receives, every day, or, rather, every night, at the house of the successor of Paul Niquet, numerous examples.

For the gents *comme il faut*, who wish to pass a part of the night at Paul Niquet's, they have constructed a small neat room, which is only arrived at by crossing the counter, and from which they can see every thing without being observed. The favour of admission to this hall is expensive. It is true, that, when once there, there is no risk of a visit from the police, whilst those who remain standing before the bar, might, at any moment, be arrested by the night patrol; but as the time of the rounds of these patrols are pretty well known, the moment the sound is recognised, the whole of this nocturnal population disperses, like a covey of partridges at the discharge of the sportsman's Manton.

And now that we have escaped from Paul Niquet's, in order that we may avoid being captured by the drunken patrol, let us enter, if you please, the house of Charles Chantôme, Rue Aubry-le-Boucher. What an infected place, and what ignoble physiognomies! From whence issue these ill-clad men, with ashen-coloured features and sinister looks—these women, who have nothing of their sex but the garments, who yell their obscene scraps, who dispute and fight, who smoke, and drink eau-de-vie? Have there ever been, in the lives of these individuals, days of innocence and purity? We can hardly believe it; they must have been born in the atmosphere in which we encounter them, since they breathe there and appear quite at their ease. But what are these men—unfortunate? Oh no! honest poverty, however frightful it may be, has not this sordid and repulsive aspect, it is vice, and not poverty which has impressed its seal on the foreheads of these men and women. In fact, the house of *Charles Chantôme* is the sewer in which those we have spoken of, get rid of the redundancy of their population of thieves and assassins.

Our readers must be fatigued with the somewhat long journey they have made through these impure bye-ways; let us hasten to put an end to it; but, previously, allow us to address a few questions to them, the solution of which, we avow it in all humility, has, until now, been beyond our reach, and to which, probably, they cannot reply in a satisfactory manner.

Why does the municipal administration tolerate the existence of establishments similar to the ones we have described—establishments which must give to strangers who visit our capital, a very sad idea of our morals, and which, in reality, are nothing less than schools of rapine and debauchery, open to every comer?

But is it possible to close these establishments, without invading the liberty of commerce? We are perfectly aware that government covers with its protection—that it bestows every imaginable security upon the smallest as well as the largest commerce; but must we give the name of commerce to the industry of these individuals, patented purveyors of the prisons and the scaffold, (let us not be thought to use too strong an expression; more than one crime, the authors of which are, at the present hour, undergoing their punishment, has been inspired by the wine of the Grand Bal Chicard, or the brandy of Charles Chantôme,) who retail to the miserable and abandoned children of our civilization, the infernal drugs which bastardize generations, brutalize them, and render them capable of committing any or every crime. And, besides, we do not absolutely demand that these houses should be closed. We are well aware that the police require fish-ponds, well stocked, in which they can at any moment give a cast with their net. We know, also, that there is no body so healthy, (and God knows whether that of our ancient society is not a little affected,) but that it requires, from time to time, a little cleansing. Let these houses remain, then, if we cannot do otherwise; but, at any rate, let them be subjected to greater surveillance than they are. Why, for example, are they not considered in the same light as houses of accommodation, that they might be closed the moment they should appear to be too dangerous? Could they not be denied the privilege of vending pernicious liquids, whose mischievous effects are incalculable?

(a) The robbery à la tire is very ancient, and has been exercised by very noble personages. 'Tis on this account, probably, that les tireurs regard themselves as composing a part of the aristocracy of thieves, and as members of la haute pègre—qualities, indeed, which no one thinks of denying them.

The Pont Neuf was formerly the rendezvous of the tireurs de laine and cutters of purses, which, at this period, the inhabitants of Paris carried suspended from a leather girdle which encircled their waist. These gentry, who were then called Mions de Boulles, have counted amongst their ranks, the brother of the King Louis XIII, Gaston d'Orleans, the poet Villon, the Chevalier de Rieux, the Count de Rochefort, the Count d'Harcourt, and many gentlemen of the first families of the court. They exercised their profession in the face of day, and under the eyes of the watch, who could do nothing. This was the good time! but now, the grand seigneurs who can dip their hands, as they please, into the chests of secret funds, which is less hazardous, and especially, more productive, than thieving a few worn-out mantles, or a few consumptive purses, have resigned the trade to the vulgar.

The tireurs are always well dressed, although from necessity they carry neither a cane or gloves in their right hand; they endeavour to imitate the manners and the language of men of good society,

in which some of them succeed to perfection. The tireurs, when at work, are three, sometimes four together; they frequent the balls, concerts, theatres, in fact every place in which they hope to meet a crowd. At exhibitions their post of choice is the waiting or cane room, because at the moment of egress, there is always a great pressure; they have relations with nearly all the pilferers and chanteurs of the street, who participate in the profits of la tire. Nothing is more easy than to recognise a tireur, he can never rest in one place, he comes and goes, he permits his hands to grope at hazard, but in such a manner, however, that they may strike the pocket or the fob, the contents of which he is desirous of ascertaining. If he fancies it is worth the trouble of robbing, two comrades, whom the tireur calls his nonnes or nonneurs, place themselves respectively at their post, namely, near the individual who is to be victimized; they hussle him, press upon him, until the operator has effected his object. The articles stolen pass into the hands of a third party, the coqueur who disappears as quickly as possible, but still, without hurry or affectation.

There are among the tireurs, light-fingered gentry expert enough to equal the celebrated Philippe himself, and the best men in the list are gifted with a sang froid really remarkable, and which never betrays them.

Readers, keep an eye on those individuals who, when all are leaving the church or exhibition, endeavour to enter; give a twist to your watch fob. Never carry a purse, a purse is the most useless piece of furniture it is possible to imagine: a purse may be lost, and consequently all it contains; if, on the contrary, your pockets are sound, you lose nothing; and in any event, the fall of a piece of money might apprise you of the danger incurred by its companions. Place nothing in the pockets of your waistcoat; let your snuff-box and your note-case be secured in a pocket with a button; let your handkerchief remain in your hat, and you may walk without fear of the tireurs.

(b) Nearly all the careurs are Bohemians, Italians, or Jews, men or women; they present themselves in a well-accustomed shop, and after purchasing, they give in payment a piece of money, the value of which far exceeds that of the purchase they have made; whilst examining the change returned to them, they remark one or two pieces dissimilar to the rest; the ancient pieces of twenty-four sous, the six-franc crown pieces à la vache, or with the double W, the five-franc pieces of Italy, Sardinia, &c., are those which they most frequently notice, because it is generally believed that these contain a certain portion of gold, and that this belief will give some value to the proposition they intend to make: "If you had many of these pieces, we would take them of you, and give you a premium," they say. The tradesman, seduced by the expectation of gain, begins searching his drawer, and sometimes even his piles of reserve, for the pieces desired by the careur; and if, to accelerate the search, the merchant gives him access to his drawer, be assured he will gauge it with a remarkable dexterity.

The careurs have at their call many ruses, which they make use of alternatively, but a change is the foundation of all; for the rest, it is very easy to recognise the careurs. When the drawer is opened, they plunge in their hand as though helping to pick, and to point out the pieces they want; if the tradesman has occasion by any chance to go into his back shop, to get a piece of gold, they follow him, and there is no species of ruse they do not employ, in order to get their fingers in the bag.

Let the merchants be persuaded that the ancient pieces of twenty-four sous, the six franc crowns à la vache or with the double W, as well as the foreign money, have no other than their intrinsic value, let them keep a sharp eye upon unknown men, women, or children, who, under any pretext whatever, propose an exchange with them, and they will be armed against the most expert ruses of the careurs.

There are among the careurs, as there are among all other thieves, nourrisseurs d'affaires; these latter, in order to gain the confidence of the individual they wish to rob, purchase from him, until the opportune moment arrives, pieces at five or six times beyond their real value.

The careurs cite amongst the celebretés of their corporation, two careuses celèbres, la Duchesse, and la mère Caron; before exercising this trade, these two women served as eclaireurs to the band of the famous Sallambier, a blacksmith of the north, executed at Bruges, with thirty of his companions.

(c) Robbery in the interior and from the counters of shops.

(d) As we have already remarked, the chanteur is a robber who levies a contribution on an individual by threatening to put the public or the authorities in the confidence of his turpitude. If it were not that sometimes honest men are the victims of the chanteurs, the latter might, without much evil resulting, be allowed to exercise peaceably their industry, for those whom they exploite are no better than themselves; men whom the laws of the middle age, unpitying laws, it is true, condemned to the worst punishment; men whose every action, every thought, is an outrage upon the imprescriptable laws of nature; men, in fact, whom we are forced to regard as anomalies, if we would not conceive a very sad idea of poor humanity.

The chanteurs have at their disposition youths endowed with a neat physiognomy, who follow some financier, some noble personage, or even a banker, who have probably forgotten their classical studies, except the odes of Anacreon to Bathylle, and the passages of the Bucolics of Virgil addressed to Alexis; if the pantre takes the bait, he is decoyed into a propitious place, and when the offence has arrived at proof, sometimes even when he has received a commencement of the execution, appears a police agent of a respectable size; "Ah! I have caught you," he says; "follow me to the commissary of police." The chanteur whines, the sinner entreats; tears, prayers, are useless. The offender produces his purse, the false agent of police is not incorruptible, all is arranged by means of a little finance, and there is no farther question of a proces verbal.

The chanteurs do not always proceed in this manner, sometimes the supposed father or brother of the youth plays the part of the police agent; the latter mode of proceeding, which, in case of a mishap, is visited with a more moderate penalty, since to the principal offence is not added that of usurpation of functions, is also the one most in vogue.

Many individuals, quite certain that they had to do with scoundrels, have, however, paid; if they had complained, the chanteurs, it is true, would have been punished, but the baseness of those complaining would have been known; they held their tongue, and acted prudently.

A little house of the Allèe des Veuves, near the Bal Mabille, has been tenanted for many years by a man named S——, called L——, who has exercised for a considerable time in Paris the trade of a chanteur, without the police having ever had an occasion to take him; his confrères, enthusiastic admirers of his audacity and address, have surnamed him the sophano des chanteurs.

(o) The word charriage, in the language of thieves, is a general term which signifies robbing an individual whilst mystified; the charrieurs are therefore both thieves and mystifiers, and they speculate generally on the bonhomie of a fripon, who only exercises the trade occasionally; they are constantly two in company, the one named l'Americain, and the other le jardinier. The gardener accosts the first individual whose exterior does not announce a very lofty conception, and finds means to enter into conversation with him; suddenly they are met by a fellow richly attired, who expresses himself with difficulty, and desires to be conducted either to the Jardin du Roi, Palais Royal, or to the plain de Grenelle, to see le petit foussillement bien choli; but always to a place at some distance from the spot at which they have met; he offers in exchange for this slight service a piece of gold, sometimes even two; he addresses himself to le jardinier, who says to the dupe; "As we are together we will divide this lucky windfall; let us conduct the stranger where he wishes to go, it will give us a walk." Ten or twenty francs are not picked up every day by a walk, so that the victim does not hesitate to accept the proposition, and behold the three started for their destination.

The stranger is communicative. He recounts his history to his companions; he has only been a few days in Paris, he was in the service of a rich foreigner, who died on arriving in France, and has left him plenty of yellow pieces, which are not current in France, and which he would gladly exchange for white pieces; he would willingly give one of his own for three or even two of those he requires.

The dupe thinks the affair excellent, a hundred per cent is to be gained by such a bargain; he consults with le jardinier, and it is agreed that they shall victimize the Americain. "But," says the jardinier, "perhaps the gold pieces are not good, we must go and have them estimated." They make the stranger understand this necessity, who confides a piece to them without hesitation, and they repair together to a money changer, who hands them four five-franc pieces in exchange for one of twenty; they give three to the Americain, who appears perfectly content, and they divide one; short accounts make long friends, the affair is all but concluded; the Americain displays his rouleaus of gold, which he places successively in a little bag secured by a padlock.

"You have made estimate de mon biece gold," he then says, "me wish to know si votre money is also de good."

"Nothing more just," replies the jardinier.

The Americain collects all the five-franc pieces of the pantre, (victim,) and leaves, accompanied by the jardinier, under the pretence of having them estimated. He also leaves, as security, the little bag which contains the rouleaus of gold.

The pantre is quite at his ease; he waits patiently in the wine shop, into which he was enticed, until it pleases his two companions to return; he waits half an hour, a whole hour, two hours; his suspicions are then aroused; at length he opens the bag, in which, in lieu of gold pieces, he finds nothing but counterfeit money.

(f) The cambriolleurs rarely travel alone; when they meditate a coup, three or four introduce themselves into a house, and mount successively every stage; one of them knocks at the doors, if no one replies, 'tis a good sign, and they prepare to operate directly; to put themselves on guard, whilst one of the associates draws the staple, or applies the padlock; another posts himself on the stage above, and a third on the one below.

When the affair is *donnèe*, or ripe, one of the thieves undertakes to *filer* or follow the person who is to be robbed, from a fear that something forgotten may bring him back to his room; in this case, the person so charged, arrives before the individual, and apprises his comrades, who can then escape before the return of the bourgeois.

If, whilst the *cambriolleurs* are at work, any one ascends or descends, and is desirous of knowing what the individuals, who are unknown to him, are about, they inquire of him for the name of some one *in the moon*, a laundress, a midwife, or a nurse. In this case, the thief who questions, or who is interrogated, stammers, rather than speaks; he does not face his interrogator, and, in a hurry to make way for him, leans against the wall, and turns his back to the staircase.

If the thieves are aware that the porter is vigilant, and that, the robbery completed, they will have heavy packets to carry off, one of them enters, carrying one under his arm, which we may well suppose contains nothing but straw, but is filled on their return by the articles stolen.

Some *cambriolleurs* are accompanied in their expeditions by women carrying a bundle or basket of linen, in which the articles stolen can be easily secreted; the presence of a woman leaving a house, and especially one without a porter, with such like apparel, is a circumstance therefore important to remark, more particularly if they think it the first time they have seen her.

There are also *cambriolleurs à la flan*, (thieves from rooms by chance,) who introduce themselves into a room without having first laid any scheme; these improvisatores are sure of nothing, they go from door to door, where there is any thing they take it; where there is nothing, the robber, like the king, loses his rights. The trade of a *cambriolleur à la flan*, which is only exercised by those who are commencing their career, is exceedingly perilous, and little lucrative.

The best means of avoiding the visits of the *cambriolleurs* is to keep the key of the apartment in a safe place, never to leave it in the door, or hang it any where, nor to lend it to any one, even to *stop a bleeding nose;* if you go out, take the key with you; secure your most valuable objects; this done, leave the other keys in their respective pieces of furniture, you will spare the thieves the trouble of breaking them open, which they will not neglect, and it will be yours to repair the damage which, without this, they would not fail to commit.

The most dangerous *cambriolleurs* are without contradiction the *nourrisseurs;* they are thus named from their nourishing or ripening the affair. To nourish an affair, is to keep it constantly in perspective, whilst waiting for the most favourable moment for its execution. The *nourrisseurs*, who never act unless certain of making a *coup sur*, are usually old cunning fellows, who know more than one trick, they know how to procure information in the place; if occasion requires, one of them will even go there to lodge, and wait, to commit the robbery, until he has acquired, in the quarter he inhabits, a character which permits no suspicion to rest upon him; this latter never executes, he limits himself simply to the furnishing his *workmen* with

indications which may be useful to them; indeed he often takes the precaution so to put himself in evidence at the time of its execution, that his presence might, at the proper time, serve to establish an incontestible alibi.

They are generally old thieves who work in this manner; the most celebrated was named *Godè*, called the *Marquis*, alias *Capdeville*, at the present moment at the *bagne* at Brest, where he is undergoing his punishment of imprisonment for life.

The robberies of chambers are generally committed on Sundays and fête days.

(ᵍ) The *roulottiers* nearly all belong to the lowest class of the people, and their costume similar to that of the commissionaires and carriers. They work always several in company. When they have observed on a carriage, an article apparently worth the trouble of stealing, one of them accosts the conductor, and amuses him at the horses' heads, whilst the others mount the vehicle and hand down the bales.

In general, the *roulottiers* proceed with an audacity really remarkable. A famous *roulottier* named *Goupil*, has frequently mounted in open day, and in the quarter of the markets or halls, to the imperial of a diligence, and brought down from it a portmanteau, as though it belonged to him.

To avoid the experiments of the *roulottiers*, there should be no baggage behind carriages, nor tied with cords or straps, but with small iron chains, which cannot be touched, without arousing, by means of a bell placed in the interior of the carriage, the passengers seated within.

Let the draymen have a small dog on the drays, the more *currish* the better; let them renounce, especially, the detestable custom of drinking a can with the first individual who invites them.

Let the guardians of laundresses' carts not sleep on their packets of dirty linen, and the industry of the *roulottiers* will vanish.

The most famous *roulottiers* were formerly the *Frances*, Mouchotte, Dorè, Cadet Harrier, César Vioque. These individuals, and especially the latter, were capable of following a post-chaise several leagues; and they have nearly all finished their existence in the bagnes and prisons. The last has corrected himself.

(ʰ) The costume of the bonjourrier, or chevalier grimpant is neat, even elegant; he is always *booted* as though ready to start for the ball, and a smile, which more resembles a grimace than any thing else, is constantly stereotyped in his countenance.

Nothing is more simple than his manner of acting. He introduces himself into a house without the knowledge of the porter, or by inquiring of him for a person whom he knows is residing there. This done, he mounts until he discovers a door with the key left in it; he does not long search, for many persons are in the unlucky habit of never withdrawing the key from the lock. The bonjourrier knocks at first softly, then a little louder, and again louder, if no one has replied, being quite certain that his victim is absent, or in a profound sleep, he turns the key, enters, and takes possession of any thing within his reach. If the person he is robbing awakes whilst he is in the apartment, he inquires for the first name he can think of, and retires, after begging him to excuse him; the robbery is often completed when this happens.

A great number of thefts au bonjour are committed at Paris every day; the *bonjourriers*, to proceed with greater facility, obtain their elements from the commercial almanac; so that they can cite at a pinch a well-known name. They do not introduce themselves into a house unless they understand that the porter is absent.

Nothing would be easier than to prevent the depredations of the *bonjourriers*. Let there be, in the lodge of the concierge, a wire, corresponding with a bell placed in each apartment, and which he must draw when an unknown comes to inquire for one of the inhabitants of the house. Never permit the domestics to hide the key of the buffet which contains the plate; however well chosen may be the cachette, the thieves will easily contrive to discover it; this measure is therefore almost useless; we should as much as possible keep the keys in our own possession.

When a *bonjourrier* has stolen a silver dish, or or any other piece of plate, he conceals it under his waistcoat; if there are covers, cups, or cruets, his hat, covered with a handkerchief, serves to conceal the booty. So that if you meet a man on the staircase, whose manner seems embarrassed, turning his back, carrying under his arm a hat covered with a handkerchief, we may presume the man is a thief. It will be prudent therefore to follow him to the lodge, and not allow him to depart till you have ascertained he is not what he appears to be.

(¹) The *ramastiques*, or *ramastiqueurs*, like many other fripons, are indebted for their success to the cupidity of their dupes.

The following is a little drama, which, despite the advertisements of the *Gazette des Tribunaux*, is rehearsed in the capital every day, so true is it that nothing is more easy than to deceive men who are governed by a passion which we all more or less possess—the thirst for gold.

The scene takes place in a thoroughfare. The principal actors examine with attention the comers and goers. At last appears on the horizon the individual they are waiting for; his physiognomy, his costume, indicate a person as credulous as he is avaricious. One of the observers accosts him, and addresses to him a few questions, the answers to which reveal to the interrogator the state of the finances of the one addressed. If the information obtained appears favourable to him, he makes a sign, one of his companions then takes the lead of them, and drops from his pocket a box or small packet, in such a manner, however, that the stranger cannot help remarking the object; and this is what happens, and at the moment he stoops to pick it up, his new acquaintance cries "Shares." They hasten to open the packet, to the great joy of the *pantre*. They find in it either a ring, or magnificent pin; a note accompanies the article, and this writing is the invoice of the jeweller, who acknowledges having received from a servant, a tolerably large sum, as the price of that which he sends Monsieur le Marquis, or M. le Comte so and so. "We will not return this," says the fripon, "a marquis, a count can well afford to lose any thing, and we should be downright fools if we did not profit from the windfall heaven has sent us." The dupe agrees with him, and nothing more remains than to sell the article, here is the difficulty. The ramastique observes that this would not be prudent, perhaps, an object of so much value cannot be so easily got rid of; what is to be done? "Listen," says the fripon at length, "you appear to me an honest fellow, and I will give you a proof of confidence, which I hope you will show yourself worthy of ; I will leave the article in your hands, but as I want money, you shall advance me a few hundred francs ; but I require that you give me your address." The dupe, who has al-

ready determined to retain the whole value of their foundling, eagerly accepts the proposition, and inwardly laughs at the simplicity of his companion; his chuckle does not cease until he has had it valued by a jeweller, who informs him that the bijoux he possesses is, at the outside, worth fifteen or twenty francs.

The ramastiques are nearly all Jews. Each of them is attired in a costume adapted to the rôle he is to play. The one who accosts is nearly always dressed as a workman; the *dropper* is distinguished by the width of his pantaloons, one of the legs of which, serves as a conductor of the object to make it fall to the ground. Many women exercise this sort of industry; but, as we may presume, they only address persons of their own sex.

Out of twenty individuals duped by the ramastiques, eighteen at least give a false name and address; if it is true that the intention ought to be punished as well as the deed, we ask if it would not be just to inflict upon them a punishment of such a kind as may serve them as a lesson for the future.

Never be fool enough to go shares with a man who finds an object, especially if, for that purpose, you must loosen the strings of your purse.

(¹) Thieves who connect themselves with any person for the purpose of afterwards cheating them in some manner. All the members of the great family of fripons may be included therefore in this class. The affair of the lingot, prejudicial to the limonadier with the gray moustaches, (who was no other than a personage of whom we have frequently made mention in this work, Ronquetti, Duke of Modena,) is a sufficient example of the mode in which the *soulasses* proceed.

(ᵏ) The *Romanichels*, originally, as we are assured, from Lower Egypt, form, like the Jews, a population wandering over the whole face of the globe. A people who have preserved the type which distinguishes it, but which diminishes every day, and of which there will soon remain nothing. The *Romanichels* then, are men with an oriental physiognomy, called in France, Bohemians; in Germany, Egyptians; in England, Gipsies; in Spain and the countries in the south of Europe, Gitanos.

After wandering for a long time in the countries in the north of Europe, a numerous troop of these men, who were called Bohemians, no doubt from the long sojourn they had made in Bohemia, arrived in France in 1427, commanded by an individual to whom they had given the title of king, and who had for lieutenants, dukes and counts. These men were ruled by a peculiar constitution and laws, we shall only cite one of these laws, which must be still in vigour. When a Bohemian had committed a crime, (a murder for example,) he wore for a year a hair-cloth, or woollen shirt, and at the expiration of the year, considered himself purified. As they had procured, we know not how, a bull from the pope, who then occupied the pontifical throne, which authorised them to travel over Europe, and to solicit charity from honest souls, they were at first well received, and had assigned them as a residence the chapel Saint Denis. But they soon abused the hospitality so generously bestowed upon them, and in 1612, a decree of the parliament of Paris, enjoined them to leave the kingdom within a stated time, if they did not wish to pass the rest of their life at the galleys.

The Bohemians did not obey this injunction, they did not quit France, but continued to *predict the future* to the credulous, and to steal when **they** found an opportunity. But to escape the pursuits which were then directed against them, they were compelled to disperse themselves; it was then they took the name of Romanichels, a name which they still retain, and which has passed into the slang of thieves.

At the time we are writing, there are not many Bohemians in France; but some are still met with, principally in the provinces of the north. As formerly, they have no fixed locality; they are constantly on the move from one village to another, and the professions they ostensibly exercise, are horse-dealers, brokers, and charlatans. The Romanichels are conversant with many plants, with which they can *sicken* domestic animals—they also know how to procure the means of administering a certain dose; they afterwards offer their services to the proprietor of the stable, whose inhabitants they have poisoned, and get well paid for the recoveries they effect.

The Romanichels have invented—or at least have exercised with great ability—the robbery, *à la care*, of which we have spoken, which they have named *Cariben*.

When the Romanichels do not themselves rob, they serve as *eclaireurs* to those who do. The *chauffeurs*, who, from the year 4, to the year 5, of the Republic, infested Belgium, a part of Holland, and most of the provinces of the north of France, had Romanichels among their band.

The *marquises* (the Romanichels thus name their wives) were usually charged to examine the position, neighbourhood, and means of defence, of the farms, or chateaus, which were to be attacked; which they did, whilst examining the hand of a young girl, to whom they failed not to predict a brilliant destiny, but who frequently went to sleep at night, and never awoke!

(¹) The first robberies, *à la vanterne*, were committed at Paris, in 1814, at the time of the entrance into France of the prisoners detained in the English depôts; such of these prisoners as had previously been sent to the islands of Rhé and Saint Marcorif, were, for the most part, old thieves; so that, at their return, they formed themselves into bands, and committed a number of robberies. In a single night, more than thirty robberies, committed by means of scaling, terrified the inhabitants of the Faubourg Saint Germain; but a short time after this memorable night, the author of this work placed in the hands of justice, three bands of famous *vanterniers*; the first composed of thirty-three men, the second of twenty-eight, and the third of sixteen. Out of this total, of seventy-six—sixty-seven were condemned to punishments, of different degrees.

It would be easy to prevent the losses from the *vanterniers*; it would be sufficient to close, at the appearance of night, and even during hot weather, all the windows, and not open them until the morning.

The *Savoyards*, of the band of the famous *Brothers Delzaives*, were mostly expert and audacious *vanterniers*.

A robbery, *à la vanterne*, is sometimes merely the preliminary to a murder. The *vanterniers* decided upon robbing an apartment, situated on the ground floor of a house of the Faubourg Saint Honorè; one of them enters, by the window, visits the bed—sees no one; presently, he is followed by one of his comrades, and both commence seeking what they hope to find; but they shortly perceive a lady, sleeping on a sofa—she has round her neck a chain and gold watch: "She sleeps," says one of the *vanterniers* to his companion—Delzaive, surnamed l'Ecrevisse; "*we must nibble the ticker, and the bit of twist!*" "But, if she *squeaks?*" replied the second *vanternier*, named *Mabon*, alias l'Apothecaire. "Why, if she squeaks," continues l'Ecrevisse, "if she squeaks, we will cut her windpipe!" The young woman, who was only feigning sleep, and who heard, without understanding the words uttered by the assassins, possessed sufficient prudence and courage to continue her apparent sleep—consequently, nothing happened to her.

The receiver of the band, of which Delzaives, or l'Ecrevisse, was the chief, was named Metral, and was *frotteur* to the Empress Josephine! In his house, at the time of his arrest, were found considerable sums.

The author of this work carried on a rude warfare with the *vanterniers* of the band of the *Brothers Delzaives*; and at length managed to procure the condemnation of the whole.

CONCLUSION.

www.ingramcontent.com/pod-product-compliance
Lightning Source LLC
Chambersburg PA
CBHW080856020726

47502CB00008B/2260